PRAISE FOR ANNE RICE

INTERVIEW WITH THE VAMPIRE

"Unrelentingly erotic . . . Sometimes beautiful, and always unforgettable."

—*The Washington Post*

"Bona fide blockbuster . . . Audacious, erotic, and unforgettable . . . An unmitigated terror trip not meant for the weak of heart . . . His ghastly initiation into the netherworld is as mesmeric as is the discovery he is not alone in the nightly search for warm fresh blood."

—*The Cincinnati Enquirer*

"If you surrender and go with her . . . you have surrendered to enchantment, as in a voluptuous dream."

—*The Boston Globe*

"A chilling, thought-provoking tale, beautifully frightening, sensuous and utterly unnerving."

—*The Hartford Courant*

"Sensational and fantastic . . . Woven with uncanny magic . . . Hypnotically poetic in tone, rich in sensory imagery, and dense with the darkness that lies behind the veil of human thought."

—*St. Louis Post-Dispatch*

"A masterful suspense story . . . [that] plumbs the deepest recesses of human sensuality . . . From the beginning we are seduced, hypnotized by the voice of the vampire."

—*Chicago Tribune*

Please turn the page for more reviews. . . .

THE VAMPIRE LESTAT

"Fiercely ambitious, nothing less than a complete unnatural history of vampires."

—*The Village Voice*

"Brilliant . . . Its undead characters are utterly alive."

—*The New York Times Book Review*

"Luxuriantly created and richly told."

—*The Cleveland Plain Dealer*

"Here, then, is the vampire Lestat . . . come to dreadful and dazzling life, holding the power to haunt our imaginations and beckoning us to some sense of magic inside ourselves. . . . *Vive* Lestat!"

—*The Houston Post*

"A worthy successor to *Interview* . . . She may very well be this century's Mary Shelley."

—*The Kansas City Star*

"Fascinating . . . A novel to be savored . . . A rich and unforgettable tale of dazzling scenes and vivid personalities."

—*Library Journal*

THE QUEEN OF THE DAMNED

"A wonderful web of dark-side mythology . . . Mesmerizing."

—*San Francisco Chronicle*

"Exhilarating . . . Rice is equally adept at evoking rainswept Paris streets, concert-hall mayhem, and ramshackle mansions in New Orleans. She's a very sensual writer."

—*Newsday*

"Imaginative . . . Intelligently written . . . This is popular fiction of the highest order."

—*USA Today*

"A welcome chance to catch up with old fiends . . . Fascinating . . . When we emerge from its folds, there's good news on the last page: 'The chronicle of the vampires will continue.' Yum."

—*The Philadelphia Inquirer*

"A tour de force."

—*The Boston Globe*

BY ANNE RICE

The Vampire Chronicles

*Interview with the Vampire**
*The Vampire Lestat**
*The Queen of the Damned**
*The Tale of the Body Thief**
*Memnoch the Devil**
*The Vampire Armand**
*Blood and Gold**

Lives of the Mayfair Witches

*The Witching Hour**
*Lasher**
*Taltos**

A Vampire/Witches Chronicle

*Merrick**

New Tales of the Vampires

*Pandora**
*Vittorio, The Vampire**
*The Feast of All Saints**
*Cry to Heaven**
*The Mummy: Or Ramses the Damned**
Servant of the Bones
*Violin**

UNDER THE NAME ANNE RAMPLING:

*Exit to Eden**
Belinda

EROTICA UNDER THE NAME A. N. ROQUELAURE:

The Claiming of Sleeping Beauty
Beauty's Punishment
Beauty's Release

*Published by Ballantine Books

THE VAMPIRE CHRONICLES COLLECTION

VOLUME I

INTERVIEW WITH THE VAMPIRE

THE VAMPIRE LESTAT

THE QUEEN OF THE DAMNED

ANNE RICE

Ballantine Books
New York

A Ballantine Book
Published by The Ballantine Publishing Group

Interview with the Vampire was originally published by Alfred A. Knopf, a division of Random House, Inc., in 1976. *The Vampire Lestat* was originally published by Alfred A. Knopf, a division of Random House, Inc., in 1985. *The Queen of the Damned* was originally published by Alfred A. Knopf, a division of Random House, Inc., in 1988.

Portions of *The Vampire Lestat* originally appeared in *The Twilight Zone* magazine.

Poems by Stan Rice quoted in *The Queen of the Damned* were originally published in:

Some Lamb by Stan Rice © 1975 by Stan Rice. Published by The Figures. Reprinted by permission of Stan Rice.
Whiteboy by Stan Rice © 1976 by Stan Rice. Published by Mudra. Reprinted by permission of Stan Rice.
Body of Work by Stan Rice © 1983 by Stan Rice. Reprinted by permission of Lost Roads Publishers.

Untitled poem by Stan Rice in *The Queen of the Damned* copyright © 1988 by Stan Rice

Ballantine and colophon are registered trademarks of Random House, Inc.

www.ballantinebooks.com

Library of Congress Control Number: 2002092626

ISBN 0-345-45634-3

Cover illustration by Tony Greco

This edition published by arrangement with Alfred A. Knopf, a division of Random House, Inc.

Manufactured in the United States of America

First Trade Paperback Edition: October 2002

10 9 8 7 6 5 4 3 2

INTERVIEW WITH THE VAMPIRE

PART I

"I SEE . . ." said the vampire thoughtfully, and slowly he walked across the room towards the window. For a long time he stood there against the dim light from Divisadero Street and the passing beams of traffic. The boy could see the furnishings of the room more clearly now, the round oak table, the chairs. A wash basin hung on one wall with a mirror. He set his briefcase on the table and waited.

"But how much tape do you have with you?" asked the vampire, turning now so the boy could see his profile. "Enough for the story of a life?"

"Sure, if it's a good life. Sometimes I interview as many as three or four people a night if I'm lucky. But it has to be a good story. That's only fair, isn't it?"

"Admirably fair," the vampire answered. "I would like to tell you the story of my life, then. I would like to do that very much."

"Great," said the boy. And quickly he removed the small tape recorder from his briefcase, making a check of the cassette and the batteries. "I'm really anxious to hear why you believe this, why you . . ."

"No," said the vampire abruptly. "We can't begin that way. Is your equipment ready?"

"Yes," said the boy.

"Then sit down. I'm going to turn on the overhead light."

"But I thought vampires didn't like light," said the boy. "If you think the dark adds to the atmosphere . . ." But then he stopped. The vampire was watching him with his back to the window. The boy could make out nothing of his face now, and something about the still figure there distracted him. He started to say something again but he said nothing. And then he sighed with relief when the vampire moved towards the table and reached for the overhead cord.

At once the room was flooded with a harsh yellow light. And the boy, staring up at the vampire, could not repress a gasp. His fingers danced backwards on the table to grasp the edge. "Dear God!" he whispered, and then he gazed, speechless, at the vampire.

The vampire was utterly white and smooth, as if he were sculpted from bleached bone, and his face was as seemingly inanimate as a statue, except for two brilliant green eyes that looked down at the boy intently like flames in a skull. But then the vampire smiled almost wistfully, and the smooth white substance of his face moved with the infinitely flexible but minimal lines of a cartoon. "Do you see?" he asked softly.

The boy shuddered, lifting his hand as if to shield himself from a powerful light. His eyes moved slowly over the finely tailored black coat he'd only glimpsed in the bar, the long folds of the cape, the black silk tie knotted at the throat, and the gleam of the white collar that was as white as the vampire's flesh. He stared at the vampire's full black hair, the waves that were combed back over the tips of the ears, the curls that barely touched the edge of the white collar.

"Now, do you still want the interview?" the vampire asked.

The boy's mouth was open before the sound came out. He was nodding. Then he said, "Yes."

The vampire sat down slowly opposite him and, leaning forward, said gently, confidentially, "Don't be afraid. Just start the tape."

And then he reached out over the length of the table. The boy recoiled, sweat running down the sides of his face. The vampire clamped a hand on the boy's shoulder and said, "Believe me, I won't hurt you. I want this opportunity. It's more important to me than you can realize now. I want you to begin." And he withdrew his hand and sat collected, waiting.

It took a moment for the boy to wipe his forehead and his lips with a handkerchief, to stammer that the microphone was in the machine, to press the button, to say that the machine was on.

"You weren't always a vampire, were you?" he began.

"No," answered the vampire. "I was a twenty-five-year-old man when I became a vampire, and the year was seventeen ninety-one."

The boy was startled by the preciseness of the date and he repeated it before he asked, "How did it come about?"

"There's a simple answer to that. I don't believe I want to give simple answers," said the vampire. "I think I want to tell the real story. . . ."

"Yes," the boy said quickly. He was folding his handkerchief over and over and wiping his lips now with it again.

"There was a tragedy . . ." the vampire started. "It was my younger brother. . . . He died." And then he stopped, so that the boy cleared his throat and wiped at his face again before stuffing the handkerchief almost impatiently into his pocket.

"It's not painful, is it?" he asked timidly.

"Does it seem so?" asked the vampire. "No." He shook his head. "It's simply that I've only told this story to one other person. And that was so long ago. No, it's not painful. . . .

"We were living in Louisiana then. We'd received a land grant and settled two indigo plantations on the Mississippi very near New Orleans. . . ."

"Ah, that's the accent . . ." the boy said softly.

For a moment the vampire stared blankly. "I have an accent?" He began to laugh.

And the boy, flustered, answered quickly. "I noticed it in the bar when I asked you what you did for a living. It's just a slight sharpness to the consonants, that's all. I never guessed it was French."

"It's all right," the vampire assured him. "I'm not as shocked as I pretend to be. It's only that I forget it from time to ime. But let me go on. . . ."

"Please . . ." said the boy.

"I was talking about the plantations. They had a great deal to do with it, really, my becoming a vampire. But I'll come to that. Our life there was both luxurious and primitive. And we ourselves found it extremely attractive. You see, we lived far better there than we could have ever lived in France. Perhaps the sheer wilderness of Louisiana only made it seem so, but seeming so, it was. I remember the imported furniture that cluttered the house." The vampire smiled. "And the harpsichord; that was lovely. My sister used to play it. On summer evenings, she would sit at the keys with her back to the open French windows. And I can still remember that thin, rapid music and the vision of the swamp rising beyond her, the moss-hung cypresses floating against the sky. And there were the sounds of the swamp, a chorus of creatures, the cry of the birds. I think we loved it. It made the rosewood furniture all the more precious, the music more delicate and desirable. Even when the wisteria tore the shutters off the attic windows and worked its tendrils right into the whitewashed brick in less than a year. . . . Yes, we loved it. All except my brother. I don't think I ever heard him complain of anything, but I knew how he felt. My father was dead then, and I was head of the family and I had to defend him constantly from my mother and sister. They wanted to take him visiting, and to New Orleans for parties, but he hated these things. I think he stopped going altogether before he was twelve. Prayer was what mattered to him, prayer and his leatherbound lives of the saints.

"Finally I built him an oratory removed from the house, and he began to spend most of every day there and often the early evening. It was ironic, really. He was so different from us, so different from everyone, and I was so regular! There was nothing extraordinary about me whatsoever." The vampire smiled.

"Sometimes in the evening I would go out to him and find him in the garden near the oratory, sitting absolutely composed on a stone bench there, and I'd tell him my troubles, the difficulties I had with the slaves, how I distrusted the overseer or the weather or my brokers . . . all the problems that made up th length and breadth of my existence. And he would listen, making only a few comments, always sympathetic, so that when I left him I had the distinct impression he had solved everything for me. I didn't think I could deny him anything, and I vowed that no matter how it would break my heart to lose him, he could enter the priesthood when the time came. Of course, I was wrong." The vampire stopped.

For a moment the boy only gazed at him and then he started as if awakened from deep thought, and he floundered, as if he could not find the right words. "Ah . . . he didn't want to be a priest?" the boy asked. The vampire studied him as if trying to discern the meaning of his expression. Then he said:

"I meant that I was wrong about myself, about my not denying him anything." His eyes moved over the far wall and fixed on the panes of the window. "He began to see visions."

"Real visions?" the boy asked, but again there was hesitation, as if he were thinking of something else.

"I didn't think so," the vampire answered. "It happened when he was fifteen. He was very handsome then. He had the smoothest skin and the largest blue eyes. He was robust, not thin as I am now and was then . . . but his eyes . . . it was as if when I looked into his eyes I was standing alone on the edge of the world . . . on a windswept ocean beach. There was nothing but the soft roar of the waves. Well," he said, his eyes still fixed on the window panes, "he began to see visions. He only hinted at this at first, and he stopped taking his meals altogether. He lived in the oratory. At any hour of day or night, I could find him on the bare flagstones kneeling before the altar. And the oratory itself was neglected. He stopped tending the candles or changing the altar cloths or even sweeping out the leaves. One night I became really alarmed when I stood in the rose arbor watching him for one solid hour, during which he never moved from his knees and never once lowered his arms, which he held outstretched in the form of a cross. The slaves all thought he was mad." The vampire raised his eyebrows in wonder. "I was convinced that he was only . . . overzealous. That in his love for God, he had perhaps gone too far. Then he told me about the visions. Both St. Dominic and the Blessed Virgin Mary had come to him in the oratory. They had told him he was to sell all our property in Louisiana, everything we owned, and use the money to do God's work in France. My brother was to be a great religious leader, to return the country to its former fervor, to turn the tide against atheism and the Revolution. Of course, he had no money of his own. I was to sell the plantations and our town houses in New Orleans and give the money to him."

Again the vampire stopped. And the boy sat motionless regarding him, astonished. "Ah . . . excuse me," he whispered. "What did you say? Did you sell the plantations?"

"No," said the vampire, his face calm as it had been from the start. "I laughed at him. And he . . . he became incensed. He insisted his command came from the Virgin herself. Who was I to disregard it? Who indeed?" he asked softly, as if he were thinking of this again. "Who indeed? And the more he tried to convince me, the more I laughed. It was nonsense, I told him, the product of an immature and even morbid mind. The oratory was a mistake, I said to him; I would have it torn down at once. He would go to school in New Orleans and get such inane notions out of his head. I don't remember all that I said. But I remember the feeling. Behind all this contemptuous dismissal on my part was a smoldering anger and a disappointment. I was bitterly disappointed. I didn't believe him at all."

"But that's understandable," said the boy quickly when the vampire paused, his expression of astonishment softening. "I mean, would anyone have believed him?"

"Is it so understandable?" The vampire looked at the boy. "I think perhaps it was vicious egotism. Let me explain. I loved my brother, as I told you, and at times I believed him to be a living saint. I encouraged him in his prayer and meditations, as I said, and I was willing to give him up to the priesthood. And if someone had told me of a saint in Arles or Lourdes who saw visions, I would have believed it. I was a Catholic; I believed in saints. I lit tapers before their marble statues in churches; I knew their pictures, their symbols, their names. But I didn't, couldn't believe my brother. Not only did I not believe he saw visions, I couldn't entertain the notion for a moment. Now, why? Because he was my brother. Holy he might be, peculiar most definitely; but Francis of Assisi, no. Not *my* brother. No brother of mine could be such. That is egotism. Do you see?"

The boy thought about it before he answered and then he nodded and said that yes, he thought that he did.

"Perhaps he saw the visions," said the vampire.

"Then you . . . you don't claim to know . . . now . . . whether he did or not?"

"No, but I do know that he never wavered in his conviction for a second. That I know now and knew then the night he left my room crazed and grieved. He never wavered for an instant. And within minutes, he was dead."

"How?" the boy asked.

"He simply walked out of the French doors onto the gallery and stood for a moment at the head of the brick stairs. And then he fell. He was dead when I reached the bottom, his neck broken." The vampire shook his head in consternation, but his face was still serene.

"Did you see him fall?" asked the boy. "Did he lose his footing?"

"No, but two of the servants saw it happen. They said that he had looked up as if he had just seen something in the air. Then his entire body moved forward as if being swept by a wind. One of them said he was about to say something when he fell. I thought that he was about to say something too, but it was at that moment I turned away from the window. My back was turned when I heard the noise." He glanced at the tape recorder. "I could not forgive myself. I felt responsible for his death," he said. "And everyone else seemed to think I was responsible also."

"But how could they? You said they saw him fall."

"It wasn't a direct accusation. They simply knew that something had passed between us that was unpleasant. That we had argued minutes before the fall. The servants had heard us, my mother had heard us. My mother would not stop asking me what had happened and why my brother, who was so quiet, had been shouting. Then my sister joined in, and of course I refused to say. I was so bitterly shocked and miserable that I had no patience with anyone, only the vague determination they would not know about his 'visions.' They would not know that he had become, finally, not a saint, but only a . . . fanatic. My sister went to bed rather than face the funeral, and my mother told everyone in the parish that something horrible had happened in my room which I would not reveal; and even the police questioned me, on the word of my own mother. Finally the priest came to see me and demanded to know what had gone on. I told no one. It was only a discussion, I said. I was not on the gallery when he fell, I protested, and they all stared at me as if I'd killed him. And I felt that I'd killed him. I sat in the parlor beside his coffin for two days thinking, I have killed him. I stared at his face until spots appeared before my eyes and I nearly fainted. The back of his skull had been shattered on the pavement, and his head had the wrong shape on the pillow. I forced myself to stare at it, to study it simply because I could hardly endure the pain and the smell of decay, and I was tempted over and over to try to open his eyes. All these were mad thoughts, mad impulses. The main thought was this: I had laughed at him; I had not believed him; I had not been kind to him. He had fallen because of me."

"This really happened, didn't it?" the boy whispered. "You're telling me something . . . that's true."

"Yes," said the vampire, looking at him without surprise. "I want to go on telling you." But as his eyes passed over the boy and returned to the window, he showed only faint interest in the boy, who seemed engaged in some silent inner struggle.

"But you said you didn't know about the visions, that you, a vampire . . . didn't know for certain whether . . ."

"I want to take things in order," said the vampire, "I want to go on telling you things as they happened. No, I don't know about the visions. To this day." And again he waited until the boy said:

"Yes, please, please go on."

"Well, I wanted to sell the plantations. I never wanted to see the house or the oratory again. I leased them finally to an agency which would work them for me and manage things so I need never go there, and I moved my mother and sister to one of the town houses in New Orleans. Of course, I did not escape my brother for a moment. I could think of nothing but his body rotting in the ground. He was buried in the St. Louis cemetery in New Orleans, and I did everything to avoid passing those gates; but still I thought of him constantly. Drunk or sober, I saw his body rotting in the coffin, and I couldn't bear it. Over and over I dreamed that he was at the head of the steps and I was holding his arm, talking kindly to him, urging him back into the bedroom, telling him gently that I did believe him, that he must pray for me to have faith. Meantime, the slaves on Pointe du Lac (that was my plantation) had begun to talk of seeing his ghost on the gallery, and the overseer couldn't keep order. People in society asked my sister offensive questions about the whole incident, and she became an hysteric. She wasn't really an hysteric. She simply thought she ought to react that way, so she did. I drank all the time and was at home as little as possible. I lived like a man who wanted to die but who had no courage to do it himself. I walked black streets and alleys alone; I passed out in cabarets. I backed out of two duels more from apathy than cowardice and truly wished to be murdered. And then I was attacked. It might have been anyone—and my invitation was open to sailors, thieves, maniacs, anyone. But it was a vampire. He caught me just a few steps from my door one night and left me for dead, or so I thought."

"You mean . . . he sucked your blood?" the boy asked.

"Yes," the vampire laughed. "He sucked my blood. That is the way it's done."

"But you lived," said the young man. "You said he left you for dead."

"Well, he drained me almost to the point of death, which was for him sufficient. I was put to bed as soon as I was found, confused and really unaware of what had happened to me. I suppose I thought that drink had finally caused a stroke. I expected to die now and had no interest in eating or drinking or talking to the doctor. My mother sent for the priest. I was feverish by then and I told the priest everything, all about my brother's visions and what I had done. I remember I clung to his arm, making him swear over and over he would tell no one. 'I know I didn't kill him,' I said to the priest finally. 'It's that I cannot live now that he's dead. Not after the way I treated him.'

" 'That's ridiculous,' he answered me. 'Of course you can live. There's nothing wrong with you but self-indulgence. Your mother needs you, not to mention your sister. And as for this brother of yours, he was possessed of the devil.' I was so stunned when he said this I couldn't protest. The devil made the visions, he went on to explain. The devil was rampant. The entire country of France was under the influence of the devil, and the Revolution had been his greatest triumph. Nothing would have saved my brother but exorcism, prayer, and fasting, men to hold him down while the devil raged in his body and tried to throw him about. 'The devil threw him down the steps; it's perfectly obvious,' he declared. 'You weren't talking to your brother in that room, you were talking to the devil.' Well, this enraged me. I believed before that I had been pushed to my limits, but I had not. He went on talking about the devil, about voodoo amongst the slaves and cases of possession in other parts of the world. And I went wild. I wrecked the room in the process of nearly killing him."

"But your strength . . . the vampire . . . ?" asked the boy.

"I was out of my mind," the vampire explained. "I did things I could not have done in perfect health. The scene is confused, pale, fantastical now. But I do remember that I drove him out of the back doors of the house, across the courtyard, and against the brick wall of the kitchen, where I pounded his head until I nearly killed him. When I was subdued finally, and exhausted then almost to the point of death, they bled me. The fools. But I was going to say something else. It was then that I conceived of my own egotism. Perhaps I'd seen it reflected in the priest. His contemptuous attitude towards my brother reflected my own; his immediate and shallow carping about the devil; his refusal to even entertain the idea that sanctity had passed so close."

"But he did believe in possession by the devil."

"That is a much more mundane idea," said the vampire immediately. "People who cease to believe in God or goodness altogether still believe in the devil. I don't know why. No, I do indeed know why. Evil is always possible. And goodness is eternally difficult. But you must understand, possession is really another way of saying someone is mad. I felt it was, for the priest. I'm sure he'd seen madness. Perhaps he had stood right over raving madness and pronounced it possession. You don't have to see Satan when he is exorcised. But to stand in the presence of a saint . . . To believe that the saint has seen a vision. No, it's egotism, our refusal to believe it could occur in our midst."

"I never thought of it in that way," said the boy. "But what happened to you? You said they bled you to cure you, and that must have nearly killed you."

The vampire laughed. "Yes. It certainly did. But the vampire came back that night. You see, he wanted Pointe du Lac, my plantation.

"It was very late, after my sister had fallen asleep. I can remember it as if it were yesterday. He came in from the courtyard, opening the French doors without a sound, a tall fair-skinned man with a mass of blond hair and a graceful, almost feline quality to his movements. And gently, he draped a shawl over my sister's eyes and lowered the wick of the lamp. She dozed there beside the basin and the cloth with which she'd bathed my forehead, and she never once stirred under that shawl until morning. But by that time I was greatly changed."

"What *was* this change?" asked the boy.

The vampire sighed. He leaned back against the chair and looked at the walls. "At first I thought he was another doctor, or someone summoned by the family to try to reason with me. But this suspicion was removed at once. He stepped close to my bed and leaned down so that his face was in the lamplight, and I saw that he was no ordinary man at all. His gray eyes burned with an incandescence, and the long white hands which hung by his sides were not those of a human being. I think I knew everything in that instant, and all that he told me was only aftermath. What I mean is, the moment I saw him, saw his extraordinary aura and knew him to be no creature I'd ever known, I was reduced to nothing. That ego which could not accept the presence of an extraordinary human being in its midst was crushed. All my conceptions, even my guilt and wish to die, seemed utterly unimportant. I completely forgot *myself!*" he said, now silently touching his breast with his fist. "I forgot myself totally. And in the same instant knew totally the meaning of possibility. From then on I experienced only increasing wonder. As he talked to me and told me of what I might become, of what his life had been and stood to be, my past shrank to embers. I saw my life as if I stood apart from it, the vanity, the self-serving, the constant fleeing from one petty annoyance after another, the lip service to God and the Virgin and a host of saints whose names filled my prayer books, none of whom made the slightest difference in a narrow, materialistic, and selfish existence. I saw my real gods . . . the gods of most men. Food, drink, and security in conformity. Cinders."

The boy's face was tense with a mixture of confusion and amazement. "And so you decided to become a vampire?" he asked. The vampire was silent for a moment.

"Decided. It doesn't seem the right word. Yet I cannot say it was inevitable from the moment that he stepped into that room. No, indeed, it was not inevitable. Yet I can't say I decided. Let me say that when he'd finished speaking, no other decision was possible for me, and I pursued my course without a backward glance. Except for one."

"Except for one? What?"

"My last sunrise," said the vampire. "That morning, I was not yet a vampire. And I saw my last sunrise.

"I remember it completely; yet I do not think I remember any other sunrise before it. I remember the light came first to the tops of the French windows, a paling behind the lace curtains, and then a gleam growing brighter and brighter in patches among the leaves of the trees. Finally the sun came through the windows themselves and the lace lay in shadows on the stone floor, and all over the form of my sister, who was still sleeping, shadows of lace on the shawl over her shoulders and head. As soon as she was warm, she pushed the shawl away without awakening, and then the sun shone full on her eyes and she tightened her eyelids. Then it was gleaming on the table where she rested her head on her arms, and gleaming, blazing, in the water in the pitcher. And I could feel it on my hands on the counterpane and then on my face. I lay in the bed thinking about all the things the vampire had told me, and then it was that I said good-bye to the sunrise and went out to become a vampire. It was . . . the last sunrise."

The vampire was looking out the window again. And when he stopped, the silence was so sudden the boy seemed to hear it. Then he could hear the noises from the street. The sound of a truck was deafening. The light cord stirred with the vibration. Then the truck was gone.

"Do you miss it?" he asked then in a small voice.

"Not really," said the vampire. "There are so many other things. But where were we? You want to know how it happened, how I became a vampire."

"Yes," said the boy. "How did you change, exactly?"

"I can't tell you exactly," said the vampire. "I can tell you about it, enclose it with words that will make the value of it to me evident to you. But I can't tell you exactly, any more than I could tell you exactly what is the experience of sex if you have never had it."

The young man seemed struck suddenly with still another question, but before he could speak the vampire went on. "As I told you, this vampire Lestat wanted the plantation. A mundane reason, surely, for granting me a life which will last until the end of the world; but he was not a very discriminating person. He didn't consider the world's small population of vampires as being a select club, I should say. He had human problems, a blind father who did not know his son was a vampire and must not find out. Living in New Orleans had become too difficult for him, considering his needs and the necessity to care for his father, and he wanted Pointe du Lac.

"We went at once to the plantation the next evening, ensconced the blind father in the master bedroom, and I proceeded to make the change. I cannot say that it consisted in any one step really—though one, of course, was the step beyond which I could make no return. But there were several acts involved, and the first was the death of the overseer. Lestat took him in his sleep. I was to watch and to approve; that is, to witness the taking of a human life as proof of my commitment and part of my change. This proved without doubt the most difficult part for me. I've told you I had no fear regarding my own death, only a squeamishness about taking my life myself. But I had a most high regard for the life of others, and a horror of death most recently developed because of my brother. I had to watch the overseer awake with a start, try to throw off Lestat with both hands, fail, then lie there struggling under Lestat's grasp, and finally go limp, drained of blood. And die. He did not die at once. We stood in his narrow bedroom for the better part of an hour watching him die. Part of my change, as I said. Lestat would never have stayed otherwise. Then it was necessary to get rid of the overseer's body. I was almost sick from this. Weak and feverish already, I had little reserve; and handling the dead body with such a purpose caused me nausea. Lestat was laughing, telling me callously that I would feel so different once I was a vampire that I would laugh, too. He was wrong about that. I never laugh at death, no matter how often and regularly I am the cause of it.

"But let me take things in order. We had to drive up the river road until we came to open fields and leave the overseer there. We tore his coat, stole his money, and saw to it his lips were stained with liquor. I knew his wife, who lived in New Orleans, and knew the state of desperation she would suffer when the body was discovered. But more than sorrow for her, I felt pain that she would never know what had happened, that her husband had not been found drunk on the road by robbers. As we beat the body, bruising the face and the shoulders, I became more and more aroused. Of course, you must realize that all this time the vampire Lestat was extraordinary. He was no more human to me than a biblical angel. But under this pressure, my enchantment with him was strained. I had seen my becoming a vampire in two lights: The first light was simply enchantment; Lestat had overwhelmed me on my deathbed. But the other light was my wish for self-destruction. My desire to be thoroughly damned. This was the open door through which Lestat had come on both the first and second occasion. Now I was not destroying myself but someone else. The overseer, his wife, his family. I recoiled and might have fled from Lestat, my sanity thoroughly shattered, had not he sensed with an infallible instinct what was happening. Infallible instinct . . ." The vampire mused. "Let me say the powerful instinct of a vampire to whom even the slightest change in a human's facial expression is as apparent as a gesture. Lestat had preternatural timing. He rushed me into the carriage and whipped the horses home. 'I want to die,' I began to murmur. 'This is unbearable. I want to die. You have it in your power to kill me. Let me die.' I refused to look at him, to be spellbound by the sheer beauty of his appearance. He spoke my name to me softly, laughing. As I said, he was determined to have the plantation."

"But would he have let you go?" asked the boy. "Under any circumstances?"

"I don't know. Knowing Lestat as I do now, I would say he would have killed me rather than let me go. But this was what I wanted, you see. It didn't matter. No, this was what I thought I wanted. As soon as we reached the house, I jumped down out of the carriage and walked, a zombie, to the brick stairs where my brother had fallen. The house had been unoccupied for months now, the overseer having his own cottage, and the Louisiana heat and damp were already picking apart the steps. Every crevice was sprouting grass and even small wildflowers. I remember feeling the moisture which in the night was cool as I sat down on the lower steps and even rested my head against the brick and felt the little wax-stemmed wildflowers with my hands. I pulled a clump of them out of the easy dirt in one hand. 'I want to die; kill me. Kill me,' I said to the vampire. 'Now I am guilty of murder. I can't live.' He sneered with the impatience of people listening to the obvious lies of others. And then in a flash he fastened on me just as he had on my man. I thrashed against him wildly. I dug my boot into his chest and kicked him as fiercely as I could, his teeth stinging my throat, the fever pounding in my temples. And with a movement of his entire body, much too fast for me to see, he was suddenly standing disdainfully at the foot of the steps. 'I thought you wanted to die, Louis,' he said."

The boy made a soft, abrupt sound when the vampire said his name, which the vampire acknowledged with the quick statement, "Yes, that is my name," and went on.

"Well, I lay there helpless in the face of my own cowardice and fatuousness again," he said. "Perhaps so directly confronted with it, I might in time have gained the courage to truly take my life, not to whine and beg for others to take it. I saw myself turning on a knife then, languishing in a day-to-day suffering which I found as necessary as penance from the confessional, truly hoping death would find me unawares and render me fit for eternal pardon. And also I saw myself as if in a vision standing at the head of the stairs, just where my brother had stood, and then hurtling my body down on the bricks.

"But there was no time for courage. Or shall I say, there was no time in Lestat's plan for anything but his plan. 'Now listen to me, Louis,' he said, and he lay down beside me now on the steps, his movement so graceful and so personal that at once it made me think of a lover. I recoiled. But he put his right arm around me and pulled me close to his chest. Never had I been this close to him before, and in the dim light I could see the magnificent radiance of his eye and the unnatural mask of his skin. As I tried to move, he pressed his right fingers against my lips and said, 'Be still. I am going to drain you now to the very threshold of death, and I want you to be quiet, so quiet that you can almost hear the flow of blood through your veins, so quiet that you can hear the flow of that same blood through mine. It is your consciousness, your will, which must keep you alive.' I wanted to struggle, but he pressed so hard with his fingers that he held my entire prone body in check; and as soon as I stopped my abortive attempt at rebellion, he sank his teeth into my neck."

The boy's eyes grew huge. He had drawn farther and farther back in his chair as the vampire spoke, and now his face was tense, his eyes narrow, as if he were preparing to weather a blow.

"Have you ever lost a great amount of blood?" asked the vampire. "Do you know the feeling?"

The boy's lips shaped the word *no*, but no sound came out. He cleared his throat. "No," he said.

"Candles burned in the upstairs parlor, where we had planned the death of the overseer. An oil lantern swayed in the breeze on the gallery. All of this light coalesced and began to shimmer, as though a golden presence hovered above me, suspended in the stairwell, softly entangled with the railings, curling and contracting like smoke. 'Listen, keep your eyes wide,' Lestat whispered to me, his lips moving against my neck. I remember that the movement of his lips raised the hair all over my body, sent a shock of sensation through my body that was not unlike the pleasure of passion. . . ."

He mused, his right fingers slightly curled beneath his chin, the first finger appearing to lightly stroke it. "The result was that within minutes I was weak to paralysis. Panic-stricken, I discovered I could not even will myself to speak. Lestat still held me, of course, and his arm was like the weight of an iron bar. I felt his teeth withdraw with such a keenness that the two puncture wounds seemed enormous, lined with pain. And now he bent over my helpless head and, taking his right hand off me, bit his own wrist. The blood flowed down upon my shirt and coat, and he watched it with a narrow, gleaming eye. It seemed an eternity that he watched it, and that shimmer of light now hung behind his head like the backdrop of an apparition. I think that I knew what he meant to do even before he did it, and I was waiting in my helplessness as if I'd been waiting for years. He pressed his bleeding wrist to my mouth, said firmly, a little impatiently, 'Louis, drink.' And I did. 'Steady, Louis,' and 'Hurry,' he whispered to me a number of times. I drank, sucking the blood out of the holes, experiencing for the first time since infancy the special pleasure of sucking nourishment, the body focused with the mind upon one vital source. Then something happened." The vampire sat back, a slight frown on his face.

"How pathetic it is to describe these things which can't truly be described," he said, his voice low almost to a whisper. The boy sat as if frozen.

"I saw nothing but that light then as I drew blood. And then this next thing, this next thing was . . . sound. A dull roar at first and then a pounding like the pounding of a drum, growing louder and louder, as if some enormous creature were coming up on one slowly through a dark and alien forest, pounding as he came, a huge drum. And then there came the pounding of another drum, as if another giant were coming yards behind him, and each giant, intent on his own drum, gave no notice to the rhythm of the other. The sound grew louder and louder until it seemed to fill not just my hearing but all my senses, to be throbbing in my lips and fingers, in the flesh of my temples, in my veins. Above all, in my veins, drum and then the other drum; and then Lestat pulled his wrist free suddenly, and I opened my eyes and checked myself in a moment of reaching for his wrist, grabbing it, forcing it back to my mouth at all costs; I checked myself because I realized that the drum was my heart, and the second drum had been his." The vampire sighed. "Do you understand?"

The boy began to speak, and then he shook his head. "No . . . I mean, I do," he said. "I mean, I . . ."

"Of course," said the vampire, looking away.

"Wait, wait!" said the boy in a welter of excitement. "The tape is almost gone. I have to turn it over." The vampire watched patiently as he changed it.

"What happened then?" the boy asked. His face was moist, and he wiped it hurriedly with his handkerchief.

"I saw as a vampire," said the vampire, his voice now slightly detached. It seemed almost distracted. Then he drew himself up. "Lestat was standing again at the foot of the stairs, and I saw him as I could not possibly have seen him before. He had seemed white to me before, starkly white, so that in the night he was almost luminous; and now I saw him filled with his own life and own blood: he was radiant, not luminous. And then I saw that not only Lestat had changed, but all things had changed.

"It was as if I had only just been able to see colors and shapes for the first time. I was so enthralled with the buttons on Lestat's black coat that I looked at nothing else for a long time. Then Lestat began to laugh, and I heard his laughter as I had never heard anything before. His heart I still heard like the beating of a drum, and now came this metallic laughter. It was confusing, each sound running into the next sound, like the mingling reverberations of bells, until I learned to separate the sounds, and then they overlapped, each soft but distinct, increasing but discrete, peals of laughter." The vampire smiled with delight. "Peals of bells.

" 'Stop looking at my buttons,' Lestat said. 'Go out there into the trees. Rid yourself of all the human waste in your body, and don't fall so madly in love with the night that you lose your way!'

"That, of course, was a wise command. When I saw the moon on the flagstones, I became so enamored with it that I must have spent an hour there. I passed my brother's oratory without so much as a thought of him, and standing among the cottonwood and oaks, I heard the night as if it were a chorus of whispering women, all beckoning me to their breasts. As for my body, it was not yet totally converted, and as soon as I became the least accustomed to the sounds and sights, it began to ache. All my human fluids were being forced out of me. I was dying as a human, yet completely alive as a vampire; and with my awakened senses, I had to preside over the death of my body with a certain discomfort and then, finally, fear. I ran back up the steps to the parlor, where Lestat was already at work on the plantation papers, going over the expenses and profits for the last year. 'You're a rich man,' he said to me when I came in. 'Something's happening to me,' I shouted.

" 'You're dying, that's all; don't be a fool. Don't you have any oil lamps? All this money and you can't afford whale oil except for that lantern. Bring me that lantern.'

" 'Dying!' I shouted. 'Dying!'

" 'It happens to everyone,' he persisted, refusing to help me. As I look back on this, I still despise him for it. Not because I was afraid, but because he might have drawn my attention to these changes with reverence. He might have calmed me and told me I might watch my death with the same fascination with which I had watched and felt the night. But he didn't. Lestat was never the vampire I am. Not at all." The vampire did not say this boastfully. He said it as if he would truly have had it otherwise.

"*Alors*," he sighed. "I was dying fast, which meant that my capacity for fear was diminishing as rapidly. I simply regret I was not more attentive to the process. Lestat was being a perfect idiot. 'Oh, for the love of hell!' he began shouting. 'Do you realize I've made no provision for you? What a fool I am.' I was tempted to say, 'Yes, you are,' but I didn't. 'You'll have to bed down with me this morning. I haven't prepared you a coffin.' "

The vampire laughed. "The coffin struck such a chord of terror in me I think it absorbed all the capacity for terror I had left. Then came only my mild alarm at having to share a coffin with Lestat. He was in his father's bedroom meantime, telling the old man good-bye, that he would return in the morning. 'But where do you go, why must you live by such a schedule!' the old man demanded, and Lestat became impatient. Before this, he'd been gracious to the old man, almost to the point of sickening one, but now he became a bully. 'I take care of you, don't I? I've put a better roof over your head than you ever put over mine! If I want to sleep all day and drink all night, I'll do it, damn you!' The old man started to whine. Only my peculiar state of emotions and most unusual feeling of exhaustion kept me from disapproving. I was watching the scene through the open door, enthralled with the colors of the counterpane and the positive riot of color in the old man's face. His blue veins pulsed beneath his pink and grayish flesh. I found even the yellow of his teeth appealing to me, and I became almost hypnotized by the quivering of his lip. 'Such a son, such a son,' he said, never suspecting, of course, the true nature of his son. 'All right, then, go. I know you keep a woman somewhere; you go to see her as soon as her husband leaves in the morning. Give me my rosary. What's happened to my rosary?' Lestat said something blasphemous and gave him the rosary. . . ."

"But . . ." the boy started.

"Yes?" said the vampire. "I'm afraid I don't allow you to ask enough questions."

"I was going to ask, rosaries have crosses on them, don't they?"

"Oh, the rumor about crosses!" the vampire laughed. "You refer to our being afraid of crosses?"

"Unable to look on them, I thought," said the boy.

"Nonsense, my friend, sheer nonsense. I can look on anything I like. And I rather like looking on crucifixes in particular."

"And what about the rumor about keyholes? That you can . . . become steam and go through them."

"I wish I could," laughed the vampire. "How positively delightful. I should like to pass through all manner of different keyholes and feel the tickle of their peculiar shapes. No." He shook his head. "That is, how would you say today . . . bull-shit?"

The boy laughed despite himself. Then his face grew serious.

"You mustn't be so shy with me," the vampire said. "What is it?"

"The story about stakes through the heart," said the boy, his cheeks coloring slightly.

"The same," said the vampire. "Bull-shit," he said, carefully articulating both syllables, so that the boy smiled. "No magical power whatsoever. Why don't you smoke one of your cigarettes? I see you have them in your shirt pocket."

"Oh, thank you," the boy said, as if it were a marvellous suggestion. But once he had the cigarette to his lips, his hands were trembling so badly that he mangled the first fragile book match.

"Allow me," said the vampire. And, taking the book, he quickly put a lighted match to the boy's cigarette. The boy inhaled, his eyes on the vampire's fingers. Now the vampire withdrew across the table with a soft rustling of garments. "There's an ashtray on the basin," he said, and the boy moved nervously to get it. He stared at the few butts in it for a moment, and then, seeing the small waste basket beneath, he emptied the ashtray and quickly set it on the table. His fingers left damp marks on the cigarette when he put it down. "Is this your room?" he asked.

"No," answered the vampire. "Just a room."

"What happened then?" the boy asked. The vampire appeared to be watching the smoke gather beneath the overhead bulb.

"Ah . . . we went back to New Orleans posthaste," he said. "Lestat had his coffin in a miserable room near the ramparts."

"And you did get into the coffin?"

"I had no choice. I begged Lestat to let me stay in the closet, but he laughed, astonished. 'Don't you know what you are?' he asked. 'But is it magical? Must it have this shape?' I pleaded. Only to hear him laugh again. I couldn't bear the idea; but as we argued, I realized I had no real fear. It was a strange realization. All my life I'd feared closed places. Born and bred in French houses with lofty ceilings and floor-length windows, I had a dread of being enclosed. I felt uncomfortable even in the confessional in church. It was a normal enough fear. And now I realized as I protested to Lestat, I did not actually feel this anymore. I was simply remembering it. Hanging on to it from habit, from a deficiency of ability to recognize my present and exhilarating freedom. 'You're carrying on badly,' Lestat said finally. 'And it's almost dawn. I should let you die. You will die, you know. The sun will destroy the blood I've given you, in every tissue, every vein. But you shouldn't be feeling this fear at all. I think you're like a man who loses an arm or a leg and keeps insisting that he can feel pain where the arm or leg used to be.' Well, that was positively the most intelligent and useful thing Lestat ever said in my presence, and it brought me around at once. 'Now, I'm getting into the coffin,' he finally said to me in his most disdainful tone, 'and you will get in on top of me if you know what's good for you.' And I did. I lay face-down on him, utterly confused by my absence of dread and filled with a distaste for being so close to him, handsome and intriguing though he was. And he shut the lid. Then I asked him if I was completely dead. My body was tingling and itching all over. 'No, you're not then,' he said. 'When you are, you'll only hear and see it changing and feel nothing. You should be dead by tonight. Go to sleep.' "

"Was he right? Were you . . . dead when you woke up?"

"Yes, changed, I should say. As obviously I am alive. My body was dead. It was some time before it became absolutely cleansed of the fluids and matter it no longer needed, but it was dead. And with the realization of it came another stage in my divorce from human emotions. The first thing which became apparent to me, even while Lestat and I were loading the coffin into a hearse and stealing another coffin from a mortuary, was that I did not like Lestat at all. I was far from being his equal yet, but I was infinitely closer to him than I had been before the death of my body. I can't really make this clear to you for the obvious reason that you are now as I was before my body died. You cannot understand. But before I died, Lestat was absolutely the most overwhelming *experience* I'd ever had. Your cigarette has become one long cylindrical ash."

"Oh!" The boy quickly ground the filter into the glass. "You mean that when the gap was closed between you, he lost his . . . spell?" he asked, his eyes quickly fixed on the vampire, his hands now producing a cigarette and match much more easily than before.

"Yes, that's correct," said the vampire with obvious pleasure. "The trip back to Pointe du Lac was thrilling. And the constant chatter of Lestat was positively the most boring and disheartening thing I experienced. Of course as I said, I was far from being his equal. I had my dead limbs to contend with . . . to use his comparison. And I learned that on that very night, when I had to make my first kill."

The vampire reached across the table now and gently brushed an ash from the boy's lapel, and the boy stared at his withdrawing hand in alarm. "Excuse me," said the vampire. "I didn't mean to frighten you."

"Excuse *me*," said the boy. "I just got the impression suddenly that your arm was . . . abnormally long. You reached so far without moving!"

"No," said the vampire, resting his hands again on his crossed knees. "I moved forward much too fast for you to see. It was an illusion."

"You moved forward? But you didn't. You were sitting just as you are now, with your back against the chair."

"No," repeated the vampire firmly. "I moved forward as I told you. Here, I'll do it again." And he did it again, and the boy stared with the same mixture of confusion and fear. "You still didn't see it," said the vampire. "But, you see, if you look at my outstretched arm now, it's really not remarkably long at all." And he raised his arm, first finger pointing heavenward as if he were an angel about to give the Word of the Lord. "You have experienced a fundamental difference between the way you see and I see. My gesture appeared slow and somewhat languid to me. And the sound of my finger brushing your coat was quite audible. Well, I didn't mean to frighten you, I confess. But perhaps you can see from this that my return to Pointe du Lac was a feast of new experiences, the mere swaying of a tree branch in the wind a delight."

"Yes," said the boy; but he was still visibly shaken. The

vampire eyed him for a moment, and then he said, "I was telling you . . ."

"About your first kill," said the boy.

"Yes. I should say first, however, that the plantation was in a state of pandemonium. The overseer's body had been found and so had the blind old man in the master bedroom, and no one could explain the blind old man's presence. And no one had been able to find me in New Orleans. My sister had contacted the police, and several of them were at Pointe du Lac when I arrived. It was already quite dark, naturally, and Lestat quickly explained to me that I must not let the police see me in even minimal light, especially not with my body in its present remarkable state; so I talked to them in the avenue of oaks before the plantation house, ignoring their requests that we go inside. I explained I'd been to Pointe du Lac the night before and the blind old man was my guest. As for the overseer, he had not been here, but had gone to New Orleans on business.

"After that was settled, during which my new detachment served me admirably, I had the problem of the plantation itself. My slaves were in a state of complete confusion, and no work had been done all day. We had a large plant then for the making of the indigo dye, and the overseer's management had been most important. But I had several extremely intelligent slaves who might have done his job just as well a long time before, if I had recognized their intelligence and not feared their African appearance and manner. I studied them clearly now and gave the management of things over to them. To the best, I gave the overseer's house on a promise. Two of the young women were brought back into the house from the fields to care for Lestat's father, and I told them I wanted as much privacy as possible and they would all of them be rewarded not only for service but for leaving me and Lestat absolutely alone. I did not realize at the time that these slaves would be the first, and possibly the only ones, to ever suspect that Lestat and I were not ordinary creatures. I failed to realize that their experience with the supernatural was far greater than that of white men. In my own inexperience I still thought of them as childlike savages barely domesticated by slavery. I made a bad mistake. But let me keep to my story. I was going to tell you about my first kill. Lestat bungled it with his characteristic lack of common sense."

"Bungled it?" asked the boy.

"I should never have started with human beings. But this was something I had to learn by myself. Lestat had us plunge headlong into the swamps right after the police and the slaves were settled. It was very late, and the slave cabins were completely dark. We soon lost sight of the lights of Pointe du Lac altogether, and I became very agitated. It was the same thing again: remembered fears, confusion. Lestat, had he any native intelligence, might have explained things to me patiently and gently—that I had no need to fear the swamps, that to snakes and insects I was utterly invulnerable, and that I must concentrate on my new ability to see in total darkness. Instead, he harassed me with condemnations. He was concerned only with our victims, with finishing my initiation and getting on with it.

"And when we finally came upon our victims, he rushed me into action. They were a small camp of runaway slaves. Lestat had visited them before and picked off perhaps a fourth of their number by watching from the dark for one of them to leave the fire, or by taking them in their sleep. They knew absolutely nothing of Lestat's presence. We had to watch for well over an hour before one of the men—they were all men—finally left the clearing and came just a few paces into the trees. He unhooked his pants now and attended to an ordinary physical necessity; and as he turned to go, Lestat shook me and said, 'Take him.' " The vampire smiled at the boy's wide eyes. "I think I was about as horrorstruck as you would be," he said. "But I didn't know then that I might kill animals instead of humans. I said quickly I could not possibly take him. And the slave heard me speak. He turned, his back to the distant fire, and peered into the dark. Then quickly and silently, he drew a long knife out of his belt. He was naked except for the pants and the belt, a tall, strong-armed, sleek young man. He said something in the French patois, and then he stepped forward. I realized that, though I saw him clearly in the dark, he could not see us. Lestat stepped in back of him with a swiftness that baffled me and got a hold around his neck while he pinned his left arm. The slave cried out and tried to throw Lestat off. He sank his teeth now, and the slave froze as if from snakebite. He sank to his knees, and Lestat fed fast as the other slaves came running. 'You sicken me,' he said when he got back to me. It was as if we were black insects utterly camouflaged in the night, watching the slaves move, oblivious to us, discover the wounded man, drag him back, fan out in the foliage searching for the attacker. 'Come on, we have to get another one before they all return to camp,' he said. And quickly we set off after one man who was separated from the others. I was still terribly agitated, convinced I couldn't bring myself to attack and feeling no urge to do so. There were many things, as I mention, which Lestat might have said and done. He might have made the experience rich in so many ways. But he did not."

"What could he have done?" the boy asked. "What do you mean?"

"Killing is no ordinary act," said the vampire. "One doesn't simply glut oneself on blood." He shook his head. "It is the experience of another's life for certain, and often the experience of the loss of that life through the blood, slowly. It is again and again the experience of that loss of my own life, which I experienced when I sucked the blood from Lestat's wrist and felt his heart pound with my heart. It is again and again a celebration of that experience; because for vampires that is the ultimate experience." He said this most seriously, as if he were arguing with someone who held a different view. "I don't think Lestat ever appreciated that, though how he could not, I don't know. Let me say he appreciated something, but very little, I think, of what there is to know. In any event, he took no pains to remind me now of what I'd felt when I clamped onto his wrist for life itself and wouldn't let it go; or to pick and choose a place for me where I might experience my first kill with some measure of quiet and dignity. He rushed headlong through the encounter as if it were something to put behind us as quickly as possible, like so many yards of the road. Once he had caught the slave, he gagged him and held him, baring his neck. 'Do it,' he said. 'You can't turn back now.' Overcome with revulsion and weak with frustration, I obeyed. I knelt beside the bent, struggling man and, clamping both my hands on his shoulders, I went into his neck. My teeth had only just begun to change, and I had to tear his flesh, not puncture it; but once the wound was made, the blood flowed. And once that happened, once I was locked to it, drinking . . . all else vanished.

"Lestat and the swamp and the noise of the distant camp meant nothing. Lestat might have been an insect, buzzing, lighting, then vanishing in significance. The sucking mesmerized me; the warm struggling of the man was soothing to the tension of my hands; and there came the beating of the drum again, which was the drumbeat of his heart—only this time it beat in perfect rhythm with the drumbeat of my own heart, the two resounding in every fiber of my being, until the beat began to grow slower and slower, so that each was a soft rumble that threatened to go on without end. I was drowsing, falling into weightlessness; and then Lestat pulled me back. 'He's dead, you idiot!' he said with his characteristic charm and tact. 'You don't drink after they're dead! Understand that!' I was in a frenzy for a moment, not myself, insisting to him that the man's heart still beat, and I was in an agony to clamp onto him again. I ran my hands over his chest, then grabbed at his wrists. I would have cut into his wrist if Lestat hadn't pulled me to my feet and slapped my face. This slap was astonishing. It was not painful in the ordinary way. It was a sensational shock of another sort, a rapping of the senses, so that I spun in confusion and found myself helpless and staring, my back against a cypress, the night pulsing with insects in my ears. 'You'll die if you do that,' Lestat was saying. 'He'll suck you right down into death with him if you cling to him in death. And now you've drunk too much, besides; you'll be ill.' His voice grated on me. I had the urge to throw myself on him suddenly, but I was feeling just what he'd said. There was a grinding pain in my stomach, as if some whirlpool there were sucking my insides into itself. It was the blood passing too rapidly into my own blood, but I didn't know it. Lestat moved through the night now like a cat and I followed him, my head throbbing, this pain in my stomach no better when we reached the house of Pointe du Lac.

"As we sat at the table in the parlor, Lestat dealing a game of solitaire on the polished wood, I sat there staring at him with contempt. He was mumbling nonsense. I would get used to killing, he said; it would be nothing. I must not allow myself to be shaken. I was reacting too much as if the 'mortal coil' had not been shaken off. I would become accustomed to things all too quickly. 'Do you think so?' I asked him finally. I really had no interest in his answer. I understood now the difference between us. For me the experience of killing had been cataclysmic. So had that of sucking Lestat's wrist. These experiences so overwhelmed and so changed my view of everything around me, from the picture of my brother on the parlor wall to the sight of a single star in the topmost pane of the French window, that I could not imagine another vampire taking them for granted. I was altered, permanently; I knew it. And what I felt, most profoundly, for everything, even the sound of the playing cards being laid down one by one upon the shining rows of the solitaire, was respect. Lestat felt the opposite. Or he felt nothing. He was the sow's ear out of which nothing fine could be made. As boring as a mortal, as trivial and unhappy as a mortal, he chattered over the game, belittling my experience, utterly locked against the possibility of any experience of his own. By morning, I realized that I was his complete superior and I had been sadly cheated in having him for a teacher. He must guide me through the necessary lessons, if there were any more real lessons, and I must tolerate in him a frame of mind which was blasphemous to life itself. I felt cold towards him. I had no contempt in superiority. Only a hunger for new experience, for that which was beautiful and as devastating as my kill. And I saw that if I were to maximize every experience available to me, I must exert my own powers over my learning. Lestat was of no use.

"It was well past midnight when I finally rose out of the chair and went out on the gallery. The moon was large over the cypresses, and the candlelight poured from the open doors. The thick plastered pillars and walls of the house had been freshly whitewashed, the floorboards freshly swept, and a summer rain had left the night clean and sparkling with drops of water. I leaned against the end pillar of the gallery, my head touching the soft tendrils of a jasmine which grew there in constant battle with a wisteria, and I thought of what lay before me throughout the world and throughout time, and resolved to go about it delicately and reverently, learning that from each thing which would take me best to another. What this meant, I wasn't sure myself. Do you understand me when I say I did not wish to rush headlong into experience, that what I'd felt as a vampire was far too powerful to be wasted?"

"Yes," said the boy eagerly. "It sounds as if it was like being in love."

The vampire's eyes gleamed. "That's correct. It is like love." He smiled. "And I tell you my frame of mind that night so you can know there are profound differences between vampires, and how I came to take a different approach from Lestat. You must understand I did not snub him because he did not appreciate his experience. I simply could not understand how such feelings could be wasted. But then Lestat did something which was to show me a way to go about my learning.

"He had more than a casual appreciation of the wealth at Pointe du Lac. He'd been much pleased by the beauty of the china used for his father's supper; and he liked the feel of the velvet drapes, and he traced the patterns of the carpets with his toe. And now he took from one of the china closets a crystal glass and said, 'I do miss glasses.' Only he said this with an impish delight that caused me to study him with a hard eye. I disliked him intensely! 'I want to show you a little trick,' he said. 'That is, if you like glasses.' And after setting it on the card table he came out on the gallery where I stood and changed his manner again into that of a stalking animal, eyes piercing the dark beyond the lights of the house, peering down under the arching branches of the oaks. In an instant, he had vaulted the railing and dropped softly on the dirt below, and then lunged into the blackness to catch something in both his hands. When he stood before me with it, I gasped to see it was a rat. 'Don't be such a damned idiot,' he said. 'Haven't you ever seen a rat?' It was a huge, struggling field rat with a long tail. He held its neck so it couldn't bite. 'Rats can be quite nice,' he said. And he took the rat to the wine glass, slashed its throat, and filled the glass rapidly with blood. The rat then went hurtling over the gallery railing, and Lestat held the wine glass to the candle triumphantly. 'You may well have to live off rats from time to time, so wipe that expression off your face,' he said. 'Rats, chickens, cattle. Travelling by ship, you damn well better live off rats, if you don't wish to cause such a panic on board that they search your coffin. You damn well better keep the ship clean of rats.' And then he sipped the blood as delicately as if it were burgundy. He made a slight face. 'It gets cold so fast.'

" 'Do you mean, then, we can live from animals?' I asked.

" 'Yes.' He drank it all down and then casually threw the glass at the fireplace. I stared at the fragments. 'You don't mind, do you?' He gestured to the broken glass with a sarcastic smile. 'I surely hope you don't, because there's nothing much you can do about it if you do mind.'

" 'I can throw you and your father out of Pointe du Lac, if I mind,' I said. I believe this was my first show of temper.

" 'Why would you do that?' he asked with mock alarm. 'You don't know everything yet . . . do you?' He was laughing then and walking slowly about the room. He ran his fingers over the satin finish of the spinet. 'Do you play?' he asked.

"I said something like, 'Don't touch it!' and he laughed at me. 'I'll touch it if I like!' he said. 'You don't know, for example, all the ways you can die. And dying now would be *such* a calamity, wouldn't it?'

" 'There must be someone else in the world to teach me these things,' I said. 'Certainly you're not the only vampire! And your father, he's perhaps seventy. You couldn't have been a vampire long, so someone must have instructed you. . . .'

" 'And do you think you can find other vampires by yourself? They might see you coming, my friend, but you won't see them. No, I don't think you have much choice about things at this point, friend. I'm your teacher and you need me, and there isn't much you can do about it either way. And we both have people to provide for. My father needs a doctor, and then there is the matter of your mother and sister. Don't get any mortal notions about telling them you are a vampire. Just provide for them and for my father, which means that tomorrow night you had better kill fast and then attend to the business of your plantation. Now to bed. We both sleep in the same room; it makes for far less risk.'

" 'No, you secure the bedroom for yourself,' I said. 'I've no intention of staying in the same room with you.'

"He became furious. 'Don't do anything stupid, Louis. I warn you. There's nothing you can do to defend yourself once the sun rises, nothing. Separate rooms mean separate security. Double precautions and double chance of notice.' He then said a score of things to frighten me into complying, but he might as well have been talking to the walls. I watched him intently, but I didn't listen to him. He appeared frail and stupid to me, a man made of dried twigs with a thin, carping voice. 'I sleep alone,' I said, and gently put my hand around the candle flames one by one. 'It's almost morning!' he insisted.

" 'So lock yourself in,' I said, embracing my coffin, hoisting it and carrying it down the brick stairs. I could hear the locks snapping on the French doors above, the swoosh of the drapes. The sky was pale but still sprinkled with stars, and another light rain blew now on the breeze from the river, speckling the flagstones. I opened the door of my brother's oratory, shoving back the roses and thorns which had almost sealed it, and set the coffin on the stone floor before the priedieu. I could almost make out the images of the saints on the walls. 'Paul,' I said softly, addressing my brother, 'for the first time in my life I feel nothing for you, nothing for your death; and for the first time I feel everything for you, feel the sorrow of your loss as if I never before knew feeling.' You see . . ."

The vampire turned to the boy. "For the first time now I was fully and completely a vampire. I shut the wood blinds flat upon the small barred windows and bolted the door. Then I climbed into the satin-lined coffin, barely able to see the gleam of cloth in the darkness, and locked myself in. That is how I became a vampire."

AND THERE YOU WERE," said the boy after a pause, "with another vampire you hated."

"But I had to stay with him," answered the vampire. "As I've told you, he had me at a great disadvantage. He hinted there was much I didn't know and must know and that he alone could tell me. But in fact, the main part of what he did teach me was practical and not so difficult to figure out for oneself. How we might travel, for instance, by ship, having our coffins transported for us as though they contained the remains of loved ones being sent here or there for burial; how no one would dare to open such a coffin, and we might rise from it at night to clean the ship of rats—things of this nature. And then there were the shops and businessmen he knew who admitted us well after hours to outfit us in the finest Paris fashions, and those agents willing to transact financial matters in restaurants and cabarets. And in all of these mundane matters, Lestat was an adequate teacher. What manner of man he'd been in life, I couldn't tell and didn't care; but he was for all appearances of the same class now as myself, which meant little to me, except that it made our lives run a little more smoothly than they might have otherwise. He had impeccable taste, though my library to him was a 'pile of dust,' and he seemed more than once to be infuriated by the sight of my reading a book or writing some observations in a journal. 'That's mortal nonsense,' he would say to me, while at the same time spending so much of my money to splendidly furnish Pointe du Lac, that even I, who cared nothing for the money, was forced to wince. And in entertaining visitors at Pointe du Lac—those hapless travellers who came up the river road by horseback or carriage begging accommodations for the night, sporting letters of introduction from other planters or officials in New Orleans—to these he was so gentle and polite that it made things far easier for me, who found myself hopelessly locked to him and jarred over and over by his viciousness."

"But he didn't harm these men?" asked the boy.

"Oh yes, often, he did. But I'll tell you a little secret if I may, which applies not only to vampires, but to generals, soldiers, and kings. Most of us would much rather see somebody die than be the object of rudeness under our roofs. Strange . . . yes. But very true, I assure you. That Lestat hunted for mortals every night, I knew. But had he been savage and ugly to my family, my guests, and my slaves, I couldn't have endured it. He was not. He seemed particularly to delight in the visitors. But he said we must spare no expense where our families were concerned. And he seemed to me to push luxury upon his father to an almost ludicrous point. The old blind man must be told constantly how fine and expensive were his bed jackets and robes and what imported draperies had just been fixed to his bed and what French and Spanish wines we had in the cellar and how much the plantation yielded even in bad years when the coast talked of abandoning the indigo production altogether and going into sugar. But then at other times he would bully the old man, as I mentioned. He would erupt into such rage that the old man whimpered like a child. 'Don't I take care of you in baronial splendor!' Lestat would shout at him. 'Don't I provide for your every want! Stop whining to me about going to church or old friends! Such nonsense. Your old friends are dead. Why don't you die and leave me and my bankroll in peace!' The old man would cry softly that these things meant so little to him in old age. He would have been content on his little farm forever. I wanted often to ask him later, 'Where was this farm? From where did you come to Louisiana?' to get some clue to that place where Lestat might have known another vampire. But I didn't dare to bring these things up, lest the old man start crying and Lestat become enraged. But these fits were no more frequent than periods of near obsequious kindness when Lestat would bring his father supper on a tray and feed him patiently while talking of the weather and the New Orleans news and the activities of my mother and sister. It was obvious that a great gulf existed between father and son, both in education and refinement, but how it came about, I could not quite guess. And from this whole matter, I achieved a somewhat consistent detachment.

"Existence, as I've said, was possible. There was always the promise behind his mocking smile that he knew great things or terrible things, had commerce with levels of darkness I could not possibly guess at. And all the time, he belittled me and attacked me for my love of the senses, my reluctance to kill, and the near swoon which killing could produce in me. He laughed uproariously when I discovered that I could see myself in a mirror and that crosses had no effect upon me, and would taunt me with sealed lips when I asked about God or the devil. 'I'd like to meet the devil some night,' he said once with a malignant smile. 'I'd chase him from here to the wilds of the Pacific. I am the devil.' And when I was aghast at this, he went into peals of laughter. But what happened was simply that in my distaste for him I came to ignore and suspect him, and yet to study him with a detached fascination. Sometimes I'd find myself staring at his wrist from which I'd drawn my vampire life, and I would fall into such a stillness that my mind seemed to leave my body or rather my body to become my mind; and then he would see me and stare at me with a stubborn ignorance of what I felt and longed to know and, reaching over, shake me roughly out of it. I bore this with an overt detachment unknown to me in mortal life and came to understand this as a part of vampire nature: that I might sit at home at Pointe du Lac and think for hours of my brother's mortal life and see it short and rounded in unfathomable darkness, understanding now the vain and senseless wasting passion with which I'd mourned his loss and turned on other mortals like a maddened animal. All that confusion was then like dancers frenzied in a fog; and now, now in this strange vampire nature, I felt a profound sadness. But I did not brood over this. Let me not give you that impression, for brooding would have been to me the most terrible waste; but rather I looked around me at all the mortals that I knew and saw all life as precious, condemning all fruitless guilt and passion that would let it slip through the fingers like sand. It was only now as a vampire that I did come to know my sister, forbidding her the plantation for the city life which she so needed in order to know her own time of life and her own beauty and come to marry, not brood for our lost brother or my going away or become a nursemaid for our mother. And I provided for them all they might need or want, finding even the most trivial request worth my immediate attention. My sister laughed at the transformation in me when we would meet at night and I would take her from our flat out the narrow wooden streets to walk along the tree-lined levee in the moonlight, savoring the orange blossoms and the caressing warmth, talking for hours of her most secret thoughts and dreams, those little fantasies she dared tell no one and would even whisper to me when we sat in the dim-lit parlor entirely alone. And I would see her sweet and palpable before me, a shimmering, precious creature soon to grow old, soon to die, soon to lose these moments that in their intangibility promised to us, wrongly . . . wrongly, an immortality. As if it were our very birthright, which we could not come to grasp the meaning of until this time of middle life when we looked on only as many years ahead as already lay behind us. When every moment, every moment must be first known and then savored.

"It was detachment that made this possible, a sublime loneliness with which Lestat and I moved through the world of mortal men. And all material troubles passed from us. I should tell you the practical nature of it.

"Lestat had always known how to steal from victims chosen for sumptuous dress and other promising signs of extravagance. But the great problems of shelter and secrecy had been for him a terrible struggle. I suspected that beneath his gentleman's veneer he was painfully ignorant of the most simple financial matters. But I was not. And so he could acquire cash at any moment and I could invest it. If he were not picking the pocket of a dead man in an alley, he was at the greatest gambling tables in the richest salons of the city, using his vampire keenness to suck gold and dollars and deeds of property from young planters' sons who found him deceptive in his friendship and alluring in his charm. But this had never given him the life he wanted, and so for that he had ushered me into the preternatural world that he might acquire an investor and manager for whom these skills of mortal life became most valuable in this life after.

"But, let me describe New Orleans, as it was then, and as it was to become, so you can understand how simple our lives were. There was no city in America like New Orleans. It was filled not only with the French and Spanish of all classes who had formed in part its peculiar aristocracy, but later with immigrants of all kinds, the Irish and the German in particular. Then there were not only the black slaves, yet unhomogenized and fantastical in their different tribal garb and manners, but the great growing class of the free people of color, those marvellous people of our mixed blood and that of the islands, who produced a magnificent and unique caste of craftsmen, artists, poets, and renowned feminine beauty. And then there were the Indians, who covered the levee on summer days selling herbs and crafted wares. And drifting through all, through this medley of languages and colors, were the people of the port, the sailors of the ships, who came in great waves to spend their money in the cabarets, to buy for the night the beautiful women both dark and light, to dine on the best of Spanish and French cooking and drink the imported wines of the world. Then add to these, within years after my transformation, the Americans, who built the city up river from the old French Quarter with magnificent Grecian houses which gleamed in the moonlight like temples. And, of course, the planters, always the planters, coming to town with their families in shining landaus to buy evening gowns and silver and gems, to crowd the narrow streets on the way to the old French Opera House and the Théâtre d'Orléans and the St. Louis Cathedral, from whose open doors came the chants of High Mass over the crowds of the Place d'Armes on Sundays, over the noise and bickering of the French Market, over the silent, ghostly drift of the ships along the raised waters of the Mississippi, which flowed against the levee above the ground of New Orleans itself, so that the ships appeared to float against the sky.

"This was New Orleans, a magical and magnificent place to live. In which a vampire, richly dressed and gracefully walking through the pools of light of one gas lamp after another might attract no more notice in the evening than hundreds of other exotic creatures—if he attracted any at all, if anyone stopped to whisper behind a fan, 'That man . . . how pale, how he gleams . . . how he moves. It's not natural!' A city in which a vampire might be gone before the words had even passed the lips, seeking out the alleys in which he could see like a cat, the darkened bars in which sailors slept with their heads on the tables, great high-ceilinged hotel rooms where a lone figure might sit, her feet upon an embroidered cushion, her legs covered with a lace counterpane, her head bent under the tarnished light of a single candle, never seeing the great shadow move across the plaster flowers of the ceiling, never seeing the long white fingers reached to press the fragile flame.

"Remarkable, if for nothing else, because of this, that all of those men and women who stayed for any reason left behind them some monument, some structure of marble and brick and stone that still stands; so that even when the gas lamps went out and the planes came in and the office buildings crowded the blocks of Canal Street, something irreducible of beauty and romance remained; not in every street perhaps, but in so many that the landscape is for me the landscape of those times always, and walking now in the starlit streets of the Quarter or the Garden District I am in those times again. I suppose that is the nature of the monument. Be it a small house or a mansion of Corinthian columns and wrought-iron lace. The monument does not say that this or that man walked here. No, that what he felt in one time in one spot continues. The moon that rose over New Orleans then still rises. As long as the monuments stand, it still rises. The feeling, at least here . . . and there . . . it remains the same."

The vampire appeared sad. He sighed, as if he doubted what he had just said. "What was it?" he asked suddenly as if he were slightly tired. "Yes, money. Lestat and I had to make money. And I was telling you that he could steal. But it was investment afterwards that mattered. What we accumulated we must use. But I go ahead of myself. I killed animals. But I'll get to that in a moment. Lestat killed humans all the time, sometimes two or three a night, sometimes more. He would drink from one just enough to satisfy a momentary thirst, and then go on to another. The better the human, as he would say in his vulgar way, the more he liked it. A fresh young girl, that was his favorite food the first of the evening; but the triumphant kill for Lestat was a young man. A young man around your age would have appealed to him in particular."

"Me?" the boy whispered. He had leaned forward on his elbows to peer into the vampire's eyes, and now he drew up.

"Yes," the vampire went on, as if he hadn't observed the boy's change of expression. "You see, they represented the greatest loss to Lestat, because they stood on the threshold of the maximum possibility of life. Of course, Lestat didn't understand this himself. I came to understand it. Lestat understood nothing.

"I shall give you a perfect example of what Lestat liked. Up the river from us was the Freniere plantation, a magnificent spread of land which had great hopes of making a fortune in sugar, just shortly after the refining process had been invented. I presume you know sugar was refined in Louisiana. There is something perfect and ironic about it, this land which I loved producing refined sugar. I mean this more unhappily than I think you know. This refined sugar is a poison. It was like the essence of life in New Orleans, so sweet that it can be fatal, so richly enticing that all other values are forgotten. . . . But as I was saying, up river from us lived the Frenieres, a great old

French family which had produced in this generation five young women and one young man. Now, three of the young women were destined not to marry, but two were young enough still and all depended upon the young man. He was to manage the plantation as I had done for my mother and sister; he was to negotiate marriages, to put together dowries when the entire fortune of the place rode precariously on the next year's sugar crop; he was to bargain, fight, and keep at a distance the entire material world for the world of Freniere. Lestat decided he wanted him. And when fate alone nearly cheated Lestat, he went wild. He risked his own life to get the Freniere boy, who had become involved in a duel. He had insulted a young Spanish Creole at a ball. The whole thing was nothing, really; but like most young Creoles this one was willing to die for nothing. They were both willing to die for nothing. The Freniere household was in an uproar. You must understand, Lestat knew this perfectly. Both of us had hunted the Freniere plantation, Lestat for slaves and chicken thieves and me for animals."

"You were killing *only* animals?"

"Yes. But I'll come to that later, as I said. We both knew the plantation, and I had indulged in one of the greatest pleasures of a vampire, that of watching people unbeknownst to them. I knew the Freniere sisters as I knew the magnificent rose trees around my brother's oratory. They were a unique group of women. Each in her own way was as smart as the brother; and one of them, I shall call her Babette, was not only as smart as her brother, but far wiser. Yet none had been educated to care for the plantation; none understood even the simplest facts about its financial state. All were totally dependent upon young Freniere, and all knew it. And so, larded with their love for him, their passionate belief that he hung the moon and that any conjugal love they might ever know would only be a pale reflection of their love for him, larded with this was a desperation as strong as the will to survive. If Freniere died in the duel, the plantation would collapse. Its fragile economy, a life of splendor based on the perennial mortgaging of the next year's crop, was in his hands alone. So you can imagine the panic and misery in the Freniere household the night that the son went to town to fight the appointed duel. And now picture Lestat, gnashing his teeth like a comic-opera devil because he was not going to kill the young Freniere."

"You mean then . . . that you *felt* for the Freniere women?"

"I felt for them totally," said the vampire. "Their position was agonizing. And I felt for the boy. That night he locked himself in his father's study and made a will. He knew full well that if he fell under the rapier at four a.m. the next morning, his family would fall with him. He deplored his situation and yet could do nothing to help it. To run out on the duel would not only mean social ruin for him, but would probably have been impossible. The other young man would have pursued him until he was forced to fight. When he left the plantation at midnight, he was staring into the face of death itself with the character of a man who, having only one path to follow, has resolved to follow it with perfect courage. He would either kill the Spanish boy or die; it was unpredictable, despite all his skill. His face reflected a depth of feeling and wisdom I'd never seen on the face of any of Lestat's struggling victims. I had my first battle with Lestat then and there. I'd prevented him from killing the boy for months, and now he meant to kill him before the Spanish boy could.

"We were on horseback, racing after the young Freniere towards New Orleans, Lestat bent on overtaking him, I bent on overtaking Lestat. Well, the duel, as I told you, was scheduled for four a.m. On the edge of the swamp just beyond the city's northern gate. And arriving there just shortly before four, we had precious little time to return to Pointe du Lac, which meant our own lives were in danger. I was incensed at Lestat as never before, and he was determined to get the boy. 'Give him his chance!' I was insisting, getting hold of Lestat before he could approach the boy. It was midwinter, bitter-cold and damp in the swamps, one volley of icy rain after another sweeping the clearing where the duel was to be fought. Of course, I did not fear these elements in the sense that you might; they did not numb me, nor threaten me with mortal shivering or illness. But vampires feel cold as acutely as humans, and the blood of the kill is often the rich, sensual alleviation of that cold. But what concerned me that morning was not the pain I felt, but the excellent cover of darkness these elements provided, which made Freniere extremely vulnerable to Lestat's attack. All he need do would be to step away from his two friends towards the swamp and Lestat might take him. And so I physically grappled with Lestat. I held him."

"But towards all this you had detachment, distance?"

"Hmmm . . ." The vampire sighed. "Yes. I had it, and with it a supremely resolute anger. To glut himself upon the life of an entire family was to me Lestat's supreme act of utter contempt and disregard for all he should have seen with a vampire's depth. So I held him in the dark, where he spit at me and cursed at me; and young Freniere took his rapier from his friend and second and went out on the slick, wet grass to meet his opponent. There was a brief conversation, then the duel commenced. In moments, it was over. Freniere had mortally wounded the other boy with a swift thrust to the chest. And he knelt in the grass, bleeding, dying, shouting something unintelligible at Freniere. The victor simply stood there. Everyone could see there was no sweetness in the victory. Freniere looked on death as if it were an abomination. His companions advanced with their lanterns, urging him to come away as soon as possible and leave the dying man to his friends. Meantime, the wounded one would allow no one to touch him. And then, as Freniere's group turned to go, the three of them walking heavily towards their horses, the man on the ground drew a pistol. Perhaps I alone could see this in the powerful dark. But, in any event, I shouted to Freniere as I ran towards the gun. And this was all that Lestat needed. While I was lost in my clumsiness, distracting Freniere and going for the gun itself, Lestat, with his years of experience and superior speed, grabbed the young man and spirited him into the cypresses. I doubt his friends even knew what had happened. The pistol had gone off, the wounded man had collapsed, and I was tearing through the near-frozen marshes shouting for Lestat.

"Then I saw him. Freniere lay sprawled over the knobbed

roots of a cypress, his boots deep in the murky water, and Lestat was still bent over him, one hand on the hand of Freniere that still held the foil. I went to pull Lestat off, and that right hand swung at me with such lightning speed I did not see it, did not know it had struck me until I found myself in the water also; and, of course, by the time I recovered, Freniere was dead. I saw him as he lay there, his eyes closed, his lips utterly still as if he were just sleeping. 'Damn you!' I began cursing Lestat. And then I started, for the body of Freniere had begun to slip down into the marsh. The water rose over his face and covered him completely. Lestat was jubilant; he reminded me tersely that we had less than an hour to get back to Pointe du Lac, and he swore revenge on me. 'If I didn't like the life of a Southern planter, I'd finish you tonight. I know a way,' he threatened me. 'I ought to drive your horse into the swamps. You'd have to dig yourself a hole and smother!' He rode off.

"Even over all these years, I feel that anger for him like a white-hot liquid filling my veins. I saw then what being a vampire meant to him."

"He was just a killer," the boy said, his voice reflecting some of the vampire's emotion. "No regard for anything."

"No. Being a vampire for him meant revenge. Revenge against life itself. Every time he took a life it was revenge. It was no wonder, then, that he appreciated nothing. The nuances of vampire existence weren't even available to him because he was focused with a maniacal vengeance upon the mortal life he'd left. Consumed with hatred, he looked back. Consumed with envy, nothing pleased him unless he could take it from others; and once having it, he grew cold and dissatisfied, not loving the thing for itself; and so he went after something else. Vengeance, blind and sterile and contemptible.

"But I've spoken to you about the Freniere sisters. It was almost half past five when I reached their plantation. Dawn would come shortly after six, but I was almost home. I slipped onto the upper gallery of their house and saw them all gathered in the parlor; they had never even dressed for bed. The candles burnt low, and they sat already as mourners, waiting for the word. They were all dressed in black, as was their at-home custom, and in the dark the black shapes of their dresses massed together with their raven hair, so that in the glow of the candles their faces appeared as five soft, shimmering apparitions, each uniquely sad, each uniquely courageous. Babette's face alone appeared resolute. It was as if she had already made up her mind to take the burdens of Freniere if her brother died, and she had that same expression on her face now which had been on her brother's when he mounted to leave for the duel. What lay ahead of her was nearly impossible. What lay ahead was the final death of which Lestat was guilty. So I did something then which caused me great risk. I made myself known to her. I did this by playing the light. As you can see, my face is very white and has a smooth, highly reflective surface, rather like that of polished marble."

"Yes," the boy nodded, and appeared flustered. "It's very . . . beautiful, actually," said the boy. "I wonder if . . . but what happened?"

"You wonder if I was a handsome man when I was alive," said the vampire. The boy nodded. "I was. Nothing structurally is changed in me. Only I never knew that I was handsome. Life whirled about me a wind of petty concerns, as I've said. I gazed at nothing, not even a mirror . . . especially not a mirror . . . with a free eye. But this is what happened. I stepped near to the pane of glass and let the light touch my face. And this I did at a moment when Babette's eyes were turned towards the panes. Then I appropriately vanished.

"Within seconds all the sisters knew a 'strange creature' had been seen, a ghostlike creature, and the two slave maids steadfastly refused to investigate. I waited out these moments impatiently for just that which I wanted to happen: Babette finally took a candelabrum from a side table, lit the candles, and, scorning everyone's fear, ventured out onto the cold gallery alone to see what was there, her sisters hovering in the door like great, black birds, one of them crying that the brother was dead and she had indeed seen his ghost. Of course, you must understand that Babette, being as strong as she was, never once attributed what she saw to imagination or to ghosts. I let her come the length of the dark gallery before I spoke to her, and even then I let her see only the vague outline of my body beside one of the columns. 'Tell your sisters to go back,' I whispered to her. 'I come to tell you of your brother. Do as I say.' She was still for an instant, and then she turned to me and strained to see me in the dark. 'I have only a little time. I would not harm you for the world,' I said. And she obeyed. Saying it was nothing, she told them to shut the door, and they obeyed as people obey who not only need a leader but are desperate for one. Then I stepped into the light of Babette's candles."

The boy's eyes were wide. He put his hand to his lips. "Did you look to her . . . as you do to me?" he asked.

"You ask that with such innocence," said the vampire. "Yes, I suppose I certainly did. Only, by candlelight I always had a less supernatural appearance. And I made no pretense with her of being an ordinary creature. 'I have only minutes,' I told her at once. 'But what I have to tell you is of the greatest importance. Your brother fought bravely and won the duel—but wait. You must know now, he is dead. Death was proverbial with him, the thief in the night about which all his goodness or courage could do nothing. But this is not the principal thing which I came to tell you. It is this. You can rule the plantation and you can save it. All that is required is that you let no one convince you otherwise. You must assume his position despite any outcry, any talk of convention, any talk of propriety or common sense. You must listen to nothing. The same land is here now that was here yesterday morning when your brother slept above. Nothing is changed. You must take his place. If you do not, the land is lost and the family is lost. You will be five women on a small pension doomed to live but half or less of what life could give you. Learn what you must know. Stop at nothing until you have the answers. And take my visitation to you to be your courage whenever you waver. You must take the reins of your own life. Your brother is dead.'

"I could see by her face that she had heard every word. She would have questioned me had there been time, but she believed me when I said there was not. Then I used all my skill to leave her so swiftly I appeared to vanish. From the garden I saw her face above in the glow of her candles. I saw her search the dark for me, turning around and around. And then I saw her make the Sign of the Cross and walk back to her sisters within."

The vampire smiled. "There was absolutely no talk on the river coast of any strange apparition to Babette Freniere, but after the first mourning and sad talk of the women left all alone, she became the scandal of the neighborhood because she chose to run the plantation on her own. She managed an immense dowry for her younger sister, and was married herself in another year. And Lestat and I almost never exchanged words."

"Did he go on living at Pointe du Lac?"

"Yes. I could not be certain he'd told me all I needed to know. And great pretense was necessary. My sister was married in my absence, for example, while I had a 'malarial chill,' and something similar overcame me the morning of my mother's funeral. Meantime, Lestat and I sat down to dinner each night with the old man and made nice noises with our knives and forks, while he told us to eat everything on our plates and not to drink our wine too fast. With dozens of miserable headaches I would receive my sister in a darkened bedroom, the covers up to my chin, bid her and her husband bear with the dim light on account of the pain in my eyes, as I entrusted to them large amounts of money to invest for us all. Fortunately her husband was an idiot; a harmless one, but an idiot, the product of four generations of marriages between first cousins.

"But though these things went well, we began to have our problems with the slaves. They were the suspicious ones; and, as I've indicated, Lestat killed anyone and everyone he chose. So there was always some talk of mysterious death on that part of the coast. But it was what they saw of us which began the talk, and I heard it one evening when I was playing a shadow about the slave cabins.

"Now, let me explain first the character of these slaves. It was only about seventeen ninety-five, Lestat and I having lived there for four years in relative quiet, I investing the money which he acquired, increasing our lands, purchasing apartments and town houses in New Orleans which I rented, the work of the plantation itself producing little . . . more a cover for us than an investment. I say 'our.' This is wrong. I never signed anything over to Lestat, and, as you realize, I was still legally alive. But in seventeen ninety-five these slaves did not have the character which you've seen in films and novels of the South. They were not soft-spoken, brown-skinned people in drab rags who spoke an English dialect. They were Africans. And they were islanders; that is, some of them had come from Santo Domingo. They were very black and totally foreign; they spoke in their African tongues, and they spoke the French patois; and when they sang, they sang African songs which made the fields exotic and strange, always frightening to me in my mortal life. They were superstitious and had their own secrets and traditions. In short, they had not yet been destroyed as Africans completely. Slavery was the curse of their existence; but they had not been robbed yet of that which had been characteristically theirs. They tolerated the baptism and modest garments imposed on them by the French Catholic laws; but in the evenings, they made their cheap fabrics into alluring costumes, made jewelry of animal bones and bits of discarded metal which they polished to look like gold; and the slave cabins of Pointe du Lac were a foreign country, an African coast after dark, in which not even the coldest overseer would want to wander. No fear for the vampire.

"Not until one summer evening when, passing for a shadow, I heard through the open doors of the black foreman's cottage a conversation which convinced me that Lestat and I slept in real danger. The slaves knew now we were not ordinary mortals. In hushed tones, the maids told of how, through a crack in the door, they had seen us dine on empty plates with empty silver, lifting empty glasses to our lips, laughing, our faces bleached and ghostly in the candlelight, the blind man a helpless fool in our power. Through keyholes they had seen Lestat's coffin, and once he had beaten one of them mercilessly for dawdling by the gallery windows of his room. 'There is no bed in there,' they confided one to the other with nodding heads. 'He sleeps in the coffin, I know it.' They were convinced, on the best of grounds, of what we were. And as for me, they'd seen me evening after evening emerge from the oratory, which was now little more than a shapeless mass of brick and vine, layered with flowering wisteria in the spring, wild roses in summer, moss gleaming on the old unpainted shutters which had never been opened, spiders spinning in the stone arches. Of course, I'd pretended to visit it in memory of Paul, but it was clear by their speech they no longer believed such lies. And now they attributed to us not only the deaths of slaves found in the fields and swamps and also the dead cattle and occasional horses, but all other strange events; even floods and thunder were the weapons of God in a personal battle waged with Louis and Lestat. But worse still, they were not planning to run away. We were devils. Our power inescapable. No, we must be destroyed. And at this gathering, where I became an unseen member, were a number of the Freniere slaves.

"This meant word would get to the entire coast. And though I firmly believed the entire coast to be impervious to a wave of hysteria, I did not intend to risk notice of any kind. I hurried back to the plantation house to tell Lestat our game of playing planter was over. He'd have to give up his slave whip and golden napkin ring and move into town.

"He resisted, naturally. His father was gravely ill and might not live. He had no intention of running away from stupid slaves. 'I'll kill them all,' he said calmly, 'in threes and fours. Some will run away and that will be fine.'

" 'You're talking madness. The fact is I want you gone from here.'

" 'You want me gone! You,' he sneered. He was building a card palace on the dining room table with a pack of very fine French cards. 'You whining coward of a vampire who prowls the night killing alley cats and rats and staring for hours at candles as if they were people and standing in the rain like a zombie until your clothes are drenched and you smell like old wardrobe trunks in attics and have the look of a baffled idiot at the zoo.'

" 'You've nothing more to tell me, and your insistence on recklessness has endangered us both. I might live in that oratory alone while this house fell to ruin. I don't care about it!' I told him. Because this was quite true. 'But you must have all the things you never had of life and make of immortality a junk shop in which both of us become grotesque. Now, go look at your father and tell me how long he has to live, for that's how long you stay, and only if the slaves don't rise up against us!'

"He told me then to go look at his father myself, since I was the one who was always 'looking,' and I did. The old man was truly dying. I had been spared my mother's death, more or less, because she had died very suddenly on an afternoon. She'd been found with her sewing basket, seated quietly in the courtyard; she had died as one goes to sleep. But now I was seeing a natural death that was too slow with agony and with consciousness. And I'd always liked the old man; he was kindly and simple and made few demands. By day, he sat in the sun of the gallery dozing and listening to the birds; by night, any chatter on our part kept him company. He could play chess, carefully feeling each piece and remembering the entire state of the board with remarkable accuracy; and though Lestat would never play with him, I did often. Now he lay gasping for breath, his forehead hot and wet, the pillow around him stained with sweat. And as he moaned and prayed for death, Lestat in the other room began to play the spinet. I slammed it shut, barely missing his fingers. 'You won't play while he dies!' I said. 'The hell I won't!' he answered me. 'I'll play the drum if I like!' And taking a great sterling silver platter from a sideboard he slipped a finger through one of its handles and beat it with a spoon.

"I told him to stop it, or I would make him stop it. And then we both ceased our noise because the old man was calling his name. He was saying that he must talk to Lestat now before he died. I told Lestat to go to him. The sound of his crying was terrible. 'Why should I? I've cared for him all these years. Isn't that enough?' And he drew from his pocket a nail file, and, seating himself on the foot of the old man's bed, he began to file his long nails.

"Meantime, I should tell you that I was aware of slaves about the house. They were watching and listening. I was truly hoping the old man would die within minutes. Once or twice before I'd dealt with suspicion or doubt on the part of several slaves, but never such a number. I immediately rang for Daniel, the slave to whom I'd given the overseer's house and position. But while I waited for him, I could hear the old man talking to Lestat; Lestat, who sat with his legs crossed, filing and filing, one eyebrow arched, his attention on his perfect nails. 'It was the school,' the old man was saying. 'Oh, I know you remember . . . what can I say to you . . .' he moaned.

" 'You'd better say it,' Lestat said, 'because you're about to die.' The old man let out a terrible noise, and I suspect I made some sound of my own. I positively loathed Lestat. I had a mind now to get him out of the room. 'Well, you know that, don't you? Even a fool like you knows that,' said Lestat.

" 'You'll never forgive me, will you? Not now, not even after I'm dead,' said the old man.

" 'I don't know what you're talking about!' said Lestat.

"My patience was becoming exhausted with him, and the old man was becoming more and more agitated. He was begging Lestat to listen to him with a warm heart. The whole thing was making me shudder. Meantime, Daniel had come, and I knew the moment I saw him that everything at Pointe du Lac was lost. Had I been more attentive I'd have seen signs of it before now. He looked at me with eyes of glass. I was a monster to him. 'Monsieur Lestat's father is very ill. Going,' I said, ignoring his expression. 'I want no noise tonight; the slaves must all stay within the cabins. A doctor is on his way.' He stared at me as if I were lying. And then his eyes moved curiously and coldly away from me towards the old man's door. His face underwent such a change that I rose at once and looked in the room. It was Lestat, slouched at the foot of the bed, his back to the bedpost, his nail file working furiously, grimacing in such a way that both his great teeth showed prominently."

The vampire stopped, his shoulders shaking with silent laughter. He was looking at the boy. And the boy looked shyly at the table. But he had already looked, and fixedly, at the vampire's mouth. He had seen that the lips were of a different texture from the vampire's skin, that they were silken and delicately lined like any person's lips, only deadly white; and he had glimpsed the white teeth. Only, the vampire had such a way of smiling that they were not completely revealed; and the boy had not even thought of such teeth until now. "You can imagine," said the vampire, "what this meant.

"I had to kill him."

"You what?" said the boy.

"I had to kill him. He started to run. He would have alarmed everyone. Perhaps it might have been handled some other way, but I had no time. So I went after him, overpowering him. But then, finding myself in the act of doing what I had not done for four years, I stopped. This was a man. He had his bone-handle knife in his hand to defend himself. And I took it from him easily and slipped it into his heart. He sank to his knees at once, his fingers tightening on the blade, bleeding on it. And the sight of the blood, the aroma of it, maddened me. I believe I moaned aloud. But I did not reach for him, I would not. Then I remember seeing Lestat's figure emerge in the mirror over the sideboard. 'Why did you do this!' he demanded. I turned to face him, determined he would not see me in this weakened state. The old man was delirious, he went on, he could not understand what the old man was saying. 'The slaves, they know . . . you must go to the cabins and keep watch,' I managed to say to him. 'I'll care for the old man.'

" 'Kill him,' Lestat said.

" 'Are you mad!' I answered. 'He's your father!'

" 'I know he's my father!' said Lestat. 'That's why you have to kill him. I can't kill him! If I could, I would have done it a long time ago, damn him!' He wrung his hands. 'We've got to get out of here. And look what you've done killing this one. There's no time to lose. His wife will be wailing up here in minutes . . . or she'll send someone worse!' "

The vampire sighed. "This was all true. Lestat was right. I could hear the slaves gathering around Daniel's cottage, waiting for him. Daniel had been brave enough to come into the haunted house alone. When he didn't return, the slaves would panic, become a mob. I told Lestat to calm them, to use all his power as a white master over them and not to alarm them with horror, and then I went into the bedroom and shut the door. I had then another shock in a night of shocks. Because I'd never seen Lestat's father as he was then.

"He was sitting up now, leaning forward, talking to Lestat, begging Lestat to answer him, telling him he understood his bitterness better than Lestat did himself. And he was a living corpse. Nothing animated his sunken body but a fierce will: hence, his eyes for their gleam were all the more sunken in his skull, and his lips in their trembling made his old yellowed mouth more horrible. I sat at the foot of the bed, and, suffering to see him so, I gave him my hand. I cannot tell you how much his appearance had shaken me. For when I bring death, it is swift and consciousless, leaving the victim as if in enchanted sleep. But this was the slow decay, the body refusing to surrender to the vampire of time which had sucked upon it for years on end. 'Lestat,' he said. 'Just for once, don't be hard with me. Just for once, be for me the boy you were. My son.' He said this over and over, the words, 'My son, my son'; and then he said something I could not hear about innocence and innocence destroyed. But I could see that he was not out of his mind, as Lestat thought, but in some terrible state of lucidity. The burden of the past was on him with full force; and the present, which was only death, which he fought with all his will, could do nothing to soften that burden. But I knew I might deceive him if I used all my skill, and, bending close to him now, I whispered the word, 'Father.' It was not Lestat's voice, it was mine, a soft whisper. But he calmed at once and I thought then he might die. But he held my hand as if he were being pulled under by dark ocean waves and I alone could save him. He talked now of some country teacher, a name garbled, who found in Lestat a brilliant pupil and begged to take him to a monastery for an education. He cursed himself for bringing Lestat home, for burning his books. 'You must forgive me, Lestat,' he cried.

"I pressed his hand tightly, hoping this might do for some answer, but he repeated this again. 'You have it all to live for, but you are as cold and brutal as I was then with the work always there and the cold and hunger! Lestat, you must remember. You were the gentlest of them all! God will forgive me if you forgive me.'

"Well, at that moment, the real Esau came through the door. I gestured for quiet, but he wouldn't see that. So I had to get up quickly so the father wouldn't hear his voice from a distance. The slaves had run from him. 'But they're out there, they're gathered in the dark. I hear them,' said Lestat. And then he glared at the old man. 'Kill him, Louis!' he said to me, his voice touched with the first pleading I'd ever heard in it. Then he bit down in rage. 'Do it!'

" 'Lean over that pillow and tell him you forgive him all, forgive him for taking you out of school when you were a boy! Tell him that now.'

" 'For what!' Lestat grimaced, so that his face looked like a skull. 'Taking me out of school!' He threw up his hands and let out a terrible roar of desperation. 'Damn him! Kill him!' he said.

" 'No!' I said. 'You forgive him. Or you kill him yourself. Go on. Kill your own father.'

"The old man begged to be told what we were saying. He called out, 'Son, son,' and Lestat danced like the maddened Rumpelstiltskin about to put his foot through the floor. I went to the lace curtains. I could see and hear the slaves surrounding the house of Pointe du Lac, forms woven in the shadows, drawing near. 'You were Joseph among your brothers,' the old man said. 'The best of them, but how was I to know? It was when you were gone I knew, when all those years passed and they could offer me no comfort, no solace. And then you came back to me and took me from the farm, but it wasn't you. It wasn't the same boy.'

"I turned on Lestat now and veritably dragged him towards the bed. Never had I seen him so weak, and at the same time enraged. He shook me off and then knelt down near the pillow, glowering at me. I stood resolute, and whispered, 'Forgive!'

" 'It's all right, Father. You must rest easy. I hold nothing against you,' he said, his voice thin and strained over his anger.

"The old man turned on the pillow, murmuring something soft with relief, but Lestat was already gone. He stopped short in the doorway, his hands over his ears. 'They're coming!' he whispered; and then, turning just so he could see me, he said, 'Take him. For *God's sake!*'

"The old man never even knew what happened. He never awoke from his stupor. I bled him just enough, opening the gash so he would then die without feeding my dark passion. That thought I couldn't bear. I knew now it wouldn't matter if the body was found in this manner, because I had had enough of Pointe du Lac and Lestat and all this identity of Pointe du Lac's prosperous master. I would torch the house, and turn to the wealth I'd held under many names, safe for just such a moment.

"Meantime, Lestat was after the slaves. He would leave such ruin and death behind him no one could make a story of that night at Pointe du Lac, and I went with him. Always before, his ferocity was mysterious, but now I bared my fangs on the humans who fled from me, my steady advance overcoming their clumsy, pathetic speed as the veil of death descended, or the veil of madness. The power and the proof of the vampire was incontestable, so that the slaves scattered in all directions. And it was I who ran back up the steps to put the torch to Pointe du Lac.

"Lestat came bounding after me. 'What are you doing!' he shouted. 'Are you mad!' But there was no way to put out the flames. 'They're gone and you're destroying it, all of it.' He turned round and round in the magnificent parlor, amid his fragile splendor. 'Get your coffin out. You have three hours till dawn!' I said. The house was a funeral pyre."

"Could the fire have hurt you?" asked the boy.

"Most definitely!" said the vampire.

"Did you go back to the oratory? Was it safe?"

"No. Not at all. Some fifty-five slaves were scattered around the grounds. Many of them would not have desired the life of a runaway and would most certainly go right to Freniere or south to the Bel Jardin plantation down river. I had no intention of staying there that night. But there was little time to go anywhere else."

"The woman, Babette!" said the boy.

The vampire smiled. "Yes, I went to Babette. She lived now at Freniere with her young husband. I had enough time to load my coffin into the carriage and go to her."

"But what about Lestat?"

The vampire sighed. "Lestat went with me. It was his intention to go on to New Orleans, and he was trying to persuade me to do just that. But when he saw I meant to hide at Freniere, he opted for that also. We might not have ever made it to New Orleans. It was growing light. Not so that mortal eyes would have seen it, but Lestat and I could see it.

"Now, as for Babette, I had visited her once again. As I told you, she had scandalized the coast by remaining alone on the plantation without a man in the house, without even an older woman. Babette's greatest problem was that she might succeed financially only to suffer the isolation of social ostracism. She had such a sensibility that wealth itself meant nothing to her; family, a line . . . this meant something to Babette. Though she was able to hold the plantation together, the scandal was wearing on her. She was giving up inside. I came to her one night in the garden. Not permitting her to look on me, I told her in a most gentle voice that I was the same person she'd seen before. That I knew of her life and her suffering. 'Don't expect people to understand it,' I told her. 'They are fools. They want you to retire because of your brother's death. They would use your life as if it were merely oil for a proper lamp. You must defy them, but you must defy them with purity and confidence.' She was listening all the while in silence. I told her she was to give a ball for a cause. And the cause to be religious. She might pick a convent in New Orleans, any one, and plan for a philanthropic ball. She would invite her deceased mother's dearest friends to be chaperones and she would do all of this with perfect confidence. Above all, perfect confidence. It was confidence and purity which were all-important.

"Well, Babette thought this to be a stroke of genius. 'I don't know what you are, and you will not tell me,' she said. (This was true, I would not.) 'But I can only think that you are an angel.' And she begged to see my face. That is, she begged in the manner of such people as Babette, who are not given to truly begging anyone for anything. Not that Babette was proud. She was simply strong and honest, which in most cases makes begging . . . I see you want to ask me a question." The vampire stopped.

"Oh, no," said the boy, who had meant to hide it.

"But you mustn't be afraid to ask me anything. If I held something too close . . ." And when the vampire said this his face darkened for an instant. He frowned, and as his brows drew together a small well appeared in the flesh of his forehead over his left brow, as though someone had pressed it with a finger. It gave him a peculiar look of deep distress. "If I held something too close for you to ask about it, I would not bring it up in the first place," he said.

The boy found himself staring at the vampire's eyes, at the eyelashes which were like fine black wires in the tender flesh of the lids.

"Ask me," he said to the boy.

"Babette, the way you speak of her," said the boy. "As if your feeling was special."

"Did I give you the impression I could not feel?" asked the vampire.

"No, not at all. Obviously you felt for the old man. You stayed to comfort him when you were in danger. And what you felt for young Freniere when Lestat wanted to kill him . . . all this you explained. But I was wondering . . . did you have a special feeling for Babette? Was it feeling for Babette all along that caused you to protect Freniere?"

"You mean love," said the vampire. "Why do you hesitate to say it?"

"Because you spoke of detachment," said the boy.

"Do you think that angels are detached?" asked the vampire.

The boy thought for a moment. "Yes," he said.

"But aren't angels capable of love?" asked the vampire. "Don't angels gaze upon the face of God with complete love?"

The boy thought for a moment. "Love or adoration," he said.

"What is the difference?" asked the vampire thoughtfully. "What is the difference?" It was clearly not a riddle for the boy. He was asking himself. "Angels feel love, and pride . . . the pride of The Fall . . . and hatred. The strong overpowering emotions of detached persons in whom emotion and will are one," he said finally. He stared at the table now, as though he were thinking this over, were not entirely satisfied with it. "I had for Babette . . . a strong feeling. It was not the strongest I've ever known for a human being." He looked up at the boy. "But it was very strong. Babette was to me in her own way an ideal human being. . . ."

He shifted in his chair, the cape moving softly about him, and turned his face to the windows. The boy bent forward and checked the tape. Then he took another cassette from his brief case and, begging the vampire's pardon, fitted it into place. "I'm afraid I did ask something too personal. I didn't mean . . ." he said anxiously to the vampire.

"You asked nothing of the sort," said the vampire, looking at him suddenly. "It is a question right to the point. I feel love, and I felt some measure of love for Babette, though not the greatest love I've ever felt. It was foreshadowed in Babette.

"To return to my story, Babette's charity ball was a success and her re-entry in social life assured by it. Her money generously underwrote any doubts in the minds of her suitors' families, and she married. On summer nights, I used to visit her never letting her see me or know that I was there. I came to see that she was happy, and seeing her happy I felt a happiness as the result.

"And to Babette I came now with Lestat. He would have killed the Frenieres long ago if I hadn't stopped him, and he thought now that was what I meant to do. 'And what peace would that bring?' I asked. 'You call me the idiot, and you've been the idiot all along. Do you think I don't know why you made me a vampire? You couldn't live by yourself, you couldn't manage even the simplest things. For years now, I've managed everything while you sat about making a pretense of superiority. There's nothing left for you to tell me about life. I have no need of you and no use for you. It's you who need me, and if you touch but one of the Freniere slaves, I'll get rid of you. It will be a battle between us, and I needn't point out to you I have more wit to fare better in my little finger than you in your entire frame. Do as I say.'

"Well, this startled him, though it shouldn't have; and he protested he had much to tell me, of things and types of people I might kill who would cause sudden death and places in the world I must never go and so forth and so on, nonsense that I could hardly endure. But I had no time for him. The overseer's lights were lit at Freniere; he was trying to quell the excitement of the runaway slaves and his own. And the fire of Pointe du Lac could be seen still against the sky. Babette was dressed and attending to business, having sent carriages to Pointe du Lac and slaves to help fight the blaze. The frightened runaways were kept away from the others, and at that point no one regarded their stories as any more than slave foolishness. Babette knew something dreadful had happened and suspected murder, never the supernatural. She was in the study making a note of the fire in the plantation diary when I found her. It was almost morning. I had only a few minutes to convince her she must help. I spoke to her at first, refusing to let her turn around, and calmly she listened. I told her I must have a room for the night, to rest. 'I've never brought you harm. I ask you now for a key, and your promise that no one will try to enter that room until tonight.

Then I'll tell you all.' I was nearly desperate now. The sky was paling. Lestat was yards off in the orchard with the coffins. 'But why have you come to me tonight?' she asked. 'And why not to you?' I replied. 'Did I not help you at the very moment when you most needed guidance, when you alone stood strong among those who are dependent and weak? Did I not twice offer you good counsel? And haven't I watched over your happiness ever since?' I could see the figure of Lestat at the window. He was in a panic. 'Give me the key to a room. Let no one come near it till nightfall. I swear to you I would never bring you harm.' 'And if I don't . . . if I believe you come from the devil!' she said now, and meant to turn her head. I reached for the candle and put it out. She saw me standing with my back to the graying windows. 'If you don't, and if you believe me to be the devil, I shall die.' I said. 'Give me the key. I could kill you now if I chose, do you see?' And now I moved close to her and showed myself to her more completely, so that she gasped and drew back, holding to the arm of her chair. 'But I would not. I would die rather than kill you. I will die if you don't give me such a key as I ask.'

"It was accomplished. What she thought, I don't know. But she gave me one of the ground-floor storage rooms where wine was aged, and I am sure she saw Lestat and me bringing the coffins. I not only locked the door but barricaded it.

"Lestat was up the next evening when I awoke."

"Then she kept her word."

"Yes. Only she had gone a step further. She had not only respected our locked door; she had locked it again from without."

"And the stories of the slaves . . . she'd heard them."

"Yes, she had. Lestat was the first to discover we were locked in, however. He became furious. He had planned to get to New Orleans as fast as possible. He was now completely suspicious of me. 'I only needed you as long as my father lived,' he said, desperately trying to find some opening somewhere. The place was a dungeon.

" 'Now I won't put up with anything from you, I warn you.' He didn't even wish to turn his back on me. I sat there straining to hear voices in the rooms above, wishing that he would shut up, not wishing to confide for a moment my feeling for Babette or my hopes.

"I was also thinking something else. You ask me about feeling and detachment. One of its aspects—detachment with feeling, I should say—is that you can think of two things at the same time. You can think that you are not safe and may die, and you can think of something very abstract and remote. And this was definitely so with me. I was thinking at that moment, wordlessly and rather deeply, how sublime friendship between Lestat and me might have been; how few impediments to it there would have been, and how much to be shared. Perhaps it was the closeness of Babette which caused me to feel it, for how could I truly ever come to know Babette, except, of course, through the one final way; to take her life, to become one with her in an embrace of death when my soul would become one with her heart and nourished with it. But my soul wanted to know Babette without my need to kill, without robbing her of every breath of life, every drop of blood. But Lestat, how we might have known each other, had he been a man of character, a man of even a little thought. The old man's words came back to me; Lestat a brilliant pupil, a lover of books that had been burned. I knew only the Lestat who sneered at my library, called it a pile of dust, ridiculed relentlessly my reading, my meditations.

"I became aware now that the house over our heads was quieting. Now and then feet moved and the boards creaked and the light in the cracks of the boards gave a faint, uneven illumination. I could see Lestat feeling along the brick walls, his hard enduring vampire face a twisted mask of human frustration. I was confident we must part ways at once, that I must if necessary put an ocean between us. And I realized that I'd tolerated him this long because of self-doubt. I'd fooled myself into believing I stayed for the old man, and for my sister and her husband. But I stayed with Lestat because I was afraid he did know essential secrets as a vampire which I could not discover alone and, more important, because he was the only one of my kind whom I knew. He had never told me how he had become a vampire or where I might find a single other member of our kind. This troubled me greatly then, as much as it had for four years. I hated him and wanted to leave him; yet could I leave him?

"Meantime, as all this passed through my thoughts, Lestat continued his diatribe: he didn't need me; he wasn't going to put up with anything, especially not any threat from the Frenieres. We had to be ready when that door opened. 'Remember!' he said to me finally. 'Speed and strength; they cannot match us in that. And fear. Remember always, to strike fear. Don't be sentimental now! You'll cost us everything.'

" 'You wish to be on your own after this?' I asked him. I wanted him to say it. I did not have the courage. Or, rather, I did not know my own feelings.

" 'I want to get to New Orleans!' he said. 'I was simply warning you I don't need you. But to get out of here we need each other. You don't begin to know how to use your powers! You have no innate sense of what you are! Use your persuasive powers with this woman if she comes. But if she comes with others, then be prepared to act like what you are.'

" 'Which is what?' I asked him, because it had never seemed such a mystery to me as it did at that time. 'What am I?' He was openly disgusted. He threw up his hands.

" 'Be prepared . . .' he said, now baring his magnificent teeth, 'to kill!' He looked suddenly at the boards overhead. 'They're going to bed up there, do you hear them?' After a long silent time during which Lestat paced and I sat there musing, plumbing my mind for what I might do or say to Babette or, deeper still, for the answer to a harder question—what did I feel for Babette?—after a long time, a light flared beneath the door. Lestat was poised to jump whoever should open it. It was Babette alone and she entered with a lamp, not seeing Lestat, who stood behind her, but looking directly at me.

"I had never seen her as she looked then; her hair was down for bed, a mass of dark waves behind her white dressing gown; and her face was tight with worry and fear. This gave it a feverish radiance and made her large brown eyes all the more huge.

As I have told you, I loved her strength and honesty, the greatness of her soul. And I did not feel passion for her as you would feel it. But I found her more alluring than any woman I'd known in mortal life. Even in the severe dressing gown, her arms and breasts were round and soft; and she seemed to me an intriguing soul clothed in rich, mysterious flesh. I who am hard and spare and dedicated to a purpose, felt drawn to her irresistibly; and, knowing it could only culminate in death, I turned away from her at once, wondering if when she gazed into my eyes she found them dead and soulless.

" 'You are the one who came to me before,' she said now, as if she hadn't been sure. 'And you are the owner of Pointe du Lac. You are!' I knew as she spoke that she must have heard the wildest stories of last night, and there would be no convincing her of any lie. I had used my unnatural appearance twice to reach her, to speak to her; I could not hide it or minimize it now.

" 'I mean you no harm,' I said to her. 'I need only a carriage and horses . . . the horses I left last night in the pasture.' She didn't seem to hear my words; she drew closer, determined to catch me in the circle of her light.

"And then I saw Lestat behind her, his shadow merging with her shadow on the brick wall; he was anxious and dangerous. 'You will give me the carriage?' I insisted. She was looking at me now, the lamp raised; and just when I meant to look away, I saw her face change. It went still, blank, as if her soul were losing its consciousness. She closed her eyes and shook her head. It occurred to me that I had somehow caused her to go into a trance without any effort on my part. 'What are you!' she whispered. 'You're from the devil. You were from the devil when you came to me!'

" 'The devil!' I answered her. This distressed me more than I thought I could be distressed. If she believed this, then she would think my counsel bad; she would question herself. Her life was rich and good, and I knew she mustn't do this. Like all strong people, she suffered always a measure of loneliness; she was a marginal outsider, a secret infidel of a certain sort. And the balance by which she lived might be upset if she were to question her own goodness. She stared at me with undisguised horror. It was as if in horror she forgot her own vulnerable position. And now Lestat, who was drawn to weakness like a parched man to water, grabbed her wrist, and she screamed and dropped the lamp. The flames leaped in the splattered oil, and Lestat pulled her backwards towards the open door. 'You get the carriage!' he said to her. 'Get it now, and the horses. You are in mortal danger; don't talk of devils!'

"I stomped on the flames and went for Lestat, shouting at him to leave her. He held her by both wrists, and she was furious. 'You'll rouse the house if you don't shut up!' he said to me. 'And I'll kill her! Get the carriage . . . lead us. Talk to the stable boy!' he said to her, pushing her into the open air.

"We moved slowly across the dark court, my distress almost unbearable, Lestat ahead of me; and before us both Babette, who moved backwards, her eyes peering at us in the dark. Suddenly she stopped. One dim light burned in the house above. 'I'll get you nothing!' she said. I reached for Lestat's arm and told him I must handle this. 'She'll reveal us to everyone unless you let me talk to her,' I whispered to him.

" 'Then get yourself in check,' he said disgustedly. 'Be strong. Don't quibble with her.'

" 'You go as I talk . . . go to the stables and get the carriage and the horses. But don't kill!' Whether he'd obey me or not I didn't know, but he darted away just as I stepped up to Babette. Her face was a mixture of fury and resolution. She said, '*Get thee behind me, Satan.*' And I stood there before her then, speechless, just holding her in my glance as surely as she held me. If she could hear Lestat in the night she gave no indication. Her hatred for me burned me like fire.

" 'Why do you say this to me?' I asked. 'Was the counsel I gave you bad? Did I do you harm? I came to help you, to give you strength. I thought only of you, when I had no need to think of you at all.'

"She shook her head. 'But why, why do you talk to me like this?' she asked. 'I know what you've done at Pointe du Lac; you've lived there like a devil! The slaves are wild with stories!

All day men have been on the river road on the way to Pointe du Lac; my husband was there! He saw the house in ruins, the bodies of slaves throughout the orchards, the fields. *What are you!* Why do you speak to me gently! What do you want of *me?*' She clung now to the pillars of the porch and was backing slowly to the staircase. Something moved above in the lighted window.

" 'I cannot give you such answers now,' I said to her. 'Believe me when I tell you I came to you only to do you good. And would not have brought worry and care to you last night for anything, had I the choice!' "

The vampire stopped.

The boy sat forward, his eyes wide. The vampire was frozen, staring off, lost in his thoughts, his memory. And the boy looked down suddenly, as if this were the respectful thing to do. He glanced again at the vampire and then away, his own face as distressed as the vampire's; and then he started to say something, but he stopped.

The vampire turned towards him and studied him, so that the boy flushed and looked away again anxiously. But then he raised his eyes and looked into the vampire's eyes. He swallowed, but he held the vampire's gaze.

"Is this what you want?" the vampire whispered. "Is this what you wanted to hear?"

He moved the chair back soundlessly and walked to the window. The boy sat as if stunned looking at his broad shoulders and the long mass of the cape. The vampire turned his head slightly. "You don't answer me. I'm not giving you what you want, am I? You wanted an interview. Something to broadcast on the radio."

"That doesn't matter. I'll throw the tapes away if you want!" The boy rose. "I can't say I understand all you're telling me. You'd know I was lying if I said I did. So how can I ask you to go on, except to say what I do understand . . . what I do understand is like nothing I've ever understood before." He took a step towards the vampire. The vampire appeared to be looking down into Divisadero Street. Then he turned his head slowly and looked at the boy and smiled. His face was serene and almost affectionate. And the boy suddenly felt uncomfortable. He shoved his hands into his pockets and turned towards the table. Then he looked at the vampire tentatively and said, "Will you . . . please go on?"

The vampire turned with folded arms and leaned against the window. "Why?" he asked.

The boy was at a loss. "Because I want to hear it." He shrugged. "Because I want to know what happened."

"All right," said the vampire, with the same smile playing on his lips. And he went back to the chair and sat opposite the boy and turned the recorder just a little and said, "Marvellous contraption, really . . . so let me go on.

"You must understand that what I felt for Babette now was a desire for communication, stronger than any other desire I then felt . . . except for the physical desire for . . . blood. It was so strong in me, this desire, that it made me feel the depth of my capacity for loneliness. When I'd spoken to her before, there had been a brief but direct communication which was as simple and as satisfying as taking a person's hand. Clasping it. Letting it go gently. All this in a moment of great need and distress. But now we were at odds. To Babette, I was a monster; and I found it horrible to myself and would have done anything to overcome her feeling. I told her the counsel I'd given her was right, that no instrument of the devil could do right even if he chose.

" 'I know!' she answered me. But by this she meant that she could no more trust me than the devil himself. I approached her and she moved back. I raised my hand and she shrank, clutching for the railing. 'All right, then,' I said, feeling a terrible exasperation. 'Why did you protect me last night! Why have you come to me alone!' What I saw in her face was cunning. She had a reason, but she would by no means reveal it to me. It was impossible for her to speak to me freely, openly, to give me the communication I desired. I felt weary looking at her. The night was already late, and I could see and hear that Lestat had stolen into the wine cellar and taken our caskets, and I had a need to get away; and other needs besides . . . the need to kill and drink.

But it wasn't that which made me weary. It was something else, something far worse. It was as if this night were only one of thousands of nights, world without end, night curving into night to make a great arching line of which I couldn't see the end, a night in which I roamed alone under cold, mindless stars. I think I turned away from her and put my hand to my eyes. I felt oppressed and weak suddenly. I think I was making some sound without my will. And then on this vast and desolate landscape of night, where I was standing alone and where Babette was only an illusion, I saw suddenly a possibility that I'd never considered before, a possibility from which I'd fled, rapt as I was with the world, fallen into the senses of the vampire, in love with color and shape and sound and singing and softness and infinite variation. Babette was moving, but I took no note of it. She was taking something from her pocket; her great ring of household keys jingled there. She was moving up the steps. Let her go away, I was thinking. 'Creature of the devil!' I whispered. 'Get thee behind me, Satan,' I repeated. I turned to look at her now. She was frozen on the steps, with wide suspicious eyes. She'd reached the lantern which hung on the wall, and she held it in her hands just staring at me, holding it tight, like a valuable purse. 'You think I come from the devil?' I asked her.

"She quickly moved her left fingers around the hook of the lantern and with her right hand made the Sign of the Cross, the Latin words barely audible to me; and her face blanched and her eyebrows rose when there was absolutely no change because of it. 'Did you expect me to go up in a puff of smoke?' I asked her. I drew closer now, for I had gained detachment from her by virtue of my thoughts. 'And where would I go?' I asked her. 'And where would I go, to hell, from whence I came? To the devil, from whom I came?' I stood at the foot of the steps. 'Suppose I told you I know nothing of the devil. Suppose I told you that I do not even know if he exists!' It was the devil I'd seen upon the landscape of my thoughts; it was the devil about whom I thought now. I turned away from her. She wasn't hearing me as you are now. She wasn't listening. I looked up at the stars.

Lestat was ready, I knew it. It was as if he'd been ready there with the carriage for years; and she had stood upon the step for years. I had the sudden sensation my brother was there and had been there for ages also, and that he was talking to me low in an excited voice, and what he was saying was desperately important but it was going away from me as fast as he said it, like the rustle of rats in the rafters of an immense house. There was a scraping sound and a burst of light. 'I don't know whether I come from the devil or not! I don't know what I am!' I shouted at Babette, my voice deafening in my own sensitive ears. 'I am to live to the end of the world, and I do not even know what I am!' But the light flared before me; it was the lantern which she had lit with a match and held now so I couldn't see her face. For a moment I could see nothing but the light, and then the great weight of the lantern struck me full force in the chest and the glass shattered on the bricks and the flames roared on my legs, in my face. Lestat was shouting from the darkness, 'Put it out, put it out, idiot. It will consume you!' And I felt something thrashing me wildly in my blindness. It was Lestat's jacket. I'd fallen helpless back against the pillar, helpless as much from the fire and the blow as from the knowledge that Babette meant to destroy me, as from the knowledge that I did not know what I was.

"All this happened in a matter of seconds. The fire was out and I knelt in the dark with my hands on the bricks. Lestat at the top of the stairs had Babette again, and I flew up after him, grabbing him about the neck and pulling him backwards. He turned on me, enraged, and kicked me; but I clung to him and pulled him down on top of me to the bottom. Babette was petrified. I saw her dark outline against the sky and the glint of light in her eyes. 'Come on then!' Lestat said, scrambling to his feet. Babette was putting her hand to her throat. My injured eyes strained to gather the light to see her. Her throat bled. 'Remember!' I said to her. 'I might have killed you! Or let him kill you! I did not. You called me devil. You are wrong.' "

"Then you'd stopped Lestat just in time," said the boy.

"Yes. Lestat could kill and drink like a bolt of lightning. But I had saved only Babette's physical life. I was not to know that until later."

"In an hour and a half Lestat and I were in New Orleans, the horses nearly dead from exhaustion, the carriage parked on a side street a block from a new Spanish hotel. Lestat had an old man by the arm and was putting fifty dollars into his hand. 'Get us a suite,' he directed him, 'and order some champagne. Say it is for two gentlemen, and pay in advance. And when you come back I'll have another fifty for you. And I'll be watching for you, I wager.' His gleaming eyes held the man in thrall. I knew he'd kill him as soon as he returned with the hotel room keys, and he did. I sat in the carriage watching wearily as the man grew weaker and weaker and finally died, his body collapsing like a sack of rocks in a doorway as Lestat let him go. 'Good night, sweet prince,' said Lestat 'and here's your fifty dollars.' And he shoved the money into his pocket as if it were a capital joke.

"Now we slipped in the courtyard doors of the hotel and went up to the lavish parlor of our suite. Champagne glistened in a frosted bucket. Two glasses stood on the silver tray. I knew Lestat would fill one glass and sit there staring at the pale yellow color. And I, a man in a trance, lay on the settee staring at him as if nothing he could do mattered. I have to leave him or die, I thought. It would be sweet to die, I thought. Yes, die. I wanted to die before. Now I wish to die. I saw it with such sweet clarity, such dead calm.

" 'You're being morbid!' Lestat said suddenly. 'It's almost dawn.' He pulled the lace curtains back, and I could see the rooftops under the dark blue sky, and above, the great constellation Orion. 'Go kill!' said Lestat, sliding up the glass. He stepped out of the sill, and I heard his feet land softly on the rooftop beside the hotel. He was going for the coffins, or at least one. My thirst rose in me like fever, and I followed him. My desire to die was constant, like a pure thought in the mind, devoid of emotion. Yet I needed to feed. I've indicated to you I would not then kill people. I moved along the rooftop in search of rats."

"But why . . . you've said Lestat shouldn't have made you *start* with people. Did you mean . . . do you mean for you it was an aesthetic choice, not a moral one?"

"Had you asked me then, I would have told you it was aesthetic, that I wished to understand death in stages. That the death of an animal yielded such pleasure and experience to me that I had only begun to understand it, and wished to save the experience of human death for my mature understanding. But it was moral. Because all aesthetic decisions are moral, really."

"I don't understand," said the boy. "I thought aesthetic decisions could be completely immoral. What about the cliché of the artist who leaves his wife and children so he can paint? Or Nero playing the harp while Rome burned?"

"Both were moral decisions. Both served a higher good, in the mind of the artist. The conflict lies between the morals of the artist and the morals of society, not between aesthetics and morality. But often this isn't understood; and here comes the waste, the tragedy. An artist, stealing paints from a store, for example, imagines himself to have made an inevitable but immoral decision, and then he sees himself as fallen from grace; what follows is despair and petty irresponsibility, as if morality were a great glass world which can be utterly shattered by one act. But this was not my great concern then. I did not know these things then. I believed I killed animals for aesthetic reasons only, and I hedged against the great moral question of whether or not by my very nature I was damned.

"Because, you see, though Lestat had never said anything about devils or hell to me, I believed I was damned when I went over to him, just as Judas must have believed it when he put the noose around his neck. You understand?"

The boy said nothing. He started to speak but didn't. The color burned for a moment in blotches on his cheeks. "Were you?" he whispered.

The vampire only sat there, smiling, a small smile that played on his lips like the light. The boy was staring at him now as if he were just seeing him for the first time.

"Perhaps . . ." said the vampire drawing himself up and crossing his legs ". . . we should take things one at a time. Perhaps I should go on with my story."

"Yes, please . . ." said the boy.

"I was agitated that night, as I told you. I had hedged against this question as a vampire and now it completely overwhelmed me, and in that state I had no desire to live. Well, this produced in me, as it can in humans, a craving for that which will satisfy at least physical desire. I think I used it as an excuse. I have told you what the kill means to vampires; you can imagine from what I've said the difference between a rat and a man.

"I went down into the street after Lestat and walked for blocks. The streets were muddy then, the actual blocks islands above the gutters, and the entire city so dark compared to the cities of today. The lights were as beacons in a black sea. Even with morning rising slowly, only the dormers and high porches of the houses were emerging from the dark, and to a mortal man the narrow streets I found were like pitch. Am I damned? Am I from the devil? Is my very nature that of a devil? I was asking myself over and over. And if it is, why then do I revolt against it, tremble when Babette hurls a flaming lantern at me, turn away in disgust when Lestat kills? What have I become in becoming a vampire? Where am I to go? And all the while, as the death wish caused me to neglect my thirst, my thirst grew hotter; my veins were veritable threads of pain in my flesh; my temples throbbed; and finally I could stand it no longer. Torn apart by the wish to take no action—to starve, to wither in thought on the one hand; and driven to kill on the other—I stood in an empty, desolate street and heard the sound of a child crying.

"She was within. I drew close to the walls, trying in my habitual detachment only to understand the nature of her cry. She was weary and aching and utterly alone. She had been crying for so long now, that soon she would stop from sheer exhaustion. I slipped my hand up under the heavy wooden shutter and pulled it so the bolt slipped. There she sat in the dark room beside a dead woman, a woman who'd been dead for some days. The room itself was cluttered with trunks and packages as though a number of people had been packing to leave; but the mother lay half clothed, her body already in decay, and no one else was there but the child. It was moments before she saw me, but when she did she began to tell me that I must do something to help her mother. She was only five at most, and very thin, and her face was stained with dirt and tears. She begged me to help. They had to take a ship, she said, before the plague came; their father was waiting. She began to shake her mother now and to cry in the most pathetic and desperate way; and then she looked at me again and burst into the greatest flow of tears.

"You must understand that by now I was burning with physical need to drink. I could not have made it through another day without feeding. But there were alternatives: rats abounded in the streets, and somewhere very near a dog was howling hopelessly. I might have fled the room had I chosen and fed and gotten back easily. But the question pounded in me: Am I damned? If so, why do I feel such pity for her, for her gaunt face? Why do I wish to touch her tiny, soft arms, hold her now on my knee as I am doing, feel her bend her head to my chest as I gently touch the satin hair? Why do I do this? If I am damned I must want to kill her, I must want to make her nothing but food for a cursed existence, because being damned I must hate her.

"And when I thought of this, I saw Babette's face contorted with hatred when she had held the lantern waiting to light it, and I saw Lestat in my mind and hated him, and I felt, yes, damned and this is hell, and in that instant I had bent down and driven hard into her soft, small neck and, hearing her tiny cry, whispered even as I felt the hot blood on my lips, 'It's only for a moment and there'll be no more pain.' But she was locked to me, and I was soon incapable of saying anything. For four years I had not savored a human; for four years I hadn't really known; and now I heard her heart in that terrible rhythm, and such a heart—not the heart of a man or an animal, but the rapid, tenacious heart of the child, beating harder and harder, refusing to die, beating like a tiny fist beating on a door, crying, 'I will not die, I will not die, I cannot die, I cannot die. . . .' I think I rose to my feet still locked to her, the heart pulling my heart faster with no hope of cease, the rich blood rushing too fast for me, the room reeling, and then, despite myself, I was staring over her bent head, her open mouth, down through the gloom at the mother's face; and through the half-mast lids her eyes gleamed at me as if they were alive! I threw the child down. She lay like a jointless doll. And turning in blind horror of the mother to flee, I saw the window filled with a familiar shape. It was Lestat, who backed away from it now laughing, his body bent as he danced in the mud street. 'Louis, Louis,' he taunted me, and pointed a long, bone-thin finger at me, as if to say he'd caught me in the act. And now he bounded over the sill, brushing me aside, and grabbed the mother's stinking body from the bed and made to dance with her."

"Good God!" whispered the boy.

"Yes, I might have said the same," said the vampire. "He stumbled over the child as he pulled the mother along in widening circles, singing as he danced, her matted hair falling in her face, as her head snapped back and a black fluid poured out of her mouth. He threw her down. I was out of the window and running down the street, and he was running after me. 'Are you afraid of me, Louis?' he shouted. 'Are you afraid? The child's alive, Louis, you left her breathing. Shall I go back and make her a vampire? We could use her, Louis, and think of all the pretty dresses we could buy for her. Louis, wait, Louis! I'll go back for her if you say!' And so he ran after me all the way back to the hotel, all the way across the rooftops, where I hoped to lose him, until I leaped in the window of the parlor and turned in rage and slammed the window shut. He hit it, arms outstretched, like a bird who seeks to fly through glass, and shook the frame. I was utterly out of my mind. I went round and round the room looking for some way to kill him. I pictured his body burned to a crisp on the roof below. Reason had altogether left me, so that I was consummate rage, and when he came through the broken glass, we fought as we'd never fought before. It was hell that stopped me, the thought of hell, of us being two souls in hell that grappled in hatred. I lost my confidence, my purpose, my grip. I was down on the floor then, and he was standing over me, his eyes cold, though his chest heaved. 'You're a fool, Louis,' he said. His voice was calm. It was so calm it brought me around. 'The sun's coming up,' he said, his chest heaving slightly from the struggle, his eyes narrow as he looked at the window. I'd never seen him quite like this. The fight had got the better of him in some way; or something had. 'Get in your coffin,' he said to me, without even the slightest anger. 'But tomorrow night . . . we talk.'

"Well, I was more than slightly amazed. Lestat talk! I couldn't imagine this. Never had Lestat and I really talked. I think I have described to you with accuracy our sparring matches, our angry go-rounds."

"He was desperate for the money, for your houses," said the boy. "Or was it that he was as afraid to be alone as you were?"

"These questions occurred to me. It even occurred to me that Lestat meant to kill me, some way that I didn't know. You see, I wasn't sure then why I awoke each evening when I did, whether it was automatic when the deathlike sleep left me, and why it happened sometimes earlier than at other times. It was one of the things Lestat would not explain. And he was often up before me. He was my superior in all the mechanics, as I've indicated. And I shut the coffin that morning with a kind of despair.

"I should explain now, though, that the shutting of the coffin is always disturbing. It is rather like going under a modern anesthetic on an operating table. Even a casual mistake on the part of an intruder might mean death."

"But how could he have killed you? He couldn't have exposed you to the light; he couldn't have stood it himself."

"This is true, but rising before me he might have nailed my

coffin shut. Or set it afire. The principal thing was, I didn't know what he might do, what he might know that I still did not know.

"But there was nothing to be done about it then, and with thoughts of the dead woman and child still in my brain, and the sun rising, I had no energy left to argue with him, and lay down to miserable dreams."

"You do dream!" said the boy.

"Often," said the vampire. "I wish sometimes that I did not. For such dreams, such long and clear dreams I never had as a mortal; and such twisted nightmares I never had either. In my early days, these dreams so absorbed me that often it seemed I fought waking as long as I could and lay sometimes for hours thinking of these dreams until the night was half gone; and dazed by them I often wandered about seeking to understand their meaning. They were in many ways as elusive as the dreams of mortals. I dreamed of my brother, for instance, that he was near me in some state between life and death, calling to me for help. And often I dreamed of Babette; and often—almost always—there was a great wasteland backdrop to my dreams, that wasteland of night I'd seen when cursed by Babette as I've told you. It was as if all figures walked and talked on the desolate home of my damned soul. I don't remember what I dreamed that day, perhaps because I remember too well what Lestat and I discussed the following evening. I see you're anxious for that, too.

"Well, as I've said, Lestat amazed me in his new calm, his thoughtfulness. But that evening I didn't wake to find him the same way, not at first. There were women in the parlor. The candles were a few, scattered on the small tables and the carved buffet, and Lestat had his arm around one woman and was kissing her. She was very drunk and very beautiful, a great drugged doll of a woman with her careful coif falling slowly down on her bare shoulders and over her partially bared breasts. The other woman sat over a ruined supper table drinking a glass of wine. I could see that the three of them had dined (Lestat pretending to dine . . . you would be surprised how people do not notice that a vampire is only pretending to eat), and the woman at the table was bored. All this put me in a fit of agitation. I did not know what Lestat was up to. If I went into the room, the woman would turn her attentions to me. And what was to happen, I couldn't imagine, except that Lestat meant for us to kill them both. The woman on the settee with him was already teasing about his kisses, his coldness, his lack of desire for her. And the woman at the table watched with black almond eyes that seemed to be filled with satisfaction; when Lestat rose and came to her, putting his hands on her bare white arms, she brightened. Bending now to kiss her, he saw me through the crack in the door. And his eyes just stared at me for a moment, and then he went on talking with the ladies. He bent down and blew out the candles on the table. 'It's too dark in here,' said the woman on the couch. 'Leave us alone,' said the other woman. Lestat sat down and beckoned her to sit in his lap. And she did, putting her left arm around his neck, her right hand smoothing back his yellow hair. 'Your skin's icy,' she said, recoiling slightly. 'Not always,' said Lestat; and then he buried his face in the flesh of her neck. I was watching all this with fascination. Lestat was masterfully clever and utterly vicious, but I didn't know how clever he was until he sank his teeth into her now, his thumb pressing down on her throat, his other arm locking her tight, so that he drank his fill without the other woman even knowing. 'Your friend has no head for wine,' he said, slipping out of the chair and seating the unconscious woman there, her arms folded under her face on the table. 'She's stupid,' said the other woman, who had gone to the window and had been looking out at the lights. New Orleans was then a city of many low buildings, as you probably know. And on such clear nights as this, the lamplit streets were beautiful from the high windows of this new Spanish hotel; and the stars of those days hung low over such dim light as they do at sea. 'I can warm that cold skin of yours better than she can.' She turned to Lestat, and I must confess I was feeling some relief that he would now take care of her as well. But he planned nothing so simple. 'Do you think so?' he said to her. He took her hand, and she said, 'Why, you're warm.' "

"You mean the blood had warmed him," said the boy.

"Oh, yes," said the vampire. "After killing, a vampire is as warm as you are now." And he started to resume; then, glancing at the boy, he smiled. "As I was saying . . . Lestat now held the woman's hand in his and said that the other had warmed him. His face, of course, was flushed; much altered. He drew her close now, and she kissed him, remarking through her laughter that he was a veritable furnace of passion.

" 'Ah, but the price is high,' he said to her, affecting sadness. 'Your pretty friend . . .' He shrugged his shoulders. 'I exhausted her.' And he stood back as if inviting the woman to walk to the table. And she did, a look of superiority on her small features. She bent down to see her friend, but then lost interest—until she saw something. It was a napkin. It had caught the last drops of blood from the wound in the throat. She picked it up, straining to see it in the darkness. 'Take down your hair,' said Lestat softly. And she dropped it, indifferent, and took down the last tresses, so that her hair fell blond and wavy down her back. 'Soft,' he said, 'so soft. I picture you that way, lying on a bed of satin.'

" 'Such things you say!' she scoffed and turned her back on him playfully.

" 'Do you know what manner of bed?' he asked. And she laughed and said *his* bed, she could imagine. She looked back at him as he advanced; and, never once looking away from her, he gently tipped the body of her friend, so that it fell backwards from the chair and lay with staring eyes upon the floor. The woman gasped. She scrambled away from the corpse, nearly upsetting a small end table. The candle went over and went out. 'Put out the light . . . and then put out the light,' Lestat said softly. And then he took her into his arms like a struggling moth and sank his teeth into her."

"But what were you thinking as you watched?" asked the

boy. "Did you want to stop him the way you wanted to stop him from killing Freniere?"

"No," said the vampire. "I could not have stopped him. And you must understand I knew that he killed humans every night. Animals gave him no satisfaction whatsoever. Animals were to be banked on when all else failed, but never to be chosen. If I felt any sympathy for the women, it was buried deep in my own turmoil. I still felt in my chest the little hammer heart of that starving child; I still burned with the questions of my own divided nature. I was angry that Lestat had staged this show for me, waiting till I woke to kill the women; and I wondered again if I might somehow break loose from him and felt both hatred and my own weakness more than ever.

"Meantime, he propped their lovely corpses at the table and went about the room lighting all the candles until it blazed as if for a wedding. 'Come in, Louis,' he said. 'I would have arranged an escort for you, but I know what a man you are about choosing your own. Pity Mademoiselle Freniere likes to hurl flaming lanterns. It makes a party unwieldy, don't you think? Especially for a hotel?' He seated the blond-haired girl so that her head lay to one side against the damask back of the chair, and the darker woman lay with her chin resting just above her breasts; this one had blanched, and her features had a rigid look to them already, as though she was one of those women in whom the fire of personality makes beauty. But the other looked only as if she slept; and I was not sure that she was even dead. Lestat had made two gashes, one in her throat and one above her left breast, and both still bled freely. He lifted her wrist now, and slitting it with a knife, filled two wine glasses and bade me to sit down.

" 'I'm leaving you,' I said to him at once. 'I wish to tell you that now.'

" 'I thought as much,' he answered, sitting back in the chair, 'and I thought as well that you would make a flowery announcement. Tell me what a monster I am; what a vulgar fiend.'

" 'I make no judgments upon you. I'm not interested in

you. I am interested in my own nature now, and I've come to believe I can't trust you to tell me the truth about it. You use knowledge for personal power,' I told him. And I suppose, in the manner of many people making such an announcement, I was not looking to him for an honest response. I was not looking to him at all. I was mainly listening to my own words. But now I saw that his face was once again the way it had been when he'd said we would talk. He was *listening* to me. I was suddenly at a loss. I felt that gulf between us as painfully as ever.

" 'Why did you become a vampire?' I blurted out. 'And why such a vampire as you are! Vengeful and delighting in taking human life even when you have no need. This girl . . . why did you kill her when one would have done? And why did you frighten her so before you killed her? And why have you propped her here in some grotesque manner, as if tempting the gods to strike you down for your blasphemy?'

"All this he listened to without speaking, and in the pause that followed I again felt at a loss. Lestat's eyes were large and thoughtful; I'd seen them that way before, but I couldn't remember when, certainly not when talking to me.

" 'What do you think a vampire is?' he asked me sincerely.

" 'I don't pretend to know. You pretend to know. What is it?' I asked. And to this he answered nothing. It was as if he sensed the insincerity of it, the spite. He just sat there looking at me with the same still expression. Then I said, 'I know that after leaving you, I shall try to find out. I'll travel the world, if I have to, to find other vampires. I know they must exist; I don't know of any reasons why they shouldn't exist in great numbers. And I'm confident I shall find vampires who have more in common with me than I with you. Vampires who understand knowledge as I do and have used their superior vampire nature to learn secrets of which you don't even dream. If you haven't told me everything, I shall find things out for myself or from them, when I find them.'

"He shook his head. 'Louis!' he said. 'You are in love with your mortal nature! You chase after the phantoms of your former self. Freniere, his sister . . . these are images for you of what you were and what you still long to be. And in your romance with mortal life, you're dead to your vampire nature!'

"I objected to this at once. 'My vampire nature has been for me the greatest adventure of my life; all that went before it was confused, clouded; I went through mortal life like a blind man groping from solid object to solid object. It was only when I became a vampire that I respected for the first time all of life. I never saw a living, pulsing human being until I was a vampire; I never knew what life was until it ran out in a red gush over my lips, my hands!' I found myself staring at the two women, the darker one now turning a terrible shade of blue. The blonde was breathing. 'She's not dead!' I said to him suddenly.

" 'I know. Let her alone,' he said. He lifted her wrist and made a new gash by the scab of the other and filled his glass. 'All that you say makes sense,' he said to me, taking a drink. 'You are an intellect. I've never been. What I've learned I've learned from listening to men talk, not from books. I never went to school long enough. But I'm not stupid, and you must listen to me because you are in danger. You do not know your vampire nature. You are like an adult who, looking back on his childhood, realizes that he never appreciated it. You cannot, as a man, go back to the nursery and play with your toys, asking for the love and care to be showered on you again simply because now you know their worth. So it is with you and mortal nature. You've given it up. You no longer look "through a glass darkly." But you cannot pass back to the world of human warmth with your new eyes.'

" 'I know that well enough!' I said. 'But what is it that is our nature! If I can live from the blood of animals, why should I not live from the blood of animals rather than go through the world bringing misery and death to human creatures!'

" 'Does it bring you happiness?' he asked. 'You wander through the night, feeding on rats like a pauper and then moon at Babette's window, filled with care, yet helpless as the goddess who came by night to watch Endymion sleep and could not have him. And suppose you could hold her in your arms and she would look on you without horror or disgust, what then? A few short years to watch her suffer every prick of mortality and then die before your eyes? Does this give happiness? This is insanity, Louis. This is vain. And what truly lies before you is vampire nature, which is killing. For I guarantee you that if you walk the streets tonight and strike down a woman as rich and beautiful as Babette and suck her blood until she drops at your feet you will have no hunger left for Babette's profile in the candlelight or for listening by the window for the sound of her voice. You will be filled, Louis, as you were meant to be, with all the life that you can hold; and you will have hunger when that's gone for the same, and the same, and the same. The red in this glass will be just as red; the roses on the wallpaper just as delicately drawn. And you'll see the moon the same way, and the same the flicker of a candle. And with that same sensibility that you cherish you will see death in all its beauty, life as it is only known on the very point of death. Don't you understand that, Louis? You alone of all creatures can see death that way with impunity. You . . . alone . . . under the rising moon . . . can strike like the hand of God!'

"He sat back now and drained the glass, and his eyes moved over the unconscious woman. Her breasts heaved and her eyebrows knit as if she were coming around. A moan escaped her lips. He'd never spoken such words to me before, and I had not thought him capable of it. 'Vampires are killers,' he said now. 'Predators. Whose all-seeing eyes were meant to give them detachment. The ability to see a human life in its entirety, not with any mawkish sorrow but with a thrilling satisfaction in being the end of that life, in having a hand in the divine plan.'

" 'That is how *you* see it!' I protested. The girl moaned again; her face was very white. Her head rolled against the back of the chair.

" 'That is the way it is,' he answered. 'You talk of finding other vampires! Vampires are killers! They don't want you or your sensibility! They'll see you coming long before you see them, and they'll see your flaw; and, distrusting you, they'll seek to kill you. They'd seek to kill you even if you were like me. Because they are lone predators and seek for companionship no more than cats in the jungle. They're jealous of their secret and of their territory; and if you find one or more of them together it will be for safety only, and one will be the slave of the other, the way you are of me.'

" 'I'm not your slave,' I said to him. But even as he spoke I realized I'd been his slave all along.

" 'That's how vampires increase . . . through slavery. How else?' he asked. He took the girl's wrist again, and she cried out as the knife cut. She opened her eyes slowly as he held her wrist over the glass. She blinked and strained to keep them open. It was as if a veil covered her eyes. 'You're tired, aren't you?' he asked her. She gazed at him as if she couldn't really see him. 'Tired!' he said, now leaning close and staring into her eyes. 'You want to sleep.' 'Yes . . .' she moaned softly. And he picked her up and took her into the bedroom. Our coffins rested on the carpet and against the wall; there was a velvet-draped bed. Lestat did not put her on the bed; he lowered her slowly into his coffin. 'What are you doing?' I asked him, coming to the door sill. The girl was looking around like a terrified child. 'No . . .' she was moaning. And then, as he closed the lid, she screamed. She continued to scream within the coffin.

" 'Why do you *do this*, Lestat?' I asked.

" 'I like to do it,' he said. 'I enjoy it.' He looked at me. 'I don't say that you have to enjoy it. Take your aesthete's tastes to purer things. Kill them swiftly if you will, but do it! Learn that you're a killer! Ah!' He threw up his hands in disgust. The girl had stopped screaming. Now he drew up a little curved-legged chair beside the coffin and, crossing his legs, he looked at the coffin lid. His was a black varnished coffin, not a pure rectangular box as they are now, but tapered at both ends and widest where the corpse might lay his hands upon his chest. It suggested the human form. It opened, and the girl sat up astonished, wild-eyed, her lips blue and trembling. 'Lie down, love,' he said to her, and pushed her back; and she lay, near-hysterical, staring up at him. 'You're dead, love,' he said to her; and she screamed and turned desperately in the coffin like a fish, as if her body could escape through the sides, through the bottom. 'It's a coffin, a coffin!' she cried. 'Let me out.'

" 'But we all must lie in coffins, eventually,' he said to her. 'Lie still, love. This is your coffin. Most of us never get to know what it feels like. You know what it feels like!' he said to her. I couldn't tell whether she was listening or not, or just going wild. But she saw me in the doorway, and then she lay still, looking at Lestat and then at me. 'Help me!' she said to me.

"Lestat looked at me. 'I expected you to feel these things instinctually, as I did,' he said. 'When I gave you that first kill, I thought you would hunger for the next and the next, that you would go to each human life as if to a full cup, the way I had. But you didn't. And all this time I suppose I kept from straightening you out because you were best weaker. I'd watch you playing shadow in the night, staring at the falling rain, and I'd think, He's easy to manage, he's simple. But you're weak, Louis. You're a mark. For vampires and now for humans alike. This thing with Babette has exposed us both. It's as if you want us both to be destroyed.'

" 'I can't stand to watch what you're doing,' I said, turning my back. The girl's eyes were burning into my flesh. She lay, all the time he spoke, staring at me.

" 'You can stand it!' he said. 'I saw you last night with that child. You're a vampire, the same as I am!'

"He stood up and came towards me, but the girl rose again and he turned to shove her down. 'Do you think we should make her a vampire? Share our lives with her?' he asked. Instantly I said, 'No!'

" 'Why, because she's nothing but a whore?' he asked. 'A damned expensive whore at that,' he said.

" 'Can she live now? Or has she lost too much?' I asked him.

" 'Touching!' he said. 'She can't live.'

" 'Then kill her.' She began to scream. He just sat there. I turned around. He was smiling, and the girl had turned her face to the satin and was sobbing. Her reason had almost entirely left her; she was crying and praying. She was praying to the Virgin to save her, her hands over her face now, now over her head, the wrist smearing blood in her hair and on the satin. I bent over the coffin. She was dying, it was true; her eyes were burning, but the tissue around them was already bluish and now she smiled. 'You won't let me die, will you?' she whispered. 'You'll save me.' Lestat reached over and took her wrist. 'But it's too late, love,' he said. 'Look at your wrist, your breast.' And then he touched the wound in her throat. She put her hands to her throat and gasped, her mouth open, the scream strangled. I stared at Lestat. I could not understand why he did this. His face was as smooth as mine is now, more animated for the blood, but cold and without emotion.

"He did not leer like a stage villain, nor hunger for her suffering as if the cruelty fed him. He simply watched her. 'I never meant to be bad,' she was crying. 'I only did what I had to do. You won't let this happen to me. You'll let me go. I can't die like this, I can't!' She was sobbing, the sobs dry and thin. 'You'll let me go. I have to go to the priest. You'll let me go.'

" 'But my friend is a priest,' said Lestat, smiling. As if he'd just thought of it as a joke. 'This is your funeral, dear. You see, you were at a dinner party and you died. But God has given you another chance to be absolved. Don't you see? Tell him your sins.'

"She shook her head at first, and then she looked at me again with those pleading eyes. 'Is it true?' she whispered. 'Well,' said Lestat, 'I suppose you're not contrite, dear. I shall have to shut the lid!'

" 'Stop this, Lestat!' I shouted at him. The girl was screaming again, and I could not stand the sight of it any longer. I bent down to her and took her hand. 'I can't remember my sins,' she said, just as I was looking at her wrist, resolved to kill her. 'You mustn't try. Tell God only that you are sorry,' I said, 'and then you'll die and it will be over.' She lay back, and her eyes shut. I sank my teeth into her wrist and began to suck her dry. She stirred once as if dreaming and said a name; and then, when I felt her heartbeat reach that hypnotic slowness, I drew back from her, dizzy, confused for the moment, my hands reaching for the door frame. I saw her as if in a dream. The candles glared in the corner of my eye. I saw her lying utterly still. And

Lestat sat composed beside her, like a mourner. His face was still. 'Louis,' he said to me. 'Don't you understand? Peace will only come to you when you can do this every night of your life. There is nothing else. But this is everything!' His voice was almost tender as he spoke, and he rose and put both his hands on my shoulders. I walked into the parlor, shying away from his touch but not resolute enough to push him off. 'Come with me, out into the streets. It's late. You haven't drunk enough. Let me show you what you are. Really! Forgive me if I bungled it, left too much to nature. Come!'

" 'I can't bear it, Lestat,' I said to him. 'You chose your companion badly.'

" 'But Louis,' he said, 'you haven't tried!'

The vampire stopped. He was studying the boy. And the boy, astonished, said nothing.

"It was true what he'd said. I had not drunk enough; and shaken by the girl's fear, I let him lead me out of the hotel, down the back stairs. People were coming now from the Condé Street ballroom, and the narrow street was jammed. There were supper parties in the hotels, and the planter families were lodged in town in great numbers and we passed through them like a nightmare. My agony was unbearable. Never since I was a human being had I felt such mental pain. It was because all of Lestat's words had made sense to me. I knew peace only when I killed, only for that minute; and there was no question in my mind that the killing of anything less than a human being brought nothing but a vague longing, the discontent which had brought me close to humans, to watch their lives through glass. I was no vampire. And in my pain, I asked irrationally, like a child, Could I not return? Could I not be human again? Even as the blood of that girl was warm in me and I felt that physical thrill and strength, I asked that question. The faces of humans passed me like candle flames in the night dancing on dark waves. I was sinking into the darkness. I was weary of longing. I was turning around and around in the street, looking at the stars and thinking, Yes, it's true. I know what he is saying is true, that when I kill there is no longing; and I can't bear this truth, I can't bear it.

"Suddenly there was one of those arresting moments. The street was utterly quiet. We had strayed far from the main part of the old town and were near the ramparts. There were no lights, only the fire in a window and the far-off sound of people laughing. But no one here. No one near us. I could feel the breeze suddenly from the river and the hot air of the night rising and Lestat near me, so still he might have been made of stone. Over the long, low row of pointed roofs were the massive shapes of oak trees in the dark, great swaying forms of myriad sounds under the low-hung stars. The pain for the moment was gone; the confusion was gone. I closed my eyes and heard the wind and the sound of water flowing softly, swiftly in the river. It was enough, for one moment. And I knew that it would not endure, that it would fly away from me like something torn out of my arms, and I would fly after it, more desperately lonely than any creature under God, to get it back. And then a voice beside me rumbled deep in the sound of the night, a drumbeat as the moment ended, saying, 'Do what it is your nature to do. This is but a taste of it. Do what it is your nature to do.' And the moment was gone. I stood like the girl in the parlor in the hotel, dazed and ready for the slightest suggestion. I was nodding at Lestat as he nodded at me. 'Pain is terrible for you,' he said. 'You feel it like no other creature because you are a vampire. You don't want it to go on.'

" 'No,' I answered him. 'I'll feel as I felt with her, wed to her and weightless, caught as if by a dance.'

" 'That and more.' His hand tightened on mine. 'Don't turn away from it, come with me.'

"He led me quickly through the street, turning every time I hesitated, his hand out for mine, a smile on his lips, his presence as marvellous to me as the night he'd come in my mortal life and told me we would be vampires. 'Evil is a point of view,' he whispered now. 'We are immortal. And what we have before us are the rich feasts that conscience cannot appreciate and mortal men cannot know without regret. God kills, and so shall we; indiscriminately He takes the richest and the poorest, and so shall we; for no creatures under God are as we are, none so like Him as ourselves, dark angels not confined to the stinking limits of hell but wandering His earth and all its kingdoms. I want a child tonight. I am like a mother . . . I want a child!'

"I should have known what he meant. I did not. He had me mesmerized, enchanted. He was playing to me as he had when I was mortal; he was leading me. He was saying, 'Your pain will end.'

"We'd come to a street of lighted windows. It was a place of rooming houses, sailors, flatboat men. We entered a narrow door; and then, in a hollow stone passage in which I could hear my own breath like the wind, he crept along the wall until his shadow leapt out in the light of a doorway beside the shadow of another man, their heads bent together, their whispers like the rustling of dry leaves. 'What is it?' I drew near him as he came back, afraid suddenly this exhilaration in me would die. I saw again that nightmare landscape I'd seen when I spoke with Babette; I felt the chill of loneliness, the chill of guilt. 'She's there!' he said. 'Your wounded one. Your daughter.'

" 'What do you say, what are you talking about!'

" 'You've saved her,' he whispered. 'I knew it. You left the window wide on her and her dead mother, and people passing in the street brought her here.'

" 'The child. The little girl!' I gasped. But he was already leading me through the door to stand at the end of the long ward of wooden beds, each with a child beneath a narrow white blanket, one candle at the end of the ward, where a nurse bent over a small desk. We walked down the aisle between the rows. 'Starving children, orphans,' he said. 'Children of plague and fever.' He stopped. I saw the little girl lying in the bed. And then the man was coming, and he was whispering with Lestat; such care for the sleeping little ones. Someone in another room was crying. The nurse rose and hurried away.

"And now the doctor bent and wrapped the child in the blanket. Lestat had taken money from his pocket and set it on the foot of the bed. The doctor was saying how glad he was we'd come for her, how most of them were orphans; they came in on the ships, sometimes orphans too young even to tell which body was that of their mother. He thought Lestat was the father.

"And in moments, Lestat was running through the streets with her, the white of the blanket gleaming against his dark coat and cape; and even to my expert vision, as I ran after him it seemed sometimes as if the blanket flew through the night with no one holding it, a shifting shape travelling on the wind like a leaf stood upright and sent scurrying along a passage, trying to gain the wind all the while and truly take flight. I caught him finally as we approached the lamps near the Place d'Armes. The child lay pale on his shoulder, her cheeks still full like plums, though she was drained and near death. She opened her eyes, or rather the lids slid back; and beneath the long curling lashes I saw a streak of white. 'Lestat, what are you doing? Where are you taking her?' I demanded. But I knew too well. He was heading for the hotel and meant to take her into our room.

"The corpses were as we left them, one neatly set in the coffin as if an undertaker had already attended her, the other in her chair at the table. Lestat brushed past them as if he didn't see them, while I watched him in fascination. The candles had all burned down, and the only light was that of the moon and the street. I could see his iced and gleaming profile as he set the child down on the pillow. 'Come here, Louis, you haven't fed enough, I know you haven't,' he said with that same calm, convincing voice he had used skillfully all evening. He held my hand in his, his own warm and tight. 'See her, Louis, how plump and sweet she looks, as if even death can't take her freshness; the will to live is too strong! He might make a sculpture of her tiny lips and rounded hands, but he cannot make her fade! You remember, the way you wanted her when you saw her in that room.' I resisted him. I didn't want to kill her. I hadn't wanted to last night. And then suddenly I remembered two conflicting things and was torn in agony: I remembered the powerful beating of her heart against mine and I hungered for it, hungered for it so badly I turned my back on her in the bed and would have rushed out of the room had not Lestat held me fast; and I remembered her mother's face and that moment of horror when I'd dropped the child and he'd come into the room. But he wasn't mocking me now; he was confusing me. 'You want her, Louis. Don't you see, once you've taken her, then you can take whomever you wish. You wanted her last night but you weakened, and that's why she's not dead.' I could feel it was true, what he said. I could feel again that ecstasy of being pressed to her, her little heart going and going. 'She's too strong for me . . . her heart, it wouldn't give up,' I said to him. 'Is she so strong?' he smiled. He drew me close to him. 'Take her, Louis, I know you want her.' And I did. I drew close to the bed now and just watched her. Her chest barely moved with her breath, and one small hand was tangled in her long, gold hair. I couldn't bear it, looking at her, wanting her not to die and wanting her; and the more I looked at her, the more I could taste her skin, feel my arm sliding under her back and pulling her up to me, feel her soft neck. Soft, soft, that's what she was, so soft. I tried to tell myself it was best for her to die—what was to become of her?—but these were lying thoughts. I wanted her! And so I took her in my arms and held her, her burning cheek on mine, her hair falling down over my wrists and brushing my eyelids, the sweet perfume of a child strong and pulsing in spite of sickness and death. She moaned now, stirred in her sleep, and that was more than I could bear. I'd kill her before I'd let her wake and know it. I went into her throat and heard Lestat saying to me strangely, 'Just a little tear. It's just a little throat.' And I obeyed him.

"I won't tell you again what it was like, except that it caught me up just as it had done before, and as killing always does, only more; so that my knees bent and I half lay on the bed, sucking her dry, that heart pounding again that would not slow, would not give up. And suddenly, as I went on and on, the instinctual part of me waiting, waiting for the slowing of the heart which would mean death, Lestat wrenched me from her. 'But she's not dead,' I whispered. But it was over. The furniture of the room emerged from the darkness. I sat stunned, staring at her, too weak to move, my head rolling back against the headboard of the bed, my hands pressing down on the velvet spread. Lestat was snatching her up, talking to her, saying a name. 'Claudia, Claudia, listen to me, come round, Claudia.' He was carrying her now out of the bedroom into the parlor, and his voice was so soft I barely heard him. 'You're ill, do you hear me? You must do as I tell you to get well.' And then, in the pause that followed, I came to my senses. I realized what he was doing, that he had cut his wrist and given it to her and she was drinking. 'That's it, dear; more,' he was saying to her. 'You must drink it to get well.'

" 'Damn you!' I shouted, and he hissed at me with blazing eyes. He sat on the settee with her locked to his wrist. I saw her white hand clutching at his sleeve, and I could see his chest heaving for breath and his face contorted the way I'd never seen it. He let out a moan and whispered again to her to go on; and when I moved from the threshold, he glared at me again, as if to say, 'I'll kill you!'

" 'But why, Lestat?' I whispered to him. He was trying now to push her off, and she wouldn't let go. With her fingers locked around his fingers and arm she held the wrist to her mouth, a growl coming out of her. 'Stop, stop!' he said to her. He was clearly in pain. He pulled back from her and held her shoulders with both hands. She tried desperately to reach his wrist with her teeth, but she couldn't; and then she looked at him with the most innocent astonishment. He stood back, his hand out lest she move. Then he clapped a handkerchief to his wrist and backed away from her, towards the bell rope. He pulled it sharply, his eyes still fixed on her.

" 'What have you done, Lestat?' I asked him. *'What have you done?'* I stared at her. She sat composed, revived, filled with life, no sign of pallor or weakness in her, her legs stretched out straight on the damask, her white gown soft and thin like an angel's gown around her small form. She was looking at Lestat. 'Not me,' he said to her, 'ever again. Do you understand? But I'll show you what to do!' When I tried to make him look at me and answer me as to what he was doing, he shook me off. He gave me such a blow with his arm that I hit the wall. Someone was knocking now. I knew what he meant to do. Once more I tried to reach out for him, but he spun so fast I didn't even see him hit me. When I did see him, I was sprawled in the chair and he was opening the door. 'Yes, come in, please, there's been an accident,' he said to the young slave boy. And then, shutting the door, he took him from behind, so that the boy never knew what happened. And even as he knelt over the body drinking, he beckoned for the child, who slid from the couch and went down on her knees and took the wrist offered her, quickly pushing back the cuff of the shirt. She gnawed first, as if she meant to devour his flesh, and then Lestat showed her what to do. He sat back and let her have the rest, his eye on the boy's chest, so that when the time came, he bent forward and said, 'No more, he's dying. . . . You must never drink after the heart stops or you'll be sick again, sick to death. Do you understand?' But she'd had enough and she sat next to him, their backs against the legs of the settee, their legs stretched out on the floor. The boy died in seconds. I felt weary and sickened, as if the night had lasted a thousand years. I sat there watching them, the child drawing close to Lestat now, snuggling near him as he slipped his arm around her, though his indifferent eyes remained fixed on the corpse. Then he looked up at me.

" 'Where is Mamma?' asked the child softly. She had a voice equal to her physical beauty, clear like a little silver bell. It was sensual. She was sensual. Her eyes were as wide and clear as Babette's. You understand that I was barely aware of what all this meant. I knew what it might mean, but I was aghast. Now Lestat stood up and scooped her from the floor and came towards me. 'She's our daughter,' he said. 'You're going to live with us now.' He beamed at her, but his eyes were cold, as if it were all a horrible joke; then he looked at me, and his face had conviction. He pushed her towards me. I found her on my lap, my arms around her, feeling again how soft she was, how plump her skin was, like the skin of warm fruit, plums warmed by sunlight; her huge luminescent eyes were fixed on me with trusting curiosity. 'This is Louis, and I am Lestat,' he said to her, dropping down beside her. She looked about and said that it was a pretty room, very pretty, but she wanted her mamma. He had his comb out and was running it through her hair, holding the locks so as not to pull with the comb; her hair was untangling and becoming like satin. She was the most beautiful child I'd ever seen, and now she glowed with the cold fire of a vampire. Her eyes were a woman's eyes, I could see it already. She would become white and spare like us but not lose her shape. I understood now what Lestat had said about death, what he meant. I touched her neck where the two red puncture wounds were bleeding just a little. I took Lestat's handkerchief from the floor and touched it to her neck. 'Your mamma's left you with us. She wants you to be happy,' he was saying with that same immeasurable confidence. 'She knows we can make you very happy.'

" 'I want some more,' she said, turning to the corpse on the floor.

" 'No, not tonight; tomorrow night,' said Lestat. And he went to take the lady out of his coffin. The child slid off my lap, and I followed her. She stood watching as Lestat put the two ladies and the slave boy into the bed. He brought the covers up to their chins. 'Are they sick?' asked the child.

" 'Yes, Claudia,' he said. 'They're sick and they're dead. You see, they die when we drink from them.' He came towards her and swung her up into his arms again. We stood there with her between us. I was mesmerized by her, by her *transformed*, by her every gesture. She was not a child any longer, she was a vampire child. 'Now, Louis was going to leave us,' said Lestat, his eyes moving from my face to hers. 'He was going to go away. But now he's not. Because he wants to stay and take care of you and make you happy.' He looked at me. 'You're not going, are you, Louis?'

" 'You bastard!' I whispered to him. 'You fiend!'

" 'Such language in front of your daughter,' he said.

" 'I'm not your daughter,' she said with the silvery voice. 'I'm my mamma's daughter.'

" 'No, dear, not anymore,' he said to her. He glanced at the window, and then he shut the bedroom door behind us and turned the key in the lock. 'You're our daughter, Louis's daughter and my daughter, do you see? Now, whom should you sleep with? Louis or me?' And then looking at me, he said, 'Perhaps you should sleep with Louis. After all, when I'm tired . . . I'm not so kind.' "

THE VAMPIRE STOPPED. The boy said nothing. "A child vampire!" he whispered finally. The vampire glanced up suddenly as though startled, though his body made no movement. He glared at the tape recorder as if it were something monstrous.

The boy saw that the tape was almost out. Quickly, he opened his briefcase and drew out a new cassette, clumsily fitting it into place. He looked at the vampire as he pressed the record button. The vampire's face looked weary, drawn, his cheekbones more prominent and his brilliant green eyes enormous. They had begun at dark, which had come early on this San Francisco winter night, and now it was just before ten p.m. The vampire straightened and smiled and said calmly, "We are ready to go on?"

"He'd done this to the little girl just to keep you with him?" asked the boy.

"That is difficult to say. It was a statement. I'm convinced that Lestat was a person who preferred not to think or talk about his motives or beliefs, even to himself. One of those people who must act. Such a person must be pushed considerably before he will open up and confess that there is method and thought to the way he lives. That is what had happened that night with Lestat. He'd been pushed to where he had to discover even for himself why he lived as he did. Keeping me with him, that was undoubtedly part of what pushed him. But I think, in retrospect, that he himself wanted to know his own reasons for killing, wanted to examine his own life. He was discovering when he spoke what he did believe. But he did indeed want me to remain. He lived with me in a way he could never have lived alone. And, as I've told you, I was careful never to sign any property over to him, which maddened him. That, he could not persuade me to do." The vampire laughed suddenly. "Look at all the other things he persuaded me to do! How strange. He could persuade me to kill a child, but not to part with my money." He shook his head. "But," he said, "it wasn't greed, really, as you can see. It was fear of him that made me tight with him."

"You speak of him as if he were dead. You say Lestat *was* this or *was* that. Is he dead?" asked the boy.

"I don't know," said the vampire. "I think perhaps he is. But I'll come to that. We were talking of Claudia, weren't we? There was something else I wanted to say about Lestat's motives that night. Lestat trusted no one, as you see. He was like a cat, by his own admission, a lone predator. Yet he had communicated with me that night; he had to some extent exposed himself simply by telling the truth. He had dropped his mockery, his condescension. He had forgotten his perpetual anger for just a little while. And this for Lestat was exposure. When we stood alone in that dark street, I felt in him a communion with another I hadn't felt since I died. I rather think that he ushered Claudia into vampirism for revenge."

"Revenge, not only on you but on the world," suggested the boy.

"Yes. As I said, Lestat's motives for everything revolved around revenge."

"Was it all started with the father? With the school?"

"I don't know. I doubt it," said the vampire. "But I want to go on."

"Oh, please go on. You have to go on! I mean, it's only ten o'clock." The boy showed his watch.

The vampire looked at it, and then he smiled at the boy. The boy's face changed. It went blank as if from some sort of shock. "Are you still afraid of me?" asked the vampire.

The boy said nothing, but he shrank slightly from the edge

of the table. His body elongated, his feet moved out over the bare boards and then contracted.

"I should think you'd be very foolish if you weren't," said the vampire. "*But don't be.* Shall we go on?"

"Please," said the boy. He gestured towards the machine.

"Well," the vampire began, "our life was much changed with Mademoiselle Claudia, as you can imagine. Her body died, yet her senses awakened much as mine had. And I treasured in her the signs of this. But I was not aware for quite a few days how much I wanted her, wanted to talk with her and be with her. At first, I thought only of protecting her from Lestat. I gathered her into my coffin every morning and would not let her out of my sight with him if possible. This was what Lestat wanted, and he gave little suggestions that he might do her harm. 'A starving child is a frightful sight,' he said to me, 'a starving vampire even worse.' They'd hear her screams in Paris, he said, were he to lock her away to die. But all this was meant for me, to draw me close and keep me there. Afraid of fleeing alone, I would not conceive of risking it with Claudia. She was a child. She needed care.

"And there was much pleasure in caring for her. She forgot her five years of mortal life at once, or so it seemed, for she was mysteriously quiet. And from time to time I even feared that she had lost all sense, that the illness of her mortal life, combined with the great vampire shock, might have robbed her of reason; but this proved hardly the case. She was simply unlike Lestat and me to such an extent I couldn't comprehend her; for little child she was, but also fierce killer now capable of the ruthless pursuit of blood with all a child's demanding. And though Lestat still threatened me with danger to her, he did not threaten her at all but was loving to her, proud of her beauty, anxious to teach her that we must kill to live and that we ourselves could never die.

"The plague raged in the city then, as I've indicated, and he took her to the stinking cemeteries where the yellow fever and plague victims lay in heaps while the sounds of shovels never ceased all through the day and night. 'This is death,' he told her, pointing to the decaying corpse of a woman, 'which we cannot suffer. Our bodies will stay always as they are, fresh and alive; but we must never hesitate to bring death, because it is how we live.' And Claudia gazed on this with inscrutable liquid eyes.

"If there was not understanding in the early years, there was no smattering of fear. Mute and beautiful, she played with dolls, dressing, undressing them by the hour. Mute and beautiful, she killed. And I, transformed by Lestat's instruction, was now to seek out humans in much greater numbers. But it was not only the killing of them that soothed some pain in me which had been constant in the dark, still nights on Pointe du Lac, when I sat with only the company of Lestat and the old man; it was their great, shifting numbers everywhere in streets which never grew quiet, cabarets which never shut their doors, balls which lasted till dawn, the music and laughter streaming out of the open windows; people all around me now, my pulsing victims, not seen with that great love I'd felt for my sister and Babette, but with some new detachment and need. And I did kill them, kills infinitely varied and great distances apart, as I walked with the vampire's sight and light movement through this teeming, burgeoning city, my victims surrounding me, seducing me, inviting me to their supper tables, their carriages, their brothels. I lingered only a short while, long enough to take what I must have, soothed in my great melancholy that the town gave me an endless train of magnificent strangers.

"For that was it. I fed on strangers. I drew only close enough to see the pulsing beauty, the unique expression, the new and passionate voice, then killed before those feelings of revulsion could be aroused in me, that fear, that sorrow.

"Claudia and Lestat might hunt and seduce, stay long in the company of the doomed victim, enjoying the splendid humor in his unwitting friendship with death. But I still could not bear it. And so to me, the swelling population was a mercy, a forest in which I was lost, unable to stop myself, whirling too fast for thought or pain, accepting again and again the invitation to death rather than extending it.

"We lived meantime in one of my new Spanish town houses

in the Rue Royale, a long, lavish upstairs flat above a shop I rented to a tailor, a hidden garden court behind us, a wall secure against the street, with fitted wooden shutters and a barred carriage door—a place of far greater luxury and security than Pointe du Lac. Our servants were free people of color who left us to solitude before dawn for their own homes, and Lestat bought the very latest imports from France and Spain: crystal chandeliers and Oriental carpets, silk screens with painted birds of paradise, canaries singing in great domed, golden cages, and delicate marble Grecian gods and beautifully painted Chinese vases. I did not need the luxury any more than I had needed it before, but I found myself enthralled with the new flood of art and craft and design, could stare at the intricate pattern of the carpets for hours, or watch the gleam of the lamplight change the somber colors of a Dutch painting.

"All this Claudia found wondrous, with the quiet awe of an unspoiled child, and marvelled when Lestat hired a painter to make the walls of her room a magical forest of unicorns and golden birds and laden fruit trees over sparkling streams.

"An endless train of dressmakers and shoemakers and tailors came to our flat to outfit Claudia in the best of children's fashions, so that she was always a vision, not just of child beauty, with her curling lashes and her glorious yellow hair, but of the taste of finely trimmed bonnets and tiny lace gloves, flaring velvet coats and capes, and sheer white puffed-sleeve gowns with gleaming blue sashes. Lestat played with her as if she were a magnificent doll, and I played with her as if she were a magnificent doll; and it was her pleading that forced me to give up my rusty black for dandy jackets and silk ties and soft gray coats and gloves and black capes. Lestat thought the best color at all times for vampires was black, possibly the only aesthetic principle he steadfastly maintained, but he wasn't opposed to anything which smacked of style and excess. He loved the great figure we cut, the three of us in our box at the new French Opera House or the Théâtre d'Orléans, to which we went as often as possible, Lestat having a passion for Shakespeare which surprised me, though he often dozed through the operas and woke just in time to invite some lovely lady to midnight supper, where he would use all his skill to make her love him totally, then dispatch her violently to heaven or hell and come home with her diamond ring to give to Claudia.

"And all this time I was educating Claudia, whispering in her tiny seashell ear that our eternal life was useless to us if we did not see the beauty around us, the creation of mortals everywhere; I was constantly sounding the depth of her still gaze as she took the books I gave her, whispered the poetry I taught her, and played with a light but confident touch her own strange, coherent songs on the piano. She could fall for hours into the pictures in a book and listen to me read until she sat so still the sight of her jarred me, made me put the book down, and just stare back at her across the lighted room; then she'd move, a doll coming to life, and say in the softest voice that I must read some more.

"And then strange things began to happen, for though she said little and was the chubby, round-fingered child still, I'd find her tucked in the arm of my chair reading the work of Aristotle or Boethius or a new novel just come over the Atlantic. Or pecking out the music of Mozart we'd only heard the night before with an infallible ear and a concentration that made her ghostly as she sat there hour after hour discovering the music—the melody, then the bass, and finally bringing it together. Claudia was mystery. It was not possible to know what she knew or did not know. And to watch her kill was chilling. She would sit alone in the dark square waiting for the kindly gentleman or woman to find her, her eyes more mindless than I had ever seen Lestat's. Like a child numbed with fright she would whisper her plea for help to her gentle, admiring patrons, and as they carried her out of the square, her arms would fix about their necks, her tongue between her teeth, her vision glazed with consuming hunger. They found death fast in those first years, before she learned to play with them, to lead them to the doll shop or the café where they gave her steaming cups of chocolate or tea to ruddy her pale cheeks, cups she pushed away, waiting, waiting, as if feasting silently on their terrible kindness.

"But when that was done, she was my companion, my pupil, her long hours spent with me consuming faster and faster the knowledge I gave her, sharing with me some quiet understanding which could not include Lestat. At dawn she lay with me, her heart beating against my heart, and many times when I looked at her—when she was at her music or painting and didn't know I stood in the room—I thought of that singular experience I'd had with her and no other, that I had killed her, taken her life from her, had drunk all of her life's blood in that fatal embrace I'd lavished on so many others, others who lay now moldering in the damp earth. But she lived, she lived to put her arms around my neck and press her tiny Cupid's bow to my lips and put her gleaming eye to my eye until our lashes touched and, laughing, we reeled about the room as if to the wildest waltz. Father and Daughter. Lover and Lover. You can imagine how well it was Lestat did not envy us this, but only smiled on it from afar, waiting until she came to him. Then he would take her out into the street and they would wave to me beneath the window, off to share what they shared: the hunt, the seduction, the kill.

"Years passed in this way. Years and years and years. Yet it wasn't until some time had passed that an obvious fact occurred to me about Claudia. I suppose from the expression on your face you've already guessed, and you wonder why I didn't guess. I can only tell you, time is not the same for me, nor was it for us then. Day did not link to day making a taut and jerking chain; rather, the moon rose over lapping waves."

"Her body!" the boy said. "She was never to grow up."

The vampire nodded. "She was to be the demon child forever," he said, his voice soft as if he wondered at it. "Just as I am the young man I was when I died. And Lestat? The same. But her mind. It was a vampire's mind. And I strained to know how she moved towards womanhood. She came to talk more, though she was never other than a reflective person and could listen to me patiently by the hour without interruption. Yet more and more her doll-like face seemed to possess two totally aware adult eyes, and innocence seemed lost somewhere with neglected toys and the loss of a certain patience. There was something dreadfully sensual about her lounging on the settee in a tiny nightgown of lace and stitched pearls; she became an eerie and powerful seductress, her voice as clear and sweet as ever, though it had a resonance which was womanish, a sharpness sometimes that proved shocking. After days of her usual quiet, she would scoff suddenly at Lestat's predictions about the war; or drinking blood from a crystal glass say that there were no books in the house, we must get more even if we had to steal them, and then coldly tell me of a library she'd heard of, in a palatial mansion in the Faubourg Ste.-Marie, a woman who collected books as if they were rocks or pressed butterflies. She asked if I might get her into the woman's bedroom.

"I was aghast at such moments; her mind was unpredictable, unknowable. But then she would sit on my lap and put her fingers in my hair and doze there against my heart, whispering to me softly I should never be as grown up as she until I knew that killing was the more serious thing, not the books, the music. 'Always the music . . .' she whispered. 'Doll, doll,' I called her. That's what she was. A magic doll. Laughter and infinite intellect and then the round-cheeked face, the bud mouth. 'Let me dress you, let me brush your hair,' I would say to her out of old habit, aware of her smiling and watching me with the thin veil of boredom over her expression. 'Do as you like,' she breathed into my ear as I bent down to fasten her pearl buttons. 'Only kill with me tonight. You never let me see you kill, Louis!'

"She wanted a coffin of her own now, which left me more wounded than I would let her see. I walked out after giving my gentlemanly consent; for how many years had I slept with her as if she were part of me I couldn't know. But then I found her near the Ursuline Convent, an orphan lost in the darkness, and she ran suddenly towards me and clutched at me with a human desperation. 'I don't want it if it hurts you,' she confided so softly that a human embracing us both could not have heard her or felt her breath. 'I'll stay with you always. But I must see it, don't you understand? A coffin for a child.'

"We were to go to the coffinmaker's. A play, a tragedy in one act: I to leave her in his little parlor and confide to him in the anteroom that she was to die. Talk of love, she must have the best, but she must not know; and the coffinmaker, shaken with the tragedy of it, must make it for her, picturing her laid there on the white satin, dabbing a tear from his eye despite all the years. . . .

" 'But, why, Claudia . . .' I pleaded with her. I loathed to do it, loathed cat and mouse with the helpless human. But hopelessly her lover, I took her there and set her on the sofa, where she sat with folded hands in her lap, her tiny bonnet bent down, as if she didn't know what we whispered about her in the foyer. The undertaker was an old and greatly refined man of color who drew me swiftly aside lest 'the baby' should hear. 'But why must she die?' he begged me, as if I were God who ordained it. 'Her heart, she cannot live,' I said, the words taking on for me a peculiar power, a disturbing resonance. The emotion in his narrow, heavily lined face disturbed me; something came to my mind, a quality of light, a gesture, the sound of something . . . a child crying in a stench-filled room. Now he unlocked one after another of his long rooms and showed me the coffins, black lacquer and silver, she wanted that. And suddenly I found myself backing away from him out of the coffin-house, hurriedly taking her hand. 'The order's been taken,' I said to her. 'It's driving me mad!' I breathed the fresh air of the street as though I'd been suffocated and then I saw her compassionless face studying mine. She slipped her small gloved hand back into my own. 'I want it, Louis,' she explained patiently.

"And then one night she climbed the undertaker's stairs, Lestat beside her, for the coffin, and left the coffinmaker, unawares, dead across the dusty piles of papers on his desk. And there the coffin lay in our bedroom, where she watched it often by the hour when it was new, as if the thing were moving or alive or unfolded some mystery to her little by little, as things do which change. But she did not sleep in it. She slept with me.

"There were other changes in her. I cannot date them or put them in order. She did not kill indiscriminately. She fell into demanding patterns. Poverty began to fascinate her; she begged Lestat or me to take a carriage out through the Faubourg Ste.-Marie to the riverfront places where the immigrants lived. She seemed obsessed with the women and children. These things Lestat told me with great amusement, for I was loath to go and would sometimes not be persuaded under any circumstance. But Claudia had a family there which she took one by one. And she had asked to enter the cemetery of the suburb city of Lafayette and there roam the high marble tombs in search of those desperate men who, having no place else to sleep, spend what little they have on a bottle of wine, and crawl into a rotting vault. Lestat was impressed, overcome. What a picture he made of her, the infant death, he called her. Sister death, and sweet death; and for me, mockingly, he had the term with a sweeping bow, Merciful Death! which he said like a woman clapping her hands and shouting out a word of exciting gossip: oh, merciful heavens! so that I wanted to strangle him.

"But there was no quarrelling. We kept to ourselves. We had our adjustments. Books filled our long flat from floor to ceiling in row after row of gleaming leather volumes, as Claudia and I pursued our natural tastes and Lestat went about his lavish acquisitions. Until she began to ask questions."

The vampire stopped. And the boy looked as anxious as before, as if patience took the greatest effort. But the vampire had brought his long, white fingers together as if to make a church steeple and then folded them and pressed his palms tight. It was as if he'd forgotten the boy altogether. "I should have known," he said, "that it was inevitable, and I should have seen the signs of it coming. For I was so attuned to her; I loved her so completely; she was so much the companion of my every waking hour, the only companion that I had, other than death. I should have known. But something in me was conscious of an enormous gulf of darkness very close to us, as though we walked always near a sheer cliff and might see it suddenly but too late if we made the wrong turn or became too lost in our thoughts.

Sometimes the physical world about me seemed insubstantial except for that darkness. As if a fault in the earth were about to open and I could see the great crack breaking down the Rue Royale, and all the buildings were falling to dust in the rumble. But worst of all, they were transparent, gossamer, like stage drops made of silk. Ah . . . I'm distracted. What do I say? That I ignored the signs in her, that I clung desperately to the happiness she'd given me. And still gave me; and ignored all else.

"But these were the signs. She grew cold to Lestat. She fell to staring at him for hours. When he spoke, often she didn't answer him, and one could hardly tell if it was contempt or that she didn't hear. And our fragile domestic tranquillity erupted with his outrage. He did not have to be loved, but he would not be ignored; and once he even flew at her, shouting that he would slap her, and I found myself in the wretched position of fighting him as I'd done years before she'd come to us. 'She's not a child any longer,' I whispered to him. 'I don't know what it is. She's a woman.' I urged him to take it lightly, and he affected disdain and ignored her in turn. But one evening he came in flustered and told me she'd followed him—though she'd refused to go with him to kill, she'd followed him afterwards. 'What's the matter with her!' he flared at me, as though I'd given birth to her and must know.

"And then one night our servants vanished. Two of the best maids we'd ever retained, a mother and daughter. The coachman was sent to their house only to report they'd disappeared, and then the father was at our door, pounding the knocker. He stood back on the brick sidewalk regarding me with that grave suspicion that sooner or later crept into the faces of all mortals who knew us for any length of time, the forerunner of death, as pallor might be to a fatal fever; and I tried to explain to him they had not been here, mother or daughter, and we must begin some search.

" 'It's she!' Lestat hissed from the shadows when I shut the gate. 'She's done something to them and brought risk for us all. I'll make her tell me!' And he pounded up the spiral stairs from the courtyard. I knew that she'd gone, slipped out while I was at the gate, and I knew something else also: that a vague stench came across the courtyard from the shut, unused kitchen, a stench that mingled uneasily with the honeysuckle—the stench of graveyards. I heard Lestat coming down as I approached the warped shutters, locked with rust to the small brick building. No food was ever prepared there, no work ever done, so that it lay like an old brick vault under the tangles of honeysuckle. The shutters came loose, the nails having turned to dust, and I heard Lestat's gasp as we stepped into the reeking dark. There they lay on the bricks, mother and daughter together, the arm of the mother fastened around the waist of the daughter, the daughter's head bent against the mother's breast, both foul with feces and swarming with insects. A great cloud of gnats rose as the shutter fell back, and I waved them away from me in a convulsive disgust. Ants crawled undisturbed over the eyelids, the mouths of the dead pair, and in the moonlight I could see the endless map of silvery paths of snails. 'Damn her!' Lestat burst out, and I grabbed his arm and held him fast, pitting all my strength against him. 'What do you mean to do with her!' I insisted. 'What can you do? She's not a child anymore that will do what we say simply because we say it. We must teach her.'

" 'She knows!' He stood back from me brushing his coat. 'She knows! She's known for years what to do! What can be risked and what cannot. I won't have her do this without my permission! I won't tolerate it.'

" 'Then, are you master of us all? You didn't teach her that. Was she supposed to imbibe it from my quiet subservience? I don't think so. She sees herself as equal to us now, and us as equal to each other. I tell you we must reason with her, instruct her to respect what is ours. As all of us should respect it.'

"He stalked off, obviously absorbed in what I'd said, though he would give no admission of it to me. And he took his vengeance to the city. Yet when he came home, fatigued and satiated, she was still not there. He sat against the velvet arm of the couch and stretched his long legs out on the length of it. 'Did you bury them?' he asked me.

" 'They're gone,' I said. I did not care to say even to myself that I had burned their remains in the old unused kitchen stove. 'But there is the father to deal with, and the brother,' I said to him. I feared his temper. I wished at once to plan some way to quickly dispose of the whole problem. But he said now that the father and the brother were no more, that death had come to dinner in their small house near the ramparts and stayed to say grace when everyone was done. 'Wine,' he whispered now, running his finger on his lip. 'Both of them had drunk too much wine. I found myself tapping the fence posts with a stick to make a tune,' he laughed. 'But I don't like it, the dizziness. Do you like it?' And when he looked at me I had to smile at him because the wine was working in him and he was mellow; and in that moment when his face looked warm and reasonable, I leaned over and said, 'I hear Claudia's tap on the stairs. Be gentle with her. It's all done.'

"She came in then, with her bonnet ribbons undone and her little boots caked with dirt. I watched them tensely, Lestat with a sneer on his lips, she as unconscious of him as if he weren't there. She had a bouquet of white chrysanthemums in her arms, such a large bouquet it made her all the more a small child. Her bonnet fell back now, hung on her shoulder for an instant, and then fell to the carpet. And all through her golden hair I saw the narrow petals of the chrysanthemums. 'Tomorrow is the Feast of All Saints,' she said. 'Do you know?'

" 'Yes,' I said to her. It is the day in New Orleans when all the faithful go to the cemeteries to care for the graves of their loved ones. They whitewash the plaster walls of the vaults, clean the names cut into the marble slabs. And finally they deck the tombs with flowers. In the St. Louis Cemetery, which was very near our house, in which all the great Louisiana families were buried, in which my own brother was buried, there were even little iron benches set before the graves where the families might sit to receive the other families who had come to the cemetery for the same purpose. It was a festival in New Orleans; a celebration of death, it might have seemed to tourists who didn't understand it, but it was a celebration of the life after. 'I bought this from one of the vendors,' Claudia said. Her voice was soft and inscrutable. Her eyes opaque and without emotion.

" 'For the two you left in the kitchen!' Lestat said fiercely. She turned to him for the first time, but she said nothing. She stood there staring at him as if she'd never seen him before. And then she took several steps towards him and looked at him, still as if she were positively examining him. I moved forward. I could feel his anger. Her coldness. And now she turned to me. And then, looking from one to the other of us, she asked:

" 'Which of you did it? *Which of you made me what I am?*'

"I could not have been more astonished at anything she might have said or done. And yet it was inevitable that her long silence would thus be broken. She seemed very little concerned with me, though. Her eyes fixed on Lestat. 'You speak of us as if we always existed as we are now,' she said, her voice soft, measured, the child's tone rounded with the woman's seriousness. 'You speak of them out there as mortals, us as vampires. But it was not always so. Louis had a mortal sister, I remember her. And there is a picture of her in his trunk. I've seen him look at it! He was mortal the same as she; and so was I. Why else this size, this shape?' She opened her arms now and let the chrysanthemums fall to the floor. I whispered her name. I think I meant to distract her. It was impossible. The tide had turned. Lestat's eyes burned with a keen fascination, a malignant pleasure.

" 'You made us what we are, didn't you?' she accused him.

"He raised his eyebrows now in mock amazement. 'What you are?' he asked. 'And would you be something other than what you are!' He drew up his knees and leaned forward, his eyes narrow. 'Do you know how long it's been? Can you picture yourself? Must I find a hag to show you your mortal countenance now if I had let you alone?'

"She turned away from him, stood for a moment as if she had no idea what she would do, and then she moved towards the chair beside the fireplace and, climbing on it, curled up like the most helpless child. She brought her knees up close to her, her velvet coat open, her silk dress tight around her knees, and she stared at the ashes in the hearth. But there was nothing helpless about her stare. Her eyes had independent life, as if the body were possessed.

" 'You could be dead by now if you were mortal!' Lestat insisted to her, pricked by her silence. He drew his legs around and set his boots on the floor. 'Do you hear me? Why do you ask me this now? Why do you make such a thing of it? You've known all your life you're a vampire.' And so he went on in a tirade, saying much the same things he'd said to me many times over: know your nature, kill, be what you are. But all of this seemed strangely beside the point. For Claudia had no qualms about killing. She sat back now and let her head roll slowly to where she could see him across from her. She was studying him again, as if he were a puppet on strings. 'Did you do it to me? And how?' she asked, her eyes narrowing. 'How did you do it?'

" 'And why should I tell you? It's my power.'

" 'Why yours alone?' she asked, her voice icy, her eyes heartless. *'How was it done?'* she demanded suddenly in rage.

"It was electric. He rose from the couch, and I was on my feet immediately, facing him. 'Stop her!' he said to me. He wrung his hands. 'Do something about her! I can't endure her!' And then he started for the door, but turned and, coming back, drew very close so that he towered over Claudia, putting her in a deep shadow. She glared up at him fearlessly, her eyes moving back and forth over his face with total detachment. 'I can undo what I did. Both to you and to him,' he said to her, his finger pointing at me across the room. 'Be glad I made you what you are,' he sneered. 'Or I'll break you in a thousand pieces!' "

"Well, the peace of the house was destroyed, though there was quiet. Days passed and she asked no questions, though now she was deep into books of the occult, of witches and witchcraft, and of vampires. This was mostly fancy, you understand. Myth, tales, sometimes mere romantic horror tales. But she read it all. Till dawn she read, so that I had to go and collect her and bring her to bed.

"Lestat, meantime, hired a butler and maid and had a team of workers in to make a great fountain in the courtyard with a stone nymph pouring water eternal from a widemouthed shell. He had goldfish brought and boxes of rooted water lilies set into the fountain so their blossoms rested upon the surface and shivered in the ever-moving water.

"A woman had seen him kill on the Nyades Road, which ran to the town of Carrolton, and there were stories of it in the papers, associating him with a haunted house near Nyades and Melpomene, all of which delighted him. He was the Hyades Road ghost for some time, though it finally fell to the back pages; and then he performed another grisly murder in another public place and set the imagination of New Orleans to working. But all this had about it some quality of fear. He was pensive, suspicious, drew close to me constantly to ask where Claudia was, where she'd gone, and what she was doing.

" 'She'll be all right,' I assured him, though I was estranged from her and in agony, as if she'd been my bride. She hardly saw me now, as she'd not seen Lestat before, and she might walk away while I spoke to her.

" 'She had better be all right!' he said nastily.

" 'And what will you do if she's not?' I asked, more in fear than accusation.

"He looked up at me with his cold gray eyes. 'You take care of her, Louis. You talk to her!' he said. 'Everything was perfect, and now this. There's no need for it.'

"But it was my choice to let her come to me, and she did. It was early one evening when I'd just awakened. The house was dark. I saw her standing by the French windows; she wore puffed sleeves and a pink sash and was watching with lowered lashes the evening rush in the Rue Royale. I could hear Lestat in his room, the sound of water splashing from his pitcher. The faint smell of his cologne came and went like the sound of music from the café two doors down from us. 'He'll tell me nothing,' she said softly. I hadn't realized she knew that I had opened my eyes. I came towards her and knelt beside her. 'You'll tell me, won't you? How it was done.'

" 'Is this what you truly want to know?' I asked, searching her face. 'Or is it why it was done to you . . . and what you were before? I don't understand what you mean by "how," for if you mean how was it done so that you in turn may do it. . . .'

" 'I don't even know what it is. What you're saying,' she said with a touch of coldness. Then she turned full around and put her hands on my face. 'Kill with me tonight,' she whispered as sensuously as a lover. 'And tell me all that you know. What are we? Why are we not like them?' She looked down into the street.

" 'I don't know the answers to your questions,' I said to her. Her face contorted suddenly, as if she were straining to hear me over a sudden noise. And then she shook her head. But I went on. 'I wonder the same things you wonder. I do not know. How I was made, I'll tell you that . . . that Lestat did it to me. But the real "how" of it, I don't know!' Her face had that same look of strain. I was seeing in it the first traces of fear, or something worse and deeper than fear. 'Claudia,' I said to her, putting my hands over her hands and pressing them gently against my skin. 'Lestat has one wise thing to tell you. Don't ask these questions. You've been my companion for countless years in my search for all that I could learn of mortal life and mortal creation. Don't be my companion now in this anxiety. He can't give us the answers. And I have none.'

"I could see she could not accept this, but I hadn't expected the convulsive turning away, the violence with which she tore at her own hair for an instant and then stopped as if the gesture were useless, stupid. It filled me with apprehension. She was looking at the sky. It was smoky, starless, the clouds blowing fast from the direction of the river. She made a sudden movement of her lips as if she'd bitten into them, then she turned to me and, still whispering, she said, 'Then he made me . . . he did it . . . you did not!' There was something so dreadful about her expression, I'd left her before I meant to do it. I was standing before the fireplace lighting a single candle in front of the tall mirror. And there suddenly, I saw something which startled me, gathering out of the gloom first as a hideous mask, then becoming its three-dimensional reality: a weathered skull. I stared at it. It smelled faintly of the earth still, but had been scrubbed. 'Why don't you answer me?' she was asking. I heard Lestat's door open. He would go out to kill at once, at least to find the kill. I would not.

"I would let the first hours of the evening accumulate in quiet, as hunger accumulated in me, till the drive grew almost too strong, so that I might give myself to it all the more completely, blindly. I heard her question again clearly, as though it had been floating in the air like the reverberation of a bell . . . and felt my heart pounding. 'He did make me, of course! He said so himself. But you hide something from me. Something he hints at when I question him. He says that it could not have been done without you!'

"I found myself staring at the skull, yet hearing her as if the words were lashing me, lashing me to make me turn around and face the lash. The thought went through me more like a flash of cold than a thought, that nothing should remain of me now but such a skull. I turned around and saw in the light from the street her eyes, like two dark flames in her white face. A doll from whom someone had cruelly ripped the eyes and replaced them with a demonic fire. I found myself moving towards her, whispering her name, some thought forming on my lips, then dying, coming towards her, then away from her, fussing for her coat and her hat. I saw a tiny glove on the floor which was phosphorescent in the shadows, and for just a moment I thought it a tiny, severed hand.

" 'What's the matter with you . . . ?' She drew nearer, looking up into my face. 'What has *always* been the matter? Why do you stare at the skull like that, at the glove?' She asked this gently, but . . . not gently enough.

"There was a slight calculation in her voice, an unreachable detachment.

" 'I need you,' I said to her, without wanting to say it. 'I cannot bear to lose you. You're the only companion I have in immortality.'

" 'But surely there must be others! Surely we are not the

only vampires on earth!' I heard her saying it as I had said it, heard my own words coming back to me now on the tide of her self-awareness, her searching. But there's no pain, I thought suddenly. There's urgency, heartless urgency. I looked down at her. 'Aren't you the same as I?' She looked at me. 'You've taught me all I know!'

" 'Lestat taught you to kill.' I fetched the glove. 'Here, come . . . let's go out. I want to go out. . . .' I was stammering, trying to force the gloves on her. I lifted the great curly mass of her hair and placed it gently over her coat. 'But you taught me to see!' she said. 'You taught me the words *vampire eyes*,' she said. 'You taught me to drink the world, to hunger for more than . . .'

" 'I never meant those words that way, *vampire eyes*,' I said to her. 'It has a different ring when you say it. . . .' She was tugging at me, trying to make me look at her. 'Come,' I said to her, 'I've something to show you. . . .' And quickly I led her down the passage and down the spiral stairs through the dark courtyard. But I no more knew what I had to show her, really, than I knew where I was going. Only that I had to move towards it with a sublime and doomed instinct.

"We rushed through the early evening city, the sky overhead a pale violet now that the clouds were gone, the stars small and faint, the air around us sultry and fragrant even as we moved away from the spacious gardens, towards those mean and narrow streets where the flowers erupt in the cracks of the stones and the huge oleander shoots out thick, waxen stems of white and pink blooms, like a monstrous weed in the empty lots. I heard the staccato of Claudia's steps as she rushed beside me, never once asking me to slacken my pace; and she stood finally, her face infinitely patient, looking up at me in a dark and narrow street where a few old slope-roofed French houses remained among the Spanish façades, ancient little houses, the plaster blistered from the moldering brick beneath. I had found the house now by a blind effort, aware that I had always known where it was and avoided it, always turned before this dark lampless corner, not wishing to pass the low window where I'd first heard Claudia cry. The house was standing still. Sunk lower than it was in those days, the alleyway crisscrossed with sagging cords of laundry, the weeds high along the low foundation, the two dormer windows broken and patched with cloth. I touched the shutters. 'It was here I first saw you,' I said to her, thinking to tell it to her so she would understand, yet feeling now the chill of her gaze, the distance of her stare. 'I heard you crying. You were there in a room with your mother. And your mother was dead. Dead for days, and you didn't know. You clung to her, whining . . . crying pitifully, your body white and feverish and hungry. You were trying to wake her from the dead, you were hugging her for warmth, for fear. It was almost morning and . . .'

"I put my hand to my temples. 'I opened the shutters . . . I came into the room. I felt pity for you. Pity. But . . . something else.'

"I saw her lips slack, her eyes wide. 'You . . . fed on me?' she whispered. 'I was your victim!'

" 'Yes!' I said to her. 'I did it.'

"There was a moment so elastic and painful as to be unbearable. She stood stark-still in the shadows, her huge eyes gathering the light, the warm air rising suddenly with a soft noise. And then she turned. I heard the clicking of her slippers as she ran. And ran. And ran. I stood frozen, hearing the sound grow smaller and smaller; and then I turned, the fear in me unravelling, growing huge and insurmountable, and I ran after her. It was unthinkable that I not catch her, that I not overtake her at once and tell her that I loved her, must have her, must keep her, and every second that I ran headlong down the dark street after her was like her slipping away from me drop by drop; my heart was pounding, unfed, pounding and rebelling against the strain. Until I came suddenly to a dead stop. She stood beneath a lamppost, staring mutely, as if she didn't know me. I took her small waist in both hands and lifted her into the light. She studied me, her face contorted, her head turning as if she wouldn't give me her direct glance, as if she must deflect an overpowering feeling of revulsion. 'You killed me,' she whispered. 'You took my life!'

" 'Yes,' I said to her, holding her so that I could feel her heart pounding. 'Rather, I tried to take it. To drink it away. But you had a heart like no other heart I've ever felt, a heart that beat and beat until I had to let you go, had to cast you away from me lest you quicken my pulse till I would die. And it was Lestat who found me out; Louis the sentimentalist, the fool, feasting on a golden-haired child, a Holy Innocent, *a little girl.* He brought you back from the hospital where they'd put you, and I never knew what he meant to do except teach me my nature. "Take her, finish it," he said. And I felt that passion for you again. Oh, I know I've lost you now forever. I can see it in your eyes! You look at me as you look on mortals, from aloft, from some region of cold self-sufficiency I can't understand. But I did it. I felt it for you again, a vile unsupportable hunger for your hammering heart, this cheek, this skin. You were pink and fragrant as mortal children are, sweet with the bite of salt and dust. I held you again, I took you again. And when I thought your heart would kill me and I didn't care, he parted us and, gashing his own wrist, gave it to you to drink. And drink you did. And drink and drink until you nearly drained him and he was reeling. But you were a vampire then. And that very night you drank a human's blood and have every night thereafter.'

"Her face had not changed. The flesh was like the wax of ivory candles; only the eyes showed life. There was nothing more to say to her. I set her down. 'I took your life,' I said. 'He gave it back to you.'

" 'And here it is,' she said under her breath. 'And I hate you both!' "

The vampire stopped.

"But why did you tell her?" asked the boy after a respectful pause.

"How could I not tell her?" The vampire looked up in mild

astonishment. "She had to know it. She had to weigh one thing against the other. It was not as if Lestat had taken her full from life as he had taken me; I had stricken her. She would have died! There would have been no mortal life for her. But what's the difference? For all of us it's a matter of years, dying! So what she saw more graphically then was what all men know: that death will come inevitably, unless one chooses . . . this!" He opened his white hands now and looked at the palms.

"And did you lose her? Did she go?"

"Go! Where would she have gone? She was a child no bigger than that. Who would have sheltered her? Would she have found some vault, like a mythical vampire, lying down with worms and ants by day and rising to haunt some small cemetery and its surroundings? But that's not why she didn't go. Something in her was as akin to me as anything in her could have been. That thing in Lestat was the same. We could not bear to live alone! We needed our little company! A wilderness of mortals surrounded us, groping, blind, preoccupied, and the brides and bridegrooms of death.

" 'Locked together in hatred,' she said to me calmly afterwards. I found her by the empty hearth, picking the small blossoms from a long stem of lavender. I was so relieved to see her there that I would have done anything, said anything. And when I heard her ask me in a low voice if I would tell her all I knew, I did this gladly. For all the rest was nothing compared to that old secret, that I had claimed her life. I told her of myself as I've told you, of how Lestat came to me and what went on the night he carried her from the little hospital. She asked no questions and only occasionally looked up from her flowers. And then, when it was finished and I was sitting there, staring again at that wretched skull and listening to the soft slithering of the petals of the flowers on her dress and feeling a dull misery in my limbs and mind, she said to me, 'I don't despise you!' I wakened. She slipped off the high, rounded damask cushion and came towards me, covered with the scent of flowers, the petals in her hand. 'Is this the aroma of mortal child?' she whispered. 'Louis. Lover.' I remember holding her and burying my head in her small chest, crushing her bird-shoulders, her small hands working into my hair, soothing me, holding me. 'I was mortal to you,' she said, and when I lifted my eyes I saw her smiling; but the softness on her lips was evanescent, and in a moment she was looking past me like someone listening for faint, important music. 'You gave me your immortal kiss,' she said, though not to me, but to herself. 'You loved me with your vampire nature.'

" 'I love you now with my human nature, if ever I had it,' I said to her.

" 'Ah yes . . .' she answered, still musing. 'Yes, and that's your flaw, and why your face was miserable when I said as humans say, "I hate you," and why you look at me as you do now. Human nature. I have no human nature. And no short story of a mother's corpse and hotel rooms where children learn monstrosity can give me one. I have none. Your eyes grow cold with fear when I say this to you. Yet I have your tongue. Your passion for the truth. Your need to drive the needle of the mind right to the heart of it all, like the beak of the hummingbird, who beats so wild and fast that mortals might think he had no tiny feet, could never set, just go from quest to quest, going again and again for the heart of it. I am your vampire self more than you are. And now the sleep of sixty-five years has ended.'

"*The sleep of sixty-five years has ended!* I heard her say it, disbelieving, not wanting to believe she knew and meant precisely what she'd said. For it had been exactly that since the night I tried to leave Lestat and failed and, falling in love with her, forgot my teeming brain, my awful questions. And now she had the awful questions on her lips and must know. She'd strolled slowly to the center of the room and strewn the crumpled lavender all around her. She broke the brittle stem and touched it to her lips. And having heard the whole story said, 'He made me then . . . to be your companion. No chains could have held you in your loneliness, and he could give you nothing. He gives me nothing. . . . I used to think him charming. I liked the way he walked, the way he tapped the flagstones with his walking stick and swung me in his arms. And the abandon with which he killed, which was as I felt. But I no longer find him charming. And you never have. And we've been his puppets, you and I; you remaining to take care of him, and I your saving companion. Now's time to end it, Louis. Now's time to leave him.'

"Time to leave him.

"I hadn't thought of it, dreamed of it in so long; I'd grown accustomed to him, as if he were a condition of life itself. I could hear a vague mingling of sounds now, which meant he had entered the carriage way, that he would soon be on the back stairs. And I thought of what I always felt when I heard him coming, a vague anxiety, a vague need. And then the thought of being free of him forever rushed over me like water I'd forgotten, waves and waves of cool water. I was standing now, whispering to her that he was coming.

" 'I know,' she smiled. 'I heard him when he turned the far corner.'

" 'But he'll never let us leave,' I whispered, though I'd caught the implication of her words; her vampire sense was keen. She stood *en garde* magnificently. 'But you don't know him if you think he'll let us leave,' I said to her, alarmed at her self-confidence. 'He will not let us go.'

"And she, still smiling, said, 'Oh . . . *really?*' "

"It was agreed then to make plans. At once. The following night my agent came with his usual complaints about doing business by the light of one wretched candle and took my explicit orders for an ocean crossing. Claudia and I would go to Europe, on the first available ship, regardless of what port we had to settle for. And paramount was that an important chest be shipped with us, a chest which might have to be fetched carefully from our house during the day and put on board, not in the freight but in our cabin. And then there were arrangements for Lestat. I had planned to leave him the rents from several shops and town houses and a small construction company operating in the Faubourg Marigny. I put my signature to these things readily. I wanted to buy our freedom: to convince Lestat we wanted only to take a trip together and that he could remain in the style to which he was accustomed; he would have his own money and need come to me for nothing. For all these years, I'd kept him dependent on me. Of course, he demanded his funds from me as if I were merely his banker, and thanked me with the most acrimonious words at his command; but he loathed his dependence. I hoped to deflect his suspicion by playing to his greed. And, convinced that he could read any emotion in my face, I was more than fearful. I did not believe it would be possible to escape him. Do you understand what that means? I acted as though I believed it, but I did not.

"Claudia, meantime, was flirting with disaster, her equanimity overwhelming to me as she read her vampire books and asked Lestat questions. She remained undisturbed by his caustic outbursts, sometimes asking the same question over and over again in different ways and carefully considering what little information he might let escape in spite of himself. 'What vampire made you what you are?' she asked, without looking up from her book and keeping her lids lowered under his onslaught. 'Why do you never talk about him?' she went on, as if his fierce objections were thin air. She seemed immune to his irritation.

" 'You're greedy, both of you!' he said the next night as he paced back and forth in the dark of the center of the room, turning a vengeful eye on Claudia, who was fitted into her corner, in the circle of her candle flame, her books in stacks about her. 'Immortality is not enough for you! No, you would look the Gift Horse of God in the mouth! I could offer it to any man out there in the street and he would jump for it . . .'

" 'Did you jump for it?' she asked softly, her lips barely moving.

" '. . . but you, you would know the *reason* for it. Do you want to end it? I can give you death more easily than I gave you life!' He turned to me, her fragile flame throwing his shadow across me. It made a halo around his blond hair and left his face, except for the gleaming cheekbone, dark. 'Do you want death?'

" 'Consciousness is not death,' she whispered.

" 'Answer me! Do you want death!'

" 'And you give all these things. They proceed from you. Life and death,' she whispered, mocking him.

" 'I have,' he said. 'I do.'

" 'You know nothing,' she said to him gravely, her voice so low that the slightest noise from the street interrupted it, might carry her words away, so that I found myself straining to hear her against myself as I lay with my head back against the chair. 'And suppose the vampire who made you knew nothing, and the vampire who made that vampire knew nothing, and the vampire before him knew nothing, and so it goes back and back, nothing proceeding from nothing, until there is nothing! And we must live with the knowledge that there is no knowledge.'

" 'Yes!' he cried out suddenly, his hands out, his voice tinged with something other than anger.

"He was silent. She was silent. He turned, slowly, as if I'd made some movement which alerted him, as if I were rising behind him. It reminded me of the way humans turn when they feel my breath against them and know suddenly that where they thought themselves to be utterly alone . . . that moment of awful suspicion before they see my face and gasp. He was looking at me now, and I could barely see his lips moving. And then I sensed it. He was afraid. Lestat afraid.

"And she was staring at him with the same level gaze, evincing no emotion, no thought.

" 'You infected her with this . . .' he whispered.

"He struck a match now with a sharp crackle and lit the mantel candles, lifted the smoky shades of the lamps, went around the room making light, until Claudia's small frame took on a solidity and he stood with his back to the marble mantel looking from light to light as if they restored some peace. 'I'm going out,' he said.

"She rose the instant he had reached the street, and suddenly she stopped in the center of the room and stretched, her tiny back arched, her arms straight up into small fists, her eyes squeezed shut for a moment and then wide open as if she were waking to the room from a dream. There was something obscene about her gesture; the room seemed to shimmer with Lestat's fear, echo with his last response. It *demanded* her attention. I must have made some involuntary movement to turn away from her, because she was standing at the arm of my chair now and pressing her hand flat upon my book, a book I hadn't been reading for hours. 'Come out with me.'

" 'You were right. He knows nothing. There is nothing he can tell us,' I said to her.

" 'Did you ever really think that he did?' she asked me in that same small voice. 'We'll find others of our kind,' she said. 'We'll find them in central Europe. That is where they live in such numbers that the stories, both fiction and fact, fill volumes. I'm convinced it was from there that all vampires came, if they came from any place at all. We've tarried too long with him. Come out. Let the flesh instruct the mind.'

"I think I felt a tremor of delight when she said these words, *Let the flesh instruct the mind.* 'Put books aside and kill,' she was whispering to me. I followed her down the stairs, across the courtyard and down a narrow alley to another street. Then she turned with outstretched arms for me to pick her up and carry her, though, of course, she was not tired; she wanted only to be near my ear, to clutch my neck. 'I haven't told him my plan, about the voyage, the money,' I was saying to her, conscious of something about her that was beyond me as she rode my measured steps, weightless in my arms.

" 'He killed the other vampire,' she said.

" 'No, why do you say this?' I asked her. But it wasn't the saying of it that disturbed me, stirred my soul as if it were a pool of water longing to be still. I felt as if she were moving me slowly towards something, as if she were the pilot of our slow walk through the dark street. 'Because I know it now,' she said with authority. 'The vampire made a slave of him, and he would no more be a slave than I would be a slave, and so he killed him. Killed him before he knew what he might know, and then in panic made a slave of you. And you've been his slave.'

" 'Never really . . .' I whispered to her. I felt the press of her cheek against my temple. She was cold and needed the kill. 'Not a slave. Just some sort of mindless accomplice,' I confessed to her, confessed to myself. I could feel the fever for the kill rising in me, a knot of hunger in my insides, a throbbing in the temples, as if the veins were contracting and my body might become a map of tortured vessels.

" 'No, slave,' she persisted in her grave monotone, as though thinking aloud, the words revelations, pieces of a puzzle. 'And I shall free us both.'

"I stopped. Her hand pressed me, urged me on. We were walking down the long wide alley beside the cathedral, towards the lights of Jackson Square, the water rushing fast in the gutter down the center of the alley, silver in the moonlight. She said, *'I will kill him.'*

"I stood still at the end of the alley. I felt her shift in my arm, move down as if she could accomplish being free of me without the awkward aid of my hands. I set her on the stone sidewalk. I said no to her, I shook my head. I had that feeling then which I described before, that the buildings around me—the Cabildo, the cathedral, the apartments along the square—all this was silk and illusion and would ripple suddenly in a horrific wind, and a chasm would open in the earth that was the reality. 'Claudia,' I gasped, turning away from her.

" 'And why not kill him!' she said now, her voice rising, silvery and finally shrill. 'I have no use for him! I can get nothing from him! And he causes me pain, which I will not abide!'

" 'And if he had so little use for us!' I said to her. But the vehemence was false. Hopeless. She was at a distance from me now, small shoulders straight and determined, her pace rapid, like a little girl who, walking out on Sundays with her parents, wants to walk ahead and pretend she is all alone. 'Claudia!' I called after her, catching up with her in a stride. I reached for the small waist and felt her stiffen as if she had become iron. 'Claudia, you cannot kill him!' I whispered. She moved backwards, skipping, clicking on the stones, and moved out into the open street. A cabriolet rolled past us with a sudden surge of laughter and the clatter of horses and wooden wheels. The street was suddenly silent. I reached out for her and moved forward over an immense space and found her standing at the gate of Jackson Square, hands gripping the wrought-iron bars. I drew down close to her. 'I don't care what you feel, what you say, you cannot mean to kill him,' I said to her.

" 'And why not? Do you think him so strong!' she said, her eyes on the statue in the square, two immense pools of light.

" 'He is stronger than you know! Stronger than you dream! How do you mean to kill him? You can't measure his skill. You don't know!' I pleaded with her but could see her utterly unmoved, like a child staring in fascination through the window of a toy shop. Her tongue moved suddenly between her teeth and touched her lower lip in a strange flicker that sent a mild shock through my body. I tasted blood. I felt something palpable and helpless in my hands. I wanted to kill. I could smell and hear humans on the paths of the square, moving about the market, along the levee. I was about to take her, make her look at me, shake her if I had to, to make her listen, when she turned to me with her great liquid eyes. 'I love you, Louis,' she said.

" 'Then listen to me, Claudia, I beg you,' I whispered, holding her, pricked suddenly by a nearby collection of whispers, the slow, rising articulation of human speech over the mingled sounds of the night. 'He'll destroy you if you try to kill him. There is no way you can do such a thing for sure. You don't know how. And pitting yourself against him you'll lose everything. Claudia, I can't bear this.'

"There was a barely perceptible smile on her lips. 'No, Louis,' she whispered. 'I can kill him. And I want to tell you something else now, a secret between you and me.'

"I shook my head but she pressed even closer to me, lowering her lids so that her rich lashes almost brushed the roundness of her cheeks. 'The secret is, Louis, that I want to kill him. I will enjoy it!'

"I knelt beside her, speechless, her eyes studying me as they'd done so often in the past; and then she said, 'I kill humans every night. I seduce them, draw them close to me, with an insatiable hunger, a constant never-ending search for something . . . something, I don't know what it is . . .' She brought her fingers to her lips now and pressed her lips, her mouth partly open so I could see the gleam of her teeth. 'And I care nothing about them—where they came from, where they would go—if I did not meet them on the way. But I dislike him! I *want* him dead and will have him dead. I shall enjoy it.'

" 'But Claudia, he is not mortal. He's immortal. No illness can touch him. Age has no power over him. You threaten a life which might endure to the end of the world!'

" 'Ah, yes, that's it, precisely!' she said with reverential awe. 'A lifetime that might have endured for centuries. Such blood, such power. Do you think I'll possess his power and my own power when I take him?'

"I was enraged now. I rose suddenly and turned away from her. I could hear the whispering of humans near me. They were whispering of the father and the daughter, of some frequent sight of loving devotion. I realized they were talking of us.

" 'It's not necessary,' I said to her. 'It goes beyond all need, all common sense, all . . .'

" 'What! Humanity? He's a killer!' she hissed. 'Lone predator!' She repeated his own term, mocking it. 'Don't interfere with me or seek to know the time I choose to do it, nor try to come between us. . . .' She raised her hand now to hush me and caught mine in an iron grasp, her tiny fingers biting into my tight, tortured flesh. 'If you do, you will bring me destruction by your interference. I can't be discouraged.'

"She was gone then in a flurry of bonnet ribbons and clicking slippers. I turned, paying no attention to where I went, wishing the city would swallow me, conscious now of the hunger rising to overtake reason. I was almost loath to put an end to it. I needed to let the lust, the excitement blot out all consciousness, and I thought of the kill over and over and over, walking slowly up this street and down the next, moving inexorably towards it, saying, 'It's a string which is pulling me through the labyrinth. I am not pulling the string. The string is pulling me. . . .' And then I stood in the Rue Conti listening to a dull thundering, a familiar sound. It was the fencers above in the salon, advancing on the hollow wooden floor, forward, back again, scuttling, and the silver zinging of the foils. I stood back against the wall, where I could see them through the high naked windows, the young men duelling late into the night, left arm poised like the arm of a dancer, grace advancing towards death, grace thrusting for the heart, images of the young Freniere now driving the silver blade forward, now being pulled by it towards hell. Someone had come down the narrow wooden steps to the street—a young boy, a boy so young he had the smooth, plump cheeks of a child; his face was pink and flushed from the fencing, and beneath his smart gray coat and ruffled shirt there was the sweet smell of cologne and salt. I could feel his heat as he emerged from the dim light of the stairwell. He was laughing to himself, talking almost inaudibly to himself, his brown hair falling down over his eyes as he went along, shaking his head, the whispers rising, then falling off. And then he stopped short, his eyes on me. He stared, and his eyelids quivered and he laughed quickly, nervously. 'Excuse me!' he said now in French. 'You gave me a start!' And then, just as he moved to make a ceremonial bow and perhaps go around me, he stood still, and the shock spread over his flushed face. I could see the heart beating in the pink flesh of his cheeks, smell the sudden sweat of his young, taut body.

" 'You saw me in the lamplight,' I said to him. 'And my face looked to you like the mask of death.'

"His lips parted and his teeth touched and involuntarily he nodded, his eyes dazed.

" 'Pass by!' I said to him. 'Fast!' "

The vampire paused, then moved as if he meant to go on. But he stretched his long legs under the table and, leaning back, pressed his hands to his head as if exerting a great pressure on his temples.

The boy, who had drawn himself up into a crouched position, his hands hugging his arms, unwound slowly. He glanced at the tapes and then back at the vampire. "But you killed someone that night," he said.

"Every night," said the vampire.

"Why did you let him go then?" asked the boy.

"I don't know," said the vampire, but it did not have the tone of truly I don't know, but rather, let it be. "You look tired," said the vampire. "You look cold."

"It doesn't matter," said the boy quickly. "The room's a little cold; I don't care about that. You're not cold, are you?"

"No." The vampire smiled and then his shoulders moved with silent laughter.

A moment passed in which the vampire seemed to be thinking and the boy to be studying the vampire's face. The vampire's eyes moved to the boy's watch.

"She didn't succeed, did she?" the boy asked softly.

"What do you honestly think?" asked the vampire. He had settled back in his chair. He looked at the boy intently.

"That she was . . . as you said, destroyed," said the boy; and he seemed to feel the words, so that he swallowed after he'd said the word *destroyed*. "Was she?" he asked.

"Don't you think that she could do it?" asked the vampire.

"But he was so powerful. You said yourself you never knew what powers he had, what secrets he knew. How could she even be sure how to kill him? How did she try?"

The vampire looked at the boy for a long time, his expression unreadable to the boy, who found himself looking away, as though the vampire's eyes were burning lights. "Why don't you drink from that bottle in your pocket?" asked the vampire. "It will make you warm."

"Oh, that . . ." said the boy. "I was going to. I just. . . ."

The vampire laughed. "You didn't think it was polite!" he said, and he suddenly slapped his thigh.

"That's true," the boy shrugged, smiling now; and he took the small flask out of his jacket pocket, unscrewed the gold cap, and took a sip. He held the bottle, now looking at the vampire.

"No," the vampire smiled and raised his hand to wave away the offer.

Then his face became serious again and, sitting back, he went on.

"Lestat had a musician friend in the Rue Dumaine. We had seen him at a recital in the home of a Madame LeClair, who lived there also, which was at that time an extremely fashionable street; and this Madame LeClair, with whom Lestat was also occasionally amusing himself, had found the musician a room in another mansion nearby, where Lestat visited him often. I told you he played with his victims, made friends with them, seduced them into trusting and liking him, even loving him, before he killed. So he apparently played with this young boy, though it had gone on longer than any other such friendship I had ever observed. The young boy wrote good music, and often Lestat brought fresh sheets of it home and played the songs on the square grand in our parlor. The boy had a great talent, but you could tell that this music would not sell, because it was too disturbing. Lestat gave him money and spent evening after evening with him, often taking him to restaurants the boy could have never afforded, and he bought him all the paper and pens which he needed for the writing of his music.

"As I said, it had gone on far longer than any such friendship Lestat had ever had. And I could not tell whether he had actually become fond of a mortal in spite of himself or was simply moving towards a particularly grand betrayal and cruelty. Several times he'd indicated to Claudia and me that he was headed out to kill the boy directly, but he had not. And, of course, I never asked him what he felt because it wasn't worth the great uproar my question would have produced. Lestat entranced with a mortal! He probably would have destroyed the parlor furniture in a rage.

"The next night—after that which I just described to you—he jarred me miserably by asking me to go with him to the boy's flat. He was positively friendly, in one of those moods when he wanted my companionship. Enjoyment could bring that out of him. Wanting to see a good play, the regular opera, the ballet. He always wanted me along. I think I must have seen *Macbeth* with him fifteen times. We went to every performance, even those by amateurs, and Lestat would stride home afterwards, repeating the lines to me and even shouting out to passers-by with an outstretched finger, 'Tomorrow and tomorrow and tomorrow!' until they skirted him as if he were drunk. But this effervescence was frenetic and likely to vanish in an instant; just a word or two of amiable feeling on my part, some suggestion that I found his companionship pleasant, could banish all such affairs for months. Even years. But now he came to me in such a mood and asked me to go to the boy's room. He was not above pressing my arm as he urged me. And I, dull, catatonic, gave him some miserable excuse—thinking only of Claudia, of the agent, of imminent disaster. I could feel it and wondered that he did not feel it. And finally he picked up a book from the floor and threw it at me, shouting, 'Read your damn poems, then! Rot!' And he bounded out.

"This disturbed me. I cannot tell you how it disturbed me. I wished him cold, impassive, gone. I resolved to plead with Claudia to drop this. I felt powerless, and hopelessly fatigued. But her door had been locked until she left, and I had glimpsed her only for a second while Lestat was chattering, a vision of lace and loveliness as she slipped on her coat; puffed sleeves again and a violet ribbon on her breast, her white lace stockings showing beneath the hem of the little gown, and her white slippers immaculate. She cast a cold look at me as she went out.

"When I returned later, satiated and for a while too sluggish for my own thoughts to bother me, I gradually began to sense that this was the night. She would try tonight.

"I cannot tell you how I knew this. Things about the flat disturbed me, alerted me. Claudia moved in the back parlor behind closed doors. And I fancied I heard another voice there, a whisper. Claudia never brought anyone to our flat; no one did except Lestat, who brought his women of the streets. But I knew there was someone there, yet I got no strong scent, no proper sounds. And then there were aromas in the air of food and drink. And chrysanthemums stood in the silver vase on the square grand—flowers which, to Claudia, meant death.

"Then Lestat came, singing something soft under his breath, his walking stick making a rat-tat-tat on the rails of the spiral stairs. He came down the long hall, his face flushed from the kill, his lips pink; and he set his music on the piano. 'Did I kill him or did I not kill him!' He flashed the question at me now with a pointing finger. 'What's your guess?'

" 'You did not,' I said numbly. 'Because you invited me to go with you, and would never have invited me to share that kill.'

" 'Ah, but! Did I kill him in a rage because you would not go with me!' he said and threw back the cover from the keys. I could see that he would be able to go on like this until dawn. He was exhilarated. I watched him flip through the music, thinking, Can he die? Can he actually die? And does she mean to do this? At one point, I wanted to go to her and tell her we must abandon everything, even the proposed trip, and live as we had before. But I had the feeling now that there was no retreat. Since the day she'd begun to question him, this—whatever it was to be—was inevitable. And I felt a weight on me, holding me in the chair.

"He pressed two chords with his hands. He had an immense reach and even in life could have been a fine pianist. But he played without feeling; he was always outside the music, drawing it out of the piano as if by magic, by the virtuosity of his vampire senses and control; the music did not come through him, was not drawn through him by himself. 'Well, did I kill him?' he asked me again.

" 'No, you did not,' I said again, though I could just as easily have said the opposite. I was concentrating on keeping my face a mask.

" 'You're right. I did not,' he said. 'It excites me to be close to him, to think over and over, I can kill him and I will kill him but not now. And then to leave him and find someone who looks as nearly like him as possible. If he had brothers . . . why, I'd kill them one by one. The family would succumb to a mysterious fever which dried up the very blood in their bodies!' he said, now mocking a barker's tone. 'Claudia has a taste for families. Speaking of families, I suppose you heard. The Freniere place is supposed to be haunted; they can't keep an overseer and the slaves run away.'

"This was something I did not wish to hear in particular. Babette had died young, insane, restrained finally from wandering towards the ruins of Pointe du Lac, insisting she had seen the devil there and must find him; I'd heard of it in wisps of gossip. And then came the funeral notices. I'd thought occasionally of going to her, of trying some way to rectify what I had done; and other times I thought it would all heal itself; and in my new life of nightly killing, I had grown far from the attachment I'd felt for her or for my sister or any mortal. And I watched the tragedy finally as one might from a theater balcony, moved from time to time, but never sufficiently to jump the railing and join the players on the stage.

" 'Don't talk of her,' I said.

" 'Very well. I was talking of the plantation. Not her. Her! Your lady love, your fancy.' He smiled at me. 'You know, I had it all my way finally in the end, didn't I? But I was telling you about my young friend and how . . .'

" 'I wish you would play the music,' I said softly, unobtrusively, but as persuasively as possible. Sometimes this worked with Lestat. If I said something just right he found himself doing what I'd said. And now he did just that: with a little snarl, as if to say, 'You fool,' he began playing the music. I heard the doors of the back parlor open and Claudia's steps move down the hall. Don't come, Claudia, I was thinking, feeling; go away from it before we're all destroyed. But she came on steadily until she reached the hall mirror. I could hear her opening the small table drawer, and then the zinging of her hairbrush. She was wearing a floral perfume. I turned slowly to face her as she appeared in the door, still all in white, and moved across the carpet silently towards the piano. She stood at the end of the keyboard, her hands folded on the wood, her chin resting on her hands, her eyes fixed on Lestat.

"I could see his profile and her small face beyond, looking up at him. 'What is it now!' he said, turning the page and letting his hand drop to his thigh. 'You irritate me. Your very presence irritates me!' His eyes moved over the page.

" 'Does it?' she said in her sweetest voice.

" 'Yes, it does. And I'll tell you something else. I've met someone who would make a better vampire than you do.'

"This stunned me. But I didn't have to urge him to go on. 'Do you get my meaning?' he said to her.

" 'Is it supposed to frighten me?' she asked.

" 'You're spoiled because you're an only child,' he said. 'You need a brother. Or rather, I need a brother. I get weary of you both. Greedy, brooding vampires that haunt our own lives. I dislike it.'

" 'I suppose we could people the world with vampires, the three of us,' she said.

" 'You think so!' he said, smiling, his voice with a note of triumph. 'Do you think you could do it? I suppose Louis has told you how it was done or how he thinks it was done. You don't have the power. *Either* of you,' he said.

"This seemed to disturb her. Something she had not accounted for. She was studying him. I could see she did not entirely believe him.

" 'And what gave you the power?' she asked softly, but with a touch of sarcasm.

" 'That, my dear, is one of those things which you may never know. For even the Erebus in which we live must have its aristocracy.'

" 'You're a liar,' she said with a short laugh. And just as he touched his fingers to the keys again, she said, 'But you upset my plans.'

" 'Your plans?' he asked.

" 'I came to make peace with you, even if you are the father of lies. You're my father,' she said. 'I want to make peace with you. I want things to be as they were.'

"Now he was the one who did not believe. He threw a glance at me, then looked at her. 'That can be. Just stop asking me questions. Stop following me. Stop searching in every alleyway for other vampires. There are no other vampires! And this is where you live and this is where you stay!' He looked confused for the moment, as if raising his own voice had confused him. 'I take care of you. You don't need anything.'

" 'And you don't know anything, and that is why you detest my questions. All that's clear. So now let's have peace, because there's nothing else to be had. I have a present for you.'

" 'And I hope it's a beautiful woman with endowments you'll never possess,' he said, looking her up and down. Her face changed when he did this. It was as if she almost lost some control I'd never seen her lose. But then she just shook her head and reached out one small, rounded arm and tugged at his sleeve.

" 'I meant what I said. I'm weary of arguing with you. Hell is hatred, people living together in eternal hatred. We're not in hell. You can take the present or not, I don't care. It doesn't matter. Only let's have an end to all this. Before Louis, in disgust, leaves us both.' She was urging him now to leave the piano, bringing down the wooden cover again over the keys, turning him on the piano stool until his eyes followed her to the door.

" 'You're serious. Present, what do you mean, present?'

" 'You haven't fed enough, I can tell by your color, by your eyes. You've never fed enough at this hour. Let's say that I can give you a precious moment. *Suffer the little children to come unto me,*' she whispered, and was gone. He looked at me. I said nothing. I might as well have been drugged. I could see the curiosity in his face, the suspicion. He followed her down the hall. And then I heard him let out a long, conscious moan, a perfect mingling of hunger and lust.

"When I reached the door, and I took my time, he was bending over the settee. Two small boys lay there, nestled among the soft velvet pillows, totally abandoned to sleep as children can be, their pink mouths open, their small round faces utterly smooth. Their skin was moist, radiant, the curls of the darker of the two damp and pressed to the forehead. I saw at once by their pitiful and identical clothes that they were orphans. And they had ravaged a meal set before them on our best china. The tablecloth was stained with wine, and a small bottle stood half full among the greasy plates and forks. But there was an aroma in the room I did not like. I moved closer, better to see the sleeping ones, and I could see their throats were bare but untouched. Lestat had sunk down beside the darker one; he was by far the more beautiful. He might have been lifted to the painted dome of a cathedral. No more than seven years old, he had that perfect beauty that is of neither sex, but angelic. Lestat brought his hand down gently on the pale throat, and then he touched the silken lips. He let out a sigh which had again that longing, that sweet, painful anticipation. 'Oh . . . Claudia . . .' he sighed. 'You've outdone yourself. Where did you find them?'

"She said nothing. She had receded to a dark armchair and sat back against two large pillows, her legs out straight on the rounded cushion, her ankles drooping so that you did not see the bottom of her white slippers but the curved insteps and the tight, delicate little straps. She was staring at Lestat. 'Drunk on brandy wine,' she said. 'A thimbleful!' and gestured to the table. 'I thought of you when I saw them . . . I thought if I share this with him, even he will forgive.'

"He was warmed by her flattery. He looked at her now and reached out and clutched her white lace ankle. 'Ducky!' he whispered to her and laughed, but then he hushed, as if he didn't wish to wake the doomed children. He gestured to her, intimately, seductively, 'Come sit beside him. You take him, and I'll take this one. Come.' He embraced her as she passed and nestled beside the other boy. He stroked the boy's moist hair, he ran his fingers over the rounded lids and along the fringe of lashes. And then he put his whole softened hand across the boy's face and felt at the temples, cheeks, and jaw, massaging the unblemished flesh. He had forgotten I was there or she was there, but he withdrew his hand and sat still for a moment, as though his desire was making him dizzy. He glanced at the ceiling and then down at the perfect feast. He turned the boy's head slowly against the back of the couch, and the boy's eyebrows tensed for an instant and a moan escaped his lips.

"Claudia's eyes were steady on Lestat, though now she

raised her left hand and slowly undid the buttons of the child who lay beside her and reached inside the shabby little shirt and felt the bare flesh. Lestat did the same, but suddenly it was as if his hand had life itself and drew his arm into the shirt and around the boy's small chest in a tight embrace; and Lestat slid down off the cushions of the couch to his knees on the floor, his arm locked to the boy's body, pulling it up close to him so that his face was buried in the boy's neck. His lips moved over the neck and over the chest and over the tiny nipple of the chest and then, putting his other arm into the open shirt, so that the boy lay hopelessly wound in both arms, he drew the boy up tight and sank his teeth into his throat. The boy's head fell back, the curls loose as he was lifted, and again he let out a small moan and his eyelids fluttered—but never opened. And Lestat knelt, the boy pressed against him, sucking hard, his own back arched and rigid, his body rocking back and forth carrying the boy, his long moans rising and falling in time with the slow rocking, until suddenly his whole body tensed, and his hands seemed to grope for some way to push the boy away, as if the boy himself in his helpless slumber were clinging to Lestat; and finally he embraced the boy again and moved slowly forward over him, letting him down among the pillows, the sucking softer, now almost inaudible.

"He withdrew. His hands pressed the boy down. He knelt there, his head thrown back, so the wavy blond hair hung loose and dishevelled. And then he slowly sank to the floor, turning, his back against the leg of the couch. 'Ah . . . God . . .' he whispered, his head back, his lids half-mast. I could see the color rushing to his cheeks, rushing into his hands. One hand lay on his bent knee, fluttering, and then it lay still.

"Claudia had not moved. She lay like a Botticelli angel beside the unharmed boy. The other's body already withered, the neck like a fractured stem, the heavy head falling now at an odd angle, the angle of death, into the pillow.

"But something was wrong. Lestat was staring at the ceiling. I could see his tongue between his teeth. He lay too still, the tongue, as it were, trying to get out of the mouth, trying to move past the barrier of the teeth and touch the lip. He appeared to shiver, his shoulders convulsing . . . then relaxing heavily; yet he did not move. A veil had fallen over his clear gray eyes. He was peering at the ceiling. Then a sound came out of him. I stepped forward from the shadows of the hallway, but Claudia said in a sharp hiss, 'Go back!'

" 'Louis . . .' he was saying. I could hear it now . . . 'Louis . . . Louis. . . .'

" 'Don't you like it, Lestat?' she asked him.

" 'Something's wrong with it,' he gasped, and his eyes widened as if the mere speaking were a colossal effort. He could not move. I saw it. He could not move at all. 'Claudia!' He gasped again, and his eyes rolled towards her.

" 'Don't you like the taste of children's blood . . . ?' she asked softly.

" 'Louis . . .' he whispered, finally lifting his head just for an instant. It fell back on the couch. 'Louis, it's . . . it's absinthe! Too much absinthe!' he gasped. 'She's poisoned them with it. She's poisoned me. Louis. . . .' He tried to raise his hand. I drew nearer, the table between us.

" 'Stay back!' she said again. And now she slid off the couch and approached him, peering down into his face as he had peered at the child. 'Absinthe, Father,' she said, 'and laudanum!'

" 'Demon!' he said to her. 'Louis . . . put me in my coffin.' He struggled to rise. 'Put me in my coffin!' His voice was hoarse, barely audible. The hand fluttered, lifted, and fell back.

" 'I'll put you in your coffin, Father,' she said, as though she were soothing him. 'I'll put you in it forever.' And then, from beneath the pillows of the couch, she drew a kitchen knife.

" 'Claudia! Don't do this thing!' I said to her. But she flashed at me a virulency I'd never seen in her face, and as I stood there paralyzed, she gashed his throat, and he let out a sharp, choking cry. 'God!' he shouted out. 'God!'

"The blood poured out of him, down his shirt front, down his coat. It poured as it might never pour from a human being, all the blood with which he had filled himself before the child and from the child; and he kept turning his head, twisting, making the bubbling gash gape. She sank the knife into his chest now and he pitched forward, his mouth wide, his fangs exposed, both hands convulsively flying towards the knife, fluttering around its handle, slipping off its handle. He looked up at me, the hair falling down into his eyes. 'Louis! Louis!' He let out one more gasp and fell sideways on the carpet. She stood looking down at him. The blood flowed everywhere like water. He was groaning, trying to raise himself, one arm pinned beneath his chest, the other shoving at the floor. And now, suddenly, she flew at him and clamping both arms about his neck, bit deep into him as he struggled. 'Louis, Louis!' he gasped over and over, struggling, trying desperately to throw her off; but she rode him, her body lifted by his shoulder, hoisted and dropped, hoisted and dropped, until she pulled away; and, finding the floor quickly, she backed away from him, her hands to her lips, her eyes for the moment clouded, then clear. I turned away from her, my body convulsed by what I'd seen, unable to look any longer. 'Louis!' she said; but I only shook my head. For a moment, the whole house seemed to sway. But she said, 'Look what's happening to him!'

"He had ceased to move. He lay now on his back. And his entire body was shrivelling, drying up, the skin thick and wrinkled, and so white that all the tiny veins showed through it. I gasped, but I could not take my eyes off it, even as the shape of the bones began to show through, his lips drawing back from his teeth, the flesh of his nose drying to two gaping holes. But his eyes, they remained the same, staring wildly at the ceiling, the irises dancing from side to side, even as the flesh cleaved to the bones, became nothing but a parchment wrapping for the bones, the clothes hollow and limp over the skeleton that remained. Finally the irises rolled to the top of his head, and the whites of his eyes went dim. The thing lay still. A great mass of wavy blond hair, a coat, a pair of gleaming boots; and this horror that had been Lestat, and I staring helplessly at it."

. . .

"For a long time, Claudia merely stood there. Blood had soaked the carpet, darkening the woven wreaths of flowers. It gleamed sticky and black on the floorboards. It stained her dress, her white shoes, her cheek. She wiped at it with a crumpled napkin, took a swipe at the impossible stains of the dress, and then she said, 'Louis, you must help me get him out of here!'

"I said, 'No!' I'd turned my back on her, on the corpse at her feet.

" 'Are you mad, Louis? It can't remain here!' she said to me. 'And the boys. You must help me! The other one's dead from the absinthe! Louis!'

"I knew that this was true, necessary; and yet it seemed impossible.

"She had to prod me then, almost lead me every step of the way. We found the kitchen stove still heaped with the bones of the mother and daughter she'd killed—a dangerous blunder, a stupidity. So she scraped them out now into a sack and dragged the sack across the courtyard stones to the carriage. I hitched the horse myself, shushing the groggy coachman, and drove the hearse out of the city, fast in the direction of the Bayou St. Jean, towards the dark swamp that stretched to Lake Pontchartrain. She sat beside me, silent, as we rode on and on until we'd passed the gas-lit gates of the few country houses, and the shell road narrowed and became rutted, the swamp rising on either side of us, a great wall of seemingly impenetrable cypress and vine. I could smell the stench of the muck, hear the rustling of the animals.

"Claudia had wrapped Lestat's body in a sheet before I would even touch it, and then, to my horror, she had sprinkled it over with the long-stemmed chrysanthemums. So it had a sweet, funereal smell as I lifted it last of all from the carriage. It was almost weightless, as limp as something made of knots and cords, as I put it over my shoulder and moved down into the dark water, the water rising and filling my boots, my feet seeking some path in the ooze beneath, away from where I'd laid the two boys. I went deeper and deeper in with Lestat's remains, though why, I did not know. And finally, when I could barely see the pale space of the road and the sky which was coming dangerously close to dawn, I let his body slip down out of my arms into the water. I stood there shaken, looking at the amorphous form of the white sheet beneath the slimy surface. The numbness which had protected me since the carriage left the Rue Royale threatened to lift and leave me flayed suddenly, staring, thinking: This is Lestat. This is all of transformation and mystery, dead, gone into eternal darkness. I felt a pull suddenly, as if some force were urging me to go down with him, to descend into the dark water and never come back. It was so distinct and so strong that it made the articulation of voices seem only a murmur by comparison. It spoke without language, saying, 'You know what you must do. Come down into the darkness. Let it all go away.'

"But at that moment I heard Claudia's voice. She was calling my name. I turned, and, through the tangled vines, I saw her distant and tiny, like a white flame on the faint luminescent shell road.

"That morning, she wound her arms around me, pressed her head against my chest in the closeness of the coffin, whispering she loved me, that we were free now of Lestat forever. 'I love you, Louis,' she said over and over as the darkness finally came down with the lid and mercifully blotted out all consciousness.

"When I awoke, she was going through his things. It was a tirade, silent, controlled, but filled with a fierce anger. She pulled the contents from cabinets, emptied drawers onto the carpets, pulled one jacket after another from his armoires, turning the pockets inside out, throwing the coins and theater tickets and bits and pieces of paper away. I stood in the door of his room, astonished, watching her. His coffin lay there, heaped with scarves and pieces of tapestry. I had the compulsion to open it. I had the wish to see him there. 'Nothing!' she finally said in disgust. She wadded the clothes into the grate. 'Not a hint of where he came from, who made him!' she said. 'Not a scrap.' She looked to me as if for sympathy. I turned away from her. I was unable to look at her. I moved back into that bedroom which I kept for myself, that room filled with my own books and what things I'd saved from my mother and sister, and I sat on the bed. I could hear her at the door, but I would not look at her. 'He deserved to die!' she said to me.

" 'Then we deserve to die. The same way. Every night of our lives,' I said back to her. 'Go away from me.' It was as if my words were my thoughts, my mind alone only formless confusion. 'I'll care for you because you can't care for yourself. But I don't want you near me. Sleep in that box you bought for yourself. Don't come near me.'

" 'I told you I was going to do it. I told you . . .' she said. Never had her voice sounded so fragile, so like a little silvery bell. I looked up at her, startled but unshaken. Her face seemed not her face. Never had anyone shaped such agitation into the features of a doll. 'Louis, I told you!' she said, her lips quivering. 'I did it for us. So we could be free.' I couldn't stand the sight of her. Her beauty, her seeming innocence, and this terrible agitation. I went past her, perhaps knocking her backwards, I don't know. And I was almost to the railing of the steps when I heard a strange sound.

"Never in all the years of our life together had I heard this sound. Never since the night long ago when I had first found her, a mortal child, clinging to her mother. She was crying!

"It drew me back now against my will. Yet it sounded so unconscious, so hopeless, as though she meant no one to hear it, or didn't care if it were heard by the whole world. I found her lying on my bed in the place where I often sat to read, her knees drawn up, her whole frame shaking with her sobs. The sound of it was terrible. It was more heartfelt, more awful than her mortal crying had ever been. I sat down slowly, gently, beside her and put my hand on her shoulder. She lifted her head, startled, her eyes wide, her mouth trembling. Her face was stained with tears, tears that were tinted with blood. Her eyes brimmed with them, and the faint touch of red stained her tiny hand. She didn't seem to be conscious of this, to see it. She pushed her hair back from her forehead. Her body quivered then with a long, low, pleading sob. 'Louis . . . if I lose you, I have nothing,' she whispered. 'I would undo it to have you back. I can't undo what I've done.' She put her arms around me, climbing up against me, sobbing against my heart. My hands were reluctant to touch her; and then they moved as if I couldn't stop them, to enfold her and hold her and stroke her hair. 'I can't live without you . . .' she whispered. 'I would die rather than live without you. I would die the same way he died. I can't bear you to look at me the way you did. I cannot bear it if you do not love me!' Her sobs grew worse, more bitter, until finally I bent and kissed her soft neck and cheeks. Winter plums. Plums from an enchanted wood where the fruit never falls from the boughs. Where the flowers never wither and die. 'All right, my dear . . .' I said to her. 'All right, my love . . .' And I rocked her slowly, gently in my arms, until she dozed, murmuring something about our being eternally happy, free of Lestat forever, beginning the great adventure of our lives."

"The great adventure of our lives. What does it mean to die when you can live until the end of the world? And what is 'the end of the world' except a phrase, because who knows even what is the world itself? I had now lived in two centuries, seen the illusions of one utterly shattered by the other, been eternally young and eternally ancient, possessing no illusions, living moment to moment in a way that made me picture a silver clock ticking in a void: the painted face, the delicately carved hands looked upon by no one, looking out at no one, illuminated by a light which was not a light, like the light by which God made the world before He had made light. Ticking, ticking, ticking, the precision of the clock, in a room as vast as the universe.

"I was walking the streets again, Claudia gone her way to kill, the perfume of her hair and dress lingering on my fingertips, on my coat, my eyes moving far ahead of me like the pale beam of a lantern. I found myself at the cathedral. What does it mean to die when you can live until the end of the world? I was thinking of my brother's death, of the incense and the rosary. I had the desire suddenly to be in that funeral room, listening to the sound of the women's voices rising and falling with the *Aves*, the clicking of the beads, the smell of the wax. I could remember the crying. It was palpable, as if it were just yesterday, just behind a door. I saw myself walking fast down a corridor and gently giving the door a shove.

"The great façade of the cathedral rose in a dark mass opposite the square, but the doors were open and I could see a soft, flickering light within. It was Saturday evening early, and the people were going to confession for Sunday Mass and Communion. Candles burned dim in the chandeliers. At the far end of the nave the altar loomed out of the shadows, laden with white flowers. It was to the old church on this spot that they had brought my brother for the final service before the cemetery. And I realized suddenly that I hadn't been in this place since, never once come up the stone steps, crossed the porch, and passed through the open doors.

"I had no fear. If anything, perhaps, I longed for something to happen, for the stones to tremble as I entered the shadowy foyer and saw the distant tabernacle on the altar. I remembered now that I had passed here once when the windows were ablaze and the sound of singing poured out into Jackson Square. I had hesitated then, wondering if there were some secret Lestat had never told me, something which might destroy me were I to enter. I'd felt compelled to enter, but I had pushed this out of my mind, breaking loose from the fascination of the open doors, the throng of people making one voice. I had had something for Claudia, a doll I was taking to her, a bridal doll I'd lifted from a darkened toy shop window and placed in a great box with ribbons and tissue paper. A doll for Claudia. I remembered pressing on with it, hearing the heavy vibrations of the organ behind me, my eyes narrow from the great blaze of the candles.

"Now I thought of that moment; that fear in me at the very sight of the altar, the sound of the *Pange Lingua*. And I thought again, persistently, of my brother. I could see the coffin rolling along up the center aisle, the procession of mourners behind it. I felt no fear now. As I said, I think if anything I felt a longing for some fear, for some reason for fear as I moved slowly along the dark, stone walls. The air was chill and damp in spite of summer. The thought of Claudia's doll came back to me. Where was that doll? For years Claudia had played with that doll. Suddenly I saw myself searching for the doll, in the relentless and meaningless manner one searches for something in a nightmare, coming on doors that won't open or drawers that won't shut, struggling over and over against the same meaningless thing, not knowing why the effort seems so desperate, why the sudden sight of a chair with a shawl thrown over it inspires the mind with horror.

"I was in the cathedral. A woman stepped out of the confessional and passed the long line of those who waited. A man who should have stepped up next did not move; and my eye, sensitive even in my vulnerable condition, noted this, and I turned to see him. He was staring at me. Quickly I turned my back on him. I heard him enter the confessional and shut the door. I walked up the aisle of the church and then, more from exhaustion than from any conviction, went into an empty pew and sat down. I had almost genuflected from old habit. My mind seemed as muddled and tortured as that of any human. I closed my eyes for a moment and tried to banish all thoughts. Hear and see, I said to myself. And with this act of will, my senses emerged from the torment. All around me in the gloom I heard the whisper of prayers, the tiny click of the rosary beads; soft the sighing of the woman who knelt now at the Twelfth Station. Rising from the sea of wooden pews came the scent of rats. A rat moving somewhere near the altar, a rat in the great wood-carved side altar of the Virgin Mary. The gold candlesticks shimmered on the altar; a rich white chrysanthemum bent suddenly on its stem, droplets glistening on the crowded petals, a sour fragrance rising from a score of vases, from altars and side altars, from statues of Virgins and Christs and saints. I stared at the statues; I became obsessed suddenly and completely with the lifeless profiles, the staring eyes, the empty hands, the frozen folds. Then my body convulsed with such violence that I found myself pitched forward, my hand on the pew before me.

It was a cemetery of dead forms, of funereal effigy and stone angels. I looked up and saw myself in a most palpable vision ascending the altar steps, opening the tiny sacrosanct tabernacle, reaching with monstrous hands for the consecrated ciborium, and taking the Body of Christ and strewing Its white wafers all over the carpet; and walking then on the sacred wafers, walking up and down before the altar, giving Holy Communion to the dust. I rose up now in the pew and stood there staring at this vision. I knew full well the meaning of it.

"God did not live in this church; these statues gave an image to nothingness. *I* was the supernatural in this cathedral. I was the only supermortal thing that stood conscious under this roof! Loneliness. Loneliness to the point of madness. The cathedral crumbled in my vision; the saints listed and fell. Rats ate the Holy Eucharist and nested on the sills. A solitary rat with an enormous tail stood tugging and gnawing at the rotted altar cloth until the candlesticks fell and rolled on the slime-covered stones. And I remained standing. Untouched. Undead—reaching out suddenly for the plaster hand of the Virgin and seeing it break in my hand, so that I held the hand crumbling in my palm, the pressure of my thumb turning it to powder.

"And then suddenly through the ruins, up through the open door through which I could see a wasteland in all directions, even the great river frozen over and stuck with the encrusted ruins of ships, up through these ruins now came a funeral procession, a band of pale, white men and women, monsters with gleaming eyes and flowing black clothes, the coffin rumbling on the wooden wheels, the rats scurrying across the broken and buckling marble, the procession advancing, so that I could see then Claudia in the procession, her eyes staring from behind a thin black veil, one gloved hand locked upon a black prayer book, the other on the coffin as it moved beside her. And there now in the coffin, beneath a glass cover, I saw to my horror the skeleton of Lestat, the wrinkled skin now pressed into the very texture of his bones, his eyes but sockets, his blond hair billowed on the white satin.

"The procession stopped. The mourners moved out, filling the dusty pews without a sound, and Claudia, turning with her book, opened it and lifted the veil back from her face, her eyes fixed on me as her finger touched the page. 'And now art thou cursed from the earth,' she whispered, her whisper rising in echo in the ruins. 'And now art thou cursed from the earth, which hath opened her mouth to receive thy brother's blood from thy hand. When thou tillest the ground, it shall not henceforth yield unto thee her strength. A fugitive and a vagabond shalt thou be in the earth . . . and whoever slayeth thee, vengeance shall be taken on him seven-fold.'

"I shouted at her, I screamed, the scream rising up out of the depths of my being like some great rolling black force that broke from my lips and sent my body reeling against my will. A terrible sighing rose from the mourners, a chorus growing louder and louder as I turned to see them all about me, pushing me into the aisle against the very sides of the coffin, so that I turned to get my balance and found both my hands upon it. And I stood there staring down not at the remains of Lestat, but at the body of my mortal brother. A quiet descended, as if a veil had fallen over all and made their forms dissolve beneath its soundless folds. There was my brother, blond and young and sweet as he had been in life, as real and warm to me now as he'd been years and years beyond which I could never have remembered him thus, so perfectly was he re-created, so perfectly in every detail. His blond hair brushed back from his forehead, his eyes closed as if he slept, his smooth fingers around the crucifix on his breast, his lips so pink and silken I could hardly bear to see them and not touch them. And as I reached out just to touch the softness of his skin, *the vision ended.*

"I was sitting still in the Saturday night cathedral, the smell of the tapers thick in the motionless air, the woman of the stations gone and darkness gathering—behind me, across from me, and now above me. A boy appeared in the black cassock of a lay brother, with a long extinguisher on a golden pole, putting its little funnel down upon one candle and then another and then another. I was stupefied. He glanced at me and then away, as if not to disturb a man deep in prayer. And then, as he moved on up to the next chandelier, I felt a hand on my shoulder.

"That two humans should pass this close to me without my hearing, without my even caring, registered somewhere within me that I was in danger, but I did not care. I looked up now and saw a gray-haired priest. 'You wish to go to confession?' he asked. 'I was about to lock up the church.' He narrowed his eyes behind his thick glasses. The only light now came from the racks of little red-glass candles which burned before the saints; and shadows leaped upon the towering walls. 'You *are* troubled, aren't you? Can I help you?'

" 'It's too late, too late,' I whispered to him, and rose to go. He backed away from me, still apparently unaware of anything about my appearance that should alarm him, and said kindly, to reassure me, 'No, it's still early. Do you want to come into the confessional?'

"For a moment I just stared at him. I was tempted to smile. And then it occurred to me to do it. But even as I followed him down the aisle, in the shadows of the vestibule, I knew this would be nothing, that it was madness. Nevertheless, I knelt down in the small wooden booth, my hands folded on the priedieu as he sat in the booth beside it and slid back the panel to show me the dim outline of his profile. I stared at him for a moment. And then I said it, lifting my hand to make the Sign of the Cross. 'Bless me, father, for I have sinned, sinned so often and so long I do not know how to change, nor how to confess before God what I've done.'

" 'Son, God is infinite in His capacity to forgive,' he whispered to me. 'Tell Him in the best way you know how and from your heart.'

" 'Murders, father, death after death. The woman who died two nights ago in Jackson Square, I killed her, and thousands of others before her, one and two a night, father, for seventy years. I have walked the streets of New Orleans like the Grim Reaper and fed on human life for my own existence. I am not mortal, father, but immortal and damned, like angels put in hell by God. I am a vampire.'

"The priest turned. 'What is this, some sort of sport for you? Some joke? You take advantage of an old man!' he said. He slid the wooden panel back with a *splat.* Quickly I opened the door and stepped out to see him standing there. 'Young man, do you fear God at all? Do you know the meaning of sacrilege?' He glared at me. Now I moved closer to him, slowly, very slowly, and at first he merely stared at me, outraged. Then, confused, he took a step back. The church was hollow, empty, black, the sacristan gone and the candles throwing ghastly light only on the distant altars. They made a wreath of soft, gold fibers about his gray head and face. 'Then there is no mercy!' I said to him and suddenly clamping my hands on his shoulders, I held him in a preternatural lock from which he couldn't hope to move and held him close beneath my face. His mouth fell open in horror. 'Do you see what I am! Why, if God exists, does He suffer me to exist!' I said to him. 'You talk of sacrilege!' He dug his nails into my hands, trying to free himself, his missal dropping to the floor, his rosary clattering in the folds of his cassock. He might as well have fought the animated statues of the saints. I drew my lips back and showed him my virulent teeth. 'Why does He suffer me to live!' I said. His face infuriated me, his fear, his contempt, his rage. I saw in it all the hatred I'd seen in Babette, and he hissed at me, 'Let me go! Devil!' in sheer mortal panic.

"I released him, watching with a sinister fascination as he floundered, moving up the center aisle as if he plowed through snow. And then I was after him, so swift that I surrounded him in an instant with my outstretched arms, my cape throwing him into darkness, his legs scrambling still. He was cursing me, calling on God at the altar. And then I grabbed him on the very steps to the Communion rail and pulled him down to face me there and sank my teeth into his neck."

The vampire stopped.

Sometime before, the boy had been about to light a cigarette. And he sat now with the match in one hand, the cigarette in the other, still as a store dummy, staring at the vampire. The vampire was looking at the floor. He turned suddenly, took the book of matches from the boy's hand, struck the match, and held it out. The boy bent the cigarette to receive it. He inhaled and let the smoke out quickly. He uncapped the bottle and took a deep drink, his eyes always on the vampire.

He was patient again, waiting until the vampire was ready to resume.

"I didn't remember Europe from my childhood. Not even the voyage to America, really. That I had been born there was an abstract idea. Yet it had a hold over me which was as powerful as the hold France can have on a colonial. I spoke French, read French, remembered waiting for the reports of the Revolution and reading the Paris newspaper accounts of Napoleon's victories. I remember the anger I felt when he sold the colony of Louisiana to the United States. How long the mortal Frenchman lived in me I don't know. He was gone by this time, really, but there was in me that great desire to see Europe and to know it, which comes not only from the reading of all the literature and the philosophy, but from the feeling of having been shaped by Europe more deeply and keenly than the rest of Americans. I was a Creole who wanted to see where it had all begun.

"And so I turned my mind to this now. To divesting my closets and trunks of everything that was not essential to me. And very little was essential to me, really. And much of that might remain in the town house, to which I was certain I would return sooner or later, if only to move my possessions to another similar one and start a new life in New Orleans. I couldn't conceive of leaving it forever. Wouldn't. But I fixed my mind and heart on Europe.

"It began to penetrate for the first time that I might see the world if I wanted. That I was, as Claudia said, free.

"Meantime, she made a plan. It was her idea most definitely that we must go first to central Europe, where the vampire seemed most prevalent. She was certain we could find something there that would instruct us, explain our origins. But she seemed anxious for more than answers: a communion with her own kind. She mentioned this over and over, 'My own kind,' and she said it with a different intonation than I might have used. She made me feel the gulf that separated us. In the first years of our life together, I had thought her like Lestat, imbibing his instinct to kill, though she shared my tastes in everything else. Now I knew her to be less human than either of us, less human than either of us might have dreamed. Not the faintest conception bound her to the sympathies of human existence. Perhaps this explained why—despite everything I had done or failed to do—she clung to me. I was not her *own kind.* Merely the closest thing to it."

"But wouldn't it have been possible," asked the boy suddenly, "to instruct her in the ways of the human heart the way you'd instructed her in everything else?"

"To what avail?" asked the vampire frankly. "So she might suffer as I did? Oh, I'll grant you I should have taught her something to prevail against her desire to kill Lestat. For my own sake, I should have done that. But you see, I had no *confidence* in anything else. Once fallen from grace, I had confidence in nothing."

The boy nodded. "I didn't mean to interrupt you. You were coming to something," he said.

"Only to the point that it was possible to forget what had happened to Lestat by turning my mind to Europe. And the thought of the other vampires inspired me also. I had not been cynical for one moment about the existence of God. Only lost from it. Drifting, preternatural, through the natural world.

"But we had another matter before we left for Europe. Oh, a great deal happened indeed. It began with the musician. He had called while I was gone that evening to the cathedral, and the next night he was to come again. I had dismissed the servants and went down to him myself. And his appearance startled me at once.

"He was much thinner than I'd remembered him and very pale, with a moist gleam about his face that suggested fever. And he was perfectly miserable. When I told him Lestat had gone away, he refused at first to believe me and began insisting Lestat would have left him some message, something. And then he went off up the Rue Royale, talking to himself about it, as if he had little awareness of anyone around him. I caught up with him under a gas lamp. 'He did leave you something,' I said, quickly feeling for my wallet. I didn't know how much I had in it, but I planned to give it to him. It was several hundred dollars. I put it into his hands. They were so thin I could see the blue veins pulsing beneath the watery skin. Now he became exultant, and I sensed at once that the matter went beyond the money. 'Then he spoke of me, he told you to give this to me!' he said, holding onto it as though it were a relic. 'He must have said something else to you!' He stared at me with bulging, tortured eyes. I didn't answer him at once, because during these moments I had seen the puncture wounds in his neck. Two red scratch-like marks to the right, just above his soiled collar. The money flapped in his hand; he was oblivious to the evening traffic of the street, the people who pushed close around us. 'Put it away,' I whispered. 'He did speak of you, that it was important you go on with your music.'

"He stared at me as if anticipating something else. 'Yes? Did he say anything else?' he asked me. I didn't know what to tell him. I would have made up anything if it would have given him comfort, and also kept him away. It was painful for me to speak of Lestat; the words evaporated on my lips. And the puncture wounds amazed me. I couldn't fathom this. I was saying nonsense to the boy finally—that Lestat wished him well, that he had to take a steamboat up to St. Louis, that he would be back, that war was imminent and he had business there . . . the boy hungering after every word, as if he couldn't possibly get enough and was pushing on with it for the thing he wanted. He was trembling; the sweat broke out fresh on his forehead as he stood there pressing me, and suddenly he bit his lip hard and said, 'But why did he go!' as if nothing had sufficed.

" 'What is it?' I asked him. 'What did you need from him? I'm sure he would want me to . . .'

" 'He was my friend!' He turned on me suddenly, his voice dropping with repressed outrage.

" 'You're not well,' I said to him. 'You need rest. There's something . . .' and now I pointed to it, attentive to his every move '. . . on your throat.' He didn't even know what I meant. His fingers searched for the place, found it, rubbed it.

" 'What does it matter? I don't know. The insects, they're everywhere,' he said, turning away from me. 'Did he say anything else?'

"For a long while I watched him move up the Rue Royale, a frantic, lanky figure in rusty black, for whom the bulk of the traffic made way.

"I told Claudia at once about the wound on his throat.

"It was our last night in New Orleans. We'd board the ship just before midnight tomorrow for an early-morning departure. We had agreed to walk out together. She was being solicitous, and there was something remarkably sad in her face, something which had not left after she had cried. 'What could the marks mean?' she asked me now. 'That he fed on the boy when the boy slept, that the boy allowed it? I can't imagine . . .' she said.

" 'Yes, that must be what it is.' But I was uncertain. I remembered now Lestat's remark to Claudia that he knew a boy who would make a better vampire than she. Had he planned to do that? Planned to make another one of us?

" 'It doesn't matter now, Louis,' she reminded me. We had to say our farewell to New Orleans. We were walking away from the crowds of the Rue Royale. My senses were keen to all around me, holding it close, reluctant to say this was the last night.

"The old French city had been for the most part burned a long time ago, and the architecture of these days was as it is now, Spanish, which meant that, as we walked slowly through the very narrow street where one cabriolet had to stop for another, we passed whitewashed walls and great courtyard gates that revealed distant lamplit courtyard paradises like our own, only each seemed to hold such promise, such sensual mystery.

Great banana trees stroked the galleries of the inner courts, and masses of fern and flower crowded the mouth of the passage. Above, in the dark, figures sat on the balconies, their backs to the open doors, their hushed voices and the flapping of their fans barely audible above the soft river breeze; and over the walls grew wisteria and passiflora so thick that we could brush against it as we passed and stop occasionally at this place or that to pluck a luminescent rose or tendrils of honeysuckle. Through the high windows we saw again and again the play of candlelight on richly embossed plaster ceilings and often the bright iridescent wreath of a crystal chandelier. Occasionally a figure dressed for evening appeared at the railings, the glitter of jewels at her throat, her perfume adding a lush evanescent spice to the flowers in the air.

"We had our favorite streets, gardens, corners, but inevitably we reached the outskirts of the old city and saw the rise of swamp. Carriage after carriage passed us coming in from the Bayou Road bound for the theater or the opera. But now the lights of the city lay behind us, and its mingled scents were drowned in the thick odor of swamp decay. The very sight of the tall, wavering trees, their limbs hung with moss, had sickened me, made me think of Lestat. I was thinking of him as I'd thought of my brother's body. I was seeing him sunk deep among the roots of cypress and oak, that hideous withered form folded in the white sheet. I wondered if the creatures of the dark shunned him, knowing instinctively the parched, crackling thing there was virulent, or whether they swarmed about him in the reeking water, picking his ancient dried flesh from the bones.

"I turned away from the swamps, back to the heart of the old city, and felt the gentle press of Claudia's hand comforting. She had gathered a natural bouquet from all the garden walls, and she held it crushed to the bosom of her yellow dress, her face buried in its perfume. Now she said to me in such a whisper that I bent my ear to her, 'Louis, it troubles you. You know the remedy. Let the flesh . . . let the flesh instruct the mind.' She let my hand go, and I watched her move away from me, turning once to whisper the same command. 'Forget him. Let the flesh instruct the mind. . . .' It brought back to me that book of poems I'd held in my hand when she first spoke these words to me, and I saw the verse upon the page:

> *Her* lips were red, *her* looks were free,
> Her locks were yellow as gold:
> Her skin was as white as leprosy,
> The Night-mare LIFE-IN-DEATH was she,
> Who thicks man's blood with cold.

"She was smiling from the far corner, a bit of yellow silk visible for a moment in the narrowing dark, then gone. My companion, my companion forever.

"I was turning into the Rue Dumaine, moving past darkened windows. A lamp died very slowly behind a broad scrim of heavy lace, the shadow of the pattern on the brick expanding, growing fainter, then vanishing into blackness. I moved on, nearing the house of Madame LeClair, hearing faint but shrill the violins from the upstairs parlor and then the thin metallic laughter of the guests. I stood across from the house in the shadows, seeing a small handful of them moving in the lighted rooms; from window to window to window moved one guest, a pale lemon-colored wine in his stem glass, his face turned towards the moon as if he sought something from a better vantage and found it finally at the last window, his hand on the dark drape.

"Across from me a door stood open in the brick wall, and a light fell on the passage at the far end. I moved silently over the narrow street and met the thick aromas of the kitchen rising on the air past the gate. The slightly nauseating smell of cooking meat. I stepped into the passage. Someone had just walked fast across the courtyard and shut a rear door. But then I saw another figure. She stood by the kitchen fire, a lean black woman with a brilliant tignon around her head, her features delicately chiselled and gleaming in the light like a figure in diorite. She stirred the mixture in the kettle. I caught the sweet smell of the spices and the fresh green of marjoram and bay leaf; and then in a wave came the horrid smell of the cooking meat, the blood and flesh decaying in the boiling fluids. I drew near and saw her set down her long iron spoon and stand with her hands on her generous, tapered hips, the white of her apron sash outlining her small, fine waist. The juices of the pot foamed on the lip and spit in the glowing coals below. Her dark odor came to me, her dusky spiced perfume, stronger than the curious mixture from the pot, tantalizing as I drew nearer and rested back against a wall of matted vine. Upstairs the thin violins began a waltz, and the floorboards groaned with the dancing couples. The jasmine of the wall enclosed me and then receded like water leaving the clean-swept beach; and again I sensed her salt perfume. She had moved to the kitchen door, her long black neck gracefully bent as she peered into the shadows beneath the lighted window. 'Monsieur!' she said, and stepped out now into the shaft of yellow light. It fell on her great round breasts and long sleek silken arms and now on the long cold beauty of her face. 'You're looking for the party, Monsieur?' she asked. 'The party's upstairs. . . .'

" 'No, my dear, I wasn't looking for the party,' I said to her, moving forward out of the shadows. 'I was looking for you.' "

"Everything was ready when I awoke the next evening: the wardrobe trunk on its way to the ship as well as a chest which contained a coffin; the servants gone; the furnishings draped in white. The sight of the tickets and a collection of notes of credit and some other papers all placed together in a flat black wallet made the trip emerge into the bright light of reality. I would have forgone killing had that been possible, and so I took care of this early, and perfunctorily, as did Claudia; and as it neared time for us to leave, I was alone in the flat, waiting for her. She had been gone too long for my nervous frame of mind. I feared for her—though she could bewitch almost anyone into assisting her if she found herself too far away from home, and had many times persuaded strangers to bring her to her very door, to her father, who thanked them profusely for returning his lost daughter.

"When she came now she was running, and I fancied as I put my book down that she had forgotten the time. She thought it later than it was. By my pocket watch we had an hour. But the instant she reached the door, I knew that this was wrong. 'Louis, the doors!' she gasped, her chest heaving, her hand at her heart. She ran back down the passage with me behind her and, as she desperately signalled me, I shut up the doors to the gallery. 'What is it?' I asked her. 'What's come over you?' But she was moving to the front windows now, the long French windows which opened onto the narrow balconies over the street. She lifted the shade of the lamp and quickly blew out the flame. The room went dark, and then lightened gradually with the illumination of the street. She stood panting, her hand on her breast, and then she reached out for me and drew me close to her beside the window.

" 'Someone followed me,' she whispered now. 'I could hear him block after block behind me. At first, I thought it was nothing!' She stopped for breath, her face blanched in the bluish light that came from the windows across the way. 'Louis, it was the musician,' she whispered.

" 'But what does that matter? He must have seen you with Lestat.'

" 'Louis, he's down there. Look out the window. Try to see him.' She seemed so shaken, almost afraid. As if she would not stand exposed on the threshold. I stepped out on the balcony, though I held her hand as she hovered by the drape; and she held me so tightly that it seemed she feared for me. It was eleven o'clock and the Rue Royale for the moment was quiet: shops shut, the traffic of the theater just gone away. A door slammed somewhere to my right, and I saw a woman and a man emerge and hurry towards the corner, the woman's face hidden beneath an enormous white hat. Their steps died away. I could see no one, sense no one. I could hear Claudia's labored breathing. Something stirred in the house; I started, then recognized it as the jingling and rustling of the birds. We'd forgotten the birds. But Claudia had started worse than I, and she pulled near to me. 'There is no one, Claudia . . .' I started to whisper to her.

"Then I saw the musician.

"He had been standing so still in the doorway of the furniture shop that I had been totally unaware of him, and he must have wanted this to be so. For now he turned his face upwards, towards me, and it shone from the dark like a white light. The frustration and care were utterly erased from his stark features; his great dark eyes peered at me from the white flesh. He had become a vampire.

" 'I see him,' I murmured to her, my lips as still as possible, my eyes holding his eyes. I felt her move closer, her hand trembling, a heart beating in the palm of her hand. She let out a gasp when she saw him now. But at the same moment, something chilled me even as I stared at him and he did not move. Because I heard a step in the lower passage. I heard the gate-hinge groan. And then that step again, deliberate, loud, echoing under the arched ceiling of the carriage way, deliberate, familiar. That step advancing now up the spiral stairs. A thin scream rose from Claudia, and then she caught it at once with her hand. The vampire in the furniture shop door had not moved. And I knew the step on the stairs. I knew the step on the porch. It was Lestat. Lestat pulling on the door, now pounding on it, now ripping at it, as if to tear it loose from the very wall. Claudia moved back into the corner of the room, her body bent, as if someone had struck her a sharp blow, her eyes moving frantically from the figure in the street to me. The pounding on the door grew louder. And then I heard his voice. 'Louis!' he called to me. 'Louis!' he roared against the door. And then came the smash of the back parlor window. And I could hear the latch turning from within. Quickly, I grabbed the lamp, struck a match hard and broke it in my frenzy, then got the flame as I wanted it and held the small vessel of kerosene poised in my hand. 'Get away from the window. Shut it,' I told her. And she obeyed as if the sudden clear, spoken command released her from a paroxysm of fear. 'And light the other lamps, now, at once.' I heard her crying as she struck the match. Lestat was coming down the hallway.

"And then he stood at the door. I let out a gasp, and, not meaning to, I must have taken several steps backwards when I saw him. I could hear Claudia's cry. It was Lestat beyond question, restored and intact as he hung in the doorway, his head thrust forward, his eyes bulging, as if he were drunk and needed the door jamb to keep him from plunging headlong into the room. His skin was a mass of scars, a hideous covering of injured flesh, as though every wrinkle of his 'death' had left its mark upon him. He was seared and marked as if by the random strokes of a hot poker, and his once clear gray eyes were shot with hemorrhaged vessels.

" 'Stay back . . . for the love of God . . .' I whispered. 'I'll throw it at you. I'll burn you alive,' I said to him. And at the same moment I could hear a sound to my left, something scraping, scratching against the façade of the town house. It was the other one. I saw his hands now on the wrought-iron balcony. Claudia let out a piercing scream as he threw his weight against the glass doors.

"I cannot tell you all that happened then. I cannot possibly recount it as it was. I remember heaving the lamp at Lestat; it smashed at his feet and the flames rose at once from the carpet. I had a torch then in my hands, a great tangle of sheet I'd pulled from the couch and ignited in the flames. But I was struggling with him before that, kicking and driving savagely at his great strength. And somewhere in the background were Claudia's panicked screams. And the other lamp was broken. And the drapes of the windows blazed. I remember that his clothes reeked of kerosene and that he was at one point smacking wildly at the flames. He was clumsy, sick, unable to keep his balance; but when he had me in his grip, I even tore at his fingers with my teeth to get him off. There was noise rising in the street, shouts, the sound of a bell. The room itself had fast become an inferno, and I did see in one clear blast of light Claudia battling the fledgling vampire. He seemed unable to close his hands on her, like a clumsy human after a bird. I remember rolling over and over with Lestat in the flames, feeling the suffocating heat in my face, seeing the flames above his back when I rolled under him. And then Claudia rose up out of the confusion and was striking at him over and over with the poker until his grip broke and I scrambled loose from him. I saw the poker coming down again and again on him and could hear the snarls rising from Claudia in time with the poker, like the stress of an unconscious animal. Lestat was holding his hand, his face a grimace of pain. And there, sprawled on the smoldering carpet, lay the other one, blood flowing from his head.

"What happened then is not clear to me. I think I grabbed the poker from her and gave him one fine blow with it to the side of the head. I remember that he seemed unstoppable, invulnerable to the blows. The heat, by this time, was singeing my clothes, had caught Claudia's gossamer gown, so that I grabbed her up and ran down the passage trying to stifle the flames with my body. I remember taking off my coat and beating at the flames in the open air, and men rushing up the stairs and past me. A great crowd swelled from the passage into the courtyard, and someone stood on the sloped roof of the brick kitchen. I had Claudia in my arms now and was rushing past them all, oblivious to the questions, thrusting a shoulder through them, making them divide. And then I was free with her, hearing her pant and sob in my ear, running blindly down the Rue Royale, down the first narrow street, running and running until there was no sound but the sound of my running. And her breath. And we stood there, the man and the child, scorched and aching, and breathing deep in the quiet of night."

PART II

ALL NIGHT LONG I stood on the deck of the French ship *Mariana*, watching the gangplanks. The long levee was crowded, and parties lasted late in the lavish staterooms, the decks rumbling with passengers and guests. But finally, as the hours moved towards dawn, the parties were over one by one, and carriages left the narrow riverfront streets. A few late passengers came aboard, a couple lingered for hours at the rail nearby. But Lestat and his apprentice, if they survived the fire (and I was convinced that they had) did not find their way to the ship. Our luggage had left the flat that day; and if anything had remained to let them know our destination, I was sure it had been destroyed. Yet still I watched. Claudia sat securely locked in our stateroom, her eyes fixed on the porthole. But Lestat did not come.

"Finally, as I'd hoped, the commotion of putting out commenced before daylight. A few people waved from the pier and the grassy hump of the levee as the great ship began first to shiver, then to jerk violently to one side, and then to slide out in one great majestic motion into the current of the Mississippi.

"The lights of New Orleans grew small and dim until there appeared behind us only a pale phosphorescence against the lightening clouds. I was fatigued beyond my worst memory, yet I stood on the deck for as long as I could see that light, knowing that I might never see it again. In moments we were carried downstream past the piers of Freniere and Pointe du Lac and then, as I could see the great wall of cottonwood and cypress growing green out of the darkness along the shore, I knew it was almost morning. Too perilously close.

"And as I put the key into the lock of the cabin I felt the greatest exhaustion perhaps that I'd ever known. Never in all the years I'd lived in our select family had I known the fear I'd experienced tonight, the vulnerability, the sheer terror. And there was to be no sudden relief from it. No sudden sense of safety. Only that relief which weariness at last imposes, when neither mind nor body can endure the terror any longer. For though Lestat was now miles away from us, he had in his resurrection awakened in me a tangle of complex fears which I could not escape. Even as Claudia said to me, 'We're safe, Louis, safe,' and I whispered the word *yes* to her, I could see Lestat hanging in that doorway, see those bulbous eyes, that scarred flesh. How had he come back, how had he triumphed over death? How could any creature have survived that shrivelled ruin he'd become? Whatever the answer, what did it mean—not only for him, but for Claudia, for me? Safe from him we were, but safe from ourselves?

"The ship was struck by a strange 'fever.' It was amazingly clean of vermin, however, though occasionally their bodies might be found, weightless and dry, as if the creatures had been dead for days. Yet there was this fever. It struck a passenger first in the form of weakness and a soreness about the throat; occasionally there were marks there, and occasionally the marks were someplace else; or sometimes there were no recognizable marks at all, though an old wound was reopened and painful again. And sometimes the passenger who fell to sleeping more and more as the voyage progressed and the fever progressed died in his sleep. So there were burials at sea on several occasions as we crossed the Atlantic. Naturally afraid of fever, I shunned the passengers, did not wish to join them in the smoking room, get to know their stories, hear their dreams and expectations. I took my 'meals' alone. But Claudia liked to watch the passengers, to stand on deck and see them come and go in the early evening, to say softly to me later as I sat at the porthole, 'I think she'll fall prey. . . .'

"I would put the book down and look out the porthole, feeling the gentle rocking of the sea, seeing the stars, more clear and brilliant than they had ever been on land, dipping down to touch the waves. It seemed at moments, when I sat alone in the dark stateroom, that the sky had come down to meet the sea and that some great secret was to be revealed in that meeting, some great gulf miraculously closed forever. But who was to make this revelation when the sky and sea became indistinguishable and neither any longer was chaos? God? Or Satan? It struck me suddenly what consolation it would be to know Satan, to look upon his face, no matter how terrible that countenance was, to know that I belonged to him totally, and thus put to rest forever the torment of this ignorance. To step through some veil that would forever separate me from all that I called human nature.

"I felt the ship moving closer and closer to this secret. There was no visible end to the firmament; it closed about us with breathtaking beauty and silence. But then the words *put to rest* became horrible. Because there would be no rest in damnation, could be no rest; and what was this torment compared to the restless fires of hell? The sea rocking beneath those constant stars—those stars themselves—what had this to do with Satan? And those images which sound so static to us in childhood when we are all so taken up with mortal frenzy that we can scarce imagine them desirable: seraphim gazing forever upon the face of God—and the face of God itself—this was rest eternal, of which this gentle, cradling sea was only the faintest promise.

"But even in these moments, when the ship slept and all the world slept, neither heaven nor hell seemed more than a tormenting fancy. To know, to believe, in one or the other . . . that was perhaps the only salvation for which I could dream.

"Claudia, with Lestat's liking for light, lit the lamps when she rose. She had a marvellous pack of playing cards, acquired from a lady on board; the picture cards were in the fashion of Marie Antoinette, and the backs of the cards bore gold fleurs-de-lis on gleaming violet. She played a game of solitaire in which the cards made the numbers of a clock. And she asked me until I finally began to answer her, how Lestat had accomplished it. She was no longer shaken. If she remembered her screams in the fire she did not care to dwell on them. If she remembered that, before the fire, she had wept real tears in my arms, it made no change in her; she was, as always in the past, a person of little indecision, a person for whom habitual quiet did not mean anxiety or regret.

" 'We should have burned him,' she said. 'We were fools to think from his appearance that he was dead.'

" 'But how could he have survived?' I asked her. 'You saw him, you know what became of him.' I had no taste for it, really. I would have gladly pushed it to the back of my mind, but my mind would not allow me to. And it was she who gave me the answers now, for the dialogue was really with herself. 'Suppose, though, he had ceased to fight us,' she explained, 'that he was still living, locked in that helpless dried corpse, conscious and calculating. . . .'

" 'Conscious in that state!' I whispered.

" 'And suppose, when he reached the swamp waters and heard the sounds of our carriage going away, that he had strength enough to propel those limbs to move. There were creatures all around him in the dark. I saw him once rip the head of a small garden lizard and watch the blood run down into a glass. Can you imagine the tenacity of the will to live in him, his hands groping in that water for anything that moved?'

" 'The will to live? Tenacity?' I murmured. 'Suppose it was something else. . . .'

" 'And then, when he'd felt the resuscitation of his strength, just enough perhaps to have sustained him to the road, somewhere along that road he found someone. Perhaps he crouched, waiting for a passing carriage; perhaps he crept, gathering still what blood he could until he came to the shacks of those immigrants or those scattered country houses. And what a spectacle he must have been!' She gazed at the hanging lamp, her eyes narrow, her voice muted, without emotion. 'And then what did he do? It's clear to me. If he could not have gotten back to New Orleans in time, he could most definitely have reached the Old Bayou cemetery. The charity hospital feeds it fresh coffins every day. And I can see him clawing his way through the moist earth for such a coffin, dumping the fresh contents out in the swamps, and securing himself until the next nightfall in that shallow grave where no manner of man would be wont to disturb him. Yes . . . that is what he did, I'm certain.'

"I thought of this for a long time, picturing it, seeing that it must have happened. And then I heard her add thoughtfully, as she laid down her card and looked at the oval face of a white-coiffed king, '*I* could have done it.

" 'And why do you look that way at me?' she asked, gathering up her cards, her small fingers struggling to make a neat pack of them and then to shuffle them.

" 'But you do believe . . . that had we burned his remains he would have died?' I asked.

" 'Of course I believe it. If there is nothing to rise, there is nothing to rise. What are you driving at?' She was dealing out the cards now, dealing a hand for me on the small oak table. I looked at the cards, but I did not touch them.

" 'I don't know . . .' I whispered to her. 'Only that perhaps there was no will to live, no tenacity . . . because very simply there was no need of either.'

"Her eyes gazed at me steadily, giving no hint of her thoughts or that she understood mine.

" 'Because perhaps he was incapable of dying . . . perhaps he is, and we are . . . truly immortal?'

"For a long time she sat there looking at me.

" 'Consciousness in that state . . .' I finally added, as I looked away from her. 'If it were so, then mightn't there be consciousness in any other? Fire, sunlight . . . what does it matter?'

" 'Louis,' she said, her voice soft. 'You're afraid. You don't stand *en garde* against fear. You don't understand the danger of fear itself. We'll know these answers when we find those who can tell us, those who've possessed knowledge for centuries, for however long creatures such as ourselves have walked the earth. That knowledge was our birthright, and he deprived us. He earned his death.'

" 'But he didn't die . . .' I said.

" 'He's dead,' she said. 'No one could have escaped that house unless they'd run with us, at our very side. No. He's dead, and so is that trembling aesthete, his friend. Consciousness, what does it matter?'

"She gathered up the cards and put them aside, gesturing for me to hand her the books from the table beside the bunk, those books which she'd unpacked immediately on board, the few select records of vampire lore which she'd taken to be her guides. They included no wild romances from England, no stories of Edgar Allan Poe, no fancy. Only those few accounts of the vampires of eastern Europe, which had become for her a sort of Bible. In those countries indeed they did burn the remains of the vampire when they found him, and the heart was staked and the head severed. She would read these now for hours, these ancient books which had been read and reread before they ever found their way across the Atlantic; they were travellers' tales, the accounts of priests and scholars. And she would plan our trip, not with the need of any pen or paper, only in her mind. A trip that would take us at once away from the glittering capitals of Europe towards the Black Sea, where we would dock at Varna and begin that search in the rural countryside of the Carpathians.

"For me it was a grim prospect, bound as I was to it, for there were longings in me for other places and other knowledge which Claudia did not begin to comprehend. Seeds of these longings had been planted in me years ago, seeds which came to bitter flower as our ship passed through the Straits of Gibraltar and into the waters of the Mediterranean Sea.

"I wanted those waters to be blue. And they were not. They were the nighttime waters, and how I suffered then, straining to remember the seas that a young man's untutored senses had taken for granted, that an undisciplined memory had let slip away for eternity. The Mediterranean was black, black off the coast of Italy, black off the coast of Greece, black always, black when, in the small cold hours before dawn, as even Claudia slept, weary of her books and the meager fare that caution allowed her vampire hunger, I lowered a lantern down, down through the rising vapor until the fire blazed right over the lapping waters; and nothing came to light on that heaving surface but the light itself, the reflection of that beam travelling constant with me, a steady eye which seemed to fix on me from the depths and say, 'Louis, your quest is for darkness only. This sea is not your sea. The myths of men are not your myths. Men's treasures are not yours.'

"But oh, how the quest for the Old World vampires filled me with bitterness in those moments, a bitterness I could all but taste, as if the very air had lost its freshness. For what secrets, what truths had those monstrous creatures of night to give us? What, of necessity, must be their terrible limits, if indeed we were to find them at all? What can the damned really say to the damned?

"I never stepped ashore at Piraeus. Yet in my mind I roamed the Acropolis at Athens, watching the moon rise through the open roof of the Parthenon, measuring my height by the grandeur of those columns, walking the streets of those Greeks who died at Marathon, listening to the sound of wind in the ancient olives. These were the monuments of men who could not die, not the stones of the living dead; here the secrets that had endured the passage of time, which I had only dimly begun to understand. And yet nothing turned me from our quest and nothing could turn me, but over and over, committed as I was, I pondered the great risk of our questions, the risk of any question that is truthfully asked; for the answer must carry an incalculable price, a tragic danger. Who knew that better than I, who had presided over the death of my own body, seeing all I called human wither and die only to form an unbreakable chain which held me fast to this world yet made me forever its exile, a specter with a beating heart?

"The sea lulled me to bad dreams, to sharp remembrances. A winter night in New Orleans when I wandered through the St. Louis cemetery and saw my sister, old and bent, a bouquet of white roses in her arms, the thorns carefully bound in an old parchment, her gray head bowed, her steps carrying her steadily along through the perilous dark to the grave where the stone of her brother Louis was set, side by side with that of his younger brother . . . Louis, who had died in the fire of Pointe du Lac leaving a generous legacy to a godchild and namesake she never knew. Those flowers were for Louis, as if it had not been half a century since his death, as if her memory, like Louis's memory, left her no peace. Sorrow sharpened her ashen beauty, sorrow bent her narrow back. And what I would not have given, as I watched her, to touch her silver hair, to whisper love to her, if love would not have loosed on her remaining years a horror worse than grief. I left her with grief. Over and over and over.

"And I dreamed now too much. I dreamed too long, in the prison of this ship, in the prison of my body, attuned as it was to the rise of every sun as no mortal body had ever been. And my heart beat faster for the mountains of eastern Europe, finally, beat faster for the one hope that somewhere we might find in that primitive countryside the answer to why under God this suffering was allowed to exist—why under God it was allowed to begin, and how under God it might be ended. I had not the courage to end it, I knew, without that answer. And in time the waters of the Mediterranean became, in fact, the waters of the Black Sea."

THE VAMPIRE SIGHED. The boy was resting on his elbow, his face cradled in his right palm; and his avid expression was incongruous with the redness of his eyes.

"Do you think I'm playing with you?" the vampire asked, his fine dark eyebrows knitted for an instant.

"No," the boy said quickly. "I know better than to ask you any more questions. You'll tell me everything in your own time." And his mouth settled, and he looked at the vampire as though he were ready for him to begin again.

There was a sound then from far off. It came from somewhere in the old Victorian building around them, the first such sound they'd heard. The boy looked up towards the hallway door. It was as if he'd forgotten the building existed. Someone walked heavily on the old boards. But the vampire was undisturbed. He looked away as if he were again disengaging himself from the present.

"That village. I can't tell you the name of it; the name's gone. I remember it was miles from the coast, however, and we'd been travelling alone by carriage. And such a carriage! It was Claudia's doing, that carriage, and I should have expected it; but then, things are always taking me unawares. From the first moment we arrived in Varna, I had perceived certain changes in her which made me at once aware she was Lestat's daughter as well as my own. From me she had learned the value of money, but from Lestat she had inherited a passion for spending it; and she wasn't to leave without the most luxurious black coach we could manage, outfitted with leather seats that might have accommodated a band of travellers, let alone a man and a child who used the magnificent compartment only for the transportation of an ornately carved oak chest. To the back were strapped two trunks of the finest clothes the shops there could provide, and we went speeding along, those light enormous wheels and fine springs carrying that bulk with a frightening ease over the mountain roads. There was a thrill to that when there was nothing else in this strange country, those horses at a gallop and the gentle listing of that carriage.

"And it was strange country. Lonely, dark, as rural country is always dark, its castles and ruins often obscured when the moon passed behind the clouds, so that I felt an anxiety during those hours I'd never quite experienced in New Orleans. And the people themselves were no relief. We were naked and lost in their tiny hamlets, and conscious always that amongst them we were in grave danger.

"Never in New Orleans had the kill to be disguised. The ravages of fever, plague, crime—these things competed with us always there, and outdid us. But here we had to go to great lengths to make the kill unnoticed. Because these simple country people, who might have found the crowded streets of New Orleans terrifying, believed completely that the dead did walk and did drink the blood of the living. They knew our names: vampire, devil. And we, who were on the lookout for the slightest rumor, wanted under no circumstances to create rumor ourselves.

"We travelled alone and fast and lavishly amongst them, struggling to be safe within our ostentation, finding talk of vampires all too cheap by the inn fires, where, my daughter sleeping peacefully against my chest, I invariably found someone amongst the peasants or guests who spoke enough German or, at times, even French to discuss with me the familiar legends.

"But finally we came to that village which was to be the turning point in our travels. I savor nothing about that journey, not the freshness of the air, the coolness of the nights. I don't talk of it without a vague tremor even now.

"We had been at a farmhouse the night before, and so no news prepared us—only the desolate appearance of the place: because it wasn't late when we reached it, not late enough for all the shutters of the little street to be bolted or for a darkened lantern to be swinging idly from the broad archway of the inn.

"Refuse was collected in the doorways. And there were other signs that something was wrong. A small box of withered flowers beneath a shuttered shop window. A barrel rolling back and forth in the center of the inn yard. The place had the aspect of a town under siege by the plague.

"But even as I was setting Claudia down on the packed earth beside the carriage, I saw the crack of light beneath the inn door. 'Put the hood of your cape up,' she said quickly. 'They're coming.' Someone inside was pulling back the latch.

"At first all I saw was the light behind the figure in the very narrow margin she allowed. Then the light from the carriage lanterns glinted in her eye.

" 'A room for the night!' I said in German. 'And my horses need tending, badly!'

" 'The night's no time for travelling . . .' she said to me in a peculiar, flat voice. 'And with a child.' As she said this, I noticed others in the room behind her. I could hear their murmurings and see the flickering of a fire. From what I could see there were mostly peasants gathered around it, except for one man who was dressed much like myself in a tailored coat, with an overcoat over his shoulders; but his clothes were neglected and shabby. His red hair gleamed in the firelight. He was a foreigner, like ourselves, and he was the only one not looking at us. His head wagged slightly as if he were drunk.

" 'My daughter's tired,' I said to the woman. 'We've no place to stay but here.' And now I took Claudia into my arms. She turned her face towards me, and I heard her whisper, 'Louis, the garlic, the crucifix above the door!'

"I had not seen these things. It was a small crucifix, with the body of Christ in bronze fixed to the wood, and the garlic was wreathed around it, a fresh garland entwined with an old one, in which the buds were withered and dried. The woman's eyes followed my eyes, and then she looked at me sharply and I could see how exhausted she was, how red were her pupils, and how the hand which clutched at the shawl at her breast trembled. Her black hair was completely dishevelled. I pressed nearer until I was almost at the threshold, and she opened the door wide suddenly as if she'd only just decided to let us in. She said a prayer as I passed her, I was sure of it, though I couldn't understand the Slavic words.

"The small, low-beamed room was filled with people, men and women along the rough, panelled walls, on benches and even on the floor. It was as if the entire village were gathered there. A child slept in a woman's lap and another slept on the staircase, bundled in blankets, his knees tucked in against one step, his arms making a pillow for his head on the next. And everywhere there was the garlic hanging from nails and hooks, along with the cooking pots and flagons. The fire was the only light, and it threw distorting shadows on the still faces as they watched us.

"No one motioned for us to sit or offered us anything, and

finally the woman told me in German I might take the horses into the stable if I liked. She was staring at me with those slightly wild, red-rimmed eyes, and then her face softened. She told me she'd stand at the inn door for me with a lantern, but I must hurry and leave the child here.

"But something else had distracted me, a scent I detected beneath the heavy fragrance of burning wood and the wine. It was the scent of death. I could feel Claudia's hand press my chest, and I saw her tiny finger pointing to a door at the foot of the stairs. The scent came from there.

"The woman had a cup of wine waiting when I returned, and a bowl of broth. I sat down, Claudia on my knee, her head turned away from the fire towards that mysterious door. All eyes were fixed on us as before, except for the foreigner. I could see his profile now clearly. He was much younger than I'd thought, his haggard appearance stemming from emotion. He had a lean but very pleasant face actually, his light, freckled skin making him seem like a boy. His wide, blue eyes were fixed on the fire as though he were talking to it, and his eyelashes and eyebrows were golden in the light, which gave him a very innocent, open expression. But he was miserable, disturbed, drunk. Suddenly he turned to me, and I saw he'd been crying. 'Do you speak English?' he said, his voice booming in the silence.

" 'Yes, I do,' I said to him. And he glanced at the others triumphantly. They stared at him stonily.

" 'You speak English!' he cried, his lips stretching into a bitter smile, his eyes moving around the ceiling and then fixing on mine. 'Get out of this country,' he said. 'Get out of it now. Take your carriage, your horses, drive them till they drop, but get out of it!' Then his shoulders convulsed as if he were sick. He put his hand to his mouth. The woman who stood against the wall now, her arms folded over her soiled apron, said calmly in German, 'At dawn you can go. At dawn.'

" 'But what is it?' I whispered to her; and then I looked to him. He was watching me, his eyes glassy and red. No one spoke. A log fell heavily in the fire.

" 'Won't you tell me?' I asked the Englishman gently. He stood up. For a moment I thought he was going to fall. He loomed over me, a much taller man than myself, his head pitching forward, then backward, before he right himself and put his hands on the edge of the table. His black coat was stained with wine, and so was his shirt cuff. 'You want to see?' he gasped as he peered into my eyes. 'Do you want to see for yourself?' There was a soft, pathetic tone to his voice as he spoke these words.

" 'Leave the child!' said the woman abruptly, with a quick, imperious gesture.

" 'She's sleeping,' I said. And, rising, I followed the Englishman to the door at the foot of the stairs.

"There was a slight commotion as those nearest the door moved away from it. And we entered a small parlor together.

"Only one candle burned on the sideboard, and the first thing I saw was a row of delicately painted plates on a shelf. There were curtains on the small window, and a gleaming picture of the Virgin Mary and Christ child on the wall. But the walls and chairs barely enclosed a great oak table, and on that table lay the body of a young woman, her white hands folded on her breast, her auburn hair mussed and tucked about her thin, white throat and under her shoulders. Her pretty face was already hard with death. Amber rosary beads gleamed around her wrist and down the side of her dark wool skirt. And beside her lay a very pretty red felt hat with a wide, soft brim and a veil, and a pair of dark gloves. It was all laid there as if she would very soon rise and put these things on. And the Englishman patted the hat carefully now as he drew close to her. He was on the verge of breaking down altogether. He'd drawn a large handkerchief out of his coat, and he had put it to his face. 'Do you know what they want to do with her?' he whispered as he looked at me. 'Do you have any idea?'

"The woman came in behind us and reached for his arm, but he roughtly shook her off. 'Do you know?' he demanded of me with his eyes fierce. 'Savages!'

" 'You stop now!' she said under her breath.

"He clenched his teeth and shook his head, so that a shock of his red hair loosened in his eyes. 'You get away from her,' he said to the woman in German. 'Get away from me.' Someone was whispering in the other room. The Englishman looked again at the young woman, and his eyes filled with tears. 'So innocent,' he said softly; and then he glanced at the ceiling and, making a fist with his right hand, he gasped, 'Damn you . . . God! Damn you!'

" 'Lord,' the woman whispered, and quickly she made the Sign of the Cross.

" 'Do you see this?' he asked me. And he pried very carefully at the lace of the dead woman's throat, as though he could not, did not wish to actually touch the hardening flesh. There on her throat, unmistakable, were the two puncture wounds, as I'd seen them a thousand times upon a thousand, engraved in the yellowing skin. The man drew his hands up to his face, his tall, lean body rocking on the balls of his feet. 'I think I'm going mad!' he said.

" 'Come now,' said the woman, holding onto him as he struggled, her face suddenly flushed.

" 'Let him be,' I said to her. 'Just let him be. I'll take care of him.'

"Her mouth contorted. 'I'll throw you all out of here, out into that dark, if you don't stop.' She was too weary for this, too close to some breaking point herself. But then she turned her back on us, drawing her shawl tight around her, and padded softly out, the men who'd gathered at the door making way for her.

"The Englishman was crying.

"I could see what I must do, but it wasn't only that I wanted so much to learn from him, my heart pounding with silent excitement. It was heartrending to see him this way. Fate brought me too mercilessly close to him.

" 'I'll stay with you,' I offered. And I brought two chairs up beside the table. He sat down heavily, his eyes on the flickering candle at his side. I shut the door, and the walls seemed to recede and the circle of the candle to grow brighter around his bowed head. He leaned back against the sideboard and wiped his face with his handkerchief. Then he drew a leatherbound flask from his pocket and offered it to me, and I said no.

" 'Do you want to tell me what happened?'

"He nodded. 'Perhaps you can bring some sanity to this place,' he said. 'You're a Frenchman, aren't you? You know, I'm English.'

" 'Yes,' I nodded.

"And then, pressing my hand fervently, the liquor so dulling his senses that he never felt the coldness of it, he told me his name was Morgan and he needed me desperately, more than he'd ever needed anyone in his life. And at that moment, holding that hand, feeling the fever of it, I did a strange thing. I told him my name, which I confided to almost no one. But he was looking at the dead woman as if he hadn't heard me, his lips forming what appeared to be the faintest smile, the tears standing in his eyes. His expression would have moved any human being; it might have been more than some could bear.

" 'I did this,' he said, nodding. 'I brought her here.' And he raised his eyebrows as if wondering at it.

" 'No,' I said quickly. 'You didn't do it. Tell me who did.'

"But then he seemed confused, lost in thought. 'I'd never been out of England,' he started. 'I was painting, you see . . . as if it mattered now . . . the paintings, the book! I thought it all so quaint! So picturesque!' His eyes moved over the room, his voice trailing off. For a long time he looked at her again, and then softly he said to her, 'Emily,' and I felt I'd glimpsed something precious he held to his heart.

"Gradually, then, the story began to come. A honeymoon journey, through Germany, into this country, wherever the regular coaches would carry them, wherever Morgan found scenes to paint. And they'd come to this remote place finally because there was a ruined monastery nearby which was said to be a very well-preserved place.

"But Morgan and Emily had never reached that monastery. Tragedy had been waiting for them here.

"It turned out the regular coaches did not come this way, and Morgan had paid a farmer to bring them by cart. But the afternoon they arrived, there was a great commotion in the cemetery outside of town. The farmer, taking one look, refused to leave his cart to see further.

" 'It was some kind of procession, it seemed,' Morgan said, 'with all the people outfitted in their best, and some with flowers; and the truth was I thought it quite fascinating. I wanted to see it. I was so eager I had the fellow leave us, bags and all. We could see the village just up ahead. Actually it was I more than Emily, of course, but she was so agreeable, you see. I left her, finally, seated on our suitcases, and I went on up the hill without her. Did you see it when you were coming, the cemetery? No, of course you didn't. Thank God that carriage of yours brought you here safe and sound. Though, if you'd driven on, no matter how bad off your horses were . . .' He stopped.

" 'What's the danger?' I urged him, gently.

" 'Ah . . . danger! Barbarians!' he murmured. And he glanced at the door. Then he took another drink from his flask and capped it.

" 'Well, it was no procession. I saw that right off,' he said. 'The people wouldn't even speak to me when I came up—you know what they are; but they had no objection to letting me watch. The truth was, you wouldn't have thought I was standing there at all. You won't believe me when I tell you what I saw, but you must believe me; because if you don't, I'm mad, I know it.'

" 'I will believe you, go on,' I said.

" 'Well, the cemetery was full of fresh graves, I saw that at once, some of them with new wooden crosses and some of them just mounds of earth with the flowers still fresh; and the peasants there, they were holding flowers, a few of them, as though they meant to be trimming these graves; but all of them were standing stock-still, their eyes on these two fellows who had a white horse by the bridle—and what an animal that was! It was pawing and stomping and shying to one side, as if it wanted no part of the place; a beautiful thing it was, though, a splendid animal—a stallion, and pure white. Well, at some point—and I couldn't tell you how they agreed upon it, because not a one of them said a word—one fellow, the leader, I think, gave the horse a tremendous whack with the handle of a shovel, and it took off up the hill, just wild. You can imagine, I thought that was the last we'd see of that horse for a while for sure. But I was wrong. In a minute it had slowed to a gallop, and it was turning around amongst the old graves and coming back down the hill towards the newer ones. And the people all stood there watching it. No one made a sound. And here it came trotting right over the mounds, right through the flowers, and no one made a move to get hold of the bridle. And then suddenly it came to a stop, right on one of the graves.'

"He wiped at his eyes, but his tears were almost gone. He seemed fascinated with his tale, as I was.

" 'Well, here's what happened,' he continued. 'The animal just stood there. And suddenly a cry went up from the crowd. No, it wasn't a cry, it was as though they were all gasping and moaning, and then everything went quiet. And the horse was just standing there, tossing its head; and finally this fellow who was the leader burst forward and shouted to several of the others; and one of the women—she screamed, and threw herself on the grave almost under the horse's hooves. I came up then as close as I could. I could see the stone with the deceased's name on it; it was a young woman, dead only six months, the dates carved right there, and there was this miserable woman on her knees in the dirt, with her arms around the stone now, as if she meant to pull it right up out of the earth. And these fellows trying to pick her up and get her away.

" 'Now I almost turned back, but I couldn't, not until I saw what they meant to do. And, of course, Emily was quite safe, and none of these people took the slightest notice of either of us. Well, two of them finally did have that woman up, and then the others had come with shovels and had begun to dig right into the grave. Pretty soon one of them was down in the grave, and everyone was so still you could hear the slightest sound, that shovel digging in there and the earth thrown up in a heap. I can't tell you what it was like. Here was the sun high above us and not a cloud in the sky, and all of them standing around, holding onto one another now, and even that pathetic woman . . .' He stopped now, because his eyes had fallen on Emily. I just sat there waiting for him. I could hear the whiskey when he lifted the flask again, and I felt glad for him that there was so much there, that he could drink it and deaden this pain. 'It might as well have been midnight on that hill,' he said, looking at me, his voice very low. 'That's how it felt. And then I could hear this fellow in the grave. He was cracking the coffin lid with his shovel! Then out came the broken boards. He was just tossing them out, right and left. And suddenly he let out an awful cry! The other fellows drew up close, and all at once there was a rush to the grave; and then they all fell back like a wave, all of them crying out, and some of them turning and trying to push away. And the poor woman, she was wild, bending her knees, and trying to get free of those men that were holding onto her. Well, I couldn't help but go up. I don't suppose anything could have kept me away; and I'll tell you that's the first time I've ever done such a thing, and, God help me, it's to be the last. Now, you must believe me, you must! But there, right there in that coffin, with that fellow standing on the broken boards over her feet, was the dead woman, and I tell you . . . I tell you she was as fresh, as pink'—his voice cracked, and he sat there, his eyes wide, his hand poised as if he held something invisible in his fingers, pleading with me to believe him—'as pink as if she were alive! Buried six months! And there she lay! The shroud was thrown back off her, and her hands lay on her breast just as if she were asleep.'

"He sighed. His hand dropped to his leg and he shook his head, and for a moment he just sat staring. 'I swear to you!' he said. 'And then this fellow who was in the grave, he bent down and lifted the dead woman's hand. I tell you that arm moved as freely as my arm! And he held her hand out as if he were looking at her nails. Then he shouted; and that woman beside the grave, she was kicking at those fellows and shoving at the earth with her foot, so it fell right down in the corpse's face and hair.

And oh, she was so pretty, that dead woman; oh, if you could have seen her, and what they did then!'

" 'Tell me what they did,' I said to him softly. But I knew before he said it.

" 'I tell you . . .' he said. 'We don't know the meaning of something like that until we see it!' And he looked at me, his eyebrow arched as if he were confiding a terrible secret. 'We just don't know.'

" 'No, we don't,' I said.

" 'I'll tell you. They took a stake, a wooden stake, mind you; and this one in the grave, he took the stake with a hammer and he put it right to her breast. I didn't believe it! And then with one great blow he drove it right into her. I tell you, I couldn't have moved even if I'd wanted to; I was rooted there. And then that fellow, that beastly fellow, he reached up for his shovel and with both his arms he drove it sharp, right into the dead woman's throat. The head was off like that.' He shut his eyes, his face contorted, and put his head to the side.

"I looked at him, but I wasn't seeing him at all. I was seeing this woman in her grave with the head severed, and I was feeling the most keen revulsion inside myself, as if a hand were pressing on my throat and my insides were coming up inside me and I couldn't breathe. Then I felt Claudia's lip against my wrist. She was staring at Morgan, and apparently she had been for some time.

"Slowly Morgan looked up at me, his eyes wild. 'It's what they want to do with *her*,' he said. 'With Emily! Well I won't let them.' He shook his head adamantly. 'I won't let them. You've got to help me, Louis.' His lips were trembling, and his face so distorted now by his sudden desperation that I might have recoiled from it despite myself. 'The same blood flows in our veins, you and I. I mean, French, English, we're civilized men, Louis. They're savages!'

" 'Try to be calm now, Morgan,' I said, reaching out for him. 'I want you to tell me what happened then. You and Emily . . .'

"He was struggling for his bottle. I drew it out of his

pocket, and he took off the cap. 'That's a fellow, Louis; that's a friend,' he said emphatically. 'You see, I took her away fast. They were going to burn that corpse right there in the cemetery; and Emily was not to see that, not while I . . .' He shook his head. 'There wasn't a carriage to be found that would take us out of here; not a single one of them would leave now for the two days' drive to get us to a decent place!'

" 'But how did they explain it to you, Morgan?' I insisted. I could see he did not have much time left.

" 'Vampires!' he burst out, the whiskey sloshing on his hand. 'Vampires, Louis. Can you believe that!' And he gestured to the door with the bottle. 'A plague of vampires! All this in whispers, as if the devil himself were listening at the door! Of course, God have mercy, they put a stop to it. That unfortunate woman in the cemetery, they'd stopped her from clawing her way up nightly to feed on the rest of us!' He put the bottle to his lips. 'Oh . . . God . . .' he moaned.

"I watched him drink, patiently waiting.

" 'And Emily . . .' he continued. 'She thought it fascinating. What with the fire out there and a decent dinner and a proper glass of wine. She hadn't seen that woman! She hadn't seen what they'd done,' he said desperately. 'Oh, I wanted to get out of here; I offered them money. "If it's over," I kept saying to them, "one of you ought to want this money, a small fortune just to drive us out of here.' "

" 'But it wasn't over . . .' I whispered.

"And I could see the tears gathering in his eyes, his mouth twisting with pain.

" 'How did it happen to her?' I asked him.

" 'I don't know,' he gasped, shaking his head, the flask pressed to his forehead as if it were something cool, refreshing, when it was not.

" 'It came into the inn?'

" 'They said she went out to it,' he confessed, the tears coursing down his cheeks. 'Everything was locked! They saw to that. Doors, windows! Then it was morning and they were all shouting, and she was gone. The window stood wide open, and she wasn't there. I didn't even take time for my robe. I was running. I came to a dead halt over her, out there, behind the inn. My foot all but came down on her . . . she was just lying there under the peach trees. She held an empty cup. Clinging to it, an empty cup! They said it lured her . . . she was trying to give it water. . . .'

"The flask slipped from his hands. He clapped his hands over his ears, his body bent, his head bowed.

"For a long time I sat there watching him; I had no words to say to him. And when he cried softly that they wanted to desecrate her, that they said she, Emily, was now a vampire, I assured him softly, though I don't think he ever heard me, that she was not.

"He moved forward finally, as if he might fall. He appeared to be reaching for the candle, and before his arm rested on the buffet, his finger touched it so the hot wax extinguished the tiny bit that was left of the wick. We were in darkness then, and his head had fallen on his arm.

"All of the light of the room seemed gathered now in Claudia's eyes. But as the silence lengthened and I sat there, wondering, hoping Morgan wouldn't lift his head again, the woman came to the door. Her candle illuminated him, drunk, asleep.

" 'You go now,' she said to me. Dark figures crowded around her, and the old wooden inn was alive with the shuffling of men and women. 'Go by the fire!'

" 'What are you going to do!' I demanded of her, rising and holding Claudia. 'I want to know what you propose to do!'

" 'Go by the fire,' she commanded.

" 'No, don't do this,' I said. But she narrowed her eyes and bared her teeth. 'You go!' she growled.

" 'Morgan,' I said to him; but he didn't hear me, he couldn't hear me.

" 'Leave him be,' said the woman fiercely.

" 'But it's stupid, what you're doing; don't you understand? This woman's dead!' I pleaded with her.

" 'Louis,' Claudia whispered, so that they couldn't hear her, her arm tightening around my neck beneath the fur of my hood. 'Let these people alone.'

"The others were moving into the room now, encircling the table, their faces grim as they looked at us.

" 'But where do these vampires come from!' I whispered. 'You've searched your cemetery! If it's vampires, where do they hide from you? This woman can't do you harm. Hunt your vampires if you must.'

" 'By day,' she said gravely, winking her eye and slowly nodding her head. 'By day. We get them, by day.'

" 'Where, out there in the graveyard, digging up the graves of your own villagers?'

"She shook her head. 'The ruins,' she said. 'It was always the ruins. We were wrong. In my grandfather's time it was the ruins, and it is the ruins again. We'll take them down stone by stone if we have to. But you . . . you go now. Because if you don't go, we'll drive you out there into that dark now!'

"And then out from behind her apron she drew her clenched fist with the stake in it and held it up in the flickering light of the candle. 'You hear me, you go!' she said; and the men pressed in close behind her, their mouths set, their eyes blazing in the light.

" 'Yes . . .' I said to her. 'Out there. I would prefer that. Out there.' And I swept past her, almost throwing her aside, seeing them scuttle back to make way. I had my hand on the latch of the inn door and slid it back with one quick gesture.

" 'No!' cried the woman in her guttural German. 'You're mad!' And she rushed up to me and then stared at the latch, dumfounded. She threw her hands up against the rough boards of the door. 'Do you know what you do!'

" 'Where are the ruins?' I asked her calmly. 'How far? Do they lie to the left of the road, or to the right?'

" 'No, no.' She shook her head violently. I pried the door back and felt the cold blast of air on my face. One of the women said something sharp and angry from the wall, and one of the children moaned in its sleep. 'I'm going. I want one thing from you. Tell me where the ruins lie, so I may stay clear of them. Tell me.'

" 'You don't know, you don't know,' she said; and then I laid my hand on her warm wrist and drew her slowly through the door, her feet scraping on the boards, her eyes wild. The men moved nearer but, as she stepped out against her will into the night, they stopped. She tossed her head, her hair falling down into her eyes, her eyes glaring at my hand and at my face. 'Tell me . . .' I said.

"I could see she was staring not at me but at Claudia. Claudia had turned towards her, and the light from the fire was on her face. The woman did not see the rounded cheeks nor the pursed lips, I knew, but Claudia's eyes, which were gazing at her with a dark, demonic intelligence. The woman's teeth bit down into the flesh of her lip.

" 'To the north or south?'

" 'To the north . . .' she whispered.

" 'To the left or the right?'

" 'The left.'

" 'And how far?'

"Her hand struggled desperately. 'Three miles,' she gasped. And I released her, so that she fell back against the door, her eyes wide with fear and confusion. I had turned to go, but suddenly behind me she cried out for me to wait. I turned to see she'd ripped the crucifix from the beam over her head, and she had it thrust out towards me now. And out of the dark nightmare landscape of my memory I saw Babette gazing at me as she had so many years ago, saying those words, '*Get thee behind me, Satan.*' But the woman's face was desperate. 'Take it, please, in the name of God,' she said. 'And ride fast.' And the door shut, leaving Claudia and me in total darkness."

"In minutes the tunnel of the night closed upon the weak lanterns of our carriage, as if the village had never existed. We lurched forward, around a bend, the springs creaking, the dim moon revealing for an instant the pale outline of the mountains beyond the pines. I could not stop thinking of Morgan, stop hearing his voice. It was all tangled with my own horrified anticipation of meeting the thing which had killed Emily, the thing which was unquestionably one of our own. But Claudia was in a frenzy. If she could have driven the horses herself, she would have taken the reins. Again and again she urged me to use the whip. She struck savagely at the few low branches that dipped suddenly into the lamps before our faces; and the arm that clung to my waist on the rocking bench was as firm as iron.

"I remember the road turning sharply, the lanterns clattering, and Claudia calling out over the wind: 'There, Louis, do you see it?' And I jerked hard on the reins.

"She was on her knees, pressed against me, and the carriage was swaying like a ship at sea.

"A great fleecy cloud had released the moon, and high above us loomed the dark outline of the tower. One long window showed the pale sky beyond it. I sat there, clutching the bench, trying to steady a motion that continued in my head as the carriage settled on its springs. One of the horses whinnied. Then everything was still.

"Claudia was saying. 'Louis, come. . . .'

"I whispered something, a swift irrational negation. I had the distinct and terrifying impression that Morgan was near to me, talking to me in that low, impassioned way he'd pleaded with me in the inn. Not a living creature stirred in the night around us. There was only the wind and the soft rustling of the leaves.

" 'Do you think he knows we're coming?' I asked, my voice unfamiliar to me over this wind. I was in that little parlor, as if there were no escape from it, as if this dense forest were not real. I think I shuddered. And then I felt Claudia's hand very gently touch the hand I lifted to my eyes. The thin pines were billowing behind her and the rustle of the leaves grew louder, as if a great mouth sucked the breeze and began a whirlwind. 'They'll bury her at the crossroads? Is that what they'll do? An Englishwoman!' I whispered.

" 'Would that I had your size . . .' Claudia was saying. 'And would that you had my heart. Oh, Louis. . . .' And her head inclined to me now, so like the attitude of the vampire bending to kiss that I shrank back from her; but her lips only gently pressed my own, finding a part there to suck the breath and let it flow back into me as my arms enclosed her. 'Let me lead you . . .' she pleaded. 'There's no turning back now. Take me in your arms,' she said, 'and let me down, on the road.'

"But it seemed an eternity that I just sat there feeling her lips on my face and on my eyelids. Then she moved, the softness of her small body suddenly snatched from me, in a movement so graceful and swift that she seemed now poised in the air beside the carriage, her hand clutching mine for an instant, then letting it go. And then I looked down to see her looking up at me, standing on the road in the shuddering pool of light beneath the lantern. She beckoned to me, as she stepped backwards, one small boot behind the other. 'Louis, come down . . .' until she threatened to vanish into the darkness. And in a second I'd unfastened the lamp from its hook, and I stood beside her in the tall grass.

" 'Don't you sense the danger?' I whispered to her. 'Can't you breathe it like the air?' One of those quick, elusive smiles played on her lips, as she turned towards the slope. The lantern pitched a pathway through the rising forest. One small, white hand drew the wool of her cape close, and she moved forward.

" 'Wait only for a moment. . . .'

" 'Fear's your enemy . . .' she answered, but she did not stop.

"She proceeded ahead of the light, feet sure, even as the tall grass gave way gradually to low heaps of rubble, and the forest thickened, and the distant tower vanished with the fading of the moon and the great weaving of the branches overhead. Soon the sound and scent of the horses died on the low wind. 'Be *en garde*,' Claudia whispered, as she moved, relentlessly, pausing only now and again where the tangled vines and rock made it seem for moments there was a shelter. But the ruins were ancient. Whether plague or fire or a foreign enemy had ravaged the town, we couldn't know. Only the monastery truly remained.

"Now something whispered in the dark that was like the wind and the leaves, but it was neither. I saw Claudia's back straighten, saw the flash of her white palm as she slowed her step. Then I knew it was water, winding its way slowly down the mountain, and I saw it far ahead through the black trunks, a straight, moonlit waterfall descending to a boiling pool below. Claudia emerged silhouetted against the fall, her hand clutching a bare root in the moist earth beside it; and now I saw her climbing hand over hand up the overgrown cliff, her arm trembling ever so slightly, her small boots dangling, then digging in to hold, then swinging free again. The water was cold, and it made the air fragrant and light all around it, so that for a moment I rested. Nothing stirred around me in the forest. I listened, senses quietly separating the tune of the water from the tune of the leaves, but nothing else stirred. And then it struck me gradually, like a chill coming over my arms and my throat and finally my face, that the night was too desolate, too lifeless. It was as if even the birds had shunned this place, as well as all the myriad creatures that should have been moving about the banks of this stream. But Claudia, above me on the ledge, was reaching for the lantern, her cape brushing my face. I lifted it, so that suddenly she sprang into light, like an eerie cherub. She put her hand out for me as if, despite her small size, she could help me up the embankment. In a moment we were moving on again, over the stream, up the mountain. 'Do you sense it?' I whispered. 'It's too still.'

"But her hand tightened on mine, as if to say, 'Quiet.' The hill was growing steeper, and the quiet was unnerving. I tried to stare at the limits of the light, to see each new bark as it loomed before us. Something did move, and I reached for Claudia, almost pulling her sharply near to me. But it was only a reptile, shooting through the leaves with a whip of his tail. The leaves settled. But Claudia moved back against me, under the folds of my cape, a hand firmly clasping the cloth of my coat;

and she seemed to propel me forward, my cape falling over the loose fabric of her own.

"Soon the scent of the water was gone, and when the moon shone clear for an instant I could see right ahead of us what appeared to be a break in the woods. Claudia firmly clasped the lantern and shut its metal door. I moved to stop this, my hand struggling with hers; but then she said to me quietly, 'Close your eyes for an instant, and then open them slowly. And when you do, you will see it.'

"A chill rose over me as I did this, during which I held fast to her shoulder. But then I opened my eyes and saw beyond the distant bark of the trees the long, low walls of the monastery and the high square top of the massive tower. Far beyond it, above an immense black valley, gleamed the snow-capped peaks of the mountains. 'Come,' she said to me, 'quiet, as if your body has no weight.' And she started without hesitation right towards those walls, right towards whatever might have been waiting in their shelter.

"In moments we had found the gap that would admit us, the great opening that was blacker still than the walls around it, the vines encrusting its edges as if to hold the stones in place. High above, through the open roof, the damp smell of the stones strong in my nostrils, I saw, beyond the streaks of clouds, a faint sprinkling of stars. A great staircase moved upward, from corner to corner, all the way to the narrow windows that looked out upon the valley. And beneath the first rise of the stair, out of the gloom emerged the vast, dark opening to the monastery's remaining rooms.

"Claudia was still now, as if she had become the stones. In the damp enclosure not even the soft tendrils of her hair moved. She was listening. And then I was listening with her. There was only the low backdrop of the wind. She moved, slowly, deliberately, and with one pointed foot gradually cleared a space in the moist earth in front of her. I could see a flat stone there, and it sounded hollow as she gently tapped it with her heel. Then I could see the broad size of it and how it rose at one distant corner; and an image came to mind, dreadful in its sharpness, of that band of men and women from the village surrounding the stone, raising it with a giant lever. Claudia's eyes moved over the staircase and then fixed on the crumbling doorway beneath it. The moon shone for an instant through a lofty window. Then Claudia moved, so suddenly that she stood beside me without having made a sound. 'Do you hear it?' she whispered. 'Listen.'

"It was so low no mortal could have heard it. And it did not come from the ruins. It came from far off, not the long, meandering way that we had come up the slope, but another way, up the spine of the hill, directly from the village. Just a rustling now, a scraping, but it was steady; and then slowly the round tramping of a foot began to distinguish itself. Claudia's hand tightened on mine, and with a gentle pressure she moved me silently beneath the slope of the stairway. I could see the folds of her dress heave slightly beneath the edge of her cape. The tramp of the feet grew louder, and I began to sense that one step preceded the other very sharply, the second dragging slowly across the earth. It was a limping step, drawing nearer and nearer over the low whistling of the wind. My own heart beat hard against my chest, and I felt the veins in my temples tighten, a tremor passing through my limbs, so that I could feel the fabric of my shirt against me, the stiff cut of the collar, the very scraping of the buttons against my cape.

"Then a faint scent came with the wind. It was the scent of blood, at once arousing me, against my will, the warm, sweet scent of human blood, blood that was spilling, flowing; and then I sensed the smell of living flesh and I heard in time with the feet a dry, hoarse breathing. But with it came another sound, faint and intermingled with the first, as the feet tramped closer and closer to the walls, the sound of yet another creature's halting, strained breath. And I could hear the heart of that creature, beating irregularly, a fearful throbbing; but beneath that was another heart, a steady, pulsing heart growing louder and louder, a heart as strong as my own! Then, in the jagged gap through which we'd come, I saw him.

"His great, huge shoulder emerged first and one long, loose

arm and hand, the fingers curved; then I saw his head. Over his other shoulder he was carrying a body. In the broken doorway he straightened and shifted the weight and stared directly into the darkness towards us. Every muscle in me became iron as I looked at him, saw the outline of his head looming there against the sky. But nothing of his face was visible except the barest glint of the moon on his eye as if it were a fragment of glass. Then I saw it glint on his buttons and heard them rustle as his arm swung free again and one long leg bent as he moved forward and proceeded into the tower right towards us.

"I held fast to Claudia, ready in an instant to shove her behind me, to step forward to meet him. But then I saw with astonishment that his eyes did not see me as I saw him, and he was trudging under the weight of the body he carried towards the monastery door. The moon fell now on his bowed head, on a mass of wavy black hair that touched his bent shoulder, and on the full black sleeve of his coat. I saw something about his coat; the flap of it was badly torn and the sleeve appeared to be ripped from the seam. I almost fancied I could see his flesh through the shoulder. The human in his arms stirred now, and moaned miserably. And the figure stopped for a moment and appeared to stroke the human with his hand. And at that moment I stepped forward from the wall and went towards him.

"No words passed my lips: I knew none to say. I only knew that I moved into the light of the moon before him and that his dark, wavy head rose with a jerk, and that I saw his eyes.

"For one full instant he looked at me, and I saw the light shining in those eyes and then glinting on two sharp canine teeth; and then a low strangled cry seemed to rise from the depths of his throat which, for a second, I thought to be my own. The human crashed to the stones, a shuddering moan escaping his lips. And the vampire lunged at me, that strangled cry rising again as the stench of fetid breath rose in my nostrils and the clawlike fingers cut into the very fur of my cape. I fell backwards, my head cracking against the wall, my hands grabbing at his head, clutching a mass of tangled filth that was his hair. At once the wet, rotting fabric of his coat ripped in my grasp, but the arm that held me was like iron; and, as I struggled to pull the head backwards, the fangs touched the flesh of my throat. Claudia screamed behind him. Something hit his head hard, which stopped him suddenly; and then he was hit again. He turned as if to strike her a blow, and I sent my fist against his face as powerfully as I could. Again a stone struck him as she darted away, and I threw my full weight against him and felt his crippled leg buckling. I remember pounding his head over and over, my fingers all but pulling that filthy hair out by the roots, his fangs projected towards me, his hands scratching, clawing at me. We rolled over and over, until I pinned him down again and the moon shone full on his face. And I realized, through my frantic sobbing breaths, what it was I held in my arms. The two huge eyes bulged from naked sockets and two small, hideous holes made up his nose; only a putrid, leathery flesh enclosed his skull, and the rank, rotting rags that covered his frame were thick with earth and slime and blood. I was battling a mindless, animated corpse. But no more.

"From above him, a sharp stone fell full on his forehead, and a fount of blood gushed from between his eyes. He struggled, but another stone crashed with such force I heard the bones shatter. Blood seeped out beneath the matted hair, soaking into the stones and grass. The chest throbbed beneath me, but the arms shuddered and grew still. I drew up, my throat knotted, my heart burning, every fiber of my body aching from the struggle. For a moment the great tower seemed to tilt, but then it righted itself. I lay against the wall, staring at the thing, the blood rushing in my ears. Gradually I realized that Claudia knelt on his chest, that she was probing the mass of hair and bone that had been his head. She was scattering the fragments of his skull. We had met the European vampire, the creature of the Old World. He was dead."

"For a long time I lay on the broad stairway, oblivious to the thick earth that covered it, my head feeling very cool against the earth, just looking at him. Claudia stood at his feet, hands hanging limply at her sides. I saw her eyes close for an instant, two tiny lids that made her face like a small, moonlit white statue as she stood there. And then her body began to rock very slowly. 'Claudia,' I called to her. She awakened. She was gaunt such as I had seldom seen her. She pointed to the human who lay far across the floor of the tower near the wall. He was still motionless, but I knew that he was not dead. I'd forgotten him completely, my body aching as it was, my senses still clouded with the stench of the bleeding corpse. But now I saw the man. And in some part of my mind I knew what his fate would be, and I cared nothing for it. I knew it was only an hour at most before dawn.

" 'He's moving,' she said to me. And I tried to rise off the steps. Better that he not wake, better that he never wake at all, I wanted to say; she was walking towards him, passing indifferently the dead thing that had nearly killed us both. I saw her back and the man stirring in front of her, his foot twisting in the grass. I don't know what I expected to see as I drew nearer, what terrified peasant or farmer, what miserable wretch that had already seen the face of that thing that had brought it here. And for a moment I did not realize who it was that lay there, that it was Morgan, whose pale face showed now in the moon, the marks of the vampire on his throat, his blue eyes staring mute and expressionless before him.

"Suddenly they widened as I drew close to him. 'Louis!' he whispered in astonishment, his lips moving as if he were trying to frame words but could not. 'Louis . . .' he said again; and then I saw he was smiling. A dry, rasping sound came from him as he struggled to his knees, and he reached out for me. His blanched, contorted face strained as the sound died in his throat, and he nodded desperately, his red hair loose and dishevelled, falling into his eyes. I turned and ran from him. Claudia shot past me, gripping me by the arm. 'Do you see the color of the sky!' she hissed at me. Morgan fell forward on his hands behind her. 'Louis,' he called out again, the light gleaming in his eyes. He seemed blind to the ruins, blind to the night, blind to everything but a face he recognized, that one word again issuing from his lips. I put my hands to my ears, backing away from him. His hand was bloody now as he lifted it. I could smell the blood as well as see it. And Claudia could smell it, too.

"Swiftly she descended on him, pushing him down against the stones, her white fingers moving through his red hair. He tried to raise his head. His outstretched hands made a frame about her face, and then suddenly he began to stroke her yellow curls. She sank her teeth, and the hands dropped helpless at his side.

"I was at the edge of the forest when she caught up with me. 'You must go to him, take him,' she commanded. I could smell the blood on her lips, see the warmth in her cheeks. Her wrist burned against me, yet I did not move. 'Listen to me, Louis,' she said, her voice at once desperate and angry. 'I left him for you, but he's dying . . . there's no time.'

"I swung her up into my arms and started the long descent. No need for caution, no need for stealth, no preternatural host waiting. The door to the secrets of eastern Europe was shut against us. I was plowing through the dark to the road. 'Will you listen to me,' she cried out. But I went on in spite of her, her hands clutching at my coat, my hair. 'Do you see the sky, do you see it!' she railed.

"She was all but sobbing against my breast as I splashed through the icy stream and ran headlong in search of the lantern at the road.

"The sky was a dark blue when I found the carriage. 'Give me the crucifix,' I shouted to Claudia as I cracked the whip. 'There's only one place to go.' She was thrown against me as the carriage rocked into its turn and headed for the village.

"I had the eeriest feeling then as I could see the mist rising amongst the dark brown trees. The air was cold and fresh and the birds had begun. It was as if the sun were rising. Yet I did not care. And yet I knew that it was not rising, that there was still time. It was a marvellous, quieting feeling. The scrapes and cuts burned my flesh and my heart ached with hunger, but my head felt marvellously light. Until I saw the gray shapes of the inn and the steeple of the church; they were too clear. And the stars above were fading fast.

"In a moment I was hammering on the door of the inn. As it opened, I put my hood up around my face tightly and held Claudia beneath my cape in a bundle. 'Your village is rid of the vampire!' I said to the woman, who stared at me in astonishment. I was clutching the crucifix which she'd given me. 'Thanks be to God he's dead. You'll find the remains in the tower. Tell this to your people at once.' I pushed past her into the inn.

"The gathering was roused into commotion instantly, but I insisted that I was tired beyond endurance. I must pray and rest. They were to get my chest from the carriage and bring it to a decent room where I might sleep. But a message was to come for me from the bishop at Varna and for this, and this only, was I to be awakened. 'Tell the good father when he arrives that the vampire is dead, and then give him food and drink and have him wait for me,' I said. The woman was crossing herself. 'You understand,' I said to her, as I hurried towards the stairs, 'I couldn't reveal my mission to you until after the vampire had been. . . .' 'Yes, yes,' she said to me. 'But you are not a priest . . . the child!' 'No, only too well-versed in these matters. The Unholy One is no match for me,' I said to her. I stopped. The door of the little parlor stood open, with nothing but a white square of cloth on the oak table. 'Your friend,' she said to me, and she looked at the floor. 'He rushed out into the night . . . he was mad.' I only nodded.

"I could hear them shouting when I shut the door of the room. They seemed to be running in all directions; and then came the sharp sound of the church bell in the rapid peal of alarm. Claudia had slipped down from my arms, and she was staring at me gravely as I bolted the door. Very slowly I unlatched the shutter of the window. An icy light seeped into the room. Still she watched me. Then I felt her at my side. I looked down to see she was holding out her hand to me. 'Here,' she said. She must have seen I was confused. I felt so weak that her face was shimmering as I looked at it, the blue of her eyes dancing on her white cheeks.

" 'Drink,' she whispered, drawing nearer. 'Drink.' And she

held the soft, tender flesh of the wrist towards me. 'No, I know what to do; haven't I done it in the past?' I said to her. It was she who bolted the window tight, latched the heavy door. I remember kneeling by the small grate and feeling the ancient panelling. It was rotten behind the varnished surface, and it gave under my fingers. Suddenly I saw my fist go through it and felt the sharp jab of splinters in my wrist. And then I remember feeling in the dark and catching hold of something warm and pulsing. A rush of cold, damp air hit my face and I saw a darkness rising about me, cool and damp as if this air were a silent water that seeped through the broken wall and filled the room. The room was gone. I was drinking from a never-ending stream of warm blood that flowed down my throat and through my pulsing heart and through my veins, so that my skin warmed against this cool, dark water. And now the pulse of the blood I drank slackened, and all my body cried out for it not to slacken, my heart pounding, trying to make that heart pound with it. I felt myself rising, as if I were floating in the darkness, and then the darkness, like the heartbeat, began to fade. Something glimmered in my swoon; it shivered ever so slightly with the pounding of feet on the stairs, on the floorboards, the rolling of wheels and horses' hooves on the earth, and it gave off a tinkling sound as it shivered. It had a small wooden frame around it, and in that frame there emerged, through the glimmer, the figure of a man. He was familiar. I knew his long, slender build, his black, wavy hair. Then I saw that his green eyes were gazing at me. And in his teeth, in his teeth, he was clutching something huge and soft and brown, which he pressed tightly with both his hands. It was a rat. A great loathsome brown rat he held, its feet poised, its mouth agape, its great curved tail frozen in the air. Crying out, he threw it down and stared aghast, blood flowing from his open mouth.

"A searing light hit my eyes. I struggled to open them against it, and the entire room was glowing. Claudia was right in front of me. She was not a tiny child, but someone much larger who drew me forward towards her with both hands. She was on her knees, and my arms encircled her waist. Then darkness descended, and I had her folded against me. The lock slid into place. Numbness came over my limbs, and then the paralysis of oblivion."

AND THAT WAS HOW it was throughout Transylvania and Hungary and Bulgaria, and through all those countries where the peasants know that the living dead walk, and the legends of the vampires abound. In every village where we did encounter the vampire, it was the same."

"A mindless corpse?" the boy asked.

"Always," said the vampire. "When we found these creatures at all. I remember a handful at most. Sometimes we only watched them from a distance, all too familiar with their wagging, bovine heads, their haggard shoulders, their rotted, ragged clothing. In one hamlet it was a woman, only dead for perhaps a few months; the villagers had glimpsed her and knew her by name. It was she who gave us the only hope we were to experience after the monster in Transylvania, and that hope came to nothing. She fled from us through the forest and we ran after her, reaching out for her long, black hair. Her white burial gown was soaked with dried blood, her fingers caked with the dirt of the grave. And her eyes . . . they were mindless, empty, two pools that reflected the moon. No secrets, no truths, only despair."

"But what were these creatures? Why were they like this?" asked the boy, his lips grimacing with disgust. "I don't understand. How could they be so different from you and Claudia, yet exist?"

"I had my theories. So did Claudia. But the main thing which I had then was despair. And in despair the recurring fear that we had killed the only other vampire like us, Lestat. Yet it seemed unthinkable. Had he possessed the wisdom of a sorcerer, the powers of a witch . . . I might have come to understand that he had somehow managed to wrest a conscious life from the same forces that governed these monsters. But he was only Lestat, as I've described him to you: devoid of mystery, finally, his limits as familiar to me in those months in eastern Europe as his charms. I wanted to forget him, and yet it seemed I thought of him always. It was as if the empty nights were made for thinking of him. And sometimes I found myself so vividly aware of him it was as if he had only just left the room and the ring of his voice were still there. And somehow there was a disturbing comfort in that, and, despite myself, I'd envision his face—not as it had been the last night in the fire, but on other nights, that last evening he spent with us at home, his hand playing idly with the keys of the spinet, his head tilted to one side. A sickness rose in me more wretched than anguish when I saw what my dreams were doing. I wanted him alive! In the dark nights of eastern Europe, Lestat was the only vampire I'd found.

"But Claudia's waking thoughts were of a far more practical nature. Over and over, she had me recount that night in the hotel in New Orleans when she'd become a vampire, and over and over she searched the process for some clue to why these things we met in the country graveyards had no mind. What if, after Lestat's infusion of blood, she'd been put in a grave, closed up in it until the preternatural drive for blood caused her to break the stone door of the vault that held her, what then would her mind have been, starved, as it were, to the breaking point? Her body might have saved itself when no mind remained. And through the world she would have blundered, ravaging where she could, as we saw these creatures do. That was how she explained them. But what had fathered them, how had they begun? That was what she couldn't explain and what gave her hope of discovery when I, from sheer exhaustion, had none. 'They spawn their own kind, it's obvious, but where does it begin?' she asked. And then, somewhere near the outskirts of Vienna, she put the question to me which had never before passed her lips. Why could I not do what Lestat had done with both of us? Why could I not make another vampire? I don't know why at first I didn't even understand her, except that in loathing what I was with every impulse in me I had a particular fear of that question, which was almost worse than any other. You see, I didn't understand something strong in myself. Loneliness had caused me to think on that very possibility years before, when I had fallen under the spell of Babette Freniere. But I held it locked inside of me like an unclean passion. I shunned mortal life after her. I killed strangers. And the Englishman Morgan, because I knew him, was as safe from my fatal embrace as Babette had been. They both caused me too much pain. Death I couldn't think of giving them. Life in death—it was monstrous. I turned away from Claudia. I wouldn't answer her. But angry as she was, wretched as was her impatience, she could not stand this turning away. And she drew near to me, comforting me with her hands and her eyes as if she were my loving daughter.

" 'Don't think on it, Louis,' she said later, when we were comfortably situated in a small suburban hotel. I was standing at the window, looking at the distant glow of Vienna, so eager for that city, its civilization, its sheer size. The night was clear and the haze of the city was on the sky. 'Let me put your conscience at ease, though I'll never know precisely what it is,' she said into my ear, her hand stroking my hair.

" 'Do that, Claudia,' I answered her. 'Put it at ease. Tell me that you'll never speak to me of making vampires again.'

" 'I want no orphans such as ourselves!' she said, all too quickly. My words annoyed her. My feeling annoyed her. 'I want answers, knowledge,' she said. 'But tell me, Louis, what makes you so certain that you've never done this without your knowing it?'

"Again there was that deliberate obtuseness in me. I must look at her as if I didn't know the meaning of her words. I wanted her to be silent and to be near me, and for us to be in Vienna. I drew her hair back and let my fingertips touch her long lashes and looked away at the light.

" 'After all, what does it take to make those creatures?' she went on. 'Those vagabond monsters? How many drops of your blood intermingled with a man's blood . . . and what kind of heart to survive that first attack?'

"I could feel her watching my face, and I stood there, my arms folded, my back to the side of the window, looking out.

" 'That pale-faced Emily, that miserable Englishman . . .' she said, oblivious to the flicker of pain in my face. 'Their hearts were nothing, and it was the fear of death as much as the drawing of blood that killed them. The idea killed them. But what of the hearts that survive? Are you sure you haven't fathered a league of monsters who, from time to time, struggled vainly and instinctively to follow in your footsteps? What was their life span, these orphans you left behind you—a day there, a week here, before the sun burnt them to ashes or some mortal victim cut them down?'

" 'Stop it,' I begged her. 'If you knew how completely I envision everything you describe, you would not describe it. I tell you it's never happened! Lestat drained me to the point of death to make me a vampire. And gave back all that blood mingled with his own. That is how it was done!'

"She looked away from me, and then it seemed she was looking down at her hands. I think I heard her sigh, but I wasn't certain. And then her eyes moved over me, slowly, up and down, before they finally met mine. Then it seemed she smiled. 'Don't be frightened of my fancy,' she said softly. 'After all, the final decision will always rest with you. Is that not so?'

" 'I don't understand,' I said. And a cold laughter erupted from her as she turned away.

" 'Can you picture it?' she said, so softly I scarcely heard. 'A coven of children? That is all I could provide. . . .'

" 'Claudia,' I murmured.

" 'Rest easy,' she said abruptly, her voice still low. 'I tell you that as much as I hated Lestat . . .' She stopped.

" 'Yes . . .' I whispered. 'Yes. . . .'

" 'As much as I hated him, with him we were . . . complete.' She looked at me, her eyelids quivering, as if the slight rise in her voice had disturbed her even as it had disturbed me.

" 'No, only you were complete . . .' I said to her. 'Because there were two of us, one on either side of you, from the beginning.'

"I thought I saw her smile then, but I was not certain. She bowed her head, but I could see her eyes moving beneath the lashes, back and forth, back and forth. Then she said, 'The two of you at my side. Do you picture that as you say it, as you picture everything else?'

"One night, long gone by, was as material to me as if I were in it still, but I didn't tell her. She was desperate in that night, running away from Lestat, who had urged her to kill a woman in the street from whom she'd backed off, clearly alarmed. I was sure the woman had resembled her mother. Finally she'd escaped us entirely, but I'd found her in the armoire, beneath the jackets and coats, clinging to her doll. And, carrying her to her crib, I sat beside her and sang to her, and she stared at me as she clung to that doll, as if trying blindly and mysteriously to calm a pain she herself did not begin to understand. Can you picture it, this splendid domesticity, dim lamps, the vampire father singing to the vampire daughter? Only the doll had a human face, only the doll.

" 'But we must get away from here!' said the present Claudia suddenly, as though the thought had just taken shape in her mind with a special urgency. She had her hand to her ear, as if clutching it against some awful sound. 'From the roads behind us, from what I see in your eyes now, because I give voice to thoughts which are nothing more to me than plain considerations . . .'

" 'Forgive me,' I said as gently as I could, withdrawing slowly from that long-ago room, that ruffled crib, that frightened monster child and monster voice. And Lestat, where was Lestat? A match striking in the other room, a shadow leaping suddenly into life, as light and dark come alive where there was only darkness.

" 'No, you forgive me . . .' she was saying to me now, in this little hotel room near the first capital of western Europe. 'No, we forgive each other. But we don't forgive him; and, without him, you see what things are between us.'

" 'Only now because we are tired, and things are dreary . . .' I said to her and to myself, because there was no one else in the world to whom I could speak.

" 'Ah, yes; and that is what must end. I tell you, I begin to understand that we have done it all wrong from the start. We must bypass Vienna. We need our language, our people. I want to go directly now to Paris.' "

PART III

I THINK the very name of Paris brought a rush of pleasure to me that was extraordinary, a relief so near to well-being that I was amazed, not only that I could feel it, but that I'd so nearly forgotten it.

"I wonder if you can understand what it meant. My expression can't convey it now, for what Paris means to me is very different from what it meant then, in those days, at that hour; but still, even now, to think of it, I feel something akin to that happiness. And I've more reason now than ever to say that happiness is not what I will ever know, or will ever deserve to know. I am not so much in love with happiness. Yet the name Paris makes me feel it.

"Mortal beauty often makes me ache, and mortal grandeur can fill me with that longing I felt so hopelessly in the Mediterranean Sea. But Paris, Paris drew me close to her heart, so I forgot myself entirely. Forgot the damned and questing preternatural thing that doted on mortal skin and mortal clothing. Paris overwhelmed, and lightened and rewarded more richly than any promise.

"It was the mother of New Orleans, understand that first; it had given New Orleans its life, its first populace; and it was what New Orleans had for so long tried to be. But New Orleans, though beautiful and desperately alive, was desperately fragile. There was something forever savage and primitive there, something that threatened the exotic and sophisticated life both from within and without. Not an inch of those wooden streets nor a brick of the crowded Spanish houses had not been bought from the fierce wilderness that forever surrounded the city, ready to engulf it. Hurricanes, floods, fevers, the plague—and the damp of the Louisiana climate itself worked tirelessly on every hewn plank or stone façade, so that New Orleans seemed at all times like a dream in the imagination of her striving populace, a dream held intact at every second by a tenacious, though unconscious, collective will.

"But Paris, Paris was a universe whole and entire unto herself, hollowed and fashioned by history; so she seemed in this age of Napoleon III with her towering buildings, her massive cathedrals, her grand boulevards and ancient winding medieval streets—as vast and indestructible as nature itself. All was embraced by her, by her volatile and enchanted populace thronging the galleries, the theaters, the cafés, giving birth over and over to genius and sanctity, philosophy and war, frivolity and the finest art; so it seemed that if all the world outside her were to sink into darkness, what was fine, what was beautiful, what was essential might there still come to its finest flower. Even the majestic trees that graced and sheltered her streets were attuned to her—and the waters of the Seine, contained and beautiful as they wound through her heart; so that the earth on that spot, so shaped by blood and consciousness, had ceased to be the earth and had become Paris.

"We were alive again. We were in love, and so euphoric was I after those hopeless nights of wandering in eastern Europe that I yielded completely when Claudia moved us into the Hôtel Saint-Gabriel on the Boulevard des Capucines. It was rumored to be one of the largest hotels in Europe, its immense rooms dwarfing the memory of our old town house, while at the same time recalling it with a comfortable splendor. We were to have one of the finest suites. Our windows looked out over the gas-lit boulevard itself where, in the early evening, the asphalt sidewalks teemed with strollers and an endless stream of carriages flowed past, taking lavishly dressed ladies and their gentlemen to the Opéra or the Opéra Comique, the ballet, the theaters, the balls and receptions without end at the Tuileries.

"Claudia put her reasons for expense to me gently and logically, but I could see that she became impatient ordering everything through me; it was wearing for her. The hotel, she said, quietly afforded us complete freedom, our nocturnal habits going unnoticed in the continual press of European tourists, our rooms immaculately maintained by an anonymous staff, while the immense price we paid guaranteed our privacy and our security. But there was more to it than that. There was a feverish purpose to her buying.

" 'This is my world,' she explained to me as she sat in a small velvet chair before the open balcony, watching the long row of broughams stopping one by one before the hotel doors. 'I must have it as I like,' she said, as if speaking to herself. And so it was as she liked, stunning wallpaper of rose and gold, an abundance of damask and velvet furniture, embroidered pillows and silk trappings for the fourposter bed. Dozens of roses appeared daily for the marble mantels and the inlaid tables, crowding the curtained alcove of her dressing room, reflected endlessly in tilted mirrors. And finally she crowded the high French windows with a veritable garden of camellia and fern. 'I miss the flowers; more than anything else I miss the flowers,' she mused. And sought after them even in the paintings which we brought from the shops and the galleries, magnificent canvases such as I'd never seen in New Orleans—from the classically executed lifelike bouquets, tempting you to reach for the petals that fell on a three-dimensional tablecloth, to a new and disturbing style in which the colors seemed to blaze with such intensity they destroyed the old lines, the old solidity, to make a vision like to those states when I'm nearest my delirium and flowers grow before my eyes and crackle like the flames of lamps. Paris flowed into these rooms.

"I found myself at home there, again forsaking dreams of ethereal simplicity for what another's gentle insistence had given me, because the air was sweet like the air of our courtyard in the Rue Royale, and all was alive with a shocking profusion of gas light that rendered even the ornate lofty ceilings devoid of shadows. The light raced on the gilt curlicues, flickered in the baubles of the chandeliers. Darkness did not exist. Vampires did not exist.

"And even bent as I was on my quest, it was sweet to think that, for an hour, father and daughter climbed into the cabriolet from such civilized luxury only to ride along the banks of the Seine, over the bridge into the Latin Quarter to roam those darker, narrower streets in search of history, not victims. And then to return to the ticking clock and the brass andirons and the playing cards laid out upon the table. Books of poets, the program from a play, and all around the soft humming of the vast hotel, distant violins, a woman talking in a rapid, animated voice above the zinging of a hairbrush, and a man high above on the top floor repeating over and over to the night air, 'I understand, I am just beginning, I am just beginning to understand. . . .'

" 'Is it as you would have it?' Claudia asked, perhaps just to let me know she hadn't forgotten me, for she was quiet now for hours; no talk of vampires. But something was wrong. It was not the old serenity, the pensiveness that was recollection. There was a brooding there, a smoldering dissatisfaction. And though it would vanish from her eyes when I would call to her or answer her, anger seemed to settle very near the surface.

" 'Oh, you know how I would have it,' I answered, persisting in the myth of my own will. 'Some garret near the Sorbonne, near enough to the noise of the Rue St. Michel, far enough away. But I would mainly have it as you would have it.' And I could see her warmed, but looking past me, as if to say, 'You have no remedy; don't draw too near; don't ask of me what I ask of you: are you content?'

"My memory is too clear; too sharp; things should wear at the edges, and what is unresolved should soften. So, scenes are near my heart like pictures in lockets, yet monstrous pictures no artist or camera would ever catch; and over and over I would see Claudia at the piano's edge that last night when Lestat was playing, preparing to die, her face when he was taunting her, that contortion that at once became a mask; attention might have saved his life, if, in fact, he were dead at all.

"Something was collecting in Claudia, revealing itself slowly to the most unwilling witness in the world. She had a new passion for rings and bracelets children did not wear. Her jaunty, straight-backed walk was not a child's, and often she entered small boutiques ahead of me and pointed a commanding finger at the perfume or the gloves she would then pay for herself. I was never far away, and always uncomfortable—not because I feared anything in this vast city, but because I feared her. She'd always been the 'lost child' to her victims, the 'orphan,' and now it seemed she would be something else, something wicked and shocking to the passers-by who succumbed to her. But this was often private; I was left for an hour haunting the carved edifices of Notre-Dame, or sitting at the edge of a park in the carriage.

"And then one night, when I awoke on the lavish bed in the suite of the hotel, my book crunched uncomfortably under me, I found her gone altogether. I didn't dare ask the attendants if they'd seen her. It was our practice to spirit past them; we had no name. I searched the corridors for her, the side streets, even the ballroom, where some almost inexplicable dread came over me at the thought of her there alone. But then I finally saw her coming through the side doors of the lobby, her hair beneath her bonnet brim sparkling from the light rain, the child rushing as if on a mischievous escapade, lighting the faces of doting men and women as she mounted the grand staircase and passed me, as if she hadn't seen me at all. An impossibility, a strange graceful slight.

"I shut the door behind me just as she was taking off her cape, and, in a flurry of golden raindrops, she shook it, shook her hair. The ribbons crushed from the bonnet fell loose and I felt a palpable relief to see the childish dress, those ribbons, and something wonderfully comforting in her arms, a small china doll. Still she said nothing to me; she was fussing with the doll. Jointed somehow with hooks or wire beneath its flouncing dress, its tiny feet tinkled like a bell. 'It's a lady doll,' she said, looking up at me. 'See? A lady doll.' She put it on the dresser.

" 'So it is,' I whispered.

" 'A woman made it,' she said. 'She makes baby dolls, all the same, baby dolls, a shop of baby dolls, until I said to her, "I want a lady doll.' "

"It was taunting, mysterious. She sat there now with the wet strands of hair streaking her high forehead, intent on that doll. 'Do you know why she made it for me?' she asked. I was wishing now the room had shadows, that I could retreat from the warm circle of the superfluous fire into some darkness, that I wasn't sitting on the bed as if on a lighted stage, seeing her before me and in her mirrors, puffed sleeves and puffed sleeves.

" 'Because you are a beautiful child and she wanted to make you happy,' I said, my voice small and foreign to myself.

"She was laughing soundlessly. 'A beautiful child,' she said, glancing up at me. 'Is that what you still think I am?' And her face went dark as again she played with the doll, her fingers pushing the tiny crocheted neckline down toward the china breasts. 'Yes, I resemble her baby dolls, I am her baby dolls. You should see her working in that shop; bent on her dolls, each with the same face, lips.' Her finger touched her own lip. Something seemed to shift suddenly, something within the very walls of the room itself, and the mirrors trembled with her image as if the earth had sighed beneath the foundations. Carriages rumbled in the streets; but they were too far away. And then I saw what her still childish figure was doing: in one hand she held the doll, the other to her lips; and the hand that held the doll was crushing it, crushing it and popping it so it bobbed and broke in a heap of glass that fell now from her open, bloody hand onto the carpet. She wrung the tiny dress to make a shower of littering particles as I averted my eyes, only to see her in the tilted mirror over the fire, see her eyes scanning me from my feet to the top of my head. She moved through that mirror towards me and drew close on the bed.

" 'Why do you look away, why don't you look at me?' she asked, her voice very smooth, very like a silver bell. But then she laughed softly, a woman's laugh, and said, 'Did you think I'd be your daughter forever? Are you the father of fools, the fool of fathers?'

" 'Your tone is unkind with me,' I answered.

" 'Hmmm . . . unkind.' I think she nodded. She was a blaze in the corner of my eye, blue flames, golden flames.

" 'And what do they think of you,' I asked as gently as I could, 'out there?' I gestured to the open window.

" 'Many things.' She smiled. 'Many things. Men are marvellous at explanations. Have you see the "little people" in the parks, the circuses, the freaks that men pay money to laugh at?'

" 'I was a sorcerer's apprentice only!' I burst out suddenly, despite myself. 'Apprentice!' I said. I wanted to touch her, to stroke her hair, but I sat there afraid of her, her anger like a match about to kindle.

"Again she smiled, and then she drew my hand into her lap and covered it as best she could with her own. 'Apprentice, yes,' she laughed. 'But tell me one thing, one thing from that lofty height. What was it like . . . making love?'

"I was walking away from her before I meant to, I was searching like a dim-witted mortal man for cape and gloves. 'You don't remember?' she asked with perfect calm, as I put my hand on the brass door handle.

"I stopped, feeling her eyes on my back, ashamed, and then I turned around and made as if to think, Where am I going, what shall I do, why do I stand here?

" 'It was something hurried,' I said, trying now to meet her eyes. How perfectly, coldly blue they were. How earnest. 'And . . . it was seldom savored . . . something acute that was quickly lost. I think that it was the pale shadow of killing.'

" 'Ahhh . . .' she said. 'Like hurting you as I do now . . . that is also the pale shadow of killing.'

" 'Yes, madam,' I said to her. 'I am inclined to believe that is correct.' And bowing swiftly, I bade her good-night."

"It was a long time after I'd left her that I slowed my pace. I'd crossed the Seine. I wanted darkness. To hide from her and the feelings that welled up in me, and the great consuming fear that

I was utterly inadequate to make her happy, or to make myself happy by pleasing her.

"I would have given the world to please her, the world we now possessed, which seemed at once empty and eternal. Yet I was injured by her words and by her eyes, and no amount of explanations to her—which passed through and through my mind now, even forming on my lips in desperate whispers as I left the Rue St. Michel and went deeper and deeper into the older, darker streets of the Latin Quarter—no amount of explanations seemed to soothe what I imagined to be her grave dissatisfaction, or my own pain.

"Finally I left off words except for a strange chant. I was in the black silence of a medieval street, and blindly I followed its sharp turns, comforted by the height of its narrow tenements, which seemed at any moment capable of falling together, closing this alleyway under the indifferent stars like a seam. 'I cannot make her happy, I do not make her happy; and her unhappiness increases every day.' This was my chant, which I repeated like a rosary, a charm to change the facts, her inevitable disillusionment with our quest, which left us in this limbo where I felt her drawing away from me, dwarfing me with her enormous need. I even conceived a savage jealousy of the dollmaker to whom she'd confided her request for that tinkling diminutive lady, because that dollmaker had for a moment given her something which she held close to herself in my presence as if I were not there at all.

"What did it amount to, where could it lead?

"Never since I'd come to Paris months before did I so completely feel the city's immense size, how I might pass from this twisting, blind street of my choice into a world of delights; and never had I so keenly felt its uselessness. Uselessness to her if she could not abide this anger, if she could not somehow grasp the limits of which she seemed so angrily, bitterly aware. I was helpless. She was helpless. But she was stronger than me. And I knew, had known even at the moment when I turned away from her in the hotel, that behind her eyes there was for me her continuing love.

"And dizzy and weary and now comfortably lost, I became aware with a vampire's inextinguishable senses that I was being followed.

"My first thought was irrational. She'd come out after me. And, cleverer than I, had tracked me at a great distance. But as surely as this came to mind, another thought presented itself, a rather cruel thought in light of all that had passed between us. The steps were too heavy for hers. It was just some mortal walking in this same alley, walking unwarily towards death.

"So I continued on, almost ready to fall into my pain again because I deserved it, when my mind said, You are a fool; listen. And it dawned on me that these steps, echoing as they were at a great distance behind me, were in perfect time with my own. An accident. Because if mortal they were, they were too far off for mortal hearing. But as I stopped now to consider that, they stopped. And as I turned saying, Louis, you deceive yourself, and started up, they started up. Footfall with my footfall, gaining speed now as I gained speed. And then something remarkable, undeniable occurred. *En garde* as I was for the steps that were behind me, I tripped on a fallen roof tile and was pitched against the wall. And behind me, those steps echoed to perfection the sharp shuffling rhythm of my fall.

"I was astonished. And in a state of alarm well beyond fear. To the right and left of me the street was dark. Not even a tarnished light shone in a garret window. And the only safety afforded me, the great distance between myself and these steps, was as I said the guarantee that they were not human. I was at a complete loss as to what I might do. I had the near-irresistible desire to call out to this being and welcome it, to let it know as quickly and as completely as possible that I awaited it, had been searching for it, would confront it. Yet I was afraid. What seemed sensible was to resume walking, waiting for it to gain on me; and as I did so I was again mocked by my own pace, and the distance between us remained the same. The tension mounted in me, the dark around me becoming more and more menacing; and I said over and over, measuring these steps, Why do you track me, why do you let me know you are there?

"Then I rounded a sharp turn in the street, and a gleam of light showed ahead of me at the next corner. The street sloped up towards it, and I moved on very slowly, my heart deafening in my ears, reluctant to eventually reveal myself in that light.

"And as I hesitated—stopped, in fact—right before the turn, something rumbled and clattered above, as if the roof of the house beside me had all but collapsed. I jumped back just in time, before a load of tiles crashed into the street, one of them brushing my shoulder. All was quiet now. I stared at the tiles, listening, waiting. And then slowly I edged around the turn into the light, only to see there looming over me at the top of the street beneath the gas lamp the unmistakable figure of another vampire.

"He was enormous in height though gaunt as myself, his long, white face very bright under the lamp, his large, black eyes staring at me in what seemed undisguised wonder. His right leg was slightly bent as though he'd just come to a halt in mid-step. And then suddenly I realized that not only was his black hair long and full and combed precisely like my own, and not only was he dressed in identical coat and cape to my own, but he stood imitating my stance and facial expression to perfection. I swallowed and let my eyes pass over him slowly, while I struggled to hide from him the rapid pace of my pulse as his eyes in like manner passed over me. And when I saw him blink I realized I had just blinked, and as I drew my arms up and folded them across my chest he slowly did the same. It was maddening. Worse than maddening. Because, as I barely moved my lips, he barely moved his lips, and I found the words dead and I couldn't make other words to confront this, to stop it. And all the while, there was that height and those sharp black eyes and that powerful attention which was, of course, perfect mockery, but nevertheless riveted to myself. *He* was the vampire; *I* seemed the mirror.

" 'Clever,' I said to him shortly and desperately, and, of course, he echoed that word as fast as I said it. And maddened as I was more by that than anything else, I found myself yielding to a slow smile, defying the sweat which had broken from every pore and the violent tremor in my legs. He also smiled, but his eyes had a ferocity that was animal, unlike my own, and the smile was sinister in its sheer mechanical quality.

"Now I took a step forward and so did he; and when I stopped short, staring, so did he. But then he slowly, very slowly, lifted his right arm, though mine remained poised and, gathering his fingers into a fist, he now struck at his chest in quickening time to mock my heartbeat. Laughter erupted from him. He threw back his head, showing his canine teeth, and the laughter seemed to fill the alleyway. I loathed him. Completely.

" 'You mean me harm?' I asked, only to hear the words mockingly obliterated.

" 'Trickster!' I said sharply. 'Buffoon!'

"That word stopped him. Died on his lips even as he was saying it, and his face went hard.

"What I did then was impulse. I turned my back on him and started away, perhaps to make him come after me and demand to know who I was. But in a movement so swift I couldn't possibly have seen it, he stood before me again, as if he had materialized there. Again I turned my back on him—only to face him under the lamp again, the settling of his dark, wavy hair the only indication that he had in fact moved.

" 'I've been looking for you! I've come to Paris looking for you!' I forced myself to say the words, seeing that he didn't echo them or move, only stood staring at me.

"Now he moved forward slowly, gracefully, and I saw his own body and his own manner had regained possession of him and, extending his hand as if he meant to ask for mine, he very suddenly pushed me backwards, off-balance. I could feel my shirt drenched and sticking to my flesh as I righted myself, my hand grimed from the damp wall.

"And as I turned to confront him, he threw me completely down.

"I wish I could describe to you his power. You would know, if I were to attack you, to deal you a sharp blow with an arm you never saw move towards you.

"But something in me said, Show him your own power; and

I rose up fast, going right for him with both arms out. And I hit the night, the empty night swirling beneath that lamppost, and stood there looking about me, alone and a complete fool. This was a test of some sort, I knew it then, though consciously I fixed my attention on the dark street, the recesses of the doorways, anyplace he might have hidden. I wanted no part of this test, but saw no way out of it. And I was contemplating some way to disdainfully make that clear when suddenly he appeared again, jerking me around and flinging me down the sloping cobblestones where I'd fallen before. I felt his boot against my ribs. And, enraged, I grabbed hold of his leg, scarcely believing it when I felt the cloth and the bone. He'd fallen against the stone wall opposite and let out a snarl of unrepressed anger.

"What happened then was pure confusion. I held tight to that leg, though the boot strained to get at me. And at some point, after he'd toppled over me and pulled loose from me, I was lifted into the air by strong hands. What might have happened I can well imagine. He could have flung me several yards from himself, he was easily that strong. And battered, severely injured, I might have lost consciousness. It was violently disturbing to me even in that melee that I didn't know whether I could lose consciousness. But it was never put to a test. For, confused as I was, I was certain someone else had come between us, someone who was battling him decisively, forcing him to relinquish his hold.

"When I looked up, I was in the street, and I saw two figures only for an instant, like the flicker of an image after the eye is shut. Then there was only a swirling of black garments, a boot striking the stones, and the night was empty. I sat, panting, the sweat pouring down my face, staring around me and then up at the narrow ribbon of faint sky. Slowly, only because my eye was totally concentrated upon it now, a figure emerged from the darkness of the wall above me. Crouched on the jutting stones of the lintel, it turned so that I saw the barest gleam of light on the hair and then the stark, white face. A strange face, broader and not so gaunt as the other, a large dark eye that was holding me steadily. A whisper came from the lips, though they never appeared to move. 'You are all right.'

"I was more than all right. I was on my feet, ready to attack. But the figure remained crouched, as if it were part of the wall. I could see a white hand working in what appeared to be a waistcoat pocket. A card appeared, white as the fingers that extended it to me. I didn't move to take it. 'Come to us, tomorrow night,' said that same whisper from the smooth, expressionless face, which still showed only one eye to the light. 'I won't harm you,' he said. 'And neither will that other. I won't allow it.' And his hand did that thing which vampires can make happen; that is, it seemed to leave his body in the dark to deposit the card in my hand, the purple script immediately shining in the light. And the figure, moving upwards like a cat on the wall, vanished fast between the garret gables overhead.

"I knew I was alone now, could feel it. And the pounding of my heart seemed to fill the empty little street as I stood under the lamp reading that card. The address I knew well enough, because I had been to theaters along that street more than once. But the name was astonishing: 'Théâtre des Vampires,' and the time noted, nine p.m.

"I turned it over and discovered written there the note, 'Bring the petite beauty with you. You are most welcome. Armand.'

"There was no doubt that the figure who'd given it to me had written this message. And I had only a very short time to get to the hotel and to tell Claudia of these things before dawn. I was running fast, so that even the people I passed on the boulevards did not actually see the shadow that brushed them."

The Théâtre des Vampires was by invitation only, and the next night the doorman inspected my card for a moment while the rain fell softly all around us: on the man and the woman stopped at the shut-up box office; on the crinkling posters of penny-dreadful vampires with their outstretched arms and cloaks resembling bat wings ready to close on the naked shoulders of a mortal victim; on the couples that pressed past us into the packed lobby, where I could easily perceive that the crowd was all human, no vampires among them, not even this boy who admitted us finally into the press of conversation and damp wool and ladies' gloved fingers fumbling with felt-brimmed hats and wet curls. I pressed for the shadows in a feverish excitement. We had fed earlier only so that in the bustling street of this theater our skin would not be too white, our eyes too unclouded. And that taste of blood which I had not enjoyed had left me all the more uneasy; but I had no time for it. This was no night for killing. This was to be a night of revelations, no matter how it ended. I was certain.

"Yet here we stood with this all-too-human crowd, the doors opening now on the auditorium, and a young boy pushing towards us, beckoning, pointing above the shoulders of the crowd to the stairs. Ours was a box, one of the best in the house, and if the blood had not dimmed my skin completely nor made Claudia into a human child as she rode in my arms, this usher did not seem at all to notice it nor to care. In fact, he smiled all too readily as he drew back the curtain for us on two chairs before the brass rail.

" 'Would you put it past them to have human slaves?' Claudia whispered.

" 'But Lestat never trusted human slaves,' I answered. I watched the seats fill, watched the marvellously flowered hats navigating below me through the rows of silk chairs. White shoulders gleamed in the deep curve of the balcony spreading out from us; diamonds glittered in the gas light. 'Remember, be sly for once,' came Claudia's whisper from beneath her bowed blond head. 'You're too much of a gentleman.'

"The lights were going out, first in the balcony, and then along the walls of the main floor. A knot of musicians had gathered in the pit below the stage, and at the foot of the long, green velvet curtain the gas flickered, then brightened, and the audience receded as if enveloped by a gray cloud through which only the diamonds sparkled, on wrists, on throats, on fingers. And a hush descended like that gray cloud until all the sound was collected in one echoing persistent cough. Then silence. And the slow, rhythmical beating of a tambourine. Added to that was the thin melody of a wooden flute, which seemed to pick up the sharp metallic tink of the bells of the tambourine, winding them into a haunting melody that was medieval in sound. Then the strumming of strings that emphasized the tambourine. And the flute rose, in that melody singing of something melancholy, sad. It had a charm to it, this music, and the whole audience seemed stilled and united by it, as if the music of that flute were a luminous ribbon unfurling slowly in the dark. Not even the rising curtain broke the silence with the slightest sound. The lights brightened, and it seemed the stage was not the stage but a thickly wooded place, the light glittering on the roughened tree trunks and the thick clusters of leaves beneath the arch of darkness above; and through the trees could be seen what appeared the low, stone bank of a river and above that, beyond that, the glittering waters of the river itself, this whole three-dimensional world produced in painting upon a fine silk scrim that shivered only slightly in a faint draft.

"A sprinkling of applause greeted the illusion, gathering adherents from all parts of the auditorium until it reached its short crescendo and died away. A dark, draped figure was moving on the stage from tree trunk to tree trunk, so fast that as he stepped into the lights he seemed to appear magically in the center, one arm flashing out from his cloak to show a silver scythe and the other to hold a mask on a slender stick before the invisible face, a mask which showed the gleaming countenance of Death, a painted skull.

"There were gasps from the crowd. It was Death standing before the audience, the scythe poised, Death at the edge of a dark wood. And something in me was responding now as the audience responded, not in fear, but in some human way, to the magic of that fragile painted set, the mystery of the lighted world there, the world in which this figure moved in his billowing black cloak, back and forth before the audience with the grace of a great panther, drawing forth, as it were, those gasps, those sighs, those reverent murmurs.

"And now, behind this figure, whose very gestures seemed to have a captivating power like the rhythm of the music to which it moved, came other figures from the wings. First an old woman, very stooped and bent, her gray hair like moss, her arm hanging down with the weight of a great basket of flowers. Her shuttling steps scraped on the stage, and her head bobbed with the rhythm of the music and the darting steps of the Grim Reaper. And then she started back as she laid eyes on him and, slowly setting down her basket, made her hands into the attitude of prayer. She was tired; her head leaned now on her hands as if in sleep, and she reached out for him, supplicating. But as he came towards her, he bent to look directly into her face, which was all shadows to us beneath her hair, and started back then, waving his hand as if to freshen the air. Laughter erupted uncertainly from the audience. But as the old woman rose and took after Death, the laughter took over.

"The music broke into a jig with their running, as round and round the stage the old woman pursued Death, until he finally flattened himself into the dark of a tree trunk, bowing his masked face under his wing like a bird. And the old woman, lost, defeated, gathered up her basket as the music softened and slowed to her pace, and made her way off the stage. I did not like it. I did not like the laughter. I could see the other figures moving in now, the music orchestrating their gestures, cripples on crutches and beggars with rags the color of ash, all reaching out for Death, who whirled, escaping this one with a sudden arching of the back, fleeing from that one with an effeminate gesture of disgust, waving them all away finally in a foppish display of weariness and boredom.

"It was then I realized that the languid, white hand that made these comic arcs was not painted white. It was a vampire hand which wrung laughter from the crowd. A vampire hand lifted now to the grinning skull, as the stage was finally clear, as if stifling a yawn. And then this vampire, still holding the mask before his face, adopted marvellously the attitude of resting his weight against a painted silken tree, as if he were falling gently to sleep. The music twittered like birds, rippled like the flowing of the water; and the spotlight, which encircled him in a yellow pool, grew dim, all but fading away as he slept.

"And another spot pierced the scrim, seeming to melt it altogether, to reveal a young woman standing alone far upstage. She was majestically tall and all but enshrined by a voluminous mane of golden blond hair. I could feel the awe of the audience as she seemed to flounder in the spotlight, the dark forest rising on the perimeter, so that she seemed to be lost in the trees. And she was lost; and not a vampire. The soil on her mean blouse and skirt was not stage paint, and nothing had touched her perfect face, which gazed into the light now, as beautiful and finely chiselled as the face of a marble Virgin, that hair her haloed veil. She could not see in the light, though all could see her. And the moan which escaped her lips as she floundered seemed to echo over the thin, romantic singing of the flute, which was a tribute to that beauty. The figure of Death woke with a start in his pale spotlight and turned to see her as the audience had seen her, and to throw up his free hand in tribute, in awe.

"The twitter of laughter died before it became real. She was too beautiful, her gray eyes too distressed. The performance too perfect. And then the skull mask was thrown suddenly into the wings and Death showed a beaming white face to the audience, his hurried hands stroking his handsome black hair, straightening a waistcoat, brushing imaginary dust from his lapels. Death in love. And clapping rose for the luminous countenance, the gleaming cheekbones, the winking black eye, as if it were all masterful illusion when in fact it was merely and certainly the face of a vampire, the vampire who had accosted me in the Latin Quarter, that leering, grinning vampire, harshly illuminated by the yellow spot.

"My hand reached for Claudia's in the dark and pressed it tightly. But she sat still, as if enrapt. The forest of the stage, through which that helpless mortal girl stared blindly towards the laughter, divided in two phantom halves, moving away from the center, freeing the vampire to close in on her.

"And she who had been advancing towards the footlights, saw him suddenly and came to a halt, making a moan like a child. Indeed, she was very like a child, though clearly a full-grown woman. Only a slight wrinkling of the tender flesh around her eyes betrayed her age. Her breasts though small were beautifully shaped beneath her blouse, and her hips though narrow gave her long, dusty skirt a sharp, sensual angularity. As she moved back from the vampire, I saw the tears standing in her eyes like glass in the flicker of the lights, and I felt my spirit contract in fear for her, and in longing. Her beauty was heartbreaking.

"Behind her, a number of painted skulls suddenly moved against the blackness, the figures that carried the masks invisible in their black clothes, except for free white hands that clasped the edge of a cape, the folds of a skirt. Vampire women were there, moving in with the men towards the victim, and now they all, one by one, thrust the masks away so they fell in an artful pile, the sticks like bones, the skulls grinning into the darkness above. And there they stood, seven vampires, the women vampires three in number, their molded white breasts shining over the tight black bodices of their gowns, their hard luminescent faces staring with dark eyes beneath curls of black hair. Starkly beautiful, as they seemed to float close around that florid human figure, yet pale and cold compared to that sparkling golden hair, that petal-pink skin. I could hear the breath of the audience, the halting, the soft sighs. It was a spectacle, that circle of white faces pressing closer and closer, and that leading figure, that Gentleman Death, turning to the audience now with his hands crossed over his heart, his head bent in longing to elicit their sympathy: was she not irresistible! A murmur of assenting laughter, of sighs.

"But it was she who broke the magic silence.

" 'I don't want to die . . .' she whispered. Her voice was like a bell.

" 'We *are* death,' he answered her; and from around her came the whisper, 'Death.' She turned, tossing her hair so it became a veritable shower of gold, a rich and living thing over the dust of her poor clothing. 'Help me!' she cried out softly, as if afraid even to raise her voice. 'Someone . . .' she said to the crowd she knew must be there. A soft laughter came from Claudia. The girl onstage only vaguely understood where she was, what was happening, but knew infinitely more than this house of people that gaped at her.

" 'I don't want to die! I don't want to!' Her delicate voice broke, her eyes fixed on the tall, malevolent leader vampire, that demon trickster who now stepped out of the circle of the others towards her.

" 'We all die,' he answered her. 'The one thing you share with every mortal is death.' His hand took in the orchestra, the distant faces of the balcony, the boxes.

" 'No,' she protested in disbelief. 'I have so many years, so many. . . .' Her voice was light, lilting in her pain. It made her irresistible, just as did the movement of her naked throat and the hand that fluttered there.

" 'Years!' said the master vampire. 'How do you know you have so many years? Death is no respecter of age! There could be a sickness in your body now, already devouring you from within. Or, outside, a man might be waiting to kill you simply for your yellow hair!' And his fingers reached for it, the sound of his deep, preternatural voice sonorous. 'Need I tell you what fate may have in store for you?'

" 'I don't care . . . I'm not afraid,' she protested, her clarion voice so fragile after him. 'I would take my chance. . . .'

" 'And if you do take that chance and live, live for years, what would be your heritage? The humpbacked, toothless visage of old age?' And now he lifted her hair behind her back, exposing her pale throat. And slowly he drew the string from the loose gathers of her blouse. The cheap fabric opened, the sleeves slipping off her narrow, pink shoulders; and she clasped it, only to have him take her wrists and thrust them sharply away. The audience seemed to sigh in a body, the women behind their opera glasses, the men leaning forward in their chairs. I could see the cloth falling, see the pale, flawless skin pulsing with her heart and the tiny nipples letting the cloth slip precariously, the vampire holding her right wrist tightly at her side, the tears coursing down her blushing cheeks, her teeth biting into the flesh of her lip. 'Just as sure as this flesh is pink, it will turn gray, wrinkled with age,' he said.

" 'Let me live, please,' she begged, her face turning away from him. 'I don't care . . . I don't care!'

" 'But then, why should you care if you die now? If these things don't frighten you . . . these horrors?'

"She shook her head, baffled, outsmarted, helpless. I felt the anger in my veins, as sure as the passion. With a bowed head she bore the whole responsibility for defending life, and it was unfair, monstrously unfair that she should have to pit logic against his for what was obvious and sacred and so beautifully embodied in her. But he made her speechless, made her overwhelming instinct seem petty, confused. I could feel her dying inside, weakening, and I hated him.

"The blouse slipped to her waist. A murmur moved through the titillated crowd as her small, round breasts stood exposed. She struggled to free her wrist, but he held it fast.

" 'And suppose we were to let you go . . . suppose the Grim Reaper had a heart that could resist your beauty . . . to whom would he turn his passion? Someone must die in your place. Would you pick the person for us? The person to stand here and suffer as you suffer now?' He gestured to the audience. Her confusion was terrible. 'Have you a sister . . . a mother . . . a child?'

" 'No,' she gasped. 'No . . .' shaking the mane of hair.

" 'Surely someone could take your place, a friend? Choose!'

" 'I can't. I wouldn't. . . .' She writhed in his tight grasp. The vampires around her looked on, still, their faces evincing no emotion, as if the preternatural flesh were masks. 'Can't you do it?' he taunted her. And I knew, if she said she could, how he would only condemn her, say she was as evil as he for marking someone for death, say that she deserved her fate.

" 'Death waits for you everywhere.' He sighed now as if he were suddenly frustrated. The audience could not perceive it; I could. I could see the muscles of his smooth face tightening. He was trying to keep her gray eyes on his eyes, but she looked desperately, hopefully away from him. On the warm, rising air I could smell the dust and perfume of her skin, hear the soft beating of her heart. 'Unconscious death . . . the fate of all mortals.' He bent closer to her, musing, infatuated with her, but struggling. 'Hmmm. . . . but we are *conscious* death! That would make you a bride. Do you know what it means to be loved by Death?' He all but kissed her face, the brilliant stain of her tears. 'Do you know what it means to have Death know your name?'

"She looked at him, overcome with fear. And then her eyes seemed to mist over, her lips to go slack. She was staring past him at the figure of another vampire who had emerged slowly from the shadows. For a long time he had stood on the periphery of the gathering, his hands clasped, his large, dark eyes very still. His attitude was not the attitude of hunger. He did not appear rapt. But she was looking into his eyes now, and her pain bathed her in a beauteous light, a light which made her irresistibly alluring. It was this that held the jaded audience, this terrible pain. I could feel her skin, feel the small, pointed breasts, feel my arms caressing her. I shut my eyes against it and saw her starkly against that private darkness. It was what they felt all around her, this community of vampires. She had no chance.

"And, looking up again, I saw her shimmering in the smoky light of the footlamps, saw her tears like gold, as softly from that other vampire who stood at a distance came the words . . . 'No pain.'

"I could see the trickster stiffen, but no one else would see it. They would see only the girl's smooth, childlike face, those parted lips, slack with innocent wonder as she gazed at that distant vampire, hear her soft voice repeat after him, 'No pain?'

" 'Your beauty is a gift to us.' His rich voice effortlessly filled the house, seemed to fix and subdue the mounting wave of excitement. And slightly, almost imperceptibly, his hand moved. The trickster was receding, becoming one of those patient, white faces, whose hunger and equanimity were strangely one. And slowly, gracefully, the other moved towards her. She was languid, her nakedness forgotten, those lids fluttering, a sigh escaping her moist lips. 'No pain,' she assented. I could hardly bear it, the sight of her yearning towards him, seeing her dying now, under this vampire's power. I wanted to cry out to her, to break her swoon. And I wanted her. Wanted her, as he was moving in on her, his hand out now for the drawstring of her skirt as she inclined towards him, her head back, the black cloth slipping over her hips, over the golden gleam of the hair between her legs—a child's down, that delicate curl—the skirt dropping to her feet. And this vampire opened his arms, his back to the flickering footlights, his auburn hair seeming to tremble as the gold of her hair fell around his black coat. 'No pain . . . no pain . . .' he was whispering to her, and she was giving herself over.

"And now, turning her slowly to the side so that they could all see her serene face, he was lifting her, her back arching as her naked breasts touched his buttons, her pale arms enfolded his neck. She stiffened, cried out as he sank his teeth, and her face was still as the dark theater reverberated with shared passion. His white hand shone on her florid buttocks, her hair dusting it, stroking it. He lifted her off the boards as he drank, her throat gleaming against his white cheek. I felt weak, dazed, hunger rising in me, knotting my heart, my veins. I felt my hand gripping the brass bar of the box, tighter, until I could feel the metal creaking in its joints. And that soft, wrenching sound which none of those mortals might hear seemed somehow to hook me to the solid place where I was.

"I bowed my head; I wanted to shut my eyes. The air seemed fragrant with her salted skin, and close and hot and sweet. Around her the other vampires drew in, the white hand that held her tight quivered, and the auburn-haired vampire let her go, turning her, displaying her, her head fallen back as he gave her over, one of those starkly beautiful vampire women rising behind her, cradling her, stroking her as she bent to drink.

They were all about her now, as she was passed from one to another and to another, before the enthralled crowd, her head thrown forward over the shoulder of a vampire man, the nape of her neck as enticing as the small buttocks or the flawless skin of her long thighs, the tender creases behind her limply bent knees.

"I was sitting back in the chair, my mouth full of the taste of her, my veins in torment. And in the corner of my eye was that auburn-haired vampire who had conquered her, standing apart as he had been before, his dark eyes seeming to pick me from the darkness, seeming to fix on me over the currents of warm air.

"One by one the vampires were withdrawing. The painted forest came back, sliding soundlessly into place. Until the mortal girl, frail and very white, lay naked in that mysterious wood, nestled in the silk of a black bier as if on the floor of the forest itself; and the music had begun again, eerie and alarming, growing louder as the lights grew dimmer. All the vampires were gone, except the trickster, who had gathered his scythe from the shadows and also his handheld mask. And he crouched near the sleeping girl as the lights slowly faded, and the music alone had power and force in the enclosing dark. And then that died also.

"For a moment, the entire crowd was utterly still.

"Then applause began here and there and suddenly united everyone around us. The lights rose in the sconces on the walls and heads turned to one another, conversation erupting all round. A woman rising in the middle of a row to pull her fox fur sharply from the chair, though no one had yet made way for her; someone else pushing out quickly to the carpeted aisle; and the whole body was on its feet as if driven to the exits.

"But then the hum became the comfortable, jaded hum of the sophisticated and perfumed crowd that had filled the lobby and the vault of the theater before. The spell was broken. The doors were flung open on the fragrant rain, the clop of horses' hooves, and voices calling for taxis. Down in the sea of slightly askew chairs, a white glove gleamed on a green silk cushion.

"I sat watching, listening, one hand shielding my lowered

face from anyone and no one, my elbow resting on the rail, the passion in me subsiding, the taste of the girl on my lips. It was as though on the smell of the rain came her perfume still, and in the empty theater I could hear the throb of her beating heart. I sucked in my breath, tasted the rain, and glimpsed Claudia sitting infinitely still, her gloved hands in her lap.

"There was a bitter taste in my mouth, and confusion. And then I saw a lone usher moving on the aisle below, righting the chairs, reaching for the scattered programs that littered the carpet. I was aware that this ache in me, this confusion, this blinding passion which only let me go with a stubborn slowness would be obliterated if I were to drop down to one of those curtained archways beside him and draw him up fast in the darkness and take him as that girl was taken. I wanted to do it, and I wanted nothing. Claudia said near my bowed ear, 'Patience, Louis. Patience.'

"I opened my eyes. Someone was near, on the periphery of my vision; someone who had outsmarted my hearing, my keen anticipation, which penetrated like a sharp antenna even this distraction, or so I thought. But there he was, soundless, beyond the curtained entrance of the box, that vampire with the auburn hair, that detached one, standing on the carpeted stairway looking at us. I knew him now to be, as I'd suspected, the vampire who had given me the card admitting us to the theater. Armand.

"He would have startled me, except for his stillness, the remote dreamy quality of his expression. It seemed he'd been standing against that wall for the longest time, and betrayed no sign of change as we looked at him, then came towards him. Had he not so completely absorbed me, I would have been relieved he was not the tall, black-haired one; but I didn't think of this. Now his eyes moved languidly over Claudia with no tribute whatsoever to the human habit of disguising the stare. I placed my hand on Claudia's shoulder. 'We've been searching for you a very long time,' I said to him, my heart growing calmer, as if his calm were drawing off my trepidation, my care, like the sea drawing something into itself from the land. I cannot exaggerate this quality in him. Yet I can't describe it and couldn't then; and the fact that my mind sought to describe it even to myself unsettled me. He gave me the very feeling that he knew what I was doing, and his still posture and his deep, brown eyes seemed to say there was no use in what I was thinking, or particularly the words I was struggling to form now. Claudia said nothing.

"He moved away from the wall and began to walk down the stairs, while at the same time he made a gesture that welcomed us and bade us follow; but all this was fluid and fast. My gestures were the caricature of human gestures compared to his. He opened a door in the lower wall and admitted us to the rooms below the theater, his feet only brushing the stone stairway as we descended, his back to us with complete trust.

"And now we entered what appeared to be a vast subterranean ballroom, carved, as it were, out of a cellar more ancient than the building overhead. Above us, the door that he had opened fell shut, and the light died away before I could get a fair impression of the room. I heard the rustle of his garments in the dark and then the sharp explosion of a match. His face appeared like a great flame over the match. And then a figure moved into the light beside him, a young boy, who brought him a candle. The sight of the boy brought back to me in a shock the teasing pleasure of the naked woman on the stage, her prone body, the pulsing blood. And he turned and gazed at me now, much in the manner of the auburn-haired vampire, who had lit the candle and whispered to him, 'Go.' The light expanded to the distant walls, and the vampire held the light up and moved along the wall, beckoning us both to follow.

"I could see a world of frescoes and murals surrounded us, their colors deep and vibrant above the dancing flame, and gradually the theme and content beside us came clear. It was the terrible 'Triumph of Death' by Breughel, painted on such a massive scale that all the multitude of ghastly figures towered over us in the gloom, those ruthless skeletons ferrying the helpless dead in a fetid moat or pulling a cart of human skulls, beheading an outstretched corpse or hanging humans from the gallows. A bell tolled over the endless hell of scorched and smoking land, towards which great armies of men came with the hideous, mindless march of soldiers to a massacre. I turned away, but the auburn-haired one touched my hand and led me further along the wall to see 'The Fall of the Angels' slowly materializing, with the damned being driven from the celestial heights into a lurid chaos of feasting monsters. So vivid, so perfect was it, I shuddered. The hand that had touched me did the same again, and I stood still despite it, deliberately looking above to the very height of the mural, where I could make out of the shadows two beautiful angels with trumpets to their lips. And for a second the spell was broken. I had the strong sense of the first evening I had entered Notre-Dame; but then that was gone, like something gossamer and precious snatched away from me.

"The candle rose. And horrors rose all around me: the dumbly passive and degraded damned of Bosch, the bloated, coffined corpses of Traini, the monstrous horsemen of Dürer, and blown out of all endurable scale a promenade of medieval woodcut, emblem, and engraving. The very ceiling writhed with skeletons and moldering dead, with demons and the instruments of pain, as if this were the cathedral of death itself.

"Where we stood finally in the center of the room, the candle seemed to pull the images to life everywhere around us. Delirium threatened, that awful shifting of the room began, that sense of falling. I reached out for Claudia's hand. She stood musing, her face passive, her eyes distant when I looked to her, as if she'd have me let her alone; and then her feet shot off from me with a rapid tapping on the stone floor that echoed all along the walls, like fingers tapping on my temples, on my skull. I held my temples, staring dumbly at the floor in search of shelter, as if to lift my eyes would force me to look on some wretched suffering I would not, could not endure. Then again I saw the vampire's face floating in his flame, his ageless eyes circled in dark lashes. His lips were very still, but as I stared at him he seemed to smile without making even the slightest movement. I watched him all the harder, convinced it was some powerful illusion I could penetrate with keen attention; and the more I watched, the more he seemed to smile and finally to be animated with a soundless whispering, musing, singing. I could hear it like something curling in the dark, as wallpaper curls in the blast of a fire or paint peels from the face of a burning doll. I had the urge to reach for him, to shake him violently so that his still face would move, admit to this soft singing; and suddenly I found him pressed against me, his arm around my chest, his lashes so close I could see them matted and gleaming above the incandescent orb of his eye, his soft, tasteless breath against my skin. It *was* delirium.

"I moved to get away from him, and yet I was drawn to him and I didn't move at all, his arm exerting its firm pressure, his candle blazing now against my eye, so that I felt the warmth of it; all my cold flesh yearned for that warmth, but suddenly I waved to snuff it but couldn't find it, and all I saw was his radiant face, as I had never seen Lestat's face, white and poreless and sinewy and male. The other vampire. All other vampires. An infinite procession of my own kind.

"The moment ended.

"I found myself with my hand outstretched, touching his face; but he was a distance away from me, as if he'd never moved near me, making no attempt to brush my hand away. I drew back, flushed, stunned.

"Far away in the Paris night a bell chimed, the dull, golden circles of sound seeming to penetrate the walls, the timbers that carried that sound down into the earth like great organ pipes. Again came that whispering, that inarticulate singing. And through the gloom I saw that mortal boy watching me, and I smelled the hot aroma of his flesh. The vampire's facile hand beckoned him, and he came towards me, his eyes fearless and exciting, and he drew up to me in the candlelight and put his arms around my shoulders.

"Never had I felt this, never had I experienced it, this yielding of a conscious mortal. But before I could push him away for his own sake, I saw the bluish bruise on his tender neck. He was offering it to me. He was pressing the length of his body against me now, and I felt the hard strength of his sex beneath his clothes pressing against my leg. A wretched gasp escaped my lips, but he bent close, his lips on what must have been so cold, so lifeless for him; and I sank my teeth into his skin, my body rigid, that hard sex driving against me, and I lifted him in passion off the floor. Wave after wave of his beating heart passed into me as, weightless, I rocked with him, devouring him, his ecstasy, his conscious pleasure.

"Then, weak and gasping, I saw him at a distance from me, my arms empty, my mouth still flooded with the taste of his blood. He lay against that auburn-haired vampire, his arm about the vampire's waist, and he gazed at me in that same pacific manner of the vampire, his eyes misted over and weak from the loss of life. I remember moving mutely forward, drawn to him and seemingly unable to control it, that gaze taunting me, that conscious life defying me; he should die and would not die; he would live on, comprehending, surviving that intimacy! I turned. The host of vampires moved in the shadows, their candles whipped and fleeting on the cool air; and above them loomed a great broadcast of ink-drawn figures: the sleeping corpse of a woman ravaged by a vulture with a human face; a naked man bound hand and foot to a tree, beside him hanging the torso of another, his severed arms tied still to another branch, and on a spike this dead man's staring head.

"The singing came again, that thin, ethereal singing. Slowly the hunger in me subsided, obeyed, but my head throbbed and the flames of the candles seemed to merge in burnished circles of light. Someone touched me suddenly, pushed me roughly, so that I almost lost my balance, and when I straightened I saw the thin, angular face of the trickster vampire I despised. He reached out for me with his white hands. But the other one, the distant one, moved forward suddenly and stood between us. It seemed he struck the other vampire, that I saw him move, and then again I did not see him move; both stood still like statues, eyes fixed on one another, and time passed like wave after wave of water rolling back from a still beach. I cannot say how long we stood there, the three of us in those shadows, and how utterly still they seemed to me, only the shimmering flames seeming to have life behind them. Then I remember floundering along the wall and finding a large oak chair into which I all but collapsed. It seemed Claudia was near and speaking to someone in a hushed but sweet voice. My forehead teemed with blood, with heat.

" 'Come with me,' said the auburn-haired vampire. I was searching his face for the movement of his lips that must have preceded the sound, yet it was so hopelessly long after the sound. And then we were walking, the three of us, down a long stone stairway deeper beneath the city, Claudia ahead of us, her shadow long against the wall. The air grew cool and refreshing with the fragrance of water, and I could see the droplets bleeding through the stones like beads of gold in the light of the vampire's candle.

"It was a small chamber we entered, a fire burning in a deep fireplace cut into the stone wall. A bed lay at the other end, fitted into the rock and enclosed with two brass gates. At first I saw these things clearly, and saw the long wall of books opposite the fireplace and the wooden desk that was against it, and the coffin to the other side. But then the room began to waver, and the auburn-haired vampire put his hands on my shoulders and guided me down into a leather chair. The fire was intensely hot against my legs, but this felt good to me, sharp and clear, something to draw me out of this confusion. I sat back, my eyes only half open, and tried to see again what was about me. It was as if that distant bed were a stage and on the linen pillows of the little stage lay that boy, his black hair parted in the middle and curling about his ears, so that he looked now in his dreamy, fevered state like one of those lithe androgynous creatures of a Botticelli painting; and beside him, nestled against him, her tiny white hand stark against his ruddy flesh, lay Claudia, her face buried in his neck. The masterful auburn-haired vampire looked on, his hands clasped in front of him; and when Claudia rose now, the boy shuddered. The vampire picked her up, gently, as I might pick her up, her hands finding a hold on his neck, her eyes half shut with the swoon, her lips rouged with blood. He set her gently on the desk, and she lay back against the leatherbound books, her hands falling gracefully into the lap of her lavender dress. The gates closed on the boy and, burying his face in the pillows, he slept.

"There was something disturbing to me in the room, and I didn't know what it was. I didn't in truth know what was wrong with me, only that I'd been drawn forcefully either by myself or someone else from two fierce, consuming states: an absorption with those grim paintings, and the kill to which I'd abandoned myself, obscenely, in the eyes of others.

"I didn't know what it was that threatened me now, what it was that my mind sought escape from. I kept looking at Claudia, the way she lay against the books, the way she sat amongst the objects of the desk, the polished white skull, the candleholder, the open parchment book whose hand-painted script gleamed in the light; and then above her there emerged into focus the lacquered and shimmering painting of a medieval devil, horned and hoofed, his bestial figure looming over a coven of worshipping witches. Her head was just beneath it, the loose curling strands of her hair just stroking it; and she watched the brown-eyed vampire with wide, wondering eyes. I wanted to pick her up suddenly, and frightfully, horribly, I saw her in my kindled imagination flopping like a doll. I was gazing at the devil, that monstrous face preferable to the sight of her in her eerie stillness.

" 'You won't awaken the boy if you speak,' said the brown-eyed vampire. 'You've come from so far, you've travelled so long.' And gradually my confusion subsided, as if smoke were rising and moving away on a current of fresh air. And I lay awake and very calm, looking at him as he sat in the opposite chair. Claudia, too, looked at him. And he looked from one to the other of us, his smooth face and pacific eyes very like they'd been all along, as though there had never been any change in him at all.

" 'My name is Armand,' he said. 'I sent Santiago to give you the invitation. I know your names. I welcome you to my house.'

"I gathered my strength to speak, my voice sounding strange to me when I told him that we had feared we were alone.

" 'But how did you come into existence?' he asked. Claudia's hand rose ever so slightly from her lap, her eyes moving mechanically from his face to mine. I saw this and knew that he must have seen it, and yet he gave no sign. I knew at once what she meant to tell me. 'You don't want to answer,' said Armand, his voice low and even more measured than Claudia's voice, far less human than my own. I sensed myself slipping away again into contemplation of that voice and those eyes, from which I had to draw myself up with great effort.

" 'Are you the leader of this group?' I asked him.

" 'Not in the way you mean *leader*,' he answered. 'But if there were a leader here, I would be that one.'

" 'I haven't come . . . you'll forgive me . . . to talk of how I came into being. Because that's no mystery to me, it presents no question. So if you have no power to which I might be required to render respect, I don't wish to talk of those things.'

" 'If I told you I did have such power, would you respect it?' he asked.

"I wish I could describe his manner of speaking, how each time he spoke he seemed to arise out of a state of contemplation very like that state into which I felt I was drifting, from which it took so much to wrench myself; and yet he never moved, and seemed at all times alert. This distracted me while at the same time I was powerfully attracted by it, as I was by this room, its simplicity, its rich, warm combination of essentials: the books, the desk, the two chairs by the fire, the coffin, the pictures. The luxury of those rooms in the hotel seemed vulgar, but more than that, meaningless, beside this room. I understood all of it except for the mortal boy, the sleeping boy, whom I didn't understand at all.

" 'I'm not certain,' I said, unable to keep my eyes off that awful medieval Satan. 'I would have to know from what . . . from whom it comes. Whether it came from other vampires . . . or elsewhere.'

" 'Elsewhere . . .' he said. 'What is elsewhere?'

" 'That!' I pointed to the medieval picture.

" 'That is a picture,' he said.

" 'Nothing more?'

" 'Nothing more.'

" 'Then Satan . . . some satanic power doesn't give you your power here, either as leader or as vampire?'

" 'No,' he said calmly, so calmly it was impossible for me to know what he thought of my questions, if he thought of them at all in the manner which I knew to be thinking.

" 'And the other vampires?'

" 'No,' he said.

" 'Then we are not . . .' I sat forward, '. . . the children of Satan?'

" 'How could we be the children of Satan?' he asked. 'Do you believe that Satan made this world around you?'

" 'No, I believe that God made it, if anyone made it. But He also must have made Satan, and I want to know if we are his children!'

" 'Exactly, and consequently if you believe God made Satan, you must realize that all Satan's power comes from God and that Satan is simply God's child, and that we are God's children also. There are no children of Satan, really.'

"I couldn't disguise my feelings at this. I sat back against the leather, looking at that small woodcut of the devil, released for the moment from any sense of obligation to Armand's presence, lost in my thoughts, in the undeniable implications of his simple logic.

" 'But why does this concern you? Surely what I say doesn't surprise you,' he said. 'Why do you let it affect you?'

" 'Let me explain,' I began. 'I know that you're a master vampire. I respect you. But I'm incapable of your detachment. I know what it is, and I do not possess it and I doubt that I ever will. I accept this.'

" 'I understand,' he nodded. 'I saw you in the theater, your suffering, your sympathy with that girl. I saw your sympathy for Denis when I offered him to you; you die when you kill, as if you feel that you deserve to die, and you stint on nothing. But why, with this passion and this sense of justice, do you wish to call yourself the child of Satan!'

" 'I'm evil, evil as any vampire who ever lived! I've killed over and over and will do it again. I took that boy, Denis, when you gave him to me, though I was incapable of knowing whether he would survive or not.'

" 'Why does that make you as evil as any vampire? Aren't there gradations of evil? Is evil a great perilous gulf into which one falls with the first sin, plummeting to the depth?'

" 'Yes, I think it is,' I said to him. 'It's not logical, as you would make it sound. But it's that dark, that empty. And it is without consolation.'

" 'But you're not being fair,' he said with the first glimmer of expression in his voice. 'Surely you attribute great degrees and variations to goodness. There is the goodness of the child which is innocence, and then there is the goodness of the monk who has given up everything to others and lives a life of self-deprivation and service. The goodness of saints, the goodness of good housewives. Are all these the same?'

" 'No. But equally and infinitely different from evil.' I answered.

"I didn't know I thought these things. I spoke them now as my thoughts. And they were my most profound feelings taking a shape they could never have taken had I not spoken them, had I not thought them out this way in conversation with another. I thought myself then possessed of a passive mind, in a sense. I mean that my mind could only pull itself together, formulate thought out of the muddle of longing and pain, when it was touched by another mind; fertilized by it; deeply excited by that other mind and driven to form conclusions. I felt now the rarest, most acute alleviation of loneliness. I could easily visualize and suffer that moment years before in another century, when I had stood at the foot of Babette's stairway, and feel the perpetual metallic frustration of years with Lestat; and then that passionate and doomed affection for Claudia which made loneliness retreat behind the soft indulgence of the senses, the same senses that longed for the kill. And I saw the desolate mountaintop in eastern Europe where I had confronted that mindless vampire and killed him in the monastery ruins. And it was as if the great feminine longing of my mind were being awakened again to be satisfied. And this I felt despite my own words: 'But it's that dark, that empty. And it is without consolation.'

"I looked at Armand, at his large brown eyes in that taut, timeless face, watching me again like a painting; and I felt the slow shifting of the physical world I'd felt in the painted ballroom, the pull of my old delirium, the wakening of a need so terrible that the very promise of its fulfillment contained the unbearable possibility of disappointment. And yet there was the question, the awful, ancient, hounding question of evil.

"I think I put my hands to my head as mortals do when so deeply troubled that they instinctively cover the face, reach for the brain as if they could reach through the skull and massage the living organ out of its agony.

" 'And how is this evil achieved?' he asked. 'How does one fall from grace and become in one instant as evil as the mob tribunal of the Revolution or the most cruel of the Roman emperors? Does one merely have to miss Mass on Sunday, or bite down on the Communion Host? Or steal a loaf of bread . . . or sleep with a neighbor's wife?'

" 'No. . . .' I shook my head. 'No.'

" 'But if evil is without gradation, and it does exist, this state of evil, then only one sin is needed. Isn't that what you are saying? That God exists and. . . .'

" 'I don't know if God exists,' I said. 'And for all I do know . . . He doesn't exist.'

" 'Then no sin matters,' he said. 'No sin achieves evil.'

" 'That's not true. Because if God doesn't exist we are the creatures of highest consciousness in the universe. We alone understand the passage of time and the value of every minute of human life. And what constitutes evil, real evil, is the taking of a single human life. Whether a man would have died tomorrow or the day after or eventually . . . it doesn't matter. Because if God does not exist, this life . . . every second of it . . . is all we have.'

"He sat back, as if for the moment stopped, his large eyes narrowing, then fixing on the depths of the fire. This was the first time since he had come for me that he had looked away from me, and I found myself looking at him unwatched. For a long time he sat in this manner and I could all but feel his thoughts, as if they were palpable in the air like smoke. Not read them, you understand, but feel the power of them. It seemed he possessed an aura and even though his face was very young, which I knew meant nothing, he appeared infinitely old, wise. I could not define it, because I could not explain how the youthful lines of his face, how his eyes expressed innocence and this age and experience at the same time.

"He rose now and looked at Claudia, his hands loosely clasped behind his back. Her silence all this time had been understandable to me. These were not her questions, yet she was fascinated with him and was waiting for him and no doubt learning from him all the while that he spoke to me. But I understood something else now as they looked at each other. He had moved to his feet with a body totally at his command, devoid of the habit of human gesture, gesture rooted in necessity, ritual, fluctuation of mind; and his stillness now was unearthly. And she, as I'd never seen before, possessed the same stillness. And they were gazing at each other with a preternatural understanding from which I was simply excluded.

"I was something whirling and vibrating to them, as mortals were to me. And I knew when he turned towards me again that he'd come to understand she did not believe or share my concept of evil.

"His speech commenced without the slightest warning. 'This is the only real evil left,' he said to the flames.

" 'Yes,' I answered, feeling that all-consuming subject alive again, obliterating all concerns as it always had for me.

" 'It's true,' he said, shocking me, deepening my sadness, my despair.

" 'Then God does not exist . . . you have no knowledge of His existence?'

" 'None,' he said.

" 'No knowledge!' I said it again, unafraid of my simplicity, my miserable human pain.

" 'None.'

" 'And no vampire here has discourse with God or with the devil!'

" 'No vampire that I've ever known,' he said, musing, the fire dancing in his eyes. 'And as far as I know today, after four hundred years, I am the oldest living vampire in the world.'

"I stared at him, astonished.

"Then it began to sink in. It was as I'd always feared, and it was as lonely, it was as totally without hope. Things would go on as they had before, on and on. My search was over. I sat back listlessly watching those licking flames.

"It was futile to leave him to continue it, futile to travel the world only to hear again the same story. 'Four hundred years'—I think I repeated the words—'four hundred years.' I remember staring at the fire. There was a log falling very slowly in the fire, drifting downwards in a process that would take it the night, and it was pitted with tiny holes where some substance that had larded it through and through had burned away fast, and in each of these tiny holes there danced a flame amid the larger flames: and all of these tiny flames with their black mouths seemed to me faces that made a chorus; and the chorus sang without singing. The chorus had no need of singing; in one breath in the fire, which was continuous, it made its soundless song.

"All at once Armand moved in a loud rustling of garments, a descent of crackling shadow and light that left him kneeling at my feet, his hands outstretched holding my head, his eyes burning.

" 'This evil, this concept, it comes from disappointment, from bitterness! Don't you see? Children of Satan! Children of God! Is this the only question you bring to me, is this the only power that obsesses you, so that you must make us gods and devils yourself when the only power that exists is inside ourselves? How could you believe in these old fantastical lies, these myths, these emblems of the supernatural?' He snatched the devil from above Claudia's still countenance so swiftly that I couldn't see the gesture, only the demon leering before me and then crackling in the flames.

"Something was broken inside me when he said this; something ripped aside, so that a torrent of feeling became one with my muscles in every limb. I was on my feet now, backing away from him.

" 'Are you mad?' I asked, astonished at my own anger, my own despair. 'We stand here, the two of us, immortal, ageless, rising nightly to feed that immortality on human blood; and there on your desk against the knowledge of the ages sits a flawless child as demonic as ourselves; and you ask me how I could believe I would find a meaning in the supernatural! I tell you, after seeing what I have become, I could damn well believe anything! Couldn't you? And believing thus, being thus confounded, I can now accept the most fantastical truth of all: that there is no meaning to any of this!'

"I backed towards the door, away from his astonished face, his hand hovering before his lips, the fingers curling to dig into his palm. 'Don't! Come back . . .' he whispered.

" 'No, not now. Let me go. Just a while . . . let me go. . . . Nothing's changed; it's all the same. Let that sink into me . . . just let me go.'

"I looked back before I shut the door. Claudia's face was turned towards me, though she sat as before, her hands clasped on her knee. She made a gesture then, subtle as her smile, which was tinged with the faintest sadness, that I was to go on.

"It was my desire to escape the theater then entirely, to find the streets of Paris and wander, letting the vast accumulation of shocks gradually wear away. But, as I groped along the stone passage of the lower cellar, I became confused. I was perhaps incapable of exerting my own will. It seemed more than ever absurd to me that Lestat should have died, if in fact he had; and looking back on him, as it seemed I was always doing, I saw him more kindly than before. Lost like the rest of us. Not the jealous protector of any knowledge he was afraid to share. He knew nothing. There was nothing to know.

"Only, that was not quite the thought that was gradually coming clear to me. I had hated him for all the wrong reasons; yes, that was true. But I did not fully understand it yet. Confounded, I found myself sitting finally on those dark steps, the light from the ballroom throwing my own shadow on the rough floor, my hands holding my head, a weariness overcoming me. My mind said, Sleep. But more profoundly, my mind said, Dream. And yet I made no move to return to the Hôtel Saint-Gabriel, which seemed a very secure and airy place to me now, a place of subtle and luxurious mortal consolation where I might lie in a chair of puce velvet, put one foot on an ottoman and watch the fire lick the marble tile, looking for all the world to myself in the long mirrors like a thoughtful human. Flee to that, I thought, flee all that is pulling you. And again came that thought: I have wronged Lestat, I have hated him for all the wrong reasons. I whispered it now, trying to withdraw it from the dark, inarticulate pool of my mind, and the whispering made a scratching sound in the stone vault of the stairs.

"But then a voice came softly to me on the air, too faint for mortals: 'How is this so? How did you wrong him?'

"I turned round so sharp that my breath left me. A vampire sat near me, so near as to almost brush my shoulder with the tip of his boot, his legs drawn up close to him, his hands clasped around them. For a moment I thought my eyes deceived me. It was the trickster vampire, whom Armand had called Santiago.

"Yet nothing in his manner indicated his former self, that devilish, hateful self that I had seen, even only a few hours ago when he had reached out for me and Armand had struck him. He was staring at me over his drawn-up knees, his hair dishevelled, his mouth slack and without cunning.

" 'It makes no difference to anyone else,' I said to him, the fear in me subsiding.

" 'But you said a name; I heard you say a name,' he said.

" 'A name I don't want to say again,' I answered, looking away from him. I could see now how he'd fooled me, why his shadow had not fallen over mine; he crouched in my shadow. The vision of him slithering down those stone stairs to sit behind me was slightly disturbing. Everything about him was disturbing, and I reminded myself that he could in no way be trusted. It seemed to me then that Armand, with his hypnotic power, aimed in some way for the maximum truth in presentation of himself: he had drawn out of me without words my state of mind. But this vampire was a liar. And I could feel his power, a crude, pounding power that was almost as strong as Armand's.

" 'You come to Paris in search of us, and then you sit alone on the stairs . . .' he said, in a conciliatory tone. 'Why don't you come up with us? Why don't you speak to us and talk to us of this person whose name you spoke; I know who it was, I know the name.'

" 'You don't know, couldn't know. It was a mortal,' I said now, more from instinct than conviction. The thought of Lestat disturbed me, the thought that this creature should know of Lestat's death.

" 'You came here to ponder mortals, justice done to mortals?' he asked; but there was no reproach or mockery in his tone.

" 'I came to be alone, let me not offend you. It's a fact,' I murmured.

" 'But alone in this frame of mind, when you don't even hear my steps. . . . I like you. I want you to come upstairs.' And as he said this, he slowly pulled me to my feet beside him.

"At that moment the door of Armand's cell threw a long light into the passage. I heard him coming, and Santiago let me go. I was standing there baffled. Armand appeared at the foot of the steps, with Claudia in his arms. She had that same dull expression on her face which she'd had all during my talk with Armand. It was as if she were deep in her own considerations and saw nothing around her; and I remember noting this, though not knowing what to think of it, that it persisted even now. I took her quickly from Armand, and felt her soft limbs against me as if we were both in the coffin, yielding to that paralytic sleep.

"And then, with a powerful thrust of his arm, Armand pushed Santiago away. It seemed he fell backwards, but was up again only to have Armand pull him towards the head of the steps, all of this happening so swiftly I could only see the blur of their garments and hear the scratching of their boots. Then Armand stood alone at the head of the steps, and I went upward towards him.

" 'You cannot safely leave the theater tonight,' he whispered to me. 'He is suspicious of you. And my having brought you here, he feels that it is his right to know you better. Our security depends on it.' He guided me slowly into the ballroom. But then he turned to me and pressed his lips almost to my ear: 'I must warn you. Answer no questions. Ask and you open one bud of truth for yourself after another. But give nothing, nothing, especially concerning your origin.'

"He moved away from us now, but beckoning for us to follow him into the gloom where the others were gathered, clustered like remote marble statues, their faces and hands all too like our own. I had the strong sense then of how we were all made from the same material, a thought which had only occurred to me occasionally in all the long years in New Orleans; and it disturbed me, particularly when I saw one or more of the others reflected in the long mirrors that broke the density of those awful murals.

"Claudia seemed to awaken as I found one of the carved oak chairs and settled into it. She leaned towards me and said something strangely incoherent, which seemed to mean that I must do as Armand said: say nothing of our origin. I wanted to talk with her now, but I could see that tall vampire, Santiago, watching us, his eyes moving slowly from us to Armand. Several women vampires had gathered around Armand, and I felt a tumult of feeling as I saw them put their arms around his waist. And what appalled me as I watched was not their exquisite form, their delicate features and graceful hands made hard as glass by vampire nature, or their bewitching eyes which fixed on me now in a sudden silence; what appalled me was my own fierce jealousy. I was afraid when I saw them so close to him, afraid when he turned and kissed them each. And, as he brought them near to me now, I was unsure and confused.

"Estelle and Celeste are the names I remember, porcelain beauties, who fondled Claudia with the license of the blind, running their hands over her radiant hair, touching even her lips, while she, her eyes still misty and distant, tolerated it all, knowing what I also knew and what they seemed unable to grasp: that a woman's mind as sharp and distinct as their own lived within that small body. It made me wonder as I watched her turning about for them, holding out her lavender skirts and smiling coldly at their adoration, how many times I must have forgotten, spoken to her as if she were the child, fondled her too freely, brought her into my arms with an adult's abandon. My mind went in three directions: that last night in the Hôtel Saint-Gabriel, which seemed a year ago, when she talked of love with rancor; my reverberating shock at Armand's revelations or lack of them; and a quiet absorption of the vampires around me, who whispered in the dark beneath the grotesque murals. For I could learn much from the vampires without ever asking a question, and vampire life in Paris was all that I'd feared it to be, all that the little stage in the theater above had indicated it was.

"The dim lights of the house were mandatory, and the paintings appreciated in full, added to almost nightly when some vampire brought a new engraving or picture by a contemporary artist into the house. Celeste, with her cold hand on my arm, spoke with contempt of men as the originators of these pictures, and Estelle, who now held Claudia on her lap, emphasized to me, the naïve colonial, that vampires had not made such horrors themselves but merely collected them, confirming over and over that men were capable of far greater evil than vampires.

" 'There is evil in making such paintings?' Claudia asked softly in her toneless voice.

"Celeste threw back her black curls and laughed. 'What can

be imagined can be done,' she answered quickly, but her eyes reflected a certain contained hostility. 'Of course, we strive to rival men in kills of all kinds, do we not!' She leaned forward and touched Claudia's knee. But Claudia merely looked at her, watching her laugh nervously and continue. Santiago drew near, to bring up the subject of our rooms in the Hôtel Saint-Gabriel; frightfully unsafe, he said, with an exaggerated stage gesture of the hands. And he showed a knowledge of those rooms which was amazing. He knew the chest in which we slept; it struck him as vulgar. 'Come here!' he said to me, with that near childlike simplicity he had evinced on the steps. 'Live with us and such disguise is unnecessary. We have our guards. And tell me, where do you come from!' he said, dropping to his knees, his hand on the arm of my chair. 'Your voice, I know that accent; speak again.'

"I was vaguely horrified at the thought of having an accent to my French, but this wasn't my immediate concern. He was strong-willed and blatantly possessive, throwing back at me an image of that possessiveness which was flowering in me more fully every moment. And meanwhile, the vampires around us talked on, Estelle explaining that black was the color for a vampire's clothes, that Claudia's lovely pastel dress was beautiful but tasteless. 'We blend with the night,' she said. 'We have a funereal gleam.' And now, bending her cheek next to Claudia's cheek, she laughed to soften her criticism; and Celeste laughed, and Santiago laughed, and the whole room seemed alive with unearthly tinkling laughter, preternatural voices echoing against the painted walls, rippling the feeble candle flames. 'Ah, but to cover up such curls,' said Celeste, now playing with Claudia's golden hair. And I realized what must have been obvious: that all of them had dyed their hair black, but for Armand; and it was that, along with the black clothes, that added to the disturbing impression that we were statues from the same chisel and paint brush. I cannot emphasize too much how disturbed I was by that impression. It seemed to stir something in me deep inside, something I couldn't fully grasp.

"I found myself wandering away from them to one of the

narrow mirrors and watching them all over my shoulder. Claudia gleamed like a jewel in their midst; so would that mortal boy who slept below. The realization was coming to me that I found them dull in some awful way: dull, dull everywhere that I looked, their sparkling vampire eyes repetitious, their wit like a dull, brass bell.

"Only the knowledge I needed distracted me from these thoughts. 'The vampires of eastern Europe . . .' Claudia was saying. 'Monstrous creatures, what have they to do with us?'

" 'Revenants,' Armand answered softly over the distance that separated them, playing on faultless preternatural ears to hear what was more muted than a whisper. The room fell silent. 'Their blood is different, vile. They increase as we do but without skill or care. In the old days—' Abruptly he stopped. I could see his face in the mirror. It was strangely rigid.

" 'Oh, but tell us about the old days,' said Celeste, her voice shrill, at human pitch. There was something vicious in her tone.

"And now Santiago took up the same baiting manner. 'Yes, tell us of the covens, and the herbs that would render us invisible.' He smiled. 'And the burnings at the stake!'

"Armand fixed his eyes on Claudia. 'Beware those monsters,' he said, and calculatedly his eyes passed over Santiago and then Celeste. 'Those revenants. They will attack you as if you were human.'

"Celeste shuddered, uttering something in contempt, an aristocrat speaking of vulgar cousins who bear the same name. But I was watching Claudia because it seemed her eyes were misted again as before. She looked away from Armand suddenly.

"The voices of the others rose again, affected party voices, as they conferred with one another on the night's kills, describing this or that encounter without a smattering of emotion, challenges to cruelty erupting from time to time like flashes of white lightning: a tall, thin vampire being accosted in one corner for a needless romanticizing of mortal life, a lack of spirit, a refusal to do the most entertaining thing at the moment it was available to him. He was simple, shrugging, slow at words, and would fall for long periods into a stupefied silence, as if, near-choked with blood, he would as soon have gone to his coffin as remained here. And yet he remained, held by the pressure of this unnatural group who had made of immortality a conformist's club. How would Lestat have found it? Had he been here? What had caused him to leave? No one had dictated to Lestat—he was master of his small circle; but how they would have praised his inventiveness, his catlike toying with his victims. And waste . . . that word, that value which had been all-important to me as a fledgling vampire, was spoken of often. You 'wasted' the opportunity to kill this child. You 'wasted' the opportunity to frighten this poor woman or drive that man to madness, which only a little prestidigitation would have accomplished.

"My head was spinning. A common mortal headache. I longed to get away from these vampires, and only the distant figure of Armand held me, despite his warnings. He seemed remote from the others now, though he nodded often enough and uttered a few words here and there so that he seemed a part of them, his hand only occasionally rising from the lion's paw of his chair. And my heart expanded when I saw him this way, saw that no one amongst the small throng caught his glance as I caught his glance, and no one held it from time to time as I held it. Yet he remained aloof from me, his eyes alone returning to me. His warning echoed in my ears, yet I disregarded it. I longed to get away from the theater altogether and stood listlessly, garnering information at last that was useless and infinitely dull.

" 'But is there no crime amongst you, no cardinal crime?' Claudia asked. Her violet eyes seemed fixed on me, even in the mirror, as I stood with my back to her.

" 'Crime! Boredom!' cried out Estelle, and she pointed a white finger at Armand. He laughed softly with her from his distant position at the end of the room. 'Boredom is death!' she cried and bared her vampire fangs, so that Armand put a languid hand to his forehead in a stage gesture of fear and falling.

"But Santiago, who was watching with his hands behind his back, intervened. 'Crime!' he said. 'Yes, there is a crime. A crime for which we would hunt another vampire down until we destroyed him. Can you guess what that is?' He glanced from Claudia to me and back again to her masklike face. 'You should know, who are so secretive about the vampire that made you.'

" 'And why is that?' she asked, her eyes widening ever so slightly, her hands resting still in her lap.

"A hush fell over the room, gradually, then completely, all those white faces turned to face Santiago as he stood there, one foot forward, his hands clasped behind his back, towering over Claudia. His eyes gleamed as he saw he had the floor. And then he broke away and crept up behind me, putting his hand on my shoulder. 'Can you guess what that crime is? Didn't your vampire master tell you?'

"And drawing me slowly around with those invading familiar hands, he tapped my heart lightly in time with its quickening pace.

" 'It is the crime that means death to any vampire anywhere who commits it. It is to kill your own kind!'

" 'Aaaaah!' Claudia cried out, and lapsed into peals of laughter. She was walking across the floor now with swirling lavender silk and crisp resounding steps. Taking my hand, she said, 'I was so afraid it was to be born like Venus out of the foam, as we were! Master vampire! Come, Louis, let's go!' she beckoned, as she pulled me away.

"Armand was laughing. Santiago was still. And it was Armand who rose when we reached the door. 'You're welcome tomorrow night,' he said. 'And the night after.'

"I don't think I caught my breath until I'd reached the street. The rain was still falling, and all of the street seemed sodden and desolate in the rain, but beautiful. A few scattered bits of paper blowing in the wind, a gleaming carriage passing slowly with the thick, rhythmic clop of the horse. The sky was pale violet. I sped fast, with Claudia beside me leading the way, then finally frustrated with the length of my stride, riding in my arms.

" 'I don't like them,' she said to me with a steel fury as we neared the Hôtel Saint-Gabriel. Even its immense, brightly lit lobby was still in the pre-dawn hour. I spirited past the sleepy clerks, the long faces at the desk. 'I've searched for them the world over, and I despise them!' She threw off her cape and walked into the center of the room. A volley of rain hit the French windows. I found myself turning up the lights one by one and lifting the candelabrum to the gas flames as if I were Lestat or Claudia. And then, seeking the puce velvet chair I'd envisioned in that cellar, I slipped down into it, exhausted. It seemed for the moment as if the room blazed about me; as my eyes fixed on a gilt-framed painting of pastel trees and serene waters, the vampire spell was broken. They couldn't touch us here, and yet I knew this to be a lie, a foolish lie.

" 'I am in danger, danger,' Claudia said with that smoldering wrath.

" 'But how can they know what we did to him? Besides, *we* are in danger! Do you think for a moment I don't acknowledge my own guilt! And if you were the only one . . .' I reached out for her now as she drew near, but her fierce eyes settled on me and I let my hands drop back limp. 'Do you think I would leave you in danger?'

"She was smiling. For a moment I didn't believe my eyes. 'No, you would not, Louis. You would not. Danger holds you to me. . . .'

" 'Love holds me to you,' I said softly.

" 'Love?' she mused. 'What do you mean by love?' And then, as if she could see the pain in my face, she came close and put her hands on my cheek. She was cold, unsatisfied, as I was cold and unsatisfied, teased by that mortal boy but unsatisfied.

" 'That you take my love for granted always,' I said to her. 'That we are wed. . . .' But even as I said these words I felt my old conviction waver; I felt that torment I'd felt last night when she had taunted me about mortal passion. I turned away from her.

" 'You would leave me for Armand if he beckoned to you. . . .'

" 'Never . . .' I said to her.

" 'You would leave me, and he wants you as you want him. He's been waiting for you. . . .'

" 'Never. . . .' I rose now and made my way to that chest. The doors were locked, but they would not keep those vampires out. Only we could keep them out by rising as early as the light would let us. I turned to her and told her to come. And she was at my side. I wanted to bury my face in her hair, I wanted to beg her forgiveness. Because, in truth, she was right; and yet I loved her, loved her as always. And now, as I drew her in close to me, she said: 'Do you know what it was that he told me over and over without ever speaking a word; do you know what was the kernel of the trance he put me in so my eyes could only look at him, so that he pulled me as if my heart were on a string?'

" 'So you felt it . . .' I whispered. 'So it was the same.'

" 'He rendered me powerless!' she said. I saw the image of her against those books above his desk, her limp neck, her dead hands.

" 'But what are you saying? That he spoke to you, that he . . .'

" 'Without words!' she repeated. I could see the gas lights going dim, the candle flames too solid in their stillness. The rain beat on the panes. 'Do you know what he said . . . that I should die!' she whispered. 'That I should let you go.'

"I shook my head, and yet in my monstrous heart I felt a surge of excitement. She spoke the truth as she believed it. There was a film in her eyes, glassy and silver. 'He draws life out of me into himself,' she said, her lovely lips trembling so, I couldn't bear it. I held her tight, but the tears stood in her eyes. 'Life out of the boy who is his slave, life out of me whom he would make his slave. He loves you. He loves you. He would have you, and he would not have me stand in the way.'

" 'You don't understand him!' I fought it, kissing her; I wanted to shower her with kisses, her cheek, her lips.

" 'No, I understand him only too well,' she whispered to my lips, even as they kissed her. 'It is you who don't understand him. Love's blinded you, your fascination with his knowledge, his power. If you knew how he drinks death you'd hate him more than you ever hated Lestat. Louis, you must never return to him. I tell you, I'm in danger!' "

"Early the next night, I left her, convinced that Armand alone among the vampires of the theater could be trusted. She let me go reluctantly, and I was troubled, deeply, by the expression in her eyes. Weakness was unknown to her, and yet I saw fear and something beaten even now as she let me go. And I hurried on my mission, waiting outside the theater until the last of the patrons had gone and the doormen were tending to the locks.

"What they thought I was, I wasn't certain. An actor, like the others, who did not take off his paint? It didn't matter. What mattered was that they let me through, and I passed them and the few vampires in the ballroom, unaccosted, to stand at last at Armand's open door. He saw me immediately, no doubt had heard my step a long way off, and he welcomed me at once and asked me to sit down. He was busy with his human boy, who was dining at the desk on a silver plate of meats and fish. A decanter of white wine stood next to him, and though he was feverish and weak from last night, his skin was florid and his heat and fragrance were a torment to me. Not apparently to Armand, who sat in the leather chair by the fire opposite me, turned to the human, his arms folded on the leather arm. The boy filled his glass and held it up now in a salute. 'My master,' he said, his eyes flashing on me as he smiled; but the toast was to Armand.

" 'Your slave,' Armand whispered with a deep intake of breath that was passionate. And he watched, as the boy drank deeply. I could see him savoring the wet lips, the mobile flesh of the throat as the wine went down. And now the boy took a morsel of white meat, making that same salute, and consumed it slowly, his eyes fixed on Armand. It was as though Armand feasted upon the feast, drinking in that part of life which he could not share any longer except with his eyes. And lost though he seemed to it, it was calculated; not that torture I'd felt years ago when I stood outside Babette's window longing for her human life.

"When the boy had finished, he knelt with his arms around Armand's neck as if he actually savored the icy flesh. And I could remember the night Lestat first came to me, how his eyes seemed to burn, how his white face gleamed. You know what I am to you now.

"Finally, it was finished. He was to sleep, and Armand locked the brass gates against him. And in minutes, heavy with his meal, he was dozing, and Armand sat opposite me, his large, beautiful eyes tranquil and seemingly innocent. When I felt them pull me towards him, I dropped my eyes, wished for a fire in the grate, but there were only ashes.

" 'You told me to say nothing of my origin, why was this?' I asked, looking up at him. It was as if he could sense my holding back, yet wasn't offended, only regarding me with a slight wonder. But I was weak, too weak for his wonder, and again I looked away from him.

" 'Did you kill this vampire who made you? Is that why you are here without him, why you won't say his name? Santiago thinks that you did.'

" 'And if this is true, or if we can't convince you otherwise, you would try to destroy us?' I asked.

" 'I would not try to do anything to you,' he said, calmly. 'But as I told you, I am not the leader here in the sense that you asked.'

" 'Yet they believe you to be the leader, don't they? And Santiago, you shoved him away from me twice.'

" 'I'm more powerful than Santiago, older. Santiago is younger than you are,' he said. His voice was simple, devoid of pride. These were facts.

" 'We want no quarrel with you.'

" 'It's begun,' he said. 'But not with me. With those above.'

" 'But what reason has he to suspect us?'

"He seemed to be thinking now, his eyes cast down, his chin resting on his closed fist. After a while which seemed interminable, he looked up. 'I could give you reasons,' he said. 'That you are too silent. That the vampires of the world are a small number and live in terror of strife amongst themselves and choose their fledglings with great care, making certain that they respect the other vampires mightily. There are fifteen vampires in this house, and the number is jealously guarded. And weak vampires are feared; I should say this also. That you are flawed is obvious to them: you feel too much, you think too much. As you said yourself, vampire detachment is not of great value to you. And then there is this mysterious child: a child who can never grow, never be self-sufficient. I would not make a vampire of that boy there now if his life, which is so precious to me, were in serious danger, because he is too young, his limbs not strong enough, his mortal cup barely tasted: yet you bring with you this child. What manner of vampire made her, they ask; did you make her? So, you see, you bring with you these flaws and this mystery and yet you are completely silent. And so you cannot be trusted. And Santiago looks for an excuse. But there is another reason closer to the truth than all those things which I've just said to you. And that is simply this: that when you first encountered Santiago in the Latin Quarter you . . . unfortunately . . . called him a buffoon.'

" 'Aaaaah.' I sat back.

" 'It would perhaps have been better all around if you had said nothing.' And he smiled to see that I understood with him the irony of this.

"I sat reflecting upon what he'd said, and what weighed as heavily upon me through all of it were Claudia's strange admonitions, that this gentle-eyed young man had said to her, 'Die,' and beyond that my slowly accumulating disgust with the vampires in the ballroom above.

"I felt an overwhelming desire to speak to him of these things. Of her fear, no, not yet, though I couldn't believe when I looked into his eyes that he'd tried to wield this power over her: his eyes said, Live. His eyes said, Learn. And oh, how much I wanted to confide to him the breadth of what I didn't understand; how, searching all these years, I'd been astonished to discover those vampires above had made of immortality a club of fads and cheap conformity. And yet through this sadness, this confusion, came the clear realization: Why should it be otherwise? What had I expected? What right had I to be so bitterly disappointed in Lestat that I would let him die! Because he wouldn't show me what I must find in myself? Armand's words, what had they been? *The only power that exists is inside ourselves. . . .*

" 'Listen to me,' he said now. 'You must stay away from them. Your face hides nothing. You would yield to me now were I to question you. Look into my eyes.'

"I didn't do this. I fixed my eyes firmly on one of those small paintings above his desk until it ceased to be the Madonna and Child and became a harmony of line and color. Because I knew what he was saying to me was true.

" 'Stop them if you will, advise them that we don't mean any harm. Why can't you do this? You say yourself we're not your enemies, no matter what we've done. . . .'

"I could hear him sigh, faintly. 'I have stopped them for the time being,' he said. 'But I don't want such power over them as would be necessary to stop them entirely. Because if I exercise such power, then I must protect it. I will make enemies. And I would have forever to deal with my enemies when all I want here is a certain space, a certain peace. Or not to be here at all. I accept the scepter of sorts they've given me, but not to rule over them, only to keep them at a distance.'

" 'I should have known,' I said, my eyes still fixed on that painting.

" 'Then, you must stay away. Celeste has a great deal of power, being one of the oldest, and she is jealous of the child's beauty. And Santiago, as you can see, is only waiting for a shred of proof that you're outlaws.'

"I turned slowly and looked at him again where he sat with

that eerie vampire stillness, as if he were in fact not alive at all. The moment lengthened. I heard his words just as if he were speaking them again: 'All I want here is a certain space, a certain peace. Or not to be here at all.' And I felt a longing for him so strong that it took all my strength to contain it, merely to sit there gazing at him, fighting it. I wanted it to be this way: Claudia safe amongst these vampires somehow, guilty of no crime they might ever discover from her or anyone else, so that I might be free, free to remain forever in this cell as long as I could be welcome, even tolerated, allowed here on any condition whatsoever.

"I could see that mortal boy again as if he were not asleep on the bed but kneeling at Armand's side with his arms around Armand's neck. It was an icon for me of love. The love I felt. Not physical love, you must understand. I don't speak of that at all, though Armand was beautiful and simple, and no intimacy with him would ever have been repellent. For vampires, physical love culminates and is satisfied in one thing, the kill. I speak of another kind of love which drew me to him completely as the teacher which Lestat had never been. Knowledge would never be withheld by Armand, I knew it. It would pass through him as through a pane of glass so that I might bask in it and absorb it and grow. I shut my eyes. And I thought I heard him speak, so faintly I wasn't certain. It seemed he said, 'Do you know why I am here?'

"I looked up at him again, wondering if he knew my thoughts, could actually read them, if such could conceivably be the extent of that power. Now after all these years I could forgive Lestat for being nothing but an ordinary creature who could not show me the uses of my powers; and yet I still longed for this, could fall into it without resistance. A sadness pervaded it all, sadness for my own weakness and my own awful dilemma. Claudia waited for me. Claudia, who was my daughter and my love.

" 'What am I to do?' I whispered. 'Go away from them, go away from you? After all these years . . .'

" '*They* don't matter to you,' he said.

"I smiled and nodded.

" 'What is it you want to do?' he asked. And his voice assumed the most gentle, sympathic tone.

" 'Don't you know, don't you have that power?' I asked. 'Can't you read my thoughts as if they were words?'

"He shook his head. 'Not the way you mean. I only know the danger to you and the child is real because it's real to you. And I know your loneliness even with her love is almost more terrible than you can bear.'

"I stood up then. It would seem a simple thing to do, to rise, to go to the door, to hurry quickly down that passage; and yet it took every ounce of strength, every smattering of that curious thing I've called my detachment.

" 'I ask you to keep them away from us,' I said at the door; but I couldn't look back at him, didn't even want the soft intrusion of his voice.

" 'Don't go,' he said.

" 'I have no choice.'

"I was in the passage when I heard him so close to me that I started. He stood beside me, eye level with my eye, and in his hand he held a key which he pressed into mine.

" 'There is a door there,' he said, gesturing to the dark end, which I'd thought to be merely a wall. 'And a stairs to the side street which no one uses but myself. Go this way now, so you can avoid the others. You are anxious and they will see it.' I turned around to go at once, though every part of my being wanted to remain there. 'But let me tell you this,' he said, and lightly he pressed the back of his hand against my heart. 'Use the power inside you. Don't abhor it anymore. Use that power! And when they see you in the streets above, use that power to make your face a mask and think as you gaze on them as on anyone: beware. Take that word as if it were an amulet I'd given you to wear about your neck. And when your eyes meet Santiago's eyes, or the eyes of any other vampire, speak to them politely what you will, but think of that word and that word only. Remember what I say. I speak to you simply because you respect what is simple. You understand this. That's your strength.'

"I took the key from him, and I don't remember actually putting it into the lock or going up the steps. Or where he was or what he'd done. Except that, as I was stepping into the dark side street behind the theater, I heard him say very softly to me from someplace close to me: 'Come here, to me, when you can.' I looked around for him but was not surprised that I couldn't see him. He had told me also sometime or other that I must not leave the Hôtel Saint-Gabriel, that I must not give the others the shred of evidence of guilt they wanted. 'You see,' he said, 'killing other vampires is very exciting; that is why it is forbidden under penalty of death.'

"And then I seemed to awake. To the Paris street shining with rain, to the tall, narrow buildings on either side of me, to the fact that the door had shut to make a solid dark wall behind me and that Armand was no longer there.

"And though I knew Claudia waited for me, though I passed her in the hotel window above the gas lamps, a tiny figure standing among waxen petaled flowers, I moved away from the boulevard, letting the darker streets swallow me, as so often the streets of New Orleans had done.

"It was not that I did not love her; rather, it was that I knew I loved her only too well, that the passion for her was as great as the passion for Armand. And I fled them both now, letting the desire for the kill rise in me like a welcome fever, threatening consciousness, threatening pain.

"Out of the mist which had followed the rain, a man was walking towards me. I can remember him as roaming on the landscape of a dream, because the night around me was dark and unreal. The hill might have been anywhere in the world, and the soft lights of Paris were an amorphous shimmering in the fog. And sharp-eyed and drunk, he was walking blindly into the arms of death itself, his pulsing fingers reaching out to touch the very bones of my face.

"I was not crazed yet, not desperate. I might have said to him, 'Pass by.' I believe my lips did form the word Armand had given me, 'Beware.' Yet I let him slip his bold, drunken arm around my waist; I yielded to his adoring eyes, to the voice that begged to paint me now and spoke of warmth, to the rich, sweet smell of the oils that streaked his loose shirt. I was following him, through Montmartre, and I whispered to him, 'You are not a member of the dead.' He was leading me through an overgrown garden, through the sweet, wet grasses, and he was laughing as I said, 'Alive, alive,' his hand touching my cheek, stroking my face, clasping finally my chin as he guided me into the light of the low doorway, his reddened face brilliantly illuminated by the oil lamps, the warmth seeping about us as the door closed.

"I saw the great sparkling orbs of his eyes, the tiny red veins that reached for the dark centers, that warm hand burning my cold hunger as he guided me to a chair. And then all around me I saw faces blazing, faces rising in the smoke of the lamps, in the shimmer of the burning stove, a wonderland of colors on canvases surrounding us beneath the small, sloped roof, a blaze of beauty that pulsed and throbbed. 'Sit down, sit down . . .' he said to me, those feverish hands against my chest, clasped by my hands, yet sliding away, my hunger rising in waves.

"And now I saw him at a distance, eyes intent, the palette in his hand, the huge canvas obscuring the arm that moved. And mindless and helpless, I sat there drifting with his paintings, drifting with those adoring eyes, letting it go on and on till Armand's eyes were gone and Claudia was running down that stone passage with clicking heels away from me, away from me.

" 'You are alive . . .' I whispered. 'Bones,' he answered me. 'Bones . . .' And I saw them in heaps, taken from those shallow graves in New Orleans as they are and put in chambers behind the sepulcher so that another can be laid in that narrow plot. I felt my eyes close; I felt my hunger become agony, my heart crying out for a living heart; and then I felt him moving forward, hands out to right my face—that fatal step, that fatal lurch. A sigh escaped my lips. 'Save yourself,' I whispered to him. 'Beware.'

"And then something happened in the moist radiance of his

face, something drained the broken vessels of his fragile skin. He backed away from me, the brush falling from his hands. And I rose over him, feeling my teeth against my lip, feeling my eyes fill with the colors of his face, my ears fill with his struggling cry, my hands fill with that strong, fighting flesh until I drew him up to me, helpless, and tore that flesh and had the blood that gave it life. 'Die,' I whispered when I held him loose now, his head bowed against my coat, 'die,' and felt him struggle to look up at me. And again I drank and again he fought, until at last he slipped, limp and shocked and near to death, on the floor. Yet his eyes did not close.

"I settled before his canvas, weak, at peace, gazing down at him, at his vague, graying eyes, my own hands florid, my skin so luxuriously warm. 'I am mortal again,' I whispered to him. 'I am alive. With your blood I am alive.' His eyes closed. I sank back against the wall and found myself gazing at my own face.

"A sketch was all he'd done, a series of bold black lines that nevertheless made up my face and shoulders perfectly, and the color was already begun in dabs and splashes: the green of my eyes, the white of my cheek. But the horror, the horror of seeing my expression! For he had captured it perfectly, and there was nothing of horror in it. Those green eyes gazed at me from out of that loosely drawn shape with a mindless innocence, the expressionless wonder of that overpowering craving which he had not understood. Louis of a hundred years ago lost in listening to the sermon of the priest at Mass, lips parted and slack, hair careless, a hand curved in the lap and limp. A mortal Louis. I believe I was laughing, putting my hands to my face and laughing so that the tears nearly rose in my eyes; and when I took my fingers down, there was the stain of the tears, tinged with mortal blood. And already there was begun in me the tingling of the monster that had killed, and would kill again, who was gathering up the painting now and starting to flee with it from the small house.

"When suddenly, up from the floor, the man rose with an animal groan and clutched at my boot, his hands sliding off the leather. With some colossal spirit that defied me, he reached up for the painting and held fast to it with his whitening hands. 'Give it back!' he growled at me. 'Give it back!' And we held fast, the two of us, I staring at him and at my own hands that held so easily what he sought so desperately to rescue, as if he would take it to heaven or hell; I the thing that his blood could not make human, he the man that my evil had not overcome. And then, as if I were not myself, I tore the painting loose from him and, wrenching him up to my lips with one arm, gashed his throat in rage."

"Entering the rooms of the Hôtel Saint-Gabriel, I set the picture on the mantel above the fire and looked at it a long time. Claudia was somewhere in the rooms, and some other presence intruded, as though on one of the balconies above a woman or a man stood near, giving off an unmistakable personal perfume. I didn't know why I had taken the picture, why I'd fought for it so that it shamed me now worse than the death, and why I still held onto it at the marble mantel, my head bowed, my hands visibly trembling. And then slowly I turned my head. I wanted the rooms to take shape around me; I wanted the flowers, the velvet, the candles in their sconces. To be mortal and trivial and safe. And then, as if in a mist, I saw a woman there.

"She was seated calmly at that lavish table where Claudia attended to her hair; and so still she sat, so utterly without fear, her green taffeta sleeves reflected in the tilted mirrors, her skirts reflected, that she was not one still woman but a gathering of women. Her dark-red hair was parted in the middle and drawn back to her ears, though a dozen little ringlets escaped to make a frame for her pale face. And she was looking at me with two calm, violet eyes and a child's mouth that seemed almost obdurately soft, obdurately the Cupid's bow unsullied by paint or personality; and the mouth smiled now and said, as those eyes seemed to fire: 'Yes, he's as you said he would be, and I love him already. He's as you said.' She rose now, gently lifting that abundance of dark taffeta, and the three small mirrors emptied at once.

"And utterly baffled and almost incapable of speech, I turned to see Claudia far off on the immense bed, her small face rigidly calm, though she clung to the silk curtain with a tight fist. 'Madeleine,' she said under her breath, 'Louis is shy.' And she watched with cold eyes as Madeleine only smiled when she said this and, drawing closer to me, put both of her hands to the lace fringe around her throat, moving it back so I could see the two small marks there. Then the smile died on her lips, and they became at once sullen and sensual as her eyes narrowed and she breathed the word, 'Drink.'

"I turned away from her, my fist rising in a consternation for which I couldn't find words. But then Claudia had hold of that fist and was looking up at me with relentless eyes. 'Do it, Louis,' she commanded. 'Because I cannot do it.' Her voice was painfully calm, all the emotion under the hard, measured tone. 'I haven't the size, I haven't the strength! You saw to that when you made me! Do it!'

"I broke away from her, clutching my wrist as if she'd burned it. I could see the door, and it seemed to me the better part of wisdom to leave by it at once. I could feel Claudia's strength, her will, and the mortal woman's eyes seemed afire with that same will. But Claudia held me, not with a gentle pleading, a miserable coaxing that would have dissipated that power, making me feel pity for her as I gathered my own forces. She held me with the emotion her eyes had evinced even through her coldness and the way that she turned away from me now, almost as if she'd been instantly defeated. I did not understand the manner in which she sank back on the bed, her head bowed, her lips moving feverishly, her eyes rising only to scan the walls. I wanted to touch her and say to her that what she asked was impossible; I wanted to soothe that fire that seemed to be consuming her from within.

"And the soft, mortal woman had settled into one of the velvet chairs by the fire, with the rustling and iridescence of her taffeta dress surrounding her like part of the mystery of her, of her dispassionate eyes which watched us now, the fever of her pale face. I remember turning to her, spurred on by that childish, pouting mouth set against the fragile face. The vampire kiss had left no visible trace except the wound, no inalterable change on the pale-pink flesh. 'How do we appear to you?' I asked, seeing her eyes on Claudia. She seemed excited by the diminutive beauty, the awful woman's-passion knotted in the small dimpled hands.

"She broke her gaze and looked up at me. 'I ask you . . . how do we appear? Do you think us beautiful, magical, our white skin, our fierce eyes? Oh, I remember perfectly what mortal vision was, the dimness of it, and how the vampire's beauty burned through that veil, so powerfully alluring, so utterly deceiving! Drink, you tell me. You haven't the vaguest conception under God of what you ask!'

"But Claudia rose from the bed and came towards me. 'How dare you!' she whispered. 'How dare you make this decision for both of us! Do you know how I despise you! Do you know that I despise you with a passion that eats at me like a canker!' Her small form trembled, her hands hovering over the pleated bodice of her yellow gown. 'Don't you look away from me! I am sick at heart with your looking away, with your suffering. You understand nothing. Your evil is that you cannot be evil, and I must suffer for it. I tell you, I will suffer no longer!' Her fingers bit into the flesh of my wrist; I twisted, stepping back from her, floundering in the face of the hatred, the rage rising like some dormant beast in her, looking out through her eyes. 'Snatching me from mortal hands like two grim monsters in a nightmare fairy tale, you idle, blind parents! Fathers!' She spat the word. 'Let tears gather in your eyes. You haven't tears enough for what you've done to me. Six more mortal years, seven, eight . . . I might have had that shape!' Her pointed finger flew at Madeleine, whose hands had risen to her face, whose eyes were clouded over. Her moan was almost Claudia's name. But Claudia did not hear her. 'Yes, that shape, I might have known what it was to walk at your side. Monsters! To give me immortality in this hopeless guise, this helpless form!' The tears stood in her eyes. The words had died away, drawn in, as it were, on her breast.

" 'Now, you give her to me!' she said, her head bowing, her curls tumbling down to make a concealing veil. 'You give her to me. You do this, or you finish what you did to me that night in the hotel in New Orleans. I will not live with this hatred any longer, I will not live with this rage! I cannot. I will not abide it!' And tossing her hair, she put her hands to her ears as if to stop the sound of her own words, her breath drawn in rapid gasps, the tears seeming to scald her cheeks.

"I had sunk to my knees at her side, and my arms were outstretched as if to enfold her. Yet I dared not touch her, dared not even say her name, lest my own pain break from me with the first syllable in a monstrous outpouring of hopelessly inarticulate cries. 'Oooh.' She shook her head now, squeezing the tears out onto her cheeks, her teeth clenched tight together. 'I love you still, that's the torment of it. Lestat I never loved. But you! The measure of my hatred is that love. They are the same! Do you know now how much I hate you!' She flashed at me through the red film that covered her eyes.

" 'Yes,' I whispered. I bowed my head. But she was gone from me into the arms of Madeleine, who enfolded her desperately, as if she might protect Claudia from me—the irony of it, the pathetic irony—protect Claudia from herself. She was whispering to Claudia, 'Don't cry, don't cry!' her hands stroking Claudia's face and hair with a fierceness that would have bruised a human child.

"But Claudia seemed lost against her breast suddenly, her eyes closed, her face smooth, as if all passion were drained away from her, her arm sliding up around Madeleine's neck, her head falling against the taffeta and lace. She lay still, the tears staining her cheeks, as if all this that had risen to the surface had left her weak and desperate for oblivion, as if the room around her, as if I, were not there.

"And there they were together, a tender mortal crying unstintingly now, her warm arms holding what she could not possibly understand, this white and fierce and unnatural childthing she believed she loved. And if I had not felt for her, this mad and reckless woman flirting with the damned, if I had not felt all the sorrow for her I felt for my mortal self, I would have wrested the demon thing from her arms, held it tight to me, denying over and over the words I'd just heard. But I knelt there still, thinking only, The love is equal to the hatred; gathering that selfishly to my own breast, holding onto that as I sank back against the bed.

"A long time before Madeleine was to know it, Claudia had ceased crying and sat still as a statue on Madeleine's lap, her liquid eyes fixed on me, oblivious to the soft, red hair that fell around her or the woman's hand that still stroked her. And I sat slumped against the bedpost, staring back at those vampire eyes, unable and unwilling to speak in my defense. Madeleine was whispering into Claudia's ear, she was letting her tears fall into Claudia's tresses. And then gently, Claudia said to her, 'Leave us.'

" 'No.' She shook her head, holding tight to Claudia. And then she shut her eyes and trembled all over with some terrible vexation, some awful torment. But Claudia was leading her from the chair, and she was now pliant and shocked and white-faced, the green taffeta ballooning around the small yellow silk dress.

"In the archway of the parlor they stopped, and Madeleine stood as if confused, her hand at her throat, beating like a wing, then going still. She looked about her like that hapless victim on the stage of the Théâtre des Vampires who did not know where she was. But Claudia had gone for something. And I saw her emerge from the shadows with what appeared to be a large doll. I rose on my knees to look at it. It was a doll, the doll of a little girl with raven hair and green eyes, adorned with lace and ribbons, sweet-faced and wide-eyed, its porcelain feet tinkling as Claudia put it into Madeleine's arms. And Madeleine's eyes appeared to harden as she held the doll, and her lips drew back from her teeth in a grimace as she stroked its hair. She was laughing low under her breath. 'Lie down,' Claudia said to her; and together they appeared to sink into the cushions of the couch, the green taffeta rustling and giving way as Claudia lay with her and put her arms around her neck. I saw the doll sliding, dropping to the floor, yet Madeleine's hand groped for it and held it dangling, her own head thrown back, her eyes shut tight, and Claudia's curls stroking her face.

"I settled back on the floor and leaned against the soft siding of the bed. Claudia was speaking now in a low voice, barely above a whisper, telling Madeleine to be patient, to be still. I dreaded the sound of her step on the carpet; the sound of the doors sliding closed to shut Madeleine away from us, and the hatred that lay between us like a killing vapor.

"But when I looked up to her, Claudia was standing there as if transfixed and lost in thought, all rancor and bitterness gone from her face, so that she had the blank expression of that doll.

" 'All you've said to me is true,' I said to her. 'I deserve your hatred. I've deserved it from those first moments when Lestat put you in my arms.'

"She seemed unaware of me, and her eyes were infused with a soft light. Her beauty burned into my soul so that I could hardly stand it, and then she said, wondering, 'You could have killed me then, despite him. You could have done it.' Then her eyes rested on me calmly. 'Do you wish to do it now?'

" 'Do it now!' I put my arm around her, moved her close to me, warmed by her softened voice. 'Are you mad, to say such things to me? Do I want to do it now!'

" 'I want you to do it,' she said. 'Bend down now as you did then, draw the blood out of me drop by drop, all you have the strength for; push my heart to the brink. I am small, you can take me. I won't resist you, I am something frail you can crush like a flower.'

" 'You mean these things? You mean what you say to me?' I asked. 'Why don't you place the knife here, why don't you turn it?'

" 'Would you die with me?' she asked, with a sly, mocking smile. 'Would you in fact die with me?' she pressed. 'Don't you understand what is happening to me? That he's killing me, that master vampire who has you in thrall, that he won't share your love with me, not a drop of it? I see his power in your eyes. I see your misery, your distress, the love for him you can't hide. Turn around, I'll make you look at me with those eyes that want him, I'll make you listen.'

" 'Don't anymore, don't . . . I won't leave you. I've sworn to you, don't you see? I cannot give you that woman.'

" 'But I'm fighting for my life! Give her to me so she can care for me, complete the guise I must have to live! And he can have you then! I am fighting for my life!'

"I all but shoved her off. 'No, no, it's madness, it's witchery,' I said, trying to defy her. 'It's you who will not share me with him, it's you who want every drop of that love. If not from me, from her. He overpowers you, he disregards you, and it's you who wish him dead the way that you killed Lestat. Well, you won't make me a party to this death, I tell you, not this death! I will not make her one of us, I will not damn the legions of mortals who'll die at her hands if I do! Your power over me is broken. I will not!'

"Oh, if she could only have understood!

"Not for a moment could I truly believe her words against Armand, that out of that detachment which was beyond revenge he could selfishly wish for her death. But that was nothing to me now; something far more terrible than I could grasp was happening, something I was only beginning to understand, against which my anger was nothing but a mockery, a hollow attempt to oppose her tenacious will. She hated me, she loathed me, as she herself had confessed, and my heart shrivelled inside me, as if, in depriving me of that love which had sustained me a lifetime, she had dealt me a mortal blow. The knife was there. I was dying for her, dying for that love as I was that very first night when Lestat gave her to me, turned her eyes to me, and told her my name; that love which had warmed me in my self-hatred, allowed me to exist. Oh, how Lestat had understood it, and now at last his plan was undone.

"But it went beyond that, in some region from which I was shrinking as I strode back and forth, back and forth, my hands opening and closing at my sides, feeling not only that hatred in her liquid eyes: It was her pain. She had shown me her pain! *To give me immortality in this hopeless guise, this helpless form.* I put my hands to my ears, as if she spoke the words yet, and the tears flowed. For all these years I had depended utterly upon her cruelty, her absolute lack of pain! And pain was what she showed to me, undeniable pain. Oh, how Lestat would have laughed at us. That was why she had put the knife to him, because he would have laughed. To destroy me utterly she need only show me that pain. The child I made a vampire suffered. Her agony was as my own.

"There was a coffin in that other room, a bed for Madeleine, to which Claudia retreated to leave me alone with what I could not abide. I welcomed the silence. And sometime during the few hours that remained of the night I found myself at the open window, feeling the slow mist of the rain. It glistened on the fronds of the ferns, on sweet white flowers that listed, bowed, and finally broke from their stems. A carpet of flowers littering the little balcony, the petals pounded softly by the rain. I felt weak now, and utterly alone. What had passed between us tonight could never be undone, and what had been done to Claudia by me could never be undone.

"But I was somehow, to my own bewilderment, empty of all regret. Perhaps it was the night, the starless sky, the gas lamps frozen in the mist that gave some strange comfort for which I never asked and didn't know how, in this emptiness and aloneness, to receive. I am alone, I was thinking. I am alone. It seemed just, perfectly, and so to have a pleasing, inevitable form. And I pictured myself then forever alone, as if on gaining that vampire strength the night of my death I had left Lestat and never looked back for him, as if I had moved on away from him, beyond the need of him and anyone else. As if the night had said to me, 'You are the night and the night alone understands you and enfolds you in its arms.' One with the shadows. Without nightmare. An inexplicable peace.

"Yet I could feel the end of this peace as surely as I'd felt my brief surrender to it, and it was breaking like the dark clouds.

The urgent pain of Claudia's loss pressed in on me, behind me, like a shape gathered from the corners of this cluttered and oddly alien room. But outside, even as the night seemed to dissolve in a fierce driving wind, I could feel something calling to me, something inanimate which I'd never known. And a power within me seemed to answer that power, not with resistance but with an inscrutable, chilling strength.

"I moved silently through the rooms, gently dividing the doors until I saw, in the dim light cast by the flickering gas flames behind me, that sleeping woman lying in my shadow on the couch, the doll limp against her breast. Sometime before I knelt at her side I saw her eyes open, and I could feel beyond her in the collected dark those other eyes watching me, that breathless tiny vampire face waiting.

" 'Will you care for her, Madeleine?' I saw her hands clutch at the doll, turning its face against her breast. And my own hand went out for it, though I did not know why, even as she was answering me.

" 'Yes!' She repeated it again desperately.

" 'Is this what you believe her to be, a doll?' I asked her, my hand closing on the doll's head, only to feel her snatch it away from me, see her teeth clenched as she glared at me.

" 'A child who can't die! That's what she is,' she said, as if she were pronouncing a curse.

" 'Aaaaah . . .' I whispered.

" 'I've done with dolls,' she said, shoving it away from her into the cushions of the couch. She was fumbling with something on her breast, something she wanted me to see and not to see, her fingers catching hold of it and closing over it. I knew what it was, had noticed it before. A locket fixed with a gold pin. I wish I could describe the passion that infected her round features, how her soft baby mouth was distorted.

" 'And the child who did die?' I guessed, watching her. I was picturing a doll shop, dolls with the same face. She shook her head, her hand pulling hard on the locket so the pin ripped the taffeta. It was fear I saw in her now, a consuming panic. And her hand bled as she opened it from the broken pin. I took the locket from her fingers. 'My daughter,' she whispered, her lip trembling.

"It was a doll's face on the small fragment of porcelain, Claudia's face, a baby face, a saccharine, sweet mockery of innocence an artist had painted there, a child with raven hair like the doll. And the mother, terrified, was staring at the darkness in front of her.

" 'Grief . . .' I said gently.

" 'I've done with grief,' she said, her eyes narrowing as she looked up at me. 'If you knew how I long to have your power; I'm ready for it, I hunger for it.' And she turned to me, breathing deeply, so that her breast seemed to swell under her dress.

"A violent frustration rent her face then. She turned away from me, shaking her head, her curls. 'If you were a mortal man; man *and* monster!' she said angrily. 'If I could only show you my power . . .' and she smiled malignantly, defiantly at me '. . . I could make you want me, desire me! But you're unnatural!' Her mouth went down at the corners. 'What can I give you! What can I do to make you give me what you have!' Her hand hovered over her breasts, seeming to caress them like a man's hand.

"It was strange, that moment; strange because I could never have predicted the feeling her words incited in me, the way that I saw her now with that small enticing waist, saw the round, plump curve of her breasts and those delicate, pouting lips. She never dreamed what the mortal man in me was, how tormented I was by the blood I'd only just drunk. Desire her I did, more than she knew; because she didn't understand the nature of the kill. And with a man's pride I wanted to prove that to her, to humiliate her for what she had said to me, for the cheap vanity of her provocation and the eyes that looked away from me now in disgust. But this was madness. These were not the reasons to grant eternal life.

"And cruelly, surely, I said to her, 'Did you love this child?'

"I will never forget her face then, the violence in her, the absolute hatred. 'Yes.' She all but hissed the words at me. 'How dare you!' She reached for the locket even as I clutched it. It was guilt that was consuming her, not love. It was guilt—that shop of dolls Claudia had described to me, shelves and shelves of the effigy of that dead child. But guilt that absolutely understood the finality of death. There was something as hard in her as the evil in myself, something as powerful. She had her hand out towards me. She touched my waistcoat and opened her fingers there, pressing them against my chest. And I was on my knees, drawing close to her, her hair brushing my face.

" 'Hold fast to me when I take you,' I said to her, seeing her eyes grow wide, her mouth open. 'And when the swoon is strongest, listen all the harder for the beating of my heart. Hold and say over and over, "I will live." '

" 'Yes, yes,' she was nodding, her heart pounding with her excitement.

"Her hands burned on my neck, fingers forcing their way into my collar. 'Look beyond me at that distant light; don't take your eyes off of it, not for a second, and say over and over, "I will live." '

"She gasped as I broke the flesh, the warm current coming into me, her breasts crushed against me, her body arching up, helpless, from the couch. And I could see her eyes, even as I shut my own, see that taunting, provocative mouth. I was drawing on her, hard, lifting her, and I could feel her weakening, her hands dropping limp at her sides. 'Tight, tight,' I whispered over the hot stream of her blood, her heart thundering in my ears, her blood swelling my satiated veins. 'The lamp,' I whispered, 'look at it!' Her heart was slowing, stopping, and her head dropped back from me on the velvet, her eyes dull to the point of death. It seemed for a moment I couldn't move, yet I knew I had to, that someone else was lifting my wrist to my mouth as the room turned round and round, that I was focusing on that light as I had told her to do, as I tasted my own blood from my own wrist, and then forced it into her mouth. 'Drink it. Drink,' I said to her. But she lay as if dead. I gathered her close to me, the blood pouring over her lips. Then she opened her eyes, and I felt the gentle pressure of her mouth, and then her hands closing tight on the arm as she began to suck. I was rocking her, whispering to her, trying desperately to break my swoon; and then I felt her powerful pull. Every blood vessel felt it. I was threaded through and through with her pulling, my hand holding fast to the couch now, her heart beating fierce against my heart, her fingers digging deep into my arm, my outstretched palm. It was cutting me, scoring me, so I all but cried out as it went on and on, and I was backing away from her, yet pulling her with me, my life passing through my arm, her moaning breath in time with her pulling. And those strings which were my veins, those searing wires pulled at my very heart harder and harder until, without will or direction, I had wrenched free of her and fallen away from her, clutching that bleeding wrist tight with my own hand.

"She was staring at me, the blood staining her open mouth. An eternity seemed to pass as she stared. She doubled and tripled in my blurred vision, then collapsed into one trembling shape. Her hand moved to her mouth, yet her eyes did not move but grew large in her face as she stared. And then she rose slowly, not as if by her own power but as if lifted from the couch bodily by some invisible force which held her now, staring as she turned round and round, her massive skirt moving stiff as if she were all of a piece, turning like some great carved ornament on a music box that dances helplessly round and round to the music. And suddenly she was staring down at the taffeta, grabbing hold of it, pressing it between her fingers so it zinged and rustled, and she let it fall, quickly covering her ears, her eyes shut tight, then opened wide again. And then it seemed she saw the lamp, the distant, low gas lamp of the other room that gave a fragile light through the double doors. And she ran to it and stood beside it, watching it as if it were alive. 'Don't touch it . . .' Claudia said to her, and gently guided her away. But Madeleine had seen the flowers on the balcony and she was drawing close to them now, her outstretched palms brushing the petals and then pressing the droplets of rain to her face.

"I was hovering on the fringes of the room, watching her every move, how she took the flowers and crushed them in her hands and let the petals fall all around her and how she pressed her fingertips to the mirror and stared into her own eyes. My own pain had ceased, a handkerchief bound the wound, and I was waiting, waiting, seeing now that Claudia had no knowledge from memory of what was to come next. They were dancing together, as Madeleine's skin grew paler and paler in the unsteady golden light. She scooped Claudia into her arms, and Claudia rode round in circles with her, her own small face alert and wary behind her smile.

"And then Madeleine weakened. She stepped backwards and seemed to lose her balance. But quickly she righted herself and let Claudia go gently down to the ground. On tiptoe, Claudia embraced her. 'Louis.' She signalled to me under her breath. 'Louis. . . .'

"I beckoned for her to come away. And Madeleine, not seeming even to see us, was staring at her own outstretched hands. Her face was blanched and drawn, and suddenly she was scratching at her lips and staring at the dark stains on her fingertips. 'No, no!' I cautioned her gently, taking Claudia's hand and holding her close to my side. A long moan escaped Madeleine's lips.

" 'Louis,' Claudia whispered in that preternatural voice which Madeleine could not yet hear.

" 'She is dying, which your child's mind can't remember. You were spared it, it left no mark on you,' I whispered to her, brushing the hair back from her ear, my eyes never leaving Madeleine, who was wandering from mirror to mirror, the tears flowing freely now, the body giving up its life.

" 'But, Louis, if she dies . . .' Claudia cried.

" 'No.' I knelt down, seeing the distress in her small face. 'The blood was strong enough, she will live. But she will be afraid, terribly afraid.' And gently, firmly, I pressed Claudia's hand and kissed her cheek. She looked at me then with mingled wonder and fear. And she watched me with that same expression as I wandered closer to Madeleine, drawn by her cries. She reeled now, her hands out, and I caught her and held her close. Her eyes already burned with unnatural light, a violet fire reflected in her tears.

" 'It's mortal death, only mortal death,' I said to her gently.

'Do you see the sky? We must leave it now and you must hold tight to me, lie by my side. A sleep as heavy as death will come over my limbs, and I won't be able to solace you. And you will lie there and you will struggle with it. But you hold tight to me in the darkness, do you hear? You hold tight to my hands, which will hold your hands as long as I have feeling.'

"She seemed lost for the moment in my gaze, and I sensed the wonder that surrounded her, how the radiance of my eyes was the radiance of all colors and how all those colors were all the more reflected for her in my eyes. I guided her gently to the coffin, telling her again not to be afraid. 'When you arise, you will be immortal,' I said. 'No natural cause of death can harm you. Come, lie down.' I could see her fear of it, see her shrink from the narrow box, its satin no comfort. Already her skin began to glisten, to have that brilliance that Claudia and I shared. I knew now she would not surrender until I lay with her.

"I held her and looked across the long vista of the room to where Claudia stood, with that strange coffin, watching me. Her eyes were still but dark with an undefined suspicion, a cool distrust. I set Madeleine down beside her bed and moved towards those eyes. And, kneeling calmly beside her, I gathered Claudia in my arms. 'Don't you recognize me?' I asked her. 'Don't you know who I am?'

"She looked at me. 'No,' she said.

"I smiled. I nodded. 'Bear me no ill will,' I said. 'We are even.'

"At that she moved her head to one side and studied me carefully, then seemed to smile despite herself and to nod in assent.

" 'For you see,' I said to her in that same calm voice, 'what died tonight in this room was not that woman. It will take her many nights to die, perhaps years. What has died in this room tonight is the last vestige in me of what was human.'

"A shadow fell over her face; clear, as if the composure were rent like a veil. And her lips parted, but only with a short intake of breath. Then she said, 'Well, then you are right. Indeed. We are even.' "

. . .

" 'I want to burn the doll shop!'

"Madeleine told us this. She was feeding to the fire in the grate the folded dresses of that dead daughter, white lace and beige linen, crinkled shoes, bonnets that smelled of camphor balls and sachet. 'It means nothing now, any of it.' She stood back watching the fire blaze. And she looked at Claudia with triumphant, fiercely devoted eyes.

"I did not believe her, so certain I was—even though night after night I had to lead her away from men and women she could no longer drain dry, so satiated was she with the blood of earlier kills, often lifting her victims off their feet in her passion, crushing their throats with her ivory fingers as surely as she drank their blood—so certain I was that sooner or later this mad intensity must abate, and she would take hold of the trappings of this nightmare, her own luminescent flesh, these lavish rooms of the Hôtel Saint-Gabriel, and cry out to be awakened; to be free. She did not understand it was no experiment; showing her fledgling teeth to the gilt-edged mirrors, she was mad.

"But I still did not realize how mad she was, and how accustomed to dreaming; and that she would not cry out for reality, rather would feed reality to her dreams, a demon elf feeding her spinning wheel with the reeds of the world so she might make her own weblike universe.

"I was just beginning to understand her avarice, her magic.

"She had a dollmaker's craft from making with her old lover over and over the replica of her dead child, which I was to understand crowded the shelves of this shop we were soon to visit. Added to that was a vampire's skill and a vampire's intensity, so that in the space of one night when I had turned her away from killing, she, with that same insatiable need, created out of a few sticks of wood, with her chisel and knife, a perfect rocking chair, so shaped and proportioned for Claudia that seated in it by the fire, she appeared a woman. To that must be added, as the nights passed, a table of the same scale; and from a toy shop a tiny oil lamp, a china cup and saucer; and from a lady's purse a little leather-bound book for notes which in Claudia's hands became a large volume. The world crumbled and ceased to exist at the boundary of the small space which soon became the length and breadth of Claudia's dressing room: a bed whose posters reached only to my breast buttons, and small mirrors that reflected only the legs of an unwieldy giant when I found myself lost among them; paintings hung low for Claudia's eye; and finally, upon her little vanity table, black evening gloves for tiny fingers, a woman's low-cut gown of midnight velvet, a tiara from a child's masked ball. And Claudia, the crowning jewel, a fairy queen with bare white shoulders wandering with her sleek tresses among the rich items of her tiny world while I watched from the doorway, spellbound, ungainly, stretched out on the carpet so I could lean my head on my elbow and gaze up into my paramour's eyes, seeing them mysteriously softened for the time being by the perfection of this sanctuary. How beautiful she was in black lace, a cold, flaxen-haired woman with a kewpie doll's face and liquid eyes which gazed at me so serenely and so long that, surely, I must have been forgotten; the eyes must be seeing something other than me as I lay there on the floor dreaming; something other than the clumsy universe surrounding me, which was now marked off and nullified by someone who had suffered in it, someone who had suffered always, but who was not seeming to suffer now, listening as it were to the tinkling of a toy music box, putting a hand on the toy clock. I saw a vision of shortened hours and little golden minutes. I felt I was mad.

"I put my hands under my head and gazed at the chandelier; it was hard to disengage myself from one world and enter the other. And Madeleine, on the couch, was working with that regular passion, as if immortality could not conceivably mean rest, sewing cream lace to lavender satin for the small bed, only stopping occasionally to blot the moisture tinged with blood from her white forehead.

"I wondered, if I shut my eyes, would this realm of tiny things consume the rooms around me, and would I, like Gulliver, awake to discover myself bound hand and foot, an unwelcome giant? I had a vision of houses made for Claudia in whose garden mice would be monsters, and tiny carriages, and flowery shrubbery become trees. Mortals would be so entranced, and drop to their knees to look into the small windows. Like the spider's web, it would attract.

"I *was* bound hand and foot here. Not only by that fairy beauty—that exquisite secret of Claudia's white shoulders and the rich luster of pearls, bewitching languor, a tiny bottle of perfume, now a decanter, from which a spell is released that promises Eden—I was bound by fear. That outside these rooms, where I supposedly presided over the education of Madeleine—erratic conversations about killing and vampire nature in which Claudia could have instructed so much more easily than I, if she had ever showed the desire to take the lead—that outside these rooms, where nightly I was reassured with soft kisses and contented looks that the hateful passion which Claudia had shown once and once only would not return—that outside these rooms, I would find that I was, according to my own hasty admission, truly changed: the mortal part of me was that part which had loved, I was certain. So what did I feel then for Armand, the creature for whom I'd transformed Madeleine, the creature for whom I had wanted to be free? A curious and disturbing distance? A dull pain? A nameless tremor? Even in this worldly clutter, I saw Armand in his monkish cell, saw his dark-brown eyes, and felt that eerie magnetism.

"And yet I did not move to go to him. I did not dare discover the extent of what I might have lost. Nor try to separate that loss from some other oppressive realization: that in Europe I'd found no truths to lessen loneliness, transform despair. Rather, I'd found only the inner workings of my own small soul, the pain of Claudia's, and a passion for a vampire who was perhaps more evil than Lestat, for whom I became as evil as Lestat, but in whom I saw the only promise of good in evil of which I could conceive.

"It was all beyond me, finally. And so the clock ticked on the mantel; and Madeleine begged to see the performances of the Théâtre des Vampires and swore to defend Claudia against any vampire who dared insult her; and Claudia spoke of strategy and said, 'Not yet, not now,' and I lay back observing with some measure of relief Madeleine's love for Claudia, her blind covetous passion. Oh, I have so little compassion in my heart or memory for Madeleine. I thought she had only seen the first vein of suffering; she had no understanding of death. She was so easily sharpened, so easily driven to wanton violence. I supposed in my colossal conceit and self-deception that my own grief for my dead brother was the only true emotion. I allowed myself to forget how totally I had fallen in love with Lestat's iridescent eyes, that I'd sold my soul for a many-colored and luminescent thing, thinking that a highly reflective surface conveyed the power to walk on water.

"What would Christ need have done to make me follow Him like Matthew or Peter? Dress well, to begin with. And have a luxurious head of pampered yellow hair.

"I hate myself. And it seemed, lulled half to sleep as I was so often by their conversation—Claudia whispering of killing and speed and vampire craft, Madeleine bent over her singing needle—it seemed then the only emotion of which I was still capable: hatred of self. I love them. I hate them. I do not care if they are there. Claudia puts her hands on my hair as if she wants to tell me with the old familiarity that her heart's at peace. I do not care. And there is the apparition of Armand, that power, that heartbreaking clarity. Beyond a glass, it seems. And taking Claudia's playful hand, I understand for the first time in my life what she feels when she forgives me for being myself whom she says she hates and loves: *she feels almost nothing.*"

IT WAS A WEEK before we accompanied Madeleine on her errand, to torch a universe of dolls behind a plate-glass window. I remember wandering up the street away from it, round a turn into a narrow cavern of darkness where the falling rain was the only sound. But then I saw the red glare against the clouds. Bells clanged and men shouted, and Claudia beside me was talking softly of the nature of fire. The thick smoke rising in that flickering glare unnerved me. I was feeling fear. Not a wild, mortal fear, but something cold like a hook in my side. This fear—it was the old town house burning in the Rue Royale, Lestat in the attitude of sleep on the burning floor.

" 'Fire purifies . . .' Claudia said. And I said, 'No, fire merely destroys. . . .'

"Madeleine had gone past us and was roaming at the top of the street, a phantom in the rain, her white hands whipping the air, beckoning to us, white arcs of white fireflies. And I remember Claudia leaving me for her. The sight of wilted, writhing yellow hair as she told me to follow. A ribbon fallen underfoot, flapping and floating in a swirl of black water. It seemed they were gone. And I bent to retrieve that ribbon. But another hand reached out for it. It was Armand who gave it to me now.

"I was shocked to see him there, so near, the figure of Gentleman Death in a doorway, marvellously real in his black cape and silk tie, yet ethereal as the shadows in his stillness. There was the faintest glimmer of the fire in his eyes, red warming the blackness there to the richer brown.

"And I woke suddenly as if I'd been dreaming, woke to the sense of him, to his hand enclosing mine, to his head inclined as if to let me know he wanted me to follow—awoke to my own excited experience of his presence, which consumed me as surely as it had consumed me in his cell. We were walking together now, fast, nearing the Seine, moving so swiftly and artfully through a gathering of men that they scarce saw us, that we scarce saw them. That I could keep up with him easily amazed me. He was forcing me into some acknowledgment of my powers, that the paths I'd normally chosen were human paths I no longer need follow.

"I wanted desperately to talk to him, to stop him with both my hands on his shoulders, merely to look into his eyes again as I'd done that last night, to fix him in some time and place, so that I could deal with the excitement inside me. There was so much I wanted to tell him, so much I wanted to explain. And yet I didn't know what to say or why I would say it, only that the fullness of the feeling continued to relieve me almost to tears. This was what I'd feared lost.

"I didn't know where we were now, only that in my wanderings I'd passed here before: a street of ancient mansions, of garden walls and carriage doors and towers overhead and windows of leaded glass beneath stone arches. Houses of other centuries, gnarled trees, that sudden thick and silent tranquillity which means that the masses are shut out; a handful of mortals inhabit this vast region of high-ceilinged rooms; stone absorbs the sound of breathing, the space of whole lives.

"Armand was atop a wall now, his arm against the overhanging bough of a tree, his hand reaching for me; and in an instant I stood beside him, the wet foliage brushing my face. Above, I could see story after story rising to a lone tower that barely emerged from the dark, teeming rain. 'Listen to me; we are going to climb to the tower,' Armand was saying.

" 'I cannot . . . it's impossible . . . !'

" 'You don't begin to know your own powers. You can climb easily. Remember, if you fall you will not be injured. Do as I do. But note this. The inhabitants of this house have known me for a hundred years and think me a spirit; so if by chance they see you, or you see them through those windows, remember what they believe you to be and show no consciousness of them lest you disappoint them or confuse them. Do you hear? You are perfectly safe.'

"I wasn't sure what frightened me more, the climb itself or the notion of being seen as a ghost; but I had no time for comforting witticisms, even to myself. Armand had begun, his boots finding the crack between the stones, his hands sure as claws in the crevices; and I was moving after him, tight to the wall, not daring to look down, clinging for a moment's rest to the thick, carved arch over a window, glimpsing inside, over a licking fire, a dark shoulder, a hand stroking with a poker, some figure that moved completely without knowledge that it was watched. Gone. Higher and higher we climbed, until we had reached the window of the tower itself, which Armand quickly wrenched open, his long legs disappearing over the sill; and I rose up after him, feeling his arm out around my shoulders.

"I sighed despite myself, as I stood in the room, rubbing the backs of my arms, looking around this wet, strange place. The rooftops were silver below, turrets rising here and there through the huge, rustling treetops; and far off glimmered the broken chain of a lighted boulevard. The room seemed as damp as the night outside. Armand was making a fire.

"From a molding pile of furniture he was picking chairs, breaking them into wood easily despite the thickness of their rungs. There was something grotesque about him, sharpened by his grace and the imperturbable calm of his white face. He did what any vampire could do, cracking these thick pieces of wood into splinters, yet he did what only a vampire could do. And there seemed nothing human about him; even his handsome features and dark hair became the attributes of a terrible angel who shared with the rest of us only a superficial resemblance. The tailored coat was a mirage. And though I felt drawn to him, more strongly perhaps than I'd ever been drawn to any living creature save Claudia, he excited me in other ways which resembled fear. I was not surprised that, when he finished, he set a heavy oak chair down for me, but retired himself to the marble mantelpiece and sat there warming his hands over the fire, the flames throwing red shadows into his face.

" 'I can hear the inhabitants of the house,' I said to him. The warmth was good. I could feel the leather of my boots drying, feel the warmth in my fingers.

" 'Then you know that I can hear them,' he said softly; and though this didn't contain a hint of reproach, I realized the implications of my own words.

" 'And if they come?' I insisted, studying him.

" 'Can't you tell by my manner that they won't come?' he asked. 'We could sit here all night and never speak of them. I want you to know that if we speak of them it is because you want to do so.' And when I said nothing, when perhaps I looked a little defeated, he said gently that they had long ago sealed off this tower and left it undisturbed; and if in fact they saw the smoke from the chimney or the light in the window, none of them would venture up until tomorrow.

"I could see now there were several shelves of books at one side of the fireplace, and a writing table. The pages on top were wilted, but there was an inkstand and several pens. I could imagine the room a very comfortable place when it was not storming, as it was now, or after the fire had dried out the air.

" 'You see,' Armand said, 'you really have no need of the rooms you have at the hotel. You really have need of very little. But each of us must decide how much he wants. These people in this house have a name for me; encounters with me cause talk for twenty years. They are only isolated instants in my time which mean nothing. They cannot hurt me, and I use their house to be alone. No one of the Théâtre des Vampires knows of my coming here. This is my secret.'

"I had watched him intently as he was speaking, and thoughts which had occurred to me in the cell at the theater occurred to me again. Vampires do not age, and I wondered how his youthful face and manner might differ now from what he had been a century before or a century before that; for his face, though not deepened by the lessons of maturity, was certainly no mask. It seemed powerfully expressive as was his unobtrusive voice, and I was at a loss finally to fully anatomize why. I knew only I was as powerfully drawn to him as before; and to some extent the words I spoke now were a subterfuge. 'But what holds you to the Théâtre des Vampires?' I asked.

" 'A need, naturally. But I've found what I need,' he said. 'Why do you shun me?'

" 'I never shunned you,' I said, trying to hide the excitement these words produced in me. 'You understand I have to protect Claudia, that she has no one but me. Or at least she had no one until . . .'

" 'Until Madeleine came to live with you. . . .'

" 'Yes . . .' I said.

" 'But now Claudia has released you, yet still you stay with her, and stay bound to her as your paramour,' he said.

" 'No, she's no paramour of mine; you don't understand,' I said. 'Rather, she's my child, and I don't know that she can release me. . . .' These were thoughts I'd gone over and over in my mind. 'I don't know if the child possesses the power to release the parent. I don't know that I won't be bound to her for as long as she . . .'

"I stopped. I was going to say, 'for as long as she lives.' But I realized it was a hollow mortal cliché. She would live forever, as I would live forever. But wasn't it so for mortal fathers? Their daughters live forever because these fathers die first. I was at a loss suddenly; but conscious all the while of how Armand listened; that he listened in the way that we dream of others listening, his face seeming to reflect on everything said. He did not start forward to seize on my slightest pause, to assert an understanding of something before the thought was finished, or to argue with a swift, irresistible impulse—the things which often make dialogue impossible.

"And after a long interval he said, 'I want you. I want you more than anything in the world.'

"For a moment I doubted what I'd heard. It struck me as unbelievable. And I was hopelessly disarmed by it, and the wordless vision of our living together expanded and obliterated every other consideration in my mind.

" 'I said that I want you. I want you more than anything in the world,' he repeated, with only a subtle change of expression. And then he sat waiting, watching. His face was as tranquil as always, his smooth, white forehead beneath the shock of his auburn hair without a trace of care, his large eyes reflecting on me, his lips still.

" 'You want this of me, yet you don't come to me,' he said. 'There are things you want to know, and you don't ask. You see Claudia slipping away from you, yet you seem powerless to prevent it, and then you would hasten it, and yet you do nothing.'

" 'I don't understand my own feelings. Perhaps they are clearer to you than they are to me. . . .'

" 'You don't begin to know what a mystery you are!' he said.

" 'But at least you know yourself thoroughly. I can't claim that,' I said. 'I love her, yet I am not close to her. I mean that when I am with you as I am now, I know that I know nothing of her, nothing of anyone.'

" 'She's an era for you, an era of your life. If and when you break with her, you break with the only one alive who has shared that time with you. You fear that, the isolation of it, the burden, the scope of eternal life.'

" 'Yes, that's true, but that's only a small part of it. The era, it doesn't mean much to me. She made it mean something. Other vampires must experience this and survive it, the passing of a hundred eras.'

" 'But they don't survive it,' he said. 'The world would be choked with vampires if they survived it. How do you think I come to be the eldest here or anywhere?' he asked.

"I thought about this. And then I ventured, 'They die by violence?'

" 'No, almost never. It isn't necessary. How many vampires do you think have the stamina for immortality? They have the most dismal notions of immortality to begin with. For in becoming immortal they want all the forms of their life to be fixed as they are and incorruptible: carriages made in the same dependable fashion, clothing of the cut which suited their prime, men attired and speaking in the manner they have always understood and valued. When, in fact, all things change except the vampire himself; everything except the vampire is subject to constant corruption and distortion. Soon, with an inflexible mind, and often even with the most flexible mind, this immortality becomes a penitential sentence in a madhouse of figures and forms that are hopelessly unintelligible and without value. One evening a vampire rises and realizes what he has feared perhaps for decades, that he simply wants no more of life at any cost. That whatever style or fashion or shape of existence made immortality attractive to him has been swept off the face of the earth. And nothing remains to offer freedom from despair except the act of killing. And that vampire goes out to die. No one will find his remains. No one will know where he has gone. And often no one around him—should he still seek the company of other vampires—no one will know that he is in despair. He will have ceased long ago to speak of himself or of anything. He will vanish.'

"I sat back impressed by the obvious truth of it, and yet at the same time, everything in me revolted against that prospect. I became aware of the depth of my hope and my terror; how very different those feelings were from the alienation that he described, how very different from that awful wasting despair. There was something outrageous and repulsive in that despair suddenly. I couldn't accept it.

" 'But you wouldn't allow such a state of mind in yourself. Look at you,' I found myself answering. 'If there weren't one single work of art left in this world . . . and there are thousands . . . if there weren't a single natural beauty . . . if the world were reduced to one empty cell and one fragile candle, I can't help but see you studying that candle, absorbed in the flicker of its light, the change of its colors . . . how long could that sustain you . . . what possibilities would it create? Am I wrong? Am I such a crazed idealist?'

" 'No,' he said. There was a brief smile on his lips, an evanescent flush of pleasure. But then he went on simply. 'But you feel an obligation to a world you love because that world for you is still intact. It is conceivable your own sensitivity might become the instrument of madness. You speak of works of art and natural beauty. I wish I had the artist's power to bring alive for you the Venice of the fifteenth century, my master's palace there, the love I felt for him when I was a mortal boy, and the love he felt for me when he made me a vampire. Oh, if I could make those times come alive for either you or me . . . for only an instant! What would that be worth? And what a sadness it is to me that time doesn't dim the memory of that period, that it becomes all the richer and more magical in light of the world I see today.'

" 'Love?' I asked. 'There was love between you and the vampire who made you?' I leaned forward.

" 'Yes,' he said. 'A love so strong he couldn't allow me to grow old and die. A love that waited patiently until I was strong enough to be born to darkness. Do you mean to tell me there was no bond of love between you and the vampire who made you?'

" 'None,' I said quickly. I couldn't repress a bitter smile.

"He studied me. 'Why then did he give you these powers?' he asked.

"I sat back. 'You see these powers as a gift!' I said. 'Of course you do. Forgive me, but it amazes me, how in your complexity you are so profoundly simple.' I laughed.

" 'Should I be insulted?' he smiled. And his whole manner only confirmed me in what I'd just said. He seemed so innocent. I was only beginning to understand him.

" 'No, not by me,' I said, my pulse quickening as I looked at him. 'You're everything I dreamed of when I became a vampire. You see these powers as a gift!' I repeated it. 'But tell me . . . do you now feel love for this vampire who gave you eternal life? Do you feel this now?'

"He appeared to be thinking, and then he said slowly, 'Why does this matter?' But went on: 'I don't think I've been fortunate in feeling love for many people or many things. But yes, I love him. Perhaps I do not love him as you mean. It seems you confuse me, rather effortlessly. You are a mystery. I do not need him, this vampire, anymore.'

" 'I was gifted with eternal life, with heightened perception, and with the need to kill,' I quickly explained, 'because the vampire who made me wanted the house I owned and my money. Do you understand such a thing?' I asked. 'Ah, but there is so much else behind what I say. It makes itself known to me so slowly, so incompletely! You see, it's as if you've cracked a door for me, and light is streaming from that door and I'm yearning to get to it, to push it back, to enter the region you say exists beyond it! When, in fact, I don't believe it! The vampire who made me was everything that I truly believed evil to be: He was as dismal, as literal, as barren, as inevitably eternally disappointing as I believed evil had to be! I know that now. But you, you are something totally beyond that conception! Open the door for me, push it back all the way. Tell me about this palace in Venice, this love affair with damnation. I want to understand it.'

" 'You trick yourself. The palace means nothing to you,' he said. 'The doorway you see leads to me, now. To your coming to live with me as I am. I am evil with infinite gradations and without guilt.'

" 'Yes, exactly,' I murmured.

" 'And this makes you unhappy,' he said. 'You, who came to me in my cell and said there was only one sin left, the willful taking of an innocent human life.'

" 'Yes . . .' I said. 'How you must have been laughing at me. . . .'

" 'I never laughed at you,' he said. 'I cannot afford to laugh at you. It is through you that I can save myself from the despair which I've described to you as our death. It is through you that I must make my link with this nineteenth century and come to understand it in a way that will revitalize me, which I so desperately need. It is for you that I've been waiting at the Théâtre des Vampires. If I knew a mortal of that sensitivity, that pain, that focus, I would make him a vampire in an instant. But such can rarely be done. No, I've had to wait and watch for you. And now I'll fight for you. Do you see how ruthless I am in love? Is this what you meant by love?'

" 'Oh, but you'd be making a terrible mistake,' I said, looking him in the eyes. His words were only slowly sinking in. Never had I felt my all-consuming frustration to be so clear. I could not conceivably satisfy him. I could not satisfy Claudia. I'd never been able to satisfy Lestat. And my own mortal brother, Paul: How dismally, mortally I had disappointed him!

" 'No. I must make contact with the age,' he said to me

calmly. 'And I can do this through you . . . not to learn things from you which I can see in a moment in an art gallery or read in an hour in the thickest books . . . you are the spirit, you are the heart,' he persisted.

" 'No, no.' I threw up my hands. I was on the point of a bitter, hysterical laughter. 'Don't you see? I'm not the spirit of any age. I'm at odds with everything and always have been! I have never belonged anywhere with anyone at any time!' It was too painful, too perfectly true.

"But his face only brightened with an irresistible smile. He seemed on the verge of laughing at me, and then his shoulders began to move with this laughter. 'But Louis,' he said softly. 'This is the very spirit of your age. Don't you see that? Everyone else feels as you feel. Your fall from grace and faith has been the fall of a century.'

"I was so stunned by this, that for a long time I sat there staring into the fire. It had all but consumed the wood and was a wasteland of smoldering ash, a gray and red landscape that would have collapsed at the touch of the poker. Yet it was very warm, and still gave off powerful light. I saw my life in complete perspective.

" 'And the vampires of the Théâtre . . .' I asked softly.

" 'They reflect the age in cynicism which cannot comprehend the death of possibilities, fatuous sophisticated indulgence in the parody of the miraculous, decadence whose last refuge is self-ridicule, a mannered helplessness. You saw them; you've known them all your life. You reflect your age differently. You reflect its broken heart.'

" 'This is unhappiness. Unhappiness you don't begin to understand.'

" 'I don't doubt it. Tell me what you feel now, what makes you unhappy. Tell me why for a period of seven days you haven't come to me, though you were burning to come. Tell me what holds you still to Claudia and the other woman.'

"I shook my head. 'You don't know what you ask. You see, it was immensely difficult for me to perform the act of making

Madeleine into a vampire. I broke a promise to myself that I would never do this, that my own loneliness would never drive me to do it. I don't see our life as powers and gifts. I see it as a curse. I haven't the courage to die. But to make another vampire! To bring this suffering on another, and to condemn to death all those men and women whom that vampire must subsequently kill! I broke a grave promise. And in so doing . . .'

" 'But if it's any consolation to you . . . surely you realize I had a hand in it.'

" 'That I did it to be free of Claudia, to be free to come to you . . . yes, I realize that. But the ultimate responsibility lies with me!' I said.

" 'No. I mean, directly. I made you do it! I was near you the night you did it. I exerted my strongest power to persuade you to do it. Didn't you know this?

" 'No!'

"I bowed my head.

" 'I would have made this woman a vampire,' he said softly. 'But I thought it best you have a hand in it. Otherwise you would not give Claudia up. You must know you wanted it. . . .'

" 'I loathe what I did!' I said.

" 'Then loathe me, not yourself.'

" 'No. You don't understand. You nearly destroyed the thing you value in me when this happened! I resisted you with all my power when I didn't even know it was your force which was working on me. Something nearly died in me! Passion nearly died in me! I was all but destroyed when Madeleine was created!'

" 'But that thing is no longer dead, that passion, that humanity, whatever you wish to name it. If it were not alive there wouldn't be tears in your eyes now. There wouldn't be rage in your voice,' he said.

"For the moment, I couldn't answer. I only nodded. Then I struggled to speak again. 'You must never force me to do something against my will! You must never exert such power . . .' I stammered.

" 'No,' he said at once. 'I must not. My power stops somewhere inside you, at some threshold. There I am powerless. However . . . this creation of Madeleine is done. You are free.'

" 'And you are satisfied,' I said, gaining control of myself. 'I don't mean to be harsh. You have me. I love you. But I'm mystified. You're satisfied?'

" 'How could I not be?' he asked. 'I am satisfied, of course.'

"I stood up and went to the window. The last embers were dying. The light came from the gray sky. I heard Armand follow me to the window ledge. I could feel him beside me now, my eyes growing more and more accustomed to the luminosity of the sky, so that now I could see his profile and his eye on the falling rain. The sound of the rain was everywhere and different: flowing in the gutter along the roof, tapping the shingles, falling softly through the shimmering layers of tree branches, splattering on the sloped stone sill in front of my hands. A soft intermingling of sounds that drenched and colored all of the night.

" 'Do you forgive me . . . for forcing you with the woman?' he asked.

" 'You don't need my forgiveness.'

" 'You need it,' he said. 'Therefore, I need it.' His face was as always utterly calm.

" 'Will she care for Claudia? Will she endure?' I asked.

" 'She is perfect. Mad; but for these days that is perfect. She will care for Claudia. She has never lived a moment of life alone; it is natural to her that she be devoted to her companions. She need not have particular reasons for loving Claudia. Yet, in addition to her needs, she does have particular reasons. Claudia's beautiful surface, Claudia's quiet, Claudia's dominance and control. They are perfect together. But I think . . . that as soon as possible they should leave Paris.'

" 'Why?'

" 'You know why. Because Santiago and the other vampires watch them with suspicion. All the vampires have seen Madeleine. They fear her because she knows about them and they don't know her. They don't let others alone who know about them.'

" 'And the boy, Denis? What do you plan to do with him?'

" 'He's dead,' he answered.

"I was astonished. Both at his words and his calm. 'You killed him?' I gasped.

"He nodded. And said nothing. But his large, dark eyes seemed entranced with me, with the emotion, the shock I didn't try to conceal. His soft, subtle smile seemed to draw me close to him; his hand closed over mine on the wet window sill and I felt my body turning to face him, drawing nearer to him, as though I were being moved not by myself but by him. 'It was best,' he conceded to me gently. And then said, 'We must go now. . . .' And he glanced at the street below.

" 'Armand,' I said. 'I can't. . . .'

" 'Louis, come after me,' he whispered. And then on the ledge, he stopped. 'Even if you were to fall on the cobblestones there,' he said, 'you would only be hurt for a while. You would heal so rapidly and so perfectly that in days you would show no sign of it, your bones healing as your skin heals; so let this knowledge free you to do what you can so easily do already. Climb down, now.'

" 'What can kill me?' I asked.

"Again he stopped. 'The destruction of your remains,' he said. 'Don't you know this? Fire, dismemberment . . . the heat of the sun. Nothing else. You can be scarred, yes; but you are resilient. You are immortal.'

"I was looking down through the quiet silver rain into darkness. Then a light flickered beneath the shifting tree limbs, and the pale beams of the light made the street appear. Wet cobblestones, the iron hook of the carriage-house bell, the vines clinging to the top of the wall. The huge black hulk of a carriage brushed the vines, and then the light grew weak, the street went from yellow to silver and vanished altogether, as if the dark trees had swallowed it up. Or, rather, as if it had all been subtracted from the dark. I felt dizzy. I felt the building move. Armand was seated on the window sill looking down at me.

" 'Louis, come with me tonight,' he whispered suddenly, with an urgent inflection.

" 'No,' I said gently. 'It's too soon. I can't leave them yet.'

"I watched him turn away and look at the dark sky. He appeared to sigh, but I didn't hear it. I felt his hand close on mine on the window sill. 'Very well . . .' he said.

" 'A little more time . . .' I said. And he nodded and patted my hand as if to say it was all right. Then he swung his legs over and disappeared. For only a moment I hesitated, mocked by the pounding of my heart. But then I climbed over the sill and commenced to hurry after him, never daring to look down."

IT WAS VERY NEAR DAWN when I put my key into the lock at the hotel. The gas light flared along the walls. And Madeleine, her needle and thread in her hands, had fallen asleep by the grate. Claudia stood still, looking at me from among the ferns at the window, in shadow. She had her hairbrush in her hands. Her hair was gleaming.

"I stood there absorbing some shock, as if all the sensual pleasures and confusions of these rooms were passing over me like waves and my body were being permeated with these things, so different from the spell of Armand and the tower room where we'd been. There was something comforting here, and it was disturbing. I was looking for my chair. I was sitting in it with my hands on my temples. And then I felt Claudia near me, and I felt her lips against my forehead.

" 'You've been with Armand,' she said. 'You want to go with him.'

"I looked up at her. How soft and beautiful her face was,

and, suddenly, so much mine. I felt no compunction in yielding to my urge to touch her cheeks, to lightly touch her eyelids—familiarities, liberties I hadn't taken with her since the night of our quarrel. 'I'll see you again; not here, in other places. Always I'll know where you are!' I said.

"She put her arms around my neck. She held me tight, and I closed my eyes and buried my face in her hair. I was covering her neck with my kisses. I had hold of her round, firm little arms. I was kissing them, kissing the soft indentation of the flesh in the crooks of her arms, her wrists, her open palms. I felt her fingers stroking my hair, my face. 'Whatever you wish,' she vowed. 'Whatever you wish.'

" 'Are you happy? Do you have what you want?' I begged her.

" 'Yes, Louis.' She held me against her dress, her fingers clasping the back of my neck. 'I have all that I want. But do you truly know what you want?' She was lifting my face so I had to look into her eyes. 'It's you I fear for, you who might be making the mistake. Why don't you leave Paris with us!' she said suddenly. 'We have the world, come with us!'

" 'No.' I drew back from her. 'You want it to be as it was with Lestat. It can't be that way again, ever. It won't be.'

" 'It will be something new and different with Madeleine. I don't ask for that again. It was I who put an end to that,' she said. 'But do you truly understand what you are choosing in Armand?'

"I turned away from her. There was something stubborn and mysterious in her dislike of him, in her failure to understand him. She would say again that he wished her death, which I did not believe. She didn't realize what I realized: He could not want her death, because I didn't want it. But how could I explain this to her without sounding pompous and blind in my love of him. 'It's meant to be. It's almost that sort of direction,' I said, as if it were just coming clear to me under the pressure of her doubts. 'He alone can give me the strength to be what I am. I can't continue to live divided and consumed with misery. Either I go with him, or I die,' I said. 'And it's something else, which is irrational and unexplainable and which satisfies only me. . . .'

"'. . . which is?' she asked.

"'That I love him,' I said.

"'No doubt you do,' she mused. 'But then, you could love even me.'

"'Claudia, Claudia.' I held her close to me, and felt her weight on my knee. She drew up close to my chest.

"'I only hope that when you have need of me, you can find me . . .' she whispered. 'That I can get back to you . . . I've hurt you so often, I've caused you so much pain.' Her words trailed off. She was resting still against me. I felt her weight, thinking, In a little while, I won't have her anymore. I want now simply to hold her. There has always been such pleasure in that simple thing. Her weight against me, this hand resting against my neck.

"It seemed a lamp died somewhere. That from the cool, damp air that much light was suddenly, soundlessly subtracted. I was sitting on the verge of dream. Had I been mortal I would have been content to sleep there. And in that drowsy, comfortable state I had a strange, habitual mortal feeling, that the sun would wake me gently later and I would have that rich, habitual vision of the ferns in the sunshine and the sunshine in the droplets of rain. I indulged that feeling. I half closed my eyes.

"Often afterwards I tried to remember those moments. Tried over and over to recall just what it was in those rooms as we rested there, that began to disturb me, should have disturbed me. How, being off my guard, I was somehow insensible to the subtle changes which must have been taking place there. Long after, bruised and robbed and embittered beyond my wildest dreams, I sifted through those moments, those drowsy quiet early-hour moments when the clock ticked almost imperceptibly on the mantelpiece, and the sky grew paler and paler; and all I could remember—despite the desperation with which I lengthened and fixed that time, in which I held out my hands to stop the clock—all I could remember was the soft changing of light.

"On guard, I would never have let it pass. Deluded with larger concerns, I made no note of it. A lamp gone out, a candle extinguished by the shiver of its own hot pool of wax. My eyes half shut, I had the sense then of impending darkness, of being shut up in darkness.

"And then I opened my eyes, not thinking of lamps or candles. And it was too late. I remember standing upright, Claudia's hand slipping on my arm, and the vision of a host of black-dressed men and women moving through the rooms, their garments seeming to garner light from every gilt edge or lacquered surface, seeming to drain all light away. I shouted out against them, shouted for Madeleine, saw her wake with a start, terrified fledgling, clinging to the arm of the couch, then down on her knees as they reached out for her. There was Santiago and Celeste coming towards us, and behind them, Estelle and others whose names I didn't know filling the mirrors and crowding together to make walls of shifting, menacing shadow. I was shouting to Claudia to run, having pulled back the door. I was shoving her through it and then was stretched across it, kicking out at Santiago as he came.

"That weak defensive position I'd held against him in the Latin Quarter was nothing compared to my strength now. I was too flawed perhaps to ever fight with conviction for my own protection. But the instinct to protect Madeleine and Claudia was overpowering. I remember kicking Santiago backwards and then striking out at that powerful, beautiful Celeste, who sought to get by me. Claudia's feet sounded on the distant marble stairway. Celeste was reeling, clawing at me, catching hold of me and scratching my face so the blood ran down over my collar. I could see it blazing in the corner of my eye. I was on Santiago now, turning with him, aware of the awful strength of the arms that held me, the hands that sought to get a hold on my throat. 'Fight them, Madeleine,' I was shouting to her. But all I could hear was her sobbing. Then I saw her in the whirl, a fixed, frightened thing, surrounded by other vampires. They were laughing that hollow vampire laughter which is like tinsel or silverbells. Santiago was clutching at his face. My teeth had drawn blood there. I struck at his chest, at his head, the pain searing through my arm, something enclosing my chest like two arms, which I shook off, hearing the crash of broken glass behind me. But something else, someone else had hold of my arm with two arms and was pulling me with tenacious strength.

"I don't remember weakening. I don't remember any turning point when anyone's strength overcame my own. I remember simply being outnumbered. Hopelessly, by sheer numbers and persistence, I was stilled, surrounded, and forced out of the rooms. In a press of vampires, I was being forced along the passageway; and then I was falling down the steps, free for a moment before the narrow back doors of the hotel, only to be surrounded again and held tight. I could see Celeste's face very near me and, if I could have, I would have wounded her with my teeth. I was bleeding badly, and one of my wrists was held so tightly that there was no feeling in that hand. Madeleine was next to me sobbing still. And all of us were pressed into a carriage. Over and over I was struck, and still I did not lose consciousness. I remember clinging tenaciously to consciousness, feeling these blows on the back of my head, feeling the back of my head wet with blood that trickled down my neck as I lay on the carriage floor. I was thinking only, I can feel the carriage moving; I am alive; I am conscious.

"And as soon as we were dragged into the Théâtre des Vampires, I was crying out for Armand.

"I was let go, only to stagger on the cellar steps, the horde of them behind me and in front of me, pushing me with menacing hands. At one point I got hold of Celeste, and she screamed and someone struck me from behind.

"And then I saw Lestat—the blow that was more crippling than any blow. Lestat, standing there in the center of the ballroom, erect, his gray eyes sharp and focused, his mouth lengthening in a cunning smile. Impeccably dressed he was, as always, and as splendid in his rich black cloak and fine linen. But those scars still scored every inch of his white flesh. And how they distorted the taut, handsome face, the fine, hard threads cutting the delicate skin above his lip, the lids of his eyes, the smooth rise of his forehead. And the eyes, they burned with a silent rage that seemed infused with vanity, an awful relentless vanity that said, 'See what I am!'

" 'This is the one?' said Santiago, thrusting me forward.

"But Lestat turned sharply to him and said in a harsh low voice, 'I told you I wanted Claudia, the child! She was the one!' And now I saw his head moving involuntarily with his outburst, and his hand reaching out as if for the arm of a chair only to close as he drew himself up again, eyes to me.

" 'Lestat,' I began, seeing now the few straws left to me. 'You are alive! You have your life! Tell them how you treated us. . . .'

" 'No,' he shook his head furiously. 'You come back to me, Louis,' he said.

"For a moment I could not believe my ears. Some saner, more desperate part of me said, Reason with him, even as the sinister laughter erupted from my lips. 'Are you mad!'

" 'I'll give you back your life!' he said, his eyelids quivering with the stress of his words, his chest heaving, that hand going out again and closing impotently in the dark. 'You promised me,' he said to Santiago, 'I could take him back with me to New Orleans.' And then, as he looked from one to the other of them as they surrounded us, his breath became frantic, and he burst out, 'Claudia, where is she? She's the one who did it to me, I told you!'

" 'By and by,' said Santiago. And when he reached out for Lestat, Lestat drew back and almost lost his balance. He had found the chair arm he needed and stood holding fast to it, his eyes closed, regaining his control.

" 'But he helped her, aided her . . .' said Santiago, drawing nearer to him. Lestat looked up.

" 'No,' he said. 'Louis, you must come back to me. There's something I must tell you . . . about that night in the swamp.' But then he stopped and looked about again, as though he were caged, wounded, desperate.

" 'Listen to me, Lestat,' I began now. 'You let her go, you free her . . . and I will . . . I'll return to you,' I said, the words sounding hollow, metallic. I tried to take a step towards him, to make my eyes hard and unreadable, to feel my power emanating from them like two beams of light. He was looking at me, studying me, struggling all the while against his own fragility. And Celeste had her hand on my wrist. 'You must tell them,' I went on, 'how you treated us, that we didn't know the laws, that she didn't know of other vampires,' I said. And I was thinking steadily, as that mechanical voice came out of me: Armand must return tonight, Armand must come back. He will stop this, he won't let it go on.

"There was a sound then of something dragging across the floor. I could hear Madeleine's exhausted crying. I looked around and saw her in a chair, and when she saw my eyes on her, her terror seemed to increase. She tried to rise but they stopped her. 'Lestat,' I said. 'What do you want of me? I'll give it to you. . .'

"And then I saw the thing that was making the noise. And Lestat had seen it too. It was a coffin with large iron locks on it that was being dragged into the room. I understood at once. 'Where is Armand?' I said desperately.

" 'She did it to me, Louis. She did it to me. You didn't! She has to die!' said Lestat, his voice becoming thin, rasping, as if it were an effort for him to speak. 'Get that thing away from here, he's coming home with me,' he said furiously to Santiago. And Santiago only laughed, and Celeste laughed, and the laughter seemed to infect them all.

" 'You promised me,' said Lestat to them.

" 'I promised you nothing,' said Santiago.

" 'They've made a fool of you,' I said to him bitterly as they were opening the coffin. 'A fool of you! You must reach Armand, Armand is the leader here,' I burst out. But he didn't seem to understand.

"What happened then was desperate and clouded and miserable, my kicking at them, struggling to free my arms, raging against them that Armand would stop what they were doing, that they dare not hurt Claudia. Yet they forced me down into the coffin, my frantic efforts serving no purpose against them except to take my mind off the sound of Madeleine's cries, her awful wailing cries, and the fear that at any moment Claudia's cries might be added to them. I remember rising against the crushing lid, holding it at bay for an instant before it was forced shut on me and the locks were being shut with the grinding of metal and keys. Words of long ago came back to me, a strident and smiling Lestat in that faraway, trouble-free place where the three of us had quarrelled together: 'A starving child is a frightful sight . . . a starving vampire even worse. They'd hear her screams in Paris.' And my wet and trembling body went limp in the suffocating coffin, and I said, Armand will not let it happen; there isn't a place secure enough for them to place us.

"The coffin was lifted, there was the scraping of boots, the swinging from side to side; my arms braced against the sides of the box, my eyes shut perhaps for a moment, I was uncertain. I told myself not to reach out for the sides, not to feel the thin margin of air between my face and the lid; and I felt the coffin swing and tilt as their steps found the stairs. Vainly I tried to make out Madeleine's cries, for it seemed that she was crying for Claudia, calling out to her as if she could help us all. Call for Armand; he must come home this night, I thought desperately. And only the thought of the awful humiliation of hearing my own cry closed in with me, flooding my ears, yet locked in with me, prevented me from calling out.

"But another thought had come over me even as I'd phrased those words: What if he did not come? What if somewhere in that mansion he had a coffin hidden to which he returned . . . ? And then it seemed my body broke suddenly, without warning, from the control of my mind, and I flailed at the wood around me, struggling to turn over and pit the strength of my back against the coffin lid. Yet I could not: it was too close; and my head fell back on the boards, and the sweat poured down my back and sides.

"Madeleine's cries were gone. All I heard were the boots, and my own breathing. Then, tomorrow night he will come—

yes, tomorrow night—and they will tell him, and he will find us and release us. The coffin swayed. The smell of water filled my nostrils, its coolness palpable through the close heat of the coffin; and then with the smell of the water was the smell of the deep earth. The coffin was set down roughly, and my limbs ached and I rubbed the backs of my arms with my hands, struggling not to touch the coffin lid, not to sense how close it was, afraid of my own fear rising to panic, to terror.

"I thought they would leave me now, but they did not. They were near at hand and busy, and another odor came to my nostrils which was raw and not known to me. But then, as I lay very still, I realized they were laying bricks and that the odor came from the mortar. Slowly, carefully, I brought my hand up to wipe my face. All right, then, tomorrow night, I reasoned with myself, even as my shoulders seemed to grow large against the coffin walls. All right, then, tomorrow night he will come; and until then this is merely the confines of my own coffin, the price I've paid for all of this, night after night after night.

"But the tears were welling in my eyes, and I could see myself flailing again at the wood; and my head was turning from side to side, my mind rushing on to tomorrow and the night after and the night after that. And then, as if to distract myself from this madness, I thought of Claudia—only to feel her arms around me in the dim light of those rooms in the Hôtel Saint-Gabriel, only to see the curve of her cheek in the light, the soft, languid flutter of her eyelashes, the silky touch of her lip. My body stiffened, my feet kicked at the boards. The sound of the bricks was gone, and the muffled steps were gone. And I cried out for her, 'Claudia,' until my neck was twisted with pain as I tossed, and my nails had dug into my palms; and slowly, like an icy stream, the paralysis of sleep came over me. I tried to call out to Armand—foolishly, desperately, only dimly aware as my lids grew heavy and my hands lay limp that the sleep was on him too somewhere, that he lay still in his resting place. One last time I struggled. My eyes saw the dark, my hands felt the wood. But I was weak. And then there was nothing."

I AWOKE TO A VOICE. It was distant but distinct. It said my name twice. For an instant I didn't know where I was. I'd been dreaming, something desperate which was threatening to vanish completely without the slightest clue to what it had been, and something terrible which I was eager, willing to let go. Then I opened my eyes and felt the top of the coffin. I knew where I was at the same instant that, mercifully, I knew it was Armand who was calling me. I answered him, but my voice was locked in with me and it was deafening. In a moment of terror, I thought, He's searching for me, and I can't tell him that I am here. But then I heard him speaking to me, telling me not to be afraid. And I heard a loud noise. And another. And there was a cracking sound, and then the thunderous falling of the bricks. It seemed several of them struck the coffin. And then I heard them lifted off one by one. It sounded as though he were pulling off the locks by the nails.

"The hard wood of the top creaked. A pinpoint of light sparkled before my eyes. I drew breath from it, and felt the sweat break out on my face. The lid creaked open and for an instant I was blinded; then I was sitting up, seeing the bright light of a lamp through my fingers.

" 'Hurry,' he said to me. 'Don't make a sound.'

" 'But where are we going?' I asked. I could see a passage of rough bricks stretching out from the doorway he'd broken down. And all along that passage were doors which were sealed, as this door had been. I had a vision at once of coffins behind those bricks, of vampires starved and decayed there. But Armand was pulling me up, telling me again to make no sound; we were creeping along the passage. He stopped at a wooden door, and then he extinguished the lamp. It was completely black for an instant until the seam of light beneath the door brightened. He opened the door so gently the hinges did not make a sound. I could hear my own breathing now, and I tried to stop it. We were entering that lower passageway which led to his cell. But as I raced along behind him I became aware of one awful truth. He was rescuing me, but me alone. I put out my hand to stop him, but he only pulled me after him. Only when we stood in the alleyway beside the Théâtre des Vampires was I able to make him stop. And even then, he was on the verge of going on. He began shaking his head even before I spoke.

" 'I can't save her!' he said.

" 'You don't honestly expect me to leave without her! They have her in there!' I was horrified. 'Armand, you must save her! You have no choice!'

" 'Why do you say this?' he answered. 'I don't have the power, you must understand. They'll rise against me. There is no reason why they should not. Louis, I tell you, I cannot save her. I will only risk losing you. You can't go back.'

"I refused to admit this could be true. I had no hope other than Armand. But I can truthfully say that I was beyond being afraid. I knew only that I had to get Claudia back or die in the effort. It was really very simple; not a matter of courage at all. And I knew also, could tell in everything about Armand's passivity, the manner in which he spoke, that he would follow me if I returned, that he would not try to prevent me.

"I was right. I was rushing back into the passage and he was just behind me, heading for the stairway to the ballroom. I could hear the other vampires. I could hear all manner of sounds. The Paris traffic. What sounded very much like a congregation in the vault of the theater above. And then, as I reached the top of the steps, I saw Celeste in the door of the ballroom. She held one of those stage masks in her hand. She was merely looking at me. She did not appear alarmed. In fact, she appeared strangely indifferent.

"If she had rushed at me, if she had sounded a general alarm, these things I could have understood. But she did nothing. She stepped backwards into the ballroom; she turned, seeming to enjoy the subtle movement of her skirts, seeming to turn for the love of making her skirts flare out, and she drifted in a widening circle to the center of the room. She put the mask to her face, and said softly behind the painted skull, 'Lestat . . . it is your friend Louis come calling. Look sharp, Lestat!' She dropped the mask, and there was a ripple of laughter from somewhere. I saw they were all about the room, shadowy things, seated here and there, standing together. And Lestat, in an armchair, sat with his shoulders hunched and his face turned away from me. It seemed he was working something with his hands, something I couldn't see; and slowly he looked up, his full yellow hair falling into his eyes. There was fear in them. It was undeniable. Now he was looking at Armand. And Armand was moving silently through the room with slow, steady steps, and all of the vampires moved back away from him, watching him. 'Bonsoir, Monsieur,' Celeste bowed to him as he passed her, that mask in her hand like a scepter. He did not look at her in particular. He looked down at Lestat. 'Are you satisfied?' he asked him.

"Lestat's gray eyes seemed to regard Armand with wonder, and his lips struggled to form a word. I could see that his eyes were filling with tears. 'Yes . . .' he whispered now, his hand struggling with the thing he concealed beneath his black cloak. But then he looked at me, and the tears spilled down his face. 'Louis,' he said, his voice deep and rich now with what seemed an unbearable struggle. 'Please, you must listen to me. You must come back. . . .' And then, bowing his head, he grimaced with shame.

"Santiago was laughing somewhere. Armand was saying softly to Lestat that he must get out, leave Paris; he was outcast.

"And Lestat sat there with his eyes closed, his face transfigured with his pain. It seemed the double of Lestat, some wounded, feeling creature I'd never known. 'Please,' he said, the voice eloquent and gentle as he implored me.

" 'I can't talk to you here! I can't make you understand. You'll come with me . . . for only a little while . . . until I am myself again?'

" 'This is madness! . . .' I said, my hands rising suddenly to my temples. 'Where is she! Where is she! I looked about me, at their still, passive faces, those inscrutable smiles. 'Lestat.' I turned him now, grabbing at the black wool of his lapels.

"And then I saw the thing in his hands. I knew what it was. And in an instant I'd ripped it from him and was staring at it, at the fragile silken thing that it was—Claudia's yellow dress. His hand rose to his lips, his face turned away. And the soft, subdued sobs broke from him as he sat back while I stared at him, while I stared at the dress. My fingers moved slowly over the tears in it, the stains of blood, my hands closing, trembling as I crushed it against my chest.

"For a long moment it seemed I simply stood there; time had no bearing upon me nor upon those shifting vampires with their light, ethereal laughter filling my ears. I remember thinking that I wanted to put my hands over my ears, but I wouldn't let go of the dress, couldn't stop trying to make it so small that it was hidden within my hands. I remember a row of candles burning, an uneven row coming to light one by one against the painted walls. A door stood open to the rain, and all the candles spluttered and blew on the wind as if the flames were being lifted from the wicks. But they clung to the wicks and were all right. I knew that Claudia was through the doorway. The candles moved. The vampires had hold of them. Santiago had a candle and was bowing to me and gesturing for me to pass through the door. I was barely aware of him. I didn't care about him or the others at all. Something in me said, If you care about them you will go mad. And they don't matter, really. She matters. Where is she? Find her. And their laughter was remote, and it seemed to have a color and a shape but to be part of nothing.

"Then I saw something through the open doorway which was something I'd seen before, a long, long time ago. No one knew of this thing I'd seen years before except myself. No. Lestat knew. But it didn't matter. He wouldn't know now or understand. That he and I had seen this thing, standing at the door of that brick kitchen in the Rue Royale, two wet shrivelled things that had been alive, mother and daughter in one another's arms, the murdered pair on the kitchen floor. But these two lying under the gentle rain were Madeleine and Claudia, and Madeleine's lovely red hair mingled with the gold of Claudia's hair, which stirred and glistened in the wind that sucked through the open doorway. Only that which was living had been burnt away—not the hair, not the long, empty velvet dress, not the small blood-stained chemise with its eyelets of white lace. And the blackened, burnt, and drawn thing that was Madeleine still bore the stamp of her living face, and the hand that clutched at the child was whole like a mummy's hand. But the child, the ancient one, my Claudia, was ashes.

"A cry rose in me, a wild, consuming cry that came from the bowels of my being, rising up like the wind in that narrow place, the wind that swirled the rain teeming on those ashes, beating at the trace of a tiny hand against the bricks, that golden hair lifting, those loose strands rising, flying upwards. And a blow struck me even as I cried out; and I had hold of something that I believed to be Santiago, and I was pounding against him, destroying him, twisting that grinning white face around with hands from which he couldn't free himself, hands against which he railed, crying out, his cries mingling with my cries, his boots coming down into those ashes, as I threw him backwards away from them, my own eyes blinded with the rain, with my tears, until he lay back away from me, and I was reaching out for him even as he held out his hand. And the one I was struggling against was Armand. Armand, who was forcing me out of the tiny graveyard into the whirling colors of the ballroom, the cries, the mingling voices, that searing, silver laughter.

"And Lestat was calling out, 'Louis, wait for me; Louis, I must talk to you!'

"I could see Armand's rich, brown eyes close to mine, and I felt weak all over and vaguely aware that Madeleine and Claudia were dead, his voice saying softly, perhaps soundlessly, 'I could not prevent it, I could not prevent it. . . .' And they were dead, simply dead. And I was losing consciousness. Santiago was near them somewhere, there where they were still, that hair lifted on the wind, swept across those bricks, unraveling locks. But I was losing consciousness.

"I could not gather their bodies up with me, could not take them out. Armand had his arm around my back, his hand under my arm, and he was all but carrying me through some hollow wooden echoing place, and the smells of the street were rising, the fresh smell of the horses and the leather, and there were the gleaming carriages stopped there. And I could see myself clearly running down the Boulevard des Capucines with a small coffin under my arm and the people making way for me and dozens of people rising around the crowded tables of the open café and a man lifting his arm. It seemed I stumbled then, the Louis whom Armand held in his arm, and again I saw his brown eyes looking at me, and felt that drowsiness, that sinking. And yet I walked, I moved, I saw the gleam of my own boots on the pavement. 'Is he mad, that he says these things to me?' I was asking of Lestat, my voice shrill and angry, even the sound of it giving me some comfort. I was laughing, laughing loudly. 'He's stark-raving mad to speak to me in this manner! Did you hear him?' I demanded. And Armand's eye said, Sleep. I wanted to say something about Madeleine and Claudia, that we could not leave them there, and I felt that cry again rising inside of me, that cry that pushed everything else out of its way, my teeth clenched to keep it in, because it was so loud and so full it would destroy me if I let it go.

"And then I conceived of everything too clearly. We were walking now, a belligerent, blind sort of walking that men do when they are wildly drunk and filled with hatred for others, while at the same time they feel invincible. I was walking in such a manner through New Orleans the night I'd first encountered Lestat, that drunken walking which is a battering against things, which is miraculously sure-footed and finds its path. I saw a drunken man's hands fumbling miraculously with a match. Flame touched to the pipe, the smoke drawn in. I was standing at a café window. The man was drawing on his pipe. He was not at all drunk. Armand stood beside me waiting, and we were in the crowded Boulevard des Capucines. Or was it the Boulevard du Temple? I wasn't sure. I was outraged that their bodies remained there in that vile place. I saw Santiago's foot touching the blackened burned thing that had been my child! I was crying out through clenched teeth, and the man had risen from his table and steam spread out on the glass in front of his face. 'Get away from me,' I was saying to Armand. 'Damn you into hell, don't come near me. I warn you, don't come near me.' I was walking away from him up the boulevard, and I could see a man and a woman stepping aside for me, the man with his arm out to protect the woman.

"Then I was running. People saw me running. I wondered how it appeared to them, what wild, white thing they saw that moved too fast for their eyes. I remember that by the time I stopped, I was weak and sick, and my veins were burning as if I were starved. I thought of killing, and the thought filled me with revulsion. I was sitting on the stone steps beside a church, at one of those small side doors, carved into the stone, which was bolted and locked for the night. The rain had abated. Or so it seemed. And the street was dreary and quiet, though a man passed a long way off with a bright, black umbrella. Armand stood at a distance under the trees. Behind him it seemed there was a great expanse of trees and wet grasses and mist rising as if the ground were warm.

"By thinking of only one thing, the sickness in my stomach and head and the tightening in my throat, was I able to return to a state of calm. By the time these things had died away and I was feeling clear again, I was aware of all that had happened, the great distance we'd come from the theater, and that the remains of Madeleine and Claudia were still there. Victims of a holocaust in each other's arms. And I felt resolute and very near to my own destruction.

" 'I could not prevent it,' Armand said softly to me. And I looked up to see his face unutterably sad. He looked away from me as if he felt it was futile to try to convince me of this, and I could feel his overwhelming sadness, his near defeat. I had the feeling that if I were to vent all my anger on him he would do little to resist me. And I could feel that detachment, that passivity in him as something pervasive which was at the root of what he insisted to me again, 'I could not have prevented it.'

" 'Oh, but you could have prevented it!' I said softly. 'You know full well that you could have. You were the leader! *You* were the only one who knew the limits of your own power. They didn't know. They didn't understand. Your understanding surpassed theirs.'

"He looked away still. But I could see the effect of my words on him. I could see the weariness in his face, the dull lusterless sadness of his eyes.

" 'You held sway over them. They feared you!' I went on. 'You could have stopped them if you'd been willing to use that power even beyond your own self-prescribed limits. It was your sense of yourself you would not violate. Your own precious conception of truth! I understand you perfectly. I see in you the reflection of myself!'

"His eyes moved gently to engage mine. But he said nothing. The pain of his face was terrible. It was softened and desperate with pain and on the verge of some terrible explicit emotion he would not be able to control. He was in fear of that emotion. I was not. He was feeling my pain with that great spellbinding power of his which surpassed mine. I was not feeling his pain. It did not matter to me.

" 'I understand you only too well . . .' I said. 'That passivity in me has been the core of it all, the real evil. That weakness, that refusal to compromise a fractured and stupid morality, that awful pride! For that, I let myself become the thing I am, when I knew it was wrong. For that, I let Claudia become the vampire she became, when I knew it was wrong. For that, I stood by and let her kill Lestat, when I knew that was wrong, the very thing that was her undoing. I lifted not a finger to prevent it. And Madeleine, Madeleine, I let her come to that, when I should never have made her a creature like ourselves. I knew that was wrong! Well, I tell you I am no longer that passive, weak creature that has spun evil from evil till the web is vast and thick while I remain its stultified victim. It's over! I know now what I must do. And I warn you, for whatever mercy you've shown me in digging me out of that grave tonight where I would have died: Do not seek your cell in the Théâtre des Vampires again. Do not go near it.' "

"I didn't wait to hear his answer. Perhaps he never attempted one. I don't know. I left him without looking back. If he followed me I was not conscious of it. I did not seek to know. I did not care.

"It was to the cemetery in Montmartre that I retreated. Why that place, I'm not certain, except that it wasn't far from the Boulevard des Capucines, and Montmartre was countryfied then, and dark and peaceful compared to the metropolis. Wandering among the low houses with their kitchen gardens, I killed without the slightest measure of satisfaction, and then sought out the coffin where I was to lie by day in the cemetery. I scraped the remains out of it with my bare hands and lay down to a bed of foulness, of damp, of the stench of death. I cannot say this gave me comfort. Rather, it gave me what I wanted. Closeted in that dark, smelling the earth, away from all humans and all living human forms, I gave myself over to everything that invaded and stifled my senses. And, in so doing, gave myself over to my grief.

"But that was short.

"When the cold, gray winter sun had set the next night, I was awake, feeling the tingling numbness leave me soon, as it does in winter, feeling the dark, living things that inhabited the coffin scurrying around me, fleeing my resurrection. I emerged slowly under the faint moon, savoring the coldness, the utter smoothness of the marble slab I shifted to escape. And, wandering out of the graves and out of the cemetery, I went over a plan in my mind, a plan on which I was willing to gamble my life with the powerful freedom of a being who truly does not care for that life, who has the extraordinary strength of being willing to die.

"In a kitchen garden I saw something, something that had

only been vague in my thoughts until I had my hands on it. It was a small scythe, its sharp curved blade still caked with green weeds from the last mowing. And once I'd wiped it clean and run my finger along the sharp blade, it was as if my plan came clear to me and I could move fast to my other errands: the getting of a carriage and a driver who could do my bidding for days—dazzled by the cash I gave him and the promises of more; the removing of my chest from the Hôtel Saint-Gabriel to the inside of that carriage; and the procuring of all the other things which I needed. And then there were the long hours of the night, when I could pretend to drink with my driver and talk with him and obtain his expensive cooperation in driving me at dawn from Paris to Fontainebleau. I slept within the carriage, where my delicate health required I not be disturbed under any circumstances—this privacy being so important that I was more than willing to add a generous sum to the amount I was already paying him simply for his not touching even the door handle of the carriage until I emerged from it.

"And when I was convinced he was in agreement and quite drunk enough to be oblivious to almost everything but the gathering up of the reins for the journey to Fountainebleau, we drove slowly, cautiously, into the street of the Théâtre des Vampires and waited some distance away for the sky to begin to grow light.

"The theater was shut up and locked against the coming day. I crept towards it when the air and the light told me I had at most fifteen minutes to execute my plan. I knew that, closeted far within, the vampires of the theater were in their coffins already. And that even if one late vampire lingered on the verge of going to bed, he would not hear these first preparations. Quickly I put pieces of wood against the bolted doors. Quickly I drove in the nails, which then locked these doors from the outside. A passer-by took some note of what I did but went on, believing me perhaps to be boarding up the establishment with the authority of the owner. I didn't know. I did know, however, that before I was finished I might encounter those ticket-sellers, those ushers, those men who swept up after, and might well remain inside to guard the vampires in their daily sleep.

"It was of those men I was thinking as I led the carriage up to Armand's alley and left it there, taking with me two small barrels of kerosene to Armand's door.

"The key admitted me easily as I'd hoped, and once inside the lower passage, I opened the door of his cell to find he was not there. The coffin was gone. In fact, everything was gone but the furnishings, including the dead boy's enclosed bed. Hastily I opened one barrel and, rolling the other before me towards the stairs, I hurried along, splashing the exposed beams with kerosene and flinging it on the wooden doors of the other cells. The smell of it was strong, stronger and more powerful than any sound I might have made to alert anyone. And, though I stood stark still at the stairs with the barrels and the scythe, listening, I heard nothing, nothing of those guards I presumed to be there, nothing of the vampires themselves. And clutching the handle of the scythe I ventured slowly upwards until I stood in the door of the ballroom. No one was there to see me splash the kerosene on the horsehair chairs or on the draperies, or to see me hesitate just for an instant at that doorway of the small yard where Madeleine and Claudia had been killed. Oh, how I wanted to open that door. It so tempted me that for a minute I almost forgot my plan. I almost dropped the barrels and turned the knob. But I could see the light through the cracks of the old wood of the door. And I knew I had to go on. Madeleine and Claudia were not there. They were dead. And what would I have done had I opened that doorway, had I been confronted again with those remains, that matted, dishevelled golden hair? There was no time, no purpose. I was running through dark corridors I hadn't explored before, bathing old wooden doors with the kerosene, certain that the vampires lay closeted within, rushing on cat feet into the theater itself, where a cold, gray light, seeping from the bolted front entrance, sped me on to fling a dark stain across the great velvet stage curtain, the padded chairs, the draperies of the lobby doors.

"And finally the barrel was empty and thrown away, and I was pulling out the crude torch I'd made, putting my match to its kerosene-drenched rags, and setting the chairs alight, the flames licking their thick silk and padding as I ran towards the stage and sent the fire rushing up that dark curtain into a cold, sucking draft.

"In seconds the theater blazed as with the light of day, and the whole frame of it seemed to creak and groan as the fire roared up the walls, licking the great proscenium arch, the plaster curlicues of the overhanging boxes. But I had no time to admire it, to savor the smell and the sound of it, the sight of the nooks and crannies coming to light in the fierce illumination that would soon consume them. I was fleeing to the lower floor again, thrusting the torch into the horsehair couch of the ballroom, into the curtains, into anything that would burn.

"Someone thundered on the boards above—in rooms I'd never seen. And then I heard the unmistakable opening of a door. But it was too late, I told myself, gripping both the scythe and the torch. The building was alight. They would be destroyed. I ran for the stairs, a distant cry rising over the crackling and roaring of the flames, my torch scraping the kerosene-soaked rafters above me, the flames enveloping the old wood, curling against the damp ceiling. It was Santiago's cry, I was sure of it; and then, as I hit the lower floor, I saw him above, behind me, coming down the stairs, the smoke filling the stairwell around him, his eyes watering, his throat thickened with his choking, his hand out towards me as he stammered, 'You . . . you . . . damn you!' And I froze, narrowing my eyes against the smoke, feeling the water rising in them, burning in them, but never letting go of his image for an instant, the vampire using all his power now to fly at me with such speed that he would become invisible. And as the dark thing that was his clothes rushed down, I swung the scythe and saw it strike his neck and felt the weight of his neck and saw him fall sideways, both hands reaching for the appalling wound. The air was full of cries, of screams, and a white face loomed above Santiago, a mask of terror. Some other vampire ran through the passage ahead of me towards that secret alleyway door. But I stood there poised, staring at Santiago, seeing him rise despite the wound. And I swung the scythe again, catching him easily. And there was no wound. Just two hands groping for a head that was no longer there.

"And the head, blood coursing from the torn neck, the eyes staring wild under the flaming rafters, the dark silky hair matted and wet with blood, fell at my feet. I struck it hard with my boot, I sent it flying along the passage. And I ran after it, the torch and the scythe thrown aside as my arms went up to protect me from the blaze of white light that flooded the stairs to the alley.

"The rain descended in shimmering needles into my eyes, eyes that squinted to see the dark outline of the carriage flicker against the sky. The slumped driver straightened at my hoarse command, his clumsy hand going instinctively for the whip, and the carriage lurched as I pulled open the door, the horses driving forward fast as I grappled with the lid of the chest, my body thrown roughly to one side, my burnt hands slipping down into the cold protecting silk, the lid coming down into concealing darkness.

"The pace of the horses increased driving away from the corner of the burning building. Yet I could still smell the smoke; it choked me; it burnt my eyes and my lungs, even as my hands were burnt and my forehead was burnt from the first diffused light of the sun.

"But we were driving on, away from the smoke and the cries. We were leaving Paris. I had done it. The Théâtre des Vampires was burning to the ground.

"And as I felt my head fall back, I saw Claudia and Madeleine again in one another's arms in that grim yard, and I said to them softly, bending down to the soft heads of hair that glistened in the candlelight, 'I couldn't take you away. I couldn't take you. But they will lie ruined and dead all around you. If the fire doesn't consume them, it will be the sun. If they are not burnt out, then it will be the people who will come to fight the fire who will find them and expose them to the light of day. But

I promise you, they will all die as you have died, everyone who was closeted there this dawn will die. And they are the only deaths I have caused in my long life which are both exquisite and good.' "

TWO NIGHTS LATER I returned. I had to see that rain-flooded cellar where every brick was scorched, crumbling, where a few skeletal rafters jabbed at the sky like stakes. Those monstrous murals that once enclosed the ballroom were blasted fragments in the rubble, a painted face here, a patch of angel's wing there, the only identifiable things that remained.

"With the evening newspapers, I pushed my way to the back of a crowded little theater café across the street; and there, under the cover of the dim gas lamps and thick cigar smoke, I read the accounts of the holocaust. Few bodies were found in the burnt-out theater, but clothing and costumes had been scattered everywhere, as though the famous vampire mummers had in fact vacated the theater in haste long before the fire. In other words, only the younger vampires had left their bones; the ancient ones had suffered total obliteration. No mention of an eye-witness or a surviving victim. How could there have been?

"Yet something bothered me considerably. I did not fear any vampires who had escaped. I had no desire to hunt them out if they had. That most of the crew had died I was certain. But why had there been no human guards? I was certain Santiago had mentioned guards, and I'd supposed them to be the ushers and doormen who staffed the theater before the performance. And I had even been prepared to encounter them with my scythe. But they had not been there. It was strange. And my mind was not entirely comfortable with the strangeness.

"But, finally, when I put the papers aside and sat thinking

these things over, the strangeness of it didn't matter. What mattered was that I was more utterly alone in the world than I had ever been in all my life. That Claudia was gone beyond reprieve. And I had less reason to live than I'd ever had, and less desire.

"And yet my sorrow did not overwhelm me, did not actually visit me, did not make of me the wracked and desperate creature I might have expected to become. Perhaps it was not possible to sustain the torment I'd experienced when I saw Claudia's burnt remains. Perhaps it was not possible to know that and exist over any period of time. I wondered vaguely, as the hours passed, as the smoke of the café grew thicker and the faded curtain of the little lamplit stage rose and fell, and robust women sang there, the light glittering on their paste jewels, their rich, soft voices often plaintive, exquisitely sad—I wondered vaguely what it would be to feel this loss, this outrage, and be justified in it, be deserving of sympathy, of solace. I would not have told my woe to a living creature. My own tears meant nothing to me.

"Where to go then, if not to die? It was strange how the answer came to me. Strange how I wandered out of the café then, circling the ruined theater, wandering finally towards the broad Avenue Napoléon and following it towards the palace of the Louvre. It was as if that place called to me, and yet I had never been inside its walls. I'd passed its long façade a thousand times, wishing that I could live as a mortal man for one day to move through those many rooms and see those many magnificent paintings. I was bent on it now, possessed only of some vague notion that in works of art I could find some solace while bringing nothing of death to what was inanimate and yet magnificently possessed of the spirit of life itself.

"Somewhere along the Avenue Napoléon, I heard the step behind me which I knew to be Armand's. He was signalling, letting me know that he was near. Yet I did nothing other than slow my pace and let him fall into step with me, and for a long while we walked, saying nothing. I dared not look at him. Of course, I'd been thinking of him all the while, and how if we were men and Claudia had been my love I might have fallen helpless in his arms finally, the need to share some common grief so strong, so consuming. The dam threatened to break now; and yet it did not break. I was numbed and I walked as one numbed.

" 'You know what I've done,' I said finally. We had turned off the avenue and I could see ahead of me the long row of double columns on the façade of the Royal Museum. 'You removed your coffin as I warned you. . . .'

" 'Yes,' he answered. There was a sudden, unmistakable comfort in the sound of his voice. It weakened me. But I was simply too remote from pain, too tired.

" 'And yet you are here with me now. Do you mean to avenge them?'

" 'No,' he said.

" 'They were your fellows, you were their leader,' I said. 'Yet you didn't warn them I was out for them, as I warned you?'

" 'No,' he said.

" 'But surely you despise me for it. Surely you respect some rule, some allegiance to your own kind.'

" 'No,' he said softly.

"It was amazing to me how logical his response was, even though I couldn't explain it or understand it.

"And something came clear to me out of the remote regions of my own relentless considerations. 'There were guards; there were those ushers who slept in the theater. Why weren't they there when I entered? Why weren't they there to protect the sleeping vampires?'

" 'Because they were in my employ and I discharged them. I sent them away,' Armand said.

"I stopped. He showed no concern at my facing him, and as soon as our eyes met I wished the world were not one black empty ruin of ashes and death. I wished it were fresh and beautiful, and that we were both living and had love to give each other. 'You did this, knowing what I planned to do?'

" 'Yes,' he said.

" 'But you were their leader! They trusted you. They believed in you. They lived with you!' I said. 'I don't understand you . . . why . . . ?'

" 'Think of any answer you like,' he said calmly and sensitively, as if he didn't wish to bruise me with any accusation or disdain, but wanted me merely to consider this literally. 'I can think of many. Think of the one you need and believe it. It's as likely as any other. I shall give you the real reason for what I did, which is the least true: I was leaving Paris. The theater belonged to me. So I discharged them.'

" 'But with what you knew . . .'

" 'I told you, it was the actual reason and it was the least true,' he said patiently.

" 'Would you destroy me as easily as you let them be destroyed?' I demanded.

" 'Why should I?' he asked.

" 'My God,' I whispered.

" 'You're much changed,' he said. 'But in a way, you are much the same.'

"I walked on for a while and then, before the entrance to the Louvre, I stopped. At first it seemed to me that its many windows were dark and silver with the moonlight and the thin rain. But then I thought I saw a faint light moving within, as though a guard walked among the treasures. I envied him completely. And I fixed my thoughts on him obdurately, that guard, calculating how a vampire might get to him, how take his life and his lantern and his keys. The plan was confusion. I was incapable of plans. I had made only one real plan in my life, and it was finished.

"And then finally I surrendered. I turned to Armand again and let my eyes penetrate his eyes, and let him draw close to me as if he meant to make me his victim, and I bowed my head and felt his firm arm around my shoulder. And, remembering suddenly and keenly Claudia's words, what were very nearly her last words—that admission that she knew that I could love Armand because I had been able to love even her—those words struck me as rich and ironical, more filled with meaning than she could have guessed.

" 'Yes,' I said softly to him, 'that is the crowning evil, that we can even go so far as to love each other, you and I. And who else would show us a particle of love, a particle of compassion or mercy? Who else, knowing us as we know each other, could do anything but destroy us? Yet we can love each other.'

"And for a long moment, he stood there looking at me, drawing nearer, his head gradually inclining to one side, his lips parted as if he meant to speak. But then he only smiled and shook his head gently to confess he didn't understand.

"But I wasn't thinking of him anymore. I had one of those rare moments when it seemed I thought of nothing. My mind had no shape. I saw that the rain had stopped. I saw that the air was clear and cold. That the street was luminous. And I wanted to enter the Louvre. I formed words to tell Armand this, to ask him if he might help me do what was necessary to have the Louvre till dawn.

"He thought it a very simple request. He said only he wondered why I had waited so long."

WE LEFT PARIS very soon after that. I told Armand that I wanted to return to the Mediterranean—not to Greece, as I had so long dreamed. I wanted to go to Egypt. I wanted to see the desert there and, more importantly, I wanted to see the pyramids and the graves of the kings. I wanted to make contact with those grave-thieves who know more of the graves than do scholars, and I wanted to go down into the graves yet unopened and see the kings as they were buried, see those furnishings and works of art stored with them, and the paintings on their walls. Armand was more than willing. And we took leave of Paris early one evening by carriage without the slightest hint of ceremony.

"I had done one thing which I should note. I had gone back

to my rooms in the Hôtel Saint-Gabriel. It was my purpose to take up some things of Claudia and Madeleine and put them into coffins and have graves prepared for them in the cemetery of Montmartre. I did not do this. I stayed a short while in the rooms, where all was neat and put right by the staff, so that it seemed Madeleine and Claudia might return at any time. Madeleine's embroidery ring lay with her bundles of thread on a chair-side table. I looked at that and at everything else, and my task seemed meaningless. So I left.

"But something had occurred to me there; or, rather, something I had already been aware of merely became clearer. I had gone to the Louvre that night to lay down my soul, to find some transcendent pleasure that would obliterate pain and make me utterly forget even myself. I'd been upheld in this. As I stood on the sidewalk before the doors of the hotel waiting for the carriage that would take me to meet Armand, I saw the people who walked there—the restless boulevard crowd of well-dressed ladies and gentlemen, the hawkers of papers, the carriers of luggage, the drivers of carriages—all these in a new light. Before, all art had held for me the promise of a deeper understanding of the human heart. Now the human heart meant nothing. I did not denigrate it. I simply forgot it. The magnificent paintings of the Louvre were not for me intimately connected with the hands that had painted them. They were cut loose and dead like children turned to stone. Like Claudia, severed from her mother, preserved for decades in pearl and hammered gold. Like Madeleine's dolls. And of course, like Claudia and Madeleine and myself, they could all be reduced to ashes."

PART IV

AND THAT IS THE END of the story, really.

"Of course, I know you wonder what happened to us afterwards. What became of Armand? Where did I go? What did I do? But I tell you nothing really happened. Nothing that wasn't merely inevitable. And my journey through the Louvre that last night I've described to you, that was merely prophetic.

"I never changed after that. I sought for nothing in the one great source of change which is humanity. And even in my love and absorption with the beauty of the world, I sought to learn nothing that could be given back to humanity. I drank of the beauty of the world as a vampire drinks. I was satisfied. I was filled to the brim. But I was dead. And I was changeless. The story ended in Paris, as I've said.

"For a long time I thought that Claudia's death had been the cause of the end of things. That if I had seen Madeleine and Claudia leave Paris safely, things might have been different with me and Armand. I might have loved again and desired again, and sought some semblance of mortal life which would have been rich and varied, though unnatural. But now I have come to see that was false. Even if Claudia had not died, even if I had not despised Armand for letting her die, it would have all turned out the same. Coming slowly to know his evil, or being catapulted into it . . . it was all the same. I wanted none of it finally. And, deserving nothing better, I closed up like a spider in the flame of a match. And even Armand who was my constant companion, and my only companion, existed at a great distance from me, beyond that veil which separated me from all living things, a veil which was a form of shroud.

"But I know you are eager to hear what became of Armand. And the night is almost ended. I want to tell you this because it is very important. The story is incomplete without it.

"We travelled the world after we left Paris, as I've told you; first Egypt, then Greece, then Italy, Asia Minor—wherever I chose to lead us, really, and wherever my pursuit of art led me. Time ceased to exist on any meaningful basis during these years, and I was often absorbed in very simple things—a painting in a museum, a cathedral window, one single beautiful statue—for long periods of time.

"But all during these years I had a vague but persistent desire to return to New Orleans. I never forgot New Orleans. And when we were in tropical places and places of those flowers and trees that grow in Louisiana, I would think of it acutely and I would feel for my home the only glimmer of desire I felt for anything outside my endless pursuit of art. And, from time to time, Armand would ask me to take him there. And I, being aware in a gentlemanly manner that I did little to please him and often went for long periods without really speaking to him or seeking him out, wanted to do this because he asked me. It seemed his asking caused me to forget some vague fear that I might feel pain in New Orleans, that I might experience again the pale shadow of my former unhappiness and longing. But I put it off. Perhaps the fear was stronger than I knew. We came to America and lived in New York for a long time. I continued to put it off. Then, finally, Armand urged me in another way. He told me something he'd concealed from me since the time we were in Paris.

"Lestat had not died in the Théâtre des Vampires. I had believed him to be dead, and when I asked Armand about those vampires, he told me they all had perished. But he told me now that this wasn't so. Lestat had left the theater the night I had run away from Armand and sought out the cemetery in Montmartre. Two vampires who had been made with Lestat by the same master had assisted him in booking passage to New Orleans.

"I cannot convey to you the feeling that came over me when I heard this. Of course, Armand told me he had protected me from this knowledge, hoping that I would not undertake a long journey merely for revenge, a journey that would have caused me pain and grief at the time. But I didn't really care. I hadn't thought of Lestat at all the night I'd torched the theater. I'd thought of Santiago and Celeste and the others who had destroyed Claudia. Lestat, in fact, had aroused in me feelings which I hadn't wished to confide in anyone, feelings I'd wished to forget, despite Claudia's death. Hatred had not been one of them.

"But when I heard this now from Armand it was as if the veil that protected me were thin and transparent, and though it still hung between me and the world of feeling, I perceived through it Lestat, and that I wanted to see him again. And with that spurring me on, we returned to New Orleans.

"It was late spring of this year. And as soon as I emerged from the railway station, I knew that I had indeed come home. It was as if the very air were perfumed and peculiar there, and I felt an extraordinary ease walking on those warm, flat pavements, under those familiar oaks, and listening to the ceaseless vibrant living sounds of the night.

"Of course, New Orleans was changed. But far from lamenting those changes, I was grateful for what seemed still the same. I could find in the uptown Garden District, which had been in my time the Faubourg Ste.-Marie, one of the stately old mansions that dated back to those times, so removed from the quiet brick street that, walking out in the moonlight under its magnolia trees, I knew the same sweetness and peace I'd known in the old days; not only in the dark, narrow streets of the Vieux Carré but in the wilderness of Pointe du Lac. There were the honeysuckle and the roses, and the glimpse of Corinthian columns against the stars; and outside the gate were dreamy streets, other mansions . . . it was a citadel of grace.

"In the Rue Royale, where I took Armand past tourists and antique shops and the bright-lit entrances of fashionable restaurants, I was astonished to discover the town house where Lestat and Claudia and I had made our home, the façade little changed by fresh plaster and whatever repairs had been done within. Its two French windows still opened onto the small balconies over the shop below, and I could see in the soft brilliance of the electric chandeliers an elegant wallpaper that would not have been unfamiliar in those days before the war. I had a strong sense of Lestat there, more of a sense of him than of Claudia, and I felt certain, though he was nowhere near this town house, that I'd find him in New Orleans.

"And I felt something else; it was a sadness that came over me then, after Armand had gone on his way. But this sadness was not painful, nor was it passionate. It was something rich, however, and almost sweet, like the fragrance of the jasmine and the roses that crowded the old courtyard garden which I saw through the iron gates. And this sadness gave a subtle satisfaction and held me a long time in that spot; and it held me to the city; and it didn't really leave me that night when I went away.

"I wonder now what might have come of this sadness, what it might have engendered in me that could have become stronger than itself. But I jump ahead of my story.

"Because shortly after that I saw a vampire in New Orleans, a sleek white-faced young man walking alone on the broad sidewalks of St. Charles Avenue in the early hours before dawn. And I was at once convinced that if Lestat still lived here that vampire might know him and might even lead me to him. Of course, the vampire didn't see me. I had long ago learned to spot my own kind in large cities without their having a chance to see me. Armand, in his brief visits with vampires in London and Rome, had learned that the burning of the Théâtre des Vampires was known throughout the world, and that both of us were considered outcasts. Battles over this meant nothing to me, and I have avoided them to this day. But I began to watch for this vampire in New Orleans and to follow him, though often he led me merely to theaters or other pastimes in which I had no interest. But one night, finally, things changed.

"It was a very warm evening, and I could tell as soon as I saw him on St. Charles that he had someplace to go. He was not only walking fast, but he seemed a little distressed. And when he turned off St. Charles finally on a narrow street which became at once shabby and dark, I felt sure he was headed for something that would interest me.

"But then he entered one side of a small wooden duplex and brought death to a woman there. This he did very fast, without a trace of pleasure; and after he was finished, he gathered her child up from the bassinet, wrapped it gently in a blue wool blanket, and came out again into the street.

"Only a block or two after that, he stopped before a vine-covered iron fence that enclosed a large overgrown yard. I could see an old house beyond the trees, dark, the paint peeling, the ornate iron railings of its long upper and lower galleries caked with orange rust. It seemed a doomed house, stranded here among the numerous small wooden houses, its high empty windows looking out on what must have been a dismal clutter of low roofs, a corner grocery, and a small adjacent bar. But the broad, dark grounds protected the house somewhat from these things, and I had to move along the fence quite a few feet before I finally spotted a faint glimmer in one of the lower windows through the thick branches of the trees. The vampire had gone through the gate. I could hear the baby wailing, and then nothing. And I followed, easily mounting the old fence and dropping down into the garden and coming up quietly onto the long front porch.

"It was an amazing sight I saw when I crept up to one of the long, floor-length windows. For despite the heat of this breezeless evening when the gallery, even with its warped and broken boards, might have been the only tolerable place for human or vampire, a fire blazed in the grate of the parlor and all its windows were shut, and the young vampire sat by that fire talking to another vampire who hovered very near it, his slippered feet right up against the hot grate, his trembling fingers pulling over and over at the lapels of his shabby blue robe. And, though a frayed electric cord dangled from a plaster wreath of roses in the ceiling, only an oil lamp added its dim light to the fire, an oil lamp which stood by the wailing child on a nearby table.

"My eyes widened as I studied this stooped and shivering vampire whose rich blond hair hung down in loose waves covering his face. I longed to wipe away the dust on the window glass which would not let me be certain of what I suspected. 'You all leave me!' he whined now in a thin, high-pitched voice.

" 'You can't keep us with you!' said the stiff young vampire sharply. He sat with his legs crossed, his arms folded on his narrow chest, his eyes looking around the dusty, empty room disdainfully. 'Oh, hush!' he said to the baby, who let out a sharp cry. 'Stop it, stop it.'

" 'The wood, the wood,' said the blond vampire feebly, and, as he motioned to the other to hand him the fuel by his chair, I saw clearly, unmistakably, the profile of Lestat, that smooth skin now devoid of even the faintest trace of his old scars.

" 'If you'd just go out,' said the other angrily, heaving the chunk of wood into the blaze. 'If you'd just hunt something other than these miserable animals. . . .' And he looked about himself in disgust. I saw then, in the shadows, the small furry bodies of several cats, lying helter-skelter in the dust. A most remarkable thing, because a vampire can no more endure to be near his dead victims than any mammal can remain near any place where he has left his waste. 'Do you know that it's summer?' demanded the young one. Lestat merely rubbed his hands. The baby's howling died off, yet the young vampire added, 'Get on with it, take it so you'll be warm.'

" 'You might have brought me something else!' said Lestat bitterly. And, as he looked at the baby, I saw his eyes squinting against the dull light of the smoky lamp. I felt a shock of recognition at those eyes, even at the expression beneath the shadow of the deep wave of his yellow hair. And yet to hear that whining voice, to see that bent and quivering back! Almost without thinking I rapped hard on the glass. The young vampire was up at once affecting a hard, vicious expression; but I merely motioned for him to turn the latch. And Lestat, clutching his bathrobe to his throat, rose from the chair.

" 'It's Louis! Louis!' he said. 'Let him in.' And he gestured frantically, like an invalid, for the young 'nurse' to obey.

"As soon as the window opened I breathed the stench of the room and its sweltering heat. The swarming of the insects on the rotted animals scratched at my senses so that I recoiled despite myself, despite Lestat's desperate pleas for me to come to him. There, in the far corner, was the coffin where he slept, the lacquer peeling from the wood, half covered with piles of yellow newspapers. And bones lay in the corners, picked clean except for bits and tufts of fur. But Lestat had his dry hands on mine now, drawing me towards him and towards the warmth, and I could see the tears welling in his eyes; and only when his mouth was stretched in a strange smile of desperate happiness that was near to pain did I see the faint traces of the old scars. How baffling and awful it was, this smooth-faced, shimmering immortal man bent and rattled and whining like a crone.

" 'Yes, Lestat,' I said softly. 'I've come to see you.' I pushed his hand gently, slowly away and moved towards the baby, who was crying desperately now from fear as well as hunger. As soon as I lifted it up and loosened the covers, it quieted a little, and then I patted it and rocked it. Lestat was whispering to me now in quick, half-articulated words I couldn't understand, the tears streaming down his cheeks, the young vampire at the open window with a look of disgust on his face and one hand on the window latch, as if he meant at any minute to bolt.

" 'So you're Louis,' said the young vampire. This seemed to increase Lestat's inexpressible excitement, and he wiped frantically at his tears with the hem of his robe.

"A fly lit on the baby's forehead, and involuntarily I gasped as I pressed it between two fingers and dropped it dead to the floor. The child was no longer crying. It was looking up at me with extraordinary blue eyes, dark-blue eyes, its round face glistening from the heat, and a smile played on its lips, a smile that grew brighter like a flame. I had never brought death to anything so young, so innocent, and I was aware of this now as I held the child with an odd feeling of sorrow, stronger even than that feeling which had come over me in the Rue Royale. And, rocking the child gently, I pulled the young vampire's chair to the fire and sat down.

" 'Don't try to speak . . . it's all right,' I said to Lestat, who dropped down gratefully into his chair and reached out to stroke the lapels of my coat with both hands.

" 'But I'm so glad to see you,' he stammered through his tears. 'I've dreamed of your coming . . . coming . . .' he said. And then he grimaced, as if he were feeling a pain he couldn't identify, and again the fine map of scars appeared for an instant. He was looking off, his hand up to his ear, as if he meant to cover it to defend himself from some terrible sound. 'I didn't . . .' he started; and then he shook his head, his eyes clouding as he opened them wide, strained to focus them. 'I didn't mean to let them do it, Louis . . . I mean that Santiago . . . that one, you know, he didn't tell me what they planned to do.'

" 'That's all past, Lestat,' I said.

" 'Yes, yes,' he nodded vigorously. 'Past. She should never . . . why, Louis, *you know*. . . .' And he was shaking his head, his voice seeming to gain in strength, to gain a little in resonance with his effort. 'She should have never been one of us, Louis.' And he rapped his sunken chest with his fist as he said 'Us' again softly.

"She. It seemed then that she had never existed. That she had been some illogical, fantastical dream that was too precious and too personal for me ever to confide in anyone. And too long gone. I looked at him. I stared at him. And tried to think, Yes, the three of us together.

" 'Don't fear me, Lestat,' I said, as though talking to myself. 'I bring you no harm.'

" 'You've come back to me, Louis,' he whispered in that thin, high-pitched voice. 'You've come home again to me, Louis, haven't you?' And again he bit his lip and looked at me desperately.

" 'No, Lestat.' I shook my head. He was frantic for a moment, and again he commenced one gesture and then another and finally sat there with his hands over his face in a paroxysm of distress. The other vampire, who was studying me coldly, asked:

" 'Are you . . . have you come back to him?'

" 'No, of course not,' I answered. And he smirked, as if this was as he expected, that everything fell to him again, and he walked out onto the porch. I could hear him there very near, waiting.

" 'I only wanted to see you, Lestat,' I said. But Lestat didn't seem to hear me. Something else had distracted him. And he was gazing off, his eyes wide, his hands hovering near his ears. Then I heard it also. It was a siren. And as it grew louder, his eyes shut tight against it and his fingers covered his ears. And it grew louder and louder, coming up the street from downtown. 'Lestat!' I said to him, over the baby's cries, which rose now in the same terrible fear of the siren. But his agony obliterated me. His lips were drawn back from his teeth in a terrible grimace of pain. 'Lestat, it's only a siren!' I said to him stupidly. And then he came forward out of the chair and took hold of me and held tight to me, and, despite myself, I took his hand. He bent down, pressing his head against my chest and holding my hand so tight that he caused me pain. The room was filled with the flashing red light of the siren, and then it was going away.

" 'Louis, I can't bear it, I can't bear it,' he growled through his tears. 'Help me, Louis, stay with me.'

" 'But why are you afraid?' I asked. 'Don't you know what these things are?' And as I looked down at him, as I saw his yellow hair pressed against my coat, I had a vision of him from long ago, that tall, stately gentleman in the swirling black cape, with his head thrown back, his rich, flawless voice singing the lilting air of the opera from which we'd only just come, his walking stick tapping the cobblestones in time with the music, his large, sparkling eye catching the young woman who stood by, enrapt, so that a smile spread over his face as the song died on his lips; and for one moment, that one moment when his eye met hers, all evil seemed obliterated in that flush of pleasure, that passion for merely being alive.

"Was this the price of that involvement? A sensibility shocked by change, shrivelling from fear? I thought quietly of all the things I might say to him, how I might remind him that he was immortal, that nothing condemned him to this retreat save himself, and that he was surrounded with the unmistakable signs of inevitable death. But I did not say these things, and I knew that I would not.

"It seemed the silence of the room rushed back around us, like a dark sea that the siren had driven away. The flies swarmed on the festering body of a rat, and the child looked quietly up at me as though my eyes were bright baubles, and its dimpled hand closed on the finger that I poised above its tiny petal mouth.

"Lestat had risen, straightened, but only to bend over and slink into the chair. 'You won't stay with me,' he sighed. But then he looked away and seemed suddenly absorbed.

" 'I wanted to talk to you so much,' he said. 'That night I came home to the Rue Royale I only wanted to talk to you!' He shuddered violently, eyes closed, his throat seeming to contract. It was as if the blows I'd struck him then were falling now. He stared blindly ahead, his tongue moistening his lip, his voice low, almost natural. 'I went to Paris after you. . .'

" 'What was it you wanted to tell me?' I asked. 'What was it you wanted to talk about?'

"I could well remember his mad insistence in the Théâtre des Vampires. I hadn't thought of it in years. No, I had never thought of it. And I was aware that I spoke of it now with great reluctance.

"But he only smiled at me, an insipid, near apologetic smile. And shook his head. I watched his eyes fill with a soft, bleary despair.

"I felt a profound, undeniable relief.

" 'But you will stay!' he insisted.

" 'No,' I answered.

" 'And neither will I!' said that young vampire from the

darkness outside. And he stood for a second in the open window looking at us. Lestat looked up at him and then sheepishly away, and his lower lip seemed to thicken and tremble. 'Close it, close it,' he said, waving his finger at the window. Then a sob burst from him and, covering his mouth with his hand, he put his head down and cried.

"The young vampire was gone. I heard his steps moving fast on the walk, heard the heavy chink of the iron gate. And I was alone with Lestat, and he was crying. It seemed a long time before he stopped, and during all that time I merely watched him. I was thinking of all the things that had passed between us. I was remembering things which I supposed I had completely forgotten. And I was conscious then of that same overwhelming sadness which I'd felt when I saw the place in the Rue Royale where we had lived. Only, it didn't seem to me to be a sadness for Lestat, for that smart, gay vampire who used to live there then. It seemed a sadness for something else, something beyond Lestat that only included him and was part of the great awful sadness of all the things I'd ever lost or loved or known. It seemed then I was in a different place, a different time. And this different place and time was very real, and it was a room where the insects had hummed as they were humming here and the air had been close and thick with death and with the spring perfume. And I was on the verge of knowing that place and knowing with it a terrible pain, a pain so terrible that my mind veered away from it, said, No, don't take me back to that place—and suddenly it was receding, and I was with Lestat here now. Astonished, I saw my own tear fall onto the face of the child. I saw it glisten on the child's cheek, and I saw the cheek become very plump with the child's smile. It must have been seeing the light in the tears. I put my hand to my face and wiped at the tears that were in fact there and looked at them in amazement.

" 'But Louis . . .' Lestat was saying softly. 'How can you be as you are, how can you stand it?' He was looking up at me, his mouth in that same grimace, his face wet with tears. 'Tell me, Louis, help me to understand! How can you understand it all, how can you endure?' And I could see by the desperation in his eyes and the deeper tone which his voice had taken that he, too, was pushing himself towards something that for him was very painful, towards a place where he hadn't ventured in a long time. But then, even as I looked at him, his eyes appeared to become misty, confused. And he pulled the robe up tight, and shaking his head, he looked at the fire. A shudder passed through him and he moaned.

" 'I have to go now, Lestat,' I said to him. I felt weary, weary of him and weary of this sadness. And I longed again for the stillness outside, that perfect quiet to which I'd become so completely accustomed. But I realized, as I rose to my feet, that I was taking the little baby with me.

"Lestat looked up at me now with his large, agonized eyes and his smooth, ageless face. 'But you'll come back . . . you'll come to visit me . . . Louis?' he said.

"I turned away from him, hearing him calling after me, and quietly left the house. When I reached the street, I looked back and I could see him hovering at the window as if he were afraid to go out. I realized he had not gone out for a long, long time, and it occurred to me then that perhaps he would never go out again.

"I returned to the small house from which the vampire had taken the child, and left it there in its crib."

"Not very long after that I told Armand I'd seen Lestat. Perhaps it was a month, I'm not certain. Time meant little to me then, as it means little to me now. But it meant a great deal to Armand. He was amazed that I hadn't mentioned this before.

"We were walking that night uptown where the city gives way to the Audubon Park and the levee is a deserted, grassy slope that descends to a muddy beach heaped here and there with driftwood, going out to the lapping waves of the river. On the far bank were the very dim lights of industries and riverfront companies, pinpoints of green or red that flickered in the distance like stars. And the moon showed the broad, strong current moving fast between the two shores; and even the summer heat was gone here, with the cool breeze coming off the water and gently lifting the moss that hung from the twisted oak where we sat. I was picking at the grass, and tasting it, though the taste was bitter and unnatural. The gesture seemed natural. I was feeling almost that I might never leave New Orleans. But then, what are such thoughts when you can live forever? Never leave New Orleans 'again'? *Again* seemed a human word.

" 'But didn't you feel any desire for revenge?' Armand asked. He lay on the grass beside me, his weight on his elbow, his eyes fixed on me.

" 'Why?' I asked calmly. I was wishing, as I often wished, that he was not there, that I was alone. Alone with this powerful and cool river under the dim moon. 'He's met with his own perfect revenge. He's dying, dying of rigidity, of fear. His mind cannot accept this time. Nothing as serene and graceful as that vampire death you once described to me in Paris. I think he is dying as clumsily and grotesquely as humans often die in this century . . . of old age.'

" 'But you . . . what did you feel?' he insisted softly. And I was struck by the personal quality of that question, and how long it had been since either of us had spoken to the other in that way. I had a strong sense of him then, the separate being that he was, the calm and collected creature with the straight auburn hair and the large, sometimes melancholy eyes, eyes that seemed often to be seeing nothing but their own thoughts. Tonight they were lit with a dull fire that was unusual.

" 'Nothing,' I answered.

" 'Nothing one way or the other?'

"I answered no. I remembered palpably that sorrow. It was as if the sorrow hadn't left me suddenly, but had been near me all this time, hovering, saying, 'Come.' But I wouldn't tell this to Armand, wouldn't reveal this. And I had the strangest sensation of feeling his need for me to tell him this . . . this, or something . . . a need strangely akin to the need for living blood.

" 'But did he tell you anything, anything that made you feel the old hatred . . .' he murmured. And it was at this point that I became keenly aware of how distressed he was.

" 'What is it, Armand? Why do you ask this?' I said.

"But he lay back on the steep levee then, and for a long time he appeared to be looking at the stars. The stars brought back to me something far too specific, the ship that had carried Claudia and me to Europe, and those nights at sea when it seemed the stars came down to touch the waves.

" 'I thought perhaps he would tell you something about Paris . . .' Armand said.

" 'What should he say about Paris? That he didn't want Claudia to die?' I asked. Claudia again; the name sounded strange. Claudia spreading out that game of solitaire on the table that shifted with the shifting of the sea, the lantern creaking on its hook, the black porthole full of the stars. She had her head bent, her fingers poised above her ear as if about to loosen strands of her hair. And I had the most disconcerting sensation: that in my memory she would look up from that game of solitaire, and the sockets of her eyes would be empty.

" 'You could have told me anything you wanted about Paris, Armand,' I said. 'Long before now. It wouldn't have mattered.'

" 'Even that it was I who . . . ?'

"I turned to him as he lay there looking at the sky. And I saw the extraordinary pain in his face, in his eyes. It seemed his eyes were huge, too huge, and the white face that framed them too gaunt.

" 'That it was you who killed her? Who forced her out into that yard and locked her there?' I asked. I smiled. 'Don't tell me you have been feeling pain for it all these years, not you.'

"And then he closed his eyes and turned his face away, his hand resting on his chest as if I'd struck him an awful, sudden blow.

" 'You can't convince me you care about this,' I said to him coldly. And I looked out towards the water, and again that feeling came over me . . . that I wished to be alone. In a little while I knew I would get up and go off by myself. That is, if he didn't leave me first. Because I would have liked to remain there actually. It was a quiet, secluded place.

" 'You care about nothing . . .' he was saying. And then he

sat up slowly and turned to me so again I could see that dark fire in his eyes. 'I thought you would at least care about that. I thought you would feel the old passion, the old anger if you were to see him again. I thought something would quicken and come alive in you if you saw him . . . if you returned to this place.'

" 'That I would come back to life?' I said softly. And I felt the cold metallic hardness of my words as I spoke, the modulation, the control. It was as if I were cold all over, made of metal, and he were fragile suddenly; fragile, as he had been, actually, for a long time.

" 'Yes!' he cried out. 'Yes, back to life!' And then he seemed puzzled, positively confused. And a strange thing occurred. He bowed his head at that moment as if he were defeated. And something in the way that he felt that defeat, something in the way his smooth white face reflected it only for an instant, reminded me of someone else I'd seen defeated in just that way. And it was amazing to me that it took me such a long moment to see Claudia's face in that attitude; Claudia, as she stood by the bed in the room at the Hôtel Saint-Gabriel pleading with me to transform Madeleine into one of us. That same helpless look, that defeat which seemed to be so heartfelt that everything beyond it was forgotten. And then he, like Claudia, seemed to rally, to pull on some reserve of strength. But he said softly to the air, 'I am dying!'

"And I, watching him, hearing him, the only creature under God who heard him, knowing completely that it was true, said nothing.

"A long sigh escaped his lips. His head was bowed. His right hand lay limp beside him in the grass. 'Hatred . . . that is passion,' he said. 'Revenge, that is passion. . . .'

" 'Not from me . . .' I murmured softly. 'Not now.'

"And then his eyes fixed on me and his face seemed very calm. 'I used to believe you would get over it—that when the pain of all of it left you, you would grow warm again and filled with love, and filled with that wild and insatiable curiosity with which you first came to me, that inveterate conscience, and that hunger for knowledge that brought you all the way to Paris to my cell. I thought it was a part of you that couldn't die. And I thought that when the pain was gone you would forgive me for what part I played in her death. She never loved you, you know. Not in the way that I loved you, and the way that you loved us both. I knew this! I understood it! And I believed I would gather you to me and hold you. And time would open to us, and we would be the teachers of one another. All the things that gave you happiness would give me happiness; and I would be the protector of your pain. My power would be your power. My strength the same. But you're dead inside to me, you're cold and beyond my reach! It is as if I'm not here, beside you. And, not being here with you, I have the dreadful feeling that I don't exist at all. And you are as cold and distant from me as those strange modern paintings of lines and hard forms that I cannot love or comprehend, as alien as those hard mechanical sculptures of this age which have no human form. I shudder when I'm near you. I look into your eyes and my reflection isn't there. . . .'

" 'What you asked was impossible!' I said quickly. 'Don't you see? What I asked was impossible, too, from the start.'

"He protested, the negation barely forming on his lips, his hand rising as if to thrust it away.

" 'I wanted love and goodness in this which is living death,' I said. 'It was impossible from the beginning, because you cannot have love and goodness when you do what you know to be evil, what you know to be wrong. You can only have the desperate confusion and longing and the chasing of phantom goodness in its human form. I knew the real answer to my quest before I ever reached Paris. I knew it when I first took a human life to feed my craving. It was my death. And yet I would not accept it, could not accept it, because like all creatures I don't wish to die! And so I sought for other vampires, for God, for the devil, for a hundred things under a hundred names. And it was all the same, all evil. And all wrong. Because no one could in any guise convince me of what I myself knew to be true, that I was damned in my own mind and soul. And when I came to Paris I thought you were powerful and beautiful and without regret, and I wanted that desperately. But you were a destroyer just as I was a destroyer, more ruthless and cunning even than I. You showed me the only thing that I could really hope to become, what depth of evil, what degree of coldness I would have to attain to end my pain. And I accepted that. And so that passion, that love you saw in me, was extinguished. And you see now simply a mirror of yourself.'

"A very long time passed before he spoke. He'd risen to his feet, and he stood with his back to me looking down the river, head bowed as before, his hands at his sides. I was looking at the river also. I was thinking quietly, There is nothing more I can say, nothing more I can do.

" 'Louis,' he said now, lifting his head, his voice very thick and unlike itself.

" 'Yes, Armand,' I said.

" 'Is there anything else you want of me, anything else you require?'

" 'No,' I said. 'What do you mean?'

"He didn't answer this. He began to slowly walk away. I think at first I thought he only meant to walk a few paces, perhaps to wander by himself along the muddy beach below. And by the time I realized that he was leaving me, he was a mere speck down there against the occasional flickering in the water under the moon. I never saw him again.

"Of course, it was several nights later before I realized he was gone. His coffin remained. But he did not return to it. And it was several months before I had that coffin taken to the St. Louis cemetery and put into the crypt beside my own. The grave, long neglected because my family was gone, received the only thing he'd left behind. But then I began to be uncomfortable with that. I thought of it on waking, and again at dawn right before I closed my eyes. And I went downtown one night and took the coffin out, and broke it into pieces and left it in the narrow aisle of the cemetery in the tall grass.

"That vampire who was Lestat's latest child accosted me one evening not long after. He begged me to tell him all I knew of the world, to become his companion and his teacher. I remember telling him that what I chiefly knew was that I'd destroy him if I ever saw him again. 'You see, someone must die every night that I walk, until I've the courage to end it,' I told him. 'And you're an admirable choice for that victim, a killer as evil as myself.'

"And I left New Orleans the next night because the sorrow wasn't leaving me. And I didn't want to think of that old house where Lestat was dying. Or that sharp, modern vampire who'd fled me. Or of Armand.

"I wanted to be where there was nothing familiar to me. And nothing mattered.

"And that's the end of it. There's nothing else."

THE BOY SAT MUTE, staring at the vampire. And the vampire sat collected, his hands folded on the table, his narrow, red-rimmed eyes fixed on the turning tapes. His face was so gaunt now that the veins of his temples showed as if carved out of stone. And he sat so still that only his green eyes evinced life, and that life was a dull fascination with the turning of the tapes.

Then the boy drew back and ran the fingers of his right hand loosely through his hair. "No," he said with a short intake of breath. Then he said it again louder, "No!"

The vampire didn't appear to hear him. His eyes moved away from the tapes towards the window, towards the dark, gray sky.

"It didn't have to end like that!" said the boy, leaning forward.

The vampire, who continued to look at the sky, uttered a short, dry laugh.

"All the things you felt in Paris!" said the boy, his voice increasing in volume. "The love of Claudia, the feeling, even the feeling for Lestat! It didn't have to end, not in this, not in despair! Because that's what it is, isn't it? Despair!"

"Stop," said the vampire abruptly, lifting his right hand. His eyes shifted almost mechanically to the boy's face. "I tell you and I have told you, that it could not have ended any other way."

"I don't accept it," said the boy, and he folded his arms across his chest, shaking his head emphatically. "I can't!" And the emotion seemed to build in him, so that without meaning to, he scraped his chair back on the bare boards and rose to pace the floor. But then, when he turned and looked at the vampire's face again, the words he was about to speak died in his throat. The vampire was merely staring at him, and his face had that long drawn expression of both outrage and bitter amusement.

"Don't you see how you made it sound? It was an adventure like I'll never know in my whole life! You talk about passion, you talk about longing! You talk about things that millions of us won't ever taste or come to understand. And then you tell me it ends like that. I tell you . . ." And he stood over the vampire now, his hands outstretched before him. "If you were to give me that power! The power to see and feel and live forever!"

The vampire's eyes slowly began to widen, his lips parting. "What!" he demanded softly. "*What!*"

"Give it to me!" said the boy, his right hand tightening in a fist, the fist pounding his chest. "Make me a vampire now!" he said as the vampire stared aghast.

What happened then was swift and confused, but it ended abruptly with the vampire on his feet holding the boy by the shoulders, the boy's moist face contorted with fear, the vampire glaring at him in rage. "This is what you want?" he whispered, his pale lips manifesting only the barest trace of movement. "This . . . after all I've told you . . . is what you ask for?"

A small cry escaped the boy's lips, and he began to tremble all over, the sweat breaking out on his forehead and on the skin above his upper lip. His hand reached gingerly for the vampire's arm. "You don't know what human life is like!" he said, on the edge of breaking into tears. "You've forgotten. You don't even understand the meaning of your own story, what it means to a human being like me." And then a choked sob interrupted his words, and his fingers clung to the vampire's arm.

"God," the vampire uttered and, turning away from him, almost pushed the boy off-balance against the wall. He stood with his back to the boy, staring at the gray window.

"I beg you . . . give it all one more chance. One more chance in me!" said the boy.

The vampire turned to him, his face as twisted with anger as before. And then, gradually, it began to become smooth. The lids came down slowly over his eyes and his lips lengthened in a smile. He looked again at the boy. "I've failed," he sighed, smiling still. "I have completely failed. . . ."

"No . . ." the boy protested.

"Don't say any more," said the vampire emphatically. "I have but one chance left. Do you see the reels? They still turn. I have but one way to show you the meaning of what I've said." And then he reached out for the boy so fast that the boy found himself grasping for something, pushing against something that was not there, so his hand was outstretched still when the vampire had him pressed to his chest, the boy's neck bent beneath his lips. "Do you see?" whispered the vampire, and the long, silky lips drew up over his teeth and two long fangs came down into the boy's flesh. The boy stuttered, a low guttural sound coming out of his throat, his hand struggling to close on something, his eyes widening only to become dull and gray as the vampire drank. And the vampire meantime looked as tranquil as someone in sleep. His narrow chest heaved so subtly with his sigh that he seemed to be rising slowly from the floor and then settling again with that same somnambulistic grace. There was a whine coming from the boy, and when the vampire let him go he held him out with both hands and looked at the damp white face, the limp hands, the eyes half closed.

The boy was moaning, his lower lip loose and trembling as if in nausea. He moaned again louder, and his head fell back and his eyes rolled up into his head. The vampire set him down gently in the chair. The boy was struggling to speak, and the tears which sprang now to his eyes seemed to come as much from that effort to speak as from anything else. His head fell forward, heavily, drunkenly, and his hand rested on the table. The vampire stood looking down at him, and his white skin became a soft luminous pink. It was as if a pink light were shining on him and his entire being seemed to give back that light. The flesh of his lips was dark, almost rose in color, and the veins of his temples and his hands were mere traces on his skin, and his face was youthful and smooth.

"Will I . . . die?" the boy whispered as he looked up slowly, his mouth wet and slack. "Will I die?" he groaned, his lip trembling.

"I don't know," the vampire said, and he smiled.

The boy seemed on the verge of saying something more, but the hand that rested on the table slid forward on the boards, and his head lay down beside it as he lost consciousness.

When next he opened his eyes, the boy saw the sun. It filled the dirty, undressed window and was hot on the side of his face and his hand. For a moment, he lay there, his face against the table and then with a great effort, he straightened, took a long deep breath and closing his eyes, pressed his hand to that place where the vampire had drawn blood. When his other hand accidentally touched a band of metal on the top of the tape recorder, he let out a sudden cry because the metal was hot.

Then he rose, moving clumsily, almost falling, until he rested both his hands on the white wash basin. Quickly he turned on the tap, splashed his face with cold water, and wiped it with a soiled towel that hung there on a nail. He was breathing regularly now and he stood still, looking into the mirror without any support. Then he looked at his watch. It was as if the watch shocked him, brought him more to life than the sun or the water. And he made a quick search of the room, of the hallway, and, finding nothing and no one, he settled again into the chair. Then, drawing a small white pad out of his pocket, and a pen, he set these on the table and touched the button of the recorder. The tape spun fast backwards until he shut it off. When he heard the vampire's voice, he leaned forward, listening very carefully, then hit the button again for another place, and, hearing that, still another. But then at last his face brightened, as the reels turned and the voice spoke in an even modulated tone: "It was a very warm evening, and I could tell as soon as I saw him on St. Charles that he had someplace to go . . ."

And quickly the boy noted:

"Lestat . . . off St. Charles Avenue. Old house crumbling . . . shabby neighborhood. Look for rusted railings."

And then, stuffing the notebook quickly in his pocket, he gathered the tapes into his briefcase, along with the small recorder, and hurried down the long hallway and down the stairs to the street, where in front of the corner bar his car was parked.

THE VAMPIRE LESTAT

Downtown Saturday Night in the Twentieth Century

1984

I AM the vampire Lestat. I'm immortal. More or less. The light of the sun, the sustained heat of an intense fire—these things might destroy me. But then again, they might not.

I'm six feet tall, which was fairly impressive in the 1780s when I was a young mortal man. It's not bad now. I have thick blond hair, not quite shoulder length, and rather curly, which appears white under fluorescent light. My eyes are gray, but they absorb the colors blue or violet easily from surfaces around them. And I have a fairly short narrow nose, and a mouth that is well shaped but just a little too big for my face. It can look very mean, or extremely generous, my mouth. It always looks sensual. But emotions and attitudes are always reflected in my entire expression. I have a continuously animated face.

My vampire nature reveals itself in extremely white and highly reflective skin that has to be powdered down for cameras of any kind.

And if I'm starved for blood I look like a perfect horror—skin shrunken, veins like ropes over the contours of my bones. But I don't let that happen now. And the only consistent indication that I am not human is my fingernails. It's the same with all vampires. Our fingernails look like glass. And some people notice that when they don't notice anything else.

Right now I am what America calls a Rock Superstar. My first album has sold 4 million copies. I'm going to San Francisco for the first spot on a nationwide concert tour that will take my band from coast to coast. MTV, the rock music cable channel, has been playing my video clips night and day for two weeks. They're also being shown in England on "Top of the Pops" and on the Continent, probably in some parts of Asia, and in Japan. Video cassettes of the whole series of clips are selling worldwide.

I am also the author of an autobiography which was published last week.

Regarding my English—the language I use in my autobiography—I first learned it from the flatboatmen who came down the Mississippi to New Orleans about two hundred years ago. I learned more after that from the English language writers—everybody from Shakespeare through Mark

Twain to H. Rider Haggard, whom I read as the decades passed. The final infusion I received from the detective stories of the early twentieth century in the *Black Mask* magazine. The adventures of Sam Spade by Dashiell Hammett in *Black Mask* were the last stories I read before I went literally and figuratively underground.

That was in New Orleans in 1929.

When I write I drift into a vocabulary that would have been natural to me in the eighteenth century, into phrases shaped by the authors I've read. But in spite of my French accent, I talk like a cross between a flatboatman and detective Sam Spade, actually. So I hope you'll bear with me when my style is inconsistent. When I blow the atmosphere of an eighteenth-century scene to smithereens now and then.

I came out into the twentieth century last year.

What brought me up were two things.

First—the information I was receiving from amplified voices that had begun their cacophony in the air around the time I lay down to sleep.

I'm referring here to the voices of radios, of course, and phonographs and later television machines. I heard the radios in the cars that passed in the streets of the old Garden District near the place where I lay. I heard the phonographs and TVs from the houses that surrounded mine.

Now, when a vampire goes underground as we call it—when he ceases to drink blood and he just lies in the earth—he soon becomes too weak to resurrect himself, and what follows is a dream state.

In that state, I absorbed the voices sluggishly, surrounding them with my own responsive images as a mortal does in sleep. But at some point during the past fifty-five years I began to "remember" what I was hearing, to follow the entertainment programs, to listen to the news broadcasts, the lyrics and rhythms of the popular songs.

And very gradually, I began to understand the caliber of the changes that the world had undergone. I began listening for specific pieces of information about wars or inventions, certain new patterns of speech.

Then a self-consciousness developed in me. I realized I was no longer dreaming. I was thinking about what I heard. I was wide awake. I was lying in the ground and I was starved for living blood. I started to believe that maybe all the old wounds I'd sustained had been healed by now. Maybe my strength had come back. Maybe my strength had actually increased as it would have done with time if I'd never been hurt. I wanted to find out.

I started to think incessantly of drinking human blood.

The second thing that brought me back—the decisive thing really—was the sudden presence near me of a band of young rock singers who called themselves Satan's Night Out.

They moved into a house on Sixth Street—less than a block away from where I slumbered under my own house on Prytania near the Lafayette Cemetery—and they started to rehearse their rock music in the attic some time in 1984.

I could hear their whining electric guitars, their frantic singing. It was as good as the radio and stereo songs I heard, and it was more melodic than most. There was a romance to it in spite of its pounding drums. The electric piano sounded like a harpsichord.

I caught images from the thoughts of the musicians that told me what they looked like, what they saw when they looked at each other and into mirrors. They were slender, sinewy, and altogether lovely young mortals —beguilingly androgynous and even a little savage in their dress and movements—two male and one female.

They drowned out most of the other amplified voices around me when they were playing. But that was perfectly all right.

I wanted to rise and join the rock band called Satan's Night Out. I wanted to sing and to dance.

But I can't say that in the very beginning there was great thought behind my wish. It was rather a ruling impulse, strong enough to bring me up from the earth.

I was enchanted by the world of rock music—the way the singers could scream of good and evil, proclaim themselves angels or devils, and mortals would stand up and cheer. Sometimes they seemed the pure embodiment of madness. And yet it was technologically dazzling, the intricacy of their performance. It was barbaric and cerebral in a way that I don't think the world of ages past had ever seen.

Of course it was metaphor, the raving. None of them believed in angels or devils, no matter how well they assumed their parts. And the players of the old Italian commedia had been as shocking, as inventive, as lewd.

Yet it was entirely new, the extremes to which they took it, the brutality and the defiance—and the way that they were embraced by the world from the very rich to the very poor.

Also there was something vampiric about rock music. It must have sounded supernatural even to those who don't believe in the supernatural. I mean the way the electricity could stretch a single note forever; the way harmony could be layered upon harmony until you felt yourself dissolving in the sound. So eloquent of dread it was, this music. The world just didn't have it in any form before.

Yes, I wanted to get closer to it. I wanted to *do* it. Maybe make the little unknown band of Satan's Night Out famous. I was ready to come up.

It took a week to rise, more or less. I fed on the fresh blood of the little animals who live under the earth when I could catch them. Then I started clawing for the surface, where I could summon the rats. From there it wasn't too difficult to take felines and finally the inevitable human victim, though I had to wait a long time for the particular kind I wanted—a man who had killed other mortals and showed no remorse.

One came along eventually, walking right by the fence, a young male with a grizzled beard who had murdered another in some far-off place on the other side of the world. True killer, this one. And oh, that first taste of human struggle and human blood!

Stealing clothes from nearby houses, getting some of the gold and jewels I'd hidden in the Lafayette Cemetery, that was no problem.

Of course I was scared from time to time. The stench of chemicals and gasoline sickened me. The drone of air conditioners and the whine of the jet planes overhead hurt my ears.

But after the third night up, I was roaring around New Orleans on a big black Harley-Davidson motorcycle making plenty of noise myself. I was looking for more killers to feed on. I wore gorgeous black leather clothes that I'd taken from my victims, and I had a little Sony Walkman stereo in my pocket that fed Bach's Art of the Fugue through tiny earphones right into my head as I blazed along.

I was the vampire Lestat again. I was back in action. New Orleans was once again my hunting ground.

As for my strength, well, it was three times what it had once been. I could leap from the street to the top of a four-story building. I could pull iron gratings off windows. I could bend a copper penny double. I could hear human voices and thoughts, when I wanted to, for blocks around.

By the end of the first week I had a pretty female lawyer in a downtown glass and steel skyscraper who helped me procure a legal birth certificate, Social Security card, and driver's license. A good portion of my old wealth was on its way to New Orleans from coded accounts in the immortal Bank of London and the Rothschild Bank.

But more important, I was swimming in realizations. I knew that everything the amplified voices had told me about the twentieth century was true.

As I roamed the streets of New Orleans in 1984 this is what I beheld:

The dark dreary industrial world that I'd gone to sleep on had burnt itself out finally, and the old bourgeois prudery and conformity had lost their hold on the American mind.

People were adventurous and erotic again the way they'd been in the old days, before the great middle-class revolutions of the late 1700s. They even *looked* the way they had in those times.

The men didn't wear the Sam Spade uniform of shirt, tie, gray suit, and gray hat any longer. Once again, they costumed themselves in velvet and silk and brilliant colors if they felt like it. They did not have to clip their hair like Roman soldiers anymore; they wore it any length they desired.

And the women—ah, the women were glorious, naked in the spring warmth as they'd been under the Egyptian pharaohs, in skimpy short skirts and tuniclike dresses, or wearing men's pants and shirts skintight over their curvaceous bodies if they pleased. They painted, and decked themselves out in gold and silver, even to walk to the grocery store. Or they went fresh scrubbed and without ornament—it didn't matter. They curled their hair like Marie Antoinette or cut it off or let it blow free.

For the first time in history, perhaps, they were as strong and as interesting as men.

And these were the common people of America. Not just the rich who've always achieved a certain androgyny, a certain joie de vivre that the middle-class revolutionaries called decadence in the past.

The old aristocratic sensuality now belonged to everybody. It was wed to the promises of the middle-class revolution, and all people had a right to love and to luxury and to graceful things.

Department stores had become palaces of near Oriental loveliness—merchandise displayed amid soft tinted carpeting, eerie music, amber light. In the all-night drugstores, bottles of violet and green shampoo gleamed like gems on the sparkling glass shelves. Waitresses drove sleek leather-lined automobiles to work. Dock laborers went home at night to swim in their heated backyard pools. Charwomen and plumbers changed at the end of the day into exquisitely cut manufactured clothes.

In fact the poverty and filth that had been common in the big cities of the earth since time immemorial were almost completely washed away.

You just didn't see immigrants dropping dead of starvation in the alleyways. There weren't slums where people slept eight and ten to a room. Nobody threw the slops in the gutters. The beggars, the cripples, the orphans, the hopelessly diseased were so diminished as to constitute no presence in the immaculate streets at all.

Even the drunkards and lunatics who slept on the park benches and in the bus stations had meat to eat regularly, and even radios to listen to, and clothes that were washed.

But this was just the surface. I found myself astounded by the more profound changes that moved this awesome current along.

For example, something altogether magical had happened to time.

The old was not being routinely replaced by the new anymore. On the contrary, the English spoken around me was the same as it had been in the 1800s. Even the old slang ("the coast is clear" or "bad luck" or "that's the thing") was still "current." Yet fascinating new phrases like "they brainwashed you" and "it's so Freudian" and "I can't relate to it" were on everyone's lips.

In the art and entertainment worlds all prior centuries were being "recycled." Musicians performed Mozart as well as jazz and rock music; people went to see Shakespeare one night and a new French film the next.

In giant fluorescent-lighted emporiums you could buy tapes of medieval madrigals and play them on your car stereo as you drove ninety miles an hour down the freeway. In the bookstores Renaissance poetry sold side by side with the novels of Dickens or Ernest Hemingway. Sex manuals lay on the same tables with the Egyptian *Book of the Dead.*

Sometimes the wealth and the cleanliness everywhere around me became like an hallucination. I thought I was going out of my head.

Through shop windows I gazed stupefied at computers and telephones as pure in form and color as nature's most exotic shells. Gargantuan silver limousines navigated the narrow French Quarter streets like indestructible sea beasts. Glittering office towers pierced the night sky like Egyptian obelisks above the sagging brick buildings of old Canal Street. Countless television programs poured their ceaseless flow of images into every air-cooled hotel room.

But it was no series of hallucinations. This century had inherited the earth in every sense.

And no small part of this unpredicted miracle was *the curious innocence* of these people in the very midst of their freedom and their wealth. The Christian god was as dead as he had been in the 1700s. *And no new mythological religion had arisen to take the place of the old.*

On the contrary, the simplest people of this age were driven by a vigorous secular morality as strong as any religious morality I had ever known. The intellectuals carried the standards. But quite ordinary individuals all over America cared passionately about "peace" and "the poor" and "the planet" as if driven by a mystical zeal.

Famine they intended to wipe out in this century. Disease they would destroy no matter what the cost. They argued ferociously about the execution of condemned criminals, the abortion of unborn babies. And the threats of "environmental pollution" and "holocaustal war" they battled as fiercely as men have battled witchcraft and heresy in ages past.

As for sexuality, it was no longer a matter of superstition and fear. The last religious overtones were being stripped from it. That was why the people went around half naked. That was why they kissed and hugged each other in the streets. They talked ethics now and responsibility and the beauty of the body. Procreation and venereal disease they had under control.

. . .

AH, THE twentieth century. Ah, the turn of the great wheel.

It had outdistanced my wildest dreams of it, this future. It had made fools of grim prophets of ages past.

I did a lot of thinking about this sinless secular morality, this optimism. This brilliantly lighted world where the value of human life was greater than it had ever been before.

IN THE amber electric twilight of a vast hotel room I watched on the screen before me the stunningly crafted film of war called *Apocalypse Now.* Such a symphony of sound and color it was, and it sang of the age-old battle of the Western world against evil. "You must make a friend of horror and moral terror," says the mad commander in the savage garden of Cambodia, to which the Western man answers as he has always answered: No.

No. Horror and moral terror can never be exonerated. They have no real value. Pure evil has no real place.

And that means, doesn't it, that *I* have no place.

Except, perhaps, in the art that repudiates evil—the vampire comics, the horror novels, the old gothic tales—or in the roaring chants of the rock stars who dramatize the battles against evil that each mortal fights within himself.

IT WAS enough to make an Old World monster go back into the earth, this stunning irrelevance to the mighty scheme of things, enough to make him lie down and weep. Or enough to make him become a rock singer, when you think about it. . . .

BUT where were the other Old World monsters? I wondered. How did other vampires exist in a world in which each death was recorded in giant electronic computers, and bodies were carried away to refrigerated crypts? Probably concealing themselves like loathsome insects in the shadows, as they have always done, no matter how much philosophy they talked or how many covens they formed.

Well, when I raised my voice with the little band called Satan's Night Out, I would bring them all into the light soon enough.

. . .

I CONTINUED my education. I talked to mortals at bus stops and at gas stations and in elegant drinking places. I read books. I decked myself out in the shimmering dream skins of the fashionable shops. I wore white turtleneck shirts and crisp khaki safari jackets, or lush gray velvet blazers with cashmere scarves. I powdered down my face so that I could "pass" beneath the chemical lights of the all-night supermarkets, the hamburger joints, the carnival thoroughfares called nightclub strips.

I was learning. I was in love.

And the only problem I had was that murderers to feed upon were scarce. In this shiny world of innocence and plenty, of kindness and gaiety and full stomachs, the common cutthroat thieves of the past and their dangerous waterfront hangouts were almost gone.

And so I had to work for a living. But I'd always been a hunter. I liked the dim smoky poolrooms with the single light shining on the green felt as the tattooed ex-convicts gathered around it as much as I liked the shiny satin-lined nightclubs of the big concrete hotels. And I was learning more all the time about my killers—the drug dealers, the pimps, the murderers who fell in with the motorcycle gangs.

And more than ever, I was resolute that I would not drink innocent blood.

FINALLY it was time to call upon my old neighbors, the rock band called Satan's Night Out.

AT SIX thirty on a hot sticky Saturday night I rang the doorbell of the attic music studio. The beautiful young mortals were all lying about in their rainbow-colored silk shirts and skintight dungarees smoking hashish cigarettes and complaining about their rotten luck getting "gigs" in the South.

They looked like biblical angels, with their long clean shaggy hair and feline movements; their jewelry was Egyptian. Even to rehearse they painted their faces and their eyes.

I was overcome with excitement and love just looking at them, Alex and Larry and the succulent little Tough Cookie.

And in an eerie moment in which the world seemed to stand still beneath me, I told them what I was. Nothing new to them, the word "vampire." In the galaxy in which they shone, a thousand other singers had worn the theatrical fangs and the black cape.

And yet it felt so strange to speak it aloud to mortals, the forbidden truth. Never in two hundred years had I spoken it to anyone who had not been marked to become one of us. Not even to my victims did I confide it before their eyes closed.

And now I said it clearly and distinctly to these handsome young creatures. I told them that I wanted to sing with them, that if they were to trust to me, we would all be rich and famous. That on a wave of preternatural and remorseless ambition, I should carry them out of these rooms and into the great world.

Their eyes misted as they looked at me. And the little twentieth-century chamber of stucco and pasteboard rang with their laughter and delight.

I was patient. Why shouldn't I be? I knew I was a demon who could mimic almost any human sound or movement. But how could they be expected to understand? I went to the electric piano and began to play and to sing.

I imitated the rock songs as I started, and then old melodies and lyrics came back to me—French songs buried deep in my soul yet never abandoned—and I wound these into brutal rhythms, seeing before me a tiny crowded little Paris theater of centuries ago. A dangerous passion welled in me. It threatened my equilibrium. Dangerous that this should come so soon. Yet I sang on, pounding the slick white keys of the electric piano, and something in my soul was broken open. Never mind that these tender mortal creatures gathered around me should never know.

It was sufficient that they were jubilant, that they loved the eerie and disjointed music, that they were screaming, that they saw prosperity in the future, the impetus that they had lacked before. They turned on the tape machines and we began singing and playing together, jamming as they called it. The studio swam with the scent of their blood and our thunderous songs.

But then came a shock I had never in my strangest dreams anticipated—something that was as extraordinary as my little revelation to these creatures had been. In fact, it was so overwhelming that it might have driven me out of their world and back underground.

I don't mean I would have gone into the deep slumber again. But I might have backed off from Satan's Night Out and roamed about for a few years, stunned and trying to gather my wits.

The men—Alex, the sleek delicate young drummer, and his taller blond-haired brother, Larry—recognized my name when I told them it was Lestat.

Not only did they recognize it, but they connected it with a body of information about me that they had read in a book.

In fact, they thought it was delightful that I wasn't just pretending to be any vampire. Or Count Dracula. Everybody was sick of Count Dracula. They thought it was marvelous that I was pretending to be the vampire Lestat.

"*Pretending* to be the vampire Lestat?" I asked.

They laughed at my exaggeration, my French accent.

I looked at all of them for a long moment, trying to scan their thoughts. Of course I hadn't expected them to believe I was a real vampire. But to have read of a fictional vampire with a name as unusual as mine? How could this be explained?

But I was losing my confidence. And when I lose my confidence, my powers drain. The little room seemed to be getting smaller. And there was something insectile and menacing about the instruments, the antenna, the wires.

"Show me this book," I said.

From the other room they brought it, a small pulp paper "novel" that was falling to pieces. The binding was gone, the cover ripped, the whole held together by a rubber band.

I got a preternatural chill of sorts at the sight of the cover. *Interview with the Vampire.* Something to do with a mortal boy getting one of the undead to tell the tale.

With their permission, I went into the other room, stretched out on their bed, and began to read. When I was halfway finished, I took the book with me and left the house. I stood stock-still beneath a street lamp with the book until I finished it. Then I placed it carefully in my breast pocket.

I didn't return to the band for seven nights.

DURING much of that time, I was roaming again, crashing through the night on my Harley-Davidson motorcycle with the Bach Goldberg Variations turned up to full volume. And I was asking myself, Lestat, what do you want to do now?

And the rest of the time I studied with a renewed purpose. I read the fat paperback histories and lexicons of rock music, the chronicles of its stars. I listened to the albums and pondered in silence the concert video tapes.

And when the night was empty and still, I heard the voices of *Interview with the Vampire* singing to me, as if they sang from the grave. I read the book over and over. And then in a moment of contemptible anger, I shredded it to bits.

FINALLY, I came to my decision.

I met my young lawyer, Christine, in her darkened skyscraper office with only the downtown city to give us light. Lovely she looked against the glass wall behind her, the dim buildings beyond forming a harsh and primitive terrain in which a thousand torches burned.

"It is not enough any longer that my little rock band be successful," I told her. "We must create a fame that will carry my name and my voice to the remotest parts of the world."

Quietly, intelligently, as lawyers are wont to do, she advised me against risking my fortune. Yet as I continued with maniacal confidence, I could feel her seduction, the slow dissolution of her common sense.

"The best French directors for the rock video films," I said. "You must lure them from New York and Los Angeles. There is ample money for that. And here you can find the studios, surely, in which we will do our work. The young record producers who mix the sound after—again, you must hire the best. It does not matter what we spend on this venture. What is important is that it be orchestrated, that we do our work in secret until the moment of revelation when our albums and our films are released with the book that I propose to write."

Finally her head was swimming with dreams of wealth and power. Her pen raced as she made her notes.

And what did I dream of as I spoke to her? Of an unprecedented rebellion, a great and horrific challenge to my kind all over the world.

"These rock videos," I said. "You must find directors who'll realize my visions. The films are to be sequential. They must tell the story that is in the book I want to create. And the songs, many of them I've already written. You must obtain superior instruments—synthesizers, the finest sound systems, electric guitars, violins. Other details we can attend to later. The designing of vampire costumes, the method of presentation to the rock television stations, the management of our first public appearance in San Francisco—all that in good time. What is important now is that you make the phone calls, get the information you need to begin."

I DIDN'T go back to Satan's Night Out until the first agreements were struck and signatures had been obtained. Dates were fixed, studios rented, letters of agreement exchanged.

Then Christine came with me, and we had a great leviathan of a limousine for my darling young rock players, Larry and Alex and Tough Cookie. We had breathtaking sums of money, we had papers to be signed.

Under the drowsy oaks of the quiet Garden District street, I poured the champagne into the glistening crystal glasses for them:

"To The Vampire Lestat," we all sang in the moonlight. It was to be the new name of the band, of the book I'd write. Tough Cookie threw her succulent little arms around me. We kissed tenderly amid the laughter and the reek of wine. Ah, the smell of innocent blood!

AND when they had gone off in the velvet-lined motor coach, I moved alone through the balmy night towards St. Charles Avenue, and thought about the danger facing them, my little mortal friends.

It didn't come from me, of course. But when the long period of secrecy was ended, they would stand innocently and ignorantly in the international limelight with their sinister and reckless star. Well, I would surround them with bodyguards and hangers-on for every conceivable purpose. I would protect them from other immortals as best I could. And if the immortals were anything like they used to be in the old days, they'd never risk a vulgar struggle with a human force like that.

As I walked up to the busy avenue, I covered my eyes with mirrored sunglasses. I rode the rickety old St. Charles streetcar downtown.

And through the early evening crowd I wandered into the elegant double-decker bookstore called de Ville Books, and there stared at the small paperback of *Interview with the Vampire* on the shelf.

I wondered how many of our kind had "noticed" the book. Never mind for the moment the mortals who thought it was fiction. What about other vampires? Because if there is one law that all vampires hold sacred it is that *you do not tell mortals about us.*

You never pass on our "secrets" to humans unless you mean to bequeath the Dark Gift of our powers to them. You never name other immortals. You never tell where their lairs might be.

My beloved Louis, the narrator of *Interview with the Vampire,* had done all this. He had gone far beyond my secret little disclosure to my rock singers. He had told hundreds of thousands of readers. He had all but drawn them a map and placed an X on the very spot in New Orleans where I slumbered, though what he really knew about that, and what his intentions were, was not clear.

Regardless, for what he'd done, others would surely hunt him down. And there are very simple ways to destroy vampires, especially now. If he was still in existence, he was an outcast and lived in a danger from our kind that no mortal could ever pose.

All the more reason for me to bring the book and the band called The Vampire Lestat to fame as quickly as possible. I had to find Louis. I had to talk to him. In fact, after reading his account of things, I ached for him, ached for his romantic illusions, and even his dishonesty. I ached even for his gentlemanly malice and his physical presence, the deceptively soft sound of his voice.

Of course I hated him for the lies he told about me. But the love was far greater than the hate. He had shared the dark and romantic years of the nineteenth century with me, he was my companion as no other immortal had ever been.

And I ached to write my story for him, not an answer to his malice in *Interview with the Vampire,* but the tale of all the things I'd seen and learned before I came to him, the story I could not tell him before.

Old rules didn't matter to me now, either.

I wanted to break every one of them. And I wanted my band and my book to draw out not only Louis but all the other demons that I had ever known and loved. I wanted to find my lost ones, awaken those who slept as I had slept.

Fledglings and ancient ones, beautiful and evil and mad and heartless —they'd all come after me when they saw those video clips and heard those records, when they saw the book in the windows of the bookstores, and they'd know exactly where to find me. I'd be Lestat, the rock superstar. Just come to San Francisco for my first live performance. I'll be there.

But there was another reason for the whole adventure—a reason even more dangerous and delicious and mad.

And I knew Louis would understand. It must have been behind his interview, his confessions. I wanted mortals *to know* about us. I wanted to proclaim it to the world the way I'd told it to Alex and Larry and Tough Cookie, and my sweet lawyer, Christine.

And it didn't matter that they didn't believe it. It didn't matter that they thought it was art. The fact was that, after two centuries of concealment, I was visible to mortals! I spoke my name aloud. I told my nature. I was there!

But again, I was going farther than Louis. His story, for all its peculiarities, had passed for fiction. In the mortal world, it was as safe as the tableaux of the old Theater of the Vampires in the Paris where the fiends had pretended to be actors pretending to be fiends on a remote and gas-lighted stage.

I'd step into the solar lights before the cameras, I'd reach out and touch with my icy fingers a thousand warm and grasping hands. I'd scare the hell out of them if it was possible, and charm them and lead them into the truth of it if I could.

And suppose—just suppose—that when the corpses began to turn up in ever greater numbers, that when those closest to me began to hearken to their inevitable suspicions—just suppose that the art ceased to be art and became real!

I mean what if they really believed it, really understood that this world still harbored the Old World demon thing, the vampire—oh, what a great and glorious war we might have then!

We would be known, and we would be hunted, and we would be fought in this glittering urban wilderness as no mythic monster has ever been fought by man before.

How could I not love it, the mere idea of it? How could it not be worth the greatest danger, the greatest and most ghastly defeat? Even at the moment of destruction, I would be alive as I have never been.

But to tell the truth, I didn't think it would ever come to that—I mean, mortals believing in us. Mortals have never made me afraid.

It was the other war that was going to happen, the one in which we'd all come together, or they would all come to fight me.

That was the real reason for The Vampire Lestat. That was the kind of game I was playing.

But that other lovely possibility of real revelation and disaster . . . Well, that added a hell of a lot of spice!

OUT of the gloomy waste of Canal Street, I went back up the stairs to my rooms in the old-fashioned French Quarter hotel. Quiet it was, and suited to me, with the Vieux Carré spread out beneath its windows, the narrow little streets of Spanish town houses I'd known for so long.

On the giant television set I played the cassette of the beautiful Visconti film *Death in Venice.* An actor said at one point that evil was a necessity. It was food for genius.

I didn't believe that. But I wish it were true. Then I could just be Lestat, the monster, couldn't I? And I was always so good at being a monster! Ah, well . . .

I put a fresh disk into the portable computer word processor and I started to write the story of my life.

THE EARLY EDUCATION AND ADVENTURES OF THE VAMPIRE LESTAT

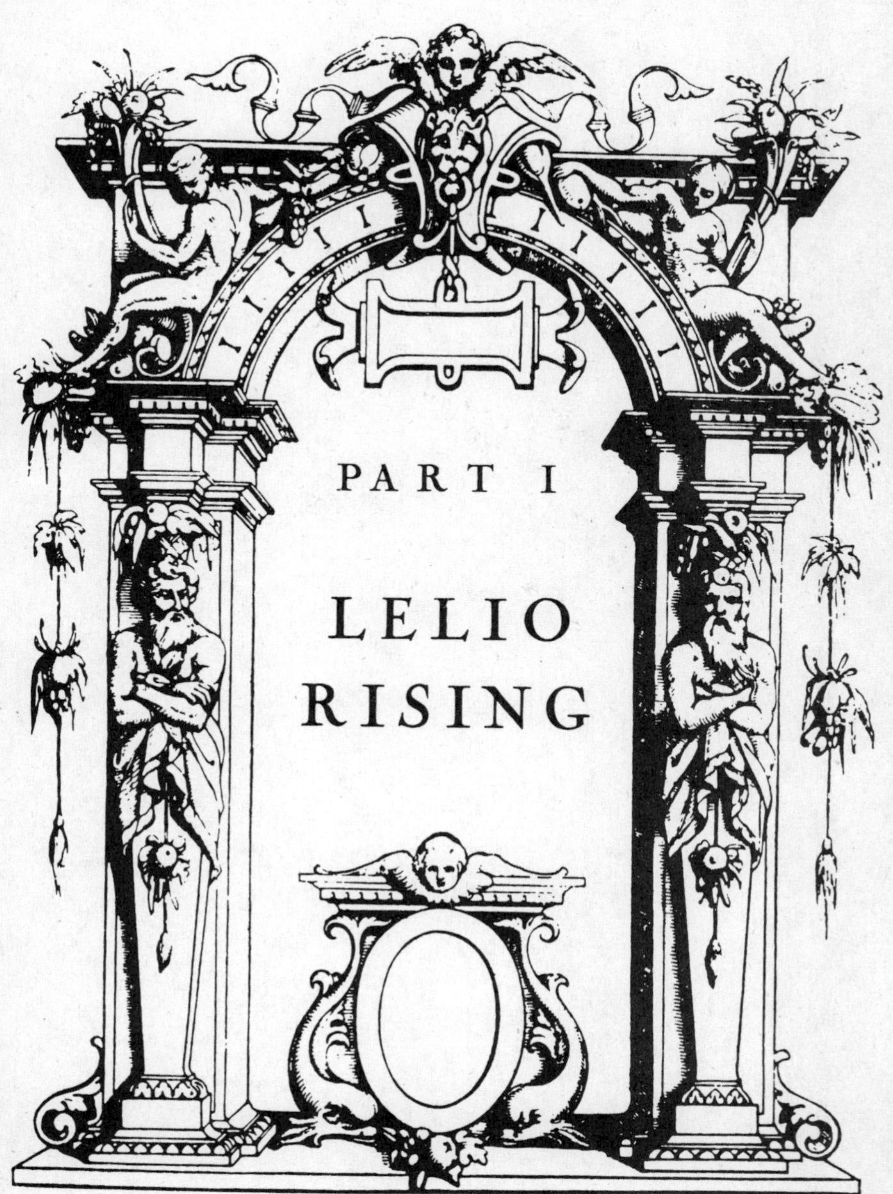

PART I

LELIO RISING

1

N THE winter of my twenty-first year, I went out alone on horseback to kill a pack of wolves.

This was on my father's land in the Auvergne in France, and these were the last decades before the French Revolution.

It was the worst winter that I could remember, and the wolves were stealing the sheep from our peasants and even running at night through the streets of the village.

These were bitter years for me. My father was the Marquis, and I was the seventh son and the youngest of the three who had lived to manhood. I had no claim to the title or the land, and no prospects. Even in a rich family, it might have been that way for a younger boy, but our wealth had been used up long ago. My eldest brother, Augustin, who was the rightful heir to all we possessed, had spent his wife's small dowry as soon as he married her.

My father's castle, his estate, and the village nearby were my entire universe. And I'd been born restless—the dreamer, the angry one, the complainer. I wouldn't sit by the fire and talk of old wars and the days of the Sun King. History had no meaning for me.

But in this dim and old-fashioned world, I had become the hunter. I brought in the pheasant, the venison, and the trout from the mountain streams—whatever was needed and could be got—to feed the family. It had become my life by this time—and one I shared with no one else—and it was a very good thing that I'd taken it up, because there were years when we might have actually starved to death.

Of course this was a noble occupation, hunting one's ancestral lands, and we alone had the right to do it. The richest of the bourgeois couldn't lift his gun in my forests. But then again he didn't have to lift his gun. He had money.

Two times in my life I'd tried to escape this life, only to be brought back with my wings broken. But I'll tell more on that later.

Right now I'm thinking about the snow all over those mountains and the wolves that were frightening the villagers and stealing my sheep. And

I'm thinking of the old saying in France in those days, that if you lived in the province of Auvergne you could get no farther from Paris.

Understand that since I was the lord and the only lord anymore who could sit a horse and fire a gun, it was natural that the villagers should come to me, complaining about the wolves and expecting me to hunt them. It was my duty.

I wasn't the least afraid of the wolves either. Never in my life had I seen or heard of a wolf attacking a man. And I would have poisoned them if I could, but meat was simply too scarce to lace with poison.

So early on a very cold morning in January, I armed myself to kill the wolves one by one. I had three flintlock guns and an excellent flintlock rifle, and these I took with me as well as my muskets and my father's sword. But just before leaving the castle, I added to this little arsenal one or two ancient weapons that I'd never bothered with before.

Our castle was full of old armor. My ancestors had fought in countless noble wars since the times of the Crusades with St. Louis. And hung on the walls above all this clattering junk were a good many lances, battleaxes, flails, and maces.

It was a very large mace—that is, a spiked club—that I took with me that morning, and also a good-sized flail: an iron ball attached to a chain that could be swung with immense force at an attacker.

Now remember this was the eighteenth century, the time when white-wigged Parisians tiptoed around in high-heeled satin slippers, pinched snuff, and dabbed at their noses with embroidered handkerchiefs.

And here I was going out to hunt in rawhide boots and buckskin coat, with these ancient weapons tied to the saddle, and my two biggest mastiffs beside me in their spiked collars.

That was my life. And it might as well have been lived in the Middle Ages. And I knew enough of the fancy-dressed travelers on the post road to feel it rather keenly. The nobles in the capital called us country lords "harecatchers." Of course we could sneer at them and call them lackeys to the king and queen. Our castle had stood for a thousand years, and not even the great Cardinal Richelieu in his war on our kind had managed to pull down our ancient towers. But as I said before, I didn't pay much attention to history.

I was unhappy and ferocious as I rode up the mountain.

I wanted a good battle with the wolves. There were five in the pack according to the villagers, and I had my guns and two dogs with jaws so strong they could snap a wolf's spine in an instant.

Well, I rode for an hour up the slopes. Then I came into a small valley I knew well enough that no snowfall could disguise it. And as I started across the broad empty field towards the barren wood, I heard the first howling.

Within seconds there had come another howling and then another, and now the chorus was in such harmony that I couldn't tell the number of the pack, only that they had seen me and were signaling to each other to come together, which was just what I had hoped they would do.

I don't think I felt the slightest fear then. But I felt something, and it caused the hair to rise on the backs of my arms. The countryside for all its vastness seemed empty. I readied my guns. I ordered my dogs to stop their growling and follow me, and some vague thought came to me that I had better get out of the open field and into the woods and hurry.

My dogs gave their deep baying alarm. I glanced over my shoulder and saw the wolves hundreds of yards behind me and streaking straight towards me over the snow. Three giant gray wolves they were, coming on in a line.

I broke into a run for the forest.

It seemed I would make it easily before the three reached me, but wolves are extremely clever animals, and as I rode hard for the trees I saw the rest of the pack, some five full-grown animals, coming out ahead of me to my left. It was an ambush, and I could never make the forest in time. And the pack was eight wolves, not five as the villagers had told me.

Even then I didn't have sense enough to be afraid. I didn't ponder the obvious fact that these animals were starving or they'd never come near the village. Their natural reticence with men was completely gone.

I got ready for battle. I stuck the flail in my belt, and with the rifle I took aim. I brought down a big male yards away from me and had time to reload as my dogs and the pack attacked each other.

They couldn't get my dogs by the neck on account of the spiked collars. And in this first skirmish my dogs brought down one of the wolves in their powerful jaws immediately. I fired and brought down a second.

But the pack had surrounded the dogs. As I fired again and again, reloading as quickly as I could and trying to aim clear of the dogs, I saw the smaller dog go down with its hind legs broken. Blood streamed over the snow; the second dog stood off the pack as it tried to devour the dying animal, but within two minutes, the pack had torn open the second dog's belly and killed it.

Now these were powerful beasts, as I said, these mastiffs. I'd bred them and trained them myself. And each weighed upwards of two hundred pounds. I always hunted with them, and though I speak of them as dogs now, they were known only by their names to me then, and when I saw them die, I knew for the first time what I had taken on and what might happen.

But all this had occurred in minutes.

Four wolves lay dead. Another was crippled fatally. But that left three, one of whom had stopped in the savage feasting upon the dogs to fix its slanted eyes on me.

I fired the rifle, missed, fired the musket, and my horse reared as the wolf shot towards me.

As if pulled on strings, the other wolves turned, leaving the fresh kill. And jerking the reins hard, I let my horse run as she wanted, straight for the cover of the forest.

I didn't look back even when I heard the growling and snapping. But then I felt the teeth graze my ankle. I drew the other musket, turned to the left, and fired. It seemed the wolf went up on his hind legs, but it was too quickly out of sight and my mare reared again. I almost fell. I felt her back legs give out under me.

We were almost to the forest and I was off her before she went down. I had one more loaded gun. Turning and steadying it with both hands, I took dead aim at the wolf who bore down on me and blasted away the top of his skull.

It was now two animals. The horse was giving off a deep rattling whinny that rose to a trumpeting shriek, the worst sound I have ever heard from any living thing. The two wolves had her.

I bolted over the snow, feeling the hardness of the rocky land under me, and made it to the trees. If I could reload I could shoot them down from there. But there was not a single tree with limbs low enough for me to catch hold of.

I leapt up trying to catch hold, my feet slipping on the icy bark, and fell back down as the wolves closed in. There was no time to load the one gun I had left to me. It was the flail and the sword because the mace I had lost a long way back.

I think as I scrambled to my feet, I knew I was probably going to die. But it never even occurred to me to give up. I was maddened, wild. Almost snarling, I faced the animals and looked the closest of the two wolves straight in the eye.

I spread my legs to anchor myself. With the flail in my left hand, I drew the sword. The wolves stopped. The first, after staring back, bowed its head and trotted several paces to the side. The other waited as if for some invisible signal. The first looked at me again in that uncannily calm fashion and then plunged forward.

I started swinging the flail so that the spiked ball went round in a circle. I could hear my own growling breaths, and I know I was bending my knees as if I would spring forward, and I aimed the flail for the side of the animal's jaw, bashing it with all my strength and only grazing it.

The wolf darted off and the second ran round me in a circle, dancing towards me and then back again. They both lunged in close enough to make me swing the flail and slash with the sword, then they ran off again.

I don't know how long this went on, but I understood the strategy. They meant to wear me down and they had the strength to do it. It had become a game to them.

I was pivoting, thrusting, struggling back, and almost falling to my knees. Probably it was no more than half an hour that this went on. But there is no measuring time like that.

And with my legs giving out, I made one last desperate gamble. I stood stock-still, weapons at my sides. And they came in for the kill this time just as I hoped they would.

At the last second I swung the flail, felt the ball crack the bone, saw the head jerked upwards to the right, and with the broadsword I slashed the wolf's neck open.

The other wolf was at my side. I felt its teeth rip into my breeches. In one second it would have torn my leg out of the socket. But I slashed at the side of its face, gashing open its eye. The ball of the flail crashed down on it. The wolf let go. And springing back, I had enough room for the sword again and thrust it straight into the animal's chest to the hilt before I drew it out again.

That was the end of it.

The pack was dead. I was alive.

And the only sound in the empty snow-covered valley was my own breathing and the rattling shriek of my dying mare who lay yards away from me.

I'm not sure I had my reason. I'm not sure the things that went through my mind were thoughts. I wanted to drop down in the snow, and yet I was walking away from the dead wolves towards the dying horse.

As I came close to her, she lifted her neck, straining to rise up on her front legs, and gave one of those shrill trumpeting pleas again. The sound bounced off the mountains. It seemed to reach heaven. And I stood staring at her, staring at her dark broken body against the whiteness of the snow, the dead hindquarters and the struggling forelegs, the nose lifted skyward, ears pressed back, and the huge innocent eyes rolling up into her head as the rattling cry came out of her. She was like an insect half mashed into a floor, but she was no insect. She was my struggling, suffering mare. She tried to lift herself again.

I took my rifle from the saddle. I loaded it. And as she lay tossing her head, trying vainly to lift herself once more with that shrill trumpeting, I shot her through the heart.

Now she looked all right. She lay still and dead and the blood ran out of her and the valley was quiet. I was shuddering. I heard an ugly choking noise come from myself, and I saw the vomit spewing out onto the snow before I realized it was mine. The smell of wolf was all over me, and the smell of blood. And I almost fell over when I tried to walk.

But not even stopping for a moment, I went among the dead wolves, and back to the one who had almost killed me, the last one, and slung him up to carry over my shoulders, and started the trek homeward.

It took me probably two hours.

Again, I don't know. But whatever I had learned or felt when I was fighting those wolves went on in my mind even as I walked. Every time I stumbled and fell, something in me hardened, became worse.

By the time I reached the castle gates, I think I was not Lestat. I was someone else altogether, staggering into the great hall, with that wolf over my shoulders, the heat of the carcass very much diminished now and the sudden blaze of the fire an irritant in my eyes. I was beyond exhaustion.

And though I began to speak as I saw my brothers rising from the table and my mother patting my father, who was blind already then and wanted to know what was happening, I don't know what I said. I know my voice was very flat, and there was some sense in me of the simplicity of describing what had happened:

"And then . . . and then . . ." Sort of like that.

But my brother Augustin suddenly brought me to myself. He came towards me, with the light of the fire behind him, and quite distinctly broke the low monotone of my words with his own:

"You little bastard," he said coldly. "You didn't kill eight wolves!" His face had an ugly disgusted look to it.

But the remarkable thing was this: Almost as soon as he spoke these words, he realized for some reason that he had made a mistake.

Maybe it was the look on my face. Maybe it was my mother's murmured outrage or my other brother not speaking at all. It was probably my face. Whatever it was, it was almost instantaneous, and the most curious look of embarrassment came over him.

He started to babble something about how incredible, and I must have been almost killed, and would the servants heat some broth for me immediately, and all of that sort of thing, but it was no good. What had happened in that one single moment was irreparable, and the next thing I knew I was lying alone in my room. I didn't have the dogs in bed with me as always in winter because the dogs were dead, and though there was no fire lighted, I climbed, filthy and bloody, under the bed covers and went into deep sleep.

For days I stayed in my room.

I knew the villagers had gone up the mountain, found the wolves, and brought them back down to the castle, because Augustin came and told me these things, but I didn't answer.

Maybe a week passed. When I could stand having other dogs near me, I went down to my kennel and brought up two pups, already big animals, and they kept me company. At night I slept between them.

The servants came and went. But no one bothered me.

And then my mother came quietly and almost stealthily into the room.

2

IT WAS evening. I was sitting on the bed, with one of the dogs stretched out beside me and the other stretched out under my knees. The fire was roaring.

And there was my mother coming at last, as I supposed I should have expected.

I knew her by her particular movement in the shadows, and whereas if anyone else had come near me I would have shouted "Go away," I said nothing at all to her.

I had a great and unshakable love of her. I don't think anyone else did. And one thing that endeared her to me always was that she never said anything ordinary.

"Shut the door," "Eat your soup," "Sit still," things like that never passed her lips. She read all the time; in fact, she was the only one in our family who had any education, and when she did speak it was really to speak. So I wasn't resentful of her now.

On the contrary she aroused my curiosity. What would she say, and would it conceivably make a difference to me? I had not wanted her to come, nor even thought of her, and I didn't turn away from the fire to look at her.

But there was a powerful understanding between us. When I had tried to escape this house and been brought back, it was she who had shown me the way out of the pain that followed. Miracles she'd worked for me, though no one around us had ever noticed.

Her first intervention had come when I was twelve, and the old parish priest, who had taught me some poetry by rote and to read an anthem or two in Latin, wanted to send me to school at the nearby monastery.

My father said no, that I could learn all I needed in my own house. But it was my mother who roused herself from her books to do loud and vociferous battle with him. I would go, she said, if I wanted to. And she sold one of her jewels to pay for my books and clothing. Her jewels had all come down to her from an Italian grandmother and each had its story, and this was a hard thing for her to do. But she did it immediately.

My father was angry and reminded her that if this had happened before he went blind, his will would have prevailed surely. My brothers assured him that his youngest son wouldn't be gone long. I'd come running home as soon as I was made to do something I didn't want to do.

Well, I didn't come running home. I loved the monastery school.

I loved the chapel and the hymns, the library with its thousands of old books, the bells that divided the day, the ever repeated rituals. I loved the cleanliness of the place, the overwhelming fact that all things here were well kept and in good repair, that work never ceased throughout the great house and the gardens.

When I was corrected, which wasn't often, I knew an intense happiness because someone for the first time in my life was trying to make me into a good person, one who could learn things.

Within a month I declared my vocation. I wanted to enter the order. I wanted to spend my life in those immaculate cloisters, in the library writing on parchment and learning to read the ancient books. I wanted to be enclosed forever with people who believed I could be good if I wanted to be.

I was liked there. And that was a most unusual thing. I didn't make other people there unhappy or angry.

The Father Superior wrote immediately to ask my father's permission. And frankly I thought my father would be glad to be rid of me.

But three days later my brothers arrived to take me home with them. I cried and begged to stay, but there was nothing the Father Superior could do.

And as soon as we reached the castle, my brothers took away my books and locked me up. I didn't understand why they were so angry. There was the hint that I had behaved like a fool for some reason. I couldn't stop crying. I was walking round and round and smashing my fist into things and kicking the door.

Then my brother Augustin started coming in and talking to me. He'd circle the point at first, but what came clear finally was that no member of a great French family was going to be a poor teaching brother. How could I have misunderstood everything so completely? I was sent there to learn to read and write. Why did I always have to go to extremes? Why did I behave habitually like a wild creature?

As for becoming a priest with real prospects within the Church, well, I was the youngest son of this family, now, wasn't I? I ought to think of my duties to my nieces and nephews.

Translate all that to mean this: We have no money to launch a real ecclesiastical career for you, to make you a bishop or cardinal as befits our rank, so you have to live out your life here as an illiterate and a beggar. Come in the great hall and play chess with your father.

AFTER I got to understand it, I wept right at the supper table, and mumbled words no one understood about this house of ours being "chaos," and was sent back to my room for it.

Then my mother came to me.

She said: "You don't know what chaos is. Why do you use words like that?"

"I know," I said. I started to describe to her the dirt and the decay that was everywhere here and to tell how the monastery had been, clean and orderly, a place where if you set your mind to it, you could accomplish something.

She didn't argue. And young as I was, I knew that she was warming to the unusual quality of what I was saying to her.

The next morning, she took me on a journey.

We rode for half a day before we reached the impressive château of a neighboring lord, and there she and the gentleman took me out to the kennel, where she told me to choose my favorites from a new litter of mastiff puppies.

I had never seen anything as tender and endearing as these little mastiff pups. And the big dogs were like drowsy lions as they watched us. Simply magnificent.

I was too excited almost to make the choice. I brought back the male and female that the lord advised me to pick, carrying them all the way home on my lap in a basket.

And within a month, my mother also bought for me my first flintlock musket and my first good horse for riding.

She never did say why she'd done all this. But I understood in my own way what she had given me. I raised those dogs, trained them, and founded a great kennel upon them.

I became a true hunter with those dogs, and by the age of sixteen I lived in the field.

But at home, I was more than ever a nuisance. Nobody really wanted to hear me talk of restoring the vineyards or replanting the neglected fields, or of making the tenants stop stealing from us.

I could affect nothing. The silent ebb and flow of life without change seemed deadly to me.

I went to church on all the feast days just to break the monotony of life. And when the village fairs came round, I was always there, greedy for the little spectacles I saw at no other time, anything really to break the routine.

It might be the same old jugglers, mimes, and acrobats of years past, but it didn't matter. It was something more than the change of the seasons and the idle talk of past glories.

But that year, the year I was sixteen, a troupe of Italian players came through, with a painted wagon in back of which they set up the most elaborate stage I'd ever seen. They put on the old Italian comedy with Pantaloon and Pulcinella and the young lovers, Lelio and Isabella, and the old doctor and all the old tricks.

I was in raptures watching it. I'd never seen anything like it, the cleverness of it, the quickness, the vitality. I loved it even when the words went so fast I couldn't follow them.

When the troupe had finished and collected what they could from the crowd, I hung about with them at the inn and stood them all to wine I couldn't really afford, just so that I could talk to them.

I felt inexpressible love for these men and women. They explained to me how each actor had his role for life, and how they did not use memorized words, but improvised everything on the stage. You knew your name, your character, and you understood him and made him speak and act as you thought he should. That was the genius of it.

It was called the commedia dell'arte.

I was enchanted. I fell in love with the young girl who played Isabella. I went into the wagon with the players and examined all the costumes and the painted scenery, and when we were drinking again at the tavern, they let me act out Lelio, the young lover to Isabella, and they clapped their hands and said I had the gift. I could make it up the way they did.

I thought this was all flattery at first, but in some very real way, it didn't matter whether or not it was flattery.

The next morning when their wagon pulled out of the village, I was in it. I was hidden in the back with a few coins I'd managed to save and all my clothes tied in a blanket. I was going to be an actor.

Now, Lelio in the old Italian comedy is supposed to be quite handsome; he's the lover, as I have explained, and he doesn't wear a mask. If he has manners, dignity, aristocratic bearing, so much the better because that's part of the role.

Well, the troupe thought that in all these things I was blessed. They trained me immediately for the next performance they would give. And the day before we put on the show, I went about the town—a much larger and more interesting place than our village, to be certain—advertising the play with the others.

I was in heaven. But neither the journey nor the preparations nor the camaraderie with my fellow players came near to the ecstasy I knew when I finally stood on that little wooden stage.

I went wildly into the pursuit of Isabella. I found a tongue for verses and wit I'd never had in life. I could hear my voice bouncing off the stone walls around me. I could hear the laughter rolling back at me from the crowd. They almost had to drag me off the stage to stop me, but everyone knew it had been a great success.

That night, the actress who played my inamorata gave me her own very special and intimate accolades. I went to sleep in her arms, and the last thing I remember her saying was that when we got to Paris we'd play the St.-Germain Fair, and then we'd leave the troupe and we'd stay in Paris working on the boulevard du Temple until we got into the Comédie-Française itself and performed for Marie Antoinette and King Louis.

When I woke up the next morning, she was gone and so were all the players, and my brothers were there.

I never knew if my friends had been bribed to give me over, or just frightened off. More likely the latter. Whatever the case, I was taken back home again.

Of course my family was perfectly horrified at what I'd done. Wanting to be a monk when you are twelve is excusable. But the theater had the taint of the devil. Even the great Molière had not been given a Christian burial. And I'd run off with a troupe of ragged vagabond Italians, painted my face white, and acted with them in a town square for money.

I was beaten severely, and when I cursed everyone, I was beaten again.

The worst punishment, however, was seeing the look on my mother's face. I hadn't even told her I was going. And I had wounded her, a thing that had never really happened before.

But she never said anything about it.

When she came to me, she listened to me cry. I saw tears in her eyes. And she laid her hand on my shoulder, which for her was something a little remarkable.

I didn't tell her what it had been like, those few days. But I think she knew. Something magical had been lost utterly. And once again, she defied my father. She put an end to the condemnations, the beatings, the restrictions.

She had me sit beside her at the table. She deferred to me, actually talked to me in conversation that was perfectly unnatural to her, until she had subdued and dissolved the rancor of the family.

Finally, as she had in the past, she produced another of her jewels and she bought the fine hunting rifle that I had taken with me when I killed the wolves.

This was a superior and expensive weapon, and in spite of my misery, I was fairly eager to try it. And she added to that another gift, a sleek chestnut mare with strength and speed I'd never known in an animal before. But these things were small compared to the general consolation my mother had given me.

Yet the bitterness inside me did not subside.

I never forgot what it had been like when I was Lelio. I became a little crueler for what had happened, and I never, never went again to the village fair. I conceived of the notion that I should never get away from here, and oddly enough as my despair deepened, so my usefulness increased.

I alone put the fear of God into the servants or tenants by the time I was eighteen. I alone provided the food for us. And for some strange reason this gave me satisfaction. I don't know why, but I liked to sit at the table and reflect that everyone there was eating what I had provided.

SO THESE moments had bound me to my mother. These moments had given us a love for each other unnoticed and probably unequaled in the lives of those around us.

And now she had come to me at this odd time, when for reasons I didn't understand myself, I could not endure the company of any other person.

WITH my eyes on the fire, I barely saw her climb up and sink down into the straw mattress beside me.

Silence. Just the crackling of the fire, and the deep respiration of the sleeping dogs beside me.

Then I glanced at her, and I was vaguely startled.

She'd been ill all winter with a cough, and now she looked truly sickly, and her beauty, which was always very important to me, seemed vulnerable for the first time.

Her face was angular and her cheekbones perfect, very high and broadly spaced but delicate. Her jawline was strong yet exquisitely feminine. And she had very clear cobalt blue eyes fringed with thick ashen lashes.

If there was any flaw in her it was perhaps that all her features were too small, too kittenish, and made her look like a girl. Her eyes became even smaller when she was angry, and though her mouth was sweet, it often appeared hard. It did not turn down, it wasn't twisted in any way, it was like a little pink rose on her face. But her cheeks were very smooth and her face narrow, and when she looked very serious, her mouth, without changing at all, looked mean for some reason.

Now she was slightly sunken. But she still looked beautiful to me. She still was beautiful. I liked looking at her. Her hair was full and blond, and that I had inherited from her.

In fact I resemble her at least superficially. But my features are larger, cruder, and my mouth is more mobile and can be very mean at times. And you can see my sense of humor in my expression, my capacity for mischievousness and near hysterical laughing, which I've always had no matter how unhappy I was. She did not laugh often. She could look profoundly cold. Yet she had always a little girl sweetness.

Well, I looked at her as she sat on my bed—I even stared at her, I suppose—and immediately she started to talk to me.

"I know how it is," she said to me. "You hate them. Because of what you've endured and what they don't know. They haven't the imagination to know what happened to you out there on the mountain."

I felt a cold delight in these words. I gave her the silent acknowledgment that she understood it perfectly.

"It was the same the first time I bore a child," she said. "I was in agony for twelve hours, and I felt trapped in the pain, knowing the only release was the birth or my own death. When it was over, I had your brother Augustin in my arms, but I didn't want anyone else near me. And it wasn't because I blamed them. It was only that I'd suffered like that, hour after hour, that I'd gone into the circle of hell and come back out. They hadn't been in the circle of hell. And I felt quiet all over. In this common occurrence, this vulgar act of giving birth, I understood the meaning of utter loneliness."

"Yes, that's it," I answered. I was a little shaken.

She didn't respond. I would have been surprised if she had. Having said what she'd come to say, she wasn't going to converse, actually. But she did lay her hand on my forehead—very unusual for her to do that—and when she observed that I was wearing the same bloody hunting clothes after all this time, I noticed it too, and realized the sickness of it.

She was silent for a while.

And as I sat there, looking past her at the fire, I wanted to tell her a lot of things, how much I loved her particularly.

But I was cautious. She had a way of cutting me off when I spoke to her, and mingled with my love was a powerful resentment of her.

All my life I'd watched her read her Italian books and scribble letters to people in Naples, where she had grown up, yet she had no patience even to teach me or my brothers the alphabet. And nothing had changed after I came back from the monastery. I was twenty and I couldn't read or write more than a few prayers and my name. I hated the sight of her books; I hated her absorption in them.

And in some vague way, I hated the fact that only extreme pain in me could ever wring from her the slightest warmth or interest.

Yet she'd been my savior. And there was no one but her. And I was as tired of being alone, perhaps, as a young person can be.

She was here now, out of the confines of her library, and she was attentive to me.

Finally I was convinced that she wouldn't get up and go away, and I found myself speaking to her.

"Mother," I said in a low voice, "there is more to it. Before it happened, there were times when I felt terrible things." There was no change in her expression. "I mean I dream sometimes that I might kill all of them," I said. "I kill my brothers and my father in the dream. I go from room to room slaughtering them as I did the wolves. I feel in myself the desire to murder . . ."

"So do I, my son," she said. "So do I." And her face was lighted with the strangest smile as she looked at me.

I bent forward and looked at her more closely. I lowered my voice.

"I see myself screaming when it happens," I went on. "I see my face twisted into grimaces and I hear bellowing coming out of me. My mouth is a perfect O, and shrieks, cries, come out of me."

She nodded with that same understanding look, as if a light were flaring behind her eyes.

"And on the mountain, Mother, when I was fighting the wolves . . . it was a little like that."

"Only a little?" she asked.

I nodded.

"I felt like someone different from myself when I killed the wolves. And now I don't know who is here with you—your son Lestat, or that other man, the killer."

She was quiet for a long time.

"No," she said finally. "It was you who killed the wolves. You're the hunter, the warrior. You're stronger than anyone else here, that's your tragedy."

I shook my head. That was true, but it didn't matter. It couldn't account for unhappiness such as this. But what was the use of saying it?

She looked away for a moment, then back to me.

"But you're many things," she said. "Not only one thing. You're the killer and the man. And don't give in to the killer in you just because you hate them. You don't have to take upon yourself the burden of murder or madness to be free of this place. Surely there must be other ways."

Those last two sentences struck me hard. She had gone to the core. And the implications dazzled me.

Always I'd felt that I couldn't be a good human being and fight them. To be good meant to be defeated by them. Unless of course I found a more interesting idea of goodness.

We sat still for a few moments. And there seemed an uncommon intimacy even for us. She was looking at the fire, scratching at her thick hair which was wound into a circle on the back of her head.

"You know what I imagine," she said, looking towards me again. "Not so much the murdering of them as an abandon which disregards them completely. I imagine drinking wine until I'm so drunk I strip off my clothes and bathe in the mountain streams naked."

I almost laughed. But it was a sublime amusement. I looked up at her, uncertain for a moment that I was hearing her correctly. But she had said these words and she wasn't finished.

"And then I imagine going into the village," she said, "and up into the inn and taking into my bed any men that come there—crude men, big men, old men, boys. Just lying there and taking them one after another, and feeling some magnificent triumph in it, some absolute release without a thought of what happens to your father or your brothers, whether they are alive or dead. In that moment I am purely myself. I belong to no one."

I was too shocked and amazed to say anything. But again this was terribly terribly amusing. When I thought of my father and brothers and the pompous shopkeepers of the village and how they would respond to such a thing, I found it damn near hilarious.

If I didn't laugh aloud it was probably because the image of my mother naked made me think I shouldn't. But I couldn't keep altogether quiet. I laughed a little, and she nodded, half smiling. She raised her eyebrows, as if to say We understand each other.

Finally I roared laughing. I pounded my knee with my fist and hit my head on the wood of the bed behind me. And she almost laughed herself. Maybe in her own quiet way she was laughing.

Curious moment. Some almost brutal sense of her as a human being quite removed from all that surrounded her. We did understand each other, and all my resentment of her didn't matter too much.

She pulled the pin out of her hair and let it tumble down to her shoulders.

We sat quiet for perhaps an hour after that. No more laughter or talk, just the fire blazing, and her near to me.

She had turned so she could see the fire. Her profile, the delicacy of her nose and lips, were beautiful to look at. Then she looked back at me and in the same steady voice without undue emotion she said:

"I'll never leave here. I am dying now."

I was stunned. The little shock before was nothing to this.

"I'll live through this spring," she continued, "and possibly the summer as well. But I won't survive another winter. I know. The pain in my lungs is too bad."

I made some little anguished sound. I think I leaned forward and said, "Mother!"

"Don't say any more," she answered.

I think she hated to be called mother, but I hadn't been able to help it.

"I just wanted to speak it to another soul," she said. "To hear it out loud. I'm perfectly horrified by it. I'm afraid of it."

I wanted to take her hands, but I knew she'd never allow it. She disliked to be touched. She never put her arms around anyone. And so it was in our glances that we held each other. My eyes filled with tears looking at her.

She patted my hand.

"Don't think on it much," she said. "I don't. Just only now and then. But you must be ready to live on without me when the time comes. That may be harder for you than you realize."

I tried to say something; I couldn't make the words come.

She left me just as she'd come in, silently.

And though she'd never said anything about my clothes or my beard or how dreadful I looked, she sent the servants in with clean clothes for me, and the razor and warm water, and silently I let myself be taken care of by them.

3

I BEGAN to feel a little stronger. I stopped thinking about what happened with the wolves and I thought about her.

I thought about the words "perfectly horrified," and I didn't know what to make of them except they sounded exactly true. I'd feel that way if I were dying slowly. It would have been better on the mountain with the wolves.

But there was more to it than that. She had always been silently unhappy. She hated the inertia and the hopelessness of our life here as much as I did. And now, after eight children, three living, five dead, she was dying. This was the end for her.

I determined to get up if it would make her feel better, but when I tried I couldn't. The thought of her dying was unbearable. I paced the floor of my room a lot, ate the food brought to me, but still I wouldn't go to her.

But by the end of the month, visitors came to draw me out.

My mother came in and said I must receive the merchants from the village who wanted to honor me for killing the wolves.

"Oh, hell with it," I answered.

"No, you must come down," she said. "They have gifts for you. Now do your duty."

I hated all this.

When I reached the hall, I found the rich shopkeepers there, all men I knew well, and all dressed for the occasion.

But there was one startling young man among them I didn't recognize immediately.

He was my age perhaps, and quite tall, and when our eyes met I remembered who he was. Nicolas de Lenfent, eldest son of the draper, who had been sent to school in Paris.

He was a vision now.

Dressed in a splendid brocade coat of rose and gold, he wore slippers with gold heels, and layers of Italian lace at his collar. Only his hair was what it used to be, dark and very curly, and boyish looking for some reason though it was tied back with a fine bit of silk ribbon.

Parisian fashion, all this—the sort that passed as fast as it could through the local post house.

And here I was to meet him in threadbare wool and scuffed leather boots and yellowed lace that had been seventeen times mended.

We bowed to each other, as he was apparently the spokesman for the town, and then he unwrapped from its modest covering of black serge a great red velvet cloak lined in fur. Gorgeous thing. His eyes were positively shining when he looked at me. You would have thought he was looking at a sovereign.

"Monsieur, we beg you to accept this," he said very sincerely. "The finest fur of the wolves has been used to line it and we thought it would stand you well in the winter, this fur-lined cloak, when you ride out to hunt."

"And these too, Monsieur," said his father, producing a finely sewn pair of fur-lined boots in black suede. "For the hunt, Monsieur," he said.

I was a little overcome. They meant these gestures in the kindest way, these men who had the sort of wealth I only dreamed of, and they paid me respect as the aristocrat.

I took the cloak and the boots. I thanked them as effusively as I'd ever thanked anybody for anything.

And behind me, I heard my brother Augustin say:

"Now he will really be impossible!"

I felt my face color. Outrageous that he should say this in the presence of these men, but when I glanced to Nicolas de Lenfent I saw the most affectionate expression on his face.

"I too am impossible, Monsieur," he whispered as I gave him the parting kiss. "Someday, will you let me come to talk to you and tell me how you killed them all? Only the impossible can do the impossible."

None of the merchants ever spoke to me like that. We were boys again for a moment. And I laughed out loud. His father was disconcerted. My brothers stopped whispering, but Nicolas de Lenfent kept smiling with a Parisian's composure.

As SOON as they had left I took the red velvet cloak and the suede boots up into my mother's room.

She was reading as always while very lazily she brushed her hair. In the weak sunlight from the window, I saw gray in her hair for the first time. I told her what Nicolas de Lenfent had said.

"Why is he impossible?" I asked her. "He said this with feeling, as if it meant something."

She laughed.

"It means something all right," she said. "He's in disgrace." She stopped looking at her book for a moment and looked at me. "You know how he's been educated all his life to be a little imitation aristocrat. Well, during his first term studying law in Paris, he fell madly in love with the violin, of all things. Seems he heard an Italian virtuoso, one of those geniuses from Padua who is so great that men say he has sold his soul to the devil. Well, Nicolas dropped everything at once to take lessons from Wolfgang Mozart. He sold his books. He did nothing but play and play until he failed his examinations. He wants to be a musician. Can you imagine?"

"And his father is beside himself."

"Exactly. He even smashed the instrument, and you know what a piece of expensive merchandise means to the good draper."

I smiled.

"And so Nicolas has no violin now?"

"He has a violin. He promptly ran away to Clermont and sold his watch to buy another. He's impossible all right, and the worst part of it is that he plays rather well."

"You've heard him?"

She knew good music. She grew up with it in Naples. All I'd ever heard were the church choir, the players at the fairs.

"I heard him Sunday when I went to mass," she said. "He was playing in the upstairs bedroom over the shop. Everyone could hear him, and his father was threatening to break his hands."

I gave a little gasp at the cruelty of it. I was powerfully fascinated! I think I loved him already, doing what he wanted like that.

"Of course he'll never be anything," she went on.

"Why not?"

"He's too old. You can't take up the violin when you're twenty. But what do I know? He plays magically in his own way. And maybe he can sell his soul to the devil."

I laughed a little uneasily. It sounded tragic.

"But why don't you go down to the town and make a friend of him?" she asked.

"Why the hell should I do that?" I asked.

"Lestat, really. Your brothers will hate it. And the old merchant will be beside himself with joy. His son and the Marquis's son."

"Those aren't good enough reasons."

"He's been to Paris," she said. She watched me for a long moment. Then she went back to her book, brushing her hair now and then lazily.

I watched her reading, hating it. I wanted to ask her how she was, if her cough was very bad that day. But I couldn't broach the subject to her.

"Go on down and talk to him, Lestat," she said, without another glance at me.

4

IT TOOK me a week to make up my mind that I would seek out Nicolas de Lenfent.

I put on the red velvet fur-lined cloak and the fur-lined suede boots, and I went down the winding main street of the village towards the inn.

The shop owned by Nicolas's father was right across from the inn, but I didn't see or hear Nicolas.

I had no more than enough for one glass of wine and I wasn't sure just how to proceed when the innkeeper came out, bowed to me, and set a bottle of his best vintage before me.

Of course these people had always treated me like the son of the lord. But I could see that things had changed on account of the wolves, and strangely enough, this made me feel even more alone than I usually felt.

But as soon as I poured the first glass, Nicolas appeared, a great blaze of color in the open doorway.

He was not so finely dressed as before, thank heaven, yet everything about him exuded wealth. Silk and velvet and brand-new leather.

But he was flushed as if he'd been running and his hair was windblown and messy, and his eyes full of excitement. He bowed to me, waited for me to invite him to sit down, and then he asked me:

"What was it like, Monsieur, killing the wolves?" And folding his arms on the table, he stared at me.

"Why don't you tell me what's it like in Paris, Monsieur?" I said, and I realized right away that it sounded mocking and rude. "I'm sorry," I said immediately. "I would really like to know. Did you go to the university? Did you really study with Mozart? What do people in Paris do? What do they talk about? What do they think?"

He laughed softly at the barrage of questions. I had to laugh myself. I signaled for another glass and pushed the bottle towards him.

"Tell me," I said, "did you go to the theaters in Paris? Did you see the Comédie-Française?"

"Many times," he answered a little dismissively. "But listen, the diligence will be coming in any minute. There'll be too much noise. Allow me the honor of providing your supper in a private room upstairs. I should so like to do it—"

And before I could make a gentlemanly protest, he was ordering everything. We were shown up to a crude but comfortable little chamber.

I was almost never in small wooden rooms, and I loved it immediately. The table was laid for the meal that would come later on, the fire was truly warming the place, unlike the roaring blazes in our castle, and the thick glass of the window was clean enough to see the blue winter sky over the snow-covered mountains.

"Now, I shall tell you everything you want to know about Paris," he said agreeably, waiting for me to sit first. "Yes, I did go to the university." He made a little sneer as if it had all been contemptible. "And I did study with Mozart, who would have told me I was hopeless if he hadn't needed pupils. Now where do you want me to begin? The stench of the city, or the infernal noise of it? The hungry crowds that surround you everywhere? The thieves in every alley ready to cut your throat?"

I waved all that away. His smile was very different from his tone, his manner open and appealing.

"A really big Paris theater . . ." I said. "Describe it to me . . . what is it like?"

* * *

I THINK we stayed in that room for four solid hours and all we did was drink and talk.

He drew plans of the theaters on the tabletop with a wet finger, described the plays he had seen, the famous actors, the little houses of the boulevards. Soon he was describing all of Paris and he'd forgotten to be cynical, my curiosity firing him as he talked of the Ile de la Cité, and the Latin Quarter, the Sorbonne, the Louvre.

We went on to more abstract things, how the newspapers reported events, how his student cronies gathered in cafés to argue. He told me men were restless and out of love with the monarchy. That they wanted a change in government and wouldn't sit still for very long. He told me about the philosophers, Diderot, Voltaire, Rousseau.

I couldn't understand everything he said. But in rapid, sometimes sarcastic speech he gave me a marvelously complete picture of what was going on.

Of course, it didn't surprise me to hear that educated people didn't believe in God, that they were infinitely more interested in science, that the aristocracy was much in ill favor, and so was the Church. These were times of reason, not superstition, and the more he talked the more I understood.

Soon he was outlining the Encyclopédie, the great compilation of knowledge supervised by Diderot. And then it was the salons he'd gone to, the drinking bouts, his evenings with actresses. He described the public balls at the Palais Royal, where Marie Antoinette appeared right along with the common people.

"I'll tell you," he said finally, "it all sounds a hell of a lot better in this room than it really is."

"I don't believe you," I said gently. I didn't want him to stop talking. I wanted it to go on and on.

"It's a secular age, Monsieur," he said, filling our glasses from the new bottle of wine. "Very dangerous."

"Why dangerous?" I whispered. "An end to superstition? What could be better than that?"

"Spoken like a true eighteenth-century man, Monsieur," he said with a faint melancholy to his smile. "But no one values anything anymore. Fashion is everything. Even atheism is a fashion."

I had always had a secular mind, but not for any philosophical reason. No one in my family much believed in God or ever had. Of course they said they did, and we went to mass. But this was duty. Real religion had long ago died out in our family, as it had perhaps in the families of thousands of aristocrats. Even at the monastery I had not believed in God. I had believed in the monks around me.

I tried to explain this in simple language that would not give offense to Nicolas, because for his family it was different.

Even his miserable money-grubbing father (whom I secretly admired) was fervently religious.

"But can men live without these beliefs?" Nicolas asked almost sadly. "Can children face the world without them?"

I was beginning to understand why he was so sarcastic and cynical. He had only recently lost that old faith. He was bitter about it.

But no matter how deadening was this sarcasm of his, a great energy poured out of him, an irrepressible passion. And this drew me to him. I think I loved him. Another two glasses of wine and I might say something absolutely ridiculous like that.

"I've always lived without beliefs," I said.

"Yes. I know," he answered. "Do you remember the story of the witches? The time you cried at the witches' place?"

"Cried over the witches?" I looked at him blankly for a moment. But it stirred something painful, something humiliating. Too many of my memories had that quality. And now I had to remember crying over witches. "I don't remember," I said.

"We were little boys. And the priest was teaching us our prayers. And the priest took us out to see the place where they burnt the witches in the old days, the old stakes and the blackened ground."

"Ah, that place." I shuddered. "That horrid, horrid place."

"You began to scream and to cry. They sent someone for the Marquise herself because your nurse couldn't quiet you."

"I was a dreadful child," I said, trying to shrug it off. Of course I did remember now—screaming, being carried home, nightmares about the fires. Someone bathing my forehead and saying, "Lestat, wake up."

But I hadn't thought of that little scene in years. It was the place itself I thought about whenever I drew near it—the thicket of blackened stakes, the images of men and women and children burnt alive.

Nicolas was studying me. "When your mother came to get you, she said it was all ignorance and cruelty. She was so angry with the priest for telling us the old tales."

I nodded.

The final horror to hear they had all died for nothing, those long-forgotten people of our own village, that they had been innocent. "Victims of superstition,'" she had said. "There were no real witches." No wonder I had screamed and screamed.

"But my mother," Nicolas said, "told a different story, that the witches had been in league with the devil, that they'd blighted the crops, and in the guise of wolves killed the sheep and the children—"

"And won't the world be better if no one is ever again burnt in the name of God?" I asked. "If there is no more faith in God to make men do that to each other? What is the danger in a secular world where horrors like that don't happen?"

He leaned forward with a mischievous little frown.

"The wolves didn't wound you on the mountain, did they?" he asked playfully. "You haven't become a werewolf, have you, Monsieur, unbeknownst to the rest of us?" He stroked the furred edge of the velvet cloak I still had over my shoulders. "Remember what the good father said, that they had burnt a good number of werewolves in those times. They were a regular menace."

I laughed.

"If I turn into a wolf," I answered, "I can tell you this much. I won't hang around here to kill the children. I'll get away from this miserable little hellhole of a village where they still terrify little boys with tales of burning witches. I'll get on the road to Paris and never stop till I see her ramparts."

"And you'll find Paris is a miserable hellhole," he said. "Where they break the bones of thieves on the wheel for the vulgar crowds in the place de Grève."

"No," I said. "I'll see a splendid city where great ideas are born in the minds of the populace, ideas that go forth to illuminate the darkened corners of this world."

"Ah, you are a dreamer!" he said, but he was delighted. He was beyond handsome when he smiled.

"And I'll know people like you," I went on, "people who have thoughts in their heads and quick tongues with which to voice them, and we'll sit in cafés and we'll drink together and we'll clash with each other violently in words, and we'll talk for the rest of our lives in divine excitement."

He reached out and put his arm around my neck and kissed me. We almost upset the table we were so blissfully drunk.

"My lord, the wolfkiller," he whispered.

When the third bottle of wine came, I began to talk of my life, as I'd never done before—of what it was like each day to ride out into the mountains, to go so far I couldn't see the towers of my father's house anymore, to ride above the tilled land to the place where the forest seemed almost haunted.

The words began to pour out of me as they had out of him, and soon we were talking about a thousand things we had felt in our hearts, varieties of secret loneliness, and the words seemed to be essential words the way they did on those rare occasions with my mother. And as we came to describe our longings and dissatisfactions, we were saying things to each other with great exuberance, like "Yes, yes," and "Exactly," and "I know completely what you mean," and "And yes, of course, you felt that you could not bear it," etc.

Another bottle, and a new fire. And I begged Nicolas to play his violin for me. He rushed home immediately to get it.

It was now late afternoon. The sun was slanting through the window and the fire was very hot. We were very drunk. We had never ordered supper. And I think I was happier than I had ever been in my life. I lay on the lumpy straw mattress of the little bed with my hands under my head watching him as he took out the instrument.

He put the violin to his shoulder and began to pluck at it and twist the pegs.

Then he raised the bow and drew it down hard over the strings to bring out the first note.

I sat up and pushed myself back against the paneled wall and stared at him because I couldn't believe the sound I was hearing.

He ripped into the song. He tore the notes out of the violin and each note was translucent and throbbing. His eyes were closed, his mouth a little distorted, his lower lip sliding to the side, and what struck my heart almost as much as the song itself was the way that he seemed with his whole body to lean into the music, to press his soul like an ear to the instrument.

I had never known music like it, the rawness of it, the intensity, the rapid glittering torrents of notes that came out of the strings as he sawed away. It was Mozart that he was playing, and it had all the gaiety, the velocity, and the sheer loveliness of everything Mozart wrote.

When he'd finished, I was staring at him and I realized I was gripping the sides of my head.

"Monsieur, what's the matter!" he said, almost helplessly, and I stood up and threw my arms around him and kissed him on both cheeks and kissed the violin.

"Stop calling me Monsieur," I said. "Call me by my name." I lay back down on the bed and buried my face on my arm and started to cry, and once I'd started I couldn't stop it.

He sat next to me, hugging me and asking me why I was crying, and though I couldn't tell him, I could see that he was overwhelmed that his music had produced this effect. There was no sarcasm or bitterness in him now.

I think he carried me home that night.

And the next morning I was standing in the crooked stone street in front of his father's shop, tossing pebbles up at his window.

When he stuck his head out, I said:

"Do you want to come down and go on with our conversation?"

5

ROM then on, when I was not hunting, my life was with Nicolas and "our conversation."

Spring was approaching, the mountains were dappled with green, the apple orchard starting back to life. And Nicolas and I were always together.

We took long walks up the rocky slopes, had our bread and wine in the sun on the grass, roamed south through the ruins of an old monastery. We hung about in my rooms or sometimes climbed to the battlements. And we went back to our room at the inn when we were too drunk and too loud to be tolerated by others.

And as the weeks passed we revealed more and more of ourselves to each other. Nicolas told me about his childhood at school, the little disappointments of his early years, those whom he had known and loved.

And I started to tell him the painful things—and finally the old disgrace of running off with the Italian players.

It came to that one night when we were in the inn again, and we were drunk as usual. In fact we were at that moment of drunkenness that the two of us had come to call the Golden Moment, when everything made sense. We always tried to stretch out that moment, and then inevitably one of us would confess, "I can't follow anymore, I think the Golden Moment's passed."

On this night, looking out the window at the moon over the mountains, I said that at the Golden Moment it was not so terrible that we weren't in Paris, that we weren't at the Opéra or the Comédie, waiting for the curtain to rise.

"You and the theaters of Paris," he said to me. "No matter what we're talking about you bring it back to the theaters and the actors—"

His brown eyes were very big and trusting. And even drunk as he was, he looked spruce in his red velvet Paris frock coat.

"Actors and actresses make magic," I said. "They make things happen on the stage; they invent; they create."

"Wait until you see the sweat streaming down their painted faces in the glare of the footlights," he answered.

"Ah, there you go again," I said. "And you, the one who gave up everything to play the violin."

He got terribly serious suddenly, looking off as if he were weary of his own struggles.

"That I did," he confessed.

Even now the whole village knew it was war between him and his father. Nicki wouldn't go back to school in Paris.

"You make life when you play," I said. "You create something from nothing. You make something good happen. And that is blessed to me."

"I make music and it makes me happy," he said. "What is blessed or good about that?"

I waved it away as I always did his cynicism now.

"I've lived all these years among those who create nothing and change nothing," I said. "Actors and musicians—they're saints to me."

"Saints?" he asked. "Blessedness? Goodness? Lestat, your language baffles me."

I smiled and shook my head.

"You don't understand. I'm speaking of the character of human beings, not what they believe in. I'm speaking of those who won't accept a useless life, just because they were born to it. I mean those who would be something better. They work, they sacrifice, they do things . . ."

He was moved by this, and I was a little surprised that I'd said it. Yet I felt I had hurt him somehow.

"There is blessedness in that," I said. "There's sanctity. And God or no God, there is goodness in it. I know this the way I know the mountains are out there, that the stars shine."

He looked sad for me. And he looked hurt still. But for the moment I didn't think of him.

I was thinking of the conversation I had had with my mother and my perception that I couldn't be good and defy my family. But if I believed what I was saying . . .

As if he could read my mind, he asked:

"But do you really believe those things?"

"Maybe yes. Maybe no," I said. I couldn't bear to see him look so sad.

And I think more on account of that than anything else I told him the whole story of how I'd run off with the players. I told him what I'd never told anyone, not even my mother, about those few days and the happiness they'd given me.

"Now, how could it not have been good," I asked, "to give and receive such happiness? We brought to life that town when we put on our play. Magic, I tell you. It could heal the sick, it could."

He shook his head. And I knew there were things he wanted to say, which out of respect for me he was leaving to silence.

"You don't understand, do you?" I asked.

"Lestat, sin always feels good," he said gravely. "Don't you see that? Why do you think the Church has always condemned the players? It was from Dionysus, the wine god, that the theater came. You can read that in

Aristotle. And Dionysus was a god that drove men to debauchery. It felt good to you to be on that stage because it was abandoned and lewd—the age-old service of the god of the grape—and you were having a high time of it defying your father—"

"No, Nicki. No, a thousand times no."

"Lestat, we're partners in sin," he said, smiling finally. "We've always been. We've both behaved badly, both been utterly disreputable. It's what binds us together."

Now it was my turn to look sad and hurt. And the Golden Moment was gone beyond reprieve—unless something new was to happen.

"Come on," I said suddenly. "Get your violin, and we'll go off somewhere in the woods where the music won't wake up anybody. We'll see if there isn't some goodness in it."

"You're a madman!" he said. But he grabbed the unopened bottle by the neck and headed for the door immediately.

I was right behind him.

When he came out of his house with the violin, he said:

"Let's go to the witches' place! Look, it's a half moon. Plenty of light. We'll do the devil's dance and play for the spirits of the witches."

I laughed. I had to be drunk to go along with that. "We'll reconsecrate the spot," I insisted, "with good and pure music."

It had been years and years since I'd walked in the witches' place.

The moon was bright enough, as he'd said, to see the charred stakes in their grim circle and the ground in which nothing ever grew even one hundred years after the burnings. The new saplings of the forest kept their distance. And so the wind struck the clearing, and above, clinging to the rocky slope, the village hovered in darkness.

A faint chill passed over me, but it was the mere shadow of the anguish I'd felt as a child when I'd heard those awful words "roasted alive," when I had imagined the suffering.

Nicki's white lace shone in the pale light, and he struck up a gypsy song at once and danced round in a circle as he played it.

I sat on a broad burned stump of tree and drank from the bottle. And the heartbreaking feeling came as it always did with the music. What sin was there, I thought, except to live out my life in this awful place? And pretty soon I was silently and unobtrusively crying.

Though it seemed the music had never stopped, Nicki was comforting me. We sat side by side and he told me that the world was full of inequities and that we were prisoners, he and I, of this awful corner of France, and someday we would break out of it. And I thought of my mother in the castle high up the mountain, and the sadness numbed me until I couldn't bear it, and Nicki started playing again, telling me to dance and to forget everything.

Yes, that's what it could make you do, I wanted to say. Is that sin? How can it be evil? I went after him as he danced in a circle. The notes seemed to be flying up and out of the violin as if they were made of gold. I could almost see them flashing. I danced round and round him now and he sawed away into a deeper and more frenzied music. I spread the wings of the fur-lined cape and threw back my head to look at the moon. The music rose all around me like smoke, and the witches' place was no more. There was only the sky above arching down to the mountains.

We were closer for all this in the days that followed.

BUT a few nights later, something altogether extraordinary happened.

It was late. We were at the inn again and Nicolas, who was walking about the room and gesturing dramatically, declared what had been on our minds all along.

That we should run away to Paris, even if we were penniless, that it was better than remaining here. Even if we lived as beggars in Paris! It had to be better.

Of course we had both been building up to this.

"Well, beggars in the streets it might be, Nicki," I said. "Because I'll be damned in hell before I'll play the penniless country cousin begging at the big houses."

"Do you think I want you to do that?" he demanded. "I mean run away, Lestat," he said. "Spite them, every one of them."

Did I want to go on like this? So our fathers would curse us. After all, our life was *meaningless* here.

Of course, we both knew this running off together would be a thousand times more serious than what I had done before. We weren't boys anymore, we were men. Our fathers *would* curse us, and this was something neither of us could laugh off.

Also we were old enough to know what poverty meant.

"What am I going to do in Paris when we get hungry?" I asked. "Shoot rats for supper?"

"I'll play my violin for coins on the boulevard du Temple if I have to, and you can go to the theaters!" Now he was really challenging me. He was saying, Is it all words with you, Lestat? "With your looks, you know, you'd be on the stage in the boulevard du Temple in no time."

I loved this change in "our conversation"! I loved seeing him believe we could do it. All his cynicism had vanished, even though he did throw in the word "spite" every ten words or so. It seemed possible suddenly to do all this.

And this notion of the meaninglessness of our lives here began to enflame us.

I took up the theme again that music and acting were good because they drove back chaos. Chaos was the meaninglessness of day-to-day life, and if we were to die now, our lives would have been nothing but meaninglessness. In fact, it came to me that my mother dying soon was meaningless and I confided in Nicolas what she had said. "I'm perfectly *horrified.* I'm afraid."

Well, if there had been a Golden Moment in the room it was gone now. And something different started to happen.

I should call it the Dark Moment, but it was still high-pitched and full of eerie light. We were talking rapidly, cursing this meaninglessness, and when Nicolas at last sat down and put his head in his hands, I took some glamorous and hearty swigs of wine and went to pacing and gesturing as he had done before.

I realized aloud in the midst of saying it that even when we die we probably don't find out the answer as to why we were ever alive. Even the avowed atheist probably thinks that in death he'll get some answer. I mean God will be there, or there won't be anything at all.

"But that's just it," I said, "we don't make any discovery at that moment! We merely stop! We pass into nonexistence without ever knowing a thing." I saw the universe, a vision of the sun, the planets, the stars, black night going on forever. And I began to laugh.

"Do you realize that! We'll never know why the hell any of it happened, not even when it's over!" I shouted at Nicolas, who was sitting back on the bed, nodding and drinking his wine out of a flagon. "We're going to die and not even know. We'll never know, and all this meaninglessness will just go on and on and on. And we won't any longer be witnesses to it. We won't have even that little bit of power to give meaning to it in our minds. We'll just be gone, dead, dead, dead, without ever knowing!"

But I had stopped laughing. I stood still and I understood perfectly what I was saying!

There was no judgment day, no final explanation, no luminous moment in which all terrible wrongs would be made right, all horrors redeemed.

The witches burnt at the stake would never be avenged.

No one was ever going to tell us anything!

No, I didn't understand it at this moment. I *saw* it! And I began to make the single sound: "Oh!" I said it again "Oh!" and then I said it louder and louder and louder, and I dropped the wine bottle on the floor. I put my hands to my head and I kept saying it, and I could see my mouth opened in that perfect circle that I had described to my mother and I kept saying, "Oh, oh, oh!"

I said it like a great hiccuping that I couldn't stop. And Nicolas took hold of me and started shaking me, saying:

"Lestat, stop!"

I couldn't stop. I ran to the window, unlatched it and swung out the heavy little glass, and stared at the stars. I couldn't stand seeing them. I couldn't stand seeing the pure emptiness, the silence, the absolute absence of any answer, and I started roaring as Nicolas pulled me back from the windowsill and pulled shut the glass.

"You'll be all right," he said over and over. Someone was beating on the door. It was the innkeeper, demanding why we had to carry on like this.

"You'll feel all right in the morning," Nicolas kept insisting. "You just have to sleep."

We had awakened everyone. I couldn't be quiet. I kept making the same sound over again. And I ran out of the inn with Nicolas behind me, and down the street of the village and up towards the castle with Nicolas trying to catch up with me, and through the gates and up into my room.

"Sleep, that's what you need," he kept saying to me desperately. I was lying against the wall with my hands over my ears, and that sound kept coming. "Oh, oh, oh."

"In the morning," he said, "it will be better."

WELL, it was not better in the morning.

And it was no better by nightfall, and in fact it got worse with the coming of the darkness.

I walked and talked and gestured like a contented human being, but I was flayed. I was shuddering. My teeth were chattering. I couldn't stop it. I was staring at everything around me in horror. The darkness terrified me. The sight of the old suits of armor in the hall terrified me. I stared at the mace and the flail I'd taken out after the wolves. I stared at the faces of my brothers. I stared at everything, seeing behind every configuration of color and light and shadow the same thing: death. Only it wasn't just death as I'd thought of it before, it was death the way I saw it now. Real death, total death, inevitable, irreversible, and resolving nothing!

And in this unbearable state of agitation I commenced to do something I'd never done before. I turned to those around me and questioned them relentlessly.

"But do you believe in God?" I asked my brother Augustin. "How can you live if you don't!"

"But do you really believe in anything?" I demanded of my blind father. "If you knew you were dying at this very minute, would you expect to see God or darkness! Tell me."

"You're mad, you've always been mad!" he shouted. "Get out of this house! You'll drive us all crazy."

He stood up, which was hard for him, being crippled and blind, and he tried to throw his goblet at me and naturally he missed.

I couldn't look at my mother. I couldn't be near her. I didn't want to make her suffer with my questions. I went down to the inn. I couldn't bear to think of the witches' place. I would not have walked to that end of the village for anything! I put my hands over my ears and shut my eyes. "Go away!" I said at the thought of those who'd died like that without ever, ever understanding anything.

The second day it was no better.

And it wasn't any better by the end of the week either.

I ate, drank, slept, but every waking moment was pure panic and pure pain. I went to the village priest and demanded did he really believe the Body of Christ was present on the altar at the Consecration. And after hearing his stammered answers, and seeing the fear in his eyes, I went away more desperate than before.

"But how do you live, how do you go on breathing and moving and doing things when you know there is no explanation?" I was raving finally. And then Nicolas said maybe the music would make me feel better. He would play the violin.

I was afraid of the intensity of it. But we went to the orchard and in the sunshine Nicolas played every song he knew. I sat there with my arms folded and my knees drawn up, my teeth chattering though we were right in the hot sun, and the sun was glaring off the little polished violin, and I watched Nicolas swaying into the music as he stood before me, the raw pure sounds swelling magically to fill the orchard and the valley, though it wasn't magic, and Nicolas put his arms around me finally and we just sat there silent, and then he said very softly, "Lestat, believe me, this will pass."

"Play again," I said. "The music is innocent."

Nicolas smiled and nodded. Pamper the madman.

And I knew it wasn't going to pass, and nothing for the moment could make me forget, but what I felt was inexpressible gratitude for the music, that in this horror there could be something as beautiful as that.

You couldn't understand anything; and you couldn't change anything. But you could make music like that. And I felt the same gratitude when I saw the village children dancing, when I saw their arms raised and their knees bent, and their bodies turning to the rhythm of the songs they sang. I started to cry watching them.

I wandered into the church and on my knees I leaned against the wall and I looked at the ancient statues and I felt the same gratitude looking at the finely carved fingers and the noses and the ears and the expressions on their faces and the deep folds in their garments, and I couldn't stop myself from crying.

At least we had these beautiful things, I said. Such goodness.

But nothing natural seemed beautiful to me now! The very sight of a great tree standing alone in a field could make me tremble and cry out. Fill the orchard with music.

And let me tell you a little secret. It *never did pass, really.*

6

WHAT caused it? Was it the late night drinking and talking, or did it have to do with my mother and her saying she was going to die? Did the wolves have something to do with it? Was it a spell cast upon the imagination by the witches' place?

I don't know. It had come like something visited upon me from outside. One minute it was an idea, and the next it was *real.* I think you can invite that sort of thing, but you can't make it come.

Of course it was to slacken. But the sky was never quite the same shade of blue again. I mean the world looked different forever after, and even in moments of exquisite happiness there was the darkness lurking, the sense of our frailty and our hopelessness.

Maybe it was a presentiment. But I don't think so. It was more important than that, and frankly I don't believe in presentiments.

BUT to return to the story, during all this misery I kept away from my mother. I wasn't going to say these monstrous things about death and chaos to her. But she heard from everyone else that I'd lost my reason.

And finally, on the first Sunday night in Lent, she came to me.

I was alone in my room and the whole household had gone down to the village at twilight for the big bonfire that was the custom every year on this evening.

I had always hated the celebration. It had a ghastly aspect to it—the roaring flames, the dancing and singing, the peasants going afterwards through the orchards with their torches to the tune of their strange chanting.

We had had a priest for a little while who called it pagan. But they got rid of him fast enough. The farmers of our mountains kept to their old rituals. It was to make the trees bear and the crops grow, all this. And on this occasion, more than any other, I felt I saw the kind of men and women who could burn witches.

In my present frame of mind, it struck terror. I sat by my own little fire, trying to resist the urge to go to the window and look down on the big fire that drew me as strongly as it scared me.

My mother came in, closed the door behind her, and told me that she must talk to me. Her whole manner was tenderness.

"Is it on account of my dying, what's come over you?" she asked. "Tell me if it is. And put your hands in mine."

She even kissed me. She was frail in her faded dressing gown, and her hair was undone. I couldn't stand to see the streaks of gray in it. She looked starved.

But I told her the truth. I didn't know, and then I explained some of what had happened in the inn. I tried not to convey the horror of it, the strange logic of it. I tried not to make it so absolute.

She listened and then she said, "You're such a fighter, my son. You never *accept.* Not even when it's the fate of all mankind, will you accept it."

"I can't!" I said miserably.

"I love you for it," she said. "It's all too like you that you should see this in a tiny bedroom in the inn late at night when you're drinking wine. And it's entirely like you to rage against it the way you rage against everything else."

I started to cry again though I knew she wasn't condemning me. And then she took out a handkerchief and opened it to reveal several gold coins.

"You'll get over this," she said. "For the moment, death is spoiling life for you, that's all. But life is more important than death. You'll realize it soon enough. Now listen to what I have to say. I've had the doctor here and the old woman in the village who knows more about healing than he knows. Both agree with me I won't live too long."

"Stop, Mother," I said, aware of how selfish I was being, but unable to hold back. "And this time there'll be no gifts. Put the money away."

"Sit down," she said. She pointed to the bench near the hearth. Reluctantly I did as I was told. She sat beside me.

"I know," she said, "that you and Nicolas are talking of running away."

"I won't go, Mother . . ."

"What, until I'm dead?"

I didn't answer her. I can't convey to you my frame of mind. I was still raw, trembling, and we had to talk about the fact that this living, breathing woman was going to stop living and breathing and start to putrefy and rot away, that her soul would spin into an abyss, that everything she had suffered in life, including the end of it, would come to nothing at all. Her little face was like something painted on a veil.

And from the distant village came the thinnest sound of the singing villagers.

"I want you to go to Paris, Lestat," she said. "I want you to take this money, which is all I have left from my family. I want to know you're in Paris, Lestat, when my time comes. I want to die knowing you are in Paris."

I was startled. I remembered her stricken expression years ago when they'd brought me back from the Italian troupe. I looked at her for a long moment. She sounded almost angry in her persuasiveness.

"I'm terrified of dying," she said. Her voice went almost dry. "And I swear I will go mad if I don't know you're in Paris and you're free when it finally comes."

I questioned her with my eyes. I was asking her with my eyes, "Do you really mean this?"

"I have kept you here as surely as your father has," she said. "Not on account of pride, but on account of selfishness. And now I'm going to atone for it. I'll see you go. And I don't care what you do when you reach Paris, whether you sing while Nicolas plays the violin, or turn somersaults on the stage at the St.-Germain Fair. But go, and do what you will do as best you can."

I tried to take her in my arms. She stiffened at first but then I felt her weaken and she melted against me, and she gave herself over so completely to me in that moment that I think I understood why she had always been so restrained. She cried, which I'd never heard her do. And I loved this moment for all its pain. I was ashamed of loving it, but I wouldn't let her go. I held her tightly, and maybe kissed her for all the times she'd never let me do it. We seemed for the moment like two parts of the same thing.

And then she grew calm. She seemed to settle into herself, and slowly but very firmly she released me and pushed me away.

She talked for a long time. She said things I didn't understand then, about how when she would see me riding out to hunt, she felt some wondrous pleasure in it, and she felt that same pleasure when I angered everyone and thundered my questions at my father and brothers as to why we had to live the way we lived. She spoke in an almost eerie way of my being a secret part of her anatomy, of my being the organ for her which women do not really have.

"You are the man in me," she said. "And so I've kept you here, afraid of living without you, and maybe now in sending you away, I am only doing what I have done before."

She shocked me a little. I never thought a woman could feel or articulate anything quite like this.

"Nicolas's father knows about your plans," she said. "The innkeeper overheard you. It's important you leave right away. Take the diligence at dawn, and write to me as soon as you reach Paris. There are letter writers at the cemetery of les Innocents near the St.-Germain Market. Find one who can write Italian for you. And then no one will be able to read the letter but me."

When she left the room, I didn't quite believe what had happened. For a long moment I stood staring before me. I stared at my bed with its mattress of straw, at the two coats I owned and the red cloak, and my one pair of leather shoes by the hearth. I stared out the narrow slit of a window at the black hulk of the mountains I'd known all my life. The darkness, the gloom, slid back from me for a precious moment.

And then I was rushing down the stairs and down the mountain to the village to find Nicolas and to tell him we were going to Paris! We were going to do it. Nothing could stop us this time.

He was with his family watching the bonfire. And as soon as he saw me, he threw his arm around my neck, and I hooked my arm around his waist and I dragged him away from the crowds and the blaze, and towards the end of the meadow.

The air smelled fresh and green as it does only in spring. Even the villagers' singing didn't sound so horrible. I started dancing around in a circle.

"Get your violin!" I said. "Play a song about going to Paris, we're on our way. We're going in the morning!"

"And how are we going to feed ourselves in Paris?" he sang out as he made with his empty hands to play an invisible violin. "Are you going to shoot rats for our supper?"

"Don't ask what we'll do when we get there!" I said. "The important thing is just to get there."

7

NOT even a fortnight passed before I stood in the midst of the noonday crowds in the vast public cemetery of les Innocents, with its old vaults and stinking open graves—the most fantastical marketplace I had ever beheld—and, amid the stench and the noise, bent over an Italian letter writer dictating my first letter to my mother.

Yes, we had arrived safely after traveling day and night, and we had rooms in the Ile de la Cité, and we were inexpressibly happy, and Paris was warm and beautiful and magnificent beyond all imagining.

I wished I could have taken the pen myself and written to her.

I wished I could have told her what it was like, seeing these towering mansions, ancient winding streets aswarm with beggars, peddlers, noblemen, houses of four and five stories banking the crowded boulevards.

I wished I could have described the carriages to her, the rumbling confections of gilt and glass bullying their way over the Pont Neuf and the Pont Notre Dame, streaming past the Louvre, the Palais Royal.

I wished I could describe the people, the gentlemen with their clocked stockings and silver walking sticks, tripping through the mud in pastel slippers, the ladies with their pearl-encrusted wigs and swaying panniers of silk and muslin, my first certain glimpse of Queen Marie Antoinette herself walking boldly through the gardens of the Tuileries.

Of course she'd seen it all years and years before I was born. She'd lived in Naples and London and Rome with her father. But I wanted to tell her what she had given to me, how it was to hear the choir in Notre Dame, to push into the jam-packed cafés with Nicolas, talk with his old student cronies over English coffee, what it was like to get dressed up in Nicolas's fine clothes—he made me do it—and stand below the footlights at the Comédie-Française gazing up in adoration at the actors on the stage.

But all I wrote in this letter was perhaps the very best of it, the address of the garret rooms we called our home in the Ile de la Cité, and the news:

"I have been hired in a real theater to study as an actor with a fine prospect of performing very soon."

What I didn't tell her was that we had to walk up six flights of stairs to our rooms, that men and women brawled and screamed in the alleyways beneath our windows, that we had run out of money already, thanks to my dragging us to every opera, ballet, and drama in town. And that the establishment where I worked was a shabby little boulevard theater, one step up from a platform at the fair, and my jobs were to help the players dress, sell tickets, sweep up, and throw out the troublemakers.

But I was in paradise again. And so was Nicolas though no decent orchestra in the city would hire him, and he was now playing solos with the little bunch of musicians in the theater where I worked, and when we were really pinched he did play right on the boulevard, with me beside him, holding out the hat. We were shameless!

We ran up the steps each night with our bottle of cheap wine and a loaf of fine sweet Parisian bread, which was ambrosia after what we'd eaten in the Auvergne. And in the light of our one tallow candle, the garret was the most glorious place I'd ever inhabited.

As I mentioned before, I'd seldom been in a little wooden room except in the inn. Well, this room had plaster walls and a plaster ceiling! It was really Paris! It had polished wood flooring, and even a tiny little fireplace with a new chimney which actually made a draft.

So what if we had to sleep on lumpy pallets, and the neighbors woke us up fighting. We were waking up in Paris, and could roam arm in arm for hours through streets and alleyways, peering into shops full of jewelry and plate, tapestries and statues, wealth such as I'd never seen. Even the reeking meat markets delighted me. The crash and clatter of the city, the tireless busyness of its thousands upon thousands of laborers, clerks, craftsmen, the comings and goings of an endless multitude.

By day I almost forgot the vision of the inn, and the darkness. Unless, of course, I glimpsed some uncollected corpse in a filthy alleyway, of which there were many, or I happened upon a public execution in the place de Grève.

And I was *always* happening upon a public execution in the place de Grève.

I'd wander out of the square shuddering, almost moaning. I could become obsessed with it if not distracted. But Nicolas was adamant.

"Lestat, no talk of the eternal, the immutable, the unknowable!" He threatened to hit me or shake me if I should start.

And when twilight came on—the time I hated more than ever—whether I had seen an execution or not, whether the day had been glorious or vexing, the trembling would start in me. And only one thing saved me from it: the warmth and excitement of the brightly lighted theater, and I made sure that before dusk I was safely inside.

Now, in the Paris of those times, the theaters of the boulevards weren't even legitimate houses at all. Only the Comédie-Française and the Théâtre des Italiens were government-sanctioned theaters, and to them all serious drama belonged. This included tragedy as well as comedy, the plays of Racine, Corneille, the brilliant Voltaire.

But the old Italian commedia that I loved—Pantaloon, Harlequin, Scaramouche, and the rest—lived on as they always had, with tightrope walkers, acrobats, jugglers, and puppeteers, in the platform spectacles at the St.-Germain and the St.-Laurent fairs.

And the boulevard theaters had grown out of these fairs. By my time, the last decades of the eighteenth century, they were permanent establishments along the boulevard du Temple, and though they played to the poor who couldn't afford the grand houses, they also collected a very well-to-do crowd. Plenty of the aristocracy and the rich bourgeoisie crowded into the loges to see the boulevard performances, because they were lively and full of good talent, and not so stiff as the plays of the great Racine or the great Voltaire.

We did the Italian comedy just as I'd learned it before, full of improvisation so that every night it was new and different yet always the same. And we also did singing and all kinds of nonsense, not just because the people loved it, but because we had to: we couldn't be accused of breaking the monopoly of the state theaters on straight plays.

The house itself was a rickety wooden rattrap, seating no more than three hundred, but its little stage and props were elegant, it had a luxurious blue velvet stage curtain, and its private boxes had screens. And its actors and actresses were seasoned and truly talented, or so it seemed to me.

Even if I hadn't had this newly acquired dread of the dark, this "malady of mortality," as Nicolas persisted in calling it, it couldn't have been more exciting to go through that stage door.

For five to six hours every evening, I lived and breathed in a little universe of shouting and laughing and quarreling men and women, struggling for this one and against that one, all of us comrades in the wings even if we weren't friends. Maybe it was like being in a little boat on the ocean, all of us pulling together, unable to escape each other. It was divine.

Nicolas was slightly less enthusiastic, but then that was to be expected. And he got even more ironical when his rich student friends came around to talk to him. They thought he was a lunatic to live as he did. And for me, a nobleman shoveling actresses into their costumes and emptying slop buckets, they had no words at all.

Of course all that these young bourgeois really wanted was to be aristocrats. They bought titles, married into aristocratic families whenever they could. And it's one of the little jokes of history that they got mixed up in the Revolution, and helped to abolish the class which in fact they really wanted to join.

I didn't care if we ever saw Nicolas's friends again. The actors didn't know about my family, and in favor of the very simple Lestat de Valois, which meant nothing actually, I'd dropped my real name, de Lioncourt.

I was learning everything I could about the stage. I memorized, I mimicked. I asked endless questions. And only stopped my education long enough each night for that moment when Nicolas played his solo on the violin. He'd rise from his seat in the tiny orchestra, the spotlight would pick him out from the others, and he would rip into a little sonata, sweet enough and just short enough to bring down the house.

And all the while I dreamed of my own moment, when the old actors, whom I studied and pestered and imitated and waited upon like a lackey, would finally say: "All right, Lestat, tonight we need you as Lelio. Now you ought to know what to do."

It came in late August at last.

Paris was at its warmest, and the nights were almost balmy and the house was full of a restless audience fanning itself with handkerchiefs and handbills. The thick white paint was melting on my face as I put it on.

I wore a pasteboard sword with Nicolas's best velvet coat, and I was trembling before I stepped on the stage thinking, This is like waiting to be executed or something.

But as soon as I stepped out there, I turned and looked directly into the jam-packed hall and the strangest thing happened. The fear evaporated.

I beamed at the audience and very slowly I bowed. I stared at the lovely Flaminia as if I were seeing her for the first time. I had to win her. The romp began.

The stage belonged to me as it had years and years ago in that far-off country town. And as we pranced madly together across the boards—quarreling, embracing, clowning—laughter rocked the house.

I could feel the attention as if it were an embrace. Each gesture, each line brought a roar from the audience—it was too easy almost—and we could have worked it for another half hour if the other actors, eager to get into the next trick as they called it, hadn't forced us finally towards the wings.

The crowd was standing up to applaud us. And it wasn't that country audience under the open sky. These were *Parisians* shouting for Lelio and Flaminia to come back out.

In the shadows of the wings, I reeled. I almost collapsed. I could not see anything for the moment but the vision of the audience gazing up at me over the footlights. I wanted to go right back on stage. I grabbed Flaminia and kissed her and realized that she was kissing me back passionately.

Then Renaud, the old manager, pulled her away.

"All right, Lestat," he said as if he were cross about something. "All right, you've done tolerably well, I'm going to let you go on regularly from now on."

But before I could start jumping up and down for joy, half the troupe materialized around us. And Luchina, one of the actresses, immediately spoke up.

"Oh no, you'll not *let* him go on regularly!" she said. "He's the handsomest actor on the boulevard du Temple and you'll hire him outright for it, and pay him outright for it, and he doesn't touch another broom or mop." I was terrified. My career had just started and it was about to be over, but to my amazement Renaud agreed to all her terms.

Of course I was very flattered to be called handsome, and I understood as I had years ago that Lelio, the lover, is supposed to have considerable style. An aristocrat with any breeding whatsoever was perfect for the part.

But if I was going to make the Paris audiences really notice me, if I was going to have them talking about me at the Comédie-Française, I had to be more than some yellow-haired angel fallen out of a marquis's family onto the stage. I had to be a great actor, and that is exactly what I determined to be.

THAT night Nicolas and I celebrated with a colossal drunk. We had all the troupe up to our rooms for it, and I climbed out on the slippery rooftops and opened my arms to Paris and Nicolas played his violin in the window until we'd awakened the whole neighborhood.

The music was rapturous, yet people were snarling and screaming up the alleyways, and banging on pots and pans. We paid no attention. We were dancing and singing as we had in the witches' place. I almost fell off the window ledge.

The next day, bottle in hand, I dictated the whole story to the Italian letter writer in the stinking sunshine in les Innocents and saw that the letter went off to my mother at once. I wanted to embrace everybody I saw in the streets. I was Lelio. I was an actor.

By September I had my name on the handbills. And I sent those to my mother, too.

And we weren't doing the old commedia. We were performing a farce by a famous writer who, on account of a general playwrights' strike, couldn't get it performed at the Comédie-Française.

Of course we couldn't say his name, but everyone knew it was his work, and half the court was packing Renaud's House of Thesbians every night.

I wasn't the lead, but I was the young lover, a sort of Lelio again really, which was almost better than the lead, and I stole every scene in which I appeared. Nicolas had taught me the part, bawling me out constantly for not learning to read. And by the fourth performance, the playwright had written extra lines for me.

Nicki was having his own moment at the intermezzo, when his latest rendering of a frothy little Mozart sonata was keeping the house in its seats. Even his student friends were back. We were getting invitations to private balls. I went tearing off to les Innocents every few days to write to my mother, and finally I had a clipping from an English paper, *The Spectator*, to send her, which praised our little play and in particular the blond-haired rogue who steals the hearts of the ladies in the third and fourth acts. Of course I couldn't read this clipping. But the gentleman who'd brought it to me said it was complimentary, and Nicolas swore it was too.

When the first chill nights of fall came on, I wore the fur-lined red cloak on the stage. You could have seen it in the back row of the gallery even if you were almost blind. I had more skill now with the white makeup, shading it here and there to heighten the contours of my face, and though my eyes were ringed in black and my lips reddened a little, I looked both startling and human at the same time. I got love notes from the women in the crowd.

Nicolas was studying music in the mornings with an Italian maestro. Yet we had money enough for good food, wood, and coal. My mother's letters came twice a week and said her health had taken a turn for the better. She wasn't coughing as badly as last winter. She wasn't in pain. But our fathers had disowned us and would not acknowledge any mention of our names.

We were too happy to worry about that. But the dark dread, the "malady of mortality," was with me a lot when the cold weather came on.

THE cold seemed worse in Paris. It wasn't clean as it had been in the mountains. The poor hovered in doorways, shivering and hungry, the crooked unpaved streets were thick with filthy slush. I saw barefoot children suffering before my very eyes, and more neglected corpses lying about than ever before. I was never so glad of the fur-lined cape as I was then. I wrapped it around Nicolas and held him close to me when we went out together, and we walked in a tight embrace through the snow and the rain.

Cold or no cold, I can't exaggerate the happiness of these days. Life was exactly what I thought it could be. And I knew I wouldn't be long in Renaud's theater. Everybody was saying so. I had visions of the big stages, of touring London and Italy and even America with a great troupe of actors. Yet there was no reason to hurry. My cup was full.

8

BUT in the month of October when Paris was already freezing, I commenced to see, quite regularly, a strange face in the audience that invariably distracted me. Sometimes it almost made me forget what I was doing, this face. And then it would be gone as if I'd imagined it. I must have seen it off and on for a fortnight before I finally mentioned it to Nicki.

I felt foolish and found it hard to put into words:

"There is someone out there watching me," I said.

"Everyone's watching you," Nicki said. "That's what you want."

He was feeling a little sad that evening, and his answer was slightly sharp.

Earlier when he was making the fire, he had said he would never amount to much with the violin. In spite of his ear and his skill, there was too much he didn't know. And I would be a great actor, he was sure. I had said this was nonsense, but it was a shadow falling over my soul. I remembered my mother telling me that it was too late for him.

He wasn't envious, he said. He was just unhappy a little, that's all.

I decided to drop the matter of the mysterious face. I tried to think of some way to encourage him. I reminded him that his playing produced profound emotions in people, that even the actors backstage stopped to listen when he played. He had an undeniable talent.

"But I want to be a great violinist," he said. "And I'm afraid it will never be. As long as we were at home, I could pretend that it was going to be."

"You can't give up on it!" I said.

"Lestat, let me be frank with you," he said. "Things are easy for you. What you set your sights on you get for yourself. I know what you're thinking, about all the years you were miserable at home. But even then, what you really set your mind to, you accomplished. And we left for Paris the very day that you decided to do it."

"You don't regret coming to Paris, do you?" I asked.

"Of course not. I simply mean that you think things are possible which aren't possible! At least not for the rest of us. Like killing the wolves . . ."

A coldness passed over me when he said this. And for some reason I thought of that mysterious face again in the audience, the one watching. Something to do with the wolves. Something to do with the sentiments Nicki was expressing. Didn't make sense. I tried to shrug it off.

"If you'd set out to play the violin, you'd probably be playing for the Court by now," he said.

"Nicki, this kind of talk is poison," I said under my breath. "You can't do anything but try to get what you want. You knew the odds were against you when you started. There isn't anything else . . . except . . ."

"I know." He smiled. "Except the meaninglessness. Death."

"Yes," I said. "All you can do is make your life have meaning, make it good—"

"Oh, not goodness again," he said. "You and your malady of mortality, and your malady of goodness." He had been looking at the fire and he turned to me with a deliberately scornful expression. "We're a pack of actors and entertainers who can't even be buried in consecrated ground. We're outcasts."

"God, if you could only believe in it," I said, "that we do good when we make others forget their sorrow, make them forget for a little while that . . ."

"What? That they are going to die?" He smiled in a particularly vicious way. "Lestat, I thought all this would change with you when you got to Paris."

"That was foolish of you, Nick," I answered. He was making me angry now. "I do good in the boulevard du Temple. I feel it—"

I stopped because I saw the mysterious face again and a dark feeling had passed over me, something of foreboding. Yet even that startling face was usually smiling, that was the odd thing. Yes, smiling . . . enjoying . . .

"Lestat, I love you," Nicki said gravely. "I love you as I have loved few people in my life, but in a real way you're a fool with all your ideas about goodness."

I laughed.

"Nicolas," I said, "I can live without God. I can even come to live with the idea there is no life after. But I do not think I could go on if I did not believe in the possibility of goodness. Instead of mocking me for once, why don't you tell me what you believe?"

"As I see it," he said, "there's weakness and there's strength. And there is good art and bad art. And that is what I believe in. At the moment we are engaged in making what is rather bad art and it has *nothing* to do with goodness!"

"Our conversation" could have turned into a full-scale fight here if I had said all that was on my mind about bourgeois pomposity. For I fully believed that our work at Renaud's was in many ways finer than what I saw at the grand theaters. Only the framework was less impressive. Why couldn't a bourgeois gentleman forget about the frame? How could he be made to look at something other than the surface?

I took a deep breath.

"If goodness does exist," he said, "then I'm the opposite of it. I'm evil and I revel in it. I thumb my nose at goodness. And if you must know, I don't play the violin for the idiots who come to Renaud's to make them happy. I play it for me, for Nicolas."

I didn't want to hear any more. It was time to go to bed. But I was bruised by this little talk and he knew it, and as I started to pull off my boots, he got up from the chair and came and sat next to me.

"I'm sorry," he said in the most broken voice. It was so changed from the posture of a minute ago that I looked up at him, and he was so young and so miserable that I couldn't help putting my arm around him and telling him that he must not worry about it anymore.

"You have a radiance in you, Lestat," he said. "And it draws everyone to you. It's there even when you're angry, or discouraged—"

"Poetry," I said. "We're both tired."

"No, it's true," he said. "You have a light in you that's almost blinding. But in me there's only darkness. Sometimes I think it's like the darkness that infected you that night in the inn when you began to cry and to tremble. You were so helpless, so unprepared for it. I try to keep that darkness from you because I need your light. I need it desperately, but you don't need the darkness."

"You're the mad one," I said. "If you could see yourself, hear your own voice, your music—which of course you play for yourself—you wouldn't see darkness, Nicki. You'd see an illumination that is all your own. Somber, yes, but light and beauty come together in you in a thousand different patterns."

THE next night the performance went especially well. The audience was a lively one, inspiring all of us to extra tricks. I did some new dance steps that for some reason never proved interesting in private rehearsal but worked miraculously on the stage. And Nicki was extraordinary with the violin, playing one of his own compositions.

But towards the end of the evening I glimpsed the mysterious face again. It jarred me worse than it ever had, and I almost lost the rhythm of my song. In fact it seemed my head for a moment was swimming.

When Nicki and I were alone I had to talk about it, about the peculiar sensation that I had fallen asleep on the stage and had been dreaming.

We sat by the hearth together with our wine on the top of a little barrel, and in the firelight Nicki looked as weary and dejected as he had the night before.

I didn't want to trouble him, but I couldn't forget about the face.

"Well, what does he look like?" Nicolas asked. He was warming his hands. And over his shoulder, I saw through the window a city of snow-covered rooftops that made me feel more cold. I didn't like this conversation.

"That's the worst part of it," I said. "All I see is a face. He must be wearing something black, a cloak and even a hood. But it looks like a mask to me, the face, very white and strangely clear. I mean the lines in his face are so deep they seemed to be etched with black greasepaint. I see it for a moment. It veritably glows. Then when I look again, there's no one there.

Yet this is an exaggeration. It's more subtle than that, the way he looks and yet . . ."

The description seemed to disturb Nicki as much as it disturbed me. He didn't say anything. But his face softened somewhat as if he were forgetting his sadness.

"Well, I don't want to get your hopes up," he said. He was very kind and sincere now. "But maybe it *is* a mask you're seeing. And maybe it's someone from the Comédie-Française come to see you perform."

I shook my head. "I wish it was, but no one would wear a mask like that. And I'll tell you something else, too."

He waited, but I could see I was passing on to him some of my own apprehension. He reached over and took the wine bottle by the neck and poured a little in my glass.

"Whoever he is," I said, "he knows about the wolves."

"He what?"

"He knows about the wolves." I was very unsure of myself. It was like recounting a dream I had all but forgotten. "He knows I killed the wolves back home. He knows the cloak I wear is lined with their fur."

"What are you talking about? You mean you've spoken to him?"

"No, that's just it," I said. This was so confusing to me, so vague. I felt that swimming sensation again. "That's what I'm trying to tell you. I've never spoken to him, never been near him. But he knows."

"Ah, Lestat," he said. He sat back on the bench. He was smiling at me in the most endearing way. "Next you'll be seeing ghosts. You have the strongest imagination of anyone I've ever known."

"There are no ghosts," I answered softly. I scowled at our little fire. I laid a few more lumps of coal on it.

All the humor went out of Nicolas.

"How in the hell could he know about the wolves? And how could you . . ."

"I told you already, I don't know!" I said. I sat thinking and not saying anything, disgusted, maybe, at how ridiculous it all seemed.

And then as we remained silent together, and the fire was the only sound or movement in the room, the name *Wolfkiller* came to me very distinctly as if someone had spoken it.

But nobody had.

I looked at Nicki, painfully aware that his lips had never moved, and I think all the blood drained from my face. I felt not the dread of death as I had on so many other nights, but an emotion that was really alien to me: fear.

I was still sitting there, too unsure of myself to say anything, when Nicolas kissed me.

"Let's go to bed," he said softly.

PART II

THE LEGACY OF MAGNUS

1

IT MUST have been three o'clock in the morning; I'd heard the church bells in my sleep.

And like all sensible men in Paris, we had our door barred and our window locked. Not good for a room with a coal fire, but the roof was a path to our window. And we were locked in.

I was dreaming of the wolves. I was on the mountain and surrounded and I was swinging the old medieval flail. Then the wolves were dead again, and the dream was better, only I had all those miles to walk in the snow. The horse screamed in the snow. My mare turned into a loathsome insect half smashed on the stone floor.

A voice said "Wolfkiller" long and low, a whisper that was like a summons and a tribute at the same time.

I opened my eyes. Or I thought I did. And there was someone standing in the room. A tall, bent figure with its back to the little hearth. Embers still glowed on the hearth. The light moved upwards, etching the edges of the figure clearly, then dying out before it reached the shoulders, the head. But I realized I was looking right at the white face I'd seen in the audience at the theater, and my mind, opening, sharpening, realized the room was locked, that Nicolas lay beside me, that this figure stood over our bed.

I heard Nicolas's breathing. I looked into the white face.

"Wolfkiller," came the voice again. But the lips hadn't moved, and the figure drew nearer and I saw that the face was no mask. Black eyes, quick and calculating black eyes, and white skin, and some appalling smell coming from it, like the smell of moldering clothes in a damp room.

I think I rose up. Or perhaps I was lifted. Because in an instant I was standing on my feet. The sleep was slipping off me like garments. I was backing up into the wall.

The figure had my red cloak in its hand. Desperately I thought of my sword, my muskets. They were under the bed on the floor. And the thing thrust the red cloak towards me and then, through the fur-lined velvet, I felt its hand close on the lapel of my coat.

I was torn forward. I was drawn off my feet across the room. I shouted for Nicolas. I screamed, "Nicki, Nicki!" as loud as I could. I saw the partially opened window, and then suddenly the glass burst into thousands of fragments and the wooden frame was broken out. I was flying over the alleyway, six stories above the ground.

I screamed. I kicked at this thing that was carrying me. Caught up in the red cloak, I twisted, trying to get loose.

But we were flying over the rooftop, and now going up the straight surface of a brick wall! I was dangling in the arm of the creature, and then very suddenly on the surface of a high place, I was thrown down.

I lay for a moment seeing Paris spread out before me in a great circle —the white snow, and chimney pots and church belfries, and the lowering sky. And then I rose up, stumbling over the fur-lined cloak, and I started to run. I ran to the edge of the roof and looked down. Nothing but a sheer drop of hundreds of feet, and then to another edge and it was exactly the same. I almost fell!

I turned desperate, panting. We were on the top of some square tower, no more than fifty feet across! And I could see nothing higher in any direction. And the figure stood staring at me, and I heard come out of it a low rasping laughter just like the whisper before.

"Wolfkiller," it said again.

"Damn you!" I shouted. "Who the hell are you!" And in a rage I flew at it with my fists.

It didn't move. I struck it as if I were striking the brick wall. I veritably bounced off it, losing my footing in the snow and scrambling up and attacking it again.

Its laughter grew louder and louder, and deliberately mocking, but with a strong undercurrent of pleasure that was even more maddening than the mockery. I ran to the edge of the tower and then turned on the creature again.

"What do you want with me!" I demanded. "Who are you!" And when it gave nothing but this maddening laughing, I went for it again. But this time I went for the face and the neck, and I made my hands like claws to do it, and I pulled off the hood and saw the creature's black hair and the full shape of its human-looking head. Soft skin. Yet it was as immovable as before.

It backed up a little, raising its arms to play with me, to push me back and forth as a man would push a little child. Too fast for my eyes, it moved its face away from me, turning to one side and then the other, and all of these movements with seeming effortlessness, as I frantically tried to hurt it and could feel nothing but that soft white skin sliding under my fingers and maybe once or twice its fine black hair.

"Brave strong little Wolfkiller," it said to me now in a rounder, deeper voice.

I stopped, panting and covered with sweat, staring at it and seeing the details of its face. The deep lines I had only glimpsed in the theater, its mouth drawn up in a jester's smile.

"Oh, God help me, help me . . ." I said as I backed away. It seemed impossible that such a face should move, show expression, and gaze with such affection on me as it did. "God!"

"What god is that, Wolfkiller?" it asked.

I turned my back on it, and let out a terrible roar. I felt its hands close on my shoulders like things forged of metal, and as I went into a last frenzy of struggling, it whipped me around so that its eyes were right before me, wide and dark, and the lips were closed yet still smiling, and then it bent down and I felt the prick of its teeth on my neck.

Out of all the childhood tales, the old fables, the name came to me, like a drowned thing shooting to the surface of black water and breaking free in the light.

"Vampire!" I gave one last frantic cry, shoving at the creature with all I had.

Then there was silence. Stillness.

I knew that we were still on the roof. I knew that I was being held in the thing's arms. Yet it seemed we had risen, become weightless, were traveling through the darkness even more easily than we had traveled before.

"Yes, yes," I wanted to say, "exactly."

And a great noise was echoing all around me, enveloping me, the sound of a deep gong perhaps, being struck very slowly in perfect rhythm, its sound washing through me so that I felt the most extraordinary pleasure through all my limbs.

My lips moved, but nothing came out of them; yet this didn't really matter. All the things I had ever wanted to say were clear to me and that is what mattered, not that they be expressed. And there was so much time, so much sweet time in which to say anything and do anything. There was no urgency at all.

Rapture. I said the word, and it seemed clear to me, that one word, though I couldn't speak or really move my lips. And I realized I was no longer breathing. Yet something was making me breathe. It was breathing for me and the breaths came with the rhythm of the gong which was nothing to do with my body, and I loved it, the rhythm, the way that it went on and on, and I no longer had to breathe or speak or know anything.

My mother smiled at me. And I said, "I love you . . ." to her, and she said, "Yes, always loved, always loved . . ." And I was sitting in the monastery library and I was twelve years old and the monk said to me, "A great scholar," and I opened all the books and could read everything, Latin, Greek, French. The illuminated letters were indescribably beautiful, and I turned around and faced the audience in Renaud's theater and saw all of them on their feet, and a woman moved the painted fan from in front of her face, and it was Marie Antoinette. She said "Wolfkiller," and Nicolas was running towards me, crying for me to come back. His face was full of anguish. His hair was loose and his eyes were rimmed with blood. He tried to catch me. I said, "Nicki, get away from me!" and I realized in agony, positive agony, that the sound of the gong was fading away.

I cried out, I begged. Don't stop it, please, please. I don't want to . . . I don't . . . please.

"Lelio, the Wolfkiller," said the thing, and it was holding me in its arms and I was crying because the spell was breaking.

"Don't, don't."

I was heavy all over, my body had come back to me with its aches and its pains and my own choking cries, and I was being lifted, thrown upwards, until I fell over the creature's shoulder and I felt its arm around my knees.

I wanted to say God protect me, I wanted to say it with every particle of me but I couldn't say it, and there was the alleyway below me again, that drop of hundreds of feet, and the whole of Paris tilted at an appalling angle, and there was the snow and the searing wind.

2

I WAS awake and I was very thirsty.

I wanted a great deal of very cold white wine, the way it is when you bring it up out of the cellar in autumn. I wanted something fresh and sweet to eat, like a ripe apple.

It did occur to me that I had lost my reason, though I couldn't have said why.

I opened my eyes and knew it was early evening. The light might have been morning light, but too much time had passed for that. It was evening.

And through a wide, heavily barred stone window I saw hills and woods, blanketed with snow, and the vast tiny collection of rooftops and towers that made up the city far away. I hadn't seen it like this since the day I came in the post carriage. I closed my eyes and the vision of it remained as if I'd never opened my eyes at all.

But it was no vision. It was there. And the room was warm in spite of the window. There had been a fire in the room, I could smell it, but the fire had gone out.

I tried to reason. But I couldn't stop thinking about cold white wine, and apples in the basket. I could see the apples. I felt myself drop down out of the branches of the tree, and I smelled all around me the freshly cut grass.

The sunlight was blinding on the green fields. It shone on Nicolas's brown hair, and on the deep lacquer of the violin. The music climbed up to the soft, rolling clouds. And against the sky I saw the battlements of my father's house.

Battlements.

I opened my eyes again.

And I knew I was lying in a high tower room several miles from Paris.

And just in front of me, on a crude little wooden table, was a bottle of cold white wine, precisely as I had dreamed it.

For a long time I looked at it, looked at the frost of droplets covering it, and I could not believe it possible to reach for it and drink.

Never had I known the thirst I was suffering now. My whole body thirsted. And I was so weak. And I was getting a little cold.

The room moved when I moved. The sky gleamed in the window.

And when at last I did reach for the bottle and pull the cork from it and smell the tart, delicious aroma, I drank and drank without stopping, not caring what would happen to me, or where I was, or why the bottle had been set here.

My head swung forward. The bottle was almost empty and the faraway city was vanishing in the black sky, leaving a little sea of lights behind it.

I put my hands to my head.

The bed on which I'd been sleeping was no more than stone with straw strewn upon it, and it was coming to me slowly that I might be in some sort of jail.

But the wine. It had been too good for a jail. Who would give a prisoner wine like that, unless of course the prisoner was to be executed.

And another aroma came to me, rich and overpowering and so delicious that it made me moan. I looked about, or I should say, I tried to look about because I was almost too weak to move. But the source of this aroma was near to me, and it was a large bowl of beef broth. The broth was thick with bits of meat, and I could see the steam rising from it. It was still hot.

I grabbed it in both hands immediately and I drank it as thoughtlessly and greedily as I'd drunk the wine.

It was so satisfying it was as if I'd never known any food like it, that rich boiled-down essence of the meat, and when the bowl was empty I fell back, full, almost sick, on the straw.

It seemed something moved in the darkness near me. But I was not sure. I heard the chink of glass.

"More wine," said a voice to me, and I knew the voice.

Gradually, I began remembering everything. Scaling the walls, the small square rooftop, that smiling white face.

For one moment, I thought, No, quite impossible, it must have been a nightmare. But this just wasn't so. It had happened, and I remembered the rapture suddenly, the sound of the gong, and I felt myself grow dizzy as though I were losing consciousness again.

I stopped it. I wouldn't let it happen. And fear crept over me so that I didn't dare to move.

"More wine," said the voice again.

Turning my head slightly I saw a new bottle, corked, but ready for me, outlined against the window's luminous glow.

I felt the thirst again, and this time it was heightened by the salt of the broth. I wiped my lips and then I reached for the bottle and again I drank.

I fell back against the stone wall, and I struggled to look clearly through the darkness, half afraid of what I knew I would see.

Of course I was very drunk now.

I saw the window, the city. I saw the little table. And as my eyes moved slowly over the dusky corners of the room, I saw *him* there.

He no longer wore his black hooded cape, and he didn't sit or stand as a man might.

Rather he leaned to rest, it seemed, upon the thick stone frame of the window, one knee bent a little towards it, the other long spindly leg sprawled out to the other side. His arms appeared to hang at his sides.

And the whole impression was of something limp and lifeless, and yet his face was as animated as it had been the night before. Huge black eyes seeming to stretch the white flesh in deep folds, the nose long and thin, and the mouth the jester's smile. There were the fang teeth, just touching the colorless lip, and the hair, a gleaming mass of black and silver growing up high from the white forehead, and flowing down over his shoulders and his arms.

I think that he laughed.

I was beyond terror. I could not even scream.

I had dropped the wine. The glass bottle was rolling on the floor. And as I tried to move forward, to gather my senses and make my body more than something drunken and sluggish, his thin, gangly limbs found animation all at once.

He advanced on me.

I didn't cry out. I gave a low roar of angry terror and scrambled up off the bed, tripping over the small table and running from him as fast as I could.

But he caught me in long white fingers that were as powerful and as cold as they had been the night before.

"Let me go, damn you, damn you, damn you!" I was stammering. My reason told me to plead, and I tried. "I'll just go away, please. Let me out of here. You have to. Let me go."

His gaunt face loomed over me, his lips drawn up sharply into his white cheeks, and he laughed a low riotous laugh that seemed endless. I struggled, pushing at him uselessly, pleading with him again, stammering nonsense and apologies, and then I cried, "God help me!" He clapped one of those monstrous hands over my mouth.

"No more of that in my presence, Wolfkiller, or I'll feed you to the wolves of hell," he said with a little sneer. "Hmmmm? Answer me. Hmmmm?"

I nodded and he loosened his grip.

His voice had had a momentary calming effect. He sounded capable of reason when he spoke. He sounded almost sophisticated.

He lifted his hands and stroked my head as I cringed.

"Sunlight in the hair," he whispered, "and the blue sky fixed forever in your eyes." He seemed almost meditative as he looked at me. His breath had no smell whatsoever, nor did his body, it seemed. The smell of mold was coming from his clothes.

I didn't dare to move, though he was not holding me. I stared at his garments.

A ruined silk shirt with bag sleeves and smocking at the neck of it. And worsted leggings and short ragged pantaloons.

In sum he was dressed as men had been centuries before. I had seen such clothes in tapestries in my home, in the paintings of Caravaggio and La Tour that hung in my mother's rooms.

"You're perfect, my Lelio, my Wolfkiller," he said to me, his long mouth opening wide so that again I saw the small white fangs. They were the only teeth he possessed.

I shuddered. I felt myself dropping to the floor.

But he picked me up easily with one arm and laid me down gently on the bed.

In my mind I was praying fiercely, God help me, the Virgin Mary help me, help me, help me, as I peered up into his face.

What was it I was seeing? What had I seen the night before? The mask of old age, this grinning thing cut deeply with the marks of time and yet frozen, it seemed, and hard as his hands. He wasn't a living thing. He was a monster. A vampire was what he was, a blood-sucking corpse from the grave gifted with intellect!

And his limbs, why did they so horrify me? He looked like a human, but he didn't move like a human. It didn't seem to matter to him whether he walked or crawled, bent over or knelt. It filled me with loathing. Yet he fascinated me. I had to admit it. He fascinated me. But I was in too much danger to allow such a strange state of mind.

He gave a deep laugh now, his knees wide apart, his fingers resting on my cheek as he made a great arc over me.

"Yeeeees, lovely one, I'm hard to look at!" he said. His voice was still a whisper and he spoke in long gasps. "I was old when I was made. And you're perfect, my Lelio, my blue-eyed young one, more beautiful even without the lights of the stage."

The long white hand played with my hair again, lifting up the strands and letting them drop as he sighed.

"Don't weep, Wolfkiller," he said. "You're chosen, and your tawdry little triumphs in the House of Thesbians will be nothing once this night comes to its close."

Again came that low riot of laughter.

There was no doubt in my mind, at least at this moment, that he was from the devil, that God and the devil existed, that beyond the isolation I'd known only hours ago lay this vast realm of dark beings and hideous meanings and I had been swallowed into it somehow.

It occurred to me quite clearly I was being punished for my life, and yet that seemed absurd. Millions believed as I believed the world over. Why the hell was this happening to me? And a grim possibility started irresistibly to take shape, that the world was no more meaningful than before, and this was but another horror . . .

"In God's name, get away!" I shouted. I *had* to believe in God now. I had to. That was absolutely the only hope. I went to make the Sign of the Cross.

For one moment he stared at me, his eyes wide with rage. And then he remained still.

He watched me make the Sign of the Cross. He listened to me call upon God again and again.

He only smiled, making his face a perfect mask of comedy from the proscenium arch.

And I went into a spasm of crying like a child. "Then the devil reigns in heaven and heaven is hell," I said to him. "Oh, God, don't desert me . . ." I called on all the saints I had ever for a little while loved.

He struck me hard across the face. I fell to one side and almost slipped from the bed to the floor. The room went round. The sour taste of the wine rose in my mouth.

And I felt his fingers again on my neck.

"Yes, fight, Wolfkiller," he said. "Don't go into hell without a battle. Mock God."

"I don't mock!" I protested.

Once again he pulled me to himself.

And I fought him harder than I had ever fought anyone or anything in my existence, even the wolves. I beat on him, kicked him, tore at his hair. But I might as well have fought the animated gargoyles from a cathedral, he was that powerful.

He only smiled.

Then all the expression went out of his face. It seemed to become very long. The cheeks were hollow, the eyes wide and almost wondering, and he opened his mouth. The lower lip contracted. I saw the fangs.

"Damn you, damn you, damn you!" I was roaring and bellowing. And he drew closer and the teeth went through my flesh.

Not this time, I was raging, not this time. I will not feel it. I will resist. I will fight for my soul *this* time.

But it was happening again.

The sweetness and the softness and the world far away, and even he in his ugliness was curiously outside of me, like an insect pressed against a glass who causes no loathing in us because he cannot touch us, and the sound of the gong, and the exquisite pleasure, and then I was altogether lost. I was incorporeal and the pleasure was incorporeal. I was nothing but pleasure. And I slipped into a web of radiant dreams.

A catacomb I saw, a rank place. And a white vampire creature waking in a shallow grave. Bound in heavy chains he was, the vampire; and over him bent this monster who had abducted me, and I knew that his name was Magnus, and that he was mortal still in this dream, a great and powerful alchemist. And he had unearthed and bound this slumbering vampire right before the crucial hour of dusk.

And now as the light died out of the heavens, Magnus drank from his helpless immortal prisoner the magical and accursed blood that would make him one of the living dead. Treachery it was, the theft of immortality. A dark Prometheus stealing a luminescent fire. Laughter in the darkness. Laughter echoing in the catacomb. Echoing as if down the centuries. And the stench of the grave. And the ecstasy, absolutely fathomless, and irresistible, and then drawing to a finish.

I was crying. I lay on the straw and I said:

"Please, don't stop it . . ."

Magnus was no longer holding me and my breathing was once again my own, and the dreams were dissolved. I fell down and down as the nightful of stars slid upwards, jewels affixed to a dark purple veil. "Clever that. I had thought the sky was . . . real."

The cold winter air was moving just a little in this room. I felt the tears on my face. I was consumed with thirst!

And far, far away from me, Magnus stood looking down at me, his hands dangling low beside his thin legs.

I tried to move. I was craving. My whole body was thirsty.

"You're dying, Wolfkiller," he said. "The light's going out of your blue eyes as if all the summer days are gone . . ."

"No, please . . ." This thirst was unbearable. My mouth was open, gaping, my back arched. And it was here at last, the final horror, death itself, like this.

"Ask for it, child," he said, his face no longer the grinning mask, but utterly transfigured with compassion. He looked almost human, almost naturally old. "Ask and you shall receive," he said.

I saw water rushing down all the mountain streams of my childhood. "Help me. Please."

"I shall give you the water of all waters," he said in my ear, and it seemed he wasn't white at all. He *was* just an old man, sitting there beside me. His face *was* human, and almost sad.

But as I watched his smile and his gray eyebrows rise in wonder, I knew it wasn't true. He wasn't human. He was that same ancient monster only he was filled with my blood!

"The wine of all wines," he breathed. "This is my Body, this is my Blood." And then his arms surrounded me. They drew me to him and I felt a great warmth emanating from him, and he seemed to be filled not with blood but with love for me.

"Ask for it, Wolfkiller, and you will live forever," he said, but his voice sounded weary and spiritless, and there was something distant and tragic in his gaze.

I felt my head turn to the side, my body a heavy and damp thing that I couldn't control. I will not ask, I will die without asking, and then the great despair I feared so much lay before me, the emptiness that was death, and still I said No. In pure horror I said No. I will not bow down to it, the chaos and the horror. I said No.

"Life everlasting," he whispered.

My head fell on his shoulder.

"Stubborn Wolfkiller." His lips touched me, warm, odorless breath on my neck.

"Not stubborn," I whispered. My voice was so weak I wondered if he could hear me. "Brave. Not stubborn." It seemed pointless not to say it.

What was vanity now? What was anything at all? And such a trivial word was stubborn, so cruel . . .

He lifted my face, and holding me with his right hand, he lifted his left hand and gashed his own throat with his nails.

My body bent double in a convulsion of terror, but he pressed my face to the wound, as he said: "Drink."

I heard my scream, deafening in my own ears. And the blood that was flowing out of the wound touched my parched and cracking lips.

The thirst seemed to hiss aloud. My tongue licked at the blood. And a great whiplash of sensation caught me. And my mouth opened and locked itself to the wound. I drew with all my power upon the great fount that I knew would satisfy my thirst as it had never been satisfied before.

Blood and blood and blood. And it was not merely the dry hissing coil of the thirst that was quenched and dissolved, it was all my craving, all the want and misery and hunger that I had ever known.

My mouth widened, pressed harder to him. I felt the blood coursing down the length of my throat. I felt his head against me. I felt the tight enclosure of his arms.

I was against him and I could feel his sinews, his bones, the very contour of his hands. I *knew* his body. And yet there was this numbness creeping through me and a rapturous tingling as each sensation penetrated the numbness, and was amplified in the penetration so that it became fuller, keener, and I could almost see what I felt.

But the supreme part of it remained the sweet, luscious blood filling me, as I drank and drank.

More of it, more, this was all I could think, if I thought at all, and for all its thick substance, it was like light passing into me, so brilliant did it seem to the mind, so blinding, that red stream, and all the desperate desires of my life were a thousandfold fed.

But his body, the scaffolding to which I clung, was weakening beneath me. I could hear his breath in feeble gasps. Yet he didn't make me stop.

Love you, I wanted to say, Magnus, my unearthly master, ghastly thing that you are, love you, love you, this was what I had always so wanted, wanted, and could never have, this, and you've given it to me!

I felt I would die if it went on, and on it did go, and I did not die.

But quite suddenly I felt his gentle loving hands caressing my shoulders and with his incalculable strength, he forced me backwards.

I let out a long mournful cry. Its misery alarmed me. But he was pulling me to my feet. He still held me in his arms.

He brought me to the window, and I stood looking out, with my hands out to the stone on either side. I was shaking and the blood in me pulsed in all my veins. I leaned my forehead against the iron bars.

Far far below lay the dark cusp of a hill, overgrown with trees that appeared to shimmer in the faint light of the stars.

And beyond, the city with its wilderness of little lights sunk not in darkness but in a soft violet mist. The snow everywhere was luminescent, melting. Rooftops, towers, walls, all were myriad facets of lavender, mauve, rose.

This was the sprawling metropolis.

And as I narrowed my eyes, I saw a million windows like so many projections of beams of light, and then as if this were not enough, in the very depths I saw the unmistakable movement of the people. Tiny mortals on tiny streets, heads and hands touching in the shadows, a lone man, no more than a speck ascending a windblown belfry. A million souls on the tessellated surface of the night, and coming soft on the air a dim mingling of countless human voices. Cries, songs, the faintest wisps of music, the muted throb of bells.

I moaned. The breeze seemed to lift my hair and I heard my own voice as I had never heard it before crying.

The city dimmed. I let it go, its swarming millions lost again in the vast and wondrous play of lilac shadow and fading light.

"Oh, what have you done, what is this that you've given to me!" I whispered.

And it seemed my words did not stop one after another, rather they ran together until all of my crying was one immense and coherent sound that perfectly amplified my horror and my joy.

If there was a God, he did not matter now. He was part of some dull and dreary realm whose secrets had long ago been plundered, whose lights had long ago gone out. This was the pulsing center of life itself round which all true complexity revolved. Ah, the allure of that complexity, the sense of being *there* . . .

Behind me the scratch of the monster's feet came on the stones.

And when I turned I saw him white and bled dry and like a great husk of himself. His eyes were stained with blood-red tears and he reached out to me as if in pain.

I gathered him to my chest. I felt such love for him as I had never known before.

"Ah, don't you see?" came the ghastly voice with its long words, whispers without end, "My heir chosen to take the Dark Gift from me with more fiber and courage than ten mortal men, what a Child of Darkness you are to be."

I kissed his eyelids. I gathered his soft black hair in my hands. He was no ghastly thing to me now but merely that which was strange and white, and full of some deeper lesson perhaps than the sighing trees below or the shimmering city calling me over the miles.

His sunken cheeks, his long throat, the thin legs . . . these were but the natural parts of him.

"No, fledgling," he sighed. "Save your kisses for the world. My time has come and you owe me but one obeisance only. Follow me now."

3

DOWN a winding stairs he drew me. And everything I beheld absorbed me. The rough-cut stones seemed to give forth their own light, and even the rats shooting past in the dark had a curious beauty.

Then he unlocked a thick iron-studded wooden door and, giving over his heavy key ring to me, led me into a large and barren room.

"You are now my heir, as I told you," he said. "You'll take possession of this house and all my treasure. But you'll do as I say first."

The barred windows gave a limitless view of the moonlit clouds, and I saw the soft shimmering city again as if it were spreading its arms.

"Ah, later you may drink your fill of all you see," he said. He turned me towards him as he stood before a huge heap of wood that lay in the center of the floor.

"Listen carefully," he said. "For I'm about to leave you." He gestured to the wood offhandedly. "And there are things you must know. You're immortal now. And your nature shall lead you soon enough to your first human victim. Be swift and show no mercy. But stop your feasting, no matter how delicious, before the victim's heart ceases to beat.

"In years to come, you'll be strong enough to feel that great moment, but for the present pass the cup to time just before it's empty. Or you may pay heavily for your pride."

"But why are you leaving me!" I asked desperately. I clung to him. Victims, mercy, feasting . . . I felt myself bombarded by these words as if I were being physically beaten.

He pulled away so easily that my hands were hurt by his movement, and I wound up staring at them, marveling at the strange quality of the pain. It wasn't like mortal pain.

He stopped, however, and pointed to the stones of the wall opposite. I could see that one very large stone had been dislodged and lay a foot from the unbroken surface around it.

"Grasp that stone," he said, "and pull it out of the wall."

"But I can't," I said. "It must weigh—"

"Pull it out!" He pointed with one of his long bony fingers and grimaced so that I tried to do it as he said.

To my pure astonishment I was able to move the stone easily, and I saw beyond it a dark opening just large enough for a man to enter if he crawled on his face.

He gave a dry cackling laugh and nodded his head.

"There, my son, is the passageway that leads to my treasure," he said. "Do with my treasure as you like, and with all my earthly property. But for now, I must have my vows."

And again astonishing me, he snatched up two twigs from the wood and rubbed them together so fiercely they were soon burning with bright small flames.

This he tossed at the heap, and the pitch in it caused the fire to leap up at once, throwing an immense light over the curved ceiling and the stone walls.

I gasped and stepped back. The riot of yellow and orange color enchanted and frightened me, and the heat, though I felt it, did not cause me a sensation I understood. There was no natural alarm that I should be burned by it. Rather the warmth was exquisite and I realized for the first time how cold I had been. The cold was an icing on me and the fire melted it and I almost moaned.

He laughed again, that hollow, gasping laugh, and started to dance about in the light, his thin legs making him look like a skeleton dancing, with the white face of a man. He crooked his arms over his head, bent his torso and his knees, and turned round and round as he circled the fire.

"*Mon Dieu!*" I whispered. I was reeling. Horrifying it might have been only an hour ago to see him dancing like this, but now in the flickering glare he was a spectacle that drew me after it step by step. The light exploded on his satin rags, the pantaloons he wore, the tattered shirt.

"But you can't leave me!" I pleaded, trying to keep my thoughts clear, trying to realize what he had been saying. My voice was monstrous in my ears. I tried to make it lower, softer, more like it should have been. "Where will you go!"

He gave his loudest laugh then, slapping his thigh and dancing faster and farther away from me, his hands out as if to embrace the fire.

The thickest logs were only now catching. The room for all its size was like a great clay oven, smoke pouring out its windows.

"Not the fire." I flew backwards, flattening myself against the wall. "You can't go into the fire!"

Fear was overwhelming me, as every sight and sound had overwhelmed me. It was like every sensation I had known so far. I couldn't resist it or deny it. I was half whimpering and half screaming.

"Oh, yes I can," he laughed. "Yes, I can!" He threw back his head and let his laughter stretch into howls. "But from you, fledgling," he said, stopping before me with his finger out again, "promises now. Come, a little mortal honor, my brave Wolfkiller, or though it will cleave my heart in two, I shall throw you into the fire and claim for myself another offspring. Answer me!"

I tried to speak. I nodded my head.

In the raging light I could see my hands had become white. And I felt a stab of pain in my lower lip that almost made me cry out.

My eyeteeth had become fangs already! I felt them and looked to him in panic, but he was leering at me as if he enjoyed my terror.

"Now, after I am burned up," he said, snatching my wrist, "and the fire is out, you *must* scatter the ashes. Hear me, little one. Scatter the ashes. Or else I might return, and in what shape that would be, I dare not contemplate. But mark my words, if you allow me to come back, more hideous than I am now, I shall hunt you down and burn you till you are scarred the same as I, do you hear me?"

I still couldn't bring myself to answer. This was not fear. It was hell. I could feel my teeth growing and my body tingling all over. Frantically, I nodded my head.

"Ah, yes." He smiled, nodding too, the fire licking the ceiling behind him, the light leaking all about the edges of his face. "It's only mercy I ask, that I go now to find hell, if there is a hell, or sweet oblivion which surely I do not deserve. If there is a Prince of Darkness, then I shall set eyes upon him at last. I shall spit in his face.

"So scatter what is burned, as I command you, and when that is done, take yourself to my lair through that low passage, being most careful to replace the stone behind you as you enter there. Within you will find my coffin. And in that box or the like of it, you must seal yourself by day or the sun's light shall burn you to a cinder. Mark my words, nothing on earth can end your life save the sun, or a blaze such as you see before you, and even then, only, and I say, only if your ashes are scattered when it is done."

I turned my face away from him and away from the flames. I had begun to cry and the only thing that kept me from sobbing was the hand I clapped to my mouth.

But he pulled me about the edge of the fire until we stood before the loose stone, his finger pointing at it again.

"Please stay with me, please," I begged him. "Only a little while, only one night, I beg you!" Again the volume of my voice terrified me. It wasn't my voice at all. I put my arms around him. I held tight to him. His gaunt white face was inexplicably beautiful to me, his black eyes filled with the strangest expression.

The light flickered on his hair, his eyes, and then again he made his mouth into a jester's smile.

"Ah, greedy son," he said. "Is it not enough to be immortal with all the world your repast? Good-bye, little one. Do as I say. Remember, the ashes! And beyond this stone the inner chamber. Therein lies all that you will need to prosper."

I struggled to hold on to him. And he laughed low in my ear, marveling at my strength. "Excellent, excellent," he whispered. "Now, live forever, beautiful Wolfkiller, with the gifts nature gave you, and discover for yourself all those most unnatural gifts which I have added to the lot."

He sent me stumbling away from him. And he leapt so high and so far into the very middle of the flames he appeared to be flying.

I saw him descend. I saw the fire catch his garments.

It seemed his head became a torch, and then all of a sudden his eyes grew wide and his mouth became a great black cavern in the radiance of the flames and his laughter rose in such piercing volume, I covered my ears.

He appeared to jump up and down on all fours in the flames, and suddenly I realized that my cries had drowned out his laughter.

The spindly black arms and legs rose and fell, rose and fell and then suddenly appeared to wither. The fire shifted, roared. And in the heart of it I could see nothing now but the blaze itself.

Yet still I cried. I fell down upon my knees, my hands over my eyes. But against my closed lids I could still see it, one vast explosion of sparks after another until I pressed my forehead on the stones.

4

FOR years it seemed I lay on the floor watching the fire burn itself out to charred timbers.

The room had cooled. The freezing air moved through the open window. And again and again I wept. My own sobs reverberated in my ears until I felt I couldn't endure the sound of them. And it was no comfort to know that all things were magnified in this state, even the misery that I felt.

Now and then I prayed again. I begged for forgiveness, though forgiveness for what I couldn't have said. I prayed to the Blessed Mother, to the saints. I murmured the Aves over and over until they became a senseless chant.

And my tears were blood, and they left their stain on my hands when I wiped at my face.

Then I lay flat on the stones, murmuring not prayers any longer but those inarticulate pleas we make to all that is powerful, all that is holy, all that may or may not exist by any and all names. Do not leave me alone here. Do not abandon me. I am in the witches' place. It's the witches' place. Do not let me fall even farther than I have already fallen this night. Do not let it happen . . . *Lestat, wake up.*

But Magnus's words came back to me, over and over: *To find hell, if there is a hell . . . If there is a Prince of Darkness . . .*

Finally I rose on my hands and knees. I felt light-headed and mad, and almost giddy. I looked at the fire and saw that I might still bring it back to a roaring blaze and throw myself into it.

But even as I forced myself to imagine the agony of this, I knew that I had no intention of doing it.

After all, why should I do it? What had I done to deserve the witches' fate? I didn't want to be in hell, even for a moment. I sure as hell wasn't going there just to spit in the face of the Prince of Darkness, whoever he might be!

On the contrary, if I was a damned thing, then let the son of a bitch come for me! Let him tell me why I was meant to suffer. I would truly like to know.

As for oblivion, well, we can wait a little while for that. We can think this over for a little while . . . at least.

An alien calm crept slowly over me. It was dark, full of bitterness and growing fascination.

I wasn't human anymore.

And as I crouched there thinking about it, and looking at the dying embers, an immense strength was gathering in me. Gradually my boyish sobs died away. And I commenced to study the whiteness of my skin, the sharpness of the two evil little teeth, and the way that my fingernails gleamed in the dark as though they'd been lacquered.

All the little familiar aches were gone out of my body. And the remaining warmth that came from the smoking wood was good to me, as something laid over me or wrapped about me.

Time passed; yet it did not pass.

Each change in the moving air was caressing. And when there came from the softly lighted city beyond a chorus of dim church bells ringing the hour, they did not mark the passage of mortal time. They were only the purest music, and I lay stunned, my mouth open, as I stared at the passing clouds.

But in my chest I started to feel a new pain, very hot and mercurial.

It moved through my veins, tightened about my head, and then seemed to collect itself in my bowels and belly. I narrowed my eyes. I cocked my head to one side. I realized I wasn't afraid of this pain, rather I was feeling it as if I were listening to it.

And I saw the cause of it then. My waste was leaving me in a small torrent. I found myself unable to control it. Yet as I watched the foulness stain my clothes, this didn't disgust me.

Rats creeping into the very room, approaching this filth on their tiny soundless feet, even these did not disgust me.

These things couldn't touch me, even as they crawled over me to devour the waste.

In fact, I could imagine nothing in the dark, not even the slithering insects of the grave, that could bring about revulsion in me. Let them crawl on my hands and face, it wouldn't matter now.

I wasn't part of the world that cringed at such things. And with a smile, I realized that I was of that dark ilk that makes others cringe. Slowly and with great pleasure, I laughed.

And yet my grief was not entirely gone from me. It lingered like an idea, and the idea had a pure truth to it.

I am dead, I am a vampire. And things will die so that I may live; I will drink their blood so that I may live. And I will never, never see Nicolas again, nor my mother, nor any of the humans I have known and loved, nor any of my human family. I'll drink blood. And I'll live forever. That is exactly what will *be.* And what will *be* is only beginning; it is just born! And the labor that brought it forth was rapture such as I have never known.

I climbed to my feet. I felt myself light and powerful, and strangely numbed, and I went to the dead fire, and walked through the burnt timbers.

There were no bones. It was as if the fiend had disintegrated. What ashes I could gather in my hands I took to the window. And as the wind caught them, I whispered a farewell to Magnus, wondering if he could yet hear me.

At last only charred logs were left and the soot that I wiped up with my hands and dusted off into the darkness.

It was time now to examine the inner room.

5

HE stone moved out easily enough, as I'd seen before, and it had a hook on the inside of it by which I could pull it closed behind me.

But to get into the narrow dark passage I had to lie on my belly. And when I dropped down on my knees and peered into it, I could see no visible light at the end. I didn't like the look of it.

I knew that if I'd been mortal still, nothing could have induced me to crawl into a passage like this.

But the old vampire had been plain enough in telling me the sun could destroy me as surely as the fire. I had to get to the coffin. And I felt the fear coming back in a deluge.

I got down flat on the ground, and crawled as a lizard might into the passage. As I feared, I could not really raise my head. And there was no room to turn and reach for the hook in the stone. I had to slip my foot into the hook and crawl forward to pull the stone behind me.

Total darkness. With room to rise only a few inches on my elbows.

I gasped, and the fear welled and I almost went mad thinking about the fact that I couldn't raise my head and finally I smacked it against the stone and lay still, whimpering.

But what was I to do? I must reach the coffin.

So telling myself to stop this whining, I commenced to crawl, faster and faster. My knees scraped the stone. My hands sought crevices and cracks to pull me along. My neck ached with the strain as I struggled not to try to lift my head again in panic.

And when my hand suddenly felt solid stone ahead, I pushed upon it with all my strength. I felt it move as a pale light seeped in.

I scrambled out of the passage, and found myself standing in a small room.

The ceiling was low, curved, and the high window was narrow with the familiar heavy grid of iron bars. But the sweet, violet light of the night poured in revealing a great fireplace cut in the far wall, the wood ready for the torch, and beside it, beneath the window, an ancient stone sarcophagus.

My red velvet fur-lined cape lay over the sarcophagus. And on a rude bench I glimpsed a splendid suit of red velvet worked with gold, and much Italian lace, as well as red silk breeches and white silk hose and red-heeled slippers.

I smoothed back my hair from my face and wiped the thin film of sweat from my upper lip and my forehead. It was bloody, this sweat, and when I saw this on my hands, I felt a curious excitement.

Ah, what am I, I thought, and what lies before me? For a long moment I looked at this blood and then I licked my fingers. A lovely zinging pleasure passed through me. It was a moment before I could collect myself sufficiently to approach the fireplace.

I lifted two sticks of kindling as the old vampire had done and, rubbing them very hard and fast, saw them almost disappear as the flame shot up from them. There was no magic in this, only skill. And as the fire warmed me, I took off my soiled clothes, and with my shirt wiped every last trace of human waste away, and threw all this in the fire, before putting on the new garments.

Red, dazzling red. Not even Nicolas had had such clothes as these. They were clothes for the Court at Versailles, with pearls and tiny rubies worked into their embroidery. The lace of the shirt was Valenciennes, which I had seen on my mother's wedding gown.

I put the wolf cape over my shoulders. And though the white chill was gone from my limbs, I felt like a creature carved from ice. My smile felt hard and glittering to me and strangely slow as I allowed myself to feel and to see these garments.

In the blaze of the fire, I looked at the coffin. The effigy of an old man was carved upon its heavy lid, and I realized immediately it was the likeness of Magnus.

But here he lay in tranquillity, his jester's mouth sealed, his eyes staring mildly at the ceiling, his hair a neat mane of deeply carved waves and ringlets.

Three centuries old was this thing surely. He lay with his hands folded on his chest, his garments long robes, and from his sword that had been carved into the stone, someone had broken out the hilt and part of the scabbard.

I stared at this for an interminable length of time, seeing that it had been carefully chipped away with much effort.

Was it the shape of the cross that someone had sought to remove? I traced it over with my finger. Nothing happened of course, any more than when I'd murmured all those prayers. And squatting in the dust beside the coffin, I drew a cross there.

Again, nothing.

Then to the cross I added a few strokes to suggest the body of Christ, his arms, the crook of his knees, his bowed head. I wrote "The Lord Jesus Christ," the only words I could write well, save for my own name, and again nothing.

And still glancing back uneasily at the words and the little crucifix, I tried to lift the lid of the coffin.

Even with this new strength, it was not easy. And no mortal man alone could have done it.

But what perplexed me was the extent of my difficulty. I did not have limitless strength. And certainly I didn't have the strength of the old vampire. Maybe the strength of three men was what I now possessed, or the strength of four; it was impossible to calculate.

It seemed pretty damned impressive to me at the moment.

I looked into the coffin. Nothing but a narrow place, full of shadows, where I couldn't imagine myself lying. There were Latin words inscribed around the rim, and I couldn't read them.

This tormented me. I wished the words weren't there, and my longing for Magnus, my helplessness, threatened to close in on me. I hated him for leaving me! And it struck me with full ironic force that I'd felt love for him before he'd leapt into the fire. I'd felt love for him when I saw the red garments.

Do devils love each other? Do they walk arm in arm in hell saying, "Ah, you are my friend, how I love you," things like that to each other? It was a rather detached intellectual question I was asking, as I did not believe in hell. But it was a matter of a concept of evil, wasn't it? All creatures in hell are supposed to hate one another, as all the saved hate the damned, without reservation.

I'd known that all my life. It had terrified me as a child, the idea that I might go to heaven and my mother might go to hell and that I should hate her. I couldn't hate her. And what if we were in hell together?

Well, now I know, whether I believe in hell or not, that vampires can love each other, that in being dedicated to evil, one does not cease to love. Or so it seemed for that brief instant. But don't start crying again. I can't abide all this crying.

I turned my eyes to a large wooden chest that was partially hidden at the head of the coffin. It wasn't locked. Its rotted wooden lid fell almost off the hinges when I opened it.

And though the old master had said he was leaving me his treasure, I was flabbergasted by what I saw here. The chest was crammed with gems and gold and silver. There were countless jeweled rings, diamond necklaces, ropes of pearls, plate and coins and hundreds upon hundreds of miscellaneous valuables.

I ran my fingers lightly over the heap and then held up handfuls of it, gasping as the light ignited the red of the rubies, the green of the emeralds. I saw refractions of color of which I'd never dreamed, and wealth beyond any calculation. It was the fabled Caribbean pirates' chest, the proverbial king's ransom.

And it was mine now.

More slowly I examined it. Scattered throughout were personal and perishable articles. Satin masks rotting away from their trimming of gold, lace handkerchiefs and bits of cloth to which were fixed pins and brooches. Here was a strip of leather harness hung with gold bells, a moldering bit of lace slipped through a ring, snuffboxes by the dozens, lockets on velvet ribbon.

Had Magnus taken all this from his victims?

I lifted up a jewel-encrusted sword, far too heavy for these times, and a worn slipper saved perhaps for its rhinestone buckle.

Of course he had taken what he wanted. Yet he himself had worn rags, the tattered costume of another age, and he lived here as a hermit might have lived in some earlier century. I couldn't understand it.

But there were other objects scattered about in this treasure. Rosaries made up of gorgeous gems, and they still had their crucifixes! I touched the small sacred images. I shook my head and bit my lip, as if to say, How awful that he should have stolen these! But I also found it very funny. And further proof that God had no power over me.

And as I was thinking about this, trying to decide if it was as fortuitous as it seemed for the moment, I lifted from the treasure an exquisite pearl-handled mirror.

I looked into it almost unconsciously as one often glances in mirrors. And there I saw myself as a man might expect, except that my skin was very white, as the old fiend's had been white, and my eyes had been transformed from their usual blue to a mingling of violet and cobalt that was softly iridescent. My hair had a high luminous sheen, and when I ran my fingers back through it I felt a new and strange vitality there.

In fact, this was not Lestat in the mirror at all, but some replica of him made of other substances! And the few lines time had given me by the age of twenty years were gone or greatly simplified and just a little deeper than they had been.

I stared at my reflection. I became frantic to discover *myself* in it. I rubbed my face, even rubbed the mirror and pressed my lips together to keep from crying.

Finally I closed my eyes and opened them again, and I smiled very gently at the creature. He smiled back. That was Lestat, all right. And there seemed nothing in his face that was any way malevolent. Well, not very malevolent. Just the old mischief, the impulsiveness. He could have been an angel, in fact, this creature, except that when his tears did rise, they were red, and the entire image was tinted red because his vision was red. And he had these evil little teeth that he could press into his lower lip when he smiled that made him look absolutely terrifying. A good enough face with one thing horribly, horribly wrong with it!

But it suddenly occurred to me, I am looking at my own reflection! And hadn't it been said enough that ghosts and spirits and those who have lost their souls to hell have no reflections in mirrors?

A lust to know all things about what I was came over me. A lust to know how I should walk among mortal men. I wanted to be in the streets of Paris, seeing with my new eyes all the miracles of life that I'd ever glimpsed. I wanted to see the faces of the people, to see the flowers in bloom, and the butterflies. To see Nicki, to hear Nicki play his music—no.

Forswear that. But there were a thousand forms of music, weren't there? And as I closed my eyes I could almost hear the orchestra of the Opéra, the arias rising in my ears. So sharp the recollection, so clear.

But nothing would be ordinary now. Not joy or pain, or the simplest memory. All would possess this magnificent luster, even grief for the things that were forever lost.

I put down the mirror, and taking one of the old yellowed lace handkerchiefs from the chest, I wiped my tears. I turned and sat down slowly before the fire. Delicious the warmth on my face and hands.

A great sweet drowsiness came over me and as I closed my eyes again I felt myself immersed suddenly in the strange dream of Magnus stealing the blood. A sense of enchantment returned, of dizzying pleasure—Magnus holding me, connected to me, my blood flowing into him. But I heard the chains scraping the floor of the old catacomb, I saw the defenseless vampire thing in Magnus's arms. Something more to it . . . something important. A meaning. About theft, treachery, about surrendering to no one, not God, not demon, and never man.

I thought and thought about it, half awake, half dreaming again, and the maddest thought came to me, that I would tell Nicki all about this, that as soon as I got home I would lay it all out, the dream, the possible meaning and we would talk—

With an ugly shock, I opened my eyes. The human in me looked helplessly about this chamber. He started to weep again and the newborn fiend was too young yet to rein him in. The sobs came up like hiccups, and I put my hand over my mouth.

Magnus, why did you leave me? Magnus, what I am supposed to do, how do I go on?

I drew up my knees and rested my head on them, and slowly my head began to clear.

Well, it has been great fun pretending you will be this vampire creature, I thought, wearing these splendid clothes, running your fingers through all that glorious lucre. But you can't live as this! You can't feed on living beings! Even if you are a monster, you have a conscience in you, natural to you . . . Good and Evil, good and evil. You cannot live without believing in—You cannot abide the acts that— Tomorrow you will . . . you will . . . you will what?

You will drink blood, won't you?

The gold and the precious stones glowed like embers in the nearby chest, and beyond the bars of the window, there rose against the gray clouds the violet shimmer of the distant city. What *is* their blood like? Hot living blood, not monster blood. My tongue pushed at the roof of my mouth, at my fangs.

Think on it, Wolfkiller.

I ROSE to my feet slowly. It was as if the will made it happen rather than the body, so easy was it. And I picked up the iron key ring which I'd brought with me from the outer chamber and I went to inspect the rest of my tower.

6

EMPTY chambers. Barred windows. The great endless sweep of the night above the battlements. That is all I found aboveground.

But on the lower floor of the tower, just outside the door to the dungeon stairs, there was a resin torch in the sconce, and a tinderbox in the niche beside it. Tracks in the dust. The lock well oiled and easy to turn when I finally found the right key for it.

I shone the torch before me on a narrow screw stairway and started down, a little repelled by a stench that rose from somewhere quite far below me.

Of course I knew that stench. It was common enough in every cemetery in Paris. In les Innocents it was thick as noxious gas, and you had to live with it to shop the stalls there, deal with the letter writers. It was the stench of decomposing bodies.

And though it sickened me, made me back up a few steps, it wasn't all that strong, and the odor of the burning resin helped to subdue it.

I went on down. If there were dead mortals here, well, I couldn't run away from them.

But on the first level beneath the ground, I found no corpses. Only a vast cool burial chamber with its rusted iron doors open to the stairs, and three giant stone sarcophagi in the center of it. It was very like Magnus's cell above, only much larger. It had the same low curved ceiling, the same crude and gaping fireplace.

And what could that mean, except that other vampires had once slept here? No one puts fireplaces in burial vaults. At least not that I had ever known. And there were even stone benches here. And the sarcophagi were like the one above, with great figures carved on them.

But years of dust overlay everything. And there were so many spiderwebs. Surely no vampires dwelled here now. Quite impossible. Yet it was very strange. Where were those who had lain in these coffins? Had they burnt themselves up like Magnus? Or were they still existing somewhere?

I went in and opened the sarcophagi one by one. Nothing but dust inside. No evidence of other vampires at all, no indication that any other vampires existed.

I went out and continued down the stairway, even though the smell of the decay grew stronger and stronger. In fact, it very quickly became unbearable.

It was coming from behind a door that I could see below, and I had real difficulty in making myself approach it. Of course as a mortal man I'd loathed this smell, but that was nothing to the aversion I felt now. My new body wanted to run from it. I stopped, took a deep breath, and forced myself towards the door, determined to see what the fiend had done here.

Well, the stench was nothing to the sight of it.

In a deep prison cell lay a heap of corpses in all states of decay, the bones and rotted flesh crawling with worms and insects. Rats ran from the light of the torch, brushing past my legs as they made for the stairs. And my nausea became a knot in my throat. The stench suffocated me.

But I couldn't stop staring at these bodies. There was something important here, something terribly important, to be realized. And it came to me suddenly that all these dead victims had been men—their boots and ragged clothing gave evidence of that—and every single one of them had yellow hair, very much like my own hair. The few who had features left appeared to be young men, tall, slight of build. And the most recent occupant here—the wet and reeking corpse that lay with its arms outstretched through the bars—so resembled me that he might have been a brother.

In a daze, I moved forward until the tip of my boot touched his head. I lowered the torch, my mouth opening as if to scream. The wet sticky eyes that swarmed with gnats were blue eyes!

I stumbled backwards. A wild fear gripped me that the thing would move, grab hold of my ankle. And I knew why it would. As I drew up against the wall, I tripped on a plate of rotted food and a pitcher. The pitcher went over and broke, and out of it the curdled milk spilled like vomit.

Pain circled my ribs. Blood came up like liquid fire into my mouth and it shot out of my lips, splashing on the floor in front of me. I had to reach for the open door to steady myself.

But through the haze of nausea, I stared at the blood. I stared at the gorgeous crimson color of it in the light of the torch. I watched the blood darken as it sank into the mortar between the stones. The blood was alive and the sweet smell of it cut like a blade through the stench of the dead. Spasms of thirst drove away the nausea. My back was arching. I was bending lower and lower to the blood with astonishing elasticity.

And all the while, my thoughts raced: This young man had been alive in this cell; this rotted food and milk were here either to nourish or torment him. He had died in the cell, trapped with those corpses, knowing full well he would soon be one of them.

God, to suffer that! To suffer that! And how many others had known exactly the same fate, young men with yellow hair, all of them.

I was down on my knees and bending over. I held the torch low with my left hand and my head went all the way down to the blood, my tongue flashing out of my mouth so that I saw it like the tongue of a lizard. It scraped at the blood on the floor. Shivers of ecstasy. Oh, too lovely!

Was I doing this? Was I lapping up this blood not two inches from this dead body? Was my heart heaving with every taste not two inches from this dead boy whom Magnus had brought here as he brought me? This boy that Magnus had then condemned to death instead of immortality?

The filthy cell flickered on and off like a flame as I licked up the blood. The dead man's hair touched my forehead. His eye like a fractured crystal stared at me.

Why wasn't I locked in this cell? What test had I passed that I was not screaming now as I shook the bars, the horror that I had foreseen in the village inn slowly closing in on me?

The blood tremors passed through my arms and legs. And the sound I heard—the gorgeous sound, as enthralling as the crimson of the blood, the blue of the boy's eye, the glistening wings of the gnat, the sliding opaline body of the worm, the blaze of the torch—was my own raw and guttural screaming.

I dropped the torch and struggled backwards on my knees, crashing against the tin plate and the broken pitcher. I climbed to my feet and ran up the stairway. And as I slammed shut the dungeon door, my screams rose up and up to the very top of the tower.

I was lost in the sound as it bounced off the stones and came back at me. I couldn't stop, couldn't close my mouth or cover it.

But through the barred entranceway and through a dozen narrow windows above I saw the unmistakable light of morning coming. My screams died. The stones had begun to glow. The light seeped around me like scalding steam, burning my eyelids.

I made no decision to run. I was simply doing it, running up and up to the inner chamber.

As I came out of the passage, the room was full of a dim purple fire. The jewels overflowing the chest appeared to be moving. I was almost blind as I lifted the lid of the sarcophagus.

Quickly, it fell into place above me. The pain in my face and hands died away, and I was still and I was safe, and fear and sorrow melted into a cool and fathomless darkness.

7

IT WAS thirst that awakened me.

And I knew at once where I was, and what I was, too.

There were no sweet mortal dreams of chilled white wine or the fresh green grass beneath the apple trees in my father's orchard.

In the narrow darkness of the stone coffin, I felt of my fangs with my fingers and found them dangerously long and keen as little knife blades.

And a mortal was in the tower, and though he hadn't reached the door of the outer chamber I could *hear* his thoughts.

I *heard* his consternation when he discovered the door to the stairs unlocked. That had never happened before. I heard his fear as he discovered the burnt timbers on the floor and called out "Master." A servant was what he was, and a somewhat treacherous one at that.

It fascinated me, this soundless hearing of his mind, but something else was disturbing me. It was his scent!

I lifted the stone lid of the sarcophagus and climbed out. The scent was faint, but it was almost irresistible. It was the musky smell of the first whore in whose bed I had spent my passion. It was the roasted venison after days and days of starvation in winter. It was new wine, or fresh apples, or water roaring over a cliff's edge on a hot day when I reached out to gulp it in handfuls.

Only it was immeasurably richer than that, this scent, and the appetite that wanted it was infinitely keener and more simple.

I moved through the secret tunnel like a creature swimming through the darkness and, pushing out the stone in the outer chamber, rose to my feet.

There stood the mortal, staring at me, his face pale with shock.

An old, withered man he was, and by some indefinable tangle of considerations in his mind, I knew he was a stable master and a coachman. But the hearing of this was maddeningly imprecise.

Then the immediate malice he felt towards me came like the heat of a stove. And there was no misunderstanding that. His eyes raced over my face and form. The hatred boiled, crested. It was he who had procured the fine clothes I wore. He who had tended the unfortunates in the dungeon while they had lived. And why, he demanded in silent outrage, was I not there?

This made me love him very much, as you can imagine. I could have crushed him to death in my bare hands for this.

"The master!" he said desperately. "Where is he? Master!"

But what did he think the master was? A sorcerer of some kind, that was what he thought. And now I had the power. In sum, he didn't know anything that would be of use to me.

But as I comprehended all this, as I drank it up from his mind, quite against his will, I was becoming entranced with the veins in his face and in his hands. And that smell was intoxicating me.

I could feel the dim throbbing of his heart, and then I could taste his blood, just what it would be like, and there came to me some full-blown sense of it, rich and hot as it filled me.

"The master's gone, burned in the fire," I murmured, hearing a strange monotone coming from myself. I moved slowly towards him.

He glanced at the blackened floor. He looked up at the blackened ceiling. "No, this is a lie," he said. He was outraged, and his anger pulsed like a light in my eye. I felt the bitterness of his mind and its desperate reasoning.

Ah, but that living flesh could look like this! I was in the grip of remorseless appetite.

And he knew it. In some wild and unreasoning way, he sensed it; and throwing me one last malevolent glance he ran for the stairway.

Immediately I caught him. In fact, I enjoyed catching him, so simple it was. One instant I was willing myself to reach out and close the distance between us. The next I had him helpless in my hands, holding him off the floor so that his feet swung free, straining to kick me.

I held him as easily as a powerful man might hold a child, that was the proportion. His mind was a jumble of frantic thoughts, and he seemed unable to decide upon any course to save himself.

But the faint humming of these thoughts was being obliterated by the vision he presented to me.

His eyes weren't the portals of his soul anymore. They were gelatinous orbs whose colors tantalized me. And his body was nothing but a writhing morsel of hot flesh and blood, that I must have or die without.

It horrified me that this food should be alive, that delicious blood should flow through these struggling arms and fingers, and then it seemed perfect that it should. He was what he was, and I was what I was, and I was going to feast upon him.

I pulled him to my lips. I tore the bulging artery in his neck. The blood hit the roof of my mouth. I gave a little cry as I crushed him against me. It wasn't the burning fluid the master's blood had been, not that lovely elixir I had drunk from the stones of the dungeon. No, that had been light itself made liquid. Rather this was a thousand times more luscious, tasting of the thick human heart that pumped it, the very essence of that hot, almost smoky scent.

I could feel my shoulders rising, my fingers biting deeper into his flesh, and almost a humming sound rising out of me. No vision but that of his tiny gasping soul, but a swoon so powerful that he himself, what he was, had no part in it.

It was with all my will that, before the final moment, I forced him away. How I wanted to feel his heart stop. How I wanted to feel the beats slow and cease and know I *possessed* him.

But I didn't dare.

He slipped heavily from my arms, his limbs sprawling out on the stones, the whites of his eyes showing beneath his half-closed eyelids.

And I found myself unable to turn away from his death, mutely fascinated by it. Not the smallest detail must escape me. I heard his breath give out, I saw the body relax into death without struggle.

The blood warmed me. I felt it beating in my veins. My face was hot against the palms of my hands, and my vision had grown powerfully sharp. I felt strong beyond all imagining.

I PICKED up the corpse and dragged it down and down the winding steps of the tower, into the stinking dungeon, and threw it to rot with the rest there.

8

IT WAS time to go out, time to test my powers.

I filled my purse and my pockets with as much money as they would comfortably hold, and I buckled on a jeweled sword that was not too old-fashioned, and then went down, locking the iron gate to the tower behind me.

The tower was obviously all that remained of a ruined house. But I picked up the scent of horses on the wind—strong, very nice smell, perhaps the way an animal would pick up the scent—and I made my way silently around the back to a makeshift stable.

It contained not only a handsome old carriage, but four magnificent black mares. Perfectly wonderful that they weren't afraid of me. I kissed their smooth flanks and their long soft noses. In fact, I was so in love with them I could have spent hours just learning all I could of them through my new senses. But I was eager for other things.

There was a human in the stable also, and I'd caught his scent too as soon as I entered. But he was sound asleep, and when I roused him, I saw he was a dull-witted boy who posed no danger to me.

"I'm your master now," I said, as I gave him a gold coin, "but I won't be needing you tonight, except to saddle a horse for me."

He understood well enough to tell me there was no saddle in the stable before he fell back to dozing.

All right. I cut the long carriage reins from one of the bridles, put it on the most beautiful of the mares myself, and rode out bareback.

I can't tell you what it was like, the burst of the horse under me, the chilling wind, and the high arch of the night sky. My body was melded to animal. I was flying over the snow, laughing aloud and now and then singing. I hit high notes I had never reached before, then plunged into a lustrous baritone. Sometimes I was simply crying out in something like joy. It had to be joy. But how could a monster feel joy?

I wanted to ride to Paris, of course. But I knew I wasn't ready. There was too much I didn't know about my powers yet. And so I rode in the opposite direction, until I came to the outskirts of a small village.

There were no humans about, and as I approached the little church, I felt a human rage and impulsiveness breaking through my strange, translucent happiness.

I dismounted quickly and tried the sacristy door. Its lock gave and I walked through the nave to the Communion rail.

I don't know what I felt at this moment. Maybe I wanted something to happen. I felt murderous. And lightning did not strike. I stared at the red glare of the vigil lights on the altar. I looked up at the figures frozen in the unilluminated blackness of the stained glass.

And in desperation, I went up over the Communion rail and put my hands on the tabernacle itself. I broke open its tiny little doors, and I reached in and took out the jeweled ciborium with its consecrated Hosts. No, there was no power here, nothing that I could feel or see or know with any of my monstrous senses, nothing that responded to me. There were wafers and gold and wax and light.

I bowed my head on the altar. I must have looked like the priest in the middle of mass. Then I shut up everything in the tabernacle again. I closed it all up just fine, so nobody would know a sacrilege had been committed.

And then I made my way down one side of the church and up the other, the lurid paintings and statues captivating me. I realized I was seeing the process of the sculptor and the painter, not merely the creative miracle. I was seeing the way the lacquer caught the light. I was seeing little mistakes in perspective, flashes of unexpected expressiveness.

What will the great masters be to my eyes, I was thinking. I found myself staring at the simplest designs painted in the plaster walls. Then I knelt down to look at the patterns in the marble, until I realized I was stretched out, staring wide-eyed at the floor under my nose.

This is getting out of hand, surely. I got up, shivering a little and crying a little, and looking at the candles as if they were alive, and getting very sick of this.

Time to get out of this place and go into the village.

For two hours I was in the village, and for most of that time I was not seen or heard by anyone.

I found it absurdly easy to jump over the garden walls, to spring from the earth to low rooftops. I could leap from a height of three stories to the ground, and climb the side of a building digging my nails and my toes into the mortar between the stones.

I peered in windows. I saw couples asleep in their ruffled beds, infants dozing in cradles, old women sewing by feeble light.

And the houses looked like dollhouses to me in their completeness. Perfect collections of toys with their dainty little wooden chairs and polished mantelpieces, mended curtains and well-scrubbed floors.

I saw all this as one who had never been a part of life, gazing lovingly at the simplest details. A starched white apron on its hook, worn boots on the hearth, a pitcher beside a bed.

And the people . . . oh, the people were marvels.

Of course I picked up their scent, but I was satisfied and it didn't make me miserable. Rather I doted upon their pink skin and delicate limbs, the precision with which they moved, the whole process of their lives as if I had never been one of them at all. That they had five fingers on each hand seemed remarkable. They yawned, cried, shifted in sleep. I was entranced with them.

And when they spoke, the thickest walls could not prevent me from hearing their words.

But the most beguiling aspect of my explorations was that I *heard the thoughts of these people*, just as I had heard the evil servant whom I killed. Unhappiness, misery, expectation. These were currents in the air, some weak, some frighteningly strong, some no more than a glimmer gone before I knew the source.

But I could not, strictly speaking, read minds.

Most trivial thought was veiled from me, and when I lapsed into my own considerations, even the strongest passions did not intrude. In sum, it was intense feeling that carried thought to me and only when I wished to receive it, and there were some minds that even in the heat of anger gave me nothing.

These discoveries jolted me and almost bruised me, as did the common beauty everywhere I looked, the splendor in the ordinary. But I knew perfectly well there was an abyss behind it into which I might quite suddenly and helplessly drop.

After all, I wasn't one of these warm and pulsing miracles of complication and innocence. They were my victims.

Time to leave the village. I'd learned enough here. But just before I left, I performed one final act of daring. I couldn't help myself. I just had to do it.

Pulling up the high collar of my red cloak, I went into the inn, sought a corner away from the fire, and ordered a glass of wine. Everyone in the little place gave me the eye, but not because they knew there was a supernatural being in their midst. They were merely glancing at the richly dressed gentleman! And for twenty minutes I remained, testing it even further. No one, not even the man who served me, detected anything! Of course I didn't touch the wine. One whiff of it and I knew that my body could not abide it. But the point was, *I could fool mortals!* I could move among them!

I was jubilant when I left the inn. As soon as I reached the woods, I started to run. And then I was running so fast that the sky and the trees had become a blur. I was almost flying.

Then I stopped, leapt, danced about. I gathered up stones and threw them so far I could not see them land. And when I saw a fallen tree limb, thick and full of sap, I picked it up and broke it over my knee as if it were a twig.

I shouted, then sang at the top of my lungs again. I collapsed on the grass laughing.

And then I rose, tore off my cloak and my sword, and commenced to turn cartwheels. I turned cartwheels just like the acrobats at Renaud's. And then I somersaulted perfectly. I did it again, and this time backwards, and then forward, and then I turned double somersaults and triple somersaults, and leapt straight up in the air some fifteen feet off the ground before landing squarely on my feet, somewhat out of breath, and wanting to do these tricks some more.

But the morning was coming.

Only the subtlest change in the air, the sky, but I knew it as if Hell's Bells were ringing. Hell's Bells calling the vampire home to the sleep of death. Ah, the melting loveliness of the sky, the loveliness of the vision of dim belfries. And an odd thought came to me, that in hell the light of the fires would be so bright it would be like sunlight, and this would be the only sunlight I would ever see again.

But what have I done? I thought. I didn't ask for this, I didn't give in. Even when Magnus told me I was dying, I fought him, and yet I am hearing Hell's Bells now.

Well, who gives a damn?

WHEN I reached the churchyard, quite ready for the ride home, something distracted me.

I stood holding the rein of my horse and looking at the small field of graves and could not quite figure what it was. Then again it came, and I knew. I felt a distinct *presence* in the churchyard.

I stood so still I heard the blood thundering in my veins.

It wasn't human, this *presence*! It had no scent. And there were no human thoughts coming from it. Rather it seemed veiled and defended and it knew I was here. It was watching me.

Could I be imagining this?

I stood listening, looking. A scattering of gray tombstones poked through the snow. And far away stood a row of old crypts, larger, ornamented, but just as ruined as the stones.

It seemed *the presence* lingered somewhere near the crypts, and then I felt it distinctly as it moved towards the enclosing trees.

"Who are you!" I demanded. I heard my voice like a knife. "Answer me!" I called out even louder.

I felt a great tumult in it, this *presence*, and I was certain that it was moving away very rapidly.

I dashed across the churchyard after it, and I could feel it receding. Yet I saw nothing in the barren forest. And I realized I was stronger than it, and that it had been afraid of me!

Well, fancy that. Afraid of me.

And I had no idea whether or not it was corporeal, vampire the same as I was, or something without a body.

"Well, one thing is sure," I said. "You're a coward!"

Tingling in the air. The forest seemed to breathe for an instant.

A sense of my own might came over me that had been brewing all along. I was in fear of nothing. Not the church, not the dark, not the worms swarming over the corpses in my dungeon. Not even this strange eerie force that had retreated into the forest, and seemed to be near at hand again. Not even of men.

I was an extraordinary fiend! If I'd been sitting on the steps of hell with my elbows on my knees and the devil had said, "Lestat, come, choose the form of the fiend you wish to be to roam the earth," how could I have chosen a better fiend than what I was? And it seemed suddenly that suffering was an idea I'd known in another existence and would never know again.

I CAN'T help but laugh now when I think of that first night, especially of that particular moment.

9

THE next night I went tearing into Paris with as much gold as I could carry. The sun had just sunk beneath the horizon when I opened my eyes, and a clear azure light still emanated from the sky as I mounted and rode off to the city.

I was starving.

And as luck would have it, I was attacked by a cutthroat before I ever reached the city walls. He came thundering out of the woods, pistol blazing, and I actually saw the ball leave the barrel of the gun and go past me as I leapt off my horse and went at him.

He was a powerful man, and I was astonished at how much I enjoyed his cursing and struggling. The vicious servant I'd taken last night had been old. This was a hard young body. Even the roughness of his badly shaven beard tantalized me, and I loved the strength in his hands as he struck at me. But it was no sport. He froze as I sank my teeth into the artery, and when the blood came it was pure voluptuousness. In fact, it was so exquisite that I forgot completely about drawing away before the heart stopped.

We were on our knees in the snow together, and it was a wallop, the life going into me with the blood. I couldn't move for a long moment. Hmmm, broke the rules already, I thought. Am I supposed to die now? Doesn't look like that is going to happen. Just this rolling delirium.

And the poor dead bastard in my arms who would have blown my face off with his pistol if I had let him.

I kept staring at the darkening sky, at the great spangled mass of shadows ahead that was Paris. And there was only this warmth after, and obviously increasing strength.

So far so good. I climbed to my feet and wiped my lips. Then I pitched the body as far as I could across the unbroken snow. I was more powerful than ever.

And for a little while I stood there, feeling gluttonous and murderous, just wanting to kill again so this ecstasy would go on forever. But I couldn't have drunk any more blood, and gradually I grew calm and changed somewhat. A desolate feeling came over me. An aloneness as though the thief had been a friend to me or kin to me and had deserted me. I couldn't understand it, except that the drinking had been so intimate. His scent was on me now, and I sort of liked it. But there he lay yards away on the crumpled crust of the snow, hands and face looking gray under the rising moon.

Hell, the son of a bitch was going to kill me, wasn't he?

WITHIN an hour I had found a capable attorney, name of Pierre Roget, at his home in the Marais, an ambitious young man with a mind that was completely open to me. Greedy, clever, conscientious. Exactly what I wanted. Not only could I read his thoughts when he wasn't talking, but he believed everything I told him.

He was most eager to be of service to the husband of an heiress from Saint-Domingue. And certainly he would put out all the candles, save one, if my eyes were still hurting from tropical fever. As for my fortune in gems, he dealt with the most reputable jewelers. Bank accounts and letters of exchange for my family in the Auvergne—yes, immediately.

This was easier than playing Lelio.

But I was having a hell of a time concentrating. Everything was a distraction—the smoky flame of the candle on the brass inkstand, the gilded pattern of the Chinese wallpaper, and Monsieur Roget's amazing little face, with its eyes glistening behind tiny octagonal spectacles. His teeth kept making me think of clavier keys.

Ordinary objects in the room appeared to dance. A chest stared at me with its brass knobs for eyes. And a woman singing in an upstairs room over the low rumble of a stove seemed to be saying something in a low and vibrant secret language, such as Come to me.

But it was going to be this way forever apparently, and I had to get myself in hand. Money must be sent by courier this very night to my father and my brothers, and to Nicolas de Lenfent, a musician with Renaud's House of Thesbians, who was to be told only that the wealth had come from his friend Lestat de Lioncourt. It was Lestat de Lioncourt's wish that Nicolas de Lenfent move at once to a decent flat on the Ile St.-Louis or some other proper place, and Roget should, of course, assist in this, and thereafter Nicolas de Lenfent should study the violin. Roget should buy for Nicolas de Lenfent the best available violin, a Stradivarius.

And finally a separate letter was to be written to my mother, the Marquise Gabrielle de Lioncourt, in Italian, so that no one else could read it, and a special purse was to be sent to her. If she could undertake a journey to southern Italy, the place where she'd been born, maybe she could stop the course of her consumption.

It made me positively dizzy to think of her with the freedom to escape. I wondered what she would think about it.

For a long moment I didn't hear anything Roget said. I was picturing her dressed for once in her life as the marquise she was, and riding out of the gates of our castle in her own coach and six. And then I remembered her ravaged face and heard the cough in her lungs as if she were here with me.

"Send the letter and the money to her tonight," I said. "I don't care what it costs. Do it." I laid down enough gold to keep her in comfort for a lifetime, if she had a lifetime.

"Now," I said, "do you know of a merchant who deals in fine furnishings—paintings, tapestries? Someone who might open his shops and storehouses to us this very evening?"

"Of course, Monsieur. Allow me to get my coat. We shall go immediately."

We were headed for the faubourg St.-Denis within minutes.

And for hours after that, I roamed with my mortal attendants through a paradise of material wealth, claiming everything that I wanted. Couches and chairs, china and silver plate, drapery and statuary—all things were mine for the taking. And in my mind I transformed the castle where I'd grown up as more and more goods were carried out to be crated and shipped south immediately. To my little nieces and nephews I sent toys of which they'd never dreamed—tiny ships with real sails, dollhouses of unbelievable craft and perfection.

I learned from each thing that I touched. And there were moments when all the color and texture became too lustrous, too overpowering. I wept inwardly.

But I would have got away with playing human to the hilt during all this time, except for one very unfortunate mishap.

At one point as we wandered through the warehouse, a rat appeared as bold city rats will, racing along the wall very close to us. I stared at it. Nothing unusual of course. But there amid plaster and hardwood and embroidered cloth, the rat looked marvelously particular. And the men, misunderstanding of course, began mumbling frantic apologies for the rat and stamping their feet to drive it away from us.

To me, their voices became a mixture of sounds like stew bubbling in a pot. All I could think was that the rat had very tiny feet, and that I had not yet examined a rat nor any small warm-blooded creature. I went and caught the rat, rather too easily I think, and looked at its feet. I wanted to see what kind of little toenails it had, and what was the flesh like between its little toes, and I forgot the men entirely.

It was their sudden silence that brought me back to myself. They were both staring dumbfounded at me.

I smiled at them as innocently as I could, let the rat go, and went back to purchasing.

Well, they never said anything about it. But there was a lesson in this. I had really frightened them.

Later that night, I gave my lawyer one last commission: He must send a present of one hundred crowns to a theater owner by the name of Renaud with a note of thanks from me for his kindness.

"Find out the situation with this little playhouse," I said. "Find out if there are any debts against it."

Of course, I'd never go near the theater. They must never guess what had happened, never be contaminated by it. And for now I had done what I could for all those I loved, hadn't I?

AND when all this was finished, when the church clocks struck three over the white rooftops and I was hungry enough to smell blood everywhere that I turned, I found myself standing in the empty boulevard du Temple.

The dirty snow had turned to slush under the carriage wheels, and I was looking at the House of Thesbians with its spattered walls and its torn playbills and the name of the young mortal actor, Lestat de Valois, still written there in red letters.

10

THE following nights were a rampage. I began to drink up Paris as if the city were blood. In the early evening I raided the worst sections, tangling with thieves and killers, often giving them a playful chance to defend themselves, then snarling them in a fatal embrace and feasting to the point of gluttony.

I savored different types of kills: big lumbering creatures, small wiry ones, the hirsute and the dark-skinned, but my favorite was the very young scoundrel who'd kill you for the coins in your pocket.

I loved their grunting and cursing. Sometimes I held them with one hand and laughed at them till they were in a positive fury, and I threw their knives over the rooftops and smashed their pistols to pieces against the walls. But in all this my full strength was like a cat never allowed to spring. And the one thing I loathed in them was fear. If a victim was really afraid I usually lost interest.

As time went on, I learned to postpone the kill. I drank a little from one, and more from another, and then took the grand wallop of the death itself from the third or the fourth one. It was the chase and the struggle that I was multiplying for my own pleasure. And when I'd had enough of all this hunting and drinking in an evening to content some six healthy vampires, I turned my eyes to the rest of Paris, all the glorious pastimes I couldn't afford before.

But not before going to Roget's house for news of Nicolas or my mother.

Her letters were brimming with happiness at my good fortune, and she promised to go to Italy in the spring if only she could get the strength to do it. Right now she wanted books from Paris, of course, and newspapers, and keyboard music for the harpsichord I'd sent. And she had to know, Was I truly happy? Had I fulfilled my dreams? She was leery of wealth. I had been so happy at Renaud's. I must confide in her.

It was agony to hear these words read to me. Time to become a liar in earnest, which I had never been. But for her I would do it.

As for Nicki, I should have known he wouldn't settle for gifts and vague tales, that he would demand to see me and keep on demanding it. He was frightening Roget a little bit.

But it didn't do any good. There was nothing the attorney could tell him except what I've explained. And I was so wary of seeing Nicki that I didn't even ask for the location of the house into which he'd moved. I told the lawyer to make certain he studied with his Italian maestro and that he had everything he could possibly desire.

But I did manage somehow to hear quite against my will that Nicolas hadn't quit the theater. He was still playing at Renaud's House of Thesbians.

Now this maddened me. Why the hell, I thought, should he do that?

Because he loved it there, the same as I had, that was why. Did anybody really have to tell me this? We had all been kindred in that little rattrap playhouse. Don't think about the moment when the curtain goes up, when the audience begins to clap and shout . . .

No. Send cases of wine and champagne to the theater. Send flowers for Jeannette and Luchina, the girls I had fought with the most and most loved, and more gifts of gold for Renaud. Pay off the debts he had.

But as the nights passed and these gifts were dispatched, Renaud became embarrassed about all this. A fortnight later, Roget told me Renaud had made a proposal,

He wanted me to buy the House of Thesbians and keep him on as manager with enough capital to stage larger and more wondrous spectacles than he'd ever before attempted. With my money and his cleverness, we could make the house the talk of Paris.

I didn't answer right away. It took me more than a moment to realize that I could own the theater just like that. Own it like the gems in the chest, or the clothes I wore, or the dollhouse I'd sent to my nieces. I said no, and went out slamming the door.

Then I came right back.

"All right, buy the theater," I said, "and give him ten thousand crowns to do whatever he wants." This was a fortune. And I didn't even know why I had done this.

This pain will pass, I thought, it has to. And I must gain some control over my thoughts, realize that these things cannot affect me.

After all, where did I spend my time now? At the grandest theaters in Paris. I had the finest seats for the ballet and the opera, for the dramas of Molière and Racine. I was hanging about before the footlights gazing up at the great actors and actresses. I had suits made in every color of the rainbow, jewels on my fingers, wigs in the latest fashion, shoes with diamond buckles as well as gold heels.

And I had eternity to be drunk on the poetry I was hearing, drunk on the singing and the sweep of the dancer's arms, drunk on the organ throbbing in the great cavern of Notre Dame and drunk on the chimes that counted out the hours to me, drunk on the snow falling soundlessly on the empty gardens of the Tuileries.

And each night I was becoming less wary among mortals, more at ease with them.

Not even a month had passed before I got up the courage to plunge right into a crowded ball at the Palais Royal. I was warm and ruddy from the kill and at once I joined the dance. I didn't arouse the slightest suspicion. Rather the women seemed drawn to me, and I loved the touch of their hot fingers and the soft crush of their arms and their breasts.

After that, I bore right into the early evening crowds in the boulevards. Rushing past Renaud's, I squeezed into the other houses to see the puppet shows, the mimes, and the acrobats. I didn't flee from street lamps anymore. I went into cafés and bought coffee just to feel the warmth of it against my fingers, and I spoke to men when I chose.

I even argued with them about the state of the monarchy, and I went madly into mastering billiards and card games, and it seemed to me I might go right into the House of Thesbians if I wanted to, buy a ticket, and slip up into the balcony and see what was going on. See Nicolas!

Well, I didn't do that. What was I dreaming of to go near to Nicki? It was one thing to fool strangers, men and women who'd never known me, but what would Nicolas see if he looked into my eyes? What would he see when he looked at my skin? Besides I had too much to do, I told myself.

I was learning more and more about my nature and my powers.

MY HAIR, for example, was lighter, yet thicker, and grew not at all. Nor did my fingernails and toenails, which had a greater luster, though if I filed them away, they would regenerate during the day to the length they had been when I died. And though people couldn't discern such secrets on inspection, they sensed other things, an unnatural gleam to my eyes, too many reflected colors in them, and a faint luminescence to my skin.

When I was hungry this luminescence was very marked. All the more reason to feed.

And I was learning that I could put people in thrall if I stared at them too hard, and my voice required very strict modulation. I might speak too low for mortal hearing, and were I to shout or laugh too loud, I could shatter another's ears. I could hurt my own ears.

There were other difficulties: my movements. I tended to walk, to run, to dance, and to smile and gesture like a human being, but if surprised, horrified, grieved, my body could bend and contort like that of an acrobat.

Even my facial expressions could be wildly exaggerated. Once forgetting myself as I walked in the boulevard du Temple, thinking of Nicolas naturally, I sat down beneath a tree, drew up my knees, and put my hands to the side of my head like a stricken elf in a fairy tale. Eighteenth-century gentlemen in brocade frock coats and white silk stockings didn't do things like that, at least not on the street.

And another time, while deep in contemplation of the changing of the light on surfaces, I hopped up and sat with my legs crossed on the top of a carriage, with my elbows on my knees.

Well, this startled people. It frightened them. But more often than not, even when frightened by the whiteness of my skin, they merely looked away. They deceived themselves, I quickly realized, that everything was explainable. It was the rational eighteenth-century habit of mind.

After all there hadn't been a case of witchcraft in a hundred years, the last that I knew of being the trial of La Voisin, a fortune-teller, burnt alive in the time of Louis the Sun King.

And this was Paris. So if I accidentally crushed crystal glasses when I lifted them, or slammed doors back into the walls when opening them, people assumed I was drunk.

But now and then I answered questions before mortals had asked them of me. I fell into stuporous states just looking at candles or tree branches, and didn't move for so long that people asked if I was ill.

And my worst problem was laughter. I would go into fits of laughter and I couldn't stop. Anything could set me off. The sheer madness of my own position might set me off.

This can still happen to me fairly easily. No loss, no pain, no deepening understanding of my predicament changes it. Something strikes me as funny. I begin to laugh and I can't stop.

It makes other vampires furious, by the way. But I jump ahead of the tale.

As you have probably noticed, I have made no mention of other vampires. The fact was I could not find any.

I could find no other supernatural being in all of Paris.

Mortals to the left of me, mortals to the right of me, and now and then —just when I'd convinced myself it wasn't happening at all—I'd feel that vague and maddeningly elusive *presence.*

It was never any more substantial than it had been the first night in the village churchyard. And invariably it was in the vicinity of a Paris cemetery.

Always, I'd stop, turn, and try to draw it out. But it was never any good, the thing was gone before I could be certain of it. I could never find it on my own, and the stench of city cemeteries was so revolting I wouldn't, couldn't, go into them.

This was coming to seem more than fastidiousness or bad memories of my own dungeon beneath the tower. Revulsion at the sight or smell of death seemed part of my nature.

I couldn't watch executions any more than when I was that trembling boy from the Auvergne, and corpses made me cover my face. I think I was offended by death unless I was the cause of it! And I had to get clean away from my dead victims almost immediately.

But to return to the matter of *the presence.* I came to wonder if it wasn't some other species of haunt, something that couldn't commune with me. On the other hand, I had the distinct impression that *the presence* was watching me, maybe even deliberately revealing itself to me.

Whatever the case, I saw no other vampires in Paris. And I was beginning to wonder if there could be more than one of us at any given time. Maybe Magnus destroyed the vampire from whom he stole the blood. Maybe he had to perish once he passed on his powers. And I too would die if I were to make another vampire.

But no, that didn't make sense. Magnus had had great strength even after giving me his blood. And he had bound his vampire victim in chains when he stole his powers.

An enormous mystery, and a maddening one. But for the moment, ignorance was truly bliss. And I was doing very well discovering things without the help of Magnus. And maybe this was what Magnus had intended. Maybe this had been his way of learning centuries ago.

I remembered his words, that in the secret chamber of the tower I would find all that I needed to prosper.

THE hours flew as I roamed the city. And only to conceal myself in the tower by day did I ever deliberately leave the company of human beings.

Yet I was beginning to wonder: "If you can dance with them, and play billiards with them and talk with them, then why can't you dwell among them, just the way you did when you were living? Why couldn't you *pass* for one of them? And enter again into the very fabric of life where there is . . . what? Say it!"

And here it was nearly spring. And the nights were getting warmer, and the House of Thesbians was putting on a new drama with new acrobats between the acts. And the trees were in bloom again, and every waking moment I thought of Nicki.

ONE night in March, I realized as Roget read my mother's letter to me that I could read as well as he could. I had learned from a thousand sources how to read without even trying. I took the letter home with me.

Even the inner chamber was no longer really cold. And I sat by the window reading my mother's words for the first time in private. I could almost hear her voice speaking to me:

"Nicolas writes that you have purchased Renaud's. So you own the little theater on the boulevard where you were so happy. But do you possess the happiness still? When will you answer me?"

I folded up the letter and put it in my pocket. The blood tears were coming into my eyes. Why must she understand so much, yet so little?

11

THE wind had lost its sting. All the smells of the city were coming back. And the markets were full of flowers. I dashed to Roget's house without even thinking of what I was doing and demanded that he tell me where Nicolas lived.

I would just have a look at him, make certain he was in good health, be certain the house was fine enough.

It was on the Ile St.-Louis, and very impressive just as I'd wanted, but the windows were all shuttered along the quais.

I stood watching it for a long time, as one carriage after another roared over the nearby bridge. And I knew that I had to see Nicki.

I started to climb the wall just as I had climbed walls in the village, and I found it amazingly easy. One story after another I climbed, much higher than I had ever dared to climb in the past, and then I sped over the roof, and down the inside of the courtyard to look for Nicki's flat.

I passed a handful of open windows before I came to the right one. And then there was Nicolas in the glare of the supper table and Jeannette and Luchina were with him, and they were having the late night meal that we used to take together when the theater closed.

At the first sight of him, I drew back away from the casement and closed my eyes. I might have fallen if my right hand hadn't held fast to the wall as if with a will of its own. I had seen the room for only an instant, but every detail was fixed in my mind.

He was dressed in old green velvet, finery he'd worn so casually in the crooked streets at home. But everywhere around him were signs of the wealth I'd sent him, leather-bound books on the shelves, and an inlaid desk with an oval painting above it, and the Italian violin gleaming atop the new pianoforte.

He wore a jeweled ring I'd sent, and his brown hair was tied back with a black silk ribbon, and he sat brooding with his elbows on the table eating nothing from the expensive china plate before him.

Carefully I opened my eyes and looked at him again. All his natural gifts were there in a blaze of light: the delicate but strong limbs, large sober brown eyes, and his mouth that for all the irony and sarcasm that could come out of it was childlike and ready to be kissed.

There seemed in him a frailty I'd never perceived or understood. Yet he looked infinitely intelligent, my Nicki, full of tangled uncompromising thoughts, as he listened to Jeannette, who was talking rapidly.

"Lestat's married," she said as Luchina nodded, "the wife's rich, and he can't let her know he was a common actor, it's simple enough."

"I say we let him in peace," Luchina said. "He saved the theater from closing, and he showers us with gifts . . ."

"I don't believe it," Nicolas said bitterly. "He wouldn't be ashamed of us." There was a suppressed rage in his voice, an ugly grief. "And why did he leave the way he did? I heard him calling me! The window was smashed to pieces! I tell you I was half awake, and I heard his voice . . ."

An uneasy silence fell among them. They didn't believe his account of things, how I'd vanished from the garret, and telling it again would only isolate him and embitter him further. I could sense this from all their thoughts.

"You didn't really know Lestat," he said now, almost in a surly fashion, returning to the manageable conversation that other mortals would allow him. "Lestat would spit in the face of anyone who would be ashamed of us! He sends me money. What am I supposed to do with it? He plays games with us!"

No answer from the others, the solid, practical beings who would not speak against the mysterious benefactor. Things were going too well.

And in the lengthening silence, I felt the depth of Nicki's anguish, I *knew* it as if I were peering into his skull. And I couldn't bear it.

I couldn't bear delving into his soul without his knowing it. Yet I couldn't stop myself from sensing a vast secret terrain inside him, grimmer perhaps than I had ever dreamed, and his words came back to me that the darkness in him was like the darkness I'd seen at the inn, and that he tried to conceal it from me.

I could almost see it, this terrain. And in a real way it was beyond his mind, as if his mind were merely a portal to a chaos stretching out from the borders of all we know.

Too frightening that. I didn't want to see it. I didn't want to feel what he felt!

But what could I do *for* him? That was the important thing. What could I do to stop this torment once and for all?

Yet I wanted so to touch him—his hands, his arms, his face. I wanted to feel his flesh with these new immortal fingers. And I found myself whispering the word "Alive." Yes, you are alive and that means you can die. And everything I see when I look at you is utterly insubstantial. It is a commingling of tiny movements and indefinable colors as if you haven't a body at all, but are a collection of heat and light. You are light itself, and what am I now?

Eternal as I am, I curl like a cinder in that blaze.

But the atmosphere of the room had changed. Luchina and Jeannette were taking their leave with polite words. He was ignoring them. He had turned to the window, and he was rising as if he'd been called by a secret voice. The look on his face was indescribable.

He knew I was there!

Instantly, I shot up the slippery wall to the roof.

But I could still *hear* him below. I looked down and I saw his naked hands on the window ledge. And through the silence I heard his panic. He'd sensed that I was there! My presence, mind you, that is what he sensed, just as I sensed *the presence* in the graveyards, but how, he argued with himself, could Lestat have been here?

I was too shocked to do anything. I clung to the roof gutter, and I could feel the departure of the others, feel that he was now alone. And all I could think was, What in the name of hell is this presence that he felt?

I mean I wasn't Lestat anymore, I was this demon, this powerful and greedy vampire, and yet he felt my presence, the presence of Lestat, the young man he knew!

It was a very different thing from a mortal seeing my face and blurting out my name in confusion. He had recognized in my monster self something that he knew and loved.

I stopped listening to him. I merely lay on the roof.

But I knew he was moving below. I knew it when he lifted the violin from its place on the pianoforte, and I knew he was again at the window.

And I put my hands over my ears.

Still the sound came. It came rising out of the instrument and cleaving the night as if it were some shining element, other than air and light and matter, that might climb to the very stars.

He bore down on the strings, and I could almost see him against my eyelids, swaying back and forth, his head bowed against the violin as if he meant to pass into the music, and then all sense of him vanished and there was only the sound.

The long vibrant notes, and the chilling glissandos, and the violin singing in its own tongue to make every other form of speech seem false. Yet as the song deepened, it became the very essence of despair as if its beauty were a horrid coincidence, grotesquery without a particle of truth.

Was this what he believed, what he had always believed when I talked on and on about goodness? Was he making the violin say it? Was he deliberately creating those long, pure liquid notes to say that beauty meant nothing because it came from the despair inside him, and it had nothing to do with the despair finally, because the despair wasn't beautiful, and beauty then was a horrid irony?

I didn't know the answer. But the sound went beyond him as it always had. It grew bigger than the despair. It fell effortlessly into a slow melody, like water seeking its own downward mountain path. It grew richer and darker still and there seemed something undisciplined and chastening in it, and heartbreaking and vast. I lay on my back on the roof now with my eyes on the stars.

Pinpoints of light mortals could not have seen. Phantom clouds. And the raw, piercing sound of the violin coming slowly with exquisite tension to a close.

I didn't move.

I was in some silent understanding of the language the violin spoke to me. Nicki, if we could talk again . . . If "our conversation" could only continue.

Beauty wasn't the treachery he imagined it to be, rather it was an uncharted land where one could make a thousand fatal errors, a wild and indifferent paradise without signposts of evil or good.

In spite of all the refinements of civilization that conspired to make art —the dizzying perfection of the string quartet or the sprawling grandeur of Fragonard's canvases—beauty was savage. It was as dangerous and lawless as the earth had been eons before man had one single coherent thought in his head or wrote codes of conduct on tablets of clay. Beauty was a Savage Garden.

So why must it wound him that the most despairing music is full of beauty? Why must it hurt him and make him cynical and sad and untrusting?

Good and evil, those are concepts man has made. And man is better, really, than the Savage Garden.

But maybe deep inside Nicki had always dreamed of a harmony among all things that I had always known was impossible. Nicki had dreamed not of goodness, but of justice.

But we could never discuss these things now with each other. We could never again be in the inn. Forgive me, Nicki. Good and evil exist still, as they always will. But "our conversation" is over forever.

* * *

YET even as I left the roof, as I stole silently away from the Ile St.-Louis, I knew what I meant to do.

I didn't admit it to myself but I knew.

THE next night it was already late when I reached the boulevard du Temple. I'd fed well in the Ile de la Cité, and the first act at Renaud's House of Thesbians was already under way.

12

I'D DRESSED as if I were going to Court, in silver brocade with a lavender velvet roquelaure over my shoulders. I had a new sword with a deep-carved silver handle and the usual heavy, ornate buckles on my shoes, the usual lace, gloves, tricorne. And I came to the theater in a hired carriage.

But as soon as I paid the driver I went back the alley and opened the stage door exactly as I used to do.

At once the old atmosphere surrounded me, the smell of the thick greasepaint and the cheap costumes full of sweat and perfume, and the dust. I could see a fragment of the lighted stage burning beyond the helter-skelter of hulking props and hear bursts of laughter from the hall. A group of acrobats waited to go on at the intermezzo, a crowd of jesters in red tights, caps and dagged collars studded with little gold bells.

I felt dizzy, and for a moment afraid. The place felt close and dangerous over my head, and yet it was wonderful to be inside it again. And a sadness was swelling inside me, no, a panic, actually.

Luchina saw me and she let out a shriek. Doors opened everywhere on the cluttered little dressing rooms. Renaud plunged towards me and pumped my hand. Where there had been nothing but wood and drapery a moment before, there was now a little universe of excited human beings, faces full of high color and dampness, and I found myself drawing back from a smoking candelabra with the quick words, "My eyes . . . put it out."

"Put out the candles, they hurt his eyes, can't you see that?" Jeannette insisted sharply. I felt her wet lips open against my face. Everyone was around me, even the acrobats who didn't know me, and the old scene painters and carpenters who had taught me so many things. Luchina said, "Get Nicki," and I almost cried No.

Applause was shaking the little house. The curtain was being pulled closed from either side. At once the old actors were upon me, and Renaud was calling for champagne.

I was holding my hands over my eyes as if like the basilisk I'd kill every one of them if I looked at them, and I could feel tears and knew that before they saw the blood in the tears, I had to wipe the tears away. But they were so close I couldn't get to my handkerchief, and with a sudden terrible weakness, I put my arms around Jeannette and Luchina, and I pressed my face against Luchina's face. Like birds they were, with bones full of air, and hearts like beating wings, and for one second I listened with a vampire's ear to the blood in them, but that seemed an obscenity. And I just gave in to the hugging and the kissing, ignoring the thump of their hearts, and holding them and smelling their powdered skin, and feeling again the press of their lips.

"You don't know how you worried us!" Renaud was booming. "And then the stories of your good fortune! Everyone, everyone!" He was clapping his hands. "It's Monsieur de Valois, the owner of this great theatrical establishment . . ." and he said a lot of other pompous and playful things, dragging up the new actors and actresses to kiss my hand, I suppose, or my feet. I was holding tight to the girls as if I'd explode into fragments if I let them go, and then I heard Nicki, and knew he was only a foot away, staring at me, and that he was too glad to see me to be hurt anymore.

I didn't open my eyes but I felt his hand on my face, then holding tight to the back of my neck. They must have made way for him and when he came into my arms, I felt a little convulsion of terror, but the light was dim here, and I had fed furiously to be warm and human-looking, and I thought desperately I don't know to whom I pray to make the deception work. And then there was only Nicolas and I didn't care.

I looked up and into his face.

How to describe what humans look like to us! I've tried to describe it a little, when I spoke of Nicki's beauty the night before as a mixture of movement and color. But you can't imagine what it's like for us to look on living flesh. There are those billions of colors and tiny configurations of movement, yes, that make up a living creature on whom we concentrate. But the radiance mingles totally with the carnal scent. Beautiful, that's what any human being is to us, if we stop to consider it, even the old and the diseased, the downtrodden that one doesn't really "see" in the street. They are all like that, like flowers ever in the process of opening, butterflies ever unfolding out of the cocoon.

Well, I saw all this when I saw Nicki, and I smelled the blood pumping in him, and for one heady moment I felt love and only love obliterating every recollection of the horrors that had deformed me. Every evil rapture, every new power with its gratification, seemed unreal. Maybe I felt a profound joy, too, that I could still love, if I'd ever doubted it, and that a tragic victory had been confirmed.

All the old mortal comfort intoxicated me, and I could have closed my eyes and slipped from consciousness carrying him with me, or so it seemed.

But something else stirred in me, collecting strength so fast my mind raced to catch up with it and deny it even as it threatened to grow out of control. And I knew it for what it was, something monstrous and enormous and natural to me as the sun was unnatural. I wanted Nicki. I wanted him as surely as any victim I'd ever struggled with in the Ile de la Cité. I wanted his blood flowing into me, wanted its taste and its smell and its heat.

The little place shook with shouts and laughter, Renaud telling the acrobats to get on with the intermezzo and Luchina opening the champagne. But we were closed off in this embrace.

The hard heat of his body made me stiffen and draw back, though it seemed I didn't move at all. And it maddened me suddenly that this one whom I loved even as I loved my mother and my brothers—this one who had drawn from me the only tenderness I'd ever felt—was an unconquerable citadel, holding fast in ignorance against my thirst for blood when so many hundreds of victims had so easily given it up.

This was what I'd been made for. This was the path I had been meant to walk. What were those others to me now—the thieves and killers I'd cut down in the wilderness of Paris? This was what I wanted. And the great awesome possibility of Nicki's death exploded in my brain. The darkness against my closed eyelids had become blood red. Nicki's mind emptying in that last moment, giving up its complexity with its life.

I couldn't move. I could feel the blood as if it were passing into me and I let my lips rest against his neck. Every particle in me said, "Take him, spirit him out of this place and away from it and feed on him and feed on him . . . until . . ." Until what! Until he's dead!

I broke loose and pushed him away. The crowd around us roared and rattled. Renaud was shouting at the acrobats, who stood staring at these proceedings. The audience outside demanded the intermezzo entertainment with a steady rhythmic clap. The orchestra was fiddling away at the lively ditty that would accompany the acrobats. Bones and flesh poked and pushed at me. A shambles it had become, rank with the smell of those ready for the slaughter. I felt the all too human rise of nausea.

Nicki seemed to have lost his equilibrium, and when our eyes met, I felt the accusations emanating from him. I felt the misery and, worse, the near despair.

I pushed past all of them, past the acrobats with the jingling bells, and I don't know why I went forward to the wings instead of out the side door. I wanted to see the stage. I wanted to see the audience. I wanted to penetrate deeper into something for which I had no name or word.

But I was mad in these moments. To say I wanted or I thought makes no sense at all.

My chest was heaving and the thirst was like a cat clawing to get out. And as I leaned against the wooden beam beside the curtain, Nicki, hurt and misunderstanding everything, came to me again.

I let the thirst rage. I let it tear at my insides. I just clung to the rafter and I saw in one great recollection all my victims, the scum of Paris, scraped up from its gutters, and I knew the madness of the course I'd chosen, and the lie of it, and what I really was. What a sublime idiocy that I had dragged that paltry morality with me, striking down the damned ones only—seeking to be saved in spite of it all? What had I thought I was, a righteous partner to the judges and executioners of Paris who strike down the poor for crimes that the rich commit every day?

Strong wine I'd had, in chipped and broken vessels, and now the priest was standing before me at the foot of the altar with the golden chalice in his hands, and the wine inside it was the Blood of the Lamb.

Nicki was talking rapidly:

"Lestat, what is it? Tell me!" as if the others couldn't hear us. "Where have you been? What's happened to you? Lestat!"

"Get on that stage!" Renaud thundered at the gaping acrobats. They trotted past us into the smoky blaze of the footlamps and went into a chain of somersaults.

The orchestra made its instruments into twittering birds. A flash of red, harlequin sleeves, bells jangling, taunts from the unruly crowd, "Show us something, really show us something!"

Luchina kissed me and I stared at her white throat, her milky hands. I could see the veins in Jeannette's face and the soft cushion of her lower lip coming ever closer. The champagne, splashed into dozens of little glasses, was being drunk. Some speech was issuing forth from Renaud about our "partnership" and how tonight's little farce was but the beginning and we would soon be the grandest theater on the boulevards. I saw myself decked out for the part of Lelio, and heard the ditty I had sung to Flaminia on bended knee.

Before me, little mortals flipflopped heavily and the audience was howling as the leader of the acrobats made some vulgar movement with his hind end.

Before I even meant to do it, I had gone out on the stage.

I was standing in the very center, feeling the heat of the footlights, the smoke stinging my eyes. I stared at the crowded gallery, the screened boxes, the rows and rows of spectators to the back wall. And I heard myself snarl a command for the acrobats to get away.

It seemed the laughter was deafening, and the taunts and shouts that greeted me were spasms and eruptions, and quite plainly behind every face in the house was a grinning skull. I was humming the little ditty I'd sung as Lelio, no more than a fragment of the part, but the one I'd carried in the streets afterwards with me, "lovely, lovely, Flaminia," and on and on, the words forming meaningless sounds.

Insults were cutting through the din.

"On with the performance!" and "You're handsome enough, now let's see some action!" From the gallery someone threw a half-eaten apple that came thumping just past my feet.

I unclasped the violet roquelaure and let it fall. I did the same with the silver sword.

The song had become an incoherent humming behind my lips, but mad poetry was pounding in my head. I saw the wilderness of beauty and its savagery, the way I'd seen it last night when Nicki was playing, and the moral world seemed some desperate dream of rationality that in this lush and fetid jungle had not the slightest chance. It was a vision and I *saw* rather than understood, except that I was part of it, natural as the cat with her exquisite and passionless face digging her claws into the back of the screaming rat.

" 'Handsome enough' is this Grim Reaper," I half uttered, "who can snuff all these 'brief candles,' every fluttering soul sucking the air, from this hall."

But the words were really beyond my reach. They floated in some stratum perhaps where a god existed who understood the colors patterned on a cobra's skin and the eight glorious notes that make up the music erupting out of Nicki's instrument, but never the principle, beyond ugliness or beauty, "Thou shalt not kill."

Hundreds of greasy faces peered back at me from the gloom. Shabby wigs and paste jewels and filthy finery, skin like water flowing over crooked bones. A crew of ragged beggars whistled and hooted from the gallery, humpback and one eye, and stinking underarm crutch, and teeth the color of the skull's teeth you sift from the dirt of the grave.

I threw out my arms. I crooked my knee, and I began turning as the acrobats and dancers could turn, round and round on the ball of one foot, effortlessly, going faster and faster, until I broke, flipping over backwards into a circle of cartwheels, and then somersaults, imitating everything I had ever seen the players at the fairs perform.

Applause came immediately. I was agile as I'd been in the village, and the stage was tiny and hampering, and the ceiling seemed to press down on me, and the smoke from the footlights to close me in. The little song to Flaminia came back to me and I started singing it loudly as I turned and jumped and spun again, and then gazing at the ceiling I willed my body upwards as I bent my knees to spring.

In an instant I touched the rafters and I was dropping down gracefully, soundlessly to the boards.

Gasps rose from the audience. The little crowd in the wings was stunned. The musicians in the pit who had been silent all the while were turning to one another. They could see there was no wire.

But I was soaring again to the delight of the audience, this time somersaulting all the way up, beyond the painted arch again to descend in even slower, finer turns.

Shouts and cheers broke out over the clapping, but those backstage were mute. Nicki stood at the very edge, his lips silently shaping my name.

"It has to be trickery, an illusion." The same avowals came from all directions. People demanded agreement from those around them. Renaud's face shone before me for an instant with gaping mouth and squinting eyes.

But I had gone into a dance again. And this time the grace of it no longer mattered to the audience. I could feel it, because the dance became a parody, each gesture broader, longer, slower than a human dancer could have sustained.

Someone shouted from the wings and was told to be still. And little cries burst from the musicians and those in the front rows. People were growing uneasy and whispering to one another, but the rabble in the gallery continued to clap.

I dashed suddenly towards the audience as if I meant to admonish it for its rudeness. Several persons were so startled they rose and tried to escape into the aisles. One of the hornplayers dropped his instrument and climbed out of the pit.

I could see the agitation, even the anger in their faces. What were these illusions? It wasn't amusing them suddenly; they couldn't comprehend the skill of it; and something in my serious manner made them afraid. For one terrible moment, I felt their helplessness.

And I felt their doom.

A great horde of jangling skeletons snared in flesh and rags, that's what they were, and yet their courage blazed out of them, they shouted at me in their irrepressible pride.

I raised my hands slowly to command their attention, and very loudly and steadily I sang the ditty to Flaminia, my lovely Flaminia, a dull little couplet spilling into another couplet, and I let my voice grow louder and louder until suddenly people were rising and screaming before me, but louder still I sang it until it obliterated every other noise and in the intolerable roar I saw them all, hundreds of them, overturning the benches as they stood up, their hands clamped to the sides of their heads.

Their mouths were grimaces, toneless screams.

Pandemonium. Shrieks, curses, all stumbling and struggling towards the doors. Curtains were pulled from their fastenings. Men dropped down from the gallery to rush for the street.

I stopped the horrid song.

I stood watching them in a ringing silence, the weak, sweating bodies straining clumsily in every direction. The wind gusted from the open doorways, and I felt a strange coldness over all my limbs and it seemed my eyes were made of glass.

Without looking, I picked up the sword and put it on again, and hooked my finger into the velvet collar of my crumpled and dusty roquelaure. All these gestures seemed as grotesque as everything else I had done, and it seemed of no import that Nicolas was trying to get loose from two of the actors who held him in fear of his life as he shouted my name.

But something out of the chaos caught my attention. It did seem to matter—to be terribly, terribly important, in fact—that there was a figure standing above in one of the open boxes who did not struggle to escape or even move.

I turned slowly and looked up at him, daring him, it seemed, to remain there. An old man he was, and his dull gray eyes were boring into me with stubborn outrage, and as I glared at him, I heard myself let out a loud open-mouthed roar. Out of my soul it seemed to come, this sound. It grew louder and louder until those few left below cowered again with their ears stopped, and even Nicolas, rushing forward, buckled beneath the sound of it, both hands clasped to his head.

And yet the man stood there in the loge glowering, indignant and old, and stubborn, with furrowed brows under his gray wig.

I stepped back and leapt across the empty house, landing in the box directly before him, and his jaw fell in spite of himself and his eyes grew hideously wide.

He seemed deformed with age, his shoulders rounded, his hands gnarled, but the spirit in his eyes was beyond vanity and beyond compromise. His mouth hardened and his chin jutted. And from under his frock coat he pulled his pistol and he aimed it at me with both hands.

"Lestat!" Nicki shouted.

But the shot exploded and the ball hit me with full force. I didn't move. I stood as steady as the old man had stood before, and the pain rolled through me and stopped, leaving in its wake a terrible pulling in all my veins.

The blood poured out. It flowed as I have never seen blood flow. It drenched my shirt and I could feel it spilling down my back. But the pulling grew stronger and stronger, and a warm tingling sensation had commenced to spread across the surface of my back and chest.

The man stared, dumbfounded. The pistol dropped out of his hand. His head went back, eyes blind, and his body crumpled as if the air had been let out of it, and he lay on the floor.

Nicki had raced up the stairs and was now rushing into the box. A low hysterical murmuring was issuing from him. He thought he was witnessing my death.

And I stood still hearkening to my body in that terrible solitude that had been mine since Magnus made me the vampire. And I knew the wounds were no longer there.

The blood was drying on the silk vest, drying on the back of my torn coat. My body throbbed where the bullet had passed through me and my veins were alive with that same pulling, but the injury was no more.

And Nicolas, coming to his senses as he looked at me, realized I was unharmed, though his reason told him it couldn't be true.

I pushed past him and made for the stairs. He flung himself against me and I threw him off. I couldn't stand the sight of him, the smell of him.

"Get away from me!" I said.

But he came back again and he locked his arm around my neck. His face was bloated and there was an awful sound coming out of him.

"Let go of me, Nicki!" I threatened him. If I shoved him off too roughly, I'd tear his arms out of the sockets, break his back.

Break his back . . .

He moaned, stuttered. And for one harrowing split second the sounds he made were as terrible as the sound that had come from my dying animal on the mountain, my horse, crushed like an insect into the snow.

I scarcely knew what I was doing when I pried loose his hands.

The crowd broke, screaming, when I walked out onto the boulevard.

Renaud ran forward, in spite of those trying to restrain him.

"Monsieur!" He grabbed my hand to kiss it and stopped, staring at the blood.

"Nothing, my dear Renaud," I said to him, quite surprised at the steadiness of my voice and its softness. But something distracted me as I started to speak again, something I should hearken to, I thought vaguely, yet I went on.

"Don't give it a thought, my dear Renaud," I said. "Stage blood, nothing but an illusion. It was all an illusion. A new kind of theatrical. Drama of the grotesque, yes, the grotesque."

But again came that distraction, something I was sensing in the melee around me, people shuffling and pushing to get close but not too close, Nicolas stunned and staring.

"Go on with your plays," I was saying, almost unable to concentrate on my own words, "your acrobats, your tragedies, your more civilized theatricals, if you like."

I pulled the bank notes out of my pocket and put them in his unsteady hand. I spilled gold coins onto the pavement. The actors darted forward fearfully to gather them up. I scanned the crowd around for the source of this strange distraction, *what was it,* not Nicolas in the door of the deserted theater, watching me with a broken soul.

No, something else both familiar and unfamiliar, having to do with the dark.

"Hire the finest mummers"—I was half babbling—"the best musicians, the great scene painters." More bank notes. My voice was getting loud again, the vampire voice, I could see the grimaces again and the hands going up, but they were afraid to let me see them cover their ears. "There is no limit, NO LIMIT, to what you can do here!"

I broke away, dragging my roquelaure with me, the sword clanking awkwardly because it was not buckled right. Something of the dark.

And I knew when I hurried into the first alleyway and started to run what it was that I had heard, what had distracted me, it had been *the presence,* undeniably, in the crowd!

I knew it for one simple reason: I was running now in the back streets faster than a mortal can run. And *the presence* was keeping time with me and *the presence* was more than one!

I came to a halt when I knew it for certain.

I was only a mile from the boulevard and the crooked alley around me narrow and black as any in which I had ever been. And I heard *them* before they seemed, quite purposefully and abruptly, to silence themselves.

I was too anxious and miserable to play with them! I was too dazed. I shouted the old question, "Who are you, speak to me!" The glass panes rattled in the nearby windows. Mortals stirred in their little chambers. There was no cemetery here. "Answer me, you pack of cowards. Speak if you have a voice or once and for all get away from me!"

And then I knew, though how I knew, I can't tell you, that they could hear me and they could answer me, if they chose. And I knew that what I had always heard was the irrepressible evidence of their proximity and their intensity, which they couldn't disguise. But their thoughts they could cloak and they had. I mean, they had intellect, and they had words.

I let out a long low breath.

I was stung by their silence, but I was stung a thousand times more by what had just happened, and as I'd done so many times in the past I turned my back on them.

They followed me. This time they followed, and no matter how swiftly I moved, they came on.

And I did not lose that strange toneless shimmer of them until I reached the place de Grève and went into the Cathedral of Notre Dame.

I SPENT the remainder of the night in the cathedral, huddled in a shadowy place by the right wall. I hungered for the blood I'd lost, and each time a mortal drew near I felt a strong pulling and tingling where the wounds had been.

But I waited.

And when a young beggar woman with a little child approached, I knew the moment had come. She saw the dried blood, and became frantic to get me to the nearby hospital, the Hôtel-Dieu. Her face was thin with hunger, but she tried to lift me herself with her little arms.

I looked into her eyes until I saw them glaze over. I felt the heat of her breasts swelling beneath her rags. Her soft, succulent body tumbled against me, giving itself to me, as I nestled her in all the bloodstained brocade and lace. I kissed her, feeding on her heat as I pushed the dirty cloth away from her throat, and I bent for the drink so skillfully that the sleepy child never saw it. Then I opened with careful trembling fingers the child's ragged shirt. This was mine, too, this little neck.

There weren't any words for the rapture. Before I'd had all the ecstasy that rape could give. But these victims had been taken in the perfect semblance of love. The very blood seemed warmer with their innocence, richer with their goodness.

I looked at them afterwards, as they slept together in death. They had found no sanctuary in the cathedral on this night.

And I knew my vision of the garden of savage beauty had been a true vision. There was meaning in the world, yes, and laws, and inevitability, but they had only to do with the aesthetic. And in this Savage Garden, these innocent ones belonged in the vampire's arms. A thousand other things can be said about the world, but only aesthetic principles can be verified, and these things alone remain the same.

I was now ready to go home. And as I went out in the early morning, I knew that the last barrier between my appetite and the world had been dissolved.

No one was safe from me now, no matter how innocent. And that included my dear friends at Renaud's and it included my beloved Nick.

13

I WANTED them gone from Paris. I wanted the playbills down, the doors shut; I wanted silence and darkness in the little rattrap theater where I had known the greatest and most sustained happiness of my mortal life.

Not a dozen innocent victims a night could make me stop thinking about them, could make this ache in me dissolve. Every street in Paris led to their door.

And an ugly shame came over me when I thought of my frightening them. How could I have done that to them? Why did I need to prove to myself with such violence that I could never be part of them again?

No. I'd bought Renaud's. I'd turned it into the showcase of the boulevard. Now I would close it down.

It was not that they suspected anything, however. They believed the simple stupid excuses Roget gave them, that I was just back from the heat of the tropical colonies, that the good Paris wine had gone right to my head. Plenty of money again to repair the damage.

God only knows what they really thought. The fact was, they went back to regular performances the following evening, and the jaded crowds of the boulevard du Temple undoubtedly put upon the mayhem a dozen sensible explanations. There was a queue under the chestnut trees.

Only Nicki was having none of it. He had taken to heavy drinking and refused to return to the theater or study his music anymore. He insulted Roget when he came to call. To the worst cafés and taverns he went, and wandered alone through the dangerous nighttime streets.

Well, we have that in common, I thought.

All this Roget told me as I paced the floor a good distance from the candle on his table, my face a mask of my true thoughts.

"Money doesn't mean very much to the young man, Monsieur," he said. "The young man has had plenty of money in his life, he reminds me. He says things that disturb me, Monsieur. I don't like the sound of them."

Roget looked like a nursery rhyme figure in his flannel cap and gown, legs and feet naked because I had roused him again in the middle of the night and given him no time to put on his slippers even or to comb his hair.

"What does he say?" I demanded.

"He talks about sorcery, Monsieur. He says that you possess unusual powers. He speaks of La Voisin and the *Chambre Ardente*, an old case of sorcery under the Sun King, the witch who made charms and poisons for members of the Court."

"Who would believe that trash now?" I affected absolute bewilderment. The truth was, the hair was standing up on the back of my neck.

"Monsieur, he says bitter things," he went on. "That your kind, as he puts it, has always had access to great secrets. He keeps speaking of some place in your town, called the witches' place."

"My kind!"

"That you are an aristocrat, Monsieur," Roget said. He was a little embarrassed. "When a man is angry as Monsieur de Lenfent is angry, these things come to be important. But he doesn't whisper his suspicions to the others. He tells only me. He says that you will understand why he despises you. You have refused to share with him your discoveries! Yes, Monsieur, your discoveries. He goes on about La Voisin, about things between heaven and earth for which there are no rational explanations. He says he knows now why you cried at the witches' place."

I couldn't look at Roget for a moment. It was such a lovely perversion of everything! And yet it hit right at the truth. How gorgeous, and how perfectly irrelevant. In his own way, Nicki was right.

"Monsieur, you are the kindest man—" Roget said.

"Spare me, please . . ."

"But Monsieur de Lenfent says fantastical things, things he should not say even in this day and age, that he saw a bullet pass through your body that should have killed you."

"The bullet missed me," I said. "Roget, don't go on with it. Get them out of Paris, all of them."

"Get them out?" he asked. "But you've put so much money into this little enterprise . . ."

"So what? Who gives a damn?" I said. "Send them to London, to Drury Lane. Offer Renaud enough for his own London theater. From there they might go to America—Saint-Domingue, New Orleans, New York. Do it, Monsieur. I don't care what it takes. Close up my theater and get them gone!"

And then the ache will be gone, won't it? I'll stop seeing them gathered around me in the wings, stop thinking about Lelio, the boy from the provinces who emptied their slop buckets and loved it.

Roget looked so profoundly timid. What is it like, working for a well-dressed lunatic who pays you triple what anyone else would pay you to forget your better judgment?

I'll never know. I'll never know what it is like to be human in any way, shape, or form again.

"As for Nicolas," I said. "You're going to persuade him to go to Italy and I'll tell you how."

"Monsieur, even persuading him to change his clothes would take some doing."

"This will be easier. You know how ill my mother is. Well, get him to take her to Italy. It's the perfect thing. He can very well study music at the conservatories in Naples, and that is exactly where my mother should go."

"He does write to her . . . is very fond of her."

"Precisely. Convince him she'll never make the journey without him. Make all the arrangements for him. Monsieur, you must accomplish this. He must leave Paris. I give you till the end of the week, and then I'll be back for the news that he's gone."

It was asking a lot of Roget, of course. But I could think of no other way. Nobody would believe Nicki's ideas about sorcery, that was no worry. But I knew now that if Nicki didn't leave Paris, he would be driven slowly out of his mind.

As the nights passed, I fought with myself every waking hour not to seek him out, not to risk one last exchange.

I just waited, knowing full well that I was losing him forever and that he would never know the reasons for anything that had come to pass. I, who had once railed against the meaninglessness of our existence, was driving him off without explanation, an injustice that might torment him to the end of his days.

Better that than the truth, Nicki. Maybe I understand all illusions a little better now. And if you can only get my mother to go to Italy, if there is only time for my mother still . . .

Meantime I could see for myself that Renaud's House of Thesbians was closed down. In the nearby café, I heard talk of the troupe's departure for England. So that much of the plan had been accomplished.

It was near dawn on the eighth night when I finally wandered up to Roget's door and pulled the bell.

He answered sooner than I expected, looking befuddled and anxious in the usual white flannel nightshirt.

"I'm getting to like that garb of yours, Monsieur," I said wearily. "I don't think I'd trust you half as much if you wore a shirt and breeches and a coat . . ."

"Monsieur," he interrupted me. "Something quite unexpected—"

"Answer me first. Renaud and the others went happily to England?"

"Yes, Monsieur. They're in London by now, but—"

"And Nicki? Gone to my mother in the Auvergne. Tell me I'm right. It's done."

"But Monsieur!" he said. And then he stopped. And quite unexpectedly, I saw the image of my mother in his mind.

Had I been thinking, I would have known what it meant. This man had never to my knowledge laid eyes upon my mother, so how could he picture her in his thoughts? But I wasn't using my reason. In fact my reason had flown.

"She hasn't . . . you're not telling me that it's too late," I said.

"Monsieur, let me get my coat . . ." he said inexplicably. He reached for the bell.

And there it was, her image again, her face, drawn and white, and all too vivid for me to stand it.

I took Roget by the shoulders.

"You've seen her! She's here."

"Yes, Monsieur. She's in Paris. I'll take you to her now. Young de Lenfent told me she was coming. But I couldn't reach you, Monsieur! I never know where to reach you. And yesterday she arrived."

I was too stunned to answer. I sank down into the chair, and my own images of her blazed hot enough to eclipse everything that was emanating from him. She was alive and she was in Paris. And Nicki was still here and he was with her.

Roget came close to me, reached out as if he wanted to touch me:

"Monsieur, you go ahead while I dress. She is in the Ile St.-Louis, three doors to the right of Monsieur Nicolas. You must go at once."

I looked up at him stupidly. I couldn't even really see him. I was seeing her. There was less than an hour before sunrise. And it would take me three-quarters of that time to reach the tower.

"Tomorrow . . . tomorrow night," I think I stammered. That line came back to me from Shakespeare's *Macbeth* . . . "Tomorrow and tomorrow and tomorrow . . ."

"Monsieur, you don't understand! There will be no trips to Italy for your mother. She has made her last journey in coming here to see you."

When I didn't answer he grabbed hold of me and tried to shake me. I'd never seen him like this before. I was a boy to him and he was the man who had to bring me to my senses.

"I've gotten lodgings for her," he said. "Nurses, doctors, all that you could wish. But they aren't keeping her alive. You are keeping her alive, Monsieur. She must see you before she closes her eyes. Now forget the hour and go to her. Even a will as strong as hers can't work miracles."

I couldn't answer. I couldn't form a coherent thought.

I stood up and went to the door, pulling him along with me. "Go to her now," I said, "and tell her I'll be there tomorrow night."

He shook his head. He was angry and disgusted. And he tried to turn his back on me.

I wouldn't let him.

"You go there at once, Roget," I said. "Sit with her all day, do you understand, and see that she waits—that she waits for me to come! Watch her if she sleeps. Wake her and talk to her if she starts to go. But don't let her die before I get there!"

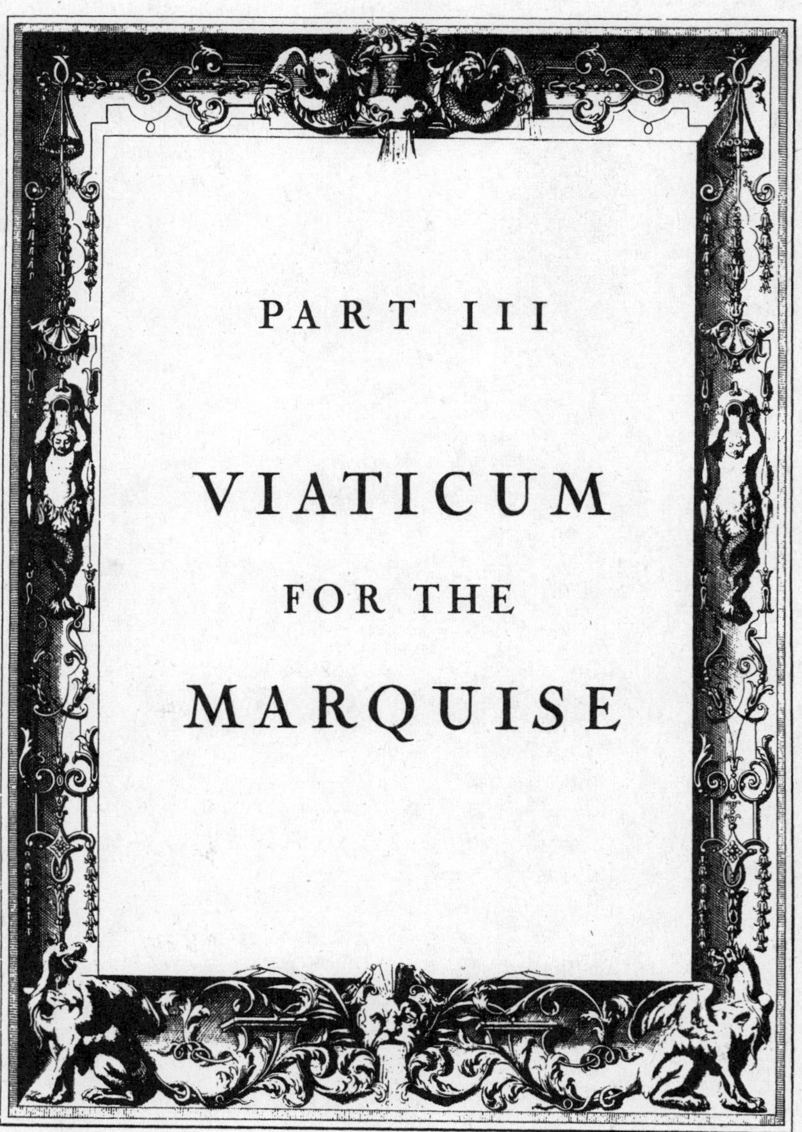

PART III

VIATICUM FOR THE MARQUISE

1

IN VAMPIRE parlance, I am an early riser. I rise when the sun has just sunk below the horizon and there is still red light in the sky. Many vampires don't rise until there is full darkness, and so I have a tremendous advantage in this, and in that they must return to the grave a full hour or more before I do. I haven't mentioned it before because I didn't know it then, and it didn't come to matter until much later.

But the next night, I was on the road to Paris when the sky was on fire.

I'd clothed myself in the most respectable garments I possessed before I slipped into the sarcophagus, and I was chasing the sun west into Paris.

It looked like the city was burning, so bright was the light to me and so terrifying, until finally I came pounding over the bridge behind Notre Dame, into the Ile St.-Louis.

I didn't think about what I would do or say, or how I might conceal myself from her. I knew only I had to see her and hold her and be with her while there was still time. I couldn't truly think of her death. It had the fullness of catastrophe, and belonged to the burning sky. And maybe I was being the common mortal, believing if I could grant her last wish, then somehow the horror was under my command.

Dusk was just bleeding the light away when I found her house on the quais.

It was a stylish enough mansion. Roget had done well, and a clerk was at the door waiting to direct me up the stairs. Two maids and a nurse were in the parlor of the flat when I came in.

"Monsieur de Lenfent is with her, Monsieur," the nurse said. "She insisted on getting dressed to see you. She wanted to sit in the window and look at the towers of the cathedral, Monsieur. She saw you ride over the bridge."

"Put out the candles in the room, except for one," I said. "And tell Monsieur de Lenfent and my lawyer to come out."

Roget came out at once, and then Nicolas appeared.

He too had dressed for her, all in brilliant red velvet, with his old fancy linen and his white gloves. The recent drinking had left him thinner, almost haggard. Yet it made his beauty all the more vivid. When our eyes met, the malice leapt out of him, scorching my heart.

"The Marquise is a little stronger today, Monsieur," Roget said, "but she's hemorrhaging badly. The doctor says she will not—"

He stopped and glanced back at the bedroom. I got it clear from his thought. She won't last through the night.

"Get her back to bed, Monsieur, as fast you can."

"For what purpose do I get her back to bed?" I said. My voice was dull, a murmur. "Maybe she wants to die at the damned window. Why the hell not?"

"Monsieur!" Roget implored me softly.

I wanted to tell him to leave with Nicki.

But something was happening to me. I went into the hall and looked towards the bedroom. She was in there. I felt a dramatic physical change in myself. I couldn't move or speak. She was in there and she was really dying.

All the little sounds of the flat became a hum. I saw a lovely bedroom through the double doors, a white painted bed with gold hangings, and the windows draped in the same gold, and the sky in the high panes of the windows with only the faintest wisps of gold cloud. But all this was indistinct and faintly horrible, the luxury I'd wanted to give her and she about to feel her body collapse beneath her. I wondered if it maddened her, made her laugh.

The doctor appeared. The nurse came to tell me only one candle remained, as I had ordered. The smell of medicines intruded and mingled with a rose perfume, and *I realized I was hearing her thoughts.*

It was the dull throb of her mind as she waited, her bones aching in her emaciated flesh so that to sit at the window even in the soft velvet chair with the comforter surrounding her was almost unendurable pain.

But what was she thinking, beneath her desperate anticipation? Lestat, Lestat, and Lestat, I could hear that. But beneath it:

"Let the pain get worse, because only when the pain is really dreadful do I want to die. If the pain would just get bad enough so that I'd be glad to die and I wouldn't be so frightened. I want it to be so terrible that I'm not frightened."

"Monsieur." The doctor touched my arm. "She will not have the priest come."

"No . . . she wouldn't."

She had turned her head towards the door. If I didn't come in now, she would get up, no matter how it hurt her, and come to me.

It seemed I couldn't move. And yet I pushed past the doctor and the nurse, and I went into the room and closed the doors.

Blood scent.

In the pale violet light of the window she sat, beautifully dressed in dark blue taffeta, her hand in her lap and the other on the arm of the chair, her thick yellow hair gathered behind her ears so that the curls spilled over her shoulders from the pink ribbons. There was the faintest bit of rouge on her cheeks.

For one eerie moment she looked to me as she had when I was a little boy. So pretty. The symmetry of her face was unchanged by time or illness, and so was her hair. And a heartbreaking happiness came over me, a warm delusion that I was mortal again, and innocent again, and with her, and everything was all right, really truly all right.

There was no death and no terror, just she and I in her bedroom, and she would take me in her arms. I stopped.

I'd come very close to her, and she was crying as she looked up. The girdle of the Paris dress bound her too tightly, and her skin was so thin and colorless over her throat and her hands that I couldn't bear to look at them, and her eyes looked up at me from flesh that was almost bruised. I could smell death on her. I could smell decay.

But she was radiant, and she was mine; she was as she'd always been, and I told her so silently with all my power, that she was lovely as my earliest memory of her when she had had her old fancy clothes still, and she would dress up so carefully and carry me on her lap in the carriage to church.

And in this strange moment when I gave her to know this, how much I cherished her, I realized she *heard* me and she answered me that she loved me and always had.

It was the answer to a question I hadn't even asked. And she knew the importance of it; her eyes were clear, unentranced.

If she realized the oddity of this, that we could talk to each other without words, she gave no clue. Surely she didn't grasp it fully. She must have felt only an outpouring of love.

"Come here so I can see you," she said, "as you are now."

The candle was by her arm on the windowsill. And quite deliberately I pinched it out. I saw her frown, a tightening of her blond brows, and her blue eyes grew just a little larger as she looked at me, at the bright silk brocade and the usual lace I'd chosen to wear for her, and the sword on my hip with its rather imposing jeweled hilt.

"Why don't you want me to see you?" she asked. "I came to Paris to see you. Light the candle again." But there was no real chastisement in the words. I was here with her and that was enough.

I knelt down before her. I had some mortal conversation in mind, that she should go to Italy with Nicki, and quite distinctly, before I could speak, she said:

"Too late, my darling, I could never finish the journey. I've come far enough."

A clamp of pain stopped her, circling her waist where the girdle bound it, and to hide it from me, she made her face very blank. She looked like a girl when she did this, and again I smelt the sickness in her, the decay in her lungs, and the clots of blood.

Her mind became a riot of fear. She wanted to scream out to me that she was afraid. She wanted to beg me to hold on to her and remain with her until it was finished, but she couldn't do this, and to my astonishment, I realized she thought I would refuse her. That I was too young and too thoughtless to ever understand.

This was agony.

I wasn't even conscious of moving away from her, but I'd walked across the room. Stupid little details embedded themselves in my consciousness: nymphs playing on the painted ceiling, the high gilt door handles and the melted wax in brittle stalactites on the white candles that I wanted to break off and crumple in my hand. The place looked hideous, overdressed. Did she hate it? Did she want those barren stone rooms again?

I was thinking about her as if there were "tomorrow and tomorrow and tomorrow . . ." I looked back at her, her stately figure holding to the windowsill. The sky had deepened behind her and a new light, the light of house lamps and passing carriages and nearby windows, gently touched the small inverted triangle of her thin face.

"Can't you talk to me," she said softly. "Can't you tell me how it's come about? You've brought such happiness to all of us." Even talking hurt her. "But how does it go with you? With you!"

I think I was on the verge of deceiving her, of creating some strong emanation of contentment with all the powers I had. I'd tell mortal lies with immortal skill. I'd start talking and talking and testing my every word to make it perfect. But something happened in the silence.

I don't think I stood still more than a moment, but something changed inside of me. An awesome shift took place. In one instant I saw a vast and terrifying possibility, and in that same instant, without question, I made up my mind.

It had no words to it or scheme or plan. And I would have denied it had anyone questioned me at that moment. I would have said, "No, never, farthest from my thoughts. What do you think I am, what sort of monster" . . . And yet the choice had been made.

I understood something absolute.

Her words had completely died away, she was afraid again and in pain again, and in spite of the pain, she rose from her chair.

I saw the comforter slip away from her, and I knew she was coming towards me and that I should stop her, but I didn't do it. I saw her hands close to me, reaching for me, and the next thing I knew she had leapt backwards as if blown by a mighty wind.

She had scuffed backwards across the carpet, and fallen past the chair against the wall. But she grew very still quickly as though she willed it, and there wasn't fear in her face, even though her heart was racing. Rather there was wonder and then a baffled calm.

If I had thoughts at that moment, I don't know what they were. I came towards her just as steadily as she had come towards me. Gauging her every reaction, I drew closer until we were as near to each other as we had been when she leapt away. She was staring at my skin and my eyes, and quite suddenly she reached out again and touched my face.

"Not alive!" That was the horrifying perception that came from her silently. "Changed into something. But NOT ALIVE."

Quietly I said no. That was not right. And I sent a cool torrent of images to her, a procession of glimpses of what my existence had become. Bits, pieces of the fabric of the nighttime Paris, the sense of a blade cutting through the world soundlessly.

With a little hiss she let out her breath. The pain balled its fist in her, opened its claw. She swallowed, sealing her lips against it, her eyes veritably burning into me. She knew now these were not sensations, these communications, but that they were thoughts.

"How then?" she demanded.

And without questioning what I meant to do I gave her the tale link by link, the shattered window through which I'd been torn by the ghostly figure who had stalked me at the theater, the tower and the exchange of blood. I revealed to her the crypt in which I slept, and its treasure, my wanderings, my powers, and above all, the nature of the thirst. The taste of blood and the feel of blood, and what it meant for all passion, all greed to be sharpened in that one desire, and that one desire to be satisfied over and over with the feeding and the death.

The pain ate at her but she no longer felt it. Her eyes were all that was left of her as she stared at me. And though I didn't mean to reveal all these things, I found I had taken hold of her and was turning so that the light of the carriages crashing along the quai below fell full on my face.

Without taking my eyes from her, I reached for the silver candelabra on the windowsill, and lifting it I slowly bent the metal, working it with my fingers into loops and twists.

The candles fell to the floor.

Her eyes rolled up into her head. She slipped backwards and away from me, and as she caught the curtains of the bed in her left hand, the blood came up out of her mouth.

It was coming from her lungs in a great silent cough. She was slipping down on her knees, and the blood was all over the side of the draped bed.

I looked at the twisted silver thing in my hands, the idiotic loops that meant nothing, and I let it drop. And I stared at her, her struggling against unconsciousness and pain, and wiping her mouth suddenly in sluggish gestures, like a vomiting drunk, on the bedclothes, as she sank unable to support herself to the floor.

I was standing over her. I was watching her, and her momentary pain meant nothing in light of the vow that I was speaking to her now. No words again, just the silent thrust of it, and the question, more immense than could ever be put into words, *Do you want to come with me now? DO YOU WANT TO COME WITH ME INTO THIS NOW?*

I hide nothing from you, not my ignorance, not my fear, not the simple terror that if I try I might fail. I do not even know if it is mine to give more than once, or what is the price of giving it, but I will risk this for you, and we will discover it together, whatever the mystery and the terror, just as I've discovered alone all else.

With her whole being she said Yes.

"Yes!" she screamed aloud suddenly, drunkenly, the voice maybe that had always been her voice yet one that I had never heard. Her eyes closed and tightened and her head turned from the left and to the right. "Yes!"

I leant forward and kissed the blood on her open lips. It sent a zinging through all my limbs and the thirst leapt out for her and tried to transform her into mere flesh. My arms slipped around her light little form and I lifted her up and up, until I was standing with her against the window, and her hair was falling down behind her, and the blood came up in her out of her lungs again, but it didn't matter now.

All the memories of my life with her surrounded us; they wove their shroud around us and closed us off from the world, the soft poems and songs of childhood, and the sense of her before words when there had only been the flicker of the light on the ceiling above her pillows and the smell of her all around me and her voice silencing my crying, and then the hatred of her and the need of her, and the losing of her behind a thousand closed doors, and cruel answers, and the terror of her and her complexity and her indifference and her indefinable strength.

And jetting up into the current came the thirst, not obliterating but heating every concept of her, until she was flesh and blood and mother and lover and all things beneath the cruel pressure of my fingers and my lips, everything I had ever desired. I drove my teeth into her, feeling her stiffen and gasp, and I felt my mouth grow wide to catch the hot flood when it came.

Her heart and soul split open. There was no age to her, no single moment. My knowledge dimmed and flickered and there was no mother anymore, no petty need and petty terror; she was simply who she was. She was Gabrielle.

And all her life came to her defense, the years and years of suffering and loneliness, the waste in those damp, hollow chambers to which she'd been condemned, and the books that were her solace, and the children who devoured her and abandoned her, and the pain and disease, her final enemy, which had, in promising release, pretended to be her friend. Beyond words and images there came the secret thudding of her passion, her seeming madness, her refusal to despair.

I was holding her, holding her off her feet, my arms crossed behind her narrow back, my hand cradling her limp head, and I was groaning so loud against her with the pumping of the blood that it was a song in time with her heart. But the heart was slowing too quickly. Her death was coming, and with all her will she pumped against it, and in a final burst of denial I pushed her away from me and held her still.

I was almost swooning. The thirst wanted her heart. It was no alchemist, the thirst. And I was standing there with my lips parted and my eyes glazed and I held her far, far away from me as if I were two beings, the one wanting to crush her and the other to bring her to me.

Her eyes were open and seemingly blind. For a moment she was in some place beyond all suffering, where there was nothing but sweetness and even something that might be understanding, but then I heard her calling to me by name.

I lifted my right wrist to my mouth and slashed the vein and pushed it against her lips. She didn't move as the blood spilled over her tongue. "Mother, drink," I said frantically, and pushed it harder, but some change had already commenced.

Her lips quivered, and her mouth locked to me and the pain whipped through me suddenly encircling my heart.

Her body lengthened, tensed, her left hand rising to grasp my wrist as she swallowed the first spurt. And the pain grew stronger and stronger so that I almost cried out. I could see it as if it were molten metal coursing through my vessels, branching through every sinew and limb. Yet it was only her pulling, her sucking, her taking the blood out of me that I had taken from her. She was standing now on her own feet, her head barely leaning against my chest. And a numbness crept over me with the pulling burning through the numbness, and my heart thundered against it, feeding the pain as it fed her pulling with every beat.

Harder and harder she drew and faster, and I felt her grip tighten and her body grow hard. I wanted to force her away, but I would not do it, and when my legs gave under me it was she who held me up. I was swaying and the room was tilting, but she went on with it and a vast silence stretched out in all directions from me and then without will or conviction, I thrust her backwards away.

She stumbled and stood before the window, her long fingers pressed flat against her open mouth. And before I turned and collapsed into the nearby chair I looked full at her white face for an instant, and her form swelling, it seemed, under the thin peeling of dark blue taffeta, her eyes like two crystal orbs gathering the light.

I think I said, "Mother," in that instant like some stupid mortal, and I closed my eyes.

2

I WAS sitting in the chair. It seemed I'd been asleep forever, but I hadn't been asleep at all. I was home in my father's house.

I looked around for the fire poker and my dogs, and to see if there was any wine left, and then I saw the gold drapery around the windows and the back of Notre Dame against the evening stars, and I saw her there.

We were in Paris. And we were going to live forever.

She had something in her hands. Another candelabra. A tinderbox. She stood very straight and her movements were quick. She made a spark and touched it to the candles one by one. And the little flames rose, and the painted flowers on the walls rolled up to the ceiling and the dancers on the ceiling moved for one moment and then were frozen in their circle again.

She was standing in front of me, the candelabra to the right of her. And her face was white and perfectly smooth. The dark bruises under her eyes had gone away; in fact every blemish or flaw she had ever had had gone away, though what those flaws had been I couldn't have told you. She was perfect now.

And the lines given her by age had been reduced and curiously deepened, so that there were tiny laugh lines at the edge of each eye, and a very tiny crease on either side of her mouth. The barest fold of extra flesh remained to each eyelid, heightening her symmetry, the sense of triangles in her face, and her lips were the softest shade of pink. She looked delicate as a diamond can look delicate when preyed upon by the light.

I closed my eyes and opened them again and saw it was no delusion, any more than her silence was a delusion. And I saw that her body was even more profoundly changed. She had the fullness of young womanhood again, the breasts that the illness had withered away. They were swelling above the dark blue taffeta of her corset, the pale pink tint of her flesh so subtle it might have been reflected light. But her hair was even more astonishing because it appeared to be alive. So much color moved in it that the hair itself appeared to be writhing, billions of tiny strands stirring around the flawless white face and throat.

The wounds on her throat were gone.

Now nothing remained but the final act of courage. Look into her eyes.

Look with these vampire eyes at another being like yourself for the first time since Magnus leapt into the fire.

I must have made some sound because she responded ever so slightly as if I had. Gabrielle, that was the only name I could ever call her now. "Gabrielle," I said to her, never having called her that except in some very private thoughts, and I saw her almost smile.

I looked down at my wrist. The wound was gone but the thirst gnashed in me. My veins spoke to me as if I had spoken to them. And I stared at her and saw her lips move in a tiny gesture of hunger. And she gave me a strange, meaningful expression as if to say, "Don't you understand?"

But I heard nothing from her. Silence, only the beauty of her eyes looking full at me and the love perhaps with which we saw each other, but silence stretching in all directions, ratifying nothing. I couldn't fathom it. Was she closing her mind? I asked her silently and she didn't appear to comprehend.

"Now," she said, and her voice startled me. It was softer, more resonant than before. For one moment we were in Auvergne, the snow was falling, and she was singing to me and it was echoing as if in a great cave. But that was finished. She said, "Go . . . done with all of this, quickly—now!" She nodded to coax me and she came closer and she tugged at my hand. "Look at yourself in the mirror," she whispered.

But I knew. I had given her more blood than I had taken from her. I was starved. I hadn't even fed before I came to her.

But I was so taken with the sound of the syllables and that glimpse of snow falling and the memory of the singing that for a moment I didn't respond. I looked at her fingers touching mine. I saw our flesh was the same. I rose up out of the chair and held her two hands and then I felt of her arms and her face. It was done and I was alive still! She was *with* me now. She had come through that awful solitude and she was with me, and I could think of nothing suddenly except holding her, crushing her to me, never letting her go.

I lifted her off her feet. I swung her up in my arms and we turned round and round.

She threw back her head and her laughter shook loose from her, growing louder and louder, until I put my hand over her mouth.

"You can shatter all the glass in the room with your voice," I whispered. I glanced towards the doors. Nicki and Roget were out there.

"Then let me shatter it!" she said, and there was nothing playful in her expression. I set her on her feet. I think we embraced again and again almost foolishly. I couldn't keep myself from it.

But other mortals were moving in the flat, the doctor and the nurses thinking that they should come in.

I saw her look to the door. She was hearing them too. But why wasn't I hearing her?

She broke away from me, eyes darting from one object to another. She snatched up the candles again and brought them to the mirror where she looked at her face.

I understood what was happening to her. She needed time to see and to measure with her new vision. But we had to get out of the flat.

I could hear Nicki's voice through the wall, urging the doctor to knock on the door.

How was I to get her out of here, get rid of them?

"No, not that way," she said when she saw me look at the door.

She was looking at the bed, the objects on the table. She went to the bed and took her jewels from under the pillow. She examined them and put them back into the worn velvet purse. Then she fastened the purse to her skirt so that it was lost in the folds of cloth.

There was an air of importance to these little gestures. I knew even though her mind was giving me nothing that this was all she wanted from this room. She was taking leave of things, the clothes she'd brought with her, her ancient silver brush and comb, and the tattered books that lay on the table by the bed.

There was knocking at the door.

"Why not this way?" she asked, and turning to the window, she threw open the glass. The breeze gusted into the gold draperies and lifted her hair off the back of her neck, and when she turned I shivered at the sight of her, her hair tangling around her face, and her eyes wide and filled with myriad fragments of color and an almost tragic light. She was afraid of nothing.

I took hold of her and for a moment wouldn't let her go. I nestled my face into her hair, and all I could think again was that we were together and nothing was ever going to separate us now. I didn't understand her silence, why I couldn't *bear* her, but I knew it wasn't her doing, and perhaps I believed it would pass. She was with me. That was the world. Death was my commander and I gave him a thousand victims, but I'd snatched her right out of his hand. I said it aloud. I said other desperate and nonsensical things. We were the same terrible and deadly beings, the two of us, we were wandering in the Savage Garden and I tried to make it real for her with images, the meaning of the Savage Garden, but it didn't matter if she didn't understand.

"The Savage Garden," she repeated the words reverently, her lips making a soft smile.

It was pounding in my head. I felt her kissing me and making some little whisper as if in accompaniment to her thoughts.

She said, "But help me, now, I want to see you *do it,* now, and we have forever to hold to each other. Come."

Thirst. I should have been burning. I positively required the blood, and she wanted the taste, I knew she did. Because I remembered that I had wanted it that very first night. It struck me then that the pain of her physical death . . . the fluids leaving her . . . might be lessened if she could first drink.

The knocking came again. The door wasn't locked.

I stepped up on the sill of the window and reached for her, and immediately she was in my arms. She weighed nothing, but I could feel her power, the tenacity of her grip. Yet when she saw the alley below, the top of the wall and the quai beyond, she seemed for a moment to doubt.

"Put your arms around my neck," I said, "and hold tight."

I climbed up the stones, carrying her with her feet dangling, her face turned upwards to me, until we had reached the slippery slates of the roof.

Then I took her hand and pulled her after me, running faster and faster, over the gutters and the chimney pots, leaping across the narrow alleys until we had reached the other side of the island. I'd been ready any moment for her to cry out or cling to me, but she wasn't afraid.

She stood silent, looking over the rooftops of the Left Bank, and down at the river crowded with thousands of dark little boats full of ragged beings, and she seemed for the moment simply to feel the wind unraveling her hair. I could have fallen in a stupor looking at her, studying her, all the aspects of the transformation, but there was an immense excitement in me to take her through the entire city, to reveal all things to her, to teach her everything I'd learned. She knew nothing of physical exhaustion now any more than I did. And she wasn't stunned by any horror such as I had been when Magnus went into the fire.

A carriage came speeding along the quai below, listing badly towards the river, the driver hunched over, trying to keep his balance on the high bench. I pointed to it as it drew near and I clasped her hand.

We leapt as it came beneath us, landing soundlessly on the leather top. The busy driver never looked around. I held tight to her, steadying her, until we were both riding easily, ready to jump off the vehicle when we chose.

It was indescribably thrilling, doing this with her.

We were thundering over the bridge and past the cathedral, and on through the crowds on the Pont Neuf. I heard her laughter again. I wondered what those in the high windows saw when they looked down on us, two gaily dressed figures clinging to the unsteady roof of the carriage like mischievous children as if it were a raft.

The carriage swerved. We were racing towards St.-Germain-des-Prés, scattering the crowds before us and roaring past the intolerable stench of the cemetery of les Innocents as towering tenements closed in.

For one second, I felt the shimmer of *the presence,* but it was gone so quickly I doubted myself. I looked back and could catch no glimmer of it. And I realized with extraordinary vividness that Gabrielle and I would talk about *the presence* together, that we would talk about everything together, and approach all things together. This night was as cataclysmic in its own way as the night Magnus had changed me, and this night had only begun.

The neighborhood was perfect now. I took her hand again, and pulled her after me, off the carriage, down into the street.

She stared dazed at the spinning wheels, but they were immediately gone. She didn't even look disheveled so much as she looked impossible, a woman torn out of time and place, clad only in slippers and dress, no chains on her, free to soar.

We entered a narrow alleyway and ran together, arms around each other, and now and then I looked down to see her eyes sweeping the walls above us, the scores of shuttered windows with their little streaks of escaping light.

I knew what she was seeing. I knew the sounds that pressed in on her. But still I could hear nothing from her, and this frightened me a little to think maybe she was deliberately shutting me out.

But she had stopped. She was having the first spasm of her death. I could see it in her face.

I reassured her, and reminded her in quick words of the vision I'd given her before.

"This is brief pain, nothing compared to what you've known. It will be gone in a matter of hours, maybe less if we drink now."

She nodded, more impatient with it than afraid.

We came out into a little square. In the gateway to an old house a young man stood, as if waiting for someone, the collar of his gray cloak up to shield his face.

Was she strong enough to take him? Was she as strong as I? This was the time to find out.

"If the thirst doesn't carry you into it, then it's too soon," I told her.

I glanced at her and a coldness crept over me. Her look of concentration was almost purely human, so intent was it, so fixed; and her eyes were shadowed with that same sense of tragedy I'd glimpsed before. Nothing was lost on her. But when she moved towards the man she wasn't human at all. She had become a pure predator, as only a beast can be a predator, and yet she was a woman walking slowly towards a man—a lady, in fact, stranded here without cape or hat or companions, and approaching a gentleman as if to beg for his aid. She was all that.

It was ghastly to watch it, the way that she moved over the stones as if she did not even touch them, and the way that everything, even the wisps of her hair blown this way and that by the breeze, seemed somehow under her command. She could have moved through the wall itself with that relentless step.

I drew back into the shadows.

The man quickened, turned to her with the faint grind of his boot heel on the stones, and she rose on tiptoe as if to whisper in his ear. I think for one moment she hesitated. Perhaps she was faintly horrified. If she was, then the thirst had not had time enough to grow strong. But if she did question it, it was for no more than that second. She was taking him and he was powerless and I was too fascinated to do anything but watch.

But it came to me quite unexpectedly that I hadn't warned her about the heart. How could I have forgotten such a thing? I rushed towards her, but she had already let him go. And he had crumpled against the wall, his head to one side, his hat fallen at his feet. He was dead.

She stood looking down at him, and I saw the blood working in her, heating her and deepening her color and the red of her lips. Her eyes were a flash of violet when she glanced at me, almost exactly the color the sky had been when I'd come into her bedroom. I was silent watching her as she looked down at the victim with a curious amazement as if she did not completely accept what she saw. Her hair was tangled again and I lifted it back for her.

She slipped into my arms. I guided her away from the victim. She glanced back once or twice, then looked straight forward.

"It's enough for this night. We should go home to the tower," I said. I wanted to show her the treasure, and just to be with her in that safe place, to hold her and comfort her if she began to go mad over it all. She was feeling the death spasms again. There she could rest by the fire.

"No, I don't want to go yet," she said. "The pain won't go on long, you promised it wouldn't. I want it to pass and then to be here." She looked up at me, and she smiled. "I came to Paris to die, didn't I?" she whispered.

Everything was distracting her, the dead man back there, slumped in his gray cape, the sky shimmering on the surface of a puddle of water, a cat streaking atop a nearby wall. The blood was hot in her, moving in her.

I clasped her hand and urged her to follow me. "I have to drink," I said.

"Yes, I see it," she whispered. "You should have taken him. I should have thought . . . And you are the gentleman, even still."

"The starving gentleman." I smiled. "Let's not stumble over ourselves devising an etiquette for monsters." I laughed. I would have kissed her, but I was suddenly distracted. I squeezed her hand too tightly.

Far away, from the direction of les Innocents, I heard *the presence* as strongly as ever before.

She stood as still as I was, and inclining her head slowly to one side, moved the hair back from her ear.

"Do you hear it?" I asked.

She looked up at me. "Is it *another one*!" She narrowed her eyes and glanced again in the direction from which the emanation had come.

"Outlaw!" she said aloud.

"What?" *Outlaw, outlaw, outlaw.* I felt a wave of light-headedness, something of a dream remembered. Fragment of a dream. But I couldn't think. I'd been damaged by doing it to her. I *had* to drink.

"It called us outlaws," she said. "Didn't you hear it?" And she listened again, but it was gone and neither of us heard it, and I couldn't be certain that I had received that clear pulse, *outlaw,* but it seemed I had!

"Never mind it, whatever it is," I said. "It never comes any closer than that." But even as I spoke I knew it had been more virulent this time. I wanted to get away from les Innocents. "It lives in graveyards," I murmured. "It may not be able to live elsewhere . . . for very long."

But before I finished speaking, I felt it again, and it seemed to expand and to exude the strongest malevolence I'd received from it yet.

"It's laughing!" she whispered.

I studied her. Without doubt, she was hearing it more clearly than I.

"Challenge it!" I said. "Call it a coward! Tell it to come out!"

She gave me an amazed look.

"Is that really what you want to do?" she questioned me under her breath. She was trembling slightly, and I steadied her. She put her arm around her waist as if one of the spasms had come again.

"Not now then," I said. "This isn't the time. And we'll hear it again, just when we've forgotten all about it."

"It's gone," she said. "But it hates us, this thing . . ."

"Let's get away from it," I said contemptuously, and putting my arm around her I hurried her along.

I didn't tell her what I was thinking, what weighed on me far more than *the presence* and its usual tricks. If she could hear *the presence* as well as I could, better in fact, then she had all my powers, including the ability to send and hear images and thoughts. Yet we could no longer *hear* each other!

3

I FOUND a victim as soon as we had crossed the river, and as soon as I spotted the man, there came the deepening awareness that everything I had done alone I would now do with her. She would watch this act, learn from it. I think the intimacy of it made the blood rush to my face.

And as I lured the victim out of the tavern, as I teased him, maddened him, and then took him, I knew I was showing off for her, making it a little crueler, more playful. And when the kill came, it had an intensity to it that left me spent afterwards.

She loved it. She watched everything as if she could suck up the very vision as she sucked blood. We came together again and I took her in my arms and I felt her heat and she felt my heat. The blood was flooding my brain. And we just held each other, even the thin covering of our garments seeming alien, two burning statues in the dark.

After that, the night lost all ordinary dimensions. In fact, it remains one of the longest nights I have ever endured in my immortal life.

It was endless and fathomless and dizzying, and there were times when I wanted some defense against its pleasures and its surprises, and I had none.

And though I said her name over and over, to make it natural, she wasn't really Gabrielle yet to me. She was simply *she,* the one I had needed all of my life with all of my being. The only woman I had ever loved.

Her actual death didn't take long.

We sought out an empty cellar room where we remained until it was finished. And there I held on to her and talked to her as it went on. I told her everything that had happened to me again, in words this time.

I told her all about the tower. I told everything that Magnus had said. I explained all the occurrences of *the presence.* And how I had become almost used to it and contemptuous of it, and not willing to chase it down. Over and over again I tried to send her images, but it was useless. I didn't say anything about it. Neither did she. But she listened very attentively.

I talked to her about Nicki's suspicions, which of course he had not mentioned to her at all. And I explained that I feared for him even more now. Another open window, another empty room, and this time witnesses to verify the strangeness of it all.

But never mind, I should tell Roget some story that would make it plausible. I should find some means to do right by Nicki, to break the chain of suspicions that was binding him to me.

She seemed dimly fascinated by all of this, but it didn't really matter to her. What mattered to her was what lay before her now.

And when her death was finished, she was unstoppable. There was no wall that she could not climb, no door she wouldn't enter, no rooftop terrain too steep.

It was as if she did not believe she would live forever; rather she thought she had been granted this one night of supernatural vitality and all things must be known and accomplished before death would come for her at dawn.

Many times I tried to persuade her to go home to the tower. As the hours passed, a spiritual exhaustion came over me. I needed to be quiet there, to think on what had happened. I'd open my eyes and see only blackness for an instant. But she wanted only experiment, adventure.

She proposed that we enter the private dwellings of mortals now to search for the clothes she needed. She laughed when I said that I always purchased my clothes in the proper way.

"We can hear if a house is empty," she said, moving swiftly through the streets, her eyes on the windows of the darkened mansions. "We can hear if the servants are asleep."

It made perfect sense, though I'd never attempted such a thing. And I was soon following her up narrow back stairs and down carpeted corridors, amazed at the ease of it all, and fascinated by the details of the informal chambers in which mortals lived. I found I liked to touch personal things: fans, snuffboxes, the newspaper the master of the house had been reading, his boots on the hearth. It was as much fun as peering into windows.

But she had her purpose. In a lady's dressing room in a large St.-Germain house, she found a fortune in lavish clothes to fit her new and fuller form. I helped to peel off the old taffeta and to dress her up in pink velvet, gathering her hair in tidy curls under an ostrich-plume hat. I was shocked again by the sight of her, and the strange eerie feeling of wandering with her through this overfurnished house full of mortal scents. She gathered objects from the dressing table. A vial of perfume, a small gold pair of scissors. She looked at herself in the glass.

I went to kiss her again and she didn't stop me. We were lovers kissing. And that was the picture we made together, white-faced lovers, as we rushed down the servants' stairs and out into the late evening streets.

We wandered in and out of the Opéra and the Comédie before they closed, then through the ball in the Palais Royal. It delighted her the way mortals saw us, but did not see us, how they were drawn to us, and completely deceived.

We heard *the presence* very sharply after that, as we explored the churches, then again it was gone. We climbed belfries to survey our kingdom, and afterwards huddled in crowded coffeehouses for a little while merely to feel and smell the mortals around us, to exchange secret glances, to laugh softly, tête-à-tête.

She fell into dream states, looking at the steam rising from the mug of coffee, at the layers of cigarette smoke hovering around the lamps.

She loved the dark empty streets and the fresh air more than anything else. She wanted to climb up into the limbs of the trees and onto the rooftops again. She marveled that I didn't always travel through the city by means of the rooftops, or ride about atop carriages as we had done.

Some time after midnight, we were in the deserted market, just walking hand in hand.

We had just heard *the presence* again but neither of us could discern a disposition in it as we had before. It was puzzling me.

But everything around us was astonishing her still—the refuse, the cats that chased the vermin, the bizarre stillness, the way that the darkest corners of the metropolis held no danger for us. She remarked on that. Perhaps it was that which enchanted her most of all, that we could slip past the dens of thieves unheard, that we could easily defeat anyone who should be fool enough to trouble us, that we were both visible and invisible, palpable and utterly unaccountable.

I didn't rush her or question her. I was merely borne along with her and content and sometimes lost in my own thoughts about this unfamiliar content.

And when a handsome, slightly built young man came riding through the darkened stalls I watched him as if he were an apparition, something coming from the land of the living into the land of the dead. He reminded me of Nicolas because of his dark hair and dark eyes, and something innocent yet brooding in the face. He shouldn't have been in the market alone. He was younger than Nicki and very foolish, indeed.

But just how foolish he was I didn't realize until she moved forward like a great pink feline, and brought him down almost silently from the horse.

I was shaken. The innocence of her victims didn't trouble her. She didn't fight my moral battles. But then I didn't fight them anymore either, so why should I judge her? Yet the ease with which she slew the young man—gracefully breaking his neck when the little drink she took was not enough to kill him—angered me though it had been extremely exciting to watch.

She was colder than I. She was better at all of it, I thought. Magnus had said, "Show no mercy." But had he meant us to kill when we did not have to kill?

It came clear in an instant why she'd done it. She tore off the pink velvet girdle and skirts right there and put on the boy's clothes. She'd chosen him for the fit of the clothes.

And to describe it more truly, as she put on his garments, she became the boy.

She put on his cream silk stockings and scarlet breeches, the lace shirt and the yellow waistcoat and then the scarlet frock coat, and even took the scarlet ribbon from the boy's hair.

Something in me rebelled against the charm of it, her standing so boldly in these new garments with all her hair still full over her shoulders looking more the lion's mane now than the lovely mass of woman's tresses it had been moments before. Then I wanted to ravage her. I closed my eyes.

When I looked at her again, my head was swimming with all that we'd seen and done together. I couldn't endure being so near to the dead boy.

She tied all of her blond hair together with the scarlet ribbon and let the long locks hang down her back. She laid the pink dress over the body of the boy to cover him, and she buckled on his sword, and drew it once and sheathed it again, and took his cream-colored roquelaure.

"Let's go, then, darling," she said, and she kissed me.

I couldn't move. I wanted to go back to the tower, and just be close to her. She looked at me and pressed my hand to spur me on. And she was almost immediately running ahead.

She had to feel the freedom of her limbs, and I found myself pounding after her, having to exert myself to catch up.

That had never happened with me and any mortal, of course. She seemed to be flying. And the sight of her flashing through the boarded-up stalls and the heaps of garbage made me almost lose my balance. Again I stopped.

She came back to me and kissed me. "But there's no real reason for me to dress that way anymore, is there?" she asked. She might have been talking to a child.

"No, of course there isn't," I said. Maybe it was a blessing that she couldn't read my thoughts. I couldn't stop looking at her legs, so perfect in the cream-colored stockings. And the way that the frock coat gathered at her small waist. Her face was like a flame.

Remember in those times you never saw a woman's legs like that. Or the silk of breeches tight over her small belly, or thighs.

But she was not really a woman now, was she? Any more than I was a man. For one silent second the horror of it all bled through.

"Come, I want to take to the roofs again," she said. "I want to go to the boulevard du Temple. I should like to see the theater, the one that you purchased and then shut up. Will you show that to me?" She was studying me as she asked this.

"Of course," I said. "Why not?"

WE HAD two hours left of the endless night when we finally returned to the Ile St.-Louis and stood on the moonlit quais. Far down the paved street I saw my mare tethered where I'd left her. Perhaps she had gone unnoticed in the confusion that must have followed our departure.

We listened carefully for any sign of Nicki or Roget, but the house appeared deserted and dark.

"They are near, however," she whispered. "I think somewhere further down . . ."

"Nicki's flat," I said. "And from Nicki's flat someone could be watching the mare, a servant posted to watch in case we came back."

"Better to leave the horse and steal another," she said.

"No, it's mine," I said. But I felt her grip on my hand tighten.

Our old friend again, *the presence,* and this time it was moving along the Seine on the other side of the island and towards the Left Bank.

"Gone," she said. "Let's go. We can steal another mount."

"Wait. I'm going to try to get her to come to me. To break the tether."

"Can you do that?"

"We'll see." I concentrated all my will on the mare, telling her silently to back up, to pull loose from the bond holding her and come.

In a second, the horse was prancing, jerking at the leather. Then she reared and the tether broke.

She came clattering towards us over the stones, and we were on her immediately, Gabrielle leaping up first and I right behind her, gathering up what was left of the rein as I urged the horse to go into a dead run.

As we crossed the bridge I felt something behind us, a commotion, the tumult of mortal minds.

But we were lost in the black echo chamber of the Ile de la Cité.

WHEN we reached the tower, I lighted the resin torch and took her down with me into the dungeon. There was no time now to show her the upper chamber.

Her eyes were glassy and she looked about herself sluggishly as we descended the screw stairs. Her scarlet clothes gleamed against the dark stones. Ever so slightly she recoiled from the dampness.

The stench from the lower prison cells disturbed her, but I told her gently it was nothing to do with us. And once we had entered the huge burial crypt, the smell was shut out by the heavy iron-studded door.

The torchlight spread out to reveal the low arches of the ceiling, the three great sarcophagi with their deeply graven images.

She did not seem afraid. I told her that she must see if she could lift the stone lid of the one she chose for herself. I might have to do it for her.

She studied the three carved figures. And after a moment's reflection, she chose not the woman's sarcophagus but the one with the knight in armor carved on the top of it. And slowly she pushed the stone lid out of place so she could look into the space within.

Not as much strength as I possessed but strong enough.

"Don't be frightened," I said.

"No, you mustn't ever worry on that account," she answered softly. Her voice had a lovely frayed sound to it, a faint timbre of sadness. She appeared to be dreaming as she ran her hands over the stone.

"By this hour," she said, "she might have already been laid out, your mother. And the room would be full of evil smells and the smoke of hundreds of candles. Think how humiliating it is, death. Strangers would have taken off her clothes, bathed her, dressed her—strangers seen her emaciated and defenseless in the final sleep. And those whispering in the corridors would have talked of their good health, and how they have never had the slightest illness in their families, no, no consumption in their families. 'The poor Marquise,' they would have said. They would have been wondering, did she have any money of her own? Did she leave it to her sons? And the old woman when she came to collect the soiled sheets, she would have stolen one of the rings off the dead woman's hand."

I nodded. And so we stand in this dungeon crypt, I wanted to say, and we prepare to lie down on stone beds, with only rats to keep us company. But it's infinitely better than that, isn't it? It has its dark splendor, to walk the nightmare terrain forever.

She looked wan, cold all over. Sleepily, she drew something out of her pocket.

It was the golden scissors she'd taken from the lady's table in the faubourg St.-Germain. Sparkling in the light of the torch like a bauble.

"No, Mother," I said. My own voice startled me. It leapt out echoing too sharply under the arched ceiling. The figures on the other sarcophagi seemed merciless witnesses. The hurt in my heart stunned me.

Evil sound, the snipping, the shearing. Her hair fell down in great long locks on the floor.

"Ooooh, Mother."

She looked down at it, scattering it silently with the tip of her boot, and then she looked up at me, and she was a young man now certainly, the short hair curling against her cheek. But her eyes were closing. She reached out to me and the scissors fell out of her hands.

"Rest now," she whispered.

"It's only the rising sun," I said to reassure her. She was weakening sooner than I did. She turned away from me and moved towards the coffin. I lifted her and her eyes shut. Pushing the lid of the sarcophagus even farther to the right, I laid her down inside, letting her pliant limbs arrange themselves naturally and gracefully.

Her face had already smoothed itself into sleep, her hair framing her face with a young boy's locks.

Dead, she seemed, and gone, the magic undone.

I kept looking at her.

I let my teeth cut into the tip of my tongue until I felt the pain and tasted the hot blood there. Then bending low I let the blood fall in tiny shining droplets on her lips. Her eyes opened. Violet blue and glittering, they stared up at me. The blood flowed into her opening mouth and slowly she lifted her head to meet my kiss. My tongue passed into her. Her lips were cold. My lips were cold. But the blood was hot and it flowed between us.

"Good night, my darling one," I said. "My dark angel Gabrielle."

She sank back into stillness as I let her go. I closed the stone over her.

4

I DID not like rising in the black underground crypt. I didn't like the chill in the air, and that faint stench from the prison below, the feeling that this was where all the dead things lay.

A fear overcame me. What if she didn't rise? What if her eyes never opened again? What did I know of what I'd done?

Yet it seemed an arrogant thing, an obscene thing to move the lid of the coffin again and gaze at her in her sleep as I had done last night. A mortal shame came over me. At home, I would never have dared to open her door without knocking, never dared to draw back the curtains of her bed.

She would rise. She had to. And better that she should lift the stone for herself, know how to rise, and that the thirst should drive her to it at the proper moment as it had driven me.

I lighted the torch on the wall for her, and went out for a moment to breathe the fresh air. Then leaving gates and doors unlocked behind me, I went up into Magnus's cell to watch the twilight melt from the sky.

I'd hear her, I thought, when she awakened.

An hour must have passed. The azure light faded, the stars rose, and the distant city of Paris lighted its myriad tiny beacons. I left the windowsill where I had sat against the iron bars and I went to the chest and began to select jewels for her.

Jewels she still loved. She had taken her old keepsakes with her when we left her room. I lighted the candles to help me see, though I didn't really need them. The illumination was beautiful to me. Beautiful on the jewels. And I found very delicate and lovely things for her—pearl-studded pins that she might wear in the lapels of her mannish little coat, and rings that would look masculine on her small hands if that was what she wanted.

I listened now and then for her. And this chill would clutch my heart. What if she did not rise? What if there had been only that one night for her? Horror thudding in me. And the sea of jewels in the chest, the candlelight dancing in the faceted stones, the gold settings—it meant nothing.

But I didn't hear her. I heard the wind outside, the great soft rustle of the trees, the faint distant whistling of the stable boy as he moved about the barn, the neighing of my horses.

Far off a village church bell rang.

Then very suddenly there came over me the feeling that someone was watching me. This was so unfamiliar to me that I panicked. I turned, almost stumbling into the chest, and stared at the mouth of the secret tunnel. No one there.

No one in this small empty sanctum with the candlelight playing on the stones and Magnus's grim countenance on the sarcophagus.

Then I looked straight in front of me at the barred window.

And I saw her looking back at me.

Floating in the air she seemed to be, holding to the bars with both hands, and she was smiling.

I almost cried out. I backed up and the sweat broke out all over my body. I was embarrassed suddenly to be caught off guard, to be so obviously startled.

But she remained motionless, smiling still, her expression gradually changing from serenity to mischievousness. The candlelight made her eyes too brilliant.

"It's not very nice to frighten other immortals like that," I said.

She laughed more freely and easily than she ever had when she was alive.

Relief coursed through me as she moved, made sounds. I knew I was blushing.

"How did you get there!" I said. I went to the window and reached through the bars and clasped both her wrists.

Her little mouth was all sweetness and laughter. Her hair was a great shimmering mane around her face.

"I climbed the wall, of course," she said. "How do you think I got here?"

"Well, go down. You can't come through the bars. I'll go to meet you."

"You're very right about that," she said. "I've been to all the windows. Meet me on the battlements above. It's faster."

She started climbing, hooking her boots easily into the bars, then she vanished.

She was all exuberance as she'd been the night before as we came down the stairs together.

"Why are we lingering here?" she said. "Why don't we go on now to Paris?"

Something was wrong with her, lovely as she was, something not right . . . what was it?

She didn't want kisses now, or even talk, really. And that had a little sting to it.

"I want to show you the inner room," I said. "And the jewels."

"The jewels?" she asked.

She hadn't seen them from the window. The cover of the chest had blocked her view. She walked ahead of me into the room where Magnus had burned, and then she lay down to crawl through the tunnel.

As soon as she saw the chest, she was shocked by it.

She tossed her hair a little impatiently over her shoulder and bent to study the brooches, the rings, the small ornaments so like those heirlooms she'd had to sell long ago one by one.

"Why, he must have been collecting them for centuries," she said. "And such exquisite things. He chose what he would take, didn't he? What a creature he must have been."

Again, almost angrily, she pushed her hair out of her way. It seemed paler, more luminous, fuller. A glorious thing.

"The pearls, look at them," I said. "And these rings." I showed her the ones I'd already chosen for her. I took her hand and slipped the rings on her fingers. Her fingers moved as if they had life of their own, could feel delight, and again she laughed.

"Ah, but we are splendid devils, aren't we?"

"Hunters of the Savage Garden," I said.

"Then let's go into Paris," she said. Faint touch of pain in her face, the thirst. She ran her tongue over her lips. Was I half as fascinating to her as she was to me?

She raked her hair back from her forehead, and her eyes darkened with the intensity of her words.

"I want to feed quickly tonight," she said, "then go out of the city, into the woods. Go where there are no men and women about. Go where there is only the wind and the dark trees, and the stars overhead. Blessed silence."

She went to the window again. Her back was narrow and straight, and her hands at her sides, alive with the jeweled rings. And coming as they did out of the thick cuffs of the man's coat, her hands looked all the more slender and exquisite. She must have been looking at the high dim clouds, the stars that burned through the purple layer of evening mist.

"I have to go to Roget," I said under my breath. "I have to take care of Nicki, tell them some lie about what's happened to you."

She turned, and her face looked small and cold suddenly, the way it could at home when she was disapproving. But she'd never really look that way again.

"Why tell them anything about me?" she asked. "Why ever even bother with them again?"

I was shocked by this. But it wasn't a complete surprise to me. Perhaps I'd been waiting for it. Perhaps I'd sensed it in her all along, the unspoken questions.

I wanted to say Nicki sat by your bed when you were dying, does that mean nothing? But how sentimental, how mortal that sounded, how positively foolish.

Yet it wasn't foolish.

"I don't mean to judge you," she said. She folded her arms and leaned against the window. "I simply don't understand. Why did you write to us? Why did you send us all the gifts? Why didn't you take this white fire from the moon and go where you wanted with it?"

"But where should I want to go?" I said. "Away from all those I'd known and loved? I did not want to stop thinking of you, of Nicki, even of my father and my brothers. I did what I wanted," I said.

"Then conscience played no role in it?"

"If you follow your conscience, you do what you want," I said. "But it was simpler than that. I wanted you to have the wealth I gave you. I wanted you . . . to be happy."

She reflected for a long time.

"Would you have had me forget *you*?" I demanded. It sounded spiteful, angry.

She didn't answer immediately.

"No, of course not," she said. "And had it been the other way around, I would never have forgotten you either. I'm sure of it. But the rest of them? I don't give a damn about them. I shall never exchange words with them again. I shall never lay eyes on them."

I nodded. But I hated what she was saying. She frightened me.

"I cannot overcome this notion that I've died," she said. "That I am utterly cut off from all living creatures. I can taste, I can see, I can feel. I can drink blood. But I am like something that cannot be seen, cannot affect things."

"It's not so," I said. "And how long do you think it will sustain you, feeling and seeing and touching and tasting, if there is no love? No one with you?"

The same uncomprehending expression.

"Oh, why do I bother to tell you this?" I said. "I am with you. We're together. You don't know what it was like when I was alone. You can't imagine it."

"I trouble you and I don't mean to," she said. "Tell them what you will. Maybe you can somehow make up a palatable story. I don't know. If you want me to go with you, I'll go. I'll do what you ask of me. But I have one more question for you." She dropped her voice. "Surely you don't mean to share this power with them!"

"No, never." I shook my head as if to say the thought was incredible. I was looking at the jewels, thinking of all the gifts I'd sent, thinking of the dollhouse. I had sent them a dollhouse. I thought of Renaud's players safely across the Channel.

"Not even with Nicolas?"

"No, God, no!" I looked at her.

She nodded slightly as if she approved of this answer. And she pushed at her hair again in a distracted way.

"Why not with Nicolas?" she asked.

I wanted this to stop.

"Because he's young," I said, "and he has life before him. He's not on the brink of death." Now I was more than uneasy. I was miserable. "In time, he'll forget about us . . . " I wanted to say "about our conversation."

"He could die tomorrow," she said. "A carriage could crush him in the streets . . . "

"Do you want me to do it!" I glared at her.

"No. I don't want you to do it. But who am I to tell you what to do? I am trying to understand you."

Her long heavy hair had slipped over her shoulders again, and exasperated, she took hold of it in both hands.

Then suddenly she made a low hissing sound, and her body went rigid. She was holding her long tresses and staring at them.

"My God," she whispered. And then in a spasm, she let go of her hair and screamed.

The sound paralyzed me. It sent a flash of white pain through my head. I had never heard her scream. And she screamed again as if she were on fire. She had fallen back against the window and she was screaming louder as she looked at her hair. She went to touch it and then pulled her fingers back from it as if it were blazing. And she struggled against the window, screaming and twisting from side to side, as if she were trying to get away from her own hair.

"Stop it!" I shouted. I grabbed hold of her shoulders and shook her. She was gasping. I realized instantly what it was. Her hair had grown back! It had grown back as she slept until it was as long as it had been before. And it was thicker even, more lustrous. That is what was wrong with the way she looked, what I had noticed and not noticed! And what she herself had just seen.

"Stop it, stop it now!" I shouted louder, her body shaking so violently I could hardly keep her in my arms. "It's grown back, that's all!" I insisted. "It's natural to you, don't you see? It's nothing!"

She was choking, trying to calm herself, touching it and then screaming as if her fingertips were blistered. She tried to get away from me, and then ripped at her hair in pure terror.

I shook her hard this time.

"Gabrielle!" I said. "Do you understand me? It's grown back, and it will every time you cut it! There's no horror in it, for the love of hell, stop!" I thought if she didn't stop, I'd start to rave myself. I was trembling as badly as she was.

She stopped screaming and she was giving little gasps. I'd never seen her like this, not in all the years and years in Auvergne. She let me guide her towards the bench by the hearth, where I made her sit down. She put her hands to her temples and tried to catch her breath, her body rocking back and forth slowly.

I looked about for a scissors. I had none. The little gold scissors had fallen on the floor of the crypt below. I took out my knife.

She was sobbing softly in her hands.

"Do you want me to cut it off again?" I asked.

She didn't answer.

"Gabrielle, listen to me." I took her hands from her face. "I'll cut it again if you like. Each night, cut it, and burn it. That's all."

She stared at me in such perfect stillness suddenly that I didn't know what to do. Her face was smeared with blood from her tears, and there was blood on her linen. Blood all over her linen.

"Shall I cut it?" I asked her again.

She looked exactly as if someone had hit her and made her bleed. Her eyes were wide and wondering, the blood tears seeping out of them down her smooth cheeks. And as I watched, the flow stopped and the tears darkened and dried to a crust on her white skin.

I wiped her face carefully with my lace handkerchief. I went to the clothing I kept in the tower, the garments made for me in Paris that I'd brought back and kept here now.

I took off her coat. She made no move to help me or stop me and I unhooked the linen shirt that she wore.

I saw her breasts and they were perfectly white except for the palest pink tint to the small nipples. Trying not to look at them, I put the fresh shirt on her and buttoned it quickly. Then I brushed her hair, brushed it and brushed it, and not wanting to hack at it with the knife, I braided it for her in one long plait, and I put her coat back on her.

I could feel her composure and her strength coming back. She didn't seem ashamed of what had happened. And I didn't want her to be. She was merely considering things. But she didn't speak. She didn't move.

I started talking to her.

"When I was little, you used to tell me about all the places you'd been. You showed me pictures of Naples and Venice, remember? Those old books? And you had things, little keepsakes from London and St. Petersburg, all the places you'd seen."

She didn't answer.

"I want us to go to all those places. I want to see them now. I want to see them and live in them. I want to go farther even, places I never dreamed of seeing when I was alive."

Something changed in her face.

"Did you know it would grow back?" she asked in a whisper.

"No. I mean yes. I mean, I didn't think. I should have known it would do that."

For a long time she stared at me again in that same still, listless fashion.

"Does nothing about it all . . . ever . . . frighten you?" she asked. Her voice was guttural and unfamiliar. "Does nothing . . . ever . . . stop you?" she asked. Her mouth was open and perfect and looked like a human mouth.

"I don't know," I whispered helplessly. "I don't see the point," I said. But I felt confused now. Again I told her to cut it each night and to burn it. Simple.

"Yes, burn it," she sighed. "Otherwise it should fill all the rooms of the tower in time, shouldn't it? It would be like Rapunzel's hair in the fairy tale. It would be like the gold that the miller's daughter had to spin from straw in the fairy tale of the mean dwarf, Rumpelstiltskin."

"We write our own fairy tales, my love," I said. "The lesson in this is that nothing can destroy what you are now. Every wound will heal. You are a goddess."

"And the goddess thirsts," she said.

HOURS later, as we walked arm in arm like two students through the boulevard crowds, it was already forgotten. Our faces were ruddy, our skin warm.

But I did not leave her to go to my lawyer. And she did not seek the quiet open country as she had wanted to do. We stayed close to each other, the faintest shimmer of *the presence* now and then making us turn our heads.

5

Y THE hour of three, when we reached the livery stables, we knew we were being stalked by *the presence.*

For half an hour, forty-five minutes at a time, we wouldn't hear it. Then the dull hum would come again. It was maddening me.

And though we tried hard to hear some intelligible thoughts from it, all we could discern was malice, and an occasional tumult like the spectacle of dry leaves disintegrated in the roar of the blaze.

She was glad that we were riding home. It wasn't that the thing annoyed her. It was only what she had said earlier—she wanted the emptiness of the country, the quiet.

When the open land broke before us, we were going so fast that the wind was the only sound, and I think I heard her laughing but I wasn't sure. She loved the feel of the wind as I did, she loved the new brilliance of the stars over the darkened hills.

But I wondered if there had been moments tonight when she had wept inwardly and I had not known. There had been times when she was obscure and silent, and her eyes quivered as if they were crying, but there were absolutely no tears.

I was deep into thoughts of that, I think, when we neared a dense wood that grew along the banks of a shallow stream, and quite suddenly the mare reared and lurched to the side.

I was almost thrown, it was so unexpected. Gabrielle held on tight to my right arm.

Every night I rode into this little glade, crashing over the narrow wooden bridge above the water. I loved the sound of the horse's hooves on the wood and the climb up the sloping bank. And my mare knew the path. But now, she would have none of it.

Shying, threatening to rear again, she turned of her own and galloped back towards Paris until, with all the power of my will, I commanded her, reining her in.

Gabrielle was staring back at the thick copse, the great mass of dark, swaying branches that concealed the stream. And there came over the thin howling of the wind and that soft volume of rustling leaves, the definite pulse of *the presence* in the trees.

We heard it at the same moment, surely, because I tightened my arm around Gabrielle as she nodded, gripping my hand.

"It's stronger!" she said to me quickly. "And it is not one alone."

"Yes," I said, enraged, "and it stands between me and my lair!" I drew my sword, bracing Gabrielle in my left arm.

"You're not riding into it," she cried out.

"The hell I'm not!" I said, trying to steady the horse. "We don't have two hours before sunrise. Draw your sword!"

She tried to turn to speak to me, but I was already driving the horse forward. And she drew her sword as I'd told her to do, her little hand knotted around it as firmly as that of a man.

Of course, the thing would flee as soon as we reached the copse, I was sure of that. I mean the damned thing had never done anything but turn tail and run. And I was furious that it had frightened my mount, and that it was frightening Gabrielle.

With a sharp kick, and the full force of my mental persuasion, I sent the horse racing straight ahead to the bridge.

I locked my hand to the weapon. I bent low with Gabrielle beneath me. I was breathing rage as if I were a dragon, and when the mare's hooves hit the hollow wood over the water, I saw them, the demons, for the first time!

White faces and white arms above us, glimpsed for no more than a second, and out of their mouths the most horrid shrieking as they shook the branches sending down on us a shower of leaves.

"Damn you, you pack of harpies!" I shouted as we reached the sloping bank on the other side, but Gabrielle had let out a scream.

Something had landed on the horse behind me, and the horse was slipping in the damp earth, and the thing had hold of my shoulder and the arm with which I tried to swing the sword.

Whipping the sword over Gabrielle's head and down past my left arm, I chopped at the creature furiously, and saw it fly off, a white blur in the darkness, while another one sprang at us with hands like claws. Gabrielle's blade sliced right through its outstretched arm. I saw the arm go up into the air, the blood spurting as if from a fountain. The screams became a searing wail. I wanted to slash every one of them to pieces. I turned the horse back too sharply so that it reared and almost fell.

But Gabrielle had hold of the horse's mane and she drove it again towards the open road.

As we raced for the tower, we could hear them screaming as they came on. And when the mare gave out, we abandoned her and ran, hand in hand, towards the gates.

I knew we had to get through the secret passage to the inner chamber before they climbed the outside wall. They must not see us take that stone out of place.

And locking the gates and doors behind me as fast as I could, I carried Gabrielle up the stairs.

By the time we reached the secret room and pushed the stone into place again, I heard their howling and shrieking below and their first scraping against the walls.

I snatched up an armful of firewood and threw it beneath the window.

"Hurry, the kindling," I said.

But there were half a dozen white faces already at the bars. Their shrieks echoed monstrously in the little cell. For one moment I could only stare at them as I backed away.

They clung to the iron grating like sc many bats, but they weren't bats. They were vampires, and vampires as we were vampires, in human form.

Dark eyes peered at us from under mops of filthy hair, howls growing louder and fiercer, the fingers that clung to the grating caked with filth. Such clothing as I could see was no more than colorless rags. And the stench coming from them was the graveyard stench.

Gabrielle pitched the kindling at the wall, and she jumped away as they reached to catch hold of her. They bared their fangs. They screeched. Hands struggled to pick up the firewood and throw it back at us. All together they pulled at the grating as if they might free it from the stone.

"Get the tinderbox," I shouted. I grabbed up one of the stouter pieces of wood and thrust it right at the closest face, easily flinging the creature out and off the wall. Weak things. I heard its scream as it fell, but the others had clamped their hands on the wood and they struggled with me now as I dislodged another dirty little demon. But by this time Gabrielle had lighted the kindling.

The flames shot upwards. The howling stopped in a frenzy of ordinary speech:

"It's fire, get back, get down, get out of the way, you idiots! Down, down. The bars are hot! Move away quickly!"

Perfectly regular French! In fact an ever increasing flood of pretty vernacular curse words.

I burst out laughing, stomping my foot and pointing to them, as I looked at Gabrielle.

"A curse on you, blasphemer!" one of them screamed. Then the fire licked at his hands and he howled, falling backwards.

"A curse on the profaners, the outlaws!" came screams from below. It caught on quickly and became a regular chorus. "A curse on the outlaws who dared to enter the House of God!" But they were scrambling down to the ground. The heavy timbers were catching, and the fire was roaring to the ceiling.

"Go back to the graveyard where you came from, you pack of pranksters!" I said. I would have thrown the fire down on them if I could have gotten near the window.

Gabrielle stood still with her eyes narrow, obviously listening.

Cries and howls continued from below. A new anthem of curses upon those who broke the sacred laws, blasphemed, provoked the wrath of God and Satan. They were pulling on the gates and lower windows. They were doing stupid things like throwing rocks at the wall.

"They can't get in," Gabrielle said in a low monotone, her head still cocked attentively. "They can't break the gate."

I wasn't so certain. The gate was rusted, very old. Nothing to do but wait.

I collapsed on the floor, leaning against the side of the sarcophagus, my arms around my chest and my back bent. I wasn't even laughing anymore.

She too sat down against the wall with her legs sprawled out before her. Her chest heaved a little, and her hair was coming loose from the braid. It was a cobra's hood around her face, loose strands clinging to her white cheeks. Soot clung to her garments.

The heat of the fire was crushing. The airless room shimmered with vapors and the flames rose to shut out the night. But we could breathe the little air that was there. We suffered nothing except the heat and the exhaustion.

And gradually I realized she was right about the gate. They hadn't managed to break it down. I could hear them drawing away.

"May the wrath of God punish the profane!"

There was some faint commotion near the stables. I saw in my mind my poor half-witted mortal stable boy dragged in terror from his hiding place, and my rage was redoubled. They were sending me images of it from their thoughts, the murder of that poor boy. Damn them.

"Be still," Gabrielle said. "It's too late."

Her eyes widened and then grew small again as she listened. He was dead, the poor miserable creature.

I felt the death just as if I had seen a small dark bird suddenly rising from the stables. And she sat forward as though seeing it too, and then settled back as if she had lost consciousness, though she had not. She murmured and it sounded like "red velvet," but it was under her breath and I didn't catch the words.

"I'll punish you for this, you gang of ruffians!" I said aloud. I sent it out towards them. "You trouble my house. I swear you'll pay for this."

But my limbs were getting heavier and heavier. The heat of the fire was almost drugging. All the night's strange happenings were taking their toll.

In my exhaustion and in the glare of the fire I could not guess the hour. I think I fell to dreaming for an instant, and woke myself with a shiver, unsure of how much time had passed.

I looked up and saw the figure of an unearthly young boy, an exquisite young boy, pacing the floor of the chamber.

Of course it was only Gabrielle.

6

SHE gave the impression of almost rampant strength as she walked back and forth. Yet all of it was contained in an unbroken grace. She kicked at the timbers and watched the blackened ruin of the fire flare for a moment before settling into itself again. I could see the sky. An hour perhaps remained.

"But who are they?" she asked. She stood over me, her legs apart, her hands in two liquid summoning gestures. "Why do they call us outlaws and blasphemers?"

"I've told you everything I know," I confessed. "Until tonight I didn't think they possessed faces or limbs or real voices."

I climbed to my feet and brushed off my clothes.

"They damned us for entering the churches!" she said. "Did you catch it, those images coming from them? And they don't know how we managed to do it. They themselves would not dare."

For the first time I observed that she was trembling. There were other small signs of alarm, the way the flesh quivered around her eyes, the way that she kept pushing the loose strands of her hair out of her eyes again.

"Gabrielle," I said. I tried to make my tone authoritative, reassuring. "The important thing is to get out of here now. We don't know how early those creatures rise, or how soon after sunset they'll return. We have to discover another hiding place."

"The dungeon crypt," she said.

"A worse trap than this," I said, "if they break through the gate." I glanced at the sky again. I pulled the stone out of the low passage. "Come on," I said.

"But where are we going?" she asked. For the first time tonight she looked almost fragile.

"To a village east of here," I said. "It's perfectly obvious that the safest place is within the village church itself."

"Would you do that?" she asked. "In the church?"

"Of course I would. As you just said, the little beasts would never dare to enter! And the crypts under the altar will be as deep and dark as any grave."

"But Lestat, to rest under the very altar!"

"Mother, you astonish me," I said. "I have taken victims under the very roof of Notre Dame." But another little idea came to me. I went to Magnus's chest and started picking at the heap of treasure. I pulled out two rosaries, one of pearls, another of emeralds, both having the usual small crucifix.

She watched me, her face white, pinched.

"Here, you take this one," I said, giving her the emerald rosary. "Keep it on you. If and when we do meet with them, show them the crucifix. If I am right, they'll run from it."

"But what happens if we don't find a safe place in the church?"

"How the hell should I know? We'll come back here!"

I could feel a fear collecting in her and radiating from her as she hesitated, looking through the window at the fading stars. She had passed through the veil into the promise of eternity and now she was in danger again.

Quickly, I took the rosary from her and kissed her and slipped the rosary into the pocket of her frock coat.

"Emeralds mean eternal life, Mother," I said.

She appeared the boy standing there again, the last glow of the fire just tracing the line of her cheek and mouth.

"It's as I said before," she whispered. "You aren't afraid of anything, are you?"

"What does it matter if I am or not?" I shrugged. I took her arm and drew her to the passage. "We are the things that others fear," I said. "Remember that."

WHEN we reached the stable, I saw the boy had been hideously murdered. His broken body lay twisted on the hay-strewn floor as if it had been flung there by a Titan. The back of his head was shattered. And to mock him, it seemed, or to mock me, they had dressed him in a gentleman's fancy velvet frock coat. Red velvet. Those were the words she'd murmured when they had done the crime. I'd seen only the death. I looked away now in disgust. All the horses were gone.

"They'll pay for that," I said.

I took her hand. But she stared at the miserable boy's body as if it drew her against her will. She glanced at me.

"I feel cold," she whispered. "I'm losing the strength in my limbs. I must, I must get to where it's dark. I can feel it."

I led her fast over the rise of the nearby hill and towards the road.

THERE were no howling little monsters hidden in this village churchyard, of course. I didn't think there would be. The earth hadn't been turned up on the old graves in a long time.

Gabrielle was past conferring with me on this.

I half carried her to the side door of the church and quietly broke the latch.

"I'm cold all over. My eyes are burning," she said again under her breath. "Someplace dark."

But as I started to take her in, she stopped.

"What if they're right," she said. "And we don't belong in the House of God."

"Gibberish and nonsense. God isn't in the House of God."

"Don't! . . ." She moaned.

I pulled her through the sacristy and out before the altar. She covered her face, and when she looked up it was at the crucifix over the tabernacle. She let out a long low gasp. But it was from the stained-glass windows that she shielded her eyes, turning her head towards me. The rising sun that I could not even feel yet was already burning her!

I picked her up as I had done last night. I had to find an old burial crypt, one that hadn't been used in years. I hurried towards the Blessed Virgin's altar, where the inscriptions were almost worn away. And kneeling, I hooked my fingernails around a slab and quickly lifted it to reveal a deep sepulcher with a single rotted coffin.

I pulled her down into the sepulcher with me and moved the slab back into place.

Inky blackness, and the coffin splintering under me so that my right hand closed on a crumbling skull. I felt the sharpness of other bones under my chest. Gabrielle spoke as if in a trance:

"Yes. Away from the light."

"We're safe," I whispered.

I pushed the bones out of the way, making a nest of the rotted wood and the dust that was too old to contain any smell of human decay.

But I did not fall into the sleep for perhaps an hour or more.

I kept thinking over and over of the stable boy, mangled and thrown there in that fancy red velvet frock coat. I had seen that coat before and I couldn't remember where I had seen it. Had it been one of my own? Had they gotten into the tower? No, that was not possible, they couldn't have gotten in. Had they had a coat made up identical to one of my own? Gone to such lengths to mock me? No. How could such creatures do a thing like that? But still . . . that particular coat. Something about it . . .

7

I HEARD the softest, loveliest singing when I opened my eyes. And as sound can often do, even in the most precious fragments, it took me back to childhood, to some night in winter when all my family had gone down to the church in our village and stood for hours among the blazing candles, breathing the heavy, sensual smell of the incense as the priest walked in procession with the monstrance lifted high.

I remembered the sight of the round white Host behind the thick glass, the starburst of gold and jewels surrounding it, and overhead the embroidered canopy, swaying dangerously as the altar boys in their lace surplices tried to steady it as they moved on.

A thousand Benedictions after that one had engraved into my mind the words of the old hymn.

O Salutaris Hostia
Quae caeli pandis ostium
Bella premunt hostilia,
Da robur, fer auxilium . . .

And as I lay in the remains of this broken coffin under the white marble slab at the side altar in this large country church, Gabrielle clinging to me still in the paralysis of sleep, I realized very slowly that above me were hundreds upon hundreds of humans who were singing this very hymn right now.

The church was full of people! And we could not get out of this damned nest of bones until all of them went away.

Around me in the dark, I could feel creatures moving. I could smell the shattered, crumbling skeleton on which I lay. I could smell the earth, too, and feel dampness and the harshness of the cold.

Gabrielle's hands were dead hands holding to me. Her face was as inflexible as bone.

I tried not to brood on this, but to lie perfectly still.

Hundreds of humans breathed and sighed above. Perhaps a thousand of them. And now they moved on into the second hymn.

What comes now, I thought dismally. The litany, the blessings? On this of all nights, I had no time to lie here musing. I must get out. The image of that red velvet coat came to me again with an irrational sense of urgency, and a flash of equally inexplicable pain.

And quite suddenly, it seemed, Gabrielle opened her eyes. Of course I didn't see it. It was utterly black here. I felt it. I felt her limbs come to life.

And no sooner had she moved than she grew positively rigid with alarm. I slipped my hand over her mouth.

"Be still," I whispered, but I could feel her panic.

All the horrors of the preceding night must be coming back to her, that she was now in a sepulcher with a broken skeleton, that she lay beneath a stone she could hardly lift.

"We're in the church!" I whispered. "And we're safe."

The singing surged on. "*Tantum ergo Sacramentum, Veneremur cernui.*"

"No, it's a Benediction," Gabrielle gasped. She was trying to lie still, but abruptly she lost the struggle, and I had to grip her firmly in both arms.

"We *must* get out," she whispered. "Lestat, the Blessed Sacrament is on the altar, for the love of God!"

The remains of the wooden coffin clattered and creaked against the stone beneath it, causing me to roll over on top of her and force her flat with my weight.

"Now lie still, do you hear me!" I said. "We have no choice but to wait."

But her panic was infecting me. I felt the fragments of bone crunching beneath my knees and smelled the rotting cloth. It seemed the death stench was penetrating the walls of the sepulcher, and I knew I could not bear to be shut up with that stench.

"We can't," she gasped. "We can't remain here. I have to get out!" She was almost whimpering. "Lestat, I can't." She was feeling the walls with both hands, and then the stone above us. I heard a pure toneless sound of terror issue from her lips.

Above the hymn had stopped. The priest would go up the altar steps, lift the monstrance in both hands. He would turn to the congregation and raise the Sacred Host in blessing. Gabrielle knew that of course, and Gabrielle suddenly went mad, writhing under me, almost heaving me to the side.

"All right, listen to me!" I hissed. I could control this no longer. "We are going out. But we shall do it like proper vampires, do you hear! There are one thousand people in the church and we are going to scare them to death. I will lift the stone and we will rise up together, and when we do, raise your arms and make the most horrible face you can muster and cry out if you can. That will make them fall back, instead of pouncing upon us and dragging us off to prison, and then we'll rush to the door."

She couldn't even stop to answer, she was already struggling, slamming the rotted boards with her heels.

I rose up, giving the marble slab a great shove with both hands, and leapt out of the vault just as I had said I would do, pulling my cloak up in a giant arc.

I landed upon the floor of the choir in a blaze of candlelight, letting out the most powerful cry I could make.

Hundreds rose to their feet before me, hundreds of mouths opening to scream.

Giving another shout, I grabbed Gabrielle's hand and lunged towards them, leaping over the Communion rail. She gave a lovely high-pitched wail, her left hand raised as a claw as I pulled her down the aisle. Everywhere there was panic, men and women clutching for children, shrieking and falling backwards.

The heavy doors gave at once on the black sky and the gusting breeze. I threw Gabrielle ahead of me and, turning back, made the loudest shriek that I could. I bared my fangs at the writhing, screaming congregation, and unable to tell whether some pursued or merely fell towards me in panic, I reached into my pockets and showered the marble floor with gold coins.

"The devil throws money!" someone screeched.

We tore through the cemetery and across the fields.

Within seconds, we had gained the woods and I could smell the stables of a large house that lay ahead of us beyond the trees.

I stood still, bent almost double in concentration, and summoned the horses. And we ran towards them, hearing the dull thunder of their hooves against the stalls.

Bolting over the low hedge with Gabrielle beside me, I pulled the door off its hinges just as a fine gelding raced out of his broken stall, and we sprang onto his back, Gabrielle scrambling into place before me as I threw my arm around her.

I dug my heels into the animal and rode south into the woods and towards Paris.

8

I TRIED to form a plan as we approached the city, but in truth I was not sure at all how to proceed.

There was no avoiding these filthy little monsters. We were riding towards a battle. And it was little different from the morning on which I'd gone out to kill the wolves, counting upon my rage and my will to carry me through.

We had scarcely entered the scattered farmhouses of Montmartre when we heard for a split second their faint murmuring. Noxious as a vapor, it seemed.

Gabrielle and I knew we had to drink at once, in order to be prepared for them.

We stopped at one of the small farms, crept through the orchard to the back door, and found inside the man and wife dozing at an empty hearth.

When it was finished, we came out of the house together and into the little kitchen garden where we stood still for a moment, looking at the pearl gray sky. No sound of the others. Only the stillness, the clarity of the fresh blood, and the threat of rain as the clouds gathered overhead.

I turned and silently bid the gelding to come to me. And gathering the reins, I turned to Gabrielle.

"I see no other way but to go into Paris," I told her, "to face these little beasts head on. And until they show themselves and start the war all over again, there are things that I must do. I have to think about Nicki. I have to talk to Roget."

"This isn't the time for that mortal nonsense," she said.

The dirt of the church sepulcher still clung to the cloth of her coat and to her blond hair, and she looked like an angel dragged in the dust.

"I won't have them come between me and what I mean to do," I said.

She took a deep breath.

"Do you want to lead these creatures to your beloved Monsieur Roget?" she asked.

That was too dreadful to contemplate.

The first few drops of rain were falling and I felt cold in spite of the blood. In a moment it would be raining hard.

"All right," I said. "Nothing can be done until this is finished!" I said. I mounted the horse and reached for her hand.

"Injury only spurs you on, doesn't it?" she asked. She was studying me. "It would only strengthen you, whatever they did or tried to do."

"Now this is what *I* call mortal nonsense!" I said. "Come on!"

"Lestat," she said soberly. "They put your stable boy in a gentleman's frock coat after they killed him. Did you see the coat? Hadn't you seen it before?"

That damned red velvet coat . . .

"I have seen it," she said. "I had looked at it for hours at my bedside in Paris. It was Nicolas de Lenfent's coat."

I looked at her for a long moment. But I don't think I saw her at all. The rage building in me was absolutely silent. It will be rage until I have proof that it must be grief, I thought. Then I wasn't thinking.

Vaguely, I knew she had no notion yet how strong our passions could be, how they could paralyze us. I think I moved my lips, but nothing came out.

"I don't think they've killed him, Lestat," she said.

Again I tried to speak. I wanted to ask, Why do you say that, but I couldn't. I was staring forward into the orchard.

"I think he is alive," she said. "And that he is their prisoner. Otherwise they would have left his body there and never bothered with that stable boy."

"Perhaps, perhaps not." I had to force my mouth to form the words. "The coat was a message."

I couldn't stand this any longer.

"I'm going after them," I said. "Do you want to return to the tower? If I fail at this . . ."

"I have no intention of leaving you," she said.

* * *

THE rain was falling in earnest by the time we reached the boulevard du Temple, and the wet paving stones magnified a thousand lamps.

My thoughts had hardened into strategies that were more instinct than reason. And I was as ready for a fight as I have ever been. But we had to find out where we stood. How many of them were there? And what did they really want? Was it to capture and destroy us, or to frighten us and drive us off? I had to quell my rage, I had to remember they were childish, susperstitious, conceivably easy to scatter or scare.

As soon as we reached the high ancient tenements near Notre Dame, I *heard* them near us, the vibration coming as in a silver flash and vanishing as quickly again.

Gabrielle drew herself up, and I felt her left hand on my wrist. I saw her right hand on the hilt of her sword.

We had entered a crooked alleyway that turned blindly in the dark in front of us, the iron clatter of the horse's shoes shattering the silence, and I struggled not to be unnerved by the sound itself.

It seemed we saw them at the same moment.

Gabrielle pressed back against me, and I swallowed the gasp that would have given an impression of fear.

High above us, on either side of the narrow thoroughfare, were their white faces just over the eaves of the tenements, a faint gleam against the lowering sky and the soundless drifts of silver rain.

I drove the horse forward in a rush of scraping and clattering. Above they streaked like rats over the roof. Their voices rose in a faint howling mortals could never have heard.

Gabrielle stifled a little cry as we saw their white arms and legs descending the walls ahead of us, and behind I heard the soft thud of their feet on the stones.

"Straight on," I shouted, and drawing my sword, I drove right over the two ragged figures who'd dropped down in our path. "Damnable creatures, out of my way," I shouted, hearing their screams underfoot.

I glimpsed anguished faces for a moment. Those above vanished and those behind us seemed to weaken and we bore ahead, putting yards between us and our pursuers as we came into the deserted place de Grève.

But they were regathering on the edges of the square, and this time I was hearing their distinct thoughts, one of them demanding what power was it we had, and why should they be frightened, and another insisting that they close in.

Some force surely came from Gabrielle at that moment because I could see them visibly fall back when she threw her glance in their direction and tightened her grip on the sword.

"Stop, stand them off!" she said under her breath. "They're terrified." Then I heard her curse. Because flying towards us out of the shadows of the Hôtel-Dieu, there came at least six more of the little demons, their thin white limbs barely swathed in rags, their hair flying, those dreadful wails coming out of their mouths. They were rallying the others. The malice that surrounded us was gaining force.

The horse reared, and almost threw us. They were commanding it to halt as surely as I commanded it to go on.

I grabbed Gabrielle about the waist, leapt off the horse, and ran top speed for the doors of Notre Dame.

A horrid derisive babble rose silently in my ears, wails and cries and threats:

"You dare not, you dare not!" Malice like the heat of a blast furnace opened upon us, as their feet came thumping and splashing around us, and I felt their hands struggling to grab hold of my sword and my coat.

But I was certain of what would happen when we reached the church. I gave it one final spurt, heaving Gabrielle ahead of me so that together we slid through the doors across the threshold of the cathedral and landed sprawling within on the stones.

Screams. Dreadful dry screams curling upwards and then an upheaval, as if the entire mob had been scattered by a cannon blast.

I scrambled to my feet, laughing out loud at them. But I was not waiting so near the door to hear more. Gabrielle was on her feet and pulling me after her and together we hurried deep into the shadowy nave, past one lofty archway after another until we were near to the dim candles of the sanctuary, and then seeking a dark and empty corner by a side altar, we sank down together on our knees.

"Just like those damned wolves!" I said. "A bloody ambush."

"Shhhhh, be quiet a moment," Gabrielle said as she clung to me. "Or my immortal heart will burst."

9

AFTER a long moment, I felt her stiffen. She was looking towards the square.

"Don't think of Nicolas," she said. "They are waiting and they are listening. They are hearing everything that goes on in our minds."

"But what are *they* thinking?" I whispered. "What is going on in *their* heads?"

I could feel her concentration.

I pressed her close, and looked straight at the silver light that came through the distant open doors. I could hear them too now, but just that low shimmer of sound coming from all of them collected there.

But as I stared at the rain, there came over me the strongest sense of peace. It was almost sensuous. It seemed to me we should yield to them, that it was foolish to resist them further. All things would be resolved were we merely to go out to them and give ourselves over. They would not torture Nicolas, whom they had in their power; they would not tear him limb from limb.

I saw Nicolas in their hands. He wore only his lace shirt and breeches because they had taken the coat. And I heard his screams as they pulled his arms from the sockets. I cried out No, putting my own hand over my mouth so that I did not rouse the mortals in the church.

Gabrielle reached up and touched my lips with her fingers.

"It's not being done to him," she said under her breath. "It's merely a threat. Don't think of him."

"He's still alive, then," I whispered.

"So they want us to believe. Listen!"

There came again the sense of peace, the summons, that's what it was, to join them, the voice saying *Come out of the church. Surrender to us, we welcome you, and we will not harm either of you if only you come.*

I turned towards the door and rose to my feet. Anxiously Gabrielle rose beside me, cautioning me again with her hand. She seemed wary of even speaking to me as we both looked at that great archway of silvery light.

You are lying to us, I said. *You have no power over us!* It was a rolling current of defiance moving through the distant door. *Surrender to you? If we do that then what's to stop you from holding the three of us! Why should we come out? Within this church we are safe; we can conceal ourselves in its deepest burial vaults. We could hunt among the faithful, drink their blood in the chapels and niches so skillfully we'd never be discovered, sending our victims out confused to die in the streets afterwards. And what would you do, you who cannot even cross the door! Besides, we don't believe you have Nicolas. Show him to us. Let him come to the door and speak.*

Gabrielle was in a welter of confusion. She was scanning me, desperate to know what I said. And she was clearly hearing them, which I could not do when I was sending these impulses.

It seemed their pulse weakened, but it had not stopped.

It went on as it had before, as if I'd not answered it, as if it were someone humming. It was promising truce again, and now it seemed to speak of rapture, that in the great pleasure of joining with it, all conflict would be resolved. It was sensuous again, it was beautiful.

"Miserable cowards, the lot of you." I sighed. I said the words aloud this time, so that Gabrielle could hear as well. "Send Nicolas into the church."

The hum of the voice became thin. It went on, but beyond it there was a hollow silence as if other voices had been withdrawn and only one or two remained now. Then I heard the thin, chaotic strains of argument and rebellion.

Gabrielle's eyes narrowed.

Silence. Only mortals out there now, weaving their way against the wind across the place de Grève. I didn't believe they would withdraw. Now what do we do to save Nicki?

I blinked my eyes. I felt weary suddenly; it was almost a feeling of despair. And I thought confusedly, This is ridiculous, I never despair! Others do that, not me. I go on fighting no matter what happens. Always. And in my exhaustion and anger, I saw Magnus leaping and jumping in the fire, I saw the grimace on his face before the flames consumed him and he disappeared. Was that despair?

The thought paralyzed me. Horrified me as the reality of it had done then. And I had the oddest feeling that someone else was speaking to me of Magnus. That is why the thought of Magnus had come into my head!

"Too clever . . ." Gabrielle whispered.

"Don't listen to it. It's playing tricks with our very thoughts," I said.

But as I stared past her at the open doorway, I saw a small figure appear. Compact it was, the figure of a young boy, not a man.

I ached for it to be Nicolas, but knew immediately that it was not. It was smaller than Nicolas, though rather heavier of build. And the creature was not human.

Gabrielle made some soft wondering sound. It sounded almost like a prayer in its reference.

The creature wasn't dressed as men dress now. Rather he wore a belted tunic, very graceful, and stockings on his well-shaped legs. His sleeves were deep, hanging at his sides. He was clothed like Magnus, actually, and for one moment I thought madly that by some magic it was Magnus returned.

Stupid thought. This was a boy, as I had said, and he had a head of long curly hair, and he walked very straight and very simply through the silvery light and into the church. He hesitated for a moment. And by the tilt of the head, it seemed he was looking up. And then he came on through the nave and towards us, his feet making not the faintest sound on the stones.

He moved into the glow of the candles on the side altar. His clothes were black velvet, once beautiful, and now eaten away by time, and crusted with dirt. But his face was shining white, and perfect, the countenance of a god it seemed, a Cupid out of Caravaggio, seductive yet ethereal, with auburn hair and dark brown eyes.

I held Gabrielle closer as I looked at him, and nothing so startled me about him, this inhuman creature, as the manner in which he was staring at us. He was inspecting every detail of our persons, and then he reached out very gently and touched the stone of the altar at his side. He stared at the altar, at its crucifix and its saints, and then he looked back to us.

He was only a few yards away, and the soft inspection of us yielded to an expression that was almost sublime. And the voice I'd heard before came out of this creature, summoning us again, calling upon us to yield, saying with indescribable gentleness that we must love one another, he and Gabrielle, whom he didn't call by name, and I.

There was something naive about it, his sending the summons as he stood there.

I held fast against him. Instinctively. I felt my eyes becoming opaque as if a wall had gone up to seal off the windows of my thoughts. And yet I felt such a longing for him, such a longing to fall into him and follow him and be led by him, that all my longings of the past seemed nothing at all. He was all mystery to me as Magnus had been. Only he was beautiful, indescribably beautiful, and there seemed in him an infinite complexity and depth which Magnus had not possessed.

The anguish of my immortal life pressed in on me. He said, *Come to me. Come to me because only I, and my like, can end the loneliness you feel.* It touched a well of inexpressible sadness. It sounded the depth of the sadness, and my throat went dry with a powerful little knot where my voice might have been, yet I held fast.

We two are together, I insisted, tightening my grip on Gabrielle. And then I asked him, *Where is Nicolas?* I asked that question and clung to it, yielding to nothing that I heard or saw.

He moistened his lips; very human thing to do. And silently he approached us until he was standing no more than two feet from us, looking from one of us to the other. And in a voice very unlike a human voice, he spoke.

"Magnus," he said. It was unobtrusive. It was caressing. "He went into the fire as you said?"

"I never said it," I answered. The human sound of my own voice startled me. But I knew now he meant my thoughts of only moments before. "It's quite true," I answered. "He went into the fire." Why should I deceive anyone on that account?

I tried to penetrate his mind. He knew I was doing it and he threw up against me such strange images that I gasped.

What was it I'd seen for an instant? I didn't even know. Hell and heaven, or both made one, vampires in a paradise drinking blood from the very flowers that hung, pendulous and throbbing, from the trees.

I felt a wave of disgust. It was as if he had come into my private dreams like a succubus.

But he had stopped. He let his eyes pucker slightly and he looked down out of some vague respect. My disgust was withering him. He hadn't anticipated my response. He hadn't expected . . . what? Such strength?

Yes, and he was letting me know it in an almost courteous way.

I returned the courtesy. I let him see me in the tower room with Magnus; I recalled Magnus's words before he went into the fire. I let him know all of it.

He nodded and when I told the words Magnus had said, there was a slight change in his face as if his forehead had gone smooth, or all of his skin had tightened. He gave me no such knowledge of himself in answer.

On the contrary, much to my surprise, he looked away from us to the main altar of the church. He glided past us, turning his back to us as if he had nothing to fear from us and had for the moment forgotten us.

He moved towards the great aisle and slowly up it, but he did not appear to walk in a human way. Rather he moved so swiftly from one bit of shadow to another that he seemed to vanish and reappear. Never was he visible in the light. And those scores of souls milling in the church had only to glance at him for him to instantly disappear.

I marveled at his skill, because that is all it was. And curious to see if I could move like that, I followed him to the choir. Gabrielle came after without a sound.

I think we both found it simpler than we had imagined it would be. Yet he was clearly startled when he saw us at his side.

And in the very act of being startled, he gave me a glimpse of his great weakness, pride. He was humiliated that we had crept up on him, moving so lightly and managing at the same time to conceal our thoughts.

But worse was to come. When he realized I had perceived this . . . it was revealed for a split second . . . he was doubly enraged. A withering heat emanated from him that wasn't heat at all.

Gabrielle made a little scornful sound. Her eyes flashed on him for a second in some shimmer of communication between them that excluded me. He seemed puzzled.

But he was in the grip of some greater battle I was struggling to understand. He looked at the faithful around him, and at the altar and all the emblems of the Almighty and the Virgin Mary everywhere that he turned. He was perfectly the god out of Caravaggio, the light playing on the hard whiteness of his innocent-looking face.

Then he put his arm about my waist, slipping it under my cloak. His touch was so strange, so sweet and enticing, and the beauty of his face so entrancing that I didn't move away. He put his other arm around Gabrielle's waist, and the sight of them together, angel and angel, distracted me.

He said: *You must come.*

"Why, where?" Gabrielle asked. I felt an immense pressure. He was attempting to move me against my will, but he could not. I planted myself on the stone floor. I saw Gabrielle's face harden as she looked at him. And again, he was amazed. He was maddened and he couldn't conceal it from us.

So he had underestimated our physical strength as well as our mental strength. Interesting.

"You must come now," he said, giving me the great force of his will, which I could see much too clearly to be fooled. "Come out and my followers won't harm you."

"You're lying to us," I said. "You sent your followers away, and you want us to come out before your followers return, because you don't want them to see you come out of the church. You don't want them to know you came into it!"

Again Gabrielle gave a little scornful laugh.

I put my hand on his chest and tried to move him away. He might have been as strong as Magnus. But I refused to be afraid. "Why don't you want them to see?" I whispered, peering into his face.

The change in him was so startling and so ghastly that I found myself holding my breath. His angelic countenance appeared to wither, his eyes widening and his mouth twisting down in consternation. His entire body became quite deformed as if he were trying not to grit his teeth and clench his fists.

Gabrielle drew away. I laughed. I didn't really mean to, but I couldn't help it. It was horrifying. But it was also very funny.

With stunning suddenness this awful illusion, if that is what it was, faded, and he came back to himself. Even the sublime expression returned. He told me in a steady stream of thought that I was infinitely stronger than he supposed. But it would frighten the others to see him emerge from the church, and so we should go at once.

"Lies again," Gabrielle whispered.

And I knew this much pride would forgive nothing. God help Nicolas if we couldn't trick this one!

Turning, I took Gabrielle's hand and we started down the aisle to the front doors, Gabrielle glancing back at him and to me questioningly, her face white and tense.

"Patience," I whispered. I turned to see him far away from us, his back to the main altar, and his eyes were so big as he stared that he looked horrible to me, loathsome, like a ghost.

When I reached the vestibule I sent out my summons to the others with all my power. And I whispered aloud for Gabrielle as I did so. I told them to come back and into the church if they wanted to, that nothing could harm them, their leader was inside the church standing at the very altar, unharmed.

I spoke the words louder, pumping the summons under the words, and Gabrielle joined me, repeating the phrases in unison with me.

I felt him coming towards us from the main altar, and then suddenly I lost him. I didn't know where he was behind us.

He grabbed hold of me suddenly, materializing at my side, and Gabrielle was thrown to the floor. He was attempting to lift me and pitch me through the door.

But I fought him. And desperately collecting everything I remembered of Magnus—his strange walk, and this creature's strange manner of moving—I hurled him, not off balance as one might do to a heavy mortal, but straight up in the air.

Just as I suspected, he went over in a somersault, crashing into the wall.

Mortals stirred. They saw movement, heard noises. But he'd vanished again. And Gabrielle and I looked no different from other young gentlemen in the shadows.

I motioned for Gabrielle to get out of the way. Then he appeared, shooting towards me, but I perceived what was to happen and stepped aside.

Some twenty feet away from me, I saw him sprawled on the stones staring at me with positive awe, as if I were a god. His long auburn hair was tossed about, his brown eyes enormous as he looked up. And for all the gentle innocence of his face, his will was rolling over me, a hot stream of commands, telling me I was weak and imperfect and a fool, and I would be torn limb from limb by his followers as soon as they appeared. They would roast my mortal lover slowly till he died.

I laughed silently. This was as ludicrous as a fight out of the old commedia.

Gabrielle was staring from one to the other of us.

I sent the summons again to the others, and this time when I sent it, I heard them answering, questioning.

"Come into the church." I repeated it over and over, even as he rose and ran at me again in blind and clumsy rage. Gabrielle caught him just as I did, and we both had hold of him and he couldn't move.

In a moment of absolute horror for me he tried to sink his fangs into my neck. I saw his eyes round and empty as the fangs descended over his drawn lip. I flung him back and again he vanished.

They were coming nearer, the others.

"He's in the church, your leader, look at him!" I repeated it. "And any of you can come into the church. You won't be hurt."

I heard Gabrielle let out a scream of warning. And too late. He rose up right in front of me, as if out of the floor itself, and struck my jaw, jerking my head back so that I saw the church ceiling. And before I could recover, he had dealt me one fine blow in the middle of the back that sent me flying out the door and onto the stones of the square.

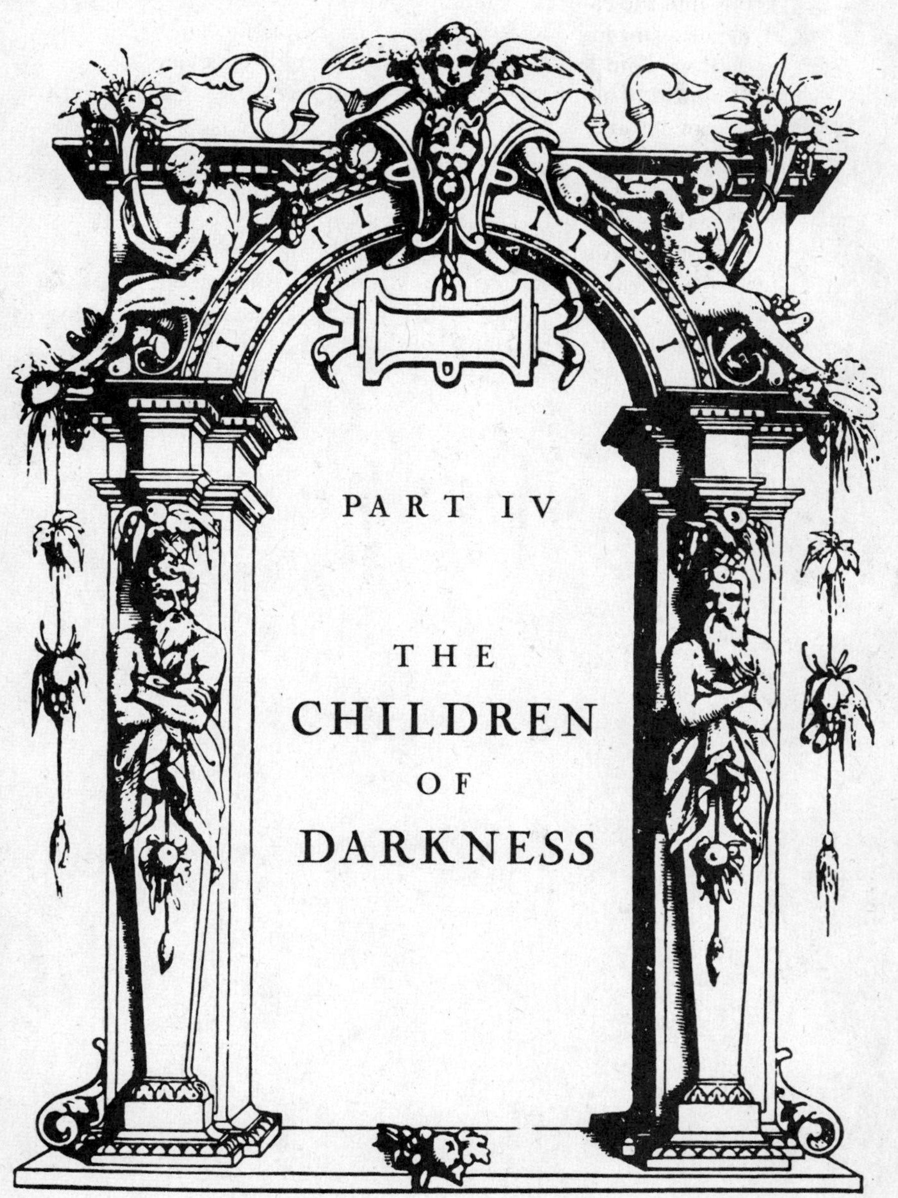

PART IV

THE CHILDREN OF DARKNESS

1

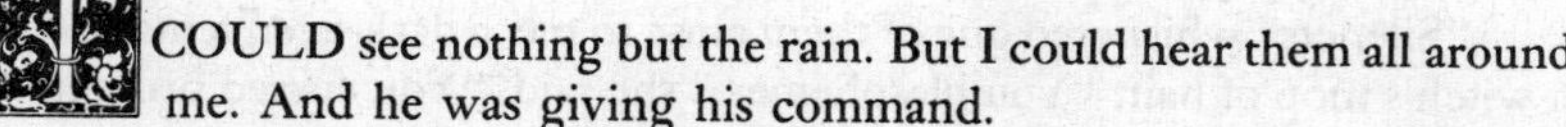

I COULD see nothing but the rain. But I could hear them all around me. And he was giving his command.

"They have no great power, these two," he was telling them in thoughts that had a curious simplicity to them, as if he were commanding vagrant children. "Take them both prisoner."

Gabrielle said: "Lestat, don't fight. It's useless to prolong it."

And I knew she was right. But I'd never surrendered to anybody in my life. And pulling her with me past the Hôtel-Dieu, I made for the bridge.

We tore through the press of wet cloaks and mud-spattered carriages, yet they were gaining upon us, rushing so fast they were almost invisible to mortals, and with only a little fear of us now.

In the dark streets of the Left Bank, the game was finished.

White faces appeared above and below me as though they were demonic cherubs, and when I tried to draw my weapon, I felt their hands on my arms. I heard Gabrielle say, "Let it be done."

I held fast to my sword but I couldn't stop them from lifting me off the ground. They were lifting Gabrielle too.

And in a blaze of hideous images, I understood where they were taking us. It was to les Innocents, only yards away. I could already see the flicker of the bonfires that burned each night among the stinking open graves, the flames that were supposed to drive away the effluvia.

I locked my arm around Gabrielle's neck and cried out that I couldn't bear that stench, but they were carrying us on swiftly through the darkness, through the gates and past the white marble crypts.

"Surely you can't endure it," I said, struggling. "So why do you live among the dead when you were made to feed on life?"

But I felt such revulsion now I couldn't keep it up, the verbal or physical struggle. All around us lay bodies in various states of decomposition, and even from the rich sepulchers there came that reek.

And as we moved into the darker part of the cemetery, as we entered an enormous sepulcher, I realized that they too hated the stench, as much as I. I could feel their disgust, and yet they opened their mouths and their lungs as if they were eating it. Gabrielle was trembling against me, her fingers digging into my neck.

Through another doorway we passed, and then, by dim torchlight, down an earthen stairs.

The smell grew stronger. It seemed to ooze from the mud walls. I turned my face down and vomited a thin stream of glittering blood upon the steps beneath me, which vanished as we moved swiftly on.

"Live among graves," I said furiously. "Tell me, why do you suffer hell already by your own choice?"

"Silence," whispered one of them close to me, a dark-eyed female with a witch's mop of hair. "You blasphemer," she said. "You cursed profaner."

"Don't be a fool for the devil, darling!" I sneered. We were eye to eye. "Unless he treats you a damn sight better than the Almighty!"

She laughed. Or rather she started to laugh, and she stopped as if she weren't allowed to laugh. What a gay and interesting little get-together this was going to be!

We were going lower and lower into the earth.

Flickering light, the scrape of their bare feet on the dirt, filthy rags brushing my face. For an instant, I saw a grinning skull. Then another, then a heap of them filling a niche in the wall.

I tried to wrench free and my foot hit another heap and sent the bones clattering on the stairs. The vampires tightened their grip, trying to lift us higher. Now we passed the ghastly spectacle of rotted corpses fixed in the walls like statues, bones swathed in rotted rags.

"This is too disgusting!" I said with my teeth clenched.

We had come to the foot of the steps and were being carried through a great catacomb. I could hear the low rapid beat of kettledrums.

Torches blazed ahead, and over a chorus of mournful wails, there came other cries, distant but filled with pain. Yet something beyond these puzzling cries had caught my attention.

Amid all the foulness, I sensed a mortal was near. It was Nicolas and he was alive and I could hear him, the warm, vulnerable current of his thoughts mingled with his scent. And something was terribly wrong with his thoughts. They were chaos.

I couldn't know if Gabrielle had caught it.

We were quite suddenly thrown down together, in the dust. And the others backed away from us.

I climbed to my feet, lifting Gabrielle with me. And I saw that we were in a great domed chamber, scarcely illuminated by three torches which the vampires held to form a triangle, in the center of which we stood.

Something huge and black to the back of the chamber; smell of wood and pitch, smell of damp, moldering cloth, smell of living mortal. Nicolas there.

Gabrielle's hair had come loose entirely from the ribbon, and it fell around her shoulders as she cleaved to me, looking about with seemingly calm, cautious eyes.

Wails rose all around us, but the most piercing supplications came from those other beings we had heard before, creatures somewhere deep in the earth.

And I realized these were entombed vampires screaming, screaming for blood, and screaming for forgiveness and release, screaming even for the fires of hell. The sound was as unbearable as the stench.

No real thoughts from Nicki, only the formless shimmer of his mind. Was he dreaming? Was he mad?

The roll of the drums was very loud and very close, and yet those screams pierced the rumbling again and again without rhythm or warning. The wailing of those nearest us died away, but the drums went on, the pounding suddenly coming from inside my head.

Trying desperately not to clamp my hands to my ears, I looked about.

A great circle had been formed, and there were ten of them at least, these creatures. I saw young ones, old ones, men and women, a young boy—and all clothed in the remnants of human garments, caked with earth, feet bare, hair tangled with filth. There was the woman I had spoken to on the stairs, her well-shaped body clothed in a filthy robe, her quick black eyes glinting like jewels in the dirt as she studied us. And beyond these, the advance guard, were a pair in the shadows beating the kettledrums.

I begged silently for strength. I tried to hear Nicolas without actually thinking of him. Solemn vow: *I shall get us all out of here, though at the moment I do not know exactly how.*

The drumbeat was slowing, becoming an ugly cadence that made the alien feeling of fear a fist against my throat. One of the torchbearers approached.

I could feel the anticipation of the others, a palpable excitement as the flames were thrust at me.

I snatched the torch from the creature, twisting his right hand until he was flung down on his knees. With a hard kick, I sent him sprawling, and as the others rushed in, I swung the torch wide driving them back.

Then defiantly, I threw down the torch.

This caught them off guard and I sensed a sudden quietness. The excitement was drained away, or rather it had lapsed into something more patient and less volatile.

The drums beat insistently, but it seemed they were ignoring the drums. They were staring at the buckles on our shoes, at our hair, and at our faces, with such distress they appeared menacing and hungry. And the young boy, with a look of anguish, reached out to touch Gabrielle.

"Get back!" I hissed. And he obeyed, snatching up the torch from the ground as he did.

But I knew it for certain now—we were surrounded by envy and curiosity, and this was the strongest advantage we possessed.

I looked from one to the other of them. And quite slowly, I commenced to brush the filth from my frock coat and breeches. I smoothed my cloak as I straightened my shoulders. Then I ran a hand through my hair, and stood with my arms folded, the picture of righteous dignity, gazing about.

Gabrielle gave a faint smile. She stood composed, her hand on the hilt of her sword.

The effect of this on the others was universal amazement. The dark-eyed female was enthralled. I winked at her. She would have been gorgeous if someone had thrown her into a waterfall and held her there for half an hour and I told her so silently. She took two steps backwards and pulled closed her robe over her breasts. Interesting. Very interesting indeed.

"What is the explanation for all this?" I asked, staring at them one by one as if they were quite peculiar. Again Gabrielle gave her faint smile.

"What are you meant to be?" I demanded. "The images of chain-rattling ghosts who haunt cemeteries and ancient castles?"

They were glancing to one another, getting uneasy. The drums had stopped.

"My childhood nurse many a time thrilled me with tales of such fiends," I said. "Told me they might at any moment leap out of the suits of armor in our house to carry me away screaming." I stomped my foot and dashed forward. "IS THAT WHAT YOU ARE!" They shrieked and shrank back.

The black-eyed woman didn't move, however.

I laughed softly.

"And your bodies are just like ours, aren't they?" I asked slowly. "Smooth, without flaw, and in your eyes I can see evidence of my own powers. Most strange . . ."

Confusion coming from them. And the howling in the walls seemed fainter as if the entombed were listening in spite of their pain.

"Is it great fun living in filth and stench such as this?" I asked. "Is that why you do it?"

Fear. Envy again. How had we managed to escape their fate?

"Our leader is Satan," said the dark-eyed woman sharply. Cultured voice. She'd been something to reckon with when she was mortal. "And we serve Satan as we are meant to do."

"Why?" I asked politely.

Consternation all around.

Faint shimmer of Nicolas. Agitation without direction. Had he heard my voice?

"You will bring down the wrath of God on all of us with your defiance," said the boy, the smallest of them, who couldn't have been more than sixteen when he was made. "In vanity and wickedness you disregard the Dark Ways. You live among mortals! You walk in the places of light."

"And why don't you?" I asked. "Are you to go to heaven on white wings when this penitential sojourn of yours is ended? Is that what Satan promises? Salvation? I wouldn't count on it, if I were you."

"You will be thrown into the pit of hell for your sins!" said one of the others, a tiny hag of a woman. "You will have power to do evil on earth no more."

"When is that supposed to happen?" I asked. "For half a year I've been what I am. God and Satan have not troubled me! It is you who trouble me!"

They were paralyzed for the moment. Why hadn't we been struck dead when we entered the churches? How could we be what we were?

It was very likely they could have been scattered now and beaten. But what about Nicki? If only his thoughts were directed, I could have gained some image of exactly what lay behind that great heap of moldering black cloth.

I kept my eyes on the vampires.

Wood, pitch, a pyre there surely. And these damned torches.

The dark-eyed woman edged in. No malice, only fascination. But the boy pushed her to the side, infuriating her. He stepped so close I could feel his breath on my face:

"Bastard!" he said. "You were made by the outcast, Magnus, in defiance of the coven, and in defiance of the Dark Ways. And so you gave the Dark Gift to this woman in rashness and vanity as it was given to you."

"If Satan does not punish," said the tiny woman, "we will punish as is our duty and our right!"

The boy pointed to the black draped pyre. He motioned for the others to draw back.

The kettledrums came up again, fast and loud. The circle widened, the torchbearers drawing near to the cloth.

Two of the others tore down the ragged drapery, great sheets of black serge that sent up the dust in a suffocating cloud.

The pyre was as big as the one that had consumed Magnus.

And on top of the pyre in a crude wooden cage, Nicolas knelt slumped against the bars. He stared blindly at us, and I could find no recognition in his face or his thoughts.

The vampires held their torches high for us to see. And I could feel their excitement rising again as it had when they had first brought us into the room.

Gabrielle was cautioning me with the press of her hand to be calm. Nothing changed in her expression.

There were bluish marks on Nicki's throat. The lace of his shirt was filthy as were their rags, and his breeches were snagged and torn. He was in fact covered with bruises and drained almost to the point of death.

The fear silently exploded in my heart, but I knew this was what they wanted to see. And I sealed it within.

The cage is nothing, I can break it. And there are only three torches. The question is when to move, how. We would not perish like this, not like this.

I found myself staring coldly at Nicolas, coldly at the bundles of kindling, the crude chopped wood. The anger rolled out of me. Gabrielle's face was a perfect mask of hate.

The group seemed to feel this and to move ever so slightly away from it, and then to draw in, confused and uncertain again.

But something else was happening. The circle was tightening.

Gabrielle touched my arm.

"The leader is coming," she said.

A door had opened somewhere. The drums surged and it seemed those imprisoned in the walls went into agony, pleading to be forgiven and released. The vampires around us took up the cries in a frenzy. It was all I could do not to cover my ears.

A strong instinct told me not to look at the leader. But I couldn't resist him, and slowly I turned to look at him and measure his powers again.

2

HE WAS moving towards the center of this great circle, his back to the pyre, a strange woman vampire at his side.

And when I looked full at him in the torchlight I felt the same shock I had experienced when he entered Notre Dame.

It wasn't merely his beauty; it was the astonishing innocence of his boyish face. He moved so lightly and swiftly I could not see his feet actually take steps. His huge eyes regarded us without anger, his hair, for all the dust in it, giving off faint reddish glints.

I tried to feel his mind, what it was, why such a sublime being should command these sad ghosts when it had the world to roam. I tried to discover again what I had almost discovered when we stood before the altar of the cathedral, this creature and I. If I knew that, maybe I could defeat him and defeat him I would.

I thought I saw him respond to me, some silent answer, some flash of heaven in the very pit of hell in his innocent expression, as if the devil still retained the face and form of the angel after the fall.

But something was very wrong. The leader was not speaking. The drums beat on anxiously, yet there was no communal conviction. The dark-eyed woman vampire was not joined with the others in their wailing. And others had stopped as well.

And the woman who had come in with the leader, a strange creature clothed as an ancient queen might have been in ragged gown and braided girdle, commenced to laugh.

The coven or whatever it called itself was quite understandably stunned. One of the kettledrums stopped.

The queen creature laughed louder and louder. Her white teeth flashed through the filthy veil of her snarled hair.

Beautiful she'd been once. And it wasn't mortal age that had ravaged her. Rather, she appeared the lunatic, her mouth a horrid grimace, her eyes staring wildly before her, her body bent suddenly in an arc with her laughing, as Magnus had bent when he danced around his own funeral pyre.

"Did I not warn you?" she screamed. "Did I not?"

Far behind her, Nicolas moved in the little cage. I felt the laughter scorching him. But he was looking steadily at me, and the old sensibility was stamped on his features in spite of their distortion. Fear struggled with malice in him, and this was tangled with wonder and near despair.

The auburn-haired leader stared at the queen vampire, his expression unreadable, and the boy with the torch stepped forward and shouted for the woman to be silent at once. He made himself rather regal now, in spite of his rags.

The woman turned her back on him and faced us. She sang her words in a hoarse, sexless voice that gave way to a galloping laughter.

"A thousand times I said it, yet you would not listen to me," she declared. Her gown shivered about her as she trembled. "And you called me mad, time's martyr, a vagrant Cassandra corrupted by too long a vigil on this earth. Well, you see, every one of my predictions has come true."

The leader gave her not the slightest recognition.

"And it took this creature"—she approached me, her face a hideous comic mask as Magnus's face had been—"this romping cavalier to prove it to you once and for all."

She hissed, drew in her breath, and stood erect. And for one moment in perfect stillness she passed into beauty. I longed to comb her hair, to wash it with my own hands, and to clothe her in modern dress, to see her in the mirror of my time. In fact, my mind went suddenly wild with the idea of it, the reclaiming of her and the washing away of her evil disguise.

I think for one second the concept of eternity burned in me. I knew then what immortality was. All things were possible with her, or so for that one moment it seemed.

She gazed at me and caught the visions, and the loveliness of her face deepened, but the mad humor was coming back.

"Punish them," the boy stormed. "Call down the judgment of Satan. Light the fire."

But no one moved in the vast room.

The old woman hummed with her lips closed, some eerie melody with the cadence of speech. The leader stared as before.

But the boy in panic advanced upon us. He bared his fangs, raised his hand in a claw.

I snatched the torch from him and dealt him an indifferent blow to the chest that sent him across the dusty circle, sliding into the kindling banked against the pyre. I ground out the torch in the dirt.

The queen vampire let out a shriek of laughter that seemed to terrify the others, but nothing changed in the leader's face.

"I won't stand here for any judgment of Satan!" I said, glancing around the circle. "Unless you bring Satan here."

"Yes, tell them, child! Make them answer to you!" the old woman said triumphantly.

The boy was on his feet again.

"You know the crimes," he roared as he reentered the circle. He was furious now, and he exuded power, and I realized how impossible it was to judge any of them by the mortal form they retained. He might well have been an elder, the tiny old woman a fledgling, the boyish leader the eldest of them all.

"Behold," he said, stepping closer, his gray eyes gleaming as he felt the attention of the others. "This fiend was no novice here or anywhere; he did not beg to be received. He made no vows to Satan. He did not on his deathbed give up his soul, and in fact, he did not die!" His voice went higher, grew louder. "He was not buried! He has not risen from the grave as a Child of Darkness! Rather he dares to roam the world in the guise of a living being! And in the very midst of Paris conducts business as a mortal man!"

Shrieks answered him from the walls. But the vampires of the circle were silent as he gazed at them. His jaw trembled.

He threw up his arms and wailed. One or two of the others answered. His face was disfigured with rage.

The old queen vampire gave a shiver of laughter and looked at me with the most maniacal smile.

But the boy wasn't giving up.

"He seeks the comforts of the hearth, strictly forbidden," he screamed, stamping his foot and shaking his garments. "He goes into the very palaces of carnal pleasure, and mingles there with mortals as they play music! As they dance!"

"Stop your raving!" I said. But in truth, I wanted to hear him out.

He plunged forward, sticking his finger in my face.

"No rituals can purify him!" he shouted. "Too late for the Dark Vows, the Dark Blessings . . . "

"Dark Vows? Dark Blessings?" I turned to the old queen. "What do you say to all this? You're as old as Magnus was when he went into the fire . . . Why do you suffer this to go on?"

Her eyes moved in her head suddenly as if they alone possessed life, and there came that racing laughter out of her again.

"I shall never harm you, young one," she said. "Either of you." She looked lovingly at Gabrielle. "You are on the Devil's Road to a great adventure. What right have I to intervene in what the centuries have in store for you?"

The Devil's Road. It was the first phrase from any of them that had rung a clarion in my soul. An exhilaration took hold of me merely looking at her. In her own way, she was Magnus's twin.

"Oh yes, I am as old as your progenitor!" She smiled, her white fangs just touching her lower lip, then vanishing. She glanced at the leader, who watched her without the slightest interest or spirit. "I was here," she said, "within this coven when Magnus stole our secrets from us, that crafty one, the alchemist, Magnus . . . when he drank the blood that would give him life everlasting in a manner which the World of Darkness had never witnessed before. And now three centuries have passed and he has given his pure and undiluted Dark Gift to you, beautiful child!"

Her face became again that leering, grinning mask of comedy, so much like Magnus's face.

"Show it to me, child," she said, "the strength he gave you. Do you know what it means to be made a vampire by one that powerful, who has never given the Gift before? It's forbidden here, child, no one of such age conveys his power! For if he should, the fledgling born of him should easily overcome this gracious leader and his coven here."

"Stop this ill-conceived lunacy!" the boy interrupted.

But everyone was listening. The pretty dark-eyed woman had come nearer to us, the better to see the old queen, and completely forgetting to fear or hate us now.

"One hundred years ago you'd said enough," the boy roared at the old queen, with his hand up to command her silence. "You're mad as all the old ones are mad. It's the death you suffer. I tell you all this outlaw must be punished. Order shall be restored when he and the woman he made are destroyed before us all."

With renewed fury, he turned on the others.

"I tell you, you walk this earth as all evil things do, by the will of God, to make mortals suffer for his Divine Glory. And by the will of God you can be destroyed if you blaspheme, and thrown in the vats of hell now, for you are damned souls, and your immortality is given you only at the price of suffering and torment."

A burst of wailing commenced uncertainly.

"So there it is finally," I said. "The whole philosophy—and the whole is founded upon a lie. And you cower like peasants, in hell already by your own choosing, enchained more surely than the lowest mortal, and you wish to punish us because we do not? Follow our examples because we do not!"

The vampires were some of them staring at us, others in frantic conversations that broke out all around. Again and again they glanced to the leader and to the old queen.

But the leader would say nothing.

The boy screamed for order:

"It is not enough that he has profaned holy places," he said, "not enough that he goes about as a mortal man. This very night in a village in the banlieue he terrified the congregation of an entire church. All of Paris is talking of this horror, the ghouls rising from the graves beneath the very altar, he and this female vampire on whom he worked the Dark Trick without consent or ritual, just as he was made."

There were gasps, more murmurs. But the old queen screamed with delight.

"These are high crimes," he said. "I tell you, they cannot go unpunished. And who among you does not know of his mockeries on the stage of the boulevard theater which he himself holds as property as a mortal man! There to a thousand Parisians he flaunted his powers as a Child of Darkness! And the secrecy we have protected for centuries was broken for his amusement and the amusement of a common crowd."

The old queen rubbed her hands together, cocking her head to the side as she looked at me.

"Is it all true, child?" she asked. "Did you sit in a box at the Opéra? Did you stand before the footlights of the Théâtre-Française? Did you dance with the king and queen in the palace of the Tuileries, you and this beauty you made so perfectly? Is it true you travel the boulevards in a golden coach?"

She laughed and laughed, her eyes now and then scanning the others, subduing them as if she gave forth a beam of warm light.

"Ah, such finery and such dignity," she continued. "What happened in the great cathedral when you entered it? Tell me now!"

"Absolutely nothing, madam!" I declared.

"High crimes!" roared the outraged boy vampire. "These are frights enough to rouse a city, if not a kingdom against us. And after centuries in which we have preyed upon this metropolis in stealth, giving birth only to the gentlest whispers of our great power. Haunts we are, creatures of the night, meant to feed the fears of man, not raving demons!"

"Ah, but it is too sublime," sang the old queen with her eyes on the domed ceiling. "From my stone pillow I have dreamed dreams of the mortal world above. I have heard its voices, its new music, as lullabies as I lie in my grave. I have envisioned its fantastical discoveries, I have known its courage in the timeless sanctum of my thoughts. And though it shuts me out with its dazzling forms, I long for one with the strength to roam it fearlessly, to ride the Devil's Road through its heart."

The gray-eyed boy was beside himself.

"Dispense with the trial," he said, glaring at the leader. "Light the pyre now."

The queen stepped back out of my way with an exaggerated gesture, as the boy reached for the torch nearest him, and I rushed at him, snatching the torch away from him, and heaving him up towards the ceiling, head over heels, so that he came tumbling in that manner all the way down. I stamped out the torch.

That left one more. And the coven was in perfect disorder, several rushing to aid the boy, the others murmuring to one another, the leader stock-still as if in a dream.

And in this interval I went forward, climbed up the pyre and tore loose the front of the little wooden cage.

Nicolas looked like an animated corpse. His eyes were leaden, and his mouth twisted as if he were smiling at me, hating me, from the other side of the grave. I dragged him free of the cage and brought him down to the dirt floor. He was feverish, and though I ignored it and would have concealed it if I could, he shoved at me and cursed me under his breath.

The old queen watched in fascination. I glanced at Gabrielle, who watched without a particle of fear. I drew out the pearl rosary from my waistcoat and letting the crucifix dangle, I placed the rosary around Nicolas's neck. He stared stuporously down at the little cross, and then he began to laugh. The contempt, the malice, came out of him in this low metallic sound. It was the very opposite of the sounds made by the vampires. You could hear the human blood in it, the human thickness of it, echoing against the walls. Ruddy and hot and strangely unfinished he seemed suddenly, the only mortal among us, like a child thrown among porcelain dolls.

The coven was more confused than ever. The two burnt-out torches still lay untouched.

"Now, by your own rules, you cannot harm him," I said. "Yet it's a vampire who has given him the supernatural protection. Tell me, how to compass that?"

I carried Nicki forward. And Gabrielle at once reached out to take him in her arms.

He accepted this, though he stared at her as if he didn't know her and even lifted his fingers to touch her face. She took his hand away as she might the hand of a baby, and kept her eyes fixed on the leader and on me.

"If your leader has no words for you now, I have words," I said. "Go wash yourselves in the waters of the Seine, and clothe yourselves like humans if you can remember how, and prowl among men as you are obviously meant to do."

The defeated boy vampire stumbled back into the circle, pushing roughly away those who had helped him to his feet.

"Armand," he implored the silent auburn-haired leader. "Bring the coven to order! Armand! Save us now!"

"Why in the name of hell," I outshouted him, "did the devil give you beauty, agility, eyes to see visions, minds to cast spells?"

Their eyes were fixed on me, all of them. The gray-haired boy cried out the name "Armand" again, but in vain.

"You waste your gifts!" I said. "And worse, you waste your immortality! Nothing in all the world is so nonsensical and contradictory, save mortals, that is, who live in the grip of the superstitions of the past."

Perfect silence reigned. I could hear Nicki's slow breathing. I could feel his warmth. I could feel his numbed fascination struggling against death itself.

"Have you no cunning?" I asked the others, my voice swelling in the stillness. "Have you no craft? How did I, an orphan, stumble upon so much possibility, when you, nurtured as you are by these evil parents"—I broke off to stare at the leader and the furious boy—"grope like blind things under the earth?"

"The power of Satan will blast you into hell," the boy bellowed, gathering all his remaining strength.

"You keep saying that!" I said. "And it keeps not happening, as we can all see!"

Loud murmurs of assent!

"And if you really thought it would happen," I said, "you would never have bothered to bring me here."

Louder voices in agreement.

I looked at the small forlorn figure of the leader. And all eyes turned away from me to him. Even the mad queen vampire looked at him.

And in the stillness I heard him whisper:

"It is finished."

Not even the tormented ones in the wall made a sound.

And the leader spoke again:

"Go now, all of you, it is at an end."

"Armand, no!" the boy pleaded.

But the others were backing away, faces concealed behind hands as they whispered. The drums were cast aside, the single torch was hung upon the wall.

I watched the leader. I knew his words weren't meant to release us.

And after he had silently driven out the protesting boy with the others, so that only the queen remained with him, he turned his gaze once again to me.

3

THE great empty room beneath its immense dome, with only the two vampires watching us, seemed all the more ghastly, the one torch giving a feeble and gloomy light.

Silently I considered: Will the others leave the cemetery, or hover at the top of the stairs? Will any of them allow me to take Nicki alive from this place? The boy will remain near, but the boy is weak; the old queen will do nothing. That leaves only the leader, really. But I must not be impulsive now.

He was still staring at me and saying nothing.

"Armand?" I said respectfully. "May I address you in this way?" I drew closer, scanning him for the slightest change of expression. "You are obviously the leader. And you are the one who can explain all this to us."

But these words were a poor cover for my thoughts. I was appealing to him. I was asking him how he had led them in all this, he who appeared as ancient as the old queen, compassing some depth they would not understand. I pictured him standing before the altar of Notre Dame again, that ethereal expression on his face. And I found myself believing perfectly in him, and the possibility of him, this ancient one who had stood silent all this while.

I think I searched him now for just an instant of human feeling! That's what I thought wisdom would reveal. And the mortal in me, the vulnerable one who had cried in the inn at the vision of the chaos, said:

"Armand, what is the meaning of all this?"

It seemed the brown eyes faltered. But then the face so subtly transformed itself to rage, that I drew back.

I didn't believe my senses. The sudden changes he had undergone in Notre Dame were nothing to this. And such a perfect incarnation of malice I'd never seen. Even Gabrielle moved away. She raised her right hand to shield Nicki, and I stepped back until I was beside her and our arms touched.

But in the same miraculous way, the hatred melted. The face was again that of a sweet and fresh mortal boy.

The old queen vampire smiled almost wanly and ran her white claws through her hair.

"You turn to me for explanations?" the leader asked.

His eyes moved over Gabrielle and the dazed figure of Nicolas against her shoulder. Then returned to me.

"I could speak until the end of the world," he said, "and I could never tell you what you have destroyed here."

I thought the old queen made some derisive sound, but I was too engaged with him, the softness of his speech and the great raging anger within.

"Since the beginning of time," he said, "these mysteries have existed." He seemed small standing in this vast chamber, the voice issuing from him effortlessly, his hands limp at his sides. "Since the ancient days there have been our kind haunting the cities of man, preying upon him by night as God and the devil commanded us to do. The chosen of Satan we are, and those admitted to our ranks had first to prove themselves through a hundred crimes before the Dark Gift of immortality was given to them."

He came just a little nearer to me, the torchlight glimmering in his eyes.

"Before their loved ones they appeared to die," he said, "and with only a small infusion of our blood did they endure the terror of the coffin as they waited for us to come. Then and only then was the Dark Gift given, and they were sealed again in the grave after, until their thirst should give them the strength to break the narrow box and rise."

His voice grew slightly louder, more resonant.

"It was death they knew in those dark chambers," he said. "It was death and the power of evil they understood as they rose, breaking open the coffin, and the iron doors that held them in. And pity the weak, those who couldn't break out. Those whose wails brought mortals the day after —for none would answer by night. We gave no mercy to them.

"But those who rose, ah, those were the vampires who walked the earth, tested, purified, Children of Darkness, born of a fledgling's blood, never the full power of an ancient master, so that time would bring the wisdom to use the Dark Gifts before they grew truly strong. And on these were imposed the Rules of Darkness. To live among the dead, for we are dead things, returning always to one's own grave or one very nearly like it. To shun the places of light, luring victims away from the company of others to suffer death in unholy and haunted places. And to honor forever the power of God, the crucifix about the neck, the Sacraments. And never never to enter the House of God, lest he strike you powerless, casting you into hell, ending your reign on earth in blazing torment."

He paused. He looked at the old queen for the first time, and it seemed, though I could not truly tell, that her face maddened him.

"You scorn these things," he said to her. "Magnus scorned these things!" He commenced to tremble. "It was the nature of his madness, as it is the nature of yours, but I tell you you do not understand these mysteries! You shatter them like so much glass, but you have no strength, no power save ignorance. You break and that is all."

He turned away, hesitating as if he would not go on, and looking about at the vast crypt.

I heard the old vampire queen very softly singing.

She was chanting something under her breath, and she began to rock back and forth, her head to one side, her eyes dreamy. Once again, she looked beautiful.

"It is finished for my children," the leader whispered. "It is finished and done, for they know now they can disregard all of it. The things that bound us together, gave us the strength to endure as damned things! The mysteries that protected us here."

Again he looked at me.

"And you ask me for explanations as if it were inexplicable!" he said. "You, for whom the working of the Dark Trick is an act of shameless greed. You gave it to the very womb that bore you! Why not to this one, the devil's fiddler, whom you worship from afar every night?"

"Have I not told you?" sang the vampire queen. "Haven't we always known? There is nothing to fear in the Sign of the Cross, nor the Holy Water, nor the Sacrament itself . . ." She repeated the words, varying the melody under her breath, adding as she went on. "And the old rites, the incense, the fire, the vows spoken, when we thought we saw the Evil One in the dark, whispering . . ."

"Silence!" said the leader, dropping his voice. His hands almost went to his ears in a strangely human gesture. Like a boy he looked, almost lost. God, that our immortal bodies could be such varied prisons for us, that our immortal faces should be such masks for our true souls.

Again he fixed his eyes on me. I thought for a moment there would be another of those ghastly transformations or that some uncontrollable violence would come from him, and I hardened myself.

But he was imploring me silently.

Why did this come about! His voice almost dried in his throat as he repeated it aloud, as he tried to curb his rage. "You explain to me! Why you, you with the strength of ten vampires and the courage of a hell full of devils, crashing through the world in your brocade and your leather boots! Lelio, the actor from the House of Thesbians, making us into grand drama on the boulevard! Tell me! Tell me why!"

"It was Magnus's strength, Magnus's genius," sang the woman vampire with the most wistful smile.

"No!" He shook his head. "I tell you, he is beyond all account. He knows no limit and so he has no limit. But why!"

He moved just a little closer, not seeming to walk but to come more clearly into focus as an apparition might.

"Why you," he demanded, "with the boldness to walk their streets, break their locks, call them by name. They dress your hair, they fit your clothes! You gamble at their tables! Deceiving them, embracing them, drinking their blood only steps from where other mortals laugh and dance. You who shun cemeteries and burst from crypts in churches. Why you! Thoughtless, arrogant, ignorant, and disdainful! You give *me* the explanation. Answer me!"

My heart was racing. My face was warm and pulsing with blood. I was in no fear of him now, but I was angry beyond all mortal anger, and I didn't fully understand why.

His mind—I had wanted to pierce his mind—and this is what I heard, this superstition, this absurdity. He was no sublime spirit who understood what his followers had not. He had not believed it. He had believed *in* it, a thousand times worse!

And I realized quite clearly what he was—not demon or angel at all, but a sensibility forged in a dark time when the small orb of the sun traveled the dome of the heavens, and the stars were no more than tiny lanterns describing gods and goddesses upon a closed night. A time when man was the center of this great world in which we roam, a time when for every question there had been an answer. That was what he was, a child of olden days when witches had danced beneath the moon and knights had battled dragons.

Ah, sad lost child, roaming the catacombs beneath a great city and an incomprehensible century. Maybe your mortal form is more fitting than I supposed.

But there was no time to mourn for him, beautiful as he was. Those entombed in the walls suffered at his command. Those he had sent out of the chamber could be called back.

I had to think of a reply to his question that he would be able to accept. The truth wasn't enough. It had to be arranged poetically the way that the old thinkers would have arranged it in the world before the age of reason had come to be.

"My answer?" I said softly. I was gathering my thoughts and I could almost feel Gabrielle's warning, Nicki's fear. "I'm no dealer in mysteries," I said, "no lover of philosophy. But it's plain enough what has happened here."

He studied me with a strange earnestness.

"If you fear so much the power of God," I said, "then the teachings of the Church aren't unknown to you. You must know that the forms of goodness change with the ages, that there are saints for all times under heaven."

Visibly he hearkened to this, warmed to the words I used.

"In ancient days," I said, "there were martyrs who quenched the flames that sought to burn them, mystics who rose into the air as they heard the voice of God. But as the world changed, so changed the saints. What are they now but obedient nuns and priests? They build hospitals and orphanages, but they do not call down the angels to rout armies or tame the savage beast."

I could see no change in him but I pressed on.

"And so it is with evil, obviously. It changes its form. How many men in this age believe in the crosses that frighten your followers? Do you think mortals above are speaking to each other of heaven and hell? Philosophy is what they talk about, and science! What does it matter to them if white-faced haunts prowl a churchyard after dark? A few more murders in a wilderness of murders? How can this be of interest to God or the devil or to man?"

I heard again the old queen vampire laughing.

But Armand didn't speak or move.

"Even your playground is about to be taken from you," I continued. "This cemetery in which you hide is about to be removed altogether from Paris. Even the bones of our ancestors are no longer sacred in this secular age."

His face softened suddenly. He couldn't conceal his shock.

"Les Innocents destroyed!" he whispered. "You're lying to me . . ."

"I never lie," I said offhand. "At least not to those I don't love. The people of Paris don't want the stench of graveyards around them anymore. The emblems of the dead don't matter to them as they matter to you. Within a few years, markets, streets, and houses will cover this spot. Commerce. Practicality. That is the eighteenth-century world."

"Stop!" he whispered. "Les Innocents has existed as long as I have existed!" His boyish face was strained. The old queen was undisturbed.

"Don't you see?" I said softly. "It is a new age. It requires a new evil. And I *am* that new evil." I paused, watching him. "I am the vampire for these times."

He had not foreseen my point. And I saw in him for the first time a glimmer of terrible understanding, the first glimmer of real fear.

I made a small accepting gesture.

"This incident in the village church tonight," I said cautiously, "it was vulgar, I'm inclined to agree. My actions on the stage of theater, worse still. But these were blunders. And you know they aren't the source of your rancor. Forget them for the moment and try to envision my beauty and my power. Try to see the evil that I am. I stalk the world in mortal dress—the worst of fiends, the monster who looks exactly like everyone else."

The woman vampire made a low song of her laughter. I could feel only pain from him, and from her the warm emanation of her love.

"Think of it, Armand," I pressed carefully. "Why should Death lurk in the shadows? Why should Death wait at the gate? There is no bedchamber, no ballroom that I cannot enter. Death in the glow of the hearth, Death on tiptoe in the corridor, that is what I am. Speak to me of the Dark Gifts—I use them. I'm Gentleman Death in silk and lace, come to put out the candles. The canker in the heart of the rose."

There was a faint moan from Nicolas.

I think I heard Armand sigh.

"There is no place where they can hide from me," I said, "these godless and powerful ones who would destroy les Innocents. There is no lock that can keep me out."

He stared back at me silently. He appeared sad and calm. His eyes were darkened slightly, but they were untroubled by malice or rage. He didn't speak for a long moment, and then:

"A splendid mission, that," he said, "to devil them mercilessly as you live among them. But it's you still who don't understand."

"How so?" I asked.

"You can't endure in the world, living among men, you cannot survive."

"But I do," I said simply. "The old mysteries have given way to a new *style.* And who knows what will follow? There's no romance in what you are. There is great romance in what I am!"

"You can't be that strong," he said. "You don't know what you're saying, you have only just come into being, you are young."

"He is very strong, however, this child," mused the queen, "and so is his beautiful newborn companion. They are fiends of high-blown ideas and great reason, these two."

"You can't live among men!" Armand insisted again.

His face colored for one second. But he wasn't my enemy now; rather he was some wondering elder struggling to tell me a critical truth. And at the same moment he seemed a child imploring me, and in that struggle lay his essence, parent and child, pleading with me to listen to what he had to say.

"And why not? I tell you I belong among men. It is their blood that makes me immortal."

"Ah, yes, immortal, but you have not begun to understand it," he said. "It's no more than a word. Study the fate of your maker. Why did Magnus go into the flames? It's an age-old truth among us, and you haven't even guessed it. Live among men, and the passing years will drive you to madness. To see others grow old and die, to see kingdoms rise and fall, to lose all you understand and cherish—who can endure it? It will drive you to idiot raving and despair. Your own immortal kind is your protection, your *salvation.* The ancient ways, don't you see, which *never changed*!"

He stopped, shocked that he had used this word, salvation, and it reverberated through the room, his lips shaping it again.

"Armand," the old queen sang softly. "Madness may come to the eldest we know, whether they keep to the old ways or abandon them." She made a gesture as if to attack him with her white claws, screeching with laughter as he stared coldly back. "I have kept to the old ways as long as you have and I am mad, am I not? Perhaps that is why I have kept them so well!"

He shook his head angrily in protest. Was he not the living proof it need not be so?

But she drew near to me and took hold of my arm, turning my face towards her.

"Did Magnus tell you nothing, child?" she asked.

I felt an immense power flowing from her.

"While others prowled this sacred place," she said, "I went alone across the snow-covered fields to find Magnus. My strength is so great now it is as if I have wings. I climbed to his window to find him in his chamber, and together we walked the battlements unseen by all save the distant stars."

She drew even closer, her grip tightening.

"Many things, Magnus knew," she said. "And it is not madness which is your enemy, not if you are really strong. The vampire who leaves his coven to dwell among human beings faces a dreadful hell long before madness comes. He grows irresistibly to love mortals! He comes to *understand* all things in love."

"Let me go," I whispered softly. Her glance was holding me as surely as her hands.

"With the passage of time he comes to know mortals as they may never know each other," she continued, undaunted, her eyebrows rising, "and finally there comes the moment when he cannot bear to take life, or bear to make suffering, and nothing but madness or his own death will ease his pain. That is the fate of the old ones which Magnus described to me, Magnus who suffered all afflictions in the end."

At last she released me. She receded from me as if she were an image in a sailor's glass.

"I don't believe what you're saying," I whispered. But the whisper was like a hiss. "Magnus? Love mortals?"

"Of course you do not," she said with her graven jester's smile.

Armand, too, was looking at her as if he did not understand.

"My words have no meaning now," she added. "But you have *all the time in the world* to understand!"

Laughter, howling laughter, scraping the ceiling of the crypt. Cries again from within the walls. She threw back her head with her laughter.

Armand was horror-stricken as he watched her. It was as if he saw the laughter emanating from her like so much glittering light.

"No, but it's a lie, a hideous simplification!" I said. My head was throbbing suddenly. My eyes were throbbing. "I mean it's a concept born out of moral idiocy, this idea of love!"

I put my hands to my temples. A deadly pain in me was growing. The pain was dimming my vision, sharpening my memory of Magnus's dungeon, the mortal prisoners who had died among the rotted bodies of those condemned before them in the stinking crypt.

Armand looked to me now as if I were torturing him as the old queen tortured him with her laughter. And her laughter went right on, rising and falling away. Armand's hands went out towards me as if he would touch me but did not dare.

All the rapture and pain I'd known in these past months came together inside me. I felt quite suddenly as if I would begin to roar as I had that night on Renaud's stage. I was aghast at these sensations. I was murmuring nonsense syllables again aloud.

"Lestat!" Gabrielle whispered.

"Love mortals?" I said. I stared at the old queen's inhuman face, horrified suddenly to see the black eyelashes like spikes about her glistening eyes, her flesh like animated marble. "Love mortals? Does it take you three hundred years!" I glared at Gabrielle. "From the first nights when I held them close to me, I loved them. Drinking up their life, their death, I love them. Dear God, is that not the very essence of the Dark Gift?"

My voice was growing in volume as it had that night in the theater. "Oh, what are you that you do not? What vile things that this is the sum of your wisdom, the simple capacity to feel!"

I backed away from them, looking about me at this giant tomb, the damp earth arching over our heads. The place was passing out of the material into an hallucination.

"God, do you lose your reason with the Dark Trick," I asked, "with your rituals, your sealing up of the fledglings in the grave? Or were you monsters when you were living? How could we not all of us love mortals with every breath we take!"

No answer. Except the senseless cries of the starving ones. No answer. Just the dim beating of Nicki's heart.

"Well, hear me, whatever the case," I said.

I pointed my finger at Armand, at the old queen.

"I never promised my soul to the devil for this! And when I made this one it was to save her from the worms that eat the corpses around here. If loving mortals is the hell you speak of, I am already in it. I have met my fate. Leave me to it and all scores are settled now."

My voice had broken. I was gasping. I ran my hands back through my hair. Armand seemed to shimmer as he came close to me. His face was a miracle of seeming purity and awe.

"Dead things, dead things . . ." I said. "Come no closer. Talking of madness and love, in this reeking place! And that old monster, Magnus, locking them up in his dungeon. How did he love them, his captives? The way boys love butterflies when they rip off their wings!"

"No, child, you think you understand but you do not," sang the woman vampire unperturbed. "You have only just begun your loving." She gave a soft lilting laugh. "You feel sorry for them, that is all. And for yourself that you cannot be both human and inhuman. Isn't it so?"

"Lies!" I said. I moved closer to Gabrielle. I put my arm around her.

"You will come to understand all things in love," the old queen went on, "when you are a vicious and hateful thing. This is your immortality, child. Ever deeper understanding of it." And throwing up her arms, again she howled.

"Damn you," I said. I picked up Gabrielle and Nicki and carried them backwards towards the door. "You're in hell already," I said, "and I intend to leave you in hell now."

I took Nicolas out of Gabrielle's arms and we ran through the catacomb towards the stairs.

The old queen was in a frenzy of keening laughter behind us.

And human as Orpheus perhaps, I stopped and glanced back.

"Lestat, hurry!" Nicolas whispered in my ear. And Gabrielle gave a desperate gesture for me to come.

Armand had not moved, and the old woman stood beside him laughing still.

"Good-bye, brave children," she cried. "Ride the Devil's Road bravely. Ride the Devil's Road as long as you can."

THE coven scattered like frightened ghosts in the cold rain as we burst out of the sepulcher. And baffled, they watched as we sped out of les Innocents into the crowded Paris streets.

Within moments we had stolen a carriage and were on our way out of the city into the countryside.

I DROVE the team on relentlessly. Yet I was so mortally tired that preternatural strength seemed purely an idea. At every thicket and turn of the road I expected to see the filthy demons surrounding us again.

But somehow I managed to get from a country inn the food and drink Nicolas would need, and the blankets to keep him warm.

He was unconscious long before we reached the tower, and I carried him up the stairs to that high cell where Magnus had first kept me.

His throat was still swollen and bruised from their feasting on him. And though he slept deeply as I laid him on the straw bed, I could feel the thirst in him, the awful craving that I'd felt after Magnus had drunk from me.

Well, there was plenty of wine for him when he awakened, and plenty of food. And I knew—though how I couldn't tell—that he wouldn't die.

What his daylight hours would be like, I could hardly imagine. But he would be safe once I turned the key in the lock. And no matter what he had been to me, or what he stood to be in the future, no mortal could wander free in my lair while I slept.

Beyond that I couldn't reason. I felt like a mortal walking in his sleep.

I was still staring down at him, hearing his vague jumbled dreams—dreams of the horrors of les Innocents—when Gabrielle came in. She had finished burying the poor unfortunate stable boy, and she looked like a dusty angel again, her hair stiff and tangled and full of delicate fractured light.

She looked down at Nicki for a long moment and then she drew me out of the room. After I had locked the door, she led me down to the lower crypt. There she put her arms tightly around me and held me, as if she too were worn almost to collapse.

"Listen to me," she said finally, drawing back and putting her hands up to hold my face. "We'll get him out of France as soon as we rise. No one will ever believe his mad tales."

I didn't answer. I could scarce understand her, her reasoning or her intentions. My head swam.

"You can play the puppeteer with him," she said, "as you did with Renaud's actors. You can send him off to the New World."

"Sleep," I whispered. I kissed her open mouth. I held her with my eyes closed. I saw the crypt again, heard their strange, inhuman voices. All this would not stop.

"After he's gone, then we can talk about these others," she said calmly. "Whether to leave Paris altogether for a while . . . "

I let her go, and I turned away from her and I went to the sarcophagus and rested for a moment against the stone lid. For the first time in my immortal life I wanted the silence of the tomb, the feeling that all things were out of my hands.

It seemed she said something else then. *Do not do this thing!*

4

WHEN I awoke I heard his cries. He was beating on the oaken door, cursing me for keeping him prisoner. The sound filled the tower, and the scent of him came through the stone walls: succulent, oh so succulent, smell of living flesh and blood, his flesh and blood.

She slept still.

Do not do this thing.

Symphony of malice, symphony of madness coming through the walls, philosophy straining to contain the ghastly images, the torture, to surround it with language . . .

When I stepped into the stairwell, it was like being caught in a whirlwind of his cries, his human smell.

And all the remembered scents mingled with it—the afternoon sunshine on a wooden table, the red wine, the smoke of the little fire.

"Lestat! Do you hear me! Lestat!" Thunder of fists against the door.

Memory of childhood fairy tale: the giant says he smells the blood of a human in his lair. Horror. I knew the giant was going to find the human. I could hear him coming after the human, step by step. I was the human.

Only no more.

Smoke and salt of flesh and pumping blood.

"This is the witches' place! Lestat, do you hear me! This is the witches' place!"

Dull tremor of the old secrets between us, the love, the things that only we had known, felt. Dancing in the witches' place. Can you deny it? Can you deny everything that passed between us?

Get him out of France. Send him to the New World. And then what? All his life he is one of those slightly interesting but generally tiresome mortals who have seen spirits, talk of them incessantly, and no one believes him. Deepening madness. Will he be a comical lunatic finally, the kind that even the ruffians and bullies look after, playing his fiddle in a dirty coat for the crowds on the streets of Port-au-Prince?

"Be the puppeteer again," she had said. Is that what I was? *No one will ever believe his mad tales.*

But he knows the place where we lie, Mother. He knows our names, the name of our kin—too many things about us. And he will never go quietly to another country. And *they* may go after him; *they* will never let him live now.

Where are *they*?

I went up the stairs in the whirlwind of his echoing cries, looked out the little barred window at the open land. They'll be coming again. They have to come. First I was alone, then I had her with me, and now I have them!

But what was the crux? That he wanted it? That he had screamed over and over that I had denied him the power?

Or was it that I now had the excuses I needed to bring him to me as I had wanted to do from the first moment? My Nicolas, my love. Eternity waits. All the great and splendid pleasures of being dead.

I went further up the stairs towards him and the thirst sang in me. To hell with his cries. The thirst sang and I was an instrument of its singing.

And his cries had become inarticulate—the pure essence of his curses, a dull punctuation to the misery that I could hear without need of any sound. Something divinely carnal in the broken syllables coming from his lips, like the low gush of the blood through his heart.

I lifted the key and put it in the lock and he went silent, his thoughts washing backwards and into him as if the ocean could be sucked back into the tiny mysterious coils of a single shell.

I tried to see *him* in the shadows of the room, and not *it*—the love for him, the aching, wrenching months of longing for him, the hideous and unshakable human need for him, the lust. I tried to see the mortal who didn't know what he was saying as he glared at me:

"You, and your talk of goodness"—low seething voice, eyes glittering—"your talk of good and evil, your talk of what was right and what was wrong and death, oh yes, death, the horror, the tragedy . . ."

Words. Borne on the ever swelling current of hatred, like flowers opening in the current, petals peeling back, then falling apart:

". . . and you shared it with her, the lord's son giveth to the lord's wife his great gift, the Dark Gift. Those who live in the castle share the Dark Gift—never were they dragged to the witches' place where the human grease pools on the ground at the foot of the burnt stake, no, kill the old crone who can no longer see to sew, and the idiot boy who cannot till the field. And what does he give us, the lord's son, the wolfkiller, the one who screamed in the witches' place? Coin of the realm! That's good enough for us!"

Shuddering. Shirt soaked with sweat. Gleam of taut flesh through the torn lace. Tantalizing, the mere sight of it, the narrow tightly muscled torso that sculptors so love to represent, nipples pink against the dark skin.

"This power"—sputtering as if all day long he had been saying the words over with the same intensity, and it does not really matter that now I am present—"this power that made all the lies meaningless, this dark power that soared over everything, this truth that obliterated . . ."

No. Language. Not truth.

The wine bottles were empty, the food devoured. His lean arms were hardened and tense for the struggle—but what struggle?—his brown hair fallen out of its ribbon, his eyes enormous and glazed.

But suddenly he pushed against the wall as if he'd go through it to get away from me—dim remembrance of their drinking from him, the paralysis, the ecstasy—yet he was drawn immediately forward again, staggering, putting his hands out to steady himself by taking hold of things that were not there.

But his voice had stopped.

Something breaking in his face.

"How could you keep it from me!" he whispered. Thoughts of old magic, luminous legend, some great eerie strata in which all the shadowy things thrived, an intoxication with forbidden knowledge in which the natural things become unimportant. No miracle anymore to the leaves falling from the autumn trees, the sun in the orchard.

No.

The scent was rising from him like incense, like the heat and the smoke of church candles rising. Heart thumping under the skin of his naked chest. Tight little belly glistening with sweat, sweat staining the thick leather belt. Blood full of salt. I could scarce breathe.

And we do breathe. We breathe and we taste and we smell and we feel and we thirst.

"You have misunderstood everything." Is this Lestat speaking? It sounded like some other demon, some loathsome thing for whom the voice was the imitation of a human voice. "You have misunderstood everything that you have seen and heard."

"I would have shared anything I possessed with you!" Rage building again. He reached out. "It was you who never understood," he whispered.

"Take your life and leave with it. Run."

"Don't you see it's the confirmation of everything? That it exists is the confirmation—pure evil, sublime evil!" Triumph in his eyes. He reached out suddenly and closed his hand on my face.

"Don't taunt me!" I said. I struck him so hard he fell backwards, chastened, silent. "When it was offered me I said no. I tell you I said no. With my last breath, I said no."

"You were always the fool," he said. "I told you that." But he was breaking down. He was shuddering and the rage was alchemizing into desperation. He lifted his arms again and then stopped. "You believed things that didn't matter," he said almost gently. "There was something you failed to see. Is it possible you don't know yourself what you possess now?" The glaze over his eyes broke instantly into tears.

His face knotted. Unspoken words coming from him of love.

And an awful self-consciousness came over me. Silent and lethal, I felt myself flooded with the power I had over him and his knowledge of it, and my love for him heated the sense of power, driving it towards a scorching embarrassment which suddenly changed into something else.

We were in the wings of the theater again; we were in the village in Auvergne in that little inn. I smelled not merely the blood in him, but the sudden terror. He had taken a step back. And the very movement stoked the blaze in me, as much as the vision of his stricken face.

He grew smaller, more fragile. Yet he'd never seemed stronger, more alluring than he was now.

All the expression drained from his face as I drew nearer. His eyes were wondrously clear. And his mind was opening as Gabrielle's mind had opened, and for one tiny second there flared a moment of us together in the garret, talking and talking as the moon glared on the snow-covered roofs, or walking through the Paris streets, passing the wine back and forth, heads bowed against the first gust of winter rain, and there had been the eternity of growing up and growing old before us, and so much joy even in misery, even in the misery—the real eternity, the real forever—the mortal mystery of that. But the moment faded in the shimmering expression of his face.

"Come to me, Nicki," I whispered. I lifted both hands to beckon. "If you want it, you must come . . . "

I SAW a bird soaring out of a cave above the open sea. And there was something terrifying about the bird and the endless waves over which it flew. Higher and higher it went and the sky turned to silver and then gradually the silver faded and the sky went dark. The darkness of evening, nothing to fear, really, nothing. Blessed darkness. But it was falling gradually and inexorably over nothing save this one tiny creature cawing in the wind above a great wasteland that was the world. Empty caves, empty sands, empty sea.

All I had ever loved to look upon, or listen to, or felt with my hands was gone, or never existed, and the bird, circling and gliding, flew on and on, upwards past me, or more truly past no one, holding the entire landscape, without history or meaning, in the flat blackness of one tiny eye.

I screamed but without a sound. I felt my mouth full of blood and each swallow passing down my throat and into fathomless thirst. And I wanted to say, yes, I understand now, I understand how terrible, how unbearable, this darkness. I didn't know. Couldn't know. The bird sailing on through the darkness over the barren shore, the seamless sea. Dear God, stop it. Worse than the horror in the inn. Worse than the helpless trumpeting of the fallen horse in the snow. But the blood was the blood after all, and the heart—the luscious heart that was all hearts—was right there, on tiptoe against my lips.

Now, my love, now's the moment. I can swallow the life that beats from your heart and send you into the oblivion in which nothing may ever be understood or forgiven, or I can bring you to me.

I pushed him backwards. I held him to me like a crushed thing. But the vision wouldn't stop.

His arms slipped around my neck, his face wet, eyes rolling up into his head. Then his tongue shot out. It licked hard at the gash I had made for him in my own throat. Yes, eager.

But please stop this vision. Stop the upward flight and the great slant of the colorless landscape, the cawing that meant nothing over the howl of the wind. The pain is nothing compared to this darkness. I don't want to . . . I don't want to . . .

But it was dissolving. Slowly dissolving.

And finally it was finished. The veil of silence had come down, as it had with her. Silence. He was separate. And I was holding him away from me, and he was almost falling, his hands to his mouth, the blood running down his chin in rivulets. His mouth was open and a dry sound came out of it, in spite of the blood, a dry scream.

And beyond him, and beyond the remembered vision of the metallic sea and the lone bird who was its only witness—I saw her in the doorway and her hair was a Virgin Mary veil of gold around her shoulders, and she said with the saddest expression on her face:

"Disaster, my son."

BY MIDNIGHT it was clear that he would not speak or answer to any voice, or move of his own volition. He remained still and expressionless in the places to which he was taken. If the death pained him he gave no sign. If the new vision delighted him, he kept it to himself. Not even the thirst moved him.

And it was Gabrielle who, after studying him quietly for hours, took him in hand, cleaning him and putting new clothes on him. Black wool she chose, one of the few somber coats I owned. And modest linen that made him look oddly like a young cleric, a little too serious, a little naive.

And in the silence of the crypt as I watched them, I knew without doubt that they could hear each other's thoughts. Without a word she guided him through the grooming. Without a word she sent him back to the bench by the fire.

Finally, she said, "He should hunt now," and when she glanced at him, he rose without looking at her as if pulled by a string.

Numbly I watched them going. Heard their feet on the stairs. And then I crept up after them, stealthily, and holding to the bars of the gate I watched them move, two feline spirits, across the field.

The emptiness of the night was an indissoluble cold settling over me, closing me in. Not even the fire on the hearth warmed me when I returned to it.

Emptiness here. And the quiet I had told myself that I wanted—just to be alone after the grisly struggle in Paris. Quiet, and the realization, which I could not bring myself to confess to her, the realization gnawing at my insides like a starved animal—*that I couldn't stand the sight of him now.*

5

WHEN I opened my eyes the next night, I knew what I meant to do. Whether or not I could stand to look at him wasn't important. I had made him this, and I had to rouse him from his stupor somehow.

The hunt hadn't changed him, though apparently he'd drunk and killed well enough. And now it was up to me to protect him from the revulsion I felt, and to go into Paris and get the one thing that might bring him around.

The violin was all he'd ever loved when he was alive. Maybe now it would awaken him. I'd put it in his hands, and he'd want to play it again, he'd want to play it with his new skill, and everything would change and the chill in my heart would somehow melt.

As SOON as Gabrielle rose I told her what I meant to do.

"But what about the others?" she said. "You can't go riding into Paris alone."

"Yes, I can," I said. "You're needed here with him. If the little pests should come round, they could lure him into the open, the way he is now. And besides, I want to know what's happening under les Innocents. If we have a real truce, I want to know."

"I don't like your going," she said, shaking her head. "I tell you, if I didn't believe we should speak to the leader again, that we had things to learn from him and the old woman, I'd be for leaving Paris tonight."

"And what could they possibly teach us?" I said coldly. "That the sun really revolves around the earth? That the earth is flat?" But the bitterness of my words made me feel ashamed.

One thing they could tell me was why the vampires I'd made could hear each other's thoughts when I could not. But I was too crestfallen over my loathing of Nicki to think of all these things.

I only looked at her and thought how glorious it had been to see the Dark Trick work its magic in her, to see it restore her youthful beauty, render her again the goddess she'd been to me when I was a little child. To see Nicki change had been to see him die.

Maybe without reading the words in my soul she understood it only too well.

We embraced slowly. "Be careful," she said.

* * *

I SHOULD have gone to the flat right away to look for his violin. And there was still my poor Roget to deal with. Lies to tell. And this matter of getting out of Paris—it seemed more and more the thing for us to do.

But for hours I did just what I wanted. I hunted the Tuileries and the boulevards, pretending there was no coven under les Innocents, that Nicki was alive still and safe somewhere, that Paris was all mine again.

But I was listening for them every moment. I was thinking about the old queen. And I heard them when I least expected it, on the boulevard du Temple, as I drew near to Renaud's.

Strange that they'd be in the places of light, as they called them. But within seconds, I knew that several of them were hiding behind the theater. And there was no malice this time, only a desperate excitement when they sensed that I was near.

Then I saw the white face of the woman vampire, the dark-eyed pretty one with the witch's hair. She was in the alleyway beside the stage door, and she darted forward to beckon to me.

I rode back and forth for a few moments. The boulevard was the usual spring evening panorama: hundreds of strollers amid the stream of carriage traffic, lots of street musicians, jugglers and tumblers, the lighted theaters with their doors open to invite the crowd. Why should I leave it to talk to these creatures? I listened. There were four of them actually, and they were desperately waiting for me to come. They were in terrible fear.

All right. I turned the horse and rode into the alley and all the way to the back where they hovered together against the stone wall.

The gray-eyed boy was there, which surprised me, and he had a dazed expression on his face. A tall blond male vampire stood behind him with a handsome woman, both of them swathed in rags like lepers. It was the pretty one, the dark-eyed one who had laughed at my little jest on the stairs under les Innocents, who spoke:

"You have to help us!" she whispered.

"I do?" I tried to steady the mare. She didn't like their company. "Why do I have to help you?" I demanded.

"He's destroying the coven," she said.

"Destroying us . . ." the boy said. But he didn't look at me. He was staring at the stones in front of him, and from his mind I caught flashes of what was happening, of the pyre lighted, of Armand forcing his followers into the fire.

I tried to get this out of my head. But the images were now coming from all of them. The dark-eyed pretty one looked directly into my eyes as she strove to sharpen the pictures—Armand swinging a great charred beam of wood as he drove the others into the blaze, then stabbing them down into the flames with the beam as they struggled to escape.

"Good Lord, there were twelve of you!" I said. "Couldn't you fight?"

"We did and we are here," said the woman. "He burned six together, and the rest of us fled. In terror, we sought strange resting places for the day. We had never done this before, slept away from our sacred graves. We didn't know what would happen to us. And when we rose he was there. Another two he managed to destroy. So we are all that is left. He has even broken open the deep chambers and burned the starved ones. He has broken loose the earth to block the tunnels to our meeting place."

The boy looked up slowly.

"You did this to us," he whispered. "You have brought us all down."

The woman stepped in front of him.

"You must help us," she said. "Make a new coven with us. Help us to exist as you exist." She glanced impatiently at the boy.

"But the old woman, the great one?" I asked.

"It was she who commenced it," said the boy bitterly. "She threw herself into the fire. She said she would go to join Magnus. She was laughing. It was then that he drove the others into the flames as we fled."

I bowed my head. So she was gone. And all she had known and witnessed had gone with her, and what had she left behind but the simple one, the vengeful one, the wicked child who believed what she had known to be false.

"You must help us," said the dark-eyed woman. "You see, it's his right as coven master to destroy those who are weak, those who can't survive."

"He couldn't let the coven fall into chaos," said the other woman vampire who stood behind the boy. "Without the faith in the Dark Ways, the others might have blundered, alarmed the mortal populace. But if you help us to form a new coven, to perfect ourselves in new ways . . ."

"We are the strongest of the coven," said the man. "And if we can fend him off long enough, and manage to continue without him, then in time he may leave us alone."

"He will destroy us," the boy muttered. "He will never leave us alone. He will lie in wait for the moment when we separate . . ."

"He isn't invincible," said the tall male. "And he's lost all conviction. Remember that."

"And you have Magnus's tower, a safe place . . ." said the boy despairingly as he looked up at me.

"No, that I can't share with you," I said. "You have to win this battle on your own."

"But surely you can guide us . . ." said the man.

"You don't need me," I said. "What have you already learned from my example? What did you learn from the things I said last night?"

"We learned more from what you said to him afterwards," said the dark-eyed woman. "We heard you speak to him of a new evil, an evil for these times destined to move through the world in handsome human guise."

"So take on the guise," I said. "Take the garments of your victims, and take the money from their pockets. And you can then move among mortals as I do. In time you can gain enough wealth to acquire your own little fortress, your secret sanctuary. Then you will no longer be beggars or ghosts."

I could see the desperation in their faces. Yet they listened attentively.

"But our skin, the timbre of our voices . . ." said the dark-eyed woman.

"You can fool mortals. It's very easy. It just takes a little skill."

"But how do we start?" said the boy dully, as if he were only reluctantly being brought into it. "What sort of mortals do we pretend to be?"

"Choose for yourself!" I said. "Look around you. Masquerade as gypsies if you will—that oughtn't to be too difficult—or better yet mummers," I glanced towards the lights of the boulevard.

"Mummers!" said the dark-eyed woman with a little spark of excitement.

"Yes, actors. Street performers. Acrobats. Make yourselves acrobats. Surely you've seen them out there. You can cover your white faces with greasepaint, and your extravagant gestures and facial expressions won't even be noticed. You couldn't choose a more nearly perfect disguise than that. On the boulevard you'll see every manner of mortal that dwells in this city. You'll learn all you need to know."

She laughed and glanced at the others. The man was deep in thought, the other woman musing, the boy unsure.

"With your powers, you can become jugglers and tumblers easily," I said. "It would be nothing for you. You could be seen by thousands who'd never guess what you are."

"That isn't what happened with you on the stage of this little theater," said the boy coldly. "You put terror into their hearts."

"Because I chose to do it," I said. Tremor of pain. "That's my tragedy. But I can fool anyone when I want to and so can you."

I reached into my pockets and drew out a handful of gold crowns. I gave them to the dark-eyed woman. She took them in both hands and stared at them as if they were burning her. She looked up and in her eyes I saw the image of myself on Renaud's stage performing those ghastly feats that had driven the crowd into the streets.

But she had another thought in her mind. She knew the theater was abandoned, that I'd sent the troupe off.

And for one second, I considered it, letting the pain double itself and pass through me, wondering if the others could feel it. What did it really matter, after all?

"Yes, please," said the pretty one. She reached up and touched my hand with her cool white fingers. "Let us inside the theater! Please." She turned and looked at the back doors of Renaud's.

Let them inside. Let them dance on my grave.

But there might be old costumes there still, the discarded trappings of a troupe that had had all the money in the world to buy itself new finery. Old pots of white paint. Water still in the barrels. A thousand treasures left behind in the haste of departure.

I was numb, unable to consider all of it, unwilling to reach back to embrace all that had happened there.

"Very well," I said, looking away as if some little thing had distracted me. "You can go into the theater if you wish. You can use whatever is there."

She drew closer and pressed her lips suddenly to the back of my hand.

"We won't forget this," she said. "My name is Eleni, this boy is Laurent, the man here is Félix, and the woman with him, Eugénie. If Armand moves against you, he moves against us."

"I hope you prosper," I said, and strangely enough, I meant it. I wondered if any of them, with all their Dark Ways and Dark Rituals, had ever really wanted this nightmare that we all shared. They'd been drawn into it as I had, really. And we were all Children of Darkness now, for better or worse.

"But be wise in what you do here," I warned. "Never bring victims here or kill near here. Be clever and keep your hiding place safe."

It was three o'clock before I rode over the bridge on to the Ile St.-Louis. I had wasted enough time. And now I had to find the violin.

But as soon as I approached Nicki's house on the quai I saw that something was wrong. The windows were empty. All the drapery had been pulled down, and yet the place was full of light, as if candles were burning inside by the hundreds. Most strange. Roget couldn't have taken possession of the flat yet. Not enough time had passed to assume that Nicki had met with foul play.

Quickly, I went up over the roof and down the wall to the courtyard window, and saw that the drapery had been stripped away there too.

And candles were burning in all the candelabra and in the wall sconces. And some were even stuck in their own wax on the pianoforte and the desk. The room was in total disarray.

Every book had been pulled off the shelf. And some of the books were in fragments, pages broken out. Even the music had been emptied sheet by sheet onto the carpet, and all the pictures were lying about on the tables with other small possessions—coins, money, keys.

Perhaps the demons had wrecked the place when they took Nicki. But who had lighted all these candles? It didn't make sense.

I listened. No one in the flat. Or so it seemed. But then I heard not thoughts, but tiny sounds. I narrowed my eyes for a moment, just concentrating, and it came to me that I was hearing pages turn, and then something being dropped. More pages turning, stiff, old parchment pages. Then again the book dropped.

I raised the window as quietly as I could. The little sounds continued, but no scent of human, no pulse of thought.

Yet there was a smell here. Something stronger than the stale tobacco and the candle wax. The smell the vampires carried with them from the cemetery soil.

More candles in the hallway. Candles in the bedroom and the same disarray, books open as they lay in careless piles, the bedclothes snarled, the pictures in a heap. Cabinets emptied, drawers pulled out.

And no violin anywhere, I managed to note that.

And those little sounds coming from another room, pages being turned very fast.

Whoever he was—and of course I knew who he had to be—he did not give a damn that I was there! He had not even stopped to take a breath.

I went farther down the hall and stood in the door of the library and found myself staring right at him as he continued with his task.

It was Armand, of course. Yet I was hardly prepared for the sight he presented here.

Candle wax dripped down the marble bust of Caesar, flowed over the brightly painted countries of the world globe. And the books, they lay in mountains on the carpet, save for those of the very last shelf in the corner where he stood, in his old rags still, hair full of dust, ignoring me as he ran his hand over page after page, his eyes intent on the words before him, his lips half open, his expression like that of an insect in its concentration as it chews through a leaf.

Perfectly horrible he looked, actually. He was sucking everything out of the books!

Finally he let this one drop and took down another, and opened it and started devouring it in the same manner, fingers moving down the sentences with preternatural speed.

And I realized that he had been examining everything in the flat in this fashion, even the bed sheets and curtains, the pictures that had been taken off their hooks, the contents of cupboards and drawers. But from the books, he was taking concentrated knowledge. Everything from Caesar's *Gallic Wars* to modern English novels lay on the floor.

But his manner wasn't the entire horror. It was the havoc he was leaving behind him, the utter disregard of everything he used.

And his utter disregard of me.

He finished his latest book, or broke off from it, and went to the old newspapers stacked on a lower shelf.

I found myself backing out of the room and away from him, staring numbly at his small dirty figure. His auburn hair shimmered despite the dirt in it; his eyes burned like two lights.

Grotesque he seemed, among all the candles and the swimming colors of the flat, this filthy waif of the netherworld, and yet his beauty held sway. He hadn't needed the shadows of Notre Dame or the torchlight of the crypt to flatter him. And there was a fierceness in him in this bright light that I hadn't seen before.

I felt an overwhelming confusion. He was both dangerous and compelling. I could have looked on him forever, but an overpowering instinct said: Get away. Leave the place to him if he wants it. What does it matter now?

The violin. I tried desperately to think about the violin. To stop watching the movement of his hands over the words in front of him, the relentless focus of his eyes.

But these things were putting me in a trance.

I turned my back on him and went into the parlor. My hands were trembling. I could hardly endure knowing he was there. I searched everywhere and didn't find the damned violin. What could Nicki have done with it? I couldn't think.

Pages turning, paper crinkling. Soft sound of the newspaper dropping to the floor.

Go back to the tower at once.

I went to pass the library quickly, when without warning his soundless voice shot out and stopped me. It was like a hand touching my throat. I turned and saw him staring at me.

Do you love them, your silent children? Do they love you? That was what he asked, the sense disentangling itself from an endless echo.

I felt the blood rise to my face. The heat spread out over me like a mask as I looked at him.

All the books in the room were now on the floor. He was a haunt standing in the ruins, a visitant from the devil he believed in. Yet his face was so tender, so young.

The Dark Trick never brings love, you see, it brings only the silence. His voice seemed softer in its soundlessness, clearer, the echo dissipated. *We used to say it was Satan's will, that the master and the fledgling not seek comfort in each other. It was Satan who had to be served, after all.*

Every word penetrated me. Every word was received by a secret, humiliating curiosity and vulnerability. But I refused to let him see this. Angrily I said:

"What do you want of me?"

It was shattering something to speak. I was feeling more fear of him at this moment than ever during the earlier battles and arguments, and I hate those who make me feel fear, those who know things that I need to know, who have that power over me.

"It is like not knowing how to read, isn't it?" he said aloud. "And your maker, the outcast Magnus, what did he care for your ignorance? He did not tell you the simplest things, did he?"

Nothing in his expression moved as he spoke.

"Hasn't it always been this way? Has anyone ever cared to teach you anything?"

"You're taking these things from my mind . . ." I said. I was appalled. I saw the monastery where I'd been as a boy, the rows and rows of books that I could not read, Gabrielle bent over her books, her back to all of us. "Stop this!" I whispered.

It seemed the longest time had passed. I was becoming disoriented. He was speaking again, but in silence.

They never satisfy you, the ones you make. In silence the estrangement and the resentment only grow.

I willed myself to move but I wasn't moving. I was merely looking at him as he went on.

You long for me and I for you, and we alone in all this realm are worthy of each other. Don't you know this?

The toneless words seemed to be stretched, amplified, like a note on the violin drawn out forever and ever.

"This is madness," I whispered. I thought of all the things he had said to me, what he had blamed me for, the horrors the others had described—that he had thrown his followers into the fire.

"Is it madness?" he asked. "Go then to your silent ones. Even now they say to each other what they cannot say to you."

"You're lying . . ." I said.

"And time will only strengthen their independence. But learn for yourself. You will find me easily enough when you want to come to me. After all, where can I go? What can I do? You have made me an orphan again."

"I didn't—" I said.

"Yes, you did," he said. "You did it. You brought it down." Still there was no anger. "But I can wait for you to come, wait for you to ask the questions that only I can answer."

I stared at him for a long moment. I don't know how long. It was as if I couldn't move, and I couldn't see anything else but him, and the great sense of peace I'd known in Notre Dame, the spell he cast, was again working. The lights of the room were too bright. There was nothing else but light surrounding him, and it was as if he were coming closer to me and I to him, yet neither of us was moving. He was drawing me, drawing me towards him.

I turned away, stumbling, losing my balance. But I was out of the room. I was running down the hallway, and then I was climbing out of the back window and up to the roof.

I rode into the Ile de la Cité as if he were chasing me. And my heart didn't stop its frantic pace until I had left the city behind.

HELL's Bells ringing.

The tower was in darkness against the first glimmer of the morning light. My little coven had already gone to rest in their dungeon crypt.

I didn't open the tombs to look at them, though I wanted desperately to do it, just to see Gabrielle and touch her hand.

I climbed alone towards the battlements to look out at the burning miracle of the approaching morning, the thing I should never see to its finish again. Hell's Bells ringing, my secret music . . .

But another sound was coming to me. I knew it as I went up the stairs. And I marveled at its power to reach me. It was like a song arching over an immense distance, low and sweet.

Once years ago, I had heard a young farm boy singing as he walked along the high road out of the village to the north. He hadn't known anyone was listening. He had thought himself alone in the open country, and his voice had a private power and purity that gave it unearthly beauty. Never mind the words of his old song.

This was the voice that was calling to me now. The lone voice, rising over the miles that separated us to gather all sounds into itself.

I was frightened again. Yet I opened the door at the top of the staircase and went out onto the stone roof. Silken the morning breeze, dreamlike the twinkling of the last stars. The sky was not so much a canopy as it was a mist rising endlessly above me, and the stars drifted upwards, growing ever smaller, in the mist.

The faraway voice sharpened, like a note sung in the high mountains, touching my chest where I had laid my hand.

It pierced me as a beam pierces darkness, singing *Come to me; all things will be forgiven if only you come to me. I am more alone than I have ever been.*

And there came in time with the voice a sense of limitless possibility, of wonder and expectation that brought with it the vision of Armand standing alone in the open doors of Notre Dame. Time and space were illusions. He was in a pale wash of light before the main altar, a lissome shape in regal tatters, shimmering as he vanished, and nothing but patience in his eyes. There was no crypt under les Innocents now. There was no grotesquery of the ragged ghost in the glare of Nicki's library, throwing down the books when he had finished with them as if they were empty shells.

I think I knelt down and rested my head against the jagged stones. I saw the moon like a phantom dissolving, and the sun must have touched her because she hurt me and I had to close my eyes.

But I felt an elation, an ecstasy. It was as if my spirit could know the glory of the Dark Trick without the blood flowing, in the intimacy of the voice dividing me and seeking the tenderest, most secret part of my soul.

What do you want of me, I wanted to say again. How can there be this forgiveness when there was such rancor only a short while ago? Your coven destroyed. Horrors I don't want to imagine . . . I wanted to say it all again.

But I couldn't shape the words now any more than I could before. And this time, I knew that if I dared to try, the bliss would melt and leave me and the anguish would be worse than the thirst for blood.

Yet even as I remained still, in the mystery of this feeling, I knew strange images and thoughts that weren't my own.

I saw myself retreat again to the dungeon and lift up the inanimate bodies of those kindred monsters I loved. I saw myself carrying them up to the roof of the tower and leaving them there in their helplessness at the mercy of the rising sun. Hell's Bells rang the alarm in vain for them. And the sun took them up and made them cinders with human hair.

My mind recoiled from this; it recoiled in the most heartbreaking disappointment.

"Child, still," I whispered. Ah, the pain of this disappointment, the possibility diminishing . . . "How foolish you are to think that such things could be done by me."

The voice faded; it withdrew itself from me. And I felt my aloneness in every pore of my skin. It was as if all covering had been taken from me forever and I would always be as naked and miserable as I was now.

And I felt far off a convulsion of power, as if the spirit that had made the voice was curling upon itself like a great tongue.

"Treachery!" I said louder. "But oh, the sadness of it, the miscalculation. How can you say that you desire *me*!"

Gone it was. Absolutely gone. And desperately, I wanted it back even if it was to fight with me. I wanted that sense of possibility, that lovely flare again.

And I saw his face in Notre Dame, boyish and almost sweet, like the face of an old da Vinci saint. A horrid sense of fatality passed over me.

6

AS SOON as Gabrielle rose, I drew her away from Nicki, out into the quiet of the forest, and I told her all that had taken place the preceding night. I told her all that Armand had suggested and said. In an embarrassed way, I spoke of the silence that existed between her and me, and of how I knew now that it wasn't to change.

"We should leave Paris as soon as possible," I said finally. "This creature is too dangerous. And the ones to whom I gave the theater—they don't know anything other than what they've been taught by him. I say let them have Paris. And let's take the Devil's Road, to use the old queen's words."

I had expected anger from her, and malice towards Armand. But through the whole story she remained calm.

"Lestat, there are too many unanswered questions," she said. "I want to know how this old coven started, I want to know all that Armand knows about *us*."

"Mother, I'm tempted to turn my back on it. I don't care how it started. I wonder if he himself even knows."

"I understand, Lestat," she said quietly. "Believe me, I do. When all is said and done, I care less about these creatures than I do about the trees in this forest or the stars overhead. I'd rather study the currents of wind or the patterns in the falling leaves . . ."

"Exactly."

"But we mustn't be hasty. The important thing now is for the three of us to remain together. We should go into the city together and prepare slowly for our departure together. And together, we must try your plan to rouse Nicolas with the violin."

I wanted to talk about Nicki. I wanted to ask her what lay behind his silence, what could she divine? But the words dried up in my throat. I thought as I had all along of her judgment in those first moments: "Disaster, my son."

She put her arm around me and led me back towards the tower.

"I don't have to read your mind," she said, "to know what's in your heart. Let's take him into Paris. Let's try to find the Stradivarius." She stood on tiptoe to kiss me. "We were on the Devil's Road together before all this happened," she said. "We'll be on it soon again."

It was as easy to take Nicolas into Paris as to lead him in everything else. Like a ghost he mounted his horse and rode alongside of us, only his dark hair and cape seemingly animate, whipped about as they were by the wind.

When we fed in the Ile de la Cité, I found I could not watch him hunt or kill.

It gave me no hope to see him doing these simple things with the sluggishness of a somnambulist. It proved nothing more than that he could go like this forever, our silent accomplice, little more than a resuscitated corpse.

Yet an unexpected feeling came over me as we moved through the alleyways together. We were not two, but three, now. A coven. And if only I could bring him around—

But the visit to Roget had to come first. I alone had to confront the lawyer. So I left them to wait only a few doors from his house, and as I pounded the knocker, I braced myself for the most grueling performance yet of my theatrical career.

Well, I was very quickly to learn an important lesson about mortals and their willingness to be convinced that the world is a safe place. Roget was overjoyed to see me. He was so relieved that I was "alive and in good health" and still wanted his services, that he was nodding his acceptance before my preposterous explanations had even begun.

(And this lesson about mortal peace of mind I never forgot. Even if a ghost is ripping a house to pieces, throwing tin pans all over, pouring water on pillows, making clocks chime at all hours, mortals will accept almost any "natural explanation" offered, no matter how absurd, rather than the obvious supernatural one, for what is going on.)

Also it became clear almost at once that he believed Gabrielle and I had slipped out of the flat by the servants' door to the bedroom, a nice possibility I hadn't considered before. So all I did about the twisted-up candelabra was mumble something about having been mad with grief when I saw my mother, which he understood right off.

As for the reason for our leaving, well, Gabrielle insisted upon being removed from everyone and taken to a convent, and there she was right now.

"Ah, Monsieur, it's a miracle, her improvement," I said. "If you could only see her—but never mind. We're going on to Italy immediately with Nicolas de Lenfent, and we need currency, letters of credit, whatever, and a traveling coach, a huge traveling coach, and a good team of six. You take care of it. Have it all ready by Friday evening early. And write to my father and tell him we're taking my mother to Italy. My father is all right, I presume?"

"Yes, yes, of course, I didn't tell him anything but the most reassuring—"

"How clever of you. I knew I could trust you. What would I do without you? And what about these rubies, can you turn them into money for me immediately? And I have here some Spanish coins to sell, quite old, I think."

He scribbled like a madman, his doubts and suspicions fading in the heat of my smiles. He was so glad to have something to do!

"Hold my property in the boulevard du Temple vacant," I said. "And of course, you'll manage everything for me. And so forth and so on."

My property in the boulevard du Temple, the hiding place of a ragged and desperate band of vampires unless Armand had already found them and burnt them up like old costumes. I should find the answer to that question soon enough.

I came down the steps whistling to myself in strictly human fashion, overjoyed that this odious task had been accomplished. And then I realized that Nicki and Gabrielle were nowhere in sight.

I stopped and turned around in the street.

I saw Gabrielle just at the moment I heard her voice, a young boyish figure emerging full blown from an alleyway as if she had just made herself material on the spot.

"Lestat, he's gone—vanished," she said.

I couldn't answer her. I said something foolish, like "What do you mean, vanished!" But my thoughts were more or less drowning out the words in my own head. If I had doubted up until this moment that I loved him, I had been lying to myself.

"I turned my back, and it was that quick, I tell you," she said. She was half aggrieved, half angry.

"Did you hear any other . . ."

"No. Nothing. He was simply too quick."

"Yes, if he moved on his own, if he wasn't taken . . ."

"I would have heard his fear if Armand had taken him," she insisted.

"But does he feel fear? Does he feel anything at all?" I was utterly terrified and utterly exasperated. He'd vanished in a darkness that spread out all around us like a giant wheel from its axis. I think I clenched my fist. I must have made some uncertain little gesture of panic.

"Listen to me," she said. "There are only two things that go round and round in his mind . . ."

"Tell me!"

"One is the pyre under les Innocents where he was almost burned. And the other is a small theater—footlights, a stage."

"Renaud's," I said.

SHE and I were archangels together. It didn't take us a quarter of an hour to reach the noisy boulevard and to move through its raucous crowd past the neglected facade of Renaud's and back to the stage door.

The boards had all been ripped down and the locks broken. But I heard no sound of Eleni or the others as we slipped quietly into the hallway that went round the back of the stage. No one here.

Perhaps Armand had gathered his children home after all, and that was my doing because I would not take them in.

Nothing but the jungle of props, the great painted scrims of night and day and hill and dale, and the open dressing rooms, those crowded little closets where here and there a mirror glared in the light that seeped through the open door we had left behind.

Then Gabrielle's hand tightened on my sleeve. She gestured towards the wings proper. And I knew by her face that it wasn't the other ones. Nicki was there.

I went to the side of the stage. The velvet curtain was drawn back to both sides and I could see his dark figure plainly in the orchestra pit. He was sitting in his old place, his hands folded in his lap. He was facing me but he didn't notice me. He was staring off as he had done all along.

And the memory came back to me of Gabrielle's strange words the night after I had made her, that she could not get over the sensation that she had died and could affect nothing in the mortal world.

He appeared that lifeless and that translucent. He was the still, expressionless specter one almost stumbles over in the shadows of the haunted house, all but melded with the dusty furnishings—the fright that is worse perhaps than any other kind.

I looked to see if the violin was there—on the floor, or against his chair —and when I saw that it wasn't, I thought, Well, there is still a chance.

"Stay here and watch," I said to Gabrielle. But my heart was knocking in my throat when I looked up at the darkened theater, when I let myself breathe in the old scents. Why did you have to bring us here, Nicki? To this haunted place? But then, who am I to ask that? I had come back, had I not?

I lighted the first candle I found in the old prima donna's dressing room. Open pots of paint were scattered everywhere, and there were many discarded costumes on the hooks. All the rooms I passed were full of cast-off clothing, forgotten combs and brushes, withered flowers still in the vases, powder spilled on the floor.

I thought of Eleni and the others again, and I realized that the faintest smell of les Innocents lingered here. And I saw very distinct naked footprints in the spilled powder. Yes, they'd come in. And they had lighted candles, too, hadn't they? Because the smell of the wax was too fresh.

Whatever the case, they hadn't entered my old dressing room, the room that Nicki and I had shared before every performance. It was locked still. And when I broke open the door, I got an ugly shock. The room was exactly the way I'd left it.

It was clean and orderly, even the mirror polished, and it was filled with my belongings as it had been on the last night I had been here. There was my old coat on the hook, the cast-off I'd worn from the country, and a pair of wrinkled boots, and my pots of paint in perfect order, and my wig, which I had worn only at the theater, on its wooden head. Letters from Gabrielle in a little stack, the old copies of English and French newspapers in which the play had been mentioned, and a bottle of wine still half full with a dried cork.

And there in the darkness beneath the marble dressing table, partly covered by a bundled black coat, lay a shiny violin case. It was not the one we'd carried all the way from home with us. No. It must hold the precious gift I'd bought for him with the "coin of the realm" after, the Stradivarius violin.

I bent down and opened the lid. It was the beautiful instrument all right, delicate and darkly lustrous, and lying here among all these unimportant things.

I wondered whether Eleni and the others would have taken it had they come into this room. Would they have known what it could do?

I set down the candle for a moment and took it out carefully, and I tightened the horsehair of the bow as I'd seen Nicki do a thousand times. And then I brought the instrument and the candle back to the stage again, and I bent down and commenced to light the long string of candle footlights.

Gabrielle watched me impassively. Then she came to help me. She lit one candle after another and then lighted the sconce in the wings.

It seemed Nicki stirred. But maybe it was only the growing illumination on his profile, the soft light that emanated out from the stage into the darkened hall. The deep folds of velvet came alive everywhere; the ornate little mirrors affixed to the front of the gallery and the loges became lights themselves.

Beautiful this little place, our place. The portal to the world for us as mortal beings. And the portal finally to hell.

When I was finished, I stood on the boards looking at the gilded railings, the new chandelier that hung from the ceiling, and up at the arch overhead with its masks of comedy and tragedy like two faces stemming from the same neck.

It seemed so much smaller when it was empty, this house. No theater in Paris seemed larger when it was full.

Outside was the low thunder of the boulevard traffic, tiny human voices rising now and then like sparks over the general hum. A heavy carriage must have passed then because everything within the theater shivered slightly: the candle flames against their reflectors, the giant stage curtain gathered to right and left, the scrim behind of a finely painted garden with clouds overhead.

I went past Nicki, who never once looked up at me, and down the little stairs behind him, and came towards him with the violin.

Gabrielle stood back in the wings again, her small face cold but patient. She rested against the beam beside her in the easy manner of a strange long-haired man.

I lowered the violin over Nicki's shoulder and held it in his lap. I felt him move, as if he had taken a great breath. The back of his head pressed against me. And slowly he lifted his left hand to take the neck of the violin and he took the bow with his right.

I knelt and put my hands on his shoulders. I kissed his cheek. No human scent. No human warmth. Sculpture of my Nicolas.

"Play it," I whispered. "Play it here just for us."

Slowly he turned to face me, and for the first time since the moment of the Dark Trick, he looked into my eyes. He made some tiny sound. It was so strained it was as if he couldn't speak anymore. The organs of speech had closed up. But then he ran his tongue along his lip, and so low I scarcely heard him, he said:

"The devil's instrument."

"Yes," I said. If you must believe that, then believe it. But play.

His fingers hovered above the strings. He tapped the hollow wood with his fingertip. And now, trembling, he plucked at the strings to tune them and wound the pegs very slowly as if he were discovering the process with perfect concentration for the first time.

Somewhere out on the boulevard children laughed. Wooden wheels made their thick clatter over the cobblestones. The staccato notes were sour, dissonant, and they sharpened the tension.

He pressed the instrument to his ear for a moment. And it seemed to me he didn't move again for an eternity, and then he slowly rose to his feet. I went back out of the pit and into the benches, and I stood staring at his black silhouette against the glow of the lighted stage.

He turned to face the empty theater as he had done so many times at the moment of the intermezzo, and he lifted the violin to his chin. And in a movement so swift it was like a flash of light in my eye, he brought the bow down across the strings.

The first full-throated chords throbbed in the silence and were stretched as they deepened, scraping the bottom of sound itself. Then the notes rose, rich and dark and shrill, as if pumped out of the fragile violin by alchemy, until a raging torrent of melody suddenly flooded the hall.

It seemed to roll through my body, to pass through my very bones.

I couldn't see the movement of his fingers, the whipping of the bow; all I could see was the swaying of his body, his tortured posture as he let the music twist him, bend him forward, throw him back.

It became higher, shriller, faster, yet the tone of each note was perfection. It was execution without effort, virtuosity beyond mortal dreams. And the violin was talking, not merely singing, the violin was insisting. The violin was telling a tale.

The music was a lamentation, a fugue of terror looping itself into hypnotic dance rhythms, jerking Nicki even more wildly from side to side. His hair was a glistening mop against the footlights. The blood sweat had broken out on him. I could smell the blood.

But I too was doubling over; I was backing away from him, slumping down on the bench as if to cower from it, as once before in this house terrified mortals had cowered before me.

And I knew, knew in some full and simultaneous fashion, that the violin was telling everything that had happened to Nicki. It was the darkness exploded, the darkness molten, and the beauty of it was like the glow of smoldering coals; just enough illumination to show how much darkness there really was.

Gabrielle too was straining to keep her body still under the onslaught, her face constricted, her hands to her head. Her lion's mane of hair had shaken loose around her, her eyes were closed.

But another sound was coming through the pure inundation of song. *They* were here. They had come into the theater and were moving towards us through the wings.

The music reached impossible peaks, the sound throttled for an instant and then released again. The mixture of feeling and pure logic drove it past the limits of the bearable. And yet it went on and on.

And the others appeared slowly from behind the stage curtain—first the stately figure of Eleni, then the boy Laurent, and finally Félix and Eugénie. Acrobats, street players, they had become, and they wore the clothes of such players, the men in white tights beneath dagged harlequin jerkins, the women in full bloomers and ruffled dresses and with dancing slippers on their feet. Rouge gleamed on their immaculate white faces; kohl outlined their dazzling vampire eyes.

They glided towards Nicki as if drawn by a magnet, their beauty flowering ever more fully as they came into the glare of the stage candles, their hair shimmering, their movements agile and feline, their expressions rapt.

Nicki turned slowly to face them as he writhed, and the song went into frenzied supplication, lurching and climbing and roaring along its melodic path.

Eleni stared wide-eyed at him as if horrified or enchanted. Then her arms rose straight up above her head in a slow dramatic gesture, her body tensing, her neck becoming ever more graceful and long. The other woman had made a pivot and lifted her knee, toe pointed down, in the first step of a dance. But it was the tall man who suddenly caught the pace of Nicki's music as he jerked his head to the side and moved his legs and arms as if he were a great marionette controlled from the rafters above by four strings.

The others saw it. They had seen the marionettes of the boulevard. And suddenly they all went into the mechanical attitude, their sudden movements like spasms, their faces like wooden faces, utterly blank.

A great cool rush of delight passed through me, as if I could breathe suddenly in the blasted heat of the music, and I moaned with pleasure watching them flip and flop and throw up their legs, toes to the ceiling, and twirl on their invisible strings.

They had found the grotesque heart of the music, the very balance between its hideous pleading and its insistent singing, and it was Nicki who commanded their strings.

But it was changing. He was playing to them now even as they danced to him.

He took a stride towards the stage, and leapt up over the smoky trough of the footlights, and landed in their midst. The light slithered off the instrument, off his glistering face.

A new element of mockery infected the never ending melody, a syncopation that staggered the song and made it all the more bitter and all the more sweet at the same time.

The jerking stiff-jointed puppets circled him, shuffling and bobbing along the floorboards. Fingers splayed, heads rocking from side to side, they jigged and twisted until all of them broke their rigid form as Nicki's melody melted into harrowing sadness, the dance becoming immediately liquid and heartbroken and slow.

It was as if one mind controlled them, as if they danced to Nicki's thoughts as well as his music, and he began to dance with them as he played, the beat coming faster, as he became the country fiddler at the Lenten bonfire, and they leapt in pairs like country lovers, the skirts of the women flaring, the men bowing their legs as they lifted the women, all creating postures of tenderest love.

Frozen, I stared at the image: the preternatural dancers, the monster violinist, limbs moving with inhuman slowness, tantalizing grace. The music was like a fire consuming us all.

Now it screamed of pain, of horror, of the pure rebellion of the soul against all things. And they again carried it into the visual, faces twisted in torment, like the mask of tragedy graven on the arch above them, and I knew that if I didn't turn my back on this I would cry.

I didn't want to hear any more or see any more. Nicki was swinging to and fro as if the violin were a beast he could no longer control. And he was stabbing at the strings with short rough strokes of the bow.

The dancers passed in front of him, in back of him, embraced him, and caught him suddenly as he threw up his hands, the violin held high over his head.

A loud piercing laughter erupted from him. His chest shivered with it, his arms and legs quaking with it. And then he lowered his head and he fixed his eyes on me. And at the top of his voice he screamed:

"I GIVE YOU THE THEATER OF THE VAMPIRES! THE THEATER OF THE VAMPIRES! THE GREATEST SPECTACLE OF THE BOULEVARD!"

Astonished, the others stared at him. But again, all of one mind, they clapped their hands and roared. They leapt into the air, giving out shrieks of joy. They threw their arms about his neck and kissed him. And dancing around him in a circle, they turned him with their arms. The laughter rose, bubbling out of all of them, as he brought them close in his arms and answered their kisses, and with their long pink tongues they licked the blood sweat off his face.

"The Theater of the Vampires!" They broke from him and bawled it to the nonexistent audience, to the world. They bowed to the footlights, and frolicking and screaming they leapt up to the rafters and then let themselves drop down with a storm of reverberation on the boards.

The last shimmer of the music was gone, replaced by this cacophony of shrieking and stomping and laughter, like the clang of bells.

I do not remember turning my back on them. I don't remember walking up the steps to the stage and going past them. But I must have.

Because I was suddenly sitting on the long narrow table of my little dressing room, my back against the corner, my knee crooked, my head against the cold glass of the mirror, and Gabrielle was there.

I was breathing hoarsely and the sound of it bothered me. I saw things —the wig I'd worn on the stage, the pasteboard shield—and these evoked thundering emotions. But I was suffocating. I could not think.

Then Nicki appeared in the door, and he moved Gabrielle to the side with a strength that astonished her and astonished me, and he pointed his finger at me:

"Well, don't you like it, my lord patron?" he asked, advancing, his words flowing in an unbroken stream so that they sounded like one great word. "Don't you admire its splendor, its perfection? Won't you endow the Theater of the Vampires with the coin of the realm which you possess in such great abundance? Won't you see your playhouse come to its final magnificent purpose? How was it now, 'the new evil, the canker in the heart of the rose, death in the very midst of things' . . ."

From a mute he had passed into mania, and even when he broke off talking, the low senseless frenzied sounds still issued from his lips like water from a spring. His face was drawn and hard and glistening with the blood droplets clinging to it, and staining the white linen at his neck.

And behind him there came an almost innocent laughter from the others, except for Eleni, who watched over his shoulder, trying very hard to comprehend what was really happening between us.

He drew closer, half laughing, grinning, stabbing at my chest with his finger:

"Well, speak. Don't you see the splendid mockery, the genius?" He struck his own chest with his fist. "They'll come to our performances, fill our coffers with gold, and never guess what they harbor, what flourishes right in the corner of the Parisian eye. In the back alleys we feed on them and they clap for us before the lighted stage . . ."

Laughter from the boy behind him. The tink of a tambourine, the thin sound of the other woman singing. A long streak of the man's laughter—like a ribbon unfurling, charting his movement as he rushed around in a circle through the rattling scrims.

Nicki drew in so that the light behind him vanished. I couldn't see Eleni.

"Magnificent evil!" he said. He was full of menace and his white hands looked like the claws of a sea creature that could at any given moment move to tear me to bits. "To serve the god of the dark wood as he has not been served ever and here in the very center of civilization. And for this you saved the theater. Out of your gallant patronage this sublime offering is born."

"It is petty!" I said. "It is merely beautiful and clever and nothing more."

My voice had not been very loud but it brought him to silence, and it brought the others to silence. And the shock in me melted slowly into another emotion, no less painful, merely easier to contain.

Nothing but the sounds again from the boulevard. A glowering anger flowed out of him, his pupils dancing as he looked at me.

"You're a liar, a contemptible liar," he said.

"There is no splendor in it," I answered. "There is nothing sublime. Fooling helpless mortals, mocking them, and then going out from here at night to take life in the same old petty manner, one death after another in all its inevitable cruelty and shabbiness so that we can live. Any man can kill another man! Play your violin forever. Dance as you wish. Give them their money's worth if it keeps you busy and eats up eternity! It's simply clever and beautiful. A grove in the Savage Garden. Nothing more."

"Vile liar!" he said between his teeth. "You are God's fool, that's what you are. You who possessed the dark secret that soared above everything, rendered everything meaningless, and what did you do with it, in those months when you ruled alone from Magnus's tower, but try to live like a good man! A good man!"

He was close enough to kiss me, the blood of his spittle hitting my face.

"Patron of the arts," he sneered. "Giver of gifts to your family, giver of gifts to us!" He stepped back, looking down on me contemptuously.

"Well, we will take the little theater that you painted in gold, and hung with velvet," he said, "and it will serve the forces of the devil more splendidly than he was ever served by the old coven." He turned and glanced at Eleni. He glanced back at the others. "We will make a mockery of all things sacred. We will lead them to ever greater vulgarity and profanity. We will astonish. We will beguile. But above all, we will thrive on their gold as well as their blood and in their midst we will grow strong."

"Yes," said the boy behind him. "We will become invincible." His face had a crazed look, the look of the zealot as he gazed at Nicolas. "We will have names and places in their very world."

"And power over them," said the other woman, "and a vantage point from which to study them and know them and perfect our methods of destroying them when we choose."

"I want the theater," Nicolas said to me. "I want it from you. The deed, the money to reopen it. My assistants here are ready to listen to me."

"You may have it, if you wish," I answered. "It is yours if it will take you and your malice and your fractured reason off my hands."

I got up off the dressing table and went towards him and I think that he meant to block my path, but something unaccountable happened. When I saw he wouldn't move, my anger rose up and out of me like an invisible fist. And I saw him moved backwards as if the fist had struck him. And he hit the wall with sudden force.

I could have been free of the place in an instant. I knew Gabrielle was only waiting to follow me. But I didn't leave. I stopped and I looked back at him, and he was still against the wall as if he couldn't move. And he was watching me and the hatred was as pure, as undiluted by remembered love, as it had been all along.

But I wanted to understand, I wanted really to know what had happened. And I came towards him again in silence and this time it was I who was menacing, and my hands looked like claws and I could feel his fear. They were all, except for Eleni, full of fear.

I stopped when I was very close to him and he looked directly at me, and it was as if he knew exactly what I was asking him.

"All a misunderstanding, my love," he said. Acid on the tongue. The blood sweat had broken out again, and his eyes glistened as if they were wet. "It was to hurt others, don't you see, the violin playing, to anger them, to secure for me an island where they could not rule. They would watch my ruin, unable to do anything about it."

I didn't answer. I wanted him to go on.

"And when we decided to go to Paris, I thought we would starve in Paris, that we would go down and down and down. It was what I wanted, rather than what *they* wanted, that I, the favored son, should rise for them. I thought we would go down! We were supposed to go down."

"Oh, Nicki . . ." I whispered.

"But you didn't go down, Lestat," he said, his eyebrows rising. "The hunger, the cold—none of it stopped you. You were a triumph!" The rage thickened his voice again. "You didn't drink yourself to death in the gutter. You turned everything upside down! And for every aspect of our proposed damnation you found exuberance, and there was no end to your enthusiasms and the passion coming out of you—and the light, always the light. And in exact proportion to the light coming out of you, there was the darkness in me! Every exuberance piercing me and creating its exact proportion of darkness and despair! And then, the magic, when you got the magic, irony of ironies, you protected me from it! And what did you do with it but use your Satanic powers to simulate the actions of a good man!"

I turned around. I saw them scattered in the shadows, and farthest away, the figure of Gabrielle. I saw the light on her hand as she raised it, beckoning for me to come away.

Nicki reached up and touched my shoulders. I could feel the hatred coming through his touch. Loathsome to be touched in hate.

"Like a mindless beam of sunlight you routed the bats of the old coven!" he whispered. "And for what purpose? What does it mean, the murdering monster who is filled with light!"

I turned and smacked him and sent him hurtling into the dressing room, his right hand smashing the mirror, his head cracking against the far wall.

For one moment he lay like something broken against the mass of old clothing, and then his eyes gathered their determination again, and his face softened into a slow smile. He righted himself and slowly, as an indignant mortal might, he smoothed his coat and his rumpled hair.

It was like my gestures under les Innocents when my captors had set me down in the dirt.

And he came forward with the same dignity, and the smile was as ugly as any I had ever seen.

"I despise you," he said. "But I am done with you. I have the power from you and I know how to use it, which you do not. I am in a realm at last where *I* choose to triumph! In darkness, we're equal now. And you will give me the theater, that because you owe it to me, and you are a giver of things, aren't you—a giver of gold coins to hungry children—and then I won't ever look upon your light again."

He stepped around me and stretched out his arms to the others:

"Come, my beauties, come, we have plays to write, business to attend to. You have things to learn from me. I know what mortals really are. We must get down to the serious invention of our dark and splendid art. We will make a coven to rival all covens. We will do what has never been done."

The others looked at me, frightened, hesitant. And in this still and tense moment I heard myself take a deep breath. My vision broadened. I saw the wings around us again, the high rafters, the walls of scenery transecting the darkness, and beyond, the little blaze along the foot of the dusty stage. I saw the house veiled in shadow and knew in one limitless recollection all that had happened here. And I saw a nightmare hatch another nightmare, and I saw a story come to an end.

"The Theater of the Vampires," I whispered. "We have worked the Dark Trick on this little place." No one of the others dared to answer. Nicolas only smiled.

And as I turned to leave the theater I raised my hand in a gesture that urged them all towards him. I said my farewell.

* * *

WE WERE not far from the lights of the boulevard when I stopped in my tracks. Without words a thousand horrors came to me—that Armand would come to destroy him, that his newfound brothers and sisters would tire of his frenzy and desert him, that morning would find him stumbling through the streets unable to find a hiding place from the sun. I looked up at the sky. I couldn't speak or breathe.

Gabrielle put her arms around me and I held her, burying my face in her hair. Like cool velvet was her skin, her face, her lips. And her love surrounded me with a monstrous purity that had nothing to do with human hearts and human flesh.

I lifted her off her feet embracing her. And in the dark, we were like lovers carved out of the same stone who had no memory of a separate life at all.

"He's made his choice, my son," she said. "What's done is done, and you're free of him now."

"Mother, how can you say it?" I whispered. "He didn't know. He doesn't know still . . ."

"Let him go, Lestat," she said. "They will care for him."

"But now I have to find that devil, Armand, don't I?" I said wearily. "I have to make him leave them alone."

THE following evening when I came into Paris, I learned that Nicki had already been to Roget.

He had come an hour earlier pounding on the doors like a madman. And shouting from the shadows, he had demanded the deed to the theater, and money that he said I had promised to him. He had threatened Roget and his family. He had also told Roget to write to Renaud and his troupe in London and to tell them to come home, that they had a new theater awaiting them, and he expected them back at once. When Roget refused, he demanded the address of the players in London, and began to ransack Roget's desk.

I went into a silent fury when I heard this. So he would make them all vampires, would he, this demon fledgling, this reckless and frenzied monster?

This would not come to pass.

I told Roget to send a courier to London, with word that Nicolas de Lenfent had lost his reason. The players must not come home.

And then I went to the boulevard du Temple and I found him at his rehearsals, excited and mad as he had been before. He wore his fancy clothes again and his old jewels from the time when he had been his father's favorite son, but his tie was askew, his stockings crooked, and his hair was as wild and unkempt as the hair of a prisoner in the Bastille who hadn't seen himself in a mirror in twenty years.

Before Eleni and the others I told him he would get nothing from me unless I had the promise that no actor or actress of Paris would ever be slain or seduced by the new coven, that Renaud and his troupe would never be brought into the Theater of the Vampires now or in the years to come, that Roget, who would hold the purse strings of the theater, must never come to the slightest harm.

He laughed at me, he ridiculed me as he had before. But Eleni silenced him. She was horrified to learn of his impulsive designs. It was she who gave the promises, and exacted them from the others. It was she who intimidated him and confused him with jumbled language of the old ways, and made him back down.

AND it was to Eleni finally that I gave control of the Theater of the Vampires, and the income, to pass through Roget, which would allow her to do with it what she pleased.

BEFORE I left her that night, I asked her what she knew of Armand. Gabrielle was with us. We were in the alleyway again, near the stage door.

"He watches," Eleni answered. "Sometimes he lets himself be seen." Her face was very confusing to me. Sorrowful. "But God only knows what he will do," she added fearfully, "when he discovers what is really going on here."

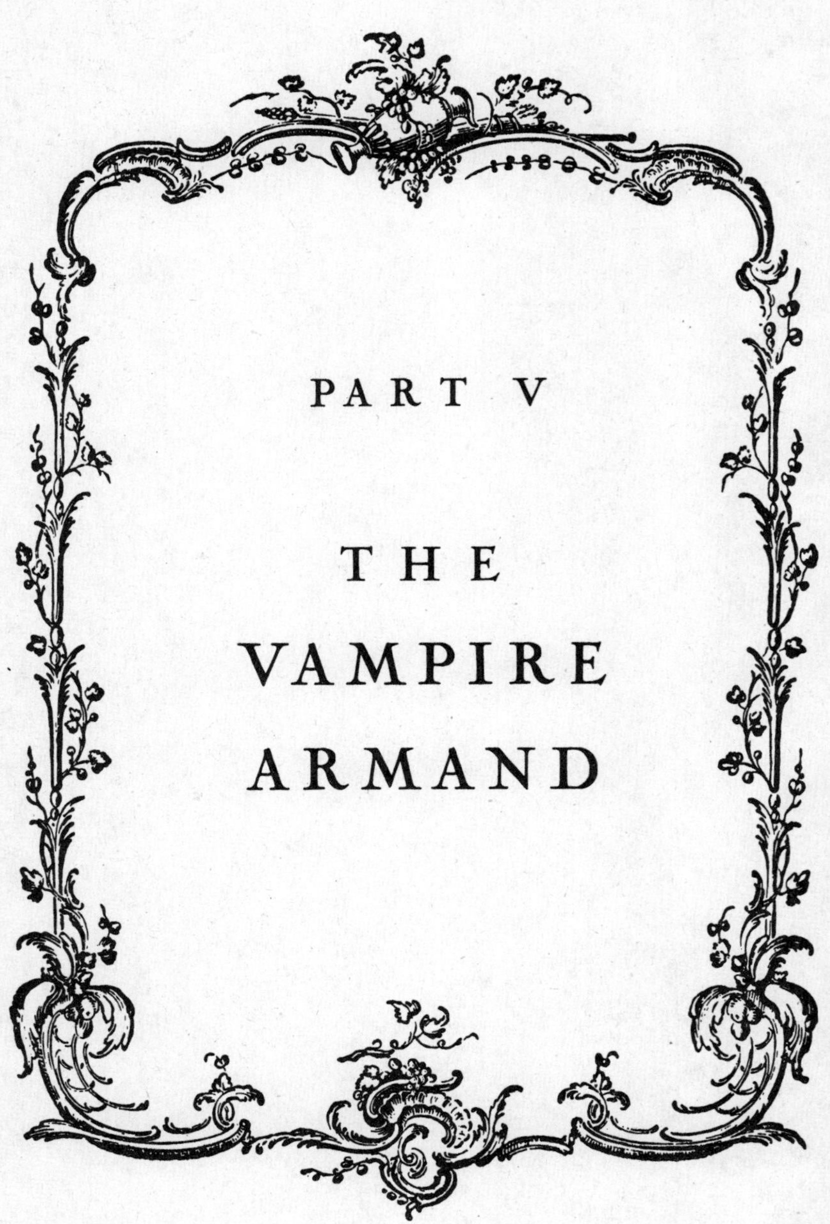

PART V

THE VAMPIRE ARMAND

1

SPRING rain. Rain of light that saturated every new leaf of the trees in the street, every square of paving, drift of rain threading light through the empty darkness itself.

And the ball in the Palais Royal.

The king and queen were there, dancing with the people. Talk in the shadows of intrigue. Who cares? Kingdoms rise and fall. Just don't burn the paintings in the Louvre, that's all.

Lost in a sea of mortals again; fresh complexions and ruddy cheeks, mounds of powdered hair atop feminine heads with all manner of millinery nonsense in them, even minute ships with three masts, tiny trees, little birds. Landscapes of pearl and ribbon. Broad-chested men like cocks in satin coats like feathered wings. The diamonds hurt my eyes.

The voices touched the surface of my skin at times, the laughter the echo of unholy laughter, wreaths of candles blinding, the froth of music positively lapping the walls.

Gust of rain from the open doors.

Scent of humans gently stoking my hunger. White shoulders, white necks, powerful hearts running at that eternal rhythm, so many gradations among these naked children hidden in riches, savages laboring beneath a swaddling of chenille, encrustations of embroidery, feet aching over high heels, masks like scabs about their eyes.

The air comes out of one body and is breathed into another. The music, does it pass out of one ear and into another, as the old expression goes? We breathe the light, we breathe the music, we breathe the moment as it passes through us.

Now and then eyes settled on me with some vague air of expectation. My white skin made them pause, but what was that when they let blood out of their veins themselves to keep their delicate pallor? (Let me hold the basin for you and drink it afterwards.) And my eyes, what were those, in this sea of paste jewels?

Yet their whispers slithered around me. And those scents, ah, not a one was like another. And as clearly as if spoken aloud it came, the summons from mortals here and there, sensing what I was, and the lust.

In some ancient language they welcomed death; they ached for death as death was passing through the room. But did they really know? Of course they didn't know. And I did not know! That was the perfect horror! And who am I to bear this secret, to hunger so to impart it, to want to take that slender woman there and suck the blood right out of the plump flesh of her round little breast.

The music rushed on, human music. The colors of the room flamed for an instant as if the whole would melt. The hunger sharpened. It was no longer an idea. My veins were throbbing with it. Someone would die. Sucked dry in less than a moment. I cannot stand it, thinking of it, knowing it's about to happen, fingers on the throat feeling the blood in the vein, feeling the flesh give, give it to me! Where? *This is my body, this is my blood.*

Send out your power, Lestat, like a reptile tongue to gather in a flick the appropriate heart.

Plump little arms ripe for the squeezing, men's faces on which the close-shaven blond beard all but glitters, muscle struggling in my fingers, you haven't got a chance!

And beneath this divine chemistry suddenly, this panorama of the denial of decay, I saw the bones!

Skulls under these preposterous wigs, two gaping holes peering from behind the uplifted fan. A room of wobbling skeletons waiting only for the tolling of the bell. Just as I had seen the audience that night in the pit of Renaud's when I had done the tricks that terrified them. The horror should be visited upon every other being in this room.

I had to get out. I'd made a terrible miscalculation. *This* was death and I could get away from it, if I could just get out! But I was tangled in mortal beings as if this monstrous place were a snare for a vampire. If I bolted, I'd send the entire ballroom into panic. As gently as I could I pushed to the open doors.

And against the far wall, a backdrop of satin and filigree, I saw, out of the corner of my eye, like something imagined, Armand.

Armand.

If there had been a summons, I never heard it. If there was a greeting, I didn't sense it now. He was merely looking at me, a radiant creature in jewels and scalloped lace. And it was Cinderella revealed at the ball, this vision, Sleeping Beauty opening her eyes under a mesh of cobwebs and wiping them all away with one sweep of her warm hand. The sheer pitch of incarnate beauty made me gasp.

Yes, perfect mortal raiment, and yet he seemed all the more supernatural, his face too dazzling, his dark eyes fathomless and just for a split second glinting as if they were windows to the fires of hell. And when his voice came it was low and almost teasing, forcing me to concentrate to hear it: *All night you've been searching for me,* he said, *and here I am, waiting for you. I have been waiting for you all along.*

I think I sensed even then, as I stood unable to look away, that never in my years of wandering this earth would I ever have such a rich revelation of the true horror that we are.

Heartbreakingly innocent he seemed in the midst of the crowd.

Yet I saw crypts when I looked at him, and I heard the beat of the kettledrums. I saw torchlit fields where I had never been, heard vague incantations, felt the heat of raging fires on my face. And they didn't come out of him, these visions. Rather I drew them out on my own.

Yet never had Nicolas, mortal or immortal, been so alluring. Never had Gabrielle held me so in thrall.

Dear God, this is love. This is desire. And all my past amours have been but the shadow of this.

And it seemed in a murmuring pulse of thought he gave me to know that I had been very foolish to think it would not be so.

Who can love us, you and I, as we can love each other, he whispered and it seemed his lips actually moved.

Others looked at him. I saw them drifting with a ludicrous slowness; I saw their eyes pass over him, I saw the light fall on him at a rich new angle as he lowered his head.

I was moving towards him. It seemed he raised his right hand and beckoned and then he didn't, and he had turned and I saw the figure of a young boy ahead of me, with narrow waist and straight shoulders and high firm calves under silk stockings, a boy who turned as he opened a door and beckoned again.

A mad thought came to me.

I was moving after him, and it seemed that none of the other things had happened. There was no crypt under les Innocents, and he had not been that ancient fearful fiend. We were somehow safe.

We were the sum of our desires and this was saving us, and the vast untasted horror of my own immortality did not lie before me, and we were navigating calm seas with familiar beacons, and it was time to be in each other's arms.

A dark room surrounded us, private, cold. The noise of the ball was far away. He was heated with the blood he'd drunk and I could hear the strong force of his heart. He drew me closer to him, and beyond the high windows there flashed the passing lights of the carriages, with dim incessant sounds that spoke of safety and comfort, and all the things that Paris was.

I had never died. The world was beginning again. I put out my arms and felt his heart against me, and calling out to my Nicolas, I tried to warn him, to tell him we were all of us doomed. Our life was slipping inch by inch from us, and seeing the apple trees in the orchard, drenched in green sunlight, I felt I would go mad.

"No, no, my dearest one," he was whispering, "nothing but peace and sweetness and your arms in mine."

"You know it was the damnedest luck!" I whispered suddenly. "I am an unwilling devil. I cry like some vagrant child. I want to go home."

Yes, yes, his lips tasted like blood, but it was not human blood. It was that elixir that Magnus had given me, and I felt myself recoil. I could get away this time. I had another chance. The wheel had turned full round.

I was crying out that I wouldn't drink; I wouldn't, and then I felt the two hot shafts driven hard through my neck and down to my soul.

I couldn't move. It was coming as it had come that night, the rapture, a thousandfold what it was when I held mortals in my arms. And I knew what he was doing! He was feeding upon me! He was draining me.

And going down on my knees, I felt myself held by him, the blood pouring out of me with a monstrous volition I couldn't stop.

"Devil!" I tried to scream. I forced the word up and up until it broke from my lips and the paralysis broke from my limbs. "Devil!" I roared again and I caught him in his swoon and hurled him backwards to the floor.

In an instant, I had my hands upon him and, shattering the French doors, had dragged him out with me into the night.

His heels were scraping on the stones, his face had become pure fury. I clutched his right arm and swung him from side to side so that his head snapped back and he could not see nor gauge where he was, nor catch hold of anything, and with my right hand I beat him and beat him, until the blood was running out of his ears and his eyes and his nose.

I dragged him through the trees away from the lights of the Palais. And as he struggled, as he sought to resurrect himself with a burst of force, he shot his declaration at me that he would kill me because he had my strength now. He'd drunk it out of me and coupled with his own strength it would make him impossible to defeat.

Maddened, I clutched at his neck, pushing his head down against the path beneath me. I pinned him down, strangling him, until the blood in great gushes poured out of his open mouth.

He would have screamed if he could. My knees drove into his chest. His neck bulged under my fingers and the blood spurted and bubbled out of him and he turned his head from side to side, his eyes growing bigger and bigger, but seeing nothing, and then when I felt him weak and limp, I let him go.

I beat him again, turning him this way and that. And then I drew my sword to sever his head.

Let him live like that if he can. Let him be immortal like that if he can. I raised the sword and when I looked down at him, the rain was pelting his face, and he was staring up at me, as one half alive, unable to plead for mercy, unable to move.

I waited. I wanted him to beg. I wanted him to give me that powerful voice full of lies and cunning, the voice that had made me believe for one pure and dazzling instant that I was alive and free and in the state of grace again. Damnable, unforgivable lie. Lie I'd never forget for as long as I walked the earth. I wanted the rage to carry me over the threshold to his grave.

But nothing came from him.

And in this moment of stillness and misery for him, his beauty slowly returned.

He lay a broken child on the gravel path, only yards from the passing traffic, the ring of the horses' hooves, the rumble of the wooden wheels.

And in this broken child were centuries of evil and centuries of knowledge, and out of him there came no ignominious entreaty but merely the soft and bruised sense of what he was. Old, old evil, eyes that had seen dark ages of which I only dream.

I let him go, and I stood up and sheathed my sword.

I walked a few paces from him, and collapsed upon a wet stone bench.

Far away, busy figures labored about the shattered window of the palace.

But the night lay between us and those confused mortals, and I looked at him listlessly as he lay still.

His face was turned to me, but not by design, his hair a tangle of curls and blood. And with his eyes closed, and his hand open beside him, he appeared the abandoned offspring of time and supernatural accident, someone as miserable as myself.

What had he done to become what he was? Could one so young so long ago have guessed the meaning of any decision, let alone the vow to become this?

I rose, and walking slowly to him, I stood over him and looked at him, at the blood that soaked his lace shirt and stained his face.

It seemed he sighed, that I heard the passage of his breath.

He didn't open his eyes, and to mortals perhaps there would have been no expression there. But I felt his sorrow. I felt its immensity, and I wished I didn't feel it, and for one moment I understood the gulf that divided us, and the gulf that divided his attempt to overpower me from my rather simple defense of myself.

Desperately he had tried to vanquish what he did not comprehend.

And impulsively and almost effortlessly I had beaten him back.

All my pain with Nicolas came back to me and Gabrielle's words and Nicolas's denunciations. My anger was nothing to his misery, his despair.

And this perhaps was the reason that I reached down and gathered him up. And maybe I did it because he was so exquisitely beautiful and so lost, and we were after all of the same ilk.

Natural enough, wasn't it, that one of his own should take him away from this place where mortals would sooner or later have approached him, driven him stumbling away.

He gave no resistance to me. In a moment he was standing on his own feet. And then he walked drowsily beside me, my arm about his shoulder, bolstering him and steadying him until we were moving away from the Palais Royal, towards the rue St.-Honoré.

I only half glanced at the figures passing us, until I saw a familiar shape under the trees, with no scent of mortality coming from it, and I realized that Gabrielle had been there for some time.

She came forward hesitantly and silently, her face stricken when she saw the blood-drenched lace and the lacerations on his white skin, and she reached out as if to help me with the burden of him though she did not seem to know how.

Somewhere far off in the darkened gardens, the others were near. I *heard* them before I saw them. Nicki was there too.

They had come as Gabrielle had come, drawn over the miles, it seemed, by the tumult, or what vague messages I could not imagine, and they merely waited and watched as we moved away.

2

WE TOOK him with us to the livery stables, and there I put him on my mare. But he looked as if he would let himself fall off at any moment, and so I mounted behind him, and the three of us rode out.

All the way through the country, I wondered what I would do. I wondered what it meant to bring him to my lair. Gabrielle didn't give any protest. Now and then she glanced over at him. I heard nothing from him, and he was small and self-contained as he sat in front of me, light as a child but not a child.

Surely he had always known where the tower was, but had its bars kept him out? Now I meant to take him inside it. And why didn't Gabrielle say something to me? It was the meeting we had wanted, it was the thing for which we had waited, but surely she knew what he had just done.

When we finally dismounted, he walked ahead of me, and he waited for me to reach the gate. I had taken out the iron key to the lock and I studied him, wondering what promises one exacts from such a monster before opening one's door. Did the ancient laws of hospitality mean anything to the creatures of the night?

His eyes were large and brown and defeated. Almost drowsy they seemed. He regarded me for a long silent moment and then he reached out with his left hand, and his fingers curled around the iron crossbar in the center of the gate.

I stared helplessly as with a loud grinding noise the gate started to rip loose from the stone. But he stopped and contented himself with merely bending the iron bar a little. The point had been made. He could have entered this tower anytime that he wished.

I examined the iron bar that he'd twisted. I had beaten him. Could I do what he had just done? I didn't know. And unable to calculate my own powers, how could I ever calculate his?

"Come," Gabrielle said a little impatiently. And she led the way down the stairs to the dungeon crypt.

It was cold here as always, the fresh spring air never touching the place. She made a big fire in the old hearth while I lighted the candles. And as he sat on the stone bench watching us, I saw the effect of the warmth on him, the way that his body seemed to grow slightly larger, the way that he breathed it in.

As he looked about, it was as if he were absorbing the light. His gaze was clear.

Impossible to overestimate the effect of warmth and light on vampires. Yet the old coven had forsworn both.

I settled on another bench, and I let my eyes roam about the broad low chamber as his eyes roamed.

Gabrielle had been standing all this while. And now she approached him. She had taken out a handkerchief and she touched this to his face.

He stared at her in the same way that he stared at the fire and the candles, and the shadows leaping on the curved ceiling. This seemed to interest him as simply as anything else.

And I felt a shudder when I realized the bruises on his face were now almost gone! The bones were whole again, the shape of the face having been fully restored, and he was only a little gaunt from the blood he had lost.

My heart expanded slightly, against my will, as it had on the battlements when I had heard his voice.

I thought of the pain only half an hour ago in the Palais when the lie had broken with the stab of his fangs into my neck.

I hated him.

But I couldn't stop looking at him. Gabrielle combed his hair for him. She took his hands and wiped the blood from them. And he seemed helpless as all this was done. And she had not so much the expression of a ministering angel as an expression of curiosity, a desire to be near him and to touch him and examine him. In the quavering illumination they looked at one another.

He hunched forward a little, eyes darkening and full of expression now as they turned again to the grate. Had it not been for the blood on his lace ruff, he might have looked human. Might . . .

"What will you do now?" I asked. I spoke to make it clear to Gabrielle. "Will you remain in Paris and let Eleni and the others go on?"

No answer from him. He was studying me, studying the stone benches, the sarcophagi. Three sarcophagi.

"Surely you know what they're doing," I said. "Will you leave Paris or remain?"

It seemed he wanted to tell me again the magnitude of what I had done to him and the others, but this faded away. For one moment his face was wretched. It was defeated and warm and full of human misery. How old was he, I wondered. How long ago had he been a human who looked like that?

He heard me. But he didn't give an answer. He looked to Gabrielle, who stood near the fire, and then to me. And silently, he said, *Love me. You have destroyed everything! But if you love me, it can all be restored in a new form. Love me.*

This silent entreaty had an eloquence, however, that I can't put into words.

"What can I do to make you love me?" he whispered. "What can I give? The knowledge of all I have witnessed, the secrets of our powers, the mystery of what I am?"

It seemed blasphemous to answer. And as I had on the battlements, I found myself on the edge of tears. For all the purity of his silent communications, his voice gave a lovely resonance to his sentiments when he actually spoke.

It occurred to me as it had in Notre Dame that he spoke the way angels must speak, if they exist.

But I was awakened from this irrelevant thought, this obviating thought, by the fact that he was now beside me. He was closing his arm round me, and pressing his forehead against my face. He gave that summons again, not the rich, thudding seduction of that moment in the Palais

Royal, but the voice that had sung to me over the miles, and he told me there were things the two of us would know and understand as mortals never could. He told me that if I opened to him and gave him my strength and my secrets that he would give me his. He had been driven to try to destroy me, and he loved me all the more that he could not.

That was a tantalizing thought. Yet I felt danger. The word that came unbidden to me was Beware.

I don't know what Gabrielle saw or heard. I don't know what she felt.

Instinctively I avoided his eyes. There seemed nothing in the world I wanted more at this moment than to look right at him and understand him, and yet I *knew* I must not. I saw the bones under les Innocents again, the flickering hellfires I had imagined in the Palais Royal. And all the lace and velvet in the eighteenth century could not give him a human face.

I couldn't keep this from him, and it pained me that it was impossible for me to explain it to Gabrielle. And the awful silence between me and Gabrielle was at that moment almost too much to bear.

With him, I could speak, yes, with him I could dream dreams. Some reverence and terror in me made me reach out and embrace him, and I held him, battling my confusion and my desire.

"Leave Paris, yes," he whispered. "But take me with you. I don't know how to exist here now. I stumble through a carnival of horrors. Please . . ."

I heard myself say: "No."

"Have I no value to you?" he asked. He turned to Gabrielle. Her face was anguished and still as she looked at him. I couldn't know what went on in her heart, and to my sadness, I realized that he was speaking to her and locking me out. What was her answer?

But he was imploring both of us now. "Is there nothing outside yourself you would respect?"

"I might have destroyed you tonight," I said. "It was respect which kept me from that."

"No." He shook his head in a startlingly human fashion. "That you never could have done."

I smiled. It was probably true. But we were destroying him quite completely in another way.

"Yes," he said, "that's true. You are destroying me. Help me," he whispered. "Give me but a few short years of all you have before you, the two of you. I beg you. That is all I ask."

"No," I said again.

He was only a foot from me on the bench. He was looking at me. And there came the horrible spectacle again of his face narrowing and darkening and caving in upon itself in rage. It was as if he had no real substance. Only will kept him robust and beautiful. And when the flow of his will was interrupted, he melted like a wax doll.

But, as before, he recovered himself almost instantly. The "hallucination" was past.

He stood up and backed away from me until he was in front of the fire.

The will coming from him was palpable. His eyes were like something that didn't belong to him, nor to anything on earth. And the fire blazing behind him made an eerie nimbus around his head.

"I curse you!" he whispered.

I felt a jet of fear.

"I curse you," he said again and came closer. "Love mortals then, and live as you have lived, recklessly, with appetite for everything and love for everything, but there will come a time when only the love of your own kind can save you." He glanced at Gabrielle. "And I don't mean children such as this!"

This was so strong that I couldn't conceal its effect on me, and I realized I was rising from the bench and slipping away from him towards Gabrielle.

"I don't come empty-handed to you," he pressed, his voice deliberately softening. "I don't come begging with nothing to give of my own. Look at me. Tell me you don't need what you see in me, one who has the strength to take you through the ordeals that lie ahead."

His eyes flashed on Gabrielle and for one moment he remained locked to her and I saw her harden and begin to tremble.

"Let her be!" I said.

"You don't know what I say to her," he said coldly. "I do not try to hurt her. But in your love of mortals, what have you already done?"

He would say something terrible if I didn't stop him, something to wound me or Gabrielle. He knew all that had happened with Nicki. I knew that he did. If, somewhere deep down in my soul, I wished for the end of Nicki, he would know that too! Why had I let him in? Why had I not known what he could do?

"Oh, but it's always a travesty, don't you see?" he said with that same gentleness. "Each time the death and the awakening will ravage the mortal spirit, so that one will hate you for taking his life, another will run to excesses that you scorn. A third will emerge mad and raving, another a monster you cannot control. One will be jealous of your superiority, another shut you out." And here he shot his glance to Gabrielle again and half smiled. "And the veil will always come down between you. Make a legion. You will be, always and forever, alone!"

"I don't want to hear this. It means nothing," I said.

Gabrielle's face had undergone some ugly change. She was staring at him with hatred now, I was sure of it.

He made that bitter little noise that is a laugh but isn't a laugh at all.

"Lovers with a human face," he mocked me. "Don't you see your error? The other one hates you beyond all reason, and she—why, the dark blood has made her even colder, has it not? But even for her, strong as she is, there will come moments when she fears to be immortal, and who will she blame for what was done to her?"

"You are a fool," Gabrielle whispered.

"You tried to protect the violinist from it. But you never sought to protect her."

"Don't say any more," I answered. "You make me hate you. Is that what you want?"

"But I speak the truth and you know it. And what you will never know, either of you, is the full depth of each other's hatreds and resentments. Or suffering. Or love."

He paused and I could say nothing. He was doing exactly what I feared he would, and I didn't know how to defend myself.

"If you leave me now with this one," he continued, "you will do it again. Nicolas you never possessed. And she already wonders how she will ever get free of you. And unlike her, you cannot stand to be alone."

I couldn't answer. Gabrielle's eyes became smaller, her mouth a little more cruel.

"So the time will come when you will seek other mortals," he went on, "hoping once more that the Dark Trick will bring you the love you crave. And of these newly mutilated and unpredictable children you'll try to fashion your citadels against time. Well, they will be prisons if they last for half a century. I warn you. It is only with those as powerful and wise as yourself that the true citadel against time can be built."

The citadel against time. Even in my ignorance the words had their power. And the fear in me expanded, reached out to compass a thousand other causes.

He seemed distant for a moment, indescribably beautiful in the firelight, the dark auburn strands of his hair barely touching his smooth forehead, his lips parted in a beatific smile.

"If we cannot have the old ways, can't we have each other?" he asked, and now his voice was the voice of the summons again. "Who else can understand your suffering? Who else knows what passed through your mind the night you stood on the stage of your little theater and you frightened all those you had loved?"

"Don't speak about that," I whispered. But I was softening all over, drifting into his eyes and his voice. Very near to me was the ecstasy I'd felt that night on the battlements. With all my will I reached out for Gabrielle.

"Who understands what passed through your mind when my renegade followers, reveling in the music of your precious fiddler, devised their ghastly boulevard enterprise?" he asked.

I didn't speak.

"The Theater of the Vampires!" His lips lengthened in the saddest smile. "Does she comprehend the irony of it, the cruelty? Does she know what it was like when you stood on that stage as a young man and you heard the audience screaming for you? When time was your friend, not your enemy as it is now? When in the wings, you put out your arms and your mortal darlings came to you, your little family, folding themselves against you . . ."

"Stop, please. I ask you to stop."

"Does anyone else know the size of your soul?"

Witchcraft. Had it ever been used with more skill? And what was he really saying to us beneath this liquid flow of beautiful language: *Come to me, and I shall be the sun round which you are locked in orbit, and my rays shall lay bare the secrets you keep from each other, and I, who possess charms and powers of which you have no inkling, shall control and possess and destroy you!*

"I asked you before," I said. "What do you want? Really want?"

"You!" he said. "You and her! That we become three at this crossroads!"

Not that we surrender to you?

I shook my head. And I saw the same wariness and recoiling in Gabrielle.

He was not angry; there was no malice now. Yet he said again, in the same beguiling voice:

"I curse you," and I felt it as if he'd declaimed it.

"I offered myself to you at the moment you vanquished me," he said. "Remember that when your dark children strike out at you, when they rise up against you. Remember me."

I was shaken, more shaken even than I had been in the sad and awful finish with Nicolas at Renaud's. I had never once known fear in the crypt under les Innocents. But I had known it in this room since we came in.

And some anger boiled in him again, something too dreadful for him to control.

I watched him bow his head and turn away. He became small, light, and held his arms close to himself as he stood before the blaze and he thought of threats now to hurt me, and I heard them though they died before they ever reached his lips.

But something disturbed my vision for a fraction of a second. Maybe it was a candle guttering. Maybe it was the blink of my eye. Whatever it was, he vanished. Or he tried to vanish, and I saw him leaping away from the fire in a great dark streak.

"No!" I cried out. And lunging at something I couldn't even see, I held him, material again, in my hands.

He had only moved very fast, and I had moved faster, and we stood facing each other in the doorway of the crypt, and again I said that single negation and I wouldn't let him go.

"Not like this, we can't part. We can't leave each other in hatred, we can't." And my will dissolved suddenly as I embraced him and held tight to him so that he couldn't free himself nor even move.

I didn't care what he was, or what he had done in that doomed moment of lying to me, or even trying to overpower me, I didn't care that I was no longer mortal and would never be again.

I wanted only that he should remain. I wanted to be with him, what he was, and all the things he had said were true. Yet it could never be as he wished it to be. He could not have this power over us. He could not divide Gabrielle from me.

Yet I wondered, did he himself really understand what he was asking? Was it possible that he believed the more innocent words he spoke?

Without speaking, without asking his consent, I led him back to the bench by the fire. I felt danger again, terrible danger. But it didn't really matter. He had to remain here with us now.

Gabrielle was murmuring to herself. She was walking back and forth and her cloak hung from one shoulder and she seemed almost to have forgotten we were there.

Armand watched her, and when she turned to him, quite suddenly and unexpectedly, she spoke aloud.

"You come to him and you say, 'Take me with you.' You say, 'Love me,' and you hint of superior knowledge, secrets, yet you give us nothing, either of us, except lies."

"I showed my power to understand," he answered in a soft murmur.

"No, you did tricks with your understanding," she replied. "You made pictures. And rather childish pictures. You have done this all along. You lure Lestat in the Palais with the most gorgeous illusions only to attack him. And here, when there is a respite in the struggle, what do you do but try to sow dissension between us . . ."

"Yes, illusions before, I admit it," he answered. "But the things I've spoken here are true. Already you despise your son for his love of mortals, his need to be ever near them, his yielding to the violinist. *You* knew the Dark Gift would madden that one, and that it will finally destroy him. You do wish for your freedom, from all the Children of Darkness. You can't hide that from me."

"Ah, but you're so simple," she said. "You see, but you don't see. How many mortal years did you live? Do you remember anything of them? What you've perceived is not the sum total of the passion I feel for my son. I have loved him as I have never loved any other being in creation. In my loneliness, my son is everything to me. How is it you can't interpret what you see?"

"It's you who fail to interpret," he answered in the same soft manner. "If you had ever felt real longing for any other one, you would know that what you feel for your son is nothing at all."

"This is futile," I said, "to talk like this."

"No," she said to him without the slightest wavering. "My son and I are kin to each other in more ways than one. In fifty years of life, I've never known anyone as strong as myself, except my son. And what divides us we can always mend. But how are we to make you one of us when you use these things like wood for fire! But understand my larger point: what is it of yourself that you can give that we should want you?"

"My guidance is what you need," he answered. "You've only begun your adventure and you have no beliefs to hold you. You cannot live without some guidance . . ."

"Millions live without belief or guidance. It is you who cannot live without it," she said.

Pain coming from him. Suffering.

But she went on, her voice so steady and without expression it was almost a monologue:

"I have my questions," she asked. "There are things I must know. I cannot live without some embracing philosophy, but it has nothing to do with old beliefs in gods or devils." She started pacing again, glancing to him as she spoke.

"I want to know, for example, why beauty exists," she said, "why nature continues to contrive it, and what is the link between the life of a tree and its beauty, and what connects the mere existence of the sea or a lightning storm with the feelings these things inspire in us? If God does not exist, if these things are not unified into one metaphorical system, then why do they retain for us such symbolic power? Lestat calls it the Savage Garden, but for me that is not enough. And I must confess that this, this maniacal curiosity or call it what you will, leads me away from my human victims. It leads me into the open countryside, away from human creation.

And maybe it will lead me away from my son, who is under the spell of all things human."

She came up to him, nothing in her manner suggesting a woman now, and she narrowed her eyes as she looked into his face.

"But that is the lantern by which I see the Devil's Road," she said. "By what lantern have you traveled it? What have you really learned besides devil worship and superstition? What do you know about us, and how we came into existence? Give that to us, and it might be worth something. And then again, it might be worth nothing."

He was speechless. He had no art to hide his amazement.

He stared at her in innocent confusion. Then he rose and he slipped away, obviously trying to escape her, a battered spirit as he stared blankly before him.

The silence closed in. And I felt for the moment strangely protective for him. She had spoken the unadorned truth about the things that interested her as had been her custom ever since I could remember, and as always, there was something violently disregarding about it. She spoke of what mattered to her with no thought of what had befallen him.

Come to a different plane, she had said, my plane. And he was stymied and belittled. The degree of his helplessness was becoming alarming. He was not recovering from her attack.

He turned and he moved towards the benches again, as if he would sit, then towards the sarcophagi, then towards the wall. It seemed these solid surfaces repelled him as though his will confronted them first in an invisible field and he was buffeted about.

He drifted out of the room and into the narrow stone stairwell and then he turned and came back.

His thoughts were locked inside himself or, worse, there were no thoughts!

There were only the tumbling images of what he saw before him, simple material things glaring back at him, the iron-studded door, the candles, the fire. Some full-blown evocation of the Paris streets, the vendors and the hawkers of papers, the cabriolets, the blended sound of an orchestra, a horrid din of words and phrases from the books he had so recently read.

I couldn't bear this, but Gabrielle gestured sternly that I should stay where I was.

Something was building in the crypt. Something was happening in the very air itself.

Something changed even as the candles melted, and the fire crackled and licked at the blackened stones behind it, and the rats moved in the chambers of the dead below.

Armand stood in the arched doorway, and it seemed hours had passed though they hadn't and Gabrielle was a long distance away in the corner of the room, her face cool in its concentration, her eyes as radiant as they were small.

Armand was going to speak to us, but it was no explanation he was going to give. There was no direction even to the things he would say, and it was as if we'd cut him open and the images were coming out like blood.

Armand was just a young boy in the doorway, holding the backs of his own arms. And I knew what I felt. It was a monstrous intimacy with another being, an intimacy that made even the rapt moments of the kill seem dim and under control. He was opened and could no longer contain the dazzling stream of pictures that made his old silent voice seem thin and lyrical and made up.

Had this been the danger all along, the trigger of my fear? Even as I recognized it, I was yielding, and it seemed the great lessons of my life had all been learned through the renunciation of fear. Fear was once again breaking the shell around me so that something else could spring to life.

Never, never in all my existence, not mortal or immortal, had I been threatened with an intimacy quite like this.

The STORY of ARMAND

3

THE chamber had faded. The walls were gone.

Horsemen came. A gathering cloud on the horizon. Then screams of terror. And an auburn-haired child in crude peasant's clothes running on and on, as the horsemen broke loose in a horde and the child fighting and kicking as he was caught and thrown over the saddle of a rider who bore him away beyond the end of the world. Armand was this child.

And these were the southern steppes of Russia, but Armand didn't know that it was Russia. He knew Mother and Father and Church and God and Satan, but he didn't even understand the name of home, or the name of his language, or that the horsemen who carried him away were Tatars and that he would never see anything that he knew or loved again.

Darkness, the tumultuous movement of the ship and its never ending sickness, and emerging out of the fear and the numbing despair, the vast glittering wilderness of impossible buildings that was Constantinople in the last days of the Byzantine Empire, with her fantastical multitudes and her slave-auction blocks. The menacing babble of foreign tongues, threats made in the universal language of gesture, and all around him the enemies he could not distinguish or placate or escape.

Years and years would pass, beyond a mortal lifetime, before Armand would look back on that awesome moment and give them names and histories, the Byzantine officials of the court who would have castrated him and the harem keepers of Islam who would have done the same, and the proud Mameluke warriors of Egypt who would have taken him to Cairo with them had he been fairer and stronger, and the radiant soft-spoken Venetians in their leggings and velvet doublets, the most dazzling creatures of all, Christians even as he was a Christian, yet laughing gently to one another as they examined him, as he stood mute, unable to answer, to plead, even to hope.

I saw the seas before him, the great rolling blue of the Aegean and the Adriatic, and his sickness again in the hold and his solemn vow not to live.

And then the great Moorish palaces of Venice rising from the gleaming surface of the lagoon, and the house to which he was taken, with its dozens and dozens of secret chambers, the light of the sky glimpsed only through barred windows, and the other boys speaking to him in that soft strange tongue that was Venetian and the threats and the cajoling as he was convinced, against all his fear and superstitions, of the sins that he must commit with the endless procession of strangers in this landscape of marble and torchlight, each chamber opening to a new tableau of tenderness that surrendered to the same ritual and inexplicable and finally cruel desire.

And at last one night when, for days and days he had refused to submit and he was hungry and sore and would not speak any longer to anyone, he was pushed through one of those doors again, just as he was, soiled and blind from the dark room in which he'd been locked, and the creature standing there to receive him, the tall one in red velvet, with the lean and almost luminous face, touched him so gently with cool fingers that, half dreaming, he didn't cry as he saw the coins exchange hands. But it was a great deal of money. Too much money. He was being sold off. And the face, it was too smooth, it might have been a mask.

At the final moment, he screamed. He swore he would obey, he wouldn't fight anymore. Will someone tell him where he's being taken, he won't disobey anymore, please, please. But even as he was pulled down the stairs towards the dank smell of the water, he felt the firm, delicate fingers of his new Master again, and on his neck cool and tender lips that could never, never hurt him, and that first deadly and irresistible kiss.

Love and love and love in the vampire kiss. It bathed Armand, cleansed him, *this is everything,* as he was carried into the gondola and the gondola moved like a great sinister beetle through the narrow stream into the sewers beneath another house.

Drunk on pleasure. Drunk on the silky white hands that smoothed back his hair and the voice that called him beautiful; on the face that in moments of feeling was suffused with expression only to become as serene and dazzling as something made of jewels and alabaster in repose. Like a pool of moonlit water it was. Touch it even with the fingertip and all its life rises to the surface only to vanish in quiet once again.

Drunk in the morning light on the memory of those kisses as, alone, he opened one door after another upon books and maps and statues in granite and marble, the other apprentices finding him and leading him patiently to his work—letting him watch as they ground the brilliant pigments, teaching him to blend the pure color with the yellow egg yolk, and how to spread the lacquer of the egg yolk over the panels, and taking him up on the scaffolding as they worked with careful strokes on the very edges of the vast depiction of sun and clouds, showing him those great faces and hands and angels' wings which only the Master's brush would touch.

Drunk as he sat at the long table with them, gorging himself on the delicious foods that he had never tasted before, and the wine which never ran out.

And falling asleep finally to wake at that moment of twilight when the Master stood beside the enormous bed, gorgeous as something imagined in his red velvet, with his thick white hair glistening in the lamplight, and the simplest happiness in his brilliant cobalt blue eyes. The deadly kiss.

"Ah, yes, never to be separated from you, yes, . . . not afraid."

"Soon, my darling one, we will be truly united soon."

Torches blazing throughout the house. The Master atop the scaffolding with the brush in his hand: "Stand there, in the light, don't move," and hours and hours frozen in the same position, and then before dawn, seeing his own likeness there in the paint, the face of the angel, the Master smiling as he moved down the endless corridor . . .

"No, Master, don't leave me, let me stay with you, don't go . . ."

Day again, and money in his pockets, real gold, and the grandeur of Venice with her dark green waterways walled in palaces, and the other apprentices walking arm in arm with him, and the fresh air and the blue sky over the Piazza San Marco like something he had only dreamed in childhood, and the palazzo again at twilight, and the Master coming, the Master bent over the smaller panel with the brush, working faster and faster as the apprentices gazed on half horrified, half fascinated, the Master looking up and seeing him and putting down the brush, and taking him out of the enormous studio as the others worked until the hour of midnight, his face in the Master's hands as, alone in the bedchamber again, that secret, never tell anyone, kiss.

Two years? Three years? No words to recreate it or embrace it, the glory that was those times—the fleets that sailed away to war from that port, the hymns that rose before those Byzantine altars, the passion plays and the miracle plays performed on their platforms in the churches and in the piazza with their hell's mouth and cavorting devils, and the glittering mosaics spreading out over the walls of San Marco and San Zanipolo and the Palazzo Ducale, and the painters who walked those streets, Giambono, Uccello, the Vivarini and the Bellini; and the endless feast days and processions, and always in the small hours in the vast torchlighted rooms of the palazzo, alone with the Master when the others slept safely locked away. The Master's brush racing over the panel before it as if uncovering the painting rather than creating it—sun and sky and sea spreading out beneath the canopy of the angel's wings.

And those awful inevitable moments when the Master would rise screaming, hurling the pots of paint in all directions, clutching at his eyes as if he would pull them out of his head.

"Why can I not see? Why can I not see better than mortals see?"

Holding tight to the Master. Waiting for the rapture of the kiss. Dark secret, unspoken secret. The Master slipping out of the door sometime before dawn.

"Let me go with you, Master."

"Soon, my darling, my love, my little one, when you're strong enough and tall enough, and there is no flaw in you anymore. Go now, and have all the pleasures that await you, have the love of a woman, and have the love of a man as well in the nights that follow. Forget the bitterness you knew in the brothel and taste of these things while there is still time."

And rarely did the night close that there wasn't that figure come back again, just before the rising sun, and this time ruddy and warm as it bent over him to give him the embrace that would sustain him through the daylight hours until the deadly kiss at twilight again.

He learned to read and to write. He took the paintings to their final destinations in the churches and the chapels of the great palaces, and collected the payments and bargained for the pigments and the oils. He scolded the servants when the beds weren't made and the meals weren't ready. And beloved by the apprentices, he sent them to their new service when they were finished, with tears. He read poetry to the Master as the Master painted, and he learned to play the lute and to sing songs.

And during those sad times when the Master left Venice for many nights, it was he who governed in the Master's absence, concealing his anguish from the others, knowing it would end only when the Master returned.

And one night finally, in the small hours when even Venice slept:

"This is the moment, beautiful one. For you to come to me and become like me. Is it what you wish?"

"Yes."

"Forever to thrive in secret upon the blood of the evildoer as I thrive, and to abide with these secrets until the end of the world."

"I take the vow, I surrender, I will . . . to be with you, my Master, always, you are the creator of all things that I am. There has never been any greater desire."

The Master's brush pointing to the painting that reached to the ceiling above the tiers of scaffolding.

"This is the only sun that you will ever see again. But a millennium of nights will be yours to see light as no mortal has ever seen it, to snatch from the distant stars as if you were Prometheus an endless illumination by which to understand all things."

How many months were there after? Reeling in the power of the Dark Gift.

This nighttime life of drifting through the alleyways and the canals together—at one with the danger of the dark and no longer afraid of it—and the age-old rapture of the killing, and never, never the innocent souls. No, always the evildoer, the mind pierced until Typhon, the slayer of his brother, was revealed, and then the drinking up of the evil from the mortal victim and the transmuting of it into ecstasy, the Master leading the way, the feast shared.

And the painting afterwards, the solitary hours with the miracle of the new skill, the brush sometimes moving as if by itself across the enameled surface, and the two of them painting furiously on the triptych, and the mortal apprentices asleep among the paint pots and the wine bottles, and only one mystery disturbing the serenity, the mystery that the Master, as in the past, must now and then leave Venice for a journey that seemed endless to those left behind.

All the more terrible now the parting. To hunt alone without the Master, to lie alone in the deep cellar after the hunt, waiting. Not to hear the ring of the Master's laughter or the beat of the Master's heart.

"But where do you go? Why can't I go with you?" Armand pleaded. Didn't they share the secret? Why was this mystery not explained?

"No, my lovely one, you are not ready for this burden. For now, it must be, as it has been for over a thousand years, mine alone. Someday you will help me with what I have to do, but only when you are ready for the knowledge, when you have shown that you truly wish to know, and when you are powerful enough that no one can ever take the knowledge from you against your will. Until then understand I have no choice but to leave you. I go to tend to Those Who Must Be Kept as I have always done."

Those Who Must Be Kept.

Armand brooded upon it; it frightened him. But worst of all it took the Master from him, and only did he learn not to fear it when the Master returned to him again and again.

"Those Who Must Be Kept are in peace, or in silence," he would say as he took the red velvet cloak from his shoulders. "More than that we may never know."

And to the feast again, the stalking of the evildoer through the alleys of Venice, he and the Master would go.

How long might it have continued—through one mortal lifetime? Through a hundred?

Not a half year in this dark bliss before the evening at twilight when the Master stood over his coffin in the deep cellar just above the water, and said:

"Rise, Armand, we must leave here. They have come!"

"But who are they, Master? Is it Those Who Must Be Kept?"

"No, my darling. It is the others. Come, we must hurry!"

"But how can they hurt us? Why must we go?"

The white faces at the windows, the pounding at the doors. Glass shattering. The Master turning this way and that as he looked at the paintings. The smell of smoke. The smell of burning pitch. They were coming up from the cellar. They were coming down from above.

"Run, there is no time to save anything." Up the stairs to the roof.

Black hooded figures heaving their torches through the doorways, the fire roaring in the rooms below, exploding the windows, boiling up the stairway. All the paintings were burning.

"To the roof, Armand. Come!"

Creatures like ourselves in these dark garments! Others like ourselves. The Master scattered them in all directions as he raced up the stairway, bones cracking as they struck the ceiling and the walls.

"Blasphemer, heretic!" the alien voices roared. The arms caught Armand and held him, and above at the very top of the stairway the Master turned back for him:

"Armand! Trust your strength. Come!"

But they were swarming behind the Master. They were surrounding him. For each one hurled into the plaster, three more appeared, until fifty torches were plunged into the Master's velvet garments, his long red sleeves, his white hair. The fire roared up to the ceiling as it consumed him, making of him a living torch, even as with flaming arms he defended himself, igniting his attackers as they threw the blazing torches like firewood at his feet.

But Armand was being borne down and away, out of the burning house, with the screaming mortal apprentices. And over the water and away from Venice, amid cries and wailing, in the belly of a vessel as terrifying as the slave ship, to an open clearing under the night sky.

"Blasphemer, blasphemer!" The bonfire growing, and the chain of hooded figures around it, and the chant rising and rising, "Into the fire."

"No, don't do it to me, no!"

And as he watched, petrified, he saw brought towards the pyre the mortal apprentices, his brothers, his only brothers, roaring in panic as they were hurled upwards and over into the flames.

"No . . . stop this, they're innocent! For the love of God, stop, innocent! . . ." He was screaming, but now his time had come. They were lifting him as he struggled, and he was flung up and up to fall down into the blast.

"Master, help me!" Then all words giving way to one wailing cry.

Thrashing, screaming, mad.

But he had been taken out of it. Snatched back into life. And he lay on the ground looking at the sky. The flames licked the stars, it seemed, but he was far away from them, and couldn't even feel the heat anymore. He could smell his burnt clothing and his burnt hair. The pain in his face and hands was the worst and the blood was leaking out of him and he could scarcely move his lips . . .

". . . All thy Master's vain works destroyed, all the vain creations which he made among mortals with his Dark Powers, images of angels and saints and living mortals! Wilt thou, too, be destroyed? Or serve Satan? Make thy choice. Thou hast tasted the fire, and the fire waits for thee, hungry for thee. Hell waits for thee. Wilt thou make thy choice?"

". . . yes . . ."

". . . to serve Satan as he is meant to be served."

"Yes . . ."

". . . That all things of the world are vanity, and thou shalt never use thy Dark Powers for any mortal vanity, not to paint, not to create music, not to dance, nor to recite for the amusement of mortals but only and forever in the service of Satan, thy Dark Powers to seduce and to terrify and to destroy, only to destroy . . ."

"Yes . . ."

". . . consecrated to thy one and only master, Satan, Satan forever, always and forever . . . to serve thy true master in darkness and pain and in suffering, to surrender thy mind and thy heart . . ."

"Yes."

"And to keep from thy brethren in Satan no secret, to yield all knowledge of the blasphemer and his burden . . ."

Silence.

"To yield all knowledge of the burden, child! Come now, the flames wait."

"I do not understand you . . ."

"Those Who Must Be Kept. Tell."

"Tell what? I do not know anything, except that I do not wish to suffer. I am so afraid."

"The truth, Child of Darkness. Where are they? Where are Those Who Must Be Kept?"

"I do not know. Look into my mind if you have that same power. There is nothing I can tell."

"But *what,* child, *what* are they? Did he never tell you? *What* are Those Who Must Be Kept?"

And so they did not understand it either. It was no more than a phrase to them as it was to him. *When you are powerful enough that no one can ever take the knowledge from you against your will.* The Master had been wise.

"What is its meaning! Where are they? We must have the answer."

"I swear to you, I do not have it. I swear on my fear which is all I possess now, I do not know!"

White faces appearing above him, one at a time. The tasteless lips giving hard, sweet kisses, hands stroking him, and from their wrists the glittering droplets of blood. They wanted the truth to come out in the blood. But what did it matter? The blood was the blood.

"Thou art the devil's child now."

"Yes."

"Don't weep for thy master, Marius. Marius is in hell where he belongs. Now drink the healing blood and rise and dance with thine own kind for the glory of Satan! And immortality will be truly thine!'

"Yes"—the blood burning his tongue as he lifted his head, the blood filling him with torturous slowness. "Oh, please."

All around him Latin phrases, and the low beat of drums. They were satisfied. They knew he had spoken the truth. They would not kill him and the ecstasy dimmed all considerations. The pain in his hands and his face had melted into this ecstasy—

"Rise, young one, and join the Children of Darkness."

"Yes, I do." White hands reaching for his hands. Horns and lutes shrilling over the thud of the drums, the harps plucked into an hypnotic strumming as the circle commenced to move. Hooded figures in mendicant black, robes flowing as they lifted their knees high and bent their backs.

And breaking hands, they whirled, leapt, and came down again, spinning round and round, and a humming song rose louder and louder from their closed lips.

The circle swept on faster. The humming was a great melancholy vibration without shape or continuity and yet it seemed to be a form of speaking, to be the very echo of thought. Louder and louder it came like a moan that could not break into a cry.

He was making the same sound with it, and then turning, and dizzy with turning, he leapt high into the air. Hands caught him, lips kissed him, he was whirling about and pulled along by the others, someone crying out in Latin, another answering, another crying louder, and another answer coming again.

He was flying, no longer bound to the earth and the awful pain of his Master's death, and the death of the paintings, and death of the mortals he loved. The wind sailed past him, and the heat blasted his face and eyes. But the singing was so beautiful that it didn't matter that he didn't know the words, or that he couldn't pray to Satan, didn't know how to believe or make such a prayer. No one knew that he didn't know and they were all in a chorus together and they cried and lamented and turned and leapt again and then, swaying back and forth, threw their heads back as the fire blinded them and licked them and someone shouted "Yes, YES!"

And the music surged. A barbarous rhythm broke loose all around him from drums and tambourines, voices in lurid rushing melody at last. The vampires threw up their arms, howled, figures flickering past him in riotous contortions, backs arched, heels stomping. The jubilation of imps in hell. It horrified him and it called to him, and when the hands clutched at him and swung him around, he stomped and twisted and danced like the others, letting the pain course through him, bending his limbs and giving the alarm to his cries.

And before dawn, he was delirious, and he had a dozen brothers around him, caressing him and soothing him, and leading him down a staircase that had opened in the bowels of the earth.

IT SEEMED that some time in the months that followed Armand dreamed his Master had not been burnt to death.

He dreamed his Master had fallen from the roof, a blazing comet, into the saving waters of the canal below. And deep in the mountains of northern Italy, his Master survived. His Master called to him to come. His Master was in the sanctuary of Those Who Must Be Kept.

Sometimes in the dream his Master was as powerful and radiant as he had ever been; beauty seemed his raiment. And at others he was burnt black and shriveled, a breathing cinder, his eyes huge and yellow, and only his white hair as lustrous and full as it had been. He crept along the ground in his weakness, pleading for Armand to help him. And behind him, warm light spilled from the sanctuary of Those Who Must Be Kept; there came the smell of incense, and there seemed some promise of ancient magic there, some promise of cold and exotic beauty beyond all evil and all good.

But these were vain imaginings. His Master had told him that fire and the light of the sun could destroy them, and he himself had seen his Master in flames. It was like wishing for his mortal life to come again to have these dreams.

And when his eyes were open on the moon and the stars, and the still mirror of the sea before him, he knew no hope, and no grief, and no joy. All those things had come from the Master, and the Master was no more.

"I am the devil's child." That was poetry. All will was extinguished in him, and there was nothing but the dark confraternity, and the kill was now of the innocent as well as the guilty. The kill was above all cruel.

In Rome in the great coven in the catacombs, he bowed before Santino, the leader, who came down the stone steps to receive him with outstretched arms. This great one had been Born to Darkness in the time of the Black Death, and he told Armand of the vision that had come to him in the year 1349 when the plague raged, that we were to be as the Black Death itself, a vexation without explanation, to cause man to doubt the mercy and intervention of God.

Into the sanctum lined with human skulls Santino took Armand, telling him of the history of the vampires.

From all times we have existed, as wolves have, a scourge of mortals. And in the coven of Rome, dark shadow of the Roman Church, lay our final perfection.

Armand already knew the rituals and common prohibitions; now he must learn the great laws:

One—that each coven must have its leader and only he might order the working of the Dark Trick upon a mortal, seeing that the methods and the rituals were properly observed.

Two—that the Dark Gifts must never be given to the crippled, the maimed, or to children, or to those who cannot, even with the Dark Powers, survive on their own. Be it further understood that all mortals who would receive the Dark Gifts should be beautiful in person so that the insult to God might be greater when the Dark Trick is done.

Three—that never should an old vampire work this magic lest the blood of the fledgling be too strong. For all our gifts increase naturally with age, and the old ones have too much strength to pass on. Injury, burning —these catastrophes, if they do not destroy the Child of Satan will only increase his powers when he is healed. Yet Satan guards the flock from the power of old ones, for almost all, without exception, go mad.

In this particular, let Armand observe that there was no vampire then living who was more than three hundred years old. No one alive then could remember the first Roman coven. The devil frequently calls his vampires home.

But let Armand understand here also that the effect of the Dark Trick is unpredictable, even when passed on by the very young vampire and with all due care. For reasons no one knows, some mortals when Born to Darkness become as powerful as Titans, others may be no more than corpses that move. That is why mortals must be chosen with skill. Those with great passion and indomitable will should be avoided as well as those who have none.

Four—that no vampire may ever destroy another vampire, except that the coven master has the power of life and death over all of his flock. And it is, further, his obligation to lead the old ones and the mad ones into the fire when they can longer serve Satan as they should. It is his obligation to destroy all vampires who are not properly made. It is his obligation to destroy those who are so badly wounded that they cannot survive on their own. And it is his obligation finally to seek the destruction of all outcasts and all who have broken these laws.

Five—that no vampire shall ever reveal his true nature to a mortal and allow that mortal to live. No vampire must ever reveal the history of the vampires to a mortal and let the mortal live. No vampire must commit to writing the history of the vampires or any true knowledge of vampires lest such a history be found by mortals and believed. And a vampire's name must never be known to mortals, save from his tombstone, and never must any vampire reveal to mortals the location of his or any other vampire's lair.

These then were the great commandments, which all vampires must obey. And this was the condition of existence among all the Undead.

Yet Armand should know that there had always been stories of ancient ones, heretic vampires of frightening power who submitted to no authority, not even that of the devil—vampires who had survived for thousands of years. Children of the Millennia, they were sometimes called. In the north of Europe there were tales of Mael, who dwelt in the forests of England

and Scotland; and in Asia Minor the legend of Pandora. And in Egypt, the ancient tale of the vampire Ramses, seen again in this very time.

In all parts of the world one found such tales. And one could easily dismiss them as fanciful save for one thing. The ancient heretic Marius had been found in Venice, and there punished by the Children of Darkness. The legend of Marius had been true. But Marius was no more.

Armand said nothing to this last judgment. He did not tell Santino of the dreams he had had. In truth the dreams had dimmed inside Armand as had the colors of Marius's paintings. They were no longer held in Armand's mind or heart to be discovered by others who might try to see.

When Santino spoke of Those Who Must Be Kept, Armand again confessed that he did not know the meaning of it. Neither did Santino, nor any vampire that Santino had ever known.

Dead was the secret. Dead was Marius. And so consign to silence the old and useless mystery. Satan is our Lord and Master. In Satan, all is understood and all is known.

Armand pleased Santino. He memorized the laws, perfected his performance of the ceremonial incantations, the rituals, and the prayers. He saw the greatest Sabbats he was ever to witness. And he learned from the most powerful and skillful and beautiful vampires he was ever to know. He learned so well that he became a missionary sent out to gather the vagrant Children of Darkness into covens, and guide others in the performance of the Sabbat, and the working of the Dark Trick when the world and the flesh and the devil called for it to be done.

In Spain and in Germany and in France, he had taught the Dark Blessings and Dark Rituals, and he had known savage and tenacious Children of Darkness, and dim flames had flared in him in their company and in those moments when the coven surrounded him, comforted by him, deriving its unity from his strength.

He had perfected the act of killing beyond the abilities of all the Children of Darkness that he knew. He had learned to summon those who truly wished to die. He had but to stand near the dwellings of mortals and call silently to see his victim appear.

Old, young, wretched, diseased, the ugly or the beautiful, it did not matter because he did not choose. Dazzling visions he gave, if they should want to receive, but he did not move towards them nor even close his arms around them. Drawn inexorably towards him, it was they who embraced him. And when their warm living flesh touched him, when he opened his lips and felt the blood spill, he knew the only surcease from misery that he could know.

It seemed to him in the best of these moments that his way was profoundly spiritual, uncontaminated by the appetites and confusions that made up the world, despite the carnal rapture of the kill.

In that act the spiritual and the carnal came together, and it was the spiritual, he was convinced, that survived. Holy Communion it seemed to him, the Blood of the Children of Christ serving only to bring the essence of life itself into his understanding for the split second in which death occurred. Only the great saints of God were his equals in this spirituality, this confrontation with mystery, this existence of meditation and denial.

Yet he had seen the greatest of his companions vanish, bring destruction upon themselves, go mad. He had witnessed the inevitable dissolution of covens, seen immortality defeat the most perfectly made Children of Darkness, and it seemed at times some awesome punishment that it never defeated him.

Was he destined to be one of the ancient ones? The Children of the Millennia? Could one believe those stories which persisted still?

Now and then a roaming vampire would speak of the fabled Pandora glimpsed in the far-off Russian city of Moscow, or of Mael living on the bleak English coast. The wanderers told even of Marius—that he had been seen again in Egypt, or in Greece. But these storytellers had not themselves laid eyes upon the legendary ones. They knew nothing really. These were often-repeated tales.

They did not distract or amuse the obedient servant of Satan. In quiet allegiance to the Dark Ways, Armand continued to serve.

Yet in the centuries of his long obedience, Armand kept two secrets to himself. These were his property, these secrets, more purely his than the coffin in which he locked himself by day, or the few amulets he wore.

The first was that no matter how great his loneliness, or how long the search for brothers and sisters in whom he might find some comfort, he never worked the Dark Trick himself. He wouldn't give that to Satan, no Child of Darkness made by him.

And the other secret, which he kept from his followers for their sake, was simply the extent of his ever deepening despair.

That he craved nothing, cherished nothing, believed nothing finally, and took not one particle of pleasure in his ever increasing and awesome powers, and existed from moment to moment in a void broken once every night of his eternal life by the kill—that secret he had kept from them as long as they had needed him and it had been possible to lead them because his fear would have made them afraid.

But it was finished.

A great cycle had ended, and even years ago he had felt it closing without understanding it was a cycle at all.

From Rome there came the garbled travelers' accounts, old when they were told to him, that the leader, Santino, had abandoned his flock. Some said he had gone mad into the countryside, others that he had leapt into the fire, others that "the world" had swallowed him, that he had been borne off in a black coach with mortals never to be seen again.

"We go into the fire or we go into legend," said a teller of the tale.

Then came accounts of chaos in Rome, of dozens of leaders who put on the black hood and the black robes to preside over the coven. And then it seemed there were none.

Since the year 1700 there had been no word anymore from Italy. For half a century Armand had not been able to trust to his passion or that of the others around him to create the frenzy of the true Sabbat. And he had dreamed of his old Master, Marius, in those rich robes of red velvet, and seen the palazzo full of vibrant paintings, and he had been afraid.

Then another had come.

His children rushed down into the cellars beneath les Innocents to describe to him this new vampire, who wore a fur-lined cloak of red velvet and could profane the churches and strike down those who wore crosses and walk in the places of light. Red velvet. It was mere coincidence, and yet it maddened him and seemed an insult to him, a gratuitous pain that his soul couldn't bear.

And then the woman had been made, the woman with the hair of a lion and the name of an angel, beautiful and powerful as her son.

And he had come up the stairway out of the catacomb, leading the band against us, as the hooded ones had come to destroy him and his Master in Venice centuries before.

And it had failed.

He stood dressed in these strange lace and brocade garments. He carried coins in his pockets. His mind swam with images from the thousands of books he had read. And he felt himself pierced with all he had witnessed in the places of light in the great city called Paris, and it was as if he could hear his old Master whispering in his ear:

But a millennium of nights will be yours to see light as no mortal has ever seen it, to snatch from the distant stars as if you were Prometheus an endless illumination by which to understand all things.

"All things have eluded my understanding," he said. "I am as one whom the earth has given back, and you, Lestat and Gabrielle, are like the images painted by my old Master in cerulean and carmine and gold."

He stood still in the doorway, his hands on the backs of his arms, and he was looking at us, asking silently:

What is there to know? What is there to give? We are the abandoned of God. And there is no Devil's Road spinning out before me and there are no bells of hell ringing in my ears.

4

AN HOUR passed. Perhaps more. Armand sat by the fire. No marks any longer on his face from the long-forgotten battle. He seemed, in his stillness, to be as fragile as an emptied shell.

Gabrielle sat across from him, and she too stared at the flames in silence, her face weary and seemingly compassionate. It was painful for me not to know her thoughts.

I was thinking of Marius. And Marius and Marius . . . the vampire who had painted pictures in and of the real world. Triptychs, portraits, frescoes on the walls of his palazzo.

And the real world had never suspected him nor hunted him nor cast him out. It was this band of hooded fiends who came to burn the paintings, the ones who shared the Dark Gift with him—had he himself ever called it the Dark Gift?—they were the ones who said he couldn't live and create among mortals. Not mortals.

I saw the little stage at Renaud's and I heard myself sing and the singing become a roar. Nicolas said, "It is splendid." I said, "It is petty." And it was like striking Nicolas. In my imagination he said what he had not said that night: "Let me have what I can believe in. You would never do that."

The triptychs of Marius were in churches and convent chapels, maybe on the walls of the great houses in Venice and Padua. The vampires would not have gone into holy places to pull them down. So they were there somewhere, with a signature perhaps worked into the detail, these creations of the vampire who surrounded himself with mortal apprentices, kept a mortal lover from whom he took the little drink, went out alone to kill.

I thought of the night in the inn when I had seen the meaninglessness of life, and the soft fathomless despair of Armand's story seemed an ocean in which I might drown. This was worse than the blasted shore in Nicki's mind. This was for three centuries, this darkness, this nothingness.

The radiant auburn-haired child by the fire could open his mouth again and out would come blackness like ink to cover the world.

That is, if there had not been this protagonist, this Venetian master, who had committed the heretical act of making meaning on the panels he painted—it had to be meaning—and our own kind, the elect of Satan, had made him into a living torch.

Had Gabrielle seen these paintings in the story as I had seen them? Did they burn in her mind's eye as they did in mine?

Marius was traveling some route into my soul that would let him roam there forever, along with the hooded fiends who turned the paintings into chaos again.

In a dull sort of misery, I thought of the travelers' tales—that Marius was alive, seen in Egypt or Greece.

I wanted to ask Armand, wasn't it possible? Marius must have been so very strong . . . But it seemed disrespectful of him to ask.

"Old legend," he whispered. His voice was as precise as the inner voice. Unhurriedly, he continued without ever looking away from the flames. "Legend from the olden times before they destroyed us both."

"Perhaps not," I said. Echo of the visions, paintings on the walls. "Maybe Marius is alive."

"We are miracles or horrors," he said quietly, "depending upon how you wish to see us. And when you first *know* about us, whether it's through the dark blood or promises or visitations, you think anything is possible. But that isn't so. The world closes tight around this miracle soon enough; and you don't hope for other miracles. That is, you become accustomed to the new limits and the limits define everything once again. So they say Marius continues. They all continue somewhere, that's what you *want* to believe.

"Not a single one remains in the coven in Rome from those nights when I was taught the ritual; and maybe the coven itself is no longer even there. Years and years have passed since there was any communication from the coven. But they all exist somewhere, don't they? After all, we can't die." He sighed. "Doesn't matter," he said.

Something greater and more terrible mattered, that this despair might crush Armand beneath it. That in spite of the thirst in him now, the blood lost when we had fought together, and the silent furnace of his body healing the bruises and the broken flesh, he could not will himself into the world above to hunt. Rather suffer the thirst and the heat of the silent furnace. Rather stay here and be with us.

But he already knew the answer, that he could not be with us.

Gabrielle and I didn't have to speak to let him know. We did not even have to resolve the question in our minds. He knew, the way God might know the future because God is the possessor of all the facts.

Unbearable anguish. And Gabrielle's expression all the more weary, sad.

"You know that with all my soul I do want to take you with us," I said. I was surprised at my own emotion. "But it would be disaster for us all."

No change in him. He knew. No challenge from Gabrielle.

"I cannot *stop* thinking of Marius," I confessed.

I know. And you do not think of Those Who Must Be Kept, which is most strange.

"That is merely another mystery," I said. "And there are a thousand mysteries. I think of Marius! And I'm too much the slave of my own obsessions and fascination. It's a dreadful thing to linger so on Marius, to extract that one radiant figure from the tale."

Doesn't matter. If it pleases you, take it. I do not lose what I give.

"When a being reveals his pain in such a torrent, you are bound to respect the whole of the tragedy. You have to try to comprehend. And such helplessness, such despair is almost incomprehensible to me. That's why I think of Marius. Marius I understand. You I don't understand."

Why?

Silence.

Didn't he deserve the truth?

"I've been a rebel always," I said. "You've been the slave of everything that ever claimed you."

"I was the leader of my coven!"

"No. You were the slave of Marius and then of the Children of Darkness. You fell under the spell of one and then the other. What you suffer now is the absence of a spell. I think I shudder that you caused me so to understand it for a little while, to know it as if I were a different being than I am."

"Doesn't matter," he said, eyes still on the fire. "You think too much in terms of decision and action. This tale is no explanation. And I am not a being who requires a respectful acknowledgment in your thoughts or in words. And we all know the answer you have given is too immense to be voiced and we all three of us know that it is final. What I don't know is why. So I am a creature very different from you, and so you cannot understand me. Why can't I go with you? I will do whatever you wish if you take me with you. I will be under your spell."

I thought of Marius with his brush and the pots of egg tempera.

"How could you have ever believed anything that they told you after they burned those paintings?" I asked. "How could you have given yourself over to them?"

Agitation, rising anger.

Caution in Gabrielle's face, but not fear.

"And you, when you stood on the stage and you saw the audience screaming to get out of the theater—how my followers described this to me, the vampire terrifying the crowd and the crowd streaming into the boulevard du Temple—what did you believe? That you did not belong among mortals, that's what you believed. You knew you did not. And there was no band of fiends in hooded robes to tell you. You knew. So Marius did not belong among mortals. So I did not."

"Ah, but it's different."

"No, it is not. That's why you scorn the Theater of the Vampires which is now at this very moment working out its little dramas to bring in the gold from the boulevard crowds. You do not wish to deceive as Marius deceived. It divides you ever more from mankind. You want to pretend to be mortal, but to deceive makes you angry and it makes you kill."

"In that moment on the stage," I said, "I revealed *myself.* I did the very opposite of deceiving. I wanted somehow in making manifest the monstrosity of myself to be joined with my fellow humans again. Better they should run from me than not see me. Better they should know I was something monstrous than for me to glide through the world unrecognized by those upon whom I preyed."

"But it was not better."

"No. What Marius did was better. He did not deceive."

"Of course he did. He fooled everyone!"

"No. He found a way to imitate mortal life. To be one with mortals. He slew only the evildoer, and he painted as mortals paint. Angels and blue skies, clouds, those are the things you made me see when you were telling. He created good things. And I see wisdom in him and a lack of vanity. He did not need to reveal himself. He had lived a thousand years and he believed more in the vistas of heaven that he painted than in himself."

Confusion.

Doesn't matter now, devils who paint angels.

"Those are only metaphors," I said. "And it does matter! If you are to rebuild, if you are to find the Devil's Road again, it does matter! There are ways for us to exist. If I could only imitate life, just find a way . . ."

"You say things that mean nothing to me. We are the abandoned of God."

Gabrielle glanced at him suddenly. "Do you *believe* in God?" she asked.

"Yes, always in God," he answered. "It is Satan—our master—who is the fiction and that is the fiction which has betrayed me."

"Oh, then you are truly damned," I said. "And you know full well that your retreat into the fraternity of the Children of Darkness was a retreat from a sin that was not a sin."

Anger.

"Your heart breaks for something you'll never have," he countered, his voice rising suddenly. "You brought Gabrielle and Nicolas over the barrier to you, but you could not go back."

"Why is it you don't hearken to your own story?" I asked. "Is it that you have never forgiven Marius for not warning you about them, letting you fall into their hands? You will never take anything, not example or inspiration, from Marius again? I am not Marius, but I tell you since I set my feet on the Devil's Road, I have heard of only one elder who could teach me anything, and that is Marius, your Venetian master. He is talking to me now. He is saying something to me of a way to be immortal."

"Mockery."

"No. It wasn't mockery! And you are the one whose heart breaks for what he will never have: another body of belief, another spell."

No answer.

"We cannot be Marius for you," I said, "or the dark lord, Santino. We are not artists with a great vision that will carry you forward. And we are not evil coven masters with the conviction to condemn a legion to perdition. And this domination—this glorious mandate—is what you must have."

I had risen to my feet without meaning to. I had come close to the fireplace and I was looking down at him.

And I saw, out of the corner of my eye, Gabrielle's subtle nod of approval, and the way that she closed her eyes for a moment as if she were allowing herself a sigh of relief.

He was perfectly still.

"You have to suffer through this emptiness," I said, "and find what impels you to continue. If you come with us we will fail you and you will destroy us."

"How suffer through it?" He looked up at me and his eyebrows came together in the most poignant frown. "How do I begin? You move like the right hand of God! But for me the world, the real world in which Marius lived, is beyond reach. I never lived in it. I push against the glass. But how do I get in?"

"I can't tell you that," I said.

"You have to study this age," Gabrielle interrupted. Her voice was calm but commanding.

He looked towards her as she spoke.

"You have to understand the age," she continued, "through its literature and its music and its art. You have come up out of the earth, as you yourself put it. Now live in the world."

No answer from him. Flash of Nicki's ravaged flat with all its books on the floor. Western civilization in heaps.

"And what better place is there than the center of things, the boulevard and the theater?" Gabrielle asked.

He frowned, his head turning dismissively, but she pressed on.

"Your gift is for leading the coven, and your coven is still there."

He made a soft despairing sound.

"Nicolas is a fledgling," she said. "He can teach them much about the world outside, but he cannot really lead them. The woman, Eleni, is amazingly clever, but she will make way for you."

"What is it to me, their games?" he whispered.

"It is a way to exist," she said. "And that is all that matters to you now."

"The Theater of the Vampires! I should rather the fire."

"Think of it," she said. "There's a perfection in it you can't deny. We are illusions of what is mortal, and the stage is an illusion of what is real."

"It's an abomination," he said. "What did Lestat call it? Petty?"

"That was to Nicolas because Nicolas would build fantastical philosophies upon it," she said. "You must live now without fantastical philosophies, the way you did when you were Marius's apprentice. Live to learn the age. And Lestat does not believe in the value of evil. But you do believe in it. I know that you do."

"I am evil," he said half smiling. He almost laughed. "It's not a matter of belief, is it? But do you think I could go from the spiritual path I followed for three centuries to voluptuousness and debauchery such as that? We were the saints of evil," he protested. "I will not be common evil. I will not."

"Make it uncommon," she said. She was getting too impatient. "If you are evil, how can voluptuousness and debauchery be your enemies? Don't the world, the flesh, and the devil conspire equally against man?"

He shook his head, as if to say he did not care.

"You are more concerned with what is spiritual than with evil," I interjected, watching him closely. "Is that not so?"

"Yes," he said at once.

"But don't you see, the color of wine in a crystal glass can be spiritual," I continued. "The look in a face, the music of a violin. A Paris theater can be infused with the spiritual for all its solidity. There's nothing in it that hasn't been shaped by the power of those who possessed spiritual visions of what it could be."

Something quickened in him, but he pushed it away.

"Seduce the public with voluptuousness," Gabrielle said. "For God's sake, and the devil's, use the power of the theater as you will."

"Weren't the paintings of your master spiritual?" I asked. I could feel a warming in myself now at the thought of it. "Can anyone look on the great works of that time and not call them spiritual?"

"I have asked myself that question," Armand answered, "many times.

Was it spiritual or was it voluptuous? Was the angel painted on the triptych caught in the material, or was the material transformed?"

"No matter what they did to you after, you never doubted the beauty and the value of his work," I said. "I know you didn't. And it was the material transformed. It ceased to be paint and it became magic, just as in the kill the blood ceases to be blood and becomes life."

His eyes misted, but no visions came from him. Whatever road he traveled back in his thoughts, he traveled alone.

"The carnal and the spiritual," Gabrielle said, "come together in the theater as they do in the paintings. Sensual fiends we are by our very nature. Take this as your key."

He closed his eyes for a moment as if he would shut us out.

"Go to them and listen to the music that Nicki makes," she said. "Make art with them in the Theater of the Vampires. You have to pass away from what failed you into what can sustain you. Otherwise—there is no hope."

I wished she had not said it so abruptly, brought it so to the point.

But he nodded and his lips pressed together in a bitter smile.

"The only thing really important for you," she said slowly, "is that you go to an extreme."

He stared at her blankly. He could not possibly understand what she meant by this. And I thought it too brutal a truth to say. But he didn't resist it. His face became thoughtful and smooth and childlike again.

For a long time he looked at the fire. Then he spoke:

"But why must you go at all?" he asked. "No one is at war with you now. No one is trying to drive you out. Why can't you build it with me, this little enterprise?"

Did that mean he would do it, go to the others and become part of the theater in the boulevard?

He didn't contradict me. He was asking again why couldn't I create the imitation of life, if that was what I wanted to call it, right in the boulevard?

But he was also giving up. He knew I couldn't endure the sight of the theater, or the sight of Nicolas. I couldn't even really urge him towards it. Gabrielle had done that. And he knew that it was too late to press us anymore.

Finally Gabrielle said:

"We can't live among our own kind, Armand."

And I thought, yes, that is the truest answer of all, and I don't know why I couldn't speak it aloud.

"The Devil's Road is what we want," she said. "And we are enough for each other now. Maybe years and years into the future, when we've been a thousand places and seen a thousand things, we'll come back. We'll talk then together as we have tonight."

This came as no real shock to him. But it was impossible now to know what he thought.

For a long time we didn't speak. I don't know how long we remained quiet together in the room.

I tried not to think of Marius anymore, or of Nicolas either. All sense of danger was gone now, but I was afraid of the parting, of the sadness of it, of the feeling that I had taken from this creature his astonishing story and given him precious little for it in return.

It was Gabrielle who finally broke the quiet. She rose and moved gracefully to the bench beside him.

"Armand," she said. "We are going. If I have my way we'll be miles from Paris before midnight tomorrow night."

He looked at her with calm and acceptance. Impossible to know now what he chose to conceal.

"Even if you do not go to the theater," she said, "accept the things that we can give you. My son has wealth enough to make an entrance into the world very easy for you."

"You can take this tower for your lair," I said. "Use it as long as you wish. Magnus found it safe enough."

After a moment, he nodded with a grave politeness, but he didn't say anything.

"Let Lestat give you the gold needed to make you a gentleman," Gabrielle said. "And all we ask in return is that you leave the coven in peace if you do not choose to lead it."

He was looking at the fire again, face tranquil, irresistibly beautiful. Then again he nodded in silence. And the nod itself meant no more than that he had heard, not that he would promise anything.

"If you will not go to them," I said slowly, "then do not hurt them. Do not hurt Nicolas."

And when I spoke these words, his face changed very subtly. It was almost a smile that crept over his features. And his eyes shifted slowly to me. And I saw the scorn in them.

I looked away but the look had affected me as much as a blow.

"I don't want him to be harmed," I said in a tense whisper.

"No. You want him destroyed," he whispered back. "So that you need never fear or grieve for him anymore." And the look of scorn sharpened hideously.

Gabrielle intervened.

"Armand," she said, "he is not dangerous to them. The woman alone can control him. And he has things to teach all of you about this time if you will listen."

They looked at each other for some time in silence. And again his face was soft and gentle and beautiful.

And in a strangely decorous manner he took Gabrielle's hand and held it firmly. Then they stood up together, and he let her hand go, and he drew a little away from her and squared his shoulders. He looked at both of us.

"I'll go to them," he said in the softest voice. "And I will take the gold you offer me, and I will seek refuge in this tower. And I will learn from your passionate fledgling whatever he has to teach me. But I reach for these things only because they float on the surface of the darkness in which I am drowning. And I would not descend without some finer understanding. I would not leave eternity to you without . . . without some final battle."

I studied him. But no thoughts came from him to clarify these words.

"Maybe as the years pass," he said, "desire will come again to me. I will know appetite again, even passion. Maybe when we meet in another age, these things will not be abstract and fleeting. I'll speak with a vigor that matches yours, instead of merely reflecting it. And we will ponder matters of immortality and wisdom. We will talk about vengeance or acceptance then. For now it's enough for me to say that I want to see you again. I want our paths to cross in the future. And for that reason alone, I will do as you ask and not what you want: I will spare your ill-fated Nicolas."

I gave an audible sigh of relief. Yet his tone was so changed, so strong, that it sounded a deep silent alarm in me. This was the coven master, surely, this quiet and forceful one, the one who would survive, no matter how the orphan in him wept.

But then he smiled slowly and gracefully, and there was something sad and endearing in his face. He became the da Vinci saint again, or more truly the little god from Caravaggio. And it seemed for a moment he couldn't be anything evil or dangerous. He was too radiant, too full of all that was wise and good.

"Remember my warnings," he said. "Not my curses."

Gabrielle and I both nodded.

"And when you have need of me," he said, "I will be here."

Then Gabrielle did the totally surprising thing of embracing him and kissing him. And I did the same.

He was pliant and gentle and loving in our arms. And he let us know without words that he was going to the coven, and we could find him there tomorrow night.

The next moment he was gone, and Gabrielle and I were there alone together, as if he'd never been in the room. I could hear no sound anywhere in the tower. Nothing but the wind in the forest beyond.

And when I climbed the steps, I found the gate open and the fields stretching to the woods in unbroken quiet.

I loved him. I knew it, as incomprehensible to me as he was. But I was so glad it was finished. So glad that we could go on. Yet I held to the bars for a long time just looking at the distant woods, and the dim glow far beyond that the city made upon the lowering clouds.

And the grief I felt was not only for the loss of him, it was for Nicki, and for Paris, and for myself.

5

WHEN I came back down to the crypt I saw her building up the fire again with the last of the wood. In a slow, weary fashion, she stoked the blaze, and the light was red on her profile and in her eyes.

I sat quietly on the bench watching her, watching the explosion of sparks against the blackened bricks.

"Did he give you what you wanted?" I asked.

"In his own way, yes," she said. She put the poker aside and sat down opposite, her hair spilling down over her shoulders as she rested her hands beside her on the bench. "I tell you, I don't care if I never look upon another one of our kind," she said coldly. "I am done with their legends, their curses, their sorrows. And done with their insufferable humanity, which may be the most astonishing thing they've revealed. I'm ready for the world again, Lestat, as I was on the night I died."

"But Marius—" I said excitedly. "Mother, there are ancient ones—ones who have used immortality in a wholly different way."

"Are there?" she asked. "Lestat, you're too generous with your imagination. The story of Marius has the quality of a fairy tale."

"No, that's not true."

"So the orphan demon claims descent not from the filthy peasant devils he resembles," she said, "but from a lost lord, almost a god. I tell you any dirty-faced village child dreaming at the kitchen fire can tell you tales like that."

"Mother, he couldn't have invented Marius," I said. "I may have a great deal of imagination, but he has almost none. He couldn't have made up the images. I tell you he saw those things . . ."

"I hadn't thought of it exactly that way," she admitted with a little smile. "But he could well have borrowed Marius from the legends he heard . . ."

"No," I said. "There was a Marius and there is a Marius still. And there are others like him. There are Children of the Millennia who have done better than these Children of Darkness with the gifts given them."

"Lestat, what is important is that *we* do better," she said. "All I learned from Armand, finally, was that immortals find death seductive and ultimately irresistible, that they fail to conquer death or humanity in their minds. Now I want to take that knowledge and wear it like armor as I move through the world. And luckily, I don't mean the world of change which these creatures have found so dangerous. I mean the world that for eons has been the same."

She tossed her hair back as she looked at the fire again. "It's of snow-covered mountains I dream," she said softly, "of desert wastes—of impenetrable jungles, or the great north woods of America where they say white men have never been." Her face warmed just a little as she looked at me. "Think on it," she said. "There is nowhere that we cannot go. And if the Children of the Millennia do exist, maybe that is where they are—far from the world of men."

"And how do they live if they are?" I asked. I was picturing my own world and it was full of mortal beings, and the things that mortal beings made. "It's man we feed on," I said.

"There are hearts that beat in those forests," she said dreamily. "There is blood that flows for the one who takes it . . . I can do the things now that you used to do. I could fight those wolves on my own . . ." Her voice trailed off as she was lost in her thoughts. "The important thing," she said after a long moment, "is that we can go wherever we wish now, Lestat. We're free."

"I was free before," I said. "I never cared for what Armand had to tell. But Marius—I know that Marius is alive. I feel it. I felt it when Armand told the tale. And Marius knows things—and I don't mean just about us, or about Those Who Must Be Kept or whatever the old mystery—he knows things about life itself, about how to move through time."

"So let him be your patron saint if you need it," she said.

This angered me, and I didn't say anything more. The fact was her talk of jungles and forests frightened me. And all the things Armand said to divide us came back to me, just as I'd known they would when he had spoken his well-chosen words. And so we live with our differences, I thought, just as mortals do, and maybe our divisions are exaggerated as are our passions, as is our love.

"There was one inkling . . ." she said as she watched the fire, "one little indication that the story of Marius had truth."

"There were a thousand indications," I said.

"He said that Marius slew the evildoer," she continued, "and he called the evildoer Typhon, the slayer of his brother. Do you remember this?"

"I thought that he meant Cain who had slain Abel. It was Cain I saw in the images, though I heard the other name."

"That's just it. Armand himself didn't understand the name Typhon. Yet he repeated it. But I know what it means."

"Tell me."

"It's from the Greek and Roman myths—the old story of the Egyptian god, Osiris, slain by his brother Typhon, so that he became lord of the Underworld. Of course Armand could have read it in Plutarch, but he didn't, that's the strange thing."

"Ah, you see then, Marius did exist. When he said he'd lived for a millennium he was telling the truth."

"Perhaps, Lestat, perhaps," she said.

"Mother, tell me this again, this Egyptian story . . ."

"Lestat, you have years to read all the old tales for yourself." She rose and bent to kiss me, and I sensed the coldness and sluggishness in her that always came before dawn. "As for me, I am done with books. They are what I read when I could do nothing else." She took my two hands in hers. "Tell me that we'll be on the road tomorrow. That we won't see the ramparts of Paris again until we've seen the other side of the world."

"Exactly as you wish," I said.

She started up the stairs.

"But where are you going?" I said as I followed her. She opened the gate and went out towards the trees.

"I want to see if I can sleep in the raw earth itself," she said over her shoulder. "If I don't rise tomorrow you'll know I failed."

"But this is madness," I said, coming after her. I hated the very idea of it. She went ahead into a thicket of old oaks, and kneeling, she dug into the dead leaves and damp soil with her hands. Ghastly she looked, as if she were a beautiful blond-haired witch scratching with the speed of a beast.

Then she rose and waved a farewell kiss to me. And commanding all her strength, she descended as if the earth belonged to her. And I was left staring in disbelief at the emptiness where she had been, and the leaves that had settled as if nothing had disturbed the spot.

I WALKED away from the woods. I walked south away from the tower. And as my step quickened, I started singing softly to myself some little song, maybe a bit of melody that the violins had played earlier this night in the Palais Royal.

And the sense of grief came back to me, the realization that we were really going, that it was finished with Nicolas and finished with the Children of Darkness and their leader, and I wouldn't see Paris again, or anything familiar to me, for years and years. And for all my desire to be free, I wanted to weep.

But it seems I had some purpose in my wandering that I hadn't admitted to myself. A half hour or so before the morning light I was on the post road near the ruin of an old inn. Falling down it was, this last outpost of an abandoned village, with only the heavily mortared walls left intact.

And taking out my dagger, I began to carve deep in the soft stone:

MARIUS, THE ANCIENT ONE: LESTAT IS SEARCHING FOR YOU. IT IS THE MONTH OF MAY, IN THE YEAR 1780 AND I GO SOUTH FROM PARIS TOWARDS LYONS. PLEASE MAKE YOURSELF KNOWN TO ME.

What arrogance it seemed when I stepped back from it. And I had already broken the dark commandments, telling the name of an immortal, and putting it into written words. Well, it gave me a wondrous satisfaction to do it. And after all, I had never been very good at obeying rules.

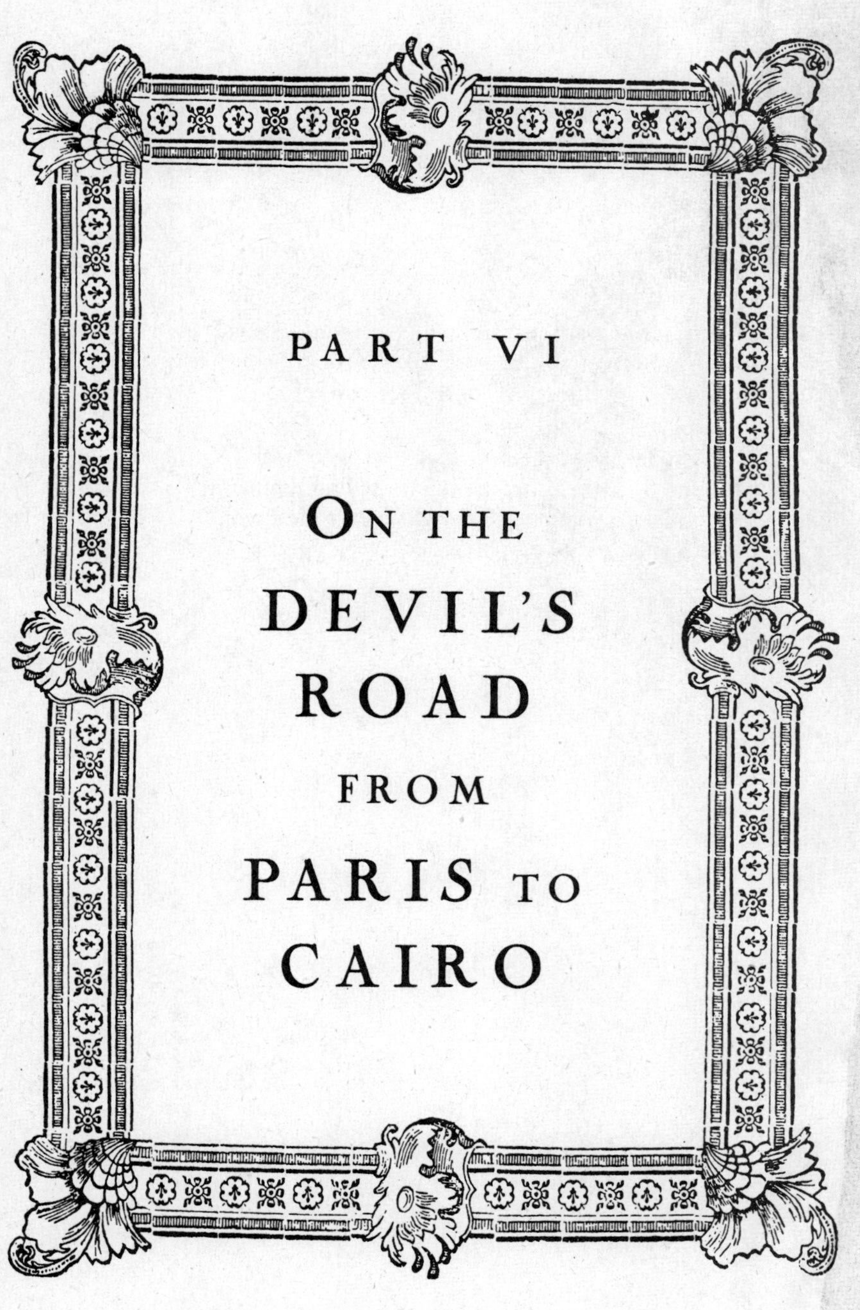

PART VI

ON THE DEVIL'S ROAD FROM PARIS TO CAIRO

1

THE last time we saw Armand in the eighteenth century, he was standing with Eleni and Nicolas and the other vampire mummers before the door of Renaud's theater, watching as our carriage made its way into the stream of traffic on the boulevard.

I'd found him earlier closeted in my old dressing room with Nicolas in the midst of a strange conversation dominated by Nicki's sarcasm and peculiar fire. He wore a wig and a somber red frock coat, and it seemed to me that he had already acquired a new opacity, as if every waking moment since the death of the old coven was giving him greater substance and strength.

Nicki and I had no words for each other in these last awkward moments, but Armand politely accepted the keys of the tower from me, and a great quantity of money, and the promise of more when he wanted it from Roget.

His mind was closed to me, but he said again that Nicolas would come to no harm from him. And as we said our farewells, I believed that Nicolas and the little coven had every chance for survival and that Armand and I were friends.

BY THE end of that first night Gabrielle and I were far from Paris, as we vowed we would be, and in the months that followed, we went on to Lyons, Turin, and Vienna, and after that to Prague and Leipzig and St. Petersburg, and then south again to Italy, where we were to settle for many years.

Eventually we went on to Sicily, then north into Greece and Turkey, and then south again through the ancient cities of Asia Minor and finally to Cairo, where we remained for some time.

And in all these places I was to write my messages to Marius on the walls.

Sometimes it was no more than a few words that I scratched with the tip of my knife. In other places, I spent hours chiseling my ruminations into the stone. But wherever I was, I wrote my name, the date, and my future destination, and my invitation: "Marius, make yourself known to me."

As for the old covens, we were to come upon them in a number of scattered places, but it was clear from the outset that the old ways were everywhere breaking down. Seldom more than three or four vampires carried on the old rituals, and when they came to realize that we wanted no part of them or their existence they let us alone.

Infinitely more interesting were the occasional rogues we glimpsed in the middle of society, lone and secretive vampires pretending to be mortal just as skillfully as we could pretend. But we never got close to these creatures. They ran from us as they must have from the old covens. And seeing nothing more than fear in their eyes, I wasn't tempted to give chase.

Yet it was strangely reassuring to know that I hadn't been the first aristocratic fiend to move through the ballrooms of the world in search of my victims—the deadly gentleman who would soon surface in stories and poetry and penny dreadful novels as the very epitome of our tribe. There were others appearing all the time.

But we were to encounter stranger creatures of darkness as we moved on. In Greece we found demons who did not know how they had been made, and sometimes even mad creatures without reason or language who attacked us as if we were mortal, and ran screaming from the prayers we said to drive them away.

The vampires in Istanbul actually dwelt in houses, safe behind high wall and gates, their graves in their gardens, and dressed as all humans do in that part of the world, in flowing robes, to hunt the nighttime streets.

Yet even they were quite horrified to see me living amongst the French and the Venetians, riding in carriages, joining the gatherings at the European embassies and homes. They menaced us, shouting incantations at us, and then ran in panic when we turned on them, only to come back and devil us again.

The revenants who haunted the Mameluke tombs in Cairo were beastly wraiths, held to the old laws by hollow-eyed masters who lived in the ruins of a Coptic monastery, their rituals full of Eastern magic and the evocation of many demons and evil spirits whom they called by strange names. They stayed clear of us, despite all their acidic threats, yet they knew our names.

As the years passed, we learned nothing from all these creatures, which of course was no great surprise to me.

And though vampires in many places had heard the legends of Marius and the other ancient ones, they had never seen such beings with their own eyes. Even Armand had become a legend to them, and they were likely to ask: "Did you really see the vampire Armand?" Nowhere did I meet a truly old vampire. Nowhere did I meet a vampire who was in any way a magnetic creature, a being of great wisdom or special accomplishment, an unusual being in whom the Dark Gift had worked any perceivable alchemy that was of interest to me.

Armand was a dark god compared to these beings. And so was Gabrielle and so was I.

But I jump ahead of my tale.

Early on, when we first came into Italy, we gained a fuller and more sympathetic knowledge of the ancient rituals. The Roman coven came out to welcome us with open arms. "Come to the Sabbat," they said. "Come into the catacombs and join in the hymns."

Yes, they knew that we'd destroyed the Paris coven, and bested the great master of dark secrets, Armand. But they didn't despise us for it. On the contrary, they could not understand the cause of Armand's resignation of his power. Why hadn't the coven changed with the times?

For even here where the ceremonies were so elaborate and sensuous that they took my breath away, the vampires, far from eschewing the ways of men, thought nothing of passing themselves off as human whenever it suited their purposes. It was the same with the two vampires we had seen in Venice, and the handful we were later to meet in Florence as well.

In black cloaks, they penetrated the crowds at the opera, the shadowy corridors of great houses during balls and banquets, and even sometimes sat amid the press in lowly taverns or wine shops, peering at humans quite close at hand. It was their habit here more than anywhere to dress in the costumes of the time of their birth, and they were often splendidly attired and most regal, possessing jewels and finery and showing it often to great advantage when they chose.

Yet they crept back to their stinking graveyards to sleep, and they fled screaming from any sign of heavenly power, and they threw themselves with savage abandon into their horrifying and beautiful Sabbats.

In comparison, the vampires of Paris had been primitive, coarse, and childlike; but I could see that it was the very sophistication and worldliness of Paris that had caused Armand and his flock to retreat so far from mortal ways.

As the French capital became secular, the vampires had clung to old magic, while the Italian fiends lived among deeply religious humans whose lives were drenched in Roman Catholic ceremony, men and women who respected evil as they respected the Roman Church. In sum the old ways of the fiends were not unlike the old ways of people in Italy, and so the Italian vampires moved in both worlds. Did they believe in the old ways? They shrugged. The Sabbat for them was a grand pleasure. Hadn't Gabrielle and I enjoyed it? Had we not finally joined in the dance?

"Come to us anytime that you wish," the Roman vampires told us.

As for this Theater of the Vampires in Paris, this great scandal which was shocking our kind the world over, well, they would believe *that* when they saw it with their own eyes. Vampires performing on a stage, vampires dazzling mortal audiences with tricks and mimicry—they thought it was too terribly Parisian! They laughed.

Of course I was hearing more directly about the theater all the time. Before I'd even reached St. Petersburg, Roget had sent me a long testament to the "cleverness" of the new troupe:

> They have gotten themselves up like giant wooden marionettes [he wrote]. Gold cords come down from the rafters to their ankles and their wrists and the tops of their heads, and by these they appear to be manipulated in the most charming dances. They wear perfect circles of rouge on their white cheeks, and their eyes are wide as glass buttons. You cannot believe the perfection with which they make themselves appear inanimate.
>
> But the orchestra is another marvel. Faces blank and painted in the very same style, the players imitate mechanical musicians—the jointed dolls one can buy that, on the winding of a key, saw away at their little instruments, or blow their little horns, to make real music!
>
> It is such an engaging spectacle that ladies and gentlemen of the audience quarrel amongst themselves as to whether or not these players are dolls or real persons. Some aver that they are all made of wood and the voices coming out of the actors' mouths are the work of ventriloquists.
>
> As for the plays themselves, they would be extremely unsettling were they not so beautiful and skillfully done.
>
> There is one most popular drama they do which features a vampiric revenant, risen from the grave through a platform in the stage. Terrifying is the creature with rag mop hair and fangs. But lo, he falls in love at once with a giant wooden puppet woman, never guessing that she is not alive. Unable to drink blood from her throat, however, the poor vampire soon perishes, at which moment the marionette reveals that she does indeed live, though she is made of wood, and with an evil smile she performs a triumphant dance upon the body of the defeated fiend.
>
> I tell you it makes the blood run cold to see it. Yet the audience screams and applauds.
>
> In another little tableau, the puppet dancers make a circle about a

human girl and entice her to let herself be bound up with golden cords as if she too were a marionette. The sorry result is that the strings make her dance till the life goes out of her body. She pleads with eloquent gestures to be released, but the real puppets only laugh and cavort as she expires.

The music is unearthly. It brings to mind the gypsies of the country fairs. Monsieur de Lenfent is the director. And it is the sound of his violin which often opens the evening fare.

I advise you as your attorney to claim some of the profits being made by this remarkable company. The lines for each performance stretch a considerable length down the boulevard.

Roget's letters always unsettled me. They left me with my heart tripping, and I couldn't help but wonder: What had I expected the troupe to do? Why did their boldness and inventiveness surprise me? We all had the power to do such things.

By the time I settled in Venice, where I spent a great deal of time looking in vain for Marius's paintings, I was hearing from Eleni directly, her letters inscribed with exquisite vampiric skill.

They were the most popular entertainment in nighttime Paris, she wrote to me. "Actors" had come from all over Europe to join them. So their troupe had swelled to twenty in number, which even that metropolis could scarce "support."

"Only the most clever artists are admitted, those who possess truly astonishing talent, but we prize discretion above all else. We do not like scandal, as you can well guess."

As for their "Dear Violinist," she wrote of him affectionately, saying he was their greatest inspiration, that he wrote the most ingenious plays, taking them from stories that he read.

"But when he is not at work, he can be quite impossible. He must be watched constantly so that he does not enlarge our ranks. His dining habits are extremely sloppy. And on occasion he says most shocking things to strangers, which fortunately they are too sensible to believe."

In other words, he tried to make other vampires. And he didn't hunt in stealth.

In the main it is Our Oldest Friend [Armand, obviously] who is relied upon to restrain him. And that he does with the most caustic threats. But I must say that these do not have an enduring effect upon Our Violinist. He talks often of old religious customs, of ritual fires, of the passage into new realms of being.

I cannot say that we do not love him. For your sake we would care for him even if we did not. But we do love him. And Our Oldest Friend, in particular, bears him great affection. Yet I should remark that in the old times, such persons would not have endured among us for very long.

As for Our Oldest Friend, I wonder if you would know him now. He has built a great manse at the foot of your tower, and there he lives among books and pictures very like a scholarly gentleman with little care for the real world.

Each night, however, he arrives at the door of the theater in his black carriage. And he watches from his own curtained box.

And he comes after to settle all disputes among us, to govern as he always did, to threaten Our Divine Violinist, but he will never, never consent to perform on the stage. It is he who accepts new members among us. As I told you, they come from all over. We do not have to solicit them. They knock upon our door. . . .

Come back to us [she wrote in closing]. You will find us more interesting than you did before. There are a thousand dark wonders which I cannot commit to paper. We are a starburst in the history of our kind. And we could not have chosen a more perfect moment in the history of this great city for our little contrivance. And it is your doing, this splendid existence we sustain. Why did you leave us? Come home.

I saved these letters. I kept them as carefully as I kept the letters from my brothers in the Auvergne. I saw the marionettes perfectly in my imagination. I heard the cry of Nicki's violin. I saw Armand, too, arriving in his dark carriage, taking his seat in the box. And I even described all of this in veiled and eccentric terms in my long messages to Marius, working in a little frenzy now and then with my chisel in a dark street while mortals slept.

But for me, there was no going back to Paris, no matter how lonely I might become. The world around me had become my lover and my teacher. I was enraptured with the cathedrals and castles, the museums and palaces that I saw. In every place I visited, I went to the heart of society: I drank up its entertainments and its gossip, its literature and its music, its architecture and its art.

I could fill volumes with the things I studied, the things I struggled to understand. I was enthralled by gypsy violinists and street puppeteers as I was by great castrati sopranos in gilded opera houses or cathedral choirs. I prowled the brothels and the gambling dens and the places where the sailors drank and quarreled. I read the newspapers everywhere I went and hung about in taverns, often ordering food I never touched, merely to have it in front of me, and I talked to mortals incessantly in public places, buying countless glasses of wine for others, smelling their pipes and cigars as they smoked, and letting all these mortal smells get into my hair and clothes.

And when I wasn't out roaming, I was traveling the realm of the books that had belonged to Gabrielle so exclusively all through those dreary mortal years at home.

Before we even got to Italy, I knew enough Latin to be studying the classics, and I made a library in the old Venetian palazzo I haunted, often reading the whole night long.

And of course it was the tale of Osiris that enchanted me, bringing back with it the romance of Armand's story and Marius's enigmatic words. As I pored over all the old versions, I was quietly thunderstruck by what I read.

Here we have an ancient king, Osiris, a man of unworldly goodness who turns the Egyptians away from cannibalism and teaches them the art of growing crops and making wine. And how is he murdered by his brother Typhon? Osiris is tricked into lying down in a box made to the exact size of his body, and his brother Typhon then nails shut the lid. He is then thrown into the river, and when his faithful Isis finds his body, he is again attacked by Typhon, who dismembers him. All parts of his body are found save one.

Now, why would Marius make reference to a myth such as this? And how could I not think on the fact that all vampires sleep in coffins which are boxes made to the size of their bodies—even the miserable rabble of les Innocents slept in their coffins. Magnus said to me, "In that box or its like you must always lie." As for the missing part of the body, the part that Isis never found, well, there is one part of us which is not enhanced by the Dark Gift, isn't there? We can speak, see, taste, breathe, move as humans move, but *we cannot procreate.* And neither could Osiris, so he became Lord of the Dead.

Was this a vampire god?

But so much puzzled me and tormented me. This god Osiris was the god of wine to the Egyptians, the one later called Dionysus by the Greeks. And Dionysus was the "dark god" of the theater, the devil god whom Nicki described to me when we were boys at home. And now we had the theater full of vampires in Paris. Oh, it was too rich.

I couldn't wait to tell all this to Gabrielle.

But she dismissed it indifferently, saying there were hundreds of such old stories.

"Osiris was the god of the corn," she said. "He was a good god to the Egyptians. What could this have to do with us?" She glanced at the books

I was studying. "You have a great deal to learn, my son. Many an ancient god was dismembered and mourned by his goddess. Read of Actaeon and Adonis. The ancients loved those stories."

And she was gone. And I was alone in the candlelighted library, leaning on my elbows amid all these books.

I brooded on Armand's dream of the sanctuary of Those Who Must Be Kept in the mountains. Was it a magic that went back to the Egyptian times? How had the Children of Darkness forgotten such things? Maybe it had all been poetry to the Venetian master, the mention of Typhon, the slayer of his brother, nothing more than that.

I went out into the night with my chisel. I wrote my questions to Marius on stones that were older than us both. Marius had become so real to me that we were talking together, the way that Nicki and I had once done. He was the confidant who received my excitement, my enthusiasm, my sublime bewilderment at all the wonders and puzzles of the world.

BUT as my studies deepened, as my education broadened, I was getting that first awesome inkling of what eternity might be. I was alone among humans, and my writing to Marius couldn't keep me from knowing my own monstrosity as I had in those first Paris nights so long ago. After all, Marius wasn't really there.

And neither was Gabrielle.

Almost from the beginning, Armand's predictions had proved true.

2

BEFORE we were even out of France, Gabrielle was breaking the journey to disappear for several nights at a time. In Vienna, she often stayed away for over a fortnight, and by the time I settled in the palazzo in Venice she was going away for months on end. During my first visit to Rome, she vanished for a half year. And after she left me in Naples, I returned to Venice without her, angrily leaving her to find her way back to the Veneto on her own, which she did.

Of course it was the countryside that drew her, the forest or the mountains, or islands on which no human beings lived. And she would return in such a tattered state—her shoes worn out, her clothes ripped, her hair in hopeless tangles—that she was every bit as frightening to look at as the ragged members of the old Paris coven had been. Then she'd walk about my rooms in her dirty neglected garments staring at the cracks in the plaster or the light caught in the distortions of the hand-blown window glass.

Why should immortals pore over newspapers, she would ask, or dwell in palaces? Or carry gold in their pockets? Or write letters to a mortal family left behind?

In an eerie, rapid undertone she'd speak of cliffs she had climbed, the drifts of snow through which she had tumbled, the caves full of mysterious markings and ancient fossils that she had found.

Then she would go as silently as she'd come, and I would be left watching for her and waiting for her—and bitter and angry at her, and resenting her when she finally came back.

One night during our first visit to Verona, she startled me in a dark street.

"Is your father still alive?" she asked. Two months she'd been gone that time. I'd missed her bitterly, and there she was asking about them as if they mattered finally. Yet when I answered, "Yes, and very ill," she seemed not to hear. I tried to tell her then that things in France were bleak indeed. There would surely be a revolution. She shook her head and waved it all away.

"Don't think about them anymore," she said. "Forget them." And once again, she was gone.

The truth was, I didn't want to forget them. I never stopped writing to Roget for news of my family. I wrote to him more often than I wrote to Eleni at the theater. I'd sent for portraits of my nieces and nephews. I sent presents back to France from every place in which I stopped. And I did worry about the revolution, as any mortal Frenchman might.

And finally, as Gabrielle's absences grew longer and our times together more strained and uncertain, I started to argue with her about these things.

"Time will take our family," I said. "Time will take the France we knew. So why should I give them up now while I can still have them? I need these things, I tell you. This is what life is to me!"

But this was only the half of it. I didn't have her any more than I had the others. She must have known what I was really saying. She must have heard the recriminations behind it all.

Little speeches like this saddened her. They brought out the tenderness in her. She'd let me get clean clothes for her, comb out her hair. And after that we'd hunt together and talk together. Maybe she would even go to the casinos with me, or to the opera. She'd be a great and beautiful lady for a little while.

And those moments still held us together. They perpetuated our belief that we were still a little coven, a pair of lovers, prevailing against the mortal world.

Gathered by the fire in some country villa, riding together on the driver's seat of the coach as I held the reins, walking together through the midnight forest, we still exchanged our various observations now and then.

We even went in search of haunted houses together—a newfound pastime that excited us both. In fact, Gabrielle would sometimes return from one of her journeys precisely because she had heard of a ghostly visitation and she wanted me to go with her to see what we could.

Of course, most of the time we found nothing in the empty buildings where spirits were supposed to appear. And those wretched persons supposed to be possessed by the devil were often no more than commonly insane.

Yet there were times when we saw fleeting apparitions or mayhem that we couldn't explain—objects flung about, voices roaring from the mouths of possessed children, icy currents that blew out the candles in a locked room.

But we never learned anything from all this. We saw no more than a hundred mortal scholars had already described.

It was just a game to us finally. And when I look back on it now, I know we went on with it because it kept us together—gave us convivial moments which otherwise we would not have had.

But Gabrielle's absences weren't the only thing destroying our affection for each other as the years passed. It was her manner when she was with me—the ideas she would put forth.

She still had that habit of speaking exactly what was on her mind and little more.

One night in our little house in the Via Ghibellina in Florence, she appeared after a month's absence and started to expound at once.

"You know the creatures of the night are ripe for a great leader," she said. "Not some superstitious mumbler of old rites, but a great dark monarch who will galvanize us according to new principles."

"What principles?" I asked. Ignoring the question, she went on.

"Imagine," she said, "not merely this stealthy and loathsome feeding on mortals, but something grand as the Tower of Babel was grand before it was brought down by the wrath of God. I mean a leader set up in a Satanic palace who sends out his followers to turn brother against brother, to cause mothers to kill their children, to put all the fine accomplishments of mankind to the torch, to scorch the land itself so that all would die of hunger, innocent and guilty! Make suffering and chaos wherever you turn, and strike down the forces of good so that men despair. Now that is something worthy of being called evil. That is what the work of a devil really is. We are nothing, you and I, except exotica in the Savage Garden, as you told me. And the world of men is no more or less now than what I saw in my books in the Auvergne years ago."

I hated this conversation. And yet I was glad she was in the room with me, that I was speaking to somebody other than a poor deceived mortal. That I wasn't alone with my letters from home.

"But what about your aesthetic questions?" I asked. "What you explained to Armand before, that you wanted to know why beauty existed and why it continues to affect us?"

She shrugged.

"When the world of man collapses in ruin, beauty will take over. The trees shall grow again where there were streets; the flowers will again cover the meadow that is now a dank field of hovels. That shall be the purpose of the Satanic master, to see the wild grass and the dense forest cover up all trace of the once great cities until nothing remains."

"And why call all this Satanic?" I asked. "Why not call it chaos? That is all it would be."

"Because," she said, "that is what men would call it. They invented Satan, didn't they? Satanic is merely the name they give to the behavior of those who would disrupt the orderly way in which men want to live."

"I don't see it."

"Well, use your preternatural brain, my blue-eyed one," she answered, "my golden-haired son, my handsome wolfkiller. It is very possible that God made the world as Armand said."

"This is what you discovered in the forest? You were told this by the leaves?"

She laughed at me.

"Of course, God is not necessarily anthropomorphic," she said. "Or what we would call, in our colossal egotism and sentimentality, 'a decent person.' But there is probably God. Satan, however, was man's invention, a name for the force that seeks to overthrow the civilized order of things. The first man who made laws—be he Moses or some ancient Egyptian king Osiris—that lawmaker created the devil. The devil meant the one who tempts you to break the laws. And we are truly Satanic in that we follow no law for man's protection. So why not truly disrupt? Why not make a blaze of evil to consume all the civilizations of the earth?"

I was too appalled to answer.

"Don't worry." She laughed. "I won't do it. But I wonder what will happen in the decades to come. Will not somebody do it?"

"I hope not!" I said. "Or let me put it this way. If one of us tries, then there shall be war."

"Why? Everyone will follow him."

"I will not. I will make the war."

"Oh, you are too amusing, Lestat," she said.

"It's petty," I said.

"Petty!" She had looked away, out into the courtyard, but she looked back and the color rose in her face. "To topple all the cities of the earth? I understood when you called the Theater of the Vampires petty, but now you are contradicting yourself."

"It is petty to destroy anything merely for the sake of the destroying, don't you think?"

"You're impossible," she said. "Sometime in the far future there may be such a leader. He will reduce man to the nakedness and fear from which he came. And we shall feed upon him effortlessly as we have always done, and the Savage Garden, as you call it, will cover the world."

"I almost hope someone does attempt it," I said. "Because I would rise up against him and do everything to defeat him. And possibly I could be saved, I could be good again in my own eyes, as I set out to save man from this."

I was very angry. I'd left my chair and walked out into the courtyard.

She came right behind me.

"You have just given the oldest argument in Christendom for the existence of evil," she said. "It exists so that we may fight it and do good."

"How dreary and stupid," I said.

"What I don't understand about you is this," she said. "You hold to your old belief in goodness with a tenacity that is virtually unshakable. Yet you are so good at being what you are! You hunt your victims like a dark angel. You kill ruthlessly. You feast all the night long on victims when you choose."

"So?" I looked at her coldly. "I don't know how to be bad at being bad."

She laughed.

"I was a good marksman when I was a young man," I said, "a good actor on the stage. And now I am a good vampire. So much for our understanding of the word 'good.' "

AFTER she had gone, I lay on my back on the flagstones in the courtyard and looked up at the stars, thinking of all the paintings and the sculptures that I had seen merely in the single city of Florence. I knew that I hated places where there are only towering trees, and the softest and sweetest music to me was the sound of human voices. But what did it matter really what I thought or felt?

But she didn't always bludgeon me with strange philosophy. Now and then when she appeared, she spoke of the practical things she'd learned. She was actually braver and more adventurous than I was. She taught me things.

We could sleep in the earth, she had ascertained that before we ever left France. Coffins and graves did not matter. And she would find herself rising naturally out of the earth at sunset even before she was awake.

And those mortals who did find us during the daylight hours, unless they exposed us to the sun at once, were doomed. For example, outside Palermo she had slept in a cellar far below an abandoned house, and when she had awakened, her eyes and face were burning as if they had been scalded, and she had in her right hand a mortal, quite dead, who had apparently attempted to disturb her rest.

"He was strangled," she said, "and my hand was still locked on his throat. And my face had been burned by the little light that leaked down from the opened door."

"What if there had been several mortals?" I asked, vaguely enchanted with her.

She shook her head and shrugged. She always slept in the earth now, not in cellars or coffins. No one would ever disturb her rest again. It did not matter to her.

I DID not say so, but I believed there was a grace in sleeping in the crypt. There was a romance to rising from the grave. I was in fact going to the very opposite extreme in that I had coffins made for myself in places where we lingered, and I slept not in the graveyard or the church, as was our most common custom, but in hiding places within the house.

I can't say that she didn't sometimes patiently listen to me when I told her these things. She listened when I described to her the great works of art I had seen in the Vatican museum, or the chorus I had heard in the cathedral, or the dreams I had in the last hour before rising, dreams that seemed to be sparked by the thoughts of mortals passing my lair. But maybe she was watching my lips move. Who could possibly tell? And then she was gone again without explanation, and I walked the streets alone, whispering aloud to Marius and writing to him the long, long messages that took the whole night sometimes to complete.

What did I want of her, that she be more human, that she be like me? Armand's predictions obsessed me. And how could she not think of them? She must have known what was happening, that we were growing ever farther apart, that my heart was breaking and I had too much pride to say it to her.

"Please, Gabrielle, I cannot endure the loneliness! Stay with me."

By the time we left Italy I was playing dangerous little games with mortals. I'd see a man, or a woman—a human being who looked perfect to me spiritually—and I would follow the human about. Maybe for a week I'd do this, then a month, sometimes even longer than that. I'd fall in love with the being. I'd imagine friendship, conversation, intimacy that we could never have. In some magical and imaginary moment I would say: "But you see what I am," and this human being, in supreme spiritual understanding, would say: "Yes, I see. I understand."

Nonsense, really. Very like the fairy tale where the princess gives her selfless love to the prince who is enchanted and he is himself again and the monster no more. Only in this dark fairy tale I would pass right into my mortal lover. We would become one being, and I would be flesh and blood again.

Lovely idea, that. Only I began to think more and more of Armand's warnings, that I'd work the Dark Trick again for the same reasons I'd done it before. And I stopped playing the game altogether. I merely went hunting with all the old vengeance and cruelty, and it wasn't merely the evildoer I brought down.

IN THE city of Athens I wrote the following message to Marius:

"I do not know why I go on. I do not search for truth. I do not believe in it. I hope for no ancient secrets from you, whatever they may be. But I believe in something. Maybe simply in the beauty of the world through which I wander or in the will to live itself. This gift was given to me too early. It was given for no good reason. And already at the age of thirty mortal years, I have some understanding as to why so many of our kind have wasted it, given it up. Yet I continue. And I search for you."

How long I could have wandered through Europe and Asia in this fashion I do not know. For all my complaints about loneliness, I was used to it all. And there were new cities as there were new victims, new languages, and new music to hear. No matter what my pain, I fixed my mind on a new destination. I wanted to know all the cities of the earth, finally, even the far-off capitals of India and China, where the simplest objects would seem alien and the minds I pierced as strange as those of creatures from another world.

But as we went south from Istanbul into Asia Minor, Gabrielle felt the allure of the new and strange land even more strongly, so that she was scarcely ever at my side.

And things were reaching a horrid climax in France, not merely with the mortal world I still grieved for, but with the vampires of the theater as well.

3

BEFORE I ever left Greece, I'd been hearing disturbing news from English and French travelers of the troubles at home. And when I reached the European hostelry in Ankara there was a large packet of letters waiting for me.

Roget had moved all of my money out of France, and into foreign banks. "You must not consider returning to Paris," he wrote. "I have advised your father and your brothers to keep out of all controversy. It is not the climate for monarchists here."

Eleni's letters spoke in their own way of the same things:

> Audiences want to see the aristocracy made fools of. Our little play featuring a clumsy queen puppet, who is trampled mercilessly by the mindless troop of puppet soldiers whom she seeks to command, draws loud laughter and screams.
>
> The clergy is also ripe for derision: In another little drama we have a bumptious priest come to chastise a group of dancing-girl marionettes for their indecent conduct. But alas, their dancing master, who is in fact a red-horned devil, turns the unfortunate cleric into a werewolf who ends his days kept by the laughing girls in a golden cage.
>
> All this is the genius of Our Divine Violinist, but we must now be with him every waking moment. To force him to write we tie him to the chair. We put ink and paper in front of him. And if this fails, we make him dictate as we write down the plays.
>
> In the streets he would accost the passers-by and tell them passionately there are horrors in this world of which they do not dream. And I assure you, if Paris were not so busy reading pamphlets that denounce Queen Marie Antoinette, he might have undone us all by now. Our Oldest Friend becomes more angry with every passing night.

Of course I wrote to her at once, begging her to be patient with Nicki, to try to help him through these first years. "Surely he can be influenced," I said. And for the first time I asked: "Would I have the power to alter things if I were to return?" I stared at the words for a long time before signing my name. My hands were trembling. Then I sealed the letter and posted it at once.

How could I go back? Lonely as I was, I couldn't bear the thought of returning to Paris, of seeing that little theater again. And what would I do for Nicolas when I got there? Armand's long-ago admonition was a din in my ears.

In fact, it seemed no matter where I was that Armand and Nicki were both with me, Armand full of grim warnings and predictions, and Nicolas taunting me with the little miracle of love turned into hate.

I had never needed Gabrielle as I did now. But she had gone ahead on our journey long ago. Now and then I remembered the way it had been before we ever left Paris. But I didn't expect anything from her anymore.

At Damascus, Eleni's answer was waiting for me.

> He despises you as much as ever. When we suggest that perhaps he should go to you, he laughs and laughs. I tell you these things not to haunt you but to let you know that we do our utmost to protect this child who should never have been Born to Darkness. He is overwhelmed by his powers, dazzled and maddened by his vision. We have seen it all and its sorry finish before.
>
> Yet he has written his greatest play this last month. The marionette dancers, *sans* strings for this one, are, in the flower of their youth, struck down by a pestilence and laid beneath tombstones and flower wreaths to rest. The priest weeps over them before he goes away. But a young violinist magician comes to the cemetery. And by means of his music makes them rise. As vampires dressed all in black silk ruffles and black satin ribbons, they come out of the graves, dancing merrily as they follow the violinist towards Paris, a beautifully rendered painting on the scrim. The crowd positively roars. I tell you we could feast on mortal victims on the stage and the Parisians, thinking it all the most novel illusion, would only cheer.

There was also a frightening letter from Roget:

Paris was in the grip of revolutionary madness. King Louis had been forced to recognize the National Assembly. The people of all classes were uniting against him as never before. Roget had sent a messenger south to see my family and try to determine the revolutionary mood in the countryside for himself.

I answered both letters with all the predictable concern and all the predictable feeling of helplessness.

But as I sent my belongings on to Cairo, I had the dread that all those things upon which I depended were in danger. Outwardly, I was unchanged as I continued my masquerade as the traveling gentleman; inwardly the demon hunter of the crooked back streets was silently and secretly lost.

Of course I told myself that it was important to go south to Egypt, that

Egypt was a land of ancient grandeur and timeless marvels, that Egypt would enchant me and make me forget the things happening in Paris which I was powerless to change.

But there was a connection in my mind. Egypt, more than any other land the world over, was a place in love with death.

Finally Gabrielle came like a spirit out of the Arabian desert, and together we set sail.

IT WAS almost a month before we reached Cairo, and when I found my belongings waiting for me in the European hostelry there was a strange package there.

I recognized Eleni's writing immediately, but I could not think why she would send me a package and I stared at the thing for a full quarter of an hour, my mind as blank as it had ever been.

There was not a word from Roget.

Why hasn't Roget written to me, I thought. What is this package? Why is it here?

At last I realized that for an hour I had been sitting in a room with a lot of trunks and packing cases and staring at a package and that Gabrielle, who had not seen fit to vanish yet, was merely watching me.

"Would you go out?" I whispered.

"If you wish," she said.

It was important to open this, yes, to open it and find out what it was. Yet it seemed just as important for me to look around the barren little room and imagine that it was a room in a village inn in the Auvergne.

"I had a dream about you," I said aloud, glancing at the package. "I dreamed that we were moving through the world together, you and I, and we were both serene and strong. I dreamed we fed on the evildoer as Marius had done, and as we looked about ourselves we felt awe and sorrow at the mysteries we beheld. But we were strong. We would go on forever. And we talked. 'Our conversation' went on and on."

I tore back the wrapping and saw the case of the Stradivarius violin.

I went to say something again, just to myself, but my throat closed. And my mind couldn't carry out the words on its own. I reached for the letter which had slipped to one side over the polished wood.

> It has come to the worst, as I feared. Our Oldest Friend, maddened by the excesses of Our Violinist, finally imprisoned him in your old residence. And though his violin was given him in his cell, his hands were taken away.
>
> But understand that with us, such appendages can always be re-

stored. And the appendages in question were kept safe by Our Oldest Friend, who allowed our wounded one no sustenance for five nights.

Finally, after the entire troupe had prevailed upon Our Oldest Friend to release N. and give back to him all that was his, it was done.

But N., maddened by the pain and the starvation—for this can alter the temperament completely—slipped into unbreakable silence and remained so for a considerable length of time.

At last he came to us and spoke only to tell us that in the manner of a mortal he had put in order his business affairs. A stack of freshly written plays was ours to have. And we must call together for him somewhere in the countryside the ancient Sabbat with its customary blaze. If we did not, then he should make the theater his funeral pyre.

Our Oldest Friend solemnly granted his wish and you have never seen such a Sabbat as this, for I think we looked all the more hellish in our wigs and fine clothes, our black ruffled vampire dancing costumes, forming the old circle, singing with an actor's bravado the old chants.

"We should have done it on the boulevard," he said. "But here, send this on to my maker," and he put the violin in my hands. We began to dance, all of us, to induce the customary frenzy, and I think we were never more moved, never more in terror, never more sad. He went into the flames.

I know how this news will affect you. But understand we did all that we could to prevent what occurred. Our Oldest Friend was bitter and grieved. And I think you should know that when we returned to Paris, we discovered that N. had ordered the theater to be named officially the Theater of the Vampires and these words had already been painted on the front. As his best plays have always included vampires and werewolves and other such supernatural creatures, the public thinks the new title very amusing, and no one has moved to change it. It is merely clever in the Paris of these times.

Hours later when I finally went down the stairs into the street, I saw a pale and lovely ghost in the shadows—image of the young French explorer in soiled white linen and brown leather boots, straw hat down over the eyes.

I knew who she was, of course, and that we had once loved each other, she and I, but it seemed for the moment to be something I could scarce remember, or truly believe.

I think I wanted to say something mean to her, to wound her and drive her away. But when she came up beside me and walked with me, I didn't say anything. I merely gave the letter to her so that we didn't have to talk.

And she read it and put it away, and then she had her arm around me again the way she used to long ago, and we were walking together through the black streets.

Smell of death and cooking fires, of sand and camel dung. Egypt smell. Smell of a place that has been the same for six thousand years.

"What can I do for you, my darling?" she whispered.

"Nothing," I said.

It was I who did it, I who seduced him, made him what he was, and left him there. It was I who subverted the path his life might have taken. And so in dark obscurity, removed from its human course, it comes to this.

LATER she stood silent as I wrote my message to Marius on an ancient temple wall. I told about the end of Nicolas, the violinist of the Theater of the Vampires, and I carved my words deep as any ancient Egyptian craftsman might have done. Epitaph for Nicki, a milestone in oblivion, which none might ever read or understand.

IT WAS strange to have her there. Strange to have her staying with me hour by hour.

"You won't go back to France, will you?" she asked me finally. "You won't go back on account of what he's done?"

"The hands?" I asked her. "The cutting off of the hands?"

She looked at me and her face smoothed out as if some shock had robbed it of expression. But she knew. She had read the letter. What shocked her? The way I said it perhaps.

"You thought I would go back to get revenge?"

She nodded uncertainly. She didn't want to put the idea in my head.

"How could I do that?" I said. "It would be hypocrisy, wouldn't it, when I left Nicolas there counting on them all to do whatever had to be done?"

The changes in her face were too subtle to describe. I didn't like to see her feel so much. It wasn't like her.

"The fact is, the little monster was trying to help when he did it, don't you think, when he cut off the hands. It must have been a lot of trouble to him, really, when he could have burnt up Nicki so easily without a backward glance."

She nodded, but she looked miserable, and as luck would have it, beautiful, too. "I rather thought so," she said. "But I didn't think you would agree."

"Oh, I'm monster enough to understand it," I said. "Do you remember what you told me years ago, before we ever left home? You said it the very day that he came up the mountain with the merchants to give me the red cloak. You said that his father was so angry with him for his violin playing that he was threatening to break his hands. Do you think we find our destiny somehow, no matter what happens? I mean, do you think that even as immortals we follow some path that was already marked for us when we were alive? Imagine it, the coven master cut off his hands."

IT WAS clear in the nights that followed that she didn't want to leave me alone. And I sensed that she would have stayed on account of Nicki's death, no matter where we were. But it made a difference that we were in Egypt. It helped that she loved these ruins and these monuments as she had loved none before.

Maybe people had to be dead six thousand years for her to love them. I thought of saying that to her, teasing her with it a little, but the thought merely came and went. These monuments were as old as the mountains she loved. The Nile had coursed through the imagination of man since the dawn of recorded time.

We scaled the pyramids together, we climbed into the arms of the giant Sphinx. We pored over inscriptions on ancient stone fragments. We studied the mummies one could buy from thieves for a pittance, bits of old jewelry, pottery, glass. We let the water of the river move through our fingers, and we hunted the tiny streets of Cairo together, and we went into the brothels to sit back on the pillows and watch the boys dance and hear the musicians play a heated erotic music that drowned out for a little while the sound of a violin that was always in my head.

I found myself rising and dancing wildly to these exotic sounds, imitating the undulations of those who urged me on, as I lost all sense of time or reason in the wail of the horns, the strumming of the lutes.

Gabrielle sat still, smiling, with the brim of her soiled white straw hat over her eyes. We did not talk to each other anymore. She was just some pale and feline beauty, cheek smudged with dirt, who drifted through the endless night at my side. Her coat cinched by a thick leather belt, her hair in a braid down her back, she walked with a queen's posture and a vampire's languor, the curve of her cheek luminous in the darkness, her small mouth a blur of rose red. Lovely and soon to be gone again, no doubt.

Yet she remained with me even when I leased a lavish little dwelling, once the house of a Mameluke lord, with gorgeously tiled floors and elaborate tentwork hanging from its ceilings. She even helped me fill the courtyard with bougainvillea and palms and every kind of tropical plant until it was a verdant little jungle. She brought in the caged parrots and finches and brilliant canaries herself.

She even nodded now and then sympathetically when I murmured there were no letters from Paris, and I was frantic for news.

Why hadn't Roget written to me? Had Paris erupted into riots and mayhem? Well, it would never touch my distant provincial family, would it? But had something happened to Roget? Why didn't he write?

She asked me to go upriver with her. I wanted to wait for letters, to question the English travelers. But I agreed. After all, it was rather remarkable really that she wanted me to come with her. She was caring for me in her own way.

I knew she'd taken to dressing in fresh white linen frock coats and breeches only to please me. For me, she brushed out her long hair.

But it did not matter at all. I was sinking. I could feel it. I was drifting through the world as if it were a dream.

It seemed very natural and reasonable that around me I should see a landscape that looked exactly as it had thousands of years ago when artists painted it on the walls of royal tombs. Natural that the palm trees in the moonlight should look exactly as they looked then. Natural that the peasant should draw his water from the river in the same manner as he had done then. And the cows he watered were the same too.

Visions of the world when the world had been new.

Had Marius ever stood in these sands?

We wandered through the giant temple of Ramses, enchanted by the millions upon millions of tiny pictures cut into the walls. I kept thinking of Osiris, but the little figures were strangers. We prowled the ruins of Luxor. We lay in the riverboat together under the stars.

On our way back to Cairo when we came to the great Colossi of Memnon, she told in a passionate whisper how Roman emperors had journeyed to marvel at these statues just as we did now.

"They were ancient in the times of the Caesars," she said, as we rode our camels through the cool sands.

The wind was not so bad as it could have been on this night. We could see the immense stone figures clearly against the deep blue sky. Faces blasted away, they seemed nevertheless to stare forward, mute witnesses to the passage of time, whose stillness made me sad and afraid.

I felt the same wonder I had known before the pyramids. Ancient gods, ancient mysteries. It made the chills rise. And yet what were these figures now but faceless sentinels, rulers of an endless waste?

"Marius," I whispered to myself. "Have you seen these? Will any one of us endure so long?"

But my reverie was broken by Gabrielle. She wanted to dismount and walk the rest of the way to the statues. I was game for it, though I didn't really know what to do with the big smelly stubborn camels, how to make them kneel down and all that.

She did it. And she left them waiting for us, and we walked through the sand.

"Come with me into Africa, into the jungles," she said. Her face was grave, her voice unusually soft.

I didn't answer for a moment. Something in her manner alarmed me. Or at least it seemed I should have been alarmed.

I should have heard a sound as sharp as the morning chime of Hell's Bells.

I didn't want to go into the jungles of Africa. And she knew I didn't. I was anxiously awaiting news of my family from Roget, and I had it in my mind to seek the cities of the Orient, to wander through India into China and on to Japan.

"I understand the existence you've chosen," she said. "And I've come to admire the perseverance with which you pursue it, you must know that."

"I might say the same of you," I said a little bitterly.

She stopped.

We were as near to the colossal statues as one should get, I suppose. And the only thing that saved them from overwhelming me was that there was nothing near at hand to put them in scale. The sky overhead was as immense as they were, and the sands endless, and the stars countless and brilliant and rising forever overhead.

"Lestat," she said slowly, measuring her words, "I am asking you to try, only once, to move through the world as I do."

The moon shone full on her, but the hat shadowed her small angular white face.

"Forget the house in Cairo," she said suddenly, dropping her voice as if in respect for the importance of what she said. "Abandon all your valuables, your clothes, the things that link you with civilization. Come south with me, up the river into Africa. Travel with me as I travel."

Still I didn't answer. My heart was pounding.

She murmured softly under her breath that we would see the secret tribes of Africa unknown to the world. We would fight the crocodile and the lion with our bare hands. We might find the source of the Nile itself.

I began to tremble all over. It was as if the night were full of howling winds. And there was no place to go.

You are saying you will leave me forever if I don't come. Isn't that it?

I looked up at these horrific statues. I think I said:

"So it comes to this."

And this was why she had stayed close to me, this was why she had done so many little things to please, this was why we were together now. It had nothing to do with Nicki gone into eternity. It was another parting that concerned her now.

She shook her head as if communing with herself, debating on how to go on. In a hushed voice she described to me the heat of tropical nights, wetter, sweeter than this heat.

"Come with me, Lestat," she said. "By day I sleep in the sand. By night I am on the wing as if I could truly fly. I need no name. I leave no footprints. I want to go down to the very tip of Africa. I will be a goddess to those I slay."

She approached and slipped her arm about my shoulder and pressed her lips to my cheek, and I saw the deep glitter of her eyes beneath the brim of her hat. And the moonlight icing her mouth.

I heard myself sigh. I shook my head.

"I can't and you know it," I said. "I can't do it any more than you can stay with me."

All the way back to Cairo, I thought on it, what had come to me in those painful moments. What I had known but not said as we stood before the Colossi of Memnon in the sand.

She was already lost to me! She had been for years. I had known it when I came down the stairs from the room in which I grieved for Nicki and I had seen her waiting for me.

It had all been said in one form or another in the crypt beneath the tower years ago. She could not give me what I wanted of her. There was nothing I could do to make her what she would not be. And the truly terrible part was this: she really didn't want anything of me!

She was asking me to come because she felt the obligation to do so. Pity, sadness—maybe those were also reasons. But what she really wanted was to be free.

She stayed with me as we returned to the city. She did and said nothing.

And I was sinking even lower, silent, stunned, knowing that another dreadful blow would soon fall. There was the clarity and the horror. She will say her farewell, and I can't prevent it. When do I start to lose my senses? When do I begin to cry uncontrollably?

Not now.

As we lighted the lamps of the little house, the colors assaulted me—Persian carpets covered with delicate flowers, the tentwork woven with a million tiny mirrors, the brilliant plumage of the fluttering birds.

I looked for a packet from Roget but there was none, and I became angry suddenly. Surely he would have written by now. I had to know what was going on in Paris! Then I became afraid.

"What the hell is happening in France?" I murmured. "I'll have to go and find other Europeans. The British, they always have information. They drag their damned Indian tea and their London *Times* with them wherever they go."

I was infuriated to see her standing there so still. It was as if something were happening in the room—that awful sense of tension and anticipation that I'd known in the crypt before Armand told us his long tale.

But nothing was happening, only that she was about to leave me forever. She was about to slip into time forever. And how would we ever find each other again!

"Damn it," I said. "I expected a letter." No servants. They hadn't known when we would be back. I wanted to send someone to hire musicians. I had just fed, and I was warm and I told myself that I wanted to dance.

She broke her stillness suddenly. She started to move in a rather deliberate way. With uncommon directness she went into the courtyard.

I watched her kneel down by the pond. There she lifted two blocks of paving, and she took out a packet and brushed the sandy earth off it, and she brought it to me.

Even before she brought it into the light I saw it was from Roget. This had come before we had ever gone up the Nile, and she had hidden it!

"But why did you do this!" I said. I was in a fury. I snatched the package from her and put it down on the desk.

I was staring at her and hating her, hating her as never before. Not even in the egotism of childhood had I hated her as I did now!

"Why did you hide this from me!" I said.

"Because I wanted one chance!" she whispered. Her chin was trembling. Her lower lip quivered and I saw the blood tears. "But without this even," she said, "you have made your choice."

I reached down and tore the packet apart. The letter slipped out of it, along with folded clippings from an English paper. I unraveled the letter, my hands shaking, and I started to read:

> Monsieur, As you must know by now, on July 14, the mobs of Paris attacked the Bastille. The city is in chaos. There have been riots all over France. For months I have sought in vain to reach your people, to get them out of the country safely if I could.
>
> But on Monday last I received the word that the peasants and tenant farmers had risen against your father's house. Your brothers, their

> wives and children, and all who tried to defend the castle were slain before it was looted. Only your father escaped.
>
> Loyal servants managed to conceal him during the siege and later to get him to the coast. He is, on this very day, in the city of New Orleans in the former French colony of Louisiana. And he begs you to come to his aid. He is grief-stricken and among strangers. He begs for you to come.

There was more. Apologies, assurances, particulars . . . it ceased to make sense.

I put the letter down on the desk. I stared at the wood and the pool of light made by the lamp.

"Don't go to him," she said.

Her voice was small and insignificant in the silence. But the silence was like an immense scream.

"Don't go to him," she said again. The tears streaked her face like clown paint, two long streams of red coming down from her eyes.

"Get out," I whispered. The word trailed off and suddenly my voice swelled again. "Get out," I said. And again my voice didn't stop. It merely went on until I said the words again with shattering violence: "GET OUT!"

4

I DREAMED a dream of family. We were all embracing one another. Even Gabrielle in a velvet gown was there. The castle was blackened, all burnt up. The treasures I had deposited were melted or turned into ashes. It always comes back to ashes. But is the old quote actually ashes to ashes or dust to dust?

Didn't matter. I had gone back and made them all into vampires, and there we were, the House de Lioncourt, white-faced beauties even to the bloodsucking baby that lay in the cradle and the mother who bent to give it the wriggling long-tailed gray rat upon which it was to feed.

We laughed and we kissed one another as we walked through the ashes, my white brothers, their white wives, the ghostly children chattering together about victims, my blind father, who like a biblical figure had risen, crying:

"I CAN SEE!"

My oldest brother put his arm around me. He looked marvelous in decent clothes. I'd never seen him look so good, and the vampiric blood had made him so spare and so spiritual in expression.

"You know it's a damn good thing you came when you did with all the Dark Gifts." He laughed cheerfully.

"The Dark Tricks, dear, the Dark Tricks," said his wife.

"Because if you hadn't," he continued, "why, we'd all be dead!"

5

THE house was empty. The trunks had been sent on. The ship would leave Alexandria in two nights. Only a small valise remained with me. On shipboard the son of the Marquis must now and then change his clothes. And, of course, the violin.

Gabrielle stood by the archway to the garden, slender, long-legged, beautifully angular in her white cotton garments, the hat on as always, her hair loose.

Was that for me, the long loose hair?

My grief was rising, a tide that included all the losses, the dead and the undead.

But it went away and the sense of sinking returned, the sense of the dream in which we navigate with or without will.

It struck me that her hair might have been described as a shower of gold, that all the old poetry makes sense when you look at one whom you have loved. Lovely the angles of her face, her implacable little mouth.

"Tell me what you need of me, Mother," I said quietly. Civilized this room. Desk. Lamp. Chair. All my brilliantly colored birds given away, probably for sale in the bazaar. Gray African parrots that live to be as old as men. Nicki had lived to be thirty.

"Do you require money from me?"

Great beautiful flush to her face, eyes a flash of moving light—blue and violet. For a moment she looked human. We might as well have been standing in her room at home. Books, the damp walls, the fire. Was she human then?

The brim of the hat covered her face completely for an instant as she bowed her head. Inexplicably she asked:

"But where will you go?"

"To a little house in the rue Dumaine in the old French city of New Orleans," I answered coldly, precisely. "And after he has died and is at rest, I haven't the slightest idea."

"You can't mean this," she said.

"I am booked on the next ship out of Alexandria," I said. "I will go to Naples, then on to Barcelona. I will leave from Lisbon for the New World."

Her face seemed to narrow, her features to sharpen. Her lips moved just a little but she didn't say anything. And then I saw the tears rising in her eyes, and I felt her emotion as if it were reaching out to touch me. I looked away, busied myself with something on the desk, then simply held my hands very still so they wouldn't tremble. I thought, I am glad Nicki took his hands with him into the fire, because if he had not, I would have to go back to Paris and get them before I could go on.

"But you can't be going to him!" she whispered.

Him? Oh. My father.

"What does it matter? I am going!" I said.

She moved her head just a little in a negative gesture. She came near to the desk. Her step was lighter than Armand's.

"Has any of our kind ever made such a crossing?" she asked under her breath.

"Not that I know of. In Rome they said no."

"Perhaps it can't be done, this crossing."

"It can be done. You know it can." We had sailed the seas before in our cork-lined coffins. Pity the leviathan who troubles me.

She came even nearer and looked down at me. And the pain in her face couldn't be concealed anymore. Ravishing she was. Why had I ever dressed her in ball gowns or plumed hats or pearls?

"You know where to reach me," I said, but the bitterness of my tone had no conviction to it. "The addresses of my banks in London and Rome. Those banks have lived as long as vampires already. They will always be there. You know all this, you've always known . . ."

"Stop," she said under her breath. "Don't say these things to me."

What a lie all this was, what a travesty. It was just the kind of exchange she had always detested, the kind of talk she could never make herself. In my wildest imaginings, I had never expected it to be like this—that I should say cold things, that she should cry. I thought I would bawl when she said she was going. I thought I would throw myself at her very feet.

We looked at each other for a long moment, her eyes tinged with red, her mouth almost quivering.

And then I lost my control.

I rose and I went to her, and I gathered her small, delicate limbs in my arms. I determined not to let her go, no matter how she struggled. But she didn't struggle, and we both cried almost silently as if we couldn't make ourselves stop. But she didn't yield to me. She didn't melt in my embrace.

And then she drew back. She stroked my hair with both her hands, and leant forward and kissed me on the lips, and then moved away lightly and soundlessly.

"All right, then, my darling," she said.

I shook my head. Words and words and words unspoken. She had no use for them, and never had.

In her slow, languid way, hips moving gracefully, she went to the door to the garden and looked up at the night sky before she looked back at me.

"You must promise me something," she said finally.

Bold young Frenchman who moved with the grace of an Arab through places in a hundred cities where only an alleycat could safely pass.

"Of course," I answered. But I was so broken in spirit now I didn't want to talk anymore. The colors dimmed. The night was neither hot nor cold. I wished she would just go, yet I was terrified of the moment when that would happen, when I couldn't get her back.

"Promise me you will never seek to end it," she said, "without first being with me, without our coming together again."

For a moment I was too surprised to answer. Then I said:

"I will *never* seek to end it." I was almost scornful. "So you have my promise. It's simple enough to give. But what about you giving a promise to me? That you'll let me know where you go from here, where I can reach you—that you won't vanish as if you were something I imagined—"

I stopped. There had been a note of urgency in my voice, of rising hysteria. I couldn't imagine her writing a letter or posting it or doing any of the things that mortals habitually did. It was as if no common nature united us, or ever had.

"I hope you're right in your estimation of yourself," she said.

"I don't believe in anything, Mother," I said. "You told Armand long ago that you believe you'll find answers in the great jungles and forests; that the stars will finally reveal a vast truth. But I don't believe in anything. And that makes me stronger than you think."

"Then why am I so afraid for you?" she asked. Her voice was little more than a gasp. I think I had to see her lips move in order to hear her.

"You sense my loneliness," I answered, "my bitterness at being shut out of life. My bitterness that I'm evil, that I don't deserve to be loved and yet I need love hungrily. My horror that I can never reveal myself to mortals. But these things don't stop me, Mother. I'm too strong for them to stop me. As you said yourself once, I am very good at being what I am. These things merely now and then make me suffer, that's all."

"I love you, my son," she said.

I wanted to say something about her promising, about the agents in Rome, that she would write. I wanted to say . . .

"Keep your promise," she said.

And quite suddenly I knew this was our last moment. I knew it and I could do nothing to change it.

"Gabrielle!" I whispered.

But she was already gone.

The room, the garden outside, the night itself, were silent and still.

Some time before dawn I opened my eyes. I was lying on the floor of the house, and I had been weeping and then I had slept.

I knew I should start for Alexandria, that I should go as far as I could and then down into the sand when the sun rose. It would feel so good to sleep in the sandy earth. I also knew that the garden gate stood open. That all the doors were unlocked.

But I couldn't move. In a cold silent way I imagined myself looking throughout Cairo for her. Calling her, telling her to come back. It almost seemed for a moment that I had done it, that, thoroughly humiliated, I had run after her, and I had tried to tell her again about destiny: that I had been meant to lose her just as Nicki had been meant to lose his hands. Somehow we had to subvert the destiny. We had to triumph after all.

Senseless that. And I hadn't run after her. I'd hunted and I had come back. She was miles from Cairo by now. And she was as lost from me as a tiny grain of sand in the air.

Finally after a long time I turned my head. Crimson sky over the garden, crimson light sliding down the far roof. The sun coming—and the warmth coming and the awakening of a thousand tiny voices all through the tangled alleyways of Cairo, and a sound that seemed to come out of the sand and the trees and the patch of grass themselves.

And very slowly, as I heard these things, as I saw the dazzle of the light moving on the roof, I realized that a mortal was near.

He was standing in the open gate of the garden, peering at my still form within the empty house. A young fair-haired European in Arab robes, he was. Rather handsome. And by the early light he saw me, his fellow European lying on the tile floor in the abandoned house.

I lay staring at him as he came into the deserted garden, the illumination of the sky heating my eyes, the tender skin around them starting to burn. Like a ghost in a white sheet he was in his clean headdress and robe.

I knew that I had to run. I had to get far away immediately and hide myself from the coming sun. No chance now to go into the crypt beneath the floor. This mortal was in my lair. There was not time enough even to kill him and get rid of him, poor unlucky mortal.

Yet I didn't move. And he came nearer, the whole sky flickering behind him, so that his figure narrowed and became dark.

"Monsieur!" The solicitous whisper, like the woman years and years ago in Notre Dame who had tried to help me before I made a victim of her and her innocent child. "Monsieur, what is it? May I be of help?"

Sunburnt face beneath the folds of the white headdress, golden eyebrows glinting, eyes gray like my own.

I knew I was climbing to my feet, but I didn't will myself to do it. I knew my lips were curling back from my teeth. And then I heard a snarl rise out of me and saw the shock on his face.

"Look!" I hissed, the fangs coming down over my lower lip. "Do you see!"

And rushing towards him, I grabbed his wrist and forced his open hand flat against my face.

"Did you think I was human?" I cried. And then I picked him up, holding him off his feet before me as he kicked and struggled uselessly. "Did you think I was your brother?" I shouted. And his mouth opened with a dry rasping noise, and then he screamed.

I hurled him up into the air and out over the garden, his body spinning round with arms and legs out before it vanished over the shimmering roof.

The sky was blinding fire.

I ran out of the garden gate and into the alleyway. I ran under tiny archways and through strange streets. I battered down gates and doorways, and hurled mortals out of my path. I bore through the very walls in front of me, the dust of the plaster rising to choke me, and shot out again into the packed mud alley and the stinking air. And the light came after me like something chasing me on foot.

And when I found a burnt-out house with its lattices in ruins, I broke into it and went down into the garden soil, digging deeper and deeper and deeper until I could not move my arms or my hands any longer.

I was hanging in coolness and in darkness.

I was safe.

6

I WAS dying. Or so I thought. I couldn't count how many nights had passed. I had to rise and go to Alexandria. I had to get across the sea. But this meant moving, turning over in the earth, giving in to the thirst.

I wouldn't give in.

The thirst came. The thirst went. It was the rack and the fire, and my brain thirsted as my heart thirsted, and my heart grew bigger and bigger, and louder and louder, and still I wouldn't give in.

Maybe mortals above could hear my heart. I saw them now and then, spurts of flame against the darkness, heard their voices, babble of foreign tongue. But more often I saw only the darkness. Heard only the darkness.

I was finally just the thirst lying in the earth, with red sleep and red dreams, and the slow knowledge that I was now too weak to push up through the soft sandy clods, too weak, conceivably, to turn the wheel again.

That's right. I couldn't rise if I wanted to. I couldn't move at all. I breathed. I went on. But not the way that mortals breathe. My heart sounded in my ears.

Yet I didn't die. I just wasted. Like those tortured beings in the walls under les Innocents, deserted metaphors of the misery that is everywhere unseen, unrecorded, unacknowledged, unused.

My hands were claws, and my flesh was shrunk to the bones, and my eyes bulged from the sockets. Interesting that we can go on like this forever, that even when we don't drink, don't surrender to the luscious and fatal pleasure, we go on. Interesting that is, if each beat of the heart wasn't such agony.

And if I could stop thinking: Nicolas de Lenfent is gone. My brothers are gone. Pale taste of wine, sound of applause. "*But don't you think it's good what we do when we are there, that we make people happy?*"

"*Good? What are you talking about? Good?*"

"*That it's good, that it does some good, that there is good in it! Dear God, even if there is no meaning in this world, surely there can still be goodness. It's good to eat, to drink, to laugh . . . to be together . . .*"

Laughter. That insane music. That din, that dissonance, that never ending shrill articulation of the meaninglessness . . .

Am I awake? Am I asleep? I am sure of one thing. I am a monster. And because I lie in torment in the earth, certain human beings move on through the narrow pass of life unmolested.

Gabrielle may be in the jungles of Africa now.

Sometime or other mortals came into the burnt-out house above, thieves hiding. Too much babble of foreign tongue. But all I had to do was sink deeper inside myself, withdraw even from the cool sand around me not to hear them.

Am I really trapped?

Stink of blood above.

Maybe they are the last hope, these two camping in the neglected garden, that the blood will draw me upwards, that it will make me turn over and stretch out these hideous—they must be—claws.

I will frighten them to death before I even drink. Shameful. I was always such a beautiful little devil, as the expression goes. Not now.

Now and then, it seems, Nicki and I are engaged in our best conversations. "I am beyond all pain and sin," he says to me. "But do you feel anything?" I ask. "Is that what it means to be free of this, that you no longer feel?" Not misery, not thirst, not ecstasy? It is interesting to me in these moments that our concept of heaven is one of ecstasy. The joys of heaven. That our concept of hell is pain. The fires of hell. So we don't think it very good not to *feel* anything, do we?

Can you give it up, Lestat? Or isn't it true that you'd rather fight the thirst with this hellish torment than die and feel nothing? At least you have the desire for blood, hot and delicious and filling every particle of you—blood.

How long are these mortals going to be here, above in my ruined garden? One night, two nights? I left the violin in the house where I lived. I have to get it, give it to some young mortal musicians, someone who will . . .

Blessed silence. Except for the playing of the violin. And Nicki's white fingers stabbing at the strings, and the bow streaking in the light, and the faces of the immortal marionettes, half entranced, half amused. One hundred years ago, the people of Paris would have got him. He wouldn't have had to burn himself. Got me too maybe. But I doubt it.

No, there never would have been any witches' place for me.

He lives on in my mind now. Pious mortal phrase. And what kind of life is that? I don't like living here myself! What does it mean to live on in the mind of another? Nothing, I think. You aren't really there, are you?

Cats in the garden. Stink of cat blood.

Thank you, but I would rather suffer, rather dry up like a husk with teeth.

7

THERE was a sound in the night. What was it like?

The giant bass drum beaten slowly in the street of my childhood village as the Italian players announced the little drama to be performed from the back of their painted wagon. The great bass drum that I myself had pounded through the streets of the town during those precious days when I, the runaway boy, had been one of them.

But it was stronger than that. The booming of a cannon echoing through valleys and mountain passes? I felt it in my bones. I opened my eyes in the dark, and I knew it was drawing nearer.

The rhythm of steps, it had, or was it the rhythm of a heart beating? The world was filled with the sound.

It was a great ominous din that drew closer and closer. And yet some part of me knew there was no real sound, nothing a mortal ear could hear, nothing that rattled the china on its shelf or the glass windows. Or made the cats streak to the top of the wall.

Egypt lies in silence. Silence covers the desert on both sides of the mighty river. There is not even the bleat of sheep or the lowing of cattle. Or a woman crying somewhere.

Yet it was deafening, this sound.

For one second I was afraid. I stretched in the earth. I forced my fingers up towards the surface. Sightless, weightless, I was floating in the soil, and I couldn't breathe suddenly, I couldn't scream, and it seemed that if I could have screamed, I would have cried out so loud all the glass for miles about me would have been shattered. Crystal goblets would have been blown to bits, windows exploded.

The sound was louder, nearer. I tried to roll over and to gain the air but I couldn't.

And it seemed then I saw the thing, the figure approaching. A glimmer of red in the dark.

It was someone coming, this sound, some creature so powerful that even in the silence the trees and the flowers and the air itself did feel it. The dumb creatures of the earth did know. The vermin ran from it, the felines darting out of its path.

Maybe this is death, I thought.

Maybe by some sublime miracle it is alive, Death, and it takes us into its arms, and it is no vampire, this thing, it is the very personification of the heavens.

And we rise up and up into the stars with it. We go past the angels and the saints, past illumination itself and into the divine darkness, into the void, as we pass out of existence. In oblivion we are forgiven all things.

The destruction of Nicki becomes a tiny pinpoint of vanishing light. The death of my brothers disintegrates into the great peace of the inevitable.

I pushed at the soil. I kicked at it, but my hands and legs were too weak. I tasted the sandy mud in my mouth. I knew I had to rise, and the sound was telling me to rise.

I felt it again like the roar of artillery: the cannon boom.

And quite completely I understood that it was looking for me, this sound, it was seeking me out. It was searching like a beam of light. I couldn't lie here anymore. I had to answer.

I sent it the wildest current of welcome. I told it I was here, and I heard my own miserable breaths as I struggled to move my lips. And the sound grew so loud that it was pulsing through every fiber of me. The earth was moving with it around me.

Whatever it was, it had come into the burnt-out ruined house.

The door had been broken away, as if the hinges had been anchored not in iron but in plaster. I saw all this against the backdrop of my closed eyes. I saw it moving under the olive trees. It was in the garden.

In a frenzy again I clawed towards the air. But the low, common noise I heard now was of a digging through the sand from above.

I felt something soft like velvet brush my face. And I saw overhead the gleam of the dark sky and the drift of the clouds like a veil over the stars, and never had the heavens in all their simplicity looked so blessed.

My lungs filled with air.

I let out a loud moan at the pleasure of it. But all these sensations were beyond pleasure. To breathe, to see light, these were miracles. And the drumming sound, the great deafening boom seemed the perfect accompaniment.

And he, the one who had been looking for me, the one from whom the sound came, was standing over me.

The sound melted; it disintegrated until it was no more than the aftersound of a violin string. And I was rising, just as if I were being lifted, up out of the earth, though this figure stood with its hands at its side.

At last, it lifted its arms to enfold me and the face I saw was beyond the realm of all possibility. What one of us could have such a face? What did we know of patience, of seeming goodness, of compassion? No, it wasn't one of us. It couldn't have been. And yet it was. Preternatural flesh and blood like mine. Iridescent eyes, gathering the light from all directions, tiny eyelashes like strokes of gold from the finest pen.

And this creature, this powerful vampire, was holding me upright and looking into my eyes, and I believe that I said some mad thing, voiced some frantic thought, that I knew now the secret of eternity.

"Then tell it to me," he whispered, and he smiled. The purest image of human love.

"O God, help me. Damn me to the pit of hell." This was my voice speaking. I can't look on this beauty.

I saw my arms like bones, hands like birds' talons. Nothing can live and be what I am now, this wraith. I looked down at my legs. They were sticks. The clothing was falling off me. I couldn't stand or move, and the remembered sensation of blood flowing in my mouth suddenly overcame me.

Like a dull blaze before me I saw his red velvet clothes, the cloak that covered him to the ground, the dark red gloved hands with which he held me. His hair was thick, white and gold strands mingled in waves fallen loosely around his face, and over his broad forehead. And the blue eyes might have been brooding under their heavy golden brows had they not been so large, so softened with the feeling expressed in the voice.

A man in the prime of life at the moment of the immortal gift. And the square face, with its slightly hollowed cheeks, its long full mouth, stamped with terrifying gentleness and peace.

"Drink," he said, eyebrows rising slightly, lips shaping the word carefully, slowly, as if it were a kiss.

As Magnus had done on that lethal night so many eons ago, he raised his hand now and moved the cloth back from his throat. The vein, dark purple beneath the translucent preternatural skin, offered itself. And the sound commenced again, that overpowering sound, and it lifted me right off the earth and drew me into it.

Blood like light itself, liquid fire. Our blood.

And my arms gathering incalculable strength, winding round his shoulders, my face pressed to his cool white flesh, the blood shooting down into my loins and every vessel in my body ignited with it. How many centuries had purified this blood, distilled its power?

It seemed beneath the roar of the flow he spoke. He said again:

"Drink, my young one, my wounded one."

I felt his heart swell, his body undulate, and we were sealed against each other.

I think I heard myself say:

"Marius."

And he answered:

"Yes."

PART VII

ANCIENT MAGIC, ANCIENT MYSTERIES

1

WHEN I awoke, I was on board a ship. I could hear the creak of the boards, smell the sea. I could smell the blood of those who manned the ship. And I knew that it was a galley because I could hear the rhythm of the oars under the low rumbling of the giant canvas sails.

I couldn't open my eyes, couldn't make my limbs move. Yet I was calm. I didn't thirst. In fact, I experienced an extraordinary sense of peace. My body was warm as if I had only just fed, and it was pleasant to lie there, to dream waking dreams on the gentle undulation of the sea.

Then my mind began to clear.

I knew that we were slipping very fast through rather still waters. And that the sun had just gone down. The early evening sky was darkening, the wind was dying away. And the sound of the oars dipping and rising was as soothing as it was clear.

My eyes were now open.

I was no longer in the coffin. I had just come out of the rear cabin of the long vessel and I was standing on the deck.

I breathed the fresh salt air and I saw the lovely incandescent blue of the twilight sky and the multitude of brilliant stars overhead. Never from land do the stars look like that. Never are they so near.

There were dark mountainous islands on either side of us, cliffs sprinkled with tiny flickering lights. The air was full of the scent of green things, of flowers, of land itself.

And the small sleek vessel was moving fast to a narrow pass through the cliffs ahead.

I felt uncommonly clearheaded and strong. There was a moment's temptation to try to figure out how I had gotten here, whether I was in the Aegean or the Mediterranean itself, to know when we had left Cairo and if the things I remembered had really taken place.

But this slipped away from me in some quiet acceptance of what was happening.

Marius was up ahead on the bridge before the mainmast.

I walked towards the bridge and stood beside it, looking up.

He was wearing the long red velvet cloak he had worn in Cairo, and his full white blond hair was blown back by the wind. His eyes were fixed on the pass before us, the dangerous rocks that protruded from the shallow water, his left hand gripping the rail of the little deck.

I felt an overpowering attraction to him, and the sense of peace in me expanded.

There was no forbidding grandeur to his face or his stance, no loftiness that might have humbled me and made me afraid. There was only a quiet nobility about him, his eyes rather wide as they looked forward, the mouth suggesting a disposition of exceptional gentleness as before.

Too smooth the face, yes. It had the sheen of scar tissue, it was so smooth, and it might have startled, even frightened, in a dark street. It gave off a faint light. But the expression was too warm, too human in its goodness to do anything but invite.

Armand might have looked like a god out of Caravaggio, Gabrielle a marble archangel at the threshold of a church.

But this figure above me was that of an immortal man.

And the immortal man, with his right hand outstretched before him, was silently but unmistakably piloting the ship through the rocks before the pass.

The waters around us shimmered like molten metal, flashing azure, then silver, then black. They sent up a great white froth as the shallow waves beat upon the rocks.

I drew closer and as quietly as I could I climbed the small steps to the bridge.

Marius didn't take his eyes off the waters for an instant, but he reached out with his left hand and took my hand, which was at my side.

Warmth. Unobtrusive pressure. But this wasn't the moment for speaking and I was surprised that he had acknowledged me at all.

His eyebrows came together and his eyes narrowed slightly, and, as if impelled by his silent command, the oarsmen slowed their stroke.

I was fascinated by what I was watching, and I realized as I deepened my own concentration that I could feel the power emanating from him, a low pulse that came in time with his heart.

I could also hear mortals on the surrounding cliffs, and on the narrow island beaches stretching out to our right and to our left. I saw them gathered on the promontories, or running towards the edge of the water with torches in their hands. I could hear thoughts ringing out like voices from them as they stood in the thin evening darkness looking out to the lanterns of our ship. The language was Greek and not known to me, but the message was clear:

The lord is passing. Come down and look: the lord is passing. And the word "lord" incorporated in some vague way the supernatural in its meaning. And a reverence, mingled with excitement, emanated like a chorus of overlapping whispers from the shores.

I was breathless listening to this! I thought of the mortal I'd terrified in Cairo, the old debacle on Renaud's stage. But for those two humiliating incidents, I'd passed through the world invisibly for ten years, and these people, these dark-clad peasants gathered to watch the passing of the ship, knew what Marius was. Or at least they knew something of what he was. They were not saying the Greek word for vampire, which I had come to understand.

But we were leaving the beaches behind. The cliffs were closing on either side of us. The ship glided with its oars above water. The high walls diminished the sky's light.

In a few moments, I saw a great silver bay opening before us, and a sheer wall of rock rising straight ahead, while gentler slopes enclosed the water on either side. The rock face was so high and so steep that I could make out nothing at the top.

The oarsmen cut their speed as we came closer. The boat was turning ever so slightly to the side. And as we drifted on towards the cliff, I saw the dim shape of an old stone embankment covered with gleaming moss. The oarsmen had lifted their oars straight towards the sky.

Marius was as still as ever, his hand exerting a gentle force on mine, as with the other he pointed towards the embankment and the cliff that rose like the night itself, our lanterns sending up their glare on the wet rock.

When we were no more than five or six feet from the embankment—dangerously close for a ship of this size and weight it seemed—I felt the ship stop.

Then Marius took my hand and we went across the deck together and mounted the side of the ship. A dark-haired servant approached and placed a sack in Marius's hand. And together, Marius and I leapt over the water to the stone embankment, easily clearing the distance without a sound.

I glanced back to see the ship rocking slightly. The oars were being lowered again. Within seconds the ship was heading for the distant lights of a tiny town on the far side of the bay.

Marius and I stood alone in the darkness, and when the ship had become only a dark speck on the glimmering water, he pointed to a narrow stairway cut into the rock.

"Go before me, Lestat," he said.

It felt good to be climbing. It felt good to be moving up swiftly, following the rough-cut steps and the zigzag turns, and feeling the wind get stronger, and seeing the water become ever more distant and frozen as if the movement of the waves had been stopped.

Marius was only a few steps behind me. And again, I could feel and hear that pulse of power. It was like a vibration in my bones.

The rough-cut steps disappeared less than halfway up the cliff, and I was soon following a path not wide enough for a mountain goat. Now and then boulders or outcroppings of stone made a margin between us and a possible fall to the water below. But most of the time the path itself was the only outcropping on the cliff face, and as we went higher and higher, even I became afraid to look down.

Once, with my hand around a tree branch, I looked back and saw Marius moving steadily towards me, the bag slung over his shoulder, his right hand hanging free. The bay, the distant little town, and the harbor, all this appeared toylike, a map made by a child on a tabletop with a mirror and sand and tiny bits of wood. I could even see beyond the pass into the open water, and the deep shadowy shapes of other islands rising out of the motionless sea. Marius smiled and waited. Then he whispered very politely:

"Go on."

I must have been spellbound. I started up again and didn't stop until I reached the summit. I crawled over a last jut of rocks and weeds and climbed to my feet in soft grass.

Higher rocks and cliffs lay ahead, and seeming to grow out of them was an immense fortress of a house. There were lights in its windows, lights on its towers.

Marius put his arm around my shoulder and we went towards the entrance.

I felt his grip loosen on me as he paused in front of the massive door. Then came the sound of a bolt sliding back inside. The door swung open and his grip became firm again. He guided me into the hallway where a pair of torches provided an ample light.

I saw with a little shock that there was no one there who could have moved the bolt or opened the door for us. He turned and he looked at the door and the door closed.

"Slide the bolt," he said.

I wondered why he didn't do it the way he had done everything else. But I put it in place immediately as he asked.

"It's easier that way, by far," he said, and a little mischief came into his expression. "I'll show you to the room where you may sleep safely, and you may come to me when you wish."

I could hear no one else in the house. But mortals had been here, that I could tell. They'd left their scent here and there. And the torches had all been lighted only a short time ago.

We went up a little stairway to the right, and when I came out into the room that was to be mine, I was stunned.

It was a huge chamber, with one entire wall open to a stone-railed terrace that hung over the sea.

When I turned around, Marius was gone. The sack was gone. But Nicki's violin and my valise of belongings lay on a stone table in the middle of the room.

A current of sadness and relief passed through me at the sight of the violin. I had been afraid that I had lost it.

There were stone benches in the room, a lighted oil lamp on a stand. And in a far niche was a pair of heavy wooden doors.

I went to these and opened them and found a little passage which turned sharply in an L. Beyond the bend was a sarcophagus with a plain lid. It had been cleanly fashioned out of diorite, which to my knowledge is one of the hardest stones on earth. The lid was immensely heavy, and when I examined the inside of it I saw that it was plated in iron and contained a bolt that could be slipped from within.

Several glittering objects lay on the bottom of the box itself. As I lifted them, they sparkled almost magically in the light that leaked in from the room.

There was a golden mask, its features carefully molded, the lips closed, the eye holes narrow but open, attached to a hood made up of layered plates of hammered gold. The mask itself was heavy but the hood was very light and very flexible, each little plate strung to the others by gold thread. And there was also a pair of leather gloves covered completely in tinier more delicate gold plates like scales. And finally a large folded blanket of the softest red wool with one side sewn with larger gold plates.

I realized that if I put on this mask and these gloves—if I laid over me the blanket—then I would be protected from the light if anyone opened the lid of the sarcophagus while I slept.

But it wasn't likely that anyone could get into the sarcophagus. And the doors of this L-shaped chamber were also covered with iron, and they too had their iron bolt.

Yet there was a charm to these mysterious objects. I liked to touch them, and I pictured myself wearing them as I slept. The mask reminded me of the Greek masks of comedy and tragedy.

All of these things suggested the burial of an ancient king.

I left these things a little reluctantly.

I came back out into the room, took off the garments I'd worn during my nights in the earth in Cairo, and put on fresh clothes. I felt rather absurd standing in this timeless place in a violet blue frock coat with pearl buttons and the usual lace shirt and diamond buckle satin shoes, but these were the only clothes I had. I tied back my hair in a black ribbon like any proper eighteenth-century gentleman and went in search of the master of the house.

2

ORCHES had been lighted throughout the house. Doors lay open. Windows were uncovered as they looked out over the firmament and the sea.

And as I left the barren little stairs that led down from my room, I realized that for the first time in my wandering I was truly in the safe refuge of an immortal being, furnished and stocked with all the things that an immortal being might want.

Magnificent Grecian urns stood on pedestals in the corridors, great bronze statues from the Orient in their various niches, exquisite plants bloomed at every window and terrace open to the sky. Gorgeous rugs from India, Persia, China covered the marble floors wherever I walked.

I came upon giant stuffed beasts mounted in lifelike attitudes—the brown bear, the lion, the tiger, even the elephant standing in his own immense chamber, lizards as big as dragons, birds of prey clutching dried branches made to look like the limbs of real trees.

But the brilliantly colored murals covering every surface from floor to ceiling dominated all.

In one chamber was a dark vibrant painting of the sunburnt Arabian desert complete with an exquisitely detailed caravan of camels and turbaned merchants moving over the sand. In another room a jungle came to life around me, swarming with delicately rendered tropical blossoms, vines, carefully drawn leaves.

The perfection of the illusion startled me, enticed me, but the more I peered into the pictures the more I saw.

There were creatures everywhere in the texture of the jungle—insects, birds, worms in the soil—a million aspects of the scene that gave me the feeling, finally, that I had slipped out of time and space into something that was more than a painting. Yet it was all quite flat upon the wall.

I was getting dizzy. Everywhere I turned walls gave out on new vistas. I couldn't name some of the tints and hues I saw.

As for the style of all this painting, it baffled me as much as it delighted me. The technique seemed utterly realistic, using the classical proportions and skills that one sees in all the later Renaissance painters: da Vinci, Raphael, Michelangelo, as well as the painters of more recent times, Watteau, Fragonard. The use of light was spectacular. Living creatures seemed to breathe as I looked on.

But the details. The details couldn't have been realistic or in proportion. There were simply too many monkeys in the jungle, too many bugs crawling on the leaves. There were thousands of tiny insects in one painting of a summer sky.

I came into a large gallery walled on either side by painted men and women staring at me, and I almost cried out. Figures from all ages these were—bedouins, Egyptians, then Greeks and Romans, and knights in armor, and peasants and kings and queens. There were Renaissance people in doublets and leggings, the Sun King with his massive mane of curls, and finally the people of our own age.

But again, the details made me feel as if I were imagining them—the droplets of water clinging to a cape, the cut on the side of a face, the spider half-crushed beneath a polished leather boot.

I started to laugh. It wasn't funny. It was just delightful. I began to laugh and laugh.

I had to force myself out of this gallery and the only thing that gave me the willpower was the sight of a library, blazing with light.

Walls and walls of books and rolled manuscripts, giant glistening world globes in their wooden cradles, busts of the ancient Greek gods and goddesses, great sprawling maps.

Newspapers in all languages lay in stacks on tables. And there were strewn everywhere curious objects. Fossils, mummified hands, exotic shells. There were bouquets of dried flowers, figurines and fragments of old sculpture, alabaster jars covered with Egyptian hieroglyphs.

And everywhere in the center of the room, scattered among the tables and the glass cases, were comfortable chairs with footstools, and candelabra or oil lamps.

In fact, the impression was one of comfortable messiness, of great long hours of pure enjoyment, of a place that was human in the extreme. Human knowledge, human artifacts, chairs in which humans might sit.

I stayed a long time here, perusing the Latin and Greek titles. I felt a little drunk, as if I'd happened on a mortal with a lot of wine in his blood.

But I had to find Marius. I went on out of this room, down a little stairs, and through another painted hallway to an even larger room that was also full of light.

I heard the singing of the birds and smelled the perfume of the flowers before I even reached this place. And then I found myself lost in a forest of cages. There were not only birds of all sizes and colors here, there were monkeys and baboons, all of them gone wild in their little prisons as I made my way around the room.

Potted plants crowded against the cages—ferns and banana trees, cabbage roses, moonflower, jasmine, and other sweetly fragrant nighttime vines. There were purple and white orchids, waxen flowers that trapped insects in their maw, little trees groaning with peaches and lemons and pears.

When I finally emerged from this little paradise, it was into a hall of sculptures equal to any gallery in the Vatican museum. And I glimpsed adjoining chambers full of paintings, Oriental furnishings, mechanical toys.

Of course I was no longer lingering on each object or new discovery. To learn the contents of this house would have taken a lifetime. And I pressed on.

I didn't know where I was going. But I knew that I was being allowed to see all these things.

Finally I heard the unmistakable sound of Marius, that low rhythmic beat of the heart which I had heard in Cairo. And I moved towards it.

3

I CAME into a brightly illuminated eighteenth-century salon. The stone walls had been covered in fine rosewood paneling with framed mirrors rising to the ceiling. There were the usual painted chests, upholstered chairs, dark and lush landscapes, porcelain clocks. A small collection of books in the glass-doored bookcases, a newspaper of recent date lying on a small table beside a brocaded winged chair.

High narrow French doors opened onto the stone terrace, where banks of white lilies and red roses gave off their powerful perfume.

And there, with his back to me, at the stone railing stood an eighteenth-century man.

It was Marius when he turned around and gestured for me to come out.

He was dressed as I was dressed. The frock coat was red, not violet, the lace Valenciennes, not Bruxelles. But he wore very much the same costume, his shining hair tied back loosely in a dark ribbon just as mine was, and he looked not at all ethereal as Armand might have, but rather like a superpresence, a creature of impossible whiteness and perfection who was nevertheless connected to everything around him—the clothes he wore, the stone railing on which he laid his hand, even the moment itself in which a small cloud passed over the bright half moon.

I savored the moment: that he and I were about to speak, that I was really here. I was still clearheaded as I had been on the ship. I couldn't feel thirst. And I sensed that it was his blood in me that was sustaining me. All the old mysteries collected in me, arousing me and sharpening me. Did Those Who Must Be Kept lie somewhere on this island? Would all these things be known?

I went up to the railing and stood beside him, glancing out over the sea. His eyes were now fixed on an island not a half mile off the shore below. He was listening to something that I could not hear. And the side of his face, in the light from the open doors behind us, looked too frighteningly like stone.

But immediately, he turned to me with a cheerful expression, the smooth face vitalized impossibly for an instant, and then he put his arm around me and guided me back into the room.

He walked with the same rhythm as a mortal man, the step light but firm, the body moving through space in the predictable way.

He led me to a pair of winged chairs that faced each other and there we sat down. This was more or less the center of the room. The terrace was to my right, and we had a clear illumination from the chandelier above as well as a dozen or so candelabra and sconces on the paneled walls.

Natural, civilized it all was. And Marius settled in obvious comfort on the brocade cushions and let his fingers curl around the arms of the chair.

As he smiled, he looked entirely human. All the lines, the animation were there until the smile melted again.

I tried not to stare at him, but I couldn't help it.

And something mischievous crept into his face.

My heart was skipping.

"What would be easier for you?" he asked in French. "That I tell you why I brought you here, or that you tell me why you asked to see me?"

"Oh, the former would be easier," I said. "You talk."

He laughed in a soft ingratiating fashion.

"You're a remarkable creature," he said. "I didn't expect you to go down into the earth so soon. Most of us experience the first death much later—after a century, maybe even two."

"The first death? You mean it's common—to go into the earth the way I did?"

"Among those who survive, it's common. We die. We rise again. Those who don't go into the earth for periods of time usually do not last."

I was amazed, but it made perfect sense. And the awful thought struck me that if only Nicki had gone down into the earth instead of into the fire— But I couldn't think of Nicki now. I would start asking inane questions if I did. Is Nicki somewhere? Has Nicki stopped? Are my brothers somewhere? Have they simply stopped?

"But I shouldn't have been so surprised that it happened when it did in your case," he resumed as if he hadn't heard these thoughts, or didn't want to address them just yet. "You've lost too much that was precious to you. You saw and learned a great deal very fast."

"How do you know what's been happening to me?" I asked.

Again, he smiled. He almost laughed. It was astonishing the warmth emanating from him, the immediacy. The manner of his speech was lively and absolutely current. That is, he spoke like a well-educated Frenchman.

"I don't frighten you, do I?" he asked.

"I didn't think that you were trying to," I said.

"I'm not." He made an offhand gesture. "But your self-possession is a little surprising, nevertheless. To answer your question, I know things that happen to our kind all over the world. And frankly I do not always understand how or why I know. The power increases with age as do all our powers, but it remains inconsistent, not easily controlled. There are moments when I can hear what is happening with our kind in Rome or even in Paris. And when another calls to me as you have done, I can hear the call over amazing distances. I can find the source of it, as you have seen for yourself.

"But information comes to me in other ways as well. I know of the messages you left for me on walls throughout Europe because I read them. And I've heard of you from others. And sometimes you and I have been near to each other—nearer than you ever supposed—and I have heard your thoughts. I can hear your thoughts now, of course, as I'm sure you realize. But I prefer to communicate with words."

"Why?" I asked. "I thought the older ones would dispense with speech altogether."

"Thoughts are imprecise," he said. "If I open my mind to you I cannot really control what you read there. And when I read your mind it is possible for me to misunderstand what I hear or see. I prefer to use speech and let my mental faculties work with it. I like the alarm of sound to announce my important communications. For my voice to be received. I do not like to penetrate the thoughts of another without warning. And quite frankly, I think speech is the greatest gift mortals and immortals share."

I didn't know what to answer to this. Again, it made perfect sense. Yet I found myself shaking my head. "And your manner," I said. "You don't move the way Armand or Magnus moved, the way I thought the ancient ones—"

"You mean like a phantom? Why should I?" He laughed again, softly, charming me. He slumped back in the chair a little further and raised his knee, resting his foot on the seat cushion just as a man might in his private study.

"There were times, of course," he said, "when all of that was very interesting. To glide without seeming to take steps, to assume physical positions that are uncomfortable or impossible for mortals. To fly short distances and land without a sound. To move objects by the mere wish to do so. But it can be crude, finally. Human gestures are *elegant.* There is wisdom in the flesh, in the way the human body does things. I like the sound of my foot touching the ground, the feel of objects in my fingers. Besides, to fly even short distances and to move things by sheer will alone is exhausting. I can do it when I have to, as you've seen, but it's much easier to use my hands to do things."

I was delighted by this and didn't try to hide it.

"A singer can shatter a glass with the proper high note," he said, "but the simplest way for anyone to break a glass is simply to drop it on the floor."

I laughed outright this time.

I was already getting used to the shifts in his face between masklike perfection and expression, and the steady vitality of his gaze that united both. The impression remained one of evenness and openness—of a startlingly beautiful and perceptive man.

But what I could not get used to was the sense of presence, that something immensely powerful, dangerously powerful, was so contained and immediately there.

I became a little agitated suddenly, a little overwhelmed. I felt the unaccountable desire to weep.

He leaned forward and touched the back of my hand with his fingers, and a shock coursed through me. We were connected in the touch. And though his skin was silky like the skin of all vampires, it was less pliant. It was like being touched by a stone hand in a silk glove.

"I brought you here because I want to tell you what I know," he said. "I want to share with you whatever secrets I possess. For several reasons, you have attracted me."

I was fascinated. And I felt the possibility of an overpowering love.

"But I warn you," he said, "there's a danger in this. I don't possess the ultimate answers. I can't tell you who made the world or why man exists. I can't tell you why we exist. I can only tell you more about us than anyone else has told you so far. I can show you Those Who Must Be Kept and tell you what I know of them. I can tell you why I *think* I have managed to survive for so long. This knowledge may change you somewhat. That's all knowledge ever really does, I suppose . . ."

"Yes—"

"But when I've given all I have to give, you will be exactly where you were before: an immortal being who must find his own reasons to exist."

"Yes," I said, "reasons to exist." My voice was a little bitter. But it was good to hear it spelled out that way.

But I felt a dark sense of myself as a hungry, vicious creature, who did a very good job of existing without reasons, a powerful vampire who always took exactly what he wanted, no matter who said what. I wondered if he knew how perfectly awful I was.

The reason to kill was the blood.

Acknowledged. The blood and the sheer ecstasy of the blood. And without it we are husks as I was in the Egyptian earth.

"Just remember my warning," he said, "that the circumstances will be the same afterwards. Only you might be changed. You might be more bereft than before you came here."

"But why have you chosen to reveal things to me?" I asked. "Surely others have gone looking for you. You must know where Armand is."

"There are several reasons, as I told you," he said. "And probably the strongest reason is the manner in which you sought me. Very few beings really seek knowledge in this world. Mortal or immortal, few really *ask.* On the contrary, they try to wring from the unknown the answers they have already shaped in their own minds—justifications, confirmations, forms of consolation without which they can't go on. To really ask is to open the door to the whirlwind. The answer may annihilate the question and the questioner. But you have been truly asking since you left Paris ten years ago."

I understood this, but only inarticulately.

"You have few preconceptions," he said. "In fact, you astound me because you admit to such extraordinary simplicity. You want a purpose. You want love."

"True," I said with a little shrug. "Rather crude, isn't it?"

He gave another soft laugh:

"No. Not really. It's as if eighteen hundred years of Western civilization have produced an innocent."

"An innocent? You can't be speaking of me."

"There is so much talk in this century of the nobility of the savage," he explained, "of the corrupting force of civilization, of the way we must find our way back to the innocence that has been lost. Well, it's all nonsense really. Truly primitive people can be monstrous in their assumptions and expectations. They cannot conceive of innocence. Neither can children. But civilization has at last created men who behave innocently. For the first time they look about themselves and say, 'What the hell is all this!' "

"True. But I'm not innocent," I said. "Godless yes. I come from godless people, and I'm glad of it. But I know what good and evil are in a very practical sense, and I am Typhon, the slayer of his brother, not the killer of Typhon, as you must know."

He nodded with a slight lift of his eyebrows. He did not have to smile anymore to look human. I was seeing an expression of emotion now even when there were no lines whatsoever in his face.

"But you don't seek any system to justify it either," he said. "That's what I mean by innocence. You're guilty of killing mortals because you've been made into something that feeds on blood and death, but you're not guilty of lying, of creating great dark and evil systems of thought within yourself."

"True."

"To be godless is probably the first step to innocence," he said, "to lose the sense of sin and subordination, the false grief for things supposed to be lost."

"So by innocence you mean not an absence of experience, but an absence of illusions."

"An absence of need for illusions," he said. "A love of and respect for what is right before your eyes."

I sighed. I sat back in the chair for the first time, thinking this over, what it had to do with Nicki and what Nicki said about the light, always the light. Had he meant this?

Marius seemed now to be pondering. He too was sitting back in his chair, as he had been all along, and he was looking off at the night sky beyond the open doors, his eyes narrow, his mouth a little tense.

"But it wasn't merely your spirit that attracted me," he said, "your honesty, if you will. It was the way you came into being as one of us."

"Then you know all that, too."

"Yes, everything," he said, dismissing that. "You have come into being at the end of an era, at a time when the world faces changes undreamed of. And it was the same with me. I was born and grew to manhood in a time when the ancient world, as we call it now, was coming to a close. Old faiths were worn out. A new god was about to rise."

"When was this time?" I asked excitedly.

"In the years of Augustus Caesar, when Rome had just become an empire, when faith in the gods was, for all lofty purposes, dead."

I let him see the shock and the pleasure spread over my face. I never doubted him for a moment. I put my hand to my head as if I had to steady myself a little.

But he went on:

"The common people of those days," he said, "still believed in religion just as they do now. And for them it was custom, superstition, elemental magic, the use of ceremonies whose origins were lost in antiquity, just as it is today. But the world of those who *originated* ideas—those who ruled and advanced the course of history—was a godless and hopelessly sophisticated world like that of Europe in this day and age."

"When I read Cicero and Ovid and Lucretius, it seemed so to me," I said.

He nodded and gave a little shrug.

"It has taken eighteen hundred years," he said, "to come back to the skepticism, the level of practicality that was our daily frame of mind then. But history is by no means repeating itself. That is the amazing thing."

"How do you mean?"

"Look around you! Completely new things are happening in Europe. The value placed upon human life is higher than ever before. Wisdom and philosophy are coupled with new discoveries in science, new inventions which will completely alter the manner in which humans live. But that is a story unto itself. That is the future. The point is that you were born on the cusp of the old way of seeing things. And so was I. You came of age without faith, and yet you aren't cynical. And so it was with me. We sprang up from a crack between faith and despair, as it were."

And Nicki fell into that crack and perished, I thought.

"That's why your questions are different," he said, "from those who were born to immortality under the Christian god."

I thought of my conversation with Gabrielle in Cairo—my last conversation. I myself had told her this was my strength.

"Precisely," he said. "So you and I have that in common. We did not grow to manhood expecting very much of others. And the burden of conscience was private, terrible though it might be."

"But was it under the Christian god . . . in the very first days of the Christian god that you were—born to immortality—as you said?"

"No," he said with a hint of disgust. "*We* never served the Christian God. That you can put out of your mind right now."

"But the forces of good and evil behind the names of Christ and Satan?"

"Again, they have very little if anything to do with *us.*"

"But the concept of evil in some form surely . . ."

"No. We are older than that, Lestat. The men that made me were worshipers of gods, true. And they believed in things that I did not believe. But their faith hearkened back to a time long before the temples of the Roman Empire, when the shedding of innocent human blood could be done on a massive scale in the name of good. And evil was the drought and the plague of the locust and the death of the crops. I was made what I am by these men in the name of good."

This was too enticing, too enthralling.

All the old myths came to my mind, in a chorus of dazzling poetry. *Osiris was a good god to the Egyptians, a god of the corn. What has this to do with us?* My thoughts were spinning. In a flash of mute pictures, I recalled the night I left my father's house in the Auvergne when the villagers had been dancing round the Lenten fire, and making their chants for the increase of the crops. Pagan, my mother had said. Pagan, had declared the angry priest they had long ago sent away.

And it all seemed more than ever the story of the Savage Garden, dancers in the Savage Garden, where no law prevailed except the law of the garden, which was the aesthetic law. That the crops shall grow high, that the wheat shall be green and then yellow, that the sun shall shine. Look at the perfectly shaped apple that the tree has made, fancy that! The villagers would run through the orchards with their burning brands from the Lenten bonfire, to make the apples grow.

"Yes, the Savage Garden," Marius said with a spark of light in his eyes. "And I had to go out of the civilized cities of the Empire to find it. I had to go into the deep woods of the northern provinces, where the garden still grew at its lushest, the very land of Southern Gaul in which you were born. I had to fall into the hands of the barbarians who gave us both our stature, our blue eyes, our fair hair. I had it through the blood of my mother, who had come from those people, the daughter of a Keltic chieftain married to a Roman patrician. And you have it through the blood of your fathers directly from those days. And by a strange coincidence, we were both chosen for immortality for the very same reason—you by Magnus and I by my captors—that we were the nonpareils of our blond and blue-eyed race, that we were taller and more finely made than other men."

"Ooooh, you have to tell me all of it! You have to explain everything!" I said.

"I *am* explaining everything," he said. "But first, I think it is time for you to see something that will be very important as we go on."

He waited a moment for the words to sink in.

Then he rose slowly in human fashion, assisting himself easily with his hands on the arms of the chair. He stood looking down at me and waiting.

"Those Who Must Be Kept?" I asked. My voice had gotten terribly small, terribly unsure of itself.

And I could see a little mischief again in his face, or rather a touch of the amusement that was never far away.

"Don't be afraid," he said soberly, trying to conceal the amusement. "It's very unlike you, you know."

I was burning to see them, to know what they were, and yet I didn't move. I'd never really thought that I would see them. I'd never really thought what it would mean . . .

"Is it . . . is it something terrible to see?" I asked.

He smiled slowly and affectionately and placed his hand on my shoulder.

"Would it stop you if I said yes?"

"No," I said. But I was afraid.

"It's only terrible as time goes on," he said. "In the beginning, it's beautiful."

He waited, watching me, trying to be patient. Then he said softly: "Come, let's go."

4

A STAIRWAY into the earth.

It was much older than the house, this stairway, though how I knew I couldn't say. Steps worn concave in the middle from the feet that have followed them. Winding deeper and deeper down into the rock.

Now and then a rough-cut portal to the sea, an opening too small for a man to climb through, and a shelf upon which birds have nested, or where the wild grass grew out of the cracks.

And then the chill, the inexplicable chill that you find sometimes in old monasteries, ruined churches, haunted rooms.

I stopped and rubbed the backs of my arms with my hands. The chill was rising through the steps.

"They don't cause it," he said gently. He was waiting for me on the steps just below.

The semidarkness broke his face into kindly patterns of light and shadow, gave the illusion of mortal age that wasn't there.

"It was here long before I brought them," he said. "Many have come to worship on this island. Maybe it was there before they came, too."

He beckoned to me again with his characteristic patience. His eyes were compassionate.

"Don't be afraid," he said again as he started down.

I was ashamed not to follow. The steps went on and on.

We came on larger portals and the noise of the sea. I could feel the cool spray on my hands and face, see the gleam of the damp on the stones. But we went on down farther and farther, the echo of our shoes swelling against the rounded ceiling, the rudely finished walls. This was deeper than any dungeon, this was the pit you dig in childhood when you brag to your mother and father that you will make a tunnel to the very center of the earth.

Finally I saw a burst of light as we rounded another bend. And at last, two lamps burning before a pair of doors.

Deep vessels of oil fed the wicks of the lamps. And the doors themselves were bolted by an enormous beam of oak. It would have taken several men to lift it, possibly levers, ropes.

Marius lifted this beam and laid it aside easily, and then he stood back and looked at the doors. I heard the sound of another beam being moved on the inside. Then the doors opened slowly, and I felt my breathing come to a halt.

It wasn't only that he'd done it without touching them. I had seen that little trick before. It was that the room beyond was full of the same lovely flowers and lighted lamps that I had seen in the house above. Here deep underground were lilies, waxen and white, and sparkling with droplets of moisture, roses in rich hues of red and pink ready to fall from their vines. It was a chapel, this chamber with the soft flicker of votive candles and the perfume of a thousand bouquets.

The walls were painted in fresco like the walls of ancient Italian churches, with gold leaf hammered into the design. But these were not the pictures of Christian saints.

Egyptian palm trees, the yellow desert, the three pyramids, the blue waters of the Nile. And the Egyptian men and women in their gracefully shaped boats sailing the river, the multicolored fishes of the deep beneath them, the purple-winged birds of the air above.

And the gold worked into it all. Into the sun that shone from the heavens, and the pyramids that gleamed in the distance, into the scales of the fishes and the feathers of the birds, and the ornaments of the lithe and delicate Egyptian figures who stood frozen looking forward, in their long narrow green boats.

I closed my eyes for a moment. I opened them slowly and saw the whole like a great shrine.

Banks of lilies on a low stone altar which held an immense golden tabernacle worked all over with fine engraving of the same Egyptian designs. And the air coming down through deep shafts in the rock above, stirring the flames of the ever burning lamps, ruffling the tall green blade-like leaves of the lilies as they stood in their vessels of water giving off their heady perfume.

I could almost hear hymns in this place. I could hear chants and ancient invocations. And I was no longer afraid. The beauty was too soothing, too grand.

But I stared at the gold doors of the tabernacle on the altar. The tabernacle was taller than I was. It was broader by three times.

And Marius, too, was looking at it. And I felt the power moving out of him, the low heat of his invisible strength, and I heard the inside lock of the tabernacle doors slide back.

I would have moved just a little closer to him had I dared. I wasn't breathing as the gold doors opened completely, folding back to reveal two splendid Egyptian figures—a man and a woman—seated side by side.

The light moved over their slender, finely sculpted white faces, their decorously arranged white limbs; it flashed in their dark eyes.

They were as severe as all the Egyptian statues I had ever seen, spare of detail, beautiful in contour, magnificent in their simplicity, only the open and childlike expression on the faces relieving the feeling of hardness and cold. But unlike all the others, they were dressed in real fabric and real hair.

I had seen saints in Italian churches dressed in this manner, velvet hung on marble, and it was not always pleasing.

But this had been done with great care.

Their wigs were of long thick black locks, cut straight across the forehead and crowned with circlets of gold. Round their naked arms were bracelets like snakes, and on their fingers were rings.

The clothes were the finest white linen, the man naked to the waist and wearing only a skirt of sorts, and the woman in a long, narrow, beautifully pleated dress. Both wore many gold necklaces, some inlaid with precious stones.

Almost the same size they were, and they sat in the very same manner, hands laid flat before them on their thighs. And this sameness astonished me somehow, as much as their stark loveliness, and the jewellike quality of their eyes.

Not in any sculpture anywhere had I ever seen such a lifelike attitude, but actually there was nothing lifelike about them at all. Maybe it was a trick of the accoutrements, the twinkling of the lights on their necklaces and rings, the reflected light in their gleaming eyes.

Were they Osiris and Isis? Was it tiny writing I saw on their necklaces, on the circlets of their hair?

Marius said nothing. He was merely gazing at them as I was, his expression unreadable, perhaps sad.

"May I go near to them," I whispered.

"Of course," he said.

I moved towards the altar like a child in a cathedral, getting ever more tentative with each step. I stopped only a few feet before them and looked directly into their eyes. Oh, too gorgeous in depth and variegation. Too real.

With infinite care each black eyelash had been fixed, each black hair of their gently curved brows.

With infinite care their mouths made partly open so that one could see the glimmer of teeth. And the faces and the arms had been so polished that not the slightest flaw disturbed the luster. And in the manner of all statues or painted figures who stare directly forward, they appeared to be looking at me.

I was confused. If they were not Osiris and Isis, who were they meant to be? Of what old truth were they the symbols, and why the imperative in that old phrase, Those Who *Must* Be Kept?

I fell into contemplating them, my head a little to the side.

The eyes were really brown, with the black deep in their centers, the whites moist looking as though covered with the clearest lacquer, and the lips were the softest shade of ashen rose.

"Is it permissible . . . ?" I whispered, turning back to Marius, but lacking confidence I stopped.

"You may touch them," he said.

Yet it seemed sacrilegious to do it. I stared at them a moment longer, at the way that their hands opened against their thighs, at the fingernails, which looked remarkably like our fingernails—as if someone had made them of inlaid glass.

I thought that I could touch the back of the man's hand, and it wouldn't seem so sacrilegious, but what I really wanted to do was to touch the woman's face. Finally I raised my fingers hesitantly to her cheek. And I just let my fingertips graze the whiteness there. And then I looked into her eyes.

It couldn't be stone I was feeling. It couldn't . . . Why, it felt exactly like . . . And the woman's eyes, something—

I jumped backwards before I could stop myself.

In fact I shot backwards, overturning the vases of lilies, and slammed against the wall beside the door.

I was trembling so violently, my legs could hardly hold me.

"They're alive!" I said. "They aren't statues! They're vampires just like us!"

"Yes," Marius said. "That word, however, they wouldn't know."

He was just ahead of me and he was still looking at them, his hands at his sides, just as he had been all along.

Slowly, he turned and came up to me and took my right hand.

The blood had rushed to my face. I wanted to say something but I couldn't. I kept staring at them. And now I was staring at him and staring at the white hand that held mine.

"It's quite all right," he said almost sadly. "I don't think they dislike your touching them."

For a moment I couldn't understand him. Then I did understand. "You mean you . . . You don't know whether . . . They just sit there and . . . Oooh God!"

And his words of hundreds of years ago, embedded in Armand's tale, came back to me: *Those Who Must Be Kept are at peace, or in silence. More than that we may never know.*

I was shuddering all over. I couldn't stop the tremors in my arms and my legs.

"They're breathing, thinking, living, as we are," I stammered. "How long have they been like this, how long?"

"Calm yourself," he said, patting my hand.

"Oh God," I said again stupidly. I kept saying it. No other words sufficed. "But who are they?" I asked finally. My voice was rising hysterically. "Are they Osiris and Isis? Is that who they are?"

"I don't know."

"I want to get away from them. I want to get out of here."

"Why?" he asked calmly.

"Because they . . . they are alive inside their bodies and they . . . they can't speak or move!"

"How do you know they can't?" he said. His voice was low, soothing as before.

"But they don't. That's the whole point. They don't—"

"Come," he said. "I want you to look at them a little more. And then I'll take you back up and I'll tell you everything, as I've already said I would."

"I don't want to look at them anymore, Marius, honestly I don't," I said, trying to get my hand free, and shaking my head. But he was holding on to me as firmly as a statue might, it seemed, and I couldn't stop thinking how much like their skin was his skin, how he was taking on the same impossible luster, how when his face was in repose, it was as smooth as theirs!

He was becoming like them. And sometime in the great yawn of eternity, I would become like him! If I survived that long.

"Please, Marius . . ." I said. I was beyond shame and vanity. I wanted to get out of the room.

"Wait for me then," he said patiently. "Stay here."

And he let my hand go. He turned and looked down at the flowers I had crushed, the spilled water.

And before my eyes these things were corrected, the flowers put back in the vase, the water gone from the floor.

He stood looking at the two before him, and then I heard his thoughts. He was greeting them in some personal way that did not require an address or a title. He was explaining to them why he had been away the last few nights. He had gone into Egypt. And he had brought back gifts for them which he would soon bring. He would take them out to look at the sea very soon.

I started to calm down a little. But my mind was now anatomizing all that had come clear to me at the moment of shock. He cared for them. He had always cared for them. He made this chamber beautiful because they were staring at it, and they just might care about the beauty of the paintings and the flowers he brought.

But he didn't know. And all I had to do was look squarely at them again to feel horror, that they were alive and locked inside themselves!

"I can't bear this," I murmured. I knew, without his ever telling me, the reason that he kept them. He could not bury them deep in the earth somewhere because they were conscious. He would not burn them because they were helpless and could not give their consent. Oh, God, it was getting worse and worse.

But he kept them as the ancient pagans kept their gods in temples that were their houses. He brought them flowers.

And now as I watched, he was lighting incense for them, a small cake that he had taken out of a silk handkerchief. This he told them had come from Egypt. And he was putting it to burn in a small bronze dish.

My eyes began to tear. I actually began to cry.

When I looked up, he was standing with his back to them, and I could see them over his shoulder. He looked shockingly like them, a statue dressed in fabric. And I felt maybe he was doing it deliberately, letting his face go blank.

"I've disappointed you, haven't I?" I whispered.

"No, not at all," he said kindly. "You have not."

"I'm sorry that I—"

"No, you have not."

I drew a little closer. I felt I had been rude to Those Who Must Be Kept. I had been rude to him. He had revealed to me this secret and I had shown horror and recoiling. I had disappointed myself.

I moved even closer. I wanted to make up for what I'd done. He turned towards them again and he put his arm around me. The incense was intoxicating. Their dark eyes were full of the eerie movement of the flames of the lamps.

No ridge of vein anywhere in the white skin, no fold or crease. Not even the penstroke lines in the lips which even Marius still had. They did not move with the rise and fall of breath.

And listening in the stillness I heard no thought from them, no heartbeat, no movement of blood.

"But it's there, isn't it?" I whispered.

"Yes, it's there."

"And do you—?" Bring the victims to them, I wanted to ask.

"They no longer drink."

Even that was ghastly! They had not even that pleasure. And yet to imagine it—how it would have been—their firing with movement long enough to take the victim and lapsing back into stillness, ah! No, I should have been relieved. But I was not.

"Long long ago, they still drank, but only once in a year. I would leave the victims in the sanctuary for them—evildoers who were weak and close to death. I would come back and find that they had been taken, and Those Who Must Be Kept would be as they were before. Only the color of the flesh was a little different. Not a drop of blood had been spilt.

"It was at the full moon always that this was done, and usually in the spring. Other victims left were never taken. And then even this yearly feast stopped. I continued to bring victims now and then. And once after a decade had passed, they took another. Again, it was the time of the full moon. It was spring. And then no more for at least half a century. I lost count. I thought perhaps they had to see the moon, that they had to know the change of the seasons. But as it turned out, this did not matter.

"They have drunk nothing since the time before I took them into Italy. That was three hundred years ago. Even in the warmth of Egypt they do not drink."

"But even when it happened, you never saw it with your own eyes?"

"No," he said.

"You've never seen them move?"

"Not since . . . the beginning."

I was trembling again. As I looked at them, I fancied I saw them breathing, fancied I saw their lips change. I knew it was illusion. But it was driving me wild. I had to get out of here. I would start crying again.

"Sometimes when I come to them," Marius said, "I find things changed."

"How? What?"

"Little things," he said. He looked at them thoughtfully. He reached out and touched the woman's necklace. "She likes this one. It is the proper kind apparently. There was another which I used to find broken on the floor."

"Then they *can* move."

"I thought at first the necklace had fallen. But after repairing it three times I realized that was foolish. She was tearing it off her neck, or making it fall with her mind."

I made some little horrified whisper. And then I felt absolutely mortified that I had done this in her presence. I wanted to go out at once. Her face was like a mirror for all my imaginings. Her lips curved in a smile but did not curve.

"It has happened with other ornaments, ornaments bearing the names of gods whom they do not like, I think. A vase I brought from a church was broken once, blown to tiny fragments as if by their glance. And then there have been more startling changes as well."

"Tell me."

"I have come into the sanctuary and found one or the other of them standing."

This was too terrifying. I wanted to tug his hand and pull him out of here.

"I found him once several paces from the chair. And the woman, another time, at the door."

"Trying to get out?" I whispered.

"Perhaps," he said thoughtfully. "But then they could easily get out if they wanted to. When you hear the whole story you can judge. Whenever I've found them moved, I've carried them back. I've arranged their limbs as they were before. It takes enormous strength to do it. They are like flexible stone, if you can imagine it. And if I have such strength, you can imagine what theirs might be."

"You say want . . . wanted to. What if they want to do everything and they no longer can? What if it was the limit of her greatest effort even to reach the door!"

"I think she could have broken the doors, had she wanted to. If I can open bolts with my mind, what can she do?"

I looked at their cold, remote faces, their narrow hollowed cheeks, their large and serene mouths.

"But what if you're wrong. And what if they can hear every word that we are saying to each other, and it angers them, outrages them . . ."

"I think they do hear," he said, trying to calm me again, his hand on mine, his tone subdued, "but I do not think they care. If they cared, they would move."

"But how can you know that?"

"They do other things that require great strength. For example, there are times when I lock the tabernacle and they at once unlock it and open the doors again. I know they are doing it because they are the only ones who could be doing it. The doors fly back and there they are. I take them out to look at the sea. And before dawn, when I come to fetch them, they are heavier, less pliant, almost impossible to move. There are times when I think they do these things to torment me as it were, to play with me."

"No. They are trying and they can't."

"Don't be so quick to judge," he said. "I have come into their chamber and found evidence of strange things indeed. And of course, there are the things that happened in the beginning . . ."

But he stopped. Something had distracted him.

"Do you hear thoughts from them?" I asked. He did seem to be listening.

He didn't answer. He was studying them. It occurred to me that something had changed! I used every bit of my will not to turn and run. I looked at them carefully. I couldn't see anything, hear anything, feel anything. I was going to start shouting and screaming if Marius didn't explain why he was staring.

"Don't be so impetuous, Lestat," he said finally, smiling a little, his eyes still fixed on the male. "Every now and then I do hear them, but it is unintelligible, it is merely the presence of them—you know the sound."

"And you heard him just then."

"Yeeesss . . . Perhaps."

"Marius, please let us go out of here, I beg you. Forgive me, I can't bear it! Please, Marius, let's go."

"All right," he said kindly. He squeezed my shoulder. "But do something for me first."

"Anything you ask."

"Talk to them. It need not be out loud. But talk. Tell them you find them beautiful."

"They know," I said. "They know I find them indescribably beautiful." I was certain that they did. But he meant tell them in a ceremonial way, and so I cleared my mind of all fear and all mad suppositions and I told them this.

"Just talk to them," Marius said, urging me on.

I did. I looked into the eyes of the man and into the eyes of the woman. And the strangest feeling crept over me. I was repeating the phrases *I find you beautiful, I find you incomparably beautiful* with the barest shape of real words. I was praying as I had when I was very very little and I would lie in the meadow on the side of the mountain and ask God please please to help me get away from my father's house.

I talked to her like this now and I said I was grateful that I had been allowed to come near her and her ancient secrets, and this feeling became physical. It was all over the surface of my skin and at the roots of my hair. I could feel tension draining from my face. I could feel it leaving my body.

I was light all over, and the incense and the flowers were enfolding my spirit as I looked into the black centers of her deep brown eyes.

"Akasha," I said aloud. I heard the name at the same moment of speaking it. And it sounded lovely to me. The hairs rose all over me. The tabernacle became like a flaming border around her, and there was only something indistinct where the male figure sat. I drew close to her without willing it, and I leaned forward and I almost kissed her lips. I wanted to. I bent nearer. Then I felt her lips.

I wanted to make the blood come up in my mouth and pass it to her as I had that time to Gabrielle when she lay in the coffin.

The spell was deepening, and I looked right into the fathomless orbs of her eyes.

I am kissing the goddess on her mouth, what is the matter with me! Am I mad to think of it!

I moved back. I found myself against the wall again, trembling, with my hands clamped to the sides of my head. At least this time I had not upset the lilies, but I was crying again.

Marius closed the tabernacle doors. He made the bolt inside slip into place.

We went into the passage and he made the inner bolt rise and go into its brackets. He put the outside bolt in with his hands.

"Come, young one," he said. "Let's go upstairs."

But we had walked only a few yards when we heard a crisp clicking sound, and then another. He turned and looked back.

"They did it again," he said. And a look of distress divided his face like a shadow.

"What?" I backed up against the wall.

"The tabernacle, they opened it. Come. I'll return later and lock it before the sun rises. Now we will go back to my drawing room and I will tell you my tale."

When we reached the lighted room, I collapsed in the chair with my head in my hands. He was standing still just looking at me, and when I realized it, I looked up.

"She told you her name," he said.

"Akasha!" I said. It was snatching a word out of the whirlpool of a dissolving dream. "She did tell me! I said Akasha out loud." I looked at him, imploring him for answers. For some explanation of the attitude with which he stared at me.

I thought I'd lose my mind if his face didn't become expressive again.

"Are you angry with me?"

"Shhh. Be quiet," he said.

I could hear nothing in the silence. Except maybe the sea. Maybe a sound from the wicks of the candles in the room. Maybe the wind. Not even their eyes had appeared more lifeless than his eyes now seemed.

"You cause something to stir in them," he whispered.

I stood up.

"What does it mean?"

"I don't know," he said. "Maybe nothing. The tabernacle is still open and they are merely sitting there as always. Who knows?"

And I felt suddenly all his long years of wanting to know. I would say centuries, but I cannot really imagine centuries. Not even now. I felt his years and years of trying to elicit from them the smallest signs and getting nothing, and I knew that he was wondering why I had drawn from her the secret of her name. Akasha. Things had happened, but that had been in the time of Rome. Dark things. Terrible things. Suffering, unspeakable suffering.

The images went white. Silence. He was stranded in the room like a saint taken down off an altar and left in the aisle of a church.

"Marius!" I whispered.

He woke and his face warmed slowly, and he looked at me affectionately, almost wonderingly.

"Yes, Lestat," he said and gave my hand a reassuring squeeze.

He seated himself and gestured for me to do the same, and we were once again facing each other comfortably. And the even light of the room was reassuring. It was reassuring to see, beyond the windows, the night sky.

His former quickness was returning, the glint of good humor in his eyes.

"It's not yet midnight," he said. "And all is well on the islands. If I'm not disturbed, I think there is time for me to tell you the whole tale."

MARIUS'S STORY

5

"IT HAPPENED in my fortieth year, on a warm spring night in the Roman Gallic city of Massilia, when in a dirty waterfront tavern I sat scribbling away on my history of the world.

"The tavern was deliciously filthy and crowded, a hangout for sailors and wanderers, travelers like me, I fancied, loving them all in a general sort of way, though most of them were poor and I wasn't poor, and they couldn't read what I wrote when they glanced over my shoulder.

"I'd come to Massilia after a long and studious journey that had taken me through all the great cities of the Empire. To Alexandria, Pergamon, Athens I'd traveled, observing and writing about the people, and now I was making my way through the cities of Roman Gaul.

"I couldn't have been more content on this night had I been in my library at Rome. In fact, I liked the tavern better. Everywhere I went I sought out such places in which to write, setting up my candle and ink and parchment at a table close to the wall, and I did my best work early in the evening when the places were at their noisiest.

"In retrospect, it's easy to see that I lived my whole life in the midst of frenzied activity. I was used to the idea that nothing could affect me adversely.

"I'd grown up an illegimate son in a rich Roman household—loved, pampered, and allowed to do what I wanted. My legitimate brothers had to worry about marriage, politics, and war. By the age of twenty, I'd become the scholar and the chronicler, the one who raised his voice at drunken banquets to settle historical and military arguments.

"When I traveled I had plenty of money, and documents that opened doors everywhere. And to say life had been good to me would be an understatement. I was an extraordinarily happy individual. But the really important point here is that life had never bored me or defeated me.

"I carried within me a sense of invincibility, a sense of wonder. And this was as important to me later on as your anger and strength have been to you, as important as despair or cruelty can be in the spirits of others.

"But to continue . . . If there was anything I'd missed in my rather eventful life—and I didn't think of this too much—it was the love and knowledge of my Keltic mother. She'd died when I was born, and all I knew of her was that she'd been a slave, daughter of the warlike Gauls who fought Julius Caesar. I was blond and blue-eyed as she was. And her people had been giants it seemed. At a very young age, I towered over my father and my brothers.

"But I had little or no curiosity about my Gallic ancestors. I'd come to Gaul as an educated Roman, through and through, and I carried with me no awareness of my barbarian blood, but rather the common beliefs of my time—that Caesar Augustus was a great ruler, and that in this blessed age of the Pax Romana, old superstition was being replaced by law and by reason throughout the Empire. There was no place too wretched for the Roman roads, and for the soldiers, the scholars, and the traders who followed them.

"On this night I was writing like a madman, scribbling down descriptions of the men who came and went in the tavern, children of all races it seemed, speakers of a dozen different languages.

"And for no apparent reason, I was possessed of a strange idea about life, a strange concern that amounted almost to a pleasant obsession. I remember that it came on me this night because it seemed somehow related to what happened after. But it wasn't related. I had had the idea before. That it came to me in these last free hours as a Roman citizen was no more than coincidence.

"The idea was simply that there was somebody who knew everything, somebody who had seen everything. I did not mean by this that a Supreme Being existed, but rather that there was on earth a continual intelligence, a continual awareness. And I thought of it in practical terms that excited me and soothed me simultaneously. There was an awareness somewhere of all things I had seen in my travels, an awareness of what it had been like in Massilia six centuries ago when the first Greek traders came, an awareness of what it had been like in Egypt when Cheops built the pyramids. Somebody knew what the light had been like in the late afternoon on the day that Troy fell to the Greeks, and someone or something knew what the peasants said to each other in their little farmhouse outside Athens right before the Spartans brought down the walls.

"My idea of who or what it was, was vague. But I was comforted by the notion that nothing spiritual—and knowing was spiritual—was lost to us. That there was this continuous knowing . . .

"And as I drank a little more wine, and thought about it, and wrote about it, I realized it wasn't so much a belief of mine as it was a prejudice. I just felt that there was a continual awareness.

"And the history that I was writing was an imitation of it. I tried to unite all things I had seen in my history, linking my observations of lands and people with all the written observations that had come down to me from the Greeks—from Xenophon and Herodotus, and Poseidonius—to make one continuous awareness of the world in my lifetime. It was a pale thing, a limited thing, compared to the true awareness. Yet I felt good as I continued writing.

"But around midnight, I was getting a little tired, and when I happened to look up after a particularly long period of unbroken concentration, I realized something had changed in the tavern.

"It was unaccountably quieter. In fact, it was almost empty. And across from me, barely illuminated by the sputtering light of my candle, there sat a tall fair-haired man with his back to the room who was watching me in silence. I was startled, not so much by the way he looked—though this was startling in itself—but by the realization that he had been there for some time, close to me, observing me, and I hadn't noticed him.

"He was a giant of a Gaul as they all were, even taller than I was, and he had a long narrow face with an extremely strong jaw and hawklike nose, and eyes that gleamed beneath their bushy blond brows with a childlike intelligence. What I mean to say is he looked very very clever, but very young and innocent also. And he wasn't young. The effect was perplexing.

"And it was made all the more so by the fact that his thick and coarse yellow hair wasn't clipped short in the popular Roman style, but was streaming down to his shoulders. And instead of the usual tunic and cloak which you saw everywhere in those times, he wore the old belted leather jerkin that had been the barbarian dress before Caesar.

"Right out of the woods this character looked, with his gray eyes burning through me, and I was vaguely delighted with him. I wrote down hurriedly the details of his dress, confident he couldn't read the Latin.

"But the stillness in which he sat unnerved me a little. His eyes were unnaturally wide, and his lips quivered slightly as if the mere sight of me excited him. His clean and delicate white hand, which casually rested on the table before him, seemed out of keeping with the rest of him.

"A quick glance about told me my slaves weren't in the tavern. Well, they're probably next door playing cards, I thought, or upstairs with a couple of women. They'll stop in any minute.

"I forced a little smile at my strange and silent friend, and went back to writing. But directly he started talking.

" 'You are an educated man, aren't you?' he asked. He spoke the universal Latin of the Empire, but with a thick accent, pronouncing each word with a care that was almost musical.

"I told him, yes, I was fortunate enough to be educated, and I started to write again, thinking this would surely discourage him. After all, he was fine to look at, but I didn't really want to talk to him.

" 'And you write both in Greek and in Latin, don't you?' he asked, glancing at the finished work that lay before me.

"I explained politely that the Greek I had written on the parchment was a quotation from another text. My text was in Latin. And again I started scribbling.

" 'But you are a Keltoi, are you not?' he asked this time. It was the old Greek word for the Gauls.

" 'Not really, no. I am a Roman,' I answered.

" 'You look like one of us, the Keltoi,' he said. 'You are tall like us, and you walk the way we do.'

"This was a strange statement. For hours I'd been sitting here, barely sipping my wine. I hadn't walked anywhere. But I explained that my mother had been Keltic, but I hadn't known her. My father was a Roman senator.

" 'And what is it you write in Greek and Latin?' he asked. 'What is it that arouses your passion?'

"I didn't answer right away. He was beginning to intrigue me. But I knew enough at forty to realize that most people you meet in taverns sound interesting for the first few minutes and then begin to weary you beyond endurance.

" 'Your slaves say,' he announced gravely, 'that you are writing a great history.'

" 'Do they?' I answered, a bit stiffly. 'And where are my slaves, I wonder!' Again I looked around. Nowhere in sight. Then I conceded to him that it was a history I was writing.

" 'And you have been to Egypt,' he said. And his hand spread itself out flat on the table.

"I paused and took another good look at him. There was something otherworldly about him, the way that he sat, the way he used this one hand to gesture. It was the decorum primitive people often have that makes them seem repositors of immense wisdom, when in fact all they possess is immense conviction.

" 'Yes,' I said a little warily. 'I've been to Egypt.'

"Obviously this exhilarated him. His eyes widened slightly, then narrowed, and he made some little movement with his lips as though speaking to himself.

" 'And you know the language and the writing of Egypt?' he asked earnestly, his eyebrows knitting. 'You know the cities of Egypt?'

" 'The language as it is spoken, yes, I do know it. But if by the writing you mean the old picture writing, no, I can't read it. I don't know anyone who can read it. I've heard that even the old Egyptian priests can't read it. Half the texts they copy they can't decipher.'

"He laughed in the strangest way. I couldn't tell whether this was exciting him or he knew something I didn't know. He appeared to take a deep breath, his nostrils dilating a little. And then his face cooled. He was actually a splendid-looking man.

" 'The gods can read it,' he whispered.

" 'Well, I wish they'd teach it to me,' I said pleasantly.

" 'You do!' he said in an astonished gasp. He leant forward over the table. 'Say this again!'

" 'I was joking,' I said. 'I only meant I wished I could read the old Egyptian writing. If I could read it, then I could know true things about the people of Egypt, instead of all the nonsense written by the Greek historians. Egypt is a misunderstood land—' I stopped myself. Why was I talking to this man about Egypt?

" 'In Egypt there are true gods still,' he said gravely, 'gods who have been there forever. Have you been to the very bottom of Egypt?'

"This was a curious way to put it. I told him I had been up the Nile quite far, that I had seen many wonders. 'But as for there being true gods,' I said, 'I can scarce accept the veracity of gods with the heads of animals—'

"He shook his head almost a little sadly.

" 'The true gods require no statues of them to be erected,' he said. 'They have the heads of man and they themselves appear when they choose, and they are living as the crops that come from the earth are living, as all things under the heavens are living, even the stones and the moon itself, which divides time in the great silence of its never changing cycles.'

" 'Very likely,' I said under my breath, not wishing to disturb him. So it was zeal, this mixture of cleverness and youthfulness I had perceived in him. I should have known it. And something came back to me from Julius Caesar's writings about Gaul, that the Keltoi had come from Dis Pater, the god of the night. Was this strange creature a believer in these things?

" 'There are old gods in Egypt,' he said softly, 'and there are old gods in this land for those who know how to worship them. I do not mean in your temples round which merchants sell the animals to defile the altars, and the butchers after sell the meat that is left over. I speak of the proper worship, the proper sacrifice for the god, the one sacrifice to which he will hearken.'

" 'Human sacrifice, you mean, don't you?' I said unobtrusively. Caesar had described well enough that practice among the Keltoi, and it rather curdled my blood to think of it. Of course I'd seen ghastly deaths in the arena in Rome, ghastly deaths at the places of execution, but human sacrifice to the gods, that we had not done in centuries. If ever.

"And now I realized what this remarkable man might actually be. A Druid, a member of the ancient priesthood of the Keltoi, whom Caesar had also described, a priesthood so powerful that nothing like it existed, so far as I knew, anywhere in the Empire. But it wasn't supposed to exist in Roman Gaul anymore either.

"Of course the Druids were always described as wearing long white robes. They went into the forests and collected mistletoe off the oak trees with ceremonial sickles. And this man looked more like a farmer, or a soldier. But then what Druid was going to wear his white robes into a waterfront tavern? And it wasn't lawful anymore for the Druids to go about being Druids.

" 'Do you really believe in this old worship?' I asked, leaning forward. 'Have you yourself been down to the bottom of Egypt?'

"If this was a real live Druid, I had made a marvelous catch, I was thinking. I could get this man to tell me things about the Keltoi that nobody knew. And what on earth did Egypt have to do with it, I wondered?

" 'No,' he said. 'I have not been to Egypt, though from Egypt our gods came to us. It is not my destiny to go there. It is not my destiny to learn to read the ancient language. The tongue I speak is enough for the gods. They give ear to it.'

" 'And what tongue is that?'

" 'The tongue of the Keltoi, of course,' he said. 'You know that without asking.'

" 'And when you speak to your gods, how do you know that they hear you?'

"His eyes widened again, and his mouth lengthened in an unmistakable look of triumph.

" 'My gods answer me,' he said quietly.

"Surely he was a Druid. And he appeared to take on a shimmer, suddenly. I pictured him in his white robes. There might have been an earthquake then in Massilia, and I doubt I would have noticed it.

" 'Then you yourself have heard them,' I said.

" 'I have laid eyes upon my gods,' he said. 'And they have spoken to me both in words and in silence.'

" 'And what do they say? What do they do that makes them different from our gods, I mean aside from the nature of the sacrifice?'

"His voice took on the lilting reverence of a song as he spoke. 'They do as gods have always done; they divide the evil from the good. They bring down blessings upon all who worship them. They draw the faithful into harmony with all the cycles of the universe, with the cycles of the moon, as I have told you. They fructify the land, the gods do. All things that are good proceed from them.'

"Yes, I thought, the old old religion in its simplest forms, and the forms that still held a great spell for the common people of the Empire.

" 'My gods sent me here,' he said. 'To search for you.'

" 'For me?' I asked. I was startled.

" 'You will understand all these things,' he said. 'Just as you will come to know the true worship of ancient Egypt. The gods will teach you.'

" 'Why ever would they do that?' I asked.

" 'The answer is simple,' he said. 'Because you are going to become one of them.'

"I was about to answer when I felt a sharp blow to the back of my head and the pain spread out in all directions over my skull as if it were water. I knew I was going out. I saw the table rising, saw the ceiling high above me. I think I wanted to say if it is ransom you want, take me to my house, to my steward.

"But I knew even then that the rules of my world had absolutely nothing to do with it.

"WHEN I awoke it was daylight and I was in a large wagon being pulled fast along an unpaved road through an immense forest. I was bound hand and foot and a loose cover was thrown over me. I could see to the left and right, through the wicker sides of the cart, and I saw the man who had talked to me, riding beside me. There were others riding with him, and all were dressed in the trousers and belted leather jerkins, and they wore iron swords and iron bracelets. Their hair was almost white in the dappled sun, and they didn't talk as they rode beside the cart together.

"This forest itself seemed made to the scale of Titans. The oaks were ancient and enormous, the interlacing of their limbs blocked out most of the light, and we moved for hours through a world of damp and dark green leaves and deep shadow.

"I do not remember towns. I do not remember villages. I remember only a crude fortress. Once inside the gates I saw two rows of thatched-roof houses, and everywhere the leather-clad barbarians. And when I was taken into one of the houses, a dark low place, and left there alone, I could hardly stand for the cramps in my legs, and I was as wary as I was furious.

"I knew now that I was in an undisturbed enclave of the ancient Keltoi, the very same fighters who had sacked the great shrine of Delphi only a few centuries ago, and Rome itself not too long after, the same warlike creatures who rode stark naked into battle against Caesar, their trumpets blasting, their cries affrighting the disciplined Roman soldiers.

"In other words, I was beyond the reach of everything I counted upon. And if all this talk about my becoming one of the gods meant I was to be slain on some blood-stained altar in an oak grove, then I had better try to get the hell out of here."

6

"WHEN my captor appeared again, he was in the fabled long white robes, and his coarse blond hair had been combed, and he looked immaculate and impressive and solemn. There were other tall white-robed men, some old, some young, and all with the same gleaming yellow hair, who came into the small shadowy room behind him.

"In a silent circle they enclosed me. And after a protracted silence, a riff of whispers passed amongst them.

" 'You are perfect for the god,' said the eldest, and I saw the silent pleasure in the one who had brought me here. 'You are what the god has asked for,' the eldest said. 'You will remain with us until the great feast of Samhain, and then you will be taken to the sacred grove and there you will drink the Divine Blood and you will become a father of gods, a restorer of all the magic that has inexplicably been taken from us.'

" 'And will my body die when this happens?' I asked. I was looking at them, their sharp narrow faces, their probing eyes, the gaunt grace with which they surrounded me. What a terror this race must have been when its warriors swept down on the Mediterranean peoples. No wonder there had been so much written about their fearlessness. But these weren't warriors. These were priests, judges, and teachers. These were the instructors of the young, the keepers of the poetry and the laws that were never written in any language.

" 'Only the mortal part of you will die,' said the one who had spoken to me all along.

" 'Bad luck,' I said. 'Since that's about all there is to me.'

" 'No,' he said. 'Your form will remain and it will become glorified. You will see. Don't fear. And besides, there is nothing you can do to change these things. Until the feast of Samhain, you will let your hair grow long, and you will learn our tongue, and our hymns and our laws. We will care for you. My name is Mael, and I myself will teach you.'

" 'But I am not willing to become the god,' I said. 'Surely the gods don't want one who is unwilling.'

" 'The old god will decide,' said Mael. 'But I know that when you drink the Divine Blood you will become the god, and all things will be clear to you.'

"ESCAPE was impossible.

"I was guarded night and day. I was allowed no knife with which I might cut off my hair or otherwise damage myself. And a good deal of the time I lay in the dark empty room, drunk on wheaten beer and satiated with the rich roasted meats they gave to me. I had nothing with which to write and this tortured me.

"Out of boredom I listened to Mael when he came to instruct me. I let him sing anthems to me and tell me old poems and talk on about laws, only now and then taunting him with the obvious fact that a god should not have to be so instructed.

"This he conceded, but what could he do but try to make me understand what would happen to me.

" 'You can help me get out of here, you can come with me to Rome,' I said. 'I have a villa all my own on the cliffs above the Bay of Naples. You have never seen such a beautiful spot, and I would let you live there forever if you would help me, asking only that you repeat all these anthems and prayers and laws to me so that I might record them.'

" 'Why do you try to corrupt me?' he would ask, but I could see he was tantalized by the world I came from. He confessed that he had searched the Greek city of Massilia for weeks before my arrival, and he loved the Roman wine and the great ships that he had seen in the port, and the exotic foods he had eaten.

" 'I don't try to corrupt you,' I said. 'I don't believe what you believe, and you've made me your prisoner.'

"But I continued to listen to his prayers out of boredom and curiosity, and the vague fear of what was in store for me.

"I began waiting for him to come, for his pale, wraithlike figure to illuminate the barren room like a white light, for his quiet, measured voice to pour forth with all the old melodious nonsense.

"It soon came clear that his verses did not unfold continuous stories of the gods as we knew them in Greek and Latin. But the identity and characteristics of the gods began to emerge in the many stanzas. Deities of all the predictable sorts belonged to the tribe of the heavens.

"But the god I was to become exerted the greatest hold over Mael and those he instructed. He had no name, this god, though he had numerous titles, and the Drinker of the Blood was the most often repeated. He was also the White One, the God of the Night, the God of the Oak, the Lover of the Mother.

"This god took blood sacrifice at every full moon. But on Samhain (the first of November in our present Christian calendar—the day that has become the Feast of All Saints or the Day of the Dead) this god would accept the greatest number of human sacrifices before the whole tribe for the increase of the crops, as well as speak all manner of predictions and judgments.

"It was the Great Mother he served, she who is without visible form, but nevertheless present in all things, and the Mother of all things, of the earth, of the trees, of the sky overhead, of all men, of the Drinker of the Blood himself who walks in her garden.

"My interest deepened but so did my apprehension. The worship of the Great Mother was certainly not unknown to me. The Mother Earth and the Mother of All Things was worshiped under a dozen names from one end of the Empire to the other, and so was her lover and son, her Dying

God, the one who grew to manhood as the crops grow, only to be cut down as the crops are cut down, while the Mother remains eternal. It was the ancient and gentle myth of the seasons. But the celebration anywhere and at any time was hardly ever gentle.

"For the Divine Mother was also Death, the earth that swallows the remains of that young lover, the earth that swallows all of us. And in consonance with this ancient truth—old as the sowing of seed itself—there came a thousand bloody rituals.

"The goddess was worshiped under the name of Cybele in Rome, and I had seen her mad priests castrating themselves in the midst of their devoted frenzy. And the gods of myth met their ends even more violently—Attis gelded, Dionysus rent limb from limb, the old Egyptian Osiris dismembered before the Great Mother Isis restored him.

"And now I was to be that God of Growing Things—the vine god, the corn god, the god of the tree, and I knew that whatever happened it was going to be something appalling.

"And what was there to do but get drunk and murmur these anthems with Mael, whose eyes would cloud with tears from time to time as he looked at me.

" 'Get me out of here, you wretch,' I said once in pure exasperation. 'Why the hell don't you become the God of the Tree? Why am I so honored?'

" 'I have told you, the god confided to me his wishes. I wasn't chosen.'

" 'And would you do it, if you were chosen?' I demanded.

"I was sick of hearing of these old rites by which any man threatened by illness or misfortune must serve up a human sacrifice to the god if he wished to be spared, and all the other sacrosanct beliefs that had to them the same childlike barbarity.

" 'I would fear but I would accept,' he whispered. 'But do you know what is so terrible about your fate? It is that your soul will be locked in your body forever. It will have no chance in natural death to pass into another body or another lifetime. No, all through time your soul will be the soul of the god. The cycle of death and rebirth will be closed in you.'

"In spite of myself and my general contempt for his belief in reincarnation, this silenced me. I felt the eerie weight of his conviction, I felt his sadness.

"My hair grew longer and fuller. And the hot summer melted into the cooler days of fall, and we were nearing the great annual feast of Samhain.

"Yet I wouldn't let up on the questions.

" 'How many have you brought to be gods in this manner? What was it in me that caused you to choose me?'

" 'I have never brought a man to be a god,' he said. 'But the god is old;

he is robbed of his magic. A terrible calamity has befallen him, and I can't speak of these things. He has chosen his successor.' He looked frightened. He was saying too much. Something was stirring the deepest fears in him.

" 'And how do you know he will want me? Have you sixty other candidates stashed in this fortress?'

"He shook his head and in a moment of uncharacteristic rawness, he said:

" 'Marius, if you fail to Drink the Blood, if you do not become the father of a new race of gods, what will become of us?'

" 'I wish I could care, my friend—' I said.

" 'Ah, calamity,' he whispered. And there followed a long subdued observation of the rise of Rome, the terrible invasions of Caesar, the decline of a people who had lived in these mountains and forests since the beginning of time, scorning the cities of the Greek and the Etruscan and the Roman for the honorable strongholds of powerful tribal leaders.

" 'Civilizations rise and fall, my friend,' I said. 'Old gods give way to new ones.'

" 'You don't understand, Marius,' he said. 'Our god was not defeated by your idols and those who tell their frivolous and lascivious stories. Our god was as beautiful as if the moon itself had fashioned him with her light, and he spoke with a voice that was as pure as the light, and he guided us in that great oneness with all things that is the only cessation of despair and loneliness. But he was stricken with terrible calamity, and all through the north country other gods have perished completely. It was the revenge of the sun god upon him, but how the sun entered into him in the hours of darkness and sleep is not known to us, nor to him. You are our salvation, Marius. You are the mortal Who Knows, and is Learned and Can Learn, and Who Can Go Down into Egypt.'

"I thought about this. I thought of the old worship of Isis and Osiris, and of those who said she was the Mother Earth and he the corn, and Typhon the slayer of Osiris was the fire of the sunlight.

"And now this pious communicator with the god was telling me that the sun had found his god of the night and caused great calamity.

"Finally my reason gave out on me.

"Too many days passed in drunkenness and solitude.

"I lay down in the dark and I sang to myself the hymns of the Great Mother. She was no goddess to me, however. Not Diana of Ephesus with her rows and rows of milk-filled breasts, or the terrible Cybele, or even the gentle Demeter, whose mourning for Persephone in the land of the dead had inspired the sacred mysteries of Eleusis. She was the strong good earth that I smelled through the small barred windows of this place, the wind that carried with it the damp and the sweetness of the dark green forest. She was the meadow flowers and the blowing grass, the water I heard now and then gushing as if from some mountain spring. She was all the things that I still had in this rude little wooden room where everything else had been taken from me. And I knew only what all men know, that the cycle of winter and spring and all growing things has within itself some sublime truth that restores without myth or language.

"I looked through the bars to the stars overhead, and it seemed to me I was dying in the most absurd and foolish way, among people I did not admire and customs I would have abolished. And yet the seeming sanctity of it all infected me. It caused me to dramatize and to dream and to give in, to see myself at the center of something that possessed its own exalted beauty.

"I sat up one morning and touched my hair, and realized it was thick and curling at my shoulders.

"And in the days that followed, there was endless noise and movement in the fortress. Carts were coming to the gates from all directions. Thousands on foot passed inside. Every hour there was the sound of people on the move, people coming.

"At last Mael and eight of the Druids came to me. Their robes were white and fresh, smelling of the spring water and sunshine in which they'd been washed and dried, and their hair was brushed and shining.

"Carefully, they shaved all the hair from my chin and upper lip. They trimmed my fingernails. They brushed my hair and put on me the same white robes. And then shielding me on all sides with white veils they passed me out of the house and into a white canopied wagon.

"I glimpsed other robed men holding back an enormous crowd, and I realized for the first time that only a select few of the Druids had been allowed to see me.

"Once Mael and I were under the canopy of the cart, the flaps were closed, and we were completely hidden. We seated ourselves on rude benches as the wagon started to move. And we rode for hours without speaking.

"Occasional rays of sun pierced the white fabric of the tentlike enclosure. And when I put my face close to the cloth I could see the forest—deeper, thicker than I remembered. And behind us came an endless train, and great wagons of men who clung to wooden bars and cried out to be released, their voices commingling in an awful chorus.

" 'Who are they? Why do they cry like that?' I asked finally. I couldn't stand the tension any longer.

"Mael roused himself as if from a dream. 'They are evildoers, thieves, murderers, all justly condemned, and they shall perish in sacred sacrifice.'

" 'Loathsome,' I muttered. But was it? We condemned our criminals to die on crosses in Rome, to be burnt at the stake, to suffer all manner of cruelties. Did it make us more civilized that we didn't call it a religious sacrifice? Maybe the Keltoi were wiser than we were in not wasting the deaths.

"But this was nonsense. My head was light. The cart was creeping along. I could hear those who passed us on foot as well as on horseback. Everyone going to the festival of Samhain. I was about to die. I didn't want it to be fire. Mael looked pale and frightened. And the wailing of the men in the prison carts was driving me to the edge of madness.

"What would I think when the fire was lighted? What would I think when I felt myself start to burn? I couldn't stand this.

" 'What is going to happen to me!' I demanded suddenly. I had the urge to strangle Mael. He looked up and his brows moved ever so slightly.

" 'What if the god is already dead . . .' he whispered.

" 'Then we go to Rome, you and I, and we get drunk together on good Italian wine!' I whispered.

"It was late afternoon when the cart came to a stop. The noise seemed to rise like steam all around us.

"When I went to look out, Mael didn't stop me. I saw we had come to an immense clearing hemmed on all sides by the giant oaks. All the carts including ours were backed into the trees, and in the middle of the clearing hundreds worked at some enterprise involving endless bundles of sticks and miles of rope and hundreds of great rough-hewn tree trunks.

"The biggest and longest logs I had ever seen were been hefted upright in two giant X's.

"The woods were alive with those who watched. The clearing could not contain the multitudes. Yet more and more carts wound their way through the press to find a spot at the edges of the forest.

"I sat back and pretended to myself that I did not know what they were doing out there, but I did. And before the sunset I heard louder and more desperate screams from those in the prison carts.

"It was almost dusk. And when Mael lifted the flap for me to see, I stared in horror at two gargantuan wicker figures—a man and a woman, it seemed, from the mass of vines that suggested dress and hair—constructed all of logs and osiers and ropes, and filled from top to bottom with the bound and writhing bodies of the condemned who screamed in supplication.

"I was speechless looking at these two monstrous giants. I could not count the number of wriggling human bodies they held, victims stuffed into the hollow framework of their enormous legs, their torsos, their arms, even their hands, and even into their immense and faceless cagelike heads, which were crowned with ivy leaves and flowers. Ropes of flowers made up the woman's gown, and stalks of wheat were stuffed into the man's great belt of ivy. The figures shivered as if they might at any moment fall, but I knew the powerful cross scaffolding of timbers supported them as they appeared to tower over the distant forest. And all around the feet of these figures were stacked the bundles of kindling and pitch-soaked wood that would soon ignite them.

" 'And all these who must die are guilty of some wrongdoing, you wish me to believe that?' I asked of Mael.

"He nodded with his usual solemnity. This didn't concern him.

" 'They have waited months, some years, to be sacrificed,' he said almost indifferently. 'They come from all over the land. And they cannot change their fate any more than we can change ours. It is to perish in the forms of the Great Mother and her Lover.'

"I was becoming ever more desperate. I should have done anything to escape. But even now some twenty Druids surrounded the cart and beyond them was a legion of warriors. And the crowd itself went so far back into the trees that I could see no end to it.

"Darkness was falling quickly, and everywhere torches were being lighted.

"I could feel the roar of excited voices. The screams of the condemned grew ever more piercing and beseeching.

"I sat still and tried to deliver my mind from panic. If I could not escape, then I would meet these strange ceremonies with some degree of calm, and when it came clear what a sham they were, I would with dignity and righteousness pronounce my judgments loud enough for others to hear them. That would be my last act—the act of the god—and it must be done with authority, or else it would do nothing in the scheme of things.

"The cart began to move. There was much noise, shouting, and Mael rose and took my arm and steadied me. When the flap was opened we had come to a stop deep in the woods many yards from the clearing. I glanced back at the lurid sight of the immense figures, torchlight glinting on the swarm of pathetic movement inside them. They seemed animate, these horrors, like things that would suddenly start to walk and crush all of us. The play of light and shadow on those stuffed into the giant heads gave a false impression of hideous faces.

"I couldn't make myself turn away from it, and from the sight of the crowd gathered all around, but Mael tightened his grip on my arm and said that I must come now to the sanctuary of the god with the elect of the priesthood.

"The others closed me in, obviously trying to conceal me. I realized the crowd did not know what was happening now. In all likelihood they knew only that the sacrifices would soon begin, and some manifestation of the god would be claimed by the Druids.

"Only one of the band carried a torch, and he led the way deeper into the evening darkness, Mael at my side, and other white-robed figures ahead of me, flanking me, and behind me.

"It was still. It was damp. And the trees rose to such dizzying heights against the vanishing glow of the distant sky that they seemed to be growing even as I looked up at them.

"I could run now, I thought, but how far would I get before this entire race of people came thundering after me?

"But we had come into a grove, and I saw, in the feeble light of the flames, dreadful faces carved into the barks of the trees and human skulls on stakes grinning in the shadows. In carved-out tree trunks were other skulls in rows, piled one row upon another. In fact, the place was a regular charnel house, and the silence that enclosed us seemed to give life to these horrid things, to let them speak suddenly.

"I tried to shake the illusion, the sense that these staring skulls were watching.

"There is no one really watching, I thought, there is no continuous awareness of anything.

"But we had paused before a gnarled oak of such enormous girth that I doubted my senses. How old it must have been, this tree, to have grown to such width I couldn't imagine. But when I looked up I saw that its soaring limbs were still alive, it was still in green leaf, and the living mistletoe everywhere decorated it.

"The Druids had stepped away to right and left. Only Mael remained near me. And I stood facing the oak, with Mael at my far right, and I saw that hundreds of bouquets of flowers had been laid at the base of the tree, their little blooms barely showing any color anymore in the gathering shadows.

"Mael had bowed his head. His eyes were closed. And it seemed the others were in the same attitude, and their bodies were trembling. I felt the cool breeze stir the green grass. I heard the leaves all around us carry the breeze in a loud and long sigh that died away as it had come in the forest.

"And then very distinctly, I heard words spoken in the dark that had no sound to them!

"They came undeniably from within the tree itself, and they asked whether or not all the conditions had been met by him who would drink the Divine Blood tonight.

"For a moment I thought that I was going mad. They had drugged me. But I had drunk nothing since morning! My head was clear, too painfully clear, and I heard the silent pulse of this personage again and it was asking questions:

"*He is a man of learning?*

"Mael's slender form seemed to shimmer as surely he expressed the answer. And the faces of the others had become rapt, their eyes fixed on the great oak, the flutter of the torch the only movement.

"*Can he go down into Egypt?*

"I saw Mael nod. And the tears rose in his eyes, and his pale throat moved as he swallowed.

"*Yes, I live, my faithful one, and I speak, and you have done well, and I shall make the new god. Send him in to me.*

"I was too astonished to speak, and I had nothing to say either. *Everything had changed.* Everything that I believed, depended upon, had suddenly been called into question. I hadn't the slightest fear; only paralyzing amazement. Mael took me by the arm. The other Druids came to assist him, and I was led around the oak, clear of the flowers heaped at its roots, until we stood behind it before a huge pile of stones banked against it.

"The grove had its carved images on this side as well, its troves of skulls, and the pale figures of Druids whom I had not seen before. And it was these men, some with long white beards, who drifted forward to lay their hands on the stones and start to remove them.

"Mael and the others worked with them, silently lifting these great rocks and casting them aside, some of the stones so heavy that three men had to lift them.

"And finally there was revealed in the base of the oak a heavy doorway of iron with huge locks over it. Mael drew out an iron key and he said some long words in the language of the Keltoi, to which the others gave responses. Mael's hand was shaking. But he soon had all the locks undone, and then it took four of the Druids to pull back the door. And then the torchbearer lighted another brand for me and placed it in my hands and Mael said:

" 'Enter, Marius.'

"In the wavering light, we glanced at each other. He seemed a helpless creature, unable to move his limbs, though his heart brimmed as he looked at me. I knew now the barest glimpse of the wonder that had shaped him and enflamed him, and was utterly humbled and baffled by its origins.

"But from within the tree, from the darkness beyond this rudely cut doorway, there came the silent one again:

"*Do not be afraid, Marius. I wait for you. Take the light and come to me.*"

7

"WHEN I stepped through the doorway, the Druids closed it. And I realized that I stood at the top of a long stone stairs. It was a configuration I was to see over and over again in the centuries that followed, and you have already seen it twice and you will see it again—the steps leading down into the Mother Earth, into the chambers where Those Who Drink the Blood always hide.

"The oak itself contained a chamber, low and unfinished, the light of my torch glinting on the rude marks left everywhere in the wood by the chisels, but the thing that called me was at the bottom of the stairs. And again, it told me that I must not be afraid.

"I was not afraid. I was exhilarated beyond my wildest dreams. I was not going to die as simply as I had imagined. I was descending to a mystery that was infinitely more interesting than I had ever thought it would be.

"But when I reached the bottom of the narrow steps and stood in the small stone chamber there, I was terrified by what I saw—terrified and repelled by it, the loathing and fear so immediate that I felt a lump rising to suffocate me or make me uncontrollably sick.

"A creature sat on a stone bench opposite the foot of the stairway, and in the full light of the torch I saw that it had the face and limbs of a man. But it was burnt black all over, horribly burnt, its skin shriveled to its very bones. In fact it appeared a yellow-eyed skeleton coated in pitch, only its flowing main of white hair untouched. It opened its mouth to speak and I saw its white teeth, its fang teeth, and I gripped the torch firmly, trying not to scream like a fool.

" 'Do not come too close to me,' it said. 'Stand there where I may really see you, not as they see you, but as my eyes can still see.'

"I swallowed, tried to breathe easily. No human being could have been burnt like that and survived. And yet the thing lived—naked and shrunken and black. And its voice was low and beautiful. It rose, and then moved slowly across the chamber.

"It pointed its finger at me, and the yellow eyes widened slightly, revealing a blood red tinge in the light.

" 'What do you want of me?' I whispered before I could stop myself. 'Why have I been brought here?'

" 'Calamity,' he said in the same voice, colored with genuine feeling —not the rasping sound I had expected from such a thing. 'I will give you my power, Marius, I will make you a god and you will be immortal. But you must leave here when it is finished. You must somehow escape our faithful worshipers, and you must go down into Egypt to find why this . . . this . . . has befallen me.'

"He appeared to be floating in the darkness, his hair a mop of white straw around him, his jaws stretching the blackened leathery skin that clung to his skull as he spoke.

" 'You see, we are the enemies of light, we gods of darkness, we serve the Holy Mother and we live and rule only by the light of the moon. But our enemy, the sun, has escaped his natural path and sought us out in darkness. All over the north country where we are worshiped, in the sacred groves from the lands of snow and ice, down into this fruitful country, and to the east, the sun has found its way into the sanctuary by day or the world by night and burned the gods alive. The youngest of these perished utterly, some exploding like comets before their worshipers! Others died in such heat that the sacred tree itself became a funeral pyre. Only the old ones—the ones who have long served the Great Mother—continued to walk and to talk as I do, but in agony, affrighting the faithful worshipers when they appeared.

" 'There must be a new god, Marius, strong and beautiful as I was, the lover of the Great Mother, but more truly there must be one strong enough to escape the worshipers, to get out of the oak somehow, and to go down into Egypt and seek out the old gods and find why this calamity has occurred. You must go to Egypt, Marius, you must go into Alexandria and into the older cities, and you must summon the gods with the silent voice that you will have after I make you, and you must find who lives still and who walks still, and why this calamity has occurred.'

"It closed its eyes now. It stood still, its light frame wavering uncontrollably as if it were a thing made of black paper, and I saw suddenly, unaccountably, a spill of violent images—these gods of the grove bursting into flame. I heard their screams. My mind, being rational, being Roman, resisted these images. It tried to memorize and contain them, rather than yield to them, but the maker of the images—this thing—was patient and the images went on. I saw the country that could only be Egypt, the burnt yellow look to all things, the sand that overlies everything and soils it and dusts it to the same color, and I saw more stairways into the earth and I saw sanctuaries . . .

" 'Find them,' he said. 'Find why and how this has come to pass. See to it that it never comes to pass again. Use your powers in the streets of Alexandria until you find the old ones. Pray the old ones are there as I am still here.'

"I was too shocked to answer, too humbled by the mystery. And perhaps there was even a moment when I accepted this destiny, accepted it completely, but I am not sure.

" 'I know,' he said. 'From me you can keep no secrets. You do not wish to be the God of the Grove, and you will seek to escape. But you see, this disaster may seek you out wherever you are unless you discover the cause and the prevention of it. So I know you will go into Egypt, else you too in the womb of the night or the womb of the dark earth may be burnt by this unnatural sun.'

"It came towards me a little, dragging its dried feet on the stone floor. 'Now mark my words, you must escape this very night,' it said. 'I will tell the worshipers that you must go down into Egypt, for the salvation of all of us, but having a new and able god, they will be loath to part with him. But you must go down. And you must not let them imprison you in the oak after the festival. You must travel fast. And before sunrise, go into the Mother Earth to escape the light. She will protect you. Now come to me. I will give you The Blood. And pray I still have the power to give you my ancient strength. It will be slow. It will be long. I will take and I will give, and I will take and I will give, but I must do it, and you must become the god, and you must do as I have said.'

"Without waiting for my compliance, it was suddenly on me, its blackened fingers clutching at me, the torch falling from my hands. I fell backwards on the stairs, but its teeth were already in my throat.

"You know what happened, you know what it was to feel the blood being drawn, to feel the swoon. I saw in those moments the tombs and temples of Egypt. I saw two figures, resplendent as they sat side by side as if on a throne. I saw and heard other voices speaking to me in other languages. And underneath it all, there came the same command: serve the Mother, take the blood of the sacrifice, preside over the worship that is the only worship, the eternal worship of the grove.

"I was struggling as one struggles in dreams, unable to cry out, unable to escape. And when I realized I was free and no longer pinned to the floor, I saw the god again, black as he had been before, but this time he was robust, as if the blaze had only baked him and he retained his full strength. His face had definition, even beauty, features well formed beneath the cracked casing of blackened leather that was his skin. The yellow eyes had round them now the natural folds of flesh that made them portals of a soul. But he was still crippled, still suffering, almost unable to move.

" 'Rise, Marius,' he said. 'You thirst and I will give you to drink. Rise and come to me.'

"And you know then the ecstasy I felt when his blood came into me, when it worked its way into every vessel, every limb. But the horrid pendulum had only begun to swing.

"Hours passed in the oak, as he took the blood out of me and gave it back over and over again. I lay sobbing on the floor when I was drained. I could see my hands like bones in front of me. I was shriveled as he had been. And again he would give me the blood to drink and I would rise in a frenzy of exquisite feeling, only to have him take it out of me again.

"With every exchange there came the lessons: that I was immortal, that only the sun and the fire could kill me, that I would sleep by day in the earth, that I should never know illness or natural death. That my soul should never migrate from my form into another, that I was the servant of the Mother, and that the moon would give me strength.

"That I would thrive on the blood of the evildoers, and even of the innocent who were sacrificed to the Mother, that I should remain in starvation between sacrifices, so that my body would become dry and empty like the dead wheat in the fields at winter, only to be filled with the blood of the sacrifice and to become full and beautiful like the new plants of the spring.

"In my suffering and ecstasy there would be the cycle of the seasons. And the powers of my mind, to read the thoughts and intentions of others, these I should use to make the judgments for my worshipers, to guide them in their justice and their laws. Never should I drink any blood but the blood of the sacrifice. Never should I seek to take my powers for my own.

"These things I learned, these things I understood. But what was really taught to me during those hours was what we all learn at the moment of the Drinking of the Blood, that I was no longer a mortal man—that I had passed away from all I knew into something so powerful that these old teachings could barely harness or explain it, that my destiny, to use Mael's words, was beyond all the knowledge that anyone—mortal or immortal—could give.

"At last the god prepared me to go out of the tree. He drained so much blood from me now that I was scarcely able to stand. I was a wraith. I was weeping from thirst, I was seeing blood and smelling blood, and would have rushed at him and caught him and drained him had I the strength. But the strength, of course, was his.

" 'You are empty, as you will always be at the commencement of the festival,' he said, 'so that you may drink your fill of the sacrificial blood. But remember what I have told you. After you preside, you must find a way to escape. As for me, try to save me. Tell them that I must be kept with you. But in all likelihood my time has come to an end.'

" 'Why, how do you mean?' I asked.

" 'You will see. There need be only one god here, one good god,' he said. 'If I could only go with you to Egypt, I could drink the blood of the old ones and it might heal me. As it is, I will take hundreds of years to heal.

And I shall not be allowed that time. But remember, go into Egypt. Do all that I have said.'

"He turned me now and pushed me towards the stairs. The torch lay blazing in the corner, and as I rose towards the door above, I smelled the blood of the Druids waiting, and I almost wept.

" 'They will give you all the blood that you can take,' he said behind me. 'Place yourself in their hands.' "

8

"YOU can well imagine how I looked when I stepped from the oak. The Druids had waited for my knock upon the door, and in my silent voice, I had said:

"*Open. It is the god.*

"My human death was long finished, I was ravenous, and surely my face was no more than a living skull. No doubt my eyes were bulging from their sockets, and my teeth were bared. The white robe hung on me as on a skeleton. And no clearer evidence of my divinity could have been given to the Druids, who stood awestruck as I came out of the tree.

"But I saw not merely their faces, I saw into their hearts. I saw the relief in Mael that the god within had not been too feeble to create me, I saw the confirmation in him of all that he believed.

"And I saw the other great vision that is ours to see—the great spiritual depth of each man buried deep within a crucible of heated flesh and blood.

"My thirst was pure agony. And summoning all my new strength, I said: 'Take me to the altars. The Feast of Samhain is to begin.'

"The Druids let out chilling screams. They howled in the forest. And far beyond the sacred grove there came a deafening roar from the multitudes who had waited for that cry.

"We walked swiftly, in procession towards the clearing, and more and more of the white-robed priests came out to greet us and I found myself pelted with fresh and fragrant flowers from all sides, blossoms I crushed under my feet as I was saluted with hymns.

"I need not tell you how the world looked to me with the new vision, how I saw each tint and surface beneath the thin veil of darkness, how these hymns and anthems assaulted my ears.

"Marius, the man, was disintegrated inside this new being.

"Trumpets blared from the clearing as I mounted the steps of the stone altar and looked out over the thousands gathered there—the sea of expectant faces, the giant wicker figures with their doomed victims still struggling and crying inside.

"A great silver caldron of water stood before the altar, and as the priests sang, a chain of prisoners was led to this caldron, their arms bound behind their backs.

"The voices were singing in concert around me as the priests placed the flowers in my hair, on my shoulders, at my feet.

" 'Beautiful one, powerful one, god of the woods and the fields, drink now the sacrifices offered to you, and as your wasted limbs fill with life, so the earth will renew itself. So you will forgive us for the cutting of the corn which is the harvest, so you will bless the seed we sow.'

"And I saw before me those selected to be my victims, three stout men, bound as the others were bound, but clean and dressed also in white robes, with flowers on their shoulders and in their hair. Youths they were, handsome and innocent and overcome with awe as they awaited the will of the god.

"The trumpets were deafening. The roaring was ceaseless. I said:

" 'Let the sacrifices begin!' And as the first youth was delivered up to me, as I prepared to drink for the very first time from that truly divine cup which is human life, as I held the warm flesh of the victim in my hands, the blood ready for my open mouth, I saw the fires lighted beneath the towering wicker giants, I saw the first two prisoners forced head down into the water of the silver caldron.

"Death by fire, death by water, death by the piercing teeth of the hungry god.

"Through the age-old ecstasy, the hymns continued: 'God of the waning and waxing moon, god of the woods and fields, you who are the very image of death in your hunger, grow strong with the blood of the victims, grow beautiful so that the Great Mother will take you to herself.'

"How long did it last? I do not know. It was forever—the blaze of the wicker giants, the screaming of the victims, the long procession of those who must be drowned. I drank and drank, not merely from the three selected for me, but from a dozen others before they were returned to the caldron, or forced into the blazing giants. The priests cut the heads from the dead with great bloody swords, stacking them in pyramids to either side of the altar, and the bodies were borne away.

"Everywhere I turned I saw rapture on sweating faces, everywhere I turned I heard the anthems and cries. But at last the frenzy was dying out. The giants were fallen into a smoldering heap upon which men poured more pitch, more kindling.

"And it was now time for the judgments, for men to stand before me and present their cases for vengeance against others, and for me to look with my new eyes into their souls. I was reeling. I had drunk too much blood, but I felt such power in me I could have leapt up and over the clearing and deep into the forest. I could have spread invisible wings, or so it seemed.

"But I carried out my 'destiny,' as Mael would have called it. I found this one just, that one in error, this one innocent, that one deserving of death.

"I don't know how long it went on because my body no longer measured time in weariness. But finally it was finished, and I realized the moment of action had come.

"I had somehow to do what the old god had commanded me, which was to escape the imprisonment in the oak. And I also had precious little time in which to do it, no more than an hour before dawn.

"As for what lay ahead in Egypt, I had not made my decision yet. But I knew that if I let the Druids enclose me in the sacred tree again, I would starve in there until the small offering at the next full moon. And all of my nights until that time would be thirst and torture, and what the old one had called 'the god's dreams' in which I'd learn the secrets of the tree and the grass that grew and the silent Mother.

"But these secrets were not for me.

"The Druids surrounded me now and we proceeded to the sacred tree again, the hymns dying to a litany which commanded me to remain within the oak to sanctify the forest, to be its guardian, and to speak kindly through the oak to those of the priesthood who would come from time to time to ask guidance of me.

"I stopped before we reached the tree. A huge pyre was blazing in the middle of the grove, casting ghastly light on the carved faces and the heaps of human skulls. The rest of the priesthood stood round it waiting. A current of terror shot through me with all the new power that such feelings have for us.

"I started talking hastily. In an authoritative voice I told them that I wished them all to leave the grove. That I should seal myself up in the oak at dawn with the old god. But I could see it wasn't working. They were staring at me coldly and glancing one to the other, their eyes shallow like bits of glass.

" 'Mael!' I said. 'Do as I command you. Tell these priests to leave the grove.'

"Suddenly, without the slightest warning, half the assemblage of priests ran towards the tree. The other took hold of my arms.

"I shouted for Mael, who led the siege on the tree, to stop. I tried to get loose but some twelve of the priests gripped my arms and my legs.

"If I had only understood the extent of my strength, I might easily have freed myself. But I didn't know. I was still reeling from the feast, too horrified by what I knew would happen now. As I struggled, trying to free my arms, even kicking at those who held me, the old god, the naked and black thing, was borne out of the tree and heaved into the fire.

"Only for a split second did I see him, and all I beheld was resignation. He did not once lift his arms to fight. His eyes were closed and he did not look at me, nor at anyone or anything, and I remembered in that moment what he had told me, of his agony, and I started to cry.

"I was shaking violently as they burned him. But from the very midst of the flames I heard his voice. 'Do as I commanded you, Marius. You are our hope.' That meant Get Out of Here Now.

"I made myself still and small in the grip of those who held me. I wept and wept and acted like I was just the sad victim of all this magic, just the poor god who must mourn his father who had gone into the flames. And when I felt their hands relax, when I saw that, one and all, they were gazing into the pyre, I pivoted with all my strength, tearing loose from their grip, and I ran as fast as I could for the woods.

"In that initial sprint, I learned for the first time what my powers were. I cleared hundreds of yards in an instant, my feet barely touching the ground.

"But the cry rang out immediately: 'THE GOD HAS FLOWN!' and within seconds the multitude in the clearing was screaming it over and over as thousands of mortals plunged into the trees.

"How on earth did this happen, I thought suddenly, that I'm a god, full of human blood, and running from thousands of Keltic barbarians through this damned woods!

"I didn't even stop to tear the white robe off me, but ripped it off while I was still running, and then I leapt up to the branches overhead and moved even faster through the tops of the oaks.

"Within minutes I was so far away from my pursuers that I couldn't hear them anymore. But I kept running and running, leaping from branch to branch, until there was nothing to fear anymore but the morning sun.

"And I learned then what Gabrielle learned so early in your wanderings, that I could easily dig into the earth to save myself from the light.

"When I awoke the heat of my thirst astonished me. I could not imagine how the old god had endured the ritual starvation. I could think only of human blood.

"But the Druids had had the day in which to pursue me. I had to proceed with great care.

"And I starved all that night as I sped through the forest, not drinking until early morning when I came upon a band of thieves in the woods which provided me with the blood of an evildoer, and a good suit of clothes.

"In those hours just before dawn, I took stock of things. I had learned a great deal about my powers, I would learn more. And I would go down to Egypt, not for the sake of the gods or their worshipers, but to find out what this was all about.

"And so even then you see, more than seventeen hundred years ago, we were questing, we were rejecting the explanations given us, we were loving the magic and the power for its own sake.

"On the third night of my new life, I wandered into my old house in Massilia and found my library, my writing table, my books all there still. And my faithful slaves overjoyed to see me. What did these things mean to me? What did it mean that I had written this history, that I had lain in this bed?

"I knew I could not be Marius, the Roman, any longer. But I would take from him what I could. I sent my beloved slaves back home. I wrote my father to say that a serious illness compelled me to live out my remaining days in the heat and dryness of Egypt. I packed off the rest of my history to those in Rome who would read it and publish it, and then I set out for Alexandria with gold in my pockets, with my old travel documents, and with two dull-witted slaves who never questioned that I traveled by night.

"And within a month of the great Samhain Feast in Gaul, I was roaming the black crooked nighttime streets of Alexandria, searching for the old gods with my silent voice.

"I was mad, but I knew the madness would pass. I had to find the old gods. And you know why I had to find them. It was not only the threat of the calamity again, the sun god seeking me out in the darkness of my daytime slumber, or visiting me with obliterating fire in the full darkness of the night.

"I had to find the old gods because I could not bear to be alone among men. The full horror of it was upon me, and though I killed only the murderer, the evildoer, my conscience was too finely tuned for self-deception. I could not bear the realization that I, Marius, who had known and enjoyed such love in his life, was the relentless bringer of death."

9

"ALEXANDRIA was not an old city. It had existed for just a little over three hundred years. But it was a great port and the home of the largest libraries in the Roman world. Scholars from all over the Empire came to study there, and I had been one of them in another lifetime, and now I found myself there again.

"Had not the god told me to come, I would have gone deeper into Egypt, 'to the bottom,' to use Mael's phrase, suspecting that the answers to all riddles lay in the older shrines.

"But a curious feeling came on me in Alexandria. I *knew* the gods were there. I knew they were guiding my feet when I sought the streets of the whorehouses and the thieves' dens, the places where men went to lose their souls.

"At night I lay on my bed in my little Roman house and I called to the gods. I grappled with my madness. I puzzled just as you have puzzled over the power and strength and crippling emotions which I now possessed. And one night just before morning, when the light of only one lamp shone through the sheer veils of the bed where I lay, I turned my eyes towards the distant garden doorway and saw a still black figure standing there.

"For one moment it seemed a dream, this figure, because it carried no scent, did not seem to breathe, did not make a sound. Then I knew it was one of the gods, but it was gone and I was left sitting up and staring after it, trying to remember what I had seen: a black naked thing with a bald head and red piercing eyes, a thing that seemed lost in its own stillness, strangely diffident, only marshaling its strength to move at the last moment before complete discovery.

"The next night in the back streets I heard a voice telling me to come. But it was a less articulate voice than that which had come from the tree. It made known to me only that the door was near. And finally there came the still and silent moment when I stood before the door.

"It was a god who opened it for me. It was a god who said Come.

"I was frightened as I descended the inevitable stairway, as I followed a steeply sloping tunnel. I lighted the candle I had brought with me, and I saw that I was entering an underground temple, a place older than the city of Alexandria, a sanctuary built perhaps under the ancient pharaohs, its walls covered with tiny colored pictures depicting the life of old Egypt.

"And then there was the writing, the magnificent picture writing with its tiny mummies and birds and embracing arms without bodies, and coiling snakes.

"I moved on, coming into a vast place of square pillars and a soaring ceiling. The same paintings decorated every inch of stone here.

"And then I saw in the corner of my eye what seemed at first a statue, a black figure standing near a pillar with one hand raised to rest against the stone. But I knew it was no statue. No Egyptian god made out of diorite ever stood in this attitude nor wore a real linen skirt about its loins.

"I turned slowly, bracing myself against the full sight of it, and saw the same burnt flesh, the same streaming hair, though it was black, the same yellow eyes. The lips were shriveled around the teeth and the gums, and the breath came out of its throat full of pain.

" 'How and whence did you come?' he asked in Greek.

"I saw myself as he saw me, luminous and strong, even my blue eyes something of an incidental mystery, and I saw my Roman garments, my linen tunic gathered in gold buckles on my shoulders, my red cloak. With my long yellow hair, I must have looked like a wanderer from the north woods, 'civilized' only on the surface, and perhaps this was now true.

"But he was the one who concerned me. And I saw him more fully, the seamed flesh burnt to his ribs and molded to his collarbone and the jutting bones of his hips. He was not starved, this thing. He had recently drunk human blood. But his agony was like heat coming from him, as though the fire still cooked him from within, as though he were a self-contained hell.

" 'How have you escaped the burning?' he asked. 'What saved you? Answer!'

" 'Nothing saved me,' I said, speaking Greek as he did.

"I approached him holding the candle to the side when he shied from it. He had been thin in life, broad-shouldered like the old pharaohs, and his long black hair was cropped straight across the forehead in that old style.

" 'I wasn't made when it happened,' I said, 'but afterwards, by the god of the sacred grove in Gaul.'

" 'Ah, then he was unharmed, this one who made you.'

" 'No, burned as you are, but he had enough strength to do it. He gave and took the blood over and over again. He said, "Go into Egypt and find why this has happened." He said the gods of the wood had burst into flames, some in their sleep and some awake. He said this had happened all over the north.'

" 'Yes.' He nodded, and he gave a dry rasping laugh that shook his entire form. 'And only the ancient had the strength to survive, to inherit the agony which only immortality can sustain. And so we suffer. But you have been made. You have come. You will make more. But is it justice to make more? Would the Father and the Mother have allowed this to happen to us if the time had not come?'

" 'But who are the Father and the Mother?' I asked. I knew he did not mean the earth when he said Mother.

" 'The first of us,' he answered, 'those from whom all of us descend.'

"I tried to penetrate his thoughts, feel the truth of them, but he knew what I was doing, and his mind folded up like a flower at dusk.

" 'Come with me,' he said. And he commenced to walk with a shuffling step out of the large room and down a long corridor, decorated as the chamber had been.

"I sensed we were in an even older place, something built before the temple from which we'd just come. I do not know how I knew it. The chill you felt on the steps here on the island was not there. You don't feel such things in Egypt. You feel something else. You feel the presence of something living in the air itself.

"But there was more palpable evidence of antiquity as we walked on. The paintings on these walls were older, the colors fainter, and here and there was damage where the colored plaster had flaked and fallen away. The style had changed. The black hair of the little figures was longer and fuller, and it seemed the whole was more lovely, more full of light and intricate design.

"Somewhere far off water dripped on stone. The sound gave a songlike echo through the passage. It seemed the walls had captured life in these delicate and tenderly painted figures, it seemed that the magic attempted again and again by the ancient religious artists had its tiny glowing kernel of power. I could hear whispers of life where there were no whispers. I could feel the great continuity of history even if there was no one who was aware.

"The dark figure beside me paused as I looked at the walls. He made an airy gesture for me to follow him through a doorway, and we entered a long rectangular chamber covered entirely with the artful hieroglyphs. It was like being encased in a manuscript to be inside it. And I saw two older Egyptian sarcophagi placed head to head against the wall.

"These were boxes carved to conform to the shape of the mummies for which they were made, and fully modeled and painted to represent the dead, with faces of hammered gold, and eyes of inlaid lapis lazuli.

"I held the candle high. And with great effort my guide opened the lids of these cases and let them fall back so that I might see inside.

"I saw what at first appeared to be bodies, but when I drew closer I realized that they were heaps of ash in manly form. Nothing of tissue remained to them except a white fang here, a chip of bone there.

" 'No amount of blood can bring them back now,' said my guide. 'They are past all resurrection. The vessels of the blood are gone. Those who could rise have risen, and centuries will pass before we are healed, before we know the cessation of our pain.'

"Before he closed the mummy cases, I saw that the lids inside were blackened by the fire that had immolated these two. I wasn't sorry to see them shut up again.

"He turned and moved towards the doorway again, and I followed with the candle, but he paused and glanced back at the painted coffins.

" 'When the ashes are scattered,' he said, 'their souls are free.'

" 'Then why don't you scatter the ashes!' I said, trying not to sound so desperate, so undone.

" 'Should I?' he asked of me, the crisped flesh around his eyes widening. 'Do you think that I should?'

" 'You ask me!' I said.

"He gave one of those dry laughs again, that seemed to carry agony with it, and he led on down the passage to a lighted room.

"It was a library we entered, where a few scattered candles revealed the diamond-shaped wooden racks of parchment and papyrus scrolls.

"This delighted me, naturally, because a library was something I could understand. It was the one human place in which I still felt some measure of my old sanity.

"But I was startled to see another one—another one of us—sitting to the side behind the writing table, his eyes on the floor.

"This one had no hair whatsoever, and though he was pitch black all over, his skin was full and well-modeled and gleamed as if it had been oiled. The planes of his face were beautiful, the hand that rested in the lap of his white linen kilt was gracefully curled, all the muscles of his naked chest well defined.

"He turned and looked up at me. And something immediately passed between us, something more silent than silence, as it can be with us.

" 'This is the Elder,' said the weaker one who'd brought me here. 'And you see for yourself how he withstood the fire. But he will not speak. He has not spoken since it happened. Yet surely he knows where are the Mother and the Father, and why this was allowed to pass.'

"The Elder merely looked forward again. But there was a curious expression on his face, something sarcastic and faintly amused, and a little contemptuous.

" 'Even before this disaster,' the other one said, 'the Elder did not often speak to us. The fire did not change him, make him more receptive. He sits in silence, more and more like the Mother and the Father. Now and then he reads. Now and then he walks in the world above. He Drinks the Blood, he listens to the singers. Now and then he will dance. He speaks to mortals in the streets of Alexandria, but he will not speak to us. He has nothing to say to us. But he knows . . . He knows why this happened to us.'

" 'Leave me with him,' I said.

"I had the feeling that all beings have in such situations. I will make the man speak. I will draw something out of him, as no one else has been able to do. But it wasn't mere vanity that impelled me. This was the one who had come to me in the bedroom of my house, I was sure of it. This was the one who had stood watching me in my door.

"And I had sensed something in his glance. Call it intelligence, call it interest, call it recognition of some common knowledge—there was something there.

"And I knew that I carried with me the possibilities of a different world, unknown to the God of the Grove and even to this feeble and wounded one beside me who looked at the Elder in despair.

"The feeble one withdrew as I had asked. I went to the writing table and looked at the Elder.

" 'What should I do?' I asked in Greek.

"He looked up at me abruptly, and I could see this thing I call intelligence in his face.

" 'Is there any point,' I asked, 'to questioning you further?'

"I had chosen my tone carefully. There was nothing formal in it, nothing reverential. It was as familiar as it could be.

" 'And just what is it you seek!' he asked in Latin suddenly, coldly, his mouth turning down at the ends, his attitude one of abruptness and challenge.

"It relieved me to switch to Latin.

" 'You heard what I told the other,' I said in the same informal manner, 'how I was made by the God of the Grove in the country of the Keltoi, and how I was told to discover why the gods had died in flames.'

" 'You don't come on behalf of the Gods of the Grove!' he said, sardonic as before. He had not lifted his head, merely looked up, which made his eyes seem all the more challenging and contemptuous.

" 'I do and I don't,' I said. 'If we can perish in this way, I would like to know why. What happened once can happen a second time. And I would like to know if we are really gods, and if we are, then what are our obligations to man. Are the Mother and the Father true beings, or are they legend? How did all this start? I would like to know that, of course.'

" 'By accident,' he said.

" 'By accident?' I leaned forward. I thought I had heard wrong.

" 'By accident it started,' he said coolly, forbiddingly, with the clear implication that the question was absurd. 'Four thousand years ago, by accident, and it has been enclosed in magic and religion ever since.'

" 'You are telling me the truth, aren't you?'

" 'Why shouldn't I? Why should I protect you from the truth? Why should I bother to lie to you? I don't even know who you are. I don't care.'

" 'Then will you explain to me what you mean, that it happened by accident,' I pressed.

" 'I don't know. I may. I may not. I have spoken more in these last few moments than I have in years. The story of the accident may be no more true than the myths that delight the others. The others have always chosen the myths. It's what you really want, is it not?' His voice rose and he rose slightly out of the chair as if his angry voice were impelling him to his feet.

" 'A story of our creation, analogous to the Genesis of the Hebrews, the tales in Homer, the babblings of your Roman poets Ovid and Virgil—a great gleaming morass of symbols out of which life itself is supposed to have sprung.' He was on his feet and all but shouting, his black forehead knotted with veins, his hand a fist on the desk. 'It is that kind of tale that fills the documents in these rooms, that emerges in fragments from the anthems and the incantations. Want to hear it? It's as true as anything else.'

" 'Tell me what you will,' I said. I was trying to keep calm. The volume of his voice was hurting my ears. And I heard things stirring in the rooms near us. Other creatures, like that dried-up wisp of a thing that had brought me in here, were prowling about.

" 'And you might begin,' I said acidly, 'by confessing why you came to me in my rooms here in Alexandria. It was you who led me here. Why did you do that? To rail at me? To curse me for asking you how it started?'

" 'Quiet yourself.'

" 'I might say the same to you.'

"He looked me up and down calmly, and then he smiled. He opened both his hands as if in greeting or offering, and then he shrugged.

" 'I want you to tell me about the accident,' I said. 'I would beg you to tell me if I thought it would do any good. What can I do for you to make you tell?'

"His face underwent several remarkable transformations. I could feel his thoughts, but not hear them, feel a high-pitched humor. And when he spoke again, his voice was thickened as if he were fighting back sorrow, as if it were strangling him.

" 'Hearken to our old story,' he said. 'The good god, Osiris, the first pharaoh of Egypt, in the eons before the invention of writing, was murdered by evil men. And when his wife, Isis, gathered together the parts of his body, he became immortal and thereafter ruled in the realm of the dead. This is the realm of the moon, and the night, in which he reigned, and to him were brought the blood sacrifices for the great goddess which he drank. But the priests tried to steal from him the secret of his immortality, and so his worship became secret, and his temples were known only to those of his cult who protected him from the sun god, who might at any time seek to destroy Osiris with the sun's burning rays. But you can see the truth in the legend. The early king discovered something—or rather he was the victim of an ugly occurrence—and he became unnatural with a power that could be used for incalculable evil by those around him, and so he made a worship of it, seeking to contain it in obligation and ceremony, seeking to limit The Powerful Blood to those who would use it for white magic and nothing else. And so here we are.'

" 'And the Mother and Father are Isis and Osiris?'

" 'Yes and no. They are the first two. Isis and Osiris are the names that were used in the myths that they told, or the old worship onto which they grafted themselves.'

" 'What was the accident, then? How was this thing discovered?'

"He looked at me for a long period of silence, and then he sat down again, turning to the side and staring off as he'd been before.

" 'But why should I tell you?' he asked, yet this time he put the question with new feeling, as though he meant it sincerely and had to answer it for himself. 'Why should I do anything? If the Mother and the Father will not rise from the sands to save themselves as the sun comes over the horizon, why should I move? Or speak? Or go on?' Again he looked up at me.

" 'This is what happened, the Mother and the Father went out into the sun?'

" 'Were left in the sun, my dear Marius,' he said, astonishing me with the knowledge of my name. 'Left in the sun. The Mother and the Father do not move of their own volition, save now and then to whisper to each other, to knock those of us down who would come to them for their healing blood. They could restore all of us who were burned, if they would let us drink the healing blood. Four thousand years the Father and Mother have existed, and our blood grows stronger with every season, every victim. It grows stronger even with starvation, for when the starvation is ended, new strength is enjoyed. But the Father and the Mother do not care for their children. And now it seems they do not care for themselves. Maybe after four thousand nights, they merely wished to see the sun!

" 'Since the coming of the Greek into Egypt, since the perversion of the old art, they have not spoken to us. They have not let us see the blink of their eye. And what is Egypt now but the granary of Rome? When the Mother and the Father strike out to drive us away from the veins in their necks, they are as iron and can crush our bones. And if they do not care anymore, then why should I?'

"I studied him for a long moment.

" 'And you are saying,' I asked, 'that this is what caused the others to burn up? That the Father and Mother were left out in the sun?'

"He nodded.

" 'Our blood comes from them!' he said. 'It is their blood. The line is direct, and what befalls them befalls us. If they are burnt, we are burnt.'

" 'We are connected to them!' I whispered in amazement.

" 'Exactly, my dear Marius,' he said, watching me, seeming to enjoy my fear. 'That is why they have been kept for a thousand years, the Mother and the Father, that is why victims are brought to them in sacrifice, that is why they are worshiped. What happens to them happens to us.'

" 'Who did it? Who put them in the sun?'

"He laughed without making a sound.

" 'The one who kept them,' he said, 'the one who couldn't endure it any longer, the one who had had this solemn charge for too long, the one who could persuade no one else to accept the burden, and finally, weeping and shivering, took them out into the desert sands and left them like two statues there.'

" 'And my fate is linked to this,' I murmured.

" 'Yes. But you see, I do not think he believed it any longer, the one who kept them. It was just an old tale. After all, they were worshiped as I told you, worshiped by us, as we are worshiped by mortals, and no one dared to harm them. No one held a torch to them to see if it made the rest of us feel pain. No. He did not believe it. He left them in the desert, and that night when he opened his eyes in his coffin and found himself a burnt and unrecognizable horror, he screamed and screamed.'

" 'You got them back underground.'

" 'Yes.'

" 'And they are blackened as you are . . .'

" 'No.' He shook his head. 'Darkened to a golden bronze, like the meat turning on the spit. No more than that. And beautiful as before, as if beauty has become part of their heritage, beauty part and parcel of what they are destined to be. They stare forward as they always have, but they no longer incline their heads to each other, they no longer hum with the rhythm of their secret exchanges, they no longer let us drink their blood. And the victims brought to them, they will not take, save now and then, and only in solitude. No one knows when they will drink, when they will not.'

"I shook my head. I moved back and forth, my head bowed, the candle fluttering in my hand, not knowing what to say to all this, needing time to think it out.

"He gestured for me to take the chair on the other side of the writing table, and without thinking of it, I did.

" 'But wasn't it meant to happen, Roman?' he asked. 'Weren't they meant to meet their death in the sands, silent, unmoving, like statues cast there after a city is sacked by the conquering army, and were we not meant to die too? Look at Egypt. What is Egypt, I ask you again, but the granary of Rome? Were they not meant to burn there day after day while all of us burned like stars the world over?'

" 'Where are they?' I asked.

" 'Why do you want to know?' he sneered. 'Why should I give you the secret? They cannot be hacked to pieces, they are too strong for that, a knife will barely pierce their skin. Yet cut them and you cut us. Burn them and you burn us. And whatever they make us feel, they feel only a particle of it because their age protects them. And yet to destroy every one of us, you have merely to bring them annoyance! The blood they do not even seem to need! Maybe their minds are connected to ours as well. Maybe the sorrow we feel, the misery, the horror at the fate of the world itself, comes from their minds, as locked in their chambers they dream! No. I cannot tell you where they are, can I? Until I decide for certain that I am indifferent, that it is time for us to die out.'

" 'Where are they?' I said again.

" 'Why should I not sink them into the very depths of sea?' he asked. 'Until such time as the earth herself heaves them up into the sunlight on the crest of a great wave?'

"I didn't answer. I was watching him, wondering at his excitement, understanding it but in awe of it just the same.

" 'Why should I not bury them in the depths of the earth, I mean the darkest depths beyond the faintest sounds of life, and let them lie in silence there, no matter what they think and feel?'

"What answer could I give? I watched him. I waited until he seemed calmer. He looked at me and his face became tranquil and almost trusting.

" 'Tell me how they became the Mother and the Father,' I said.

" 'Why?'

" 'You know damn good and well why. I want to know! Why did you come into my bedroom if you didn't mean to tell me?' I asked again.

" 'So what if I did?' he said bitterly. 'So what if I wanted to see the Roman with my own eyes? We will die and you will die with us. So I wanted to see our magic in a new form. Who worships us now, after all? Yellow-haired warriors in the northern forests? Old old Egyptians in secret crypts beneath the sands? We do not live in the temples of Greece and Rome. We never did. And yet they celebrate our myth—the only myth—they call the names of the Mother and the Father . . .'

" 'I don't give a damn,' I said. 'You know I don't. We are alike, you and I. I won't go back to the northern forests to make a race of gods for those people! But I came here to know and you must tell.'

" 'All right. So that you can understand the futility of it, so that you can understand the silence of the Mother and the Father, I will tell. But mark my words, I may yet bring us all down. I may yet burn the Mother and the Father in the heat of a kiln! But we will dispense with lengthy initiations and high-blown language. We will do away with the myths that died in the sand the day the sun shone on the Mother and the Father. I will tell you what all these scrolls left by the Father and the Mother reveal. Set down your candle. And listen to me.' "

10

" 'WHAT the scrolls will tell you,' he said, 'if you could decipher them, is that we have two human beings, Akasha and Enkil, who had come into Egypt from some other, older land. This was in the time long before the first writing, before the first pyramids, when the Egyptians were still cannibals and hunted for the bodies of enemies to eat.

" 'Akasha and Enkil directed the people away from these practices. They were worshipers of the Good Mother Earth and they taught the Egyptians how to sow seed in the Good Mother, and how to herd animals for meat and milk and skins.

" 'In all probability, they were not alone as they taught these things, but rather the leaders of a people who had come with them from older cities whose names are now lost beneath the sands of Lebanon, their monuments laid waste.

" 'Whatever is the truth, these were benevolent rulers, these two, in whom the good of others was the commanding value, as the Good Mother was the Nourishing Mother and wished for all men to live in peace, and they decided all questions of justice for the emerging land.

" 'Perhaps they would have passed into myth in some benign form had it not been for a disturbance in the house of the royal steward which began with the antics of a demon that hurled the furniture about.

" 'Now this was no more than a common demon, the kind one hears of in all lands at all times. He devils those who live in a certain place for a certain while. Perhaps he enters into the body of some innocent and roars through her mouth with a loud voice. He may cause the innocent one to belch obscenities and carnal invitations to those around her. Do you know of these things?'

"I nodded. I told him you always heard such stories. Such a demon was supposed to have possessed a vestal virgin in Rome. She made lewd overtures to all those around her, her face turning purple with exertion, then fainted. But the demon had somehow been driven out. 'I thought the girl was simply mad,' I said. 'That she was, shall we say, not suited to be a vestal virgin . . .'

" 'Of course!' he said with a note of rich irony. 'And I would assume the same thing, and so would most any intelligent man walking the streets of Alexandria above us. Yet such stories come and go. And if they are remarkable for any one thing it is that they do not affect the course of human events. These demons rather trouble some household, some person, and then they are gone into oblivion and we are right where we started again.'

" 'Precisely,' I said.

" 'But you understand this was old old Egypt. This was a time when men ran from the thunder, or ate the bodies of the dead to absorb their souls.'

" 'I understand,' I said.

" 'And this good King Enkil decided that he would himself address the demon who had come into his steward's house. This thing was out of harmony, he said. The royal magicians begged, of course, to be allowed to see to this, to drive the demon out. But this was a king who would do good for everyone. He had some vision of all things being united in good, of all forces being made to go on the same divine course. He would speak to this demon, try to harness its power, so to speak, for the general good. And only if that could not be done would he consent to the demon's being driven out.

" 'And so he went into the house of his steward, where furniture was being flung at the walls, and jars broken, and doors slammed. And he commenced to talk to this demon and invite it to talk to him. Everyone else ran away.

" 'A full night passed before he came out of the haunted house and he had amazing things to say:

" ' "These demons are mindless and childlike," he told his magicians, "but I have studied their conduct and I have learned from all the evidence why it is that they rage. They are maddened that they do not have bodies, that they cannot feel as we feel. They make the innocent scream filth because the rites of love and passion are things that they cannot possibly know. They can work the body parts but not truly inhabit them, and so they are obsessed with the flesh that they cannot invade. And with their feeble powers they bump upon objects, they make their victims twist and jump. This longing to be carnal is the origin of their anger, the indication of the suffering which is their lot." And with these pious words he prepared to lock himself in the haunted chambers to learn more.

" 'But this time his wife came between him and his purpose. She would not let him stay with the demons. He must look into the mirror, she said. He had aged remarkably in the few hours that he had remained in the house alone.

" 'And when he would not be deterred, she locked herself in with him, and all those who stood outside the house heard the crashing and banging of objects, and feared for the moment when they would hear the King and the Queen themselves screaming or raging in spirit voices. The noise from the inner chambers was alarming. Cracks were appearing in the walls.

" 'All fled as before, except for a small party of interested men. Now these men since the beginning of the reign had been the enemies of the

King. These were old warriors who had led the campaigns of Egypt in search of human flesh, and they had had enough of the King's goodness, enough of the Good Mother and farming and the like, and they saw in this spirit adventure not only more of the King's vain nonsense, but a situation that nevertheless provided a remarkable opportunity for them.

" 'When night fell, they crept into the haunted house. They were fearless of spirits, just as the grave robbers are who rifle the tombs of the pharaohs. They believe, but not enough to control their greed.

" 'And when they saw Enkil and Akasha together in the middle of this room full of flying objects, they set upon them and they stabbed the King over and over, as your Roman senators stabbed Caesar, and they stabbed the only witness, his wife.

" 'And the King cried out, "No, don't you see what you have done? You have given the spirits a way to get in! You have opened my body to them! Don't you see!" But the men fled, sure of the death of the King and the Queen, who was on her hands and knees, cradling her husband's head in her hands, both bleeding from more wounds than one could count.

" 'Now the conspirators stirred up the populace. Did everyone know that the King had been killed by the spirits? He should have left the demons to his magicians as any other king would have done. And bearing torches, all flocked to the haunted house, which had grown suddenly and totally quiet.

" 'The conspirators urged the magicians to enter, but they were afraid. "Then we will go in and see what's happened," said the evil ones, and they threw open the doors.

" 'There stood the King and the Queen, staring calmly at the conspirators, and all of their wounds were healed. And their eyes had taken on an eerie light, their skin a white shimmer, their hair a magnificent gleam. Out of the house they came as the conspirators ran in terror, and they dismissed all the people and the priests and went back to the palace alone.

" 'And though they confided in no one, they knew what had happened to them.

" 'They had been entered through their wounds by the demon at the point when mortal life itself was about to escape. But it was the blood that the demon permeated in that twilight moment when the heart almost stopped. Perhaps it was the substance that he had always sought in his ragings, the substance that he had tried to bring forth from his victims with his antics, but he had never been able to inflict enough wounds before his victim died. But now he was in the blood, and the blood was not merely the demon, or the blood of the King and Queen, but a combination of the human and the demon which was an altogether different thing.

" 'And all that was left of the King and Queen was what this blood could animate, what it could infuse and claim for its own. Their bodies were for all other purposes dead. But the blood flowed through the brain and through the heart and through the skin, and so the intelligence of the King and Queen remained. Their souls, if you will, remained, as the souls reside in these organs, though why we do not know. And though the demon blood had no mind of its own, no character of its own that the King and Queen could discover, it nevertheless enhanced their minds and their characters, for it flowed through the organs that create thought. And it added to their faculties its purely spiritual powers, so that the King and Queen could hear the thoughts of mortals, and sense things and understand things that mortals could not.

" 'In sum, the demon had added and the demon had taken away, and the King and Queen were New Things. They could no longer eat food, or grow, or die, or have children, yet they could feel with an intensity that terrified them. And the demon had what it wanted: a body to live in, a way to be in the world at last, a way to *feel.*

" 'But then came the even more dreadful discovery, that to keep their corpses animate, the blood must be fed. And all it could convert to its use was the selfsame thing of which it was made: blood. Give it more blood to enter, give it more blood to push through the limbs of the body in which it enjoyed such glorious sensations, of blood it could not get enough.

" 'And oh, the grandest of all sensations was the drinking in which it renewed itself, fed itself, enlarged itself. And in that moment of drinking it could feel the death of the victim, the moment it pulled the blood so hard out of the victim that the victim's heart stopped.

" 'The demon had them, the King and Queen. They were Drinkers of the Blood; and whether or not the demon knew of them, we will never be able to tell. But the King and Queen knew that they had the demon and could not get rid of it, and if they did they would die because their bodies were already dead. And they learned immediately that these dead bodies, animated as they were entirely by this demonic fluid, could not withstand fire or the light of the sun. On the one hand, they seemed as fragile white flowers that can be withered black in the daytime desert heat. On the other, it seemed the blood in them was so volatile that it would boil if heated, thereby destroying the fibers through which it moved.

" 'It has been said that in these very early times, they could withstand no brilliant illumination, that even a nearby fire would cause their skin to smoke.

" 'Whatever, they were of a new order of being, and their thoughts were of a new order of being, and they tried to understand the things that they saw, the dispositions that afflicted them in this new state.

" 'All discoveries are not recorded. There is nothing in writing or in the unwritten tradition about when they first chose to pass on the blood, or ascertained the method by which it must be done—that the victim must be drained to the twilight moment of approaching death, or the demonic blood given him cannot take hold.

" 'We do know through the unwritten tradition that the King and Queen tried to keep secret what had happened to them, but their disappearance by day aroused suspicions. They could not attend to the religious duties in the land.

" 'And so it came to pass that even before they had formed their clearest decisions, they had to encourage the populace to a worship of the Good Mother in the light of the moon.

" 'But they could not protect themselves from the conspirators, who still did not understand their recovery and sought to do away with them again. The attack came despite all precautions and the strength of the King and the Queen proved overwhelming to the conspirators, and they were all the more frightened by the fact that those wounds they managed to inflict upon the King and the Queen were miraculously and instantly healed. An arm was severed from the King and this he put back on his shoulder and it came to life again and the conspirators fled.

" 'And through these attacks, these battles, the secret came into the possession not only of the King's enemies but the priests as well.

" 'And no one wanted to destroy the King and the Queen now; rather they wanted to take them prisoner and gain the secret of immortality from them, and they sought to take the blood from them, but their early attempts failed.

" 'The drinkers were not near to death; and so they became hybrid creatures—half god and half human—and they perished in horrible ways. Yet some succeeded. Perhaps they emptied their veins first. It isn't recorded. But in later ages, this has always proved a way to steal the blood.

" 'And perhaps the Mother and the Father chose to make fledglings. Maybe out of loneliness and fear, they chose to pass on the secret to those of good mettle whom they could trust. Again we are not told. Whatever the case, other Drinkers of the Blood did come into being, and the method of making them was eventually known.

" 'And the scrolls tell us that the Mother and the Father sought to triumph in their adversity. They sought to find some reason in what had happened, and they believed that their heightened senses must surely serve some good. The Good Mother had allowed this to happen, had she not?

" 'And they must sanctify and contain what was done by mystery, or else Egypt might become a race of blood-drinking demons who would divide the world into Those Who Drink the Blood and those who are bred only to give it, a tyranny that once achieved might never be broken by mortal men alone.

" 'And so the good King and Queen chose the path of ritual, of myth. They saw in themselves the images of the waning and waxing moon, and in their drinking of the blood the god incarnate who takes unto himself his sacrifice, and they used their superior powers to divine and predict and judge. They saw themselves as truly accepting the blood for the god, which otherwise would run down the altar. They girded with the symbolic and the mysterious what could not be allowed to become common, and they passed out of the sight of mortal men into the temples, to be worshiped by those who would bring them blood. They took to themselves the most fit sacrifices, those that had always been made for the good of the land. Innocents, outsiders, evildoers, they drank the blood for the Mother and for the Good.

" 'They set into motion the tale of Osiris, composed in part of their own terrible suffering—the attack of the conspirators, the recovery, their need to live in the realm of darkness, the world beyond life, their inability to walk anymore in sun. And they grafted this upon the older stories of the gods who rise and fall in their love of the Good Mother, which were already there in the land from which they came.

" 'And so these stories came down to us; these stories spread beyond the secret places in which the Mother and the Father were worshiped, in which those they made with the blood were installed.

" 'And they were already old when the first pharaoh built his first pyramid. And the earliest texts record them in broken and strange form.

" 'A hundred other gods ruled in Egypt, just as they rule in all lands. But the worship of the Mother and Father and Those Who Drink the Blood remained secret and powerful, a cult to which the devoted went to hear the silent voices of the gods, to dream their dreams.

" 'We are not told who were the first fledglings of the Mother and Father. We know only that they spread the religion to the islands of the great sea, and to the lands of the two rivers, and to the north woods. That in shrines everywhere the moon god ruled and drank his blood sacrifices and used his powers to look into the hearts of men. During the periods between sacrifice, in starvation, the god's mind could leave his body; it could travel the heavens; he could learn a thousand things. And those mortals of the greatest purity of heart could come to the shrine and hear the voice of the god, and he could hear them.

" 'But even before my time, a thousand years ago, this was all an old and incoherent story. The gods of the moon had ruled in Egypt for maybe three thousand years. And the religion had been attacked again and again.

" 'When the Egyptian priests turned to the sun god Amon Ra, they opened the crypts of the moon god and let the sun burn him to cinders. And many of our kind were destroyed. The same happened when the first rude warriors rode down into Greece and broke open the sanctuaries and killed what they did not understand.

" 'Now the babbling oracle of Delphi rules where we once ruled, and statues stand where we once stood. Our last hour is enjoyed in the north woods whence you came, among those who still drench our altars with the blood of the evildoer, and in the small villages of Egypt, where one or two priests tend the god in the crypt and allow the faithful to bring to him the evildoers, for they cannot take the innocent without arousing suspicion, and of evildoers and outsiders there are always some to be had. And down in the jungles of Africa, near the ruins of old cities that no one remembers, there, too, we are still obeyed.

" 'But our history is punctuated by tales of rogues—the Drinkers of the Blood who look to no goddess for guidance and have always used their powers as they chose.

" 'In Rome they live, in Athens, in all cities of the Empire, these who hearken to no laws of right and wrong and use their powers for their own ends.

" 'And they died horribly in the heat and the flame just as did the gods in the groves and the sanctuaries, and if any have survived they probably do not even guess why they were subjected to the killing flame, of how the Mother and the Father were put into the sun.'

"He had stopped.

"He was studying my reaction. The library was quiet and if the others prowled behind the walls, I couldn't hear them anymore.

" 'I don't believe a word of it,' I said.

"He stared at me in stupefied silence for a moment and then he laughed and laughed.

"In a rage, I left the library and went out through the temple rooms and up through the tunnel and out into the street."

11

"THIS was very uncharacteristic of me, to leave in temper, to break off abruptly and depart. I had never done that sort of thing when I was a mortal man. But as I've said, I was on the edge of madness, the first madness many of us suffer, especially those who have been brought into this by force.

"I went back to my little house near the great library of Alexandria, and I lay down on my bed as if I could really let myself fall asleep there and escape from this thing.

" 'Idiot nonsense,' I murmured to myself.

"But the more I thought about the story, the more it made sense. It made sense that something was in my blood impelling me to drink more blood. It made sense that it heightened all sensations, that it kept my body —a mere imitation now of a human body—functioning when it should have come to a stop. And it made sense that this thing had no mind of its own but was nevertheless a power, an organization of force with a desire to live all its own.

"And then it even made sense that we could all be connected to the Mother and the Father because this thing was spiritual, and had no bodily limits except the limits of the individual bodies in which it had gained control. It was the vine, this thing, and we were the flowers, scattered over great distances, but connected by the twining tendrils that could reach all over the world.

"And this was why we gods could hear each other so well, why I could know the others were in Alexandria, even before they called to me. It was why they could come and find me in my house, why they could lead me to the secret door.

"All right. Maybe it was true. And it *was* an accident, this melding of an unnamed force and a human body and mind to make the New Thing as the Elder had said.

"But still—I didn't like it.

"I revolted against all of it because if I was anything, I was an individual, a particular being, with a strong sense of my own rights and prerogatives. I could not realize that I was host to an alien entity. I was still Marius, no matter what had been done to me.

"I was left finally with one thought and one thought only: if I was connected to this Mother and Father then I must see them, and I must know that they were safe. I could not live with the thought that I could die at any moment on account of some alchemy I could neither control nor understand.

"But I didn't return to the underground temple. I spent the next few nights feasting on blood until my miserable thoughts were drowned in it, and then in the early hours I roamed the great library of Alexandria, reading as I had always done.

"SOME of the madness dissolved in me. I stopped longing for my mortal family. I stopped being angry at that cursed thing in the cellar temple, and

I thought rather of this new strength I possessed. I would live for centuries: I would know the answers to all kinds of questions. I would be the continual awareness of things as time passed! And as long as I slew only the evildoer, I could endure my blood thirst, revel in it, in fact. And when the appropriate time came, I would make my companions and make them well.

"Now what remained? Go back to the Elder and find out where he had put the Mother and the Father. And see these creatures for myself. And do the very thing the Elder had threatened, sink them so deep into the earth that no mortal could ever find them and expose them to the light.

"Easy to think about this, easy to imagine them as so simply dispatched.

"Five nights after I'd left the Elder, when all these thoughts had had time to develop in me, I lay resting in my bedroom, with the lamps shining through the sheer bed curtains as before. In filtered and golden light, I listened to the sounds of sleeping Alexandria, and slipped into thin and glittering waking dreams. I wondered if the Elder would come to me again, disappointed that I had not returned—and as the thought came clear to me, I realized that someone was standing in the doorway again.

"Someone was watching me. I could feel it. To see this person I had but to turn my head. And then I would have the upper hand with the Elder. I would say, 'So you've come out of loneliness and disillusionment and now you want to tell me more, do you? Why don't you go back and sit in silence to wound your wraithlike companions, the brotherhood of the cinders?' Of course I wouldn't say such a thing to him. But I wasn't above thinking about it and letting him—if he was the one in the doorway—hear these thoughts.

"The one who was there did not go away.

"And slowly I turned my eyes in the direction of the door, and it was a woman I saw standing there. And not merely a woman, but a magnificent bronze-skinned Egyptian woman as artfully bejeweled and dressed as the old queens, in fine pleated linen, with her black hair down to her shoulders and braided with strands of gold. An immense force emanated from her, an invisible and commanding sense of her presence, her occupation of this small and insignificant room.

"I sat up and moved back the curtains, and the lamps in the room went out. I saw the smoke rising from them in the dark, gray wisps like snakes coiling towards the ceiling and then gone. She was still there, the remaining light defining her expressionless face, sparkling on the jewels around her neck and in her large almond-shaped eyes. And silently she said:

"*Marius, take us out of Egypt.*

"And then she was gone.

"My heart was knocking in me uncontrollably. I went into the garden looking for her. I leapt over the wall and stood alone listening in the empty unpaved street.

"I started to run towards the old section where I had found the door. I meant to get into the underground temple and find the Elder and tell him that he must take me to her, I had seen her, she had moved, she had spoken, she had come to me! I was delirious, but when I reached the door, I knew that I didn't have to go down. I knew that if I went out of the city into the sands I could find her. She was already leading me to where she was.

"In the hour that followed I was to remember the strength and the speed I'd known in the forests of Gaul, and had not used since. I went out from the city to where the stars provided the only light, and I walked until I came to a ruined temple, and there I began to dig in the sand. It would have taken a band of mortals several hours to discover the trapdoor, but I found it quickly, and I was able to lift it, which mortals couldn't have done.

"The twisting stairs and corridors I followed were not illuminated. And I cursed myself for not bringing a candle, for being so swept off my feet by the sight of her that I had rushed after her as if I were in love.

" 'Help me, Akasha,' I whispered. I put my hands out in front of me and tried not to feel mortal fear of the blackness in which I was as blind as an ordinary man.

"My hands touched something hard before me. And I rested, catching my breath, trying to command myself. Then my hands moved on the thing and felt what seemed the chest of a human statue, its shoulders, its arms. But this was no statue, this thing, this thing was made of something more resilient than stone. And when my hand found the face, the lips proved just a little softer than all the rest of it, and I drew back.

"I could hear my heart beat. I could feel the sheer humiliation of cowardice. I didn't dare say the name Akasha. I knew that this thing I had touched had a man's form. It was Enkil.

"I closed my eyes, trying to gather my wits, form some plan of action that didn't include turning and running like a madman, and I heard a dry, crackling sound, and against my closed lids saw fire.

"When I opened my eyes, I saw a blazing torch on the wall beyond him, and his dark outline looming before me, and his eyes animate, and looking at me without question, the black pupils swimming in a dull gray light. He was otherwise lifeless, hands limp at his sides. He was ornamented as she had been, and he wore the glorified dress of the pharaoh and his hair too was plaited with gold. His skin was bronze all over, as hers had been, enhanced, as the Elder had said. And he was the incarnation of menace in his stillness as he stood staring at me.

"In the barren chamber behind him, she sat on a stone shelf, with her head at an angle, her arms dangling, as if she were a lifeless body flung there. Her linen was smeared with sand, her sandaled feet caked with it, and her eyes were vacant and staring. Perfect attitude of death.

"And he like a stone sentinel in a royal tomb blocked my path.

"I could hear no more from either of them than you heard from them when I took you down to the chamber here on the island. And I thought I might expire on the spot from fear.

"Yet there was the sand on her feet and on her linen. She'd come to me! She had!

"But someone had come into the corridor behind me. Someone was shuffling along the passage, and when I turned, I saw one of the burnt ones —a mere skeleton, this one, with black gums showing and the fangs cutting into the shiny black raisin skin of his lower lip.

"I swallowed a gasp at the sight of him, his bony limbs, feet splayed, arms jiggling with every step. He was plowing towards us, but he did not seem to see me. He put his hands up and shoved at Enkil.

" 'No, no, back into the chamber!' he whispered in a low, crackling voice. 'No, no!' and each syllable seemed to take all he had. His withered arms shoved at the figure. He couldn't budge it.

" 'Help me!' he said to me. 'They have moved. Why did they move? Make them go back. The further they move, the harder it is to get them back.'

"I stared at Enkil and I felt the horror that you felt to see this statue with life in it, seemingly unable or unwilling to move. And as I watched the spectacle grew even more horrible, because the blackened wraith was now screaming and scratching at Enkil, unable to do anything with him. And the sight of this thing that should have been dead wearing itself out like this, and this other thing that looked so perfectly godlike and magnificent just standing there, was more than I could bear.

" 'Help me!' the thing said. 'Get him back into the chamber. Get them back where they must remain.'

"How could I do this? How could I lay hands on this being? How could I presume to push him where he did not wish to go?

" 'They will be all right, if you help me,' the thing said. 'They will be together and they will be at peace. Push on him. Do it. Push! Oh, look at her, what's happened to her. Look.'

" 'All right, damn it!' I whispered, and overcome with shame, I tried. I laid my hands again on Enkil and I pushed at him, but it was impossible. My strength meant nothing here, and the burnt one became all the more irritating with his useless ranting and shoving.

"But then he gasped and cackled and threw his skeletal arms up in the air and backed up.

" 'What's the matter with you!' I said, trying not to scream and run. But I saw soon enough.

"Akasha had appeared behind Enkil. She was standing directly behind him and looking at me over his shoulder, and I saw her fingertips come round his muscular arms. Her eyes were as empty in their glazed beauty as they had been before. But she was making him move, and now came the spectacle of these two things walking of their own volition, he backing up slowly, feet barely leaving the ground, and she shielded by him so that I saw only her hands and the top of her head and her eyes.

"I blinked, trying to clear my head.

"They were sitting on the shelf again, together, and they had lapsed into the same posture in which you saw them downstairs on this island tonight.

"The burnt creature was near to collapse. He had gone down on his knees, and he didn't have to explain to me why. He had found them many a time in different positions, but he had never witnessed their movement. And he had never seen her as she had been before.

"I was bursting with the knowledge of why she had been as she was before. She had come to me. But there was a point at which my pride and exhilaration gave way to what it should have been: overwhelming awe, and finally grief.

"I started to cry. I started to cry uncontrollably as I had not cried since I had been with the old god in the grove and my death had occurred, and this curse, this great luminous and powerful curse, had descended on me. I cried as you cried when you first saw them. I cried for their stillness and their isolation, and this horrible little place in which they stared forward at nothing or sat in darkness while Egypt died above.

"The goddess, the mother, the thing, whatever she was, the mindless and silent or helpless progenitor was looking at me. Surely it wasn't an illusion. Her great glossy eyes, with their black fringe of lashes, were fixed upon me. And there came her voice again, but it had nothing of its old power, it was merely the thought, quite beyond language, inside my head.

"*Take us out of Egypt, Marius. The Elder means to destroy us. Guard us, Marius. Or we perish here.*

" 'Do they want blood?' the burnt one cried. 'Did they move because they would have sacrifice?' the dried one begged.

" 'Go get them a sacrifice,' I said.

" 'I cannot now. I haven't the strength. And they won't give their healing blood to me. Would they but allow me a few drops, my burnt flesh might restore itself, the blood in me would be replenished, and I should bring them glorious sacrifices . . .'

"But there was an element of dishonesty in this little speech, because *they* didn't desire glorious sacrifices anymore.

" 'Try again to drink their blood,' I said and this was horribly selfish of me. I just wanted to see what would happen.

"Yet to my humiliation, he did approach them, bent over and weeping, begging them to give their powerful blood, their old blood, so that his burns might heal faster, saying that he was innocent, he had not put them in the sand—it had been the Elder—please, please, would they let him drink from the original fount.

"And then ravenous hunger consumed him. And, convulsing, he distended his fangs as a cobra might and he shot forward, his black claws out, to the neck of Enkil.

"Enkil's arm rose as the Elder said it would, and it flung the burnt one across the chamber on his back before it returned to its proper place.

"The burnt one was sobbing and I was even more ashamed. The burnt one was too weak to hunt for victims or bring victims. I had urged him on to this to see it. And the gloom of this place, the gritty sand on the floor, the barrenness, the stink of the torch, and the ugly sight of the burnt one writhing and crying, all this was dispiriting beyond words.

" 'Then drink from me,' I said, shuddering at the sight of him, the fangs distended again, the hands out to grasp me. But it was the least I could do."

12

"AS SOON as I was done with that creature, I ordered him to let no one enter the crypt. How the hell he was supposed to keep anyone out I couldn't imagine, but I told him this with tremendous authority and I hurried away.

"I went back into Alexandria, and I broke into a shop that sold antique things and I stole two fine painted and gold-plated mummy cases, and I took a great deal of linen for wrapping, and I went back to the desert crypt.

"My courage and my fear were at their peak.

"As often happens when we give the blood or take it from another of our kind, I had seen things, dreamed things as it were, when the burnt one had his teeth in my throat. And what I had seen and dreamed had to do with Egypt, the age of Egypt, the fact that for four thousand years this land had known little change in language, religion, or art. And for the first time this was understandable to me and it put me in profound sympathy with the Mother and the Father as relics of this country, as surely as the pyramids were relics. It intensified my curiosity and made it something more akin to devotion.

"Though to be honest, I would have stolen the Mother and the Father just in order to survive.

"This new knowledge, this new infatuation, inspired me as I approached Akasha and Enkil to put them in the wooden mummy cases, knowing full well that Akasha would allow it and that one blow from Enkil could probably crush my skull.

"But Enkil yielded as well as Akasha. They allowed me to wrap them in linen, to make mummies of them, and to place them into the shapely wooden coffins which bore the painted faces of others, and the endless hieroglyph instructions for the dead, and to take them with me into Alexandria, which I did.

"I left the wraith being in a terrible state of agitation as I went off dragging a mummy case under each arm.

"When I reached the city I hired men to carry these coffins properly to my house, out of a sense of fittingness, and then I buried them deep beneath the garden, explaining to Akasha and Enkil all the while aloud that their stay in the earth would not be long.

"I was in terror to leave them the next night. I hunted and killed within yards of my own garden gate. And then I sent my slaves to purchase horses and a wagon for me, and to make preparations for a journey around the coast to Antioch on the Orontes River, a city I knew and loved, and in which I felt I would be safe.

"As I feared, the Elder soon appeared. I was actually waiting for him in the shadowy bedroom, seated on my couch like a Roman, one lamp beside me, an old copy of some Roman poem in my hand. I wondered if he would sense the location of Akasha and Enkil, and deliberately imagined false things—that I had shut them up in the great pyramid itself.

"I still dreamed the dream of Egypt that had come to me from the burnt one: a land in which the laws and the beliefs had remained the same for longer than we could imagine, a land that had known the picture writing and the pyramids and the myths of Osiris and Isis when Greece had been in darkness and when there was no Rome. I saw the river Nile overflowing her banks. I saw the mountains on either side which created the valley. I saw time with a wholly different idea of it. And it was not merely the dream of the burnt one—it was all I had ever seen or known in Egypt, a sense of things beginning there which I had learned from books long before I had become the child of the Mother and the Father, whom I meant now to take.

" 'What makes you think that we would entrust them to you!' the Elder said as soon as he appeared in the doorway.

"He appeared enormous as, girded only in the short linen kilt, he walked around my room. The lamplight shone on his bald head, his round face, his bulging eyes. 'How dare you take the Mother and the Father! What have you done with them!' he said.

" 'It was you who put them in the sun,' I answered. 'You who sought to destroy them. You were the one who didn't believe the old story. You were the guardian of the Mother and the Father, and you lied to me. You brought about the death of our kind from one end of the world to the other. You, and you lied to me.'

"He was dumbfounded. He thought me proud and impossible beyond words. So did I. But so what? He had the power to burn me to ashes if and when he burnt the Mother and the Father. And she had come to me! To me!

" 'I did not know what would happen!' he said now, his veins cording against his forehead, his fists clenched. He looked like a great bald Nubian as he tried to intimidate me. 'I swear to you by all that is sacred, I didn't know. And you cannot know what it means to keep them, to look at them year after year, decade after decade, century after century, and know that they could speak, they could move, and they will not!'

"I had no sympathy for him and what he said. He was merely an enigmatic figure poised in the center of this small room in Alexandria railing at me of sufferings beyond the imagination. How could I sympathize with him?

" 'I inherited them,' he said. 'They were given to me! What was I to do?' he declared. 'And I must contend with their punishing silence, their refusal to direct the tribe they had loosed into the world. And why came this silence? Vengeance, I tell you. Vengeance on us. But for what? Who exists who can remember back a thousand years now? No one. Who understands all these things? The old gods go into the sun, into the fire, or they meet with obliteration through violence, or they bury themselves in the deepest earth never to rise again. But the Mother and the Father go on forever, and they do not speak. Why don't they bury themselves where no harm can come to them? Why do they simply watch and listen and refuse to speak? Only when one tries to take Akasha from Enkil does he move, does he strike out and then batter down his foes as if he were a stone colossus come to life. I tell you when I put them in the sand they did not try to save themselves! They stood facing the river as I ran!'

" 'You did it to see what would happen, if it would make them move!'

" 'To free myself! To say, "I will keep you no longer. Move. Speak."

To see if it was true, the old story, and if it was true, then let us all die in flames.'

"He had exhausted himself. In a feeble voice he said finally, 'You cannot take the Mother and the Father. How could you think that I would allow you to do this! You who might not last out the century, you who ran from the obligations of the grove. You don't really know what the Mother and the Father are. You have heard more than one lie from me.'

" 'I have something to tell you,' I said. 'You *are* free now. You know that we're not gods. And we're not men, either. We don't serve the Mother Earth because we do not eat her fruits and we do not naturally descend to her embrace. We are not of her. And I leave Egypt without further obligation to you, and I take them with me because it is what they have asked me to do and I will not suffer them or me to be destroyed.'

"He was again dumbfounded. How had they asked me? But he couldn't find words, he was so angry, and so full of hatred suddenly, and so full of dark wrathful secrets that I could not even glimpse. He had a mind as educated as mine, this one, but he knew things about our powers that I didn't guess. I had never slain a man when I was mortal. I did not know how to kill any living thing, save in the tender and remorseless need for blood.

"He knew how to use his supernatural strength. He closed his eyes to slits, and his body hardened. Danger radiated from him.

"He approached me and his intentions went before him, and in an instant I had risen off my couch, and I was trying to ward off his blows. He had me by the throat and he threw me against the stone wall so that the bones of my shoulder and right arm were crushed. In a moment of exquisite pain, I knew he would dash my head against the stone and crush all my limbs, and then he would pour the oil of the lamp over me and burn me, and I would be gone out of his private eternity as if I had never known these secrets or dared to intrude.

"I fought as I never could have before. But my battered arm was a riot of pain, and his strength was to me what mine would be to you. But instead of clawing at his hands as they locked round my throat, instead of trying to free my throat as was instinctive, I shot my thumbs into his eyes. Though my arm blazed with pain, I used all my strength to push his eyes backwards into his head.

"He let go of me and he wailed. Blood was pouring down his face. I ran clear of him and towards the garden door. I still could not breathe from the damage he'd done to my throat, and as I clutched at my dangling arm, I saw things out of the corner of my eye that confused me, a great spray of earth flying up from the garden, the air dense as if with smoke. I bumped the door frame, losing my balance, as if a wind had moved me, and glancing back I saw him coming on, eyes still glittering, though from deep inside his head. He was cursing me in Egyptian. He was saying that I should go into the netherworld with the demons, unmourned.

"And then his face froze in a mask of fear. He stopped in his tracks and looked almost comical in his alarm.

"Then I saw what he saw—the figure of Akasha, who moved past me to my right. The linen wrapping had been ripped from around her head, and her arms were torn free, and she was covered with the sandy earth. Her eyes had the same expressionless stare they always had, and she bore down on him slowly, drawing ever closer because he could not move to save himself.

"He went down on his knees, babbling to her in Egyptian, first with a tone of astonishment and then with incoherent fright. Still she came on, tracking the sand after her, the linen falling off her as each slow sliding step ruptured the wrappings more violently. He turned away and fell forward on his hands and started to crawl as if, by some unseen force, she prevented him from rising to his feet. Surely that was what she was doing, because he lay prone finally, his elbows jutting up, unable to move himself.

"Quietly and slowly, she stepped on the back of his right knee, crushing it flat beneath her foot, the blood squirting from under her heel. And with the next step she crushed his pelvis just as flat while he roared like a dumb beast, the blood gushing from his mangled parts. Then came her next step down upon his shoulder and the next upon his head, which exploded beneath her weight as if it had been an acorn. The roaring ceased. The blood spurted from all his remains as they twitched.

"Turning, she revealed to me no change in expression, signifying nothing of what had happened to him, indifferent even to the lone and horrified witness who shrank back against the wall. She walked back and forth over his remains with the same slow and effortless gait, and crushed the last of him utterly.

"What was left was not even the outline of a man, but mere blood-soaked pulp upon the floor, and yet it glittered, bubbled, seemed to swell and contract as if there were still life in it.

"I was petrified, knowing that there was life in it, that this was what immortality could mean.

"But she had come to a stop, and she turned to her left so slowly it seemed the revolution of a statue on a chain, and her hand rose and the lamp beside the couch rose in the air and fell down upon the bloody mass, the flame quickly igniting the oil as it spilled.

"Like grease he went up, flames dancing from one end of the dark mass to the other, the blood seeming to feed the fire, the smoke acrid but only with the stench of the oil.

"I was on my knees, with my head against the side of the doorway. I was as near to losing consciousness from shock as I have ever been. I watched him burn to nothing. I watched her standing there, beyond the flames, her bronze face giving forth not the slightest sign of intelligence or triumph or will.

"I held my breath, expecting her eyes to move to me. But they didn't. And as the moment lengthened, as the fire died, I realized that she had ceased to move. She had returned to the state of absolute silence and stillness that all the others had come to expect of her.

"The room was dark now. The fire had gone out. The smell of burning oil sickened me. She looked like an Egyptian ghost in her torn wrappings, poised there before the glittering embers, the gilded furnishings glinting in the light from the sky, bearing, for all their Roman craftsmanship, some resemblance to the elaborate and delicate furnishings of a royal burial chamber.

"I rose to my feet, and the pain in my shoulder and in my arm throbbed. I could feel the blood rushing to heal it, but the damage was considerable. I did not know how long I would have this.

"I did know, of course, that if I were to drink from her, the healing would be much faster, perhaps instantaneous, and we could start our journey out of Alexandria tonight. I could take her far far away from Egypt.

"Then I realize that *she* was telling me this. The words, far far away, were breathed in by me sensuously.

"And I answered her: *I have been all through the world and I will take you to safe places.* But then again perhaps this dialogue was all my doing. And the soft, yielding sensation of love for her was my doing. And I was going completely mad, knowing this nightmare would never, never end except in fire such as that, that no natural old age or death would ever quiet my fears and dull my pains, as I had once expected it to do.

"It ceased to matter. What mattered was that I was alone with her, and in this darkness she might have been a human woman standing there, a young god woman full of vitality and full of lovely language and ideas and dreams.

"I moved closer to her and it seemed then that she was this pliant and yielding creature, and some knowledge of her was inside me, waiting to be remembered, waiting to be enjoyed. Yet I was afraid. She could do to me what she had done to the Elder. But that was absurd. She would not. I was her guardian now. She would never let anyone hurt me. No. I was to understand that. And I came closer and closer to her, until my lips were almost at her bronze throat, and it was decided when I felt the firm cold press of her hand on the back of my head."

13

"I WON'T try to describe the ecstasy. You know it. You knew it when you took the blood from Magnus. You knew it when I gave you the blood in Cairo. You know it when you kill. And you know what it means when I say it was that, but a thousand times that.

"I neither saw nor heard nor felt anything but absolute happiness, absolute satisfaction.

"Yet I was in other places, other rooms from long ago, and voices were talking and battles were being lost. Someone was crying in agony. Someone was screaming in words I knew and didn't know: *I do not understand. I do not understand.* A great pool of darkness opened and there came the invitation to fall and to fall and to fall and she sighed and said: *I can fight no longer.*

"Then I awoke, and found myself lying on my couch. She was in the center of the room, still as before, and it was late in the night, and the city of Alexandria murmured around us in its sleep.

"I knew a multitude of other things.

"I knew so many things that it would have taken hours if not nights for me to learn them if they'd been confided in mortal words. And I had no inkling of how much time had passed.

"I knew that thousands of years ago there had been great battles among the Drinkers of the Blood, and many of them after the first creation had become ruthless and profane bringers of death. Unlike the benign lovers of the Good Mother who starved and then drank her sacrifices, these were death angels who could swoop down upon any victim at any moment, glorying in the conviction that they were part of the rhythm of all things in which no individual human life matters, in which death and life are equal —and to them belonged suffering and slaughter as they chose to mete it out.

"And these terrible gods had their devoted worshipers among men, human slaves who brought victims to them, and quaked in fear of the moment when they themselves might fall to the god's whim.

"Gods of this kind had ruled in ancient Babylon, and in Assyria, and in cities long forgotten, and in far-off India, and in countries beyond whose names I did not understand.

"And even now, as I sat silent and stunned by these images, I understood that these gods had become part of the Oriental world which was alien to the Roman world to which I'd been born. They were part of the world of the Persians whose men were abject slaves to their king, while the Greeks who had fought them had been free men.

"No matter what our cruelties and our excesses, even the lowliest peasant had value to us. Life had value. And death was merely the end of life, something to be faced with bravery when honor left no choice. Death was not grand to us. In fact, I don't think death was anything really to us. It certainly was not a state preferable to life.

"And though these gods had been revealed to me by Akasha in all their grandeur and mystery, I found them appalling. I could not now or ever embrace them and I knew that the philosophies that proceeded from them or justified them would never justify my killing, or give me consolation as a Drinker of the Blood. Mortal or immortal, I was of the West. And I loved the ideas of the West. And I should always *be guilty* of what I did.

"Nevertheless I saw the power of these gods, their incomparable loveliness. They enjoyed a freedom I would never know. And I saw their contempt for all those who challenged them. And I saw them wearing in the pantheon of other countries their glittering crowns.

"And I saw them come to Egypt to steal the original and all-powerful blood of the Father and the Mother, and to ensure that the Father and the Mother did not burn themselves to bring an end to the reign of these dark and terrible gods for whom all the good gods must be brought down.

"And I saw the Mother and the Father imprisoned. I saw them entombed with blocks of diorite and granite pressed against their very bodies in an underground crypt, only their heads and their necks free. In this manner the dark gods could feed the Mother and the Father the human blood they could not resist, and take from their necks the powerful blood against their will. And all the dark gods of the world came to drink from this oldest of founts.

"The Father and the Mother screamed in torment. They begged to be released. But this meant nothing to the dark gods, who relished such agony, who drank it as they drank human blood. The dark gods wore human skulls dangling from their girdles; their garments were dyed with human blood. The Mother and the Father refused sacrifice, but this only increased their helplessness. They did not take the very thing that might have given them the strength to move the stones, and to affect objects by mere thought.

"Nevertheless their strength increased..

"Years and years of this torment, and wars among the gods, wars among the sects that held to life and those who held to death.

"Years beyond counting, until finally the Mother and the Father became silent, and there were none in existence who could even remember a time when they begged or fought or talked. Years came when nobody could remember who had imprisoned the Mother and the Father, or why the Mother and the Father must not ever be let out. Some did not believe that the Mother and the Father were even the originals or that their immolation would harm anyone else. It was just an old tale.

"And all the while Egypt was Egypt and its religion, uncorrupted by outsiders, finally moved on towards the belief in conscience, the judgment after death of all beings, be they rich or poor, the belief in goodness on earth and life after death.

"And then the night came when the Mother and the Father were found free of their prison, and those who tended them realized that only they could have moved the stones. In silence, their strength had grown beyond all reckoning. Yet they were as statues, embracing each other in the middle of the dirty and darkened chamber where for centuries they had been kept. Naked and shimmering they were, all their clothing having long ago rotted away.

"If and when they drank from the victims offered, they moved with the sluggishness of reptiles in winter, as though time had taken on an altogether different meaning for them, and years were as nights to them, and centuries as years.

"And the ancient religion was strong as ever, not of the East and not really of the West. The Drinkers of the Blood remained good symbols, the luminous image of life in the afterworld which even the lowliest Egyptian soul might come to enjoy.

"Sacrifice could only be the evildoer in these later times. And by this means the gods drew the evil out of the people, and protected the people, and the silent voice of the god consoled the weak, telling the truths learned by the god in starvation: that the world was full of abiding beauty, that no soul here is really alone.

"The Mother and the Father were kept in the loveliest of all shrines and all the gods came to them and took from them, with their will, droplets of their precious blood.

"But then the impossible was happening. Egypt was reaching its finish. Things thought to be unchangeable were about to be utterly changed. Alexander had come, the Ptolemies were the rulers, Caesar and Antony—all rude and strange protagonists of the drama which was simply The End of All This.

"And finally the dark and cynical Elder, the wicked one, the disappointed one, who put the Mother and Father in the sun.

"I GOT up off the couch and I stood in this room in Alexandria looking at the motionless and staring figure of Akasha and the soiled linen hanging from her seemed an insult. And my head swam with old poetry. And I was overcome with love.

"There was no more pain in my body from the battle with the Elder. The bones were restored. And I went down on my knees, and I kissed the fingers of the right hand that hung at Akasha's side. I looked up and I saw her looking down at me, her head tilted, and the strangest look passed over her; it seemed as pure in its suffering as the happiness I had just known. Then her head, very slowly, inhumanly slowly, returned to its position of facing forward, and I knew in that instant that I had seen and known things that the Elder had never known.

"As I wrapped her body again in linen, I was in a trance. More than ever I felt the mandate to take care of her and Enkil, and the horror of the Elder's death was flashing before me every second, and the blood she had given me had increased my exhilaration as well as my physical strength.

"And as I prepared to leave Alexandria, I suppose I dreamed of waking Enkil and Akasha, that in the years to come they would recover all the vitality stolen from them, and we would know each other in such intimate and astonishing ways that these dreams of knowledge and experience given me in the blood would pale.

"My slaves had long ago come back with the horses and the wagons for our journey, with the stone sarcophagi and the chains and locks I had told them to procure. They waited outside the walls.

"I placed the mummy cases with the Mother and the Father in the sarcophagi side by side in the wagon, and I covered them with locks and chains and heavy blankets, and we set out, heading towards the door to the underground temple of the gods on our way to the city gates.

"When I reached the door, I left my slaves with firm orders to give a loud alarm if anyone approached, and then I took a leather sack and went down into the temple, and into the library of the Elder, and I put all the scrolls I could find into the sack. I stole every bit of portable writing that was in the place. I wished I could have taken the writing off the walls.

"There were others in the chambers, but they were too terrified to come out. Of course they knew I had stolen the Mother and the Father. And they probably knew of the Elder's death.

"It didn't matter to me. I was getting out of old Egypt, and I had the source of all our power with me. And I was young and foolish and enflamed.

"WHEN I finally reached Antioch on the Orontes—a great and wonderful city that rivaled Rome in population and wealth—I read these old papyri and they told of all the things Akasha had revealed to me.

"And she and Enkil had the first of many chapels I would build for them all over Asia and Europe, and they knew that I would always care for them and I knew that they would let no harm come to me.

"Many centuries after, when I was set afire in Venice by the band of the Children of Darkness, I was too far from Akasha for rescue, or again, she would have come. And when I did reach the sanctuary, knowing full well the agony that the burnt gods had known, I drank of her blood until I was healed.

"But by the end of the first century of keeping them in Antioch I had despaired that they would ever 'come to life,' as it were. Their silence and stillness was almost continuous as it is now. Only the skin changed dramatically with the passing years, losing the damage of the sun until it was like alabaster again.

"But by the time I realized all this I was powerfully engaged in watching the goings-on of the city and the changing of the times. I was madly in love with a beautiful brown-haired Greek courtesan named Pandora, with the loveliest arms I have ever beheld on a human being, who knew what I was from the first moment she set eyes on me and bided her time, enchanting me and dazzling me until I was ready to bring her over into the magic, at which time she was allowed the blood from Akasha and became one of the most powerful supernatural creatures I have ever known. Two hundred years I lived and fought and loved with Pandora. But that is another tale.

"There are a million tales I could tell of the centuries I have lived since then, of my journeys from Antioch to Constantinople, back to Alexandria and on to India and then to Italy again and from Venice to the bitter cold highlands of Scotland and then to this island in the Aegean, where we are now.

"I could tell you of the tiny changes in Akasha and Enkil over the years, of the puzzling things they do, and the mysteries they leave unsolved.

"Perhaps some night in the far distant future, when you've returned to me, I'll talk of the other immortals I've known, those who were made as I was made by the last of the gods who survived in various lands—some the servants of the Mother and others of the terrible gods out of the East.

"I could tell you how Mael, my poor Druid priest, finally drank from a wounded god himself and in one instant lost all his belief in the old religion, going on to become as enduring and dangerous a rogue immortal as any of us. I could tell you how the legends of Those Who Must Be Kept spread through the world. And of the times other immortals have tried to take them from me out of pride or sheer destructiveness, wanting to put an end to us all.

"I will tell you of my loneliness, of the others I made, and how they met their ends. Of how I have gone down into the earth with Those Who

Must Be Kept, and risen again, thanks to their blood, to live several mortal lifetimes before burying myself again. I will tell you of the other truly eternal ones whom I meet only now and then. Of the last time I saw Pandora in the city of Dresden, in the company of a powerful and vicious vampire from India, and of how we quarreled and separated, and of how I discovered too late her letter begging me to meet her in Moscow, a fragile piece of writing that had fallen to the bottom of a cluttered traveling case. Too many things, too many stories, stories with and without lessons . . .

"But I have told you the most important things—how I came into possession of Those Who Must Be Kept, and who we really were.

"What is crucial now is that you understand this:

"As the Roman Empire came to its close, all the old gods of the pagan world were seen as demons by the Christians who rose. It was useless to tell them as the centuries passed that their Christ was but another God of the Wood, dying and rising, as Dionysus or Osiris had done before him, and that the Virgin Mary was in fact the Good Mother again enshrined. Theirs was a new age of belief and conviction, and in it we became devils, detached from what they believed, as old knowledge was forgotten or misunderstood.

"But this had to happen. Human sacrifice had been a horror to the Greeks and Romans. I had thought it ghastly that the Keltoi burned for the god their evildoers in the wicker colossi as I described. And so it was to the Christians. So how could we, gods who fed upon human blood, have been seen as 'good'?

"But the real perversion of us was accomplished when the Children of Darkness came to believe they served the Christian devil, and like the terrible gods of the East, they tried to give value to evil, to believe in its power in the scheme of things, to give it a just place in the world.

"Hearken to me when I say: *There has never been a just place for evil in the Western world.* There has never been an easy accommodation of death.

"No matter how violent have been the centuries since the fall of Rome, no matter how terrible the wars, the persecutions, the injustices, the value placed upon human life has only increased.

"Even as the Church erected statues and pictures of her bloody Christ and her bloody martyrs, she held the belief that these deaths, so well used by the faithful, could only have come at the hands of enemies, not God's own priests.

"It is the belief in the value of human life that has caused the torture chambers and the stake and the more ghastly means of execution to be abandoned all over Europe in this time. And it is the belief in the value of human life that carries man now out of the monarchy into the republics of America and France.

"And now we stand again on the cusp of an atheistic age—an age where the Christian faith is losing its hold, as paganism once lost its hold, and the new humanism, the belief in man and his accomplishments and his rights, is more powerful than ever before.

"Of course we cannot know what will happen as the old religion thoroughly dies out. Christianity rose on the ashes of paganism, only to carry forth the old worship in new form. Maybe a new religion will rise now. Maybe without it, man will crumble in cynicism and selfishness because he really needs his gods.

"But maybe something more wonderful will take place: the world will truly move forward, past all gods and goddesses, past all devils and angels. And in such a world, Lestat, we will have less of a place than we have ever had.

"All the stories I have told you are finally as useless as all ancient knowledge is to man and to us. Its images and its poetry can be beautiful; it can make us shiver with the recognition of things we have always suspected or felt. It can draw us back to times when the earth was new to man, and wondrous. But always we come back to the way the earth is now.

"And in this world the vampire is only a Dark God. He is a Child of Darkness. He can't be anything else. And if he wields any lovely power upon the minds of men, it is only because the human imagination is a secret place of primitive memories and unconfessed desires. The mind of each man is a Savage Garden, to use your phrase, in which all manner of creatures rise and fall, and anthems are sung and things imagined that must finally be condemned and disavowed.

"Yet men love us when they come to know us. They love us even now. The Paris crowds love what they see on the stage of the Theater of the Vampires. And those who have seen your like walking through the ballrooms of the world, the pale and deadly lord in the velvet cloak, have worshiped in their own way at your feet.

"They thrill at the possibility of immortality, at the possibility that a grand and beautiful being could be utterly evil, that he could feel and know all things yet choose willfully to feed his dark appetite. Maybe they wish they could be that lusciously evil creature. How simple it all seems. And it is the simplicity of it that they want.

"But give them the Dark Gift and only one in a multitude will not be as miserable as you are.

"What can I say finally that will not confirm your worst fears? I have lived over eighteen hundred years, and I tell you life does not need us. I have never had a true purpose. We have no place."

14

MARIUS paused.

He looked away from me for the first time and towards the sky beyond the windows, as if he were listening to island voices I couldn't hear.

"I have a few more things to tell you," he said, "things which are important, though they are merely practical things . . ." But he was distracted. "And there are promises," he said, finally, "which I must exact . . ."

And he slipped into quiet, listening, his face too much like that of Akasha and Enkil.

There were a thousand questions I wanted to ask. But more significant perhaps there were a thousand statements of his I wanted to reiterate, as if I had to say them aloud to grasp them. If I talked, I wouldn't make very good sense.

I sat back against the cool brocade of the winged chair with my hands together in the form of a steeple, and I just looked ahead of me, as if his tale were spread out there for me to read over, and I thought of the truth of his statements about good and evil, and how it might have horrified me and disappointed me had he tried to convince me of the rightness of the philosophy of the terrible gods of the East, that we could somehow glory in what we did.

I too was a child of the West, and all my brief life I had struggled with the Western inability to accept evil or death.

But underneath all these considerations lay the appalling fact that Marius could annihilate all of us by destroying Akasha and Enkil. Marius could kill every single one of us in existence if he were to burn Akasha and Enkil and thereby get rid of an old and decrepit and useless form of evil in the world. Or so it seemed.

And the horror of Akasha and Enkil themselves . . . What could I say to this, except that I too had felt the first glimmer of what he once felt, that I could rouse them, I could make them speak again, I could make them move. Or more truly, I had felt when I saw them that someone should and could do it. Someone could end their open-eyed sleep.

And what would they be if they ever walked and talked again? Ancient Egyptian monsters. What would they do?

I saw the two possibilities as seductive suddenly—rousing them or destroying them. Both tempted the mind. I wanted to pierce them and commune with them, and yet I understood the irresistible madness of trying to destroy them. Of going out in a blaze of light with them that would take all our doomed species with it.

Both attitudes had to do with power. And some triumph over the passage of time.

"Aren't you ever tempted to do it?" I asked, and my voice had pain in it. I wondered if down in their chapel they heard.

He awakened from his listening and turned to me and he shook his head. No.

"Even though you know better than anyone that we have no place?"

Again he shook his head. No.

"I am immortal," he said, "*truly* immortal. To be perfectly honest, I do not know what can kill me now, if anything. But that isn't the point. I want to go on. I do not even think of it. I am a continual awareness unto myself, the intelligence I longed for years and years ago when I was alive, and I'm in love as I've always been with the great progress of mankind. I want to see what will happen now that the world has come round again to questioning its gods. Why, I couldn't be persuaded now to close my eyes for any reason."

I nodded in understanding.

"But I don't suffer what you suffer," he said. "Even in the grove in northern France, when I was made into this, I was not young. I have been lonely since, I have known near madness, indescribable anguish, but I was never immortal and young. I have done over and over what you have yet to do—the thing that must take you away from me very very soon."

"Take me away? But I don't want—"

"You have to go, Lestat," he said. "And very soon, as I said. You're not ready to remain here with me. This is one of the most important things I have left to tell you and you must listen with the same attention with which you listened to the rest."

"Marius, I can't imagine leaving now. I can't even . . ." I felt anger suddenly. Why had he brought me here to cast me out? And I remembered all Armand's admonitions to me. It is only with the old ones that we find communion, not with those we create. And I had found Marius. But these were mere words. They didn't touch the core of what I felt, the sudden misery and fear of separation.

"Listen to me," he said gently. "Before I was taken by the Gauls, I had lived a good lifetime, as long as many a man in those days. And after I took Those Who Must Be Kept out of Egypt, I lived again for years in Antioch as a rich Roman scholar might live. I had a house, slaves, and the love of Pandora. We had life in Antioch, we were watchers of all that passed. And having had that lifetime, I had the strength for others later on. I had the strength to become part of the world in Venice, as you know. I had the strength to rule on this island as I do. You, like many who go early into the fire or the sun, have had no real life at all.

"As a young man, you tasted real life for no more than six months in Paris. As a vampire, you have been a roamer, an outsider, haunting houses and other lives as you drifted from place to place.

"If you mean to survive, you must live out one complete lifetime as soon as you can. To forestall it may be to lose everything, to despair and to go into the earth again, never to rise. Or worse . . ."

"I want it. I understand," I said. "And yet when they offered it to me in Paris, to remain with the Theater, I couldn't do it."

"That was not the right place for you. Besides, the Theater of the Vampires is a coven. It isn't the world any more than this island refuge of mine is the world. And too many horrors happened to you there.

"But in this New World wilderness to which you're headed, this barbaric little city called New Orleans, you may enter into the world as never before. You may take up residence there as a mortal, just as you tried to do so many times in your wanderings with Gabrielle. There will be no old covens to bother you, no rogues to try to strike you down out of fear. And when you make others—and you will, out of loneliness, make others—make and keep them as human as you can. Keep them close to you as members of a family, not as members of a coven, and understand the age you live in, the decades you pass through. Understand the style of garment that adorns your body, the styles of dwellings in which you spend your leisure hours, the place in which you hunt. Understand what it means to feel the passage of time!"

"Yes, and feel all the pain of seeing things die . . ." All the things Armand advised against.

"Of course. You are made to triumph over time, not to run from it. And you will suffer that you harbor the secret of your monstrosity and that you must kill. And maybe you will try to feast only on the evildoer to assuage your conscience, and you may succeed, or you may fail. But you can come very close to life, if you will only lock the secret within you. You are fashioned to be close to it, as you yourself once told the members of the old Paris coven. You are the imitation of a man."

"I want it, I do want it—"

"Then do as I advise. And understand this also. In a real way, eternity is merely the living of one human lifetime after another. Of course, there may be long periods of retreat; times of slumber or of merely watching. But again and again we plunge into the stream, and we swim as long as we can, until time or tragedy brings us down as they will do mortals."

"Will you do it again? Leave this retreat and plunge into the stream?"

"Yes, definitely. When the right moment presents itself. When the world is so interesting again that I can't resist it. Then I'll walk city streets. I'll take a name. I'll do things."

"Then come now, with me!" Ah, painful echo of Armand. And of the vain plea from Gabrielle ten years after.

"It's a more tempting invitation than you know," he answered, "but I'd do you a great disservice if I came with you. I'd stand between you and the world. I couldn't help it."

I shook my head and looked away, full of bitterness.

"Do you want to continue?" he asked. "Or do you want Gabrielle's predictions to come true?"

"I want to continue," I said.

"Then you must go," he said. "A century from now, maybe less, we'll meet again. I won't be on this island. I will have taken Those Who Must Be Kept to another place. But wherever I am and wherever you are, I'll find you. And then I'll be the one who will not want you to leave me. I'll be the one who begs you to remain. I'll fall in love with your company, your conversation, the mere sight of you, your stamina and your recklessness, and your lack of belief in anything—all the things about you I already love rather too strongly."

I could scarcely listen to this without breaking down. I wanted to beg him to let me remain.

"Is it absolutely impossible now?" I asked. "Marius, can't you spare me this lifetime?"

"Quite impossible," he said. "I can tell you stories forever, but they are no substitute for life. Believe me, I've tried to spare others. I've never succeeded. I can't teach what one lifetime can teach. I never should have taken Armand in his youth, and his centuries of folly and suffering are a penance to me even now. You did him a mercy driving him into the Paris of this century, but I fear for him it is too late. Believe me, Lestat, when I say this has to happen. You must have that lifetime, for those who are robbed of it spin in dissatisfaction until they finally live it somewhere or they are destroyed."

"And what about Gabrielle?"

"Gabrielle had her life; she had her death almost. She has the strength to reenter the world when she chooses, or to live on its fringes indefinitely."

"And do you think she will ever reenter?"

"I don't know," he said. "Gabrielle defies my understanding. Not my experience—she's too like Pandora. But I never understood Pandora. The truth is most women are weak, be they mortal or immortal. But when they are strong, they are absolutely unpredictable."

I shook my head. I closed my eyes for a moment. I didn't want to think of Gabrielle. Gabrielle was gone, no matter what we said here.

And I still could not accept that I had to go. This seemed an Eden to me. But I didn't argue anymore. I knew he was resolute, and I also knew that he wouldn't force me. He'd let me start worrying about my mortal father, and he'd let me come to him and say I had to go. I had a few nights left.

"Yes," he answered softly. "And there are other things I can tell you."

I opened my eyes again. He was looking at me patiently, affectionately. I felt the ache of love as strongly as I'd ever felt it for Gabrielle. I felt the inevitable tears and did my best to suppress them.

"You've learned a great deal from Armand," he said, his voice steady as if to help me with this little silent struggle. "And you learned much more on your own. But there are still some things I might teach you."

"Yes, please," I said.

"Well, for one thing," he said, "your powers are extraordinary, but you can't expect those you make in the next fifty years to equal you or Gabrielle. Your second child didn't have half Gabrielle's strength and later children will have even less. The blood I gave you will make some difference. If you drink . . . if you drink from Akasha and Enkil, which you may choose not to do . . . that will make some difference too. But no matter, only so many children can be made by one in a century. And new offspring will be weak. However, this is not necessarily a bad thing. The rule of the old covens had wisdom in it that strength should come with time. And then again, there is the old truth: you might make titans or imbeciles, no one knows why or how.

"Whatever will happen will happen, but choose your companions with care. Choose them because you like to look at them and you like the sound of their voices, and they have profound secrets in them that you wish to know. In other words, choose them because you love them. Otherwise you will not be able to bear their company for very long."

"I understand," I said. "Make them in love."

"Exactly, make them in love. And make certain they have had some lifetime before you make them; and never never make one as young as Armand. That is the worst crime I have ever committed against my own kind, the taking of the young boy child Armand."

"But you didn't know the Children of Darkness would come when they did, and separate him from you."

"No. But still, I should have waited. It was loneliness that drove me to it. And Armand's helplessness, that his mortal life was so completely in my hands. Remember, beware of that power, and the power you have over those who are dying. Loneliness in us, and that sense of power, can be as strong as the thirst for blood. If there were not an Enkil there might be no Akasha, and if there were not an Akasha, then there would be no Enkil."

"Yes. And from everything you said, it seems Enkil covets Akasha. That Akasha is the one who now and then . . ."

"Yes, that's true." His face became very somber suddenly, and his eyes had a confidential look in them as if we were whispering to each other and fearful another might hear. He waited for a moment as if thinking what to say. "Who knows what Akasha might do if there were no Enkil to hold her?" he whispered. "And why do I pretend that he can't hear this even when I think it? Why do I whisper? He can destroy me anytime that he likes. Maybe Akasha is the only thing keeping him from it. But then what would become of them if he did away with me?"

"Why did they let themselves be burnt by the sun?" I asked.

"How can we know? Perhaps they knew it wouldn't hurt them. It would only hurt and punish those who had done it to them. Perhaps in the state they live in they are slow to realize what is going on outside them. And they did not have time to gather their forces, to wake from their dreams and save themselves. Maybe their movements after it happened—the movements of Akasha I witnessed—were only possible because they had been awakened by the sun. And now they sleep again with their eyes open. And they dream again. And they do not even drink."

"What did you mean . . . if I *choose* to drink their blood?" I asked. "How could I not choose?"

"That is something we have to think on, both of us," he said. "And there is always the possibility that they won't allow you to drink."

I shuddered thinking of one of those arms striking out at me, knocking me twenty feet across the chapel, or perhaps right through the stone floor itself.

"She told you her name, Lestat," he said. "I think she will let you drink. But if you take her blood, then you will be even more resilient than you are now. A few droplets will strengthen you, but if she gives you more than that, a full measure, hardly any force on earth can destroy you after that. You have to be certain you want it."

"Why wouldn't I want it?" I said.

"Do you want to be burnt to a cinder and live on in agony? Do you want to be slashed with knives a thousand times over, or shot through and through with guns, and yet live on, a shredded husk that cannot fend for itself? Believe me, Lestat, that can be a terrible thing. You could suffer the sun even, and live through it, burnt beyond recognition, wishing as the old gods did in Egypt that they had died."

"But won't I heal faster?"

"Not necessarily. Not without another infusion of her blood in the wounded state. Time with its constant measure of human victims or the blood of old ones—these are the restoratives. But you may wish you had died. Think on this. Take your time."

"What would you do if you were I?"

"I would drink from Those Who Must Be Kept, of course. I would drink to be stronger, more nearly immortal. I would beseech Akasha on my knees to allow it, and then I would go into her arms. But it's easy to say these things. She has never struck out at me. She has never forbidden me, and I know that I want to live forever. I would endure the fire again. I would endure the sun. And all manner of suffering in order to go on. You may not be so sure that eternity is what you want."

"I want it," I said. "I could pretend to think about it, pretend to be clever and wise as I weigh it. But what the hell? I wouldn't fool you, would I? You knew what I would say."

He smiled.

"Then before you leave we will go into the chapel and we will ask her, humbly, and we will see what she says."

"And for now, more answers?" I asked.

He gestured for me to ask.

"I've seen ghosts," I said. "Seen the pesty demons you described. I've seen them possess mortals and dwellings."

"I know no more than you do. Most ghosts seem to be mere apparitions without knowledge that they are being watched. I have never spoken to a ghost nor been addressed by one. As for the pesty demons, what can I add to Enkil's ancient explanation, that they rage because they do not have bodies. But there are other immortals that are more interesting."

"What are they?"

"There are at least two in Europe who do not and have never drunk blood. They can walk in the daylight as well as in the dark, and they have bodies and they are very strong. They look exactly like men. There was one in ancient Egypt, known as Ramses the Damned to the Egyptian court, though he was hardly damned as far as I can tell. His name was taken off all the royal monuments after he vanished. You know the Egyptians used to do that, obliterate the name as they sought to kill the being. And I don't know what happened to him. The old scrolls didn't tell."

"Armand spoke of him," I said. "Armand told of legends, that Ramses was an ancient vampire."

"He is not. But I didn't believe what I read of him till I'd seen the others with my own eyes. And again, I have not communicated with them. I have only seen them, and they were terrified of me and fled. I fear them because they walk in the sun. And they are powerful and bloodless and who knows what they might do? But you may live centuries and never see them."

"But how old are they? How long has it been?"

"They are very old, probably as old as I am. I can't tell. They live as wealthy, powerful men. And possibly there are more of them, they may have some way of propagating themselves, I'm not sure. Pandora said once that there was a woman too. But then Pandora and I couldn't agree upon anything about them. Pandora said they had been what we were, and they were ancient, and had ceased to drink as the Mother and the Father have ceased to drink. I don't think they were ever what we are. They are something else without blood. They don't reflect light as we do. They absorb it. They are just a shade darker than mortals. And they are dense, and strong. You may never see them, but I tell you to warn you. You must never let them know where you lie. They can be more dangerous than humans."

"But are humans really dangerous? I've found them so easy to deceive."

"Of course they're dangerous. Humans could wipe us out if they ever really understood about us. They could hunt us by day. Don't ever underestimate that single advantage. Again, the rules of the old covens have their wisdom. Never, never tell mortals about us. Never tell a mortal where you lie or where any vampire lies. It is absolute folly to think you can control mortals."

I nodded, though it was very hard for me to fear mortals. I never had.

"Even the vampire theater in Paris," he cautioned, "does not flaunt the simplest truths about us. It plays with folklore and illusions. Its audience is completely fooled."

I realized this was true. And that even in her letters to me Eleni always disguised her meanings and never used our full names.

And something about this secrecy oppressed me as it always had.

But I was racking my brain, trying to discover if I'd ever seen the bloodless things . . . The truth was, I might have mistaken them for rogue vampires.

"There is one other thing I should tell you about supernatural beings," Marius said.

"What is it?"

"I am not certain of this, but I'll tell you what I think. I suspect that when we are burnt—when we are destroyed utterly—that we can come back again in another form. I don't speak of man now, of human reincarnation. I know nothing of the destiny of human souls. But we do live forever and I think we come back."

"What makes you say this?" I couldn't help but think of Nicolas.

"The same thing that makes mortals talk of reincarnation. There are those who claim to remember other lives. They come to us as mortals, claiming to know all about us, to have been one of us, and asking to be given the Dark Gift again. Pandora was one of these. She knew many things, and there was no explanation for her knowledge, except perhaps that she imagined it, or drew it, without realizing it, out of my mind. That's a real possibility, that they are merely mortals with hearing that allows them to receive our undirected thoughts.

"Whatever the case, there are not many of them. If they were vampires, then surely they are only a few of those who have been destroyed. So the others perhaps do not have the strength to come back. Or they do not choose to do so. Who can know? Pandora was convinced she had died when the Mother and the Father had been put in the sun."

"Dear God, they are born again as mortals and they *want* to be vampires again?"

Marius smiled.

"You're young, Lestat, and how you contradict yourself. What do you *really* think it would be like to be mortal again? Think on this when you set eyes on your mortal father."

Silently I conceded the point. But what I had made of mortality in my imagination I didn't really want to lose. I wanted to go on grieving for my lost mortality. And I knew that my love of mortals was all bound up with my not being afraid of them.

Marius looked away, distracted once more. The same perfect attitude of listening. And then his face became attentive to me again.

"Lestat, we should have no more than two or three nights," he said sadly.

"Marius!" I whispered. I bit down on the words that wanted to spill out.

My only consolation was the expression on his face, and it seemed now he had never looked even faintly inhuman.

"You don't know how I want you to stay here," he said. "But life is out there, not here. When we meet again I'll tell you more things, but you have all you need for now. You have to go to Louisiana and see your father to the finish of his life and learn from that what you can. I've seen legions of mortals grow old and die. You've seen none. But believe me, my young friend, I want you desperately to remain with me. You don't know how much. I promise you that I will find you when the time comes."

"But why can't I return to you? Why must you leave here?"

"It's time," he said. "I've ruled too long over these people as it is. I arouse suspicions, and besides, Europeans are coming into these waters. Before I came here I was hidden in the buried city of Pompeii below Vesuvius, and mortals, meddling and digging up those ruins, drove me out. Now it's happening again. I must seek some other refuge, something more remote, and more likely to remain so. And frankly I would never have brought you here if I planned to remain."

"Why not?"

"You know why not. I can't have you or anyone else know the location of Those Who Must Be Kept. And that brings us now to something very important: the promises I must have from you."

"Anything," I said. "But what could you possibly want that I could give?"

"Simply this. *You must never tell others the things that I have told you.* Never tell of Those Who Must Be Kept. Never tell the legends of the old gods. Never tell others that you have seen me."

I nodded gravely. I had expected this, but I knew without even thinking that this might prove very hard indeed.

"If you tell even one part," he said, "another will follow, and with every telling of the secret of Those Who Must Be Kept you increase the danger of their discovery."

"Yes," I said. "But the legends, our origins . . . What about those children that I make? Can't I tell them—"

"No. As I told you, tell part and you will end up telling all. Besides, if these fledglings are children of the Christian god, if they are poisoned as Nicolas was with the Christian notion of Original Sin and guilt, they will only be maddened and disappointed by these old tales. It will all be a horror to them that they cannot accept. Accidents, pagan gods they don't believe in, customs they cannot understand. One has to be ready for this knowledge, meager as it may be. Rather listen hard to their questions and tell them what you must to make them contented. And if you find you cannot lie to them, don't tell them anything at all. Try to make them strong as godless men today are strong. But mark my words, the old legends never. Those are mine and mine alone to tell."

"What will you do to me if I tell them?" I asked.

This startled him. He lost his composure for almost a full second, and then he laughed.

"You are the damnedest creature, Lestat," he murmured. "The point is I can do anything I like to you if you tell. Surely you know that. I could crush you underfoot the way Akasha crushed the Elder. I could set you ablaze with the power of my mind. But I don't want to utter such threats. I want you to come back to me. But I will not have these secrets known. I will not have a band of immortals descend upon me again as they did in Venice. I will not be known to our kind. You must never—deliberately or accidentally—send anyone searching for Those Who Must Be Kept or for Marius. You will never utter my name to others."

"I understand," I said.

"Do you?" he asked. "Or must I threaten you after all? Must I warn you that my vengeance can be terrible? That my punishment would include those to whom you've told the secrets as well as you? Lestat, I have destroyed others of our kind who came in search of me. I have destroyed them simply because they knew the old legends and they knew the name of Marius, and they would never give up the quest."

"I can't bear this," I murmured. "I won't tell anyone, ever, I swear. But I'm afraid of what others can read in my thoughts, naturally. I fear that they might take the images out of my head. Armand could do it. What if—"

"You can conceal the images. You know how. You can throw up other images to confuse them. You can lock your mind. It's a skill you already know. But let's be done with threats and admonitions. I feel love for you."

I didn't respond for a moment. My mind was leaping ahead to all manner of forbidden possibilities. Finally I put it in words:

"Marius, don't you ever have the desire to tell all of it to all of them! I mean, to make it known to the whole world of our kind, and to draw them together?"

"Good God, no, Lestat. Why would I do that?" He seemed genuinely puzzled.

"So that we might possess our legends, might at least ponder the riddles of our history, as men do. So that we might swap our stories and share our power—"

"And combine to use it as the Children of Darkness have done, against men?"

"No . . Not like that."

"Lestat, in eternity, covens are actually rare. Most vampires are distrustful and solitary beings and they do not love others. They have no more than one or two well-chosen companions from time to time, and they guard their hunting grounds and their privacy as I do mine. They wouldn't want to come together, and if they did ever overcome the viciousness and suspicions that divide them, their convocation would end in terrible battles and struggles for supremacy like those revealed to me by Akasha, which happened thousands of years ago. We are evil things finally. We are killers. Better that those who unite on this earth be mortal and that they unite for the good."

I accepted this, ashamed of how it excited me, ashamed of all my weaknesses and all my impulsiveness. Yet another realm of possibilities was already obsessing me.

"And what about to mortals, Marius? Have you never wanted to reveal yourself to them, and tell them the whole story?"

Again, he seemed positively baffled by the notion.

"Have you never wanted the world to know about us, for better or for worse? Has it never seemed preferable to living in secret?"

He lowered his eyes for a moment and rested his chin against his closed hand. For the first time I perceived a communication of images coming from him, and I felt that he allowed me to see them because he was uncertain of his answer. He was remembering with a recall so powerful that it made my powers seem fragile. And what he remembered were the earliest times, when Rome had still ruled the world, and he was still within the range of a normal human lifetime.

"You remember wanting to tell them all," I said. "To make it known, the monstrous secret."

"Perhaps," he said, "in the very beginning, there was some desperate passion to communicate."

"Yes, communicate," I said, cherishing the word. And I remembered that long-ago night on the stage when I had so frightened the Paris audience.

"But that was in the dim beginning," he said slowly, speaking of himself. His eyes were narrow and remote as if he were looking back over all the centuries. "It would be folly, it would be madness. Were humanity ever really convinced, it would destroy us. I don't want to be destroyed. Such dangers and calamities are not interesting to me."

I didn't answer.

"You don't feel the urge yourself to reveal these things," he said to me almost soothingly.

But I do, I thought. I felt his fingers on the back of my hand. I was looking beyond him, back over my brief past—the theater, my fairy-tale fantasies. I felt paralyzed in sadness.

"What you feel is loneliness and monstrousness," he said. "And you're impulsive and defiant."

"True."

"But what would it matter to reveal anything to anyone? No one can forgive. No one can redeem. It's a childish illusion to think so. Reveal yourself and be destroyed, and what have you done? The Savage Garden would swallow your remains in pure vitality and silence. Where is there justice or understanding?"

I nodded.

I felt his hand close on mine. He rose slowly to his feet, and I stood up, reluctantly but compliantly.

"It's late," he said gently. His eyes were soft with compassion. "We've talked enough for now. And I must go down to my people. There's trouble in the nearby village, as I feared there would be. And it will take what time I have until dawn, and then more tomorrow evening. It may well be after midnight tomorrow before we can talk—"

He was distracted again, and he lowered his head and listened.

"Yes, I have to go," he said. And we embraced lightly and very comfortably.

And though I wanted to go with him and see what happened in the village—how he would conduct his affairs there—I wanted just as much to seek my rooms and look at the sea and finally sleep.

"You'll be hungry when you rise," he said. "I'll have a victim for you. Be patient till I come."

"Yes, of course . . ."

"And while you wait for me tomorrow," he said, "do as you like in the house. The old scrolls are in the cases in the library. You may look at them. Wander all the rooms. Only the sanctuary of Those Who Must Be Kept should not be approached. You must not go down the stairs alone."

I nodded.

I wanted to ask him one thing more. When would he hunt? When would he drink? His blood had sustained me for two nights, maybe more. But whose blood sustained him? Had he taken a victim earlier? Would he hunt now? I had a growing suspicion that he no longer needed the blood as much as I did. That, like Those Who Must Be Kept, he had begun to drink less and less. And I wanted desperately to know if this was true.

But he was leaving me. The village was definitely calling him. He went out onto the terrace and then he disappeared. For a moment I thought he had gone to the right or left beyond the doors. Then I came to the doors and saw the terrace was empty. I went to the rail and I looked down and I saw the speck of color that was his frock coat against the rocks far below.

And so we have all this to look forward to, I thought: that we may not need the blood, that our faces will gradually lose all human expression, that we can move objects with the strength of our minds, that we can all but fly. That some night thousands of years hence we may sit in utter silence as Those Who Must Be Kept are sitting now? How often tonight had Marius looked like them? How long did he sit without moving when no one was here?

And what would half a century mean to him, during which time I was to live out that one mortal life far across the sea?

I turned away and went back through the house to the bedchamber I'd been given. And I sat looking at the sea and the sky until the light started to come. When I opened the little hiding place of the sarcophagus, there were fresh flowers there. I put on the golden mask headdress and the gloves and I lay down in the stone coffin, and I could still smell the flowers as I closed my eyes.

The fearful moment was coming. The loss of consciousness. And on the edge of dream, I heard a woman laugh. She laughed lightly and long as though she were very happy and in the midst of conversation, and just before I went into darkness, I saw her white throat as she bent her head back.

15

WHEN I opened my eyes I had an idea. It came full blown to me, and it immediately obsessed me so that I was scarcely conscious of the thirst I felt, of the sting in my veins.

"Vanity," I whispered. But it had an alluring beauty to it, the idea.

No, forget about it. Marius said to stay away from the sanctuary, and besides he will be back at midnight and then you can present the idea to him. And he can . . . what? Sadly shake his head.

I came out in the house and all was as it had been the night before, candles burning, windows open to the soft spectacle of the dying light. It didn't seem possible that I would leave here soon. And that I would never come back to it, that he himself would vacate this extraordinary place.

I felt sorrowful and miserable. And then there was the idea.

Not to do it in his presence, but silently and secretly so that I did not feel foolish, to go all alone.

No. Don't do it. After all, it won't do any good. Nothing will happen when you do it.

But if that's the case, why not do it? Why not do it now?

I made my rounds again, through the library and the galleries and the room full of birds and monkeys, and on into other chambers where I had not been.

But that idea stayed in my head. And the thirst nagged at me, making me just a little more impulsive, a little more restless, a little less able to reflect on all the things Marius had told me and what they might mean as time went on.

He wasn't in the house. That was certain. I had been finally through all the rooms. Where he slept was his secret, and I knew there were ways to get in and out of the house that were his secret as well.

But the door to the stairway down to Those Who Must Be Kept, that I discovered again easily enough. And it wasn't locked.

I stood in the wallpapered salon with its polished furniture looking at the clock. Only seven in the evening, five hours till he came back. Five hours of the thirst burning in me. And the idea . . . The idea.

I didn't really decide to do it. I just turned my back on the clock and started walking back to my room. I knew that hundreds of others before me must have had such ideas. And how well he had described the pride he felt when he thought he could rouse them. That he might make them move.

No. I just want to do it, even if nothing happens, which is exactly how it will go. I just want to go down there alone and do it. It has something to do with Nicki maybe. I don't know. I don't know!

I went into my chamber and in the incandescent light rising from the sea, I unlocked the violin case and I looked at the Stradivarius violin.

Of course I didn't know how to play it, but we are powerful mimics. As Marius said, we have superior concentration and superior skills. And I had seen Nicki do it so often.

I tightened the bow now and rubbed the horsehair with the little piece of resin, as I had seen him do.

Only two nights ago, I couldn't have borne the idea of touching this thing. Hearing it would have been pure pain.

Now I took it out of its case and I carried it through the house, the way I'd carried it to Nicki through the wings of the Theater of the Vampires, and not even thinking of vanity, I rushed faster and faster towards the door to the secret stairs.

It was as if they were drawing me to them, as if I had no will. Marius didn't matter now. Nothing much mattered, except to be going down the narrow damp stone steps faster and faster, past the windows full of sea spray and early evening light.

In fact, my infatuation was getting so strong, so total that I stopped suddenly, wondering if it was originating with me. But that was foolishness. Who could have put it in my head? Those Who Must Be Kept? Now that was real vanity, and besides, did these creatures know what this strange, delicate little wooden instrument was?

It made a sound, did it not, that no one had ever heard in the ancient world, a sound so human and so powerfully affecting that men thought the violin the work of the devil and accused its finest players of being possessed.

I was slightly dizzy, confused.

How had I gotten so far down the steps, and didn't I remember that the door was bolted from inside? Give me another five hundred years and I might be able to open that bolt, but not just now.

Yet I went on down, these thoughts breaking up and disintegrating as fast as they'd come. I was on fire again, and the thirst was making it worse, though the thirst had nothing to do with it.

And when I came round the last turn I saw the doors to the chapel were open wide. The light of the lamps poured out into the stairwell. And the scent of the flowers and incense was suddenly overwhelming and made a knot in my throat.

I drew nearer, holding the violin with both hands to my chest, though why I didn't know. And I saw that the tabernacle doors were open, and there they sat.

Someone had brought them more flowers. Someone had laid out the incense in cakes on golden plates.

And I stopped just inside the chapel, and I looked at their faces and they seemed as before to look directly at me.

White, so white I could not imagine them bronzed, and as hard, it seemed, as the jewels they wore. Snake bracelet around her upper arm. Layered necklace on her breast. Tiniest lip of flesh from his chest covering the top of the clean linen skirt he wore.

Her face was narrower than his face, her nose just a little longer. His eyes were slightly longer, the folds of flesh defining them a little thicker. Their long black hair was very much the same.

I was breathing uneasily. I felt suddenly weak and let the scent of the flowers and the incense fill my lungs.

The light of the lamps danced in a thousand tiny specks of gold in the murals.

I looked down at the violin and tried to remember my idea, and I ran my fingers along the wood and wondered what this thing looked like to them.

In a hushed voice I explained what it was, that I wanted them to hear it, that I didn't really know how to play it but that I was going to try. I wasn't speaking loud enough to hear myself, but surely they could hear it if they chose to listen.

And I lifted the violin to my shoulder, braced it under my chin, and lifted the bow. I closed my eyes and I remembered music, Nicki's music, the way that his body had moved with it and his fingers came down with the pressure of hammers and he let the message travel to his fingers from his soul.

I plunged into it, the music suddenly wailing upwards and rippling down again as my fingers danced. It was a song, all right, I could make a song. The tones were pure and rich as they echoed off the close walls with a resounding volume, creating the wailing beseeching voice that only the violin can make. I went madly on with it, rocking back and forth, forgetting Nicki, forgetting everything but the feel of my fingers stabbing at the soundboard and the realization that I was making this, this was coming out of me, and it plummeted and climbed and overflowed ever louder and louder as I bore down upon it with the frantic sawing of the bow.

I was singing with it, I was humming and then singing loudly, and all the gold of the little room was a blur. And suddenly it seemed my own voice became louder, inexplicably louder, with a pure high note which I knew that I myself could not possibly sing. Yet it was there, this beautiful note, steady and unchanging and growing even louder until it was hurting my ears. I played harder, more frantically, and I heard my own gasps coming, and I knew suddenly that I was not the one making this strange high note!

The blood was going to come out of my ears if the note did not stop. And I wasn't making the note! Without stopping the music, without giving in to the pain that was splitting my head, I looked forward and I saw Akasha had risen and her eyes were very wide and her mouth was a perfect O. The sound was coming from her, she was making it, and she was moving off the steps of the tabernacle towards me with her arms outstretched and the note pierced my eardrums as if it were a blade of steel.

I couldn't see. I heard the violin hit the stone floor. I felt my hands on the sides of my head. I screamed and screamed, but the note absorbed my screaming.

"Stop it! Stop it!" I was roaring. But all the light was there again and she was right in front of me and she was reaching out.

"O God, Marius!" I turned and ran towards the doors. And the doors flew shut against me, knocking my face so hard I fell down on my knees. Under the high shrill continuum of the note I was sobbing,

"Marius, Marius, Marius!"

And turning to see what was about to happen to me, I saw her foot come down on the violin. It popped and splintered under her heel. But the note she sang was dying. The note was fading away.

And I was left in silence, deafness, unable to hear my own screams for Marius which were going on and on, as I scrambled to my feet.

Ringing silence, shimmering silence. She was right in front of me, and her black eyebrows came together delicately, barely creasing her white flesh, her eyes full of torment and questioning and her pale pink lips opened to reveal her fang teeth.

Help me, help me, Marius, help me, I was stammering, unable to hear myself except in the pure abstraction of intention in my mind. And then her arms enclosed me, and she drew me closer, and I felt the hand as Marius had described it, cupping my head gently, very gently, and I felt my teeth against her neck.

I did not hesitate. I did not think about the limbs that were locked around me, that could crush the life out of me in a second. I felt my fangs break through the skin as if through a glacial crust, and the blood came steaming into my mouth.

Oh, yes, yes . . . oh, yes. I had thrown my arm over her left shoulder, I was clinging to her, my living statue, and it didn't matter that she was harder than marble, that was the way it was supposed to be, it was perfect, my Mother, my lover, my powerful one, and the blood was penetrating every pulsing particle of me with the threads of its burning web. But her lips were against my throat. She was kissing me, kissing the artery through which her own blood so violently flowed. Her lips were opening on it, and as I drew upon her blood with all my strength, sucking, and feeling that gush again and again before it spread itself out into me, I felt the unmistakable sensation of her fangs going into my neck.

Out of every zinging vessel my blood was suddenly drawn into her, even as hers was being drawn into me.

I saw it, the shimmering circuit, and more divinely I felt it because nothing else existed but our mouths locked to each other's throats and the relentless pounding path of the blood. There were no dreams, there were no visions, there was just this, *this*—gorgeous and deafening and heated—and nothing mattered, absolutely nothing, except that this never stop. The world of all things that had weight and filled space and interrupted the flow of light was gone.

And yet some horrid noise intruded, something ugly, like the sound of stone cracking, like the sound of stone dragged across the floor. Marius coming. No, Marius, don't come. Go back, don't touch. Don't separate us.

But it wasn't Marius, this awful sound, this intrusion, this sudden disruption of everything, this thing grabbing hold of my hair and tearing me off her so the blood spurted out of my mouth. It was Enkil. And his powerful hands were clamped on the sides of my head.

The blood gushed down my chin. I saw her stricken face! I saw her reach out for him. Her eyes blazed with common anger, her glistening white limbs animate as she grabbed at the hands that held my head. I heard her voice rise out of her, screaming, shrieking, louder than the note she had sung, the blood drooling from the end of her mouth.

The sound took sight as well as sound with it. The darkness swirled, broken into millions of tiny specks. My skull was going to crack.

He was forcing me down on my knees. He was bent over me, and suddenly I saw his face completely and it was as impassive as ever, only the stress of the muscles in his arms evincing true life.

And even through the obliterating sound of her scream I knew the door behind me quaked with Marius's pounding, his shouts almost as loud as her cries.

The blood was coming out of my ears from her screams. I was moving my lips.

The vise of stone clamped to my head suddenly let go. I felt myself hit the floor. I was sprawled out flat, and I felt the cold pressure of his foot on my chest. He would crush my heart in a second, and she, her screams growing ever louder, ever more piercing, was on his back with her arm locked around his neck. I saw her knotted eyebrows, her flying black hair.

But it was Marius I heard through the door talking to him, cutting through the white sound of her screams.

Kill him, Enkil, and I will take her away from you forever, and she will help me to do it! I swear!

Sudden silence. Deafness again. The warmth of blood trickling down the sides of my neck.

She stepped aside and she looked straight forward and the doors flew open, smacking the side of the narrow stone passage, and Marius was suddenly standing above me with his hands on Enkil's shoulders and Enkil seemed unable to move.

The foot slid down, bruising my stomach, and then it was gone. And Marius was speaking words I could hear only as thoughts: *Get out, Lestat. Run.*

I struggled to sit up, and I saw him driving them both slowly back towards the tabernacle, and I saw them both staring not forward, but at him, Akasha clutching Enkil's arm, and I saw their faces blank again, but for the first time the blankness seemed listless and not the mask of curiosity but the mask of death.

"Lestat, run!" he said again, without turning. And I obeyed.

16

I WAS at the farthest corner of the terrace when Marius finally came into the lighted salon. There was a heat in all my veins still that breathed as if it had its own life. And I could see far beyond the dim hulking shapes of the islands. I could hear the progress of a ship along a distant coast. But all I kept thinking was that if Enkil came at me again, I could jump over this railing. I could get into the sea and swim. I kept feeling his hands on the sides of my head, his foot on my chest.

I stood against the stone railing, shivering, and there was blood all over my hands still from the bruises on my face which had already completely healed.

"I'm sorry. I'm sorry I did it," I said as soon as Marius came out of the salon. "I don't know why I did it. I shouldn't have done it. I'm sorry. I'm sorry, I swear it, I'm sorry, Marius. I'll never never do anything you tell me not to do again."

He stood with his arms folded looking at me. He was glowering.

"Lestat, what did I say last night?" he asked. "You are the *damnedest creature*!"

"Marius, forgive me. Please forgive me. I didn't think anything would happen. I was sure nothing would happen . . ."

He gestured for me to be quiet, for us to go down onto the rocks together, and he slipped over the railing and went first. I came behind him, vaguely delighted with the ease of it, but too dazed still to care about things like that. Her presence was all over me like a fragrance, only she had had no fragrance, except that of the incense and the flowers that must have somehow managed to permeate her hard white skin. How strangely fragile she had seemed in spite of that hardness.

We went down over the slippery boulders until we reached the white beach and we walked together in silence, looking out over the snow-white froth that leapt against the rocks or streaked towards us on the smooth hard-packed white sand. The wind roared in my ears, and I felt the sense of solitude this always creates in me, the roaring wind that blots out all other sensations as well as sound.

And I was getting calmer and calmer, and more and more agitated and miserable at the same time.

Marius had slipped his arm around me the way Gabrielle used to do it, and I paid no attention to where we were going, quite surprised when I saw we'd come to a small inlet of the water where a longboat lay at anchor with only a single pair of oars.

When we stopped I said again, "I'm sorry I did it! I swear I am. I didn't believe . . ."

"Don't tell me you regret it," Marius said calmly. "You are not at all sorry that it occurred, and that you were the cause of it, now that you are safe, and not crushed like an eggshell on the chapel floor."

"Oh, but that's not the point," I said. I started crying. I took out my handkerchief, grand accoutrement of an eighteenth-century gentleman, and wiped the blood off my face. I could feel her holding me, feel her blood, feel his hands. The whole thing commenced to reenact itself. If Marius hadn't come in time . . .

"But what did happen, Marius? What did you see?"

"I wish we could get beyond his hearing," Marius said wearily. "It's madness to speak or think anything that could disturb him any further. I have to let him lapse back."

And now he seemed truly furious and he turned his back on me.

But how could I not think about it? I wished I could open my head and pull the thoughts out of it. They were rocketing through me, like her blood. In her body was locked a mind still, an appetite, a blazing spiritual core whose heat had moved through me like liquid lightning, and without question Enkil had a deathhold upon her! I loathed him. I wanted to destroy him. And my brain seized upon all sorts of mad notions, that somehow he could be destroyed without endangering us as long as she remained!

But that made little sense. Hadn't the demons entered first into him? But what if that wasn't so . . .

"Stop it, young one!" Marius flashed.

I went to crying again. I felt of my neck where she had touched it, and licked my lips and tasted her blood again. I looked at the scattered stars above and even these benign and eternal things seemed menacing and senseless and I felt a scream swelling dangerously in my throat.

The effects of her blood were waning already. The first clear vision was clouded, and my limbs were once again my limbs. They might be stronger, yes, but the magic was dying. The magic had left only something stronger than memory of the circuit of the blood through us both.

"Marius, what happened!" I said, shouting over the wind. "Don't be angry with me, don't turn away from me. I can't . . ."

"Shhh, Lestat," he said. He came back and took me by the arm. "Don't worry about my anger," he said. "It's unimportant, and it is not directed at you. Give me a little more time to collect myself."

"But did you see what happened between her and me?"

He was looking out to sea. The water looked perfectly black and the foam perfectly white.

"Yes, I saw," he said.

"I took the violin and I wanted to play it for them, I was thinking—"

"Yes, I know, of course . . ."

"—that music would affect them, especially that music, that strange, unnatural-sounding music, you know how a violin . . ."

"Yes—"

"Marius, she gave me . . . she . . . and she took—"

"I know."

"And he keeps her there! He keeps her prisoner!"

"Lestat, I beg you . . ." He was smiling wearily, sadly.

Imprison him, Marius, the way that they did, and let her go!

"You dream, my child," he said. "You dream."

He turned and he left me, gesturing for me to leave him alone. He went down to the wet beach and let the water lap at him as he walked back and forth.

I tried to get calm again. It seemed unreal to me that I had ever been any place but this island, that the world of mortals was out there, that the strange tragedy and menace of Those Who Must Be Kept was unknown beyond these wet and shining cliffs.

Finally Marius made his way back.

"Listen to me," he said. "Straight west is an island that is not under my protection and there is an old Greek city on the northern tip of it where the seamen's taverns stay open all night. Go there now in the boat. Hunt and forget what has happened here. Assess the new powers you might have from her. But try not to think of her or him. Above all try not to plot against him. Before dawn, come back to the house. It won't be difficult. You'll find a dozen open doors and windows. Do as I say, now, for me."

I bowed my head. It was the one thing under heaven that could distract me, that could wipe out any noble or enervating thoughts. Human blood and human struggle and human death.

And without protest, I made my way out through the shallow water to the boat.

In the early hours I looked at my reflection in a fragment of metallic mirror pinned to the wall of a seaman's filthy bedroom in a little inn. I saw myself in my brocade coat and white lace, and my face warm from killing, and the dead man sprawled behind me across the table. He still held the knife with which he'd tried to cut my throat. And there was the bottle of wine with the drug in it which I'd kept refusing, with playful protestations, until he'd lost his temper and tried the last resort. His companion lay dead on the bed.

I looked at the young blond-haired rake in the mirror.

"Well, if it isn't the vampire Lestat," I said.

But all the blood in the world couldn't stop the horrors from coming over me when I went to my rest.

I couldn't stop thinking of her, wondering if it was her laugh I had heard in my sleep the night before. And I wondered that she had told me nothing in the blood, until I closed my eyes and quite suddenly things came back to me, of course, wonderful things, incoherent as they were magical. She and I were walking down a hallway together—not here but in a place I knew. I think it was a palace in Germany where Haydn wrote his music—and she spoke casually as she had a thousand times to me. *But tell me about all this, what do the people believe, what turns the wheels inside of them, what are these marvelous inventions . . .* She wore a fashionable black hat with a great white plume on its broad brim and a white veil tied round the top of it and under her chin, and her face was merely beginning, merely young.

* * *

WHEN I opened my eyes, I knew Marius was waiting for me. I came out into the chamber and saw him standing by the empty violin case, with his back to the open window over the sea.

"You have to go now, my young one," he said sadly. "I had hoped for more time, but that is impossible. The boat is waiting to take you away."

"Because of what I did . . ." I said miserably. So I was being cast out.

"He's destroyed the things in the chapel," Marius said, but his voice was asking for calm. He put his arm around my shoulder, and he took my valise in his other hand. We went towards the door. "I want you to go now because it is the only thing that will quiet him, and I want you to remember not his anger, but everything that I told you, and to be confident that we will meet again as we said."

"But are you afraid of him, Marius?"

"Oh, no, Lestat. Don't carry this worry away with you. He has done little things like this before, now and then. He does not know what he does, really. I am convinced of that. He only knows that someone stepped between him and Akasha. Time is all that is required for him to lapse back."

There it was, that phrase again, "lapse back."

"And she sits as if she never moved, doesn't she?" I asked.

"I want you away now so that you don't provoke him," Marius said, leading me out of the house and towards the cliffside stairs. He continued speaking:

"Whatever ability we creatures have to move objects mentally, to ignite them, to do any real harm by the power of the mind does not extend very far from the physical spot where we stand. So I want you gone from here tonight and on your way to America. All the sooner to return to me when he is no longer agitated and no longer remembers, and I will have forgotten nothing and will be waiting for you."

I saw the galley in the harbor below when we reached the edge of the cliff. The stairs looked impossible, but they weren't impossible. What was impossible was that I was leaving Marius and this island right now.

"You needn't come down with me," I said, taking the valise from him. I was trying not to sound bitter and crestfallen. After all, I had caused this. "I would rather not weep in front of others. Leave me here."

"I wish we had had a few more nights together," he said, "for us to consider in quiet what took place. But my love goes with you. And try to remember the things I've told you. When we meet again we'll have much to say to each other—" He paused.

"What is it, Marius?"

"Tell me truthfully," he asked. "Are you sorry that I came for you in Cairo, sorry that I brought you here?"

"How could I be?" I asked. "I'm only sorry that I'm going. What if I can't find you again or you can't find me?"

"When the time is right, I'll find you," he said. "And always remember: you have the power to call to me, as you did before. When I hear that call, I can bridge distances to answer that I could never bridge on my own. If the time is right, I will answer. Of that you can be sure."

I nodded. There was too much to say and I didn't speak a word.

We embraced for a long moment, and then I turned and slowly started my descent, knowing he would understand why I didn't look back.

17

I DID not know how much I wanted "the world" until my ship finally made its way up the murky Bayou St. Jean towards the city of New Orleans, and I saw the black ragged line of the swamp against the luminous sky.

The fact that none of our kind had ever penetrated this wilderness excited me and humbled me at the same time.

Before the sun rose on that first morning, I'd fallen in love with the low and damp country, as I had with the dry heat of Egypt, and as time passed I came to love it more than any spot on the globe.

Here the scents were so strong you smelled the raw green of the leaves as well as the pink and yellow blossoms. And the great brown river, surging past the miserable little Place d'Armes and its tiny cathedral, threw into eclipse every other fabled river I'd ever seen.

Unnoticed and unchallenged, I explored the ramshackle little colony with its muddy streets and gunwale sidewalks and dirty Spanish soldiers lounging about the calaboose. I lost myself in the dangerous waterfront shacks full of gambling and brawling flatboatmen and lovely dark-skinned Caribbean women, wandering out again to glimpse the silent flash of lightning, hear the dim roar of the thunder, feel the silky warmth of the summer rain.

The low-slung roofs of the little cottages gleamed under the moon. Light skittered on the iron gates of the fine Spanish town houses. It flickered behind real lace curtains hung inside freshly washed glass doors. I walked among the crude little bungalows that spread out to the ramparts, peeping through windows at gilded furniture and enameled bits of wealth and civilization that in this barbaric place seemed priceless and fastidious and even sad.

Now and then through the mire there came a vision: a real French gentleman done up in snow-white wig and fancy frock coat, his wife in panniers, and a black slave carrying clean slippers for the two high above the flowing mud.

I knew that I had come to the most forsaken outpost of the Savage Garden, and that this was my country and I would remain in New Orleans, if New Orleans could only manage to remain. Whatever I suffered should be lessened in this lawless place, whatever I craved should give me more pleasure once I had it in my grasp.

And there were moments on that first night in this fetid little paradise when I prayed that in spite of all my secret power, I was somehow kin to every mortal man. Maybe I was not the exotic outcast that I imagined, but merely the dim magnification of every human soul.

Old truths and ancient magic, revolution and invention, all conspire to distract us from the passion that in one way or another defeats us all.

And weary finally of this complexity, we dream of that long-ago time when we sat upon our mother's knee and each kiss was the perfect consummation of desire. What can we do but reach for the embrace that must now contain both heaven and hell: our doom again and again and again.

Epilogue

Interview with the Vampire

I

And so I came to the end of The Early Education and Adventures of the Vampire Lestat, the tale that I set out to tell. You have the account of Old World magic and mystery which I have chosen, despite all prohibitions and injunctions, to pass on.

But my story isn't finished, no matter how reluctant I might be to continue it. And I must consider, at least briefly, the painful events that led to my decision to go down into the earth in 1929.

That was a hundred and forty years after I left Marius's island. And I never set eyes upon Marius again. Gabrielle also remained completely lost to me. She'd vanished that night in Cairo never to be heard from by anyone mortal or immortal that I was ever to know.

And when I made my grave in the twentieth century, I was alone and weary and badly wounded in body and soul.

I'd lived out my "one lifetime" as Marius advised me to do. But I couldn't blame Marius for the way in which I'd lived it, and the hideous mistakes I'd made.

Sheer will had shaped my experience more than any other human characteristic. And advice and predictions notwithstanding, I courted tragedy and disaster as I have always done. Yet I had my rewards, I can't deny that. For almost seventy years I had my fledgling vampires Louis and Claudia, two of the most splendid immortals who ever walked the earth, and I had them on my terms.

Shortly after reaching the colony, I fell fatally in love with Louis, a young dark-haired bourgeois planter, graceful of speech and fastidious of manner, who seemed in his cynicism and self-destructiveness the very twin of Nicolas.

He had Nicki's grim intensity, his rebelliousness, his tortured capacity to believe and not to believe, and finally to despair.

Yet Louis gained a hold over me far more powerful than Nicolas had ever had. Even in his cruelest moments, Louis touched the tenderness in me, seducing me with his staggering dependence, his infatuation with my every gesture and every spoken word.

And his naiveté conquered me always, his strange bourgeois faith that God was still God even if he turned his back on us, that damnation and salvation established the boundaries of a small and hopeless world.

Louis was a sufferer, a thing that loved mortals even more than I did. And I wonder sometimes if I didn't look to Louis to punish me for what had happened to Nicki, if I didn't create Louis to be my conscience and to mete out year in and year out the penance I felt I deserved.

But I loved him, plain and simple. And it was out of the desperation to keep him, to bind him closer to me at the most precarious of moments, that I committed the most selfish and impulsive act of my entire life among the living dead. It was the crime that was to be my undoing: the creation with Louis and for Louis of Claudia, a stunningly beautiful vampire child.

Her body wasn't six years old when I took her, and though she would have died if I hadn't done it (just as Louis would have died if I hadn't taken him also), this was a challenge to the gods for which Claudia and I would both pay.

But this is the tale that was told by Louis in *Interview with the Vampire*, which for all its contradictions and terrible misunderstandings manages to capture the atmosphere in which Claudia and Louis and I came together and stayed together for sixty-five years.

During that time, we were nonpareils of our species, a silk- and velvet-clad trio of deadly hunters, glorying in our secret and in the swelling city of New Orleans that harbored us in luxury and supplied us endlessly with fresh victims.

And though Louis did not know it when he wrote his chronicle, sixty-five years is a phenomenal time for any bond in our world.

As for the lies he told, the mistakes he made, well, I forgive him his excess of imagination, his bitterness, and his vanity, which was, after all, never very great. I never revealed to him half my powers, and with reason, because he shrank in guilt and self-loathing from using even half of his own.

Even his unusual beauty and unfailing charm were something of a secret to him. When you read his statement that I made him a vampire because I coveted his plantation house, you can write that off to modesty more easily than stupidity, I suppose.

As for his belief that I was a peasant, well that was understandable. He was, after all, a discriminating and inhibited child of the middle class, aspiring as all the colonial planters did to be a genuine aristocrat though he had never met one, and I came from a long line of feudal lords who licked their fingers and threw the bones over their shoulders to the dogs as they dined.

When he says I played with innocent strangers, befriending them and then killing them, how was he to know that I hunted almost exclusively among the gamblers, the thieves, and the killers, being more faithful to my unspoken vow to kill the evildoer than even I had hoped I would be? (The young Freniere, for example, a planter whom Louis romanticizes hopelessly in his text, was in fact a wanton killer and a cheater at cards on the verge of signing over his family's plantation for debt when I struck him down. The whores I feasted upon in front of Louis once, to spite him, had drugged and robbed many a seaman who was never seen alive again.)

But little things like this don't really matter. He told the tale as he believed it.

And in a real way, Louis was always the sum of his flaws, the most beguilingly human fiend I have ever known. Even Marius could not have imagined such a compassionate and contemplative creature, always the gentleman, even teaching Claudia the proper use of table silver when she, bless her little black heart, had not the slightest need ever to touch a knife or a fork.

His blindness to the motives or the suffering of others was as much a part of his charm as his soft unkempt black hair or the eternally troubled expression in his green eyes.

And why should I bother to tell of the times he came to me in wretched anxiety, begging me never to leave him, of the times we walked together and talked together, acted Shakespeare together for Claudia's amusement, or went arm in arm to hunt the riverfront taverns or to waltz with the dark-skinned beauties of the celebrated quadroon balls?

Read between the lines.

I betrayed him when I created him, that is the significant thing. Just as I betrayed Claudia. And I forgive the nonsense he wrote, because he told the truth about the eerie contentment he and Claudia and I shared and had no right to share in those long nineteenth-century decades when the peacock colors of the ancient regime died out and the lovely music of Mozart and Haydn gave way to the bombast of Beethoven, which could sound at times too remarkably like the clang of my imaginary Hell's Bells.

I had what I wanted, what I had always wanted. I had *them.* And I could now and then forget Gabrielle and forget Nicki, and even forget Marius and the blank staring face of Akasha, or the icy touch of her hand or the heat of her blood.

But I had always wanted many things. What accounted for the duration of the life he described in *Interview with the Vampire*? Why did we last so long?

All during the nineteenth century, vampires were "discovered" by the literary writers of Europe. Lord Ruthven, the creation of Dr. Polidori, gave way to Sir Francis Varney in the penny dreadfuls, and later came Sheridan Le Fanu's magnificent and sensuous Countess Carmilla Karnstein, and finally the big ape of the vampires, the hirsute Slav Count Dracula, who though he can turn himself into a bat or dematerialize at will, nevertheless crawls down the wall of his castle in the manner of a lizard apparently for fun—all of these creations and many like them feeding the insatiable appetite for "gothic and fantastical tales."

We were the essence of that nineteenth-century conception—aristocratically aloof, unfailingly elegant, and invariably merciless, and cleaving to each other in a land ripe for, but untroubled by, others of our kind.

Maybe we had found the perfect moment in history, the perfect balance between the monstrous and the human, the time when that "vampiric romance" born in my imagination amid the colorful brocades of the ancient regime should find its greatest enhancement in the flowing black cape, the black top hat, and the little girl's luminous curls spilling down from their violet ribbon to the puffed sleeves of her diaphanous silk dress.

But what had I done to Claudia? And when would I have to pay for that? How long was she content to be the mystery that bound Louis and me so tightly together, the muse of our moonlit hours, the one object of devotion common to us both?

Was it inevitable that she who would never have a woman's form would strike out at the demon father who condemned her to the body of a little china doll?

I should have listened to Marius's warning. I should have stopped for one moment to reflect on it as I stood on the edge of that grand and intoxicating experiment: to make a vampire of "the least of these." I should have taken a deep breath.

But you know, it was like playing the violin for Akasha. I *wanted* to do it. I wanted to see what would happen, I mean, with a beautiful little girl like that!

Oh, Lestat, you deserve everything that ever happened to you. You'd better not die. You might actually go to hell.

But why was it that for purely selfish reasons, I didn't listen to some of the advice given me? Why didn't I learn from any of them—Gabrielle, Armand, Marius? But then, I never have listened to anyone, really. Somehow or other, I never can.

And I cannot say even now that I regret Claudia, that I wish I had never seen her, nor held her, nor whispered secrets to her, nor heard her laughter echoing through the shadowy gaslighted rooms of that all too human town house in which we moved amid the lacquered furniture and the darkening oil paintings and the brass flowerpots as living beings should. Claudia was my dark child, my love, evil of my evil. Claudia broke my heart.

And on a warm sultry night in the spring of the year 1860, she rose up to settle the score. She enticed me, she trapped me, and she plunged a knife over and over again into my drugged and poisoned body, until almost every drop of the vampiric blood gushed out of me before my wounds had the precious few seconds in which to heal.

I don't blame her. It was the sort of thing I might have done myself.

And those delirious moments will never be forgotten by me, never consigned to some unexplored compartment of the mind. It was her cunning and her will that laid me low as surely as the blade that slashed my throat and divided my heart. I will think on those moments every night for as long as I go on, and of the chasm that opened under me, the plunge into mortal death that was nearly mine. Claudia gave me that.

But as the blood flowed, taking with it all power to see or hear or move finally, my thoughts traveled back and back, way beyond the creation of the doomed vampire family in their paradise of wallpaper and lace curtains, to the dimly envisioned groves of mythical lands where the old Dionysian god of the wood had felt again and again his flesh torn, his blood spilled.

If there was not meaning, at least there was the luster of congruence, the stunning repetition of the *same old theme.*

And the god dies. And the god rises. But this time no one is redeemed.

With the blood of Akasha, Marius had said to me, you will survive disasters that would destroy others of our kind.

Later, abandoned in the stench and darkness of the swamp, I felt the thirst define my proportions, I felt the thirst propel me, I felt my jaws open in the rank water and my fangs seek the warm-blooded things that could put my feet on the long road back.

And three nights later, when again I had been beaten and my children left me once and for all in the blazing inferno of our town house, it was the blood of the old ones, Magnus and Marius and Akasha, that sustained me as I crawled away from the flames.

But without more of that healing blood, without a fresh infusion, I was left at the mercy of time to heal my wounds.

And what Louis could not describe in his story is what happened to me after, how for years I hunted on the edge of the human herd, a hideous and crippled monster, who could strike down only the very young or infirm. In constant danger from my victims, I became the very antithesis of the romantic demon, bringing terror rather than rapture, resembling nothing so much as the old revenants of les Innocents in their filth and rags.

The wounds I'd suffered affected my very spirit, my capacity to reason. And what I saw in the mirror every time I dared to look further shriveled my soul.

Yet not once in all this time did I call out to Marius, did I try to reach him over the miles. I could not beg for his healing blood. Better suffer purgatory for a century than Marius's condemnation. Better suffer the worst loneliness, the worst anguish, than discover that he knew everything I'd done and had long ago turned his back on me.

As for Gabrielle, who would have forgiven me anything, whose blood was powerful enough at least to hasten my recovery, I did not know even where to look.

When I had recovered sufficiently to make the long voyage to Europe, I turned to the only one that I could turn to: Armand. Armand who lived still on the land I'd given him, in the very tower where I'd been made by Magnus, Armand who still commanded the thriving coven of the Theater of the Vampires in the boulevard du Temple, which still belonged to me. After all, I owed Armand no explanations. And did he not owe something to me?

IT WAS a shock to see him when he came to answer the knock on his door.

He looked like a young man out of the novels of Dickens in his somber and sleekly tailored black frock coat, all the Renaissance curls clipped away. His eternally youthful face was stamped with the innocence of a David Copperfield and the pride of a Steerforth—anything but the true nature of the spirit within.

For one moment a brilliant light burned in him as he looked at me. Then he stared slowly at the scars that covered my face and hands, and he said softly and almost compassionately:

"Come in, Lestat."

He took my hand. And we walked together through the house he had built at the foot of Magnus's tower, a dark and dreary place fit for all the Byronic horrors of this strange age.

"You know, the rumor is that you met the end somewhere in Egypt, or the Far East," he said quickly in everyday French with an animation I'd never seen in him before. He was skilled now at pretending to be a living being. "You went with the old century, and no one has heard of you since."

"And Gabrielle?" I demanded immediately, wondering that I had not blurted it out at the door.

"No one has ever seen her or heard of her since you left Paris," he said.

Once again his eyes moved over me caressingly. And there was thinly veiled excitement in him, a fever that I could feel like the warmth of the nearby fire. I knew he was trying to read my thoughts.

"What's happened to you?" he asked.

My scars were puzzling him. They were too numerous, too intricate, scars of an attack that should have meant death. I felt a sudden panic that in my confusion I'd reveal everything to him, the things that Marius had long ago forbidden me to tell.

But it was the story of Louis and Claudia that came rushing out, in stammering and half truths, *sans* one salient fact: that Claudia had been only . . . a child.

I told briefly of the years in Louisiana, of how they had finally risen against me just as he had predicted my children might. I conceded everything to him, without guile or pride, explaining that it was his blood I needed now. Pain and pain and pain, to lay it out for him, to feel him considering it. To say, yes, you were right. It isn't the whole story. But in the main, you were right.

Was it sadness I saw in his face then? Surely it wasn't triumph. Unobtrusively, he watched my trembling hands as I gestured. He waited patiently when I faltered, couldn't find the right words.

A small infusion of his blood would hasten my healing, I whispered. A small infusion would clear my mind. I tried not to be lofty or righteous when I reminded him that I had given him this tower, and the gold he'd used to build his house, that I still owned the Theater of the Vampires, that surely he could do this little thing, this intimate thing, for me now. There was an ugly naiveté to the words I spoke to him, addled as I was, and weak and thirsting and afraid. The blaze of the fire made me anxious. The light on the dark grain of the woodwork of these stuffy rooms made imagined faces appear and disappear.

"I don't want to stay in Paris," I said. "I don't want to trouble you or the coven at the theater. I am asking this small thing. I am asking . . ." It seemed my courage and the words had run out.

A long moment passed:

"Tell me again about this Louis," he said.

The tears rose to my eyes disgracefully. I repeated some foolish phrases about Louis's indestructible humanity, his understanding of things that other immortals couldn't grasp. Carelessly I whispered things from the heart. It wasn't Louis who had attacked me. It was the woman, Claudia . . .

I saw something in him quicken. A faint blush came to his cheeks.

"They have been seen here in Paris," he said softly. "And she is no woman, this creature. She is a vampire child."

I can't remember what followed. Maybe I tried to explain the blunder. Maybe I admitted there was no accounting for what I'd done. Maybe I brought us round again to the purpose of my visit, to what I needed, what I must have. I remember being utterly humiliated as he led me out of the house and into the waiting carriage, as he told me that I must go with him to the Theater of the Vampires.

"You don't understand," I said. "I can't go there. I will not be seen like this by the others. You must stop this carriage. You must do as I ask."

"No, you have it backwards," he said in the tenderest voice. We were already in the crowded Paris streets. I couldn't see the city I remembered. This was a nightmare, this metropolis of roaring steam trains and giant concrete boulevards. Never had the smoke and filth of the industrial age seemed so hideous as it was here in the City of Light.

I scarcely remember being forced by him out of the carriage and stumbling along the broad pavements as he pushed me towards the theater doors. What was this place, this enormous building? Was this the boulevard du Temple? And then the descent into that hideous cellar full of ugly copies of the bloodiest paintings of Goya and Brueghel and Bosch.

And finally starvation as I lay on the floor of a brick-lined cell, unable even to shout curses at him, the darkness full of the vibrations of the passing omnibuses and tramcars, penetrated again and again by the distant screech of iron wheels.

Sometime in the dark, I discovered a mortal victim there. But the victim was dead. Cold blood, nauseating blood. The worst kind of feeding, lying on that clammy corpse, sucking up what was left.

And then Armand was there, standing motionless in the shadows, immaculate in his white linen and black wool. He spoke in an undertone about Louis and Claudia, that there would be some kind of trial. Down on his knees he came to sit beside me, forgetting for a moment to be human, the boy gentleman sitting in this filthy damp place. "You will declare it before the others, that she did it," he said. And the others, the new ones, came to the door to look at me one by one.

"Get clothing for him," Armand said. His hand was resting on my shoulder. "He must look presentable, our lost lord," he told them. "That was always his way."

They laughed when I begged to speak to Eleni or Félix or Laurent. They did not know those names. Gabrielle—it meant nothing.

And where was Marius? How many countries, rivers, mountains lay between us? Could he hear and see these things?

High above, in the theater, a mortal audience, herded like sheep into a corral, thundered on the wooden staircases, the wooden floors.

I dreamed of getting away from here, getting back to Louisiana, letting time do its inevitable work. I dreamed of the earth again, its cool depths which I'd known so briefly in Cairo. I dreamed of Louis and Claudia and that we were together. Claudia had grown miraculously into a beautiful woman, and she said, laughing, "You see this is what I came to Europe to discover, how to do this!"

And I feared that I was never to be allowed out of here, that I was to be entombed as those starving ones had been under les Innocents, that I had made a fatal mistake. I was stuttering and crying and trying to talk to Armand. And then I realized Armand was not even there. If he had come, he had gone as quickly. I was having delusions.

And the victim, the warm victim—"Give it to me, I beg you!"—and Armand saying:

"You will say what I have told you to say."

It was a mob tribunal of monsters, white-faced demons shouting accusations, Louis pleading desperately, Claudia staring at me mute, and my saying, yes, she was the one who did it, yes, and then cursing Armand as he shoved me back into the shadows, his innocent face radiant as ever.

"But you have done well, Lestat. You have done well."

What had I done? Borne testimony against them that they had broken the old rules? They'd risen against the coven master? What did they know of the old rules? I was screaming for Louis. And then I was drinking blood in the darkness, living blood from another victim, and it wasn't the healing blood, it was just blood.

We were in the carriage again and it was raining. We were riding through the country. And then we went up and up through the old tower to the roof. I had Claudia's bloody yellow dress in my hands. I had seen her in a narrow wet place where she had been burnt by the sun. "Scatter the ashes!" I had said. Yet no one moved to do it. The torn bloody yellow dress lay on the cellar floor. Now I held it in my hands. "They will scatter the ashes, won't they?" I said.

"Didn't you want justice?" Armand asked, his black wool cape close around him in the wind, his face dark with the power of the recent kill.

What did it have to do with justice? Why did I hold this thing, this little dress?

I looked out from Magnus's battlements and I saw the city had come to get me. It had reached out its long arms to embrace the tower, and the air stank of factory smoke.

Armand stood still at the stone railing watching me, and he seemed suddenly as young as Claudia had seemed. *And make sure they have had some lifetime before you make them; and never never make one as young as Armand.* In death she said nothing. She had looked at those around her as if they were giants jabbering in an alien tongue.

Armand's eyes were red.

"Louis—where is he?" I asked. "They didn't kill him. I saw him. He went out into the rain . . ."

"They have gone after him," he answered. "He is already destroyed."

Liar, with the face of a choirboy.

"Stop them, you have to! If there's still time . . ."

He shook his head.

"Why can't you stop them? Why did you do it, the trial, all of it, what do you care what they did to me?"

"It's finished."

Under the roar of the winds came the scream of a steam whistle. Losing the train of thought. Losing it . . . Not wanting to go back. Louis, come back.

"And you don't mean to help me, do you?" Despair.

He leaned forward, and his face transformed itself as it had done years and years ago, as if his rage were melting it from within.

"You, who destroyed all of us, you who took everything. Whatever made you think that I would help you!" He came closer, the face all but collapsed upon itself. "You who put us on the lurid posters in the boulevard du Temple, you who made us the subject of cheap stories and drawing room talk!"

"But I didn't. You know I . . . I swear . . . It wasn't me!"

"You who carried our secrets into the limelight—the fashionable one, the Marquis in the white gloves, the fiend in the velvet cape!"

"You're mad to blame it all on me. You have no right," I insisted, but my voice was faltering so badly I couldn't understand my own words.

And his voice shot out of him like the tongue of a snake.

"We had our Eden under that ancient cemetery," he hissed. "We had our faith and our purpose. And it was you who drove us out of it with a flaming sword. What do we have now! Answer me! Nothing but the love of each other and what can that mean to creatures like us!"

"No, it's not true, it was all happening already. You don't understand anything. You never did."

But he wasn't listening to me. And it didn't matter whether or not he was listening. He was drawing closer, and in a dark flash his hand went out, and my head went back, and I saw the sky and the city of Paris upside down.

I was falling through the air.

And I went down and down past the windows of the tower, until the stone walkway rose up to catch me, and every bone in my body broke within its thin case of preternatural skin.

2

Two years passed before I was strong enough to board a ship for Louisiana. And I was still badly crippled, still scarred. But I had to leave Europe, where no whisper had come to me of my lost Gabrielle or of the great and powerful Marius, who had surely rendered his judgment upon me.

I had to go home. And home was New Orleans, where the warmth was, where the flowers never stopped blooming, where I still owned, through my never ending supply of "coin of the realm," a dozen empty old mansions with rotting white columns and sagging porches round which I could roam.

And I spent the last years of the 1800s in complete seclusion in the old Garden District a block from the Lafayette Cemetery, in the finest of my houses, slumbering beneath towering oaks.

I read by candle or oil lamp all the books I could procure. I might as well have been Gabrielle trapped in her castle bedroom, save there was no furniture here. And the stacks of books reached to the ceiling in one room after another as I went on to the next. Now and then I mustered enough stamina to break into a library or an old bookstore for new volumes, but less and less I went out. I wrote off for periodicals. I hoarded candles and bottles and tin cans of oil.

I do not remember when it became the twentieth century, only that everything was uglier and darker, and the beauty I'd known in the old eighteenth-century days seemed more than ever some kind of fanciful idea. The bourgeois ran the world now upon dreary principles and with a distrust of the sensuality and the excess that the ancient regime had so loved.

But my vision and thoughts were getting ever more clouded. I no longer hunted humans. And a vampire cannot thrive without human blood, human death. I survived by luring the garden animals of the old neighborhood, the pampered dogs and cats. And when they couldn't be got easily, well, then there was always the vermin that I could call to me like the Pied Piper, fat long-tailed gray rats.

One night I forced myself to make the long trek through the quiet streets to a shabby little theater called the Happy Hour near the waterfront slums. I wanted to see the new silent moving pictures. I was wrapped in a greatcoat with a muffler hiding my gaunt face. I wore gloves to hide my skeletal hands. The sight of the daytime sky even in this imperfect film terrified me. But it seemed the dreary tones of black and white were perfect for a colorless age.

I did not think about other immortals. Yet now and then a vampire would appear—some orphaned fledgling who had stumbled on my lair, or a wanderer come in search of the legendary Lestat, begging for secrets, power. Horrid, these intrusions.

Even the timbre of the supernatural voice shattered my nerves, drove me into the farthest corner. Yet no matter how great the pain, I scanned each new mind for knowledge of my Gabrielle. I never discovered any. Nothing to do after that but ignore the poor human victims the fiend would bring in the vain hope of restoring me.

But these encounters were over soon enough. Frightened, aggrieved, shouting curses, the intruder would depart, leaving me in blessed silence.

I'd slip a little deeper away from things, just lying there in the dark.

I wasn't even reading much anymore. And when I did read, I read the *Black Mask* magazine. I read the stories of the ugly nihilistic men of the twentieth century—the gray-clad crooks and the bank robbers and the detectives—and I tried to remember things. But I was so weak. I was so tired.

And then early one evening, Armand came.

I thought at first it was a delusion. He was standing so still in the ruined parlor, looking younger than ever with his short auburn cap of twentieth-century hair and narrow little suit of dark cloth.

It had to be an illusion, this figure coming into the parlor and looking down at me as I lay on my back on the floor by the broken French window reading Sam Spade by the light of the moon. Except for one thing. If I were going to conjure up an imaginary visitor, it certainly wouldn't have been Armand.

I glanced at him and some vague shame passed over me, that I was so ugly, that I was no more than a skeleton with bulging eyes lying there. Then I went back to reading about the Maltese Falcon, my lips moving to speak Sam Spade's lines.

When I looked up again, Armand was still there. It might have been the same night, or the next night, for all I knew.

He was talking about Louis. He had been for some time.

And I realized it was a lie he'd told me in Paris about Louis. Louis had been with Armand all these years. And Louis had been looking for me. Louis had been downtown in the old city looking for me near the town house where we had lived for so long. Louis had come finally to this very place and seen me through the windows.

I tried to imagine it. Louis alive. Louis here, so close, and I had not even known it.

I think I laughed a little. I couldn't keep it clear in my mind that Louis wasn't burnt up. But it was really wonderful that Louis still lived. It was wonderful that there existed still that handsome face, that poignant expression, that tender and faintly imploring voice. My beautiful Louis surviving, instead of dead and gone with Claudia and Nick.

But then maybe he *was* dead. Why should I believe Armand? I went back to reading by the moonlight, wishing the garden out there hadn't gotten so high. A good thing for Armand to do, I told him, would be to go out there and pull down some of those vines, since Armand was so strong. The morning-glory vines and the wisteria were dripping off the upstairs porches and they blocked out the moonlight and then there were the old black oaks that had been here when there was nothing but swamp.

I don't think I actually suggested this to Armand.

And I only vaguely remember Armand letting me know that Louis was leaving him and he, Armand, did not want to go on. Hollow he sounded. Dry. Yet he gathered the moonlight to him as he stood there. And his voice still had its old resonance, its pure undertone of pain.

Poor Armand. And you told me Louis was dead. Go dig a room for yourself under the Lafayette Cemetery. It's just up the street.

No words spoken. No audible laughter, just the secret enjoyment of laughter in me. I remember one clear image of him stranded in the middle of the dirty empty room, looking at the walls of books on all sides. The rain had bled down from leaks in the roof and melded the books together like papier-mâché bricks. And I noticed it distinctly when I saw him standing there against the backdrop of it. And I knew all the rooms in the house were walled in books like this. I hadn't thought about it until that moment, when he started to look at it. I hadn't been in the other rooms in years.

It seems he came back several times after that.

I didn't see him, but I would hear him moving through the garden outside, looking for me with his mind, like a beam of light.

Louis had gone away to the west.

One time, when I was lying in the rubble under the foundations, Armand came to the grating and peered in at me, and I did see him, and he hissed at me and called me ratcatcher.

You've gone mad—you, the one who knew everything, the one who scoffed at us! You're mad and you feed on the rats. You know, in France in the old days what they called your kind, you country lords, they called you harecatchers, because you hunted the hare so you wouldn't starve. And now what are you in this house, a ragged haunt, a ratcatcher. You're mad as the ancient ones who cease to talk sense and jabber at the wind! And yet you hunt the rats as you were born to do.

Again I laughed. I laughed and laughed. I remembered the wolves and I laughed.

"You always make me laugh," I told him. "I would have laughed at you under that cemetery in Paris, except it didn't seem the kind thing to do. And even when you cursed me and blamed me for all the stories about us, that was funny too. If you hadn't been about to throw me off the tower I would have laughed. You always make me laugh."

Delicious it was, the hatred between us, or so I thought. Such unfamiliar excitement, to have him there to ridicule and despise.

Yet suddenly the scene about me began to change. I wasn't lying in the rubble. I was walking through my house. And I wore not the filthy rags that had covered me for years, but a fine black tailcoat and a satin-lined cape. And the house, why, the house was beautiful, and all the books were in their proper place upon shelves. The parquet floor glistened in the light of the chandelier and there was music coming from everywhere, the sound of a Vienna waltz, the rich harmony of violins. With each step I felt powerful again, and light, marvelously light. I could have easily taken the stairs two by two. I could have flown out and up through the darkness, the cloak like black wings.

And then I was moving up in the darkness, and Armand and I stood together on the high roof. Radiant he was, in the same old-fashioned evening clothes, and we were looking over the jungle of dark singing treetops at the distant silver curve of the river and the low heavens where the stars burned through the pearl gray clouds.

I was weeping at the sheer sight of it, at the feel of the damp wind against my face. And Armand stood beside me, with his arm around me. And he was talking of forgiveness and sadness, of wisdom and things learned through pain. "I love you, my dark brother," he whispered.

And the words moved through me like blood itself.

"It wasn't that I wanted vengeance," he whispered. His face was stricken, his heart broken. He said, "But you came to be healed, and you did not want me! A century I had waited, and you did not want me!"

And I knew, as I had all along really, that my restoration was illusion, that I was the same skeleton in rags, of course. And the house was still a ruin. And in the preternatural being who held me was the power that could give me back the sky and the wind.

"Love me and the blood is yours," he said. "This blood that I have never given to another." I felt his lips against my face.

"I can't deceive you," I answered. "I can't love you. What are you to me that I should love you? A dead thing that hungers for the power and the passion of others? The embodiment of thirst itself?"

And in a moment of incalculable power, it was I who struck him and knocked him backwards and off the roof. Absolutely weightless he was, his figure dissolving into the gray night.

But who was defeated? Who fell down and down again through the soft tree branches to the earth where he belonged? Back to the rags and filth beneath the old house. Who lay finally in the rubble, with hands and face against the cool soil?

Yet memory plays its tricks. Maybe I imagined it, his last invitation, and the anguish after. The weeping. I do know that as the months passed he was out there again. I heard him from time to time just walking those old Garden District streets. And I wanted to call to him, to tell him that it was a lie I'd spoken to him, that I did love him. I did.

But it was my time to be at peace with all things. It was my time to starve and to go down into the earth finally, and maybe at last to dream the god's dreams. And how could I tell Armand about the god's dreams?

THERE were no more candles, and there was no more oil for the lamps. Somewhere was a strongbox full of money and jewels and letters to my lawyers and bankers who would continue to administer these properties I owned forever, on account of sums I had left with them.

And so why not go now into the ground, knowing that it would never be disturbed, not in this old city with its crumbling replicas of other centuries. Everything would just go on and on and on.

By the light of the heavens I read more of the story of Sam Spade and the Maltese Falcon. I looked at the date on the magazine and I knew it was 1929, and I thought, oh, that's not possible, is it? And I drank enough from the rats to have the strength to dig really deep.

THE earth was holding me. Living things slithered through its thick and moist clods against my dried flesh. And I thought if I ever do rise again, if I ever see even one small patch of the night sky full of stars, I will never never do terrible things. I will never slay innocents. Even when I hunted the weak, it was the hopeless and the dying I took, I swear it was. I will never never work the Dark Trick again. I will just . . . you know, be the "continual awareness" for no purpose, no purpose at all.

THIRST. Pain as clear as light.

I SAW Marius. I saw him so vividly that I thought, This can't be a dream! And my heart expanded painfully. How splendid Marius looked. He wore a narrow plain modern suit of clothes, but it was made of red velvet, and his white hair was cut short and brushed back from his face. He had a glamour to him, this modern Marius, and a sprightliness that his costume of the old days had apparently concealed.

And he was doing the most remarkable things. He had before him a black camera upon three spider legs, and this he cranked with his right hand as he made motion pictures of mortals in a studio full of incandescent light. How my heart was swelling to see this, the way that he spoke to these mortal beings, told them how they must hold one another, dance, move about. Painted scenery behind them, yes. And outside the windows of his studio were high brick buildings, and the noise of motor coaches in the streets.

No, this isn't a dream, I told myself. It is happening. He is there. And if only I try I can see the city beyond the windows, know where he is. If only I try I can hear the language that he speaks to the young players. "Marius!" I said, but the earth around me devoured the sound.

The scene changed.

Marius rode in the great cage of an elevator down into a cellar. Metal doors screeched and clanked. And into the vast sanctum of Those Who Must Be Kept he went, and how different it all was. No more the Egyptian paintings, the perfume of flowers, the glitter of gold.

The high walls were covered with the dappled colors of the impressionists building out of myriad fragments a vibrant twentieth-century world. Airplanes flew over sunlit cities, towers rose beyond the arch of steel bridges, iron ships drove through silver seas. A universe it was, dissolving the walls on which it was rendered, surrounding the motionless and unchanged figures of Akasha and Enkil.

Marius moved about the chapel. He moved past dark tangled sculptures, telephone devices, typewriting machines upon wooden stands. He set before Those Who Must Be Kept a large and stately gramophone. Delicately he put the tiny needle to its task upon the revolving record. A thin and rasping Vienna waltz poured forth from the metal horn.

I laughed to see it, this sweet invention, set before them like an offering. Was the waltz like incense rising in the air?

But Marius had not completed his tasks. A white screen he had unrolled down the wall. And now from a high platform behind the seated god and goddess, he projected moving pictures of mortals onto the white screen. Those Who Must Be Kept stared mute at the flickering images. Statues in a museum, the electric light glaring on their white skin.

And then the most marvelous thing happened. The jittery little figures in the motion picture began to talk. Above the grind of the gramophone waltz they actually talked.

And as I watched, frozen in excitement, frozen in joy to see it all, a great sadness suddenly engulfed me, a great crushing realization. It was just a dream, this. Because the truth was, the little figures in the moving pictures couldn't possibly talk.

The chamber and all its little wonders lost its substance, went dim.

Ah, horrid imperfection, horrid little giveaway that I'd made it all up. And out of real bits and pieces, too—the silent movies I'd seen myself at the little theater called the Happy Hour, the gramophones I'd heard around me from a hundred houses in the dark.

And the Vienna waltz, ah, taken from the spell Armand had worked upon me, too heartbreaking to think of that.

Why hadn't I been just a little more clever in fooling myself, kept the film silent as it should have been, and I might have gone on believing it was a true vision after all.

But here was the final proof of my invention, this audacious and self-serving fancy: Akasha, my beloved, was speaking to me!

Akasha stood in the door of the chamber gazing down the length of the underground corridor to the elevator by which Marius had returned to the world above. Her black hair hung thickly and heavily about her white shoulders. She raised her cold white hand to beckon. Her mouth was red.

"Lestat!" she whispered. "Come."

Her thoughts flowed out of her soundlessly in the words of the old queen vampire who had spoken them to me under les Innocents years and years before:

From my stone pillow I have dreamed dreams of the mortal world above. I have heard its voices, its new music, as lullabies as I lie in my grave. I have envisioned its fantastical discoveries, I have known its courage in the timeless sanctum of my thoughts. And though it shuts me out with its dazzling forms, I long for one with the strength to roam it fearlessly, to ride the Devil's Road through its heart.

"Lestat!" she whispered again, her marble face tragically animate. "Come!"

"Oh, my darling," I said, tasting the bitter earth between my lips, "if only I could."

Lestat de Lioncourt
In the year of his Resurrection
1984

Dionysus in San Francisco

1985

1

The week before our record album went on sale, *they* reached out for the first time to threaten us over the telephone wires.

Secrecy regarding the rock band called *The Vampire Lestat* had been expensive but almost impenetrable. Even the book publishers of my autobiography had cooperated in full. And during the long months of recording and filmmaking, I hadn't seen a single one of *them* in New Orleans, nor heard them roaming about.

Yet somehow *they* had obtained the unlisted number and into the electronic answering machine they issued their admonitions and epithets.

"Outcast. We know what you are doing. We are ordering you to stop." "Come out where we can see you. We dare you to come out."

I had the band holed up in a lovely old plantation house north of New Orleans, pouring the Dom Pérignon for them as they smoked their hashish cigarettes, all of us weary of anticipation and preparation, eager for the first live audience in San Francisco, the first certain taste of success.

Then my lawyer, Christine, sent on the first phone messages—uncanny how the equipment captured the timbre of the unearthly voices—and in the middle of the night, I drove my musicians to the airport and we flew west.

After that, even Christine didn't know where we were hiding. The musicians themselves were not entirely sure. In a luxurious ranch house in Carmel Valley we heard our music for the first time over the radio. We danced as our first video films appeared nationwide on the television cable.

And each evening I went alone to the coastal city of Monterey to pick up Christine's communications. Then I went north to hunt.

I drove my sleek powerful black Porsche all the way to San Francisco, taking the hairpin curves of the coast road at intoxicating speed. And in the immaculate yellow gloom of the big city skid row I stalked my killers a little more cruelly and slowly than before.

The tension was becoming unbearable.

Still I didn't see the others. I didn't hear them. All I had were those phone messages from immortals I'd never known:

"We warn you. Do not continue this madness. You are playing a more dangerous game than you realize." And then the recorded whisper that mortal ears could not hear:

"Traitor!" "Outcast!" "Show yourself, Lestat!"

If they were hunting San Francisco, I didn't see them. But then San Francisco is a dense and crowded city. And I was sly and silent as I had always been.

Finally the telegrams came pouring in to the Monterey postbox. We had done it. Sales of our album were breaking records here and in Europe. We could perform in any city we wanted after San Francisco. My autobiography was in all the bookstores from coast to coast. *The Vampire Lestat* was at the top of the charts.

And after the nightly hunt in San Francisco, I started riding the long length of Divisadero Street. I let the black carapace of the Porsche crawl past the ruined Victorian houses, wondering in which one of these—if any—Louis had told the tale of *Interview with the Vampire* to the mortal boy. I was thinking constantly about Louis and Gabrielle. I was thinking about Armand. I was thinking about Marius, Marius whom I had betrayed by telling the whole tale.

Was *The Vampire Lestat* stretching its electronic tentacles far enough to touch them? Had they seen the video films: *The Legacy of Magnus, The Children of Darkness, Those Who Must Be Kept*? I thought of the other ancient ones whose names I'd revealed: Mael, Pandora, Ramses the Damned.

The fact was, Marius could have found me no matter what the secrecy or the precautions. His powers could have bridged even the vast distances of America. If he was looking, if he had heard . . .

The old dream came back to me of Marius cranking the motion picture camera, of the flickering patterns on the wall of the sanctum of Those Who Must Be Kept. Even in recollection it seemed impossibly lucid, made my heart trip.

And gradually I realized that I possessed a new concept of loneliness, a new method of measuring a silence that stretched to the end of the world. And all I had to interrupt it were those menacing recorded preternatural voices which carried no images as their virulency increased:

"Don't dare to appear on stage in San Francisco. We warn you. Your challenge is too vulgar, too contemptuous. We will risk anything, even a public scandal, to punish you."

I laughed at the incongruous combination of archaic language and the unmistakable American sound. What were they like, these modern vampires? Did they affect breeding and education once they walked with the undead? Did they assume a certain style? Did they live in covens or ride about on big black motorcycles, as I liked to do?

The excitement was building in me uncontrollably. And as I drove alone through the night with the radio blaring our music, I sensed a purely human enthusiasm mounting in me.

I wanted to perform the way my mortals, Tough Cookie and Alex and Larry, wanted to perform. After the grueling work of building the records and films, I wanted us to raise our voices together before the screaming throng. And at odd moments I remembered those long-ago nights at Renaud's little theater too clearly. The strangest details came back—the feel of the white paint as I had smoothed it over my face, the smell of the powder, the instant of stepping before the footlights.

Yes, it was all coming together, and if the wrath of Marius came with it, well, I deserved it, did I not?

San Francisco charmed me, subdued me somewhat. Not hard to imagine my Louis in this place. Almost Venetian, it seemed, the somber multicolored mansions and tenements rising wall to wall over the narrow black streets. Irresistible the lights sprinkled over hilltop and vale; and the hard brilliant wilderness of downtown skyscrapers shooting up like a fairy-tale forest out of an ocean of mist.

Each night on my return to Carmel Valley, I took out the sacks of fan mail forwarded to Monterey from New Orleans, and I looked through them for the vampire writing: characters inscribed a little too heavily, style slightly old-fashioned—maybe a more outrageous display of supernatural talent in a handwritten letter made to look as if it had been printed in Gothic style. But there was nothing but the fervent devotion of mortals.

> Dear Lestat, my friend Sheryl and I love you, and we can't get tickets for the San Francisco concert even though we stood in line for six hours. Please send us two tickets. We will be your victims. You can drink our blood.

Three o'clock in the morning on the night before the San Francisco concert:

The cool green paradise of Carmel Valley was asleep. I was dozing in the giant "den" before the glass wall that faced the mountains. I was dreaming off and on of Marius. Marius said in my dream:

"Why did you risk my vengeance?"

And I said: "You turned your back on me."

"That is not the reason," he said. "You act on impulse, you want to throw all the pieces in the air."

"I want to affect things, to make something happen!" I said. In the dream I shouted, and I felt suddenly the presence of the Carmel Valley house around me. Just a dream, a thin mortal dream.

Yet something, something else . . . a sudden "transmission" like a vagrant radio wave intruding upon the wrong frequency, a voice saying *Danger. Danger to us all.*

For one split second the vision of snow, ice. Wind howling. Something shattered on a stone floor, broken glass. *Lestat! Danger!*

I awoke.

I was not lying on the couch any longer. I was standing and looking towards the glass doors. I could hear nothing, see nothing but the dim outline of the hills, the black shape of the helicopter hovering over its square of concrete like a giant fly.

With my soul I listened. I listened so hard I was sweating. Yet no more of the "transmission." No images.

And then the gradual awareness that there was a creature outside in the darkness, that I was hearing tiny physical sounds.

Someone out there walking in the stillness. No human scent.

One of *them* was out there. One of *them* had penetrated the secrecy and was approaching beyond the distant skeletal silhouette of the helicopter, through the open field of high grass.

Again I listened. No, not a shimmer to reinforce the message of Danger. In fact the mind of the being was locked to me. I was getting only the inevitable signals of a creature passing through space.

The rambling low-roofed house slumbered around me—a giant aquarium, it seemed, with its barren white walls and the blue flickering light of the silent television set. Tough Cookie and Alex in each other's arms on the rug before the empty fireplace. Larry asleep in the cell-like bedroom with the carnally indefatigable groupie called Salamander whom they had "picked up" in New Orleans before we came west. Sleeping bodyguards in the other low-ceilinged modern chambers, and in the bunkhouse beyond the great blue oyster-shell swimming pool.

And out there under the clear black sky this creature coming, moving towards us from the highway, on foot. This thing that I sensed now was completely alone. Beat of a supernatural heart in the thin darkness. Yes, I can hear it very distinctly. The hills were like ghosts in the distance, the yellow blossoms of the acacias gleaming white under the stars.

Not afraid of anything, it seemed. Just coming. And the thoughts absolutely impenetrable. That could mean one of the old ones, the very skilled ones, except the skilled ones would never crush the grass underfoot. This thing moved almost like a human. This vampire had been "made" by me.

My heart was skipping. I glanced at the tiny lights of the alarm box half concealed by the gathered drapery in the corner. Promise of sirens if anything, mortal or immortal, tried to penetrate this house.

On the edge of the white concrete he appeared. Tall, slender figure. Short dark hair. And then he paused as if he could see me in the electric blue haze behind the glass veil.

Yes, he saw me. And he moved towards me, towards the light.

Agile, traveling just a little too lightly for a mortal. Black hair, green eyes, and the limbs shifting silkily under the neglected garments: a frayed black sweater that hung shapelessly from his shoulders, legs like long black spokes.

I felt the lump come up in my throat. I was trembling. I tried to remember what was important, even in this moment, that I must scan the night for others, must be careful. *Danger.* But none of that mattered now. I knew. I shut my eyes for a second. It did not help anything, make anything easier.

Then my hand went out to the alarm buttons and I turned them off. I opened the giant glass doors and the cold fresh air moved past me into the room.

He was past the helicopter, turning and stepping away like a dancer to look up at it, his head back, his thumbs hooked very casually in the pockets of his black jeans. When he looked at me again, I saw his face distinctly. And he smiled.

Even our memories can fail us. He was proof of that, delicate and blinding as a laser as he came closer, all the old images blown away like dust.

I flicked on the alarm system again, closed the doors on my mortals, and turned the key in the lock. For a second I thought, I cannot stand this. And this is only the beginning. And if he is here, only a few steps away from me now, then surely the others, too, will come. They will all come.

I turned and went towards him, and for a silent moment I just studied him in the blue light falling through the glass. My voice was tight when I spoke:

"Where's the black cape and the 'finely tailored' black coat and the silk tie and all that foolishness?" I asked.

Eyes locked on each other.

Then he broke the stillness and laughed without making a sound. But he went on studying me with a rapt expression that gave me a secret joy.

And with the boldness of a child, he reached out and ran his fingers down the lapel of my gray velvet coat.

"Can't always be the living legend," he said. The voice was like a whisper that wasn't a whisper. And I could hear his French accent so clearly, though I had never been able to hear my own.

I could scarcely bear the sound of the syllables, the complete familiarity of it.

And I forgot all the stiff surly things I had planned to say and I just took him in my arms.

We embraced the way we never had in the past. We held each other the way Gabrielle and I used to do. And then I ran my hands over his hair and his face, just letting myself really see him, as if he belonged to me. And he did the same. Seems we were talking and not talking. True silent voices that didn't have any words. Nodding a little. And I could feel him brimming with affection and a feverish satisfaction that seemed almost as strong as my own.

But he was quiet suddenly, and his face became a little drawn.

"I thought you were dead and gone, you know," he said. It was barely audible.

"How did you find me here?" I asked.

"You wanted me to," he answered. Flash of innocent confusion. He gave a slow shrug of the shoulders.

Everything he did was magnetizing me just the way it had over a century ago. Fingers so long and delicate, yet hands so strong.

"You let me see you and you let me follow you," he said. "You drove up and down Divisadero Street looking for me."

"And you were still there?"

"The safest place in the world for me," he said. "I never left it. They came looking for me and they didn't find me and then they went away. And now I move among them whenever I want and they don't know me. They never knew what I looked like, really."

"And they'd try to destroy you if they knew," I said.

"Yes," he answered. "But they've been trying to do that since the Theater of the Vampires and the things that happened there. Of course *Interview with the Vampire* gave them some new reasons. And they do need reasons to play their little games. They need the impetus, the excitement. They feed upon it like blood." His voice sounded labored for a second.

He took a deep breath. Hard to talk about all this. I wanted to put my arms around him again but I didn't.

"But at the moment," he said, "I think you are the one that they want to destroy. And they do know what you look like." Little smile. "Everybody knows now what you look like. Monsieur Le Rock Star."

He let his smile broaden. But the voice was polite and low as it had always been. And the face suffused with feeling. There had been not the slightest change there yet. Maybe there never would be.

I slipped my arm around his shoulder and we walked together away from the lights of the house. We walked past the great gray hulk of the copter and into the dry sunbaked field and towards the hills.

I think to be this happy is to be miserable, to feel this much satisfaction is to burn.

"Are you going to go through with it?" he asked. "The concert tomorrow night?"

Danger to us all. Had it been a warning or a threat?

"Yes, of course," I said. "What in hell could stop me from it?"

"I would like to stop you," he answered. "I would have come sooner if I could. I spotted you a week ago, then lost you."

"And why do you want to stop me?"

"You know why," he said. "I want to talk to you." So simple, the words, and yet they had such meaning.

"There'll be time after," I answered. " 'Tomorrow and tomorrow and tomorrow.' Nothing is going to happen. You'll see." I kept glancing at him and away from him, as if his green eyes were hurting me. In modern parlance he *was* a laser beam. Deadly and delicate he seemed. His victims had always loved him.

And I had always loved him, hadn't I, no matter what happened, and how strong could love grow if you had eternity to nourish it, and it took only these few moments in time to renew its momentum, its heat?

"How can you be sure of that, Lestat?" he asked. Intimate his speaking my name. And I had not brought myself to say Louis in that same natural way.

We were walking slowly now, without direction, and his arm was around me loosely as mine was around him.

"I have a battalion of mortals guarding us," I said. "There'll be bodyguards on the copter and in the limousine with my mortals. I'll travel alone from the airport in the Porsche so I can more easily defend myself, but we'll have a veritable motorcade. And just what can a handful of hateful twentieth-century fledglings do anyway? These idiot creatures use the telephone for their threats."

"There are more than a handful," he said. "But what about Marius? Your enemies out there are debating it, whether the story of Marius was true, whether Those Who Must Be Kept exist or not—"

"Naturally, and you, did you believe it?"

"Yes, as soon as I read it," he said. And there passed between us a moment of silence, in which perhaps we were both remembering the questing immortal of long ago who had asked me over and over, Where did it begin?

Too much pain to be reinvoked. It was like taking pictures from the attic, cleaning away the dust and finding the colors still vibrant. And the pictures should have been portraits of dead ancestors and they were pictures of us.

I made some little nervous mortal gesture, raked my hair back off my forehead, tried to feel the cool of the breeze.

"What makes you so confident," he asked, "that Marius won't end this experiment as soon as you step on the stage tomorrow night?"

"Do you think any of the old ones would do that?" I answered.

He reflected for a long moment, slipping deep into his thoughts the way he used to do, so deep it was as if he forgot I was there. And it seemed that old rooms took shape around him, gaslight gave off its unsteady illumination, there came the sounds and scents of a former time from outside streets. We two in that New Orleans parlor, coal fire in the grate beneath the marble mantel, everything growing older except us.

And he stood now a modern child in sagging sweater and worn denim gazing off towards the deserted hills. Disheveled, eyes sparked with an inner fire, hair mussed. He roused himself slowly as if coming back to life.

"No. I think if the old ones trouble themselves with it at all, they will be too interested to do that."

"Are you interested?"

"Yes, you know I am," he said.

And his face colored slightly. It became even more human. In fact, he looked more like a mortal man than any of our kind I've ever known. "I'm here, aren't I?" he said. And I sensed a pain in him, running like a vein of ore through his whole being, a vein that could carry feeling to the coldest depths.

I nodded. I took a deep breath and looked away from him, wishing I could say what I really wanted to say. That I loved him. But I couldn't do that. The feeling was too strong.

"Whatever happens, it will be worth it," I said. "That is, if you and I, and Gabrielle, and Armand . . . and Marius are together even for a short while, it will be worth it. Suppose Pandora chooses to show herself. And Mael. And God only knows how many others. What if all the old ones come. It will be worth it, Louis. As for the rest, I don't care."

"No, you care," he said, smiling. He was deeply fascinated. "You're just confident that it's going to be exciting, and that whatever the battle, you'll win."

I bowed my head. I laughed. I slipped my hands into the pockets of my pants the way mortal men did in this day and age, and I walked on through the grass. The field still smelled of sun even in the cool California night. I didn't tell him about the mortal part, the vanity of wanting to perform, the eerie madness that had come over me when I saw myself on the television screen, saw my face on the album covers plastered to the windows of the North Beach record store.

He followed at my side.

"If the old ones really wanted to destroy me," I said, "don't you think it would already be done?"

"No," he said. "I saw you and I followed you. But before that, I couldn't find you. As soon as I heard that you'd come out, I tried."

"How did you hear?" I asked.

"There are places in all the big cities where the vampires meet," he said. "Surely you know this by now."

"No, I don't. Tell me," I said.

"They are the bars we call the Vampire Connection," he said, smiling a little ironically as he said it. "They are frequented by mortals, of course, and known to us by their names. There is Dr. Polidori in London, and Lamia in Paris. There is Bela Lugosi in the city of Los Angeles, and Carmilla and Lord Ruthven in New York. Here in San Francisco we have the most beautiful of them all, possibly, the cabaret called Dracula's Daughter, on Castro Street."

I started laughing. I couldn't help it and I could see that he was about to laugh, too.

"And where are the names from *Interview with the Vampire*?" I asked with mock indignation.

"*Verboten,*" he said with a little lift of the eyebrows. "They are not fictional. They are real. But I will tell you they are playing your video clips on Castro Street now. The mortal customers demand it. They toast you with their vodka Bloody Marys. *The Dance of les Innocents* is pounding through the walls."

A real laughing fit was definitely coming. I tried to stop it. I shook my head.

"But you've effected something of a revolution in speech in the back room as well," he continued in the same mock sober fashion, unable to keep his face entirely straight.

"What do you mean?"

"Dark Trick, Dark Gift, Devil's Road—they're all bantering those words about, the crudest fledglings who never even styled themselves vampires. They're imitating the book even though they condemn it utterly. They are loading themselves down with Egyptian jewelry. Black velvet is once again de rigueur."

"Too perfect," I said. "But these places, what are they like?"

"They're saturated with the vampire trappings," he said. "Posters from the vampire films adorn the walls, and the films themselves are projected continuously on high screens. The mortals who come are a regular freak show of theatrical types—punk youngsters, artists, those done up in black capes and white plastic fangs. They scarcely notice *us.* We are often drab by comparison. And in the dim lights we might as well be invisible, velvet and Egyptian jewelry and all. Of course, no one preys upon these mortal customers. We come to the vampire bars for information. The vampire bar is the safest place for a mortal in all Christendom. You cannot kill in the vampire bar."

"Wonder somebody didn't think of it before," I said.

"They did think of it," he said. "In Paris, it was the Théâtre des Vampyres."

"Of course," I admitted. He went on:

"The word went out a month ago on the Vampire Connection that you were back. And the news was old then. They said you were hunting New Orleans, and then they learned what you meant to do. They had early copies of your autobiography. There was endless talk about the video films."

"And why didn't I see them in New Orleans?" I asked.

"Because New Orleans has been for half a century Armand's territory. No one dares to hunt New Orleans. They learned through mortal sources of information, out of Los Angeles and New York."

"I didn't see Armand in New Orleans," I said.

"I know," he answered. He looked troubled, confused for a moment. I felt a little tightening in the region of the heart.

"No one knows where Armand is," he said a little dully. "But when he was there, he killed the young ones. They left New Orleans to him. They say that many of the old ones do that, kill the young ones. They say it of me, but it isn't so. I haunt San Francisco like a ghost. I do not trouble anyone save my unfortunate mortal victims."

All this didn't surprise me much.

"There are too many of us," he said, "as there always have been. And there is much warring. And a coven in any given city is only a means by which three or more powerful ones agree not to destroy each other, and to share the territory according to the rules."

"The rules, always the rules," I said.

"They are different now, and more stringent. Absolutely no evidence of the kill must ever be left about. Not a single corpse must be left for mortals to investigate."

"Of course."

"And there must be no exposure whatsoever in the world of close-up photography and zoom lenses, of freeze-frame video examination—no risk that could lead to capture, incarceration, and scientific verification by the mortal world."

I nodded. But my pulse was racing. I loved being the outlaw, the one who had already broken every single law. And so they were imitating my book, were they? Oh, it was started already. Wheels set into motion.

"Lestat, you think you understand," he said patiently, "but do you? Let the world have but one tiny fragment of our tissue for their microscopes, and there will be no arguments anymore about legend or superstition. The proof will be there."

"I don't agree with you, Louis," I said. "It isn't that simple."

"They have the means to identify and classify us, to galvanize the human race against us."

"No, Louis. Scientists in this day and age are witch doctors perpetually at war. They quarrel over the most rudimentary questions. You would have to spread that supernatural tissue to every microscope in the world and even then the public might not believe a word of it."

He reflected for a moment.

"One capture then," he said. "One living specimen in their hands."

"Even that wouldn't do it," I said. "And how could they ever hold me?"

But it was too lovely to contemplate—the chase, the intrigue, the possible capture and escape. I loved it.

He was smiling now in a strange way. Full of disapproval and delight.

"You are madder than you ever were," he said under his breath. "Madder than when you used to go about New Orleans deliberately scaring people in the old days."

I laughed and laughed. But then I got quiet. We didn't have that much time before morning. And I could laugh all the way into San Francisco tomorrow night.

"Louis, I've thought this over from every angle," I said. "It will be harder to start a real war with mortals than you think—"

"—And you're bound and determined to start it, aren't you? You want everyone, mortal or immortal, to come after you."

"Why not?" I asked. "Let it begin. And let them try to destroy us the way they have destroyed their other devils. Let them try to wipe us out."

He was watching me with that old expression of awe and incredulity that I had seen a thousand times on his face. I was a fool for it, as the expression goes.

But the sky was paling overhead, the stars drifting steadily away. Only precious moments we had together before the early spring morning.

"And so you really mean for it to happen," he said earnestly, his tone gentler than before.

"Louis, I mean for something and everything to happen," I said. "I mean for all that we have been to change! What are we but leeches now —loathsome, secretive, without justification. The old romance is gone. So let us take on a new meaning. I crave the bright lights as I crave blood. I crave the divine visibility. I crave war."

"The new evil, to use your old words," he said. "And this time it is the twentieth-century evil."

"Precisely," I said. But again, I thought of the purely mortal impulse, the vain impulse, for worldly fame, acknowledgment. Faint blush of shame. It was all going to be such a pleasure.

"But why, Lestat?" he asked a little suspiciously. "Why the danger, the risk? After all, you have done it. You have come back. You're stronger than ever. You have the old fire as if it had never been lost, and you know how precious this is, this will simply to go on. Why risk it immediately? Have you forgotten what it was like when we had the world all around us, and no one could hurt us except ourselves?"

"Is this an offer, Louis? Have you come back to me, as lovers say?"

His eyes darkened and he looked away from me.

"I'm not mocking you, Louis," I said.

"You've come back to *me,* Lestat," he said evenly, looking at me again. "When I heard the first whispers of you at Dracula's Daughter, I felt something that I thought was gone forever—" He paused.

But I knew what he was talking about. He had already said it. And I had understood it centuries ago when I felt Armand's despair after the death of the old coven. Excitement, the desire to continue, these things were priceless to us. All the more reason for the rock concert, the continuation, the war itself.

"Lestat, don't go on the stage tomorrow night," he said. "Let the films and the book do what you want. But protect yourself. Let us come together and let us talk together. Let us have each other in this century the way we never did in the past. And I do mean all of us."

"Very tempting, beautiful one," I said. "There were times in the last century when I would have given almost anything to hear those words. And we will come together, and we will talk, all of us, and we will have each other. It will be splendid, better than it ever was before. But I am going on the stage. I am going to be Lelio again the way I never was in Paris. I will be the Vampire Lestat for all to see. A symbol, an outcast, a freak of nature—something loved, something despised, all of those things. I tell you I can't give it up. I can't miss it. And quite frankly I am not the least afraid."

I braced myself for a coldness or a sadness to come over him. And I hated the approaching sun as much as I ever had in the past. He turned his back to it. The illumination was hurting him a little. But his face was as full of warm expression as before.

"Very well, then," he said. "I would like to go into San Francisco with you. I would like that very much. Will you take me with you?"

I couldn't immediately answer. Again, the sheer excitement was excruciating, and the love I felt for him was positively humiliating.

"Of course I'll take you with me," I said.

We looked at each other for a tense moment. He had to leave now. The morning had come for him.

"One thing, Louis," I said.

"Yes?"

"Those clothes. Impossible. I mean, tomorrow night, as they say in the twentieth century, you will *lose* that sweater and those pants."

THE morning was too empty after he had gone. I stood still for a while thinking of that message, *Danger.* I scanned the distant mountains, the never ending fields. Threat, warning—what did it matter? The young ones dial the telephones. The old ones raise their supernatural voices. Was it so strange?

I could only think of Louis now, that he was with me. And of what it would be like when the others came.

2

THE vast sprawling parking lots of the San Francisco Cow Palace were overflowing with frenzied mortals as our motorcade pushed through the gates, my musicians in the limousine ahead, Louis in the leather-lined Porsche beside me. Crisp and shining in the black-caped costume of the band, he looked as if he'd stepped out of the pages of his own story, his green eyes passing a little fearfully over the screaming youngsters and motorcycle guards who kept them back and away from us.

The hall had been sold out for a month; the disappointed fans wanted the music broadcast outside so they could hear it. Beer cans littered the ground. Teenagers sat atop car roofs and on trunks and hoods, radios blaring *The Vampire Lestat* at appalling volume.

Alongside my window, our manager ran on foot explaining that we would have the outside video screens and speakers. The San Francisco police had given the go-ahead to prevent a riot.

I could feel Louis's mounting anxiety. A pack of youngsters broke through the police lines and pressed themselves against his window as the motorcade made its sharp turn and plowed on towards the long ugly tube-shaped hall.

I was positively enthralled with what was happening. And the recklessness in me was cresting. Again and again the fans surrounded the car before they were swept back, and I was beginning to understand how woefully I had underestimated this entire experience.

The filmed rock shows I'd watched hadn't prepared me for the crude electricity that was already coursing through me, the way the music was already surging in my head, the way the shame for my mortal vanity was evaporating.

It was mayhem getting into the hall. Through a crush of guards, we ran into the heavily secured backstage area, Tough Cookie holding tight to me, Alex pushing Larry ahead of him.

The fans tore at our hair, our capes. I reached back and gathered Louis under my wing and brought him through the doors with us.

And then in the curtained dressing rooms I heard it for the first time, the bestial sound of the crowd—fifteen thousand souls chanting and screaming under one roof.

No, I did not have this under control, this fierce glee that made my entire body shudder. When had this ever happened to me before, this near hilarity?

I pushed up to the front and looked through the peephole into the auditorium. Mortals on both sides of the long oval, up to the very rafters. And in the vast open center, a mob of thousands dancing, caressing, pumping fists into the smoky haze, vying to get close to the stage platform. Hashish, beer, human blood smell swirled on the ventilation currents.

The engineers were shouting that we were set. Face paint had been retouched, black velvet capes brushed, black ties straightened. No good to keep this crowd waiting a moment longer.

The word was given to kill the houselights. And a great inhuman cry swelled in the darkness, rolling up the walls. I could feel it in the floor beneath me. It grew stronger as a grinding electronic buzz announced the connection of "the equipment."

The vibration went through my temples. A layer of skin was being peeled off. I clasped Louis's arm, gave him a lingering kiss, and then felt him release me.

Everywhere beyond the curtain people snapped on their little chemical cigarette lighters, until thousands and thousands of tiny flames trembled in the gloom. Rhythmic clapping erupted, died out, the general roar rolling up and down, pierced by random shrieks. My head was teeming.

And yet I thought of Renaud's so long ago. I positively saw it. But this place was like the Roman Colosseum! And making the tapes, the films—it had been so controlled, so cold. It had given no taste of this.

The engineer gave the signal, and we shot through the curtain, the mortals fumbling because they couldn't see, as I maneuvered effortlessly over the cables and wires.

I was at the lip of the stage right over the heads of the swaying, shouting crowd. Alex was at the drums. Tough Cookie had her flat shimmering electric guitar in hand, Larry was at the huge circular keyboard of the synthesizer.

I turned around and glanced up at the giant video screens which would magnify our images for the scrutiny of every pair of eyes in the house. Then back at the sea of screaming youngsters.

Waves and waves of noise inundated us from the darkness. I could smell the heat and the blood.

Then the immense bank of overhead lights went on. Violent beams of silver, blue, red crisscrossed as they caught us, and the screaming reached an unbelievable pitch. The entire hall was on its feet.

I could feel the light crawling on my white skin, exploding in my yellow hair. I glanced around to see my mortals glorified and frenzied already as they perched amid the endless wires and silver scaffolding.

The sweat broke out on my forehead as I saw the fists raised everywhere in salute. And scattered all through the hall were youngsters in their Halloween vampire clothes, faces gleaming with artificial blood, some wearing floppy yellow wigs, some with black rings about their eyes to make them all the more innocent and ghastly. Catcalls and hoots and raucous cries rose above the general din.

No, this was not like making the little films. This was nothing like singing in the air-cooled cork-lined chambers of the studio. This was a human experience made vampiric, as the music itself was vampiric, as the images of the video film were the images of the blood swoon.

I was shuddering with pure exhilaration and the red-tinged sweat was pouring down my face.

The spotlights swept the audience, leaving us bathed in a mercuric twilight, and everywhere the light hit, the crowd went into convulsions, redoubling their cries.

What was it about this sound? It signaled man turned into mob—the crowds surrounding the guillotine, the ancient Romans screaming for Christian blood. And the Keltoi gathered in the grove awaiting Marius, the god. I could see the grove as I had when Marius told the tale; had the torches been any more lurid than these colored beams? Had the horrific wicker giants been larger than these steel ladders that held the banks of speakers and incandescent spotlights on either side of us?

But there was no violence here; there was no death—only this childish exuberance pouring forth from young mouths and young bodies, an energy focused and contained as naturally as it was cut loose.

Another wave of hashish from the front ranks. Long-haired leather-clad bikers with spiked leather bracelets clapping their hands above their heads—ghosts of the Keltoi, they seemed, barbarian locks streaming. And from all corners of this long hollow smoky place an uninhibited wash of something that felt like love.

The lights were flashing on and off so that the movement of the crowd seemed fragmented, to be happening in fits and jerks.

They were chanting in unison, now the volume swelling, what was it, LESTAT, LESTAT, LESTAT.

Oh, this is too divine. What mortal could withstand this indulgence, this worship? I clasped the ends of my black cloak, which was the signal. I shook out my hair to its fullest. And these gestures sent a current of renewed screaming to the very back of the hall.

The lights converged on the stage. I raised my cloak on either side like bat wings.

The screams fused into a great monolithic roar.

"I AM THE VAMPIRE LESTAT!" I shouted at the top of my lungs as I stepped way back from the microphone, and the sound was almost visible as it arched over the length of the oval theater, and the voice of the crowd rose even higher, louder, as if to devour the ringing sound.

"COME ON, LET ME HEAR YOU! YOU LOVE ME!" I shouted suddenly, without deciding to do it. Everywhere people were stomping. They were stomping not only on the concrete floors but on the wooden seats.

"HOW MANY OF YOU WOULD BE VAMPIRES?"

The roar became a thunder. Several people were trying to scramble up onto the front of the stage, the bodyguards pulling them off. One of the big dark shaggy-haired bikers was jumping straight up and down, a beer can in each hand.

The lights went brighter like the glare of an explosion. And there rose from the speakers and equipment behind me the full-throated engine of a locomotive at stultifying volume as if the train were racing onto the stage.

Every other sound in the auditorium was swallowed by it. In blaring silence the crowd danced and bobbed before me. Then came the piercing, twanging fury of the electrical guitar. The drums boomed into a marching cadence, and the grinding locomotive sound of the synthesizer crested, then broke into a bubbling caldron of noise in time with the march. It was time to begin the chant in the minor key, its puerile lyrics leaping over the accompaniment:

I AM THE VAMPIRE LESTAT
YOU ARE HERE FOR THE GRAND SABBAT
BUT I PITY YOU YOUR LOT

I grabbed the microphone from the stand and ran to one side of the stage and then to the other, the cape flaring out behind me:

YOU CAN'T RESIST THE LORDS OF NIGHT
THEY HAVE NO MERCY ON YOUR PLIGHT
IN YOUR FEAR THEY TAKE DELIGHT

They were reaching out for my ankles, throwing kisses, girls lifted by their male companions to touch my cape as it swirled over their heads.

YET IN LOVE, WE WILL TAKE YOU,
AND IN RAPTURE, WE'LL BREAK YOU
AND IN DEATH WE'LL RELEASE YOU

NO ONE CAN SAY
YOU WERE NOT WARNED.

Tough Cookie, strumming furiously, danced up beside me, gyrating wildly, the music peaking in a shrill glissando, drums and cymbals crashing, the bubbling caldron of the synthesizer rising again.

I felt the music come up into my bones. Not even at the old Roman Sabbat had it taken hold of me like this.

I pitched myself into the dance, swinging my hips elastically, then pumping them as the two of us moved towards the edge of the stage. We were performing the free and erotic contortions of Punchinello and Harlequin and all the old commedia players—improvising now as they had done, the instruments cutting loose from the thin melody, then finding it again, as we urged each other on with our dancing, nothing rehearsed, everything within character, everything utterly new.

The guards shoved people back roughly as they tried to join us. Yet we danced over the edge of the platform as if taunting them, whipping our hair around our faces, turning round to see ourselves above in an impossible hallucination on the giant screens. The sound traveled up through my body as I turned back to the crowd. It traveled like a steel ball finding one pocket after another in my hips, my shoulders, until I knew I was rising off the floor in a great slow leap, and then descending silently again, the black cape flaring, my mouth open to reveal the fang teeth.

Euphoria. Deafening applause.

And everywhere I saw pale mortal throats bared, boys and girls shoving their collars down and stretching their necks and some had made red lipstick marks like wounds on their necks. And they were gesturing to me to come and take them, inviting me and begging me, and some of the girls were crying.

The blood scent was thick as the smoke in the air. Flesh and flesh and flesh. And yet everywhere the canny innocence, the unfathomable trust that it was art, nothing but art! No one would be hurt. It was safe, this splendid hysteria.

When I screamed, they thought it was the sound system. When I leapt, they thought it was a trick. And why not, when magic was blaring at them from all sides and they could forsake our flesh and blood for the great glowing giants on the screens above us?

Marius, I wish you could behold this! Gabrielle, where are you?

The lyrics poured out, sung by the whole band again in unison, Tough Cookie's lovely soprano soaring over the others, before she wrung her head round and round in a circle, her hair flopping down to touch the boards in front of her feet, her guitar jerking lasciviously like a giant phallus, thousands and thousands stamping and clapping in unison.

"I AM TELLING YOU I AM A VAMPIRE!" I screamed suddenly.

Ecstasy, delirium.

"I AM EVIL! EVIL!"

"Yes, Yes, *Yes, Yes,* YES, YES, YES."

I threw out my arms, my hands curved upwards:

"I WANT TO DRINK UP YOUR SOULS!"

The big woolly-haired biker in the black leather jacket backed up, knocking over those behind him, and leapt on the stage next to me, fists over his head. The bodyguards went to tackle him but I had him, locking him to my chest, lifting him off his feet in one arm and closing my mouth on his neck, teeth just touching him, just touching that geyser of blood ready to spew straight upwards!

But they had torn him loose, thrown him back like a fish into the sea. Tough Cookie was beside me, the light skittering on her black satin pants, her whirling cape, her arm out to steady me, even as I tried to slip free.

Now I knew all that had been left out of the pages I had read about the rock singers—this mad marriage of the primitive and the scientific, this religious frenzy. We were in the ancient grove all right. We were all with the gods.

And we were blowing out the fuses on the first song. And rolling into the next, as the crowd picked up the rhythm, shouting the lyrics they knew from the albums and the clips. Tough Cookie and I sang, stomping in time with it:

CHILDREN OF DARKNESS
MEET THE CHILDREN OF LIGHT

CHILDREN OF MAN,
FIGHT THE CHILDREN OF NIGHT

And again they cheered and bellowed and wailed, unmindful of the words. Could the old Keltoi have cut loose with lustier ululations on the verge of massacre?

But again there was no massacre, there was no burnt offering.

Passion rolled towards the images of evil, not evil. Passion embraced the image of death, not death. I could feel it like the scalding illumination on the pores of my skin, in the roots of my hair, Tough Cookie's amplified scream carrying the next stanza, my eyes sweeping the farthest nooks and crannies, the amphitheater become a great wailing soul.

Deliver me from this, deliver me from loving it. Deliver me from forgetting everything else, and sacrificing all purpose, all resolve to it. I want you, my babies. I want your blood, innocent blood. I want your adoration at the moment when I sink my teeth. Yes, this is beyond all temptation.

But in this moment of precious stillness and shame, I saw them for the first time, the real ones out there. Tiny white faces tossed like masks on the waves of shapeless mortal faces, distinct as Magnus's face had been in that long-ago little boulevard hall. And I knew that back beyond the curtains, Louis also saw them. But all I saw in them, all I felt emanating from them, was wonder and fear.

"ALL YOU REAL VAMPIRES OUT THERE," I shouted. "REVEAL YOURSELVES!" And they remained changeless, as the painted and costumed mortals about them went wild.

For three solid hours we danced, we sang, we beat the hell out of the metallic instruments, the whiskey splashing back and forth among Alex and Larry and Tough Cookie, the crowd surging towards us over and over until the phalanx of police had doubled, and the lights had been raised. Wooden seats were breaking in the high corners of the auditorium, cans rolled on the concrete floors. The real ones never ventured a step closer. Some vanished.

That's how it was.

Unbroken screaming, like fifteen thousand drunks on the town, right up to the final moments, when it was the ballad from the last clip, *Age of Innocence.*

And then the music softening. The drums rolling out, and the guitar dying, and the synthesizer throwing up the lovely translucent notes of an electric harpsichord, notes so light yet profuse that it was as if the air were showered with gold.

One mellow spot hit the place where I stood, my clothes streaked with blood sweat, my hair wet with it and tangled, the cape dangling from one shoulder.

Into a great yawning mouth of rapt and drunken attention I raised my voice slowly, letting each phrase become clear:

This is the Age of Innocence
True Innocence
All your Demons are visible
All your Demons are material

Call them Pain
Call them Hunger
Call them War

Mythic evil you don't need anymore.

Drive out the vampires and the devils
With the gods you no longer adore

Remember:
The Man with the fangs wears a cloak.
What passes for charm
Is a charm.

Understand what you see
When you see me!

Kill us, my brothers and sisters
The war is on

Understand what you see
When you see me.

I closed my eyes on the rising walls of applause. What were they really clapping for? What were they celebrating?

Electric daylight in this giant auditorium. The real ones were vanishing in the shifting throng. The uniformed police had jumped up onto the platform to make a solid row in front of us. Alex was tugging at me as we went through the curtain:

"Man, we have to run for it. They've got the damned limo surrounded. And you'll never make it to your own car."

I said no, they had to go on, to take the limo, to get going now.

And to my left I saw the hard white face of one of the real ones as he shoved his way through the press. He wore the black leather skins of the motorcycle riders, his silken preternatural hair a gleaming black mop.

The curtains were ripping from their overhead rods, letting the house flow into the backstage area. Louis was beside me. I saw another immortal on my right, a thin grinning male with tiny dark eyes.

Blast of cold air as we pushed into the parking lot, and pandemonium of squirming, struggling mortals, the police yelling for order, the limo rocking like a boat as Tough Cookie and Alex and Larry were shoved into it. One of the bodyguards had the engine of the Porsche running for me, but the youngsters were beating on the hood and the roof as if it were a drum.

Behind the black-haired vampire male there appeared another demon, a woman, and the pair were pushing inexorably closer. What the hell did they think they were going to do?

The giant motor of the limousine was growling like a lion at the children who wouldn't make way for it, and the motorcycle guards gunned their little engines, spewing fumes and noise into the throng.

The vampire trio was suddenly surrounding the Porsche, the tall male's face ugly with fury, and one thrust of his powerful arm lifted the low-slung car in spite of the youngsters who held to it. It was going to capsize. I felt an arm around my throat suddenly. And I felt Louis's body pivot, and I heard the sound of his fist strike the preternatural skin and bone behind me, heard the whispered curse.

Mortals everywhere were suddenly screaming. A policeman exhorted the crowd over a loudspeaker to clear out.

I rushed forward, knocking down several of the youngsters, and steadied the Porsche just before it went over like a scarab on its back. As I struggled to open the door, I felt the crowd crushing against me. Any moment this would become a riot. There would be a stampede.

Whistles, screams, sirens. Bodies shoving Louis and me together, and then the leather-clad vampire male rising on the other side of the Porsche, a great silver scythe flashing in the floodlights as he swung it over his head.

I heard Louis's shout of warning. I saw another scythe gleaming in the corner of my eye.

But a preternatural screech cut through the cacophony as in a blinding flash the vampire male burst into flames. Another blaze exploded beside me. The scythe clattered to the concrete. And yards away yet another vampiric figure suddenly went up in a crackling gust.

The crowd was in utter panic, rushing back into the auditorium, streaming out into the parking lot, running anyplace it could to escape the whirling figures as they were burnt black in their own private infernos, their limbs melting in the heat to mere bones. And I saw other immortals streaking away at invisible speed through the sluggish human press.

Louis was stunned as he turned to me, and surely the look of amazement on my face only stunned him more. Neither of us had done this! Neither of us had the power! I knew but one immortal who did.

But I was suddenly slammed back by the car door opening and a small delicate white hand reached out to pull me inside.

"Hurry, both of you!" said a female voice in French suddenly. "What are you waiting for, the Church to pronounce it a miracle?" And I was jerked into the leather bucket seat before I realized what was happening, dragging Louis in on top of me so that he had to scramble over me into the compartment in back.

The Porsche lurched forward, scattering the fleeing mortals in front of its headlights. I stared at the slender figure of the driver beside me, her yellow hair streaming over her shoulders, her soiled felt hat smashed down over her eyes.

I wanted to throw my arms around her, to crush her with kisses, to press my heart against her heart and forget absolutely everything else. The hell with these idiot fledglings. But the Porsche almost went over again as she made the sharp right out of the gate and into the busy street.

"Gabrielle, stop!" I shouted, my hand closing on her arm. "You didn't do that, burn them like that—!"

"Of course not," she said, in sharp French still, barely glancing at me. She looked irresistible as with two fingers she twisted the wheel again, swinging us into yet another ninety-degree turn. We were headed for the freeway.

"Then you're driving us away from Marius!" I said. "Stop."

"So let him blow up the van that's following us!" she cried. "Then I'll stop." She had the gas pedal floored, her eyes fixed on the road in front of her, her hands locked to the leather-clad wheel.

I turned to see it over Louis's shoulder, a monster of a vehicle bearing down with surprising speed—an overgrown hearse it seemed, hulking and black, with a mouthful of chromium teeth across the snub-nosed front and four of the undead leering at us from behind the tinted windshield glass.

"We can't get clear of this traffic to outrun them!" I said. "Turn around. Go back to the auditorium. Gabrielle, turn around!"

But she bore on, weaving in and out of the motor coaches wildly, driving some of them in sheer panic to the side.

The van was gaining.

"It's a war machine, that's what it is!" Louis said. "They've rigged it with an iron bumper. They're going to try to ram us, the little monsters!"

Oh, I had played this one wrong. I had underestimated. I had envisioned my own resources in this modern age, but not theirs.

And we were moving farther and farther away from the one immortal who could blow them to Kingdom Come. Well, I would handle them with pleasure. I'd smash their windshield to pieces for starters, then tear off their heads one by one. I opened the window, climbing halfway up and out of it, the wind whipping my hair, as I glared at them, their ugly white faces behind the glass.

As we shot up the freeway ramp, they were almost on top of us. Good. Just a little closer and I would spring. But our car was skidding to a halt. Gabrielle couldn't clear the path ahead.

"Hold on, it's coming!" she screamed.

"Like hell it is!" I shouted, and in an instant I would have jumped off the roof and gone into them like a battering ram.

But I didn't have that instant. They had struck us full force, and my body flew up in the air, diving over the side of the freeway as the Porsche shot out in front of me, sailing into space.

I saw Gabrielle break through the side door before the car hit the ground. And she and I were both rolling over on the grassy slope as the car capsized and exploded with a deafening roar.

"Louis!" I shouted. I scrambled towards the blaze. I would have gone right into it after him. But the glass of the back portal splintered as he came through it. He hit the embankment just as I reached him. And with my cape I beat at his smoking garments, Gabrielle ripping off her jacket to do the same.

The van had stopped at the freeway railing high above. The creatures were dropping over the edge, like big white insects, and landing on their feet on the slope.

And I was ready for them.

But again, as the first one skidded down towards us, scythe raised, there came that ghastly preternatural scream again and the blinding combustion, the creature's face a black mask in a riot of orange flame. The body convulsed in a horrid dance.

The others turned and ran under the freeway.

I started after them, but Gabrielle had her arms around me and wouldn't let me go. Her strength maddened me and amazed me.

"Stop, damn it!" she said. "Louis, help me!"

"Let me loose!" I said furiously. "I want one of them, just one of them. I can get the hindmost in the pack!"

But she wouldn't release me, and I certainly wasn't going to fight her, and Louis had joined with her in her angry and desperate entreaties.

"Lestat, don't go after them!" he said, his polite manner strained to the fullest. "We've had quite enough. We must leave here now."

"All right!" I said, giving it up resentfully. Besides, it was too late. The burnt one had expired in smoke and sputtering flames, and the others were gone into silence and darkness without a trace.

The night around us was suddenly empty, except for the thunder of the freeway traffic high above. And there we were, the three of us, standing together in the lurid glare of the blazing car.

Louis wiped the soot from his face wearily, his stiff white shirtfront smudged, his long velvet opera cape burnt and torn.

And there was Gabrielle, the waif just as she'd been so long ago, the dusty, ragged boy in frayed khaki jungle jacket and pants, the squashed brown felt hat askew on her lovely head.

Out of the cacophony of city noises, we heard the thin whine of sirens approaching.

Yet we stood motionless, the three of us, waiting, glancing to one another. And I knew we were all scanning for Marius. Surely it was Marius. It had to be. And he was with us, not against us. And he would answer us now.

I said his name aloud softly. I peered into the dark under the freeway, and out over the endless army of little houses that crowded the surrounding slopes.

But all I could hear were the sirens growing louder and the murmur of human voices as mortals began the long climb from the boulevard below.

I saw fear in Gabrielle's face. I reached out for her, went towards her, in spite of all the hideous confusion, the mortals coming nearer and nearer, the vehicles stopped on the freeway above.

Her embrace was sudden, warm. But she gestured for me to hurry.

"We're in danger! All of us," she whispered. "Terrible danger. Come!"

3

IT WAS five o'clock in the morning and I stood alone at the glass doors of the Carmel Valley ranch house. Gabrielle and Louis had gone into the hills together to find their rest.

A phone call north had told me that my mortal musicians were safe in the new Sonoma hideaway, partying madly behind electric fences and gates. As for the police and the press and all their inevitable questions, well, that would have to wait.

And now I waited alone for the morning light as I'd always done, wondering why Marius hadn't shown himself, why he had saved us only to vanish without a word.

"AND suppose it wasn't Marius," Gabrielle had said anxiously as she paced the floor afterwards. "I tell you I felt an overwhelming sense of menace. I felt danger to us as well as to them. I felt it outside the auditorium when I drove away. I felt it when we stood by the burning car. Something about it. It wasn't Marius, I'm convinced—"

"Something almost barbaric about it," Louis had said. "Almost but not quite—"

"Yes, almost savage," she had answered, glancing to him in acknowledgment. "And even if it was Marius, what makes you think he didn't save you so that he could take his private vengeance in his own way?"

"No," I had said, laughing softly. "Marius doesn't want revenge, or he would already have it, that much I know."

But I had been too excited just watching her, the old walk, the old gestures. And ah, the frayed safari clothing. After two hundred years, she was still the intrepid explorer. She straddled the chair like a cowboy when she sat down, resting her chin on her hands on the high back.

We had so much to talk about, to tell each other, and I was simply too happy to be afraid.

And besides, being afraid was too awful, because I knew now I had made another serious miscalculation. I'd realized it for the first time when the Porsche exploded with Louis still inside it. This little war of mine would put all those I loved in danger. What a fool I'd been to think I could draw the venom to myself.

We had to talk all right. We had to be cunning. We had to take great care.

But for now we were safe. I'd told her that soothingly. She and Louis didn't feel the menace here; it had not followed us to the valley. And I had never felt it. And our young and foolish immortal enemies had scattered, believing that we possessed the power to incinerate them at will.

"You know a thousand times, a thousand times, I pictured our reunion," Gabrielle said. "And never once was it anything like this."

"I rather think it went splendidly!" I said. "And don't suppose for a moment that I couldn't have gotten us out of it! I was about to throttle that one with the scythe, toss him over the auditorium. And I saw the other one coming. I could have broken him in half. I tell you one of the frustrating things about all this is I didn't get the chance—"

"You, Monsieur, are an absolute imp!" she said. "You are impossible! You are—what did Marius himself call you—the damnedest creature! I am in full accord."

I laughed delightedly. Such sweet flattery. And how lovely the old-fashioned French.

And Louis had been so taken with her, sitting back in the shadows as he watched her, reticent, musing as he'd always been. Immaculate he was again, as if his garments were entirely at his command, and we'd just come from the last act of *La Traviata* to watch the mortals drink their champagne at the marble-top café tables as the fashionable carriages clattered past.

Feeling of the new coven formed, magnificent energy, the denial of the human reality, the three of us together against all tribes, all worlds. And a profound feeling of safety, of unstoppable momentum—how to explain that to them.

"Mother, stop worrying," I had said finally, hoping to settle it all, to create a moment of pure equanimity. "It's pointless. A creature powerful enough to burn his enemies can find us anytime that he chooses, do exactly what he likes."

"And this should stop me from worrying?" she said.

I saw Louis shake his head.

"I don't have your powers," he said unobtrusively, "nevertheless I felt this thing. And I tell you it was alien, utterly uncivilized, for want of a better word."

"Ah, you've hit it again," Gabrielle interjected. "It was completely foreign as if coming from a being so removed . . ."

"And your Marius is too civilized," Louis insisted, "too burdened with philosophy. That's why you know he doesn't want revenge."

"Alien? Uncivilized?" I glanced at both of them. "Why didn't I feel this menace!" I asked.

"*Mon Dieu,* it could have been anything," Gabrielle had said finally. "That music of yours could wake the dead."

I HAD thought of last night's enigmatic message—*Lestat! Danger*—but it had been too close to dawn for me to worry them with it. And besides, it explained nothing. It was merely another fragment of the puzzle, and one perhaps that did not belong at all.

AND now they were gone together, and I was standing alone before the glass doors watching the gleam of light grow brighter and brighter over the Santa Lucia Mountains, thinking:

"Where are you, Marius? Why the hell don't you reveal yourself?" It could damn well be true, everything that Gabrielle said. "Is it a game to you?"

And was it a game to me that I didn't really call out to him? I mean raise my secret voice with its full power, as he had told me two centuries ago that I might do?

Through all my struggles, it had become such a matter of pride not to call to him, but what did that pride matter now?

Maybe it was the call he required of me. Maybe he was demanding that call. All the old bitterness and stubbornness were gone from me now. Why not make that effort, at least?

And closing my eyes, I did what I had not done since those old eighteenth-century nights when I'd talked to him aloud in the streets of Cairo or Rome. Silently, I called. And I felt the voiceless cry rising out of me and traveling into oblivion. I could almost feel it traverse the world of visible proportions, feel it grow fainter and fainter, feel it burn out.

And there it was again for a split second, the distant unrecognizable place I had glimpsed last night. Snow, endless snow, and some sort of stone dwelling, windows encrusted with ice. And on a high promontory a curious modern apparatus, a great gray metal dish turning on an axis to draw to itself the invisible waves that crisscross the earth skies.

Television antenna! Reaching from this snowy waste to the satellite —that is what it was! And the broken glass on the floor was the glass of a television screen. I saw it. Stone bench . . . a broken television screen. Noise.

Fading.

MARIUS!

Danger, Lestat. All of us in danger. She has . . . I cannot . . . Ice. Buried in ice. Flash of shattered glass on a stone floor, the bench empty, the clang and vibration of *The Vampire Lestat* throbbing from the speakers—"*She has . . . Lestat, help me! All of us . . . danger. She has . . .*"

Silence. The connection broken.

MARIUS!

Something, but too faint. For all its intensity simply too faint!

MARIUS!

I was leaning against the window, staring right into the morning light as it grew brighter, my eyes watering, the tips of my fingers almost burning on the hot glass.

Answer me, is it Akasha? Are you telling me that it is Akasha, that she is the one, that it was she?

But the sun was rising over the mountains. The lethal rays were spilling down into the valley, ranging across the valley floor.

I ran out of the house, across the field and towards the hills, my arm up to shield my eyes.

And within moments I had reached my hidden underground crypt, pulled back the stone, and I went down the crudely dug little stairs. One more turn and then another and I was in cold and safe blackness, earth smell, and I lay on the mud floor of the tiny chamber, my heart thudding, my limbs trembling. Akasha! *That music of yours could wake the dead.*

Television set in the chamber, of course, Marius had given them that, and the broadcasts right off the satellite. They had seen the video films! I knew it, I knew it as certainly as if he had spelled it out to the last detail. He had brought the television down into their sanctum, just as he had brought the movies to them years and years ago.

And she had been awakened, she had risen. *That music of yours could wake the dead.* I'd done it again.

Oh, if only I could keep my eyes open, could only think, if the sun wasn't rising.

She had been there in San Francisco, she had been that close to us, burning our enemies. *Alien, utterly foreign,* yes.

But not uncivilized, no, not savage. She was not that. She was only just reawakened, my goddess, risen like a magnificent butterfly from its cocoon. And what was the world to her? How had she come to us? What was the state of her mind? *Danger to all of us.* No. I don't believe it! She had slain our enemies. She had come to us.

But I couldn't fight the drowsiness and heaviness any longer. Pure sensation was driving out all wonder and excitement. My body grew limp and helplessly still against the earth.

And then I felt a hand suddenly close on mine.

Cold as marble it was, and just about that strong.

My eyes snapped open in the darkness. The hand tightened its grip. A great mass of silken hair brushed my face. A cold arm moved across my chest.

Oh, please, my darling, my beautiful one, please! I wanted to say. But my eyes were closing! My lips wouldn't move. I was losing consciousness. The sun had risen above.

THE QUEEN OF THE DAMNED

TRAGIC RABBIT

Tragic rabbit, a painting.
The caked ears green like rolled corn.
The black forehead pointing at the stars.
A painting on my wall, alone

as rabbits are
and aren't. Fat red cheek,
all Art, trembling nose,
a habit hard to break as not.

You too can be a tragic rabbit; green and red
your back, blue your manly little chest.
But if you're ever goaded into being one
beware the True Flesh, it

will knock you off your tragic horse
and break your tragic colors like a ghost
breaks marble; your wounds will heal
so quickly water

will be jealous.
Rabbits on white paper painted
outgrow all charms against their breeding wild;
and their rolled corn ears become horns.

So watch out if the tragic life feels fine—
caught in that rabbit trap
all colors look like sunlight's swords,
and scissors like The Living Lord.

STAN RICE
Some Lamb (1975)

I'M THE Vampire Lestat. Remember me? The vampire who became a super rock star, the one who wrote the autobiography? The one with the blond hair and the gray eyes, and the insatiable desire for visibility and fame? You remember. I wanted to be a symbol of evil in a shining century that didn't have any place for the literal evil that I am. I even figured I'd do some good in that fashion—playing the devil on the painted stage.

And I was off to a good start when we talked last. I'd just made my debut in San Francisco—first "live concert" for me and my mortal band. Our album was a huge success. My autobiography was doing respectably with both the dead and the undead.

Then something utterly unforeseen took place. Well, at least *I* hadn't seen it coming. And when I left you, I was hanging from the proverbial cliff, you might say.

Well, it's all over now—what followed. I've survived, obviously. I wouldn't be talking to you if I hadn't. And the cosmic dust has finally settled; and the small rift in the world's fabric of rational beliefs has been mended, or at least closed.

I'm a little sadder for all of it, and a little meaner and a little more conscientious as well. I'm also infinitely more powerful, though the human in me is closer to the surface than ever—an anguished and hungry being who both loves and detests this invincible immortal shell in which I'm locked.

The blood thirst? Insatiable, though physically I have never needed the blood less. Possibly I could exist now without it altogether. But the lust I feel for everything that walks tells me that this will never be put to the test.

You know, it was never merely the need for the blood anyway, though the blood is all things sensual that a creature could desire; it's the intimacy of that moment—drinking, killing—the great heart-to-heart dance that takes place as the victim weakens and I feel myself expanding, swallowing the death which, for a split second, blazes as large as the life.

That's deceptive, however. No death can be as large as a life. And that's why I keep taking life, isn't it? And I'm as far from salvation now as I could ever get. The fact that I know it only makes it worse.

Of course I can still pass for human; all of us can, in one way or another, no matter how old we are. Collar up, hat down, dark glasses, hands in pockets—it usually does the trick. I like slim leather jackets and tight jeans for this disguise now, and a pair of plain black boots that are good for walking on any terrain. But now and then I wear the fancier silks which people like in these southern climes where I now reside.

If someone does look too closely, then there is a little telepathic razzle-dazzle: *Perfectly normal, what you see.* And a flash of the old smile, fang teeth easily concealed, and the mortal goes his way.

Occasionally I throw up all the disguises; I just go out the way I am. Hair long, a velvet blazer that makes me think of the olden times, and an emerald ring or two on my right hand. I walk fast right through the downtown crowds in this lovely corrupt southern city; or stroll slowly along the beaches, breathing the warm southern breeze, on sands that are as white as the moon.

Nobody stares for more than a second or two. There are too many other inexplicable things around us—horrors, threats, mysteries that draw you in and then inevitably disenchant you. Back to the predictable and humdrum. The prince is never going to come, everybody knows that; and maybe Sleeping Beauty's dead.

It's the same for the others who have survived with me, and who share this hot and verdant little corner of the universe—the southeastern tip of the North American continent, the glistering metropolis of Miami, a happy hunting ground for bloodthirsting immortals if ever there was such a place.

It's good to have them with me, the others; it's crucial, really—and what I always thought I wanted: a grand coven of the wise, the enduring, the ancient, and the careless young.

But ah, the agony of being anonymous among mortals has never been worse for me, greedy monster that I am. The soft murmur of preternatural voices can't distract me from it. That taste of mortal recognition was too seductive—the record albums in the windows, the fans leaping and clapping in front of the stage. Never mind that they didn't really believe I was a vampire; for that moment we were together. They were calling my name!

Now the record albums are gone, and I will never listen to those songs again. My book remains—along with *Interview with the Vampire*—safely disguised as fiction, which is, perhaps, as it should be. I caused enough trouble, as you will see.

Disaster, that's what I wrought with my little games. The vampire who would have been a hero and a martyr finally for one moment of pure relevance . . .

You'd think I'd learn something from it, wouldn't you? Well, I did, actually. I really did.

But it's just so painful to shrink back into the shadows—Lestat, the sleek and nameless gangster ghoulie again creeping up on helpless mortals who know nothing of things like me. So hurtful to be again the outsider, forever on the fringes, struggling with good and evil in the age-old private hell of body and soul.

In my isolation now I dream of finding some sweet young thing in a moonlighted chamber—one of those tender teenagers, as they call them now, who read my book and listened to my songs; one of the idealistic lovelies who wrote me fan letters on scented paper, during that brief period of ill-fated glory, talking of poetry and the power of illusion, saying she wished I was real; I dream of stealing into her darkened room, where maybe my book lies on a bedside table, with a pretty velvet marker in it, and I dream of touching her shoulder and smiling as our eyes meet. "Lestat! I always believed in you. I always knew you would come!"

I clasp her face in both hands as I bend to kiss her. "Yes, darling," I answer, "and you don't know how I need you, how I love you, how I always have."

Maybe she would find me more charming on account of what's befallen me—the unexpected horror I've seen, the inevitable pain I've endured. It's an awful truth that suffering can deepen us, give a greater luster to our colors, a richer resonance to our words. That is, if it doesn't destroy us, if it doesn't burn away the optimism and the spirit, the capacity for visions, and the respect for simple yet indispensable things.

Please forgive me if I sound bitter.

I don't have any right to be. I started the whole thing; and I got out in one piece, as they say. And so many of our kind did not. Then there were the mortals who suffered. That part was inexcusable. And surely I shall always pay for that.

But you see, I still don't really fully understand what happened. I don't know whether or not it was a tragedy, or merely a meaningless venture. Or whether or not something absolutely magnificent might have been born of my blundering, something that could have lifted me right out of irrelevance and nightmare and into the burning light of redemption after all.

I may never know, either. The point is, it's over. And our world—our little private realm—is smaller and darker and safer than ever. It will never again be what it was.

It's a wonder that I didn't foresee the cataclysm, but then I never really envision the finish of anything that I start. It's the risk that fascinates, the moment of infinite possibility. It lures me through eternity when all other charms fail.

After all, I was like that when I was alive two hundred years ago—the restless one, the impatient one, the one who was always spoiling for love and a good brawl. When I set out for Paris in the 1780s to be an actor, all I dreamed of were beginnings—the moment each night when the curtain went up.

Maybe the old ones are right. I refer now to the true immortals—the blood drinkers who've survived the millennia—who say that none of us really changes over time; we only become more fully what we are.

To put it another way, you do get wiser when you live for hundreds of years; but you also have more time to turn out as badly as your enemies always said you might.

And I'm the same devil I always was, the young man who would have center stage, where you can best see me, and maybe love me. One's no good without the other. And I want so much to amuse you, to enthrall you, to make you forgive me everything. . . . Random moments of secret contact and recognition will never be enough, I'm afraid.

But I'm jumping ahead now, aren't I?

If you've read my autobiography then you want to know what I'm talking about. What was this disaster of which I speak?

Well, let's review, shall we? As I've said, I wrote the book and made the album because I wanted to be visible, to be seen for what I am, even if only in symbolic terms.

As to the risk that mortals might really catch on, that they might realize I was exactly what I said I was—I was rather excited by that possibility as well. Let them hunt us down, let them destroy us, that was in a way my fondest wish. We don't deserve to exist; they ought to kill us. And think of the battles! Ah, fighting those who really know what I am.

But I never really expected such a confrontation; and the rock musician persona, it was too marvelous a cover for a fiend like me.

It was my own kind who took me literally, who decided to punish me for what I had done. And of course I'd counted on that too.

After all, I'd told our history in my autobiography; I'd told our deepest secrets, things I'd been sworn never to reveal. And I was strutting before the hot lights and the camera lenses. And what if some scientist had gotten hold of me, or more likely a zealous police officer on a minor traffic violation five minutes before sunup, and somehow I'd been incarcerated, inspected, identified, and classified—all during the daylight hours while I lay helpless—to the satisfaction of the worst mortal skeptics worldwide?

Granted, that wasn't very likely. Still isn't. (Though it could be such fun, it really could!)

Yet it was inevitable that my own kind should be infuriated by the risks I was taking, that they would try to burn me alive, or chop me up in little immortal pieces. Most of the young ones, they were too stupid to realize how safe we were.

And as the night of the concert approached, I'd found myself dreaming of those battles, too. Such a pleasure it was going to be to destroy those who were as evil as I was; to cut a swathe through the guilty; to cut down my own image again and again.

Yet, you know, the sheer joy of being out there, making music, making theater, making magic!—that's what it was all about in the end. I wanted to be alive, finally. I wanted to be simply human. The mortal actor who'd gone to Paris two hundred years ago and met death on the boulevard, would have his moment at last.

But to continue with the review—the concert was a success. I had my moment of triumph before fifteen thousand screaming mortal fans; and two of my greatest immortal loves were there with me—Gabrielle and Louis—my fledglings, my paramours, from whom I'd been separated for too many dark years.

Before the night was over, we licked the pesty vampires who tried to punish me for what I was doing. But we'd had an invisible ally in these little skirmishes; our enemies burst into flames before they could do us harm.

As morning approached, I was too elated by the whole night to take the question of danger seriously. I ignored Gabrielle's impassioned warnings—too sweet to hold her once again; and I dismissed Louis's dark suspicions as I always had.

And then the jam, the cliffhanger . . .

Just as the sun was rising over Carmel Valley and I was closing my eyes as vampires must do at that moment, I realized I wasn't alone in my underground lair. It wasn't only the young vampires I'd reached with my music; my songs had roused from their slumber the very oldest of our kind in the world.

And I found myself in one of those breathtaking instants of risk and possibility. What was to follow? Was I to die finally, or perhaps to be reborn?

Now, to tell you the full story of what happened after that, I must move back a little in time.

I have to begin some ten nights before the fatal concert and I have to let you slip into the minds and hearts of other beings who were responding to my music and my book in ways of which I knew little or nothing at the time.

In other words, a lot was going on which I had to reconstruct later. And it is the reconstruction that I offer you now.

So we will move out of the narrow, lyrical confines of the first person singular; we will jump as a thousand mortal writers have done into the brains and souls of "many characters." We will gallop into the world of "third person" and "multiple point of view."

And by the way, when these other characters think or say of me that I am beautiful or irresistible, etc., don't think I put these words in their heads. I didn't! It's what was told to me after, or what I drew out of their minds with infallible telepathic power; I wouldn't lie about that or anything else. I can't help being a gorgeous fiend. It's just the card I drew. The bastard monster who made me what I am picked me on account of my good looks. That's the long and short of it. And accidents like that occur all the time.

We live in a world of accidents finally, in which only aesthetic principles have a consistency of which we can be sure. Right and wrong we will struggle with forever, striving to create and maintain an ethical balance; but the shimmer of summer rain under the street lamps or the great flashing glare of artillery against a night sky—such brutal beauty is beyond dispute.

Now, be assured: though I am leaving you, I will return with full flair at the appropriate moment. The truth is, I hate not being the first person narrator all the way through! To paraphrase David Copperfield, I don't know whether I'm the hero or the victim of this tale. But either way, shouldn't I dominate it? I'm the one really telling it, after all.

Alas, my being the James Bond of vampires isn't the whole issue. Vanity must wait. I want you to know what really took place with us, even if you never believe it. In fiction if nowhere else, I must have a little meaning, a little coherence, or I will go mad.

So until we meet again, I am thinking of you always; I love you; I wish you were here . . . in my arms.

CONTENTS

PROEM

Declaration in the Form of Graffiti

—written in black felt-tip pen on a red wall in the back room of a bar called Dracula's Daughter in San Francisco—

Children of Darkness
Be Advised of the Following:

Book One: *Interview with the Vampire*, published in 1976, was a true story. Any one of us could have written it—an account of becoming what we are, of the misery and the searching. Yet Louis, the two-hundred-year-old immortal who reveals all, insists on mortal sympathy. Lestat, the villain who gave Louis the Dark Gift, gave him precious little else in the way of explanations or consolation. Sound familiar? Louis hasn't given up the search for salvation yet, though even Armand, the oldest immortal he was ever to find, could tell him nothing of why we are here or who made us. Not very surprising, is it, vampire boys and girls? After all, there has never been a Baltimore Catechism for vampires.

That is, there wasn't until the publication of:

Book Two: *The Vampire Lestat*, this very week. Subtitle: His "early education and adventures." You don't believe it? Check with the nearest mortal bookseller. Then go into the nearest record store and ask to see the album which has only just arrived—also entitled *The Vampire Lestat*, with predictable modesty. Or if all else fails, switch on your cable TV, if you don't disdain such things, and wait for one of Lestat's numerous rock video films which began to air with nauseating frequency only yesterday. You will know Lestat for what he is immediately. And it may not surprise you to be told that he plans to compound these unprecedented outrages by appearing "live" on stage in a debut concert in this very city. Yes, on Halloween, you guessed it.

But let us forget for the moment the blatant insanity of his preternatural eyes flashing from every record store window, or his powerful voice singing out the secret names and stories of the most ancient among us. Why is he doing all this? What do his songs tell us? It is spelled out in his book. He has given us not only a catechism but a Bible.

And deep into biblical times we are led to confront our first parents: Enkil and Akasha, rulers of the valley of the Nile before it was ever called Egypt. Kindly disregard the gobbledygook of how they became the first bloodsuckers on the face of the earth; it makes only a little more sense than the story of how life formed on this planet in the first place, or how human fetuses develop from microscopic cells within the wombs of their mortal mothers. The truth is we are descended from this venerable pair, and like it or no, there is considerable reason to believe that the primal generator of all our delicious and indispensable powers resides in one or the other of their ancient bodies. What does this mean? To put it bluntly, if Akasha and Enkil should ever walk hand in hand into a furnace, we should all burn with them. Crush them to glittering dust, and we are annihilated.

Ah, but there's hope. The pair haven't moved in over fifty centuries! Yes, that's correct. Except of course that Lestat claims to have wakened them both by playing a violin at the foot of their shrine. But if we dismiss his extravagant tale that Akasha took him in her arms and shared with him her primal blood, we are left with the more likely state of affairs, corroborated by stories of old, that the two have not batted an eyelash since before the fall of the Roman Empire. They've been kept all this time in a nice private crypt by Marius, an ancient Roman vampire, who certainly knows what's best for all of us. And it was he who told the Vampire Lestat never to reveal the secret.

Not a very trustworthy confidant, the Vampire Lestat. And what are his motives for the book, the album, the films, the concert? Quite impossible to know what goes on in the mind of this fiend, except that what he wants to do he does, with reliable consistency. After all, did he not make a vampire child? And a vampire of his own mother, Gabrielle, who for years was his loving companion? He may set his sights upon the papacy, this devil, out of sheer thirst for excitement!

So that's the gist: Louis, a wandering philosopher whom none of us can find, has confided our deepest moral secrets to countless strangers. And Lestat has dared to reveal our history to the world, as he parades his supernatural endowments before the mortal public.

Now the Question: Why are these two still in existence? Why have we not destroyed them already? Oh, the danger to us from the great mortal herd is by no means a certainty. The villagers are not yet at the door, torches in hand, threatening to burn the castle. But the monster is courting a change in mortal perspective. And though we are too clever to corroborate for the human record his foolish fabrications, the outrage exceeds all precedent. It cannot go unpunished.

Further observations: If the story the Vampire Lestat has told is true—and there are many who swear it is, though on what account they cannot tell you—may not the two-thousand-year-old Marius come forward to punish Lestat's disobedience? Or perhaps the King and Queen, if they have ears to hear, will waken at the sound of their names carried on radio waves around the planet. What might happen to us all if this should occur? Shall we prosper under their new reign? Or will they set the time for universal destruction? Whatever the case, might not the swift destruction of the Vampire Lestat avert it?

The Plan: Destroy the Vampire Lestat and all his cohorts as soon as they dare to show themselves. Destroy all those who show him allegiance.

A Warning: Inevitably, there are other very old blood drinkers out there. We have all from time to time glimpsed them, or felt their presence. Lestat's revelations do not shock so much as they rouse some unconscious awareness within us. And surely with their great powers, these old ones can hear Lestat's music. What ancient and terrible beings, incited by history, purpose, or mere recognition, might be moving slowly and inexorably to answer his summons?

Copies of this Declaration have to been sent to every meeting place on the Vampire Connection, and to coven houses the world over. But you must take heed and spread the word: The Vampire Lestat is to be destroyed and with him his mother, Gabrielle, his cohorts, Louis and Armand, and any and all immortals who show him loyalty.

Happy Halloween, vampire boys and girls. We shall see you at the concert. We shall see that the Vampire Lestat never leaves it.

THE blond-haired figure in the red velvet coat read the declaration over again from his comfortable vantage point in the far corner. His eyes were almost invisible behind his dark tinted glasses and the brim of his gray hat. He wore gray suede gloves, and his arms were folded over his chest as he leaned back against the high black wainscoting, one boot heel hooked on the rung of his chair.

"Lestat, you are the damnedest creature!" he whispered under his breath. "You are a brat prince." He gave a little private laugh. Then he scanned the large shadowy room.

Not unpleasing to him, the intricate black ink mural drawn with such skill, like spiderwebs on the white plaster wall. He rather enjoyed the ruined castle, the graveyard, the withered tree clawing at the full moon. It was the cliché reinvented as if it were not a cliché, an artistic gesture he invariably appreciated. Very fine too was the molded ceiling with its frieze of prancing devils and hags upon broomsticks. And the incense, sweet—an old Indian mixture which he himself had once burnt in the shrine of Those Who Must Be Kept centuries ago.

Yes, one of the more beautiful of the clandestine meeting places.

Less pleasing were the inhabitants, the scattering of slim white figures who hovered around candles set on small ebony tables. Far too many of them for this civilized modern city. And they knew it. To hunt tonight, they would have to roam far and wide, and young ones always have to hunt. Young ones have to kill. They are too hungry to do it any other way.

But they thought only of him just now—who was he, where had he come from? Was he very old and very strong, and what would he do before he left here? Always the same questions, though he tried to slip into their "vampire bars" like any vagrant blood drinker, eyes averted, mind closed.

Time to leave their questions unanswered. He had what he wanted, a fix on their intentions. And Lestat's small audio cassette in his jacket pocket. He would have a tape of the video rock films before he went home.

He rose to go. And one of the young ones rose also. A stiff silence fell, a silence in thoughts as well as words as he and the young one both approached the door. Only the candle flames moved, throwing their shimmer on the black tile floor as if it were water.

"Where do you come from, stranger?" asked the young one politely. He couldn't have been more than twenty when he died, and that could not have been ten years ago. He painted his eyes, waxed his lips, streaked his hair with barbaric color, as if the preternatural gifts were not enough. How extravagant he looked, how unlike what he was, a spare and powerful revenant who could with luck survive the millennia.

What had they promised him with their modern jargon? That he should know the Bardo, the Astral Plane, etheric realms, the music of the spheres, the sound of one hand clapping?

Again he spoke: "Where do you stand on the Vampire Lestat, on the Declaration?"

"You must forgive me. I'm going now."

"But surely you know what Lestat's done," the young one pressed, slipping between him and the door. Now, this was not good manners.

He studied this brash young male more closely. Should he do something to stir them up? To have them talking about it for centuries? He couldn't repress a smile. But no. There'd be enough excitement soon, thanks to his beloved Lestat.

"Let me give you a little piece of advice in response," he said quietly to the young inquisitor. "You cannot destroy the Vampire Lestat; no one can. But why that is so, I honestly can't tell you."

The young one was caught off guard, and a little insulted.

"But let me ask you a question now," the other continued. "Why this obsession with the Vampire Lestat? What about the content of his revelations? Have you fledglings no desire to seek Marius, the guardian of Those Who Must Be Kept? To see for yourselves the Mother and the Father?"

The young one was confused, then gradually scornful. He could not form a clever answer. But the true reply was plain enough in his soul—in the souls of all those listening and watching. Those Who Must Be Kept might or might not exist; and Marius perhaps did not exist either. But the Vampire Lestat was real, as real as anything this callow immortal knew, and the Vampire Lestat was a greedy fiend who risked the secret prosperity of all his kind just to be loved and seen by mortals.

He almost laughed in the young one's face. Such an insignificant battle. Lestat understood these faithless times so beautifully, one had to admit it. Yes, he'd told the secrets he'd been warned to keep, but in so doing, he had betrayed nothing and no one.

"Watch out for the Vampire Lestat," he said to the young one finally with a smile. "There are very few true immortals walking this earth. He may be one of them."

Then he lifted the young one off his feet and set him down out of the way. And he went out the door into the tavern proper.

The front room, spacious and opulent with its black velvet hangings and fixtures of lacquered brass, was packed with noisy mortals. Cinema vampires glared from their gilt frames on satin-lined walls. An organ poured out the passionate Toccata and Fugue of Bach, beneath a babble of conversation and violent riffs of drunken laughter. He loved the sight of so much exuberant life. He loved even the age-old smell of the malt and the wine, and the perfume of the cigarettes. And as he made his way to the front, he loved the crush of the soft fragrant humans against him. He loved the fact that the living took not the slightest notice of him.

At last the moist air, the busy early evening pavements of Castro Street. The sky still had a polished silver gleam. Men and women rushed to and fro to escape the faint slanting rain, only to be clotted at the corners, waiting for great bulbous colored lights to wink and signal.

The speakers of the record store across the street blared Lestat's voice over the roar of the passing bus, the hiss of wheels on the wet asphalt:

In my dreams, I hold her still,
Angel, lover, Mother.
And in my dreams, I kiss her lips,
Mistress, Muse, Daughter.

She gave me life
I gave her death
My beautiful Marquise.

And on the Devil's Road we walked
Two orphans then together.

And does she hear my hymns tonight
of Kings and Queens and Ancient truths?
Of broken vows and sorrow?

Or does she climb some distant path
where rhyme and song can't find her?

Come back to me, my Gabrielle
My Beautiful Marquise.
The castle's ruined on the hill
The village lost beneath the snow
But you are mine forever.

Was she here already, his mother?

The voice died away in a soft drift of electric notes to be swallowed finally by the random noise around him. He wandered out into the wet breeze and made his way to the corner. Pretty, the busy little street. The flower vendor still sold his blooms beneath the awning. The butcher was thronged with after-work shoppers. Behind the café windows, mortals took their evening meals or lingered with their newspapers. Dozens waited for a downhill bus, and a line had formed across the way before an old motion picture theater.

She was here, Gabrielle. He had a vague yet infallible sense of it.

When he reached the curb, he stood with his back against the iron street lamp, breathing the fresh wind that came off the mountain. It was a good view of downtown, along the broad straight length of Market Street. Rather like a boulevard in Paris. And all around the gentle urban slopes covered with cheerful lighted windows.

Yes, but where was she, precisely? Gabrielle, he whispered. He closed his eyes. He listened. At first there came the great boundless roar of thousands of voices, image crowding upon image. The whole wide world threatened to open up, and to swallow him with its ceaseless lamentations. *Gabrielle.* The thunderous clamor slowly died away. He caught a glimmer of pain from a mortal passing near. And in a high building on the hill, a dying woman dreamed of childhood strife as she sat listless at her window. Then in a dim steady silence, he saw what he wanted to see: Gabrielle, stopped in her tracks. She'd heard his voice. She knew that she was watched. A tall blond female, hair in a single braid down her back, standing in one of the clean deserted streets of downtown, not far from him. She wore a khaki jacket and pants, a worn brown sweater. And a hat not unlike his own that covered her eyes, only a bit of her face visible above her upturned collar. Now she closed her mind, effectively surrounding herself with an invisible shield. The image vanished.

Yes, here, waiting for her son, Lestat. Why had he ever feared for her—the cold one who fears nothing for herself, only for Lestat. All right. He was pleased. And Lestat would be also.

But what about the other? Louis, the gentle one, with the black hair and green eyes, whose steps made a careless sound when he walked, who even whistled to himself in dark streets so that mortals heard him coming. *Louis, where are you?*

Almost instantly, he saw Louis enter an empty drawing room. He had only just come up the stairs from the cellar where he had slept by day in a vault behind the wall. He had no awareness at all of anyone watching. He moved with silky strides across the dusty room, and stood looking down through the soiled glass at the thick flow of passing cars. Same old house on Divisadero Street. In fact, nothing changed much at all with this elegant and sensuous creature who had caused such a little tumult with his story in *Interview with the Vampire.* Except that now he was waiting for Lestat. He had had troubling dreams; he was fearful for Lestat, and full of old and unfamiliar longings.

Reluctantly, he let the image go. He had a great affection for that one, Louis. And the affection was not wise because Louis had a tender, educated soul and none of the dazzling power of Gabrielle or her devilish son. Yet Louis might survive as long as they, he was sure of that. Curious the kinds of courage which made for endurance. Maybe it had to do with acceptance. But then how account for Lestat, beaten, scarred, yet risen again? Lestat who never accepted anything?

They had not found each other yet, Gabrielle and Louis. But it was all right. What was he to do? Bring them together? The very idea. . . . Besides, Lestat would do that soon enough.

But now he was smiling again. "Lestat, you are the damnedest creature! Yes, a brat prince." Slowly, he reinvoked every detail of Lestat's face and form. The ice-blue eyes, darkening with laughter; the generous smile; the way the eyebrows came together in a boyish scowl; the sudden flares of high spirits and blasphemous humor. Even the catlike poise of the body he could envisage. So uncommon in a man of muscular build. Such strength, always such strength and such irrepressible optimism.

The fact was, he did not know his own mind about the entire enterprise, only that he was amused and fascinated. Of course there was no thought of vengeance against Lestat for telling his secrets. And surely Lestat had counted upon that, but then one never knew. Maybe Lestat truly did not care. He knew no more than the fools back there in the bar, on that score.

What mattered to him was that for the first time in so many years, he found himself thinking in terms of past and future; he found himself most keenly aware of the nature of this era. Those Who Must Be Kept were fiction even to their own children! Long gone were the days when fierce rogue blood drinkers searched for their shrine and their powerful blood. Nobody believed or even cared any longer!

And there lay the essence of the age; for its mortals were of an even more practical ilk, rejecting at every turn the miraculous. With unprecedented courage, they had founded their greatest ethical advances squarely upon the truths embedded in the physical.

Two hundred years since he and Lestat had discussed these very things on an island in the Mediterranean—the dream of a godless and truly moral world where love of one's fellow man would be the only dogma. *A world in which we do not belong.* And now such a world was almost realized. And the Vampire Lestat had passed into popular art where all the old devils ought to go, and would take with him the whole accused tribe, including Those Who Must Be Kept, though they might never know it.

It made him smile, the symmetry of it. He found himself not merely in awe but strongly seduced by the whole idea of what Lestat had done. He could well understand the lure of fame.

Why, it had thrilled him shamelessly to see his own name scrawled on the wall of the bar. He had laughed; but he had enjoyed the laughter thoroughly.

Leave it to Lestat to construct such an inspiring drama, and that's what it was, all right. Lestat, the boisterous boulevard actor of the ancien régime, now risen to stardom in this beauteous and innocent era.

But had he been right in his little summation to the fledgling in the bar, that no one could destroy the brat prince? That was sheer romance. Good advertising. *The fact is, any of us can be destroyed . . . one way or another. Even Those Who Must Be Kept, surely.*

They were weak, of course, those fledgling "Children of Darkness," as they styled themselves. The numbers did not increase their strength significantly. But what of the older ones? If only Lestat had not used the names of Mael and Pandora. But were there not blood drinkers older even than that, ones of whom he himself knew nothing? He thought of that warning on the wall: "ancient and terrible beings . . . moving slowly and inexorably to answer his summons."

A frisson startled him; coldness, yet for an instant he thought he saw a jungle—a green, fetid place, full of unwholesome and smothering warmth. Gone, without explanation, like so many sudden signals and messages he received. He'd learned long ago to shut out the endless flow of voices and images that his mental powers enabled him to hear; yet now and then something violent and unexpected, like a sharp cry, came through.

Whatever, he had been in this city long enough. He did not know that he meant to intervene, no matter what happened! He was angry with his own sudden warmth of feeling. He wanted to be home now. He had been away from Those Who Must Be Kept for too long.

But how he loved to watch the energetic human crowd, the clumsy parade of shining traffic. Even the poison smells of the city he did not mind. They were no worse than the stench of ancient Rome, or Antioch, or Athens—when piles of human waste fed the flies wherever you looked, and the air reeked of inevitable disease and hunger. No, he liked the clean pastel-colored cities of California well enough. He could have lingered forever among their clear-eyed and purposeful inhabitants.

But he must go home. The concert was not for many nights, and he would see Lestat then, if he chose. . . . How delicious not to know precisely what he might do, any more than others knew, others who didn't even believe in him!

He crossed Castro Street and went swiftly up the wide pavement of

Market. The wind had slackened; the air was almost warm. He took up a brisk pace, even whistling to himself the way that Louis often did. He felt good. Human. Then he stopped before the store that sold television sets and radios. Lestat was singing on each and every screen, both large and small.

He laughed under his breath at the great concert of gesture and movement. The sound was off, buried in tiny glowing seeds within the equipment. He'd have to search to receive it. But wasn't there a charm in merely watching the antics of the yellow-haired brat prince in merciless silence?

The camera drew back to render the full figure of Lestat who played a violin as if in a void. A starry darkness now and then enclosed him. Then quite suddenly a pair of doors were opened—it was the old shrine of Those Who Must Be Kept, quite exactly! And there—Akasha and Enkil, or rather actors made up to play the part, white-skinned Egyptians with long black silken hair and glittering jewelry.

Of course. Why hadn't he guessed that Lestat would carry it to this vulgar and tantalizing extreme? He leant forward, listening for the transmission of the sound. He heard the voice of Lestat above the violin:

Akasha! Enkil!
Keep your secrets
Keep your silence
It is a better gift than truth.

And now as the violin player closed his eyes and bore down on his music, Akasha slowly rose from the throne. The violin fell from Lestat's hands as he saw her; like a dancer, she wrapped her arms around him, drew him to her, bent to take the blood from him, while pressing his teeth to her own throat.

It was rather better than he had ever imagined—such clever craft. Now the figure of Enkil awakened, rising and walking like a mechanical doll. Forward he came to take back his Queen. Lestat was thrown down on the floor of the shrine. And there the film ended. The rescue by Marius was not part of it.

"Ah, so I do not become a television celebrity," he whispered with a faint smile. He went to the entrance of the darkened store.

The young woman was waiting to let him in. She had the black plastic video cassette in her hand.

"All twelve of them," she said. Fine dark skin and large drowsy brown eyes. The band of silver around her wrist caught the light. He found it enticing. She took the money gratefully, without counting it. "They've been playing them on a dozen channels. I caught them all over, actually. Finished it yesterday afternoon."

"You've served me well," he answered. "I thank you." He produced another thick fold of bills.

"No big thing," she said. She didn't want to take the extra money. *You will.*

She took it with a shrug and put it in her pocket.

No big thing. He loved these eloquent modern expressions. He loved the sudden shift of her luscious breasts as she'd shrugged, and the lithe twist of her hips beneath the coarse denim clothes that made her seem all the more smooth and fragile. An incandescent flower. As she opened the door for him, he touched the soft nest of her brown hair. Quite unthinkable to feed upon one who has served you; one so innocent. He would not do this! Yet he turned her around, his gloved fingers slipping up through her hair to cradle her head:

"The smallest kiss, my precious one."

Her eyes closed; his teeth pierced the artery instantly and his tongue lapped at the blood. Only a taste. A tiny flash of heat that burnt itself out in his heart within a second. Then he drew back, his lips resting against her frail throat. He could feel her pulse. The craving for the full draught was almost more than he could bear. Sin and atonement. He let her go. He smoothed her soft, springy curls, as he looked into her misted eyes.

Do not remember.

"Good-bye now," she said, smiling.

He stood motionless on the deserted sidewalk. And the thirst, ignored and sullen, gradually died back. He looked at the cardboard sheath of the video cassette.

"A dozen channels," she had said. "I caught them all over, actually." Now if that was so, his charges had already seen Lestat, inevitably, on the large screen positioned before them in the shrine. Long ago, he'd set the satellite dish on the slope above the roof to bring them broadcasts from all the world. A tiny computer device changed the channel each hour. For years, they'd stared expressionless as the images and colors shifted before their lifeless eyes. Had there been the slightest flicker when they heard Lestat's voice, or saw their very own image? Or heard their own names sung as if in a hymn?

Well, he would soon find out. He would play the video cassette for them. He would study their frozen, gleaming faces for something—anything—besides the mere reflection of the light.

"Ah, Marius, you never despair, do you? You are no better than Lestat, with your foolish dreams."

. . .

IT WAS midnight before he reached home.

He shut the steel door against the driving snow, and, standing still for a moment, let the heated air surround him. The blizzard through which he'd passed had lacerated his face and his ears, even his gloved fingers. The warmth felt so good.

In the quiet, he listened for the familiar sound of the giant generators, and the faint electronic pulse of the television set within the shrine many hundreds of feet beneath him. Could that be Lestat singing? Yes. Undoubtedly, the last mournful words of some other song.

Slowly he peeled off his gloves. He removed his hat and ran his hand through his hair. He studied the large entrance hall and the adjacent drawing room for the slightest evidence that anyone else had been here.

Of course that was almost an impossibility. He was miles from the nearest outpost of the modern world, in a great frozen snow-covered waste. But out of force of habit, he always observed everything closely. There were some who could breach this fortress, if only they knew where it was.

All was well. He stood before the giant aquarium, the great room-sized tank which abutted the south wall. So carefully he had constructed this thing, of the heaviest glass and the finest equipment. He watched the schools of multicolored fishes dance past him, then alter their direction instantly and totally in the artificial gloom. The giant sea kelp swayed from one side to another, a forest caught in a hypnotic rhythm as the gentle pressure of the aerator drove it this way and that. It never failed to captivate him, to lock him suddenly to its spectacular monotony. The round black eyes of the fish sent a tremor through him; the high slender trees of kelp with their tapering yellow leaves thrilled him vaguely; but it was the movement, the constant movement that was the crux.

Finally he turned away from it, glancing back once into that pure, unconscious, and incidentally beautiful world.

Yes, all was well here.

Good to be in these warm rooms. Nothing amiss with the soft leather furnishings scattered about the thick wine-colored carpet. Fireplace piled with wood. Books lining the walls. And there the great bank of electronic equipment waiting for him to insert Lestat's tape. That's what he wanted to do, settle by the fire and watch each rock film in sequence. The craft intrigued him as well as the songs themselves, the chemistry of old and new—how Lestat had used the distortions of media to disguise himself so perfectly as another mortal rock singer trying to appear a god.

He took off his long gray cloak and threw it on the chair. Why did the whole thing give him such an unexpected pleasure! Do we all long to blaspheme, to shake our fists in the faces of the gods? Perhaps so. Centuries ago, in what is now called "ancient Rome," he, the well-mannered boy, had always laughed at the antics of bad children.

He should go to the shrine before he did anything else, he knew that. Just for a few moments, to make certain things were as they should be. To check the television, the heat, and all the complex electrical systems. To place fresh coals and incense in the brazier. It was so easy to maintain a paradise for them now, with the livid lights that gave the nutrients of the sun to trees and flowers that had never seen the natural lights of heaven. But the incense, that must be done by hand, as always. And never did he sprinkle it over the coals that he did not think of the first time he'd ever done it.

Time to take a soft cloth, too, and carefully, respectfully, wipe the dust from the parents—from their hard unyielding bodies, even from their lips and their eyes, their cold unblinking eyes. And to think, it had been a full month. It seemed shameful.

Have you missed me, my beloved Akasha and Enkil? Ah, the old game.

His reason told him, as it always had, that they did not know or care whether he came or went. But his pride always teased with another possibility. Does not the crazed lunatic locked in the madhouse cell feel something for the slave who brings it water? Perhaps it wasn't an apt comparison. Certainly not one that was kind.

Yes, they had moved for Lestat, the brat prince, that was true—Akasha to offer the powerful blood and Enkil to take vengeance. And Lestat could make his video films about it forever. But had it not merely proved once and for all that there was no mind left in either of them? Surely no more than an atavistic spark had flared for an instant; it had been too simple to drive them back to silence and stillness on their barren throne.

Nevertheless, it had embittered him. After all, it had never been his goal to transcend the emotions of a thinking man, but rather to refine them, reinvent them, enjoy them with an infinitely perfectible understanding. And he had been tempted at the very moment to turn on Lestat with an all-too-human fury.

Young one, why don't you take Those Who Must Be Kept since they have shown you such remarkable favor? I should like to be rid of them now. I have only had this burden since the dawn of the Christian era.

But in truth that wasn't his finer feeling. Not then, not now. Only a temporary indulgence. Lestat he loved as he always had. Every realm needs a brat prince. And the silence of the King and Queen was as much a blessing as a curse, perhaps. Lestat's song had been quite right on that point. But who would ever settle the question?

Oh, he would go down later with the video cassette and watch for himself, of course. And if there were just the faintest flicker, the faintest shift in their eternal gaze.

But there you go again. . . . Lestat makes you young and stupid. Likely to feed on innocence and dream of cataclysm.

How many times over the ages had such hopes risen, only to leave him wounded, even heartbroken. Years ago, he had brought them color films of the rising sun, the blue sky, the pyramids of Egypt. Ah, such a miracle! Before their very eyes the sun-drenched waters of the Nile flowed. He himself had wept at the perfection of illusion. He had even feared the cinematic sun might hurt him, though of course he knew that it could not. But such had been the caliber of the invention. That he could stand there, watching the sunrise, as he had not seen it since he was a mortal man.

But Those Who Must Be Kept had gazed on in unbroken indifference, or was it wonder—great undifferentiated wonder that held the particles of dust in the air to be a source of endless fascination?

Who will ever know? They had lived four thousand years before he was ever born. Perhaps the voices of the world roared in their brains, so keen was their telepathic hearing; perhaps a billion shifting images blinded them to all else. Surely such things had almost driven him out of his mind until he'd learned to control them.

It had even occurred to him that he would bring modern medical tools to bear on the matter, that he would hook electrodes to their very heads to test the patterns of their brains! But it had been too distasteful, the idea of such callous and ugly instruments. After all, they were his King and his Queen, the Father and Mother of us all. Under his roof, they had reigned without challenge for two millennia.

One fault he must admit. He had an acid tongue of late in speaking to them. He was no longer the High Priest when he entered the chamber. No. There was something flippant and sarcastic in his tone, and that should be beneath him. Maybe it was what they called "the modern temper." How could one live in a world of rockets to the moon without an intolerable self-consciousness threatening every trivial syllable? And he had never been oblivious to the century at hand.

Whatever the case, he had to go to the shrine now. And he would purify his thoughts properly. He would not come with resentment or despair. Later, after he had seen the videos, he would play the tape for them. He would remain there, watching. But he did not have the stamina for it now.

He entered the steel elevator and pressed the button. The great electronic whine and the sudden loss of gravity gave him a faint sensuous pleasure. The world of this day and age was full of so many sounds that had never been heard before. It was quite refreshing. And then there was the lovely ease of plummeting hundreds of feet in a shaft through solid ice to reach the electrically lighted chambers below.

He opened the door and stepped into the carpeted corridor. It was Lestat again singing within the shrine, a rapid, more joyful song, his voice battling a thunder of drums and the twisted undulating electronic moans.

But something was not quite right here. Merely looking at the long corridor he sensed it. The sound was too loud, too clear. The antechambers leading to the shrine were open!

He went to the entrance immediately. The electric doors had been unlocked and thrown back. How could this be? Only he knew the code for the tiny series of computer buttons. The second pair of doors had been opened wide as well and so had the third. In fact he could see into the shrine itself, his view blocked by the white marble wall of the small alcove. The red and blue flicker of the television screen beyond was like the light of an old gas fireplace.

And Lestat's voice echoed powerfully over the marble walls, the vaulted ceilings.

Kill us, my brothers and sisters
The war is on.

Understand what you see,
When you see me.

He took a slow easy breath. No sound other than the music, which was fading now to be replaced by characterless mortal chatter. And no outsider here. No, he would have known. No one in his lair. His instincts told him that for certain.

There was a stab of pain in his chest. He even felt a warmth in his face. How remarkable.

He walked through the marble antechambers and stopped at the door of the alcove. Was he praying? Was he dreaming? He knew what he would soon see—Those Who Must be Kept—just as they had always been. And some dismal explanation for the doors, a shorted circuit or a broken fuse, would soon present itself.

Yet he felt not fear suddenly but the raw anticipation of a young mystic on the verge of a vision, that at last he would see the living Lord, or in his own hands the bloody stigmata.

Calmly, he stepped into the shrine.

For a moment it did not register. He saw what he expected to see, the long room filled with trees and flowers, and the stone bench that was the throne, and beyond it the large television screen pulsing with eyes and mouths and unimportant laughter. Then he acknowledged the fact: there was only one figure seated on the throne; and this figure was almost completely transparent! The violent colors of the distant television screen were passing right through it!

No, but this is quite out of the question! *Marius, look carefully. Even your senses are not infallible.* Like a flustered mortal he put his hands to his head as if to block out all distraction.

He was gazing at the back of Enkil, who, save for his black hair, had become some sort of milky glass statue through which the colors and the lights moved with faint distortion. Suddenly an uneven burst of light caused the figure to radiate, to become a source of faint glancing beams.

He shook his head. Not possible. Then he gave himself a little shake all over. "All right, Marius," he whispered. "Proceed slowly."

But a dozen unformed suspicions were sizzling in his mind. Someone had come, someone older and more powerful than he, someone who had discovered Those Who Must Be Kept, and done something unspeakable! And all this was Lestat's doing! Lestat, who had told the world his secret.

His knees were weak. Imagine! He had not felt such mortal debilities in so long that he had utterly forgotten them. Slowly he removed a linen handkerchief from his pocket. He wiped at the thin layer of blood sweat that covered his forehead. Then he moved towards the throne, and went round it, until he stood staring directly at the figure of the King.

Enkil as he had been for two thousand years, the black hair in long tiny plaits, hanging to his shoulders. The broad gold collar lying against his smooth, hairless chest, the linen of his kilt immaculate with its pressed pleats, the rings still on his motionless fingers.

But the body itself was glass! And it was utterly hollow! Even the huge shining orbs of the eyes were transparent, only shadowy circles defining the irises. No, wait. Observe everything. And there, you can see the bones, turned to the very same substance as the flesh, they are there, and also the fine crazing of veins and arteries, and something like lungs inside, but it is all transparent now, it is all of the same texture. But what had been done to him!

And the thing was changing still. Before his very eyes, it was losing its milky cast. It was drying up, becoming ever more transparent.

Tentatively, he touched it. Not glass at all. A husk.

But his careless gesture had upset the thing. The body teetered, then fell over onto the marble tile, its eyes locked open, its limbs rigid in their former position. It made a sound like the scraping of an insect as it settled.

Only the hair moved. The soft black hair. But it too was changed. It was breaking into fragments. It was breaking into tiny shimmering splinters. A cool ventilating current was scattering it like straw. And as the hair fell away from the throat, he saw two dark puncture wounds in it. Wounds that had not healed as they might have done because all the healing blood had been drawn out of the thing.

"Who has done this?" He whispered aloud, tightening the fingers of his right fist as if this would keep him from crying out. Who could have taken every last drop of life from him?

And the thing was dead. There wasn't the slightest doubt of it. And what was revealed by this awful spectacle?

Our King is destroyed, our Father. And I still live; I breathe. And this can only mean that *she* contains the primal power. She was the first, and it has always resided in her. *And someone has taken her!*

Search the cellar. Search the house. But these were frantic, foolish thoughts. No one had entered here, and he knew it. Only one creature could have done this deed! Only one creature would have known that such a thing was finally possible.

He didn't move. He stared at the figure lying on the floor, watching it lose the very last trace of opacity. And would that he could weep for the thing, for surely someone should. Gone now with all that it had ever known, all that it had ever witnessed. This too coming to an end. It seemed beyond his ability to accept it.

But he wasn't alone. Someone or something had just come out of the alcove, and he could feel it watching him.

For one moment—one clearly irrational moment—he kept his eyes on the fallen King. He tried to comprehend as calmly as he could everything that was occurring around him. The thing was moving towards him now, without a sound; it was becoming a graceful shadow in the corner of his eye, as it came around the throne and stood beside him.

He knew who it was, who it had to be, and that it had approached with the natural poise of a living being. Yet, as he looked up, nothing could prepare him for the moment.

Akasha, standing only three inches away from him. Her skin was white and hard and opaque as it had always been. Her cheek shone like pearl as she smiled, her dark eyes moist and enlivened as the flesh puckered ever so slightly around them. They positively glistered with vitality.

Speechless, he stared. He watched as she lifted her jeweled fingers to touch his shoulder. He closed his eyes, then opened them. Over thousands of years he had spoken to her in so many tongues—prayers, pleas, complaints, confessions—and now he said not a word. He merely looked at her mobile lips, at the flash of white fang teeth, and the cold glint of recognition in her eyes, and the soft yielding cleft of the bosom moving beneath the gold necklace.

"You've served me well," she said. "I thank you." Her voice was low, husky, beautiful. But the intonation, the words; it was what he'd said hours ago to the girl in the darkened store in the city!

The fingers tightened on his shoulder.

"Ah, Marius," she said, imitating his tone perfectly again, "you never despair, do you? You are no better than Lestat, with your foolish dreams."

His own words again, spoken to himself on a San Francisco street. She mocked him!

Was this terror? Or was it hatred that he felt—hatred that had lain waiting in him for centuries, mixed with resentment and weariness, and grief for his human heart, hatred that now boiled to a heat he could never have imagined. He didn't dare move, dare speak. The hate was fresh and astonishing and it had taken full possession of him and he could do nothing to control it or understand it. All judgment had left him.

But she knew. Of course. She knew everything, every thought, word, deed, that's what she was telling him. She had always known, everything and anything that she chose to know! And she'd known that the mindless thing beside her was past defending itself. And this, which should have been a triumphant moment, was somehow a moment of horror!

She laughed softly as she looked at him. He could not bear the sound of it. He wanted to hurt her. He wanted to destroy her, all her monstrous children be damned! Let us all perish with her! If he could have done it, he would have destroyed her!

It seemed she nodded, that she was telling him she understood. The monstrous insult of it. Well, he did not understand. And in another moment, he would be weeping like a child. Some ghastly error had been made, some terrible miscarriage of purpose.

"My dear servant," she said, her lips lengthening in a faint bitter smile. "You have never had the power to stop me."

"What do you want! What do you mean to do!"

"You must forgive me," she said, oh, so politely, just as he had said the very words to the young one in the back room of the bar. "I'm going now."

He heard the sound before the floor moved, the shriek of tearing metal. He was falling, and the television screen had blown apart, the glass piercing his flesh like so many tiny daggers. He cried out, like a mortal man, and this time it was fear. The ice was cracking, roaring, as it came down upon him.

"Akasha!"

He was dropping into a giant crevasse, he was plunging into scalding coldness.

"Akasha!" he cried again.

But she was gone, and he was still falling. Then the broken tumbling ice caught him, surrounded him, and buried him, as it crushed the bones of his arms, his legs, his face. He felt his blood pouring out against the searing surface, then freezing. He couldn't move. He couldn't breathe. And the pain was so intense that he couldn't bear it. He saw the jungle again, inexplicably for an instant, as he had seen it earlier. The hot fetid jungle, and something moving through it. Then it was gone. And when he cried out this time, it was to Lestat: *Danger. Lestat, beware. We are all in danger.*

Then there was only the cold and the pain, and he was losing consciousness. A dream coming, a lovely dream of warm sun shining on a grassy clearing. Yes, the blessed sun. The dream had him now. And the women, how lovely their red hair. But what was it, the thing that was lying there, beneath the wilted leaves, on the altar?

PART I

THE ROAD TO THE VAMPIRE LESTAT

Tempting to place in coherent collage
the bee, the mountain range, the shadow
of my hoof—
tempting to join them, enlaced by logical
vast & shining molecular thought-thread
thru all Substance—

. . . .

Tempting
to say I see in all I see
the place where the needle
began in the tapestry—but ah,
it all looks whole and *part—*
long live the eyeball and the lucid heart.

STAN RICE
from "Four Days in Another City"
Some Lamb (1975)

1

THE LEGEND OF THE TWINS

Tell it
in rhythmic
continuity.
Detail by detail
the living creatures.
Tell it
as must, the rhythm
solid in the shape.
Woman. Arms lifted. Shadow eater.

STAN RICE
from "Elegy"
Whiteboy (1976)

CALL her for me," he said. "Tell her I have had the strangest dreams, that they were about the twins. You must call her!"

His daughter didn't want to do it. She watched him fumble with the book. His hands were his enemies now, he often said. At ninety-one, he could scarcely hold a pencil or turn a page.

"Daddy," she said, "that woman's probably dead."

Everybody he had known was dead. He'd outlived his colleagues; he'd outlived his brothers and sisters, and even two of his children. In a tragic way, he had outlived the twins, because no one read his book now. No one cared about "the legend of the twins."

"No, you call her," he said. "You must call her. You tell her that I dreamed of the twins. I *saw* them in the dream."

"Why would she want to know that, Daddy?"

His daughter took the little address book and paged through it slowly. Dead all these people, long dead. The men who had worked with her father on so many expeditions, the editors and photographers who had worked with him on his book. Even his enemies who had said his life was wasted, that his research had come to nothing; even the most scurrilous, who had accused him of doctoring pictures and lying about the caves, which her father had never done.

Why should she be still alive, the woman who had financed his long-ago expeditions, the rich woman who had sent so much money for so many years?

"You must ask her to come! Tell her it's very important. I must describe to her what I've seen."

To come? All the way to Rio de Janeiro because an old man had had strange dreams? His daughter found the page, and yes, there was the name and the number. And the date beside it, only two years old.

"She lives in Bangkok, Daddy." What time was it in Bangkok? She had no idea.

"She'll come to me. I know she will."

He closed his eyes and settled back onto the pillow. He was small now, shrunken. But when he opened his eyes, there was her father looking at her, in spite of the shriveling yellowed skin, the dark spots on the backs of his wrinkled hands, the bald head.

He appeared to be listening to the music now, the soft singing of the Vampire Lestat, coming from her room. She would turn it down if it kept him awake. She wasn't much for American rock singers, but this one she'd rather liked.

"Tell her I must speak to her!" he said suddenly, as though coming back to himself.

"All right, Daddy, if you want me to." She turned off the lamp by the bed. "You go back to sleep."

"Don't give up till you find her. Tell her . . . the twins! I've seen the twins."

But as she was leaving, he called her back again with one of those sudden moans that always frightened her. In the light from the hall, she could see he was pointing to the books on the far wall.

"Get it for me," he said. He was struggling to sit up again.

"The book, Daddy?"

"The twins, the pictures . . ."

She took down the old volume and brought it to him and put it in his lap. She propped the pillows up higher for him and turned on the lamp again.

It hurt her to feel how light he was as she lifted him; it hurt her to see him struggle to put on his silver-rimmed glasses. He took the pencil in hand, to read with it, ready to write, as he had always done, but then he let it fall and she caught it and put it back on the table.

"You go call her!" he said.

She nodded. But she stayed there, just in case he needed her. The music from her study was louder now, one of the more metallic and raucous songs. But he didn't seem to notice. Very gently she opened the book for him, and turned to the first pair of color pictures, one filling the left page, the other the right.

How well she knew these pictures, how well she remembered as a little girl making the long climb with him to the cave on Mount Carmel, where he had led her into the dry dusty darkness, his flashlight lifted to reveal the painted carvings on the wall.

"There, the two figures, you see them, the red-haired women?"

It had been difficult at first to make out the crude stick figures in the dim beam of the flashlight. So much easier later to study what the close-up camera so beautifully revealed.

But she would never forget that first day, when he had shown her each small drawing in sequence: the twins dancing in rain that fell in tiny dashes from a scribble of cloud; the twins kneeling on either side of the altar upon which a body lay as if in sleep or death; the twins taken prisoner and standing before a tribunal of scowling figures; the twins running away. And then the damaged pictures of which nothing could be recovered; and finally the one twin alone weeping, her tears falling in tiny dashes, like the rain, from eyes that were tiny black dashes too.

They'd been carved in the rock, with pigments added—orange for the hair, white chalk for the garments, green for the plants that grew around them, and even blue for the sky over their heads. Six thousand years had passed since they had been created in the deep darkness of the cave.

And no less old were the near identical carvings, in a shallow rock chamber high on the slope of Huayna Picchu, on the other side of the world.

She had made that journey also with her father, a year later, across the Urubamba River and up through the jungles of Peru. She'd seen for herself the same two women in a style remarkably similar though not the same.

There again on the smooth wall were the same scenes of the rain falling, of the red-haired twins in their joyful dance. And then the somber altar scene in loving detail. It was the body of a woman lying on the altar, and in their hands the twins held two tiny, carefully drawn plates. Soldiers bore down upon the ceremony with swords uplifted. The twins were taken into bondage, weeping. And then came the hostile tribunal and the familiar escape. In another picture, faint but still discernible, the twins held an infant between them, a small bundle with dots for eyes and the barest bit of red hair; then to others they entrusted their treasure as once more the menacing soldiers appeared.

And lastly, the one twin, amid the full leafy trees of the jungle, her arms out as if reaching for her sister, the red pigment of her hair stuck to the stone wall with dried blood.

How well she could recall her excitement. She had shared her father's ecstasy, that he had found the twins a world apart from each other, in these ancient pictures, buried in the mountain caves of Palestine and Peru.

It seemed the greatest event in history; nothing could have been so important. Then a year later a vase had been discovered in a Berlin museum that bore the very same figures, kneeling, plates in hand before the stone bier. A crude thing it was, without documentation. But what did that matter? It had been dated 4000 B.C. by the most reliable methods, and there unmistakably, in the newly translated language of ancient Sumer, were the words that meant so much to all of them:

"The Legend of the Twins"

Yes, so terribly significant, it had all seemed. The foundation of a life's work, until he presented his research.

They'd laughed at him. Or ignored him. Not believable, such a link between the Old World and the New. Six thousand years old, indeed! They'd relegated him to the "crazy camp" along with those who talked of ancient astronauts, Atlantis, and the lost kingdom of Mu.

How he'd argued, lectured, begged them to believe, to journey with him to the caves, to see for themselves! How he'd laid out the specimens of pigment, the lab reports, the detailed studies of the plants in the carvings and even the white robes of the twins.

Another man might have given it up. Every university and foundation had turned him away. He had no money even to care for his children. He took a teaching position for bread and butter, and, in the evenings, wrote letters to museums all over the world. And a clay tablet, covered with drawings, was found in Manchester, and another in London, both clearly depicting the twins! On borrowed money he journeyed to photograph these artifacts. He wrote papers on them for obscure publications. He continued his search.

Then she had come, the quiet-spoken and eccentric woman who had listened to him, looked at his materials, and then given him an ancient papyrus, found early in this century in a cave in Upper Egypt, which contained some of the very same pictures, and the words "The Legend of the Twins."

"A gift for you," she'd said. And then she'd bought the vase for him from the museum in Berlin. She obtained the tablets from England as well.

But it was the Peruvian discovery that fascinated her most of all. She gave him unlimited sums of money to go back to South America and continue his work.

For years he'd searched cave after cave for more evidence, spoken to villagers about their oldest myths and stories, examined ruined cities, temples, even old Christian churches for stones taken from pagan shrines.

But decades passed and he found nothing.

It had been the ruin of him finally. Even she, his patron, had told him to give it up. She did not want to see his life spent on this. He should leave it now to younger men. But he would not listen. This was his discovery! The Legend of the Twins! And so she wrote the checks for him, and he went on until he was too old to climb the mountains and hack his way through the jungle anymore.

In the last years, he lectured only now and then. He could not interest the new students in this mystery, even when he showed the papyrus, the vase, the tablets. After all, these items did not fit anywhere really, they were of no definable period. And the caves, could anyone have found them now?

But she had been loyal, his patron. She'd bought him this house in Rio, created a trust for him which would come to his daughter when he died. Her money had paid for his daughter's education, for so many other things. Strange that they lived in such comfort. It was as if he had been successful after all.

"Call her," he said again. He was becoming agitated, empty hands scraping at the photographs. After all, his daughter had not moved. She stood at his shoulder looking down at the pictures, at the figures of the twins.

"All right, Father." She left him with his book.

It was late afternoon the next day when his daughter came in to kiss him. The nurse said that he'd been crying like a child. He opened his eyes as his daughter squeezed his hand.

"I know now what they did to them," he said. "I've seen it! It was sacrilege what they did."

His daughter tried to quiet him. She told him that she had called the woman. The woman was on her way.

"She wasn't in Bangkok, Daddy. She's moved to Burma, to Rangoon. But I reached her there, and she was so glad to hear from you. She said she'd leave within a few hours. She wants to know about the dreams."

He was so happy. She was coming. He closed his eyes and turned his head into the pillow. "The dreams will start again, after dark," he whispered. "The whole tragedy will start again."

"Daddy, rest," she said. "Until she comes."

SOMETIME during the night he died. When his daughter came in, he was already cold. The nurse was waiting for her instructions. He had the dull, half-lidded stare of dead people. His pencil was lying on the coverlet, and there was a piece of paper—the flyleaf of his precious book—crumpled under his right hand.

She didn't cry. For a moment she didn't do anything. She remembered the cave in Palestine, the lantern. "Do you see? The two women?"

Gently, she closed his eyes, and kissed his forehead. He'd written something on the piece of paper. She lifted his cold, stiff fingers and removed the paper and read the few words he'd scrawled in his uneven spidery hand:

"IN THE JUNGLES—WALKING."

What could it mean?

And it was too late to reach the woman now. She would probably arrive sometime that evening. All that long way. . . .

Well, she would give her the paper, if it mattered, and tell her the things he'd said about the twins.

2

THE SHORT HAPPY LIFE OF BABY JENKS AND THE FANG GANG

The Murder Burger
is served right here.
You need not wait
at the gate of Heaven
for unleavened death.
You can be a goner
on this very corner.
Mayonnaise, onions, dominance of flesh.
If you wish to eat it
you must feed it.
"Yall come back."
"You bet."

STAN RICE
from "Texas Suite"
Some Lamb (1975)

BABY Jenks pushed her Harley to seventy miles an hour, the wind freezing her naked white hands. She'd been fourteen last summer when they'd done it to her, made her one of the Dead, and "dead weight" she was eighty-five pounds max. She hadn't combed out her hair since it happened—didn't have to—and her two little blond braids were swept back by the wind, off the shoulders of her black leather jacket. Bent forward, scowling with her little pouting mouth turned down, she looked mean, and deceptively cute. Her big blue eyes were vacant.

The rock music of *The Vampire Lestat* was blaring through her earphones, so she felt nothing but the vibration of the giant motorcycle under her, and the mad lonesomeness she had known all the way from Gun Barrel City five nights ago. And there was a dream that was bothering her, a dream she kept having every night right before she opened her eyes.

She'd see these redheaded twins in the dream, these two pretty ladies, and then all these terrible things would go down. No, she didn't like it one damn bit and she was so lonely she was going out of her head.

The Fang Gang hadn't met her south of Dallas as they had promised. She had waited two nights by the graveyard, then she had known that something was really, really wrong. They would never have headed out to California without her. They were going to see the Vampire Lestat on stage in San Francisco, but they'd had plenty of time. No, something was wrong. She knew it.

Even when she had been alive, Baby Jenks could feel things like that. And now that she was Dead it was ten times what it had been then. She knew the Fang Gang was in deep trouble. Killer and Davis would never have dumped her. Killer said he loved her. Why the hell else would he have ever made her, if he didn't love her? She would have died in Detroit if it hadn't been for Killer.

She'd been bleeding to death, the doctor had done it to her all right, the baby was gone and all, but she was going to die too, he'd cut something in there, and she was so high on heroin she didn't give a damn. And then that funny thing happened. Floating up to the ceiling and looking down at her body! And it wasn't the drugs either. Seemed to her like a whole lot of other things were about to happen.

But down there, Killer had come into the room and from up where she was floating she could see that he was a Dead guy. Course she didn't know what he called himself then. She just knew he wasn't alive. Otherwise he just looked kind of ordinary. Black jeans, black hair, real deep black eyes. He had "Fang Gang" written on the back of his leather jacket. He'd sat down on the bed by her body and bent over it.

"Ain't you cute, little girl!" he'd said. Same damn thing the pimp had said to her when he made her braid her hair and put plastic barrettes in it before she went out on the street.

Then whoom! She was back in her body all right, and she was just full of something warmer and better than horse and she heard him say: "You're not going to die, Baby Jenks, not ever!" She had her teeth in his goddamn neck, and boy, was that heaven!

But the never dying part? She wasn't so sure now.

Before she'd lit out of Dallas, giving up on the Fang Gang for good, she'd seen the coven house on Swiss Avenue burnt to timbers. All the glass blown out of the windows. It had been the same in Oklahoma City. What the hell had happened to all those Dead guys in those houses? And they were the big city bloodsuckers, too, the smart ones that called themselves vampires.

How she'd laughed when Killer and Davis had told her that, that those Dead guys went around in three-piece suits and listened to classical music and called themselves vampires. Baby Jenks could have laughed herself to death. Davis thought it was pretty funny too, but Killer just kept warning her about them. Stay away from them.

Killer and Davis, and Tim and Russ, had taken her by the Swiss Avenue coven house just before she left them to go to Gun Barrel City.

"You got to always know where it is," Davis had said. "Then stay away from it."

They'd showed her the coven houses in every big city they hit. But it was when they showed her the first one in St. Louis that they'd told her the whole story.

She'd been real happy with the Fang Gang since they left Detroit, feeding off the men they lured out of the roadside beer joints. Tim and Russ were OK guys, but Killer and Davis were her special friends and they were the leaders of the Fang Gang.

Now and then they'd gone into town and found some little shack of a place, all deserted, with maybe two bums in there or something, men who looked kinda like her dad, wearing bill caps and with real calloused hands from the work they did. And they'd have a feast in there on those guys. You could always live off that kind, Killer told her, because nobody gives a damn what happens to them. They'd strike fast, kachoom!—drinking the blood quick, draining them right down to the last heartbeat. It wasn't fun to torture people like that, Killer said. You had to feel sorry for them. You did what you did, then you burnt down the shack, or you took them outside and dug a hole real deep and stuck them down there. And if you couldn't do anything like that to cover it up, you did this little trick: cut your finger, let your Dead blood run over the bite where you'd sucked them dry, and look at that, the little puncture wounds just like to vanished. Flash! Nobody'd ever figure it out; it looked like stroke or heart attack.

Baby Jenks had been having a ball. She could handle a full-sized Harley, carry a dead body with one arm, leap over the hood of a car, it was fantastic. And she hadn't had the damn dream then, the dream that had started up in Gun Barrel City—with those redheaded twins and that woman's body lying on an altar. *What were they doing?*

What would she do now if she couldn't find the Fang Gang? Out in California the Vampire Lestat was going on stage two nights from now. And every Dead guy in creation would be there, leastways that's how she figured it, and that's how the Fang Gang had figured it and they were all supposed to be together. So what the hell was she doing lost from the Fang Gang and headed for a jerkwater city like St. Louis?

All she wanted was for everything to be like it had been before, goddamn it. Oh, the blood was good, yum, it was so good, even now that she was alone and had to work up her nerve, the way it had been this evening, to pull into a gas station and lure the old guy out back. Oh, yeah, snap, when she'd gotten her hands on his neck, and the blood came, it had been just fine, it was hamburgers and french fries and strawberry shakes, it was beer and chocolate sundaes. It was mainline, and coke and hash. It was better than screwing! It was all of it.

But everything had been better when the Fang Gang was with her. And they had understood when she got tired of the chewed-up old guys and said she wanted to taste something young and tender. No problem. Hey, it was a nice little runaway kid she needed, Killer said. Just close your eyes and wish. And sure enough, like that, they found him hitchhiking on the main road, just five miles out of some town in northern Missouri, name of Parker. Real pretty boy with long shaggy black hair, just twelve years old, but real tall for his age, with some beard on his chin, and trying to pass for sixteen. He'd climbed on her bike and they'd taken him into the woods. Then Baby Jenks laid down with him, real gentle like, and slurp, that was it for Parker.

It was delicious all right, juicy was the word. But she didn't know really whether it was any better than the mean old guys when you got down to it. And with them it was more sport. Good ole boy blood, Davis called it.

Davis was a black Dead guy and one damned good-looking black Dead guy, as Baby Jenks saw it. His skin had a gold glow to it, the Dead glow which in the case of white Dead guys made them look like they were standing in a fluorescent light all the time. Davis had beautiful eyelashes too, just damn near unbelievably long and thick, and he decked himself out in all the gold he could find. He stole the gold rings and watches and chains and things off the victims.

Davis loved to dance. They all loved to dance. But Davis could outdance any of them. They'd go to the graveyards to dance, maybe round three a.m., after they'd all fed and buried the dead and all that jazz. They'd set the ghetto blaster radio on a tombstone and turn it way up, with the Vampire Lestat roaring. "The Grand Sabbat" song, that was the one that was good for dancing. And oh, man, how good it felt, twisting and turning and leaping in the air, or just watching Davis move and Killer move and Russ spinning in circles till he fell down. Now that was real Dead guy dancing.

Now if those big city bloodsuckers weren't hip to that, they were crazy.

God, she wished now that she could tell Davis about this dream she'd been having since Gun Barrel City. How it had come to her in her mom's trailer, zap, the first time when she'd been sitting waiting. It was so clear for a dream, those two women with the red hair, and the body lying there with its skin all black and crackled like. And what the hell was that on the plates in the dream? Yeah, it had been a heart on one plate and a brain on the other. Christ. All those people kneeling around that body and those plates. It was creepy. And she'd had it over and over again since then. Why, she was having it every goddamn time she shut her eyes and again right before she dug her way out of wherever she'd been hiding by daylight.

Killer and Davis would understand. They'd know if it meant something. They wanted to teach her everything.

When they first hit St. Louis on their way south, the Fang Gang had headed off the boulevard into one of those big dark streets with iron gates that they call "a private place" in St. Louis. It was the Central West End down here, they said. Baby Jenks had liked those big trees. There just aren't enough big trees in south Texas. There wasn't much of nothing in south Texas. And here the trees were so big their branches made a roof over your head. And the streets were full of noisy rustling leaves and the houses were big, with peaked roofs and the lights buried deep inside them. The coven house was made of brick and had what Killer called Moorish arches.

"Don't go any closer," Davis had said. Killer just laughed. Killer wasn't scared of the big city Dead. Killer had been made sixty years ago, he was old. He knew everything.

"But they will try to hurt you, Baby Jenks," he said, walking his Harley just a little farther up the street. He had a lean long face, wore a gold earring in his ear, and his eyes were small, kind of thoughtful. "See, this one's an old coven, been in St. Louis since the turn of the century."

"But why would they want to hurt us?" Baby Jenks had asked. She was real curious about that house. What did the Dead do who lived in houses? What kind of furniture did they have? Who paid the bills, for God's sakes?

Seems like she could see a chandelier in one of those front rooms, through the curtains. A big fancy chandelier. Man! Now that's living.

"Oh, they got all that down," said Davis, reading her mind. "You don't think the neighbors think they're real people? Look at that car in the drive, you know what that is? That's a Bugatti, baby. And the other one beside it, a Mercedes-Benz."

What the hell was wrong with a pink Cadillac? That's what she'd like to have, a big gas-guzzling convertible that she could push to a hundred and twenty on the open stretch. And that's what had got her into trouble, got her to Detroit, an asshole with a Cadillac convertible. But just 'cause you were Dead didn't mean you had to drive a Harley and sleep in the dirt every day, did it?

"We're free, darlin'," Davis said, reading her thoughts. "Don't you see? There's a lotta baggage goes with this big city life. Tell her, Killer. And you ain't getting me in no house like that, sleeping in a box under the floorboards."

He broke up. Killer broke up. She broke up too. But what the hell was it like in there? Did they turn on the late show and watch the vampire movies? Davis was really rolling on the ground.

"The fact is, Baby Jenks," Killer said, "we're rogues to them, they wanna run everything. Like they don't think we have a right to be Dead. Like when they make a new vampire as they call it, it's a big ceremony."

"Like what happens, like a wedding or something you mean?"

More laughter from those two.

"Not exactly," Killer said, "more like a funeral!"

They were making too much noise. Surely those Dead guys in the house were going to hear them. But Baby Jenks wasn't afraid if Killer wasn't afraid. Where were Russ and Tim, gone off hunting?

"But the point is, Baby Jenks," said Killer, "they have all these rules, and I'll tell you what, they're spreading it all over that they're going to get the Vampire Lestat the night of his concert, but you know what, they're reading his book like it was the Bible. They're using all that language he used, Dark Gift, Dark Trick, I tell you it's the stupidest thing I've ever seen, they're going to burn the guy at the stake and then use his book like it was Emily Post or Miss Manners—"

"They'll never get Lestat," Davis had sneered. "No way, man. You can't kill the Vampire Lestat, that is flat out impossible. It has been tried, you see, and it has failed. Now that is one cat who is utterly and completely immortal."

"Hell, they're going out there same as we are," Killer said, "to join up with the cat if he wants us."

Baby Jenks didn't understand the whole thing. She didn't know who Emily Post was or Miss Manners either. And weren't we all supposed to be immortal? And why would the Vampire Lestat want to be running around with the Fang Gang? I mean he was a rock star, for Chrissakes. Probably had his own limousine. And was he ever one adorable-looking guy, Dead or alive! Blond hair to die for and a smile that just made you wanna roll over and let him bite your goddamn neck!

She'd tried to read the Vampire Lestat's book—the whole history of

Dead guys back to ancient times and all—but there were just too many big words and konk, she was asleep.

Killer and Davis said she'd find out she could read real fast now if she just stuck with it. They carried copies of Lestat's book around with them, and the first one, the one with the title she could never get straight, something like "conversations with the vampire," or "talking with the vampire," or "getting to meet the vampire," or something like that. Davis would read out loud from that one sometimes, but Baby Jenks couldn't take it in, snore! The Dead Guy, Louis, or whoever he was, had been made Dead down in New Orleans and the book was full of stuff about banana leaves and iron railings and Spanish moss.

"Baby Jenks, they know everything, the old European ones," Davis had said. "They know how it started, they know we can go on and on if we hang in there, live to be a thousand years old and turn into white marble."

"Gee, that's just great, Davis," Baby Jenks said. "It's bad enough now not being able to walk into a Seven Eleven under those lights without people looking at you. Who wants to look like white marble?"

"Baby Jenks, you don't need anything anymore from the Seven Eleven," Davis said real calmly. But he got the point.

Forget the books. Baby Jenks did love the Vampire Lestat's music, and those songs just kept giving her a lot, especially that one about Those Who Must Be Kept—the Egyptian King and Queen—though to tell the truth she didn't know what the hell it meant till Killer explained.

"They're the parents of all vampires, Baby Jenks, the Mother and the Father. See, we're all an unbroken line of blood coming down from the King and the Queen in ancient Egypt who are called Those Who Must Be Kept. And the reason you gotta keep them is if you destroy them, you destroy all of us, too."

Sounded like a bunch of bull to her.

"Lestat's seen the Mother and the Father," Davis said. "Found them hidden on a Greek island, so he knows that it's the truth. That's what he's been telling everybody with these songs—and it's the truth."

"And the Mother and the Father don't move or speak or drink blood, Baby Jenks," Killer said. He looked real thoughtful, sad, almost. "They just sit there and stare like they've done for thousands of years. Nobody knows what those two know."

"Probably nothing," Baby Jenks had said disgustedly. "And I tell you, this is some kind of being immortal! What do you mean the big city Dead guys can kill us? Just how can they manage that?"

"Fire and sun can always do it," Killer answered just a touch impatient. "I told you that. Now mind me, please. You can always fight the big city Dead guys. You're tough. Fact is, the big city Dead are as scared of you as you will ever be of them. You just beat it when you see a Dead guy you don't know. That's a rule that's followed by everybody who's Dead."

After they'd left the coven house, she'd got another big surprise from Killer: he'd told her about the vampire bars. Big fancy places in New York and San Francisco and New Orleans, where the Dead guys met in the back rooms while the damn fool human beings drank and danced up front. In there, no other Dead guy could kill you, city slicker, European, or rogue like her.

"You run for one of those places," he told her, "if the big city Dead guys ever get on your case."

"I'm not old enough to go in a bar," Baby Jenks said.

That really did it. He and Davis laughed themselves sick. They were falling off their motorcycles.

"You find a vampire bar, Baby Jenks," Killer said, "you just give them the Evil Eye and say 'Let me in.'"

Yeah, she'd done that Evil Eye on people and made them do stuff, it worked OK. And truth was, they'd never seen the vampire bars. Just heard about them. Didn't know where they were. She'd had lots of questions when they finally left St. Louis.

But as she made her way north towards the same city now, the only thing in the world she cared about was getting to that same damned coven house. Big city Dead guys, here I come. She'd go clean out of her head if she had to go on alone.

The music in the earphones stopped. The tape had run out. She couldn't stand the silence in the roar of the wind. The dream came back; she saw those twins again, the soldiers coming. Jesus. If she didn't block it out, the whole damn dream would replay itself like the tape.

Steadying the bike with one hand, she reached in her jacket to open the little cassette player. She flipped the tape over. "Sing on, man!" she said, her voice sounding shrill and tiny to her over the roar of the wind, if she heard it at all.

Of Those Who Must Be Kept
What can we know?
Can any explanation save us?

Yes sir, that was the one she loved. That's the one she'd been listening to when she fell asleep waiting for her mother to come home from work in Gun Barrel City. It wasn't the words that got to her, it was the way he sang it, groaning like Bruce Springsteen into the mike and making it just break your heart.

It was kind of like a hymn in a way. It had that kind of sound, yet Lestat was right there in the middle of it, singing to her, and there was a steady drumbeat that went to her bones.

"OK, man, OK, you're the only goddamn Dead guy I've got now, Lestat, keep singing!"

Five minutes to St. Louis, and there she was thinking about her mother again, how strange it had all been, how bad.

Baby Jenks hadn't even told Killer or Davis why she was going home, though they knew, they understood.

Baby Jenks had to do it, she had to get her parents before the Fang Gang went out west. And even now she didn't regret it. Except for that strange moment when her mother was dying there on the floor.

Now Baby Jenks had always hated her mother. She thought her mother was just a real fool, making crosses every day of her life with little pink seashells and bits of glass and then taking them to the Gun Barrel City Flea Market and selling them for ten dollars. And they were ugly, too, just real ready-made junk, those things with a little twisted-up Jesus in the middle made up of tiny red and blue beads and things.

But it wasn't just that, it was everything her mother had ever done that got to Baby Jenks and made her disgusted. Going to church, that was bad enough, but talking the way she did to people so sweet and just putting up with her husband's drinking and always saying nice things about everybody.

Baby Jenks never bought a word of it. She used to lie there on her bunk in the trailer thinking to herself, What really makes that lady tick? When is she going to blow up like a stick of dynamite? Or is she just too stupid? Her mother had stopped looking Baby Jenks in the eye years ago. When Baby Jenks was twelve she'd come in and said, "You know I done it, don't you? I hope to God you don't think I'm no virgin." And her mother just faded out, like, just looked away with her eyes wide and empty and stupid, and went back to her work, humming like always as she made those seashell crosses.

One time some big city person told her mother that she made real folk art. "They're making a fool of you," Baby Jenks had said. "Don't you know that? They didn't buy one of those ugly things, did they? You know what those things look like to me? I'll tell you what they look like. They look like great big dime-store earrings!"

No arguing. Just turning the other cheek. "You want some supper, honey?"

It was like an open and shut case, Baby Jenks figured. So she had headed out of Dallas early, making Cedar Creek Lake in less than an hour, and there was the familiar sign that meant her sweet little old home town: WELCOME TO GUN BARREL CITY. WE SHOOT STRAIGHT WITH YOU.

She hid her Harley behind the trailer when she got there, nobody home, and lay down for a nap, Lestat singing in the earphones, and the steam iron ready by her side. When her mother came in, slam bam, thank you, ma'am, she'd take her out with it.

Then the dream happened. Why, she wasn't even asleep when it started. It was like Lestat faded out, and the dream pulled her down and snap:

She was in a place full of sunlight. A clearing on the side of a mountain. And these two twins were there, beautiful women with soft wavy red hair, and they knelt like angels in church with their hands folded. Lots of people around, people in long robes, like people in the Bible. And there was music, too, a creepy thumping and the sound of a horn playing, real mournful. But the worst part was the dead body, the burned body of the woman on a stone slab. Why, she looked like she'd been cooked, lying there! And on the plates, there was a fat shiny heart and a brain. Yep, sure thing, that was a heart and a brain.

Baby Jenks had woken up, scared. To hell with that. Her mother was standing in the door. Baby Jenks jumped up and banged her with the steam iron till she stopped moving. Really bashed in her head. And she should have been dead, but she wasn't yet, and then that crazy moment came.

Her mother was lying there on the floor, half dead, staring, just like her daddy would be later. And Baby Jenks was sitting in the chair, one blue jean leg thrown over the arm, leaning on her elbow, or twirling one of her braids, just waiting, thinking about the twins in the dream sort of, and the body and the things on the plates, what was it all for? But mostly just waiting. Die, you stupid bitch, go on, die, I'm not slamming you again!

Even now Baby Jenks wasn't sure what had happened. It was like her mother's thoughts had changed, grown wider, bigger. Maybe she was floating up on the ceiling somewhere the way Baby Jenks had been when she nearly died before Killer saved her. But whatever was the cause, the thoughts were just amazing. Just flat out amazing. Like her mother knew everything! All about good and bad and how important it was to love, really love, and how it was so much more than just all the rules about don't drink, don't smoke, pray to Jesus. It wasn't preacher stuff. It was just gigantic.

Her mother, lying there, had thought about how the lack of love in her daughter, Baby Jenks, had been as awful as a bad gene that made Baby Jenks blind and crippled. Yet it didn't matter. It was going to be all right.

Baby Jenks would rise out of what was going on now, just as she had almost done before Killer had got to her, and there would be a finer understanding of everything. What the hell did that mean? Something about everything around us being part of one big thing, the fibers in the carpet, the leaves outside the window, the water dripping in the sink, the clouds moving over Cedar Creek Lake, and the bare trees, and they weren't really so ugly as Baby Jenks had thought. No, the whole thing was almost too beautiful to describe suddenly. And Baby Jenks' mother had always known about this! Seen it that way. Baby Jenks' mother forgave Baby Jenks everything. Poor Baby Jenks. She didn't know. She didn't know about the green grass. Or the seashells shining in the light of the lamp.

Then Baby Jenks' mother had died. Thank God! Enough! But Baby Jenks had been crying. Then she'd carried the body out of the trailer and buried it in back, real deep, feeling how good it was to be one of the Dead and so strong and able to just heft those shovels full of dirt.

Then her father came home. This one's really for fun! She buried him while he was still alive. She'd never forget the look on his face when he came in the door and saw her with the fire ax. "Well, if it ain't Lizzie Borden."

Who the hell was Lizzie Borden?

Then the way his chin stuck out, and his fist came flying towards her, he was so sure of himself! "You little slut!" She split his goddamn forehead in half. Yeah, that part was great, feeling the skull cave—"Go down, you bastard!"—and so was shoveling dirt on his face while he was still looking at her. Paralyzed, couldn't move, thinking he was a kid again on a farm or something in New Mexico. Just baby talk. *You son of a bitch, I always knew you had shit for brains. Now I can smell it!*

But why the hell had she ever gone down there? Why had she left the Fang Gang?

If she'd never left them, she'd be with them now in San Francisco, with Killer and Davis, waiting to see Lestat on the stage. They might have even made the vampire bar out there or something. Leastways, if they had ever gotten there. If something wasn't really really wrong.

And what the hell was she doing now backtracking? Maybe she should have gone along out west. Two nights, that was all that was left.

Hell, maybe she'd rent a motel room when the concert happened, so she could watch it on TV. But before that, she had to find some Dead guys in St. Louis. She couldn't go on alone.

How to find the Central West End. Where was it?

This boulevard looked familiar. She was cruising along, praying no meddling cop would start after her. She'd outrun him of course, she always did, though she dreamed of getting just one of those damn sons-a-bitches on a lonely road. But the fact was she didn't want to be chased out of St. Louis.

Now this looked like something she knew. Yeah, this was the Central West End or whatever they called it and she turned off now to the right and went down an old street with those big cool leafy trees all around her. Made her think of her mother again, the green grass, the clouds. Little sob in her throat.

If she just wasn't so damn lonesome! But then she saw the gates, yeah, this was the street. Killer had told her that Dead guys never really forget anything. Her brain would be like a little computer. Maybe it was true. These were the gates all right, great big iron gates, opened wide and covered with dark green ivy. Guess they never really close up "a private place."

She slowed to a rumbling crawl, then cut the motor altogether. Too noisy in this dark valley of mansions. Some bitch might call the cops. She had to get off to walk her bike. Her legs weren't long enough to do it any other way. But that was OK. She liked walking in these deep dead leaves. She liked this whole quiet street.

Boy, if I was a big city vampire I'd live here too, she thought, and then far off down the street, she saw the coven house, saw the brick walls and the white Moorish arches. Her heart was really going!

Burnt up!

At first she didn't believe it! Then she saw it was true all right, big streaks of black on the bricks, and the windows all blown out, not a pane of glass left anywhere. Jesus Christ! She was going crazy. She walked her bike up closer, biting her lip so hard she could taste her own blood. Just look at it. Who the hell was doing it! Teeny bits of glass all over the lawn and even in the trees so the whole place was kind of sparkling in a way that human beings probably couldn't make out. Looked to her like nightmare Christmas decorations. And the stink of burning wood. It was just hanging there.

She was going to cry! She was going to start screaming! But then she heard something. Not a real sound, but the things that Killer had taught her to listen for. There was a Dead guy in there!

She couldn't believe her luck, and she didn't give a damn what happened, she was going in there. Yeah, somebody in there. It was real faint. She went a few more feet, crunching real loud in the dead leaves. No light but something moving in there, and it knew she was coming. And as she stood there, heart hammering, afraid, and frantic to go in, somebody came out on the front porch, a Dead guy looking right at her.

Praise the Lord, she whispered. And he wasn't no jerkoff in a three-piece suit, either. No, he was a young kid, maybe no more than two years older than her when they did it to him, and he looked real special. Like he had silver hair for one thing, just real pretty short curly gray hair, and that always looked great on a young person. And he was tall too, about six feet, and skinny, a real elegant guy, the way she saw it. He had an icy look to his skin it was so white, and he wore a dark brown turtleneck shirt, real smooth across his chest, and a fancy cut brown leather jacket and pants, nothing at all like biker leather. Really boss, this guy, and cuter than any Dead guy in the Fang Gang.

"Come inside!" he said in a hiss. "Hurry."

She like to flew up the steps. The air was still full of tiny ashes, and it hurt her eyes and made her cough. Half the porch had fallen in. Carefully she made her way into the hallway. Some of the stairs was left, but the roof way above was wide open. And the chandelier had fallen down, all crushed and full of soot. Real spooky, like a haunted house this place.

The Dead guy was in the living room or what was left of it, kicking and picking through burnt-up stuff, furniture and things, sort of in a rage, it looked like.

"Baby Jenks, is it?" he said, flashing her a weird fake smile, full of pearly teeth including his little fangs, and his gray eyes glittering kind of. "And you're lost, aren't you?"

OK, another goddamn mind reader like Davis. And one with a foreign accent.

"Yeah, so what?" she said. And real surprising, she caught his name like as if it was a ball and he'd tossed it to her: Laurent. Now that was a classy name, French sounding.

"Stay right there, Baby Jenks," he said. The accent was French too, probably. "There were three in this coven and two were incinerated. The police can't detect the remains but you will know them if you step on them and you will not like it."

Christ! And he was telling her the truth, 'cause there was one of them right there, no jive, at the back of the hall, and it looked like a half-burnt suit of clothes lying there, kind of vaguely in the outline of a man, and sure thing, she could tell by the smell, there'd been a Dead guy in the clothes, and just the sleeves and the pant legs and shoes were left. In the middle of it all there was a kind of grayish messy stuff, looked more like grease and powder than ashes. Funny the way the shirt sleeve was still neatly sticking out of the coat sleeve. Now that had been a three-piece suit maybe.

She was getting sick. Could you get sick when you were Dead? She wanted to get out of here. What if whatever had done this was coming back? Immortal, tie a can to it!

"Don't move," the Dead guy said to her, "and we'll be leaving together just as soon as we can."

"Like now, OK!" she said. She was shaking, goddamn it. This is what they meant when they said cold sweat!

He'd found a tin box and he was taking all the unburnt money out of it.

"Hey, man, I'm splitting," she said. She could feel something around here, and it had nothing to do with that grease spot on the floor. She was thinking of the burnt-up coven houses in Dallas and Oklahoma City, the way the Fang Gang had vanished on her. He got all that, she could tell. His face got soft, real cute again. He threw down the box and came towards her so fast it scared her worse.

"Yes, *ma chère,*" he said in a real nice voice, "all those coven houses, exactly. The East Coast has been burnt out like a circuit of lights. There is no answer at the coven house in Paris or the coven house in Berlin."

He took her arm as they headed for the front door.

"Who the hell's doing this!" she said.

"Who the hell knows, *chérie?* It destroys the houses, the vampire bars, whatever rogues it finds. We have got to get out of here. Now make the bike go."

But she had come to a halt. *Something out here.* She was standing at the edge of the porch. Something. She was as scared to go on as she was to go back in the house.

"What's wrong?" he asked her in a whisper.

How dark this place was with these great big trees and the houses, they all looked haunted, and she could hear something, something real low like . . . like something's breathing. Something like that.

"Baby Jenks? Move it now!"

"But where are we going?" she asked. This thing, whatever it was, it was almost a sound.

"The only place we can go. To him, darling, to the Vampire Lestat. He is out there in San Francisco waiting, unharmed!"

"Yeah?" she said, staring at the dark street in front of her. "Yeah, right, to the Vampire Lestat." Just ten steps to the bike. Take it, Baby Jenks. He was about to leave without her. "No, don't you do that, you son of a bitch, don't you touch my bike!"

But it was a sound now, wasn't it? Baby Jenks had never heard anything quite like it. But you hear a lot of things when you're Dead. You hear trains miles away, and people talking on planes over your head.

The Dead guy heard it. No, he heard her hearing it! "What is it?" he whispered. Jesus, he was scared. And now he heard it all by himself too.

He pulled her down the steps. She stumbled and almost fell, but he lifted her off her feet and put her on the bike.

The noise was getting really loud. It was coming in beats like music. And it was so loud now she couldn't even hear what this Dead guy was saying to her. She twisted the key, turned the handles to give the Harley gas, and the Dead guy was on the bike behind her, but Jesus, the noise, she couldn't think. She couldn't even hear the engine of the bike!

She looked down, trying to see what the hell was going on, was it running, she couldn't even feel it. Then she looked up and she knew she was looking towards the thing that was sending the noise. It was in the darkness, behind the trees.

The Dead guy had leaped off the bike, and he was jabbering away at it, as if he could see it. But no, he was looking around like a crazy man talking to himself. But she couldn't hear a word. She just knew it was there, it was looking at them, and the crazy guy was wasting his breath!

She was off the Harley. It had fallen over. The noise stopped. Then there was a loud ringing in her ears.

"—anything you want!" the Dead guy next to her was saying, "just anything, name it, we will do it. We are your servants—!" Then he ran past Baby Jenks, nearly knocking her over and grabbing up her bike.

"Hey!" she shouted, but just as she started for him, he burst into flames! He screamed.

And then Baby Jenks screamed too. She screamed and screamed. The burning Dead guy was turning over and over on the ground, just pinwheeling. And behind her, the coven house exploded. She felt the heat on her back. She saw stuff flying through the air. The sky looked like high noon.

Oh, sweet Jesus, let me live, let me live!

For one split second she thought her heart had burst. She meant to look down to see if her chest had broken open and her heart was spewing out blood like molten lava from a volcano, but then the heat built up inside her head and swoosh! she was gone.

She was rising up and up through a dark tunnel, and then high above she floated, looking down on the whole scene.

Oh yeah, just like before. And there it was, the thing that had killed them, a white figure standing in a thicket of trees. And there was the Dead guy's clothes smoking on the pavement. And her own body just burning away.

Through the flames she could see the pure black outline of her own skull and her bones. But it didn't frighten her. It didn't really seem that interesting at all.

It was the white figure that amazed her. It looked just like a statue, like the Blessed Virgin Mary in the Catholic church. She stared at the sparkling silver threads that seemed to move out from the figure in all directions, threads made out of some kind of dancing light. And as she moved higher, she saw that the silver threads stretched out, tangling with other threads, to make a giant net all over the whole world. All through the net were Dead guys, caught, like helpless flies in a web. Tiny pinpoints of light, pulsing, and connected to the white figure, and almost beautiful, the sight of it, except it was so sad. Oh, poor souls of all the Dead guys locked in indestructible matter unable to grow old or die.

But she was free. The net was way far away from her now. She was seeing so many things.

Like there were thousands and thousands of other dead people floating up here, too, in a great hazy gray layer. Some were lost, others were fighting with each other, and some were looking back down to where they'd died, so pitiful, like they didn't know or wouldn't believe they were dead. There was even a couple of them trying to be seen and heard by the living, but that they could not do.

She knew she was dead. This had happened before. She was just passing through this murky lair of sad lingering people. She was on her way! And the pitifulness of her life on earth caused her sorrow. But it was not the important thing now.

The light was shining again, the magnificent light she'd glimpsed when she'd almost died that first time around. She moved towards it, into it. And this was truly beautiful. Never had she seen such colors, such radiance, never had she heard the pure music that she was hearing now. There were no words to describe this; it was beyond any language she'd ever known. And this time nobody would bring her back!

Because the one coming towards her, to take her and to help her—it was her mother! And her mother wouldn't let her go.

Never had she felt such love as she felt for her mother; but then love surrounded her; the light, the color, the love—these things were utterly indistinguishable.

Ah, that poor Baby Jenks, she thought as she looked down to earth just one last time. But she wasn't Baby Jenks now. No, not at all.

3

THE GODDESS PANDORA

Once we had the words.
Ox and Falcon. Plow.
There was clarity.
Savage as horns
curved.
We lived in stone rooms.
We hung our hair out the windows and up it climbed the men.
A garden behind the ears, the curls.
On each hill a king
of that hill. At night the threads were pulled out
of the tapestries. The unravelled men screamed.
All moons revealed. We had the words.
. . . .

STAN RICE
from "The Words Once"
Whiteboy (1976)

SHE was a tall creature, clad in black, with only her eyes uncovered, her strides long as she moved with inhuman speed up the treacherous snow-covered path.

Almost clear this night of tiny stars in the high thin air of the Himalayas, and far ahead—beyond her powers of reckoning distance—loomed the massive pleated flank of Everest, splendidly visible above a thick wreath of turbulent white cloud. It took her breath away each time she glanced at it, not only because it was so beautiful, but because it was so seemingly full of meaning, though no true meaning was there.

Worship this mountain? Yes, one could do that with impunity, because the mountain would never answer. The whistling wind that chilled her skin was the voice of nothing and no one. And this incidental and utterly indifferent grandeur made her want to cry.

So did the sight of the pilgrims far below her, a thin stream of ants it seemed, winding their way up an impossibly narrow road. Too unspeakably sad their delusion. Yet she moved towards the same hidden mountain temple. She moved towards the same despicable and deceiving god.

She was suffering from the cold. Frost covered her face, her eyelids. It clung in tiny crystals to her eyelashes. And each step in the driving wind was hard even for her. Pain or death it couldn't cause her, really; she was too old for that. It was something mental, her suffering. It came from the tremendous resistance of the elements, from seeing nothing for hours but the sheer white and dazzling snows.

No matter. A deep shiver of alarm had passed through her nights ago, in the crowded stinking streets of Old Delhi, and every hour or so since had repeated itself, as if the earth had begun to tremble at its core.

At certain moments, she was sure that the Mother and the Father must be waking. Somewhere far away in a crypt where her beloved Marius had placed them, Those Who Must Be Kept had stirred at last. Nothing less than such a resurrection could transmit this powerful yet vague signal—Akasha and Enkil rising, after six thousand years of horrifying stillness, from the throne they shared.

But that was fancy, wasn't it? Might as well ask the mountain to speak. For these were no mere legend to her, the ancient parents of all blood drinkers. Unlike so many of their spawn, she had seen them with her own eyes. At the door of their shrine she had been made immortal; she had crept forward on her knees and touched the Mother; she had pierced the smooth shining surface that had once been the Mother's human skin and caught in her open mouth the gushing stream of the Mother's blood. What a miracle it had been even then, the living blood pouring forth from the lifeless body before the wounds miraculously closed.

But in those early centuries of magnificent belief she had shared Marius's conviction that the Mother and Father merely slumbered, that the time would come when they would wake and speak to their children once again.

In the candlelight, she and Marius had sung hymns to them together; she herself had burnt the incense, placed before them the flowers; she had sworn never to reveal the location of the sanctuary lest other blood drinkers come to destroy Marius, to steal his charges and feast gluttonously on the original and most powerful blood.

But that was long ago when the world was divided among tribes and empires, when heroes and emperors were made gods in a day. In that time elegant philosophical ideas had caught her fancy.

She knew now what it meant to live forever. Tell it to the mountain.

Danger. She felt it again coursing through her, a scorching current. Then gone. And then a glimpse of a green and humid place, a place of soft earth and stifling growth. But it vanished almost immediately.

She paused, the moonlit snow blinding her for a moment, and she raised her eyes to the stars, twinkling through a thin fleece of passing cloud. She listened for other immortal voices. But she heard no clear and vital transmission—only a dim throb from the temple to which she was going, and from far behind her, rising out of the dark warrens of a dirty over-crowded city, the dead, electronic recordings of that mad blood drinker, "the rock star," the Vampire Lestat.

Doomed that impetuous modern fledgling who had dared to fashion garbled songs of bits and pieces of old truths. She had seen countless young ones rise and fall.

Yet his audacity intrigued her, even as it shocked her. Could it be that the alarm she heard was somehow connected to his plaintive yet raucous songs?

Akasha, Enkil
Hearken to your children

How dare he speak the ancient names to the mortal world? It seemed impossible, an offense to reason, that such a creature not be dismissed out of hand. Yet the monster, reveling in improbable celebrity, revealed secrets he could have learned only from Marius himself. And where was Marius, who for two thousand years had taken Those Who Must Be Kept from one secret sanctuary to another? Her heart would break if she let herself think of Marius, of the quarrels that had long ago divided them.

But the recorded voice of Lestat was gone now, swallowed by other faint electric voices, vibrations rising from cities and villages, and the ever audible cry of mortal souls. As so often happened, her powerful ears could separate no one signal. The rising tide had overwhelmed her—shapeless, horrific—so that she closed herself off. Only the wind again.

Ah, what must the collective voices of the earth be to the Mother and the Father whose powers had grown, inevitably, from the dawn of recorded time? Had they the power, as she had still, to shut off the flow, or to select from time to time the voices they might hear? Perhaps they were as passive in this regard as in any other, and it was the unstoppable din that kept them fixed, unable to reason, as they heard the endless cries, mortal and immortal, of the entire world.

She looked at the great jagged peak before her. She must continue. She tightened the covering over her face. She walked on.

And as the trail led her to a small promontory, she saw her destination at last. Across an immense glacier, the temple rose from a high cliff, a stone structure of near invisible whiteness, its bell tower disappearing into the swirling snow that had just begun to fall.

How long would it take her to reach it, even fast as she could walk? She knew what she must do, yet she dreaded it. She must lift her arms, defy the laws of nature and her own reason, and rise over the gulf that separated her from the temple, gently descending only when she had reached the other side of the frozen gorge. No other power she possessed could make her feel so insignificant, so inhuman, so far from the common earthly being she had once been.

But she wanted to reach the temple. She had to. And so she did raise her arms slowly, with conscious grace. Her eyes closed for the moment as she willed herself upwards, and she felt her body rising immediately as if it were weightless, a force seemingly unfettered by substance, riding by sheer intention the wind itself.

For a long moment she let the winds buffet her; she let her body twist, drift. She rose higher and higher, allowing herself to turn away from the earth altogether, the clouds flying past her, as she faced the stars. How heavy her garments felt; was she not ready to become invisible? Would that not be the next step? A speck of dust in the eye of God, she thought. Her heart was aching. The horror of this, to be utterly unconnected. . . . The tears welled in her eyes.

And as always happened in such moments, the vague shining human past she clung to seemed more than ever a myth to be cherished as all practical belief died away. *That I lived, that I loved, that my flesh was warm.* She saw Marius, her maker, not as he was now, but then, a young immortal burning with a supernatural secret: "Pandora, my dearest . . ." "Give it to me, I beg you." "Pandora, come with me to ask the blessing of the Mother and the Father. Come into the shrine."

Unanchored, in despair, she might have forgotten her destination. She could have let herself drift towards the rising sun. But the alarm came again, the silent, pulsating signal of *Danger,* to remind her of her purpose. She spread out her arms, willed herself to face the earth again, and saw the temple courtyard with its smoking fires directly below. *Yes, there.*

The speed of her descent astonished her; momentarily, it shattered her reason. She found herself standing in the courtyard, her body aching for one flashing instant, and then cold and still.

The scream of the wind was distant. The music of the temple came through the walls, a dizzying throb, the tambourines and drums driving with it, voices melding into one gruesome and repetitive sound. And before her were the pyres, spitting, crackling, the dead bodies darkening as they lay heaped on the burning wood. The stench sickened her. Yet for a long time, she watched the flames working slowly at the sizzling flesh, the blackening stumps, the hair that gave off sudden wisps of white smoke. The smell suffocated her; the cleansing mountain air could not reach her here.

She stared at the distant wooden door to the inner sanctum. She would test the power again, bitterly. *There.* And she found herself moving over the threshold, the door opened, the light of the inner chamber dazzling her, along with the warm air and the deafening chant.

"Azim! Azim! Azim!" the celebrants sang over and over, their backs turned to her as they pressed to the center of the candle-lighted hall, their hands raised, twisting at the wrists in rhythm with their rocking heads. "Azim! Azim! Azim-Azim-Azim! Ahhhh Zeeeem!" Smoke rose from the censers; an endless swarm of figures turned, circling in place on their bare feet, but they did not see her. Their eyes were closed, their dark faces smooth, only their mouths moving as they repeated the revered name.

She pushed into the thick of them, men and women in rags, others in gorgeous colored silks and clattering gold jewelry, all repeating the invocation in horrifying monotony. She caught the smell of fever, starvation, dead bodies fallen in the press, unheeded in the common delirium. She clung to a marble column, as if to anchor herself in the turbulent stream of movement and noise.

And then she saw Azim in the middle of the crush. His dark bronze skin was moist and gleaming in the light of the candles, his head bound in a black silk turban, his long embroidered robes stained with a mingling of mortal and immortal blood. His black eyes, ringed in kohl, were enormous. To the hard underlying beat of the drums, he danced, undulating, thrusting his fists forward and drawing them back as though pounding upon an invisible wall. His slippered feet tapped the marble in frenzied rhythm. Blood oozed from the corners of his mouth. His expression was one of utter mindless absorption.

Yet he knew that she had come. And from the center of his dance, he looked directly at her, and she saw his blood-smeared lips curl in a smile.

Pandora, my beautiful immortal Pandora. . . .

Glutted with the feast he was, plump and heated with it as she had seldom ever seen an immortal become. He threw back his head, spun round, and gave a shrill cry. His acolytes came forward, slashing at his outstretched wrists with their ceremonial knives.

And the faithful surged against him, mouths uplifted to catch the sacred blood as it gushed out. The chant grew louder, more insistent over the strangled cries of those nearest him. And suddenly, she saw him being lifted, his body stretched out full length on the shoulders of his followers, golden slippers pointed to the high tessellated ceiling, the knives slashing at his ankles and again at his wrists where the wounds had already closed.

The maddened crowd seemed to expand as its movements grew more frantic, reeking bodies slamming against her, oblivious to the coldness and hardness of the ancient limbs beneath her soft shapeless wool clothes. She did not move. She let herself be surrounded, drawn in. She saw Azim lowered to the ground once more; bled, moaning, wounds already healed. He beckoned to her to join him. Silently she refused.

She watched as he reached out and snatched a victim, blindly, at random, a young woman with painted eyes and dangling golden earrings, gashing open her slender throat.

The crowd had lost the perfect shape of the syllables it chanted; it was now a simple wordless cry that came from every mouth.

Eyes wide as if in horror at his own power, Azim sucked the woman dry of blood in one great draught, then dashed the body on the stones before him where it lay mangled as the faithful surrounded it, hands out in supplication to their staggering god.

She turned her back; she went out in the cold air of the courtyard, moving away from the heat of the fires. Stink of urine, offal. She stood against the wall, gazing upwards, thinking of the mountain, paying no heed when the acolytes dragged past her the bodies of the newly dead and threw them into the flames.

She thought of the pilgrims she had seen on the road below the temple, the long chain that moved sluggishly day and night through the uninhabited mountains to this unnamed place. How many died without ever reaching this precipice? How many died outside the gates, waiting to be let in?

She loathed it. And yet it did not matter. It was an ancient horror. She waited. Then Azim called her.

She turned and moved back through the door and then through another into a small exquisitely painted antechamber where, standing on a red carpet bordered with rubies, he waited silently for her, surrounded by random treasures, offerings of gold and silver, the music in the hall lower, full of languor and fear.

"Dearest," he said. He took her face in his hands and kissed her. A heated stream of blood flowed out of his mouth into her, and for one rapturous moment her senses were filled with the song and dance of the faithful, the heady cries. Flooding warmth of mortal adoration, surrender. Love.

Yes, love. She saw Marius for one instant. She opened her eyes, and stepped back. For a moment she saw the walls with their painted peacocks, lilies; she saw the heaps of shimmering gold. Then she saw only Azim.

He was changeless as were his people, changeless as were the villages from which they had come, wandering through snow and waste to find this horrid, meaningless end. One thousand years ago, Azim had begun his rule in this temple from which no worshiper ever departed alive. His supple golden skin nourished by an endless river of blood sacrifice had paled only slightly over the centuries, whereas her own flesh had lost its human blush in half the time. Only her eyes, and her dark brown hair perhaps, gave an immediate appearance of life. She had beauty, yes, she knew that, but he had a great surpassing vigor. *Evil.* Irresistible to his followers, shrouded in legend, he ruled, without past or future, as incomprehensible to her now as he had ever been.

She didn't want to linger. The place repelled her more than she wanted him to know. She told him silently of her purpose, the alarm that she had heard. Something wrong somewhere, something changing, something that has never happened before! And she told him too of the young blood drinker who recorded songs in America, songs full of truths about the Mother and the Father, whose names he knew. It was a simple opening of her mind, without drama.

She watched Azim, sensing his immense power, the ability with which he'd glean from her any random thought or idea, and shield from her the secrets of his own mind.

"Blessed Pandora," he said scornfully. "What do I care about the Mother and the Father? What are they to me? What do I care about your precious Marius? That he calls for help over and over! This is nothing to me!"

She was stunned. Marius calling for help. Azim laughed.

"Explain what you're saying," she said.

Again laughter. He turned his back to her. There was nothing she could do but wait. Marius had made her. All the world could hear Marius's voice, but she could not hear it. Was it an echo that had reached her, dim in its deflection, of a powerful cry that the others had heard? *Tell me, Azim. Why make an enemy of me?*

When he turned to her again, he was thoughtful, his round face plump, human-looking as he yielded to her, the backs of his hands fleshy and dimpled as he pressed them together just beneath his moist lower lip. He wanted something of her. There was no scorn or malice now.

"It's a warning," he said. "It comes over and over, echoing through a chain of listeners who carry it from its origins in some far-off place. We are all in danger. Then it is followed by a call for help, which is weaker.

Help him that he may try to avert the danger. But in this there is little conviction. It is the warning above all that he would have us heed."

"The words, what are they?"

He shrugged. "I do not listen. I do not care."

"Ah!" She turned her back now on him. She heard him come towards her, felt his hands on her shoulders.

"You must answer *my* question now," he said. He turned her to face him. "It is the dream of the twins that concerns me. What does this mean?"

Dream of the twins. She didn't have an answer. The question didn't make sense to her. She had had no such dream.

He regarded her silently, as if he believed she was lying. Then he spoke very slowly, evaluating her response carefully.

"Two women, red hair. Terrible things befall them. They come to me in troubling and unwelcome visions just before I would open my eyes. I see these women raped before a court of onlookers. Yet I do not know who they are or where this outrage takes place. And I am not alone in my questioning. Out there, scattered through the world, there are other dark gods who have these dreams and would know why they come to us now."

Dark gods! We are not gods, she thought contemptuously.

He smiled at her. Were they not standing in his very temple? Could she not hear the moaning of the faithful? Could she not smell their blood?

"I know nothing of these two women," she said. Twins, red hair. No. She touched his fingers gently, almost seductively. "Azim, don't torment me. I want you to tell me about Marius. From where does his call come?"

How she hated him at this moment, that he might keep this secret from her.

"From where?" he asked her defiantly. "Ah, that is the crux, isn't it? Do you think he would dare to lead us to the shrine of the Mother and the Father? If I thought that, I would answer him, oh, yes, oh, truly. I would leave my temple to find him, of course. But he cannot fool us. He would rather see himself destroyed than reveal the shrine."

"From where is he calling?" she asked patiently.

"These dreams," he said, his face darkening with anger. "The dreams of the twins, this I would have explained!"

"And I would tell you who they are and what they mean, if only I knew." She thought of the songs of Lestat, the words she'd heard. Songs of Those Who Must Be Kept and crypts beneath European cities, songs of questing, sorrow. Nothing there of red-haired women, nothing. . . .

Furious, he gestured for her to stop. "The Vampire Lestat," he said, sneering. "Do not speak of this abomination to me. Why hasn't he been destroyed already? Are the dark gods asleep like the Mother and the Father?"

He watched her, calculating. She waited.

"Very well. I believe you," he said finally. "You've told me what you know."

"Yes."

"I close my ears to Marius. I told you. Stealer of the Mother and the Father, let him cry for help until the end of time. But you, Pandora, for you I feel love as always, and so I will soil myself with these affairs. Cross the sea to the New World. Look in the frozen north beyond the last of the woodlands near the western sea. And there you may find Marius, trapped in a citadel of ice. He cries that he is unable to move. As for his warning, it is as vague as it is persistent. We are in danger. We must help him so that he may stop the danger. So that he may go to the Vampire Lestat."

"Ah. So it is the young one who has done this!"

The shiver passed through her, violent, painful. She saw in her mind's eye the blank, senseless faces of the Mother and the Father, indestructible monsters in human form. She looked at Azim in confusion. He had paused, but he wasn't finished. And she waited for him to go on.

"No," he said, his voice dropping, having lost its sharp edge of anger. "There is a danger, Pandora, yes. Great danger, and it does not require Marius to announce it. It has to do with the red-haired twins." How uncommonly earnest he was, how unguarded. "This I know," he said, "because I was old before Marius was made. The twins, Pandora. Forget Marius. And hearken to your dreams."

She was speechless, watching him. He looked at her for a long moment, and then his eyes appeared to grow smaller, to become solid. She could feel him drawing back, away from her and all the things of which they'd spoken. Finally, he no longer saw her.

He heard the insistent wails of his worshipers; he felt thirst again; he wanted hymns and blood. He turned and started out of the chamber, then he glanced back.

"Come with me, Pandora! Join me but for an hour!" His voice was drunken, unclear.

The invitation caught her off guard. She considered. It had been years since she had sought the exquisite pleasure. She thought not merely of the blood itself, but of the momentary union with another soul. And there it was, suddenly, waiting for her, among those who had climbed the highest mountain range on earth to seek this death. She thought also of the quest that lay before her—to find Marius—and of the sacrifices it would entail.

"Come, dearest."

She took his hand. She let herself be led out of the room and into the center of the crowded hall. The brightness of the light startled her; yes, the blood again. The smell of humans pressed in on her, tormenting her.

The cry of the faithful was deafening. The stamp of human feet seemed to shake the painted walls, the glimmering gold ceiling. The incense burned her eyes. Faint memory of the shrine, eons ago, of Marius embracing her. Azim stood before her as he removed her outer cloak, revealing her face, her naked arms, the plain gown of black wool she wore, and her long brown hair. She saw herself reflected in a thousand pairs of mortal eyes.

"The goddess Pandora!" he cried out, throwing back his head.

Screams rose over the rapid thudding of drums. Countless human hands stroked her. "Pandora, Pandora, Pandora!" The chant mingled with the cries of "Azim!"

A young brown-skinned man danced before her, white silk shirt plastered to the sweat of his dark chest. His black eyes, gleaming under low dark brows, were fired with the challenge. *I am your victim! Goddess!* She could see nothing suddenly in the flickering light and drowning noise but his eyes, his face. She embraced him, crushing his ribs in her haste, her teeth sinking deep into his neck. *Alive.* The blood poured into her, reached her heart and flooded its chambers, then sent its heat through all her cold limbs. It was beyond remembrance, this glorious sensation—and the exquisite lust, the wanting again! The death shocked her, knocked the breath out of her. She felt it pass into her brain. She was blinded, moaning. Then instantly, the clarity of her vision was paralyzing. The marble columns lived and breathed. She dropped the body, and took hold of another young male, half starved, naked to the waist, his strength on the verge of death maddening her.

She broke his tender neck as she drank, hearing her own heart swell, feeling even the surface of her skin flooded with blood. She could see the color in her own hands just before she closed her eyes, yes, human hands, the death slower, resistant, and then yielding in a rush of dimming light and roaring sound. *Alive.*

"Pandora! Pandora! Pandora!"

God, is there no justice, is there no end?

She stood rocking back and forth, human faces, each discrete, lurid, dancing in front of her. The blood inside her was boiling as it sought out every tissue, every cell. She saw her third victim hurling himself against her, sleek young limbs enfolding her, so soft this hair, this fleece on the back of his arms, the fragile bones, so light, as if she were the real being and these were but creatures of the imagination.

She ripped the head half off the neck, staring at the white bones of the broken spinal cord, then swallowing the death instantly with the violent spray of blood from the torn artery. But the heart, the beating heart, she would see it, taste it. She threw the body back over her right arm, bones cracking, while with her left hand she split the breast bone and tore open the ribs, and reached through the hot bleeding cavity to pull the heart free.

Not dead yet this, not really. And slippery, glistening like wet grapes. The faithful crushed against her as she held it up over her head, squeezing it gently so that the living juice ran down her fingers and into her open mouth. Yes, this, forever and ever.

"Goddess! Goddess!"

Azim was watching her, smiling at her. But she did not look at him. She stared at the shriveled heart as the last droplets of blood left it. A pulp. She let it fall. Her hands glowed like living hands, smeared with blood. She could feel it in her face, the tingling warmth. A tide of memory threatened, a tide of visions without understanding. She drove it back. This time it wouldn't enslave her.

She reached for her black cloak. She felt it enclosing her, as warm, solicitous human hands brought the soft wool covering up over her hair, over the lower part of her face. And ignoring the heated cries of her name all around her, she turned and went out, her limbs accidentally bruising the frenzied worshipers who stumbled into her path.

So deliciously cold the courtyard. She bent her head back slightly, breathing a vagrant wind as it gusted down into the enclosure, where it fanned the pyres before carrying their bitter smoke away. The moonlight was clear and beautiful falling on the snow-covered peaks beyond the walls.

She stood listening to the blood inside her, and marveling in a crazed, despairing way that it could still refresh her and strengthen her, even now. Sad, grief-stricken, she looked at the lovely stark wilderness encircling the temple, she looked up at the loose and billowing clouds. How the blood gave her courage, how it gave her a momentary belief in the sheer rightness of the universe—fruits of a ghastly, unforgivable act.

If the mind can find no meaning, then the senses give it. Live for this, wretched being that you are.

She moved towards the nearest pyre and, careful not to singe her clothes, reached out to let the fire cleanse her hands, burn away the blood, the bits of heart. The licking flames were nothing to the heat of the blood inside her. When finally the faintest beginning of pain was there, the faintest signal of change, she drew back and looked down at her immaculate white skin.

But she must leave here now. Her thoughts were too full of anger, new resentment. Marius needed her. *Danger.* The alarm came again, stronger than ever before, because the blood made her a more powerful receptor. And it did not seem to come from one. Rather it was a communal voice, the dim clarion of a communal knowledge. She was afraid.

She allowed her mind to empty itself, as tears blurred her vision. She lifted her hands, just her hands, delicately. And the ascent was begun. Soundlessly, swiftly, as invisible to mortal eyes, perhaps, as the wind itself.

High over the temple, her body pierced a soft thin agitated mist. The degree of light astonished her. Everywhere the shining whiteness. And below the crenellated landscape of stone peak and blinding glacier descending to a soft darkness of lower forests and vale. Nestled here and there were clusters of sparkling lights, the random pattern of villages or towns. She could have gazed on this forever. Yet within seconds an undulating fleece of cloud had obscured all of it. And she was with the stars alone.

The stars—hard, glittering, embracing her as though she were one of their own. But the stars claimed nothing, really, and no one. She felt terror. Then a deepening sorrow, not unlike joy, finally. No more struggle. No more grief.

Scanning the splendid drift of the constellations, she slowed her ascent and reached out with both hands to the west.

The sunrise lay nine hours behind her. And so she commenced her journey away from it, in time with the night on its way to the other side of the world.

4

THE STORY OF DANIEL, THE DEVIL'S MINION, OR THE BOY FROM INTERVIEW WITH THE VAMPIRE

Who are these shades we wait for and believe
will come some evening in limousines
from Heaven?
The rose
though it knows
is throatless
and cannot say.
My mortal half laughs.
The code and the message are not the same.
And what is an angel
but a ghost in drag?

STAN RICE
from "Of Heaven"
Body of Work (1983)

HE WAS a tall, slender young man, with ashen hair and violet eyes. He wore a dirty gray sweat shirt and jeans, and in the icy wind whipping along Michigan Avenue at five o'clock, he was cold.

Daniel Molloy was his name. He was thirty-two, though he looked younger, a perennial student, not a man, that kind of youthful face. He murmured aloud to himself as he walked. "Armand, I need you. Armand, that concert is tomorrow night. And something terrible is going to happen, something terrible. . . ."

He was hungry. Thirty-six hours had passed since he'd eaten. There was nothing in the refrigerator of his small dirty hotel room, and besides, he had been locked out of it this morning because he had not paid the rent. Hard to remember everything at once.

Then he remembered the dream that he kept having, the dream that came every time he closed his eyes, and he didn't want to eat at all.

He saw the twins in the dream. He saw the roasted body of the woman before them, her hair singed away, her skin crisped. Her heart lay glistening like a swollen fruit on the plate beside her. The brain on the other plate looked exactly like a cooked brain.

Armand knew about it, he had to know. It was no ordinary dream, this. Something to do with Lestat, definitely. And Armand would come soon.

God, he was weak, delirious. Needed something, a drink at least. In his pocket there was no money, only an old crumpled royalty check for the book *Interview with the Vampire,* which he had "written" under a pseudonym over twelve years ago.

Another world, that, when he had been a young reporter, roaming the bars of the world with his tape recorder, trying to get the flotsam and jetsam of the night to tell him some truth. Well, one night in San Francisco he had found a magnificent subject for his investigations. And the light of ordinary life had suddenly gone out.

Now he was a ruined thing, walking too fast under the lowering night sky of Chicago in October. Last Sunday he had been in Paris, and the Friday before that in Edinburgh. Before Edinburgh, he had been in Stockholm and before that he couldn't recall. The royalty check had caught up with him in Vienna, but he did not know how long ago that was.

In all these places he frightened those he passed. The Vampire Lestat had a good phrase for it in his autobiography: "One of those tiresome mortals who has seen spirits . . ." *That's me!*

Where was that book, *The Vampire Lestat?* Ah, somebody had stolen it off the park bench this afternoon while Daniel slept. Well, let them have it. Daniel had stolen it himself, and he'd read it three times already.

But if only he had it now, he could sell it, maybe get enough for a glass of brandy to make him warm. And what was his net worth at this moment, this cold and hungry vagabond that shuffled along Michigan Avenue, hating the wind that chilled him through his worn and dirty clothes? Ten million? A hundred million? He didn't know. Armand would know.

You want money, Daniel? I'll get it for you. It's simpler than you think.

A thousand miles south Armand waited on their private island, the island that belonged in fact to Daniel alone. And if only he had a quarter now, just a quarter, he could drop it into a pay phone and tell Armand that he wanted to come home. Out of the sky, they'd come to get him. They always did. Either the big plane with the velvet bedroom on it or the smaller one with the low ceiling and the leather chairs. Would anybody on this street lend him a quarter in exchange for a plane ride to Miami? Probably not.

Armand, now! I want to be safe with you when Lestat goes on that stage tomorrow night.

Who would cash this royalty check? No one. It was seven o'clock and the fancy shops along Michigan Avenue were for the most part closed, and he had no identification because his wallet had somehow disappeared day before yesterday. So dismal this glaring gray winter twilight, the sky boiling silently with low metallic clouds. Even the stores had taken on an uncommon grimness, with their hard facades of marble or granite, the wealth within gleaming like archaeological relics under museum glass. He plunged his hands in his pockets to warm them, and he bowed his head as the wind came with greater fierceness and the first sting of rain.

He didn't give a damn about the check, really. He couldn't imagine pressing the buttons of a phone. Nothing here seemed particularly real to him, not even the chill. Only the dream seemed real, and the sense of impending disaster, that the Vampire Lestat had somehow set into motion something that even he could never control.

Eat from a garbage can if you have to, sleep somewhere even if it's a park. None of that matters. But he'd freeze if he lay down again in the open air, and besides the dream would come back.

It was coming now every time he closed his eyes. And each time, it was longer, more full of detail. The red-haired twins were so tenderly beautiful. He did not want to hear them scream.

The first night in his hotel room he'd ignored the whole thing. Meaningless. He'd gone back to reading Lestat's autobiography, and glancing up now and then as Lestat's rock video films played themselves out on the little black and white TV that came with that kind of dump.

He'd been fascinated by Lestat's audacity; yet the masquerade as rock star was so simple. Searing eyes, powerful yet slender limbs, and a mischievous smile, yes. But you really couldn't tell. Or could you? He had never laid eyes on Lestat.

But he was an expert on Armand, wasn't he, he had studied every detail of Armand's youthful body and face. Ah, what a delirious pleasure it had been to read about Armand in Lestat's pages, wondering all the while if Lestat's stinging insults and worshipful analyses had put Armand himself into a rage.

In mute fascination, Daniel had watched that little clip on MTV portraying Armand as the coven master of the old vampires beneath the Paris cemetery, presiding over demonic rituals until the Vampire Lestat, the eighteenth-century iconoclast, had destroyed the Old Ways.

Armand must have loathed it, his private history laid bare in flashing images, so much more crass than Lestat's more thoughtful written history. Armand, whose eyes scanned perpetually the living beings around him, refusing even to speak of the undead. But it was impossible that he did not know.

And all this for the multitudes—like the paperback report of an anthropologist, back from the inner circle, who sells the tribe's secrets for a slot on the best-seller list.

So let the demonic gods war with each other. This mortal has been to the top of the mountain where they cross swords. And he has come back. He has been turned away.

The next night, the dream had returned with the clarity of a hallucination. He knew that it could not have been invented by him. He had never seen people quite like that, seen such simple jewelry made of bone and wood.

The dream had come again three nights later. He'd been watching a Lestat rock video for the fifteenth time, perhaps—this one about the ancient and immovable Egyptian Father and Mother of the vampires, Those Who Must Be Kept:

Akasha and Enkil,
We are your children,
but what do you give us?
Is your silence
A better gift than truth?

And then Daniel was dreaming. And the twins were about to begin the feast. They would share the organs on the earthen plates. One would take the brain, the other the heart.

He'd awakened with a sense of urgency, dread. Something terrible going to happen, something going to happen to all of us . . . And that was the first time he'd connected it with Lestat. He had wanted to pick up the phone then. It was four o'clock in the morning in Miami. Why the hell hadn't he done it? Armand would have been sitting on the terrace of the villa, watching the tireless fleet of white boats wend its way back and forth from the Night Island. "Yes, Daniel?" That sensuous, mesmerizing voice. "Calm down and tell me where you are, Daniel."

But Daniel hadn't called. Six months had passed since he had left the

Night Island, and this time it was supposed to be for good. He had once and for all forsworn the world of carpets and limousines and private planes, of liquor closets stocked with rare vintages and dressing rooms full of exquisitely cut clothing, of the quiet overwhelming presence of his immortal lover who gave him every earthly possession he could want.

But now it was cold and he had no room and no money, and he was afraid.

You know where I am, you demon. You know what Lestat's done. And you know I want to come home.

What would Armand say to that?

But I don't know, Daniel. I listen. I try to know. I am not God, Daniel.

Never mind. Just come, Armand. Come. It's dark and cold in Chicago. And tomorrow night the Vampire Lestat will sing his songs on a San Francisco stage. And something bad is going to happen. This mortal knows.

Without slowing his pace, Daniel reached down under the collar of his sagging sweat shirt and felt the heavy gold locket he always wore—the amulet, as Armand called it with his unacknowledged yet irrepressible flair for the dramatic—which held the tiny vial of Armand's blood.

And if he had never tasted that cup would he be having this dream, this vision, this portent of doom?

People turned to look at him; he was talking to himself again, wasn't he? And the wind made him sigh loudly. He had the urge for the first time in all these years to break open the locket and the vial, to feel that blood burn his tongue. *Armand, come!*

The dream had visited him in its most alarming form this noon.

He'd been sitting on a bench in the little park near the Water Tower Place. A newspaper had been left there, and when he opened it he saw the advertisement: "Tomorrow Night: The Vampire Lestat Live on Stage in San Francisco." The cable would broadcast the concert at ten o'clock Chicago time. How nice for those who still lived indoors, could pay their rent, and had electricity. He had wanted to laugh at the whole thing, delight in it, revel in it, Lestat surprising them all. But the chill had passed through him, becoming a deep jarring shock.

And what if Armand does not know? But the record stores on the Night Island must have *The Vampire Lestat* in their windows. In the elegant lounges, they must be playing those haunting and hypnotic songs.

It had even occurred to Daniel at that moment to go on to California on his own. Surely he could work some miracle, get his passport from the hotel, go into any bank with it for identification. Rich, yes so very rich, this poor mortal boy. . . .

But how could he think of something so deliberate? The sun had been warm on his face and shoulders as he'd lain down on the bench. He'd folded the newspaper to make of it a pillow.

And there was the dream that had been waiting all the time. . . .

Midday in the world of the twins: the sun pouring down onto the clearing. Silence, except for the singing of the birds.

And the twins kneeling quite still together, in the dust. Such pale women, their eyes green, their hair long and wavy and coppery red. Fine clothes they wore, white linen dresses that had come all the way from the markets of Nineveh, bought by the villagers to honor these powerful witches, whom the spirits obey.

The funeral feast was ready. The mud bricks of the oven had been torn down and carried away, and the body lay steaming hot on the stone slab, the yellow juices running out of it where the crisp skin had broken, a black and naked thing with only a covering of cooked leaves. It horrified Daniel.

But it horrified no one present, this spectacle, not the twins or the villagers who knelt to watch the feast begin.

This feast was the right and the duty of the twins. *This was their mother, the blackened body on the stone slab.* And what was human must remain with the human. A day and night it may take to consume the feast, but all will keep watch until it is done.

Now a current of excitement passes through the crowd around the clearing. One of the twins lifts the plate on which the brain rests together with the eyes, and the other nods and takes the plate that holds the heart.

And so the division has been made. The beat of a drum rises, though Daniel cannot see the drummer. Slow, rhythmic, brutal.

"Let the banquet begin."

But the ghastly cry comes, just as Daniel knew it would. *Stop the soldiers.* But he can't. All this has happened somewhere, of that he is now certain. It is no dream, it is a vision. And he is not there. The soldiers storm the clearing, the villagers scatter, the twins set down the plates and fling themselves over the smoking feast. But this is madness.

The soldiers tear them loose so effortlessly, and as the slab is lifted, the body falls, breaking into pieces, and the heart and the brain are thrown down into the dust. The twins scream and scream.

But the villagers are screaming too, the soldiers are cutting them down as they run. The dead and the dying litter the mountain paths. The eyes of the mother have fallen from the plate into the dirt, and they, along with the heart and brain, are trampled underfoot.

One of the twins, her arms pulled behind her back, cries to the spirits for vengeance. And they come, they do. It is a whirlwind. But not enough.

If only it were over. But Daniel can't wake up.

Stillness. The air is full of smoke. Nothing stands where these people have lived for centuries. The mud bricks are scattered, clay pots are broken, all that will burn has burned. Infants with their throats slit lie naked on the ground as the flies come. No one will roast these bodies, no one will consume this flesh. It will pass out of the human race, with all its power and its mystery. The jackals are already approaching. And the soldiers have gone. Where are the twins! He hears the twins crying, but he cannot find them. A great storm is rumbling over the narrow road that twists down through the valley towards the desert. The spirits make the thunder. The spirits make the rain.

His eyes opened. Chicago, Michigan Avenue at midday. The dream had gone out like a light turned off. He sat there shivering, sweating.

A radio had been playing near him, Lestat singing in that haunting mournful voice of Those Who Must Be Kept.

Mother and Father.
Keep your silence,
Keep your secrets,
But those of you with tongues,
sing my song.

Sons and daughters
Children of darkness
Raise your voices
Make a chorus
Let heaven hear us

Come together,
Brother and sisters,
Come to me.

He had gotten up, started walking. Go into the Water Tower Place, so like the Night Island with its engulfing shops, endless music and lights, shining glass.

And now it was almost eight o'clock and he had been walking continuously, running from sleep and from the dream. He was far from any music and light. How long would it go on next time? Would he find out whether they were alive or dead? My beauties, my poor beauties. . . .

He stopped, turning his back to the wind for a moment, listening to the chimes somewhere, then spotting a dirty clock above a dime store lunch counter; yes, Lestat had risen on the West Coast. Who is with him? Is Louis there? And the concert, a little over twenty-four hours. Catastrophe! *Armand, please.*

The wind gusted, pushed him back a few steps on the pavement, left him shivering violently. His hands were frozen. Had he ever been this cold in his life? Doggedly, he crossed Michigan Avenue with the crowd at the stoplight and stood at the plate glass windows of the bookstore, where he could see the book, *The Vampire Lestat,* on display.

Surely Armand had read it, devouring every word in that eerie, horrible way he had of reading, of turning page after page without pause, eyes flashing over the words, until the book was finished, and then tossing it aside. How could a creature shimmer with such beauty yet incite such . . . what was it, revulsion? No, he had never been revolted by Armand, he had to admit it. What he always felt was ravening and hopeless desire.

A young girl inside the warmth of the store picked up a copy of Lestat's book, then stared at him through the window. His breath made steam on the glass in front of him. *Don't worry, my darling, I am a rich man. I could buy this whole store full of books and make it a present to you. I am lord and master of my own island, I am the Devil's minion and he grants my every wish. Want to come take my arm?*

It had been dark for hours on the Florida coast. The Night Island was already thronged.

The shops, restaurants, bars had opened their broad, seamless plate glass doors at sunset, on five levels of richly carpeted hallway. The silver escalators had begun their low, churning hum. Daniel closed his eyes and envisioned the walls of glass rising above the harbor terraces. He could almost hear the great roar of the dancing fountains, see the long narrow beds of daffodils and tulips blooming eternally out of season, hear the hypnotic music that beat like a heart beneath it all.

And Armand, he was probably roaming the dimly lighted rooms of the villa, steps away from the tourists and the shoppers, yet utterly cut off by steel doors and white walls—a sprawling palace of floor-length windows and broad balconies, perched over white sand. Solitary, yet near to the endless commotion, its vast living room facing the twinkling lights of the Miami shore.

Or maybe he had gone through one of the many unmarked doors into the public galleria itself. "To live and breathe among mortals" as he called it in this safe and self-contained universe which he and Daniel had made. How Armand loved the warm breezes of the Gulf, the endless springtime of the Night Island.

No lights would go out until dawn.

"Send someone for me, Armand, I need you! You know you want me to come home."

Of course it had happened this way over and over again. It did not need strange dreams, or Lestat to reappear, roaring like Lucifer from tape and film.

Everything would go all right for months as Daniel felt compelled to move from city to city, walking the pavements of New York or Chicago or New Orleans. Then the sudden disintegration. He'd realize he had not moved from his chair in five hours. Or he'd wake suddenly in a stale and unchanged bed, frightened, unable to remember the name of the city where he was, or where he'd been for days before. Then the car would come for him, then the plane would take him home.

Didn't Armand cause it? Didn't he somehow drive Daniel to these periods of madness? Didn't he by some evil magic dry up every source of pleasure, every fount of sustenance until Daniel welcomed the sight of the familiar chauffeur come to drive him to the airport, the man who was never shocked by Daniel's demeanor, his unshaven face, his soiled clothes?

When Daniel finally reached the Night Island, Armand would deny it.

"You came back to me because you wanted to, Daniel," Armand always said calmly, face still and radiant, eyes full of love. "There is nothing for you now, Daniel, except me. You know that. Madness waits out there."

"Same old dance," Daniel invariably answered. And all that luxury, so intoxicating, soft beds, music, the wine glass placed in his hand. The rooms were always full of flowers, the foods he craved came on silver trays.

Armand lay sprawled in a huge black velvet wing chair gazing at the television, Ganymede in white pants and white silk shirt, watching the news, the movies, the tapes he'd made of himself reading poetry, the idiot sitcoms, the dramas, the musicals, the silent films.

"Come in, Daniel, sit down. I never expected you back so soon."

"You son of a bitch," Daniel would say. "You wanted me here, you summoned me. I couldn't eat, sleep, nothing, just wander and think of you. You did it."

Armand would smile, sometimes even laugh. Armand had a rich, beautiful laugh, always eloquent of gratitude as well as humor. He looked and sounded mortal when he laughed. "Calm yourself, Daniel. Your heart's racing. It frightens me." Small crease to the smooth forehead, the voice for a moment deepened by compassion. "Tell me what you want, Daniel, and I'll get it for you. Why do you keep running away?"

"Lies, you bastard. Say that you wanted me. You'll torment me forever, won't you, and then you'll watch me die, and you'll find that interesting, won't you? It was true what Louis said. You watch them die, your mortal slaves, they mean nothing to you. You'll watch the colors change in my face as I die."

"That's Louis's language," Armand said patiently. "Please don't quote that book to me. I'd rather die than see you die, Daniel."

"Then give it to me! Damn you! Immortality that close, as close as your arms."

"No, Daniel, because I'd rather die than do that, too."

But even if Armand did not cause this madness that brought Daniel home, surely he always knew where Daniel was. He could hear Daniel's call. The blood connected them, it had to—the precious tiny drinks of burning preternatural blood. Never enough to do more than awaken dreams in Daniel, and the thirst for eternity, to make the flowers in the wallpaper sing and dance. Whatever, Armand could always find him, of that he had no doubt.

IN THE early years, even before the blood exchange, Armand had pursued Daniel with the cunning of a harpy. There had been no place on earth that Daniel could hide.

Horrifying yet tantalizing, their beginning in New Orleans, twelve years ago when Daniel had entered a crumbling old house in the Garden District and known at once that it was the vampire Lestat's lair.

Ten days before he'd left San Francisco after his night-long interview with the vampire Louis, suffering from the final confirmation of the frightening tale he had been told. In a sudden embrace, Louis had demonstrated his supernatural power to drain Daniel almost to the point of death. The puncture wounds had disappeared, but the memory had left Daniel near to madness. Feverish, sometimes delirious, he had traveled no more than a few hundred miles a day. In cheap roadside motels, where he forced himself to take nourishment, he had duplicated the tapes of the interview one by one, sending the copies off to a New York publisher, so that a book was in the making before he ever stood before Lestat's gate.

But that had been secondary, the publication, an event connected with the values of a dimming and distant world.

He had to find the vampire Lestat. He had to unearth the immortal who had made Louis, the one who still survived somewhere in this damp, decadent, and beautiful old city, waiting perhaps for Daniel to awaken him, to bring him out into the century that had terrified him and driven him underground.

It was what Louis wanted, surely. Why else had he given this mortal emissary so many clues as to where Lestat could be found? Yet some of the details were misleading. Was this ambivalence on Louis's part? It did not matter, finally. In the public records, Daniel had found the title to the property, and the street number, under the unmistakable name: Lestat de Lioncourt.

The iron gate had not even been locked, and once he'd hacked his way through the overgrown garden, he had managed easily to break the rusted lock on the front door.

Only a small pocket flash helped him as he entered. But the moon had been high, shining its full white light here and there through the oak branches. He had seen clearly the rows and rows of books stacked to the ceiling, making up the very walls of every room. No human could or would have done such a mad and methodical thing. And then in the upstairs bedroom, he had knelt down in the thick dust that covered the rotting carpet and found the gold pocket watch on which was written the name Lestat.

Ah, that chilling moment, that moment when the pendulum swung away from ever increasing dementia to a new passion—he would track to the ends of the earth these pale and deadly beings whose existence he had only glimpsed.

What had he wanted in those early weeks? Did he hope to possess the splendid secrets of life itself? Surely he would gain from this knowledge no purpose for an existence already fraught with disappointment. No, he wanted to be swept away from everything he had once loved. He longed for Louis's violent and sensuous world.

Evil. He was no longer afraid.

Maybe he was like the lost explorer who, pushing through the jungle, suddenly sees the wall of the fabled temple before him, its carvings overhung with spiderwebs and vines; no matter that he may not live to tell his story; he has beheld the truth with his own eyes.

But if only he could open the door a little further, see the full magnificence. If they would only let him in! Maybe he just wanted to live forever. Could anyone fault him for that?

He had felt good and safe standing alone in the ruin of Lestat's old house, with the wild roses crawling at the broken window and the four-poster bed a skeleton, its hangings rotting away.

Near them, near to their precious darkness, their lovely devouring gloom. How he had loved the hopelessness of it all, the moldering chairs with their bits of carving, shreds of velvet, and the slithering things eating the last of the carpet away.

But the relic; ah, the relic was everything, the gleaming gold watch that bore an immortal's name!

After a while, he had opened the armoire; the black frock coats fell to pieces when he touched them. Withered and curling boots lay on the cedar boards.

But Lestat, you are here. He had taken the tape recorder out, set it down, put in the first tape, and let the voice of Louis rise softly in the shadowy room. Hour by hour, the tapes played.

Then just before dawn he had seen a figure in the hallway, and known that he was meant to see it. And he had seen the moon strike the boyish face, the auburn hair. The earth tilted, the darkness came down. The last word he uttered had been the name Armand.

He should have died then. Had a whim kept him alive?

He'd awakened in a dark, damp cellar. Water oozed from the walls. Groping in the blackness, he'd discovered a bricked-up window, a locked door plated with steel.

And what was his comfort, that he had found yet another god of the secret pantheon—Armand, the oldest of the immortals whom Louis had described, Armand, the coven master of the nineteenth-century Theater of the Vampires in Paris, who had confided his terrible secret to Louis: of our origins nothing is known.

For three days and nights, perhaps, Daniel had lain in this prison. Impossible to tell. He had been near to dying certainly, the stench of his own urine sickening him, the insects driving him mad. Yet his was a religious fervor. He had come ever nearer to the dark pulsing truths that Louis had revealed. Slipping in and out of consciousness, he dreamed of Louis, Louis talking to him in that dirty little room in San Francisco, *there have always been things such as we are, always,* Louis embracing him, his green eyes darkening suddenly as he let Daniel see the fang teeth.

The fourth night, Daniel had awakened and known at once that someone or something was in the room. The door lay open to a passage. Water was flowing somewhere fast as if in a deep underground sewer. Slowly his eyes grew accustomed to the dirty greenish light from the doorway and then he saw the pale white-skinned figure standing against the wall.

So immaculate the black suit, the starched white shirt—like the imitation of a twentieth-century man. And the auburn hair clipped short and the fingernails gleaming dully even in this semidarkness. Like a corpse for the coffin—that sterile, that well prepared.

The voice had been gentle with a trace of an accent. Not European; something sharper yet softer at the same time. Arabic or Greek perhaps, that kind of music. The words were slow and without anger.

"Get out. Take your tapes with you. They are there beside you. I know of your book. No one will believe it. Now you will go and take these things."

Then you won't kill me. And you won't make me one of you either. Desperate, stupid thoughts, but he couldn't stop them. He had seen the power! No lies, no cunning here. And he'd felt himself crying, so weakened by fear and hunger, reduced to a child.

"Make you one of us?" The accent thickened, giving a fine lilt to the words. "Why would I do that?" Eyes narrowing. "I would not do that to those whom I find to be despicable, whom I would see burning in hell as a matter of course. So why should I do it to an innocent fool—like you?"

I want it. I want to live forever. Daniel had sat up, climbed to his feet slowly, struggling to see Armand more clearly. A dim bulb burned somewhere far down the hall. *I want to be with Louis and with you.*

Laughter, low, gentle. But contemptuous. "I see why he chose you for his confidant. You are naive and beautiful. But the beauty could be the only reason, you know."

Silence.

"Your eyes are an unusual color, almost violet. And you are strangely defiant and beseeching in the same breath."

Make me immortal. Give it to me!

Laughter again. Almost sad. Then silence, the water rushing fast in that distant someplace. The room had become visible, a filthy basement hole. And the figure more nearly mortal. There was even a faint pink tinge to the smooth skin.

"It was all true, what he told you. But no one will ever believe it. And you will go mad in time from this knowledge. That's what always happens. But you're not mad yet."

No. This is real, it's all happening. You're Armand and we're talking together. And I'm not mad..

"Yes. And I find it rather interesting . . . interesting that you know my name and that you're alive. I have never told my name to anyone who is alive." Armand hesitated. "I don't want to kill you. Not just now."

Daniel had felt the first touch of fear. If you looked closely enough at these beings you could see what they were. It had been the same with Louis. No, they weren't living. They were ghastly imitations of the living. And this one, the gleaming manikin of a young boy!

"I am going to let you leave here," Armand had said. So politely, softly. "I want to follow you, watch you, see where you go. As long as I find you interesting, I won't kill you. And of course, I may lose interest altogether and not bother to kill you. That's always possible. You have hope in that. And maybe with luck I'll lose track of you. I have my limitations, of course. You have the world to roam, and you can move by day. Go now. Start running. I want to see what you do, I want to know what you are."

Go now, start running!

He'd been on the morning plane to Lisbon, clutching Lestat's gold watch in his hand. Yet two nights later in Madrid, he'd turned to find Armand seated on a city bus beside him no more than inches away. A week later in Vienna he'd looked out the window of a café to see Armand watching him from the street. In Berlin, Armand slipped into a taxi beside him, and sat there staring at him, until finally Daniel had leapt out in the thick of the traffic and run away.

Within months, however, these shattering silent confrontations had given way to more vigorous assaults.

He woke in a hotel room in Prague to find Armand standing over him, crazed, violent. "Talk to me now! I demand it. Wake up. I want you to walk with me, show me things in this city. Why did you come to this particular place?"

Riding on a train through Switzerland, he looked up suddenly to see Armand directly opposite watching him over the upturned cover of his fur-lined coat. Armand snatched the book out of his hand and insisted that he explain what it was, why he read it, what did the picture on the cover mean?

In Paris Armand pursued him nightly through the boulevards and the back streets, only now and then questioning him on the places he went, the things he did. In Venice, he'd looked out of his room at the Danieli, to see Armand staring from a window across the way.

Then weeks passed without a visitation. Daniel vacillated between terror and strange expectation, doubting his very sanity again. But there was Armand waiting for him in the New York airport. And the following night in Boston, Armand was in the dining room of the Copley when Daniel came in. Daniel's dinner was already ordered. Please sit down. Did Daniel know that *Interview with the Vampire* was in the bookstores?

"I must confess I enjoy this small measure of notoriety," Armand had said with exquisite politeness and a vicious smile. "What puzzles me is that you do not want notoriety! You did not list yourself as the 'author,' which means that you are either very modest or a coward. Either explanation would be very dull."

"I'm not hungry, let's get out of here," Daniel had answered weakly. Yet suddenly dish after dish was being placed on the table; everyone was staring.

"I didn't know what you wanted," Armand confided, the smile becoming absolutely ecstatic. "So I ordered everything that they had."

"You think you can drive me crazy, don't you?" Daniel had snarled. "Well, you can't. Let me tell you. Every time I lay eyes on you, I realize that I didn't invent you, and that I'm sane!" And he had started eating, lustily, furiously—a little fish, a little beef, a little veal, a little sweetbreads, a little cheese, a little everything, put it all together, what did he care, and Armand had been so delighted, laughing and laughing like a schoolboy as he sat watching, with folded arms. It was the first time Daniel had ever heard that soft, silky laughter. So seductive. He got drunk as fast as he could.

The meetings grew longer and longer. Conversations, sparring matches, and downright fights became the rule. Once Armand had dragged Daniel out of bed in New Orleans and shouted at him: "That telephone, I want you to dial Paris, I want to see if it can really talk to Paris."

"Goddamn it, do it yourself," Daniel had roared. "You're five hundred years old and you can't use a telephone? Read the directions. What are you, an immortal idiot? I will do no such thing!"

How surprised Armand had looked.

"All right, I'll call Paris for you. But you pay the bill."

"But of course," Armand had said innocently. He had drawn dozens of hundred-dollar bills out of his coat, sprinkling them on Daniel's bed.

More and more they argued philosophy at these meetings. Pulling Daniel out of a theater in Rome, Armand had asked what did Daniel really think that death was? People who were still living knew things like that! Did Daniel know what Armand truly feared?

As it was past midnight and Daniel was drunk and exhausted and had been sound asleep in the theater before Armand found him, he did not care.

"I'll tell you what I fear," Armand had said, intense as any young student. "That it's chaos after you die, that it's a dream from which you can't wake. Imagine drifting half in and out of consciousness, trying vainly to remember who you are or what you were. Imagine straining forever for the lost clarity of the living. . . ."

It had frightened Daniel. Something about it rang true. Weren't there tales of mediums conversing with incoherent yet powerful presences? He didn't know. How in hell could he know? Maybe when you died there was flat out nothing. That terrified Armand, no effort expended to conceal the misery.

"You don't think it terrifies me?" Daniel had asked, staring at the white-faced figure beside him. "How many years do I have? Can you tell just by looking at me? Tell me."

When Armand woke him up in Port-au-Prince, it was war he wanted to talk about. What did men in this century actually think of war? Did Daniel know that Armand had been a boy when this had begun for him? Seventeen years old, and in those times that was young, very young.

Seventeen-year-old boys in the twentieth century were virtual monsters; they had beards, hair on their chests, and yet they were children. Not then. Yet children worked as if they were men.

But let us not get sidetracked. The point was, Armand didn't know what men felt. He never had. Oh, of course he'd known the pleasures of the flesh, that was par for the course. Nobody then thought children were innocent of sensuous pleasures. But of true aggression he knew little. He killed because it was his nature as a vampire; and the blood was irresistible. But why did men find war irresistible? What was the desire to clash violently against the will of another with weapons? What was the physical need to destroy?

At such times, Daniel did his best to answer: for some men it was the need to affirm one's own existence through the annihilation of another. Surely Armand knew these things.

"Know? Know? What does that matter if you don't understand," Armand had asked, his accent unusually sharp in his agitation, "if you cannot proceed from one perception to another? Don't you see, this is what I cannot do."

When he found Daniel in Frankfurt, it was the nature of history, the impossibility of writing any coherent explanation of events that was not in itself a lie. The impossibility of truth being served by generalities, and the impossibility of learning proceeding without them.

Now and then these meetings had not been entirely selfish. In a country inn in England Daniel woke to the sound of Armand's voice warning him to leave the building at once. A fire destroyed the inn in less than an hour.

Another time he had been in jail in New York, picked up for drunkenness and vagrancy when Armand appeared to bail him out, looking all too human as he always did after he had fed, a young lawyer in a tweed coat and flannel pants, escorting Daniel to a room in the Carlyle, where he left him to sleep it off with a suitcase full of new clothes waiting, and a wallet full of money hidden in a pocket.

Finally, after a year and a half of this madness, Daniel began to question Armand. What had it really been like in those days in Venice? Look at this film, set in the eighteenth century, tell me what is wrong.

But Armand was remarkably unresponsive. "I cannot tell you those things because I have no experience of them. You see, I have so little ability to synthesize knowledge; I deal in the immediate with a cool intensity. What was it like in Paris? Ask me if it rained on the night of Saturday, June 5, 1793. Perhaps I could tell you that."

Yet at other moments, he spoke in rapid bursts of the things around him, of the eerie garish cleanliness of this era, of the horrid acceleration of change.

"Behold, earthshaking inventions which are useless or obsolete within the same century—the steamboat, the railroads; yet do you know what these meant after six thousand years of galley slaves and men on horseback? And now the dance hall girl buys a chemical to kill the seed of her lovers, and lives to be seventy-five in a room full of gadgets which cool the air and veritably eat the dust. And yet for all the costume movies and the paperback history thrown at you in every drugstore, the public has no accurate memory of anything; every social problem is observed in relation to 'norms' which in fact never existed, people fancy themselves 'deprived' of luxuries and peace and quiet which in fact were never common to any people anywhere at all."

"But the Venice of your time, tell me. . . ."

"What? That it was dirty? That it was beautiful? That people went about in rags with rotting teeth and stinking breath and laughed at public executions? You want to know the key difference? There is a horrifying loneliness at work in this time. No, listen to me. We lived six and seven to a room in those days, when I was still among the living. The city streets were seas of humanity; and now in these high buildings dim-witted souls hover in luxurious privacy, gazing through the television window at a faraway world of kissing and touching. It is bound to produce some great fund of common knowledge, some new level of human awareness, a curious skepticism, to be so alone."

Daniel found himself fascinated, sometimes trying to write down the things Armand told him. Yet Armand continued to frighten him. Daniel was ever on the move.

He wasn't quite sure how long it had gone on before he stopped running, though the night itself was quite impossible to forget.

Maybe four years had passed since the game had begun. Daniel had spent a long quiet summer in southern Italy during which he had not seen his demon familiar even once.

In a cheap hotel only a half block from the ruins of ancient Pompeii, he had spent his hours reading, writing, trying to define what his glimpse of the supernatural had done to him, and how he must learn again to want, to envision, to dream. Immortality on this earth was indeed possible. This he knew without question, but what did it matter if immortality was not Daniel's to have?

By day he walked the broken streets of the excavated Roman city. And when the moon was full he wandered there, alone, by night as well. It seemed sanity had come back to him. And life might soon come back too. Green leaves smelled fresh when he crushed them in his fingers. He looked up at the stars and did not feel resentful so much as sad.

Yet at other times, he burned for Armand as if for an elixir without which he could not go on. The dark energy that had fired him for four years was now missing. He dreamed Armand was near him; he awoke weeping stupidly. Then the morning would come and he would be sad but calm.

Then Armand had returned.

It was late, perhaps ten o'clock in the evening, and the sky, as it is so often in southern Italy, was a brilliant dark blue overhead. Daniel had been walking alone down the long road that leads from Pompeii proper to the Villa of the Mysteries, hoping no guards would come to drive him away.

As soon as he'd reached the ancient house, a stillness had descended. No guards here. No one living. Only the sudden silent appearance of Armand before the entrance. Armand again.

He'd come silently out of the shadows into the moonlight, a young boy in dirty jeans and worn denim jacket, and he had slipped his arm around Daniel and gently kissed Daniel's face. Such warm skin, full of the fresh blood of the kill. Daniel fancied he could smell it, the perfume of the living clinging to Armand still.

"You want to come into this house?" Armand had whispered. No locks ever kept Armand from anything. Daniel had been trembling, on the edge of tears. And why was that? So glad to see him, touch him, ah, damn him!

They had entered the dark, low-ceilinged rooms, the press of Armand's arm against Daniel's back oddly comforting. Ah, yes, this intimacy, because that's what it is, isn't it? You, my secret . . .

Secret lover.

Yes.

Then the realization had come to Daniel as they stood together in the ruined dining room with its famous murals of ritual flagellation barely visible in the dark: He isn't going to kill me after all. He isn't going to do it. Of course he won't make me what he is, but he isn't going to kill me. The dance will not end like that.

"But how could you not know such a thing," Armand had said, reading his thoughts. "I love you. If I hadn't grown to love you, I would have killed you before now, of course."

The moonlight poured through the wooden lattices. The lush figures of the murals came to life against their red backdrop, the color of dried blood.

Daniel stared hard at the creature before him, this thing that looked human and sounded human but was not. There was a horrid shift in his consciousness; he saw this being like a great insect, a monstrous evil predator who had devoured a million human lives. And yet he loved this thing. He loved its smooth white skin, its great dark brown eyes. He loved it not because it looked like a gentle, thoughtful young man, but because it was ghastly and awful and loathsome, and beautiful all at the same time. He loved it the way people love evil, because it thrills them to the core of their souls. Imagine, killing like that, just taking life any time you want it, just doing it, sinking your teeth into another and taking all that that person can possibly give.

Look at the garments he wore. Blue cotton shirt, brass-buttoned denim jacket. Where had he gotten them? Off a victim, yes, like taking out his knife and skinning the kill while it was still warm? No wonder they reeked of salt and blood, though none was visible. And the hair trimmed just as if it weren't going to grow out within twenty-four hours to its regular shoulder length. This is evil. This is illusion. *This is what I want to be, which is why I cannot stand to look at him.*

Armand's lips had moved in a soft, slightly concealed smile. And then his eyes had misted and closed. He had bent close to Daniel, pressed his lips to Daniel's neck.

And once again, as he had in a little room on Divisadero Street in San Francisco with the vampire Louis, Daniel felt the sharp teeth pierce the surface of his skin. Sudden pain and throbbing warmth. "Are you killing me finally?" He grew drowsy, on fire, filled with love. "Do it, yes."

But Armand had taken only a few droplets. He'd released Daniel and pressed gently on his shoulders, forcing Daniel down to his knees. Daniel had looked up to see the blood flowing from Armand's wrist. Great electric shocks had passed through Daniel at the taste of that blood. It had seemed in a flash that the city of Pompeii was full of a whispering, a crying, some vague and pulsing imprint of long-ago suffering and death. Thousands perishing in smoke and ash. Thousands dying together. *Together.* Daniel had clung to Armand. But the blood was gone. Only a taste—no more.

"You are mine, beautiful boy," Armand had said.

The following morning when he awoke in bed at the Excelsier in Rome, Daniel knew that he would not run away from Armand ever again. Less than an hour after sunset, Armand came to him. They would go to London now, the car was waiting to take them to the plane. But there was time enough, wasn't there, for another embrace, another small exchange of blood. "Here from my throat," Armand had whispered, cradling Daniel's head in his hand. A fine soundless throbbing. The light of the lamps expanded, brightened, obliterated the room.

Lovers. Yes, it had become an ecstatic and engulfing affair.

"You are my teacher," Armand told him. "You will tell me everything about this century. I am learning secrets already that have eluded me since the beginning. You'll sleep when the sun rises, if you wish, but the nights are mine."

INTO the very midst of life they plunged. At pretense Armand was a genius, and killing early on any given evening, he passed for human everywhere that they went. His skin was burning hot in those early hours, his face full of passionate curiosity, his embraces feverish and quick.

It would have taken another immortal to keep up with him. Daniel nodded off at symphonies and operas or during the hundreds upon hundreds of films that Armand dragged him to see. Then there were the endless parties, the cluttered noisy gatherings from Chelsea to Mayfair where Armand argued politics and philosophy with students, or women of fashion, or anyone who would give him the slightest chance. His eyes grew moist with excitement, his voice lost its soft preternatural resonance and took on the hard human accent of the other young men in the room.

Clothes of all kinds fascinated him, not for their beauty but for what he thought they meant. He wore jeans and sweat shirts like Daniel; he wore cable-knit sweaters and workmen's brogans, leather windbreakers, and mirrored sunglasses pushed up on his head. He wore tailored suits, and dinner jackets, and white tie and tails when the fancy suited him; his hair was cut short one night so he looked like any young man down from Cambridge, and left curly and long, an angel's mane, the next.

It seemed that he and Daniel were always walking up four unlighted flights of stairs to visit some painter, sculptor, or photographer, or to see some special never-released yet revolutionary film. They spent hours in the cold-water flats of dark-eyed young women who played rock music and made herbal tea which Armand never drank.

Men and women fell in love with Armand, of course, "so innocent, so passionate, so brilliant!" You don't say. In fact, Armand's power to seduce was almost beyond his control. And it was Daniel who must bed these unfortunates, if Armand could possibly arrange it, while he watched from a chair nearby, a dark-eyed Cupid with a tender approving smile. Hot, nerve-searing, this witnessed passion, Daniel working the other body with ever greater abandon, aroused by the dual purpose of every intimate gesture. Yet he lay empty afterwards, staring at Armand, resentful, cold.

. . .

In New York they went tearing to museum openings, cafés, bars, adopted a young dancer, paying all his bills through school. They sat on the stoops in SoHo and Greenwich Village whiling the hours away with anybody who would stop to join them. They went to night classes in literature, philosophy, art history, and politics. They studied biology, bought microscopes, collected specimens. They studied books on astronomy and mounted giant telescopes on the roofs of the buildings in which they lived for a few days or a month at most. They went to boxing matches, rock concerts, Broadway shows.

Technological inventions began to obsess Armand, one after the other. First it was kitchen blenders, in which he made frightful concoctions mostly based on the colors of the ingredients; then microwave ovens, in which he cooked roaches and rats. Garbage disposers enchanted him; he fed them paper towels and whole packages of cigarettes. Then it was telephones. He called long distance all over the planet, speaking for hours with "mortals" in Australia or India. Finally television caught him up utterly, so that the flat was full of blaring speakers and flickering screens.

Anything with blue skies enthralled him. Then he must watch news programs, prime time series, documentaries, and finally every film, regardless of merit, ever taped.

At last particular movies struck his fancy. Over and over he watched Ridley Scott's *Blade Runner,* fascinated by Rutger Hauer, the powerfully built actor who, as the leader of the rebel androids, confronts his human maker, kisses him, and then crushes his skull. It would bring a slow and almost impish laugh from Armand, the bones cracking, the look in Hauer's ice-cold blue eye.

"That's your friend, Lestat, there," Armand whispered once to Daniel. "Lestat would have the . . . how do you say? . . . guts? . . . to do that!"

After *Blade Runner* it was the idiotic and hilarious *Time Bandits,* a British comedy in which five dwarfs steal a "Map of Creation" so they can travel through the holes in Time. Into one century after another they tumble, thieving and brawling, along with a little boy companion, until they all wind up in the devil's lair.

Then one scene in particular became Armand's favorite: the dwarfs on a broken-down stage in Castelleone singing "Me and My Shadow" for Napoleon really sent Armand out of his mind. He lost all supernatural composure and became utterly human, laughing till the tears rose in his eyes.

Daniel had to admit there was a horrible charm to it, the "Me and My

Shadow" number, with the dwarfs stumbling, fighting with each other, finally lousing up the whole proceedings, and the dazed eighteenth-century musicians in the pit not knowing what to make of the twentieth-century song. Napoleon was stupefied, then delighted! A stroke of comic genius, the entire scene. But how many times could a mortal watch it? For Armand there seemed no end.

Yet within six months he had dropped the movies for video cameras and must make his own films. All over New York he dragged Daniel, as he interviewed people on the nighttime streets. Armand had reels of himself reciting poetry in Italian or Latin, or merely staring with his arms folded, a gleaming white presence slipping in and out of focus in eternally dim bronze light.

Then somewhere, somehow, in a place unbeknownst to Daniel, Armand made a long tape of himself lying in the coffin during his daytime deathlike sleep. Daniel found this impossible to look at. Armand sat before the slow-moving film for hours, watching his own hair, cut at sunrise, slowly growing against the satin as he lay motionless with closed eyes.

Next it was computers. He was filling disk after disk with his secret writings. He rented additional apartments in Manhattan to house his word processors and video game machines.

Finally he turned to planes.

Daniel had always been a compulsive traveler, he had fled Armand to cities worldwide, and certainly he and Armand had taken planes together. Nothing new in that. But now it was a concentrated exploration; they must spend the entire night in the air. Flying to Boston, then Washington, then to Chicago, then back to New York City, was not unusual. Armand observed everything, passengers, stewardesses; he spoke with the pilots; he lay back in the deep first-class seats listening to the engines roar. Double-decker jets particularly enchanted him. He must try longer, more daring adventures: all the way to Port-au-Prince or San Francisco, or Rome, or Madrid or Lisbon, it didn't matter, as long as Armand was safely landed by dawn.

Armand virtually disappeared at dawn. Daniel was never to know where Armand actually slept. But then Daniel was dead on his feet by daybreak anyway. Daniel didn't see high noon for five years.

Often Armand had been in the room some time before Daniel awakened. The coffee would be perking, the music going—Vivaldi or honky-tonk piano, as Armand loved both equally—and Armand would be pacing, ready for Daniel to get up.

"Come, lover, we're going to the ballet tonight. I want to see Baryshnikov. And after that, down to the Village. You remember that jazz band

I loved last summer, well, they've come back. Come on, I'm hungry, my beloved. We must go."

And if Daniel was sluggish, Armand would push him into the shower, soap him all over, rinse him off, drag him out, dry him thoroughly, then shave his face as lovingly as an old-fashioned barber, and finally dress him after carefully selecting from Daniel's wardrobe of dirty and neglected clothes.

Daniel loved the feel of the hard gleaming white hands moving over his naked flesh, rather like satin gloves. And the brown eyes that seemed to draw Daniel out of himself; ah, the delicious disorientation, the certainty that he was being carried downwards, out of all things physical, and finally the hands closing on his throat gently, and the teeth breaking through the skin.

He closed his eyes, his body heating slowly, only to burn truly when Armand's blood touched his lips. He heard the distant sighs again, the crying, was it of lost souls? It seemed a great luminous continuity was there, as if all his dreams were suddenly connected and vitally important, yet it was all slipping away. . . .

Once he'd reached out, held Armand with all his strength, and tried to gash the skin of his throat. Armand had been so patient, making the tear for him, and letting him close his mouth on it for the longest time—yes, this—then guiding him gently away.

Daniel was past all decision. Daniel lived only in two alternating states: misery and ecstasy, united by love. He never knew when he'd be given the blood. He never knew if things looked different because of it—the carnations staring at him from their vases, skyscrapers hideously visible like plants sprung up from steel seeds overnight—or because he was just going out of his mind.

Then had come the night when Armand said he was ready to enter this century in earnest, he understood enough about it now. He wanted "incalculable" wealth. He wanted a vast dwelling full of all those things he'd come to value. And yachts, planes, cars—millions of dollars. He wanted to buy Daniel everything that Daniel might ever desire.

"What do you mean, millions!" Daniel had scoffed. "You throw your clothes away after you wear them, you rent apartments and forget where they are. Do you know what a zip code is, or a tax bracket? I'm the one who buys all the goddamned airline tickets. Millions. How are we going to get millions! Steal another Maserati and be done with it, for God's sakes!"

"Daniel, you are a gift to me from Louis," Armand had said tenderly. "What would I do without you? You misunderstand everything." His eyes were large, childlike. "I want to be in the vital center of things the way I was years ago in Paris in the Theater of the Vampires. Surely you remember. I want to be a canker in the very eye of the world."

Daniel had been dazzled by the speed with which things happened.

It had begun with a treasure find in the waters off Jamaica, Armand chartering a boat to show Daniel where salvage operations must begin. Within days a sunken Spanish galleon loaded with bullion and jewels had been discovered. Next it was an archaeological find of priceless Olmec figurines. Two more sunken ships were pinpointed in rapid succession. A cheap piece of South American property yielded a long forgotten emerald mine.

They purchased a mansion in Florida, yachts, speedboats, a small but exquisitely appointed jet plane.

And now they must be outfitted like princes for all occasions. Armand himself supervised the measurements for Daniel's custom-made shirts, suits, shoes. He chose the fabrics for an endless parade of sports coats, pants, robes, silk foulards. Of course Daniel must have for colder climes mink-lined raincoats, and dinner jackets for Monte Carlo, and jeweled cuff links, and even a long black suede cloak, which Daniel with his "twentieth-century height" could carry off quite well.

At sunset when Daniel awoke, his clothes had already been laid out for him. Heaven help him if he were to change a single item, from the linen handkerchief to the black silk socks. Supper awaited in the immense dining room with its windows open to the pool. Armand was already at his desk in the adjoining study. There was work to do: maps to consult, more wealth to be acquired.

"But how do you do it!" Daniel had demanded, as he watched Armand making notes, writing directions for new acquisitions.

"If you can read the minds of men, you can have anything that you want," Armand had said patiently. Ah, that soft reasonable voice, that open and almost trusting boyish face, the auburn hair always slipping into the eye a bit carelessly, the body so suggestive of human serenity, of physical ease.

"Give *me* what I want," Daniel had demanded.

"I'm giving you everything you could ever ask for."

"Yes, but not what I *have* asked for, not what I want!"

"Be alive, Daniel." A low whisper, like a kiss. "Let me tell you from my heart that life is better than death."

"I don't want to be alive, Armand, I want to live forever, and then *I* will tell *you* whether life is better than death."

The fact was, the riches were maddening him, making him feel his mortality more keenly than ever before. Sailing the warm Gulf Stream with Armand under a clear night sky, sprinkled with countless stars, he was desperate to possess all of this forever. With hatred and love he watched Armand effortlessly steering the vessel. Would Armand really let him die?

The game of acquisition continued.

Picassos, Degas, Van Goghs, these were but a few of the stolen paintings Armand recovered without explanation and handed over to Daniel for resales or rewards. Of course the recent owners would not dare to come forward, if in fact they had survived Armand's silent nocturnal visit to the sanctums where these stolen treasures had been displayed. Sometimes no clear title to the work in question existed. At auction, they brought millions. But even this was not enough.

Pearls, rubies, emeralds, diamond tiaras, these he brought to Daniel. "Never mind, they were stolen, no one will claim them." And from the savage narcotics traders off the Miami coast, Armand stole anything and everything, guns, suitcases full of money, even their boats.

Daniel stared at the piles and piles of green bills, as the secretaries counted them and wrapped them for coded accounts in European banks.

Often Daniel watched Armand go out alone to hunt the warm southern waters, a youth in soft black silk shirt and black pants, manning a sleek unlighted speedboat, the wind whipping his uncut long hair. Such a deadly foe. Somewhere far out there, beyond sight of land, he finds his smugglers and he strikes—the lone pirate, death. Are the victims dropped into the deep, hair billowing perhaps for one moment while the moon can still illuminate them as they look up for a last glimpse at what has been their ruin? This boy! They thought they were the evil ones. . . .

"Would you let me go with you? Would you let me see it when you do it?"

"No."

Finally enough capital had been amassed; Armand was ready for real action.

He ordered Daniel to make purchases without counsel or hesitation: a fleet of cruise ships, a chain of restaurants and hotels. Four private planes were now at their disposal. Armand had eight phones.

And then came the final dream: the Night Island, Armand's own personal creation with its five dazzling glass stories of theaters, restaurants, and shops. He drew the pictures for the architects he'd chosen. He gave them endless lists of the materials he wanted, the fabrics, the sculptures for the fountains, even the flowers, the potted trees.

Behold, the Night Island. From sunset till dawn, the tourists mobbed it, as boat after boat brought them out from the Miami docks. The music played eternally in the lounges, on the dance floors. The glass elevators never stopped their climb to heaven; ponds, streams, waterfalls glittered amid banks of moist, fragile blooms.

You could buy anything on the Night Island—diamonds, a Coca-Cola, books, pianos, parrots, designer fashions, porcelain dolls. All the fine cuisines of the world awaited you. Five films played nightly in the cinemas. Here was English tweed and Spanish leather, Indian silk, Chinese carpets, sterling silver, ice-cream cones or cotton candy, bone china, and Italian shoes.

Or you could live adjacent to it, in secret luxury, slipping in and out of the whirl at will.

"All this is yours, Daniel," Armand said, moving slowly through the spacious airy rooms of their very own Villa of the Mysteries, which covered three stories—and cellars verboten to Daniel—windows open to the distant burning nightscape of Miami, to the dim high clouds rolling above.

Gorgeous the skilled mixture of old and new. Elevator doors rolling back on broad rectangular rooms full of medieval tapestries and antique chandeliers; giant television sets in every room. Renaissance paintings filled Daniel's suite, where Persian rugs covered the parquet. The finest of the Venetian school surrounded Armand in his white carpeted study full of shining computers, intercoms, and monitors. The books, magazines, newspapers came from all over the world.

"This is your home, Daniel."

And so it had been and Daniel had loved it, he had to admit that, and what he had loved even more was the freedom, the power, and the luxury that attended him everywhere that he went.

He and Armand had gone into the depths of the Central American jungles by night to see the Mayan ruins; they had gone up the flank of Annapurna to glimpse the distant summit under the light of the moon. Through the crowded streets of Tokyo they had wandered together, through Bangkok and Cairo and Damascus, through Lima and Rio and Kathmandu. By day Daniel wallowed in comfort at the best of the local hostelries; by night he wandered fearless with Armand at his side.

Now and then, however, the illusion of civilized life would break down. Sometimes in some far-flung place, Armand sensed the presence of other immortals. He explained that he had thrown his shield around Daniel, yet it worried him. Daniel must stay at his side.

"Make me what you are and worry no more."

"You don't know what you're saying," Armand had answered. "Now you're one of a billion faceless humans. If you were one of us, you'd be a candle burning in the dark."

Daniel wouldn't accept it.

"They would spot you without fail," Armand continued. He had become angry, though not at Daniel. The fact was he disliked any talk at all of the undead. "Don't you know the old ones destroy the young ones out of hand?" he'd asked. "Didn't your beloved Louis explain that to you? It's what I do everywhere that we settle—I clean them out, the young ones, the vermin. But I am not invincible." He'd paused as though debating whether or not he should continue. Then: "I'm like any beast on the prowl. I have enemies who are older and stronger who would try to destroy me if it interested them to do so, I am sure."

"Older than you are? But I thought you were the oldest," Daniel had said. It had been years since they'd spoken of *Interview with the Vampire.* They had, in fact, never discussed its contents in detail.

"No, of course I'm not the oldest," Armand had answered. He seemed slightly uneasy. "Merely the oldest your friend Louis was ever to find. There are others. I don't know their names, I've seldom seen their faces. But at times, I feel them. You might say that we feel each other. We send our silent yet powerful signals. 'Keep away from me.' "

The following night, he'd given Daniel the locket, the amulet as he called it, to wear. He'd kissed it first and rubbed it in his hands as if to warm it. Strange to witness this ritual. Stranger still to see the thing itself with the letter A carved on it, and inside the tiny vial of Armand's blood.

"Here, snap the clasp if they come near you. Break the vial instantly. And they will feel the power that protects you. They will not dare—"

"Ah, you'll let them kill me. You know you will," Daniel had said coldly. Shut out. "Give me the power to fight for myself."

But he had worn the locket ever since. Under the lamp, he'd examined the A and the intricate carvings all over the thing to find they were tiny twisted human figures, some mutilated, others writhing as if in agony, some dead. Horrid thing actually. He had dropped the chain down into his shirt, and it was cold against his naked chest, but out of sight.

Yet Daniel was never to see or sense the presence of another supernatural being. He remembered Louis as if he'd been a hallucination, something known in a fever. Armand was Daniel's single oracle, his merciless and all-loving demonic god.

More and more his bitterness increased. Life with Armand inflamed him, maddened him. It had been years since Daniel had even thought of his family, of the friends he used to know. Checks went out to kin, of that he'd made certain, but they were just names now on a list.

"You'll never die, and yet you look at me and you watch me die, night after night, you watch it."

Ugly fights, terrible fights, finally, Armand broken down, glassy-eyed with silent rage, then crying softly but uncontrollably as if some lost emotion had been rediscovered which threatened to tear him apart. "I will not do it, I cannot do it. Ask me to kill you, it would be easier than that. You don't know what you ask for, don't you see? It is always a damnable error! Don't you realize that any one of us would give it up for one human lifetime?"

"Give up immortality, just to live one life? I don't believe you. This is the first time you have told me an out-and-out lie."

"How dare you!"

"Don't hit me. You might kill me. You're very strong."

"I'd give it up. If I weren't a coward when it gets right down to it, if I weren't after five hundred greedy years in this whirlwind still terrified to the marrow of my bones of death."

"No, you wouldn't. Fear has nothing to do with it. Imagine one lifetime back then when you were born. And all this lost? The future in which you know power and luxury of which Genghis Khan never dreamed? But forget the technical miracles. Would you settle for ignorance of the world's destiny? Ah, don't tell me you would."

No resolution in words was ever reached. It would end with the embrace, the kiss, the blood stinging him, the shroud of dreams closing over him like a great net, hunger! I love you! Give me more! Yes, more. But never enough.

It was useless.

What had these transfusions done to his body and soul? Made him see the descent of the falling leaf in greater detail? Armand was not going to give it to him!

Armand would see Daniel leave time and again, and drift off into the terrors of the everyday world, risk that, rather than do it. There was nothing Daniel could do, nothing he could give.

And the wandering started, the escaping, and Armand did not follow him. Armand would wait each time until Daniel begged to come back. Or until Daniel was beyond calling, until Daniel was on the verge of death itself. And then and only then, Armand would bring him back.

THE rain hit the wide pavements of Michigan Avenue. The bookstore was empty, the lights had gone out. Somewhere a clock had struck the hour of nine. He stood against the glass watching the traffic stream past in front of him. Nowhere to go. Drink the tiny drop of blood inside the locket. Why not?

And Lestat in California, on the prowl already, perhaps stalking a victim even now. And they were preparing the hall for the concert, weren't they? Mortal men rigging up lights, microphones, concession stands, oblivious to the secret codes being given, the sinister audience that would conceal itself in the great indifferent and inevitably hysterical human throng. Ah, maybe Daniel had made a horrible miscalculation. Maybe Armand was there!

At first it seemed an impossibility, then a certainty. Why hadn't Daniel realized this before?

Surely Armand had gone! If there was any truth at all in what Lestat had written, Armand would go for a reckoning, to witness, to search perhaps for those he'd lost over the centuries now drawn to Lestat by the same call.

And what would a mortal lover matter then, a human who'd been no more than a toy for a decade? No. Armand had gone on without him. And this time there would be no rescue.

He felt cold, small, as he stood there. He felt miserably alone. It didn't matter, his premonitions, how the dream of the twins descended upon him and then left him with foreboding. These were things that were passing him by like great black wings. You could feel the indifferent wind as they swept over. Armand had proceeded without him towards a destiny that Daniel would never fully understand.

It filled him with horror, with sadness. Gates locked. The anxiety aroused by the dream mingled with a dull sickening fear. He had come to the end of the line. What would he do? Wearily, he envisioned the Night Island locked against him. He saw the villa behind its white walls, high above the beach, impossible to reach. He imagined his past gone, along with his future. Death was the understanding of the immediate present: that there is finally nothing else.

He walked on a few steps; his hands were numb. The rain had drenched his sweat shirt. He wanted to lie down on the very pavement and let the twins come again. And Lestat's phrases ran through his head. The Dark Trick he called the moment of rebirth. The Savage Garden he called the world that could embrace such exquisite monsters, ah, yes.

But let me be a lover in the Savage Garden with you, and the light that went out of life would come back in a great burst of glory. Out of mortal flesh I would pass into eternity. I would be one of you.

Dizzy. Did he almost fall? Someone talking to him, someone asking if he was all right. No, of course not. Why should I be?

But there was a hand on his shoulder.

Daniel.

He looked up.

Armand stood at the curb.

At first he could not believe it, he wanted it so badly, but there was no denying what he saw. Armand stood there. He was peering silently from the unearthly stillness he seemed to carry with him, his face flushed beneath the faintest touch of unnatural pallor. How normal he looked, if beauty is ever normal. And yet how strangely set apart from the material things touching him, the rumpled white coat and pants he wore. Behind him the big gray hulk of a Rolls waited, like an ancillary vision, droplets teeming on its silver roof.

Come on, Daniel. You made it hard for me this time, didn't you, so hard.

Why the urgency of the command when the hand that pulled him forward was so strong? Such a rare thing to see Armand truly angry. Ah, how Daniel loved this anger! His knees went out from under him. He felt himself lifted. And then the soft velvet of the back seat of the car spread out under him. He fell over on his hands. He closed his eyes.

But Armand gently pulled him upright, held him. The car rocked gently, deliciously as it moved forward. So nice to sleep at last in Armand's arms. But there was so much he must tell Armand, so much about the dream, the book.

"Don't you think I know?" Armand whispered. A strange light in the eye, what was it? Something raw and tender in the way Armand looked, all the composure stripped away. He lifted a tumbler half full of brandy and put it in Daniel's hand.

"And you running from me," he said, "from Stockholm and Edinburgh and Paris. What do you think I am that I can follow you at such speed down so many pathways? And such danger—"

Lips against Daniel's face, suddenly, ah, that's better, I like kissing. And snuggling with dead things, yes, hold me. He buried his face in Armand's neck. *Your blood.*

"Not yet, my beloved." Armand pushed him forward, pressing his fingers to Daniel's lips. Such uncommon feeling in the low, controlled voice. "Listen to what I'm saying to you. All over the world, our kind are being destroyed."

Destroyed. It sent a current of panic through him, so that his body tensed in spite of his exhaustion. He tried to focus on Armand, but he saw the red-haired twins again, the soldiers, the blackened body of the mother being overturned in the ashes. But the meaning, the continuity . . . Why?

"I cannot tell you," Armand said. And he meant the dream when he spoke, because he'd had the dream too. He lifted the brandy to Daniel's lips.

Oh, so warm, yes. He would slip into unconsciousness if he didn't hold tight. They were racing silently along the freeway now, out of Chicago, the rain flooding the windows, locked together in this warm, velvet-lined little place. Ah, such lovely silver rain. And Armand had turned away, distracted, as if listening to some faraway music, his lips parted, frozen on the verge of speech.

I'm with you, safe with you.

"No, Daniel, not safe," he answered. "Maybe not even for a night or so much as an hour."

Daniel tried to think, to form a question, but he was too weak, too drowsy. The car was so comfortable, the motion of it so soothing. And the twins. The beautiful red-haired twins wanted in now! His eyes closed for a split second and he sank against Armand's shoulder, feeling Armand's hand on his back.

Far away he heard Armand's voice: "What do I do with you, my beloved? Especially now, when I myself am so afraid."

Darkness again. He held fast to the taste of the brandy in his mouth, to the touch of Armand's hand, but he was already dreaming.

The twins were walking in the desert; the sun was high above. It burned their white arms, their faces. Their lips were swollen and cracked from thirst. Their dresses were stained with blood.

"Make the rain fall," Daniel whispered aloud, "you can do it, make the rain fall." One of the twins fell down on her knees, and her sister knelt and put her arms around her. Red hair and red hair.

Somewhere far off he heard Armand's voice again. Armand said that they were too deep in the desert. Not even their spirits could make rain in such a place.

But why? Couldn't spirits do anything?

He felt Armand kiss him gently again.

The twins have now entered a low mountain pass. But there is no shade because the sun is directly above them, and the rocky slopes are too treacherous for them to climb. On they walk. Can't someone help them? They stumble and fall every few steps now. The rocks look too hot to touch. Finally one of them falls face down in the sand, and the other lies over her, sheltering her with her hair.

Oh, if only evening would come, with its cold winds.

Suddenly the twin who is protecting her sister looks up. Movement on the cliffs. Then stillness again. A rock falls, echoes with a soft clear shuffling sound. And then Daniel sees the men moving over the precipices, desert people as they have looked for thousands of years with their dark skin and heavy white robes.

The twins rise on their knees together as these men approach. The men offer them water. They pour the cool water over the twins. Suddenly the twins are laughing and talking hysterically, so great is their relief, but the men don't understand. Then it is gestures, so purely eloquent, as one twin points to the belly of her sister, and then folding her arms makes the universal sign for rocking a child. Ah, yes. The men lift the pregnant woman. And all move together towards the oasis, round which their tents stand.

At last by the light of a fire outside the tent, the twins sleep, safe, among the desert people, the Bedouins. Could it be that the Bedouins are so very ancient, that their history goes back thousands and thousands of years? At dawn, one of the twins rises, the one who does not carry a child. As her sister watches, she walks out towards the olive trees of the oasis. She lifts her arms, and at first it seems she is only welcoming the sun. Others have awakened; they gather to see. Then a wind rises, gently, moving the branches of the olive trees. And the rain, the light sweet rain begins to fall.

He opened his eyes. He was on the plane.

HE RECOGNIZED the small bedroom immediately by the white plastic walls and the soothing quality of the dim yellow light. Everything synthetic, hard and gleaming like the great rib bones of prehistoric creatures. Have things come full circle? Technology has recreated Jonah's chamber deep within the belly of the whale.

He was lying on the bed that had no head or foot or legs or frame to it. Someone had washed his hands and his face. He was clean-shaven. Ah, that felt so good. And the roar of the engines was a huge silence, the whale breathing, slicing through the sea. That made it possible for him to see things around him very distinctly. A decanter. Bourbon. He wanted it. But he was too exhausted to move. And something not right, something. . . . He reached up, felt his neck. The amulet was gone! But it didn't matter. He was with Armand.

Armand sat at the little table near the whale's eye window, the white plastic lid pulled all the way down. He had cut his hair. And he wore black wool now, neat and fine, like the corpse again dressed for the funeral even to the shining black shoes. Grim all this. Someone will now read the Twenty-third Psalm. Bring back the white clothes.

"You're dying," Armand said softly.

" 'And though I walk through the valley of the shadow of death,' et cetera," Daniel whispered. His throat was so dry. And his head ached. Didn't matter saying what was really on his mind. All been said long ago.

Armand spoke again silently, a laser beam touching Daniel's brain: *Shall we bother with the particulars? You weigh no more than a hundred and thirty pounds now. And the alcohol is eating at your insides. You are half mad. There is almost nothing left in the world that you enjoy.*

"Except talking to you now and then. It's so easy to hear everything you say."

If you were never to see me again, that would only make things worse. If you go on as you are, you won't live another five days.

Unbearable thought, actually. But if that's so, then why have I been running away?

No response.

How clear everything seemed. It wasn't only the roar of the engines, it was the curious movement of the plane, that never-ending irregular undulation as if it rode the air in bumps and dips and over curbs and now and then uphill. The whale speeding along on the whale path, as Beowulf called it.

Armand's hair was brushed to one side, neatly. Gold watch on his wrist, one of those high-tech numbers he so adored. Think of that thing flashing its digits inside a coffin during the day. And the black jacket, old-fashioned rather with narrow lapels. The vest was black silk, it looked like that anyway. But his face, ah, he had fed all right. Fed plenty.

Do you remember anything I said to you earlier?

"Yes," Daniel said. But the truth is he had trouble remembering. Then it came back suddenly, oppressively. "Something about destruction everywhere. But I'm dying. They're dying, I'm dying. They got to be immortal before it happened; I am merely alive. See? I remember. I would like to have the bourbon now."

There is nothing I can do to make you want to live, isn't that so?

"Not that again. I will jump out of the plane if you go on."

Will you listen to me, then? Really listen?

"How can I help it? I can't get away from your voice when you want me to listen; it's like a tiny microphone inside my head. What is this, tears? You're going to weep over me?"

For one second, he looked so young. What a travesty.

"Damn you, Daniel," he said, so that Daniel heard the words aloud.

A chill passed over Daniel. Horrid to see him suffering. Daniel said nothing.

"What we are," Armand said, "it wasn't meant to be, you know that. You didn't have to read Lestat's book to find it out. Any one of us could have told you it was an abomination, a demonic fusion—"

"Then what Lestat wrote was true." A demon going into the ancient

Egyptian Mother and the Father. Well, a spirit anyway. They had called it a demon back then.

"Doesn't matter whether or not it's true. The beginning is no longer important. What matters is that the end may be at hand."

Deep tightening of panic, the atmosphere of the dream returning, the shrill sound of the twins' screams.

"Listen to me," Armand said patiently, calling him back away from the two women. "Lestat has awakened something or someone—"

"Akasha . . . Enkil."

"Perhaps. It may be more than one or two. No one knows for certain. There is a vague repeated cry of danger, but no one seems to know whence it comes. They only know that we are being sought out and annihilated, that coven houses, meeting places, go up in flames."

"I've heard the cry of danger," Daniel whispered. "Sometimes very strong in the middle of the night, and then at other moments like an echo." Again he saw the twins. It had to be connected to the twins. "But how do you know these things, about the coven houses, about—"

"Daniel, don't try me. There isn't much time left. I know. The others know. It's like a current, running through the wires of a great web."

"Yes." Whenever Daniel had tasted the vampiric blood, he had glimpsed for one instant that great glittering mesh of knowledge, connections, half-understood visions. And it was true then. The web had begun with the Mother and the Father—

"Years ago," Armand interrupted, "it wouldn't have mattered to me, all this."

"What do you mean?"

"But I don't want it to end now. I don't want to continue unless you—" His face changed slightly. Faint look of surprise. "I don't want you to die."

Daniel said nothing.

Eerie the stillness of this moment. Even with the plane riding the air currents gently. Armand sitting there, so self-contained, so patient, with the words belying the smooth calm of the voice.

"I'm not afraid, because you're here," Daniel said suddenly.

"You're a fool then. But I will tell you another mysterious part of it."

"Yes?"

"Lestat is still in existence. He goes on with his schemes. And those who've gathered near him are unharmed."

"But how do you know for certain?"

Short little velvet laugh. "There you go again. So irrepressibly human. You overestimate me or underestimate me. Seldom do you ever hit the mark."

"I work with limited equipment. The cells in my body are subject to deterioration, to a process called aging and—"

"They're gathered in San Francisco. They crowd the back rooms of a tavern called Dracula's Daughter. Perhaps I know because others know it and one powerful mind picks up images from another and unwittingly or deliberately passes those images along. Perhaps one witness telegraphs the image to many. I can't tell. Thoughts, feelings, voices, they're just there. Traveling the web, the threads. Some are clear, others clouded. Now and then the warning overrides everything. *Danger.* It is as if our world falls silent for one instant. Then other voices rise again."

"And Lestat. Where is Lestat?"

"He's been seen but only in glimpses. They can't track him to his lair. He's too clever to let that happen. But he teases them. He races his black Porsche through the streets of San Francisco. He may not know all that's happened."

"Explain."

"The power to communicate varies. To listen to the thoughts of others is often to be heard oneself. Lestat is concealing his presence. His mind may be completely cut off."

"And the twins? The two women in the dream, who are they?"

"I don't know. Not all have had these dreams. But many know of them, and all seem to fear them, to share the conviction that somehow Lestat is to blame. For all that's happened, Lestat is to blame."

"A real devil among devils." Daniel laughed softly.

With a subtle nod, Armand acknowledged the little jest wearily. He even smiled.

Stillness. Roar of the engines.

"Do you understand what I'm telling you? There have been attacks upon our kind everywhere but there."

"Where Lestat is."

"Precisely. But the destroyer moves erratically. It seems it must be near to the thing it would destroy. It may be waiting for the concert in order to finish what it has begun."

"It can't hurt you. It would have already—"

The short, derisive laugh again, barely audible. A telepathic laugh?

"Your faith touches me as always, but don't be my acolyte just now. The thing is not omnipotent. It can't move with infinite speed. You have to understand the choice I've made. We're going to him because there isn't any other safe place to go. It has found rogues in far-flung places and burnt them to ashes—"

"And because you want to be with Lestat."

No answer.

"You know you do. You want to see him. You want to be there if he needs you. If there's going to be a battle . . ."

No answer.

"And if Lestat caused it, maybe he can stop it."

Still Armand didn't answer. He appeared confused.

"It is simpler than that," he said finally. "I *have* to go."

The plane seemed a thing suspended on a spume of sound. Daniel looked drowsily at the ceiling, at the light moving.

To see Lestat at last. He thought of Lestat's old house in New Orleans. Of the gold watch he'd recovered from the dusty floor. And now it was back to San Francisco, back to the beginning, back to Lestat. God, he wanted the bourbon. Why wouldn't Armand give it to him? He was so weak. They'd go to the concert, he'd see Lestat—

But then the sense of dread came again, deepening, the dread which the dreams inspired. "Don't let me dream any more of them," he whispered suddenly.

He thought he heard Armand say yes.

Suddenly Armand stood beside the bed. His shadow fell over Daniel. The whale's belly seemed smaller, no more than the light surrounding Armand.

"Look at me, beloved," he said.

Darkness. And then the high iron gates opening, and the moon flooding down on the garden. *What is this place?*

Oh, Italy, it had to be, with this gentle embracing warm air and a full moon shining down on the great sweep of trees and flowers, and beyond, the Villa of the Mysteries at the very edge of ancient Pompeii.

"But how did we get here!" He turned to Armand, who stood beside him dressed in strange, old-fashioned velvet clothes. For one moment he could do nothing but stare at Armand, at the black velvet tunic he wore and the leggings, and his long curling auburn hair.

"We aren't really here," Armand said. "You know we aren't." He turned and walked into the garden towards the villa, his heels making the faintest sound on the worn gray stones.

But it was real! Look at the crumbling old brick walls, and the flowers in their long deep beds, and the path itself with Armand's damp footprints! And the stars overhead, the stars! He turned around and reached up into the lemon tree and broke off a single fragrant leaf.

Armand turned, reached back to take his arm. The smell of freshly turned earth rose from the flower beds. *Ah, I could die here.*

"Yes," said Armand, "you could. And you will. And you know, I've never done it before. I told you but you never believed me. Now Lestat's told you in his book. I've never done it. Do you believe him?"

"Of course I believed you. The vow you made, you explained everything. But Armand, this is my question, to whom did you make this vow?"

Laughter.

Their voices carried over the garden. Such roses and chrysanthemums, how enormous they were. And light poured from the doorways of the Villa of the Mysteries. Was there music playing? Why, the whole ruined place was brilliantly illuminated under the incandescent blue of the night sky.

"So you would have me break my vow. You would have what you think you want. But look well at this garden, because once I do it, you'll never read my thoughts or see my visions again. A veil of silence will come down."

"But we'll be brothers, don't you see?" Daniel asked.

Armand stood so close to him they were almost kissing. The flowers were crushed against them, huge drowsing yellow dahlias and white gladioli, such lovely drenching perfume. They had stopped beneath a dying tree in which the wisteria grew wild. Its delicate blossoms shivered in clusters, its great twining arms white as bone. And beyond voices poured out of the Villa. Were there people singing?

"But where are we really?" Daniel asked. "Tell me!"

"I told you. It's just a dream. But if you want a name, let me call it the gateway of life and death. I'll bring you with me through this gateway. And why? Because I am a coward. And I love you too much to let you go."

Such joy Daniel felt, such cold and lovely triumph. And so the moment was his, and he was lost no more in the awesome free fall of time. No more one of the teeming millions who would sleep in this dank odoriferous earth, beneath the broken withered flowers, without name or knowledge, all vision lost.

"I promise you nothing. How can I? I've told you what lies ahead."

"I don't care. I'll go towards it with you."

Armand's eyes were reddened, weary, old. Such delicate clothes these were, hand sewn, dusty, like the clothes of a ghost. Were they what the mind conjured effortlessly when it wanted to be purely itself?

"Don't cry! It's not fair," Daniel said. "This is my rebirth. How can you cry? Don't you know what this means? Is it possible you never knew?" He looked up suddenly, to catch the whole sweep of this enchanted landscape, the distant Villa, the rolling land above and below. And then he turned his face upwards, and the heavens astonished him. Never had he seen so many stars.

Why, it seemed as if the sky itself went up and up forever with stars so plentiful and bright that the constellations were utterly lost. No pattern. No meaning. Only the gorgeous victory of sheer energy and matter. But then he saw the Pleiades—the constellation beloved of the doomed red-haired twins in the dream—and he smiled. He saw the twins together on a mountaintop, and they were happy. It made him so glad.

"Say the word, my love," Armand said. "I'll do it. We'll be in hell together after all."

"But don't you see," Daniel said, "all human decisions are made like this. Do you think the mother knows what will happen to the child in her womb? Dear God, we are lost, I tell you. What does it matter if you give it to me and it's wrong! There is no wrong! There is only desperation, and I would *have it!* I want to live forever with you."

He opened his eyes. The ceiling of the cabin of the plane, the soft yellow lights reflected in the warm wood-paneled walls, and then around him the garden, the perfume, the sight of the flowers almost breaking loose from their stems.

They stood beneath the dead tree twined full of airy purple wisteria blossoms. And the blossoms stroked his face, the clusters of waxy petals. Something came back to him, something he had known long ago—that in the language of an ancient people the word for flowers was the same as the word for blood. He felt the sudden sharp stab of the teeth in his neck.

His heart was caught suddenly, wrenched in a powerful grip! The pressure was more than he could bear. Yet he could see over Armand's shoulder and the night was sliding down around him, the stars growing as large as these moist and fragrant blooms. Why, they were rising into the sky!

For a split second he saw the Vampire Lestat, driving, plunging through the night in his long sleek black car. How like a lion Lestat looked with his mane of hair blown back by the wind, his eyes filled with mad humor and high spirits. And then he turned and looked at Daniel, and from his throat came a deep soft laugh.

Louis was there too. Louis was standing in a room on Divisadero Street looking out of the window, waiting, and then he said, "Yes, come, Daniel, if that is what must happen."

But they didn't know about the burnt-out coven houses! They didn't know about the twins! About the cry of danger!

They were all in a crowded room, actually, inside the Villa, and Louis was leaning against the mantel in a frock coat. Everyone was there! Even the twins were there! "Thank God, you've come," Daniel said. He kissed Louis on one cheek and then the other decorously. "Why, my skin is as pale as yours!"

He cried out suddenly as his heart was let go, and the air filled his lungs. The garden again. The grass was all around him. The garden grew up over his head. *Don't leave me here, not here against the earth.*

"Drink, Daniel." The priest said the Latin words as he poured the Holy Communion wine into his mouth. The red-haired twins took the sacred plates—the heart, the brain. "This the brain and the heart of my mother I devour with all respect for the spirit of my mother—"

"God, give it to me!" He'd knocked the chalice to the marble floor of the church, so clumsy, but God! The blood!

He sat up, crushing Armand to him, drawing it out of him, draught after draught. They had fallen over together in the soft bank of flowers. Armand lay beside him, and his mouth was open on Armand's throat, and the blood was an unstoppable fount.

"Come into the Villa of the Mysteries," said Louis to him. Louis was touching his shoulder. "We're waiting." The twins were embracing each other, stroking each other's long curling red hair.

The kids were screaming outside the auditorium because there were no more tickets. They would camp in the parking lot until tomorrow night.

"Do we have tickets?" he asked. "Armand, the tickets!"

Danger. Ice. It's coming from the one trapped beneath the ice!

Something hit him, hard. He was floating.

"Sleep, beloved."

"I want to go back to the garden, the Villa." He tried to open his eyes. His belly was hurting. Strangest pain, it seemed so far away.

"You know he's buried under the ice?"

"Sleep," Armand said, covering him with the blanket. "And when you wake, you'll be just like me. Dead."

San Francisco. He knew he was there before he even opened his eyes. And such a ghastly dream, he was glad to leave it—suffocating, blackness, and riding the rough and terrifying current of the sea! But the dream was fading. A dream without sight, and only the sound of the water, the feel of the water! A dream of unspeakable fear. He'd been a woman in it, helpless, without a tongue to scream.

Let it go away.

Something about the wintry air on his face, a white freshness that he could almost taste. San Francisco, of course. The cold moved over him like a tight garment, yet inside he was deliciously warm.

Immortal. Forever.

He opened his eyes. Armand had put him here. Through the viscid darkness of the dream, he'd heard Armand telling him to remain. Armand had told him that here he would be safe.

Here.

The French doors stood open all along the far wall. And the room itself, opulent, cluttered, one of those splendid places that Armand so often found, so dearly loved.

Look at the sheer lace panel blown back from the French doors. Look at the white feathers curling and glowing in the Aubusson carpet. He climbed to his feet and went out through the open doors.

A great mesh of branches rose between him and the wet shining sky. Stiff foliage of the Monterey cypress. And down there, through the branches, against a velvet blackness, he saw the great burning arc of the Golden Gate Bridge. The fog poured like thick white smoke past the immense towers. In fits and gusts it tried to swallow the pylons, the cables, then vanished as if the bridge itself with its glittering stream of traffic burnt it away.

Too magnificent, this spectacle—and the deep dark outline of the distant hills beneath their mantle of warm lights. Ah, but to take one tiny detail—the damp rooftops spilling downhill away from him, or the gnarled branches rising in front of him. Like elephant hide, this bark, this living skin.

Immortal . . . forever.

He ran his hands back through his hair and a gentle tingling passed through him. He could feel the soft imprint of his fingers on his scalp after he had taken his hands away. The wind stung him exquisitely. He remembered something. He reached up to find his fang teeth. Yes, they were beautifully long and sharp.

Someone touched him. He turned so quickly he almost lost his balance. Why, this was all so inconceivably different! He steadied himself, but the sight of Armand made him want to cry. Even in deep shadow, Armand's dark brown eyes were filled with a vibrant light. And the expression on his face, so loving. He reached out very carefully and touched Armand's eyelashes. He wanted to touch the tiny fine lines in Armand's lips. Armand kissed him. He began to tremble. The way it felt, the cool silky mouth, like a kiss of the brain, the electric purity of a thought!

"Come inside, my pupil," Armand said. "We have less than an hour left."

"But the others—"

Armand had gone to discover something very important. What was it? Terrible things happening, coven houses burned. Yet nothing at the moment seemed more important than the warmth inside him, and the tingling as he moved his limbs.

"They're thriving, plotting," Armand said. Was he speaking out loud? He must have been. But the voice was so clear! "They're frightened of the wholesale destruction, but San Francisco isn't touched. Some say Lestat has done it to drive everyone to him. Others that it's the work of Marius, or even the twins. Or Those Who Must Be Kept, who strike with infinite power from their shrine."

The twins! He felt the darkness of the dream again around him, a woman's body, tongueless, terror, closing him in. Ah, nothing could hurt him now. Not dreams or plots. He was Armand's child.

"But these things must wait," Armand said gently. "You must come and do as I tell you. We must finish what was begun."

"Finish?" It was finished. He was reborn.

Armand brought him in out of the wind. Glint of the brass bed in the darkness, of a porcelain vase alive with gilded dragons. Of the square grand piano with its keys like grinning teeth. Yes, touch it, feel the ivory, the velvet tassels hanging from the lampshade. . . .

The music, where did the music come from? A low, mournful jazz trumpet, playing all alone. It stopped him, this hollow melancholy song, the notes flowing slowly into one another. He did not want to move just now. He wanted to say he understood what was happening, but he was absorbing each broken sound.

He started to say thank you for the music, but again, his voice sounded so unaccountably strange—sharper, yet more resonant. Even the feel of his tongue, and out there, the fog, look at it, he pointed, the fog blowing right past the terrace, the fog eating the night!

Armand was patient. Armand understood. Armand brought him slowly through the darkened room.

"I love you," Daniel said.

"Are you certain?" Armand answered.

It made him laugh.

They had come into a long high hallway. A stairs descending in deep shadow. A polished balustrade. Armand urged him forward. He wanted to look at the rug beneath him, a long chain of medallions woven with lilies, but Armand had brought him into a brightly lighted room.

He caught his breath at the sheer flood of illumination, light moving over the low-slung leather couches, chairs. Ah, but the painting on the wall!

So vivid the figures in the painting, formless creatures who were actually great thick smears of glaring yellow and red paint. Everything that looked alive was alive, that was a distinct possibility. You painted armless beings, swimming in blinding color, and they had to exist like that forever. Could they see you with all those tiny, scattered eyes? Or did they see only the heaven and hell of their own shining realm, anchored to the studs in the wall by a piece of twisted wire?

He could have wept to think of it, wept at the deep-throated moan of the trumpet—and yet he wasn't weeping. He had caught a strong seductive aroma. *God, what is it?* His whole body seemed to harden inexplicably. Then suddenly he was staring at a young girl.

She sat in a small gilded straight-back chair watching him, ankles crossed, her thick brown hair a gleaming mop around her white face. Her scant clothes were dirty. A little runaway with her torn jeans and soiled shirt. What a perfect picture, even to the sprinkling of freckles across her nose, and the greasy backpack that lay at her feet. But the shape of her little arms, the way her legs were made! And her eyes, her brown eyes! He was laughing softly, but it was humorless, crazed. It had a sinister sound to it; how strange! He realized he had taken her face in his hands and she was staring up at him, smiling, and a faint scarlet blush came in her warm little cheeks.

Blood, that was the aroma! His fingers were burning. Why, he could even see the blood vessels beneath her skin! And the sound of her heart, he could hear it. It was getting louder, it was such a . . . a moist sound. He backed away from her.

"God, get her out of here!" he cried.

"Take her," Armand whispered. "And do it now."

5

KHAYMAN, MY KHAYMAN

No one is listening.
Now you may sing the selfsong,
as the bird does, not for territory
or dominance,
but for self-enlargement.
Let something
come from nothing.
. . .

STAN RICE
from "Texas Suite"
Body of Work (1983)

UNTIL this night, this awful night, he'd had a little joke about himself: He didn't know who he was, or where he'd come from, but he knew what he liked.

And what he liked was all around him—the flower stands on the corners, the big steel and glass buildings full of milky evening light, the trees, of course, the grass beneath his feet. And the bought things of shining plastic and metal—toys, computers, telephones—it didn't matter. He liked to figure them out, master them, then crush them into tiny hard multicolored balls which he could then juggle or toss through plate glass windows when nobody was about.

He liked piano music, the motion pictures, and the poems he found in books.

He also liked the automobiles that burnt oil from the earth like lamps. And the great jet planes that flew on the same scientific principles, above the clouds.

He always stopped and listened to the people laughing and talking up there when one of the planes flew overhead.

Driving was an extraordinary pleasure. In a silver Mercedes-Benz, he had sped on smooth empty roads from Rome to Florence to Venice in one night. He also liked television—the entire electric process of it, with its tiny bits of light. How soothing it was to have the company of television, the intimacy with so many artfully painted faces speaking to you in friendship from the glowing screen.

The rock and roll, he liked that too. He liked all music. He liked the Vampire Lestat singing "Requiem for the Marquise." He didn't pay attention to the words much. It was the melancholy, and the dark undertone of drums and cymbals. Made him want to dance.

He liked giant yellow machines that dug into the earth late at night in the big cities with men in uniforms crawling all over them; he liked the double-decker buses of London, and the people—the clever mortals everywhere—he liked them, too, of course.

He liked walking in Damascus during the evening, and seeing in sudden flashes of disconnected memory the city of the ancients. Romans, Greeks, Persians, Egyptians in these streets.

He liked the libraries where he could find photographs of ancient monuments in big smooth good-smelling books. He took his own photographs of the new cities around him and sometimes he could put images on these pictures which came from his thoughts. For example, in his photograph of Rome there were Roman people in tunics and sandals superimposed upon the modern versions in their thick ungraceful clothes.

Oh, yes, much to like all around him always—the violin music of Bartók, little girls in snow white dresses coming out of the church at midnight having sung at the Christmas mass.

He liked the blood of his victims too, of course. That went without saying. It was no part of his little joke. Death was not funny to him. He stalked his prey in silence; he didn't want to know his victims. All a mortal had to do was speak to him and he was turned away. Not proper, as he saw it, to talk to these sweet, soft-eyed beings and then gobble their blood, break their bones and lick the marrow, squeeze their limbs to a dripping pulp. And that was the way he feasted now, so violently. He felt no great need for blood anymore; but he wanted it. And the desire overpowered him in all its ravening purity, quite apart from thirst. He could have feasted upon three or four mortals a night.

Yet he was sure, absolutely sure, that he had been a human being once. Walking in the sun in the heat of the day, yes, he had once done that, even though he certainly couldn't do it now. He envisioned himself sitting at a plain wood table and cutting open a ripe peach with a small copper knife. Beautiful the fruit before him. He knew the taste of it. He knew the taste of bread and beer. He saw the sun shining on the dull yellow sand that stretched for miles and miles outside. "Lie down and rest in the heat of the day," someone had once said to him. Was this the last day that he had been alive? Rest, yes, because tonight the King and the Queen will call all the court together and something terrible, something. . .

But he couldn't really remember.

No, he just knew it, that is, until this night. This night . . .

Not even when he'd heard the Vampire Lestat did he remember. The character merely fascinated him a little—a rock singer calling himself a blood drinker. And he did look unearthly, but then that was television, wasn't it? Many humans in the dizzying world of rock music appeared unearthly. And there was such human emotion in the Vampire Lestat's voice.

It wasn't merely emotion; it was human ambition of a particular sort. The Vampire Lestat wanted to be heroic. When he sang, he said: "Allow me my significance! I am the symbol of evil; and if I am a true symbol, then I do good."

Fascinating. Only a human being could think of a paradox like that. And he himself knew this, because he'd been human, of course.

Now he did have a supernatural understanding of things. That was true. Humans couldn't look at machines and perceive their principles as he could. And the manner in which everything was "familiar" to him—that had to do with his superhuman powers as well. Why, there was nothing that surprised him really. Not quantum physics or theories of evolution or the paintings of Picasso or the process by which children were inoculated with germs to protect them from disease. No, it was as if he'd been aware of things long before he remembered being here. Long before he could say: "I think; therefore I am."

But disregarding all that, he still had a human perspective. That no one would deny. He could feel human pain with an eerie and frightening perfection. He knew what it meant to love, and to be lonely, ah, yes, he knew that above all things, and he felt it most keenly when he listened to the Vampire Lestat's songs. That's why he didn't pay attention to the words.

And another thing. The more blood he drank the more human-looking he became.

When he'd first appeared in this time—to himself and others—he hadn't looked human at all. He'd been a filthy skeleton, walking along the highway in Greece towards Athens, his bones enmeshed in tight rubbery veins, the whole sealed beneath a layer of toughened white skin. He'd terrified people. How they had fled from him, gunning the engines of their little cars. But he'd read their minds—seen himself as they saw him—and he understood, and he was so sorry, of course.

In Athens, he'd gotten gloves, a loose wool garment with plastic buttons, and these funny modern shoes that covered up your whole foot. He'd wrapped rags around his face with only holes for his eyes and mouth. He'd covered his filthy black hair with a gray felt hat.

They still stared but they didn't run screaming. At dusk, he roamed through the thick crowds in Omonia Square and no one paid him any mind. How nice the modern bustle of this old city, which in long ago ages had been just as vital, when students came there from all over the world to study philosophy and art. He could look up at the Acropolis and see the Parthenon as it had been then, perfect, the house of the goddess. Not the ruin it was today.

The Greeks as always were a splendid people, gentle and trusting, though they were darker of hair and skin now on account of their Turkish blood. They didn't mind his strange clothes. When he talked in his soft, soothing voice, imitating their language perfectly—except for a few apparently hilarious mistakes—they loved him. And in private, he had noticed that his flesh was slowly filling out. It was hard as a rock to the touch. Yet it was changing. Finally, one night when he unwrapped the ragged covering, he had seen the contours of a human face. So this is what he looked like, was it?

Big black eyes with fine soft wrinkles at the corners and rather smooth lids. His mouth was a nice, smiling mouth. The nose was neat and finely made; he didn't disdain it. And the eyebrows: he liked these best of all because they were very black and straight, not broken or bushy, and they were drawn high enough above his eyes so that he had an open expression, a look of veiled wonder that others might trust. Yes, it was a very pretty young male face.

After that he'd gone about uncovered, wearing modern shirts and pants. But he had to keep to the shadows. He was just too smooth and too white.

He said his name was Khayman when they asked him. But he didn't know where he'd gotten it. And he had been called Benjamin once, later, he knew that, too. There were other names. . . . But when? Khayman. That was the first and secret name, the one he never forgot. He could draw two tiny pictures that meant Khayman, but where these symbols had come from he had no idea.

His strength puzzled him as much as anything else. He could walk through plaster walls, lift an automobile and hurl it into a nearby field. Yet he was curiously brittle and light. He drove a long thin knife right through his own hand. Such a strange sensation! And blood everywhere. Then the wounds closed and he had to open them again to pull the knife out.

As for the lightness, well, there was nothing that he could not climb. It was as though gravity had no control over him once he decided to defy it. And one night after climbing a tall building in the middle of the city, he flew off the top of it, descending gently to the street below.

Lovely, this. He knew he could traverse great distances if only he dared. Why, surely he had once done it, moving into the very clouds. But then . . . maybe not.

He had other powers as well. Each evening as he awakened, he found himself listening to voices from all over the world. He lay in the darkness bathed in sound. He heard people speaking in Greek, English, Romanian, Hindustani. He heard laughter, cries of pain. And if he lay very still, he could hear thoughts from people—a jumbled undercurrent full of wild exaggeration that frightened him. He did not know where these voices came from. Or why one voice drowned out another. Why, it was as if he were God and he were listening to prayers.

And now and then, quite distinct from the human voices, there came to him immortal voices too. Others like him out there, thinking, feeling, sending a warning? Far away their powerful silvery cries, yet he could easily separate them from the human warp and woof.

But this receptiveness hurt him. It brought back some awful memory of being shut up in a dark place with only these voices to keep him company for years and years and years. Panic. He would not remember that. Some things one doesn't want to remember. Like being burned, imprisoned. Like remembering everything and crying, terrible anguished crying.

Yes, bad things had happened to him. He had been here on this earth under other names and at other times. But always with this same gentle and optimistic disposition, loving things. Was his a migrant soul? No, he had always had this body. That's why it was so light and so strong.

Inevitably he shut off the voices. In fact, he remembered an old admonition: If you do not learn to shut out the voices, they will drive you mad. But with him now, it was simple. He quieted them simply by rising, opening his eyes. Actually, it would have required an effort to listen. They just went on and on and became one irritating noise.

The splendor of the moment awaited him. And it was easy to drown out the thoughts of mortals close at hand. He could sing, for instance, or fix his attention hard upon anything around him. Blessed quiet. In Rome there were distractions everywhere. How he loved the old Roman houses painted ocher and burnt sienna and dark green. How he loved the narrow stone streets. He could drive a car very fast through the broad boulevard full of wreckless mortals, or wander the Via Veneto until he found a woman with whom to fall in love for a little while.

And he did so love the clever people of this time. They were still people, but they knew so much. A ruler was murdered in India, and within the hour all the world could mourn. All manner of disasters, inventions, and medical miracles weighed down upon the mind of the ordinary man. People played with fact and fancy. Waitresses wrote novels at night that would make them famous. Laborers fell in love with naked movie queens in rented cassette films. The rich wore paper jewelry, and the poor bought tiny diamonds. And princesses sallied forth onto the Champs Elysées in carefully faded rags.

Ah, he wished he was human. After all, what was he? What were the others like?—the ones whose voices he shut out. Not the First Brood, he was sure of it. The First Brood could never contact each other purely through the mind. But what the hell was the First Brood? He couldn't remember! A little panic seized him. Don't think of those things. He wrote poems in a notebook—modern and simple, yet he knew that they were in the earliest style he'd ever known.

He moved ceaselessly about Europe and Asia Minor, sometimes walking, sometimes rising into the air and willing himself to a particular place. He charmed those who would have interfered with him and slumbered carelessly in dark hiding places by day. After all, the sun didn't burn him anymore. But he could not function in the sunlight. His eyes began to close as soon as he saw light in the morning sky. Voices, all those voices, other blood drinkers crying in anguish—then nothing. And he awoke at sunset, eager to read the age-old pattern of the stars.

Finally he grew brave with his flying. On the outskirts of Istanbul he went upwards, shooting like a balloon far over the roofs. He tossed and tumbled, laughing freely, and then willed himself to Vienna, which he reached before dawn. Nobody saw him. He moved too fast for them to see him. And besides he did not try these little experiments before prying eyes.

He had another interesting power too. He could travel without his body. Well, not really travel. He could send out his vision, as it were, to look at things far away. Lying still, he would think, for example, of a distant place that he would like to see, and suddenly he was there before it. Now, there were some mortals who could do that too, either in their dreams or when they were awake, with great and deliberate concentration. Occasionally he passed their sleeping bodies and perceived that their souls were traveling elsewhere. But the souls themselves he could never see. He could not see ghosts or any kind of spirit for that matter. . . .

But he knew they were there. They *had* to be.

And some old awareness came to him, that once as a mortal man, in the temple, he had drunk a strong potion given to him by the priests, and had traveled in the very same way, up out of his body, and into the firmament. The priests had called him back. He had not wanted to come. He was with those among the dead whom he loved. But he had known he must return. That was what was expected of him.

He'd been a human being then, all right. Yes, definitely. He could remember the way the sweat had felt on his naked chest when he lay in the dusty room and they brought the potion to him. Afraid. But then they all had to go through it.

Maybe it was better to be what he was now, and be able to fly about with body and soul together.

But not knowing, not really remembering, not understanding how he could do such things or why he lived off the blood of humans—all this caused him intense pain.

In Paris, he went to "vampire" movies, puzzling over what seemed true and what was false. Familiar all this, though much of it was silly. The Vampire Lestat had taken his garments from these old black and white films. Most of the "creatures of the night" wore the same costume—the black cloak, the stiff white shirt, the fine black jacket with tails, the black pants.

Nonsense of course, yet it comforted him. After all, these were blood drinkers, beings who spoke gently, liked poetry, and yet killed mortals all the time.

He bought the vampire comics and cut out certain pictures of beautiful gentlemen blood drinkers like the Vampire Lestat. Maybe he himself should try this lovely costume; again, it would be a comfort. It would make him feel that he was part of something, even if the something didn't really exist.

In London, past midnight in a darkened store, he found his vampire clothes. Coat and pants, and shining patent leather shoes; a shirt as stiff as new papyrus with a white silk tie. And oh, the black velvet cloak, magnificent, with its lining of white satin; it hung down to the very floor.

He did graceful turns before the mirrors. How the Vampire Lestat would have envied him, and to think, he, Khayman, was no human pretending; he was real. He brushed out his thick black hair for the first time. He found perfumes and unguents in glass cases and anointed himself properly for a grand evening. He found rings and cuff links of gold.

Now he was beautiful, as he had once been in other garments long ago. And immediately in the streets of London people adored him! This had been the right thing to do. They followed him as he walked along smiling and bowing, now and then, and winking his eye. Even when he killed it was better. The victim would stare at him as if seeing a vision, as if *understanding.* He would bend—as the Vampire Lestat did in the television songs—and drink first, gently, from the throat, before ripping the victim apart.

Of course this was all a joke. There was something frightfully trivial about it. It had nothing to do with being a blood drinker, that was the dark secret, nothing to do with the faint things he only half remembered, now and then, and pushed from his mind. Nevertheless it was fun for the moment to be "somebody" and "something."

Yes, the moment, the moment was splendid. And the moment was all he ever had. After all, he would forget this time too, wouldn't he? These nights with their exquisite details would vanish from him; and in some even more complex and demanding future he would be loosed again, remembering only his name.

Home to Athens he went finally.

Through the museum by night he roamed with a stub of candle, inspecting the old tombstones with their carved figures which made him cry. The dead woman seated—always the dead are seated—reaches out for the living baby she has left behind, who is held in her husband's arm. Names came back to him, as if bats were whispering in his ear. *Go to Egypt; you'll remember.* But he would not. Too soon to beg for madness and forgetfulness. Safe in Athens, roaming the old cemetery beneath the Acropolis, from which they'd taken all the stele; never mind the traffic roaring by; the earth here is beautiful. And it still belongs to the dead.

He acquired a wardrobe of vampire garments. He even bought a coffin, but he did not like to get inside. For one thing, it was not shaped like a person, this coffin, and it had no face on it, and no writings to guide the soul of the dead. Not proper. Rather like a box for jewelry, as he saw it. But still, being a vampire, well, he thought he should have it and it was fun. Mortals who came to the flat loved it. He served them bloodred wine in crystal glasses. He recited "The Rime of the Ancient Mariner" for them or sang songs in strange tongues which they loved. Sometimes he read his poems. What good-hearted mortals. And the coffin gave them something to sit on in a flat that contained nothing else.

But gradually the songs of the American rock singer, the Vampire Lestat, had begun to disturb him. They weren't fun anymore. Neither were the silly old films. But the Vampire Lestat really bothered him. What blood drinker would dream of acts of purity and courage? Such a tragic tone to the songs.

Blood drinker. . . . Sometimes when he awoke, alone on the floor of the hot airless flat with the last light of day fading through the curtained windows, he felt a heavy dream lift from him in which creatures sighed and groaned in pain. Had he been following through a ghastly nightscape the path of two beautiful red-haired women who suffered unspeakable injustice, twin beauties to whom he reached out again and again? After they cut out her tongue, the red-haired woman in the dream snatched the tongue back from the soldiers and ate it. Her courage had astonished them—

Ah, do not look at such things!

His face hurt, as if he had been crying also or miserably anxious. He let himself relax slowly. Behold the lamp. The yellow flowers. Nothing. Just Athens with its miles and miles of undistinguished stucco buildings, and the great broken temple of Athena on the hill, looming over all despite the smoke-filled air. Evening time. The divine rush as thousands in their drab workaday clothes poured down the escalators to the underground trains. Syntagma Square scattered with the lazy drinkers of retsina or ouzo, suffering beneath the early evening heat. And the little kiosks selling magazines and papers from all lands.

He didn't listen to any more of the Vampire Lestat's music. He left the American dance halls where they played it. He moved away from the students who carried small tape players clipped to their belts.

Then one night in the heart of the Plaka, with its glaring lights and noisy taverns, he saw other blood drinkers hurrying through the crowds. His heart stopped. Loneliness and fear overcame him. He could not move or speak. Then he tracked them through the steep streets, in and out of one dancing place after another where the electronic music blared. He studied them carefully as they rushed on through the crush of tourists, not aware that he was there.

Two males and a female in scant black silk garments, the woman's feet strapped painfully into high-heeled shoes. Silver sunglasses covered their eyes; they whispered together and gave out sudden piercing bursts of laughter; decked with jewels and scent, they flaunted their shining preternatural skin and hair.

But never mind these superficial matters, they were very different from him. They were nothing as hard and white, to begin with. In fact they were made up of so much soft human tissue that they were animated corpses still. Beguilingly pink and weak. And how they needed the blood of their victims. Why, they were suffering agonies of thirst right now. And surely this was their fate nightly. Because the blood had to work endlessly on all the soft human tissue. It worked not merely to animate the tissue, but to convert it slowly into something else.

As for him, he was all made up of that something else. He had no soft human tissue left. Though he lusted for blood, it was not needed for this conversion. Rather he realized suddenly that the blood merely refreshed him, increased his telepathic powers, his ability to fly, or to travel out of his body, or his prodigious strength. Ah, he understood it! For the nameless power that worked in all of them, he was now a nearly perfected host.

Yes, that was it exactly. And they were younger, that's all. They had merely begun their journey towards true vampiric immortality. Didn't he remember—? Well, not actually, but he *knew* it, that they were fledglings, no more than one or two hundred years along the way! That was the dangerous time, when you first went mad from it, or the others got you, shut you up, burned you, that sort of thing. Many did not survive those years. And how long ago it had been for him, of the First Brood. Why, the amount of time was almost inconceivable! He stopped beside the painted wall of a garden, reaching up to rest his hand on a gnarled branch, letting the cool fleecy green leaves touch his face. He felt himself washed in sadness suddenly, sadness more terrible than fear. He heard someone crying, not here but in his head. Who was it? Stop!

Well, he would not hurt them, these tender children! No, he wanted only to know them, to embrace them. After all, we are of the same family, blood drinkers, you and I!

But as he drew nearer, as he sent out his silent yet exuberant greeting, they turned and looked at him with undisguised terror. They fled. Through a dark tangle of hillside lanes they descended, away from the lights of the Plaka, and nothing he could say or do would make them stop.

He stood rigid and silent, feeling a sharp pain he had not known before. Then a curious and terrible thing happened. He went after them till he had them in sight again. He became angry, really angry. *Damn you. Punish you that you hurt me!* And lo and behold he felt a sudden sensation in his forehead, a cold spasm just behind the bone. Out of him, a power seemed to leap as if it were an invisible tongue. Instantly it penetrated the hindmost of the fleeing trio, the female, and her body burst into flame.

Stupefied he watched this. Yet he realized what had happened. He had penetrated her with some sharply directed force. It had kindled the powerful combustible blood that he and she had in common, and at once the fire had shot through the circuit of her veins. Invading the marrow of her bones, it had caused her body to explode. In seconds, she was no more.

Ye gods! He had done this! In grief and terror, he stood staring down at her empty clothes, unburnt, yet blackened and stained with grease. Only a little of her hair was left on the stones, and this burnt away to wisps of smoke as he watched.

Maybe there was some mistake. But no, he knew he'd done it. He'd felt himself doing it. And she had been so afraid!

In shocked silence, he made his way home. He knew he'd never used this power before, or even been aware of it. Had it come to him only now, after centuries of the blood working, drying out his cells, making them thin and white and strong like the chambers of a wasps' nest?

Alone in his flat, with the candles and incense burning to comfort him, he pierced himself again with his knife and watched the blood gush. Thick and hot it was, pooling on the table before him, glittering in the light of the lamp as if it was alive. And it was!

In the mirror, he studied the darkening radiance which had returned to him after so many weeks of dedicated hunting and drinking. A faint yellow tinge to his cheeks, a trace of pink to his lips. But never mind, he was as the abandoned skin of the snake lying on the rock—dead and light and crisp save for the constant pumping of this blood. This vile blood. And his brain, ah, his brain, what did it look like now? Translucent as a thing made of crystal with the blood surging through its tiny compartments? And therein the power lived, did it not, with its invisible tongue?

Going out again, he tried this newfound force upon animals, upon the cats, for which he had an unreasonable loathing—evil things, those creatures—and upon rats, which all men disdain. Not the same. He killed these creatures with the invisible tongue flick of energy, but they didn't catch fire. Rather the brains and hearts suffered some sort of fatal rupture, but the natural blood in them, it was not combustible. And so they did not burn.

This fascinated him in a cold, harrowing fashion. "What a subject I am for study," he whispered, eyes shining suddenly with unwelcome tears. Capes, white ties, vampire movies, what was this to him! *Who in hell was he?* The fool of the gods, roaming the road from moment to moment through eternity? When he saw a great lurid poster of the Vampire Lestat mocking him in a video store window, he turned and with the tongue flick of energy shattered the glass.

Ah, lovely, lovely. Give me the forests, the stars. He went to Delphi that night, ascending soundlessly above the darkened land. Down into the moist grass he went to walk where the oracle had once sat, in this the ruin of the god's house.

But he would not leave Athens. He must find the two blood drinkers, and tell them he was sorry, that he would never, never use this power against them. They must talk to him! They must be with him—! Yes.

The next night upon awakening, he listened for them. And an hour later, he heard them as they rose from their graves. A house in the Plaka was their lair, with one of those noisy, smoky taverns open to the street. In its cellars they slept by day, he realized, and came up by dark to watch the mortals of the tavern sing and dance. Lamia, the old Greek word for vampire, was the name of this establishment in which the electric guitars played the primitive Greek music, and the young mortal men danced with one another, hips churning with all the seductiveness of women, as the retsina flowed. On the walls hung pictures from the vampire movies—Bela Lugosi as Dracula, the pale Gloria Holden as his daughter—and posters of the blond and blue-eyed Vampire Lestat.

So they too had a sense of humor, he thought gently. But the vampire pair, stunned with grief and fear, sat together, staring at the open door as he peered in. How helpless they looked!

They did not move when they saw him standing on the threshold with his back to the white glare of the street. What did they think when they saw his long cloak? A monster come alive from their own posters to bring them destruction when so little else on earth could?

I come in peace. I only wish to speak with you. Nothing shall anger me. I come in . . . love.

The pair appeared transfixed. Then suddenly one of them rose from the table, and both gave a spontaneous and horrid cry. Fire blinded him as it blinded the mortals who pushed past him in their sudden stampede to the street. The blood drinkers were in flames, dying, caught in a hideous dance with twisted arms and legs. The house itself was burning, rafters smoking, glass bottles exploding, orange sparks shooting up to the lowering sky.

Had he done this! Was he death to the others, whether he willed such a thing or not?

Blood tears flowed down his white face onto his stiff shirt front. He lifted his arm to shield his face with his cloak. It was a gesture of respect for the horror happening before him—the blood drinkers dying within.

No, couldn't have done it, couldn't. He let the mortals push him and shove him out of the way. Sirens hurt his ears. He blinked as he tried to see, despite the flashing lights.

And then in a moment of violent understanding he knew that he had not done it. Because he saw the being who had! There covered in a cloak of gray wool, and half hidden in a dark alleyway, stood the one, silently watching him.

And as their eyes met, she softly whispered his name:

"Khayman, my Khayman!"

His mind went blank. Wiped clean. It was as though a white light descended on him, burning out all detail. He felt nothing for one serene moment. He heard no noise of the raging fire, nothing of those who still jostled him as they went past.

He merely stared at this thing, this beautiful and delicate being, exquisite as ever she had been. An unsupportable horror overcame him. He remembered everything—everything he had ever seen or been or known.

The centuries opened before him. The millennia stretched out, going back and back to the very beginning. *First Brood.* He knew it all. He was shuddering, crying. He heard himself say with all the rancor of an accusation:

"You!"

Suddenly, in a great withering flash he felt the full force of her undisguised power. The heat struck him in the chest, and he felt himself staggering backwards.

Ye gods, you will kill me, too! But she could not hear his thoughts! He was knocked against the whitewashed wall. A fierce pain collected in his head.

Yet he continued to see, to feel, to think! And his heart beat steadily as before. He was not burning!

And then with sudden calculation, he gathered his strength and fought this unseen energy with a violent thrust of his own.

"Ah, it is malice again, my sovereign," he cried out in the ancient language. How human the sound of his voice!

But it was finished. The alleyway was empty. She was gone.

Or more truly she had taken flight, rising straight upwards, just as he himself had often done, and so fast that the eye could not see. Yes, he felt her receding presence. He looked up and, without effort, found her—a tiny pen stroke moving towards the west above the bits and pieces of pale cloud.

Raw sounds shocked him—sirens, voices, the crackle of the burning house as its last timbers collapsed. The little narrow street was jam-crowded; the bawling music of the other taverns had not stopped. He drew back, away from the place, weeping, with one backward glance for the domain of the dead blood drinkers. Ah, how many thousands of years he could not count, and yet it was still the same war.

For hours he wandered the dark back streets.

Athens grew quiet. People slept behind wooden walls. The pavements shone in the mist that came as thick as rain. Like a giant snail shell was his history, curling and immense above him, pressing him down to the earth with its impossible weight.

Up a hill he moved finally, and into the cool luxurious tavern of a great modern steel and glass hotel. Black and white this place, just as he was, with its checkered dance floor, black tables, black leather banquettes.

Unnoticed he sank down on a bench in the flickering dimness, and he let his tears flow. Like a fool he cried, with his forehead pressed to his arm.

Madness did not come to him; neither did forgetfulness. He was wandering the centuries, revisiting the places he had known with tender thoughtless intimacy. He cried for all those he had known and loved.

But what hurt him above all things was the great suffocating sense of the beginning, the true beginning, even before that long ago day when he had lain down in his house by the Nile in the noon stillness, knowing he must go to the palace that night.

The true beginning had been a year before when the King had said to him, "But for my beloved Queen, I would take my pleasure of these two women. I would show that they are not witches to be feared. You will do this in my stead."

It was as real as this moment; the uneasy court gathered there watching; black-eyed men and women in their fine linen skirts and elaborate black wigs, some hovering behind the carved pillars, others proudly close to the throne. And the red-haired twins standing before him, his beautiful prisoners whom he had come to love in their captivity. *I cannot do this.* But he had done it. As the court waited, as the King and the Queen waited, he had put on the King's necklace with its gold medallion, to act for the King. And he had gone down the steps from the dais, as the twins stared at him, and he had defiled them one after the other.

Surely this pain couldn't last.

Into the womb of the earth he would have crawled, if he had had the strength for it. Blessed ignorance, how he wanted it. Go to Delphi, wander in the high sweet-smelling green grass. Pick the tiny wild flowers. Ah, would they open for him, as for the light of the sun, if he held them beneath the lamp?

But then he did not want to forget at all. Something had changed; something had made this moment like no other. *She* had risen from her long slumber! He had seen her in an Athens street with his own eyes! Past and present had become one.

As his tears dried, he sat back, listening, thinking.

Dancers writhed on the lighted checkerboard before him. Women smiled at him. Was he a beautiful porcelain Pierrot to them, with his white face and red-stained cheeks? He raised his eyes to the video screen pulsing and glittering above the room. His thoughts grew strong like his physical powers.

This was now, the month of October, in the late twentieth century after the birth of Christ. And only a handful of nights ago, he had seen the twins in his dreams! No. There was no retreat. For him the true agony was just beginning, but that did not matter. He was more *alive* than he had ever been.

He wiped his face slowly with a small linen handkerchief. He washed his fingers in the glass of wine before him, as if to consecrate them. And he looked up again to the high video screen where the Vampire Lestat sang his tragic song.

Blue-eyed demon, yellow hair flung wild about him, with the powerful arms and chest of a young man. Jagged yet graceful his movements, lips seductive, voice full of carefully modulated pain.

And all this time you have been telling me, haven't you? Calling me! Calling her name!

The video image seemed to stare at him, respond to him, sing to him, when of course it could not see him at all. *Those Who Must Be Kept! My King and my Queen.* Yet he listened with his full attention to each syllable carefully articulated above the din of horns and throbbing drums.

And only when the sound and the image faded did he rise and leave the tavern to walk blindly through the cool marble corridors of the hotel and into the darkness outside.

Voices called out to him, voices of blood drinkers the world over, signaling. Voices that had always been there. They spoke of calamity, of converging to prevent some horrid disaster. *The Mother Walks.* They spoke of the dreams of the twins which they did not understand. And he had been deaf and blind to all this!

"How much you do not understand, Lestat," he whispered.

He climbed to a dim promontory finally and gazed at the High City of temples far beyond—broken white marble gleaming beneath the feeble stars.

"Damn you, my sovereign!" he whispered. "Damn you into hell for what you did, to all of us!" And to think that in this world of steel and gasoline, of roaring electronic symphonies and silent gleaming computer circuitry, we wander still.

But another curse came back to him, far stronger than his own. It had come a year after the awful moment when he had raped the two women—a curse screamed within the courtyard of the palace, under a night sky as distant and uncaring as this.

"Let the spirits witness: for theirs is the knowledge of the future—both what it would be, *and what I will:* You are the Queen of the Damned, that's what you are! Evil is your only destiny. But at your greatest hour, it is I who will defeat you. Look well on my face. It is I who will bring you down."

How many times during the early centuries had he remembered those words? In how many places across desert and mountains and through fertile river valleys had he searched for the two red-haired sisters? Among the Bedouins who had once sheltered them, among the hunters who wore skins still and the people of Jericho, the oldest city in the world. They were already legend.

And then blessed madness had descended; he had lost all knowledge, rancor, and pain. He was Khayman, filled with love for all he saw around him, a being who understood the word *joy*.

Could it be that the hour had come? That the twins had somehow endured just as he had? And for this great purpose his memory had been restored?

Ah, what a lustrous and overwhelming thought, that the First Brood would come together, that the First Brood would finally know victory.

But with a bitter smile, he thought of the Vampire Lestat's human hunger for heroism. *Yes, my brother, forgive me for my scorn. I want it too, the goodness, the glory. But there is likely no destiny, and no redemption. Only what I see before me as I stand above this soiled and ancient landscape—just birth and death, and horrors await us all.*

He took one last look at the sleeping city, the ugly and careworn modern place where he had been so content, wandering over countless old graves.

And then he went upwards, rising within seconds above the clouds. Now would come the greatest test of this magnificent gift, and how he loved the sudden sense of purpose, illusory though it might be. He moved west, towards the Vampire Lestat, and towards the voices that begged for understanding of the dreams of the twins. He moved west as she had moved before him.

His cloak flared like sleek wings, and the delicious cold air bruised him and made him laugh suddenly as if for one moment he were the happy simpleton again.

6

THE STORY OF JESSE, THE GREAT FAMILY, AND THE TALAMASCA

i.

The dead don't share.
Though they reach towards us
from the grave (I swear
they do) they do
not hand their hearts to you.
They hand their heads,
the part that stares.

STAN RICE
from "Their Share"
Body of Work (1983)

ii.

Cover her face; mine eyes dazzle; she died young.

JOHN WEBSTER

iii.

THE TALAMASCA

Investigators of the Paranormal
We watch
And we are always here.

London Amsterdam Rome

JESSE was moaning in her sleep. She was a delicate woman of thirty-five with long curly red hair. She lay deep in a shapeless feather mattress, cradled in a wooden bed which hung from the ceiling on four rusted chains.

Somewhere in the big rambling house a clock chimed. She must wake up. Two hours until the Vampire Lestat's concert. But she could not leave the twins now.

This was new to her, this part unfolding so rapidly, and the dream was maddeningly dim as all the dreams of the twins had been. Yet she knew the twins were in the desert kingdom again. The mob surrounding the twins was dangerous. And the twins, how different they looked, how pale. Maybe it was an illusion, this phosphorescent luster, but they appeared to glow in the semidarkness, and their movements were languid, almost as if they were caught in the rhythm of a dance. Torches were thrust at them as they embraced one another; but look, something was wrong, very wrong. One of them was now blind.

Her eyelids were shut tight, the tender flesh wrinkled and sunken. Yes, they have plucked out her eyes. And the other one, why does she make those terrible sounds? "Be still, don't fight anymore," said the blind one, in the ancient language which was always understandable in the dreams. And out of the other twin came a horrid, guttural moaning. She couldn't speak. They'd cut out her tongue!

I don't want to see any more, I want to wake up. But the soldiers were pushing their way through the crowd, something dreadful was to happen, and the twins became suddenly very still. The soldiers took hold of them, dragged them apart.

Don't separate them! Don't you know what this means to them? Get the torches away. Don't set them on fire! Don't burn their red hair.

The blind twin reached out for her sister, screaming her name: "Mekare!" And Mekare, the mute one, who could not answer, roared like a wounded beast.

The crowd was parting, making way for two immense stone coffins, each carried on a great heavy bier. Crude these sarcophagi, yet the lids had the roughened shape of human faces, limbs. What have the twins done to be put in these coffins? I can't stand it, the biers being set down, the twins dragged towards the coffins, the crude stone lids being lifted. Don't do it! The blind one is fighting as if she can see it, yet they are overpowering her, lifting her and putting her inside the stone box. In mute terror, Mekare is watching, though she herself is being dragged to the other bier. Don't lower the lid, or I will scream for Mekare! For both of them—

Jesse sat up, her eyes open. She had screamed.

Alone in this house, with no one to hear her, she'd screamed, and she could feel the echo still. Then nothing but the quiet settling around her, and the faint creaking of the bed as it moved on its chains. The song of the birds outside in the forest, the deep forest; and her own curious awareness that the clock had struck six.

The dream was fading rapidly. Desperately she tried to hold on to it, to see the details that always slipped away—the clothing of these strange people, the weapons the soldiers carried, the faces of the twins! But it was already gone. Only the spell remained and an acute awareness of what had happened—and the certainty that the Vampire Lestat was linked to these dreams.

Sleepily, she checked her watch. No time left. She wanted to be in the auditorium when the Vampire Lestat entered; she wanted to be at the very foot of the stage.

Yet she hesitated, staring at the white roses on the bedside table. Beyond, through the open window, she saw the southern sky full of a faint orange light. She picked up the note that lay beside the flowers and she read it through once more.

> My darling,
>
> I have only just received your letter, as I am far from home and it took some time for this to reach me. I understand the fascination which this creature, Lestat, holds for you. They are playing his music even in Rio. I have already read the books which you have enclosed. And I know of your investigation of this creature for the Talamasca. As for your dreams of the twins, this we must talk about together. It is of the utmost importance. For there are others who have had such dreams. But I beg you—no, I order you not to go to this concert. You must remain at the Sonoma compound until I get there. I am leaving Brazil as soon as I can.
>
> Wait for me. I love you.
>
> Your aunt Maharet

"Maharet, I'm sorry," she whispered. But it was unthinkable that she not go. And if anyone in the world would understand, it was Maharet.

The Talamasca, for whom she'd worked for twelve long years, would never forgive her for disobeying their orders. But Maharet knew the reason; *Maharet was the reason.* Maharet would forgive.

Dizzy. The nightmare still wouldn't let go. The random objects of the room were disappearing in the shadows, yet the twilight burned so clear suddenly that even the forested hills were giving back the light. And the roses were phosphorescent, like the white flesh of the twins in the dream.

White roses, she tried to remember something she'd heard about white roses. You send white roses for a funeral. But no, Maharet could not have meant that.

Jesse reached out, took one of the blossoms in both hands, and the petals came loose instantly. Such sweetness. She pressed them to her lips, and a faint yet shining image came back to her from that long ago summer of Maharet in this house in a candle-lighted room, lying on a bed of rose petals, so many white and yellow and pink rose petals, which she had gathered up and pressed to her face and her throat.

Had Jesse really seen such a thing? So many rose petals caught in Maharet's long red hair. Hair like Jesse's hair. Hair like the hair of the twins in the dream—thick and wavy and streaked with gold.

It was one of a hundred fragments of memory which she could never afterwards fit into a whole. But it no longer mattered, what she could or could not remember of that dreamy lost summer. The Vampire Lestat waited: there would be a finish if not an answer, not unlike the promise of death itself.

She got up. She put on the worn hacking jacket that was her second skin these days, along with the boy's shirt, open at the neck, and the jeans she wore. She slipped on her worn leather boots. Ran the brush through her hair.

Now to take leave of the empty house she'd invaded this morning. It hurt her to leave it. But it had hurt her more to come at all.

AT THE first light, she'd arrived at the edge of the clearing, quietly stunned to discover it unchanged after fifteen years, a rambling structure built into the foot of the mountain, its roofs and pillared porches veiled in blue morning glory vines. High above, half hidden in the grassy slopes, a few tiny secret windows caught the first flash of morning light.

Like a spy she'd felt as she came up the front steps with the old key in her hand. No one had been here in months, it seemed. Dust and leaves wherever she looked.

Yet there were the roses waiting in their crystal vase, and the letter for her pinned to the door, with the new key in the envelope.

For hours, she'd wandered, revisited, explored. Never mind that she was tired, that she'd driven all night. She had to walk the long shaded galleries, to move through the spacious and overwhelming rooms. Never had the place seemed so much like a crude palace with its enormous timbers shouldering the rough-sawn plank ceilings, the rusted smokestack chimneys rising from the round stone hearths.

Even the furnishings were massive—the millstone tables, chairs and couches of unfinished lumber piled with soft down pillows, bookshelves and niches carved into the unpainted adobe walls.

It had the crude medieval grandeur, this place. The bits and pieces of Mayan art, the Etruscan cups and Hittite statues, seemed to belong here, amid the deep casements and stone floors. It was like a fortress. It felt safe.

Only Maharet's creations were full of brilliant color as if they'd drawn it from the trees and sky outside. Memory hadn't exaggerated their beauty in the least. Soft and thick the deep hooked wool rugs carrying the free pattern of woodland flower and grass everywhere as if the rug were the earth itself. And the countless quilted pillows with their curious stick figures and odd symbols, and finally the giant hanging quilts—modern tapestries that covered the walls with childlike pictures of fields, streams, mountains and forests, skies full of sun and moon together, of glorious clouds and even falling rain. They had the vibrant power of primitive painting with their myriad tiny bits of fabric sewn so carefully to create the detail of cascading water or falling leaf.

It had killed Jesse to see all this again.

By noon, hungry and light-headed from the long sleepless night, she'd gotten the courage to lift the latch from the rear door that led into the secret windowless rooms within the mountain itself. Breathless, she had followed the stone passage. Her heart pounded as she found the library unlocked and switched on the lamps.

Ah, fifteen years ago, simply the happiest summer of her life. All her wonderful adventures afterwards, ghost hunting for the Talamasca, had been nothing to that magical and unforgettable time.

She and Maharet in this library together, with the fire blazing. And the countless volumes of the family history, amazing her and delighting her. The lineage of "the Great Family," as Maharet always called it—"the thread we cling to in the labyrinth which is life." How lovingly she had taken down the books for Jesse, unlocked for her the caskets that contained the old parchment scrolls.

Jesse had not fully accepted it that summer, the implications of all she'd seen. There had been a slow confusion, a delicious suspension of ordinary reality, as if the papyruses covered with a writing she could not classify belonged more truly to dream. After all, Jesse had already become a trained archaeologist by that time. She'd done her time on digs in Egypt and at Jericho. Yet she could not decipher those strange glyphs. *In the name of God, how old were these things?*

For years after, she'd tried to remember other documents she'd seen. Surely she had come into the library one morning and discovered a back room with an open door.

Into a long corridor, she'd gone past other unlighted rooms. She'd found a light switch finally, and seen a great storage place full of clay tablets—clay tablets covered with tiny pictures! Without doubt, she'd held these things in her hands.

Something else had happened; something she had never really wanted to recall. Was there another hallway? She knew for certain that there had been a curving iron stairway which took her down into lower rooms with plain earthen walls. Tiny bulbs were fixed in old porcelain light sockets. She had pulled chains to turn them on.

Surely she had done that. Surely she had opened a heavy redwood door . . .

For years after, it had come back to her in little flashes—a vast, low-ceilinged room with oak chairs, a table and benches that looked as if they were made from stone. And what else? Something that at first seemed utterly familiar. And then—

Later that night, she'd remembered nothing but the stairway. Suddenly it was ten o'clock, and she'd just awakened and Maharet was standing at the foot of her bed. Maharet had come to her and kissed her. Such a lovely warm kiss; it had sent a low throbbing sensation through her. Maharet said they'd found her down by the creek, asleep in the clearing, and at sunset, they'd brought her in.

Down by the creek? For months after, she'd actually "remembered" falling asleep there. In fact, it was a rather rich "recollection" of the peace and stillness of the forest, of the water singing over the rocks. But it had never happened, of that she was now sure.

But on this day, some fifteen years later, she had found no evidence one way or the other of these half-remembered things. Rooms were bolted against her. Even the neat volumes of the family history were in locked glass cases which she dared not disturb.

Yet never had she believed so firmly in what she could recall. Yes, clay tablets covered with nothing but tiny stick figures for persons, trees, animals. She'd seen them, taken them off the shelves and held them under the feeble overhead light. And the stairway, and the room that frightened her, no, terrified her, yes . . . all there.

Nevertheless, it had been paradise here, in those warm summer days and nights, when she had sat by the hour talking to Maharet, when she had danced with Mael and Maharet by the light of the moon. Forget for now the pain afterwards, trying to understand why Maharet had sent her back home to New York never to come here again.

> My darling,
>
> The fact is I love you too much. My life will engulf yours if we are not separated. You must have freedom, Jesse, to devise your own plans, ambitions, dreams . . .

It was not to relive the old pain that she had returned, it was to know again, for a little while, the joy that had gone before.

FIGHTING weariness this afternoon, she'd wandered out of the house finally, and down the long lane through the oaks. So easy to find the old paths through the dense redwoods. And the clearing, ringed in fern and clover on the steep rocky banks of the shallow rushing creek.

Here Maharet had once guided her through total darkness, down into the water and along a path of stones. Mael had joined them. Maharet had poured the wine for Jesse, and they had sung together a song Jesse could never recall afterwards, though now and then she would find herself humming this eerie melody with inexplicable accuracy, then stop, aware of it, unable to find the proper note again.

She might have fallen asleep near the creek in the deep mingled sounds of the forest, so like the false "recollection" of years ago.

So dazzling the bright green of the maples, catching the rare shafts of light. And the redwoods, how monstrous they seemed in the unbroken quiet. Mammoth, indifferent, soaring hundreds of feet before their somber lacy foliage closed on the frayed margin of sky.

And she'd known what the concert tonight, with Lestat's screaming fans, would demand of her. But she'd been afraid that the dream of the twins would start again.

FINALLY, she'd gone back to the house, and taken the roses and the letter with her. Her old room. Three o'clock. Who wound the clocks of this place that they knew the hour? The dream of the twins was stalking her. And she was simply too tired to fight anymore. The place felt so good to her. No ghosts here of the kind she'd encountered so many times in her work. Only the peace. She'd lain down on the old hanging bed, on the quilt that she herself had made so carefully with Maharet that summer. And sleep—and the twins—had come together.

Now she had two hours to get to San Francisco, and she must leave this house, maybe in tears, again. She checked her pockets. Passport, papers, money, keys.

She picked up her leather bag, slung it over her shoulder, and hurried through the long passage to the stairs. Dusk was coming fast, and when darkness did cover the forest, nothing would be visible at all.

There was still a bit of sunlight in the main hall when she reached it. Through the western windows, a few long dusty rays illuminated the giant tapestry quilt on the wall.

Jesse caught her breath as she looked at it. Always her favorite, for its intricacy, its size. At first it seemed a great mass of random tiny prints and patches—then gradually the wooded landscape emerged from the myriad pieces of cloth. One minute you saw it; the next it was gone. That's how it had happened over and over again that summer when, drunk with wine, she had walked back and forth before it, losing the picture, then recovering it: the mountain, the forest, a tiny village nestled in the green valley below.

"I'm sorry, Maharet," she whispered again softly. She had to go. Her journey was nearly ended.

But as she looked away, something in the quilted picture caught her eye. She turned back, studied it again. Were there figures there, which she had never seen? Once more it was a swarm of stitched-together fragments. Then slowly the flank of the mountain emerged, then the olive trees, and finally the rooftops of the village, no more than yellow huts scattered on the smooth valley floor. The figures? She could not find them. That is, until she again turned her head away. In the corner of her eye, they were visible for a split second. Two tiny figures holding each other, women with red hair!

Slowly, almost cautiously she turned back to the picture. Her heart was skipping. Yes, there. But was it an illusion?

She crossed the room until she stood directly before the quilt. She reached up and touched it. Yes! Each little rag-doll being had a tiny pair of green buttons for its eyes, a carefully sewn nose and red mouth! And the hair, the hair was red yarn, crimped into jagged waves and delicately sewn over the white shoulders.

She stared at it, half disbelieving. Yet there they were—the twins! And as she stood there, petrified, the room began to darken. The last light had slipped below the horizon. The quilt was fading before her eyes into an unreadable pattern.

In a daze, she heard the clock strike the quarter hour. Call the Talamasca. Call David in London. Tell him part of it, anything— But that was out of the question and she knew it. And it broke her heart to realize that no matter what did happen to her tonight, the Talamasca would never know the whole story.

She forced herself to leave, to lock the door behind her and walk across the deep porch and down the long path.

She didn't fully understand her feelings, why she was so shaken and on the verge of tears. It confirmed her suspicions, all she thought she knew. And yet she was frightened. She was actually crying.

Wait for Maharet.

But that she could not do. Maharet would charm her, confuse her, drive her away from the mystery in the name of love. That's what had happened in that long ago summer. The Vampire Lestat withheld nothing. The Vampire Lestat was the crucial piece in the puzzle. To see him and touch him was to validate everything.

The red Mercedes roadster started instantly. And with a spray of gravel she backed up, turned, and made for the narrow unpaved road. The convertible top was down; she'd be frozen by the time she reached San Francisco, but it didn't matter. She loved the cold air on her face, she loved to drive fast.

The road plunged at once into the darkness of the woods. Not even the rising moon could penetrate here. She pushed to forty, swinging easily into the sudden turns. Her sadness grew heavier suddenly, but there were no more tears. The Vampire Lestat . . . almost there.

When at last she hit the county road, she was speeding, singing to herself in syllables she could hardly hear above the wind. Full darkness came just as she roared through the pretty little city of Santa Rosa and connected with the broad swift current of Highway 101 south.

The coastal fog was drifting in. It made ghosts of the dark hills to the east and west. Yet the bright flow of tail lamps illuminated the road ahead of her. Her excitement was mounting. One hour to the Golden Gate. The sadness was leaving her. All her life she'd been confident, lucky; and sometimes impatient with the more cautious people she'd known. And despite her sense of fatality on this night, her keen awareness of the dangers she was approaching, she felt her usual luck might be with her. She wasn't really afraid.

SHE'D been born lucky, as she saw it, found by the side of the road minutes after the car crash that had killed her seven-months-pregnant teenaged mother—a baby spontaneously aborted from the dying womb, and screaming loudly to clear her own tiny lungs when the ambulance arrived.

She had no name for two weeks as she languished in the county hospital, condemned for hours to the sterility and coldness of machines; but the nurses had adored her, nicknaming her "the sparrow," and cuddling her and singing to her whenever allowed.

Years later they were to write to her, sending along the snapshots they'd taken, telling her little stories, which had greatly amplified her early sense of having been loved.

It was Maharet who at last came for her, identifying her as the sole survivor of the Reeves family of South Carolina and taking her to New York to live with cousins of a different name and background. There she was to grow up in a lavish old two-story apartment on Lexington Avenue with Maria and Matthew Godwin, who gave her not only love but everything she could want. An English nanny had slept in her room till Jesse was twelve years old.

She could not remember when she'd learned that her aunt Maharet had provided for her, that she could go on to any college and any career she might choose. Matthew Godwin was a doctor, Maria was a sometime dancer and teacher; they were frank about their attachment to Jesse, their dependence upon her. She was the daughter they had always wanted, and these had been rich and happy years.

The letters from Maharet started before she was old enough to read. They were wonderful, often full of colorful postcards and odd pieces of currency from the countries where Maharet lived. Jesse had a drawerful of rupees and lire by the time she was seventeen. But more important, she had a friend in Maharet, who answered every line she ever wrote with feeling and care.

It was Maharet who inspired her in her reading, encouraged her music lessons and painting classes, arranged her summer tours of Europe and finally her admission to Columbia, where Jesse studied ancient languages and art.

It was Maharet who arranged her Christmas visits with European cousins—the Scartinos of Italy, a powerful banking family who lived in a villa outside Siena, and the humbler Borchardts of Paris, who welcomed her to their overcrowded but cheerful home.

The summer that Jesse turned seventeen she went to Vienna to meet the Russian émigré branch of the family, young fervent intellectuals and musicians whom she greatly loved. Then it was off to England to meet the Reeves family, directly connected to the Reeveses of South Carolina, who had left England centuries ago.

When she was eighteen, she'd gone to visit the Petralona cousins in their villa on Santorini, rich and exotic-looking Greeks. They had lived in near feudal splendor, surrounded by peasant servants, and had taken Jesse with them on a spur-of-the-moment voyage aboard their yacht to Istanbul, Alexandria, and Crete.

Jesse had almost fallen in love with young Constantin Petralona. Maharet had let her know the marriage would have everyone's blessing, but she must make her own decision. Jesse had kissed her lover good-bye and flown back to America, the university, and preparation for her first archaeological dig in Iraq.

But even through the college years, she remained as close to the family as ever. Everyone was so good to her. But then everyone was good to everyone else. Everyone believed in the family. Visits among the various branches were common; frequent intermarriage had made endless entanglements; every family house contained rooms in constant readiness for relatives who might drop in. Family trees seemed to go back forever; people passed on funny stories about famous relatives who had been dead for three or four hundred years. Jesse had felt a great communion with these people, no matter how different they seemed.

In Rome she was charmed by the cousins who drove their sleek Ferraris at breakneck speed, stereos blaring, and went home at night to a charming old palazzo where the plumbing didn't work and the roof leaked. The Jewish cousins in southern California were a dazzling bunch of musicians, designers, and producers who had one way or the other been connected with the motion pictures and the big studios for fifty years. Their old house off Hollywood Boulevard was home to a score of unemployed actors. Jesse could live in the attic if she wanted to; dinner was served at six to anybody and everybody who walked in.

But who was this woman Maharet, who had always been Jesse's distant but ever attentive mentor, who guided her studies with frequent and thoughtful letters, who gave her the personal direction to which she so productively responded and which she secretly craved?

To all the cousins whom Jesse was ever to visit, Maharet was a palpable presence though her visits were so infrequent as to be remarkable. She was the keeper of the records of the Great Family, that is, all the branches under many names throughout the world. It was she who frequently brought members together, even arranging marriages to unite different branches, and the one who could invariably provide help in times of trouble, help that could sometimes mean the difference between life and death.

Before Maharet, there had been her mother, now called Old Maharet, and before that Great-aunt Maharet and so forth and so on as long as anybody could remember. "There will always be a Maharet" was an old family saying, rattled off in Italian as easily as in German or Russian or Yiddish or Greek. That is, a single female descendant in each generation would take the name and the record-keeping obligations, or so it seemed, anyhow, for no one save Maharet herself really knew those details.

"When will I meet you?" Jesse had written many times over the years. She had collected the stamps off the envelopes from Delhi and Rio and Mexico City, from Bangkok, and Tokyo and Lima and Saigon and Moscow.

All the family were devoted to this woman and fascinated by her, but with Jesse there was another secret and powerful connection.

From her earliest years, Jesse had had "unusual" experiences, unlike those of the people around her.

For example, Jesse could read people's thoughts in a vague, wordless way. She "knew" when people disliked her or were lying to her. She had a gift for languages because she frequently understood the "gist" even when she did not know the vocabulary.

And she saw ghosts—people and buildings that could not possibly be there.

When she was very little she often saw the dim gray outline of an elegant town house across from her window in Manhattan. She'd known it wasn't real, and it made her laugh at first, the way it came and went, sometimes transparent, other times as solid as the street itself, with lights behind its lace-curtained windows. Years passed before she learned that the phantom house had once been the property of architect Stanford White. It had been torn down decades ago.

The human images she saw were not at first so well formed. On the contrary, they were brief flickering apparitions that often compounded the inexplicable discomfort she felt in particular places.

But as she got older these ghosts became more visible, more enduring. Once on a dark rainy afternoon, the translucent figure of an old woman had ambled towards her and finally passed right through her. Hysterical, Jesse had run into a nearby shop, where clerks had called Matthew and Maria. Over and over Jesse tried to describe the woman's troubled face, her bleary-eyed stare which seemed utterly blind to the real world about her.

Friends often didn't believe Jesse when she described these things. Yet they were fascinated and begged her to repeat the stories. It left Jesse with an ugly vulnerable feeling. So she tried not to tell people about the ghosts, though by the time she was in her early teens she was seeing these lost souls more and more often.

Even walking in the dense crowds of Fifth Avenue at midday she glimpsed these pale searching creatures. Then one morning in Central Park, when Jesse was sixteen, she saw the obvious apparition of a young man sitting on a bench not far from her. The park was crowded, noisy; yet the figure seemed detached, a part of nothing around it. The sounds around Jesse began to go dim as if the thing were absorbing them. She prayed for it to go away. Instead it turned and fixed its eyes on her. It tried to speak to her.

Jesse ran all the way home. She was in a panic. These things knew her now, she told Matthew and Maria. She was afraid to leave the apartment. Finally Matthew gave her a sedative and told her she would be able to sleep. He left the door of her room open so she wouldn't be frightened.

As Jesse lay there halfway between dream and waking, a young girl came in. Jesse realized she knew this young girl; of course, she was one of the family, she'd always been here, right by Jesse, they'd talked lots of times, hadn't they, and no surprise at all that she was so sweet, so loving, and so familiar. She was just a teenager, no older than Jesse.

She sat on Jesse's bed and told Jesse not to worry, that these spirits could never hurt her. No ghost had ever hurt anybody. They didn't have the power. They were poor pitiful weak things. "You write to Aunt Maharet," the girl said, and then she kissed Jesse and brushed the hair back out of Jesse's face. The sedative was really working then. Jesse couldn't even keep her eyes open. There was a question she wanted to ask about the car wreck when she was born, but she couldn't think of it. "Good-bye, sweetheart," said the girl and Jesse was asleep before the girl had left the room.

When she woke up it was two o'clock in the morning. The flat was dark. She began her letter to Maharet immediately, recounting every strange incident that she could remember.

It wasn't until dinnertime that she thought of the young girl with a start. Impossible that such a person had been living here and was familiar and had always been around. How could she have accepted such a thing? Even in her letter she had said, "Of course Miriam was here and Miriam said . . ." And who was Miriam? A name on Jesse's birth certificate. Her mother.

Jesse told no one what had happened. Yet a comforting warmth enveloped her. She could feel Miriam here, she was sure of it.

Maharet's letter came five days later. Maharet believed her. These spirit apparitions were nothing surprising at all. Such things most certainly did exist, and Jesse was not the only person who saw them:

> Our family over the generations has contained many a seer of spirits. And as you know these were the sorcerers and witches of ages past.

Frequently this power appears in those who are blessed with your physical attributes: your green eyes, pale skin, and red hair. It would seem the genes travel together. Maybe science one day will explain this to us. But for now be assured that your powers are entirely natural.

This does not mean, however, that they are constructive. Though spirits are real, they make almost no difference in the scheme of things! They can be childish, vindictive, and deceitful. By and large you cannot help the entities who try to communicate with you, and sometimes you are merely gazing at a lifeless ghost—that is, a visual echo of a personality no longer present.

Don't fear them, but do not let them waste your time. For that they love to do, once they know that you can see them. As for Miriam, you must tell me if you see her again. But as you have done as she asked in writing to me I do not think she will find it necessary to return. In all probability she is quite above the sad antics of those whom you see most often. Write to me about these things whenever they frighten you. But try not to tell others. Those who do not see will never believe you.

This letter proved invaluable to Jesse. For years she carried it with her, in her purse or pocket wherever she went. Not only had Maharet believed her, but Maharet had given her a way to understand and survive this troublesome power. Everything that Maharet said had made sense.

After that Jesse was occasionally frightened again by spirits; and she did share these secrets with her closest friends. But by and large she did as Maharet had instructed her, and the powers ceased to bother her. They seemed to go dormant. She forgot them for long periods.

Maharet's letters came with ever greater frequency. Maharet was her confidante, her best friend. As Jesse entered college, she had to admit that Maharet was more real to her through the letters than anyone else she had ever known. But she had long come to accept that they might never see each other.

Then one evening during Jesse's third year at Columbia she had opened the door of her apartment to discover the lights burning, and a fire going under the mantel, and a tall, thin red-haired woman standing at the andirons with the poker.

Such beauty! That had been Jesse's first overwhelming impression. Skillfully powdered and painted, the face had an Oriental artifice, save for the remarkable intensity of the green eyes and the thick curly red hair pouring down over the shoulders.

"My darling," the woman said. "It's Maharet."

Jesse had rushed into her arms. But Maharet had caught her, gently holding her apart as if to look at her. Then she'd covered Jesse with kisses, as if she dared not touch her in any other way, her gloved hands barely holding Jesse's arms. It had been a lovely and delicate moment. Jesse had stroked Maharet's soft thick red hair. So like her own.

"You are my child," Maharet had whispered. "You are everything I had hoped you would be. Do you know how happy I am?"

Like ice and fire, Maharet had seemed that night. Immensely strong, yet irrepressibly warm. A thin, yet statuesque creature with a tiny waist and flowing skirts, she had the high-toned mystery of fashion manikins, the eerie glamour of women who have made of themselves sculpture, her long brown wool cape moving with sweeping grace as they left the flat together. Yet how easy with one another they had been.

It had been a long night on the town; they'd gone to galleries, the theater, and then to a late night supper though Maharet had wanted nothing. She was too excited, she said. She did not even remove her gloves. She wanted only to listen to all that Jesse had to tell her. And Jesse had talked unendingly about everything—Columbia, her work in archaeology, her dreams of fieldwork in Mesopotamia.

So different from the intimacy of letters. They had even walked through Central Park in the pitch darkness together, Maharet telling Jesse there was not the slightest reason to be afraid. And it had seemed entirely normal then, hadn't it? And so beautiful, as if they were following the paths of an enchanted forest, fearing nothing, talking in excited yet hushed voices. How divine to feel so safe! Near dawn, Maharet left Jesse at the apartment with promises to bring her to visit in California very soon. Maharet had a house there, in the Sonoma mountains.

But two years were to pass before the invitation ever came. Jesse had just finished her bachelor's degree. She was scheduled to work on a dig in Lebanon in July.

"You must come for two weeks," Maharet had written. The plane ticket was enclosed. Mael, "a dear friend," would fetch her from the airport.

THOUGH Jesse hadn't admitted it at the time, there had been strange things happening from the start.

Mael, for instance, a tall overpowering man with long wavy blond hair and deep-set blue eyes. There had been something almost eerie about the way he moved, the timbre of his voice, the precise way he handled the car as they drove north to Sonoma County. He'd worn the rawhide clothes of a rancher it seemed, even to the alligator boots, except for a pair of exquisite black kid gloves and a large pair of gold-rimmed blue-tinted glasses.

And yet he'd been so cheerful, so glad to see her, and she'd liked him immediately. She'd told him the story of her life before they reached Santa Rosa. He had the most lovely laugh. But Jesse had gotten positively dizzy looking at him once or twice. Why?

The compound itself was unbelievable. Who could have built such a place? It was at the end of an impossible unpaved road, to begin with; and its back rooms had been dug out of the mountain, as if by enormous machines. Then there were the roof timbers. Were they primeval redwood? They must have been twelve feet in girth. And the adobe walls, positively ancient. Had there been Europeans in California so long ago that they could have . . . but what did it matter? The place was magnificent, finally. She loved the round iron hearths and animal-skin rugs, and the huge library and the crude observatory with its ancient brass telescope.

She had loved the good-hearted servants who came each morning from Santa Rosa to clean, do laundry, prepare the sumptuous meals. It did not even bother her that she was alone so much. She loved walking in the forest. She went into Santa Rosa for novels and newspapers. She studied the tapestried quilts. There were ancient artifacts here she could not classify; she loved examining these things.

And the compound had every convenience. Aerials high on the mountain brought television broadcasts from far and wide. There was a cellar movie theater complete with projector, screen, and an immense collection of films. On warm afternoons she swam in the pond to the south of the house. As dusk fell bringing the inevitable northern California chill, huge fires blazed in every hearth.

Of course the grandest discovery for her had been the family history, that there were countless leather volumes tracing the lineage of all the branches of the Great Family for centuries back. She was thrilled to discover photograph albums by the hundreds, and trunks full of painted portraits, some no more than tiny oval miniatures, others large canvases now layered with dust.

At once she devoured the history of the Reeveses of South Carolina, her own people—rich before the Civil War, and ruined after. Their photographs were almost more than she could bear. Here at last were the forebears she truly resembled; she could see her features in their faces. They had her pale skin, even her expression! And two of them had her long curly red hair. To Jesse, an adopted child, this had a very special significance.

It was only towards the end of her stay that Jesse began to realize the implications of the family records, as she opened scrolls covered with ancient Latin, Greek, and finally Egyptian hieroglyphs. Never afterwards was she able to pinpoint the discovery of the clay tablets deep within the cellar room. But the memory of her conversations with Maharet were never clouded. They'd talked for hours about the family chronicles.

Jesse had begged to work with the family history. She would have given up school for this library. She wanted to translate and adapt the old records and feed them into computers. Why not publish the story of the Great Family? For surely such a long lineage was highly unusual, if not absolutely unique. Even the crowned heads of Europe could not trace themselves back before the Dark Ages.

Maharet had been patient with Jesse's enthusiasm, reminding her that it was time-consuming and unrewarding work. After all, it was only the story of one family's progress through the centuries; sometimes there were only lists of names in the record, or short descriptions of uneventful lives, tallies of births and deaths, and records of migration.

Good memories, those conversations. And the soft mellow light of the library, the delicious smells of the old leather and parchment, of the candles and the blazing fire. And Maharet by the hearth, the lovely manikin, her pale green eyes covered with large faintly tinted glasses, cautioning Jesse that the work might engulf her, keep her from better things. It was the Great Family that mattered, not the record of it, it was the vitality in each generation, and the knowledge and love of one's kin. The record merely made this possible.

Jesse's longing for this work was greater than anything she'd ever known. Surely Maharet would let her stay here! She'd have years in this library, discovering finally the very origins of the family!

Only afterwards did she see it as an astounding mystery, and one among many during that summer. Only afterwards, had so many little things preyed on her mind.

For example, Maharet and Mael simply never appeared until after dark, and the explanation—they slept all day—was no explanation at all. And where did they sleep?—that was another question. Their rooms lay empty all day with the doors open, the closets overflowing with exotic and spectacular clothes. At sunset they would appear almost as if they'd materialized. Jesse would look up. Maharet would be standing by the hearth, her makeup elaborate and flawless, her clothes dramatic, her jeweled earrings and necklace sparkling in the broken light. Mael, dressed as usual in soft brown buckskin jacket and pants, stood silently against the wall.

But when Jesse asked about their strange hours, Maharet's answers were utterly convincing! They were pale beings, they detested sunlight, and they did stay up so late! True. Why, at four in the morning, they were still arguing with each other about politics or history, and from such a bizarre and grand perspective, calling cities by their ancient names, and sometimes speaking in a rapid, strange tongue that Jesse could not classify, let alone understand. With her psychic gift, she sometimes knew what they were saying; but the strange sounds baffled her.

And something about Mael rankled Maharet, it was obvious. Was he her lover? It did not really seem so.

Then it was the way that Mael and Maharet kept speaking to each other, as if they were reading each other's minds. All of a sudden, Mael would say, "But I told you not to worry," when in fact Maharet had not said a word out loud. And sometimes they did it with Jesse too. One time, Jesse was certain, Maharet had called her, asked her to come down to the main dining hall, though Jesse could have sworn she heard the voice only in her head.

Of course Jesse was psychic. But were Mael and Maharet both powerful psychics as well?

Dinner: that was another thing—the way that Jesse's favorite dishes appeared. She didn't have to tell the servants what she liked and didn't like. They knew! Escargots, baked oysters, fettucini alla carbonara, beef Wellington, any and all her favorites were the nightly fare. And the wine, she had never tasted such delicious vintages. Yet Maharet and Mael ate like birds, or so it seemed. Sometimes they sat out the entire meal with their gloves on.

And the strange visitors, what about them? Santino, for instance, a black-haired Italian, who arrived one evening on foot, with a youthful companion named Eric. Santino had stared at Jesse as if she were an exotic animal, then he'd kissed her hand and given her a gorgeous emerald ring, which had disappeared without explanation several nights later. For two hours Santino had argued with Maharet in that same unusual language, then left in a rage, with the flustered Eric.

Then there were the strange nighttime parties. Hadn't Jesse awakened twice at three or four in the morning to find the house full of people? There had been people laughing and talking in every room. And all of these people had something in common. They were very pale with remarkable eyes, much like Mael and Maharet. But Jesse had been so sleepy. She couldn't even remember going back to bed. Only that at one point she had been surrounded by several very beautiful young men who filled a glass of wine for her, and the next thing she knew it was morning. She was in bed. The sun was pouring through the window. The house was empty.

Also, Jesse had heard things at odd hours. The roar of helicopters, small planes. Yet no one said a word about such things.

But Jesse was so happy! These things seemed of no consequence! Maharet's answers would banish Jesse's doubts in an instant. Yet how unusual that Jesse would change her mind like that. Jesse was such a confident person. Her own feelings were often known to her at once. She was actually rather stubborn. And yet she always had two attitudes towards various things Maharet told her. On the one hand, "Why, that's ridiculous," and on the other, "Of course!"

But Jesse was having too much fun to care. She spent the first few evenings of her visit talking with Maharet and Mael about archaeology. And Maharet was a fund of information though she had some very strange ideas.

For example, she maintained that the discovery of agriculture had actually come about because tribes who lived very well by hunting wanted to have hallucinogenic plants ever available to them for religious trances. And also they wanted beer. Never mind that there wasn't a shred of archaeological evidence. Just keep digging. Jesse would find out.

Mael read poetry out loud beautifully; Maharet sometimes played the piano, very slowly, meditatively. Eric reappeared for a couple of nights, joining them enthusiastically in their singing.

He'd brought films with him from Japan and Italy, and they'd had a splendid time watching these. *Kwaidan,* in particular, had been quite impressive, though frightening. And the Italian *Juliet of the Spirits* had made Jesse break into tears.

All of these people seemed to find Jesse interesting. In fact, Mael asked her incredibly odd questions. Had she ever in her life smoked a cigarette? What did chocolate taste like? How could she dare to go with young men alone in automobiles or to their apartments? Didn't she realize they might kill her? She had almost laughed. No, but seriously, that could happen, he insisted. He worked himself into a state over it. Look at the papers. Women of the modern cities were hunted by men like deer in the wood.

Best to get him off that subject, and onto his travels. His descriptions of all the places he'd been were marvelous. He'd lived for years in the jungles of the Amazon. Yet he would not fly in "an aeroplane." That was too dangerous. What if it exploded? And he didn't like "cloth garments" because they were too fragile.

Jesse had a very peculiar moment with Mael. They'd been talking together at the dining table. She'd been explaining about the ghosts she sometimes saw, and he had referred to these crossly as the addlebrained dead, or the insane dead, which had made her laugh in spite of herself. But it was true; ghosts did behave as if they were a little addlebrained, that was the horror of it. Do we cease to exist when we die? Or do we linger in a stupid state, appearing to people at odd moments and making nonsensical remarks to mediums? When had a ghost ever said anything interesting?

"But they are merely the earthbound, of course," Mael had said. "Who knows where we go when we at last let loose of the flesh and all its seductive pleasures?"

Jesse had been quite drunk by this time, and she felt a a terrible dread coming over her—thoughts of the old ghost mansion of Stanford White, and the spirits roaming the New York crowds. She'd focused sharply upon Mael, who for once was not wearing his gloves or his tinted glasses. Handsome Mael, whose eyes were very blue except for a bit of blackness at the centers.

"Besides," Mael had said, "there are other spirits who have always been here. They were never flesh and blood; and it makes them so angry."

What a curious idea. "How do you know this?" Jesse had asked, still staring at Mael. Mael was beautiful. The beauty was the sum of the faults—the hawk nose, the too prominent jaw, the leanness of the face with the wild wavy straw-colored hair around it. Even the eyes were too deep-set, yet all the more visible for it. Yes, beautiful—to embrace, to kiss, to invite to bed . . . In fact, the attraction she'd always felt to him was suddenly overwhelming.

Then, an odd realization had seized her. *This isn't a human being.* This is something pretending to be a human being. It was so clear. But it was also ridiculous! If it wasn't a human being, what the hell was it? It certainly was no ghost or spirit. That was obvious.

"I guess we don't know what's real or unreal," she had said without meaning to. "You stare at anything long enough and suddenly it looks monstrous." She had in fact turned away from him to stare at the bowl of flowers in the middle of the table. Old tea roses, falling to pieces amid the baby's breath and fern and purple zinnias. And they did look absolutely alien, these things, the way that insects always do, and sort of horrible! What were these things, really? Then the bowl broke into pieces and the water went everywhere. And Mael had said quite sincerely, "Oh, forgive me. I didn't mean to do that."

Now that had happened, without question. Yet it had made not the slightest impact. Mael had slipped away for a walk in the woods, kissing her forehead before he went, his hand trembling suddenly as he reached to touch her hair and then apparently thought the better of it.

Of course, Jesse had been drinking. In fact, Jesse drank too much the entire time she was there. And no one seemed to notice.

Now and then they went out and danced in the clearing under the moon. It was not an organized dancing. They would move singly, in circles, gazing up at the sky. Mael would hum or Maharet would sing songs in the unknown language.

What had been her state of mind to do such things for hours? And why had she never questioned, even in her mind, Mael's strange manner of wearing gloves about the house, or walking in the dark with his sunglasses on?

Then one morning well before dawn, Jesse had gone to bed drunk and had a terrible dream. Mael and Maharet were fighting with each other. Mael kept saying over and over:

"But what if she dies? What if somebody kills her, or a car hits her? What if, what if, what if . . ." It had become a deafening roar.

Then several nights later the awful and final catastrophe had begun. Mael had been gone for a while, but then he'd returned. She'd been drinking burgundy all evening long, and she was standing on the terrace with him and he had kissed her and she had lost consciousness and yet she knew what was going on. He was holding her, kissing her breasts, yet she was slipping down through a fathomless darkness. Then the girl had come again, the teenaged girl who'd come to her that time in New York when she was so afraid. Only Mael couldn't see the girl, and of course Jesse knew exactly who she was, Jesse's mother, Miriam, and that Miriam was afraid. Mael had suddenly released Jesse.

"Where is she!" he'd cried out angrily.

Jesse had opened her eyes. Maharet was there. She struck Mael so hard he flew backwards over the railing of the terrace. And Jesse screamed, pushing aside the teenaged girl accidentally as she ran to look over the edge.

Far down there in the clearing Mael stood, unhurt. Impossible, yet obviously the case. He was on his feet already, and he made Maharet a deep ceremonial bow. He stood in the light falling from the windows of the lower rooms, and he blew a kiss to Maharet. Maharet looked sad, but she smiled. She'd said something under her breath and made a little dismissive gesture to Mael, as if to say she wasn't angry.

Jesse was in a panic that Maharet would be angry with her, but when she looked into Maharet's eyes she knew that there was no cause for worry. Then Jesse looked down and saw that the front of her dress was torn. She felt a sharp pain where Mael had been kissing her, and when she turned to Maharet, she became disoriented, unable to hear her own words.

She was sitting on her bed somehow, propped against the pillows, and she wore a long flannel gown. She was telling Maharet that her mother had come again, she'd seen her on the terrace. But that was only part of what she'd been saying because she and Maharet had been talking for hours about the whole thing. But what whole thing? Maharet told her she would forget.

Oh, God, how she tried to recall after. Bits and pieces had tormented her for years. Maharet's hair was down, and it was very long and full. They had moved through the dark house together, like ghosts, she and Maharet, Maharet holding her, and now and then stopping to kiss her, and she had hugged Maharet. Maharet's body felt like stone that could breathe.

They were high up in the mountain in a secret room. Massive computers were there, with their reels and red lights, giving off a low electronic hum. And there, on an immense rectangular screen that stretched dozens of feet up the wall, was an enormous family tree drawn electronically by means of light. This was the Great Family, stretching back through all the millennia. Ah, yes, to one root! The plan was matrilineal, which had always been the way with the ancient peoples—as it had been with the Egyptians, yes, descent through the princesses of the royal house. And as it was, after a fashion, with the Hebrew tribes to this day.

All the details had been plain to Jesse at this moment—ancient names, places, the beginning!—God, had she known even the beginning?—the staggering reality of hundreds of generations charted before her eyes! She had seen the progress of the family through the ancient countries of Asia Minor and Macedonia and Italy and finally up through Europe and then to the New World! And this could have been the chart of any human family!

Never after was she able to reinvoke the details of that electronic map. No, Maharet had told her she would forget it. The miracle was that she remembered anything at all.

But what else had happened? What had been the real thrust of their long talk?

Maharet crying, that she remembered. Maharet weeping with the soft feminine sound of a young girl. Maharet had never appeared so alluring; her face had been softened, yet luminous, the lines so few and so delicate. But it had been shadowy then, and Jesse could scarcely see anything clearly. She remembered the face burning like a white ember in the darkness, the pale green eyes clouded yet vibrant, and the blond eyelashes glistening as if the tiny hairs had been stroked with gold.

Candles burning in her room. The forest rising high outside the window. Jesse had been begging, protesting. But what in God's name was the argument about?

You will forget this. You will remember nothing.

She'd known when she opened her eyes in the sunlight that it was over; they had gone. Nothing had come back to her in those first few moments, except that something irrevocable had been said.

Then she had found the note on the bedside table:

My darling,

It is no longer good for you to be around us. I fear we have all become too enamored of you and would sweep you off your feet and take you away from those things which you have set out to do.

You will forgive us for leaving so suddenly. I am confident that this is best for you. I have arranged for the car to take you to the airport. Your plane leaves at four o'clock. Your cousins Maria and Matthew will meet you in New York.

Be assured I love you more than words can say. My letter will be waiting for you when you reach home. Some night many years from now we will discuss the family history again. You may become my helper with these records if you still wish it. But for now this must not engulf you. It must not lead you away from life itself.

Yours always,
with unquestioning love,
Maharet

JESSE had never seen Maharet again.

Her letters came with the same old regularity, full of affection, concern, advice. But never again was there to be a visit. Never was Jesse invited back to the house in the Sonoma forest.

In the following months, Jesse had been showered with presents—a beautiful old town house on Washington Square in Greenwich Village, a new car, a heady increase in income, and the usual plane tickets to visit members of the family all over the world. Eventually, Maharet underwrote a substantial part of Jesse's archaeological work at Jericho. In fact, as the years passed she gave Jesse anything and everything Jesse could possibly desire.

Nevertheless, Jesse had been damaged by that summer. Once in Damascus she had dreamed of Mael and awakened crying.

SHE was in London, working at the British Museum, when the memories began to come back with full force. She never knew what triggered them. Maybe the effect of Maharet's admonition—*You will forget*—had simply worn off. But there might have been another reason. One evening in

Trafalgar Square, she'd seen Mael or a man who looked exactly like him. The man, who stood many feet away, had been staring at her when their eyes met. Yet when she'd waved, he'd turned his back and walked off without the slightest recognition. She'd run after him trying to catch up with him; but he was gone as if he'd never been there.

It had left her hurt and disappointed. Yet three days later she'd received an anonymous gift, a bracelet of hammered silver. It was an ancient Celtic relic, she soon found out, and probably priceless. Could Mael have sent her this precious and lovely thing? She wanted so to believe it.

Holding the bracelet tightly in her hand she felt his presence. She remembered the long ago night when they'd spoken of addlebrained ghosts. She smiled. It was as if he were there, holding her, kissing her. She told Maharet about the gift when she wrote. She wore the bracelet ever after that.

Jesse kept a diary of the memories that came back to her. She wrote down dreams, fragments she saw in flashes. But she did not mention any of this in her letters to Maharet.

She had a love affair while she was in London. It ended badly, and she felt rather alone. It was at that time that the Talamasca contacted her and the course of her life was changed forever.

JESSE had been living in an old house in Chelsea, not far from where Oscar Wilde had once lived. James McNeill Whistler had once shared the neighborhood and so had Bram Stoker, the author of *Dracula.* It was a place that Jesse loved. But unbeknownst to her, the house in which she'd leased her rooms had been haunted for many years. Jesse saw several strange things within the first few months. They were faint, flickering, apparitions of the kind one frequently sees in such places; echoes, as Maharet had called them, of people who'd been there years before. Jesse ignored them.

However when a reporter stopped her one afternoon, explaining that he was doing a story on the haunted house, she told him rather matter-of-factly about the things she'd seen. Common enough ghosts for London—an old woman carrying a pitcher from the pantry, a man in a frock coat and top hat who would appear for a second or more on the stair.

It made for a rather melodramatic article. Jesse had talked too much, obviously. She was called a "psychic" or "natural medium" who saw these things all the time. One of the Reeves family in Yorkshire called to tease her a little about it. Jesse thought it was funny too. But other than that, she didn't much care. She was deep into her studies at the British Museum. It just didn't matter at all.

Then the Talamasca, having read the paper, came to call.

Aaron Lightner, an old-fashioned gentleman with white hair and exquisite manners, asked to take Jesse to lunch. In an old but meticulously maintained Rolls Royce, he and Jesse were driven through London to a small and elegant private club.

Surely it was one of the strangest meetings Jesse had ever had. In fact, it reminded her of the long ago summer, not because it was like it, but because both experiences were so unlike anything else that had ever happened to Jesse.

Lightner was a bit on the glamorous side, as Jesse saw it. His white hair was quite full and neatly groomed, and he wore an impeccably tailored suit of Donegal tweed. He was the only man she'd ever seen with a silver walking stick.

Rapidly and pleasantly he explained to Jesse that he was a "psychic detective"; he worked for a "secret order called the Talamasca," whose sole purpose was to collect data on "paranormal" experiences and maintain those records for the study of such phenomena. The Talamasca held out its hand to people with paranormal powers. And to those of extremely strong ability, it now and then offered membership, a career in "psychic investigation," which was in fact more truly a vocation, as the Talamasca demanded full devotion, loyalty, and obedience to its rules.

Jesse almost laughed. But Lightner was apparently prepared for her skepticism. He had a few "tricks" he always used at such introductory meetings. And to Jesse's utter amazement, he managed to move several objects on the table without touching them. A simple power, he said, which functioned as a "calling card."

As Jesse watched the salt shaker dance back and forth of its own volition, she was too amazed to speak. But the real surprise came when Lightner confessed he knew all about her. He knew where she'd come from, where she'd studied. He knew that she'd seen spirits when she was a little girl. It had come to the attention of the order years ago through "routine channels," and a file had been created for Jesse. She must not be offended.

Please understand the Talamasca proceeded in its investigations with the utmost respect for the individual. The file contained only hearsay reports of things that Jesse had told neighbors, teachers, and school friends. Jesse could see the file any time she wanted. That was always the way it was with the Talamasca. Contact was always eventually attempted with subjects under observation. Information was freely given to the subject, though it was otherwise confidential.

Jesse questioned Lightner rather relentlessly. It soon became clear that he did know a great deal about her, but he knew nothing whatsoever about Maharet or the Great Family.

And it was this combination of knowledge and ignorance that lured Jesse. One mention of Maharet and she would have turned her back on the Talamasca forever, for to the Great Family Jesse was unfailingly loyal. But the Talamasca cared only about Jesse's abilities. And Jesse, in spite of Maharet's advice, had always cared about them, too.

Then the history of the Talamasca itself proved powerfully attractive. Was this man telling the truth? A secret order, which traced its existence back to the year 758, an order with records of witches, sorcerers, mediums, and seers of spirits going back to that remote period? It dazzled her as the records of the Great Family had once dazzled her.

And Lightner graciously withstood another round of relentless questioning. He knew his history and his geography, that was clear enough. He spoke easily and accurately of the persecution of the Cathars, the suppression of the Knights Templar, the execution of Grandier, and a dozen other historical "events." In fact, Jesse couldn't stump him. On the contrary, he referred to ancient "magicians" and "sorcerers" of whom she had never heard.

That evening, when they arrived at the Motherhouse outside London, Jesse's fate was pretty much sealed. She didn't leave the Motherhouse for a week, and then only to close up her flat in Chelsea and return to the Talamasca.

The Motherhouse was a mammoth stone structure built in the 1500s and acquired by the Talamasca "only" two hundred years ago. Though the sumptuous paneled libraries and parlors had been created in the eighteenth century, along with appropriate plasterwork and friezes, the dining room and many of the bedchambers dated back to the Elizabethan period.

Jesse loved the atmosphere immediately, the dignified furnishings, the stone fireplaces, the gleaming oak floors. Even the quiet civil members of the order appealed to her, as they greeted her cheerfully, then returned to their discussions or the reading of the evening papers, as they sat about the vast, warmly lighted public rooms. The sheer wealth of the place was startling. It lent substance to Lightner's claims. And the place felt good. Psychically good. People here were what they said they were.

But it was the libraries themselves that finally overwhelmed her, and brought her back to that tragic summer when another library and its ancient treasures had been shut against her. Here were countless volumes chronicling witch trials and hauntings and poltergeist investigations, cases of possession, of psychokinesis, reincarnation, and the like. Then there were museums beneath the building, rooms crammed with mysterious objects connected with paranormal occurrences. There were vaults to which no one was admitted except the senior members of the order. Delicious, the prospect of secrets revealed only over a period of time.

"So much work to be done, always," Aaron had said casually. "Why, all these old records, you see, are in Latin, and we can no longer demand that the new members read and write Latin. It's simply out of the question in this day and age. And these storage rooms, you see, the documentation on most of these objects hasn't been reevaluated in four centuries—"

Of course Aaron knew that Jesse could read and write not only Latin, but Greek, ancient Egyptian, and ancient Sumerian as well. What he didn't know was that here Jesse had found a replacement for the treasures of that lost summer. She had found another "Great Family."

That night a car was sent to get Jesse's clothing and whatever she might want from the Chelsea flat. Her new room was in the southwest corner of the Motherhouse, a cozy little affair with a coffered ceiling and a Tudor fireplace.

Jesse never wanted to leave this house, and Aaron knew it. On Friday of that week, only three days after her arrival, she was received into the order as a novice. She was given an impressive allowance, a private parlor adjacent to her bedroom, a full-time driver, and a comfortable old car. She left her job at the British Museum as soon as possible.

The rules and regulations were simple. She would spend two years in full-time training, traveling with other members when and where necessary throughout the world. She could talk about the order to members of her family or friends, of course. But all subjects, files, and related details remained confidential. And she must never seek to publish anything about the Talamasca. In fact, she must never contribute to any "public mention" of the Talamasca. References to specific assignments must always omit names and places, and remain vague.

Her special work would be within the archives, translating and "adapting" old chronicles and records. And in the museums she would work on organizing various artifacts and relics at least one day of each week. But fieldwork—investigations of hauntings and the like—would take precedence over research at any time.

It was a month before she wrote to Maharet of her decision. And in her letter she poured out her soul. She loved these people and their work. Of course the library reminded her of the family archive in Sonoma, and the time when she'd been so happy. Did Maharet understand?

Maharet's answer astonished her. Maharet knew what the Talamasca was. In fact, Maharet seemed quite thoroughly familiar with the history of the Talamasca. She said without preamble that she admired enormously the efforts of the order during the witchcraft persecutions of the fifteenth and sixteenth centuries to save the innocent from the stake.

Surely they have told you of their "underground railroad" by means of which many accused persons were taken from the villages and hamlets where they might have been burnt and given refuge in Amsterdam, an enlightened city, where the lies and foolishness of the witchcraft era were not long believed.

Jesse hadn't known anything about this, but she was soon to confirm every detail. However, Maharet had her reservations about the Talamasca:

Much as I admire their compassion for the persecuted of all eras, you must understand that I do not think their investigations amount to much. To clarify: spirits, ghosts, vampires, werewolves, witches, entities that defy description—all these may exist and the Talamasca may spend another millennium studying them, but what difference will this make to the destiny of the human race?

Undoubtedly there have been, in the distant past, individuals who saw visions and spoke to spirits. And perhaps as witches or shamans, these people had some value for their tribes or nations. But complex and fanciful religions have been founded upon such simple and deceptive experiences, giving mythical names to vague entities, and creating an enormous vehicle for compounded superstitious belief. Have not these religions been more evil than good?

Allow me to suggest that, however one interprets history, we are now well past the point where contact with spirits can be of any use. A crude but inexorable justice may be at work in the skepticism of ordinary individuals regarding ghosts, mediums, and like company. The supernatural, in whatever form it exists, *should not* interfere in human history.

In sum, I am arguing that, except for comforting a few confused souls here and there, the Talamasca compiles records of things that are not important and should not be important. The Talamasca is an interesting organization. But it cannot accomplish great things.

I love you. I respect your decision. But I hope for your sake that you tire of the Talamasca—and return to the real world—very soon.

Jesse thought carefully before answering. It tortured her that Maharet didn't approve of what she had done. Yet Jesse knew there was a recrimination in her decision. Maharet had turned her away from the secrets of the family; the Talamasca had taken her in.

When she wrote, she assured Maharet that the members of the order had no illusions about the significance of their work. They had told Jesse it was largely secret; there was no glory, sometimes no real satisfaction. They would agree in full with Maharet's opinions about the insignificance of mediums, spirits, ghosts.

But did not millions of people think that the dusty finds of archaeologists were of little significance as well? Jesse begged Maharet to understand what this meant to her. And lastly she wrote, much to her own surprise, the following lines:

> I will never tell the Talamasca anything about the Great Family. I will never tell them about the house in Sonoma and the mysterious things that happened to me while I was there. They would be too hungry for this sort of mystery. And my loyalty is to you. But some day, I beg you, let me come back to the California house. Let me talk to you about the things that I saw. I've remembered things lately. I have had puzzling dreams. But I trust your judgment in these matters. You've been so generous to me. I don't doubt that you love me. Please understand how much I love you.

Maharet's response was brief.

> Jesse, I am an eccentric and willful being; very little has ever been denied me. Now and then I deceive myself as to the effect I have upon others. I should never have brought you to the Sonoma house; it was a selfish thing to do, for which I cannot forgive myself. But you must soothe my conscience for me. Forget the visit ever took place. Do not deny the truth of what you recall; but do not dwell on it either. Live your life as if it had never been so recklessly interrupted. Some day I will answer all your questions, but never again will I try to subvert your destiny. I congratulate you on your new vocation. You have my unconditional love forever.

Elegant presents soon followed. Leather luggage for Jesse's travels and a lovely mink-lined coat to keep her warm in "the abominable British weather." It is a country "only a Druid could love," Maharet wrote.

Jesse loved the coat because the mink was inside and didn't attract attention. The luggage served her well. And Maharet continued to write twice and three times a week. She remained as solicitous as ever.

But as the years passed, it was Jesse who grew distant—her letters brief and irregular—because her work with the Talamasca was confidential. She simply could not describe what she did.

Jesse still visited members of the Great Family, at Christmas and Easter. Whenever cousins came to London, she met them for sight-seeing or lunch. But all such contact was brief and superficial. The Talamasca soon became Jesse's life.

A WORLD was revealed to Jesse in the Talamasca archives as she began her translations from the Latin: records of psychic families and individuals, cases of "obvious" sorcery, "real" *maleficia,* and finally the repetitive yet horribly fascinating transcripts of actual witchcraft trials which invariably involved the innocent and the powerless. Night and day she worked, translating directly into the computer, retrieving invaluable historical material from crumbling parchment pages.

But another world, even more seductive, was opening up to her in the field. Within a year of joining the Talamasca, Jesse had seen poltergeist hauntings frightening enough to send grown men running out of the house and into the street. She had seen a telekinetic child lift an oak table and send it crashing through a window. She had communicated in utter silence with mind readers who received any message she sent to them. She had seen ghosts more palpable than anything she had ever believed could exist. Feats of psychometry, automatic writing, levitation, trance mediumship—all these she witnessed, jotting down her notes afterwards, and forever marveling at her own surprise.

Would she never get used to it? Take it for granted? Even the older members of the Talamasca confessed that they were continually shocked by the things they witnessed.

And without doubt Jesse's power to "see" was exceptionally strong. With constant use it developed enormously. Two years after entering the Talamasca, Jesse was being sent to haunted houses all over Europe and the United States. For every day or two spent in the peace and quiet of the library, there was a week in some drafty hallway watching the intermittent appearances of a silent specter who had frightened others.

Jesse seldom came to any conclusions about these apparitions. Indeed, she learned what all members of the Talamasca knew: there was no single theory of the occult to embrace all the strange things one saw or heard. The work was tantalizing, but ultimately frustrating. Jesse was unsure of herself when she addressed these "restless entities," or addlebrained spirits as Mael had once rather accurately described them. Yet Jesse advised them to move on to "higher levels," to seek peace for themselves and thereby leave mortals at peace also.

It seemed the only possible course to take, though it frightened her that she might be forcing these ghosts out of the only life that remained to them.

What if death were the end, and hauntings came about only when tenacious souls would not accept it? Too awful to think of that—of the spirit world as a dim and chaotic afterglow before the ultimate darkness.

Whatever the case, Jesse dispelled any number of hauntings. And she was constantly comforted by the relief of the living. There developed in her a profound sense of the specialness of her life. It was exciting. She wouldn't have swapped it for anything in the world.

Well, not for almost anything. After all, she might have left in a minute if Maharet had appeared on her doorstep and asked her to return to the Sonoma compound and take up the records of the Great Family in earnest. And then again perhaps not.

Jesse did have one experience with the Talamasca records, however, which caused her considerable personal confusion regarding the Great Family.

In transcribing the witch documents Jesse eventually discovered that the Talamasca had monitored for centuries certain "witch families" whose fortunes appeared to be influenced by supernatural intervention of a verifiable and predictable sort. The Talamasca was watching a number of such families right now! There was usually a "witch" in each generation of such a family, and this witch could, according to the record, attract and manipulate supernatural forces to ensure the family's steady accumulation of wealth and other success in human affairs. The power appeared to be hereditary—i.e., based in the physical—but no one knew for sure. Some of these families were now entirely ignorant as to their own history; they did not understand the "witches" who had manifested in the twentieth century. And though the Talamasca attempted regularly to make "contact" with such people, they were often rebuffed, or found the work too "dangerous" to pursue. After all, these witches could work actual *maleficia.*

Shocked and incredulous, Jesse did nothing after this discovery for several weeks. But she could not get the pattern out of her mind. It was too like the pattern of Maharet and the Great Family.

Then she did the only thing she could do without violating her loyalty to anybody. She carefully reviewed the records of every witch family in the Talamasca files. She checked and double-checked. She went back to the oldest records in existence and went over them minutely.

No mention of anyone named Maharet. No mention of anyone connected to any branch or surname of the Great Family that Jesse had ever heard of. No mention of anything even vaguely suspicious.

Her relief was enormous, but in the end, she was not surprised. Her instincts had told her she was on the wrong track. Maharet was no witch. Not in this sense of the word. *There was more to it than that.*

Yet in truth, Jesse never tried to figure it all out. She resisted theories about what had happened as she resisted theories about everything. And it occurred to her, more than once, that she had sought out the Talamasca in order to lose this personal mystery in a wilderness of mysteries. Surrounded by ghosts and poltergeists and possessed children, she thought less and less about Maharet and the Great Family.

BY THE time Jesse became a full member, she was an expert on the rules of the Talamasca, the procedures, the way to record investigations, when and how to help the police in crime cases, how to avoid all contact with the press. She also came to respect that the Talamasca was not a dogmatic organization. It did not require its members to believe *anything*, merely to be honest and careful about all the phenomena that they observed.

Patterns, similarities, repetitions—these fascinated the Talamasca. Terms abounded, but there was no rigid vocabulary. The files were merely cross-referenced in dozens of different ways.

Nevertheless members of the Talamasca studied the theoreticians. Jesse read the works of all the great psychic detectives, mediums, and mentalists. She studied anything and everything related to the occult.

And many a time she thought of Maharet's advice. What Maharet had said was true. Ghosts, apparitions, psychics who could read minds and move objects telekinetically—it was all fascinating to those who witnessed it firsthand. But to the human race at large it meant very little. There was not now, nor would there ever be, any great occult discovery that would alter human history.

But Jesse never tired of her work. She became addicted to the excitement, even the secrecy. She was within the womb of the Talamasca, and though she grew accustomed to the elegance of her surroundings—to antique lace and poster beds and sterling silver, to chauffeured cars and servants—she herself became ever more simple and reserved.

At thirty she was a fragile-looking light-skinned woman with her curly red hair parted in the middle and kept long so that it would fall behind her shoulders and leave her alone. She wore no cosmetics, perfume, or jewelry, except for the Celtic bracelet. A cashmere blazer was her favorite garment, along with wool pants, or jeans if she was in America. Yet she was an attractive person, drawing a little more attention from men than she thought was best. Love affairs she had, but they were always short. And seldom very important.

What mattered more were her friendships with the other members of the order; she had so many brothers and sisters. And they cared about her as she cared about them. She loved the feeling of the community surrounding her. At any hour of the night, one could go downstairs to a lighted parlor where people were awake—reading, talking, arguing perhaps in a subdued way. One could wander into the kitchen where the night cook was ever ready to prepare an early breakfast or a late dinner, whatever one might desire.

Jesse might have gone on forever with the Talamasca. Like a Catholic religious order, the Talamasca took care of its old and infirm. To die within the order was to know every luxury as well as every medical attention, to spend your last moments the way you wanted, alone in your bed, or with other members near you, comforting you, holding your hand. You could go home to your relatives if that was your choice. But most, over the years, chose to die in the Motherhouse. The funerals were dignified and elaborate. In the Talamasca, death was a part of life. A great gathering of black-dressed men and women witnessed each burial.

Yes, these had become Jesse's people. And in the natural course of events she would have remained forever.

But when she reached the end of her eighth year, something happened that was to change everything, something that led eventually to her break with the order.

Jesse's accomplishments up to that point had been impressive. But in the summer of 1981, she was still working under the direction of Aaron Lightner and she had seldom even spoken to the governing council of the Talamasca or the handful of men and women who were really in charge.

So when David Talbot, the head of the entire order, called her up to his office in London, she was surprised. David was an energetic man of sixty-five, heavy of build, with iron-gray hair and a consistently cheerful manner. He offered Jesse a glass of sherry and talked pleasantly about nothing for fifteen minutes before getting to the point.

Jesse was being offered a very different sort of assignment. He gave her a novel called *Interview with the Vampire.* He said, "I want you to read this book."

Jesse was puzzled. "The fact is, I have read it," she said. "It was a couple of years ago. But what does a novel like this have to do with us?"

Jesse had picked up a paperback copy at the airport and devoured it on a long transcontinental flight. The story, supposedly told by a vampire to a young reporter in present-day San Francisco, had affected Jesse rather like a bad dream. She wasn't sure she liked it. Matter of fact, she'd thrown it away later, rather than leave it on a bench at the next airport for fear some unsuspecting person might find it.

The main characters of the work—rather glamorous immortals when you got right down to it—had formed an evil little family in antebellum New Orleans where they preyed on the populace for over fifty years. Lestat was the villain of the piece, and the leader. Louis, his anguished subordinate, was the hero, and the one telling the tale. Claudia, their exquisite vampire "daughter," was a truly tragic figure, her mind maturing year after year while her body remained eternally that of a little girl. Louis's fruitless quest for redemption had been the theme of the book, obviously, but Claudia's hatred for the two male vampires who had made her what she was, and her own eventual destruction, had had a much stronger effect upon Jesse.

"The book isn't fiction," David explained simply. "Yet the purpose of creating it is unclear. And the act of publishing it, even as a novel, has us rather alarmed."

"Not fiction?" Jesse asked. "I don't understand."

"The author's name is a pseudonym," David continued, "and the royalty checks go to a nomadic young man who resists all our attempts at contact. He was a reporter, however, much like the boy interviewer in the novel. But that's neither here nor there at the moment. Your job is to go to New Orleans and document the events in the story which took place there before the Civil War."

"Wait a minute. You're telling me there are vampires? That these characters—Louis and Lestat and the little girl Claudia—are real!"

"Yes, exactly," David answered. "And don't forget about Armand, the mentor of the Théâtre des Vampires in Paris. You do remember Armand."

Jesse had no trouble remembering Armand or the theater. Armand, the oldest immortal in the novel, had had the face and form of an adolescent boy. As for the theater, it had been a gruesome establishment where human beings were killed on stage before an unsuspecting Parisian audience as part of the regular fare.

The entire nightmarish quality of the book was coming back to Jesse. Especially the parts that dealt with Claudia. Claudia had died in the Theater of the Vampires. The coven, under Armand's command, had destroyed her.

"David, am I understanding you correctly? You're saying these creatures exist?"

"Absolutely," David answered. "We've been observing this type of being since we came into existence. In a very real way, the Talamasca was formed to observe these creatures, but that's another story. In all probability, there are no fictional characters in this little novel whatsoever, but that would be your assignment, you see—to document the existence of the New Orleans coven, as described here—Claudia, Louis, Lestat."

Jesse laughed. She couldn't help it. She really laughed. David's patient expression only made her laugh more. But she wasn't surprising David, any more than her laughter had surprised Aaron Lightner eight years ago when they first met.

"Excellent attitude," David said, with a little mischievous smile. "We wouldn't want you to be too imaginative or trusting. But this field requires great care, Jesse, and strict obedience to the rules. Believe me when I say that this is an area which can be extremely dangerous. You are certainly free to turn down the assignment right now."

"I'm going to start laughing again," Jesse said. She had seldom if ever heard the word "dangerous" in the Talamasca. She had seen it in writing only in the witch family files. Now, she could believe in a witch family without much difficulty. Witches were human beings, and spirits could be manipulated, most probably. But vampires?

"Well, let's approach it this way," David said. "Before you make up your mind, we'll examine certain artifacts pertaining to these creatures which we have in the vaults."

The idea was irresistible. There were scores of rooms beneath the Motherhouse to which Jesse had never been admitted. She wasn't going to pass up this opportunity.

As she and David went down the stairs together, the atmosphere of the Sonoma compound came back to her unexpectedly and rather vividly. Even the long corridor with its occasional dim electric bulbs reminded her of Maharet's cellar. She found herself all the more excited.

She followed David silently through one locked storage room after another. She saw books, a skull on a shelf, what seemed old clothing heaped on the floor, furniture, oil paintings, trunks and strongboxes, dust.

"All this paraphernalia," David said, with a dismissive gesture, "is in one way or another connected to our blood-drinking immortal friends. They tend to be a rather materialistic lot, actually. And they leave behind them all sorts of refuse. It is not unknown for them to leave an entire household, complete with furnishings, clothing, and even coffins—very ornate and interesting coffins—when they tire of a particular location or identity. But there are some specific things which I must show you. It will all be rather conclusive, I should think."

Conclusive? There was something conclusive in this work? This was certainly an afternoon for surprises.

David led her into a final chamber, a very large room, paneled in tin and immediately illuminated by a bank of overhead lights.

She saw an enormous painting against the far wall. She placed it at once as Renaissance, and probably Venetian. It was done in egg tempera on wood. And it had the marvelous sheen of such paintings, a gloss that no synthetic material can create. She read the Latin title along with the name of the artist, in small Roman-style letters painted in the lower right corner.

"The Temptation of Amadeo"
by Marius

She stood back to study it.

A splendid choir of black-winged angels hovered around a single kneeling figure, that of a young auburn-haired boy. The cobalt sky behind them, seen through a series of arches, was splendidly done with masses of gilded clouds. And the marble floor before the figures had a photographic perfection to it. One could feel its coldness, see the veins in the stone.

But the figures were the true glory of the picture. The faces of the angels were exquisitely modeled, their pastel robes and black feathered wings extravagantly detailed. And the boy, the boy was very simply alive! His dark brown eyes veritably glistened as he stared forward out of the painting. His skin appeared moist. He was about to move or speak.

In fact, it was all too realistic to be Renaissance. The figures were particular rather than ideal. The angels wore expressions of faint amusement, almost bitterness. And the fabric of the boy's tunic and leggings, it was too exactly rendered. She could even see the mends in it, a tiny tear, the dust on his sleeve. There were other such details—dried leaves here and there on the floor, and two paintbrushes lying to one side for no apparent reason.

"Who is this Marius?" she whispered. The name meant nothing. And never had she seen an Italian painting with so many disturbing elements. Black-winged angels . . .

David didn't answer. He pointed to the boy. "It's the boy I want you to observe," he said. "He's not the real subject of your investigation, merely a very important link."

Subject? Link. . . . She was too engrossed in the picture. "And look, bones in the corner, human bones covered with dust, as if someone had merely swept them out of the way. But what on earth does it all mean?"

"Yes," David murmured. "When you see the word 'temptation,' usually there are devils surrounding a saint."

"Exactly," she answered. "And the craft is exceptional." The more she stared at the picture, the more disturbed she became. "Where did you get this?"

"The order acquired it centuries ago," David answered. "Our emissary in Venice retrieved it from a burnt-out villa on the Grand Canal. These vampires are endlessly associated with fires, by the way. It is the one weapon they can use effectively against one another. There are always fires. In *Interview with the Vampire,* there were several fires, if you recall. Louis set fire to a town house in New Orleans when he was trying to destroy his maker and mentor, Lestat. And later, Louis burned the Theater of the Vampires in Paris after Claudia's death."

Claudia's death. It sent a shiver through Jesse, startling her slightly.

"But look at this boy carefully," David said. "It's the boy we're discussing now."

Amadeo. It meant "one who loves God." He was a handsome creature, all right. Sixteen, maybe seventeen, with a square, strongly proportioned face and a curiously imploring expression.

David had put something in her hand. Reluctantly she took her eyes off the painting. She found herself staring at a tintype, a late-nineteenth-century photograph. After a moment, she whispered: "This is the same boy!"

"Yes. And something of an experiment," David said. "It was most likely taken just after sunset in impossible lighting conditions which might not have worked with another subject. Notice not much is really visible but his face."

True, yet she could see the style of the hair was of the period.

"You might look at this as well," David said. And this time he gave her an old magazine, a nineteenth-century journal, the kind with narrow columns of tiny print and ink illustrations. There was the same boy again alighting from a barouche—a hasty sketch, though the boy was smiling.

"The article's about him, and about his Theater of the Vampires. Here's an English journal from 1789. That's a full eighty years earlier, I believe. But you will find another very thorough description of the establishment and the same young man."

"The Theater of the Vampires . . ." She stared up at the auburn-haired boy kneeling in the painting. "Why, this is Armand, the character in the novel!"

"Precisely. He seems to like that name. It may have been Amadeo when he was in Italy, but it became Armand by the eighteenth century and he's used Armand ever since."

"Slow down, please," Jesse said. "You're telling me that the Theater of the Vampires has been documented? By our people?"

"Thoroughly. The file's enormous. Countless memoirs describe the theater. We have the deeds to the property as well. And here we come to another link with our files and this little novel, *Interview with the Vampire.* The name of the owner of the theater was Lestat de Lioncourt, who purchased it in 1789. And the property in modern Paris is in the hands of a man by the same name even now."

"This is verified?" Jesse said.

"It's all in the file," David said, "photostats of the old records and the recent ones. You can study the signature of Lestat if you like. Lestat does everything in a big way—covers half the page with his magnificent lettering. We have photostats of several examples. We want you to take those photostats to New Orleans with you. There's a newspaper account of the fire which destroyed the theater exactly as Louis described it. The date is consistent with the facts of the story. You must go over everything, of course. And the novel, do read it again carefully."

BY THE end of the week, Jesse was on a plane for New Orleans. She was to annotate and document the novel, in every way possible, searching property titles, transfers, old newspapers, journals—anything she could find to support the theory that the characters and events were real.

But Jesse still didn't believe it. Undoubtedly there was "something here," but there had to be a catch. And the catch was in all probability a clever historical novelist who had stumbled upon some interesting research and woven it into a fictional story. After all, theater tickets, deeds, programs, and the like do not prove the existence of bloodsucking immortals.

As for the rules Jesse had to follow, she thought they were a scream.

She was not allowed to remain in New Orleans except between the hours of sunrise and four p.m. At four p.m. she had to drive north to the city of Baton Rouge and spend the nights safe within a sixteenth-story room in a modern hotel. If she should have the slightest feeling that someone was watching her or following her, she was to make for the safety of a large crowd at once. From a well-lighted and populated place, she was to call the Talamasca long distance in London immediately.

Never, under any circumstances, must she attempt a "sighting" of one of these vampire individuals. The parameters of vampiric power were not known to the Talamasca. But one thing was certain: the beings could read minds. Also, they could create mental confusion in human beings. And there was considerable evidence that they were exceptionally strong. Most certainly they could kill.

Also some of them, without doubt, knew of the existence of the Talamasca. Over the centuries, several members of the order had disappeared during this type of investigation.

Jesse was to read the daily papers scrupulously. The Talamasca had reason to believe that there were no vampires in New Orleans at present.

Or Jesse would not be going there. But at any time, Lestat, Armand, or Louis might appear. If Jesse came across an article about a suspicious death she was to get out of the city and not return.

Jesse thought all this was hilarious. Even a handful of old items about mysterious deaths did not impress her or frighten her. After all, these people could have been the victims of a satanic cult. And they were all too human.

But Jesse had wanted this assignment.

On the way to the airport, David had asked her why. "If you really can't accept what I'm telling you, then why do you want to investigate the book?"

She'd taken her time in answering. "There is something obscene about this novel. It makes the lives of these beings seem attractive. You don't realize it at first; it's a nightmare and you can't get out of it. Then all of a sudden you're comfortable there. You want to remain. Even the tragedy of Claudia isn't really a deterrent."

"And?"

"I want to prove it's fiction," Jesse said.

That was good enough for the Talamasca, especially coming from a trained investigator.

But on the long flight to New York, Jesse had realized there was something she couldn't tell David. She had only just faced it herself. *Interview with the Vampire* "reminded" her of that long ago summer with Maharet, though Jesse didn't know why. Again and again she stopped her reading to think about that summer. And little things were coming back to her. She was even dreaming about it again. Quite beside the point, she told herself. Yet there was some connection, something to do with the atmosphere of the book, the mood, even the attitudes of the characters, and the whole manner in which things seemed one way and were really not that way at all. But Jesse could not figure it out. Her reason, like her memory, was curiously blocked.

JESSE's first few days in New Orleans were the strangest in her entire psychic career.

The city had a moist Caribbean beauty, and a tenacious colonial flavor that charmed her at once. Yet everywhere Jesse went she "felt" things. The entire place seemed haunted. The awesome antebellum mansions were seductively silent and gloomy. Even the French Quarter streets, crowded with tourists, had a sensuous and sinister atmosphere that kept her forever walking out of her way or stopping for long periods to dream as she sat slumped on a bench in Jackson Square.

She hated to leave the city at four o'clock. The high-rise hotel in Baton Rouge provided a divine degree of American luxury. Jesse liked that well enough. But the soft lazy ambience of New Orleans clung to her. She awoke each morning dimly aware that she'd dreamed of the vampire characters. And of Maharet.

Then, four days into her investigation, she made a series of discoveries that sent her directly to the phone. There most certainly had been a Lestat de Lioncourt on the tax rolls in Louisiana. In fact, in 1862 he had taken possession of a Royal Street town house from his business partner, Louis de Pointe du Lac. Louis de Pointe du Lac had owned seven different pieces of Louisiana property, and one of them had been the plantation described in *Interview with the Vampire.* Jesse was flabbergasted. She was also delighted.

But there were even more discoveries. Somebody named Lestat de Lioncourt owned houses all over the city right now. And this person's signature, appearing in records dated 1895 and 1910, was identical to the eighteenth-century signatures.

Oh, this was too marvelous. Jesse was having a wonderful time.

At once she set out to photograph Lestat's properties. Two were Garden District mansions, clearly uninhabitable and falling to ruin behind rusted gates. But the rest, including the Royal Street town house—the very same deeded to Lestat in 1862—were rented by a local agency which made payment to an attorney in Paris.

This was more than Jesse could bear. She cabled David for money. She must buy out the tenants in Royal Street, for this was surely the house once inhabited by Lestat, Louis, and the child Claudia. They may or may not have been vampires, but they lived there!

David wired the money immediately, along with strict instructions that she mustn't go near the ruined mansions she'd described. Jesse answered at once that she'd already examined these places. Nobody had been in them for years.

It was the town house that mattered. By week's end she'd bought out the lease. The tenants left cheerfully with fists full of cash. And early on a Monday morning, Jesse walked into the empty second-floor flat.

Deliciously dilapidated. The old mantels, moldings, doors all there!

Jesse went to work with a screwdriver and chisel in the front rooms. Louis had described a fire in these parlors in which Lestat had been badly burnt. Well, Jesse would find out.

Within an hour she had uncovered the burnt timbers! And the plasterers—bless them—when they had come to cover up the damage, they had stuffed the holes with old newspapers dated 1862. This fitted with Louis's account perfectly. He'd signed the town house over to Lestat, made plans to leave for Paris, then came the fire during which Louis and Claudia had fled.

Of course Jesse told herself she was still skeptical, but the characters of the book were becoming curiously real. The old black telephone in the hall had been disconnected. She had to go out to call David, which annoyed her. She wanted to tell him everything right now.

But she didn't go out. On the contrary, she merely sat in the parlor for hours, feeling the warm sun on the rough floorboards around her, listening to the creaking of the building. A house of this age is never quiet, not in a humid climate. It feels like a living thing. No ghosts here, not that she could see anyway. Yet she didn't feel alone. On the contrary, there was an embracing warmth. Someone shook her to wake her up suddenly. No, of course not. No one here but her. A clock chiming four . . .

The next day she rented a wallpaper steamer and went to work in the other rooms. She must get down to the original coverings. Patterns could be dated, and besides she was looking for something in particular. But there was a canary singing nearby, possibly in another flat or shop, and the song distracted her. So lovely. Don't forget the canary. The canary will die if you forget it. Again, she fell asleep.

It was well after dark when she awakened. She could hear the nearby music of a harpsichord. For a long time, she'd listened before opening her eyes. Mozart, very fast. Too fast, but what skill. A great rippling riff of notes, a stunning virtuosity. Finally she forced herself to get up and turn on the overhead lights and plug in the steamer again.

The steamer was heavy; the hot water dripped down her arm. In each room she stripped a section of wall to the original plaster, then she moved on. But the droning noise of the thing bothered her. She seemed to hear voices in it—people laughing, talking to one another, someone speaking French in a low urgent whisper, and a child crying—or was it a woman?

She'd turn the damn thing off. Nothing. Just a trick of the noise itself in the empty echoing flat.

She went back to work with no consciousness of time, or that she had not eaten, or that she was getting drowsy. On and on she moved the heavy thing until quite suddenly in the middle bedroom she found what she'd been seeking—a hand-painted mural on a bare plaster wall.

For a moment, she was too excited to move. Then she went to work in a frenzy. Yes, it was the mural of the "magical forest" that Lestat had commissioned for Claudia. And in rapid sweeps of the dripping steamer she uncovered more and more.

"Unicorns and golden birds and laden fruit trees over sparkling streams." It was exactly as Louis had described it. Finally she had laid bare a great portion of the mural running around all four walls. Claudia's room, this, without question. Her head was spinning. She was weak from not eating. She glanced at her watch. One o'clock.

One o'clock! She'd been here half the night. She should go now, immediately! This was the first time in all these years that she'd broken a rule!

Yet she could not bring herself to move. She was so tired, in spite of her excitement. She was sitting against the marble mantel, and the light from the ceiling bulb was so dreary, and her head hurt, too. Yet she kept staring at the gilded birds, the small, wonderfully wrought flowers and trees. The sky was a deep vermilion, yet there was a full moon in it and no sun, and a great drifting spread of tiny stars. Bits of hammered silver still clinging to the stars.

Gradually she noticed a stone wall painted in the background in one corner. There was a castle behind it. How lovely to walk through the forest towards it, to go through the carefully painted wooden gate. Pass into another realm. She heard a song in her head, something she'd all but forgotten, something Maharet used to sing.

Then quite abruptly she saw that the gate was painted over an actual opening in the wall!

She sat forward. She could see the seams in the plaster. Yes, a square opening, which she had not seen, laboring behind the heavy steamer. She knelt down in front of it and touched it. A wooden door. Immediately she took the screwdriver and tried to pry it open. No luck. She worked on one edge and then the other. But she was only scarring the picture to no avail.

She sat back on her heels and studied it. A painted gate covering a wooden door. And there was a worn spot right where the painted handle was. Yes! She reached out and gave the worn spot a little jab. The door sprang open. It was as simple as that.

She lifted her flashlight. A compartment lined in cedar. And there were things there. A small white leather-bound book! A rosary, it looked like, and a doll, a very old porcelain doll.

For a moment she couldn't bring herself to touch these objects. It was like desecrating a tomb. And there was a faint scent there as of perfume. She wasn't dreaming, was she? No, her head hurt too much for this to be a dream. She reached into the compartment, and removed the doll first.

The body was crude by modern standards, yet the wooden limbs were well jointed and formed. The white dress and lavender sash were decaying, falling into bits and pieces. But the porcelain head was lovely, the large blue paperweight eyes perfect, the wig of flowing blond hair still intact.

"Claudia," she whispered.

Her voice made her conscious of the silence. No traffic now at this hour. Only the old boards creaking. And the soft soothing flicker of an oil lamp on a nearby table. And then that harpsichord from somewhere, someone playing Chopin now, the Minute Waltz, with the same dazzling skill she'd heard before. She sat still, looking down at the doll in her lap. She wanted to brush its hair, fix its sash.

The climactic events of *Interview with the Vampire* came back to her—Claudia destroyed in Paris. Claudia caught by the deadly light of the rising sun in a brick-lined airshaft from which she couldn't escape. Jesse felt a dull shock, and the rapid silent beat of her heart against her throat. Claudia gone, while the others continued. Lestat, Louis, Armand. . . .

Then with a start, she realized she was looking at the other things inside the compartment. She reached for the book.

A diary! The pages were fragile, spotted. But the old-fashioned sepia script was still readable, especially now that the oil lamps were all lighted, and the room had a cozy brightness to it. She could translate the French effortlessly. The first entry was September 21, 1836:

> This is my birthday present from Louis. Use as I like, he tells me. But perhaps I should like to copy into it those occasional poems which strike my fancy, and read these to him now and then?
>
> I do not understand entirely what is meant by birthday. Was I born into this world on the 21st of September or was it on that day that I departed all things human to become this?
>
> My gentlemen parents are forever reluctant to illuminate such simple matters. One would think it bad taste to dwell on such subjects. Louis looks puzzled, then miserable, before he returns to the evening paper. And Lestat, he smiles and plays a little Mozart for me, then answers with a shrug: "It was the day you were born *to us.*"
>
> Of course, he gave me a doll as usual, the replica of me, which as always wears a duplicate of my newest dress. To France he sends for these dolls, he wants me to know. And what should I do with it? Play with it as if I were really a child?
>
> "Is there a message here, my beloved father?" I asked him this evening. "That I shall be a doll forever myself?" He has given me thirty such dolls over the years if recollection serves me. And recollection never does anything else. Each doll has been exactly like the rest. They would crowd me out of my bedroom if I kept them. But I do not keep them. I burn them, sooner or later. I smash their china faces with the poker. I watch the fire eat their hair. I can't say that I like doing this. After all, the dolls are beautiful. And they do resemble me. Yet, it becomes the appropriate gesture. The doll expects it. So do I.

And now he has brought me another, and he stands in my doorway staring at me afterwards, as if my question cut him. And the expression on his face is so dark suddenly, I think, this cannot be my Lestat.

I wish that I could hate him. I wish that I could hate them both. But they defeat me not with their strength but with their weakness. They are so loving! And so pleasing to look at. Mon Dieu, how the women go after them!

As he stood there watching me, watching me examine this doll he had given me, I asked him sharply:

"Do you like what you see?"

"You don't want them anymore, do you?" he whispered.

"Would you want them," I asked, "if you were me?"

The expression on his face grew even darker. Never have I seen him the way he looked. A scorching heat came into his face, and it seemed he blinked to clear his vision. His perfect vision. He left me and went into the parlor. I went after him. In truth, I couldn't bear to see him the way he was, yet I pursued him. "Would you like them," I asked, "if you were me?"

He stared at me as if I frightened him, and he a man of six feet and I a child no more than half that, at best.

"Am I beautiful to you?" I demanded.

He went past me down the hall, out the back door. But I caught up with him. I held tight to his sleeve as he stood at the top of the stairs. "Answer me!" I said to him. "Look at me. What do you see?"

He was in a dreadful state. I thought he'd pull away, laugh, flash his usual brimming colors. But instead he dropped to his knees before me and took hold of both my arms. He kissed me roughly on the mouth. "I love you," he whispered. "I love you!" As if it were a curse he laid on me, and then he spoke this poetry to me:

Cover her face;
mine eyes dazzle;
she died young.

Webster it is, I am almost certain. One of those plays Lestat so loves. I wonder . . . will Louis be pleased by this little poem? I cannot imagine why not. It is small but very pretty.

Jesse closed the book gently. Her hand was trembling. She lifted the doll and held it against her breast, her body rocking slightly as she sat back against the painted wall.

"Claudia," she whispered.

Her head throbbed, but it didn't matter. The light of the oil lamps was so soothing, so different from the harsh electric bulb. She sat still, caressing the doll with her fingers almost in the manner of a blind woman, feeling its soft silken hair, its stiff starched little dress. The clock chimed again, loudly, each somber note echoing through the room. She must not faint here. She must get up somehow. She must take the little book and the doll and the rosary and leave.

The empty windows were like mirrors with the night behind them. Rules broken. Call David, yes, call David now. But the phone was ringing. At this hour, imagine. The phone ringing. And David didn't have any number for this flat because the phone. . . . She tried to ignore it, but it went on and on ringing. All right, answer it!

She kissed the doll's forehead. "Be right back, my darling," she whispered.

Where was the damn phone in this flat anyway? In the niche in the hallway, of course. She had almost reached it when she saw the wire with the frayed end, curled around it. It wasn't connected. She could see it wasn't connected. Yet it was ringing, she could hear it, and it was no auditory hallucination, the thing was giving one shrill pulse after another! And the oil lamps! My God, there were no oil lamps in this flat!

All right, you've seen things like this before. Don't panic, for the love of God. Think! What should you do? But she was about to scream. The phone would not stop ringing! If you panic, you will lose control utterly. You must turn off these lamps, stop this phone! But the lamps can't be real. And the living room at the end of the hall—the furniture's not real! The flicker of the fire, not real! And the person moving in there, who is it, a man? Don't look up at him! She reached out and shoved the phone out of the niche so that it fell to the floor. The receiver rolled on its back. Tiny and thin, a woman's voice came out of it.

"Jesse?"

In blind terror, she ran back to the bedroom, stumbling over the leg of a chair, falling against the starched drapery of a four-poster bed. Not real. Not there. Get the doll, the book, the rosary! Stuffing them in her canvas bag, she climbed to her feet and ran out of the flat to the back stairway. She almost fell as her feet hit the slippery iron. The garden, the fountain— But you know there's nothing there but weeds. There was a wrought-iron gate blocking her path. Illusion. Go through it! Run!

It was the proverbial nightmare and she was caught in it, the sounds of horses and carriages thudding in her ears as she ran down the cobblestone pavement. Each clumsy gesture stretched over eternity, her hands struggling to get the car keys, to get the door open, and then the car refusing to start.

By the time she reached the edge of the French Quarter, she was sobbing and her body was drenched with sweat. On she drove through the shabby garish downtown streets towards the freeway. Blocked at the on-ramp, she turned her head. Back seat empty. OK, they didn't follow. And the canvas bag was in her lap; she could feel the hard porcelain head of the doll against her breast. She floored it to Baton Rouge.

She was sick by the time she reached the hotel. She could barely walk to the desk. An aspirin, a thermometer. Please help me to the elevator.

When she woke up eight hours later, it was noon. The canvas bag was still in her arms. Her temperature was 104. She called David, but the connection was dreadful. He called her back; it was still no good. Nevertheless she tried to make herself understood. The diary, it was Claudia's, absolutely, it confirmed everything! And the phone, it wasn't connected, yet she heard the woman's voice! The oil lamps, they'd been burning when she ran out of the flat. The flat had been filled with furniture; there'd been fires in the grates. Could they burn down the flat, these lamps and fires? David must do something! And he was answering her, but she could barely hear him. She had the bag, she told him, he must not worry.

It was dark when she opened her eyes. The pain in her head had woken her up. The digital clock on the dresser said ten thirty. Thirst, terrible thirst, and the glass by the bed was empty. *Someone else was in the room.*

She turned over on her back. Light through the thin white curtains. Yes, there. A child, a little girl. She was sitting in the chair against the wall.

Jesse could just see the outline clearly—the long yellow hair, the puff-sleeved dress, the dangling legs that didn't touch the floor. She tried to focus. Child . . . not possible. Apparition. No. Something occupying space. Something malevolent. Menace— And the child was looking at her.

Claudia.

She scrambled out of the bed, half falling, the bag in her arms still as she backed up against the wall. The little girl got up. There was the clear sound of her feet on the carpet. The sense of menace seemed to grow stronger. The child moved into the light from the window as she came towards Jesse, and the light struck her blue eyes, her rounded cheeks, her soft naked little arms.

Jesse screamed. Clutching the bag against her, she rushed blindly in the direction of the door. She clawed at the lock and chain, afraid to look over her shoulder. The screams were coming out of her uncontrollably. Someone was calling from the other side, and finally she had the door open and she was stumbling out into the hallway.

People surrounded her; but they couldn't stop her from getting away from the room. But then someone was helping her up because apparently she'd fallen again. Someone else had gotten a chair. She cried, trying to be quiet, yet unable to stop it, and she held the bag with the doll and the diary in both hands.

When the ambulance arrived, she refused to let them take the bag away from her. In the hospital they gave her antibiotics, sedatives, enough dope to drive anyone to insanity. She lay curled up like a child in the bed with the bag beside her under the covers. If the nurse so much as touched it, Jesse woke at once.

When Aaron Lightner arrived two days later, she gave it to him. She was still sick when she got on the plane for London. The bag was in his lap, and he was so good to her, calming her, caring for her, as she slept on and off on the long flight home. It was only just before they landed that she realized her bracelet was gone, her beautiful silver bracelet. She'd cried softly with her eyes closed. Mael's bracelet gone.

THEY pulled her off the assignment.

She knew even before they told her. She was too young for this work, they said, too inexperienced. It had been their mistake, sending her. It was simply too dangerous for her to continue. Of course what she had done was of "immense value." And the haunting, it had been one of unusual power. The spirit of a dead vampire? Entirely possible. And the ringing phone, well, there were many reports of such things—entities used various means to "communicate" or frighten. Best to rest now, put it out of her mind. Others would continue the investigation.

As for the diary, it included only a few more entries, nothing more significant than what she herself had read. The psychometrics who had examined the rosary and the doll learned nothing. These things would be stored with utmost care. But Jesse really must remove her mind from all this immediately.

Jesse argued. She begged to go back. She threw a scene of sorts, finally. But it was like talking to the Vatican. Some day, ten years from now, maybe twenty, she could enter this particular field again. No one was ruling out such a possibility, but for the present the answer was no. Jesse was to rest, get better, forget what had taken place.

Forget what had taken place. . . .

She was sick for weeks. She wore white flannel gowns all day long and drank endless cups of hot tea. She sat in the window seat of her room. She looked out on the soft deep greenery of the park, at the heavy old oak trees.

She watched the cars come and go, tiny bits of soundless color moving on the distant gravel road. Lovely here, such stillness. They brought her delicious things to eat, to drink. David came and talked softly to her of anything but the vampires. Aaron filled her room with flowers. Others came.

She talked little, or not at all. She could not explain to them how deeply this hurt her, how it reminded her of the long ago summer when she'd been pushed away from other secrets, other mysteries, other documents in vaults. It was the same old story. She'd glimpsed something of inestimable importance, only to have it locked away.

And now she would never understand what she'd seen or experienced. She must remain here in silence with her regrets. Why hadn't she picked up that phone, spoken into it, listened to the voice on the other end?

And the child, what had the spirit of the child wanted! Was it the diary or the doll! No, Jesse had been meant to find them and remove them! And yet she had turned away from the spirit of the child! She who had addressed so many nameless entities, who had stood bravely in darkened rooms talking to weak flickering things when others fled in panic. She who comforted others with the old assurance: these beings, whatever they are, cannot do us harm!

One more chance, she pleaded. She went over everything that had happened. She must return to that New Orleans flat. David and Aaron were silent. Then David came to her and put his arm around her.

"Jesse, my darling," he said. "We love you. But in this area above all others, one simply does not break the rules."

At night she dreamed of Claudia. Once she woke at four o'clock and went to the window and looked out over the park straining to see past the dim lights from the lower windows. There was a child out there, a tiny figure beneath the trees, in a red cloak and hood, a child looking up at her. She had run down the stairs, only to find herself stranded finally on the empty wet grass with the cold gray morning coming.

IN THE spring they sent her to New Delhi.

She was to document evidence of reincarnation, reports from little children in India that they remembered former lives. There had been much promising work done in this field by a Dr. Ian Stevenson. And Jesse was to undertake an independent study on behalf of the Talamasca which might produce equally fruitful results.

Two elder members of the order met her in Delhi. They made her right at home in the old British mansion where they lived. She grew to love the work; and after the initial shocks and minor discomforts, she grew to love India as well. By the end of the year she was happy—and useful—again.

And something else happened, a rather small thing, yet it seemed a good omen. In a pocket of her old suitcase—the one Maharet had sent her years ago—she'd found Mael's silver bracelet.

Yes, happy she had been.

But she did not forget what had happened. There were nights when she would remember so vividly the image of Claudia that she would get up and turn on every light in the room. At other times she thought she saw around her in the city streets strange white-faced beings very like the characters in *Interview with the Vampire.* She felt she was being watched.

Because she could not tell Maharet about this strange adventure, her letters became even more hurried and superficial. Yet Maharet was as faithful as ever. When members of the family came to Delhi, they visited Jesse. They tried to keep her in the fold. They sent her news of weddings, births, funerals. They begged her to visit during the holidays. Matthew and Maria wrote from America, begging Jesse to come home soon. They missed her.

JESSE spent four happy years in India. She documented over three hundred individual cases which included startling evidence of reincarnation. She worked with some of the finest psychic investigators she had ever known. And she found her work continuously rewarding, almost comforting. Very unlike the chasing of haunts which she had done in her early years.

In the fall of her fifth year, she finally yielded to Matthew and Maria. She would come home to the States for a four-week visit. They were overjoyed.

The reunion meant more to Jesse than she had ever thought it would. She loved being back in the old New York apartment. She loved the late night dinners with her adopted parents. They didn't question her about her work. Left alone during the day, she called old college friends for lunch or took long solitary walks through the bustling urban landscape of all her childhood hopes and dreams and griefs.

Two weeks after her return, Jesse saw *The Vampire Lestat* in the window of a bookstore. For a moment, she thought she'd made a mistake. Not possible. But there it was. The bookstore clerk told her of the record album by the same name, and the upcoming San Francisco concert. Jesse bought a ticket on the way home at the record store where she purchased the album.

All day Jesse lay alone in her room reading the book. It was as if the nightmare of *Interview with the Vampire* had returned and, once again, she could not get out of it. Yet she was strangely compelled by every word. *Yes, real, all of you.* And how the tale twisted and turned as it moved back in time to the Roman coven of Santino, to the island refuge of Marius, and to the Druid grove of Mael. And finally to Those Who Must Be Kept, alive yet hard and white as marble.

Ah, yes, she had touched that stone! She had looked into Mael's eyes; she had felt the clasp of Santino's hand. She had seen the painting done by Marius in the vault of the Talamasca!

When she closed her eyes to sleep, she saw Maharet on the balcony of the Sonoma compound. The moon was high above the tips of the redwoods. And the warm night seemed unaccountably full of promise and danger. Eric and Mael were there. So were others whom she'd never seen except in Lestat's pages. All of the same tribe; eyes incandescent, shimmering hair, skin a poreless shining substance. On her silver bracelet she had traced a thousand times the old Celtic symbols of gods and goddesses to whom the Druids spoke in woodland groves like that to which Marius had once been taken prisoner. How many links did she require between these esoteric fictions and the unforgettable summer?

One more, without question. The Vampire Lestat himself—in San Francisco, where she would see him and touch him—that would be the final link. She would know then, in that physical moment, the answer to everything.

The clock ticked. Her loyalty to the Talamasca was dying in the warm quiet. She could tell them not a word of it. And such a tragedy it was, when they would have cared so much and so selflessly; they would have doubted none of it.

The lost afternoon. She was there again. Going down into Maharet's cellar by the spiral stairway. Could she not push back the door? Look. See what you saw then. Something not so horrible at first glance—merely those she knew and loved, asleep in the dark, asleep. But Mael lies on the cold floor as if dead and Maharet sits against the wall, upright like a statue. Her eyes are open!

She awoke with a start, her face flushed, the room cold and dim around her. "Miriam," she said aloud. Gradually the panic subsided. She had drawn closer, so afraid. She had touched Maharet. Cold, petrified. And Mael dead! The rest was darkness.

New York. She lay on the bed with the book in her hand. And Miriam didn't come to her. Slowly, she climbed to her feet and walked across the bedroom to the window.

There, opposite in the dirty afternoon gloom, stood the high narrow phantom town house of Stanford White. She stared until the bulky image gradually faded.

From the album cover propped on the dresser the Vampire Lestat smiled at her.

She closed her eyes. She envisioned the tragic pair of Those Who Must Be Kept. Indestructible King and Queen on their Egyptian throne, to whom the Vampire Lestat sang his hymns out of the radios and the jukeboxes and from the little tapes people carried with them. She saw Maharet's white face glowing in the shadows. Alabaster. The stone that is always full of light.

Dusk falling, suddenly as it does in the late fall, the dull afternoon fading into the sharp brightness of evening. Traffic roared through the crowded street, echoing up the sides of the buildings. Did ever traffic sound so loud as in the streets of New York? She leaned her forehead against the glass. Stanford White's house was visible in the corner of her eye. There were figures moving inside it.

JESSE left New York the next afternoon, in Matt's old roadster. She paid him for the car in spite of his arguments. She knew she'd never bring it back. Then she embraced her parents and, as casually as she could, she told them all the simple heartfelt things she'd always wanted them to know.

That morning, she had sent an express letter to Maharet, along with the two "vampire" novels. She explained that she had left the Talamasca, she was going to the Vampire Lestat's concert out west, and she wanted to stop at the Sonoma compound. She had to see Lestat, it was of crucial importance. Would her old key fit the lock of the Sonoma house? Would Maharet allow her to stop there?

It was the first night in Pittsburgh that she dreamed of the twins. She saw the two women kneeling before the altar. She saw the cooked body ready to be devoured. She saw one twin lift the plate with the heart; the other the plate with the brain. Then the soldiers, the sacrilege.

By the time she reached Salt Lake City she had dreamed of the twins three times. She had seen them raped in a hazy and terrifying scene. She had seen a baby born to one of the sisters. She had seen the baby hidden when the twins were again hunted down and taken prisoner. Had they been killed? She could not tell. The red hair. If only she could see their faces, their eyes! The red hair tormented her.

Only when she called David from a roadside pay phone did she learn that others had had these dreams—psychics and mediums the world over. Again and again the connection had been made to the Vampire Lestat. David told Jesse to come home immediately.

Jesse tried to explain gently. She was going to the concert to see Lestat for herself. She had to. There was more to tell, but it was too late now. David must try to forgive her.

"You will not do this, Jessica," David said. "What is happening is no simple matter for records and archives. You must come back, Jessica. The truth is, you are needed here. You are needed desperately. It's unthinkable that you should attempt this 'sighting' on your own. Jesse, listen to what I'm telling you."

"I can't come back, David. I've always loved you. Loved you all. But tell me. It's the last question I'll ever ask you. How can you not come yourself?"

"Jesse, you're not listening to me."

"David, the truth. Tell me the truth. Have you ever really believed in them? Or has it always been a question of artifacts and files and paintings in vaults, things you can see and touch! You know what I'm saying, David. Think of the Catholic priest, when he speaks the words of consecration at Mass. Does he really believe Christ is on the altar? Or is it just a matter of chalices and sacramental wine and the choir singing?"

Oh, what a liar she had been to keep so much from him yet press him so hard. But his answer had not disappointed her.

"Jesse, you've got it wrong. I know what these creatures are. I've always known. There's never been the slightest doubt with me. And on account of that, no power on earth could induce me to attend this concert. It is you who can't accept the truth. You'll have to see it to believe it! Jesse, the danger's real. Lestat is exactly what he professes to be, and there will be others there, even more dangerous, others who may spot you for what you are and try to hurt you. Realize this and do as I tell you. Come home now."

What a raw and painful moment. He was striving to reach her, and she was only telling him farewell. He had said other things, that he would tell her "the whole story," that he would open the files to her, that she was needed on this very matter by them all.

But her mind had been drifting. She couldn't tell him her "whole story," that was the sorrow. She'd been drowsy again, the dream threatening as she hung up the phone. She'd seen the plates, the body on the altar. Their mother. Yes, their mother. Time to sleep. The dream wants in. And then go on.

. . .

HIGHWAY 101. Seven thirty-five p.m. Twenty-five minutes until the concert.

She had just come through the mountain pass on the Waldo Grade and there was the old miracle—the great crowded skyline of San Francisco tumbling over the hills, far beyond the black glaze of the water. The towers of the Golden Gate loomed ahead of her, the ice cold wind off the Bay freezing her naked hands as she gripped the steering wheel.

Would the Vampire Lestat be on time? It made her laugh to think of an immortal creature having to be *on time.* Well, she would be on time; the journey was almost ended.

All grief was gone now, for David and Aaron and those she'd loved. There was no grief either for the Great Family. Only the gratitude for all of it. Yet maybe David was right. Perhaps she had not accepted the cold frightening truth of the matter, but had merely slipped into the realm of memories and ghosts, of pale creatures who were the proper stuff of dreams and madness.

She was walking towards the phantom town house of Stanford White, and it didn't matter now who lived there. She would be welcome. They had been trying to tell her that ever since she could remember.

PART II

ALL HALLOW'S EVE

Very little is
more worth our time
than understanding
the talent of Substance.
. . .
A bee, a living bee,
at the windowglass, trying to get out, doomed,
it can't understand.

STAN RICE
Untitled Poem
from
Pig's Progress (1976)

Daniel

LONG curving lobby; the crowd was like liquid sloshing against the colorless walls. Teenagers in Halloween costume poured through the front doors; lines were forming to purchase yellow wigs, black satin capes—"Fang teeth, fifty cents!"—glossy programs. Whiteface everywhere he looked. Painted eyes and mouths. And here and there bands of men and women carefully done up in authentic nineteenth-century clothes, their makeup and coiffed hair exquisite.

A velvet-clad woman tossed a great shower of dead rosebuds into the air above her head. Painted blood flowed down her ashen cheeks. Laughter.

He could smell the greasepaint, and the beer, so alien now to his senses: rotten. The hearts beating all around him made a low, delicious thunder against the tender tympana of his ears.

He must have laughed out loud, because he felt the sharp pinch of Armand's fingers on his arm. "Daniel!"

"Sorry, boss," he whispered. Nobody was paying a damn bit of attention anyway; every mortal within sight was disguised; and who were Armand and Daniel but two pale nondescript young men in the press, black sweaters, jeans, hair partially hidden under sailor's caps of blue wool, eyes behind dark glasses. "So what's the big deal? I can't laugh out loud, especially now that everything is so funny?"

Armand was distracted; listening again. Daniel couldn't get it through his head to be afraid. He had what he wanted now. None of you my brothers and sisters!

Armand had said to him earlier, "You take a lot of teaching." That was during the hunt, the seduction, the kill, the flood of blood through his greedy heart. But he had become a natural at being unnatural, hadn't he, after the clumsy anguish of the first murder, the one that had taken him from shuddering guilt to ecstasy within seconds. Life by the mouthful. He'd woken up thirsting.

And thirty minutes ago, they'd taken two exquisite little vagabonds in the ruins of a derelict school by the park where the kids lived in boarded-up rooms with sleeping bags and rags and little cans of Sterno to cook the food they stole from the Haight-Ashbury dumpsters. No protests this time around. No, just the thirsting and the ever increasing sense of the perfection and the inevitability of it, the preternatural memory of the taste faultless. Hurry. Yet there had been such an art to it with Armand, none of the rush of the night before when time had been the crucial element.

Armand had stood quietly outside the building, scanning it, waiting for "those who wanted to die"; that was the way he liked to do it; you called to them silently and they came out. And the death had a serenity to it. He'd tried to show that trick to Louis long ago, he'd said, but Louis had found it distasteful.

And sure enough the denim-clad cherubs had come wandering through the side door, as if hypnotized by the music of the Pied Piper. "Yes, you came, we knew you'd come. . . ." Dull flat voices welcoming them as they were led up the stairs and into a parlor made out of army blankets on ropes. To die in this garbage in the sweep of the passing headlights through the cracks in the plywood.

Hot dirty little arms around Daniel's neck; reek of hashish in her hair; he could scarcely stand it, the dance, her hips against him, then driving his fangs into the flesh. "You love me, you know you do," she'd said. And he'd answered yes with a clear conscience. Was it going to be this good forever? He'd clasped her chin with his hand, underneath, pushing her head back, and then, the death like a doubled fist going down his throat, to his gut, the heat spreading, flooding his loins and his brain.

He'd let her drop. Too much and not enough. He'd clawed at the wall for a moment thinking it must be flesh and blood, too, and were it flesh and blood it could be his. Then such a shock to know he wasn't hungry anymore. He was filled and complete and the night waited, like something made out of pure light, and the other one was dead, folded up like a baby in sleep on the grimy floor, and Armand, glowing in the dark, just watching.

It was getting rid of the bodies after that had been hard. Last night that had been done out of his sight, as he wept. Beginner's luck. This time Armand said "no trace means no trace." So they'd gone down together to bury them deep beneath the basement floor in the old furnace room, carefully putting the paving stones back in place. Lots of work even with such strength. So loathsome to touch the corpse like that. Only for a second did it flicker in his mind: *who were they?* Two fallen beings in a pit. No more *now*, no destiny. And the waif last night? Was somebody looking for her somewhere? He'd been crying suddenly. He'd heard it, then reached up and touched the tears coming out of his eyes.

"What do you think this is?" Armand had demanded, making him help with the paving stones. "A penny dreadful novel? You don't feed if you can't cover it up."

The building had been crawling with gentle humans who noticed not a thing as they'd stolen the clothes they now wore, uniforms of the young, and left by a broken door into an alley. Not my brothers and sisters anymore. The woods have always been filled with these soft doe-eyed things, with hearts beating for the arrow, the bullet, the lance. And now at last I reveal my secret identity: I have always been the huntsman.

"Is it all right, the way I am now?" he'd asked Armand. "Are you happy?" Haight Street, seven thirty-five. Bumper-to-bumper traffic, junkies screaming on the corner. Why didn't they just go on to the concert? Doors open already. He couldn't bear the anticipation.

But the coven house was near, Armand had explained, big tumble-down mansion one block from the park, and some of them were still hanging back in there plotting Lestat's ruin. Armand wanted to pass close, just for a moment, know what was going on.

"Looking for someone?" Daniel had asked. "Answer me, are you pleased with me or not?"

What had he seen in Armand's face? A sudden flare of humor, lust? Armand had hurried him along the dirty stained pavements, past the bars, the cafés, the stores crowded with stinking old clothes, the fancy clubs with their gilded letters on the greasy plate glass and overhead fans stirring the fumes with gilded wooden blades, while the potted ferns died a slow death in the heat and the semidarkness. Past the first little children—"Trick or treat!"—in their taffeta and glitter costumes.

Armand had stopped, at once surrounded by tiny upturned faces covered in store-bought masks, plastic spooks, ghouls, witches; a lovely warm light had filled his brown eyes; with both hands he'd dropped shiny silver dollars in their little candy sacks, then taken Daniel by the arm and led him on.

"I love it well enough the way you turned out," he had whispered with a sudden irrepressible smile, the warmth still there. "You're my firstborn," he'd said. Was there a catch in his throat, a sudden glancing from right to left as if he'd found himself cornered? Back to the business at hand. "Be patient. I am being afraid for us both, remember?"

Oh, we shall go to the stars together! Nothing can stop us. All the ghosts running through these streets are mortal!

Then the coven house had blown up.

He'd heard the blast before he saw it—and a sudden rolling plume of flame and smoke, accompanied by a shrill sound he would never before have detected: preternatural screams like silver paper curling in the heat. Sudden scatter of shaggy-haired humans running to see the blaze.

Armand had shoved Daniel off the street, into the stagnant air of a narrow liquor store. Bilious glare; sweat and reek of tobacco; mortals, oblivious to the nearby conflagration, reading the big glossy girlie magazines. Armand had pushed him to the very rear of the tiny corridor. Old lady buying tiny carton of milk and two cans of cat food out of the icebox. No way out of here.

But how could one hide from the thing that was passing over, from the deafening sound that mortals could not even hear? He'd lifted his hands to his ears, but that was foolish, useless. Death out there in alleyways. Things like him running through the debris of backyards, caught, burnt in their tracks. He saw it in sputtering flashes. Then nothing. Ringing silence. The clanging bells and squealing tires of the mortal world.

Yet he'd been too enthralled still to be afraid. Every second was eternal, the frost on the icebox door beautiful. The old lady with the milk in her hand, eyes like two small cobalt stones.

Armand's face had gone blank beneath the mask of his dark glasses, hands slipped into his tight pants pockets. The tiny bell on the door jangled as a young man entered, bought a single bottle of German beer, and went out.

"It's over, isn't it?"

"For now," Armand had answered.

Not until they'd gotten in the cab did he say more.

"It knew we were there; it heard us."

"Then why didn't it—?"

"I don't know. I only know it knew we were there. It knew before we found shelter."

AND now, push and shove inside the hall, and he loved it, the crowd carrying them closer and closer to the inner doors. He could not even raise his arms, so tight was the press; yet young men and women elbowed past him, buffeted him with delicious shocks; he laughed again as he saw the life-sized posters of Lestat plastered to the walls.

He felt Armand's fingers against his back; he felt a subtle change in Armand's whole body. A red-haired woman up ahead had turned around and was facing them as she was moved along towards the open door.

A soft warm shock passed through Daniel. "Armand, the red hair." So like the twins in the dream! It seemed her green eyes locked on him as he said, "Armand, the twins!"

Then her face vanished as she turned away again and disappeared inside the hall.

"No," Armand whispered. Small shake of his head. He was in a silent fury, Daniel could feel it. He had the rigid glassy look he always got when profoundly offended. "Talamasca," he whispered, with a faint uncharacteristic sneer.

"Talamasca." The word struck Daniel suddenly as beautiful. Talamasca. He broke it down from the Latin, understood its parts. Somewhere out of his memory bank it came: animal mask. Old word for witch or shaman.

"But what does it really mean?" he asked.

"It means Lestat is a fool," Armand said. Flicker of deep pain in his eyes. "But it makes no difference now."

Khayman

KHAYMAN watched from the archway as the Vampire Lestat's car entered the gates of the parking lot. Almost invisible Khayman was, even in the stylish denim coat and pants he'd stolen earlier from a shop manikin. He didn't need the silver glasses that covered his eyes. His glowing skin didn't matter. Not when everywhere he looked he saw masks and paint, glitter and gauze and sequined costumes.

He moved closer to Lestat, as if swimming through the wriggling bodies of the youngsters who mobbed the car. At last he glimpsed the creature's blond hair, and then his violet blue eyes as he smiled and blew kisses to his adorers. Such charm the devil had. He drove the car himself, gunning the motor and forcing the bumper against these tender little humans even as he flirted, winked, seduced, as if he and his foot on the gas pedal weren't connected to each other.

Exhilaration. Triumph. That's what Lestat felt and knew at this moment. And even his reticent companion, Louis, the dark-haired one in the car beside him, staring timidly at the screaming children as if they were birds of paradise, didn't understand what was truly happening.

Neither knew that the Queen had waked. Neither knew the dreams of the twins. Their ignorance was astonishing. And their young minds were so easy to scan. Apparently the Vampire Lestat, who had hidden himself quite well until this night, was now prepared to do battle with everyone. He wore his thoughts and intentions like a badge of honor.

"Hunt us down!" That's what he said aloud to his fans, though they didn't hear. "Kill us. We're evil. We're bad. It's perfectly fine to cheer and sing with us now. But when you catch on, well, then the serious business will begin. And you'll remember that I never lied to you."

For one instant his eyes and Khayman's eyes met. *I want to be good! I would die for that!* But there was no recognition of who or what received this message.

Louis, the watcher, the patient one, was there on account of love pure and simple. The two had found each other only last night, and theirs had been an extraordinary reunion. Louis would go where Lestat led him. Louis would perish if Lestat perished. But their fears and hopes for this night were heartbreakingly human.

They did not even guess that the Queen's wrath was close at hand, that she'd burnt the San Francisco coven house within the hour. Or that the infamous vampire tavern on Castro Street was burning now, as the Queen hunted down those fleeing from it.

But then the many blood drinkers scattered throughout this crowd did not know these simple facts either. They were too young to hear the warnings of the old, to hear the screams of the doomed as they perished. The dreams of the twins had only confused them. From various points, they glared at Lestat, overcome with hatred or religious fervor. They would destroy him or make of him a god. They did not guess at the danger that awaited them.

But what of the twins themselves? What was the meaning of the dreams?

Khayman watched the car move on, forcing its way towards the back of the auditorium. He looked up at the stars overhead, the tiny pinpricks of light behind the mist that hung over the city. He thought he could feel the closeness of his old sovereign.

He turned back towards the auditorium and made his way carefully through the press. To forget his strength in such a crowd as this would have been disaster. He would bruise flesh and break bones without even feeling it.

He took one last look at the sky, and then he went inside, easily befuddling the ticket taker as he went through the little turnstile and towards the nearest stairway.

The auditorium was almost filled. He looked about himself thoughtfully, savoring the moment somewhat as he savored everything. The hall itself was nothing, a shell of a place to hold light and sound—utterly modern and unredeemably ugly.

But the mortals, how pretty they were, glistering with health, their pockets full of gold, sound bodies everywhere, in which no organ had been eaten by the worms of disease, no bone ever broken.

In fact the sanitized well-being of this entire city rather amazed Khayman. True, he'd seen wealth in Europe such as he could never have imagined, but nothing equaled the flawless surface of this small and overpopulated place, even to the San Francisco peasantry, whose tiny stucco cottages were choked with luxuries of every description. Driveways here were jammed with handsome automobiles. Paupers drew their money from bank machines with magic plastic cards. No slums anywhere. Great towers the city had, and fabulous hostelries; mansions in profusion; yet girded as it was by sea and mountains and the glittering waters of the Bay, it seemed not so much a capital as a resort, an escape from the world's greater pain and ugliness.

No wonder Lestat had chosen this place to throw down the gauntlet. In the main, these pampered children were good. Deprivation had never wounded or weakened them. They might prove perfect combatants for real evil. That is, when they came to realize that the symbol and the thing were one and the same. Wake up and smell the blood, young ones.

But would there be time for that now?

Lestat's great scheme, whatever it truly was, might be stillborn; for surely the Queen had a scheme of her own, and Lestat knew nothing of it.

Khayman made his way now to the top of the hall. To the very last row of wooden seats where he had been earlier. He settled comfortably in the same spot, pushing aside the two "vampire books," which still lay on the floor, unnoticed.

Earlier, he had devoured the texts—Louis's testament: "Behold, the void." And Lestat's history: "And this and this and this, and it means nothing." They had clarified for him many things. And what Khayman had divined of Lestat's intentions had been confirmed completely. But of the mystery of the twins, of course, the book told nothing.

And as for the Queen's true intent, that continued to baffle him.

She had slain hundreds of blood drinkers the world over, yet left others unharmed.

Even now, Marius lived. In destroying her shrine, she had punished him but not killed him, which would have been simple. He called to the older ones from his prison of ice, warning, begging for assistance. And effortlessly, Khayman sensed two immortals moving to answer Marius's call, though one, Marius's own child, could not even hear it. Pandora was that one's name; she was a lone one, a strong one. The other, called Santino, did not have her power, but he could hear Marius's voice, as he struggled to keep pace with her.

Without doubt the Queen could have struck them down had she chosen to do it. Yet on and on they moved, clearly visible, clearly audible, yet unmolested.

How did the Queen make such choices? Surely there were those in this very hall whom she had spared for some purpose. . . .

Daniel

THEY had reached the doors, and now had to push the last few feet down a narrow ramp into the giant open oval of the main floor.

The crowd loosened, like marbles rolling in all directions. Daniel moved towards the center, his fingers hooked around Armand's belt so as not to lose him, his eyes roaming over the horseshoe-shaped theater, the high banks of seats rising to the ceiling. Mortals everywhere swarmed the cement stairs, or hung over iron railings, or flowed into the milling crowd around him.

A blur it was suddenly, the noise of it like the low grind of a giant machine. But then in the moment of deliberately distorted vision, he saw *the others.* He saw the simple, inescapable difference between the living and the dead. Beings like himself in every direction, concealed in the mortal forest, yet shining like the eyes of an owl in the light of the moon. No paint or dark glasses or shapeless hats or hooded capes could ever conceivably hide them from each other. And it wasn't merely the unearthly sheen to their faces or hands. It was the slow, lissome grace of their movements, as if they were more spirit than flesh.

Ah, my brothers and sisters, at last!

But it was hatred he felt around him. A rather dishonest hatred! They loved Lestat and condemned him simultaneously. They loved the very act of hating, punishing. Suddenly, he caught the eye of a powerful hulking creature with greasy black hair who bared his fangs in an ugly flash and then revealed the plan in stunning completeness. Beyond the prying eyes of mortals, they would hack Lestat's limbs from his body; they would sever his head; then the remains would be burnt on a pyre by the sea. The end of the monster and his legend. *Are you with us or against us?*

Daniel laughed out loud. "You'll never kill him," Daniel said. Yet he gaped as he glimpsed the sharpened scythe the creature held against his chest inside his coat. Then the beast turned and vanished. Daniel gazed upwards through the smoky light. *One of them now. Know all their secrets!* He felt giddy, on the verge of madness.

Armand's hand closed on his shoulder. They had come to the very center of the main floor. The crowd was getting denser by the second. Pretty girls in black silk gowns shoved and pushed against the crude bikers in their worn black leather. Soft feathers brushed his cheek; he saw a red devil with giant horns; a bony skeleton face topped with golden curls and pearl combs. Random cries rose in the bluish gloom. The bikers howled like wolves; someone shouted "Lestat" in a deafening voice, and others took up the call instantly.

Armand again had the lost expression, the expression that belonged to deep concentration, as if what he saw before him meant nothing at all.

"Thirty perhaps," he whispered in Daniel's ear, "no more than that, and one or two so old they could destroy the rest of us in an instant."

"Where, tell me where?"

"Listen," Armand said. "And see for yourself. There is no hiding from them."

Khayman

MAHARET'S child. Jessica. The thought caught Khayman off guard. *Protect Maharet's child. Somehow escape from here.*

He roused himself, senses sharpened. He'd been listening to Marius again, Marius trying to reach the young untuned ears of the Vampire Lestat, who preened backstage, before a broken mirror. What could this mean, Maharet's child, Jessica, and when the thoughts pertained, without doubt, to a mortal woman?

It came again, the unexpected communication of some strong yet unveiled mind: *Take care of Jesse. Somehow stop the Mother . . .* But there were no words really—it was no more than a shining glimpse into another's soul, a sparkling overflow.

Khayman's eyes moved slowly over the balconies opposite, over the swarming main floor. Far away in some remote corner of the city, an old one wandered, full of fear of the Queen yet longing to look upon her face. He had come here to die, but to know her face in the final instant.

Khayman closed his eyes to shut this out.

Then he heard it again suddenly. *Jessica, my Jessica.* And behind the soulful call, the knowledge of Maharet! The sudden vision of Maharet, enshrined in love, and ancient and white as he himself was. It was a moment of stunning pain. He slumped back in the wooden seat and bowed his head just a little. Then he looked out again over the steel rafters, the ugly tangles of black wire and rusted cylindrical lights. *Where are you?*

There, far away against the opposite wall, he saw the figure from whom the thoughts were coming. Ah, the oldest he had seen so far. A giant Nordic blood drinker, seasoned and cunning, dressed in coarse brown rawhide garments, with flowing straw-colored hair, his heavy brows and small deep-set eyes giving him a brooding expression.

The being was tracking a small mortal woman who fought her way through the crowds of the main floor. Jesse, Maharet's mortal daughter.

Maddened, disbelieving, Khayman focused tightly on the small woman. He felt his eyes mist with tears as he saw the astonishing resemblance. Here was Maharet's long coppery red hair, curling, thick, and the same tall birdlike frame, the same clever and curious green eyes, sweeping the scene as the female let herself be turned around and around by those who pushed against her.

Maharet's profile. Maharet's skin, which had been so pale and almost luminous in life, so like the inner lining of a seashell.

In a sudden vivid memory, he saw Maharet's skin through the mesh of his own dark fingers. As he had pushed her face to the side during the rape, his fingertips had touched the delicate folds of flesh over her eyes. Not till a year later had they plucked out her eyes and he had been there remembering the moment, the feel of the flesh. That is before he had picked up the eyes themselves and . . .

He shuddered. He felt a sharp pain in his lungs. His memory wasn't going to fail him. He would not slip away from this moment, the happy clown remembering nothing.

Maharet's child, all right. But how? Through how many generations had these characteristics survived to flower again in this small female who appeared to be fighting her way towards the stage at the end of the hall?

It was not impossible, of course. He quickly realized it. Perhaps three hundred ancestors stood between this twentieth-century woman and the long ago afternoon when he had put on the King's medallion and stepped down from the dais to commit the King's rape. Maybe even less than that. A mere fraction of this crowd, to put it more neatly in perspective.

But more astonishing than this, that Maharet knew her own descendants. And know this woman Maharet did. The tall blood drinker's mind yielded that fact immediately.

He scanned the tall Nordic one. Maharet, alive. Maharet, the guardian of her mortal family. Maharet, the embodiment of illimitable strength and will. Maharet who had given him, this blond servant, no explanation of the dreams of the twins, but had sent him here instead to do her bidding: save Jessica.

Ah, but she lives, Khayman thought. She lives, and if she lives then in a real way, they both live, the red-haired sisters!

Khayman studied the creature even more intently, probing even deeper. But all he caught now was the fierce protectiveness. Rescue Jesse, not merely from the danger of the Mother but from this place altogether, where Jesse's eyes would see what no one could ever explain away.

And how he loathed the Mother, this tall, fair being with the posture of a warrior and a priest in one. He loathed that the Mother had disrupted the serenity of his timeless and melancholy existence; loathed that his sad, sweet love for this woman, Jessica, exacerbated the alarm he felt for himself. He knew the extent of the destruction too, that every blood drinker from one end of this continent to the other had been destroyed, save for a precious few, most of whom were under this roof, never dreaming of the fate that threatened them.

He knew as well of the dreams of the twins, but he did not understand them. After all, two redheaded sisters he had never known; only one red-haired beauty ruled his life. And once again Khayman saw Maharet's face, a vagrant image of softened weary human eyes peering from a porcelain mask: *Mael, do not ask me anything more. But do as I tell you.*

Silence. The blood drinker was aware of the surveillance suddenly. With a little jerk of his head he looked around the hall, trying to spot the intruder.

The name had done it, as names so often do. The creature had felt himself known, recognized. And Khayman had recognized the name at once, connecting it with the Mael of Lestat's pages. Undoubtedly they were one and the same—this was the Druid priest who had lured Marius into the sacred grove where the blood god had made him one of its own, and sent him off to Egypt to find the Mother and the Father.

Yes, this was the same Mael. And the creature felt himself recognized and hated it.

After the initial spasm of rage, all thought and emotion vanished. A rather dizzying display of strength, Khayman conceded. He relaxed in the chair. But the creature couldn't find him. Two dozen other white faces he picked out of the crowd, but not Khayman.

Intrepid Jessica had meantime reached her destination. Ducking low, she'd slipped through the heavy-muscled motorcycle riders who claimed the space before the stage as their own, and had risen to take hold of the lip of the wooden platform.

Flash of her silver bracelet in the light. And that might as well have been a tiny dagger to the mental shield of Mael, because his love and his thoughts were wholly visible again for one fluid instant.

This one is going to die, too, if he doesn't become wise, Khayman thought. He'd been schooled by Maharet, no doubt, and perhaps nourished by her powerful blood; yet his heart was undisciplined, and his temper beyond his control, it was obvious.

Then some feet behind Jesse, in the swirling color and noise, Khayman spied another intriguing figure, much younger, yet almost as powerful in his own fashion as the Gaul, Mael.

Khayman sought for the name, but the creature's mind was a perfect blank; not so much as a glimmer of personality escaped from it. A boy he'd been when he died, with straight dark auburn hair, and eyes a little too big for his face. But it was easy, suddenly, to filch the being's name from Daniel, his newborn fledgling who stood beside him. Armand. And the fledgling, Daniel, was scarcely dead. All the tiny molecules of his body were dancing with the demon's invisible chemistry.

Armand immediately attracted Khayman. Surely he was the same Armand of whom Louis and Lestat had both written—the immortal with the form of a youth. And this meant that he was no more than five hundred years old, yet he veiled himself completely. Shrewd, cold he seemed, yet without flair—a stance that required no room in which to display itself. And now, sensing infallibly that he was watched, he turned his large soft brown eyes upward and fixed instantly upon the remote figure of Khayman.

"No harm meant to you or your young one," Khayman whispered, so that his lips might shape and control the thoughts. "No friend to the Mother."

Armand heard but gave no answer. Whatever terror he felt at the sight of one so old, he masked completely. One would have thought he was looking at the wall behind Khayman's head, at the steady stream of laughing and shouting children who poured down the steps from the topmost doorways.

And, quite inevitably, this oddly beguiling little five-hundred-year-old being fixed his eyes upon Mael as the gaunt one felt another irresistible surge of concern for his fragile Jesse.

Khayman understood this being, Armand. He felt he understood him and liked him completely. As their eyes met again, all that had been written of this creature in the two little histories was informed and balanced by the creature's innate simplicity. The loneliness which Khayman had felt in Athens was now very strong.

"Not unlike my own simple soul," Khayman whispered. "You're lost in all this because you know the terrain too well. And that no matter how far you walk, you come again to the same mountains, the same valley."

No response. Of course. Khayman shrugged and smiled. To this one he'd give anything that he could; and guilelessly, he let Armand know it.

Now the question was, how to help them, these two that might have some hope of sleeping the immortal sleep until another sunset. And most important of all, how to reach Maharet, to whom the fierce and distrusting Mael was unstintingly devoted.

To Armand, Khayman said with the slightest movement of his lips: "No friend of the Mother. I told you. And keep with the mortal crowd. She'll pick you out when you step apart. It's that simple."

Armand's face registered no change. Beside him, the fledgling Daniel was happy, glorying in the pageant that surrounded him. He knew no fear, no plans or dreams. And why not? He had this extremely powerful creature to take care of him. He was a damn sight luckier than the rest.

Khayman rose to his feet. It was the loneliness as much as anything else. He would be near to one of these two, Armand or Mael. That's what he had wanted in Athens when all this glorious remembering and knowing had begun. To be near another like himself. To speak, to touch . . . something.

He moved along the top aisle of the hall, which circled the entire room, save for a margin at the far end behind the stage which belonged to the giant video screen.

He moved with slow human grace, careful not to crush the mortals who pushed against him. And also he wanted this slow progress because he must give Mael the opportunity to see him.

He knew instinctively that if he snuck up on this proud and quarrelsome thing, the insult would never be borne. And so he proceeded, only picking up his pace when he realized Mael was now aware of his approach.

Mael couldn't hide his fear as Armand could. Mael had never seen a blood drinker of Khayman's age save for Maharet; he was gazing at a potential enemy. Khayman sent the same warm greeting he had sent to Armand—Armand who watched—but nothing in the old warrior's stance changed.

The auditorium was now full and locked; outside children screamed and beat upon the doors. Khayman heard the whine and belch of the police radios.

The Vampire Lestat and his cohorts stood spying upon the hall through the holes in a great serge curtain.

Lestat embraced his companion Louis, and they kissed on the mouth, as the mortal musicians put their arms around both of them.

Khayman paused to feel the passion of the crowd, the very air charged with it.

Jessica had rested her arms on the edge of the platform. She had rested her chin upon the back of her hands. The men behind her, hulking creatures clothed in shiny black leather, shoved her brutally, out of carelessness and drunken exuberance, but they couldn't dislodge her.

Neither could Mael, should he make the attempt.

And something else came clear to Khayman suddenly, as he looked down at her. It was the single word Talamasca. This woman belonged to them; she was part of the order.

Not possible, he thought again, then laughed silently at his own foolish innocence. This was a night of shocks, was it not? Yet it seemed quite incredible that the Talamasca should have survived from the time he had known it centuries before, when he had played with its members and tormented them, and then turned his back on them out of pity for their fatal combination of innocence and ignorance.

Ah, memory was too ghastly a thing. Let his past lives slip into oblivion! He could see the faces of those vagabonds, those secular monks of the Talamasca who had so clumsily pursued him across Europe, recording glimpses of him in great leather-bound books, their quill pens scratching late into the night. Benjamin had been his name in that brief respite of consciousness, and Benjamin the Devil they had labeled him in their fancy Latin script, sending off crackling parchment epistles with big sloppy wax seals to their superiors in Amsterdam.

It had been a game to him, to steal their letters and add his notes to them; to frighten them; to crawl out from under their beds in the night and grab them by the throats and shake them; it had been fun; and what was not? When the fun stopped, he'd always lost his memory again.

But he had loved them; not exorcists they, or witch-hunting priests, or sorcerers who hoped to chain and control his power. It had even occurred to him once that when it came time to sleep, he would choose the vaults beneath their moldy Motherhouse. For all their meddlesome curiosity, they would never have betrayed him.

And now to think that the order had survived, with the tenacity of the Church of Rome, and this pretty mortal woman with the shining bracelet on her arm, beloved of Maharet and Mael, was one of their special breed. No wonder she had fought her way to the front ranks, as if to the bottom step of the altar.

Khayman drew closer to Mael, but he stopped short of him by several feet, the crowd passing ceaselessly in front of them. This he did out of respect for Mael's apprehension, and the shame the creature felt for being afraid. It was Mael who approached and stood at Khayman's side.

The restless crowd passed them as if they were the wall itself. Mael leant close to Khayman, which in its own way was a greeting, an offering of trust. He looked out over the hall, where no empty seat was visible, and the main floor was a mosaic of flashing colors and glistening hair and tiny upthrust fists. Then he reached out and touched Khayman as if he couldn't prevent himself from doing it. With his fingertips he touched the back of Khayman's left hand. And Khayman remained still to allow this little exploration.

How many times had Khayman seen such a gesture between immortals, the young one verifying for himself the texture and hardness of the elder's flesh. Hadn't some Christian saint slipped his hand in Christ's wounds because the sight of them had not been sufficient? More mundane comparisons made Khayman smile. It was like two fierce dogs tentatively examining each other.

Far below, Armand remained impassive as he kept his eyes upon the two figures. Surely he saw Mael's sudden disdainful glance, but he did not acknowledge it.

Khayman turned and embraced Mael, and smiled at him. But this merely frightened Mael, and Khayman felt the disappointment heavily. Politely, he stepped away. For a moment he was painfully confused. He stared down at Armand. Beautiful Armand who met his gaze with utter passivity. But it was time to say now what he'd come to say.

"You must make your shield stronger, my friend," he explained to Mael gently. "Don't let your love for that girl expose you. The girl will be perfectly safe from our Queen if you curb your thoughts of the girl's origins and her protector. That name is anathema to the Queen. It always has been."

"And where is the Queen?" Mael asked, his fear surging again, along with the rage that he needed to fight it.

"She's close."

"Yes, but where?"

"I cannot say. She's burnt their tavern house. She hunts the few rogues who haven't come to the hall. She takes her time with it. And this I've learned through the minds of her victims."

Khayman could see the creature shudder. He could see subtle changes in him that marked his ever increasing anger. Well and good. The fear withered in the heat of the anger. But what a basically quarrelsome creature this one was. His mind did not make sophisticated distinctions.

"And why do you give me this warning," demanded Mael, "when she can hear every word we speak to each other?"

"But I don't think that she can," Khayman replied calmly. "I am of the First Brood, friend. To hear other blood drinkers as we hear mortal men, that curse belongs only to distant cousins. I could not read her mind if she stood on this spot; and mine is closed to her as well, you can be sure of it. And so it was with all our kind through the early generations."

That clearly fascinated the blond giant. So Maharet could not hear the Mother! Maharet had not admitted this to him.

"No," Khayman said, "and the Mother can only know of her through your thoughts, so kindly guard them. Speak to me now in a human voice, for this city is a wilderness of such voices."

Mael considered, brows puckered in a frown. He glared at Khayman as if he meant to hit him.

"And this will defeat her?"

"Remember," Khayman said, "that excess can be the very opposite of essence." He looked back at Armand as he spoke. "She who hears a multitude of voices may not hear any one voice. And she who would listen closely to one, must shut out the others. You are old enough to know the trick."

Mael didn't answer out loud. But it was clear that he understood. The telepathic gift had always been a curse to him, too, whether he was besieged by the voices of blood drinkers or humans.

Khayman gave a little nod. The telepathic gift. Such nice words for the madness that had come on him eons ago, after years of listening, years of lying motionless, covered with dust in the deep recesses of a forgotten Egyptian tomb, listening to the weeping of the world, without knowledge of himself or his condition.

"Precisely my point, my friend," he said. "And for two thousand years you have fought the voices while our Queen may well have been drowned by them. It seems the Vampire Lestat has outshouted the din; he has, as it were, snapped his fingers in the corner of her eye and brought her to attention. But do not overestimate the creature who sat motionless for so long. It isn't useful to do so."

These ideas startled Mael somewhat. But he saw the logic of them. Below, Armand remained attentive.

"She can't do all things," Khayman said, "whether she herself knows it or not. She was always one to reach for the stars, and then draw back as if in horror."

"How so?" Mael said. Excited, he leaned closer. "What is she really like!" he whispered.

"She was full of dreams and high ideals. She was like Lestat." Khayman shrugged. "The blond one down there who would be good and do good and gather to himself the needy worshipers."

Mael smiled, coldly, cynically.

"But what in the name of hell does she mean to do?" he asked. "So he has waked her with his abominable songs. Why does she destroy us?"

"There's a purpose, you can be sure of it. With our Queen there has always been a purpose. She could not do the smallest thing without a grand purpose. And you must know we do not really change over time; we are as flowers unfolding; we merely become more nearly ourselves." He glanced again at Armand. "As for what her purpose may be, I can give you only speculations . . ."

"Yes, tell me."

"This concert will take place because Lestat wants it. And when it is finished, she will slaughter more of our kind. But she will leave some, some to serve this purpose, some perhaps to witness."

Khayman gazed at Armand. Marvelous how his expressionless face conveyed wisdom, while the harried, weary face of Mael did not. And who can say which one understood the most? Mael gave a little bitter laugh.

"To witness?" Mael asked. "I think not. I think she is cruder than that. She spares those whom Lestat loves, it's that simple."

This hadn't occurred to Khayman.

"Ah, yes, think on it," Mael said, in the same sharply pronounced English. "Louis, Lestat's companion. Is he not alive? And Gabrielle, the mother of the fiend, she is near at hand, waiting to rendezvous with her son as soon as it is wise to do so. And Armand, down there, whom you so like to look at, it seems Lestat would see him again, so he is alive, and that outcast with him, the one who published the accursed book, the one the others would tear limb from limb if only they guessed . . ."

"No, there's more to it than that. There has to be," Khayman said. "Some of us she can't kill. And those who go to Marius now, Lestat knows nothing of them but their names."

Mael's face changed slightly; it underwent a deep, human flush, as his eyes narrowed. It was clear to Khayman that Mael would have gone to Marius if he could. He would have gone this very night, if only Maharet had come to protect Jessica. He tried now to banish Maharet's name from his thoughts. He was afraid of Maharet, deeply afraid.

"Ah, yes, you try to hide what you know," Khayman said. "And this is just what you must reveal to me."

"But I can't," Mael said. The wall had gone up. Impenetrable. "I am not given answers, only orders, my friend. And my mission is to survive this night, and to take my charge safely out of here."

Khayman meant to press, to demand. But he did neither. He had felt a soft, subtle change in the atmosphere around him, a change so insignificant yet pure that he couldn't call it movement or sound.

She was coming. She was moving close to the hall. He felt himself slip away from his body into pure listening; yes, it was she. All the sounds of the night rose to confuse him, yet he caught it; a low irreducible sound which she could not veil, the sound of her breathing, of the beat of her heart, of a force moving through space at tremendous and unnatural speed, causing the inevitable tumult amid the visible and the invisible.

Mael sensed it; so did Armand. Even the young one beside Armand heard it, though so many other young ones did not. Even some of the more finely tuned mortals seemed to feel it and to be distracted by it.

"I must go, friend," Khayman said. "Remember my advice." Impossible to say more now.

She was very close. Undoubtedly she scanned; she listened.

He felt the first irresistible urge to see her, to scan for the minds of those hapless souls out there in the night whose eyes might have passed over her.

"Good-bye, friend," he said. "It's no good for me to be near you."

Mael looked at him in confusion. Below, Armand gathered Daniel to him and made for the edge of the crowd.

The hall went dark suddenly; and for one split second Khayman thought it was her magic, that some grotesque and vengeful judgment would now be made.

But the mortal children all around him knew the ritual. The concert was about to begin! The hall went mad with shrieks, and cheers, and stomping. Finally it became a great collective roar. He felt the floor tremble.

Tiny flames appeared as mortals struck their matches, ignited their chemical lighters. And a drowsy beautiful illumination once again revealed the thousands upon thousands of moving forms. The screams were a chorus from all sides.

"I am no coward," Mael whispered suddenly, as if he could not remain silent. He took hold of Khayman's arm, then let it go as if the hardness of it repelled him.

"I know," Khayman said.

"Help me. Help Jessica."

"Don't speak her name again. Stay away from her as I've told you. You are conquered again, Druid. Remember? Time to fight with cunning, not rage. Stay with the mortal herd. I will help you when and if I can."

There was so much more he wanted to say! Tell me where Maharet is! But it was too late now for that. He turned away and moved along the aisle swiftly until he came to an open place above a long narrow flight of cement stairs.

Below on the darkened stage, the mortal musicians appeared, darting over wires and speakers to gather their instruments from the floor.

The Vampire Lestat came striding through the curtain, his black cloak flaring around him, as he moved to the very front of the platform. Not three feet from Jesse he stood with microphone in hand.

The crowd had gone into ecstasies. Clapping, hooting, howling, it was a noise such as Khayman had never actually heard. He laughed in spite of himself at the stupid frenzy, at the tiny smiling figure down there who loved it utterly, who was laughing even as Khayman laughed.

Then in a great white flash, light flooded the small stage. Khayman stared, not at the small figures strutting in their finery, but at the giant video screen that rose behind them to the very roof. The living image of the Vampire Lestat, thirty feet in height, blazed before Khayman. The creature smiled; he lifted his arms, and shook his mane of yellow hair; he threw back his head and howled.

The crowd was on its feet in delirium; the very structure rumbled; but it was the howl that filled all ears. The Vampire Lestat's powerful voice swallowed every other sound in the auditorium.

Khayman closed his eyes. In the heart of the monstrous cry of the Vampire Lestat, he listened again for the sound of the Mother, but he could no longer find it.

"My Queen," he whispered, searching, scanning, hopeless though it was. Did she stand up there on some grassy slope listening to the music of her troubadour? He felt the soft damp wind and saw the gray starless sky as random mortals felt and saw these things. The lights of San Francisco, its spangled hills and glowing towers, these were the beacons of the urban night, as terrible suddenly as the moon or the drift of the galaxies.

He closed his eyes. He envisioned her again as she'd been in the Athens street watching the tavern burn with her children in it; her tattered cape had hung loose over her shoulders, the hood thrown back from her plaited hair. Ah, the Queen of Heaven she'd seemed, as she had once so loved to be known, presiding over centuries of litany. Her eyes had been shining and empty in the electric light; her mouth soft, guileless. The sheer sweetness of her face had been infinitely beautiful.

The vision carried him back now over the centuries to a dim and awful moment, when he'd come, a mortal man, heart pounding to hear her will. His Queen, now cursed and consecrated to the moon, the demon in her demanding blood, his Queen who would not allow even the bright lamps to be near to her. How agitated she had been, pacing the mud floor, the colored walls around her full of silent painted sentinels.

"These twins," she'd said, "these evil sisters, they have spoken such abominations."

"Have mercy," he had pleaded. "They meant no harm, I swear they tell the truth. Let them go again, Your Highness. They cannot change it now."

Oh, such compassion he had felt for all of them! The twins, and his afflicted sovereign.

"Ah, but you see, we must put it to the test, their revolting lies," she had said. "You must come closer, my devoted steward, you who have always served me with such devotion—"

"My Queen, my beloved Queen, what do you want of me?"

And with the same lovely expression on her face, she had lifted her icy hands to touch his throat, to hold him fast suddenly with a strength that terrified him. In shock, he'd watched her eyes go blank, her mouth open. The two tiny fang teeth he'd seen, as she rose on tiptoe with the eerie grace of nightmare. *Not me. You would not do this to me! My Queen, I am Khayman!*

He should have perished long before now, as so many blood drinkers had afterwards. Gone without a trace, like the nameless multitudes dissolved within the earth of all lands and nations. But he had not perished. And the twins—at least one—had lived on also.

Did she know it? Did she know those terrible dreams? Had they come to her from the minds of all the others who had received them? Or had she traveled the night around the world, dreamless, and without cease, and bent upon one task, since her resurrection?

They live, my Queen, they live on in the one if not in the two together. *Remember the old prophecy!* If only she could hear his voice!

He opened his eyes. He was back again in the moment, with this ossified thing that was his body. And the rising music saturated him with its remorseless rhythm. It pounded against his ears. The flashing lights blinded him.

He turned his back and put his hand against the wall. Never had he been so engulfed by sound. He felt himself losing consciousness, but Lestat's voice called him back.

With his fingers splayed across his eyes, Khayman looked down at the fiery white square of the stage. Behold the devil dance and sing with such obvious joy. It touched Khayman's heart in spite of himself.

Lestat's powerful tenor needed no electric amplification. And even the immortals lost among their prey were singing with him, it was so contagious, this passion. Everywhere he looked Khayman saw them caught up, mortal and immortal alike. Bodies twisted in time with the bodies on the stage. Voices rose; the hall swayed with one wave of movement after another.

The giant face of Lestat expanded on the video screen as the camera moved in upon it. The blue eye fixed upon Khayman and winked.

"WHY DON'T YOU KILL ME! YOU KNOW WHAT I AM!"

Lestat's laughter rose above the twanging scream of the guitars.

"DON'T YOU KNOW EVIL WHEN YOU SEE IT?"

Ah, such a belief in goodness, in heroism. Khayman could see it even in the creature's eyes, a dark gray shadow there of tragic need. Lestat threw back his head and roared again; he stamped his feet and howled; he looked to the rafters as if they were the firmament.

Khayman forced himself to move; he had to escape. He made his way clumsily to the door, as if suffocating in the deafening sound. Even his sense of balance had been affected. The blasting music came after him into the stairwell, but at least he was sheltered from the flashing lights. Leaning against the wall, he tried to clear his vision.

Smell of blood. Hunger of so many blood drinkers in the hall. And the throb of the music through the wood and the plaster.

He moved down the steps, unable to hear his own feet on the concrete, and sank down finally on a deserted landing. He wrapped his arms around his knees and bowed his head.

The music was like the music of old, when all songs had been the songs of the body, and the songs of the mind had not yet been invented.

He saw himself dancing; he saw the King—the mortal king he had so loved—turn and leap into the air; he heard the beat of the drums; the rise of the pipes; the King put the beer in Khayman's hand. The table sagged beneath its wealth of roasted game and glistening fruit, its steaming loaves of bread. The Queen sat in her golden chair, immaculate and serene, a mortal woman with a tiny cone of scented wax atop her elaborate hair, melting slowly in the heat to perfume her plaited tresses.

Then someone had put the coffin in his hand; the tiny coffin that was passed now among those who feasted; the little reminder: Eat. Drink. For Death awaits all of us.

He held it tight; should he pass it now to the King?

He felt the King's lips against his face suddenly. "Dance, Khayman. Drink. Tomorrow we march north to slay the last of the flesh eaters." The King didn't even look at the tiny coffin as he took it; he slipped it into the Queen's hands and she, without looking down, gave it to another.

The last of the flesh eaters. How simple it had all seemed; how good. Until he had seen the twins kneeling before that altar.

The great rattle of drums drowned out Lestat's voice. Mortals passed Khayman, hardly noticing him huddled there; a blood drinker ran quickly by without the slightest heed of him.

The voice of Lestat rose again, singing of the Children of Darkness, hidden beneath the cemetery called Les Innocents in superstition and fear.

Into the light
We've come
My Brothers and Sisters!

KILL US!
My Brothers and Sisters!

Sluggishly, Khayman rose. He was staggering, but he moved on, downward until he had come out in the lobby where the noise was just a little muted, and he rested there, across from the inner doors, in a cooling draft of fresh air.

Calm was returning to him, but only slowly, when he realized that two mortal men had paused nearby and were staring at him as he stood against the wall with his hands in his pockets, his head bowed.

He saw himself suddenly as they saw him. He sensed their apprehension, mingled with a sudden irrepressible sense of victory. Men who had known about his kind, men who had lived for a moment such as this, yet dreaded it, and never truly hoped for it.

Slowly, he looked up. They stood some twenty feet away from him, near to the cluttered concession stand, as if it could hide them—proper British gentlemen. They were old, in fact, learned, with heavily creased faces and prim formal attire. Utterly out of place here their fine gray overcoats, the bit of starched collar showing, the gleaming knot of silk tie. They seemed explorers from another world among the flamboyant youth that moved restlessly to and fro, thriving on the barbaric noise and broken chatter.

And with such natural reticence they stared; as if they were too polite to be afraid. Elders of the Talamasca looking for Jessica.

Know us? Yes, you do of course. No harm. Don't care.

His silent words drove the one called David Talbot back a pace. The man's breathing became hurried, and there was a sudden dampness on his forehead and upper lip. Yet such elegant composure. David Talbot narrowed his eyes as if he would not be dazzled by what he saw; as if he would see the tiny dancing molecules in the brightness.

How small it seemed suddenly the span of a human life; look at this fragile man, for whom education and refinement have only increased all risks. So simple to alter the fabric of his thought, his expectations. Should Khayman tell them where Jesse was? Should he meddle? It would make no difference ultimately.

He sensed now that they were afraid to go or to remain, that he had them fixed almost as if he'd hypnotized them. In a way, it was respect that kept them there, staring at him. It seemed he had to offer something, if only to end this awful scrutiny.

Don't go to her. You'd be fools if you did. She has others like me now to look after her. Best leave here. I would if I were you.

Now, how would all this read in the archives of the Talamasca? Some night he might find out. To what modern places had they removed their old documents and treasures?

Benjamin, the Devil. That's who I am. Don't you know me? He smiled at himself. He let his head droop, staring at the floor. He had not known he possessed this vanity. And suddenly he did not care what this moment meant to them.

He thought listlessly of those olden times in France when he had played with their kind. "Allow us but to speak to you!" they'd pleaded. Dusty scholars with pale eternally red-rimmed eyes and worn velvet clothing, so unlike these two fine gentlemen, for whom the occult was a matter of science, not philosophy. The hopelessness of that time suddenly frightened him; the hopelessness of this time was equally frightening.

Go away.

Without looking up, he saw that David Talbot had nodded. Politely, he and his companion withdrew. Glancing back over their shoulders, they hurried down the curve of the lobby, and into the concert.

Khayman was alone again, with the rhythm of the music coming from the doorway, alone and wondering why he had come here, what it was he wanted; wishing that he could forget again; that he was in some lovely place full of warm breezes and mortals who didn't know what he was, and twinkling electric lights beneath the faded clouds, and flat endless city pavements to walk until morning.

Jesse

LET me alone, you son of a bitch!" Jesse kicked the man beside her, the one who had hooked his arm around her waist and lifted her away from the stage. "You bastard!" Doubled over with the pain in his foot, he was no match for her sudden shove. He toppled and went down.

Five times she'd been swept back from the stage. She ducked and pushed through the little cluster that had taken her place, sliding against their black leather flanks as if she were a fish and rising up again to grab the apron of unpainted wood, one hand taking hold of the strong synthetic cloth that decorated it, and twisting it into a rope.

In the flashing lights she saw the Vampire Lestat leap high into the air and come down without a palpable sound on the boards, his voice rising again without benefit of the mike to fill the auditorium, his guitar players prancing around him like imps.

The blood ran in tiny rivulets down his white face, as if from Christ's Crown of Thorns, his long blond hair flying out as he turned full circle, his hand ripping at his shirt, tearing it open down his chest, the black tie loose and falling. His pale crystalline blue eyes were glazed and shot with blood as he screamed the unimportant lyrics.

Jesse felt her heart knocking again as she stared up at him, at the rocking of his hips, the tight cloth of the black pants revealing the powerful muscles of his thighs. He leapt again, rising effortlessly, as if he would ascend to the very ceiling of the hall.

Yes, you see it, and there is no mistake! No other explanation!

She wiped at her nose. She was crying again. But touch him, damn it, you have to! In a daze she watched him finish the song, stomping his foot to the last three resounding notes, as the musicians danced back and forth, taunting, tossing their hair over their heads, their voices lost in his as they struggled to meet his pace.

God, how he loved it! There was not the slightest pretense. He was bathed in the adoration he was receiving. He was soaking it up as if it were blood.

And now as he went into the frenzied opening of another song, he ripped off the black velvet cloak, gave it a great twirl, and sent it flying into the audience. The crowd wailed, shifted. Jesse felt a knee in her back, a boot scraping her heel, but this was her chance, as the guards jumped down off the boards to stop the melee.

With both hands pressed down hard on the wood, she sprang up and over on her belly and onto her feet. She ran right towards the dancing figure whose eyes suddenly looked into hers.

"Yes, you! You!" she cried out. In the corner of her eye was the approaching guard. She threw her full weight at the Vampire Lestat. Shutting her eyes, she locked her arms around his waist. She felt the cold shock of his silky chest against her face, she tasted the blood suddenly on her lip!

"Oh, God, real!" she whispered. Her heart was going to burst, but she hung on. Yes, Mael's skin, like this, and Maharet's skin, like this, and all of them. Yes, this! Real, not human. Always. And it was all here in her arms and she knew and it was too late for them to stop her now!

Her left hand went up, and caught a thick tangle of his hair, and as she opened her eyes, she saw him smiling down at her, saw the poreless gleaming white skin, and the tiny fang teeth.

"You devil!" she whispered. She was laughing like a mad woman, crying and laughing.

"Love you, Jessica," he whispered back at her, smiling at her as if he were teasing her, the wet blond hair tumbling down into his eyes.

Astonished, she felt his arm around her, and then he lifted her on his hip, swinging her in a circle. The screaming musicians were a blur; the lights were violent streaks of white, red. She was moaning; but she kept looking up at him, at his eyes, yes, real. Desperately she hung on, for it seemed he meant to throw her high into the air over the heads of the crowd. And then as he set her down and bowed his head, his hair falling against her cheek, she felt his mouth close on hers.

The throbbing music went dim as if she'd been plunged into the sea. She felt him breathe into her, sigh against her, his smooth fingers sliding up her neck. Her breasts were pressed against the beat of his heart; and a voice was speaking to her, purely, the way a voice had long ago, a voice that knew her, a voice that understood her questions and knew how they must be answered.

Evil, Jesse. As you have always known.

Hands pulled her back. Human hands. She was being separated from him. She screamed.

Bewildered, he stared at her. He was reaching deep, deep into his dreams for something he only faintly remembered. The funeral feast; the red-haired twins kneeling on either side of the altar. But it was no more than a split second; then gone; he was baffled; his smile flashed again, impersonal, like one of the lights that were constantly blinding her. "Beautiful Jesse!" he said, his hand lifted as if in farewell. They were carrying her backwards away from him, off the stage.

She was laughing when they set her down.

Her white shirt was smeared with blood. Her hands were covered with it—pale streaks of salty blood. She felt she knew the taste of it. She threw back her head and laughed; and it was so curious not to be able to hear it, only to feel it, to feel the shudder running through her, to know she was crying and laughing at the same time. The guard said something rough to her, something crude, threatening. But that didn't matter.

The crowd had her again. It just swallowed her, tumbling against her, driving her out of the center. A heavy shoe crushed her right foot. She stumbled, and turned, and let herself be pushed along ever more violently, towards the doors.

Didn't matter now. *She knew.* She knew it all. Her head spun. She could not have stood upright if it were not for the shoulders knocking against her. And never had she felt such wondrous abandon. Never had she felt such release.

The crazy cacophonous music went on; faces flickered and disappeared in a wash of colored light. She smelled the marijuana, the beer. Thirst. Yes, something cold to drink. Something cold. So thirsty. She lifted her hand again and licked at the salt and the blood. Her body trembled, vibrated, the way it so often did on the verge of sleep. A soft delicious tremor that meant that dreams were coming. She licked at the blood again and closed her eyes.

Quite suddenly she felt herself pass into an open place. No one shoving her. She looked up and saw that she had come to the doorway, to the slick ramp that led some ten feet into the lobby below. The crowd was behind her, above her. And she could rest here. She was all right.

She ran her hand along the greasy wall, stepping over the crush of paper cups, a fallen wig with cheap yellow curls. She lay her head back suddenly and merely rested, the ugly light from the lobby shining in her eyes. The taste of the blood was on the tip of her tongue. It seemed she was going to cry again, and it was a perfectly fine thing to do. For the moment, there was no past or present, no necessity, and all the world was changed, from the simplest things to the grandest. She was floating, as if in the center of the most seductive state of peace and acceptance that she had ever known. Oh, if only she could tell David these things; if only somehow she could share this great and overwhelming secret.

Something touched her. Something hostile to her. Reluctantly she turned and saw a hulking figure at her side. *What?* She struggled to see it clearly.

Bony limbs, black hair slicked back, red paint on the twisted ugly mouth, but the skin, the same skin. And the fang teeth. Not human. One of them!

Talamasca?

It came at her like a hiss. It struck her in the chest. Instinctively her arms rose, crossing over her breasts, fingers locking on her shoulders.

Talamasca?

It was soundless yet deafening in its rage.

She moved to back away, but his hand caught her, fingers biting into her neck. She tried to scream as she was lifted off her feet.

Then she was flying across the lobby and she was screaming until her head slammed into the wall.

Blackness. She saw the pain. It flashed yellow and then white as it traveled down her backbone and then spread out as if into a million branches in her limbs. Her body went numb. She hit the floor with another shocking pain in her face and in the open palms of her hands and then she rolled over on her back.

She couldn't see. Maybe her eyes were closed, but the funny thing was, if they were, she couldn't open them. She heard voices, people shouting. A whistle blew, or was it the clang of a bell? There was a thunderous noise, but that was the crowd inside applauding. People near her argued.

Someone close to her ear said:

"Don't touch her. Her neck's broken!"

Broken? Can you live when your neck is broken?

Someone laid a hand on her forehead. But she couldn't really feel it so much as a tingling sensation, as if she were very cold, walking in snow, and all real feeling had left her. *Can't see.*

"Listen, honey." A young man's voice. One of those voices you could hear in Boston or New Orleans or New York City. Firefighter, cop, saver of the injured. "We're taking care of you, honey. The ambulance is on its way. Now lie still, honey, don't you worry."

Someone touching her breast. No, taking the cards out of her pocket. Jessica Miriam Reeves. Yes.

She stood beside Maharet and they were looking up at the giant map with all the tiny lights. And she understood. Jesse born of Miriam, who was born of Alice, who was born of Carlotta, who was born of Jane Marie, who was born of Anne, who was born of Janet Belle, who was born of Elizabeth, who was born of Louise, who was born of Frances, who was born of Frieda, who was born of—

"If you will allow me, please, we are her friends—"

David.

They were lifting her; she heard herself scream, but she had not meant to scream. She saw the screen again and the great tree of names. "Frieda born of Dagmar, born of . . ."

"Steady now, steady! Goddamn it!"

The air changed; it went cool and moist; she felt the breeze moving over her face; then all feeling left her hands and feet completely. She could feel her eyelids but not move them.

Maharet was talking to her. ". . . came out of Palestine, down into Mesopotamia and then up slowly through Asia Minor and into Russia and then into Eastern Europe. Do you see?"

This was either a hearse or an ambulance and it seemed too quiet to be the latter, and the siren, though steady, was too far away. What had happened to David? He wouldn't have let her go, unless she was dead. But then how could David have been there? David had told her nothing could induce him to come. David wasn't here. She must have imagined it. And the odd thing was, Miriam wasn't here either. "Holy Mary, Mother of God . . . now and at the hour of our death . . . ."

She listened: they were speeding through the city; she felt them turn the corner; but where was her body? She couldn't feel it. Broken neck. That meant surely that one had to be dead.

What was that, the light she could see through the jungle? A river? It seemed too wide to be a river. How to cross it. But it wasn't Jesse who was walking through the jungle, and now along the bank of the river. It was somebody else. Yet she could see the hands out in front of her, moving aside the vines and the wet sloppy leaves, as if they were her hands. She could see red hair when she looked down, red hair in long curling tangles, full of bits of leaf and earth. . . .

"Can you hear me, honey? We've got you. We're taking care of you. Your friends are in the car behind us. Now don't you worry."

He was saying more. But she had lost the thread. She couldn't hear him, only the tone of it, the tone of loving care. Why did he feel so sorry for her? He didn't even know her. Did he understand that it wasn't her blood all over her shirt? Her hands? *Guilty.* Lestat had tried to tell her it was evil, but that had been so unimportant to her, so impossible to relate to the whole. It wasn't that she didn't care about what was good and what was right; it was that this was bigger for the moment. *Knowing.* And he'd been talking as if she meant to do something and she hadn't meant to do anything at all.

That's why dying was probably just fine. If only Maharet would understand. And to think, David was with her, in the car behind them. David knew some of the story, anyway, and they would have a file on her: Reeves, Jessica. And it would be more evidence. "One of our devoted members, definitely the result of . . . most dangerous . . . must not under any circumstances attempt a sighting . . . ."

They were moving her again. Cool air again, and smells rising of gasoline and ether. She knew that just on the other side of this numbness, this darkness, there was terrible pain and it was best to lie very still and not try to go there. Let them carry you along; let them move the gurney down the hallway.

Someone crying. A little girl.

"Can you hear me, Jessica? I want you to know that you're in the hospital and that we are doing everything we can for you. Your friends are outside. David Talbot and Aaron Lightner. We've told them that you must lie very still. . . ."

Of course. When your neck is broken you are either dead or you die if you move. That was it. Years ago in a hospital she had seen a young girl with a broken neck. She remembered now. And the girl's body had been tied to a huge aluminum frame. Every now and then a nurse would move the frame to change the girl's position. Will you do that to me?

He was talking again but this time he was farther away. She walked a little faster through the jungle, to get closer, to hear over the sound of the river. He was saying . . . .

". . . of course we can do all that, we can run those tests, of course, but you must understand what I'm saying, this situation is terminal. The back of the skull is completely crushed. You can see the brain. And the obvious injury to the brain is enormous. Now, in a few hours the brain will begin to swell, if we even have a few hours. . . ."

Bastard, you killed me. You threw me against the wall. If I could move anything—my eyelids, my lips. But I'm trapped inside here. I have no body anymore yet I'm trapped in here! When I was little, I used to think it would be like this, death. You'd be trapped in your head in the grave, with no eyes to see and no mouth to scream. And years and years would pass.

Or you roamed the twilight realm with the pale ghosts; thinking you were alive when you were really dead. Dear God, I have to know when I'm dead. I have to know when it's begun!

Her lips. There was the faintest sensation. Something moist, warm. Something parting her lips. But there's no one here, is there? They were out in the hallway, and the room was empty. She would have known if someone was here. Yet now she could taste it, the warm fluid flowing into her mouth.

What is it? What are you giving me? I don't want to go under.

Sleep, my beloved.

I don't want to. I want to feel it when I die. I want to know!

But the fluid was filling her mouth, and she was swallowing. The muscles of her throat were alive. Delicious the taste of it, the saltiness of it. She knew this taste! She knew this lovely, tingling sensation. She sucked harder. She could feel the skin of her face come alive, and the air stirring around her. She could feel the breeze moving through the room. A lovely warmth was moving down her spine. It was moving through her legs and her arms, taking exactly the path the pain had taken, and all her limbs were coming back.

Sleep, beloved.

The back of her head tingled; and the tingling moved through the roots of her hair.

Her knees were bruised but her legs weren't hurt and she'd be able to walk again, and she could feel the sheet under her hand. She wanted to reach up, but it was too soon for that, too soon to move.

Besides she was being lifted, carried.

And it was best to sleep now. Because if this was death . . . well, it was just fine. The voices she could barely hear, the men arguing, threatening, they didn't matter now. It seemed David was calling out to her. But what did David want her to do? To die? The doctor was threatening to call the police. The police couldn't do anything now. That was almost funny.

Down and down the stairs they went. Lovely cold air.

The sound of the traffic grew louder; a bus roaring past. She had never liked these sounds before but now they were like the wind itself, that pure. She was being rocked again, gently, as if in a cradle. She felt the car move forward with a sudden lurch, and then the smooth easy momentum. Miriam was there and Miriam wanted Jesse to look at her, but Jesse was too tired now.

"I don't want to go, Mother."

"But Jesse. Please. It's not too late. You can still come!" Like David calling. "Jessica."

Daniel

ABOUT halfway through, Daniel understood. The white-faced brothers and sisters would circle each other, eye each other, even threaten each other all during the concert, but nobody would do anything. The rule was too hard and fast: leave no evidence of what we are—not victims, not a single cell of our vampiric tissue.

Lestat was to be the only kill and that was to be done most carefully. Mortals were not to see the scythes unless it was unavoidable. Snatch the bastard when he tried to take his leave, that was the scheme; dismember him before the cognoscenti only. That is, unless he resisted, in which case he must die before his fans, and the body would have to be destroyed completely.

Daniel laughed and laughed. Imagine Lestat allowing such a thing to happen.

Daniel laughed in their spiteful faces. Pallid as orchids, these vicious souls who filled the hall with their simmering outrage, their envy, their greed. You would have thought they hated Lestat if for no other reason than his flamboyant beauty.

Daniel had broken away from Armand finally. Why not?

Nobody could hurt him, not even the glowing stone figure he'd seen in the shadows, the one so hard and so old he looked like the Golem of legend. What an eerie thing that was, that stone one staring down at the wounded mortal woman who lay with her neck broken, the one with the red hair who looked like the twins in the dream. And probably some stupid human being had done that to her, broken her neck like that. And the blond vampire in the buckskin, pushing past them to reach the scene, he had been an awe-inspiring sight as well, with the hardened veins bulging on his neck and on the backs of his hands when he reached the poor broken victim. Armand had watched the men take the red-haired woman away with the most unusual expression on his face, as if he should somehow intervene; or maybe it was only that the Golem thing, standing idly by, made him wary. Finally, he'd shoved Daniel back into the singing crowd. But there was no need to fear. It was sanctuary for *them* in this place, this cathedral of sound and light.

And Lestat was Christ on the cathedral cross. How describe his overwhelming and irrational authority? His face would have been cruel if it hadn't been for the childlike rapture and exuberance. Pumping his fist into the air, he bawled, pleaded, roared at the powers that be as he sang of his downfall—Lelio, the boulevard actor turned into a creature of night against his will!

His soaring tenor seemed to leave his body utterly as he recounted his defeats, his resurrections, the thirst inside him which no measure of blood could ever quench. "Am I not the devil in you all!" he cried, not to the moonflower monsters in the crowd but to the mortals who adored him.

And even Daniel was screaming, bellowing, leaping off his feet as he cried in agreement, though the words meant nothing finally; it was merely the raw force of Lestat's defiance. Lestat cursed heaven on behalf of all who had ever been outcasts, all who had ever known violation, and then turned, in guilt and malice, on their own kind.

It seemed to Daniel at the highest moments as though it were an omen that he should find immortality on the eve of this great Mass. The Vampire Lestat was God; or the nearest thing he had ever known to it. The giant on the video screen gave his benediction to all that Daniel had ever desired.

How could the others resist? Surely the fierceness of their intended victim made him all the more inviting. The final message behind all Lestat's lyrics was simple: Lestat had the gift that had been promised to each of them; Lestat was unkillable. He devoured the suffering forced upon him and emerged all the stronger. To join with him was to live forever:

This is my Body. This is my Blood.

Yet the hate boiled among the vampire brothers and sisters. As the concert came to a close, Daniel felt it keenly—an odor rising from the crowd—an expanding hiss beneath the strum of the music.

Kill the god. Tear him limb from limb. Let the mortal worshipers do as they have always done—mourn for him who was meant to die. "Go, the Mass is ended."

The houselights went on. The fans stormed the wooden stage, tearing down the black serge curtain to follow the fleeing musicians.

Armand grabbed Daniel's arm. "Out the side door," he said. "Our only chance is to get to him quickly."

Khayman

IT WAS just as he had expected. She struck out at the first of those who struck at him. Lestat had come through the back door, Louis at his side, and made a dash for his black Porsche when the assassins set upon him. It seemed a rude circle sought to close, but at once the first, with scythe raised, went up in flames. The crowd panicked, terrified children stampeding in all directions. Another immortal assailant was suddenly on fire. And then another.

Khayman slipped back against the wall as the clumsy humans hurtled past him. He saw a tall elegant female blood drinker slice unnoticed through the mob, and slide behind the wheel of Lestat's car, calling to Louis and Lestat to join her. It was Gabrielle, the fiend's mother. And logically enough the lethal fire did not harm her. There wasn't a particle of fear in her cold blue eyes as she readied the vehicle with swift, decisive gestures.

Lestat meantime turned around and around in a rage. Maddened, robbed of the battle, he finally climbed into the car only because the others forced him to do so.

And as the Porsche plowed viciously through the rushing youngsters, blood drinkers burst into flame everywhere. In a horrid silent chorus, their cries rose, their frantic curses, their final questions.

Khayman covered his face. The Porsche was halfway to the gates before the crowd forced it to stop. Sirens screamed; voices roared commands; children had fallen with broken limbs. Mortals cried in misery and confusion.

Get to Armand, Khayman thought. But what was the use? He saw them burning everywhere he looked in great writhing plumes of orange and blue flame that changed suddenly to white in their heat as they released the charred clothes which fell to the pavements. How could he come between the fire and Armand? How could he save the young one, Daniel?

He looked up at the distant hills, at a tiny figure glowing against the dark sky, unnoticed by all who screamed and fled and cried for help around him.

Suddenly he felt the heat; he felt it touch him as it had in Athens. He felt it dance about his face, he felt his eyes watering. Steadily he regarded the distant tiny source. And then for reasons that he might never himself understand, he chose not to drive back the fire, but rather to see what it might do to him. Every fiber of his being said, Give it back. Yet he remained motionless, washed of thought, and feeling the sweat drip from him. The fire circled him, embraced him. And then it moved away, leaving him alone, cold, and wounded beyond his wildest imagining. Quietly he whispered a prayer: *May the twins destroy you.*

Daniel

FIRE!" Daniel caught the rank greasy stench just as he saw the flames themselves breaking out here and there all through the multitude. What protection was the crowd now? Like tiny explosions the fires were, as groups of frantic teenagers stumbled to get away from them, and ran in senseless circles, colliding helplessly with one another.

The sound. Daniel heard it again. It was moving above them. Armand pulled him back against the building. It was useless. They could not get to Lestat. And they had no cover. Dragging Daniel after him, Armand retreated into the hall again. A pair of terrified vampires ran past the entrance, then exploded into tiny conflagrations.

In horror, Daniel watched the skeletons glowing as they melted within the pale yellow blaze. Behind them in the deserted auditorium a fleeing figure was suddenly caught in the same ghastly flames. Twisting, turning, he collapsed on the cement floor, smoke rising from his empty clothing. A pool of grease formed on the cement, then dried up even as Daniel stared at it.

Out into the fleeing mortals, they ran again, this time towards the distant front gates over yards and yards of asphalt.

And suddenly they were traveling so fast that Daniel's feet had left the ground. The world was nothing but a smear of color. Even the piteous cries of the frightened fans were stretched, softened. Abruptly they stopped at the gates, just as Lestat's black Porsche raced out of the parking lot, past them, and onto the avenue. Within seconds it was gone, like a bullet traveling south towards the freeway.

Armand made no attempt to follow it; he seemed not even to see it. He stood near the gatepost looking back over the heads of the crowd, beyond the curved roof of the hall to the distant horizon. The eerie telepathic noise was deafening now. It swallowed every other sound in the world; it swallowed every sensation.

Daniel couldn't keep his hands from going to his ears, couldn't keep his knees from buckling. He felt Armand draw close. But he could no longer see. He knew that if it was meant to happen it would be now, yet still he couldn't feel the fear; still he couldn't believe in his own death; he was paralyzed with wonder and confusion.

Gradually the sound faded. Numb, he felt his vision clear; he saw the great red shape of a lumbering ladder truck approach, the firemen shouting for him to move out of the gateway. The siren came as if from another world, an invisible needle through his temples.

Armand was gently pulling him out of the path. Frightened people thundered past as if driven by a wind. He felt himself fall. But Armand caught him. Into the warm crush of mortals, outside the fence they passed, slipping among those who peered through the chain mesh at the melee.

Hundreds still fled. Sirens, sour and discordant, drowned out their cries. One fire engine after another roared up to the gates, to nudge its way through dispersing mortals. But these sounds were thin and distant, dulled still by the receding supernatural noise. Armand clung to the fence, his eyes closed, his forehead pressed against the metal. The fence shuddered, as if it alone could hear the thing as they heard it.

It was gone.

An icy quiet descended. The quiet of shock, emptiness. Though the pandemonium continued, it did not touch them.

They were alone, the mortals loosening, milling, moving away. And the air carried those lingering preternatural cries like burning tinsel again; more dying, but where?

Across the avenue he moved at Armand's side. Unhurried. And down a dark side street they made their way, past faded stucco houses and shabby corner stores, past sagging neon signs and over cracked pavements.

On and on, they walked. The night grew cold and still around them. The sound of the sirens was remote, almost mournful.

As they came to a broad garish boulevard, a great lumbering trolleybus appeared, flooded with a greenish light. Like a ghost it seemed, proceeding towards them, through the emptiness and the silence. Only a few forlorn mortal passengers peered from its smeared and dirty windows. The driver drove as if in his sleep.

Armand raised his eyes, wearily, as if only to watch it pass. And to Daniel's amazement the bus came to a halt for them.

They climbed aboard together, ignoring the little coin box, and sank down side by side on the long leather bench seat. The driver never turned his head from the dark windshield before him. Armand sat back against the window. Dully, he stared at the black rubber floor. His hair was tousled, his cheek smudged with soot. His lower lip protruded ever so slightly. Lost in thought, he seemed utterly unconscious of himself.

Daniel looked at the lackluster mortals: the prune-faced woman with a slit for a mouth who looked at him angrily; the drunken man, with no neck, who snored on his chest; and the small-headed teenage woman with the stringy hair and the sores at the corners of her mouth who held a giant toddler on her lap with skin like bubblegum. Why, something was horribly wrong with each of them. And there, the dead man on the back seat, with his eyes half mast and the dried spit on his chin. Did nobody know he was dead? The urine stank as it dried beneath him.

Daniel's own hands look dead, lurid. Like a corpse with one live arm, the driver seemed, as he turned the wheel. Was this a hallucination? The bus to hell?

No. Only a trolleybus like a million he had taken in his lifetime, on which the weary and the down-and-out rode the city's streets through the late hours. He smiled suddenly, foolishly. He was going to start laughing, thinking of the dead man back there, and these people just riding along, and the way the light made everyone look, but then a sense of dread returned.

The silence unnerved him. The slow rocking of the bus unnerved him; the parade of dingy houses beyond the windows unnerved him; the sight of Armand's listless face and empty stare was unbearable.

"Will she come back for us?" he asked. He could not endure it any longer.

"She knew we were there," Armand said, eyes dull, voice low. "She passed us over."

Khayman

HE HAD retreated to the high grassy slope, with the cold Pacific beyond it.

It was like a panorama now; death at a distance, lost in the lights, the vapor-thin wails of preternatural souls interwoven with the darker, richer voices of the human city.

The fiends had pursued Lestat, forcing the Porsche over the edge of the freeway. Unhurt, Lestat had emerged from the wreck, spoiling for battle; but the fire had struck again to scatter or destroy those who surrounded him.

Finally left alone with Louis and Gabrielle, he had agreed to retreat, uncertain of who or what had protected him.

And unbeknownst to the trio, the Queen pursued their enemies for them.

Over the roofs, her power moved, destroying those who had fled, those who had tried to hide, those who had lingered near fallen companions in confusion and anguish.

The night stank of their burning, these wailing phantoms that left nothing on the empty pavement but their ruined clothes. Below, under the arc lamps of the abandoned parking lots, the lawmen searched in vain for bodies; the firefighters looked in vain for those to assist. The mortal youngsters cried piteously.

Small wounds were treated; the crazed were narcotized and taken away gently. So efficient the agencies of this plentiful time. Giant hoses cleaned the lots. They washed away the scorched rags of the burnt ones.

Tiny beings down there argued and swore that they had witnessed these immolations. But no evidence remained. She had destroyed completely her victims.

And now she moved on far away from the hall, to search the deepest recesses of the city. Her power turned corners and entered windows and doorways. There would be a tiny burst of flame out there like the striking of a sulphur match; then nothing.

The night grew quieter. Taverns and shops shut their doors, winking out in the thickening darkness. Traffic thinned on the highways.

The ancient one she caught in the North Beach streets, the one who had wanted but to see her face; she had burned him slowly as he crawled along the sidewalk. His bones turned to ash, the brain a mass of glowing embers in its last moments. Another she struck down upon a high flat roof, so that he fell like a shooting star out over the glimmering city. His empty clothes took flight like dark paper when it was finished.

And south Lestat went, to his refuge in Carmel Valley. Jubilant, drunk on the love he felt for Louis and Gabrielle, he spoke of old times and new dreams, utterly oblivious to the final slaughter.

"Maharet, where are you?" Khayman whispered. The night gave no answer. If Mael was near, if Mael heard the call, he gave no sign of it. Poor, desperate Mael, who had run out into the open after the attack upon Jessica. Mael, who might have been slain now, too. Mael staring helplessly as the ambulance carried Jesse away from him.

Khayman could not find him.

He combed the light-studded hills, the deep valleys in which the beat of souls was like a thunderous whisper. "Why have I witnessed these things?" he asked. "Why have the dreams brought me here?"

He stood listening to the mortal world.

The radios chattered of devil worship, riots, random fires, mass hallucinations. They whined of vandalism and crazed youth. But it was a big city for all its geographic smallness. The rational mind had already encapsulated the experience and disregarded it. Thousands took no notice. Others slowly and painstakingly revised in memory the impossible things they had seen. The Vampire Lestat was a human rock star and nothing more, his concert the scene of predictable though uncontrollable hysteria.

Perhaps it was part of the Queen's design to so smoothly abort Lestat's dreams. To burn his enemies off the earth before the frail blanket of human assumptions could be irreparably damaged. If this was so, would she punish the creature himself finally?

No answer came to Khayman.

His eyes moved over the sleepy terrain. An ocean fog had swept in, settling in deep rosy layers beneath the tops of the hills. The whole had a fairy-tale sweetness to it now in the first hour past midnight.

Collecting his strongest power, he sought to leave the confines of his body, to send his vision out of himself like the wandering *ka* of the Egyptian dead, to see those whom the Mother might have spared, to draw close to them.

"Armand," he said aloud. And then the lights of the city went dim. He felt the warmth and illumination of another place, and Armand was there before him.

He and his fledgling, Daniel, had come safely again to the mansion where they would sleep beneath the cellar floor unmolested. Groggily the young one danced through the large and sumptuous rooms, his mind full of Lestat's songs and rhythms. Armand stared out into the night, his youthful face as impassive as before. He saw Khayman! He saw him standing motionless on the faraway hill, yet felt him near enough to touch. Silently, invisibly, they studied one another.

It seemed Khayman's loneliness was more than he could bear; but the eyes of Armand held no emotion, no trust, no welcome.

Khayman moved on, drawing on ever greater strength, rising higher and higher in his search, so far from his body now that he could not for the moment even locate it. To the north he went, calling the names Santino, Pandora.

In a blasted field of snow and ice he saw them, two black figures in the endless whiteness—Pandora's garments shredded by the wind, her eyes full of blood tears as she searched for the dim outline of Marius's compound. She was glad of Santino at her side, this unlikely explorer in his fine clothes of black velvet. The long sleepless night through which Pandora had circled the world had left her aching in every limb and near to collapsing. All creatures must sleep; must dream. If she did not lie down soon in some dark place, her mind would be unable to fight the voices, the images, the madness. She did not want to take to the air again, and this Santino could not do such things, and so she walked beside him.

Santino cleaved to her, feeling only her strength, his heart shrunken and bruised from the distant yet inescapable cries of those whom the Queen had slaughtered. Feeling the soft brush of Khayman's gaze, he pulled his black cloak tight around his face. Pandora took no notice whatsoever.

Khayman veered away. Softly, it hurt him to see them touch; it hurt him to see the two of them together.

In the mansion on the hill, Daniel slit the throat of a wriggling rat and let its blood flow into a crystal glass. "Lestat's trick," he said studying it in the light. Armand sat still by the fire, watching the red jewel of blood in the glass as Daniel lifted it to his lips lovingly.

Back into the night Khayman moved, wandering higher again, far from the city lights as if in a great orbit.

Mael, answer me. Let me know where you are. Had the Mother's cold fiery beam struck him, too? Or did he mourn now so deeply for Jesse that he hearkened to nothing and no one? Poor Jesse, dazzled by miracles, struck down by a fledgling in the blink of an eye before anyone could prevent it.

Maharet's child, my child!

Khayman was afraid of what he might see, afraid of what he dared not seek to alter. But maybe the Druid was simply too strong for him now; the Druid concealed himself and his charge from all eyes and all minds. Either that or the Queen had had her way and it was finished.

Jesse

SO QUIET here. She lay on a bed that was hard and soft, and her body felt floppy like that of a rag doll. She could lift her hand but then it would drop, and still she could not see, except in a vague ghostly way things that might have been an illusion.

For example lamps around her; ancient clay lamps shaped like fish and filled with oil. They gave a thick odoriferous perfume to the room. Was this a funeral parlor?

It came again, the fear that she was dead, locked in the flesh yet disconnected. She heard a curious sound; what was it? A scissors cutting. It was trimming the edges of her hair; the feel of it traveled to her scalp. She felt it even in her intestines.

A tiny vagrant hair was plucked suddenly from her face; one of those annoying hairs, quite out of place, which women so hate. She was being groomed for the coffin, wasn't she? Who else would take such care, lifting her hand now, and inspecting her fingernails so carefully.

But the pain came again, an electric flash moving down her back and she screamed. She screamed aloud in this room where she'd been only hours before in this very bed with the chains creaking.

She heard a gasp from someone near her. She tried to see, but she only saw the lamps again. And some dim figure standing in the window. Miriam watching.

"Where?" he asked. He was startled, trying to see the vision. Hadn't this happened before?

"Why can't I open my eyes?" she asked. He could look forever and he would never see Miriam.

"Your eyes are open," he said. How raw and tender his voice sounded. "I can't give you any more unless I give it all. We are not healers. We are slayers. It's time for you to tell me what you want. There is no one to help me."

I don't know what I want. All I know is I don't want to die! I don't want to stop living. What cowards we are, she thought, what liars. A great fatalistic sadness had accompanied her all the way to this night, yet there had been the secret hope of this always! Not merely to see, to know, but to be part of . . . .

She wanted to explain, to hone it carefully with audible words, but the pain came again. A fiery brand touched to her spine, the pain shooting into her legs. And then the blessed numbness. It seemed the room she couldn't see grew dark and the flames of the ancient lamps sputtered. Outside the forest whispered. The forest writhed in the dark. And Mael's grip on her wrist was weak suddenly, not because he had let her go but because she couldn't any longer feel it.

"Jesse!"

He shook her with both his hands, and the pain was like lightning shattering the dark. She screamed through her clenched teeth. Miriam, stony-eyed and silent, glared from the window.

"Mael, do it!" she cried.

With all her strength, she sat up on the bed. The pain was without shape or limit; the scream strangled inside her. But then she opened her eyes, truly opened them. In the hazy light, she saw Miriam's cold unmerciful expression. She saw the tall bent figure of Mael towering over the bed. And then she turned to the open door. Maharet was coming.

Mael didn't know, didn't realize, till she did. With soft silky steps, Maharet came up the stairs, her long skirts moving with a dark rustling sound; she came down the corridor.

Oh, after all these years, these long years! Through her tears, Jesse watched Maharet move into the light of the lamps; she saw her shimmering face, and the burning radiance of her hair. Maharet gestured for Mael to leave them.

Then Maharet approached the bed. She lifted her hands, palms open, as if in invitation; she raised her hands as if to receive a baby.

"Yes, do it."

"Say farewell then, my darling, to Miriam."

IN OLDEN times there was a terrible worship in the city of Carthage. To the great bronze god Baal, the populace offered in sacrifice their little children. The small bodies were laid on the statue's outstretched arms, and then by means of a spring, the arms would rise and the children would fall into the roaring furnace of the god's belly.

After Carthage was destroyed, only the Romans carried the old tale, and as the centuries passed wise men came not to believe it. Too terrible, it seemed, the immolation of these children. But as the archaeologists brought their shovels and began to dig, they found the bones of the small victims in profusion. Whole necropolises they unearthed of nothing but little skeletons.

And the world knew the old legend was true; that the men and women of Carthage had brought their offspring to the god and stood in obeisance as their children tumbled screaming into the fire. It was religion.

Now as Maharet lifted Jesse, as Maharet's lips touched her throat, Jesse thought of the old legend. Maharet's arms were like the hard metal arms of the god Baal, and in one fiery instant Jesse knew unspeakable torment.

But it was not her own death that Jesse saw; it was the deaths of others—the souls of the immolated undead, rising upwards away from terror and the physical pain of the flames that consumed their preternatural bodies. She heard their cries; she heard their warnings; she saw their faces as they left the earth, dazzling as they carried with them still the stamp of human form without its substance; she felt them passing from misery into the unknown; she heard their song just beginning.

And then the vision paled, and died away, like music half heard and half remembered. She was near to death; her body gone, all pain gone, all sense of permanence or anguish.

She stood in the clearing in the sunshine looking down at the mother on the altar. "In the flesh," Maharet said. "In the flesh all wisdom begins. Beware the thing that has no flesh. Beware the gods, beware the *idea,* beware the devil."

Then the blood came; it poured through every fiber of her body; she was legs and arms again as it electrified her limbs, her skin stinging with the heat; and the hunger making her body writhe as the blood sought to anchor her soul to substance forever.

They lay in each other's arms, she and Maharet, and Maharet's hard skin warmed and softened so that they became one wet and tangled thing, hair enmeshed, Jesse's face buried in Maharet's neck as she gnawed at the fount, as one shock of ecstasy passed through her after another.

Suddenly Maharet drew away and turned Jesse's face against the pillow. Maharet's hand covered Jesse's eyes, and Jesse felt the tiny razor-sharp teeth pierce her skin; she felt it all being taken back, drawn out. Like the whistling wind, the sensation of being emptied, of being devoured; of being nothing!

"Drink again, my darling." Slowly she opened her eyes; she saw the white throat and the white breasts; she reached out and caught the throat in her hands, and this time it was she who broke the flesh, she tore it. And when the first spill of blood hit her tongue, she pulled Maharet down under her. Utterly compliant Maharet was; hers; Maharet's breasts against her breasts; Maharet's lips against her face, as she sucked the blood, sucked it harder and harder. *You are mine, you are utterly and completely mine.* All images, voices, visions, gone now.

They slept, or almost slept, folded against one another. It seemed the pleasure left its shimmer; it seemed that to breathe was to feel it again; to shift against the silken sheets or against Maharet's silken skin was to begin again.

The fragrant wind moved through the room. A great collective sigh rose from the forest. No more Miriam, no more the spirits of the twilight realm, caught between life and death. She had found her place; her eternal place.

As she closed her eyes, she saw the thing in the jungle stop and look at her. The red-haired thing saw her and saw Maharet in her arms; it saw the red hair; two women with red hair; and the thing veered and moved towards them.

Khayman

DEAD quiet the peace of Carmel Valley. So happy were the little coven in the house, Lestat, Louis, Gabrielle, so happy to be together. Lestat had rid himself of his soiled clothes and was resplendent again in shining "vampire attire," even to the black velvet cloak thrown casually over one shoulder. And the others, how animated they were, the woman Gabrielle unbraiding her yellow hair rather absently as she talked in an easy, passionate manner. And Louis, the human one, silent, yet profoundly excited by the presence of the other two, entranced, as it were, by their simplest gestures.

At any other time, how moved Khayman would have been by such happiness. He would have wanted to touch their hands, look into their eyes, tell them who he was and what he had seen, he would have wanted just to be with them.

But she was near. And the night was not finished.

The sky paled and the faintest warmth of the morning crept across the fields. Things stirred in the growing light. The trees shifted, their leaves uncurling ever so slowly.

Khayman stood beneath the apple tree, watching the color of the shadows change; listening to the morning. She was here, without question.

She concealed herself, willfully, and powerfully. But Khayman she could not deceive. He watched; he waited, listening to the laughter and talk of the small coven.

At the doorway of the house, Lestat embraced his mother, as she took leave of him. Out into the gray morning she came, with a sprightly step, in her dusty neglected khaki clothes, her thick blond hair brushed back, the picture of a carefree wanderer. And the black-haired one, the pretty one, Louis, was beside her.

Khayman watched them cross the grass, the female moving on into the open field before the woods where she meant to sleep within the earth itself, while the male entered the cool darkness of a small outbuilding. Something so refined about that one, even as he slipped beneath the floorboards, something about the way that he lay down as if in the grave; the way he composed his limbs, falling at once into utter darkness.

And the woman; with stunning violence, she made her deep and secret hiding place, the leaves settling as if she had never been there. The earth held her outstretched arms, her bent head. Into the dreams of the twins she plunged, into images of jungle and river she would never remember.

So far so good. Khayman did not want them to die, to burn up.

Exhausted, he stood with his back to the apple tree, the pungent green fragrance of the apples enveloping him.

Why was she here? And where was she hiding? When he opened himself to it, he felt the low radiant sound of her presence, rather like an engine of the modern world, giving off some irrepressible whisper of itself and its lethal power.

Finally Lestat emerged from the house and hurried towards the lair he had made for himself beneath the acacia trees against the hillside. Through a trapdoor he descended, down earthen steps, and into a dank chamber.

So it was peace for them all, peace until tonight when he would be the bringer of bad tidings.

The sun rose closer to the horizon; the first deflected rays appeared, which always dulled Khayman's vision. He focused upon the soft deepening colors of the orchard as all the rest of the world lost its distinct lines and shapes. He closed his eyes for a moment, realizing that he must go into the house, that he must seek some cool and shadowy place where mortals were unlikely to disturb him.

And when the sun set, he'd be waiting for them when they woke. He would tell them what he knew; he would tell them about the others. With a sudden stab of pain he thought of Mael, and of Jesse, whom he could not find, as if the earth had devoured them.

He thought of Maharet and he wanted to weep. But he made his way towards the house now. The sun was warm on his back; his limbs were heavy. Tomorrow night, whatever else came to pass, he wouldn't be alone. He would be with Lestat and his cohorts; and if they turned him away, he would seek out Armand. He would go north to Marius.

He heard the sound first—a loud, crackling roar. He turned, shielding his eyes from the rising sun. A great spray of earth shot up from the floor of the forest. The acacias swayed as if in a storm, limbs cracking, roots heaved up from the soil, trunks falling helter-skelter.

In a dark streak of windblown garments the Queen rose with ferocious speed, the limp body of Lestat dangling from her arms as she made for the western sky away from the sunrise.

Khayman gave a loud cry before he could stop himself. And his cry rang out over the stillness of the valley. So she had taken her lover.

Oh, poor lover, oh, poor beautiful blond-haired prince . . . .

But there was no time to think or to act or to know his own heart; he turned to the shelter of the house; the sun had struck the clouds and the horizon had become an inferno.

DANIEL stirred in the dark. The sleep seemed to lift like a blanket that had been about to crush him. He saw the gleam of Armand's eye. He heard Armand's whisper: "She's taken him."

JESSE moaned aloud. Weightless, she drifted in the pearly gloom. She saw the two rising figures as if in a dance—the Mother and the Son. Like saints ascending on the painted ceiling of a church. Her lips formed the words "the Mother."

IN THEIR deep-dug grave beneath the ice, Pandora and Santino slept in each other's arms. Pandora heard the sound. She heard Khayman's cry. She saw Lestat with his eyes closed and his head thrown back, rising in Akasha's embrace. She saw Akasha's black eyes fixed upon his sleeping face. Pandora's heart stopped in terror.

MARIUS closed his eyes. He could keep them open no longer. Above the wolves howled; the wind tore at the steel roof of the compound. Through the blizzard the feeble rays of the sun came as if igniting the swirling snow, and he could feel the dulling heat move down through layer upon layer of ice to numb him.

He saw the sleeping figure of Lestat in her arms; he saw her rising into the sky. "Beware of her, Lestat," he whispered with his last conscious breath. "Danger."

ON THE cool carpeted floor, Khayman stretched out and buried his face in his arm. And a dream came at once, a soft silky dream of a summer night in a lovely place, where the sky was big over the city lights, and they were all together, these immortals whose names he knew and held to his heart now.

PART III

AS IT WAS IN THE BEGINNING, IS NOW, AND EVER SHALL BE...

Hide me
from me.
Fill these
holes with eyes
for mine are not
mine. Hide
me head & need
for I am no good
so dead in life
so much time.
Be wing, and
shade my me
from my desire
to be
hooked fish.
That worm
wine
looks sweet and
makes my me
blind. And, too,
my heart hide
for I shall at
this rate it also
eat in time.

STAN RICE
"Cannibal"
Some Lamb (1975)

1

LESTAT: IN THE ARMS OF THE GODDESS

I CAN'T say when I awoke, when I first came to my senses.

I remember knowing that she and I had been together for a long time, that I'd been feasting on her blood with an animal abandon, that Enkil was destroyed and she alone held the primeval power; and that she was causing me to see things and understand things that made me cry like a child.

Two hundred years ago, when I'd drunk from her in the shrine, the blood had been silent, eerily and magnificently silent. Now it was an utter transport of images—ravishing the brain just as the blood itself ravished the body; I was learning everything that had happened; I was there as the others died one by one in that horrible way.

And then there were the voices: the voices that rose and fell, seemingly without purpose, like a whispering choir in a cave.

It seemed there was a lucid moment in which I connected everything—the rock concert, the house in Carmel Valley, her radiant face before me. And the knowledge that I was here now with her, in this dark snowy place. I'd waked her. Or rather I had given her the reason to rise as she had said it. The reason to turn and stare back at the throne on which she'd sat and take those first faltering steps away from it.

Do you know what it meant to lift my hand and see it move in the light? Do you know what it meant to hear the sudden sound of my own voice echoing in that marble chamber?

Surely we had danced together in the dark snow-covered wood, or was it only that we had embraced over and over again?

Terrible things had happened. Over the whole world, terrible things. The execution of those who should never have been born. *Evil spawn.* The massacre at the concert had been only the finish.

Yet I was in her arms in this chilling darkness, in the familiar scent of winter, and her blood was mine again, and it was enslaving me. When she drew away, I felt agony. I had to clear my thoughts, had to know whether or not Marius was alive, whether or not Louis and Gabrielle, and Armand, had been spared. I had to find myself again, somehow.

But the voices, the rising tide of voices! Mortals near and far. Distance made no difference. Intensity was the measure. It was a million times my old hearing, when I could pause on a city street and hear the tenants of some dark building, each in his own chamber, talking, thinking, praying, for as long and as closely as I liked.

Sudden silence when she spoke:

"Gabrielle and Louis are safe. I've told you this. Do you think I would hurt those you love? Look into my eyes now and listen only to what I say. I have spared many more than are required. And this I did for you as well as for myself, that I may see myself reflected in immortal eyes, and hear the voices of my children speaking to me. But I chose the ones you love, the ones you would see again. I could not take that comfort from you. But now you are with me, and you must see and know what is being revealed to you. You must have courage to match mine."

I couldn't endure it, the visions she was giving me—that horrid little Baby Jenks in those last moments; had it been a desperate dream the moment of her death, a string of images flickering within her dying brain? I couldn't bear it. And Laurent, my old companion Laurent, drying up in the flames on the pavement; and on the other side of the world, Felix, whom I had known also at the Theater of the Vampires, driven, burning, through the alleyways of Naples, and finally into the sea. And the others, so many others, the world over; I wept for them; I wept for all of it. Suffering without meaning.

"A life like that," I said of Baby Jenks, crying.

"That's why I showed you all of it," she answered. "That's why it is finished. The Children of Darkness are no more. And we shall have only angels now."

"But the others," I asked. "What has happened to Armand?" And the voices were starting again, the low humming that could mount to a deafening roar.

"Come now, my prince," she whispered. Silence again. She reached up and held my face in her hands. Her black eyes grew larger, the white face suddenly supple and almost soft. "If you must see it, I'll show you those who still live, those whose names will become legend along with yours and mine."

Legend?

She turned her head ever so slightly; it seemed a miracle when she closed her eyes; because then the visible life went out of her altogether. A dead and perfect thing, fine black eyelashes curling exquisitely. I looked down at her throat; at the pale blue of the artery beneath the flesh, suddenly visible as if she meant for me to see it. The lust I felt was unsupportable. The goddess, mine! I took her roughly with a strength that would have hurt a mortal woman. The icy skin seemed absolutely impenetrable and then my teeth broke through it and the hot fount was roaring into me again.

The voices came, yet they died back at my command. And there was nothing then but the low rush of the blood and her heart beating slowly next to my own.

Darkness. A brick cellar. A coffin made of oak and polished to a fine luster. Locks of gold. The magic moment; the locks opened as if sprung by an invisible key. The lid rose, revealing the satin lining. There was a faint scent of Eastern perfume. I saw Armand lying on the white satin pillow, a seraph with long full auburn hair; head to one side, eyes blank, as if to wake was unfailingly startling. I watched him rise from the coffin, with slow, elegant gestures; our gestures, for we are the only beings who routinely rise from coffins. I saw him close the lid. Across the damp brick floor, he walked to yet another coffin. And this one he opened reverently, as if it were a casket containing a rare prize. Inside, a young man lay sleeping; lifeless, yet dreaming. Dreaming of a jungle where a red-haired woman walked, a woman I could not clearly see. And then the most bizarre scene, something I'd glimpsed before, but where? Two women kneeling beside an altar. That is, I thought it was an altar. . . .

A tensing in her; a tightening. She shifted against me like a statue of the Virgin ready to crush me. I swooned; I thought I heard her speak a name. But the blood came in another gush and my body was throbbing again with the pleasure; no earth; no gravity.

The brick cellar once more. A shadow had fallen over the young man's body. Another had come into the cellar and placed a hand on Armand's shoulder. Armand knew him. Mael was his name. *Come.*

But where is he taking them?

Purple evening in the redwood forest. Gabrielle was walking in that careless, straight-backed, unstoppable way of hers, her eyes like two chips of glass, giving back nothing to what she saw around her, and there was Louis beside her, struggling gracefully to keep up. Louis looked so touchingly civilized in the wilderness; so hopelessly out of place. The vampire guise of last night had been discarded; yet he seemed even more the gentleman in his worn old clothing, merely a little down on his luck. Out of his league with her, and does she know it? Will she take care of him? *But they're both afraid, afraid for me!*

The tiny sky above was turning to polished porcelain; the trees seemed to bring the light down their massive trunks almost to the roots. I could hear a creek rushing in the shadows. Then I saw it. Gabrielle walked right into the water in her brown boots. *But where are they going?* And who was the third one with them, who came into view only as Gabrielle turned back to look at him?—my God, such a face, and so placid. Ancient, powerful, yet letting the two young ones walk before him. Through the trees I could see a clearing, a house. On a high stone veranda stood a red-haired woman; the woman whom I'd seen in the jungle? Ancient expressionless mask of a face like the face of the male in the forest who was looking up at her; face like the face of my Queen.

Let them come together. I sighed as the blood poured into me. *It will make it all the simpler.* But who were they, these ancient ones, these creatures with countenances washed as clean as her own?

The vision shifted. This time the voices were a soft wreath around us, whispering, crying. And for one moment I wanted to listen, to try to detach from the monstrous chorus one fleeting mortal song. Imagine it, voices from all over, from the mountains of India, from the streets of Alexandria, from the tiny hamlets near and far.

But another vision was coming.

Marius. Marius was climbing up out of a bloodstained pit of broken ice with Pandora and Santino to aid him. They had just managed to reach the jagged shelf of a basement floor. The dried blood was a crust covering half of Marius's face; he looked angry, bitter, eyes dull, his long yellow hair matted with blood. With a limp he went up a spiraling iron stairs, Pandora and Santino in his wake. It was like a pipe through which they ascended. When Pandora tried to help him he brushed her aside roughly.

Wind. Bitter cold. Marius's house lay open to the elements as if an earthquake had broken it apart. Sheets of glass were shattered into dangerous fragments; rare and beautiful tropical fish were frozen on the sand floor of a great ruined tank. Snow blanketed the furnishings and lay heaped against the bookshelves, against the statues, against the racks of records and tapes. The birds were dead in their cages. The green plants were dripping with icicles. Marius stared at the dead fish in the murky margin of ice in the bottom of the tank. He stared at the great dead stalks of seaweed that lay among the shards of gleaming glass.

Even as I watched, I saw him healing; the bruises seemed to melt from his face; I saw the face itself regain its natural shape. His leg was mending. He could stand almost straight. In rage he stared at the tiny blue and silver fish. He looked up at the sky, at the white wind that obliterated the stars completely. He brushed the flakes of dried blood from his face and hair.

Thousands of pages had been scattered about by the wind—pages of parchment, old crumbling paper. The swirling snow came down now lightly into the ruined parlor. There Marius took up the brass poker for a walking stick, and stared out through the ruptured wall at the starving wolves howling in their pen. No food for them since he, their master, had been buried. Ah, the sound of the wolves howling. I heard Santino speak to Marius, try to tell him that they must go, they were expected, that a woman waited for them in the redwood forest, a woman as old as the Mother, and the meeting could not begin until they had come. A chord of alarm went through me. What was this meeting? Marius understood but he didn't answer. He was listening to the wolves. To the wolves. . . .

The snow and the wolves. I dreamed of wolves. I felt myself drift away, back into my own mind, into my own dreams and memories. I saw a pack of fleet wolves racing over the newly fallen snow.

I saw myself as a young man fighting them—a pack of wolves that had come in deep winter to prey upon my father's village two hundred years ago. I saw myself, the mortal man, so close to death that I could smell it. But I had cut down the wolves one by one. Ah, such coarse youthful vigor, the pure luxury of thoughtless irresistible life! Or so it seemed. At the time it had been misery, hadn't it? The frozen valley, my horse and dogs slain. But now all I could do was remember, and ah, to see the snow covering the mountains, my mountains, my father's land.

I opened my eyes. She had let me go and forced me back a pace. For the first time I understood where we really were. Not in some abstract night, but in a real place and a place that had once, for all purposes, been mine.

"Yes," she whispered. "Look around you."

I knew it by the air, by the smell of winter, and as my vision cleared again, I saw the broken battlements high above, and the tower.

"This is my father's house!" I whispered. "This is the castle in which I was born."

Stillness. The snow shining white over the old floor. This had been the great hall, where we now stood. God, to see it in ruins; to know that it had been desolate for so long. Soft as earth the old stones seemed; and here had been the table, the great long table fashioned in the time of the Crusades; and there had been the gaping hearth, and there the front door.

The snow was not falling now. I looked up and I saw the stars. The tower had its round shape still, soaring hundreds of feet above the broken roof, though all the rest was as a fractured shell. My father's house . . . .

Lightly she stepped away from me, across the shimmering whiteness of the floor, turning slowly in a circle, her head back, as if she were dancing.

To move, to touch solid things, to pass from the realm of dreams into the real world, of all these joys she'd spoken earlier. It took my breath away, watching her. Her garments were timeless, a black silk cloak, a gown of silken folds that swirled gently about her narrow form. Since the dawn of history women have worn such garments, and they wear them now into the ballrooms of the world. I wanted to hold her again, but she forbade it with a soft sudden gesture. What had she said? *Can you imagine it? When I realized that he could no longer keep me there? That I was standing before the throne, and he had not stirred! That not the faintest response came from him?*

She turned; she smiled; the pale light of the sky struck the lovely angles of her face, the high cheekbones, the gentle slope of her chin. Alive she looked, utterly alive.

Then she vanished!

"Akasha!"

"Come to me," she said.

But where was she? Then I saw her far, far away from me at the very end of the hall. A tiny figure at the entrance to the tower. I could scarce make out the features of her face now, yet I could see behind her the black rectangle of the open door.

I started to walk towards her.

"No," she said. "Time to use the strength I've given you. Merely come!"

I didn't move. My mind was clear. My vision was clear. And I knew what she meant. But I was afraid. I'd always been the sprinter, the leaper, the player of tricks. Preternatural speed that baffled mortals, that was not new to me. But she asked for a different accomplishment. I was to leave the spot where I stood and locate myself suddenly beside her, with a speed which I myself could not track. It required a surrender, to try such a thing.

"Yes, surrender," she said gently. "Come."

For a tense moment I merely looked at her, her white hand gleaming on the edge of the broken door. Then I made the decision to be standing at her side. It was as if a hurricane touched me, full of noise and random force. Then I was there! I felt myself shudder all over. The flesh of my face hurt a little, but what did that matter! I looked down into her eyes and I smiled.

Beautiful she was, so beautiful. The goddess with her long black plaited hair. Impulsively I took her in my arms and kissed her; kissed her cold lips and felt them yield to me just a little.

Then the blasphemy of it struck me. It was like the time I'd kissed her in the shrine. I wanted to say something in apology, but I was staring at her throat again, hungry for the blood. It tantalized me that I could drink it and yet she was who she was; she could have destroyed me in a second with no more than the wish to see me die. That's what she had done to the others. The danger thrilled me, darkly. I closed my fingers round her arms, felt the flesh give ever so slightly. I kissed her again, and again. I could taste blood in it.

She drew back and placed her finger on my lips. Then she took my hand and led me through the tower door. Starlight fell through the broken roof hundreds of feet above us, through a gaping hole in the floor of the highest room.

"Do you see?" she said. "The room at the very top is still there? The stairs are gone. The room is unreachable. Except for you and me, my prince."

Slowly she started to rise. Never taking her eyes off me she traveled upwards, the sheer silk of her gown billowing only slightly. I watched in astonishment as she rose higher and higher, her cloak ruffled as if by a faint breeze. She passed through the opening and then stood on the very edge.

Hundreds of feet! Not possible for me to do this . . .

"Come to me, my prince," she said, her soft voice carrying in the emptiness. "Do as you have already done. Do it quickly, and as mortals so often say, don't look down." Whispered laughter.

Suppose I got a fifth of the way up—a good leap, the height, say, of a four-story building, which was rather easy for me but also the limit of—Dizziness. Not possible. Disorientation. How had we come to be here? It was all spinning again. I saw her but it was dreamlike, and the voices were intruding. I didn't want to lose this moment. I wanted to remain connected with time in a series of linked moments, to understand this on my terms.

"Lestat!" she whispered. "Now." Such a tender thing, her small gesture to me to be quick.

I did what I had done before; I looked at her and decided that I should instantly be at her side.

The hurricane again, the air bruising me; I threw up my arms and fought the resistance. I think I saw the hole in the broken boards as I passed through it. Then I was standing there, shaken, terrified I would fall.

It sounded as if I were laughing; but I think I was just going mad a little. Crying actually. "But how?" I said. "I have to know how I did it."

"You know the answer," she said. "The intangible thing which animates you has much more strength now than it did before. It moved you as it has always moved you. Whether you take a step or take flight, it is simply a matter of degree."

"I want to try it again," I said.

She laughed very softly, but spontaneously. "Look about this room," she said. "Do you remember it?"

I nodded. "When I was a young man, I came here all the time," I said. I moved away from her. I saw piles of ruined furniture—the heavy benches and stools that had once filled our castle, medieval work so crude and strong it was damn near indestructible, like the trees that fall in the forest and remain for centuries, the bridges over streams, their trunks covered with moss. So these things had not rotted away. Even old caskets remained, and armor. Oh, yes, the old armor, ghosts of past glory. And in the dust I saw a faint bit of color. Tapestries, but they were utterly destroyed.

In the revolution, these things must have been brought here for safekeeping and then the stairs had fallen away.

I went to one of the tiny narrow windows and I looked out on the land. Far below, nestled in the mountainside, were the electric lights of a little city, sparse, yet there. A car made its way down the narrow road. Ah, the modern world so close yet far away. The castle was the ghost of itself.

"Why did you bring me here?" I asked her. "It's so painful to see this, as painful as everything else."

"Look there, at the suits of armor," she said. "At what lies at their feet. You remember the weapons you took with you the day you went out to kill the wolves?"

"Yes. I remember them."

"Look at them again. I will give you new weapons, infinitely more powerful weapons with which you will kill for me now."

"Kill?"

I glanced down at the cache of arms. Rusted, ruined it seemed; save for the old broadsword, the fine one, which had been my father's and given to him by his father, who had got it from his father, and so forth and so on, back to the time of St. Louis. The lord's broadsword, which I, the seventh son, had used on that long ago morning when I'd gone out like a medieval prince to kill the wolves.

"But whom will I kill?" I asked.

She drew closer. How utterly sweet her face was, how brimming with innocence. Her brows came together; there was that tiny vertical fold of flesh in her forehead, just for an instant. Then all went smooth again.

"I would have you obey me without question," she said gently. "And then understanding would follow. But this is not your way."

"No," I confessed. "I've never been able to obey anyone, not for very long."

"So fearless," she said, smiling.

She opened her right hand gracefully; and quite suddenly she was holding the sword. It seemed I'd felt the thing moving towards her, a tiny change of atmosphere, no more. I stared at it, at the jeweled scabbard and the great bronze hilt that was of course a cross. The belt still hung from it, the belt I'd bought for it, during some long ago summer, of toughened leather and plaited steel.

It was a monster of a weapon, as much for battering as for slashing or piercing. I remembered the weight of it, the way it had made my arm ache when I had slashed again and again at the attacking wolves. Knights in battle had often held such weapons with two hands.

But then what did I know of such battles? I'd been no knight. I'd skewered an animal with this weapon. My only moment of mortal glory, and what had it got me? The admiration of an accursed bloodsucker who chose to make me his heir.

She placed the sword in my hands.

"It's not heavy now, my prince," she said. "You are immortal. Truly immortal. My blood is in you. And you will use your new weapons for me as you once used this sword."

A violent shudder went through me as I touched the sword; it was as if the thing held some latent memory of what it had witnessed; I saw the wolves again; I saw myself standing in the blackened frozen forest ready to kill.

And I saw myself a year later in Paris, dead, immortal; a monster, and on account of those wolves. "Wolfkiller," the vampire had called me. He had picked me from the common herd because I had slain those cursed wolves! And worn their fur so proudly through the winter streets of Paris.

How could I feel such bitterness even now? Did I want to be dead and buried down below in the village graveyard? I looked out of the window again at the snow-covered hillside. Wasn't the same thing happening now? Loved for what I'd been in those early thoughtless mortal years. Again I asked, "But whom or what will I kill?"

No answer.

I thought of Baby Jenks again, that pitiful little thing, and all the blood drinkers who were now dead. And I had wanted a war with them, a little war. And they were all dead. All who had responded to the battle call—dead. I saw the coven house in Istanbul burning; I saw an old one she had caught and burned so slowly; one who had fought her and cursed her. I was crying again.

"Yes, I took your audience from you," she said. "I burnt away the arena in which you sought to shine. I stole the battle! But don't you see?

I offer you finer things than you have ever reached for. I offer you the world, my prince."

"How so?"

"Stop the tears you shed for Baby Jenks, and for yourself. Think on the mortals you should weep for. Envision those who have suffered through the long dreary centuries—the victims of famine and deprivation and ceaseless violence. Victims of endless injustice and endless battling. How then can you weep for a race of monsters, who without guidance or purpose played the devil's gambit on every mortal they chanced to meet!"

"I know. I understand—"

"Do you? Or do you merely retreat from such things to play your symbolic games? Symbol of evil in your rock music. That is nothing, my prince, nothing at all."

"Why didn't you kill me along with the rest of them?" I asked, belligerently, miserably. I grasped the hilt of the sword in my right hand. I fancied I could see the dried blood of the wolf still on it. I pulled the blade free of the leather scabbard. Yes, the blood of the wolf. "I'm no better than they are, am I?" I said. "Why spare any of us?"

Fear stopped me suddenly. Terrible fear for Gabrielle and Louis and Armand. For Marius. Even for Pandora and Mael. Fear for myself. There isn't a thing made that doesn't fight for life, even when there is no real justification. I wanted to live; I always had.

"I would have you love me," she whispered tenderly. Such a voice. In a way, it was like Armand's voice; a voice that could caress you when it spoke to you. Draw you into itself. "And so I take time with you," she continued. She put her hands on my arms, and looked up into my eyes. "I want you to understand. You are my instrument! And so the others shall be if they are wise. Don't you see? There has been a design to all of it—your coming, my waking. For now the hopes of the millennia can be realized at last. Look on the little town below, and on this ruined castle. This could be Bethlehem, my prince, my savior. And together we shall realize all the world's most enduring dreams."

"But how could that possibly be?" I asked. Did she know how afraid I was? That her words moved me from simple fear into terror? Surely she did.

"Ah, you are so strong, princeling," she said. "But you were destined for me, surely. Nothing defeats you. You fear and you don't fear. For a century I watched you suffer, watched you grow weak and finally go down in the earth to sleep, and I then saw you rise, the very image of my own resurrection."

She bowed her head now as if she were listening to sounds from far away. The voices rising. I heard them too, perhaps because she did. I heard the ringing din. And then, annoyed, I pushed them away.

"So strong," she said. "They cannot drag you down into them, the voices, but do not ignore this power; it's as important as any other you possess. They are praying to you just as they have always prayed to me."

I understood her meaning. But I didn't want to hear their prayers; what could I do for them? What had prayers to do with the thing that I was?

"For centuries they were my only comfort," she continued. "By the hour, by the week, by the year I listened; it seemed in early times that the voices I heard had woven a shroud to make of me a dead and buried thing. Then I learned to listen more carefully. I learned to select one voice from the many as if picking a thread from the whole. To that voice alone I would listen and through it I knew the triumph and ruin of a single soul."

I watched her in silence.

"Then as the years passed, I acquired a greater power—to leave my body invisibly and to go to the single mortal whose voice I listened to, to see then through that mortal's eyes. I would walk in the body of this one, or that one. I would walk in sunshine and in darkness; I would suffer; I would hunger; I would know pain. Sometimes I walked in the bodies of immortals as I walked in the body of Baby Jenks. Often, I walked with Marius. Selfish, vain Marius, Marius who confuses greed with respect, who is ever dazzled by the decadent creations of a way of life as selfish as he is. Oh, don't suffer so. I loved him. I love him now; he cared for me. My keeper." Her voice was bitter but only for that instant. "But more often I walked with one among the poor and the sorrowful. It was the rawness of true life I craved."

She stopped; her eyes clouded; her brows came together and the tears rose in her eyes. I knew the power of which she spoke, but only slightly. I wanted so to comfort her but when I reached out to embrace her she motioned for me to be still.

"I would forget who I was, where I was," she continued. "I would be that creature, the one whose voice I had chosen. Sometimes for years. Then the horror would return, the realization that I was a motionless, purposeless thing condemned to sit forever in a golden shrine! Can you imagine the horror of waking suddenly to that realization? That all you have seen and heard and been is nothing but illusion, the observation of another's life? I would return to myself. I would become again what you see before you. This idol with a heart and brain."

I nodded. Centuries ago when I had first laid eyes upon her, I had imagined unspeakable suffering locked within her. I had imagined agonies without expression. And I had been right.

"I knew he kept you there," I said. I spoke of Enkil. Enkil who was now gone, destroyed. A fallen idol. I was remembering the moment in the shrine when I'd drunk from her and he'd come to claim her and almost finished me then and there. Had he known what he meant to do? Was all reason gone even then?

She only smiled in answer. Her eyes were dancing as she looked out into the dark. The snow had begun again, swirling almost magically, catching the light of the stars and the moon and diffusing it through all the world, it seemed.

"It was meant, what happened," she answered finally. "That I should pass those years growing ever more strong. Growing so strong finally that no one . . . no one can be my equal." She stopped. Just for a moment her conviction seemed to waver. But then she grew confident again. "He was but an instrument in the end, my poor beloved King, my companion in agony. His mind was gone, yes. And I did not destroy him, not really. I took into myself what was left of him. And at times I had been as empty, as silent, as devoid of the will even to dream as he was. Only for him there was no returning. He had seen his last visions. He was of no use anymore. He has died a god's death because it only made me stronger. And it was all meant, my prince. All meant from start to finish."

"But how? By whom?"

"Whom?" She smiled again. "Don't you understand? You need look no further for the cause of anything. I am the fulfillment and I shall from this moment on be the cause. There is nothing and no one now who can stop me." Her face hardened for a second. That wavering again. "Old curses mean nothing. In silence I have attained such power that no force in nature could harm me. Even my first brood cannot harm me though they plot against me. It was meant that those years should pass before you came."

"How did I change it?"

She came a step closer. She put her arm around me and it felt soft for the moment, not like the hard thing it truly was. We were just two beings standing near to each other, and she looked indescribably lovely to me, so pure and otherworldly. I felt the awful desire for the blood again. To bend down, to kiss her throat, to have her as I had had a thousand mortal women, yet she the goddess, she with the immeasurable power. I felt the desire rising, cresting.

Again, she put her finger on my lips, as if to say be still.

"Do you remember when you were a boy here?" she asked. "Think back now on the time when you begged them to send you to the monastery school. Do you remember the things the brothers taught you? The prayers, the hymns, the hours you worked in the library, the hours in the chapel when you prayed alone?"

"I remember, of course." I felt the tears coming again. I could see it so vividly, the monastery library, and the monks who had taught me and believed I could be a priest. I saw the cold little cell with its bed of boards; I saw the cloister and the garden veiled in rosy shadow; God, I didn't want to think now of those times. But some things can never be forgotten.

"Do you remember the morning that you went into the chapel," she continued, "and you knelt on the bare marble floor, with your arms out in the form of the cross, and you told God you would do anything if only he would make you good?"

"Yes, good . . . ." Now it was my voice that was tinged with bitterness.

"You said you would suffer martyrdom; torments unspeakable; it did not matter; if only you were to be someone who was good."

"Yes, I remember." I saw the old saints; I heard the hymns that had broken my heart. I remembered the morning my brothers had come to take me home, and I had begged them on my knees to let me stay there.

"And later, when your innocence was gone, and you took the high road to Paris, it was the same thing you wanted; when you danced and sang for the boulevard crowds, you wanted to be good."

"I was," I said haltingly. "It was a good thing to make them happy and for a little while I did."

"Yes, happy," she whispered.

"I could never explain to Nicolas, my friend, you know, that it was so important to . . . believe in a concept of goodness, even if we make it up ourselves. We don't really make it up. It's there, isn't it?"

"Oh, yes, it's there," she said. "It's there because we put it there."

Such sadness. I couldn't speak. I watched the falling snow. I clasped her hand and felt her lips against my cheek.

"You were born for me, my prince," she said. "You were tried and perfected. And in those first years, when you went into your mother's bedchamber and brought her into the world of the undead with you, it was but a prefigurement of your waking me. I am your true Mother, the Mother who will never abandon you, and I have died and been reborn, too. All the religions of the world, my prince, sing of you and of me."

"How so?" I asked. "How can that be?"

"Ah, but you know. *You know!*" She took the sword from me and examined the old belt slowly, running it across the open palm of her right hand. Then she dropped it down into the rusted heap—the last remnants on earth of my mortal life. And it was as if a wind touched these things, blowing them slowly across the snow-covered floor, until they were gone.

"Discard your old illusions," she said. "Your inhibitions. They are no more of use than these old weapons. Together, we will make the myths of the world real."

A chill cut through me, a dark chill of disbelief and then confusion; but her beauty overcame it.

"You wanted to be a saint when you knelt in that chapel," she said. "Now you shall be a god with me."

There were words of protest on the tip of my tongue; I was frightened; some dark sense overcame me. Her words, what could they possibly mean?

But suddenly I felt her arm around me, and we were rising out of the tower up through the shattered roof. The wind was so fierce it cut my eyelids. I turned towards her. My right arm went round her waist and I buried my head against her shoulder.

I heard her soft voice in my ear telling me to sleep. It would be hours before the sun set on the land to which we were going, to the place of the first lesson.

Lesson. Suddenly I was weeping again, clinging to her, weeping because I was lost, and she was all there was to cling to. And I was in terror now of what she would ask of me.

2

MARIUS: COMING TOGETHER

THEY met again at the edge of the redwood forest, their clothes tattered, their eyes tearing from the wind. Pandora stood to the right of Marius, Santino to the left. And from the house across the clearing, Mael came towards them, a lanky figure almost loping over the mown grass.

Silently, he embraced Marius.

"Old friend," Marius said. But his voice had no vitality. Exhausted, he looked past Mael towards the lighted windows of the house. He sensed a great hidden dwelling within the mountain behind the visible structure with its peaked and gabled roof.

And what lay there waiting for him? For all of them? If only he had the slightest spirit for it; if only he could recapture the smallest part of his own soul.

"I'm weary," he said to Mael. "I'm sick from the journey. Let me rest here a moment longer. Then I'll come."

Marius did not despise the power to fly, as he knew Pandora did, nevertheless it invariably chastened him. He had been defenseless against it on this night of all nights; and he had now to feel the earth under him, to smell the forest, and to scan the distant house in a moment of uninterrupted quiet. His hair was tangled from the wind and still matted with dried blood. The simple gray wool jacket and pants he had taken from the ruins of his house barely gave him warmth. He brought the heavy black cloak close around him, not because the night here required it, but because he was still chilled and sore from the wind.

Mael appeared not to like his hesitation, but to accept it. Suspiciously he gazed at Pandora, whom he had never trusted, and then with open hostility he stared at Santino, who was busy brushing off his black garments and combing his fine, neatly trimmed black hair. For one second, their eyes met, Santino bristling with viciousness, then Mael turned away.

Marius stood still listening, thinking. He could feel the last bit of healing in his body; it rather amazed him that he was once again whole. Even as mortals learn year by year that they are older and weaker, so immortals must learn that they are stronger than ever they imagined they would be. It maddened him at the moment.

Scarcely an hour had passed since he was helped from the icy pit by Santino and Pandora, and now it was as if he had never been there, crushed and helpless, for ten days and nights, visited again and again by the nightmares of the twins. Yet nothing could ever be as it had been.

The twins. The red-haired woman was inside the house waiting. Santino had told him this. Mael knew it too. But who was she? And why did he not want to know the answers? Why was this the blackest hour he had ever known? His body was fully healed, no doubt about it; but what was going to heal his soul?

Armand in this strange wooden house at the base of the mountain? Armand again after all this time? Santino had told him about Armand also, and that the others—Louis and Gabrielle—had also been spared.

Mael was studying him. "He's waiting for you," he said. "Your Amadeo." It was respectful, not cynical or impatient.

And out of the great bank of memories that Marius carried forever with him, there came a long neglected moment, startling in its purity—Mael coming to the palazzo in Venice in the contented years of the fifteenth century, when Marius and Armand had known such happiness, and Mael seeing the mortal boy at work with the other apprentices on a mural which Marius had only lately left to their less competent hands. Strange how vivid, the smell of the egg tempera, the smell of the candles, and that familiar smell—not unpleasant now in remembering—which permeated all Venice, the smell of the rottenness of things, of the dark and putrid waters of the canals. "And so you would make that one?" Mael had asked with simple directness. "When it's time," Marius had said dismissively, "when it's time." Less than a year later, he had made his little blunder. "Come into my arms, young one, I can live without you no more."

Marius stared at the distant house. *My world trembles and I think of him, my Amadeo, my Armand.* The emotions he felt were suddenly as bittersweet as music, the blended orchestral melodies of recent centuries, the tragic strains of Brahms or Shostakovich which he had come to love.

But this was no time for cherishing this reunion. No time to feel the keen warmth of it, to be glad of it, and to say all the things to Armand that he so wanted to say.

Bitterness was something shallow compared to his present state of mind. *Should have destroyed them, the Mother and the Father. Should have destroyed us all.*

"Thank the gods," Mael said, "that you did not."

"And why?" Marius demanded. "Tell me why?"

Pandora shuddered. He felt her arm come around his waist. And why did that make him so angry? He turned sharply to her; he wanted to strike her, push her away. But what he saw stopped him. She wasn't even looking at him; and her expression was so distant, so soul weary that he felt his own exhaustion all the more heavily. He wanted to weep. The well-being of Pandora had always been crucial to his own survival. He did not need to be near her—better that he was not near her—but he had to know that she was somewhere, and continuing, and that they might meet again. What he saw now in her—had seen earlier—filled him with foreboding. If he felt bitterness, then Pandora felt despair.

"Come," Santino said, "they're waiting." It was said with courtly politeness.

"I know," Marius answered.

"Ah, what a trio we are!" Pandora whispered suddenly. She was spent, fragile, hungering for sleep and dreams, yet protectively she tightened her grip on Marius's waist.

"I can walk unaided, thank you," he said with uncharacteristic meanness, and to this one, the one he most loved.

"Walk, then," she answered. And just for a second, he saw her old warmth, even a spark of her old humor. She gave him a little shove, and then started out alone towards the house.

Acid. His thoughts were acid as he followed. He could not be of use to these immortals. Yet he walked on with Mael and Santino into the light streaming from the windows beyond. The redwood forest receded into shadow; not a leaf moved. But the air was good here, warm here, full of fresh scents and without the sting of the north.

Armand. It made him want to weep.

Then he saw the woman appear in the doorway. A sylph with her long curly red hair catching the hallway light.

He did not stop, but surely he felt a little intelligent fear. Old as Akasha she was, certainly. Her pale eyebrows were all but faded into the radiance of her countenance. Her mouth had no color anymore. And her eyes . . . . Her eyes were not really her eyes. No, they had been taken from a mortal victim and they were already failing her. She could not see very well as she looked at him. Ah, the blinded twin from the dreams, she was. And she felt pain now in the delicate nerves connected to the stolen eyes.

Pandora stopped at the edge of the steps.

Marius went past her and up onto the porch. He stood before the red-haired woman, marveling at her height—she was as tall as he was—and at the fine symmetry of her masklike face. She wore a flowing gown of black wool with a high neck and full dagged sleeves. In long loose gores the cloth fell from a slender girdle of braided black cord just beneath her small breasts. A lovely garment really. It made her face seem all the more radiant and detached from everything around it, a mask with the light behind it, glowing in a frame of red hair.

But there was a great deal more to marvel at than these simple attributes which she might have possessed in one form or another six thousand years ago. The woman's vigor astonished him. It gave her an air of infinite flexibility and overwhelming menace. Was she the true immortal?—the one who had never slept, never gone silent, never been released by madness? One who had walked with a rational mind and measured steps through all the millennia since she had been born?

She let him know, for what it was worth, that this was exactly what she was.

He could see her immeasurable strength as if it were incandescent light; yet he could sense an immediate informality, the immediate receptivity of a clever mind.

How to read her expression, however. How to know what she really felt.

A deep, soft femininity emanated from her, no less mysterious than anything else about her, a tender vulnerability that he associated exclusively with women though now and then he found it in a very young man. In the dreams, her face had evinced this tenderness; now it was something invisible but no less real. At another time it would have charmed him; now he only took note of it, as he noted her gilded fingernails, so beautifully tapered, and the jeweled rings she wore.

"All those years you knew of me," he said politely, speaking in the old Latin. "You knew I kept the Mother and the Father. Why didn't you come to me? Why didn't you tell me who you were?"

She considered for a long moment before answering, her eyes moving back and forth suddenly over the others who drew close to him now.

Santino was terrified of this woman, though he knew her very well. And Mael was afraid of her too, though perhaps a little less. In fact, it seemed that Mael loved her and was bound to her in some subservient way. As for Pandora, she was merely apprehensive. She drew even closer to Marius as if to stand with him, regardless of what he meant to do.

"Yes, I knew of you," the woman said suddenly. She spoke English in the modern fashion. But it was the unmistakable voice of the twin in the dream, the blind twin who had cried out the name of her mute sister, Mekare, as both had been shut up in stone coffins by the angry mob.

Our voices never really change, Marius thought. The voice was young, pretty. It had a reticent softness as she spoke again.

"I might have destroyed your shrine if I had come," she said. "I might have buried the King and the Queen beneath the sea. I might even have destroyed them, and so doing, destroyed all of us. And this I didn't want to do. And so I did nothing. What would you have had me do? I couldn't take your burden from you. I couldn't help you. So I did not come."

It was a better answer than he had expected. It was not impossible to like this creature. On the other hand, this was merely the beginning. And her answer—it wasn't the whole truth.

"No?" she asked him. Her face revealed a tracery of subtle lines for an instant, the glimpse of something that had once been human. "What is the whole truth?" she asked. "That I owed you nothing, least of all the knowledge of my existence and that you are impertinent to suggest that I should have made myself known to you? I have seen a thousand like you. I know when you come into being. I know when you perish. What are you to me? We come together now because we have to. We are in danger. All living things are in danger! And maybe when this is finished we will love each other and respect each other. And maybe not. Maybe we'll all be dead."

"Perhaps so," he said quietly. He couldn't help smiling. She was right. And he liked her manner, the bone-hard way in which she spoke.

It had been his experience that all immortals were irrevocably stamped by the age in which they were born. And so it was true, also, of even this ancient one, whose words had a savage simplicity, though the timbre of the voice had been soft.

"I'm not myself," he added hesitantly. "I haven't survived all this as well as I should have survived it. My body's healed—the old miracle." He sneered. "But I don't understand my present view of things. The bitterness, the utter—" He stopped.

"The utter darkness," she said.

"Yes. Never has life itself seemed so senseless," he added. "I don't mean for us. I mean—to use your phrase—for all living things. It's a joke, isn't it? Consciousness, it's a kind of joke."

"No," she said. "That's not so."

"I disagree with you. Will you patronize me? Tell me now how many thousands of years you've lived before I was born? How much you know that I don't know?" He thought again of his imprisonment, the ice hurting him, the pain shooting through his limbs. He thought of the immortal voices that had answered him; the rescuers who had moved towards him, only to be caught one by one by Akasha's fire. He had heard them die, if he had not seen them! And what had sleep meant for him? The dreams of the twins.

She reached out suddenly and caught his right hand gently in both of hers. It was rather like being held in the maw of a machine; and though Marius had inflicted that very impression upon many young ones himself over the years, he had yet to feel such overpowering strength himself.

"Marius, we need you now," she said warmly, her eyes glittering for an instant in the yellow light that poured out of the door behind her, and out of the windows to the right and to the left.

"For the love of heaven, why?"

"Don't jest," she answered. "Come into the house. We must talk while we have time."

"About what?" he insisted. "About why the Mother has allowed us to live? I know the answer to that question. It makes me laugh. You she cannot kill, obviously, and we . . . we are spared because Lestat wants it. You realize this, don't you? Two thousand years I cared for her, protected her, worshiped her, and she has spared me now on account of her love for a two-hundred-year-old fledgling named Lestat."

"Don't be so sure of it!" Santino said suddenly.

"No," the woman said. "It's not her only reason. But there are many things we must consider—"

"I know you're right." he said. "But I haven't the spirit for it. My illusions are gone, you see, and I didn't even know they were illusions. I thought I had attained such wisdom! It was my principal source of pride. I was with the eternal things. Then, when I saw her standing there in the shrine, I knew that all my deepest hopes and dreams had come true! She was alive inside that body. Alive, while I played the acolyte, the slave, the eternal guardian of the tomb!"

But why try to explain it? Her vicious smile, her mocking words to him, the ice falling. The cold darkness afterwards and the twins. Ah, yes, the twins. That was at the heart of it as much as anything else, and it occurred to him suddenly that the dreams had cast a spell on him. He should have questioned this before now. He looked at her, and the dreams seemed to surround her suddenly, to take her out of the moment back to those stark times. He saw sunlight; he saw the dead body of the mother; he saw the twins poised above the body. So many questions . . .

"But what have these dreams to do with this catastrophe!" he demanded suddenly. He had been so defenseless against those endless dreams.

The woman looked at him for a long moment before answering. "This I will tell you, insofar as I know. But you must calm yourself. It's as if you've got your youth back, and what a curse it must be."

He laughed. "I was never young. But what do you mean by this?"

"You rant and rave. And I can't console you."

"And you would if you could?"

"Yes."

He laughed softly.

But very gracefully she opened her arms to him. The gesture shocked him, not because it was extraordinary but because he had seen her so often go to embrace her sister in this manner in the dreams. "My name is Maharet," she said. "Call me by my name and put away your distrust. Come into my house."

She leant forward, her hands touching the sides of his face as she kissed him on the cheek. Her red hair touched his skin and the sensation confused him. The perfume rising from her clothes confused him—the faint Oriental scent that made him think of incense, which always made him think of the shrine.

"Maharet," he said angrily. "If I am needed, why didn't you come for me when I lay in that pit of ice? Could she have stopped *you?*"

"Marius, I have come," she said. "And you are here now with us." She released him, and let her hands fall, gracefully clasped before her skirts. "Do you think I had nothing to do during these nights when all our kind were being destroyed? To the left and right of me, the world over, she slew those I had loved or known. I could not be here and there to protect these victims. Cries reached my ears from every corner of the earth. And I had my own quest, my own sorrow—" Abruptly she stopped.

A faint carnal blush came over her; in a warm flash the normal expressive lines of her face returned. She was in pain, both physical and mental, and her eyes were clouding with thin blood tears. Such a strange thing, the fragility of the eyes in the indestructible body. And the suffering emanating from her—he could not bear it—it was like the dreams themselves. He saw a great riff of images, vivid yet wholly different. And quite suddenly he realized—

"You aren't the one who sent the dreams to us!" he whispered. "You are not the source."

She didn't answer.

"Ye gods, where is your sister! What does all this mean?"

There was a subtle recoiling, as if he'd struck her heart. She tried to veil her mind from him; but he felt the unquenchable pain. In silence, she stared at him, taking in all of his face and figure slowly and obviously, as if to let him know that he had unforgivably transgressed.

He could feel the fear coming from Mael and Santino, who dared to say nothing. Pandora drew even closer to him and gave him a little warning signal as she clasped his hand.

Why had he spoken so brutally, so impatiently? *My quest, my own sorrow* . . . . But damn it all!

He watched her close her eyes, and press her fingers tenderly to her eyelids as if she would make the ache in her eyes go away, but she could not.

"Maharet," he said with a soft, honest sigh. "We're in a war and we stand about on the battlefield speaking harsh words to each other. I am the worst offender. I only want to understand."

She looked up at him, her head still bowed, her hand hovering before her face. And the look was fierce, almost malicious. Yet he found himself staring senselessly at the delicate curve of her fingers, at the gilded nails and the ruby and emerald rings which flashed suddenly as if sparked with electric light.

The most errant and awful thought came to him, that if he didn't stop being so damned stupid he might never see Armand. She might drive him out of here or worse. . . . And he wanted so—before it was over—to see Armand.

"You come in now, Marius," she said suddenly, her voice polite, forgiving. "You come with me, and be reunited with your old child, and then we'll gather with the others who have the same questions. We will begin."

"Yes, my old child . . . ." he murmured. He felt the longing for Armand again like music, like Bartók's violin phrases played in a remote and safe place where there was all the time in the world to hear. Yet he hated her; he hated all of them. He hated himself. The other twin, where was the other twin? Flashes of heated jungle. Flashes of the vines torn and the saplings breaking underfoot. He tried to reason, but he couldn't. Hatred poisoned him.

Many a time he had witnessed this black denial of life in mortals. He had heard the wisest of them say, "Life is not worth it," and he had never fathomed it; well, he understood it now.

Vaguely he knew she had turned to those around him. She was welcoming Santino and Pandora into the house.

As if in a trance, he saw her turn to lead the way. Her hair was so long it fell to her waist in back, a great mass of soft red curls. And he felt the urge to touch it, see if it was as soft as it looked. How positively remarkable that he could be distracted by something lovely at this moment, something impersonal, and that it could make him feel all right; as if nothing had happened; as if the world were good. He beheld the shrine intact again; the shrine at the center of his world. Ah, the idiot human brain, he thought, how it seizes whatever it can. And to think Armand was waiting, so near . . . .

She led them through a series of large, sparely furnished rooms. The place for all its openness had the air of a citadel; the ceiling beams were enormous; the fireplaces, each with a roaring blaze, were no more than open stone hearths.

So like the old meeting halls of Europe in the dark times, when the Roman roads had fallen to ruin and the Latin tongue had been forgotten, and the old warrior tribes had risen again. The Celts had been triumphant in the end really. They were the ones who conquered Europe; its feudal castles were no more than Celtic encampments; even in the modern states, the Celtic superstitions, more than Roman reason, lived on.

But the appointments of this place hearkened back to even earlier times. Men and women had lived in cities built like this before the invention of writing; in rooms of plaster and wood; among things woven, or hammered by hand.

He rather liked it; ah, the idiot brain again, he thought, that he could like something at such a time. But the places built by immortals always intrigued him. And this one was a place to study slowly, to come to know over a great span of time.

Now they passed through a steel door and into the mountain itself. The smell of the raw earth enclosed him. Yet they walked in new metal corridors, with walls of tin. He could hear the generators, the computers, all the sweet humming electrical sounds that had made him feel so safe in his own house.

Up an iron stairs they went. It doubled back upon itself again and again as Maharet led them higher and higher. Now roughened walls revealed the innards of the mountain, its deep veins of colored clay and rock. Tiny ferns grew here; but where did the light come from? A skylight high above. Little portal to heaven. He glanced up thankfully at the bare glimmer of blue light.

Finally they emerged on a broad landing and entered a small darkened room. A door lay open to a much larger chamber where the others waited; but all Marius could see for the moment was the bright shock of distant firelight, and it made him turn his eyes away.

Someone was waiting here in this little room for him, someone whose presence he had been unable, except by the most ordinary means, to detect. A figure who stood behind him now. And as Maharet went on into the large room, taking Pandora and Santino and Mael with her, he understood what was about to happen. To brace himself he took a slow breath and closed his eyes.

How trivial all his bitterness seemed; he thought of this one whose existence had been for centuries unbroken suffering; whose youth with all its needs had been rendered truly eternal; this one whom he had failed to save, or to perfect. How many times over the years had he dreamed of such a reunion, and he had never had the courage for it; and now on this battlefield, in this time of ruin and upheaval, they were at last to meet.

"My love," he whispered. He felt himself chastened suddenly as he had been earlier when he had flown up and up over the snowy wastes past the realm of the indifferent clouds. Never had he spoken words more heartfelt. "My beautiful Amadeo," he said.

And reaching out he felt the touch of Armand's hand.

Supple still this unnatural flesh, supple as if it were human, and cool and so soft. He couldn't help himself now. He was weeping. He opened his eyes to see the boyish figure standing before him. Oh, such an expression. So accepting, so yielding. Then he opened his arms.

Centuries ago in a palazzo in Venice, he had tried to capture in imperishable pigment the quality of this love. What had been its lesson? That in all the world no two souls contain the same secret, the same gift of devotion or abandon; that in a common child, a wounded child, he had found a blending of sadness and simple grace that would forever break his heart? This one had understood him! This one had loved him as no other ever had.

Through his tears he saw no recrimination for the grand experiment that had gone wrong. He saw the face that he had painted, now darkened slightly with the thing we naively call wisdom; and he saw the same love he had counted upon so totally in those lost nights.

If only there were time, time to seek the quiet of the forest—some warm, secluded place among the soaring redwoods—and there talk together by the hour through long unhurried nights. But the others waited; and so these moments were all the more precious, and all the more sad.

He tightened his arms around Armand. He kissed Armand's lips, and his long loose vagabond hair. He ran his hand covetously over Armand's shoulders. He looked at the slim white hand he held in his own. Every detail he had sought to preserve forever on canvas; every detail he had certainly preserved in death.

"They're waiting, aren't they?" he asked. "They won't give us more than a few moments now."

Without judgment, Armand nodded. In a low, barely audible voice, he said, "It's enough. I always knew that we would meet again." Oh, the memories that the timbre of the voice brought back. The palazzo with its coffered ceilings, beds draped in red velvet. The figure of this boy rushing up the marble staircase, his face flushed from the winter wind off the Adriatic, his brown eyes on fire. "Even in moments of the greatest jeopardy," the voice continued, "I knew we would meet before I would be free to die."

"Free to die?" Marius responded. "We are always free to die, aren't we? What we must have now is the courage to do it, if indeed it is the right thing to do."

Armand appeared to think on this for a moment. And the soft distance that crept into his face brought back the sadness again to Marius. "Yes, that's true," he said.

"I love you," Marius whispered suddenly, passionately as a mortal man might. "I have always loved you. I wish that I could believe in anything other than love at this moment; but I can't."

Some small sound interrupted them. Maharet had come to the door.

Marius slipped his arm around Armand's shoulder. There was one final moment of silence and understanding between them. And then they followed Maharet into an immense mountaintop room.

ALL of glass it was, except for the wall behind him, and the distant iron chimney that hung from the ceiling above the blazing fire. No other light here save the blaze, and above and beyond, the sharp tips of the monstrous redwoods, and the bland Pacific sky with its vaporous clouds and tiny cowardly stars.

But it was beautiful still, wasn't it? Even if it was not the sky over the Bay of Naples, or seen from the flank of Annapurna or from a vessel cast adrift in the middle of the blackened sea. The mere sweep of it was beautiful, and to think that only moments ago he had been high up there, drifting in the darkness, seen only by his fellow travelers and by the stars themselves. The joy came back to him again as it had when he looked at Maharet's red hair. No sorrow as when he thought of Armand beside him; just joy, impersonal and transcendent. A reason to remain alive.

It occurred to him suddenly that he wasn't very good at bitterness or regret, that he didn't have the stamina for them, and if he was to recapture his dignity, he had better shape up fast.

A little laugh greeted him, friendly, unobtrusive; a little drunken maybe, the laugh of a fledgling who lacked common sense. He smiled in acknowledgment, darting a glance at the amused one, Daniel. Daniel the anonymous "boy" of *Interview with the Vampire.* It hit him quickly that this was Armand's child, the only child Armand had ever made. A good start on the Devil's Road this creature had, this exuberant and intoxicated being, strengthened with all that Armand had to give.

Quickly he surveyed the others who were gathered around the oval table.

To his right and some distance away, there was Gabrielle, with her blond hair in a braid down her back and her eyes full of undisguised anguish; and beside her, Louis, unguarded and passive as always, staring at Marius mutely as if in scientific inquiry or worship or both; then came his beloved Pandora, her rippling brown hair free over her shoulders and still speckled with the tiny sparkling droplets of melted frost. Santino sat to her right, finally, looking composed once more, all the dirt gone from his finely cut black velvet clothes.

On his left sat Khayman, another ancient one, who gave his name silently and freely, a horrifying being, actually, with a face even smoother than that of Maharet. Marius found he couldn't take his eyes off this one. Never had the faces of the Mother and the Father so startled him, though they too had had these black eyes and jet black hair. It was the smile, wasn't it? The open, affable expression fixed there in spite of all the efforts of time to wash it away. The creature looked like a mystic or a saint, yet he was a savage killer. Recent feasts of human blood had softened his skin just a little, and given a faint blush to his cheeks.

Mael, shaggy and unkempt as always, had taken the chair to Khayman's left. And after him came another old one, Eric, past three thousand years by Marius's reckoning, gaunt and deceptively fragile in appearance, perhaps thirty when he died. His soft brown eyes regarded Marius thoughtfully. His handmade clothes were like exquisite replicas of the store-bought goods men of business wore today.

But what was this other being? The one who sat to the right of Maharet, who stood directly opposite Marius at the far end? Now, this one truly gave him a shock. The other twin was his first rash conjecture as he stared at her green eyes and her coppery red hair.

But this being had been alive yesterday, surely. And he could find no explanation for her strength, her frigid whiteness; the piercing manner in which she stared at him; and the overwhelming telepathic power that emanated from her, a cascade of dark and finely delineated images which she seemed unable to control. She was seeing with uncanny accuracy the painting he had done centuries ago of his Amadeo, surrounded by black-winged angels as he knelt in prayer. A chill passed over Marius.

"In the crypt of the Talamasca," he whispered. "My painting?" He laughed, rudely, venomously. "And so it's there!"

The creature was frightened; she hadn't meant to reveal her thoughts. Protective of the Talamasca, and hopelessly confused, she shrank back into herself. Her body seemed to grow smaller and yet to redouble its power. A monster. A monster with green eyes and delicate bones. Born yesterday, yes, exactly as he had figured it; there was living tissue in her; and suddenly he understood all about her. This one, named Jesse, had been made by

Maharet. This one was an actual human descendant of the woman; and now she had become the fledgling of her ancient mother. The scope of it astonished him and frightened him slightly. The blood racing through the young one's veins had a potency that was unimaginable to Marius. She was absolutely without thirst; yet she wasn't even really dead.

But he must stop this, this merciless and rummaging appraisal. They were, after all, waiting for him. Yet he could not help but wonder where in God's name were his own mortal descendants, spawn of the nephews and nieces he had so loved when he was alive? For a few hundred years, true, he had followed their progress; but finally, he could no longer recognize them; he could no longer recognize Rome itself. And he had let it all go into darkness, as Rome had passed into darkness. Yet surely there were those walking the earth today who had that old family blood in their veins.

He continued to stare at the red-haired young one. How she resembled her great mother; tall, yet frail of bone, beautiful yet severe. *Some great secret here, something to do with the lineage, the family*. . . . She wore soft dark clothes rather similar to those of the ancient one; her hands were immaculate; she wore no scent or paint.

They were all of them magnificent in their own way. The tall heavily built Santino was elegant in his priestly black, with his lustrous black eyes and a sensuous mouth. Even the unkempt Mael had a savage and overpowering presence as he glowered at the ancient woman with an obvious mixture of love and hate. Armand's angelic face was beyond description; and the boy Daniel, a vision with his ashen hair and gleaming violet eyes.

Was nobody ugly ever given immortality? Or did the dark magic simply make beauty out of whatever sacrifice was thrown into the blaze? But Gabrielle had been a lovely thing in life surely, with all her son's courage and none of his impetuosity, and Louis, ah, well, Louis of course had been picked for the exquisite bones of his face, for the depth of his green eyes. He had been picked for the inveterate attitude of somber appreciation that he revealed now. He looked like a human being lost among them, his face softened with color and feeling; his body curiously defenseless; his eyes wondering and sad. Even Khayman had an undeniable perfection of face and form, horrifying as the total effect had come to be.

As for Pandora, he saw her alive and mortal when he looked at her, he saw the eager innocent woman who had come to him so many eons ago in the ink-black nighttime streets of Antioch, begging to be made immortal, not the remote and melancholy being who sat so still now in her simple biblical robes, staring through the glass wall opposite her at the fading galaxy beyond the thickening clouds.

Even Eric, bleached by the centuries and faintly radiant, retained, as Maharet did, an air of great human feeling, made all the more appealing by a beguiling androgynous grace.

The fact was, Marius had never laid eyes on such an assemblage—a gathering of immortals of all ages from the newborn to the most ancient; and each endowed with immeasurable powers and weaknesses, even to the delirious young man whom Armand had skillfully created with all the unspent virtue of his virgin blood. Marius doubted that such a "coven" had ever come together before.

And how did he fit into the picture, he who had been the eldest of his own carefully controlled universe in which the ancients had been silent gods? The winds had cleansed him of the dried blood that had clung to his face and shoulder-length hair. His long black cloak was damp from the snows from which he'd come. And as he approached the table, as he waited belligerently for Maharet to tell him he might be seated, he fancied he looked as much the monster as the others did, his blue eyes surely cold with the animosity that was burning him from within.

"Please," she said to him graciously. She gestured to the empty wooden chair before him, a place of honor obviously, at the foot of the table; that is, if one conceded that she stood at the head.

Comfortable it was, not like so much modern furniture. Its curved back felt good to him as he seated himself, and he could rest his hand on the arm, that was good, too. Armand took the empty chair to his right.

Maharet seated herself without a sound. She rested her hands with fingers folded on the polished wood before her. She bowed her head as if collecting her thoughts to begin.

"Are we all that is left?" Marius asked. "Other than the Queen and the brat prince and—" He paused.

A ripple of silent confusion passed through the others. The mute twin, where was she? What was the mystery?

"Yes," Maharet answered soberly. "Other than the Queen, and the brat prince, and my sister. Yes, we are the only ones left. Or the only ones left who count."

She paused as if to let her words have their full effect. Her eyes gently took in the complete assembly.

"Far off," she said, "there may be others—old ones who choose to remain apart. Or those she hunts still, who are doomed. But we are what remains in terms of destiny or decision. Or intent."

"And my son," Gabrielle said. Her voice was sharp, full of emotion, and subtle disregard for those present. "Will none of you tell me what she's done with him and where he is?" She looked from the woman to Marius, fearlessly and desperately. "Surely you have the power to know where he is."

Her resemblance to Lestat touched Marius. It was from this one that Lestat had drawn his strength, without doubt. But there was a coldness in her that Lestat would never understand.

"He's with her, as I've already told you," Khayman said, his voice deep and unhurried. "But beyond that she doesn't let us know."

Gabrielle did not believe it, obviously. There was a pulling away in her, a desire to leave here, to go off alone. Nothing could have forced the others away from the table. But this one had made no such commitment to the meeting, it was clear.

"Allow me to explain this," Maharet said, "because it's of the utmost importance. The Mother is skillful at cloaking herself, of course. But we of the early centuries have never been able to communicate silently with the Mother and the Father or with each other. We are all simply too close to the source of the power that makes us what we are. We are deaf and blind to each other's minds just as master and fledgling are among you. Only as time passed and more and more blood drinkers were created did they acquire the power to communicate silently with each other as we have done with mortals all along."

"Then Akasha couldn't find you," Marius said, "you or Khayman—if you weren't with us."

"That's so. She must see us through your minds or not at all. And so we must see her through the minds of others. Except of course for a certain sound we hear now and then on the approach of the powerful, a sound that has to do with a great exertion of energy, and with breath and blood."

"Yes, that sound," Daniel murmured softly. "That awful relentless sound."

"But is there nowhere *we* can hide from her?" Eric asked. "Those of us she can hear and see?" It was a young man's voice, of course, and with a heavy undefinable accent, each word rather beautifully intoned.

"You know there isn't," Maharet answered with explicit patience. "But we waste time talking of hiding. You are here either because she cannot kill you or she chooses not to. And so be it. We must go on."

"Or she hasn't finished," Eric said disgustedly. "She hasn't made up her infernal mind on the matter of who shall die and who shall live!"

"I think you are safe here," Khayman said. "She had her chance with everyone present, did she not?"

But that was just it, Marius realized. It was not at all clear that the Mother had had her chance with Eric, Eric who traveled, apparently, in the company of Maharet. Eric's eyes locked on Maharet. There was some quick silent exchange but it wasn't telepathic. What came clear to Marius was that Maharet had made Eric, and neither knew for certain whether Eric was too strong now for the Mother. Maharet was pleading for calm.

"But Lestat, you can read *his* mind, can't you?" Gabrielle said. "Can't you discover them both through him?"

"Not even I can always cover a pure and enormous distance," Maharet answered. "If there were other blood drinkers left who could pick up Lestat's thoughts and relay them to me, well, then of course I could find him in an instant. But in the main, those blood drinkers are no more. And Lestat has always been good at cloaking his presence; it's natural to him. It's always that way with the strong ones, the ones who are self-sufficient and aggressive. Wherever he is now, he instinctively shuts us out."

"She's taken him," Khayman said. He reached across the table and laid his hand on Gabrielle's hand. "She'll reveal everything to us when she is ready. And if she chooses to harm Lestat in the meantime there is absolutely nothing that any of us can do."

Marius almost laughed. It seemed these ancient ones thought statements of absolute truth were a comfort; what a curious combination of vitality and passivity they were. Had it been so at the dawn of recorded history? When people sensed the inevitable, they stood stock-still and accepted it? It was difficult for him to grasp.

"The Mother won't harm Lestat," he said to Gabrielle, to all of them. "She loves him. And at its core it's a common kind of love. She won't harm him because she doesn't want to harm herself. And she knows all his tricks, I'll wager, just as we know them. He won't be able to provoke her, though he's probably foolish enough to try."

Gabrielle gave a little nod at that with a trace of a sad smile. It was her considered opinion that Lestat could provoke anyone, finally, given enough time and opportunity; but she let it pass.

She was neither consoled nor resigned. She sat back in the wooden chair and stared past them as if they no longer existed. She felt no allegiance to this group; she felt no allegiance to anyone but Lestat.

"All right then," she said coldly. "Answer the crucial question. If I destroy this monster who's taken my son, do we all die?"

"How the hell are you going to destroy her?" Daniel asked in amazement.

Eric sneered.

She glanced at Daniel dismissively. Eric she ignored. She looked at Maharet. "Well, is the old myth true? If I waste this bitch, to use the vernacular, do I waste the rest of us too?"

There was faint laughter in the gathering. Marius shook his head. But Maharet gave a little smile of acknowledgment as she nodded:

"Yes. It was tried in the earlier times. It was tried by many a fool who didn't believe it. The spirit who inhabits her animates us all. Destroy the host, you destroy the power. The young die first; the old wither slowly; the eldest perhaps would go last. But she is the Queen of the Damned, and the Damned can't live without her. Enkil was only her consort, and that is why it does not matter now that she has slain him and drunk his blood to the last drop."

"The Queen of the Damned." Marius whispered it aloud softly. There had been a strange inflection when Maharet had said it, as if memories had stirred in her, painful and awful, and undimmed by time. Undimmed as the dreams were undimmed. Again he had a sense of the starkness and severity of these ancient beings, for whom language perhaps, and all the thoughts governed by it, had not been needlessly complex.

"Gabrielle," Khayman said, pronouncing the name exquisitely, "we cannot help Lestat. We must use this time to make a plan." He turned to Maharet. "The dreams, Maharet. Why have the dreams come to us now? This is what we all want to know."

There was a protracted silence. All present had known, in some form, these dreams. Only lightly had they touched Gabrielle and Louis, so lightly in fact that Gabrielle had, before this night, given no thought to them, and Louis, frightened by Lestat, had pushed them out of his mind. Even Pandora, who confessed no personal knowledge of them, had told Marius of Azim's warning. Santino had called them horrid trances from which he couldn't escape.

Marius knew now that they had been a noxious spell for the young ones, Jesse and Daniel, almost as cruel as they had been for him.

Yet Maharet did not respond. The pain in her eyes had intensified; Marius felt it like a soundless vibration. He felt the spasms in the tiny nerves.

He bent forward slightly, folding his hands before him on the table.

"Maharet," he said. "Your sister is sending the dreams. Isn't this so?"

No answer.

"Where is Mekare?" he pushed.

Silence again.

He felt the pain in her. And he was sorry, very sorry once more for the bluntness of his speech. But if he was to be of use here, he must push things to a conclusion. He thought of Akasha in the shrine again, though why he didn't know. He thought of the smile on her face. He thought of Lestat—protectively, desperately. But Lestat was just a symbol now. A symbol of himself. Of them all.

Maharet was looking at him in the strangest way, as if he were a mystery to her. She looked at the others. Finally she spoke:

"You witnessed our separation," she said quietly. "All of you. You saw it in the dreams. You saw the mob surround me and my sister; you saw them force us apart; in stone coffins they placed us, Mekare unable to cry out to me because they had cut out her tongue, and I unable to see her for the last time because they had taken my eyes.

"But I saw through the minds of those who hurt us. I knew it was to the seashores that we were being taken. Mekare to the west; and I to the east.

"Ten nights I drifted on the raft of pitch and logs, entombed alive in the stone coffin. And finally when the raft sank and the water lifted the stone lid, I was free. Blind, ravenous, I swam ashore and stole from the first poor mortal I encountered the eyes to see and the blood to live.

"But Mekare? Into the great western ocean she had been cast—the waters that ran to the end of the world.

"Yet from that first night on I searched for her; I searched through Europe, through Asia, through the southern jungles and the frozen lands of the north. Century after century I searched, finally crossing the western ocean when mortals did to take my quest to the New World as well.

"I never found my sister. I never found a mortal or immortal who had set eyes upon her or heard her name. Then in this century, in the years after the second great war, in the high mountain jungles of Peru, the indisputable evidence of my sister's presence was discovered by a lone archaeologist on the walls of a shallow cave—pictures my sister had created—of stick figures and crude pigment which told the tale of our lives together, the sufferings you all know.

"But six thousand years ago these drawings had been carved into the stone. And six thousand years ago my sister had been taken from me. No other evidence of her existence was ever found.

"Yet I have never abandoned the hope of finding my sister. I have always known, as only a twin might, that she walks this earth still, that I am not here alone.

"And now, within these last ten nights, I have, for the first time, proof that my sister is still with me. It has come to me through the dreams.

"These are Mekare's thoughts; Mekare's images; Mekare's rancor and pain."

Silence. All eyes were fixed on her. Marius was quietly stunned. He feared to be the one to speak again, but this was worse than he had imagined and the implications were now entirely clear.

The origin of these dreams was almost certainly not a conscious survivor of the millennia; rather the visions had—very possibly—come from one who had no more mind now than an animal in whom memory is a spur to action which the animal does not question or understand. It would explain their clarity; it would explain their repetition.

And the flashes he had seen of something moving through the jungles, this was Mekare herself.

"Yes," Maharet said immediately. " 'In the jungles. Walking,' " she whispered. "The words of the dying archaeologist, scribbled on a piece of paper and left for me to find when I came. 'In the jungles. Walking.' But where?"

It was Louis who broke the silence.

"Then the dreams may not be a deliberate message," he said, his words marked by a slight French accent. "They may simply be the outpouring of a tortured soul."

"No. They are a message," Khayman said. "They are a warning. They are meant for all of us, and for the Mother as well."

"But how can you say this?" Gabrielle asked him. "We don't know what her mind is now, or that she even knows that we are here."

"You don't know the whole story," Khayman said. "I know it. Maharet will tell it." He looked to Maharet.

"I saw her," Jesse said unobtrusively, her voice tentative as she looked at Maharet. "She's crossed a great river; she's coming. I saw her! No, that's not right. I saw as if I were she."

"Yes," Marius answered. "Through her eyes!"

"I saw her red hair when I looked down," Jesse said. "I saw the jungle giving way with each step."

"The dreams must be a communication," Mael said with sudden impatience. "For why else would the message be so strong? Our private thoughts don't carry such power. She raises her voice; she wants someone or something to know what she is thinking. . . ."

"Or she is obsessed and acting upon that obsession," Marius answered. "And moving towards a certain goal." He paused. "To be united with you, her sister! What else could she possibly want?"

"No," Khayman said. "That is not her goal." Again he looked at Maharet. "She has a promise to keep to the Mother, and that is what the dreams mean."

Maharet studied him for a moment in silence; it seemed this was almost beyond her endurance, this discussion of her sister, yet she fortified herself silently for the ordeal that lay ahead.

"We were there in the beginning," Khayman said. "We were the first children of the Mother; and in these dreams lies the story of how it began."

"Then you must tell us . . . all of it," Marius said as gently as he could.

"Yes." Maharet sighed. "And I will." She looked at each of them in turn and then back to Jesse. "I must tell you the whole story," she said, "so that you can understand what we may be powerless to avert. You see, this is not merely the story of the beginning. It may be the story of the end as well." She sighed suddenly as if the prospect were too much for her. "Our world has never seen such upheaval," she said, looking at Marius. "Lestat's music, the rising of the Mother, so much death."

She looked down for a moment, as if collecting herself again for the effort. And then she glanced at Khayman and at Jesse, who were the ones she most loved.

"I have never told it before," she said as if pleading for indulgence. "It has for me now the hard purity of mythology—those times when I was alive. When I could still see the sun. But in this mythology is rooted all the truths that I know. And if we go back, we may find the future, and the means to change it. The very least that we can do is seek to understand."

A hush fell. All waited with respectful patience for her to begin.

"In the beginning," she said, "we were witches, my sister and I. We talked to the spirits and the spirits loved us. Until she sent her soldiers into our land."

3

LESTAT: THE QUEEN OF HEAVEN

SHE let me go. Instantly I began to plummet; the wind was a roar in my ears. But the worst part was that I couldn't see! I heard her say *Rise.*

There was a moment of exquisite helplessness. I was plunging towards the earth and nothing was going to stop it; then I looked up, my eyes stinging, the clouds closing over me, and I remembered the tower, and the feeling of rising. I made the decision. *Go up!* And my descent stopped at once.

It was as if a current of air had caught me. I went up hundreds of feet in one instant, and then the clouds were below me—a white light that I could scarcely see. I decided to drift. Why did I have to go anywhere for the moment? Maybe I could open my eyes fully, and see through the wind, if I wasn't afraid of the pain.

She was laughing somewhere—in my head or over it, I didn't know which. *Come on, prince, come higher.*

I spun around and shot upwards again, until I saw her coming towards me, her garments swirling about her, her heavy plaits lifted more gently by the wind.

She caught me and kissed me. I tried to steady myself, holding onto her, to look down and really see something through the breaks in the clouds. Mountains, snow-covered and dazzling in the moonlight, with great bluish flanks that disappeared into deep valleys of fathomless snow.

"Lift me now," she whispered in my ear. "Carry me to the northwest."

"I don't know the direction."

"Yes, you do. The body knows it. Your mind knows it. Don't ask them which way it is. Tell them that is the way you wish to go. You know the principles. When you lifted your rifle, you looked at the wolf running; you didn't calculate the distance or the speed of the bullet; you fired; the wolf went down."

I rose again with that same incredible buoyancy; and then I realized she had become a great weight in my arm. Her eyes were fixed on me; she was making me carry her. I smiled. I think I laughed aloud. I lifted her and kissed her again, and continued the ascent without interruption. *To the northwest.* That is to the right and to the right again and higher. My mind did know it; it knew the terrain over which we'd come. I made a little artful turn and then another; I was spinning, clutching her close to me, rather loving the weight of her body, the press of her breasts against me, and her lips again closing delicately on mine.

She drew close to my ear. "Do you hear it?" she asked.

I listened; the wind seemed annihilating; yet there came a dull chorus from the earth, human voices chanting; some in time with each other, others at random; voices praying aloud in an Asian tongue. Far far away I could hear them, and then near at hand. Important to distinguish the two sounds. First, there was a long procession of worshipers ascending through the mountain passes and over the cliffs, chanting to keep themselves alive as they trudged on in spite of weariness and cold. And within a building, a loud, ecstatic chorus, chanting fiercely over the clang of cymbals and drums.

I gathered her head close to mine and looked down, but the clouds had become a solid bed of whiteness. Yet I could see through the minds of the worshipers the brilliant vision of a courtyard and a temple of marble arches and vast painted rooms. The procession wound towards the temple.

"I want to see it!" I said. She didn't answer, but she didn't stop me as I drifted downward, stretching out on the air as if I were a bird flying, yet descending until we were in the very middle of the clouds. She had become light again, as if she were nothing.

And as we left the sea of whiteness, I saw the temple gleaming below, a tiny clay model of itself, it seemed, the terrain buckling here and there beneath its meandering walls. The stench of burning bodies rose from its blazing pyres. And towards this cluster of roofs and towers, men and women wound their way along perilous paths from as far as I could see.

"Tell me who is inside, my prince," she said. "Tell me who is the god of this temple."

See it! Draw close to it. The old trick, but all at once I began to fall. I let out a terrible cry. She caught me.

"More care, my prince," she said, steadying me.

I thought my heart was going to burst.

"You cannot move out of your body to look into the temple and fly at the same time. Look through the eyes of the mortals the way you did it before."

I was still shaking, clutching hold of her.

"I'll drop you again if you don't calm yourself," she said gently. "Tell your heart to do as you would have it do."

I gave a great sigh. My body ached suddenly from the constant force of the wind. And my eyes, they were stinging so badly again, I couldn't see anything. But I tried to subdue these little pains; or rather to ignore them as if they didn't exist. I took hold of her firmly and started down, telling myself to go slowly; and then again I tried to find the minds of the mortals and see what they saw:

Gilded walls, cusped arches, every surface glittering with decoration; incense rising, mingling with the scent of fresh blood. In blurred snatches I saw him, "the god of the temple."

"A vampire," I whispered. "A bloodsucking devil. He draws them to himself, and slaughters them at his leisure. The place reeks of death."

"And so there shall be more death," she whispered, kissing my face again tenderly. "Now, very fast, so fast mortal eyes can't see you. Bring us down to the courtyard beside the funeral pyre."

I could have sworn it was done before I'd decided it; I'd done no more than consider the idea! And there I was fallen against a rough plaster wall, with hard stones under my feet, trembling, my head reeling, my innards grinding in pain. My body wanted to keep going down, right through solid rock.

Sinking back against the wall, I heard the chanting before I could see anything. I smelt the fire, the bodies burning; then I saw the flames.

"That was very clumsy, my prince," she said softly. "We almost struck the wall."

"I don't exactly know how it happened."

"Ah, but that's the key," she said, "the word 'exact.' The spirit in you obeys swiftly and completely. Consider a little more. You don't cease to hear and see as you descend; it merely happens faster than you realize. Do you know the pure mechanics of snapping your fingers? No, you do not. Yet you can do it. A mortal child can do it."

I nodded. The principle was clear all right, as it had been with the target and the gun.

"Merely a matter of degrees," I said.

"And of surrender, fearless surrender."

I nodded. The truth was I wanted to fall on a soft bed and sleep. I blinked my eyes at the roaring fire, the sight of the bodies going black in the flames. One of them wasn't dead; an arm was raised, fingers curled. Now he was dead. Poor devil. All right.

Her cold hand touched my cheek. It touched my lips, and then she smoothed back the tangled hair of my head.

"You've never had a teacher, have you?" she asked. "Magnus orphaned you the night he made you. Your father and brothers were fools. As for your mother, she hated her children."

"I've always been my own teacher," I said soberly. "And I must confess I've always been my favorite pupil as well."

Laughter.

"Maybe it was a little conspiracy," I said. "Of pupil and teacher. But as you said, there was never anyone else."

She was smiling at me. The fire was playing in her eyes. Her face was luminous, frighteningly beautiful.

"Surrender," she said, "and I'll teach you things you never dreamed of. You've never known battle. Real battle. You've never felt the purity of a righteous cause."

I didn't answer. I felt dizzy, not merely from the long journey through the air, but from the gentle caress of her words, and the fathomless blackness of her eyes. It seemed a great part of her beauty was the sweetness of her expression, the serenity of it, the way that her eyes held steady even when the glistening white flesh of her face moved suddenly with a smile or a subtle frown. I knew if I let myself, I'd be terrified of what was happening. She must have known it too. She took me in her arms again. "Drink, prince," she whispered. "Take the strength you need to do as I would have you do."

I don't know how many moments passed. When she pulled away, I was drugged for an instant, then the clarity was as always overwhelming. The monotonous music of the temple was thundering through the walls.

"Azim! Azim! Azim!"

As she drew me along after her, it seemed my body didn't exist anymore except as a vision I kept in place. I felt of my own face, the bones beneath my skin, to touch something solid that was myself; but this skin, this sensation. It was utterly new. What was left of me?

The wooden doors opened as if by magic before us. We passed silently into a long corridor of slender white marble pillars and scalloped arches, but this was but the outer border of an immense central room. And the room was filled with frenzied, screaming worshipers who did not even see us or sense our presence as they continued to dance, to chant, to leap into the air in the hopes of glimpsing their one and only god.

"Keep at my side, Lestat," she said, the voice cutting through the din as if I'd been touched by a velvet glove.

The crowd parted, violently, bodies thrust to right and left. Screaming replaced the chant immediately; the room was in chaos, as a path lay open for us to the center of the room. The cymbals and drums were silenced; moans and soft piteous cries surrounded us.

Then a great sigh of wonder rose as Akasha stepped forward and threw back her veil.

Many feet away, in the center of the ornate floor stood the blood god, Azim, clothed in a black silk turban and jeweled robes. His face was disfigured with fury as he stared at Akasha, as he stared at me.

Prayers rose from the crowd around us; a shrill voice cried out an anthem to "the eternal mother."

"Silence!" Azim commanded. I didn't know the language; but I understood the word.

I could hear the sound of human blood in his voice; I could see it rushing through his veins. Never in fact had I seen any vampire or blood drinker so choked with human blood as was this one; he was as old as Marius, surely, yet his skin had a dark golden gleam. A thin veil of blood sweat covered it completely, even to the backs of his large, soft-looking hands.

"You dare to come into my temple!" he said, and again the language itself eluded me but the meaning was telepathically clear.

"You will die now!" Akasha said, the voice even softer than it had been a moment ago. "You who have misled these hopeless innocents; you who have fed upon their lives and their blood like a bloated leech."

Screams rose from the worshipers, cries for mercy. Again, Azim told them to be quiet.

"What right have you to condemn my worship," he cried, pointing his finger at us, "you who have sat silent on your throne since the beginning of time!"

"Time did not begin with you, my cursed beauty," Akasha answered. "I was old when you were born. And I am risen now to rule as I was meant to rule. And you shall die as a lesson to your people. You are my first great martyr. You shall die now!"

He tried to run at her; and I tried to step between them; but it was all too fast to be seen. She caught him by some invisible means and shoved him backwards so that his feet slid across the marble tile and he teetered, almost falling and then dancing as he sought to right himself, his eyes rolling up into his head.

A deep gurgling cry came out of him. He was burning. His garments were burning; and then the smoke rose from him gray and thin and writhing in the gloom as the terrified crowd gave way to screams and wails. He was twisting as the heat consumed him; then suddenly, bent double, he rose, staring at her, and flew at her with his arms out.

It seemed he would reach her before she thought what to do. And again, I tried to step before her, and with a quick shove of her right hand she threw me back into the human swarm. There were half-naked bodies all around, struggling to get away from me as I caught my balance.

I spun around and saw him poised not three feet from her, snarling at her, and trying to reach her over some invisible and unsurmountable force.

"Die, damnable one!" she cried out. (I clamped my hands over my ears.) "Go into the pit of perdition. I create it for you now."

Azim's head exploded. Smoke and flame poured out of his ruptured skull. His eyes turned black. With a flash, his entire frame ignited; yet he went down in a human posture, his fist raised against her, his legs curling as if he meant to try to stand again. Then his form disappeared utterly in a great orange blaze.

Panic descended upon the crowd, just as it had upon the rock fans outside the concert hall when the fires had broken out and Gabrielle and Louis and I had made our escape.

Yet it seemed the hysteria here reached a more dangerous pitch. Bodies crashed against the slender marble pillars. Men and women were crushed instantly as others rushed over them to the doors.

Akasha turned full circle, her garments caught in a brief dance of black and white silk around her; and everywhere human beings were caught as if by invisible hands and flung to the floor. Their bodies went into convulsions. The women, looking down at the stricken victims, wailed and tore their hair.

It took me a moment to realize what was happening, that she was killing the men. It wasn't fire. It was some invisible attack upon the vital organs. Blood poured from their ears and their eyes as they expired. Enraged, several of the women ran at her, only to meet the same fate. The men who attacked her were vanquished instantly.

Then I heard her voice inside my head:

Kill them, Lestat. Slaughter the males to the last one.

I was paralyzed. I stood beside her, lest one of them get close to her. But they didn't have a chance. This was beyond nightmare, beyond the stupid horrors to which I'd been a party all of my accursed life.

Suddenly she was standing in front of me, grasping my arms. Her soft icy voice had become an engulfing sound in my brain.

My prince, my love. You will do this for me. Slaughter the males so that the legend of their punishment will surpass the legend of the temple. They are the henchmen of the blood god. The women are helpless. Punish the males in my name.

"Oh, God help me, please don't ask this of me," I whispered. "They are pitiful humans!"

The crowd seemed to have lost its spirit. Those who had run into the rear yard were trapped. The dead and the mourning lay everywhere around us, while from the ignorant multitude at the front gates there rose the most piteous pleas.

"Let them go, Akasha, please," I said to her. Had I ever in my life begged for anything as I did now? What had these poor beings to do with us?

She drew closer to me. I couldn't see anything now but her black eyes.

"My love, this is divine war. Not the loathsome feeding upon human life which you have done night after night without scheme or reason save to survive. You kill now in my name and for my cause and I give you the greatest freedom ever given man: I tell you that to slay your mortal brother is right. Now use the new power I've given you. Choose your victims one by one, use your invisible strength or the strength of your hands."

My head was spinning. Had I this power to make men drop in their tracks? I looked around me in the smoky chamber where the incense still poured from the censers and bodies tumbled over one another, men and women embracing each other in terror, others crawling into corners as if there they would be safe.

"There is no life for them now, save in the lesson," she said. "Do as I command."

It seemed I saw a vision; for surely this wasn't from my heart or mind; I saw a thin emaciated form rise before me; I gritted my teeth as I glared at it, concentrating my malice as if it were a laser, and then I saw the victim rise off his feet and tumble backwards as the blood came out of his mouth. Lifeless, withered, he fell to the floor. It had been like a spasm; and then as effortless as shouting, as throwing one's voice out unseen yet powerful, over a great space.

Yes, kill them. Strike for the tender organs; rupture them; make the blood flow. You know that you have always wanted to do it. To kill as if it were nothing, to destroy without scruple or regret!

It was true, so true; but it was also forbidden, forbidden as nothing else on earth is forbidden. . . .

My love, it is as common as hunger; as common as time. And now you have my power and command. You and I shall put an end to it through what we will do now.

A young man rushed at me, crazed, hands out to catch my throat. *Kill him.* He cursed me as I drove him backwards with the invisible power, feeling the spasm deep in my throat and my belly; and then a sudden tightening in the temples; I *felt* it touching him, I felt it pouring out of me; I felt it as surely as if I had penetrated his skull with my fingers and was squeezing his brain. Seeing it would have been crude; there was no need to see it. All I needed to see was the blood spurting from his mouth and his ears, and down his naked chest.

Oh, was she ever right, how I had wanted to do it! How I had dreamed of it in my earliest mortal years! The sheer bliss of killing them, killing them under all their names which were the same name—*enemy*—those who deserved killing, those who were born for killing, killing with full force, my body turning to solid muscle, my teeth clenched, my hatred and my invisible strength made one.

In all directions they ran, but that only further inflamed me. I drove them back, the power slamming them into the walls. I aimed for the heart with this invisible tongue and heard the heart when it burst. I turned round and round, directing it carefully yet instantly at this one, and that one, and then another as he ran through the doorway, and yet another as he rushed down the corridor, and yet another as he tore the lamp from its chains and hurled it foolishly at me.

Into the back rooms of the temple I pursued them, with exhilarating ease through the heaps of gold and silver, tossing them over on their backs as if with long invisible fingers, then clamping those invisible fingers on their arteries until the blood gushed through the bursting flesh.

The women crowded together weeping; others fled. I heard bones break as I walked over the bodies. And then I realized that she too was killing them; that we were doing it together, and the room was now littered with the mutilated and the dead. A dark, rank smell of blood permeated everything; the fresh cold wind could not dispel it; the air was filled with soft, despairing cries.

A giant of a man raced at me, eyes bulging as he tried to stop me with a great curved sword. In rage I snatched the sword from him and sliced through his neck. Right through the bone the blade went, breaking as it did so, and head and broken blade fell at my feet.

I kicked aside the body. I went in the courtyard and stared at those who shrank from me in terror. I had no more reason, no more conscience. It was a mindless game to chase them, corner them, thrust aside the women behind whom they hid, or who struggled so pitifully to hide them, and aim the power at the right place, to pump the power at that vulnerable spot until they lay still.

The front gates! She was calling me. The men in the courtyard were dead; the women were tearing their hair, sobbing. I walked through the ruined temple, through the mourners and the dead they mourned. The crowd at the gates was on its knees in the snow, ignorant of what had gone on inside, voices raised in desperate entreaty.

Admit me to the chamber; admit me to the vision and the hunger of the lord.

At the sight of Akasha, their cries rose in volume. They reached out to touch her garments as the locks broke and the gates swung open. The wind howled down the mountain pass; the bell in the tower above gave a faint hollow sound.

Again I shoved them down, rupturing brains and hearts and arteries. I saw their thin arms flung out in the snow. The wind itself stank of blood. Akasha's voice cut through the horrid screams, telling the women to draw back and away and they would be safe.

Finally I was killing so fast I couldn't even see it anymore: The males. The males must die. I was rushing towards completion, that every single male thing that moved or stirred or moaned should be dead.

Like an angel I moved on down the winding path, with an invisible sword. And finally all the way down the cliff they dropped to their knees and waited for death. In a ghastly passivity they accepted it!

Suddenly I felt her holding me though she was nowhere near me. I heard her voice in my head:

Well done, my prince.

I couldn't stop. This invisible thing was one of my limbs now. I couldn't withdraw it and bring it back into myself. It was as if I was poised to take a breath, and if I did not take that breath I should die. But she held me motionless, and a great calm was coming over me, as if a drug had been fed into my veins. Finally I grew still and the power concentrated itself within me and became part of me and nothing more.

Slowly I turned around. I looked at the clear snowy peaks, the perfectly black sky, and at the long line of dark bodies that lay on the path from the temple gates. The women were clinging to one another, sobbing in disbelief, or giving off low and terrible moans. I smelled death as I have never smelled it; I looked down at the bits of flesh and gore that had splashed my garments. But my hands! My hands were so white and clean. *Dear God, I didn't do it! Not me. I didn't. And my hands, they are clean!*

Oh, but I had! And what am I that I could do it? That I loved it, loved it beyond all reason, loved it as men have always loved it in the absolute moral freedom of war—

It seemed a silence had fallen.

If the women still cried I didn't hear them. I didn't hear the wind either. I was moving, though why I didn't know. I had dropped down to my knees and I reached out for the last man I had slain, who was flung like broken sticks in the snow, and I put my hand into the blood on his mouth and then I smeared this blood all over both my hands and pressed them to my face.

Never had I killed in two hundred years that I hadn't tasted the blood, and taken it, along with the life, into myself. And that was a monstrous thing. But more had died here in these few ghastly moments than all those I'd ever sent to their untimely graves. And it had been done with the ease of thought and breath. Oh, this can never be atoned for! This can never never be justified!

I stood staring at the snow, through my bloody fingers; weeping and yet hating that as well. Then gradually I realized that some change had taken place with the women. Something was happening around me, and I could feel it as if the cold air had been warmed and the wind had risen and left the steep slope undisturbed.

Then the change seemed to enter into me, subduing my anguish and even slowing the beat of my heart.

The crying *had* ceased. Indeed the women were moving by twos and threes down the path as if in a trance, stepping over the dead. It seemed that sweet music was playing, and that the earth had suddenly yielded spring flowers of every color and description, and that the air was full of perfume.

Yet these things weren't happening, were they? In a haze of muted colors, the women passed me, in rags and silks, and dark cloaks. I shook myself all over. I had to think clearly! This was no time for disorientation. This power and these dead bodies were no dream and I could not, absolutely could not, yield to this overwhelming sense of well-being and peace.

"Akasha!" I whispered.

Then lifting my eyes, not because I wanted to, but because I had to, I saw her standing on a far promontory, and the women, young and old, were moving towards her, some so weak from the cold and from hunger that others had to carry them over the frozen ground.

A hush had fallen over all things.

Without words she began to speak to those assembled before her. It seemed she addressed them in their own language, or in something quite beyond specific language. I couldn't tell.

In a daze, I saw her stretch out her arms to them. Her black hair spilled down on her white shoulders, and the folds of her long simple gown barely moved in the soundless wind. It struck me that never in all my life had I beheld anything quite as beautiful as she was, and it was not merely the sum of her physical attributes, it was the pure serenity, the essence that I perceived with my innermost soul. A lovely euphoria came over me as she spoke.

Do not be afraid, she told them. The bloody reign of your god is over, and now you may return to the truth.

Soft anthems rose from the worshipers. Some dipped their foreheads to the ground before her. And it appeared that this pleased her or at least that she would allow it.

You must return now to your villages, she said. You must tell those who knew of the blood god that he is dead. The Queen of Heaven has destroyed him. The Queen will destroy all those males who still believe in him. The Queen of Heaven will bring a new reign of peace on earth. There will be death for the males who have oppressed you, but you must wait for my sign.

As she paused the anthems rose again. The Queen of Heaven, the Goddess, the Good Mother—the old litany sung in a thousand tongues the world over was finding a new form.

I shuddered. I made myself shudder. I had to penetrate that spell! It was a trick of the power, just as the killing had been a trick of the power—something definable and measurable, yet I remained drugged by the sight of her, and by the anthems. By the soft embrace of this feeling: all is well; all is as it should be. We are all safe.

Somewhere, from the sunlit recesses of my mortal memory a day came back, a day like many before it, when in the month of May in our village we had crowned a statue of the Virgin amid banks of sweet-smelling flowers, when we had sung exquisite hymns. Ah, the loveliness of that moment, when the crown of white lilies had been lifted to the Virgin's veiled head. I'd gone home that night singing those hymns. In an old prayer book, I'd found a picture of the Virgin, and it had filled me with enchantment and wondrous religious fervor such as I felt now.

And from somewhere deeper in me even, where the sun had never penetrated, came the realization that if I believed in her and what she was saying, then this unspeakable thing, this slaughter that I had committed against fragile and helpless mortals would somehow be redeemed.

You kill now in my name and for my cause and I give you the greatest freedom ever given man: I tell you that to slay your brother is right.

"Go on," she said aloud. "Leave this temple forever. Leave the dead to the snow and the winds. Tell the people. A new era is coming when those males who glorify death and killing shall reap their reward; and the era of peace shall be yours. I will come again to you. I will show you the way. Await my coming. And I will tell you then what you must do. For now, believe in me and what you have seen here. And tell others that they too may believe. Let the men come and see what awaits them. Wait for signs from me."

In a body they moved to obey her command; they ran down the mountain path towards those distant worshipers who had fled the massacre; their cries rose thin and ecstatic in the snowy void.

The wind gusted through the valley; high on the hill, the temple bell gave another dull peal. The wind tore at the scant garments of the dead. The snow had begun to fall, softly and then thickly, covering brown legs and arms and faces, faces with open eyes.

The sense of well-being had dissipated, and all the raw aspects of the moment were clear and inescapable again. These women, this visitation. . . . Bodies in the snow! Undeniable displays of power, disruptive and overwhelming.

Then a soft little sound broke the silence; things shattering in the temple above; things falling, breaking apart.

I turned and looked at her. She stood still on the little promontory, the cloak very loose over her shoulders, her flesh as white as the falling snow. Her eyes were fixed on the temple. And as the sounds continued, I knew what was happening within.

Jars of oil breaking; braziers falling. The soft whisper of cloth exploding into flame. Finally the smoke rose, thick and black, billowing from the bell tower, and from over the rear wall.

The bell tower trembled; a great roaring noise echoed against the far cliffs; and then the stones broke loose; the tower collapsed. It fell down into the valley, and the bell, with one final peal, disappeared into the soft white abyss.

The temple was consumed in fire.

I stared at it, my eyes watering from the smoke that blew down over the path, carrying with it tiny ashes and bits of soot.

Vaguely, I was aware that my body wasn't cold despite the snow. That it wasn't tired from the exertion of killing. Indeed my flesh was whiter than it had been. And my lungs took in the air so efficiently that I couldn't hear my own breathing; even my heart was softer, steadier. Only my soul was bruised and sore.

For the first time ever in my life, either mortal or immortal, I was afraid that I might die. I was afraid that she might destroy me and with reason, because I simply could not do again what I'd just done. I could not be part of this design. And I prayed I couldn't be made to do it, that I would have the strength to refuse.

I felt her hands on my shoulders.

"Turn and look at me, Lestat," she said.

I did as she asked. And there it was again, the most seductive beauty I'd ever beheld.

And I am yours, my love. You are my only true companion, my finest instrument. You know this, do you not?

Again, a deliberate shudder. Where in God's name are you, Lestat! Are you going to shrink from speaking your heart?

"Akasha, help me," I whispered. "Tell me. Why did you want me to do this, this killing? What did you mean when you told them that the males would be punished? That there would be a reign of peace on earth?" How stupid my words sounded. Looking into her eyes, I could believe she was the goddess. It was as if she drew my conviction out of me, as if it were merely blood.

I was quaking suddenly with fear. Quaking. I knew what the word meant for the first time. I tried to say more but I merely stammered. Finally I blurted it out:

"In the name of what morality will all this be done?"

"In the name of *my* morality!" she answered, the faint little smile as beautiful as before. "I am the reason, the justification, the right by which it is done!" Her voice was cold with anger, but her blank, sweet expression had not changed. "Now, listen to me, beautiful one," she said. "I love you. You've awakened me from my long sleep and to my great purpose; it gives me joy merely to look at you, to see the light in your blue eyes, and to hear the sound of your voice. It would wound me beyond your understanding of pain to see you die. But as the stars are my witness, you will aid me in my mission. Or you will be no more than the instrument for the commencement, as Judas was to Christ. And I shall destroy you as Christ destroyed Judas once your usefulness is past."

Rage overcame me. I couldn't help myself. The shift from fear to anger was so fast, I was boiling inside.

"But how do you dare to do these things!" I asked. "To send these ignorant souls abroad with mad lies!"

She stared at me in silence; it seemed she would strike out at me; her face became that of a statue again; and I thought, Well, the moment is now. I will die the way I saw Azim die. I can't save Gabrielle or Louis. I can't save Armand. I won't fight because it's useless. I won't move when it happens. I'll go deep into myself, perhaps, if I must run from the pain. I'll find some last illusion like Baby Jenks did and cling to it until I am no longer Lestat.

She didn't move. The fires on the hill were burning down. The snow was coming more thickly and she had become like a ghost standing there in the silent snowfall, white as the snow was white.

"You really aren't afraid of anything, are you?" she said.

"I'm afraid of you," I said.

"Oh, no, I do not think so."

I nodded. "I am. And I'll tell you what else I am. Vermin on the face of the earth. Nothing more than that. A loathsome killer of human beings. But I *know* that's what I am! I do not pretend to be what I am not! You have told these ignorant people that you are the Queen of Heaven! How do you mean to redeem those words and what they will accomplish among stupid and innocent minds?"

"Such arrogance," she said softly. "Such incredible arrogance, and yet I love you. I love your courage, even your rashness, which has always been your saving grace. I even love your stupidity. Don't you understand? There is no promise now that I cannot keep! I shall make the myths over! I *am* the Queen of Heaven. And Heaven shall reign on earth finally. I am anything that I say I am!"

"Oh, lord, God," I whispered.

"Do not speak those hollow words. Those words that have never meant anything to anyone! You stand in the presence of the only goddess you will ever know. You are the only god these people will ever know! Well, you must think like a god now, my beauty. You must reach for something beyond your selfish little ambitions. Don't you realize what's taken place?"

I shook my head. "I don't know anything. I'm going mad."

She laughed. She threw back her head and laughed. "We are what they dream of, Lestat. We cannot disappoint them. If we did, the truth implicit in the earth beneath our feet would be betrayed."

She turned away from me. She went back up again to the small outcropping of snow-covered rock where she had stood before. She was looking down into the valley, at the path that cut along the sheer cliff beneath her, at the pilgrims turning back now as the fleeing women gave them the word.

I heard cries echo off the stone face of the mountain. I heard the men dying down there, as she, unseen, struck them with that power, that great seductive and easy power. And the women stammering madly of miracles and visions. And then the wind rose, swallowing everything, it seemed; the great indifferent wind. I saw her shimmering face for an instant; she came towards me; I thought this is death again, this is death coming, the woods and the wolves coming, and no place to hide; and then my eyes closed.

WHEN I awoke I was in a small house. I didn't know how we'd gotten here, or how long ago the slaughter in the mountains had been. I'd been drowning in the voices, and now and then a dream had come to me, a terrible yet familiar dream. I had seen two redheaded women in this dream. They knelt beside an altar where a body lay waiting for them to perform some ritual, some crucial ritual. And I'd been struggling desperately to understand the dream's content, for it seemed that everything depended upon it; I must not forget it again.

But now all that faded. The voices, the unwelcome images; the moment pressed in.

The place where I lay was dark and dirty, and full of foul smells. In little dwellings all around us, mortals lived in misery, babies crying in hunger, amid the smell of cooking fires and rancid grease.

There was war in this place, true war. Not the debacle of the mountainside, but old-fashioned twentieth-century war. From the minds of the afflicted I caught it in viscid glimpses—an endless existence of butchery and menace—buses burned, people trapped inside beating upon the locked windows; trucks exploding, women and children running from machine gun fire.

I lay on the floor as if someone had flung me there. And Akasha stood in the doorway, her cloak wrapped tightly around her, even to her eyes, as she peered out into the dark.

When I had climbed to my feet and come up beside her, I saw a mud alley full of puddles and other small dwellings, some with roofs of tin and others with roofs of sagging newspaper. Against the filthy walls men slept, wrapped from head to toe as if in shrouds. But they were not dead; and the rats they sought to avoid knew it. And the rats nibbled at the wrappings, and the men twitched and jerked in their sleep.

It was hot here, and the warmth cooked the stenches of the place—urine, feces, the vomit of dying children. I could even smell the hunger of the children, as they cried in spasms. I could smell the deep dank sea smell of the gutters and the cesspools.

This was no village; it was a place of hovels and shacks, of hopelessness. Dead bodies lay between the dwellings. Disease was rampant; and the old and the sick sat silent in the dark, dreaming of nothing, or of death perhaps, which was nothing, as the babies cried.

Down the alley there came now a tottering child with a swollen belly, screaming as it rubbed with a small fist its swollen eye.

It seemed not to see us in the darkness. From door to door it went crying, its smooth brown skin glistening in the dim flicker of the cooking fires as it moved away.

"Where are we?" I asked her.

Astonished, I saw her turn and lift her hand tenderly to stroke my hair and my face. Relief washed through me. But the raw suffering of this place was too great for that relief to matter. So she had not destroyed me; she had brought me to hell. What was the purpose? All around me I felt the misery, the despair. What could alter the suffering of these abject people?

"My poor warrior," she said. Her eyes were full of blood tears. "Don't you know where we are?"

I didn't answer.

She spoke slowly, close to my ear. "Shall I recite the poetry of names?" she asked. "Calcutta, if you wish, or Ethiopia; or the streets of Bombay; these poor souls could be the peasants of Sri Lanka; of Pakistan; of Nicaragua, of El Salvador. It does not matter what it is; it matters how much there is of it; that all around the oases of your shining Western cities it exists; it is three-fourths of the world! Open your ears, my darling; listen to their prayers; listen to the silence of those who've learned to pray for nothing. For nothing has always been their portion, whatever the name of their nation, their city, their tribe."

We walked out together into the mud street; past piles of dung and filthy puddles and the starving dogs that came forth, and the rats that darted across our path. Then we came to the ruins of an ancient palace. Reptiles slithered among the stones. The blackness swarmed with gnats. Derelicts slept in a long row beside a running gutter. Beyond in the swamp, bodies rotted, bloated and forgotten.

Far away on the highway, the trucks passed, sending their rumble through the stifling heat like thunder. The misery of the place was like a gas, poisoning me as I stood there. This was the ragged edge of the savage garden of the world in which hope could not flower. This was a sewer.

"But what can we do?" I whispered. "Why have we come here?" Again, I was distracted by her beauty, the look of compassion that suddenly infected her and made me want to weep.

"We can reclaim the world," she said, "as I've told you. We can make the myths real; and the time will come when this will be a myth, that humans ever knew such degradation. We shall see to that, my love."

"But this is for them to solve, surely. It isn't only their obligation, it's their right. How can we aid in such a thing? How can our interference not lead to catastrophe?"

"We shall see that it does not," she said calmly. "Ah, but you don't begin to comprehend. You don't realize the strength we now possess. Nothing can stop us. But you must watch now. You are not ready and I would not push you again. When you kill again for me you must have perfect faith and perfect conviction. Be assured that I love you and I know that a heart can't be educated in the space of a night. But *learn* from what you see and hear."

She went back out in the street. For one moment she was merely a frail figure, moving through the shadows. Then suddenly I could hear beings roused in the tiny hovels all around us, and I saw the women and children emerge. Around me the sleeping forms began to stir. I shrank back into the dark.

I was trembling. I wanted desperately to do something, to beg her to have patience!

But again that sense of peace descended, that spell of perfect happiness, and I was traveling back through the years to the little French church of my childhood as the hymns began. Through my tears I saw the shining altar. I saw the icon of the Virgin, a gleaming square of gold above the flowers; I heard the Aves whispered as if they were a charm. Under the arches of Notre Dame de Paris I heard the priests singing "Salve Regina."

Her voice came, clear, inescapable as it had been before, as if it were inside my brain. Surely the mortals heard it with the same irresistible power. The command itself was without words; and the essence was beyond dispute—that a new order was to begin, a new world in which the abused and injured would know peace and justice finally. The women and the children were exhorted to rise, and to slay all males within this village. All males save one in a hundred should be killed, and all male babies save one in a hundred should also be slaughtered immediately. Peace on earth would follow once this had been done far and wide; there would be no more war; there would be food and plenty.

I was unable to move, or to voice my terror. In panic I heard the frenzied cries of the women. Around me, the sleeping derelicts rose from their wrappings, only to be driven back against the walls, dying as I had seen the men die in Azim's temple.

The street rang with cries. In clouded flashes, I saw people running; I saw the men rushing out of the houses, only to drop in the mud. On the distant road the trucks went up in flames, wheels screeching as the drivers lost control. Metal was hurled against metal. Gas tanks exploded; the night was full of magnificent light. Rushing from house to house, the women surrounded the men and beat them with any weapon they could find. Had the village of shanties and hovels ever known such vitality as it did now in the name of death?

And she, the Queen of Heaven, had risen and was hovering above the tin rooftops, a stark delicate figure burning against the clouds as if made of white flame.

I closed my eyes and turned towards the wall, fingers clutching at the crumbling rock. To think that we were solid as this, she and I. Yet not of it. No, never of it. And we did not belong here! We had no right.

But even as I wept, I felt the soft embrace of the spell again; the sweet drowsy sensation of being surrounded by flowers, of slow music with its inevitable and enthralling rhythm. I felt the warm air as it passed into my lungs; I felt the old stone tiles beneath my feet.

Soft green hills stretched out before me in hallucinatory perfection—a world without war or deprivation in which women roamed free and unafraid, women who even under provocation would shrink from the common violence that lurks in the heart of every man.

Against my will I lingered in this new world, ignoring the thud of bodies hitting the wet earth, and the final curses and cries of those who were being killed.

In great dreamy flashes, I saw whole cities transformed; I saw streets without fear of the predatory and the senselessly destructive; streets in which beings moved without urgency or desperation. Houses were no longer fortresses; gardens no longer needed their walls.

"Oh, Marius, help me," I whispered, even as the sun poured down on the tree-lined pathways and endless green fields. "Please, please help me."

And then another vision shocked me, crowding out the spell. I saw fields again, but there was no sunlight; this was a real place somewhere—and I was looking through the eyes of someone or something walking in a straight line with strong strides at incredible speed. But who was this someone? What was this being's destination? Now, this vision was being sent; it was powerful, refusing to be ignored. But why?

It was gone as quickly as it had come.

I was back in the crumbling palace arcade, among the scattered dead; staring through the open archway at the rushing figures; hearing the high-pitched cries of victory and jubilation.

Come out, my warrior, where they can see you. Come to me.

She stood before me with her arms extended. God, what did they think they were seeing? For a moment I didn't move, then I went towards her, stunned and compliant, feeling the eyes of the women, their worshipful gaze. They fell down on their knees as she and I came together. I felt her hand close too tightly; I felt my heart thudding. *Akasha, this is a lie, a terrible lie. And the evil sown here will flourish for a century.*

Suddenly the world tilted. We weren't standing on the ground anymore. She had me in her embrace and we were rising over the tin roofs, and the women below were bowing and waving their arms, and touching their foreheads to the mud.

"Behold the miracle, behold the Mother, behold the Mother and her Angel . . ."

Then in an instant, the village was a tiny scattering of silver roofs far below us, all that misery alchemized into images, and we were traveling once again on the wind.

I glanced back, trying in vain to recognize the specific location—the dark swamps, the lights of the nearby city, the thin strip of road where the overturned trucks still burned. But she was right, it really didn't matter.

Whatever was going to happen had now begun, and I did not know what could possibly stop it.

4

THE STORY OF THE TWINS PART I

ALL eyes were fixed on Maharet as she paused. Then she began again, her words seemingly spontaneous, though they came slowly and were carefully pronounced. She seemed not sad, but eager to reexamine what she meant to describe.

"Now, when I say that my sister and I were witches, I mean this: we inherited from our mother—as she had from her mother—the power to communicate with the spirits, to get them to do our bidding in small and significant ways. We could feel the presence of the spirits—which are in the main invisible to human eyes—and the spirits were drawn to us.

"And those with such powers as we had were greatly revered amongst our people, and sought after for advice and miracles and glimpses into the future, and occasionally for putting the spirits of the dead to rest.

"What I am saying is that we were perceived as good; and we had our place in the scheme of things.

"There have always been witches, as far as I know. And there are witches now, though most no longer understand what their powers are or how to use them. Then there are those known as clairvoyants or mediums, or channelers. Or even psychic detectives. It is all the same thing. These are people who for reasons we may never understand attract spirits. Spirits find them downright irresistible; and to get the notice of these people, the spirits will do all kinds of tricks.

"As for the spirits themselves, I know that you're curious about their nature and properties, that you did not—all of you—believe the story in Lestat's book about how the Mother and the Father were made. I'm not sure that Marius himself believed it, when he was told the old story, or when he passed it on to Lestat."

Marius nodded. Already he had numerous questions. But Maharet gestured for patience. "Bear with me," she said. "I will tell you all we knew of the spirits then, which is the same as what I know of them now. Understand of course that others may use a different name for these entities. Others may define them more in the poetry of science than I will do.

"The spirits spoke to us only telepathically; as I have said, they were invisible; but their presence could be felt; they had distinct personalities, and our family of witches had over many generations given them various names.

"We divided them as sorcerers have always done into the good and the evil; but there is no evidence that they themselves have a sense of right and wrong. The evil spirits were those who were openly hostile to human beings and who liked to play malicious tricks such as the throwing of stones, the making of wind, and other such pesty things. Those who possess humans are often 'evil' spirits; those who haunt houses and are called poltergeists fall into this category, too.

"The good spirits could love, and wanted by and large to be loved as well. Seldom did they think up mischief on their own. They would answer questions about the future; they would tell us what was happening in other, remote places; and for very powerful witches such as my sister and me, for those whom the good spirits really loved, they would do their greatest and most taxing trick: they would make the rain.

"But you can see from what I'm saying that labels such as good and evil were self-serving. The good spirits were useful; the bad spirits were dangerous and nerve-wracking. To pay attention to the bad spirits—to invite them to hang about—was to court disaster, because ultimately they could not be controlled.

"There was also abundant evidence that what we called bad spirits envied us that we were fleshly and also spiritual—that we had the pleasures and powers of the physical while possessing spiritual minds. Very likely, this mixture of flesh and spirit in human beings makes all spirits curious; it is the source of our attraction for them; but it rankles the bad spirits; the bad spirits would know sensuous pleasure, it seems; yet they cannot. The good spirits did not evince such dissatisfaction.

"Now, as to where these spirits came from—they used to tell us that they had always been here. They would brag that they had watched human beings change from animals into what they were. We didn't know what they meant by such remarks. We thought they were being playful or just lying. But now, the study of human evolution makes it obvious that the spirits had witnessed this development. As for questions about their nature—how they were made or by whom—well, these they never answered. I don't think they understood what we were asking. They seemed insulted by the questions or even slightly afraid, or even thought the questions were humorous.

"I suspect that someday the scientific nature of spirits will be known. I suspect that they are matter and energy in sophisticated balance as is everything else in our universe, and that they are no more magical than electricity or radio waves, or quarks or atoms, or voices over the telephone—the things that seemed supernatural only two hundred years ago. In fact the poetry of modern science has helped me to understand them in retrospect better than any other philosophical tool. Yet I cling to my old language rather instinctively.

"It was Mekare's contention that she could now and then see them, and that they had tiny cores of physical matter and great bodies of whirling energy which she compared to storms of lightning and wind. She said there were creatures in the sea which were equally exotic in their organization; and insects who resembled the spirits, too. It was always at night that she saw their physical bodies, and they were never visible for more than a second, and usually only when the spirits were in a rage.

"Their size was enormous, she said, but then they said this too. They told us we could not imagine how big they were; but then they love to brag; one must constantly sort from their statements the part which makes sense.

"That they exert great force upon the physical world is beyond doubt. Otherwise how could they move objects as they do in poltergeist hauntings? And how could they have brought together the clouds to make the rain? Yet very little is really accomplished by them for all the energy they expend. And that was a key, always, to controlling them. There is only so much they can do, and no more, and a good witch was someone who understood that perfectly.

"Whatever their material makeup is, they have no apparent biological needs, these entities. They do not age; they do not change. And the key to understanding their childish and whimsical behavior lies in this. They have no *need* to do anything; they drift about unaware of time, for there is no physical reason to care about it, and they do whatever strikes the fancy. Obviously they see our world; they are part of it; but how it looks to them I can't guess.

"Why witches attract them or interest them I don't know either. But that's the crux of it; they see the witch, they go to her, make themselves known to her, and are powerfully flattered when they are noticed; and they do her bidding in order to get more attention; and in some cases, in order to be loved.

"And as this relationship progresses, they are made for the love of the witch to concentrate on various tasks. It exhausts them but it also delights them to see human beings so impressed.

"But imagine now, how much fun it is for them to listen to prayers and try to answer them, to hang about altars and make thunder after sacrifices are offered up. When a clairvoyant calls upon the spirit of a dead ancestor to speak to his descendants, they are quite thrilled to start chattering away in pretense of being the dead ancestor, though of course they are not that person; and they will telepathically extract information from the brains of the descendants in order to delude them all the more.

"Surely all of you know the pattern of their behavior. It's no different now than it was in our time. But what is different is the attitude of human beings to what spirits do; and that difference is crucial.

"When a spirit in these times haunts a house and makes predictions through the vocal cords of a five-year-old child, no one much believes it except those who see and hear it. It does not become the foundation of a great religion.

"It is as if the human species has grown immune to such things; it has evolved perhaps to a higher stage where the antics of spirits no longer befuddle it. And though religions linger—old religions which became entrenched in darker times—they are losing their influence among the educated very rapidly.

"But I'll say more on this later on. Let me continue now to define the properties of a witch, as such things relate to me and my sister, and to what happened to us.

"It was an inherited thing in our family. It may be physical for it seemed to run in our family line through the women and to be coupled invariably with the physical attributes of green eyes and red hair. As all of you know—as you've come to learn in one way or another since you entered this house—my child, Jesse, was a witch. And in the Talamasca she used her powers often to comfort those who were plagued by spirits and ghosts.

"Ghosts, of course, are spirits too. But they are without question spirits of those who have been human on earth; whereas the spirits I have been speaking of are not. However, one can never be too sure on this point. A very old earthbound ghost could forget that he had ever been alive; and possibly the very malevolent spirits are ghosts; and that is why they hunger so for the pleasures of the flesh; and when they possess some poor human being they belch obscenities. For them, the flesh is filth and they would have men and women believe that erotic pleasures and malice are equally dangerous and evil.

"But the fact is, given the way spirits lie—if they don't want to tell you—there's no way to know why they do what they do. Perhaps their obsession with the erotic is merely something abstracted from the minds of men and women who have always felt guilty about such things.

"To return to the point, it was mostly the women in our family who were witches. In other families it passes through both men and women. Or it can appear full-blown in a human being for reasons we can't grasp.

"Be that as it may, ours was an old, old family of witches. We could count witches back fifty generations, to what was called The Time Before the Moon. That is, we claimed to have lived in the very early period of earth history before the moon had come into the night sky.

"The legends of our people told of the coming of the moon, and the floods, storms, and earthquakes that attended it. Whether such a thing really happened I don't know. We also believed that our sacred stars were the Pleiades, or the Seven Sisters, that all blessings came from that constellation, but why, I never knew or cannot remember.

"I talk of old myths now, beliefs that were old before I was born. And those who commune with spirits become for obvious reasons rather skeptical of things.

"Yet science even now cannot deny or verify the tales of The Time Before the Moon. The coming of the moon—its subsequent gravitational pull—has been used theoretically to explain the shifting of the polar caps and the late ice ages. Maybe there was truth in the old stories, truths that will someday be clarified for us all.

"Whatever the case, ours was an old line. Our mother had been a powerful witch to whom the spirits told numerous secrets, reading men's minds as they do. And she had a great effect upon the restless spirits of the dead.

"In Mekare and me, it seemed her power had been doubled, as is often true with twins. That is, each of us was twice as powerful as our mother. As for the power we had together, it was incalculable. We talked to the spirits when we were in the cradle. We were surrounded by them when we played. As twins, we developed our own secret language, which not even our mother understood. But the spirits knew it. The spirits would understand anything we said to them; they could even speak our secret language back to us.

"Understand, I don't tell you all this out of pride. That would be absurd. I tell you so that you will grasp what we were to each other and to our own people before the soldiers of Akasha and Enkil came into our land. I want you to understand why this evil—this making of the blood drinkers—eventually happened!

"We were a great family. We had lived in the caves of Mount Carmel for as long as anybody knew. And our people had always built their encampments on the valley floor at the foot of the mountain. They lived by herding goats and sheep. And now and then they hunted; and they grew a few crops, for the making of the hallucinogenic drugs we took to make trances—this was part of our religion—and also for the making of beer. They cut down the wild wheat which grew then in profusion.

"Small round mud-brick houses with thatched roofs made up our village, but there were others which had grown into small cities, and some in which all the houses were entered from the roofs.

"Our people made a highly distinctive pottery which they took to the markets of Jericho for trade. From there they brought back lapis lazuli, ivory, incense, and mirrors of obsidian and other such fine things. Of course we knew of many other cities, vast and beautiful as Jericho, cities which are now buried completely under the earth and which may never be found.

"But by and large we were simple people. We knew what writing was—that is, the concept of it. But it did not occur to us to use such a thing, as words had a great power and we would not have dared to write our names, or curses or truths that we knew. If a person had your name, he could call on the spirits to curse you; he could go out of his body in a trance and travel to where you were. Who could know what power you would put into his hands if he could write your name on stone or papyrus? Even for those who weren't afraid, it was distasteful at the very least.

"And in the large cities, writing was largely used for financial records which we of course could keep in our heads.

"In fact, all knowledge among our people was committed to memory; the priests who sacrificed to the bull god of our people—in whom we did not believe, by the way—committed his traditions and beliefs to memory and taught them to the young priests by rote and by verse. Family histories were told from memory, of course.

"We did however paint pictures; they covered the walls of the bull shrines in the village.

"And my family, living in the caves on Mount Carmel as we had always, covered our secret grottoes with paintings which no one saw but us. Therein we kept a kind of record. But this was done with caution. I never painted or drew the image of myself, for example, until after catastrophe had struck and I and my sister were the things which we all are.

"But to return to our people, we were peaceful; shepherds, sometime craftsmen, sometime traders, no more, no less. When the armies of Jericho went to war, sometimes our young men joined them; but that was what they wanted to do. They wanted to be young men of adventure, and to be soldiers and know glory of that sort. Others went to the cities, to see the great markets, the majesty of the courts, or the splendor of the temples. And some went to ports of the Mediterranean to see the great merchant ships. But for the most part life went on in our villages as it had for many centuries without change. And Jericho protected us, almost indifferently, because it was the magnet which drew an enemy's force unto itself.

"Never, never, did we hunt men to eat their flesh! This was not our custom! And I cannot tell you what an abomination such cannibalism would have been to us, the eating of enemy flesh. Because we were cannibals, and the eating of the flesh had a special significance—we ate the flesh of our dead."

Maharet paused for a moment as if she wanted the significance of these words to be plain to all.

Marius saw the image again of the two red-haired women kneeling before the funeral feast. He felt the warm midday stillness, and the solemnity of the moment. He tried to clear his mind and see only Maharet's face.

"Understand," Maharet said. "We believed that the spirit left the body at death; but we also believed that the residue of all living things contains some tiny amount of power after life itself is gone. For example, a man's personal belongings retain some bit of his vitality; and the body and bones, surely. And of course when we consumed the flesh of our dead this residue, so to speak, would be consumed as well.

"But the real reason we ate the dead was out of respect. It was in our view the proper way to treat the remains of those we loved. We took into ourselves the bodies of those who'd given us life, the bodies from which our bodies had come. And so a cycle was completed. And the sacred remains of those we loved were saved from the awful horror of putrefaction within the earth, or from being devoured by wild beasts, or burnt as if they were fuel or refuse.

"There is a great logic to it if you think on it. But the important thing to realize is that it was part and parcel of us as a people. The sacred duty of every child was to consume the remains of his parents; the sacred duty of the tribe was to consume the dead.

"Not a single man, woman, or child died in our village whose body was not consumed by kith or kin. Not a single man, woman, or child of our village had not consumed the flesh of the dead."

Again, Maharet paused, her eyes sweeping the group slowly before she went on.

"Now, it was not a time of great wars," she said. "Jericho had been at peace for as long as anyone could remember. And Nineveh had been at peace as well.

"But far away, to the southwest in the Nile Valley, the savage people of that land made war as they had always done upon the jungle peoples south of them so that they might bring back captives for their spits and pots. For not only did they devour their own dead with all proper respect as we did, they ate the bodies of their enemies; they gloried in it. They believed the strength of the enemy went into their bodies when they consumed his flesh. Also they liked the taste of the flesh.

"We scorned what they did, for the reasons I've explained. How could anyone want the flesh of an enemy? But perhaps the crucial difference between us and the warlike dwellers of the Nile Valley was not that they ate their enemies, but that they were warlike and we were peaceful. We did not have any enemies.

"Now, about the time that my sister and I reached our sixteenth year, a great change occurred in the Nile Valley. Or so we were told.

"The aging Queen of that realm died without a daughter to carry on the royal blood. And amongst many ancient peoples the royal blood went only through the female line. Since no male can ever be certain of the paternity of his wife's child, it was the Queen or the Princess who brought with her the divine right to the throne. This is why Egyptian pharaohs of a later age often married their sisters. It was to secure their royal right.

"And so it would have been with this young King Enkil if he had had a sister, but he did not. He did not even have a royal cousin or aunt to marry. But he was young and strong and determined to rule his land. Finally, he settled upon a new bride, not from his own people, but from those of the city of Uruk in the Tigris and Euphrates Valley.

"And this was Akasha, a beauty of the royal family, and a worshiper of the great goddess Inanna, and one who could bring into Enkil's kingdom the wisdom of her land. Or so the gossip went in the marketplaces of Jericho and Nineveh and with the caravans that came to trade for our wares.

"Now the people of the Nile were farmers already, but they tended to neglect this to hunt to make war for human flesh. And this horrified the beautiful Akasha, who set about at once to turn them away from this barbaric habit as possibly anyone of higher civilization might do.

"She probably also brought with her writing, as the people of Uruk had it—they were great keepers of records—but as writing was something largely scorned by us, I do not know this for sure. Perhaps the Egyptians had already begun to write on their own.

"You cannot imagine the slowness with which such things affect a culture. Records of taxation might be kept for generations before anyone commits to a clay tablet the words of a poem. Peppers and herbs might be cultivated by a tribe for two hundred years before anyone thinks to grow wheat or corn. As you know, the Indians of South America had toys with wheels when the Europeans swept down upon them; and jewelry they had, made of metal. But they had no wheels in use in any other form whatsoever; and they did not use metal for their weapons. And so they were defeated by the Europeans almost at once.

"Whatever the case, I don't know the full story of the knowledge Akasha brought with her from Uruk. I do know that our people heard great gossip about the ban upon all cannibalism in the Nile Valley, and how those who disobeyed were cruelly put to death. The tribes who had hunted for flesh for generations were infuriated that they could no longer enjoy this sport; but even greater was the fury of all the people that they could not eat their own dead. Not to hunt, that was one thing, but to commit one's ancestors to the earth was a horror to them as it would have been to us.

"So in order that Akasha's edict would be obeyed, the King decreed that all the bodies of the dead must be treated with unguents and wrapped up. Not only could one not eat the sacred flesh of mother or father, but it must be secured in linen wrappings at great expense, and these intact bodies must be displayed for all to see, and then placed in tombs with proper offerings and incantation of the priest.

"The sooner the wrapping was done the better; because no one could then get to the flesh.

"And to further assist the people in this new observance, Akasha and Enkil convinced them that the spirits of the dead would fare better in the realm to which they had gone if their bodies were preserved in these wrappings on earth. In other words, the people were told, 'Your beloved ancestors are not neglected; rather they are well kept.'

"We thought it was very amusing when we heard it—wrapping the dead and putting them away in furnished rooms above or below the desert sand. We thought it amusing that the spirits of the dead should be helped by the perfect maintenance of their bodies on earth. For as anyone knows who has ever communicated with the dead, it is better that they forget their bodies; it is only when they relinquish their earthly image that they can rise to the higher plane.

"And now in Egypt in the tombs of the very rich and very religious, there lay these things—these mummies in which the flesh rotted away.

"If anyone had told us that this custom of mummification would become entrenched in that culture, that for four thousand years the Egyptians would practice it, that it would become a great and enduring mystery to the entire world—that little children in the twentieth century would go into museums to gaze at mummies—we would not have believed such a thing.

"However, it did not matter to us, really. We were very far from the Nile Valley. We could not even imagine what these people were like. We knew their religion had come out of Africa, that they worshiped the god Osiris, and the sun god, Ra, and animal gods as well. But we really didn't understand these people. We didn't understand their land of inundation and desert. When we held in our hands fine objects which they had made, we knew some faint shimmer of their personalities, but it was alien. We felt sorry for them that they could not eat their dead.

"When we asked the spirits about them, the spirits seemed mightily amused by the Egyptians. They said the Egyptians had 'nice voices' and 'nice words' and that it was pleasurable to visit their temples and altars; they liked the Egyptian tongue. Then they seemed to lose interest in the question, and to drift off as was often the case.

"What they said fascinated us but it didn't surprise us. We knew how the spirits liked our words and our chants and our songs. So the spirits were playing gods there for the Egyptians. The spirits did that sort of thing all the time.

"As the years passed, we heard that Enkil, to unite his kingdom and stop the rebellion and resistance of the die-hard cannibals, had made a great army and embarked on conquests to north and south. He had launched ships in the great sea. It was an old trick: get them all to fight an enemy and they'll stop quarreling at home.

"But again, what had this to do with us? Ours was a land of serenity and beauty, of laden fruit trees and fields of wild wheat free for anyone to cut with the scythe. Ours was a land of green grass and cool breezes. But there wasn't anything that anyone would want to take from us. Or so we believed.

"My sister and I continued to live in perfect peace on the gentle slopes of Mount Carmel, often speaking to our mother and to each other silently, or with a few private words, which we understood perfectly; and learning from our mother all she knew of the spirits and men's hearts.

"We drank the dream potions made by our mother from the plants we grew on the mountain, and in our trances and dream states, we traveled back into the past and spoke with our ancestors—very great witches whose names we knew. In sum, we lured the spirits of these ancient ones back to earth long enough to give us some knowledge. We also traveled out of our bodies and high over the land.

"I could spend these hours telling what we saw in these trances; how once Mekare and I walked hand in hand through the streets of Nineveh, gazing on wonders which we had not imagined; but these things are not important now.

"Let me say only what the company of the spirits meant to us—the soft harmony in which we lived with all living things around us and with the spirits; and how at moments, the love of the spirits was palpable to us, as Christian mystics have described the love of God or his saints.

"We lived in bliss together, my sister and I and our mother. The caves of our ancestors were warm and dry; and we had all things that we needed—fine robes and jewelry and lovely combs of ivory and sandals of leather—brought to us by the people as offerings, for no one ever paid us for what we did.

"And every day the people of our village came to consult with us, and we would put their questions to the spirits. We would try to see the future, which of course the spirits can do after a fashion, insofar as certain things tend to follow an inevitable course.

"We looked into minds with our telepathic power and we gave the best wisdom that we could. Now and then those possessed were brought to us. And we drove out the demon, or the bad spirit, for that is all it was. And when a house was bedeviled, we went there and ordered the bad spirit away.

"We gave the dream potion to those who requested it. And they would fall into the trance, or sleep and dream heavily in vivid images, which we sought then to interpret or explain.

"For this we didn't really need the spirits though sometimes we sought their particular advice. We used our own powers of understanding and deep vision, and often the information handed down to us, as to what various images mean.

"But our greatest miracle—which took all our power to accomplish, and which we could never guarantee—was the bringing down of the rain.

"Now, in two basic ways we worked this miracle—'little rain,' which was largely symbolic and a demonstration of power and a great healing thing for our people's souls. Or 'big rain,' which was needed for the crops, and which was very hard, indeed, to do if we could do it at all.

"Both required a great wooing of the spirits, a great calling of their names, and demanding that they come together and concentrate and use their force at our command. 'Little rain' was often done by our most familiar spirits, those who loved Mekare and me most particularly, and had loved our mother and her mother, and all our ancestors before us, and could always be counted upon to do hard tasks out of love.

"But many spirits were required for 'big rain' and since some of these spirits seemed to loathe each other and to loathe cooperation, a great deal of flattery had to be thrown into the bargain. We had to do chants, and a great dance. For hours, we worked at it as the spirits gradually took interest, came together, became enamored of the idea, and then finally set to work.

"Mekare and I were able to accomplish 'big rain' only three times. But what a lovely thing it was to see the clouds gather over the valley, to see the great blinding sheets of rain descend. All our people ran out into the downpour; the land itself seemed to swell, to open, to give thanks.

" 'Little rain' we did often; we did it for others, we did it for joy.

"But it was the making of 'big rain' that really spread our fame far and wide. We had always been known as the witches of the mountain; but now people came to us from the cities of the far north, from lands whose names we didn't know.

"Men waited their turn in the village to come to the mountain and drink the potion and have us examine their dreams. They waited their turn to seek our counsel or sometimes merely to see us. And of course our village served them meat and drink and took an offering for this, and all profited, or so it seemed. And in this regard what we did was not so different from what doctors of psychology do in this century; we studied images; we interpreted them; we sought for some truth from the subconscious mind; and the miracles of 'little rain' and 'big rain' merely bolstered the faith of others in our abilities.

"One day, half a year I think before our mother was to die, a letter came into our hands. A messenger had brought it from the King and Queen of Kemet, which was the land of Egypt as the Egyptians called it themselves. It was a letter written on a clay tablet as they wrote in Jericho and Nineveh, and there were little pictures in the clay, and the beginnings of what men would later call cuneiform.

"Of course we could not read it; in fact, we found it frightening, and thought that it might be a curse. We did not want to touch it, but touch it we had to do if we were to understand anything about it that we should know.

"The messenger said that his sovereigns Akasha and Enkil had heard of our great power and would be honored if we would visit at their court; they had sent a great escort to accompany us to Kemet, and they would send us home with great gifts.

"We found ourselves, all three, distrustful of this messenger. He was speaking the truth as far as he knew it, but there was more to the whole thing.

"So our mother took the clay tablet into her hands. Immediately, she felt something from it, something which passed through her fingers and gave her great distress. At first she wouldn't tell us what she had seen; then taking us aside, she said that the King and Queen of Kemet were evil, great shedders of blood, and very disregarding of others' beliefs. And that a terrible evil would come to us from this man and woman, no matter what the writing said.

"Then Mekare and I touched the letter and we too caught the presentiment of evil. But there was a mystery here, a dark tangle, and caught up with the evil was an element of courage and what seemed good. In sum this was no simple plot to steal us and our power; there was some genuine curiosity and respect.

"Finally we asked the spirits—those two spirits which Mekare and I most loved. They came near to us and they read the letter which was a very easy thing for them to do. They said that the messenger had told the truth. But some terrible danger would come to us if we were to go to the King and Queen of Kemet.

" 'Why?' we asked the spirits.

" 'Because the King and Queen will ask you questions,' the spirits answered, 'and if you answer truthfully, which you will, the King and Queen will be angry with you, and you will be destroyed.'

"Of course we would never have gone to Egypt anyway. We didn't leave our mountain. But now we knew for sure that we must not. We told the messenger with all respect that we could not leave the place where we had been born, that no witch of our family had ever left here, and we begged him to tell this to the King and Queen.

"And so the messenger left and life returned to its normal routine.

"Except that several nights later, an evil spirit came to us, one which we called Amel. Enormous, powerful, and full of rancor, this thing danced about the clearing before our cave trying to get Mekare and me to take notice of him, and telling us that we might soon need his help.

"We were long used to the blandishments of evil spirits; it made them furious that we would not talk to them as other witches and wizards might. But we knew these entities to be untrustworthy and uncontrollable and we had never been tempted to use them and thought that we never would.

"This Amel, in particular, was maddened by our 'neglect' of him, as he called it. And he declared over and over again that he was 'Amel, the powerful,' and 'Amel, the invincible,' and we should show him some respect. For we might have great need of him in the future. We might need him more than we could imagine, for trouble was coming our way.

"At this point, our mother came out of the cave and demanded of this spirit what was this trouble that he saw.

"This shocked us because we had always been forbidden by her to speak to evil spirits; and when she had spoken to them it was always to curse them or drive them away; or to confuse them with riddles and trick questions so that they got angry, felt stupid, and gave up.

"Amel, the terrible, the evil, the overwhelming—whatever he called himself, and his boasting was endless—declared only that great trouble was coming and we should pay him the proper respect if we were wise. He then bragged of all the evil he had worked for the wizards of Nineveh. That he could torment people, bedevil them, and even prick them as if he were a swarm of gnats! He could draw blood from humans, he declared; and he liked the taste of it; and he would draw blood for us.

"My mother laughed at him. 'How could you do such a thing?' she demanded. 'You are a spirit; you have no body; you can taste nothing!' she said. And this is the sort of language which always made spirits furious, for they envy us the flesh, as I've said.

"Well, this spirit, to demonstrate his power, came down upon our mother like a gale; and immediately her good spirits fought him and there was a terrible commotion over the clearing, but when it had died away and Amel had been driven back by our guardian spirits, we saw that there were tiny pricks upon our mother's hand. Amel, the evil one, had drawn blood from her, exactly as he had said he would—as if a swarm of gnats had tormented her with little bites.

"My mother looked at these tiny pinprick wounds; the good spirits went mad to see her treated with such disrespect, but she told them to be still. Silently she pondered this thing, how it could be possible, and how this spirit might taste the blood that he had drawn.

"And it was then that Mekare explained her vision that these spirits had infinitesimal material cores at the very center of their great invisible bodies, and it was possibly through this core that the spirit tasted the blood. Imagine, Mekare said, the wick of a lamp, but a tiny thing within a flame. The wick might absorb blood. And so it was with the spirit who appeared to be all flame but had that tiny wick in it.

"Our mother was scornful but she did not like this thing. She said ironically that the world was full of wonders enough without evil spirits with a taste for blood. 'Be gone, Amel,' she said, and laid curses on him, that he was trivial, unimportant, did not matter, was not to be recognized, and might as well blow away. In other words the things she always said to get rid of pesty spirits—the things which priests say even now in slightly different form when they seek to exorcise children who are possessed.

"But what worried our mother more than Amel's antics was his warning, that evil was coming our way. It deepened the distress she had felt when she took hold of the Egyptian tablet. Yet she did not ask the good spirits for comfort or advice. Maybe she knew better than to ask them. But this I can never know. Whatever was the case, our mother knew something was going to happen, and clearly she felt powerless to prevent it. Perhaps she understood that sometimes, when we seek to prevent disaster, we play into its hands.

"Whatever was the truth of it, she grew sick in the days that followed, then weak, and then unable to speak.

"For months she lingered, paralyzed, half asleep. We sat by her night and day and sang to her. We brought flowers to her and we tried to read her thoughts. The spirits were in a terrible state of agitation as they loved her. And they made the wind blow on the mountain; they tore the leaves from the trees.

"All the village was in sorrow. Then one morning the thoughts of our mother took shape again; but they were fragments. We saw sunny fields and flowers and images of things she'd known in childhood; and then only brilliant colors and little more.

"We knew our mother was dying, and the spirits knew it. We did our best to calm them, but some of them had gone into a rage. When she died, her ghost would rise and pass through the realm of the spirits and they would lose her forever and go mad for a while in their grief.

"But finally it happened, as it was perfectly natural and inevitable, and we came out of the cave to tell the villagers our mother had gone to higher realms. All the trees of the mountain were caught in the wind made by the spirits; the air was full of green leaves. My sister and I wept; and for the first time in my life I thought I heard the spirits; I thought I heard their cries and lamentations over the wind.

"At once the villagers came to do what must be done.

"First our mother was laid out on a stone slab as was the custom so that all could come and pay their respects. She was dressed in the white gown she so loved in life, of Egyptian linen, and all her fine jewelry from Nineveh and the rings and necklaces of bone which contained tiny bits of our ancestors, and which would soon come to us.

"And after ten hours had passed, and hundreds had come to visit, both from our village and all the surrounding villages, we then prepared the body for the funeral feast. For any other dead person of our village, the priests would have done this honor. But we were witches and our mother was a witch; and we alone could touch her. And in privacy, and by the light of oil lamps, my sister and I removed the gown from our mother and covered her body completely with fresh flowers and leaves. We sawed open her skull and lifted the top carefully so that it remained intact at the forehead, and we removed her brain and placed it on a plate with her eyes. Then with an equally careful incision we removed the heart and placed it on another plate. Then these plates were covered with heavy domes of clay to protect them.

"And the villagers came forward and built a brick oven around the body of our mother on the stone slab, with the plates beside her, and they put the fire in the oven, beneath the slab, between the rocks upon which it rested, and the roasting began.

"All night it took place. The spirits had quieted because the spirit of our mother was gone. I don't think the body mattered to them; what we did now did not matter, but it certainly mattered to us.

"Because we were witches and our mother was a witch, we alone would partake of her flesh. It was all ours by custom and right. The villagers would not assist in the feast as they might have done at any other where only two offspring were left with the obligation. No matter how long it took we would consume our mother's flesh. And the villagers would keep watch with us.

"But as the night wore on, as the remains of our mother were prepared in the oven, my sister and I deliberated over the heart and the brain. We would divide these organs of course; and which should take which organ, that was what concerned us; for we had strong beliefs about these organs and what resided in each.

"Now to many peoples of that time, it was the heart that mattered. To the Egyptians, for example, the heart was the seat of conscience. This was even so to the people of our village; but we as witches believed that the brain was the residence of the human spirit: that is, the spiritual part of each man or woman that was like unto the spirits of the air. And our belief that the brain was important came from the fact that the eyes were connected to the brain; and the eyes were the organs of sight. And *seeing* is what we did as witches; we *saw* into hearts, we saw into the future; we saw into the past. Seer, that was the word for what we were in our language; that is what 'witch' meant.

"But again, this was largely ceremony of which we spoke; we believed our mother's spirit had gone. Out of respect for her, we consumed these organs so that they should not rot. So it was easy for us to reach agreement; Mekare would take the brain and the eyes; and I would take the heart.

"Mekare was the more powerful witch; the one born first; and the one who always took the lead in things; the one who spoke out immediately; the one who acted as the older sister, as one twin invariably does. It seemed right that she should take the brain and the eyes; and I, who had always been quieter of disposition, and slower, should take the organ which was associated with deep feeling, and love—the heart.

"We were pleased with the division and as the morning sky grew light we slept for a few hours, our bodies weak from hunger and the fasting that prepared us for the feast.

"Sometime before dawn the spirits waked us. They were making the wind come again. I went out of the cave; the fire glowed in the oven. The villagers who kept watch were asleep. Angrily I told the spirits to keep quiet. But one of them, that one which I most loved, said that strangers were gathered on the mountain, many many strangers who were most impressed with our power and dangerously curious about the feast.

" 'These men want something of you and Mekare,' the spirit told me. 'These men are not for the good.'

"I told him that strangers always came here; that this was nothing, and that he must be quiet now, and let us do what we had to do. But then I went to one of the men of our village and asked that the village be ready in case some trouble was to happen, that the men bring their arms with them when they gathered for the feast to begin.

"It wasn't such a strange request. Most men carried their weapons with them wherever they went. Those few who had been professional soldiers or could afford swords frequently wore them; those with knives kept them tucked in their belt.

"But in the main I was not concerned about such things; after all, strangers from far and wide came to our village; it was only natural that they would for this special event—the death of a witch.

"But you know what was to happen. You saw it in your dreams. You saw the villagers gather around the clearing as the sun rose towards the high point of noon. Maybe you saw the bricks taken down slowly from the cooling oven; or only the body of our mother, darkened, shriveled, yet peaceful as in sleep, revealed on the warm slab of stone. You saw the wilted flowers covering her, and you saw the heart and the brain and the eyes upon their plates.

"You saw us kneel on either side of our mother's body. And you heard the musicians begin to play.

"What you could not see, but you know now, is that for thousands of years our people had gathered at such feasts. For thousands of years we had lived in that valley and on the slopes of the mountain where the high grass grew and the fruit fell from the trees. This was our land, our custom, our moment.

"Our sacred moment.

"And as Mekare and I knelt opposite each other, dressed in the finest robes we possessed and wearing now the jewelry of our mother as well as our own adornments, we saw before us, not the warnings of the spirits, or the distress of our mother when she had touched the tablet of the King and Queen of Kemet. We saw our own lives—with hope, long and happy—to be lived here among our own.

"I don't know how long we knelt there; how long we prepared our souls. I remember that finally, in unison, we lifted the plates which contained the organs of our mother; and the musicians began to play. The music of the flute and the drum filled the air around us; we could hear the soft breath of the villagers; we could hear the song of the birds.

"And then the evil came down upon us; came so suddenly with the tramp of feet and loud shrill war cries of the Egyptian soldiers, that we scarce knew what was happening. Over our mother's body, we threw ourselves, seeking to protect the sacred feast; but at once they had pulled us up and away, and we saw the plates falling into the dirt, and the slab overturned!

"I heard Mekare screaming as I had never heard a human scream. But I too was screaming, screaming as I saw my mother's body thrown down into the ashes.

"Yet curses filled my ears; men denouncing us as flesh eaters, cannibals, men denouncing us as savages and those who must be put to the sword.

"Only no one harmed us. Screaming, struggling, we were bound and kept helpless, though all of our kith and kin were slaughtered before our eyes. Soldiers tramped on the body of our mother; they tramped on her heart and her brain and her eyes. They tramped back and forth in the ashes, while their cohorts skewered the men and women and children of our village.

"And then, through the chorus of screams, through the hideous outcry of all those hundreds dying on the side of the mountain, I heard Mekare call on our spirits for vengeance, call on them to punish the soldiers for what they had done.

"But what was wind or rain to such men as these? The trees shook; it seemed the earth itself trembled; leaves filled the air as they had the night before. Rocks rolled down the mountain; dust rose in clouds. But there was no more than a moment's hesitation, before the King, Enkil, himself stepped forth and told his men that these were but tricks that all men had witnessed, and we and our demons could do no more.

"It was all too true, this admonition; and the massacre went on unabated. My sister and I were ready to die. But they did not kill us. It was not their intention to kill us, and as they dragged us away, we saw our village burning, we saw the fields of wild wheat burning, we saw all the men and women of our tribe lying dead, and we knew their bodies would be left there for the beasts and the earth to consume, in utter disregard and abandon."

Maharet stopped. She had made a small steeple of her hands and now she touched the tips of her fingers to her forehead, and rested it seemed before she went on. When she continued, her voice was roughened slightly and lower, but steady as it had been before.

"What is one small nation of villages? What is one people—or even one life?

"Beneath the earth a thousand such peoples are buried. And so our people are buried to this day.

"All we knew, all we had been, was laid waste within the space of an hour. A trained army had slaughtered our simple shepherds, our women, and our helpless young. Our villages lay in ruins, huts pulled down; everything that could burn was burned.

"Over the mountain, over the village that lay at the foot of it, I felt the presence of the spirits of the dead; a great haze of spirits, some so agitated and confused by the violence done them that they clung to the earth in terror and pain; and others rising above the flesh to suffer no more.

"And what could the spirits do?

"All the way to Egypt, they followed our procession; they bedeviled the men who kept us bound and carried us by means of a litter on their shoulders, two weeping women, snuggling close to each other in terror and grief.

"Each night when the company made camp, the spirits sent wind to tear up their tents and scatter them. Yet the King counseled his soldiers not to be afraid. The King said the gods of Egypt were more powerful than the demons of the witches. And as the spirits were in fact doing all that they were capable of, as things got no worse, the soldiers obeyed.

"Each night the King had us brought before him. He spoke our language, which was a common one in the world then, spoken all through the Tigris and Euphrates Valley and along the flanks of Mount Carmel. 'You are great witches,' he would say, his voice gentle and maddeningly sincere. 'I have spared your life on this account though you were flesh eaters as were your people, and you were caught in the very act by me and my men. I have spared you because I would have the benefit of your wisdom. I would learn from you, and my Queen would learn as well. Tell me what I can give you to ease your suffering and I will do it. You are under my protection now; I am your King.'

"Weeping, refusing to meet his eyes, saying nothing, we stood before him until he tired of all this, and sent us back to sleep in the small crowded litter—a tiny rectangle of wood with only small windows—as we had been before.

"Alone once more, my sister and I spoke to each other silently, or by means of our language, the twin language of gestures and abbreviated words that only we understood. We recalled what the spirits had said to our mother; we remembered that she had taken ill after the letter from the King of Kemet and she had never recovered. Yet we weren't afraid.

"We were too stricken with grief to be afraid. It was as if we were already dead. We'd seen our people massacred, we'd seen our mother's body desecrated. We did not know what could be worse. We were together; maybe separation would be worse.

"But during this long journey to Egypt, we had one small consolation which we were not later to forget. Khayman, the King's steward, looked upon us with compassion, and did everything that he could, in secret, to ease our pain."

Maharet stopped again and looked at Khayman, who sat with his hands folded before him on the table and his eyes down. It seemed he was deep in his recollection of the things which Maharet described. He accepted this tribute but it didn't seem to console him. Then finally he looked to Maharet in acknowledgment. He seemed dazed and full of questions. But he didn't ask them. His eyes passed over the others, acknowledging their glances as well, acknowledging the steady stare of Armand, and of Gabrielle, but again, he said nothing.

Then Maharet continued:

"Khayman loosened our bonds whenever possible; he allowed us to walk about in the evening; he brought us meat and drink. And there was a great kindness in that he didn't speak to us when he did these things; he did not ask for our gratitude. He did these things with a pure heart. It was simply not to his taste to see people suffer.

"It seemed we traveled ten days to reach the land of Kemet. Maybe it was more; maybe it was less. Some time during that journey the spirits tired of their tricks; and we, dejected and without courage, did not call upon them. We sank into silence finally, only now and then looking into each other's eyes.

"At last we came into a kingdom the like of which we had never seen. Over scorching desert we were brought to the rich black land that bordered the Nile River, the black earth from which the word Kemet derives; and then over the mighty river itself by raft we were taken as was all the army, and into a sprawling city of brick buildings with grass roofs, of great temples and palaces built of the same coarse materials, but all very fine.

"This was long before the time of the stone architecture for which the Egyptians would become known—the temples of the pharaohs which have stood to this day.

"But already there was a great love of show and decoration, a movement towards the monumental. Unbaked bricks, river reeds, matting—all of these simple materials had been used to make high walls which were then whitewashed and painted with lovely designs.

"Before the palace into which we were taken as royal prisoners were great columns made from enormous jungle grasses, which had been dried and bound together and plastered with river mud; and within a closed court a lake had been made, full of lotus blossoms and surrounded by flowering trees.

"Never had we seen people so rich as these Egyptians, people decked out with so much jewelry, people with beautifully plaited hair and painted eyes. And their painted eyes tended to unnerve us. For the paint hardened their stare; it gave an illusion of depth where perhaps there was no depth; instinctively, we shrank from this artifice.

"But all we saw merely inspired further misery in us. How we hated everything around us. And we could sense from these people—though we didn't understand their strange tongue—that they hated and feared us too. It seemed our red hair caused great confusion among them; and that we were twins, this too produced fear.

"For it had been the custom among them now and then to kill twin children; and the red-haired were invariably sacrificed to the gods. It was thought to be lucky.

"All this came clear to us in wanton flashes of understanding; imprisoned, we waited grimly to see what would be our fate.

"As before, Khayman was our only consolation in those first hours. Khayman, the King's chief steward, saw that we had comforts in our imprisonment. He brought us fresh linen, and fruit to eat and beer to drink. He brought us even combs for our hair and clean dresses; and for the first time he spoke to us; he told us that the Queen was gentle and good, and we must not be afraid.

"We knew that he was speaking the truth, there was no doubt of it; but something was wrong, as it had been months before with the words of the King's messenger. Our trials had only begun.

"We also feared the spirits had deserted us; that maybe they did not want to come into this land on our behalf. But we didn't call upon the spirits; because to call and not to be answered—well, that would have been more than we could bear.

"Then evening came and the Queen sent for us; and we were brought before the court.

"The spectacle overwhelmed us, even as we despised it: Akasha and Enkil upon their thrones. The Queen was then as she is now—a woman of straight shoulders and firm limbs with a face almost too exquisite to evince intelligence, a being of enticing prettiness with a soft treble voice. As for the King, we saw him now not as a soldier but as a sovereign. His hair was plaited, and he wore his formal kilt and jewels. His black eyes were full of earnestness as they had always been; but it was clear, within a moment, that it was Akasha who ruled this kingdom and always had. Akasha had the language—the verbal skill.

"At once, she told us that our people had been properly punished for their abominations; that they had been dealt with mercifully, as all flesh eaters are savages, and they should have, by right, suffered a slow death. And she said that we had been shown mercy because we were great witches, and the Egyptians would learn from us; they would know what wisdom of the realms of the invisible we had to impart.

"Immediately, as if these words were nothing, she went into her questions. Who were our demons? Why were some good, if they were demons? Were they not gods? How could we make the rain fall?

"We were too horrified by her callousness to respond. We were bruised by the spiritual coarseness of her manner, and had begun to weep again. We turned away from her and into each other's arms.

"But something else was also coming clear to us—something very plain from the manner in which this person spoke. The speed of her words, their flippancy, the emphasis she put upon this or that syllable—all this made known to us that she was lying and did not herself know that she lied.

"And looking deep into the lie, as we closed our eyes, we saw the truth which she herself would surely deny:

"She had slaughtered our people in order to bring us here! She had sent her King and her soldiers upon this 'holy war' simply because we had refused her earlier invitation, and she wanted us at her mercy. *She was curious about us.*

"This was what our mother had seen when she held the tablet of the King and Queen in her hands. Perhaps the spirits in their own way had foreseen it. We only understood the full monstrousness of it now.

"Our people had died because we had attracted the interest of the Queen just as we attracted the interest of the spirits; we had brought this evil upon all.

"Why, we wondered, hadn't the soldiers merely taken us from our helpless villagers? Why had they brought to ruin all that our people were?

"But that was the horror! A moral cloak had been thrown over the Queen's purpose, a cloak through which she could not see any more than anyone else.

"She had convinced herself that our people should die, yes, that their savagery merited it, even though they were not Egyptians and our land was far from her home. And oh, wasn't it rather convenient, that then we should be shown mercy and brought here to satisfy her curiosity at last. And we should, of course, be grateful by then and willing to answer her questions.

"And even deeper beyond her deception, we beheld the mind that made such contradictions possible.

"This Queen had no true morality, no true system of ethics to govern the things which she did. This Queen was one of those many humans who sense that perhaps there is nothing and no reason to anything that can ever be known. Yet she cannot bear the thought of it. And so she created day in and day out her ethical systems, trying desperately to believe in them, and they were all cloaks for things she did for merely pragmatic reasons. Her war on the cannibals, for instance, had stemmed more from her *dislike* of such customs than anything else. Her people of Uruk hadn't eaten human flesh; and so she would not have this offensive thing happening around her; there really wasn't a whole lot more to it than that. For always in her there was a dark place full of despair. And a great driving force to make meaning because there was none.

"Understand, it was not a shallowness we perceived in this woman. It was a youthful belief that she could make the light shine if she tried; that she could shape the world to comfort herself; and it was also a lack of interest in the pain of others. She knew others felt pain, but well, she could not really dwell on it.

"Finally, unable to bear the extent of this obvious duplicity, we turned and studied her, for we must now contend with her. She was not twenty-five years old, this Queen, and her powers were absolute in this land which she had dazzled with her customs from Uruk. And she was almost too pretty to be truly beautiful, for her loveliness overcame any sense of majesty or deep mystery; and her voice contained still a childish ring to it, a ring which evokes tenderness instinctively in others, and gives a faint music to the simplest words. A ring which we found maddening.

"On and on she went with her questions. How did we work our miracles? How did we look into men's hearts? Whence came our magic, and why did we claim that we talked to beings who were invisible? Could we speak in the same manner to her gods? Could we deepen her knowledge or bring her into closer understanding of what was divine? She was willing to pardon us for our savagery if we were to be grateful; if we were to kneel at her altars and lay before her gods and before her what we knew.

"She pursued her various points with a single-mindedness that could make a wise person laugh.

"But it brought up the deepest rage from Mekare. She who had always taken the lead in anything spoke out now.

" 'Stop your questions. You speak in stupidities,' she declared. 'You have no gods in this kingdom, because there are no gods. The only invisible inhabitants of the world are spirits, and they play with you through your priests and your religion as they play with everyone else. Ra, Osiris—these are merely made-up names with which you flatter and court the spirits, and when it suits their purposes they give you some little sign to send you scurrying to flatter them some more.'

"Both the King and Queen stared at Mekare in horror. But Mekare went on:

" 'The spirits are real, but they are childlike and capricious. And they are dangerous as well. They marvel at us and envy us that we are both spiritual and fleshly, which attracts them and makes them eager to do our will. Witches such as we have always known how to use them; but it takes great skill and great power to do it, and this we have and you do not have. You are fools, and what you have done to take us prisoner is evil; it is dishonest; you live in the lie! But we will not lie to you.'

"And then, half weeping, half choking with rage, Mekare accused the Queen before the entire court of duplicity, of massacring our peaceable people simply so that we might be brought here. Our people had not hunted for human flesh in a thousand years, she told this court; and it was a funeral feast that was desecrated at our capture, and all this evil done so that the Queen of Kemet might have witches to talk to, witches of whom to ask questions, witches in her possession whose power she would seek to use for herself.

"The court was in an uproar. Never had anyone heard such disrespect, such blasphemy, and so forth and so on. But the old lords of Egypt, those who still chafed at the ban on sacred cannibalism, they were horrified by this mention of the desecrated funeral feast. And others who also feared the retribution of heaven for not devouring the remains of their parents were struck dumb with fear.

"But in the main, it was confusion. Except for the King and the Queen, who were strangely silent and strangely intrigued.

"Akasha didn't make any answer to us, and it was clear that something in our explanation had rung true for her in the deeper regions of her mind. There flared for the moment a deadly earnest curiosity. *Spirits who pretend to be gods? Spirits who envy the flesh?* As for the charge that she had sacrificed our people needlessly, she didn't even consider it. Again, it did not interest her. It was the spiritual question which fascinated her, and in her fascination the spirit was divorced from the flesh.

"Allow me to draw your attention to what I have just said. It was the spiritual question which fascinated her—you might say the abstract idea; and in her fascination the abstract idea was everything. I do not think she believed that the spirits could be childlike and capricious. But whatever was there, she meant to know of it; and she meant to know of it through us. As for the destruction of our people, she did not care!

"Meantime the high priest of the temple of Ra was demanding our execution. So was the high priest of the temple of Osiris. We were evil; we were witches; and all those with red hair should be burned as had always been done in the land of Kemet. And at once the assemblage echoed these denunciations. There should be a burning. Within moments it seemed a riot would have broken out in the palace.

"But the King ordered all to be quiet. We were taken to our cell again, and put under heavy guard.

"Mekare, enraged, paced the floor, as I begged her not to say any more. I reminded her of what the spirits had told us: that if we went to Egypt, the King and Queen would ask us questions, and if we answered truthfully, which we would, the King and Queen would be angry with us, and we would be destroyed.

"But this was like talking to myself now; Mekare wouldn't listen. Back and forth she walked, now and then striking her breast with her fist. I felt the anguish she felt.

" 'Damnable,' she was saying. 'Evil.' And then she'd fall silent and pace, and then say these words again.

"I knew she was remembering the warning of Amel, the evil one. And I also knew that Amel was near; I could hear him, sense him.

"I knew that Mekare was being tempted to call upon him; and I felt that she must not. What would his silly torments mean to the Egyptians? How many mortals could he afflict with his pinpricks? It was no more than the storms of wind and flying objects which we could already produce. But Amel heard these thoughts; and he began to grow restless.

" 'Be quiet, demon,' Mekare said. 'Wait until I need you!' Those were the first words I ever heard her speak to an evil spirit, and they sent a shiver of horror through me.

"I don't remember when we fell asleep. Only that sometime after midnight I was awakened by Khayman.

"At first I thought it was Amel doing some trick, and I awoke in a frenzy. But Khayman gestured for me to be quiet. He was in a terrible state. He wore only a simple bed gown and no sandals, and his hair was mussed. It seemed he'd been weeping. His eyes were red.

"He sat down beside me. 'Tell me, is this true, what you said of the spirits?' I didn't bother to tell him it was Mekare who said it. People always confused us or thought of us as one being. I merely told him, yes, it was true.

"I explained that there have always been these invisible entities; that they themselves had told us there were no gods or goddesses of which they knew. They had bragged to us often of the tricks they played at Sumer or Jericho or in Nineveh at the great temples. Now and then they would come booming that they *were* this or that god. But we knew their personalities, and when we called them by their old names, they gave up the new game at once.

"What I did not say was that I wished Mekare had never made known such things. What purpose could it serve now?

"He sat there defeated, listening to me, listening as if he had been a man lied to all his life and now he saw truth. For he had been deeply moved when he had seen the spirits strike up the wind on our mountain and he had seen a shower of leaves fall upon the soldiers; it had chilled his soul. And that is always what produces faith, that mixture of truth and a physical manifestation.

"But then I perceived there was an even greater burden upon his conscience, or on his reason, one might say. 'And the massacre of your people, this was a holy war; it was not a selfish thing, as you said.'

" 'Oh, no,' I told him. 'It was a selfish and simple thing, I can't say otherwise.' I told him of the tablet sent to us by the messenger, of what the spirits had said, of my mother's fear and her illness, and of my own power to hear the truth in the Queen's words, the truth which she herself might not be able to accept.

"But long before I'd finished, he was defeated again. He knew, from his own observations, that what I was saying was true. He had fought at the King's side through many a campaign against foreign peoples. That an army should fight for gain was nothing to him. He had seen massacres and cities burned; he had seen slaves taken; he had seen men return laden with booty. And though he himself was no soldier, these things he understood.

"But there had been no booty worth taking in our villages; there had been no territory which the King would retain. Yes, it had been fought for our capture, he knew it. And he too felt the distaste for the lie of a holy war against flesh eaters. And he felt a sadness that was even greater than his defeat. He was of an old family; he had eaten the flesh of his ancestors; and he found himself now punishing such traditions among those whom he had known and loved. He thought of the mummification of the dead with repugnance, but more truly he felt repugnance for the ceremony which accompanied it, for the depth of superstition in which the land had been steeped. So much wealth heaped upon the dead; so much attention to those putrefying bodies simply so men and women would not feel guilty for abandoning the older customs.

"Such thoughts exhausted him; they weren't natural to him; what obsessed him finally were the deaths he had seen; executions; massacres. Just as the Queen could not grasp such things, he could not forget them and he was a man losing his stamina; a man drawn into a mire in which he might drown.

"Finally he took his leave of me. But before he went he promised that he would do his best to see that we were released. He did not know how he could do it, but he would try to do it. And he begged me not to be afraid. I felt a great love for him at that moment. He had then the same beautiful face and form which he has now; only then he was dark-skinned and leaner and the curls had been ironed from his hair and it had been plaited and hung long to his shoulders, and he had the air of the court about him, the air of one who commands, and one who stands in the warm love of his prince.

"The following morning the Queen sent for us again. And this time we were brought privately to her chamber, where only the King was with her, and Khayman.

"It was a more lavish place even than the great hall of the palace; it was stuffed to overflowing with fine things, with a couch made of carved leopards, and a bed hung with sheer silk; and with polished mirrors of seemingly magical perfection. And the Queen herself, like a temptress she was, bedecked with finery and perfume, and fashioned by nature into a thing as lovely as any treasure around her.

"Once again she put her questions.

"Standing together, our hands bound, we had to listen to the same nonsense.

"And once again Mekare told the Queen of the spirits; she explained that the spirits have always existed; she told how they bragged of playing with the priests of other lands. She told how the spirits had said the songs and chants of the Egyptians pleased them. It was all a game to the spirits, and no more.

" 'But these spirits! They are the gods, then, that is what you are saying!' Akasha said with great fervor. 'And you speak to them? I want to see you do it! Do it for me now.'

" 'But they are not gods,' I said. 'That is what we are trying to tell you. And they do not abhor the eaters of the flesh as you say your gods do. They don't care about such things. They never have.' Painstakingly I strove to convey the difference; these spirits had no code; they were morally inferior to us. Yet I knew this woman couldn't grasp what I was telling her.

"I perceived the war inside her, between the handmaiden of the goddess Inanna who wanted to believe herself blessed, and the dark brooding soul who believed finally in nothing. A chill place was her soul; her religious fervor was nothing but a blaze which she fed constantly, seeking to warm that chill place.

" 'Everything you say is a lie!' she said finally. 'You are evil women!' She ordered our execution. We should be burnt alive the next day and together, so that we might see each other suffer and die. Why had she ever bothered with us?

"At once the King interrupted her. He told her that he had seen the power of the spirits; so had Khayman. What might not the spirits do if we were so treated? Wouldn't it be better to let us go?

"But there was something ugly and hard in the Queen's gaze. The King's words meant nothing; our lives were being taken from us. What could we do? And it seemed she was angry with us because we had not been able to frame our truths in ways which she could use or take pleasure in. Ah, it was an agony to deal with her. Yet her mind is a common mind; there are countless human beings who think and feel as she did then; and does now, in all likelihood.

"Finally Mekare seized the moment. She did the thing which I did not dare to do. She called the spirits—all of them by name, but so quickly this Queen would never remember the words. She screamed for them to come to her and do her bidding; and she told them to show their displeasure at what was happening to those mortals—Maharet and Mekare—whom they claimed to love.

"It was a gamble. But if nothing happened, if they had deserted us as I feared, well, then she could call on Amel, for he was there, lurking, waiting. And it was the only chance we had finally.

"Within an instant the wind had begun. It howled through the courtyard and whistled through the corridors of the palace. The draperies were torn by it; doors slammed; fragile vessels were smashed. The Queen was in a state of terror as she felt it surround her. Then small objects began to fly through the air. The spirits gathered up the ornaments of her dressing table and hurled them at her; the King stood beside her, striving to protect her, and Khayman was rigid with fear.

"Now, this was the very limit of the spirits' power; and they would not be able to keep it up for very long. But before the demonstration stopped, Khayman begged the King and Queen to revoke the sentence of execution. And on the spot they did.

"At once Mekare, sensing that the spirits were spent anyway, ordered them with great pomp to stop. Silence fell. And the terrified slaves ran here and there to gather up what had been thrown about.

"The Queen was overcome. The King tried to tell her that he had seen this spectacle before and it had not harmed him; but something deep had been violated within the Queen's heart. She'd never witnessed the slightest proof of the supernatural; and she was struck dumb and still now. In that dark faithless place within her, there had been a spark of light; true light. And so old and certain was her secret skepticism, that this small miracle had been for her a revelation of great magnitude; it was as if she had seen the face of her gods.

"She sent the King and Khayman away from her. She said she would speak with us alone. And then she implored us to talk to the spirits so that she could hear it. There were tears in her eyes.

"It was an extraordinary moment, for I sensed now what I'd sensed months ago when I'd touched the clay tablet—a mixture of good and evil that seemed more dangerous than evil itself.

"Of course we couldn't make the spirits speak so that she could understand it, we told her. But perhaps she would give us some questions that they might answer. At once she did.

"These were no more than the questions which people have been putting to wizards and witches and saints ever since. 'Where is the necklace I lost as a child? What did my mother want to tell me the night she died when she could no longer speak? Why does my sister detest my company? Will my son grow to manhood? Will he be brave and strong?'

"Struggling for our lives, we put these questions patiently to the spirits, cajoling them and flattering them to make them pay attention. And we got answers which veritably astonished Akasha. The spirits knew the name of her sister; they knew the name of her son. She seemed on the edge of madness as she considered these simple tricks.

"Then Amel, the evil one, appeared—obviously jealous of all these goings-on—and suddenly flung down before Akasha the lost necklace of which she'd been speaking—a necklace lost in Uruk; and this was the final blow. Akasha was thunderstruck.

"She wept now, holding on to this necklace. And then she begged us to put to the spirits the really important questions whose answers she must know.

"Yes, the gods were made up by her people, the spirits said. No, the names in the prayers didn't matter. The spirits merely liked the music and rhythm of the language—the shape of the words, so to speak. Yes, there were bad spirits who liked to hurt people, and why not? And there were good spirits who loved them, too. And would they speak to Akasha if we were to leave the kingdom? Never. They were speaking now, and she couldn't hear them, what did she expect them to do? But yes, there were witches in the kingdom who could hear them, and they would tell those witches to come to the court at once if that was what she wanted.

"But as this communication progressed, a terrible change came over Akasha.

"She went from jubilance to suspicion and then misery. Because these spirits were only telling her the same dismal things that we had already told her.

" 'What do you know of the life after?' she asked. And when the spirits said only that the souls of the dead either hovered about the earth, confused and suffering, or rose and vanished from it completely, she was brutally disappointed. Her eyes dulled; she was losing all appetite for this. When she asked what of those who had lived bad lives, as opposed to those who had lived good lives, the spirits could give no answer. They didn't know what she meant.

"Yet it continued, this interrogation. And we could sense that the spirits were tiring of it, and playing with her now, and that the answers would become more and more idiotic.

" 'What is the will of the gods?' she asked. 'That you sing all the time,' said the spirits. 'We like it.'

"Then all of a sudden, Amel, the evil one, so proud of the trick with the necklace, flung another great string of jewels before Akasha. But from this she shrank back in horror.

"At once we saw the error. It had been her mother's necklace, and lay on her mother's body in the tomb near Uruk, and of course Amel, being only a spirit, couldn't guess how bizarre and distasteful it could be to bring this thing here. Even now he did not catch on. He had seen this necklace in Akasha's mind when she had spoken of the other one. Why didn't she want it too? Didn't she like necklaces?

"Mekare told Amel this had not pleased. It was the wrong miracle. Would he please wait for her command, as she understood this Queen and he didn't.

"But it was too late. Something had happened to the Queen which was irrevocable. She had seen two pieces of evidence as to the power of the spirits, and she had heard truth and nonsense, neither of which could compare to the beauty of the mythology of her gods which she had always forced herself to believe in. Yet the spirits were destroying her fragile faith. How would she ever escape the dark skepticism in her own soul if these demonstrations continued?

"She bent down and picked up the necklace from her mother's tomb. 'How was this got!' she demanded. But her heart wasn't really in the question. She knew the answer would be more of what she'd been hearing since we had arrived. She was frightened.

"Nevertheless I explained; and she listened to every word.

"The spirits read our minds; and they are enormous and powerful. Their true size is difficult for us to imagine; and they can move with the swiftness of thought; when Akasha thought of this second necklace, the spirit saw it; he went to look for it; after all, one necklace had pleased her, so why not another? And so he had found it in her mother's tomb; and brought it out by means perhaps of some small opening. For surely it could not pass through stone. That was ridiculous.

"But as I said this last part I realized the truth. This necklace had probably been stolen from the body of Akasha's mother, and very possibly by Akasha's father. It had never been buried in any tomb. That is why Amel could find it. Maybe even a priest had stolen it. Or so it very likely seemed to Akasha, who was holding the necklace in her hand. She loathed this spirit that he made known such an awful thing to her.

"In sum, all the illusions of this woman lay now in complete ruin; yet she was left with the sterile truth she had always known. She had asked her questions of the supernatural—a very unwise thing to do—and the supernatural had given her answers which she could not accept; yet she could not refute them either.

" 'Where are the souls of the dead?' she whispered, staring at this necklace.

"As softly as I could I said, 'The spirits simply do not know.'

"Horror. Fear. And then her mind began to work, to do what it had always done—find some grand system to explain away what caused pain; some grand way to accommodate what she saw before her. The dark secret place inside her was becoming larger; it was threatening to consume her from within; she could not let such a thing happen; she had to go on. She was the Queen of Kemet.

"On the other hand, she was angry, and the rage she felt was against her parents and against her teachers, and against the priests and priestesses of her childhood, and against the gods she had worshiped and against anyone who had ever comforted her, or told her that life was good.

"A moment of silence had fallen; something was happening in her expression; fear and wonder had gone; there was something cold and disenchanted and, finally, malicious in her gaze.

"And then with her mother's necklace in hand she rose and declared that all we had said were lies. These were demons to whom we were speaking, demons who sought to subvert her and her gods, who looked with favor upon her people. The more she spoke the more she believed what she was saying; the more the elegance of her beliefs seized her; the more she surrendered to their logic. Until finally she was weeping and denouncing us, and the darkness within had been denied. She evoked the images of her gods; she evoked her holy language.

"But then she looked again at the necklace; and the evil spirit, Amel, in a great rage—furious that she was not pleased with his little gift and was once again angry with us—told us to tell her that if she did us any harm he would hurl at her every object, jewel, wine cup, looking glass, comb, or other such item that she ever so much as asked for, or imagined, or remembered, or wished for, or missed.

"I could have laughed had we not been in such danger; it was such a wonderful solution in the mind of the spirit; and so perfectly ridiculous from a human point of view. Yet it certainly wasn't something that one would want to happen.

"And Mekare told Akasha exactly what Amel had said.

" 'He that can produce this necklace can inundate you in such reminders of suffering,' Mekare said. 'And I do not know that any witch on earth can stop him, should he so begin.'

" 'Where is he?' Akasha screamed. 'Let me see this demon thing you speak to!'

"And at this, Amel, in vanity and rage, concentrated all his power and dove at Akasha, declaring 'I am Amel, the evil one, who pierces!' and he made the great gale around her that he had made around our mother; only it was ten times that. Never had I seen such fury. The room itself appeared to tremble as this immense spirit compressed himself and directed himself into this tiny place. I could hear the cracking of the brick walls. And all over the Queen's beautiful face and arms the tiny bitelike wounds appeared as so many red dots of blood.

"She screamed helplessly. Amel was in ecstasy. Amel could do wondrous things! Mekare and I were in terror.

"Mekare commanded him to stop. And now she heaped flattery upon him, and great thanks, and told him he was very simply the most powerful of all spirits, but he must obey her now, to demonstrate his great wit as well as his power; and that she would allow him to strike again at the right time.

"Meantime, the King rushed to the aid of Akasha; Khayman ran to her; all the guards ran to her. But when the guards raised their swords to strike us down, she ordered them to leave us alone. Mekare and I stood staring at her, silently threatening her with this spirit's power, for it was all that we had left. And Amel, the evil one, hovered above us, filling the air with the most eerie of all sounds, the great hollow laughter of a spirit, that seemed then to fill the entire world.

"Alone in our cell again, we could not think what to do or how to use what little advantage we now had in Amel.

"As for Amel himself, he would not leave us. He ranted and stormed in the little cell; he made the reed mats rustle, and made our garments move; he sent winds through our hair. It was a nuisance. But what frightened me was to hear the things of which he boasted. That he liked to draw blood; that it plumped him up inside and made him slow; but that it tasted good; and when the peoples of the world made blood sacrifice upon their altars he liked to come down and slurp up that blood. After all, it was there for him, was it not? More laughter.

"There was a great recoiling in the other spirits. Mekare and I both sensed this. Except for those who were faintly jealous and demanded to know what this blood tasted like, and why he liked such a thing so much.

"And then it came out—that hatred and jealousy of the flesh which is in so many evil spirits, that feeling that we are abominations, we humans, because we have both body and soul, which should not exist on this earth. Amel ranted of the times when there had been but mountains and oceans and forests and no living things such as us. He told us that to have spirit within mortal bodies was a curse.

"Now, I had heard these complaints among the evil ones before; but I had never thought much about them. For the first time I believed them, just a little, as I lay there and I saw my people put to the sword in my mind's eye. I thought as many a man or woman has thought before and since that maybe it was a curse to have the concept of immortality without the body to go with it.

"Or as you said, on this very night, Marius—life seemed not worth it; it seemed a joke. My world was darkness at that moment, darkness and suffering. All that I was no longer mattered; nothing I looked at could make me want to be alive.

"But Mekare began to speak to Amel again, informing him that she would much rather be what she was than what he was—drifting about forever with nothing important to do. And this sent Amel into a rage again. He would show her what he could do!

" 'When I command you, Amel!' she said. 'Count upon me to choose the moment. Then all men will know what you can do.' And this childish vain spirit was contented, and spread himself out again over the dark sky.

"For three nights and days we were kept prisoner. The guards would not look at us or come near us. Neither would the slaves. In fact, we would have starved had it not been for Khayman, the royal steward, who brought us food with his own hands.

"Then he told us what the spirits had already told us. A great controversy raged; the priests wanted us put to death. But the Queen was afraid to kill us, that we'd loose these spirits on her, and there would be no way she could drive them off. The King was intrigued by what had happened; he believed that more could be learned from us; he was curious about the power of the spirits, and to what uses it could be put. But the Queen feared it; the Queen had seen enough.

"Finally we were brought before the entire court in the great open atrium of the palace.

"It was high noon in the kingdom and the King and Queen made their offerings to the sun god Ra as was the custom, and this we were made to watch. It meant nothing to us to see this solemnity; we were afraid these were the last hours of our lives. I dreamed then of our mountain, our caves; I dreamed of the children we might have borne—fine sons and daughters, and some of them who would have inherited our power—I dreamed of the life that had been taken from us, of the annihilation of our kith and kindred which might soon be complete. I thanked whatever powers that be that I could see blue sky above my head, and that Mekare and I were still together.

"At last the King spoke. There was a terrible sadness and weariness in him. Young as he was, he had something of an old man's soul in these moments. Ours was a great gift, he told us, but we had misused it, clearly, and could be no use to anyone else. For lies, for the worship of demons, for black magic, he denounced us. He would have us burned, he said, to please the people; but he and his Queen felt sorry for us. The Queen in particular wanted him to have mercy on us.

"It was a damnable lie, but one look at her face told us she'd convinced herself that it was true. And of course the King believed it. But what did this matter? What was this mercy, we wondered, trying to look deeper into their souls.

"And now the Queen told us in tender words that our great magic had brought her the two necklaces she most wanted in all the world and for this and this alone she would let us live. In sum, the lie she spun grew larger and more intricate, and more distant from the truth.

"And then the King said he would release us, but first he would demonstrate to all the court that we had no power, and therefore the priests would be appeased.

"And if at any moment an evil demon should manifest himself and seek to abuse the just worshipers of Ra or Osiris, then our pardon should be revoked and we should be put to death at once. For surely the power of our demons would die with us. And we would have forfeited the Queen's mercy which we scarce deserved as it was.

"Of course we realized what was to happen; we saw it now in the hearts of the King and the Queen. A compromise had been struck. And we had been offered a bargain. As the King removed his gold chain and medallion and put it around the neck of Khayman, we knew that we were to be raped before the court, raped as common female prisoners or slaves would have been raped in any war. And if we called the spirits we'd die. That was our position.

" 'But for the love of my Queen,' said Enkil, 'I would take my pleasure of these two women, which is my right; I would do it before you all to show that they have no power and are not great witches, but are merely women, and my chief steward, Khayman, my beloved Khayman, will be given the privilege of doing it in my stead.'

"All the court waited in silence as Khayman looked at us, and prepared to obey the King's command. We stared at him, daring him in our helplessness not to do it—not to lay hands upon us or to violate us, before these uncaring eyes.

"We could feel the pain in him and the tumult. We could feel the danger that surrounded him, for were he to disobey he would surely have died. Yet this was our honor he meant to take; he meant to desecrate us; ruin us as it were; and we who had lived always in the sunshine and peace on our mountain knew nothing really of the act which he meant to perform.

"I think, as he came towards us, I believed he could not do it, that a man could not feel the pain which he felt and still sharpen his passion for this ugly work. But I knew little of men then, of how the pleasures of the flesh can combine in them with hatred and anger; of how they can hurt as they perform the act which women perform, more often than not, for love.

"Our spirits clamored against what was to happen; but for our very lives, we told them to be quiet. Silently I pressed Mekare's hand; I gave her to know that we would live when this was over; we would be free; this was not death after all; and we would leave these miserable desert people to their lies and their illusions; to their idiot customs; we would go home.

"And then Khayman set about to do what he had to do. Khayman untied our bonds; he took Mekare to himself first, forcing her down on her back against the matted floor, and lifting her gown, as I stood transfixed and unable to stop him, and then I was subjected to the same fate.

"But in his mind, we were not the women whom Khayman raped. As his soul trembled, as his body trembled, he stoked the fire of his passion with fantasies of nameless beauties and half remembered moments so that body and soul could be one.

"And we, our eyes averted, closed our souls to him and to these vile Egyptians who had done to us these terrible things; our souls were alone and untouched within our bodies; and all around us, I heard without doubt the weeping of the spirits, the sad, terrible weeping, and in the distance, the low rolling thunder of Amel.

"*You are fools to bear this, witches.*

"It was nightfall when we were left at the edge of the desert. The soldiers gave us what food and drink was allowed. It was nightfall as we started our long journey north. Our rage then was as great as it had ever been.

"And Amel came, taunting us and raging at us; why did we not want him to exact vengeance?

" 'They will come after us and kill us!' Mekare said. 'Now go away from us.' But that did not do the trick. So finally she tried to put Amel to work on something important. 'Amel, we want to reach our home alive. Make cool winds for us; and show us where we can find water.'

"But these are things which evil spirits never do. Amel lost interest. And Amel faded away, and we walked on through the cold desert wind, arm in arm, trying not to think of the miles that lay before us.

"Many things befell us on our long journey which are too numerous here to tell.

"But the good spirits had not deserted us; they made the cooling winds, and they led us to springs where we could find water and a few dates to eat; and they made 'little rain' for us as long as they could; but finally we were too deep in the desert for such a thing, and we were dying, and I knew I had a child from Khayman in my womb, and I wanted my child to live.

"It was then that the spirits led us to the Bedouin peoples, and they took us in, they cared for us.

"I was sick, and for days I lay singing to my child inside my body, and driving away my sickness and my moments of worst remembering with my songs. Mekare lay beside me, holding me in her arms.

"Months passed before I was strong enough to leave the Bedouin camps, and then I wanted my child to be born in our land and I begged Mekare that we should continue our journey.

"At last, with the food and drink the Bedouins had given us, and the spirits to guide us, we came into the green fields of Palestine, and found the foot of the mountain and the shepherd peoples—so like our own tribe—who had come down to claim our old grazing places.

"They knew us as they had known our mother and all our kindred and they called us by name, and immediately took us in.

"And we were so happy again, among the green grasses and the trees and the flowers that we knew, and my child was growing bigger inside my womb. It would live; the desert had not killed it.

"So, in my own land I gave birth to my daughter and named her Miriam as my mother had been named before me. She had Khayman's black hair but the green eyes of her mother. And the love I felt for her and the joy I knew in her were the greatest curative my soul could desire. We were three again. Mekare, who knew the birth pain with me, and who lifted the child out of my body, carried Miriam in her arms by the hour and sang to her just as I did. The child was ours, as much as it was mine. And we tried to forget the horrors we had seen in Egypt.

"Miriam thrived. And finally Mekare and I vowed to climb the mountain and find the caves in which we'd been born. We did not know yet how we would live or what we would do, so many miles from our new people. But with Miriam, we would go back to the place where we had been so happy; and we would call the spirits to us, and we would make the miracle of rain to bless my newborn child.

"But this was never to be. Not any of it.

"For before we could leave the shepherd people, soldiers came again, under the command of the King's high steward, Khayman, soldiers who had passed out gold along the way to any tribe who had seen or heard of the red-haired twins and knew where they might be.

"Once again at midday as the sun poured down on the grassy fields, we saw the Egyptian soldiers with their swords raised. In all directions the people scattered, but Mekare ran out and dropped down on her knees before Khayman and said, 'Don't harm our people again.'

"Then Khayman came with Mekare to the place where I was hiding with my daughter, and I showed him this child, which was his child, and begged him for mercy, for justice, that he leave us in peace.

"But I had only to look at him to understand that he would be put to death if he did not bring us back. His face was thin and drawn and full of misery, not the smooth white immortal face that you see here at this table tonight.

"Enemy time has washed away the natural imprint of his suffering. But it was very plain on that long ago afternoon.

"In a soft, subdued voice he spoke to us. 'A terrible evil has come over the King and the Queen of Kemet,' he said. 'And your spirits have done it, your spirits that tormented me night and day for what I did to you, until the King sought to drive them out of my house.'

"He stretched out his arms to me that I could see the tiny scars that covered him where this spirit had drawn blood. Scars covered his face and his throat.

" 'Oh, you don't know the misery in which I have lived,' he said, 'for nothing could protect me from these spirits; and you don't know the times I cursed you, and cursed the King for what he made me do to you, and cursed my mother that I'd been born.'

" 'Oh, but we have not done this!' Mekare said. 'We have kept faith with you. For our lives we left you in peace. But it is Amel, the evil one, who has done this! Oh, this evil spirit! And to think he has deviled you instead of the King and Queen who made you do what you did! We cannot stop him! I beg you, Khayman, let us go.'

" 'Whatever Amel does,' I said, 'he will tire of, Khayman. If the King and Queen are strong, he will eventually go away. You are looking now upon the mother of your child, Khayman. Leave us in peace. For the child's sake, tell the King and Queen that you could not find us. Let us go if you fear justice at all.'

"But he only stared at the child as if he did not know what it was. He was Egyptian. Was this child Egyptian? He looked at us: 'All right, you did not send this spirit,' he said. 'I believe you. For you do not understand what this spirit has done, obviously. His bedeviling has come to an end. He has gone *into* the King and Queen of Kemet! He is in their bodies! He has changed the very substance of their flesh!'

"For a long time, we looked at him and considered his words, and we understood that he did not mean by this that the King and the Queen were possessed. And we understood also that he himself had seen such things that he could not but come for us himself and try on his life to bring us back.

"But I didn't believe what he was saying. How could a spirit be made flesh!

" 'You do not understand what has happened in our kingdom,' he whispered. 'You must come and see with your own eyes.' He stopped then because there was more, much more, that he wanted to tell us, and he was afraid. Bitterly he said, 'You must undo what has been done, even if it is not your doing!'

"Ah, but we could not undo it. That was the horror. And even then we knew it; we sensed it. We remembered our mother standing before the cave gazing at the tiny wounds on her hand.

"Mekare threw back her head now and called to Amel, the evil one, to come to her, to obey her command. In our own tongue, the twin tongue, she screamed, 'Come out of the King and Queen of Kemet and come to me, Amel. Bow down before my will. You did this not by my command.'

"It seemed all the spirits of the world listened in silence; this was the cry of a powerful witch; but there was no answer; and then we felt it—a great recoiling of many spirits as if something beyond their knowledge and beyond their acceptance had suddenly been revealed. It seemed the spirits were shrinking from us; and then coming back, sad and undecided; seeking our love, yet repelled.

" 'But what is it?' Mekare screamed. 'What is it!' She called to the spirits who hovered near her, her chosen ones. And then in the stillness, as the shepherds waited in fear, and the soldiers stood in anticipation, and Khayman stared at us with tired glazed eyes, we heard the answer. It came in wonder and uncertainty.

" 'Amel has now what he has always wanted; *Amel has the flesh. But Amel is no more.*'

"What could it mean?

"We could not fathom it. Again, Mekare demanded of the spirits that they answer, but it seemed that the uncertainty of the spirits was now turning to fear.

" 'Tell me what has happened!' Mekare said. 'Make known to me what you know!' It was an old command used by countless witches. 'Give me the knowledge which is yours to give.'

"And again the spirits answered in uncertainty:

" 'Amel is in the flesh; and Amel is not Amel; he cannot answer now.'

" 'You must come with me,' Khayman said. 'You must come. The King and Queen would have you come!'

"Mutely, and seemingly without feeling, he watched as I kissed my baby girl and gave her to the shepherd women who would care for her as their own. And then Mekare and I gave ourselves up to him; but this time we did not weep. It was as if all our tears had been shed. Our brief year of happiness with the birth of Miriam was past now—and the horror that had come out of Egypt was reaching out to engulf us once more.

Maharet closed her eyes for a moment; she touched the lids with her fingers, and then looked up at the others, as they waited, each in his or her own thoughts and considerations, each reluctant for the narrative to be broken, though they all knew that it must.

The young ones were drawn and weary; Daniel's rapt expression had changed little. Louis was gaunt, and the need for blood was hurting him, though he paid it no mind. "I can tell you no more now," Maharet said. "It's almost morning; and the young ones must go down to the earth. I have to prepare the way for them.

"Tomorrow night we will gather here and continue. That is, if our Queen will allow. The Queen is nowhere near us now; I cannot hear the faintest murmur of her presence; I cannot catch the faintest flash of her countenance in another's eyes. If she knows what we do, she allows it. Or she is far away and indifferent, and we must wait to know her will.

"Tomorrow, I'll tell you what we saw when we went into Kemet."

"Until then, rest safe within the mountain. All of you. It has kept my secrets from the prying eyes of mortal men for countless years. Remember not even the Queen can hurt us until nightfall."

Marius rose as Maharet did. He moved to the far window as the others slowly left the room. It was as if Maharet's voice were still speaking to him. And what affected him most deeply was the evocation of Akasha, and the hatred Maharet felt for her; because Marius felt that hatred too; and he felt more strongly than ever that he should have brought this nightmare to a close while he'd had the power to do it.

But the red-haired woman could not have wanted any such thing to happen. None of them wanted to die any more than he did. And Maharet craved life, perhaps, more fiercely than any immortal he'd ever known.

Yet her tale seemed to confirm the hopelessness of it all. What had risen when the Queen stood up from her throne? What was this being that had Lestat in its maw? He could not imagine.

We change, but we do not change, he thought. We grow wise, but we are fallible things! We are only human for however long we endure, that was the miracle and the curse of it.

He saw again the smiling face he had seen as the ice began to fall. Is it possible that he loved as strongly still as he hated? That in his great humiliation, clarity had escaped him utterly? He honestly didn't know.

And he was tired suddenly, craving sleep, craving comfort; craving the soft sensuous pleasure of lying in a clean bed. Of sprawling upon it and burying his face in a pillow; of letting his limbs assemble themselves in the most natural and comfortable position.

Beyond the glass wall, a soft radiant blue light was filling the eastern sky, yet the stars retained their brilliance, tiny and distant though they seemed. The dark trunks of the redwoods had become visible; and a lovely green smell had come into the house from the forest as always happens near dawn.

Far below where the hillside fell away and a clearing full of clover moved out to the woods, Marius saw Khayman walking alone. His hands appeared to glow in the thin, bluish darkness, and as he turned and looked back—up at Marius—his face was an eyeless mask of pure white.

Marius found himself raising his hand in a small gesture of friendship towards Khayman. And Khayman returned the gesture and went on into the trees.

Then Marius turned and saw what he already knew, that only Louis remained with him in the room. Louis stood quite still looking at him as he had earlier, as though he were seeing a myth made real.

Then he put the question that was obsessing him, the question he could not lose sight of, no matter how great was Maharet's spell. "You know whether or not Lestat's still alive, don't you?" he asked. It had a simple human tone to it, a poignant tone, yet the voice was so reserved.

Marius nodded. "He's alive. But I don't really know that the way you think I do. Not from asking or receiving the answer. Not from using all these lovely powers which plague us. I know it simply because I know."

He smiled at Louis. Something in the manner of this one made Marius happy, though he wasn't sure why. He beckoned for Louis to come to him and they met at the foot of the table and walked together out of the room. Marius put his arm around Louis's shoulder and they went down the iron stairs together, through the damp earth, Marius walking slowly and heavily, exactly like a human being might walk.

"And you're sure of it?" Louis asked respectfully.

Marius stopped. "Oh, yes, quite sure." They looked at one another for a moment, and again Marius smiled. This one was so gifted yet not gifted at the same time; he wondered if the human light would go out of Louis's eyes if he ever gained more power, if he ever had, for instance, a little of the blood of Marius in his veins.

And this young one was hungry too; he was suffering; and he seemed to like it, to like the hunger and the pain.

"Let me tell you something," Marius said now, agreeably. "I knew the first moment I ever laid eyes on Lestat that nothing could kill him. That's the way it is with some of us. We can't die." But why was he saying this? Did he believe it again as he had before these trials had begun? He thought back to that night in San Francisco when he had walked down the broad clean-swept pavements of Market Street with his hands in his pockets, unnoticed by mortal men.

"Forgive me," Louis said, "but you remind me of the things they said of him at Dracula's Daughter, the talk among the ones who wanted to join him last night."

"I know," Marius said. "But they are fools and I'm right." He laughed softly. Yes, he did believe it. Then he embraced Louis again warmly. Just a little blood, and Louis might be stronger, true, but then he might lose the human tenderness, the human wisdom that no one could give another; the gift of knowing others' suffering with which Louis had probably been born.

But the night was over now for this one. Louis took Marius's hand, and then turned and walked down the tin-walled corridor to where Eric waited to show him the way.

Then Marius went up into the house.

He had perhaps a full hour more before the sun forced him into sleep, and tired as he was, he would not give it up. The lovely fresh smell of the woods was overpowering. And he could hear the birds now, and the clear singing of a deep creek.

He went into the great room of the adobe dwelling, where the fire had burnt down on the central hearth. He found himself standing before a giant quilt that covered almost half the wall.

Slowly he realized what he was seeing before him—the mountain, the valley, and the tiny figures of the twins as they stood together in the green clearing beneath the burning sun. The slow rhythm of Maharet's speech came back to him with the faint shimmer of all the images her words had conveyed. So immediate was that sun-drenched clearing, and how different it seemed now from the dreams. Never had the dreams made him feel close to these women! And now he knew them; he knew this house.

It was such a mystery, this mixture of feeling, where sorrow touched something that was undeniably positive and good. Maharet's soul attracted him; he loved the particular complexity of it, and he wished he could somehow tell her so.

Then it was as if he caught himself; he realized that he had forgotten for a little while to be bitter, to be in pain. Maybe his soul was healing faster than he had ever supposed it could.

Or maybe it was only that he had been thinking about others—about Maharet, and before that about Louis, and what Louis needed to believe. Well, hell, Lestat probably was immortal. In fact, the sharp and bitter fact occurred to him that Lestat might survive all this even if he, Marius, did not.

But that was a little supposition that he could do without. Where was Armand? Had Armand gone down into the earth already? If only he could see Armand just now. . . .

He went towards the cellar door again but something distracted him. Through an open doorway he saw two figures, very like the figures of the twins on the quilt. But these were Maharet and Jesse, arm in arm before an eastern window, watching motionless as the light grew brighter in the dark woods.

A violent shudder startled him. He had to grip the door frame to steady himself as a series of images flooded his mind. Not the jungle now; there was a highway in the distance, winding north, it seemed, through barren burnt land. And the creature had stopped, shaken, but by what? An image of two red-haired women? He heard the feet begin their relentless tramp again; he saw the feet caked with earth as if they were his feet; the hands caked with earth as if they were his hands. And then he saw the sky catching fire, and he moaned aloud.

When he looked up again, Armand was holding him. And with her bleary human eyes Maharet was imploring him to tell her what he had just seen. Slowly the room came alive around him, the agreeable furnishings, and then the immortal figures near him, who were of it, yet of nothing. He closed his eyes and opened them again.

"She's reached our longitude," he said, "yet she's miles to the east. The sun's just risen there with blazing force." He had felt it, that lethal heat! But she had gone into the earth; that too he had felt.

"But it's very far south of here," Jesse said to him. How frail she looked in the translucent darkness, her long thin fingers hugging the backs of her slender arms.

"Not so far," Armand said. "And she was moving very fast."

"But in what direction does she move!" Maharet asked. "Is she coming towards us?"

She didn't wait for an answer. And it didn't seem that they could give it. She lifted her hand to cover her eyes as if the pain there was now intolerable; and then gathering Jesse to her, and kissing her suddenly, she bid the others good sleep.

Marius closed his eyes; he tried to see again the figure he had seen before. The garment, what was it? A rough thing thrown over the body like a peasant poncho, with a torn opening for the head. Bound at the waist, yes, he'd felt it. He tried to see more but he could not. What he had felt was power, illimitable power and unstoppable momentum, and almost nothing other than that.

When he opened his eyes again the morning shimmered in the room around him. Armand stood close to him, embracing him still, yet Armand seemed alone and perturbed by nothing; his eyes moved only a little as he looked at the forest, which now seemed to press against the house through every window, as if it had crept to the very edge of the porch.

Marius kissed Armand's forehead. And then he did exactly what Armand was doing.

He watched the room grow lighter; he watched the light fill the windowpanes; he watched the beautiful colors brighten in the vast network of the giant quilt.

5

LESTAT: THIS IS MY BODY; THIS IS MY BLOOD

WHEN I awoke it was quiet, and the air was clean and warm, with the smell of the sea.

I was now thoroughly confused as to time. And I knew from my light-headedness that I had not slept through a day. Also I wasn't in any protective enclosure.

We'd been following the night around the world, perhaps, or rather moving at random in it, as Akasha maybe didn't need at all to sleep.

I needed it, that was obvious. But I was too curious not to want to be awake. And frankly too miserable. Also I'd been dreaming of human blood.

I found myself in a spacious bedroom with terraces to the west and to the north. I could smell the sea and I could hear it, yet the air was fragrant and rather still. Very gradually, I took stock of the room.

Lavish old furnishings, most likely Italian—delicate yet ornamented—were mingled with modern luxuries everywhere I looked. The bed on which I lay was a gilded four-poster, hung with gauzy curtains, and covered with down pillows and draperies of silk. A thick white carpet concealed the old floor.

There was a dressing table littered with glittering jars and silver objects, and a curious old-fashioned white telephone. Velvet chairs; a monster of a television set and shelves of stereo music equipment; and small polished tables everywhere, strewn with newspapers, ashtrays, decanters of wine.

People had lived here up till an hour ago; but now the people were dead. In fact, there were many dead on this island. And as I lay there for a moment, drinking in the beauty around me, I saw the village in my mind where we had been before. I saw the filth, the tin roofs, the mud. And now I lay in this bower, or so it seemed.

And there was death here too. We had brought it.

I got up off the bed and went out onto the terrace and looked down over the stone railing at a white beach. No land on the horizon, only the gently rolling sea. The lacy foam of the receding waves glistening under the moon. And I was in an old weathered palazzo, probably built some four centuries ago, decked with urns and cherubs and covered with stained plaster, a rather beautiful place. Electric lights shone through the green-painted shutters of other rooms. Nestled on a lower terrace just beneath me was a little swimming pool.

And ahead where the beach curved to the left, I saw another old graceful dwelling nestled into the cliffs. People had died in there too. This was a Greek island, I was sure of it; this was the Mediterranean Sea.

When I listened, I heard cries coming from the land behind me, over the crest of the hill. Men being slain. I leaned against the frame of the door. I tried to stop my heart from racing.

Some sudden memory of the slaughter in Azim's temple gripped me—a flash of myself walking through the human herd, using the invisible blade to pierce solid flesh. Thirst. Or was it merely lust? I saw those mangled limbs again; wasted bodies contorted in the final struggle, faces smeared with blood.

Not my doing, I couldn't have . . . But I had.

And now I could smell fires burning, fires like those fires in Azim's courtyard where the bodies were being burnt. The smell nauseated me. I turned towards the sea again and took a deep clean breath. If I let them, the voices would come, voices from all over the island, and from other islands, and from the nearby land, too. I could feel it, the sound, hovering there waiting; I had to push it back.

Then I heard more immediate noise. Women in this old mansion. They were approaching the bedchamber. I turned around just in time to see the double doors opened, and the women, dressed in simple blouses and skirts and kerchiefs, come into the room.

It was a motley crowd of all ages, including young beauties and stout older matrons, and even some rather frail creatures with darkly wrinkled skin and snow white hair. They brought vases of flowers with them; they were placing them everywhere. And then one of the women, a tentative slender thing with a beautiful long neck, moved forward with beguiling natural grace, and began to turn on the many lamps.

Smell of their blood. How could it be so strong and so enticing, when I felt no thirst?

Suddenly they all came together in the center of the room and they stared at me; it was as if they'd fallen into a trance. I was standing on the terrace, merely looking at them; then I realized what they saw. My torn costume—the vampire rags—black coat, white shirt, and the cloak—all spattered with blood.

And my skin, that had changed measurably. I was whiter, more ghastly to look at, of course. And my eyes must have been brighter; or maybe I was being deceived by their naive reactions. When had they seen one of us before?

Whatever . . . it all seemed to be some sort of dream, these still women with their black eyes and their rather somber faces—even the stout ones had rather gaunt faces—gathered there staring at me, and then their dropping one by one to their knees. Ah, to their knees. I sighed. They had the crazed expression of people who had been delivered out of the ordinary; they were seeing a vision and the irony was that they looked like a vision to me.

Reluctantly, I read their thoughts.

They had seen the Blessed Mother. That is what she was here. The Madonna, the Virgin. She'd come to their villages and told them to slaughter their sons and husbands; even the babies had been slaughtered. And they had done it, or witnessed the doing of it; and they were now carried upon a wave of belief and joy. They were witnesses to miracles; they had been spoken to by the Blessed Mother herself. And she was the ancient Mother, the Mother who had always dwelt in the grottoes of this island, even before Christ, the Mother whose tiny naked statues were now and then found in the earth.

In her name they had knocked down the columns of the ruined temples, the ones the tourists came here to see; they had burned the only church on the island; they had knocked out its windows with sticks and stones. Ancient murals had burned in the church. The marble columns, broken into fragments, had fallen into the sea.

As for me, what was I to them? Not merely a god. Not merely the chosen of the Blessed Mother. No, something else. It puzzled me as I stood there, trapped by their eyes, repelled by their convictions, yet fascinated and afraid.

Not of them, of course, but of everything that was happening. Of this delicious feeling of mortals looking at me, the way they had been looking when I'd been on the stage. Mortals looking at me and sensing my power after all the years of hiding, mortals come here to worship. Mortals like all those poor creatures strewn over the path in the mountains. But they'd been worshipers of Azim, hadn't they? They'd gone there to die.

Nightmare. Have to reverse this, have to stop it; have to stop myself from accepting it or any aspect of it!

I mean I could start believing that I was really— But I know what I am, don't I? And these are poor, ignorant women; women for whom television sets and phones are miracles, these are women for whom change itself is a form of miracle. . . . And they will wake up tomorrow and they will see what they have done!

But now the feeling of peace came over us—the women and me. The familiar scent of flowers, the spell. Silently, through their minds, the women were receiving their instructions.

There was a little commotion; two of them rose from their knees and entered an adjoining bath—one of those massive marble affairs that wealthy Italians and Greeks seem to love. Hot water was flowing; steam poured out of the open doors.

Other women had gone to the closets, to take out clean garments. Rich, whoever he was, the poor bastard who had owned this little palace, the poor bastard who had left that cigarette in the ashtray and the faint greasy fingerprints on the white phone.

Another pair of women came towards me. They wanted to lead me into the bath. I did nothing. I felt them touch me—hot human fingers touching me and all the attendant shock and excitement in them as they felt the peculiar texture of my flesh. It sent a powerful and delicious chill through me, these touches. Their dark liquid eyes were beautiful as they looked at me. They tugged at me with their warm hands; they wanted me to come with them.

All right. I allowed myself to be taken along. White marble tile, carved gold fixtures; an ancient Roman splendor, when you got right down to it, with gleaming bottles of soaps and scents lining marble shelves. And the flood of hot water in the pool, with the jets pumping it full of bubbles, it was all very inviting; or might have been at some other time.

They stripped my garments off me. Absolutely fascinating feeling. No one had ever done such a thing to me. Not since I'd been alive and then only when I was a very small child. I stood in the flood of steam from the bath, watching all these small dark hands, and feeling the hairs rise all over my body; feeling the adoration in the women's eyes.

Through the steam I looked into the mirror—a wall of mirror actually, and I saw myself for the first time since this sinister odyssey had begun. The shock was more for a moment than I could handle. *This can't be me.*

I was much paler than I'd imagined. Gently I pushed the women away and went towards the mirror wall. My skin had a pearlescent gleam to it; and my eyes were even brighter, gathering all the colors of the spectrum and mingling them with an icy light. Yet I didn't look like Marius. I didn't look like Akasha. The lines in my face were still there!

In other words I'd been bleached by Akasha's blood, but I hadn't become smooth yet. I'd kept my human expression. And the odd thing was, the contrast now made these lines all the more visible. Even the tiny lines all over my fingers were more clearly etched than before.

But what consolation was this when I was more than ever noticeable, astonishing, unlike a human being? In a way, this was worse than that first moment two hundred years ago, when an hour or so after my death I'd seen myself in a mirror, and tried to find my humanity in what I was seeing. I was just as afraid right now.

I studied my reflection—my chest was like a marble torso in a museum, that white. And the organ, the organ we don't need, poised as if ready for what it would never again know how to do or want to do, marble, a Priapus at a gate.

Dazed, I watched the women draw closer; lovely throats, breasts, dark moist limbs. I watched them touch me all over again. I was beautiful to them, all right.

The scent of their blood was stronger in here, in the rising steam. Yet I wasn't thirsty, not really. Akasha had filled me, but the blood was tormenting me a little. No, quite a lot.

I *wanted* their blood—and it had nothing to do with thirst. I wanted it the way a man can want vintage wine, though he's drunk water. Only magnify that by twenty or thirty or a hundred. In fact, it was so powerful I could imagine taking all of them, tearing at their tender throats one after another and leaving their bodies lying here on the floor.

No, this is not going to take place, I reasoned. And the sharp, dangerous quality of this lust made me want to weep. *What's been done to me!* But then I knew, didn't I? I knew I was so strong now that twenty men couldn't have subdued me. And think what I could do to them. I could rise up through the ceiling if I wanted to and get free of here. I could do things of which I'd never dreamed. Probably I had the fire gift now; I could burn things the way she could burn them, the way Marius said that he could. Just a matter of strength, that's all it was. And dizzying levels of awareness, of acceptance. . . .

The women were kissing me. They were kissing my shoulders. Just a lovely little sensation, the soft pressure of the lips on my skin. I couldn't help smiling, and gently I embraced them and kissed them, nuzzling their heated little necks and feeling their breasts against my chest. I was utterly surrounded by these malleable creatures, I was blanketed in succulent human flesh.

I stepped into the deep tub and allowed them to wash me. The hot water splashed over me deliciously, washing away easily all the dirt that never really clings to us, never penetrates us. I looked up at the ceiling and let them brush the hot water through my hair.

Yes, extraordinarily pleasurable, all of it. Yet never had I been so alone. I was sinking into these mesmerizing sensations; I was drifting. Because really, there was nothing else that I could do.

When they were finished I chose the perfumes that I wanted and told them to get rid of the others. I spoke in French but they seemed to understand. Then they dressed me with the clothes I selected from what they presented to me. The master of this house had liked handmade linen shirts, which were only a little too large for me. And he'd liked handmade shoes as well, and they were a tolerable fit.

I chose a suit of gray silk, very fine weave, and rather jaunty modern cut. And silver jewelry. The man's silver watch, and his cuff links which had tiny diamonds embedded in them. And even a tiny diamond pin for the narrow lapel of the coat. But all these clothes felt so strange on me; it was as if I could feel the surface of my own skin yet not feel it. And there came that déjà vu. Two hundred years ago. The old mortal questions. Why in the hell is this happening? How can I gain control of it?

I wondered for a moment, was it possible not to care what happened? To stand back from it and view them all as alien creatures, things upon which I fed? Cruelly I'd been ripped out of their world! Where was the old bitterness, the old excuse for endless cruelty? Why had it always focused itself upon such small things? Not that a life is small. Oh, no, never, not any life! That was the whole point actually. Why did I who could kill with such abandon shrink from the prospect of seeing their precious traditions laid waste?

Why did my heart come up in my throat now? Why was I crying inside, like something dying myself?

Maybe some other fiend could have loved it; some twisted and conscienceless immortal could have sneered at her visions, yet slipped into the robes of a god as easily as I had slipped into that perfumed bath.

But nothing could give me that freedom, nothing. Her permissions meant nothing; her power finally was but another degree of what we all possessed. And what we all possessed had never made the struggle simple; it had made it agony, no matter how often we won or lost.

It couldn't happen, the subjugation of a century to one will; the design had to be foiled somehow, and if I just maintained my calm, I'd find the key.

Yet mortals had inflicted such horrors upon others; barbarian hordes had scarred whole continents, destroying everything in their path. Was she merely human in her delusions of conquest and domination? Didn't matter. She had inhuman means to see her dreams made real!

I would start weeping again if I didn't stop reaching now for the solution; and these poor tender creatures around me would be even more damaged and confused than before.

When I lifted my hands to my face, they didn't move away from me. They were brushing my hair. Chills ran down my back. And the soft thud of the blood in their veins was deafening suddenly.

I told them I wanted to be alone. I couldn't endure the temptation any longer. And I could have sworn they knew what I wanted. Knew it, and were yielding to it. Dark salty flesh so close to me. Too much temptation. Whatever the case, they obeyed instantly, and a little fearfully. They left the room in silence, backing away as if it weren't proper to simply walk out.

I looked at the face of the watch. I thought it was pretty funny, me wearing this watch that told the time. And it made me angry suddenly. And then the watch broke! The glass shattered; everything flew out of the ruptured silver case. The strap broke and the thing fell off my wrist onto the floor. Tiny glittering wheels disappeared into the carpet.

"Good God!" I whispered. Yet why not?—if I could rupture an artery or a heart. But the point was to control this thing, to direct it, not let it escape like that.

I looked up and chose at random a small mirror, one standing on the dresser in a silver frame. I thought *Break* and it exploded into gleaming fragments. In the hollow stillness I could hear the pieces as they struck the walls and the dresser top.

Well, that was useful, a hell of a lot more useful than being able to kill people. I stared at the telephone on the edge of the dresser. I concentrated, let the power collect, then consciously subdued it and directed it to push the phone slowly across the glass that covered the marble. Yes. All right. The little bottles tumbled and fell as it was pushed into them. Then I stopped them; I couldn't right them however. I couldn't pick them up. Oh, but wait, yes I could. I imagined a hand righting them. And certainly the power wasn't literally obeying this image; but I was using it to organize the power. I righted all the little bottles. I retrieved the one which had fallen and put it back in place.

I was trembling just a little. I sat on the bed to think this over, but I was too curious to think. The important thing to realize was this: it was physical; it was energy. And it was no more than an extension of powers I'd possessed before. For example, even in the beginning, in the first few weeks after Magnus had made me, I'd managed once to move another—my beloved Nicolas with whom I'd been arguing—across a room as if I'd struck him with an invisible fist. I'd been in a rage then; I hadn't been able to duplicate the little trick later. But it was the same power; the same verifiable and measurable trait.

"You are no god," I said. But this increase of power, this new dimension, as they say so aptly in this century. . . . Hmmmm. . . .

Looking up at the ceiling, I decided I wanted to rise slowly and touch it, run my hands over the plaster frieze that ran around the cord of the chandelier. I felt a queasiness; and then I realized I was floating just beneath the ceiling. And my hand, why, it looked like my hand was going through the plaster. I lowered myself a little and looked down at the room.

Dear God, I'd done this without taking my body with me! I was still sitting there, on the side of the bed. I was staring at myself, at the top of my own head. I—my body at any rate—sat there motionless, dreamlike, staring. *Back.* And I was there again, thank God, and my body was all right, and then looking up at the ceiling, I tried to figure what this was all about.

Well, I knew what it was all about, too. Akasha herself had told me how her spirit could travel out of her body. And mortals had always done such things, or so they claimed. Mortals had written of such invisible travel from the most ancient times.

I had almost done it when I tried to see into Azim's temple, *gone there to see,* and she had stopped me because when I left my body, my body had started to fall. And long before that, there had been a couple of other times. . . . But in general, I'd never believed all the mortal stories.

Now I knew I could do this as well. But I certainly didn't want to do it by accident. I made the decision to move to the ceiling again but this time with my body, and it was accomplished at once! We were there together, pushing against the plaster and this time my hand didn't go through. All right.

I went back down and decided to try the other again. Now *only in spirit.* The queasy feeling came, I took a glance down at my body, and then I was rising right through the roof of the palazzo. I was traveling out over the sea. Yet things looked unaccountably different; I wasn't sure this was the literal sky or the literal sea. It was more like a hazy conception of both, and I didn't like this, not one bit. No, thank you. Going home now! Or should I bring my body to me? I tried, but absolutely nothing happened, and that didn't surprise me actually. This was some kind of hallucination. I hadn't really left my body, and ought to just accept that fact.

And Baby Jenks, what about the beautiful things Baby Jenks had seen when she went up? Had they been hallucinations? I would never know, would I?

Back!

Sitting. Side of the bed. Comfortable. The room. I got up and walked around for a few minutes, merely looking at the flowers, and the odd way the white petals caught the lamplight and how dark the reds looked; and how the golden light was caught on the surfaces of the mirrors, all the other lovely things.

It was overwhelming suddenly, the pure detail surrounding me; the extraordinary complexity of a single room.

Then I practically fell into the chair by the bed. I lay back against the velvet, and listened to my heart pounding. Being invisible, leaving my body, I hated it! I wasn't going to do it again!

Then I heard laughter, faint, gentle laughter. I realized Akasha was there, somewhere behind me, near the dresser perhaps.

There was a sudden surge in me of gladness to hear her voice, to feel her presence. In fact I was surprised at how strong these sensations were. I wanted to see her but I didn't move just yet.

"This traveling without your body—it's a power you share with mortals," she said. "They do this little trick of traveling out of their bodies all the time."

"I know," I said dismally. "They can have it. If I can fly with my body, that's what I intend to do."

She laughed again; soft, caressing laughter that I'd heard in my dreams.

"In olden times," she said, "men went to the temple to do this; they drank the potions given them by the priests; it was in traveling the heavens that men faced the great mysteries of life and death."

"I know," I said again. "I always thought they were drunk or stoned out of their minds as one says today."

"You're a lesson in brutality," she whispered. "Your responses to things are so swift."

"That's brutal?" I asked. I caught a whiff again of the fires burning on the island. Sickening. *Dear God.* And we talk here as if this isn't happening, as if we hadn't penetrated their world with these horrors. . . .

"And flying with your body does not frighten you?" she asked.

"It all frightens me, you know that," I said. "When do I discover the limits? Can I sit here and bring death to mortals who are miles away?"

"No," she said. "You'll discover the limits rather sooner than you think. It's like every other mystery. There really is no mystery."

I laughed. For a split second I heard the voices again, the tide rising, and then it faded into a truly audible sound—cries on the wind, cries coming from villages on the island. They had burned the little museum with the ancient Greek statues in it; and with the icons and the Byzantine paintings.

All that art going up in smoke. Life going up in smoke.

I had to see her suddenly. I couldn't find her in the mirrors, the way they were. I got up.

She was standing at the dresser; and she too had changed her garments, and the style of her hair. Even more purely lovely, yet timeless as before. She held a small hand mirror, and she was looking at herself in it; but it seemed she was not really looking at anything; she was listening to the voices; and I could hear them again too.

A shiver went through me; she resembled her old self, the frozen self sitting in the shrine.

Then she appeared to wake; to look into the mirror again, and then at me as she put the mirror aside.

Her hair had been loosened; all those plaits gone. And now the rippling black waves came down free over her shoulders, heavy, glossy, and inviting to kiss. The dress was similar to the old one, as if the women had made it for her out of dark magenta silk that she had found here. It gave a faint rosy blush to her cheeks, and to her breasts which were only half covered by the loose folds that went up over her shoulders, gathered there by tiny gold clasps.

The necklaces she wore were all modern jewelry, but the profusion made them look archaic, pearls and gold chains and opals and even rubies.

Against the luster of her skin, all this ornament appeared somehow unreal! It was caught up in the overall gloss of her person; it was like the light in her eyes, or the luster of her lips.

She was something fit for the most lavish palace of the imagination; something both sensuous and divine. I wanted her blood again, the blood without fragrance and without killing. I wanted to go to her and lift my hand and touch the skin which seemed absolutely impenetrable but which would break suddenly like the most fragile crust.

"All the men on the island are dead, aren't they?" I asked. I shocked myself.

"All but ten. There were seven hundred people on this island. Seven have been chosen to live."

"And the other three?"

"They are for you."

I stared at her. For me? The desire for blood shifted a little, revised itself, included her and human blood—the hot, bubbling, fragrant kind, the kind that— But there was no physical need. I could still call it thirst, technically, but it was actually worse.

"You don't want them?" she said, mockingly, smiling at me. "My reluctant god, who shrinks from his duty? You know all those years, when I listened to you, long before you made songs to me, I loved it that you took only the hard ones, the young men. I loved it that you hunted thieves and killers; that you liked to swallow their evil whole. Where's your courage now? Your impulsiveness? Your willingness to plunge, as it were?"

"Are they evil?" I said. "These victims who are waiting for me?"

She narrowed her eyes for a moment. "Is it cowardice finally?" she asked. "Does the grandeur of the plan frighten? For surely the killing means little."

"Oh, but you're wrong," I said. "The killing always means something. But yes, the grandeur of the plan terrifies me. The chaos, the total loss of all moral equilibrium, it means everything. But that's not cowardice, is it?" How calm I sounded. How sure of myself. It wasn't the truth, but she knew it.

"Let me release you from all obligation to resist," she said. "You cannot stop me. I love you, as I told you. I love to look at you. It fills me with happiness. But you can't influence me. Such an idea is absurd."

We stared at each other in silence. I was trying to find words to tell myself how lovely she was, how like the old Egyptian paintings of princesses with shining tresses whose names are now forever lost. I was trying to understand why my heart hurt even looking at her; and yet I didn't care that she was beautiful; I cared about what we said to each other.

"Why have you chosen this way?" I asked.

"You know why," she said with a patient smile. "It is the best way. It is the only way; it is the clear vision after centuries of searching for a solution."

"But that can't be the truth, I can't believe it."

"Of course it can. Do you think this is impulse with *me?* I don't make my decisions as you do, my prince. Your youthful exuberance is something I treasure, but such small possibilities are long gone for me. You think in terms of lifetimes; in terms of small accomplishments and human pleasures. I have thought out for thousands of years my designs for the world that is now mine. And the evidence is overwhelming that I must proceed as I have done. I cannot turn this earth into a garden, I cannot create the Eden of human imagination—unless I eliminate the males almost completely."

"And by this you mean kill forty percent of the population of the earth? Ninety percent of all males?"

"Do you deny that this will put an end to war, to rape, to violence?"

"But the point . . ."

"No, answer my question. Do you deny that it will put an end to war, to rape, and to violence?"

"Killing everyone would put an end to those things!"

"Don't play games with me. Answer my question."

"Isn't that a game? The price is unacceptable. It's madness; it's mass murder; it's against nature."

"Quiet yourself. None of what you say is true. What is natural is simply what has been done. And don't you think the peoples of this earth have limited in the past their female children? Don't you think they have killed them by the millions, because they wanted only male children so that those children could go to war? Oh, you cannot imagine the extent to which such things have been done.

"And so now they will choose female over male and there will be no war. And what of the other crimes committed by men against women? If there were any nation on earth which had committed such crimes against another nation, would it not be marked for extermination? And yet nightly, daily, throughout this earth these crimes are perpetrated without end."

"All right, that's true. Undoubtedly that's true. But is your solution any better? It's unspeakable, the slaughter of all things male. Surely if you want to rule—" But even this to me was unthinkable. I thought of Marius's old words, spoken long ago to me when we existed still in the age of powdered wigs and satin slippers—that the old religion, Christianity, was dying, and maybe no new religion would rise:

"Maybe something more wonderful will take place," Marius had said, "the world will truly move forward, past all gods and goddesses, past all devils and angels . . ."

Wasn't that the destiny of this world, really? The destiny to which it was moving without our intervention?

"Ah, you are a dreamer, my beautiful one," she said harshly. "How you pick and choose your illusions! Look to the eastern countries, where the desert tribes, now rich on the oil they have pulled up from beneath the sands, kill each other by the thousands in the name of Allah, their god! Religion is not dead on this earth; it never will be. You and Marius, what chess players you are; your ideas are nothing but chess pieces. And you cannot see beyond the board on which you place them in this or that pattern as suits your small ethical souls."

"You're wrong," I said angrily. "Not about us perhaps. We don't matter. You're wrong in all this that you've begun. You're wrong."

"No, I am not wrong," she said. "And there is no one who can stop me, male or female. And we shall see for the first time since man lifted the club to strike down his brother, the world that women would make and what women have to teach men. And only when men can be taught, will they be allowed to run free among women again!"

"There must be some other way! Ye gods, I'm a flawed thing, a weak thing, a thing no better than most of the men who've ever lived. I can't argue for their lives now. I couldn't defend my own. But, Akasha, for the love of all things living, I'm begging you to turn away from this, this wholesale murder—"

"You speak to me of murder? Tell me the value of one human life, Lestat. Is it not infinite? And how many have you sent to the grave? We have blood on our hands, all of us, just as we have it in our veins."

"Yes, exactly. And we are not all wise and all knowing. I'm begging you to stop, to consider . . . Akasha, surely Marius—"

"Marius!" Softly she laughed. "What did Marius teach you? What did he give you? Really give you!"

I didn't answer. I couldn't. And her beauty was confusing me! So confusing to see the roundness of her arms; the tiny dimple in her cheek.

"My darling," she said, her face suddenly tender and soft as her voice was. "Bring to mind your vision of the Savage Garden, in which aesthetic principles are the only enduring principles—the laws that govern the evolution of all things large and small, of colors and patterns in glorious profusion, and beauty! Beauty everywhere one looks. That is nature. And death is everywhere in it.

"And what I shall make is Eden, the Eden all long for, and it shall be better than nature! It shall take things a step further; and the utter abusive and amoral violence of nature shall be redeemed. Don't you understand that men will never do more than dream of peace? But women can realize that dream? My vision is amplified in the heart of every woman. But it cannot survive the heat of male violence! And that heat is so terrible that the earth itself may not survive."

"What if there's something you don't understand," I said. I was struggling, grasping for the words. "Suppose the duality of masculine and feminine is indispensable to the human animal. Suppose the women want the men; suppose they rise against you and seek to protect the men. The world is not this little brutal island! All women are not peasants blinded by visions!"

"Do you think men are what women want?" she asked. She drew closer, her face changing imperceptibly in the play of the light. "Is that what you're saying? If it is so, then we shall spare a few more of the men, and keep them where they may be looked at as the women looked at you, and touched as the women touched you. We'll keep them where the women may have them when they want them, and I assure you they shall not be used as women have been used by men."

I sighed. It was useless to argue. She was absolutely right and absolutely wrong.

"You do yourself an injustice," she said. "I know your arguments. For centuries I have pondered them, as I've pondered so many questions. You think I do what I do with human limitations. I do not. To understand me, you must think in terms of abilities yet unimagined. Sooner will you understand the mystery of splitting atoms or of black holes in space."

"There has to be a way without death. There has to be a way that triumphs over death."

"Now that, my beauty, is truly against nature," she said. "Even I cannot put an end to death." She paused; she seemed suddenly distracted; or rather deeply distressed by the words she'd just spoken. "An end to death," she whispered. It seemed some personal sorrow had intruded on her thoughts. "An end to death," she said again. But she was drifting away from me. I watched her close her eyes, and lift her fingers to her temples.

She was hearing the voices again; letting them come. Or maybe even unable to stop them for a moment. She said some words in an ancient tongue, and I didn't understand them. I was struck by her sudden seeming vulnerability, the way the voices seemed to be cutting her off; the way her eyes appeared to search the room and then to fix on me and brighten.

I was speechless and overwhelmed with sadness. How small had my visions of power always been! To vanquish a mere handful of enemies, to be seen and loved by mortals as an image; to find some place in the great drama of things which was infinitely larger than I was, a drama whose study could occupy the mind of one being for a thousand years. And we stood outside time suddenly; outside of justice; capable of collapsing whole systems of thought. Or was it just an illusion? How many others had reached for such power, in one form or another?

"They were not immortals, my beloved." It was almost an entreaty.

"But it's an accident that we are," I said. "We're things that never should have come into existence."

"Don't speak those words!"

"I can't help it."

"It doesn't matter now. You fail to grasp how little *anything* matters. I give you no sublime reason for what I do because the reasons are simple and practical; how we came into being is irrelevant. What matters is that we have survived. Don't you see? That is the utter beauty of it, the beauty out of which all other beauties will be born, that we have survived."

I shook my head. I was in a panic. I saw again the museum that the villagers on this island had only just burnt. I saw the statues blackened and lying on the floor. An appalling sense of loss engulfed me.

"History does not matter," she said. "Art does not matter; these things imply continuities which in fact do not exist. They cater to our need for pattern, our hunger for meaning. But they cheat us in the end. We must make the meaning."

I turned my back. I didn't want to be drugged by her resolution or her beauty; by the glimmer of light in her jet black eyes. I felt her hands on my shoulders; her lips against my neck.

"When the years have passed," she said, "when my garden has bloomed through many summers and gone to sleep through many winters; when the old ways of rape and war are nothing but memory, and women watch the old films in mystification that such things could ever have been done; when the ways of women are inculcated into every member of the population, naturally, as aggression is now inculcated, then perhaps the males can return. Slowly, their numbers can be increased. Children will be reared in an atmosphere where rape is unthinkable, where war is unimaginable. And then . . . then . . . there can be men. When the world is ready for them."

"It won't work. It can't work."

"Why do you say so? Let us look to nature, as you wanted to do only moments ago. Go out in the lush garden that surrounds this villa; study the bees in their hives and the ants who labor as they have always done. They are female, my prince, by the millions. A male is only an aberration and a matter of function. They learned the wise trick a long time before me of limiting the males.

"And we may now live in an age where males are utterly unnecessary. Tell me, my prince, what is the primary use of men now, if it is not to protect women from other men?"

"What is it that makes you want me here!" I said desperately. I turned around to face her again. "Why have you chosen me as your consort! For the love of heaven, why don't you kill me with the other men! Choose some other immortal, some ancient being who hungers for such power! There must be one. I don't want to rule the world! I don't want to rule anything! I never did."

Her face changed just a little. It seemed there was a faint, evanescent sadness in her that made her eyes even deeper in their darkness for an instant. Her lip quivered as if she wanted to say something but couldn't. Then she did answer.

"Lestat, if all the world were destroyed, I would not destroy you," she said. "Your limitations are as radiant as your virtues for reasons I don't understand myself. But more truly perhaps, I love you because you are so perfectly what is wrong with all things male. Aggressive, full of hate and recklessness, and endlessly eloquent excuses for violence—you are the essence of masculinity; and there is a gorgeous quality to such purity. But only because it can now be controlled."

"By you."

"Yes, my darling. This is what I was born for. This is why I am here. And it does not matter if no one ratifies my purpose. I shall make it so. Right now the world burns with masculine fire; it is a conflagration. But when that is corrected, your fire shall burn ever more brightly—as a torch burns."

"Akasha, you prove my point! Don't you think the souls of women crave that very fire? My God, would you tamper with the stars themselves?"

"Yes, the soul craves it. But to see it in the blaze of a torch as I have indicated, or in the flame of a candle. But not as it rages now through every forest and over every mountain and in every glen. There is no woman alive who has ever wanted to be burnt by it! They want the light, my beauty, the light! And the warmth! But not the destruction. How could they? They are only women. They are not mad."

"All right. Say you accomplish your purpose. That you begin this revolution and it sweeps the world—and mind you I don't think such a thing will happen! But if you do, is there nothing under heaven that will demand atonement for the death of so many millions? If there are no gods or goddesses, is there not some way in which humans themselves—and you and I—shall be made to pay?"

"It is the gateway to innocence and so it shall be remembered. And never again will the male population be allowed to increase to such proportions, for who would want such horrors again?"

"Force the men to obey you. Dazzle them as you've dazzled the women, as you've dazzled me."

"But Lestat, that is just the point; they would never obey. Will you obey? They would die first, as you would die. They would have another reason for rebellion, as if any were ever wanting. They would gather together in magnificent resistance. Imagine a goddess to fight. We shall see enough of that by and by as it is. They cannot help but be men. And I could rule only through tyranny, by endless killing. And there would be chaos. But this way, there shall be a break in the great chain of violence. There shall be an era of utter and perfect peace."

I was quiet again. I could think of a thousand answers but they were all short-circuited. She knew her purpose only too well. And the truth was, she was right in many things she said.

Ah, but it was fantasy! A world without males. What exactly would have been accomplished? Oh, no. No, don't even accept the idea for a moment. Don't even. . . . Yet the vision returned, the vision I'd glimpsed in that miserable jungle village, of a world without fear.

Imagine trying to explain to them what men had been like. Imagine trying to explain that there had been a time when one could be murdered in the streets of the cities; imagine trying to explain what rape meant to the male of the species . . . imagine. And I saw their eyes looking at me, the uncomprehending eyes as they tried to fathom it, tried to make that leap of understanding. I felt their soft hands touching me.

"But this is madness!" I whispered.

"Ah, but you fight me so hard, my prince," she whispered. There was a flash of anger, hurt. She came near to me. If she kissed me again I was going to start weeping. I'd thought I knew what beauty was in women; but she'd surpassed all the language I had for it.

"My prince," she said again in a low whisper. "The logic of it is elegant. A world in which only a handful of males are kept for breeding shall be a female world. And that world will be what we have never known in all our bloody miserable history, in which men now breed germs in vials with which to kill continents in chemical warfare, and design bombs which can knock the earth from its path around the sun."

"What if the women divide along principles of masculine/feminine, the way men so often divide if there are no females there?"

"You know that's a foolish objection. Such distinctions are never more than superficial. Women are women! Can you conceive of war made by women? Truly, answer me. Can you? Can you conceive of bands of roving women intent only on destruction? Or rape? Such a thing is preposterous. For the aberrant few justice will be immediate. But overall, something utterly unforeseen will take place. Don't you see? The possibility of peace on earth has always existed, and there have always been people who could realize it, and preserve it, and those people are women. If one takes away the men."

I sat down on the bed in consternation, like a mortal man. I put my elbows on my knees. Dear God, dear God! Why did those two words keep coming to me? There was no God! I was in the room with God.

She laughed triumphantly.

"Yes, precious one," she said. She touched my hand and turned me around and drew me towards her. "But tell me, doesn't it excite you even a little?"

I looked at her. "What do you mean?"

"You, the impulsive one. You who made that child, Claudia, into a blood drinker, just to see what would happen?" There was mockery in her tone but it was affectionate. "Come now, don't you want to see what will happen if all the males are gone? Aren't you even a little curious? Reach into your soul for the truth. It is a very interesting idea, isn't it?"

I didn't answer. Then I shook my head. "No," I said.

"Coward," she whispered.

No one had ever called me that, no one.

"Coward," she said again. "Little being with little dreams."

"Maybe there would be no war and no rape and no violence," I said, "if all beings were little and had little dreams, as you put it."

She laughed softly. Forgivingly.

"We could argue these points forever," she whispered. "But very soon we will know. The world will be as I would have it be; and we shall see what happens as I said."

She sat beside me. For a moment it seemed I was losing my mind. She slipped her smooth naked arms around my neck. It seemed there had never been a softer female body, never anything as yielding and luscious as her embrace. Yet she was so hard, so strong.

The lights in the room were dimming. And the sky outside seemed ever more vivid and darkly blue.

"Akasha," I whispered. I was looking beyond the open terrace at the stars. I wanted to say something, something crucial that would sweep away all arguments; but the meaning escaped me. I was so drowsy; surely it was her doing. It was a spell she was working, yet knowing it did not release me. I felt her lips again on my lips, and on my throat. I felt the cool satin of her skin.

"Yes, rest now, precious one. And when you wake, the victims will be waiting."

"Victims. . . ." Almost dreaming, as I held her in my arms.

"But you must sleep now. You are young still and fragile. My blood's working on you, changing you, perfecting you."

Yes, destroying me; destroying my heart and my will. I was vaguely conscious of moving, of lying down on the bed. I fell back into the silken pillows, and then there was the silk of her hair near me, the touch of her fingers, and again, her lips on my mouth. Blood in her kiss; blood thundering beneath it.

"Listen to the sea," she whispered. "Listen to the flowers open. You can hear them now, you know. You can hear the tiny creatures of the sea if you listen. You can hear the dolphins sing, for they do."

Drifting. Safe in her arms; she the powerful one; she was the one they all feared.

Forget the acrid smell of the burning bodies; yes, listen to the sea pounding like guns on the beach beneath us; listen to the sound of a rose petal breaking loose and falling onto marble. And the world is going to hell, and I cannot help it, and I am in her arms and I am going to sleep.

"Hasn't that happened a million times, my love?" she whispered. "On a world full of suffering and death, you turned your back as millions of mortals do every night?"

Darkness. Splendid visions taking place; a palace even more lovely than this. Victims. Servants. The mythical existence of pashas, and emperors.

"Yes, my darling, anything that you desire. All the world at your feet. I shall build you palace upon palace; they shall do it; they that worship you. That is nothing. That is the simplest part of it. And think of the hunting, my prince. Until the killing is done, think of the chase. For they would surely run from you and hide from you, yet you would find them."

In the dwindling light—just before dreams come—I could see it. I could see myself traveling through the air, like the heroes of old, over the sprawling country where their campfires flickered.

In packs like wolves they would travel, through the cities as well as the woods, daring to show themselves only by day; for only then would they be safe from us. When night fell, we would come; and we would track them by their thoughts and by their blood, and by the whispered confessions of the women who had seen them and maybe even harbored them. Out in the open they might run, firing their useless weapons. And we would swoop down; we would destroy them one by one, our prey, save for those we wanted alive, those whose blood we would take slowly, mercilessly.

And out of that war shall come peace? Out of that hideous game shall come a garden?

I tried to open my eyes. I felt her kiss my eyelids.

Dreaming.

A barren plain and the soil breaking. Something rising, pushing the dried clods of earth out of its way. I am this thing. This thing walking across the barren plain as the sun sinks. The sky is still full of light. I look down at the stained cloth that covers me, but this is not me. I'm only Lestat. And I'm afraid. I wish Gabrielle were here. And Louis. Maybe Louis could make her understand. Ah, Louis, of all of us, Louis who always knew. . . .

And there is the familiar dream again, the redheaded women kneeling by the altar with the body—their mother's body and they are ready to consume it. Yes, it's their duty, their sacred right—to devour the brain and the heart. Except that they never will because something awful always happens. Soldiers come. . . . I wish I knew the meaning.

BLOOD.

I woke up with a start. Hours had passed. The room had cooled faintly. The sky was wondrously clear through the open windows. From her came all the light that filled the room.

"The women are waiting, and the victims, they are afraid."

The victims. My head was spinning. The victims would be full of luscious blood. Males who would have died anyway. Young males all mine to take.

"Yes. But come, put an end to their suffering."

Groggily I got up. She wrapped a long cloak over my shoulders, something simpler than her own garment, but warm and soft to touch. She stroked my hair with her two hands.

"Masculine—feminine. Is that all there ever was to it?" I whispered. My body wanted to sleep some more. But the blood.

She reached up and touched my cheek with her fingers. Tears again?

We went out of the room together, and onto a long landing with a marble railing, from which a stairs descended, turning once, into an immense room. Candelabra everywhere. Dim electric lamps creating a luxurious gloom.

At the very center, the women were assembled, perhaps two hundred or more of them, standing motionless and looking up at us, their hands clasped as if in prayer.

Even in their silence, they seemed barbaric, amid the European furniture, the Italian hardwoods with their gilt edges, and the old fireplace with its marble scrolls. I thought of her words suddenly: "history doesn't matter; art doesn't matter." Dizzy. On the walls, there ran those airy eighteenth-century paintings, full of gleaming clouds and fat-cheeked angels, and skies of luminescent blue.

The women stood looking past this wealth which had never touched them and indeed meant nothing to them, looking up at the vision on the landing, which now dissolved, and in a rush of whispered noise and colored light, materialized suddenly at the foot of the stairs.

Sighs rose, hands were raised to shield bowed heads as if from a blast of unwelcome light. Then all eyes were fixed upon the Queen of Heaven and her consort, who stood on the red carpet, only a few feet above the assembly, the consort a bit shaken and biting his lip a little and trying to see this thing clearly, this awful thing that was happening, this awful mingling of worship and blood sacrifice, as the victims were brought forth.

Such fine specimens. Dark-haired, dark-skinned, Mediterranean men. Every bit as beautiful as the young women. Men of that stocky build and exquisite musculature that has inspired artists for thousands of years. Ink black eyes and darkly shaved faces; and deep cunning; and deep anger as they looked upon these hostile supernatural creatures who had decreed the death of their brothers far and wide.

With leather straps they'd been bound—probably their own belts, and the belts of dozens of others; but the women had done it well. Their ankles were tethered even, so that they could walk but not kick or run. Naked to the waist they were, and only one was trembling, as much with anger as with fear. Suddenly he began to struggle. The other two turned, stared at him, and started to struggle as well.

But the mass of women closed on them, forcing them to their knees. I felt the desire rise in me at the sight of it, at the sight of leather belts cutting into the dark naked flesh of the men's arms. Why is this so seductive! And the women's hands holding them, those tight menacing hands that could be so soft otherwise. They couldn't fight so many women. Heaving sighs, they stopped the rebellion, though the one who had started the struggle looked up, accusingly, at me.

Demons, devils, things from hell, that is what his mind told him; for who else could have done such things to his world? Oh, this is the beginning of darkness, terrible darkness!

But the desire was so strong. *You are going to die and I am going to do it!* And he seemed to hear it, and to understand it. And a savage hatred of the women rose out of him, replete with images of rape and retribution that made me smile, and yet I understood. Rather completely I understood. So easy to feel that contempt for them, to be outraged that they had dared to become the enemy, the enemy in the age-old battle, they, the women! And it was darkness, this imagined retribution, it was unspeakable darkness, too.

I felt Akasha's fingers on my arm. The feeling of bliss came back; the delirium. I tried to resist it, but I felt it as before. Yet the desire didn't go away. The desire was in my mouth now. I could taste it.

Yes, pass into the moment; pass into pure function; let the bloody sacrifice begin.

The women went down on their knees en masse, and the men who were already kneeling seemed to grow calm, their eyes glazing over as they looked at us, their lips trembling and loose.

I stared at the muscled shoulders of the first one, the one who had rebelled. I imagined as I always do at such moments the feel of his coarse rough-shaven throat when my lips would touch it, and my teeth would break through the skin—not the icy skin of the goddess—but hot, salty human skin.

Yes, beloved. Take him. He is the sacrifice that you deserve. You are a god now. Take him. Do you know how many wait for you?

It seemed the women understood what to do. They lifted him as I stepped forward; there was another struggle, but it was no more than a spasm in the muscles as I took him into my arms. My hand closed too hard on his head; I didn't know my new strength, and I heard the bones cracking even as my teeth went in. But the death came almost instantly, so great was my first draught of blood. I was burning with hunger; and the whole portion, complete and entire in one instant, had not been enough. Not nearly enough!

At once I took the next victim, trying to be slow with it, so that I would tumble into the darkness as I'd so often done, with only the soul speaking to me. Yes, telling me its secrets as the blood spurted into my mouth, as I let my mouth fill before I swallowed. *Yes, brother. I am sorry, brother.* And then staggering forward, I stepped on the corpse before me and crushed it underfoot.

"Give me the last one."

No resistance. He stared up at me in utter quiet, as if some light had dawned in him, as if he'd found in theory or belief some perfect rescue. I pulled him to me—gently, Lestat—and this was the real fount I wanted, this was the slow, powerful death I craved, the heart pumping as if it would never stop, the sigh slipping from his lips, my eyes clouded still, even as I let him go, with the fading images of his brief and unrecorded life, suddenly collapsed into one rare second of meaning.

I let him drop. Now there was no meaning.

There was only the light before me, and the rapture of the women who had at last been redeemed through miracles.

The room was hushed; not a thing stirred; the sound of the sea came in, that distant monotonous booming.

Then Akasha's voice:

The sins of the men have now been atoned for; and those who are kept now, shall be well cared for, and loved. But never give freedom to those who remain, those who have oppressed you.

And then soundlessly, without distinct words, the lesson came.

The ravening lust which they had just witnessed, the deaths they had seen at my hands—that was to be the eternal reminder of the fierceness that lived in all male things and must never be allowed free again. The males had been sacrificed to the embodiment of their own violence.

In sum, these women had witnessed a new and transcendent ritual; a new holy sacrifice of the Mass. And they would see it again; and they must always remember it.

My head swam from the paradox. And my own small designs of not very long ago were there to torment me. I had wanted the world of mortals to know of me. I had wanted to be the image of evil in the theater of the world and thereby somehow do good.

And now I was that image all right, I was its literal embodiment, passing through the minds of these few simple souls into myth as she had promised. And there was a small voice whispering in my ear, hammering me with that old adage: be careful what you wish for; your wish might come true.

Yes, that was the heart of it; all I'd ever wished for was coming true. In the shrine I had kissed her and longed to awaken her, and dreamt of her power; and now we stood together, she and I, and the hymns rose around us. Hosannas. Cries of joy.

The doors of the palazzo were thrown open.

And we were taking our leave; we were rising in splendor and in magic, and passing out of the doors, and up over the roof of the old mansion, and then out over the sparkling waters into the calm sweep of the stars.

I had no fear of falling anymore; I had no fear of anything so insignificant. Because my whole soul—petty as it was and always had been—knew fears I'd never imagined before.

6

THE STORY OF THE TWINS PART II

SHE was dreaming of killing. It was a great dark city like London or Rome, and she was hurrying through it, on an errand of killing, to bring down the first sweet human victim that would be her own. And just before she opened her eyes, she had made the leap from the things she had believed all her life, to this simple amoral act—killing. She had done what the reptile does when it hoists in its leathery slit of a mouth the tiny crying mouse that it will crush slowly without ever hearing that soft heartbreaking song.

Awake in the dark; and the house alive above her; the old ones saying Come. A television talking somewhere. The Blessed Virgin Mary had appeared on an island in the Mediterranean Sea.

No hunger. Maharet's blood was too strong. The idea was growing, beckoning like a crone in a dark alley. *Killing*.

Rising from the narrow box in which she lay, she tiptoed through the blackness until her hands felt the metal door. She went into the hallway and looked up the endless iron stairs, crisscrossing back over itself as if it were a skeleton, and she saw the sky through the glass like smoke. Mael was halfway up, at the door of the house proper, gazing down at her.

She reeled with it—*I am one of you and we are together*—and the feel of the iron rail under her hand, and some sudden grief, just a fleeting thing, for all she had been before this fierce beauty had grabbed her by the hair.

Mael came down as if to retrieve her, because it was carrying her away.

They understood, didn't they, the way the earth breathed for her now, and the forest sang, and the roots prowled the dark, coming through these earthen walls.

She stared at Mael. Faint smell of buckskin, dust. How had she ever thought such beings were human? Eyes glittering like that. And yet the time would come when she would be walking among human beings again, and she would see their eyes linger and then suddenly move away. She'd be hurrying through some dark city like London or Rome. Looking into the eyes of Mael, she saw the crone again in the alleyway; but it had not been a literal image. No, she saw the alleyway, she saw the killing, purely. And in silence, they both looked away at the same instant, but not quickly, rather respectfully. He took her hand; he looked at the bracelet he'd given her. He kissed her suddenly on the cheek. And then he led her up the stairs towards the mountaintop room.

The electronic voice of the television grew louder and louder, speaking of mass hysteria in Sri Lanka. Women killing men. Even male babies murdered. On the island of Lynkonos there had been mass hallucinations and an epidemic of unexplained deaths.

Only gradually did it dawn on her, what she was hearing. So it wasn't the Blessed Virgin Mary, and she had thought how lovely, when she first heard it, that they can believe something like that. She turned to Mael but he was looking ahead. He knew these things. The television had been playing its words to him for an hour.

Now she saw the eerie blue flicker as she came into the mountaintop room. And the strange spectacle of these her new brethren in the Secret Order of the Undead, scattered about like so many statues, glowing in the blue light, as they stared fixedly at the large screen.

". . . outbreaks in the past caused by contaminants in food or water. Yet no explanation has been found for the similarity of the reports from widely divergent places, which now include several isolated villages in the mountains of Nepal. Those apprehended claim to have seen a beautiful woman, called variously the Blessed Virgin, or the Queen of Heaven, or simply the Goddess, who commanded them to massacre the males of their village, except for a few carefully chosen to be spared. Some reports describe a male apparition also, a fair-haired deity who does not speak and who as yet has no official or unofficial title or name . . ."

Jesse looked at Maharet, who watched without expression, one hand resting on the arm of her chair.

Newspapers covered the table. Papers in French and Hindustani as well as English.

". . . from Lynkonos to several other islands before the militia was called in. Early estimates indicate some two thousand men may have been killed in this little archipelago just off the tip of Greece."

Maharet touched the small black control under her hand and the screen vanished. It seemed the entire apparatus vanished, fading into the dark wood, as the windows became transparent and the treetops appeared in endless, misted layers against the violent sky. Far away, Jesse saw the twinkling lights of Santa Rosa cradled in the dark hills. She could smell the sun that had been in this room; she could feel the heat rising slowly through the glass ceiling.

She looked at the others who were sitting there in stunned silence. Marius glared at the television screen, at the newspapers spread out before him.

"We have no time to lose," Khayman said quickly to Maharet. "You must continue the tale. We don't know when she will come here."

He made a small gesture, and the scattered newspapers were suddenly cleared away, crushed together, and hurtling soundlessly into the fire which devoured them with a gust that sent a shower of sparks up the gaping smokestack.

Jesse was suddenly dizzy. Too fast, all of that. She stared at Khayman. Would she ever get used to it? Their porcelain faces and their sudden violent expressions, their soft human voices, and their near invisible movements?

And what was the Mother doing? Males slaughtered. The fabric of life for these ignorant people utterly destroyed. A cold sense of menace touched her. She searched Maharet's face for some insight, some understanding.

But Maharet's features were utterly rigid. She had not answered Khayman. She turned towards the table slowly and clasped her hands under her chin. Her eyes were dull, remote, as if she saw nothing before her.

"The fact is, she has to be destroyed," Marius said, as if he could hold it in no longer. The color flared in his cheeks, shocking Jesse, because all the normal lines of a man's face had been there for an instant. And now they were gone, and he was visibly shaking with anger. "We've loosed a monster, and it's up to us to reclaim it."

"And how can that be done?" Santino asked. "You speak as if it's a simple matter of decision. You cannot kill her!"

"We forfeit our lives, that's how it's done," Marius said. "We act in concert, and we end this thing once and for all as it should have been ended long ago." He glanced at them all one by one, eyes lingering on Jesse. Then shifting to Maharet. "The body isn't indestructible. It isn't made of marble. It can be pierced, cut. I've pierced it with my teeth. I've drunk its blood!"

Maharet made a small dismissive gesture, as if to say I know these things and you know I know.

"And as we cut it, we cut ourselves?" Eric said. "I say we leave here. I say we hide from her. What do we gain staying in this place?"

"No!" Maharet said.

"She'll kill you one by one if you do that," Khayman said. "You're alive because you wait now for her purpose."

"Would you go on with the story," Gabrielle said, speaking directly to Maharet. She'd been withdrawn all this time, only now and then listening to the others. "I want to know the rest," she said. "I want to hear everything." She sat forward, arms folded on the table.

"You think you'll discover some way to vanquish her in these old tales?" Eric asked. "You're mad if you think that."

"Go on with the story, please," Louis said. "I want to . . ." He hesitated. "I want to *know* what happened also."

Maharet looked at him for a long moment.

"Go on, Maharet," Khayman said. "For in all likelihood, the Mother will be destroyed and we both know how and why, and all this talk means nothing."

"What can prophecy mean now, Khayman?" Maharet asked, her voice low, devitalized. "Do we fall into the same errors that ensnare the Mother? The past may instruct us. But it won't save us."

"Your sister comes, Maharet. She comes as she said she would."

"Khayman," Maharet said with a long, bitter smile.

"Tell us what happened," Gabrielle said.

Maharet sat still, as if trying to find some way to begin. The sky beyond the windows darkened in the interval. Yet a faint tinge of red appeared in the far west, growing brighter and brighter against the gray clouds. Finally, it faded, and they were wrapped in absolute darkness, except for the light of the fire, and the dull sheen of the glass walls which had become mirrors.

"Khayman took you to Egypt," Gabrielle said. "What did you see there?"

"Yes, he took us to Egypt," Maharet said. She sighed as she sat back in the chair, her eyes fixed on the table before her. "There was no escape from it; Khayman would have taken us by force. And in truth, we accepted that we had to go. Through twenty generations, we had gone between man and the spirits. If Amel had done some great evil, we would try to undo it. Or at least . . . as I said to you when we first came to this table . . . we would seek to understand.

"I left my child. I left her in the care of those women I trusted most. I kissed her. I told her secrets. And then I left her, and we set out, carried in the royal litter as if we were guests of the King and Queen of Kemet and not prisoners, just as before.

"Khayman was gentle with us on the long march, but grim and silent, and refusing to meet our gaze. And it was just as well, for we had not forgotten our injuries. Then on the very last night when we camped on the banks of the great river, which we would cross in the morning to reach the royal palace, Khayman called us into his tent and told us all that he knew.

"His manner was courteous, decorous. And we tried to put aside our personal suspicions of him as we listened. He told us of what the demon—as he called it—had done.

"Only hours after we had been sent out of Egypt, he had known that something was watching him, some dark and evil force. Everywhere that he went, he felt this presence, though in the light of day it tended to wane.

"Then things within his house were altered—little things which others did not notice. He thought at first he was going mad. His writing things were misplaced; then the seal which he used as great steward. Then at random moments—and always when he was alone—these objects came flying at him, striking him in the face, or landing at his feet. Some turned up in ridiculous places. He would find the great seal, for instance, in his beer or his broth.

"And he dared not tell the King and Queen. He knew it was our spirits who were doing it; and to tell would be a death sentence for us.

"And so he kept this awful secret, as things grew worse and worse. Ornaments which he had treasured from childhood were now rent to pieces and made to rain down upon him. Sacred amulets were hurled into the privy; excrement was taken from the well and smeared upon the walls.

"He could barely endure his own house, yet he admonished his slaves to tell no one, and when they ran off in fear, he attended to his own toilet and swept the place like a lowly servant himself.

"But he was now in a state of terror. Something was there with him in his house. He could hear its breath upon his face. And now and then he would swear that he felt its needlelike teeth.

"At last in desperation he began to talk to it, beg it to get out. But this seemed only to increase its strength. With the talking, it redoubled its power. It emptied his purse upon the stones and made the gold coins jingle against each other all night long. It upset his bed so that he landed on his face on the floor. It put sand in his food when he wasn't looking.

"Finally six months had passed since we had left the kingdom. He was growing frantic. Perhaps we were beyond danger. But he could not be sure, and he did not know where to turn, for the spirit was really frightening him.

"Then in the dead of night, as he lay wondering what the thing was up to, for it had been so quiet, he heard suddenly a great pounding at his door. He was in terror. He knew he shouldn't answer, that the knocking didn't come from a human hand. But finally he could bear it no longer. He said his prayers; he threw open the door. And what he beheld was the horror of horrors—the rotted mummy of his father, the filthy wrappings in tatters, propped against the garden wall.

"Of course, he knew there was no life in the shrunken face or dead eyes that stared at him. Someone or something had unearthed the corpse from its desert mastaba and brought it there. And this was the body of his father, putrid, stinking; the body of his father, which by all things holy, should have been consumed in a proper funeral feast by Khayman and his brothers and sisters.

"Khayman sank to his knees weeping, half screaming. And then, before his unbelieving eyes, the thing moved! The thing began to dance! Its limbs were jerked hither and thither, the wrappings breaking to bits and pieces, until Khayman ran into the house and shut the door against it. And then the corpse was flung, pounding its fist it seemed, upon the door, demanding entrance.

"Khayman called on all the gods of Egypt to be rid of this monstrosity. He called out to the palace guards; he called to the soldiers of the King. He cursed the demon thing and ordered it to leave him; and Khayman became the one flinging objects now, and kicking the gold coins about in his rage.

"All the palace rushed through the royal gardens to Khayman's house. But the demon now seemed to grow even stronger. The shutters rattled and then were torn from their pivots. The few bits of fine furniture which Khayman possessed began to skitter about.

"Yet this was only the beginning. At dawn when the priests entered the house to exorcise the demon, a great wind came out of the desert, carrying with it torrents of blinding sand. And everywhere Khayman went, the wind pursued him; and finally he looked down to see his arms covered with tiny pinpricks and tiny droplets of blood. Even his eyelids were assaulted. In a cabinet he flung himself to get some peace. And the thing tore up the cabinet. And all fled from it. And Khayman was left crying on the floor.

"For days the tempest continued. The more the priests prayed and sang, the more the demon raged.

"The King and Queen were beside themselves in consternation. The priests cursed the demon. The people blamed it upon the red-haired witches. They cried that we should never have been allowed to leave the land of Kemet. We should be found at all costs and brought back to be burnt alive. And then the demon would be quiet.

"But the old families did not agree with this verdict. To them the judgment was clear. Had not the gods unearthed the putrid body of Khayman's father, to show that the flesh eaters had always done what was pleasing to heaven? No, it was the King and Queen who were evil, the King and Queen who must die. The King and Queen who had filled the land with mummies and superstition.

"The kingdom, finally, was on the verge of civil war.

"At last the King himself came to Khayman, who sat weeping in his house, a garment drawn over him like a shroud. And the King talked to the demon, even as the tiny bites afflicted Khayman and made drops of blood on the cloth that covered Khayman.

" 'Now think what those witches told us,' the King said. 'These are but spirits; not demons. And they can be reasoned with. If only I could make them hear me as the witches could; and make them answer.'

"But this little conversation only seemed to enrage the demon. It broke what little furniture it had not already smashed. It tore the door off its pivots; it uprooted the trees from the garden and flung them about. In fact, it seemed to forget Khayman altogether for the moment, as it went tearing through the palace gardens destroying all that it could.

"And the King went after it, begging it to recognize him and to converse with him, and to impart to him its secrets. He stood in the very midst of the whirlwind created by this demon, fearless and enrapt.

"Finally the Queen appeared. In a loud piercing voice she addressed the demon too. 'You punish us for the affliction of the red-haired sisters!' she screamed. 'But why do you not serve us instead of them!' At once the demon tore at her clothes and greatly afflicted her, as it had done to Khayman before. She tried to cover her arms and her face, but it was impossible. And so the King took hold of her and together they ran back to Khayman's house.

" 'Now, go,' said the King to Khayman. 'Leave us alone with this thing for I will learn from it, I will understand what it wants.' And calling the priests to him, he told them through the whirlwind what we had said, that the spirit hated mankind because we were both spirit and flesh. But he would ensnare it and reform it and control it. For he was Enkil, King of Kemet, and he could do this thing.

"Into Khayman's house, the King and the Queen went together, and the demon went with them, tearing the place to pieces, yet there they remained. Khayman, who was now free of the thing, lay on the floor of the palace exhausted, fearing for his sovereigns but not knowing what to do.

"The entire court was in an uproar; men fought one another; women wept, and some even left the palace for fear of what was to come.

"For two whole nights and days, the King remained with the demon; and so did the Queen. And then the old families, the flesh eaters, gathered outside the house. The King and Queen were in error; it was time to seize the future of Kemet. At nightfall, they went into the house on their deadly errand with daggers raised. They would kill the King and Queen; and if the people raised any outcry, then they would say that the demon had done it; and who could say that the demon had not? And would not the demon stop when the King and Queen were dead, the King and Queen who had persecuted the red-haired witches?

"It was the Queen who saw them coming; and as she rushed forward, crying in alarm, they thrust their daggers into her breast and she sank down dying. The King ran to her aid, and they struck him down too, just as mercilessly; and then they ran out of the house, for the demon had not stopped his persecutions.

"Now Khayman, all this while, had knelt at the very edge of the garden, deserted by the guards who had thrown in with the flesh eaters. He expected to die with other servants of the royal family. Then he heard a horrid wailing from the Queen. Sounds such as he had never heard before. And when the flesh eaters heard these sounds, they deserted the place utterly.

"It was Khayman, loyal steward to the King and Queen, who snatched up a torch and went to the aid of his master and mistress.

"No one tried to stop him. All crept away in fear. Khayman alone went into the house.

"It was pitch-black now, save for the torchlight. And this is what Khayman saw:

"The Queen lay on the floor writhing as if in agony, the blood pouring from her wounds, and a great reddish cloud enveloped her; it was like a whirlpool surrounding her, or rather a wind sweeping up countless tiny drops of blood. And in the midst of this swirling wind or rain or whatever it could be called, the Queen twisted and turned, her eyes rolling up in her head. The King lay sprawled on his back.

"All instinct told Khayman to leave this place. To get as far away from it as he could. At that moment, he wanted to leave his homeland forever. But this was his Queen, who lay there gasping for breath, her back arched, her hands clawing at the floor.

"Then the great blood cloud that veiled her, swelling and contracting around her, grew denser and, all of a sudden, as if drawn into her wounds, disappeared. The Queen's body went still; then slowly she sat upright, her eyes staring forward, and a great guttural cry broke from her before she fell quiet.

"There was no sound whatsoever as the Queen stared at Khayman, except for the crackling of the torch. And then hoarsely the Queen began to gasp again, her eyes widening, and it seemed she should die; but she did not. She shielded her eyes from the bright light of the torch as though it was hurting her, and she turned and saw her husband lying as if dead at her side.

"She cried a negation in her agony; it could not be so. And at the same instant, Khayman beheld that all her wounds were healing; deep gashes were no more than scratches upon the surface of her skin.

" 'Your Highness!' he said. And he came towards her as she crouched weeping and staring at her own arms, which had been torn with the slashes of the daggers, and at her own breasts, which were whole again. She was whimpering piteously as she looked at these healing wounds. And suddenly with her long nails, she tore at her own skin and the blood gushed out and yet the wound healed!

" 'Khayman, my Khayman!' she screamed, covering her eyes so that she did not see the bright torch. 'What has befallen me!' And her screams grew louder and louder; and she fell upon the King in panic, crying, 'Enkil, help me. Enkil, do not die!' and all the other mad things that one cries in the midst of disaster. And then as she stared down at the King, a great ghastly change came over her, and she lunged at the King, as if she were a hungry beast, and with her long tongue, she lapped at the blood that covered his throat and his chest.

"Khayman had never seen such a spectacle. She was a lioness in the desert lapping the blood from a tender kill. Her back was bowed, and her knees were drawn up, and she pulled the helpless body of the King towards her and bit the artery in his throat.

"Khayman dropped the torch. He backed halfway from the open door. Yet even as he meant to run for his life, he heard the King's voice. Softly the King spoke to her. 'Akasha,' he said. 'My Queen.' And she, drawing up, shivering, weeping, stared at her own body, and at his body, at her smooth flesh, and his torn still by so many wounds. 'Khayman,' she cried. 'Your dagger. Give it to me. For they have taken their weapons with them. Your dagger. I must have it now.'

"At once Khayman obeyed, though he thought it was to see his King die once and for all. But with the dagger the Queen cut her own wrists and watched the blood pour down upon the wounds of her husband, and she saw it heal them. And crying out in her excitement, she smeared the blood all over his torn face.

"The King's wounds healed. Khayman saw it. Khayman saw the great gashes closing. He saw the King tossing, heaving his arms this way and that. His tongue lapped at Akasha's spilt blood as it ran down his face. And then rising in that same animal posture that had so consumed the Queen only moments before, the King embraced his wife, and opened his mouth on her throat.

"Khayman had seen enough. In the flickering light of the dying torch these two pale figures had become haunts to him, demons themselves. He backed out of the little house and up against the garden wall. And there it seems he lost consciousness, feeling the grass against his face as he collapsed.

"When he waked, he found himself lying on a gilded couch in the Queen's chambers. All the palace lay quiet. He saw that his clothes had been changed, and his face and hands bathed, and that there was only the dimmest light here and sweet incense, and the doors were open to the garden as if there was nothing to fear.

"Then in the shadows, he saw the King and the Queen looking down at him; only this was not his King and not his Queen. It seemed then that he would cry out; he would give voice to screams as terrible as those he had heard from others; but the Queen quieted him.

" 'Khayman, my Khayman,' she said. She handed to him his beautiful gold-handled dagger. 'You have served us well.'

"There Khayman paused in his story. 'Tomorrow night,' he said, 'when the sun sets, you will see for yourselves what has happened. For then and only then, when all the light is gone from the western sky, will they appear together in the rooms of the palace, and you will see what I have seen.'

" 'But why only in the night?' I asked him. 'What is the significance of this?'

"And then he told us, that not one hour after he'd waked, even before the sun had risen, they had begun to shrink from the open doors of the palace, to cry that the light hurt their eyes. Already they had fled from torches and lamps; and now it seemed the morning was coming after them; and there was no place in the palace that they could hide.

"In stealth they left the palace, covered in garments. They ran with a speed no human being could match. They ran towards the mastabas or tombs of the old families, those who had been forced with pomp and ceremony to make mummies of their dead. In sum, to the sacred places which no one would desecrate, they ran so fast that Khayman could not follow them. Yet once the King stopped. To the sun god, Ra, he called out for mercy. Then weeping, hiding their eyes from the sun, crying as if the sun burnt them even though its light had barely come into the sky, the King and the Queen disappeared from Khayman's sight.

" 'Not a day since have they appeared before sunset; they come down out of the sacred cemetery, though no one knows from where. In fact the people now wait for them in a great multitude, hailing them as the god and the goddess, the very image of Osiris and Isis, deities of the moon, and tossing flowers before them, and bowing down to them.

" 'For the tale spread far and wide that the King and Queen had vanquished death at the hands of their enemies by some celestial power; that they are gods, immortal and invincible; and that by that same power they can see into men's hearts. No secret can be kept from them; their enemies are immediately punished; they can hear the words one speaks only in one's head. All fear them.

" 'Yet I know as all their faithful servants know that they cannot bear a candle or a lamp too close to them; that they shriek at the bright light of a torch; and that when they execute their enemies in secret, they drink their blood! They drink it, I tell you. Like jungle cats, they feed upon these victims; and the room after is as a lion's den. And it is I, Khayman, their trusted steward, who must gather these bodies and heave them into the pit.' And then Khayman stopped and gave way to weeping.

"But the tale was finished; and it was almost morning. The sun was rising over the eastern mountains; we made ready to cross the mighty Nile. The desert was warming; Khayman walked to the edge of the river as the first barge of soldiers went across. He was weeping still as he saw the sun come down upon the river; saw the water catch fire.

" 'The sun god, Ra, is the oldest and greatest god of all Kemet,' he whispered. 'And this god has turned against them. Why? In secret they weep over their fate; the thirst maddens them; they are frightened it will become more than they can bear. You must save them. You must do it for our people. They have not sent for you to blame you or harm you. They need you. You are powerful witches. Make this spirit undo his work.' And then looking at us, remembering all that had befallen us, he gave way to despair.

"Mekare and I made no answer. The barge was now ready to carry us to the palace. And we stared across the glare of the water at the great collection of painted buildings that was the royal city, and we wondered what the consequences of this horror would finally be.

"As I stepped down upon the barge, I thought of my child, and I knew suddenly I should die in Kemet. I wanted to close my eyes, and ask the spirits in a small secret voice if this was truly meant to happen, yet I did not dare. I could not have my last hope taken from me."

MAHARET tensed.

Jesse saw her shoulders straighten; saw the fingers of her right hand move against the wood, curling and then opening again, the gold nails gleaming in the firelight.

"I do not want you to be afraid," she said, her voice slipping into monotone. "But you should know that the Mother has crossed the great eastern sea. She and Lestat are closer now . . ."

Jesse felt the current of alarm passing through all those at the table. Maharet remained rigid, listening, or perhaps seeing; the pupils of her eyes moving only slightly.

"Lestat calls," Maharet said. "But it is too faint for me to hear words; too faint for pictures. He is not harmed, however; that much I know, and that I have little time now to finish this story. . . ."

7

LESTAT: THE KINGDOM OF HEAVEN

THE CARIBBEAN. Haiti. The Garden of God.

I stood on the hilltop in the moonlight and I tried not to see this paradise. I tried to picture those I loved. Were they gathered still together in that fairy-tale wood of monster trees, where I had seen my mother walking? If only I could see their faces or hear their voices. Marius, do not be the angry father. Help me! Help us all! I do not give in, but I am losing. I am losing my soul and my mind. My heart is already gone. It belongs to her.

But they were beyond my reach; the great sweep of miles closed us off; I had not the power to overarch that distance.

I looked instead on these verdant green hills, now patched with tiny farms, a picture book world with flowers blooming in profusion, the red poinsettia as tall as trees. And the clouds, ever changing, borne like the tall sailing ships on brisk winds. What had the first Europeans thought when they looked upon this fecund land surrounded by the sparkling sea? That this was the Garden of God?

And to think, they had brought such death to it, the natives gone within a few short years, destroyed by slavery, disease, and endless cruelty. Not a single blood descendant remains of those peaceful beings who had breathed this balmy air, and plucked the fruit from the trees which ripened all year round, and thought their visitors gods perhaps, who could not but return their kindness.

Now, below in the streets of Port-au-Prince, riots and death, and not of our making. Merely the unchanging history of this bloody place, where violence has flourished for four hundred years as flowers flourish; though the vision of the hills rising into the mist could break the heart.

But we had done our work all right, she because she did it, and I because I did nothing to stop it—in the small towns strewn along the winding road that led to this wooded summit. Towns of tiny pastel houses, and banana trees growing wild, and the people so poor, so hungry. Even now the women sang their hymns and, by the light of candles and the burning church, buried the dead.

We were alone. Far beyond the end of the narrow road; where the forest grew again, hiding the ruins of this old house that had once overlooked the valley like a citadel. Centuries since the planters had left here; centuries since they danced and sang and drank their wine within these shattered rooms while the slaves wept.

Over the brick walls, the bougainvillea climbed, fluorescent in the light of the moon. And out of the flagstone floor a great tree had risen, hung with moon blossoms, pushing back with its gnarled limbs the last remnants of the old timbers that had once held the roof.

Ah, to be here forever, and with her. And for the rest to be forgotten. No death, no killing.

She sighed; she said: "This is the Kingdom of Heaven."

In the tiny hamlet below, the women had run barefoot after the men with clubs in hand. And the voodoo priest had screamed his ancient curses as they caught him in the graveyard. I had left the scene of the carnage; I'd climbed the mountain alone. Fleeing, angry, unable any longer to bear witness.

And she had come after, finding me in this ruin, clinging to something that I could understand. The old iron gate, the rusted bell; the brick pillars swathed in vines; things, fashioned by hands, which had endured. Oh, how she had mocked me.

The bell that had called the slaves, she said; this was the dwelling place of those who'd drenched this earth in blood; why was I hurt and driven here by the hymns of simple souls who had been exalted? Would that every such house had fallen to ruin. We had fought. Really fought, as lovers fight.

"Is that what you want?" she had said. "Not ever to taste blood again?"

"I was a simple thing, dangerous yes, but simple. I did what I did to stay alive."

"Oh, you sadden me. Such lies. Such lies. What must I do to make you see? Are you so blind, so selfish!"

I'd glimpsed it again, the pain in her face, the sudden flash of hurt that humanized her utterly. I'd reached out for her.

And for hours we had been in each other's arms, or so it seemed.

And now the peace and the stillness; I walked back from the edge of the cliff, and I held her again. I heard her say as she looked up at the great towering clouds through which the moon poured forth its eerie light: "This is the Kingdom of Heaven."

It did not matter anymore such simple things as lying down together, or sitting on a stone bench. Standing, my arms wound around her, this was pure happiness. And I'd drunk the nectar again, her nectar, even though I'd been weeping, and thinking ah, well, you are being dissolved as a pearl in wine. You're gone, you little devil—you're gone, you know—into her. You stood and watched them die; you stood and watched.

"There is no life without death," she whispered. "I am the way now, the way to the only hope of life without strife that there may ever be." I felt her lips on my mouth. I wondered, would she ever do what she had done in the shrine? Would we lock together like that, taking the heated blood from each other?

"Listen to the singing in the villages, you can hear it."

"Yes."

"And then listen hard for the sounds of the city far below. Do you know how much death is in that city tonight? How many have been massacred? Do you know how many more will die at the hands of men, if we do not change the destiny of this place? If we do not sweep it up into a new vision? Do you know how long this battle has gone on?"

Centuries ago, in my time, this had been the richest colony of the French crown. Rich in tobacco, indigo, coffee. Fortunes had been made here in one season. And now the people picked at the earth; barefoot they walked through the dirt streets of their towns; machine guns barked in the city of Port-au-Prince; the dead in colored cotton shirts lay in heaps on the cobblestones. Children gathered water in cans from the gutters. Slaves had risen; slaves had won; slaves had lost everything.

But it is their destiny; their world; they who are human.

She laughed softly. "And what are we? Are we useless? How do we justify what we are! How do we stand back and watch what we are unwilling to alter?"

"And suppose it is wrong," I said, "and the world is worse for it, and it is all horror finally—unrealizable, unexecutable, what then? And all those men in their graves, the whole earth a graveyard, a funeral pyre. And nothing is better. And it's wrong, wrong."

"Who's to tell you it is wrong?"

I didn't answer.

"Marius?" How scornfully she laughed. "Don't you realize there are no fathers now? Angry or no?"

"There are brothers. And there are sisters," I said. "And in each other we find our fathers and mothers, isn't that so?"

Again she laughed, but it was gentle.

"Brothers and sisters," she said. "Would you like to see your real brothers and sisters?"

I lifted my head from her shoulder. I kissed her cheek. "Yes. I want to see them." My heart was racing again. "Please," I said, even as I kissed her throat, and her cheekbones and her closed eyes. "Please."

"Drink again," she whispered. I felt her bosom swell against me. I pressed my teeth against her throat and the little miracle happened again, the sudden breaking of the crust, and the nectar poured into my mouth.

A great hot wave consumed me. No gravity; no specific time or place. *Akasha.*

Then I saw the redwood trees; the house with the lights burning in it, and in the high mountaintop room, the table and all of them around it, their faces reflected in the walls of dark glass, and the fire dancing. Marius, Gabrielle, Louis, Armand. They're together and they're safe! Am I dreaming this? They're listening to a red-haired woman. And I know this woman! I've seen this woman.

She was in the dream of the red-haired twins.

But I want to see this—these immortals gathered at the table. The young red-haired one, the one at the woman's side, I've seen her too. But she'd been alive then. At the rock concert, in the frenzy, I'd put my arm around her and looked into her crazed eyes. I'd kissed her and said her name; and it was as if a pit had opened under me, and I was falling down into those dreams of the twins that I could never really recall. Painted walls; temples.

It all faded suddenly. *Gabrielle. Mother.* Too late. I was reaching out; I was spinning through the darkness.

You have all of my powers now. You need only time to perfect them. You can bring death, you can move matter, you can make fire. You are ready now to go to them. But we will let them finish their reverie; their stupid schemes and discussion. We will show them a little more of our power—

No, please, Akasha, please, let's go to them.

She drew away from me; she struck me.

I reeled from the shock. Shuddering, cold, I felt the pain spread out through the bones of my face, as if her fingers were still splayed and pressed there. In anger I bit down, letting the pain swell and then recede. In anger I clenched my fists and did nothing.

She walked across the old flags with crisp steps, her hair swaying as it hung down her back. And then she stopped at the fallen gate, her shoulders rising slightly, her back curved as if she were folding into herself.

The voices rose; they reached a pitch before I could stop them. And then they lapsed back, like water receding after a great flood.

I saw the mountains again around me; I saw the ruined house. The pain in my face was gone; but I was shaking.

She turned and looked at me, tensely, her face sharpened, and her eyes slightly narrowed. "They mean so much to you, don't they? What do you think they will do, or say? You think Marius will turn me from my course? I know Marius as you could never know him. I know every pathway of his reason. He is greedy as you are greedy. What do you think I am that I am so easily swayed? I was born a Queen. I have always ruled; even from the shrine I ruled." Her eyes were glazed suddenly. I heard the voices, a dull hum rising. "I ruled if only in legend; if only in the minds of those who came to me and paid me tribute. Princes who played music for me; who brought me offerings and prayers. What do you want of me now? That for you, I renounce my throne, my destiny!"

What answer could I make?

"You can read my heart," I said. "You know what I want, that you go to them, that you give them a chance to speak on these things as you've given me the chance. They have words I don't have. They know things I don't know."

"Oh, but Lestat, I do not love them. I do not love them as I love you. So what does it matter to me what they say? I have no patience for them!"

"But you need them. You said that you did. How can you begin without them? I mean really begin, not with these backward villages, I mean in the cities where the people will fight. Your angels, that's what you called them."

She shook her head sadly. "I need no one," she said, "except . . . Except . . ." She hesitated, and then her face went blank with pure surprise.

I made some little soft sound before I could stop myself; some little expression of helpless grief. I thought I saw her eyes dim; and it seemed the voices were rising again, not in my ears but in hers; and that she stared at me, but that she didn't see me.

"But I will destroy you all if I have to," she said, vaguely, eyes searching for me, but not finding me. "Believe me when I say it. For this time I will not be vanquished; I will not lapse back. I will see my dreams realized."

I looked away from her, through the ruined gateway, over the broken edge of the cliff, and down over the valley. What would I have given to be released from this nightmare? Would I be willing to die by my own hand? My eyes were filled with tears, looking over the dark fields. It was cowardice to think of it; this was my doing! There was no escape now for me.

Stark still she stood, listening; and then she blinked slowly; her shoulders moved as if she carried a great weight inside her. "Why can you not believe in me?" she said.

"Abandon it!" I answered. "Turn away from all such visions." I went to her and took hold of her arms. Almost groggily she looked up. "This is a timeless place we stand in—and those poor villages we've conquered, they are the same as they've been for thousands of years. Let me show you my world, Akasha; let me show you the tiniest part of it! Come with me, like a spy into the cities; not to destroy, but to see!"

Her eyes were brightening again; the lassitude was breaking. She embraced me; and suddenly I wanted the blood again. It was all I could think of, even though I was resisting it; even though I was weeping at the pure weakness of my will. I wanted it. I wanted her and I couldn't fight it; yet my old fantasies came back to me, those long ago visions in which I imagined myself waking her, and taking her with me through the opera houses, and the museums and the symphony halls, through the great capitals and their storehouses of all things beautiful and imperishable that men and women had made over the centuries, artifacts that transcended all evil, all wrongs, all fallibility of the individual soul.

"But what have I to do with such paltry things, my love?" she whispered. "And you would teach me of your world? Ah, such vanity. I am beyond time as I have always been."

But she was gazing at me now with the most heartbroken expression. Sorrow, that's what I saw in her.

"I need you!" she whispered. And for the first time her eyes filled with tears.

I couldn't bear it. I felt the chills rise, as they always do, at moments of surprising pain. But she put her fingers to my lips to silence me.

"Very well, my love," she said. "We'll go to your brothers and sisters, if you wish it. We'll go to Marius. But first, let me hold you one more time, close to my heart. You see, I cannot be other than what I would be. This is what you waked with your singing; this is what I am!"

I wanted to protest, to deny it; I wanted again to begin the argument that would divide us and hurt her. But I couldn't find the words as I looked into her eyes. And suddenly I realized what had happened.

I had found the way to stop her; I had found the key; it had been there before me all the time. It was not her love for me; it was her need of me; the need of one ally in all the great realm; one kindred soul made of the same stuff that she was made of. And she had believed she could make me like herself, and now she knew she could not.

"Ah, but you are wrong," she said, her tears shimmering. "You are only young and afraid." She smiled. "You belong to me. And if it has to be, my prince, I'll destroy you."

I didn't speak. I couldn't. I knew what I had seen; I knew even as she couldn't accept it. Not in all the long centuries of stillness had she ever been alone; had she ever suffered the ultimate isolation. Oh, it was not such a simple thing as Enkil by her side, or Marius come to lay before her his offerings; it was something deeper, infinitely more important than that; she had never all alone waged a war of reason with those around her!

The tears were flowing down her cheeks. Two violent streaks of red. Her mouth was slack; her eyebrows knit in a dark frown, though her face would never be anything but radiant.

"No, Lestat," she said again. "You are wrong. But we must see this through now to the finish; if they must die—all of them—so that you cleave to me, so be it." She opened her arms.

I wanted to move away; I wanted to rail against her again, against her threats; but I didn't move as she came closer.

Here; the warm Caribbean breeze; her hands moving up my back; her fingers slipping through my hair. The nectar flowing into me again, flooding my heart. And her lips on my throat finally; the sudden stab of her teeth through my flesh. Yes! As it had been in the shrine, so long ago, yes! Her blood and my blood. And the deafening thunder of her heart, yes! And it was ecstasy and yet I couldn't yield; I couldn't do it; and she knew it.

8

THE STORY OF THE TWINS CONCLUSION

WE FOUND the palace the same as we remembered it, or perhaps a little more lavish, with more booty from conquered lands. More gold drapery, and even more vivid paintings; and twice as many slaves about, as if they were mere ornaments, their lean naked bodies hung with gold and jewels.

"To a royal cell we were now committed, with graceful chairs and tables, and a fine carpet, and dishes of meat and fish to eat.

"Then at sunset, we heard cheers as the King and the Queen appeared in the palace; all the court went to bow to them, singing anthems to the beauty of their pale skin and their shimmering hair; and to the bodies that had miraculously healed after the assault of the conspirators; all the palace echoed with these hymns of praise.

"But when this little spectacle was finished, we were taken into the bedchamber of the royal couple, and for the first time, by the small light of distant lamps, we beheld the transformation with our own eyes.

"We saw two pale yet magnificent beings, resembling in all particulars what they had been when they were alive; but there was an eerie luminescence surrounding them; their skin was no longer skin. And their minds were no longer entirely their minds. Yet gorgeous they were. As you can well imagine, all of you. Oh, yes, gorgeous, as though the moon had come down from heaven and fashioned them with its light. Amid their dazzling gold furniture they stood, draped in finery, and staring at us with eyes that gleamed like obsidian. And then, with a wholly different voice, a voice softly shaded by music, it seemed, the King spoke:

" 'Khayman's told you what has befallen us,' he said. 'We stand before you the beneficiaries of a great miracle; for we have triumphed over certain death. We are now quite beyond the limitations and needs of human beings; and we see and understand things which were withheld from us before.'

"But the Queen's facade gave way immediately. In a hissing whisper she said, 'You must explain this to us! *What has your spirit done?*'

"We were in worse danger than ever from these monsters; and I tried to convey this warning to Mekare, but at once the Queen laughed. 'Do you think I don't know what you are thinking?' she said.

"But the King begged her to be silent. 'Let the witches use their powers,' he said. 'You know that we have always revered you.'

" 'Yes.' The Queen sneered. 'And you sent this curse upon us.'

"At once I averred that we had not done it, that we had kept faith when we left the kingdom, that we had gone back to our home. And as Mekare studied the pair of them in silence, I begged them to understand that if the spirit had done this, he had done it of his own whim.

" 'Whim!' the Queen said. 'What do you mean by such a word as whim? What has happened to us? What are we!' she asked again. Then she drew back her lips for us to see her teeth. We beheld the fangs in her mouth, tiny, yet sharp as knives. And the King demonstrated to us this change as well.

" 'The better to draw the blood,' he whispered. 'Do you know what this thirst is to us! We cannot satisfy it! Three, four men a night die to feed us, yet we go to our bed tortured by thirst.'

"The Queen tore at her hair as if she would give in to screaming. But the King laid his hand on her arm. 'Advise us, Mekare and Maharet,' he said. 'For we would understand this transformation and how it might be used for good.'

" 'Yes,' the Queen said, struggling to recover. 'For surely such a thing cannot happen without reason . . . .' Then losing her conviction, she fell quiet. Indeed it seemed her small pragmatic view of things, ever puny and seeking for justifications, had collapsed utterly, while the King clung to his illusions as men often do, until very late in life.

"Now, as they fell silent, Mekare went forward and laid her hands upon the King. She laid her hands upon his shoulders; and closed her eyes. Then she laid her hands upon the Queen in the same manner, though the Queen glared at her with venom in her eyes.

" 'Explain to us,' Mekare said, looking at the Queen, 'what happened at the very moment. What do you remember? What did you see?'

"The Queen was silent, her face drawn and suspicious. Her beauty had been, in truth, enhanced by this transformation, yet there was something repellent in her, as if she were not the flower now but the replica of the flower made of pure white wax. And as she grew reflective she appeared somber and vicious, and instinctively I drew close to Mekare to protect her from what might take place.

"But then the Queen spoke:

" 'They came to kill us, the traitors! They would blame it on the spirits; that was the plan. And all to eat the flesh again, the flesh of their mothers and fathers, and the flesh for which they loved to hunt. They came into the house and they stabbed me with their daggers, I their sovereign Queen.' She paused as if seeing these things again before her eyes. 'I fell as they slashed at me, as they drove their daggers into my breast. One cannot live with such wounds as I received; and so as I fell to the floor, I knew that I was dead! Do you hear what I am saying? I knew that nothing could save me. My blood was pouring out onto the floor.

" 'But even as I saw it pooling before me, I realized I was not in my wounded body, that I had already left it, that death had taken me and was drawing me upwards sharply as if through a great tunnel to where I would suffer no more!

" 'I wasn't frightened; I felt nothing; I looked down and saw myself lying pale and covered with blood in that little house. Yet I did not care. I was free of it. But suddenly something took hold of me, took hold of my invisible being! The tunnel was gone; I was caught in a great mesh like a fisherman's net. With all my strength I pushed against it, and it gave with my strength but it did not break and it gripped me and held me fast and I could not rise through it.

" 'When I tried to scream I was in my body again! I felt the agony of my wounds as if the knives were cutting me afresh. But this net, this great net, it still had a hold of me, and instead of being the endless thing it had been before, it was now contracted into a tighter weave like the weave of a great silk veil.

" 'And all about me this thing—visible yet invisible—whirled as if it were wind, lifting me, casting me down, turning me about. The blood gushed from my wounds. And it ran into the weave of this veil, just as it might into the mesh of any fabric.

" 'And that which had been transparent was now drenched in blood. And a monstrous thing I saw, shapeless, and enormous, with my blood broadcast throughout it. And yet this thing had another property to it, a center, it seemed, a tiny burning center which was in me, and ran riot in my body like a frightened animal. Through my limbs it ran, thumping and beating. A heart with legs scampering. In my belly it circled as I clawed at myself. I would have cut myself open to get this thing out of me!

" 'And it seemed the great invisible part of this thing—the blood mist that surrounded me and enveloped me—was controlled by this tiny center, twisting this way and that as it scurried within me, racing into my hands one moment and into my feet the next. Up my spine it ran.

" 'I would die, surely I would die, I thought. Then came a moment of blindness! Silence. It had killed me, I was certain. I should rise again, should I not? Yet suddenly I opened my eyes; I sat up off the floor as if no attack had befallen me; and I saw so clearly! Khayman, the glaring torch in his hand!—the trees of the garden—why, it was as if I had never truly seen such simple things for what they were! The pain was gone completely, from inside and from my wounds as well. Only the light hurt my eyes; I could not endure its brilliance. Yet I had been saved from death; my body had been glorified and made perfect. Except that—' And there she stopped.

"She stared before her, indifferent for a moment. Then she said, 'Khayman has told you all the rest.' She looked to the King who stood beside her, watching her; trying to fathom the things she said, just as we tried to fathom them.

" 'Your spirit,' she said. 'It tried to destroy us. But something else had happened; some great power has intervened to triumph over its diabolical evil.' Then again her conviction deserted her. The lies stopped on her tongue. Her face was suddenly cold with menace. And sweetly she said: 'Tell us, witches, wise witches. You who know all the secrets. What is the name for what we are!'

"Mekare sighed. She looked at me. I knew she didn't want to speak now on this thing. And the old warning of the spirits came back. The Egyptian King and Queen would ask us questions and they would not like our answers. We would be destroyed. . . .

"Then the Queen turned her back. She sat down and bowed her head. And it was then, and only then, that her true sadness came to the fore. The King smiled at us, wearily. 'We are in pain, witches,' he said. 'We could bear the burden of this transformation if only we understood it better. You, who have communed with all things invisible; tell us what you know of such magic; help us, if you will, for you know that we never meant to harm you, only to spread the truth and the law.'

"We did not dwell on the stupidity of this statement—the virtue of spreading the truth through wholesale slaughter and so forth and so on. But Mekare demanded that the King now tell what he could recall.

"He spoke of things which you—all of you seated here—surely know. Of how he was dying; and how he tasted the blood from his wife which had covered his face; and of how his body quickened, and wanted this blood, and then how he took it from his wife and she gave it; and then he became as she was. But for him there was no mysterious cloud of blood. There was no thing running rampant within him. 'The thirst; it's unbearable,' he said to us. 'Unbearable.' And he too bowed his head.

"We stood in silence for a moment looking at each other, Mekare and I, and as always, Mekare spoke first:

" 'We know no name for what you are,' she said. 'We know no stories of such a thing ever happening in this world before. But it's plain enough what took place.' She fixed her eyes upon the Queen. 'As you perceived your own death, your soul sought to make its swift escape from suffering as souls so often do. But as it rose, the spirit Amel seized it, this thing being invisible as your soul was invisible; and in the normal course of things you might have easily overcome this earthbound entity and gone on to realms we do not know.

" 'But this spirit had long before wrought a change within himself; a change that was utterly new. This spirit had tasted the blood of humans whom he had pierced or tormented, as you yourself have seen him do. And your body, lying there, and full of blood despite its many wounds, had life still.

" 'And so the spirit, thirsting, plunged down into your body, his invisible form still wedded to your soul.

" 'Still you might have triumphed, fighting off this evil thing as possessed persons often do. But now the tiny core of this spirit—the thing of matter which is the roaring center of all spirits, from which their endless energy comes—was suddenly filled with blood as never in the past.

" 'And so the fusion of blood and timeless tissue was a million times magnified and accelerated; and blood flowed through all his body, both material and nonmaterial, and this was the blood cloud that you saw.

" 'But it is the pain you felt which is most significant, this pain which traveled through your limbs. For surely as inevitable death came to your body, the spirit's tiny core merged with the flesh of your body as its energy had already merged with your soul. It found some special place or organ in which matter merged with matter as spirit had already merged with spirit; and a new thing was formed.'

" 'Its heart and my heart,' the Queen whispered. 'They became one.' And closing her eyes, she lifted her hand and laid it on her breast.

"We said nothing, for this seemed a simplification, and we did not believe the heart was the center of intellect or emotion. For us, it had been the brain which controlled these things. And in that moment, both Mekare and I saw a terrible memory—our mother's heart and brain thrown down and trampled in ashes and dust.

"But we fought this memory. It was abhorrent that this pain should be glimpsed by those who had been its cause.

"The King pressed us with a question. 'Very well,' he said, 'you've explained what has happened to Akasha. This spirit is in her, core wedded perhaps to core. But what is in me? I felt no such pain, no such scurrying demon. I felt . . . I felt only the thirst when her bloodied hands touched my lips.' He looked to his wife.

"The shame, the horror, they felt over the thirst was clear.

" 'But the same spirit is in you, too,' Mekare answered. 'There is but one Amel. Its core resides in the Queen, but it is in you also.'

" 'How is such a thing possible?' asked the King.

" 'This being has a great invisible part,' Mekare said. 'Were you to have seen it in its entirety, before this catastrophe took place, you would have seen something almost without end.'

" 'Yes,' the Queen confessed. 'It was as if the net covered the whole sky.'

"Mekare explained: 'It is only by concentrating such immense size that these spirits achieve any physical strength. Left on their own, they are as clouds over the horizon; greater even; they have now and then boasted to us that they have no true boundaries, though this is not likely the truth.'

"The King stared at his wife.

" 'But how can it be released!' demanded Akasha.

" 'Yes. How can it be made to depart!' the King asked.

"Neither of us wanted to answer. We wondered that the answer was not obvious to them both. 'Destroy your body,' Mekare said to the Queen finally. 'And it will be destroyed as well.'

"The King looked at Mekare with disbelief. 'Destroy her body!' Helplessly he looked at his wife.

"But Akasha merely smiled bitterly. The words came as no surprise to her. For a long moment, she said nothing. She merely looked at us with plain hatred; then she looked at the King. When she looked to us, she put the question. 'We are dead things, aren't we? We cannot live if it departs. We do not eat; we do not drink, save for the blood it wants; our bodies throw off no waste any longer; we have not changed in one single particular since that awful night; we are not alive anymore.'

"Mekare didn't answer. I knew that she was studying them; struggling to see their forms not as a human would see them but as a witch would see them, to let the quiet and the stillness collect around them, so that she might observe the tiny imperceptible aspects of this which eluded regular gaze. Into a trance she fell as she looked at them and listened. And when she spoke her voice was flat, dull:

" 'It is working on your body; it is working and working as fire works on the wood it consumes; as worms work on the carcass of an animal. It is working and working and its work is inevitable; it is the continuance of the fusion which has taken place; that is why the sun hurts it, for it is using all of its energy to do what it must do; and it cannot endure the sun's heat coming down upon it.'

" 'Or the bright light of a torch even,' the King sighed.

" 'At times not even a candle flame,' said the Queen.

" 'Yes,' Mekare said, shaking off the trance finally. 'And you are dead,' she said in a whisper. 'Yet you are alive! If the wounds healed as you say they did; if you brought the King back as you say you did, why, you may have vanquished death. That is, if you do not go into the burning rays of the sun.'

" 'No, this cannot continue!' the King said. 'The thirst, you don't know how terrible is the thirst.'

"But the Queen only smiled bitterly again. 'These are not living bodies now. These are hosts for this demon.' Her lip trembled as she looked at us. 'Either that or we are truly gods!'

" 'Answer us, witches,' said the King. 'Could it be that we are divine beings now, blessed with gifts that only gods share?' He smiled as he said it; he so wanted to believe it. 'Could it not be that when your demon sought to destroy us, our gods intervened?'

"An evil light shone in the Queen's eye. How she loved this idea, but she didn't believe it . . . not really.

"Mekare looked at me. She wanted me to go forward and to touch them as she had done. She wanted me to look at them as she had done. There was something further that she wanted to say, yet she was not sure of it. And in truth, I had slightly stronger powers of the instinctive nature, though less of a gift for words than she.

"I went forward; I touched their white skin, though it repelled me as they repelled me for all that they had done to our people and us. I touched them and then withdrew and gazed at them; and I saw the work of which Mekare spoke, I could even hear it, the tireless churning of the spirit within. I stilled my mind; I cleared it utterly of all preconception or fear and then as the calmness of the trance deepened in me, I allowed myself to speak.

" 'It wants more humans,' I said. I looked at Mekare. This was what she had suspected.

" 'We offer to it all we can!' the Queen gasped. And the blush of shame came again, extraordinary in its brightness to her pale cheeks. And the King's face colored also. And I understood then, as did Mekare, that when they drank the blood they felt ecstasy. Never had they known such pleasure, not in their beds, not at the banquet table, not when drunk with beer or wine. That was the source of the shame. It hadn't been the killing; it had been the monstrous feeding. It had been the pleasure. Ah, these two were such a pair.

"But they had misunderstood me. 'No,' I explained. 'It wants more like you. It wants to go in and make blood drinkers of others as it did with the King; it is too immense to be contained within two small bodies. The thirst will become bearable only when you make others, for they will share the burden of it with you.'

" 'No!' the Queen screamed. 'That is unthinkable.'

" 'Surely it cannot be so simple!' the King declared. 'Why, we were both made at one and the same terrible instant, when our gods warred with this demon. Conceivably, when our gods warred and won.'

" 'I think not,' I said.

" 'You mean to say,' the Queen asked, 'that if we nourish others with this blood that they too will be so infected?' But she was recalling now every detail of the catastrophe. Her husband dying, the heartbeat gone from him, and then the blood trickling into his mouth.

" 'Why, I haven't enough blood in my body to do such a thing!' she declared. 'I am only what I am!' Then she thought of the thirst and all the bodies that had served it.

"And we realized the obvious point; that she had sucked the blood out of her husband before he had taken it back from her, and that is how the thing had been accomplished; that and the fact that the King was on the edge of death, and most receptive, his own spirit shaking loose and ready to be locked down by the invisible tentacles of Amel.

"Of course they read our thoughts, both of them.

" 'I don't believe what you say,' said the King. 'The gods would not allow it. We are the King and Queen of Kemet. Burden or blessing, this magic has been meant for us.'

"A moment of silence passed. Then he spoke again, most sincerely. 'Don't you see, witches? This was destiny. We were meant to invade your lands, to bring you and this demon here, so that this might befall us. We suffer, true, but we are gods now; this is a holy fire; and we must give thanks for what has happened to us.'

"I tried to stop Mekare from speaking. I clasped her hand tightly. But they already knew what she meant to say. Only her conviction jarred them.

" 'It could very likely pass into anyone,' she said, 'were the conditions duplicated, were the man or woman weakened and dying, so that the spirit could get its grip.'

"In silence they stared at us. The King shook his head. The Queen looked away in disgust. But then the King whispered, 'If this is so, then others may try to take this from us!'

" 'Oh, yes,' Mekare whispered. 'If it would make them immortal? Most surely, they would. For who would not want to live forever?'

"At this the King's face was transformed. He paced back and forth in the chamber. He looked at his wife, who stared forward as one about to go mad, and he said to her most carefully, 'Then we know what we must do. We cannot breed a race of such monsters! We know!'

"But the Queen threw her hands over her ears and began to scream. She began to sob, and finally to roar in her agony, her fingers curling into claws as she looked up at the ceiling above her.

"Mekare and I withdrew to the edges of the room, and held tight to each other. And then Mekare began to tremble, and to cry also, and I felt tears rise in my eyes.

" 'You did this to us!' the Queen roared, and never had we heard a human voice attain such volume. And as she went mad now, shattering everything within the chamber, we saw the strength of Amel in her, for she did things no human could do. The mirrors she hurled at the ceiling; the gilded furniture went to splinters under her fists. 'Damn you into the lower world among demons and beasts forever!' she cursed us, 'for what you have done to us. Abominations. Witches. You and your demon! You say you did not send this thing to us. But in your hearts you did. You sent this demon! And he read it from your hearts, just as I read it now, that you wished us evil!'

"But then the King caught her in his arms and hushed her and kissed her and caught her sobs against his chest.

"Finally she broke away from him. She stared at us, her eyes brimming with blood. 'You lie!' she said. 'You lie as your demons lied before. Do you think such a thing could happen if it was not meant to happen!' She turned to the King. 'Oh, don't you see, we've been fools to listen to these mere mortals, who have not such powers as we have! Ah, but we are young deities and must struggle to learn the designs of heaven. And surely our destiny is plain; we see it in the gifts we possess.'

"We didn't respond to what she had said. It seemed to me at least for a few precious moments that it was a mercy if she could believe such nonsense. For all I could believe was that Amel, the evil one, Amel, the stupid, the dull-witted, the imbecile spirit, had stumbled into this disastrous fusion and that perhaps the whole world would pay the price. My mother's warning came back to me. All our suffering came back to me. And then such thoughts—wishes for the destruction of the King and Queen—seized me that I had to cover my head with my hands and shake myself and try to clear my mind, lest I face their wrath.

"But the Queen was paying no mind to us whatsoever, except to scream to her guards that they must at once take us prisoner, and that tomorrow night she would pass judgment upon us before the whole court.

"And quite suddenly we were seized; and as she gave her orders with gritted teeth and dark looks, the soldiers dragged us away roughly and threw us like common prisoners into a lightless cell.

"Mekare took hold of me and whispered that until the sun rose we must think nothing that could bring us harm; we must sing the old songs we knew and pace the floor so that as not even to dream dreams that would offend the King and Queen, for she was mortally afraid.

"Now I had never truly seen Mekare so afraid. Mekare was always the one to rave in anger; it was I who hung back imagining the most terrible things.

"But when dawn came, when she was sure the demon King and Queen had gone to their secret retreat, she burst into tears.

" 'I did it, Maharet,' she said to me. 'I did it. I sent him against them. I tried not to do it; but Amel, he read it in my heart. It was as the Queen said, exactly.'

"There was no end to her recriminations. It was she who had spoken to Amel; she who had strengthened him and puffed him up and kept his interest; and then she had wished his wrath upon the Egyptians and he had known.

"I tried to comfort her. I told her none of us could control what was in our hearts; that Amel had saved our lives once; that no one could fathom these awful choices, these forks in the road; and we must now banish all guilts and look only to the future. How could we get free of this place? How could we make these monsters release us? Our good spirits would not frighten them now; not a chance of it; we must think; we must plan; we must do something.

"Finally, the thing for which I secretly hoped happened: Khayman appeared. But he was even more thin and drawn than before.

" 'I think you are doomed, my red-haired ones,' he said to us. 'The King and Queen were in a quandary over the things which you said to them; before morning they went to the temple of Osiris to pray. Could you not give them any hope of reclamation? Any hope this horror would come to an end?'

" 'Khayman, there is one hope,' Mekare whispered. 'Let the spirits be my witness; I don't say that you should do it. I only answer your question. If you would put an end to this, put an end to the King and Queen. Find their hiding place and let the sun come down upon them, the sun which their new bodies cannot bear.'

"But he turned away, terrified by the prospect of such treason. Only to look back and sigh and say, 'Ah, my dear witches. Such things I've seen. And yet I dare not do such a thing.'

"As the hours passed we went through agony, for surely we would be put to death. But there were no regrets any longer in us for the things we'd said, or the things we'd done. And as we lay in the dark in one another's arms, we sang the old songs again from our childhood; we sang our mother's songs; I thought of my little baby and I tried to go to her, to rise in spirit from this place and be close to her, but without the trance potion, I could not do it. I had never learned such skill.

"Finally dusk fell. And soon we heard the multitude singing hymns as the King and Queen approached. The soldiers came for us. Into the great open court of the palace we were brought as we had been before. Here it was that Khayman had laid his hands upon us and we had been dishonored, and before those very same spectators we were brought, with our hands bound again.

"Only it was night and the lamps burnt low in the arcades of the court; and an evil light played upon the gilded lotus blossoms of the pillars, and upon the painted silhouettes which covered the walls. At last the King and Queen stepped upon the dais. And all those assembled fell to their knees. The soldiers forced us into the same subservience. And then the Queen stepped forward and began to speak.

"In a quavering voice, she told her subjects that we were monstrous witches, and that we had loosed upon this kingdom the demon which had only lately plagued Khayman and tried its evil devilment upon the King and Queen themselves. But lo, the great god Osiris, oldest of all the gods, stronger even than the god Ra, had cast down this diabolical force and raised up into celestial glory the King and the Queen.

"But the great god could not look kindly upon the witches who had so troubled his beloved people. And he demanded now that no mercy be shown.

" 'Mekare, for your evil lies and your discourse with demons,' the Queen said, 'your tongue shall be torn from your mouth. And Maharet, for the evil which you have envisioned and sought to make us believe in, your eyes shall be plucked out! And all night, you shall be bound together, so that you may hear each other's weeping, the one unable to speak, the other unable to see. And then at high noon tomorrow in the public place before the palace you shall be burnt alive for all the people to see.

" 'For behold, no such evil shall ever prevail against the gods of Egypt and their chosen King and Queen. For the gods have looked upon us with benevolence and special favor, and we are as the King and Queen of Heaven, and our destiny is for the common good!'

"I was speechless as I heard the condemnation; my fear, my sorrow lay beyond my reach. But Mekare cried out at once in defiance. She startled the soldiers as she pulled away from them and stepped forward. Her eyes were on the stars as she spoke. And above the shocked whispers of the court she declared:

" 'Let the spirits witness; for theirs is the knowledge of the future—both what it would be, *and what I will!* You are the Queen of the Damned, that's what you are! Your only destiny is evil, as well you know! But I shall stop you, if I must come back from the dead to do it. At the hour of your greatest menace it is I who will defeat you! It is I who will bring you down. Look well upon my face, for you will see me again!'

"And no sooner had she spoken this oath, this prophecy, than the spirits, gathering, began their whirlwind and the doors of the palace were flung open and the sands of the desert salted the air.

"Screams rose from the panic-stricken courtiers.

"But the Queen cried out to her soldiers: 'Cut out her tongue as I have commanded you!' and though the courtiers were clinging to the walls in terror, the soldiers came forward and caught hold of Mekare and cut out her tongue.

"In cold horror I watched it happen; I heard her gasp as it was done. And then with astonishing fury, she thrust them aside with her bound hands and going down on her knees snatched up the bloody tongue and swallowed it before they would tramp upon it or throw it aside.

"Then the soldiers laid hold of me.

"The last things I beheld were Akasha, her finger pointed, her eyes gleaming. And then the stricken face of Khayman with tears streaming down his cheeks. The soldiers clamped their hands on my head and pushed back my eyelids and tore all vision from me, as I wept without a sound.

"Then suddenly, I felt a warm hand lay hold of me; and I felt something against my lips. Khayman had my eyes; Khayman was pressing them to my lips. And at once I swallowed them lest they be desecrated or lost.

"The wind grew fiercer; sand swirled about us, and I heard the courtiers running now in all directions, some coughing, others gasping, and many crying as they fled, while the Queen implored her subjects to be calm. I turned, groping for Mekare, and felt her head come down on my shoulder, her hair against my cheek.

" 'Burn them now!' declared the King.

" 'No, it is too soon,' said the Queen. 'Let them suffer.'

"And we were taken away, and bound together, and left alone finally on the floor of the little cell.

"For hours the spirits raged about the palace; but the King and Queen comforted their people, and told them not to be afraid. At noon tomorrow all evil would be expurgated from the kingdom; and until then let the spirits do what they would.

"Finally, it was still and quiet as we lay together. It seemed nothing walked in the palace save the King and the Queen. Even our guards slept.

"And these are the last hours of my life, I thought. And will her suffering be more than mine in the morning, for she shall see me burn, whereas I cannot see her, and she cannot even cry out. I held Mekare to me. She laid her head against my heartbeat. And so the minutes passed.

"Finally, it must have been three hours before morning, I heard noises outside the cell. Something violent; the guard giving a sharp cry and then falling. The man had been slain. Mekare stirred beside me. I heard the lock pulled, and the pivots creak. Then it seemed I heard a noise from Mekare, something like unto a moan.

"Someone had come into the cell, and I knew by my old instinctive power that it was Khayman. As he cut the ropes which bound us, I reached out and clasped his hand. But instantly I thought, this is not Khayman! And then I understood. 'They have done it to you! They have worked it on you.'

" 'Yes,' he whispered, and his voice was full of wrath and bitterness, and a new sound had crept into it, an inhuman sound. 'They have done it! To put it to the test, they have done it! To see if you spoke the truth! They have put this evil into *me.*' It seemed he was sobbing; a rough dry sound, coming from his chest. And I could feel the immense strength of his fingers, for though he didn't want to hurt my hand, he was.

" 'Oh, Khayman,' I said, weeping. 'Such treachery from those you've served so well.'

" 'Listen to me, witches,' he said, his voice guttural and full of rage. 'Do you want to die tomorrow in fire and smoke before an ignorant populace; or would you fight this evil thing? Would you be its equal and its enemy upon this earth? For what stays the power of mighty men save that of others of the same strength? What stops the swordsman but a warrior of the same mettle? Witches, if they could do this to me, can I not do it to you?'

"I shrank back, away from him, but he wouldn't let me go. I didn't know if it was possible. I knew only that I didn't want it.

" 'Maharet,' he said. 'They shall make a race of fawning acolytes unless they are beaten, and who can beat them save ones as powerful as themselves!'

" 'No, I would die first,' I said, yet even as the words left me I thought of the waiting flames. But no, it was unforgivable. Tomorrow I should go to my mother; I should leave here forever, and nothing could make me remain.

" 'And you, Mekare?' I heard him say. 'Will you reach now for the fulfillment of your own curse? Or die and leave it to the spirits who have failed you from the start?'

"The wind came up again, howling about the palace; I heard the outside doors rattling; I heard the sand flung against the walls. Servants ran through distant passages; sleepers rose from their beds. I could hear the faint, hollow, and unearthly wails of the spirits I most loved.

" 'Be still,' I told them, 'I will not do it. I will not let this evil in.'

"But as I knelt there, leaning my head against the wall, and reasoning that I must die, and must somehow find the courage for it, I realized that within the small confines of this cell, the unspeakable magic was being worked again. As the spirits railed against it, Mekare had made her choice. I reached out and felt these two forms, man and woman, melded like lovers; and as I struggled to part them, Khayman struck me, knocking me unconscious on the floor.

"Surely only a few minutes passed. Somewhere in the blackness, the spirits wept. The spirits knew the final outcome before I did. The winds died away; a hush fell in the blackness; the palace was still.

"My sister's cold hands touched me. I heard a strange sound like laughter; can those who have no tongue laugh? I made no decision really; I knew only that all our lives we had been the same; twins and mirror images of each other; two bodies it seemed and one soul. And I was sitting now in the hot close darkness of this little place, and I was in my sister's arms, and for the first time she was changed and we were not the same being; and yet we were. And then I felt her mouth against my throat; I felt her hurting me; and Khayman took his knife and did the work for her; and the swoon began.

"Oh, those divine seconds; those moments when I saw again within my brain the lovely light of the silver sky; and my sister there before me smiling, her arms uplifted as the rain came down. We were dancing in the rain together, and all our people were there with us, and our bare feet sank into the wet grass; and when the thunder broke and the lightning tore the sky, it was as if our souls had released all their pain. Drenched by the rain we went deep into the cave together; we lighted one small lamp and looked at the old paintings on the walls—the paintings done by all the witches before us; huddling together, with the sound of the distant rain we lost ourselves in these paintings of witches dancing; of the moon coming for the first time into the night sky.

"Khayman fed me the magic; then my sister; then Khayman again. You know what befell me, don't you? But do you know what the Dark Gift is for those who are blind? Tiny sparks flared in the gaseous gloom; then it seemed a glowing light began to define the shapes of things around me in weak pulses; like the afterimages of bright things when one closes one's eyes.

"Yes, I could move through this darkness. I reached out to verify what I beheld. The doorway, the wall; then the corridor before me; a faint map flashed for a second of the path ahead.

"Yet never had the night seemed so silent; nothing inhuman breathed in the darkness. The spirits were utterly gone.

"And never, never again did I ever hear or see the spirits. Never ever again were they to answer my questions or my call. The ghosts of the dead yes, but the spirits, gone forever.

"But I did not realize this abandonment in those first few moments, or hours, or even in the first few nights.

"So many other things astonished me; so many other things filled me with agony or joy.

"Long before the sunrise, we were hidden, as the King and Queen were hidden, deep within a tomb. It was to the grave of Khayman's own father that he took us, the grave to which the poor desecrated corpse had been restored. I had by then drunk my first draught of mortal blood. I had known the ecstasy which made the King and Queen blush for shame. But I had not dared to steal the eyes of my victim; I had not even thought such a thing might work.

"It was five nights later that I made such a discovery; and saw as a blood drinker truly sees for the first time.

"By then we had fled the royal city, moving north all night. And in place after place, Khayman had revealed the magic to various persons declaring that they must rise up against the King and Queen, for the King and Queen would have them believe they alone had the power, which was only the worst of their many lies.

"Oh, the rage Khayman felt in those early nights. To any who wanted the power he gave it, even when he was so weakened that he could scarce walk at our side. That the King and the Queen should have worthy enemies, that was his vow. How many blood drinkers were created in those thoughtless weeks, blood drinkers who would increase and multiply and create the battles of which Khayman dreamed?

"But we were doomed in this first stage of the venture—doomed in the first rebellion, doomed in our escape. We were soon to be separated forever—Khayman, Mekare, and I.

"Because the King and Queen, horrified at Khayman's defection, and suspecting that he had given us the magic, sent their soldiers after us, men who could search by day as well as night. And as we hunted ravenously to feed our newborn craving, our trail was ever easy to follow along the small villages of the riverbank or even to the encampments of the hills.

"And finally not a fortnight after we had fled the royal palace, we were caught by the mobs outside the gates of Saqqâra, less than two nights' walk from the sea.

"If only we had reached the sea. If only we had remained together. The world had been born over again to us in darkness; desperately we loved one another; desperately we had exchanged our secrets by the light of the moon.

"But a trap lay waiting for us at Saqqâra. And though Khayman did manage to fight his way to freedom, he saw that he could not possibly save us, and went deep into the hills to wait his moment, but it never came.

"Mekare and I were surrounded as you remember, as you have seen in your dreams. My eyes were torn from me again; and we feared the fire now, for surely that could destroy us; and we prayed to all things invisible for final release.

"But the King and the Queen feared to destroy our bodies. They had believed Mekare's account of the one great spirit, Amel, who infected all of us, and they feared that whatever pain we might feel would then be felt by them. Of course this was not so; but who could know it then?

"And so into the stone coffins we were put, as I've told you. One to be taken to the east and one to the west. The rafts had already been made to set us adrift in the great oceans. I had seen them even in my blindness; we were being carried away upon them; and I knew from the minds of my captors what they meant to do. I knew also that Khayman could not follow, for the march would go on by day as it had by night, and surely this was true.

"When I awoke, I was drifting on the breast of the sea. For ten nights the raft carried me as I've told you. Starvation and terror I suffered, lest the coffin sink to the bottom of the waters; lest I be buried alive forever, a thing that cannot die. But this did not happen. And when I came ashore at last on the eastern coast of lower Africa, I began my search for Mekare, crossing the continent to the west.

"For centuries I searched from one tip of the continent to the other. I went north in Europe. I traveled up and down along the rocky beaches, and even into the northern islands, until I reached the farthest wastes of ice and snow. Over and over again, however, I journeyed back to my own village, and that part of the story I will tell you in a moment, for it is very important to me that you know it, as you will see.

"But during those early centuries I turned my back upon Egypt; I turned my back upon the King and Queen.

"Only much later, did I learn that the King and Queen made a great religion of their transformation; that they took upon themselves the identity of Osiris and Isis, and darkened those old myths to suit themselves.

" 'God of the underworld' Osiris became—that is, the King who could appear only in darkness. And the Queen became Isis, the Mother, who gathers up her husband's battered and dismembered body and heals it and brings it back to life.

"You've read in Lestat's pages—in the tale Marius told to Lestat as it was told to him—of how the blood gods created by the Mother and Father took the blood sacrifice of evildoers in shrines hidden within the hills of Egypt; and how this religion endured until the time of Christ.

"And you have learned something also of how Khayman's rebellion succeeded, how the equal enemies of the King and Queen whom he had created eventually rose up against the Mother and Father; and how great wars were fought among the blood drinkers of the world. Akasha herself revealed these things to Marius, and Marius revealed them to Lestat.

"In those early centuries, the Legend of the Twins was born; for the Egyptian soldiers who had witnessed the events of our lives from the massacre of our people to our final capture were to tell the tales. The Legend of the Twins was even written by the scribes of Egypt in later times. It was believed that one day Mekare would reappear to strike down the Mother, and all the blood drinkers of the world would die as the Mother died.

"But all this happened without my knowledge, my vigilance, or my collusion, for I was long gone from such things.

"Only three thousand years later did I come to Egypt, an anonymous being, swathed in black robes, to see for myself what had become of the Mother and Father—listless, staring statues, shut up in stone in their underground temple, with only their heads and throats exposed. And to the priestly blood drinkers who guarded them, the young ones came, seeking to drink from the primal fount.

"Did I wish to drink, the young blood drinker priest asked me. Then I must go to the Elders and declare my purity and my devotion to the old worship, declare that I was not a rogue bent upon selfish ends. I could have laughed.

"But oh, the horror to see those staring things! To stand before them and whisper the names Akasha and Enkil, and see not a flicker within the eye or the tiniest twitch of the white skin.

"And so they had been for as long as anyone could remember, and so the priests told me; no one even knew anymore if the myths of the beginning were true. We—the very first children—had come to be called merely the First Brood who had spawned the rebels; but the Legend of the Twins was forgotten; and no one knew the names Khayman or Mekare or Maharet.

"Only one time later was I to see them, the Mother and the Father. Another thousand years had passed. The great burning had just happened when the Elder in Alexandria—as Lestat has told you—sought to destroy the Mother and the Father by placing them in the sun. They'd been merely bronzed by the day's heat as Lestat told it, so strong had they become; for though we all sleep helplessly by day, the light itself becomes less lethal with the passage of time.

"But all over the world blood drinkers had gone up in flames during those daylight hours in Egypt; while the very old ones had suffered and darkened but nothing more. My beloved Eric was then one thousand years; we lived together in India; and he was during those interminable hours severely burned. It took great draughts of my blood to restore him. I myself was bronzed only, and though I lived with great pain for many nights, there was a curious side effect to it: it was then easier for me to pass among human beings with this dark skin.

"Many centuries later, weary of my pale appearance, I was to burn myself in the sun deliberately. I shall probably do it again.

"But it was all a mystery to me the first time it happened. I wanted to know why I had seen fire and heard the cries of so many perishing in my dreams, and why others whom I had made—beloved fledglings—had died this unspeakable death.

"And so I journeyed from India to Egypt, which to me has always been a hateful place. It was then I heard tell of Marius, a young Roman blood drinker, miraculously unburnt, who had come and stolen the Mother and Father and taken them out of Alexandria where no one could ever burn them—or us—again.

"It was not difficult to find Marius. As I've told you, in the early years we could never hear each other. But as time passed we could hear the younger ones just as if they were human beings. In Antioch, I discovered Marius's house, a virtual palace where he lived a life of Roman splendor though he hunted the dark streets for human victims in the last hours before dawn.

"He had already made an immortal of Pandora, whom he loved above all other things on earth. And the Mother and Father he had placed in an exquisite shrine, made by his own hands of Carrara marble and mosaic flooring, in which he burned incense as if it were a temple, as if they were truly gods.

"I waited for my moment. He and Pandora went to hunt. And then I entered the house, making the locks give way from the inside.

"I saw the Mother and Father, darkened as I had been darkened, yet beautiful and lifeless as they'd been a thousand years before. On a throne he'd placed them, and so they would sit for two thousand years, as you all know. I went to them; I touched them. I struck them. They did not move. Then with a long dagger I made my test. I pierced the flesh of the Mother, which had become an elastic coating as my flesh had become. I pierced the immortal body which had become both indestructible and deceptively fragile, and my blade went right through her heart. From right to left I slashed with it, then stopped.

"Her blood poured viscous and thick for a moment; for a moment the heart ceased to beat; then the rupture began to heal; the spilt blood hardened like amber as I watched.

"But most significant, I had felt that moment when the heart failed to pump the blood; I had felt the dizziness, the vague disconnection; the very whisper of death. No doubt, all through the world blood drinkers had felt it, perhaps the young ones strongly, a shock which knocked them off their feet. The core of Amel was still within her; the terrible burning and the dagger, these things proved that the life of the blood drinkers resided within her body as it always would.

"I would have destroyed her then, if it had not been so. I would have cut her limb from limb; for no span of time could ever cool my hatred for her; my hatred for what she had done to my people; for separating Mekare from me. Mekare my other half; Mekare my own self.

"How magnificent it would have been if the centuries had schooled me in forgiveness; if my soul had opened to understand all the wrongs done me and my people.

"But I tell you, it is the soul of humankind which moves towards perfection over the centuries, the human race which learns with each passing year how better to love and forgive. I am anchored to the past by chains I cannot break.

"Before I left, I wiped away all trace of what I had done. For an hour perhaps I stared at the two statues, the two evil beings who had so long ago destroyed my kindred and brought such evil upon me and my sister; and who had known such evil in return.

" 'But you did not win, finally,' I said to Akasha. 'You and your soldiers and their swords. For my child, Miriam, survived to carry the blood of my family and my people forward in time; and this, which may mean nothing to you as you sit there in silence, means all things to me.'

"And the words I spoke were true. But I will come to the story of my family in a moment. Let me deal now with Akasha's one victory: that Mekare and I were never united again.

"For as I have told you, never in all my wanderings did I ever find a man, woman, or blood drinker who had gazed upon Mekare or heard her name. Through all the lands of the world I wandered, at one time or another, searching for Mekare. But she was gone from me as if the great western sea had swallowed her; and I was as half a being reaching out always for the only thing which can render me complete.

"Yet in the early centuries, I knew Mekare lived; there were times when the twin I was felt the suffering of the other twin; in dark dreamlike moments, I knew inexplicable pain. But these are things which human twins feel for each other. As my body grew harder, as the human in me melted away and this more powerful and resilient immortal body grew dominant, I lost the simple human link with my sister. Yet I knew, I knew that she was alive.

"I spoke to my sister as I walked the lonely coast, glancing out over the ice cold sea. And in the grottoes of Mount Carmel I made our story in great drawings—all that we had suffered—the panorama which you beheld in the dreams.

"Over the centuries many mortals were to find that grotto, and to see those paintings; and then they would be forgotten again, to be discovered anew.

"Then finally in this century, a young archaeologist, hearing tell of them, climbed Mount Carmel one afternoon with a lantern in his hand. And when he gazed on the pictures that I had long ago made, his heart leapt because he had seen these very same images on a cave across the sea, above the jungles in Peru.

"It was years before his discovery was known to me. He had traveled far and wide with his bits and pieces of evidence—photographs of the cave drawings from both the Old World and the New; and a vase he found in the storage room of a museum, an ancient artifact from those dim forgotten centuries when the Legend of the Twins was still known.

"I cannot tell you the pain and happiness I experienced when I looked at the photographs of the pictures he had discovered in a shallow cave in the New World.

"For Mekare had drawn there the very same things that I had drawn; the brain, the heart, and the hand so much like my own had given expression to the same images of suffering and pain. Only the smallest differences existed. But the proof was beyond denial.

"Mekare's bark had carried her over the great western ocean to a land unknown in our time. Centuries perhaps before man had penetrated the southern reaches of the jungle continent, Mekare had come ashore there, perhaps to know the greatest loneliness a creature can know. How long had she wandered among birds and beasts before she'd seen a human face?

"Had it been centuries, or millennia, this inconceivable isolation? Or had she found mortals at once to comfort her, or run from her in terror? I was never to know. My sister may have lost her reason long before the coffin which carried her ever touched the South American shore.

"All I knew was that she had been there; and thousands of years ago she had made those drawings, just as I had made my own.

"Of course I lavished wealth upon this archaeologist; I gave him every means to continue his research into the Legend of the Twins. And I myself made the journey to South America. With Eric and Mael beside me, I climbed the mountain in Peru by the light of the moon and saw my sister's handiwork for myself. So ancient these paintings were. Surely they had been done within a hundred years of our separation and very possibly less.

"But we were never to find another shred of evidence that Mekare lived or walked in the South American jungles, or anywhere else in this world. Was she buried deep in the earth, beyond where the call of Mael or Eric could reach her? Did she sleep in the depths of some cave, a white statue, staring mindlessly, as her skin was covered with layer upon layer of dust?

"I cannot conceive of it. I cannot bear to think on it.

"I know only, as you know now, that she has risen. She has waked from her long slumber. Was it the songs of the Vampire Lestat that waked her? Those electronic melodies that reached the far corners of the world? Was it the thoughts of the thousands of blood drinkers who heard them, interpreted them, and responded to them? Was it Marius's warning that the Mother walks?

"Perhaps it was some dim sense collected from all these signals—that the time had come to fulfill the old curse. I cannot tell you. I know only that she moves northward, that her course is erratic, and that all efforts on my part through Eric and Mael to find her have failed.

"It is not me she seeks. I am convinced of it. It is the Mother. And the Mother's wanderings throw her off course.

"But she will find the Mother if that is her purpose! She will find the Mother! Perhaps she will come to realize that she can take to the air as the Mother can, and she will cover the miles in the blink of an eye when that discovery is made.

"But she will find the Mother. I know it. And there can be but one outcome. Either Mekare will perish; or the Mother will perish, and with the Mother so shall all of us.

"Mekare's strength is equal to mine, if not greater. It is equal to the Mother's; and she may draw from her madness a ferocity which no one can now measure or contain.

"I am no believer of curses; no believer of prophecy; the spirits that taught me the validity of such things deserted me thousands of years ago. But Mekare believed the curse when she uttered it. It came from the depths of her being; she set it into motion. And her dreams now speak only of the beginning, of the sources of her rancor, which surely feed the desire for revenge.

"Mekare may bring about the fulfillment; and it may be the better thing for us all. And if she does not destroy Akasha, if we do not destroy Akasha, what will be the outcome? We know now what evils the Mother has already begun to do. Can the world stop this thing if the world understands nothing of it? That it is immensely strong, yet certainly vulnerable; with the power to crush, yet skin and bone that can be pierced or cut? This thing that can fly, and read minds, and make fire with its thoughts; yet can be burnt itself?

"How can we stop her and save ourselves, that is the question. I want to live, as I have always wanted it. I do not want to close my eyes on this world. I do not want those I love to come to harm. Even the young ones, who must take life, I struggle in my mind to find some way to protect them. Is this evil of me? Or are we not a species, and do we not share the desire of any species to live on?

"Hearken to everything that I've told you of the Mother. To what I've said of her soul, and of the nature of the demon that resides in her—its core wedded to her core. Think on the nature of this great invisible thing which animates each one of us, and every blood drinker who has ever walked.

"We are as receptors for the energy of this being; as radios are receptors for the invisible waves that bring sound. Our bodies are no more than shells for this energy. We are—as Marius so long ago described it—blossoms on a single vine.

"Examine this mystery. For if we examine it closely perhaps we can yet find a way to save ourselves.

"And I would have you examine one thing further in regard to it; perhaps the single most valuable thing which I have ever learned.

"In those early times, when the spirits spoke to my sister and me on the side of the mountain, what human being would have believed that the spirits were irrelevant things? Even we were captives of their power, thinking it our duty to use the gifts we possessed for the good of our people, just as Akasha would later believe.

"For thousands of years after that, the firm belief in the supernatural has been part of the human soul. There were times when I would have said it was natural, chemical, an indispensable ingredient in the human makeup; something without which humans could not prosper, let alone survive.

"Again and again we have witnessed the birth of cults and religions—the dreary proclamations of apparitions and miracles and the subsequent promulgation of the creeds inspired by these 'events.'

"Travel the cities of Asia and Europe—behold the ancient temples still standing, and the cathedrals of the Christian god in which his hymns are still sung. Walk through the museums of all countries; it is religious painting and sculpture that dazzles and humbles the soul.

"How great seems that achievement; the very machinery of culture dependent upon the fuel of religious belief.

"Yet what has been the price of that faith which galvanizes countries and sends army against army; which divides up the map of nations into victor and vanquished; which annihilates the worshipers of alien gods.

"But in the last few hundred years, a true miracle has happened which has nothing to do with spirits or apparitions, or voices from the heavens telling this or that zealot what he must now do!

"We have seen in the human animal a resistance finally to the miraculous; a skepticism regarding the works of spirits, or those who claim to see them and understand them and speak their truths.

"We have seen the human mind slowly abandon the traditions of law based upon revelation, to seek ethical truths through reason; and a way of life based upon respect for the physical and the spiritual as perceived by all human beings.

"And with this loss of respect for supernatural intervention; with this credulity of all things divorced from the flesh, has come the most enlightened age of all; for men and women seek for the highest inspiration not in the realm of the invisible, but in the realm of the human—the thing which is both flesh and spirit; invisible and visible; earthly and transcendent.

"The psychic, the clairvoyant, the witch, if you will, is no longer of value, I am convinced of it. The spirits can give us nothing more. In sum, we have outgrown our susceptibility to such madness, and we are moving to a perfection that the world has never known.

"The word has been made flesh at last, to quote the old biblical phrase with all its mystery; but the word is the word of reason; and the flesh is the acknowledgment of the needs and the desires which all men and women share.

"And what would our Queen do for this world with her intervention? What would she give it—she whose very existence is now irrelevant, she whose mind has been locked for centuries in a realm of unenlightened dreams?

"She must be stopped; Marius is right; who could disagree with him?

We must stand ready to help Mekare, not to thwart her, even if it means the end for us all.

"But let me lay before you now the final chapter of my tale in which lies the fullest illumination of the threat that the Mother poses to us all:

"As I've already said, Akasha did not annihilate my people. They lived on in my daughter Miriam and in her daughters, and those daughters born to them.

"Within twenty years I had returned to the village where I'd left Miriam, and found her a young woman who had grown up on the stories that would become the Legend of the Twins.

"By the light of the moon I took her with me up the mountain and revealed to her the caves of her ancestors, and gave her the few necklaces and the gold that was still hidden deep within the painted grottoes where others feared to go. And I told Miriam all the stories of her ancestors which I knew. But I adjured her: stay away from the spirits; stay away from all dealings with things invisible, whatever people call them, and especially if they are called gods.

"Then I went to Jericho, for there in the crowded streets it was easy to hunt for victims, for those who wished for death and would not trouble my conscience; and easy to hide from prying eyes.

"But I was to visit Miriam many times over the years; and Miriam gave birth to four daughters and two sons, and these gave birth in turn to some five children who lived to maturity and of these five, two were women, and of those women eight different children were born. And the legends of the family were told by their mothers to these children; the Legend of the Twins they also learned—the legend of the sisters who had once spoken to spirits, and made the rain fall, and were persecuted by the evil King and Queen.

"Two hundred years later, I wrote down for the first time all the names of my family, for they were an entire village now, and it took four whole clay tablets for me to record what I knew. I then filled tablet after tablet with the stories of the beginning, of the women who had gone back to The Time Before the Moon.

"And though I wandered sometimes for a century away from my homeland, searching for Mekare, hunting the wild coasts of northern Europe, I always came back to my people, and to my secret hiding places in the mountains and to my house in Jericho, and I wrote down again the progress of the family, which daughters had been born and the names of those daughters born to them. Of the sons, too, I wrote in detail—of their accomplishments, and personalities, and sometime heroism—as I did with the women. But of their offspring no. It was not possible to know if the children of the men were truly of my blood, and of my people's blood. And so the thread became matrilineal as it has always been since.

"But never, never, in all this time, did I reveal to my family the evil magic which had been done to me. I was determined that this evil should never touch the family; and so if I used my ever increasing supernatural powers, it was in secret, and in ways that could be naturally explained.

"By the third generation, I was merely a kinswoman who had come home after many years in another land. And when and if I intervened, to bring gold or advice to my daughters, it was as a human being might do it, and nothing more.

"Thousands of years passed as I watched the family in anonymity, only now and then playing the long lost kinswoman to come into this or that village or family gathering and hold the children in my arms.

"But by the early centuries of the Christian era, another concept had seized my imagination. And so I created the fiction of a branch of the family which kept all its records—for there were now tablets and scrolls in abundance, and even bound books. And in each generation of this fictional branch, there was a fictional woman to whom the task of recordkeeping was passed. The name of Maharet came with the honor; and when time demanded it, old Maharet would die, and young Maharet would inherit the task.

"And so I myself was within the family; and the family knew me; and I knew the family's love. I became the writer of letters; the benefactor; the unifier; the mysterious yet trusted visitor who appeared to heal breaches and right wrongs. And though a thousand passions consumed me; though I lived for centuries in different lands, learning new languages and customs, and marveling at the infinite beauty of the world, and the power of the human imagination, I always returned to the family, the family which knew me and expected things from me.

"As the centuries passed, as the millennia passed, I never went down into the earth as many of you have done. I never faced madness and loss of memory as was common among the old ones, who became often like the Mother and Father, statues buried beneath the ground. Not a night has passed since those early times that I have not opened my eyes, known my own name, and looked with recognition upon the world around me, and reached for the thread of my own life.

"But it was not that madness didn't threaten. It was not that weariness did not sometimes overwhelm. It was not that grief did not embitter me, or that mysteries did not confuse me, or that I did not know pain.

"It was that I had the records of my family to safeguard; I had my own progeny to look after, and to guide in the world. And so even in the darkest times, when all human existence seemed monstrous to me and unbearable, and the changes of the world beyond comprehension, I turned to the family as if it were the very spring of life itself.

"And the family taught me the rhythms and passions of each new age; the family took me into alien lands where perhaps I would never have ventured alone; the family took me into realms of art which might have intimidated me; the family was my guide through time and space. My teacher, my book of life. The family was all things."

Maharet paused.

For a moment it seemed she would say something more. Then she rose from the table. She glanced at each of the others, and then she looked at Jesse.

"Now I want you to come with me. I want to show you what this family has become."

Quietly, all rose and waited as Maharet walked round the table and then they followed her out of the room. They followed her across the iron landing in the earthen stairwell, and into another great mountaintop chamber, with a glass roof and solid walls.

Jesse was the last to enter, and she knew even before she had passed through the door what she would see. An exquisite pain coursed through her, a pain full of remembered happiness and unforgettable longing. It was the windowless room in which she'd stood long ago.

How clearly she recalled its stone fireplace, and the dark leather furnishings scattered over the carpet; and the air of great and secret excitement, infinitely surpassing the memory of the physical things, which had forever haunted her afterwards, engulfing her in half-remembered dreams.

Yes, there the great electronic map of the world with its flattened continents, covered with thousands and thousands of tiny glowing lights.

And the other three walls, so dark, seemingly covered by a fine black wire mesh, until you realized what you were seeing: an endless ink-drawn vine, crowding every inch between floor and ceiling, growing from a single root in one corner into a million tiny swarming branches, each branch surrounded by countless carefully inscribed names.

A gasp rose from Marius as he turned about, looking from the great glowing map to the dense and delicately drawn family tree. Armand gave a faint sad smile also, while Mael scowled slightly, though he was actually amazed.

The others stared in silence; Eric had known these secrets; Louis, the most human of them all, had tears standing in his eyes. Daniel gazed in undisguised wonder. While Khayman, his eyes dulled as if with sadness, stared at the map as if he did not see it, as if he were still looking deep into the past.

Slowly Gabrielle nodded; she made some little sound of approval, of pleasure.

"The Great Family," she said in simple acknowledgment as she looked at Maharet.

Maharet nodded.

She pointed to the great sprawling map of the world behind her, which covered the south wall.

Jesse followed the vast swelling procession of tiny lights that moved across it, out of Palestine, spreading all over Europe, and down into Africa, and into Asia, and then finally to both continents of the New World. Countless tiny lights flickering in various colors; and as Jesse deliberately blurred her vision, she saw the great diffusion for what it was. She saw the old names, too, of continents and countries and seas, written in gold script on the sheet of glass that covered the three-dimensional illusion of mountains, plains, valleys.

"These are my descendants," Maharet said, "the descendants of Miriam, who was my daughter and Khayman's daughter, and of my people, whose blood was in me and in Miriam, traced through the maternal line as you see before you, for six thousand years."

"Unimaginable!" Pandora whispered. And she too was sad almost to the point of tears. What a melancholy beauty she had, grand and remote, yet reminiscent of warmth as if it had once been there, naturally, overwhelmingly. It seemed to hurt her, this revelation, to remind her of all that she had long ago lost.

"It is but one human family," Maharet said softly. "Yet there is no nation on earth that does not contain some part of it, and the descendants of males, blood of our blood and uncounted, surely exist in equal numbers to all those now known by name. Many who went into the wastes of Great Russia and into China and Japan and other dim regions were lost to this record. As are many of whom I lost track over the centuries for various reasons. Nevertheless their descendants are there! No people, no race, no country does not contain some of the Great Family. The Great Family is Arab, Jew, Anglo, African; it is Indian; it is Mongolian; it is Japanese and Chinese. In sum, the Great Family is the human family."

"Yes," Marius whispered. Remarkable to see the emotion in his face, the faint blush of human color again and the subtle light in the eyes that always defies description. "One family and all families—" he said. He went towards the enormous map and lifted his hands irresistibly as he looked up at it, studying the course of lights moving over the carefully modeled terrain.

Jesse felt the atmosphere of that long ago night enfold her; and then unaccountably those memories—flaring for an instant—faded, as though they didn't matter anymore. She was here with all the secrets; she was standing again in this room.

She moved closer to the dark, fine engraving on the wall. She looked at the myriad tiny names inscribed in black ink; she stood back and followed the progress of one branch, one thin delicate branch, as it rose slowly to the ceiling through a hundred different forks and twists.

And through the dazzle of all her dreams fulfilled now, she thought lovingly of all those souls who had made up the Great Family that she had known; of the mystery of heritage and intimacy. The moment was timeless; quiet for her; she didn't see the white faces of her new kin, the splendid immortal forms caught in their eerie stillness.

Something of the real world was alive still for her now, something that evoked awe and grief and perhaps the finest love she had ever been capable of; and it seemed for one moment that natural and supernatural possibility were equal in their mystery. They were equal in their power. And all the miracles of the immortals could not outshine this vast and simple chronicle. The Great Family.

Her hand rose as if it had a life of its own. And as the light caught Mael's silver bracelet which she wore around her wrist still, she laid her fingers out silently on the wall. A hundred names covered by the palm of her hand.

"This is what is threatened now," Marius said, his voice softened by sadness, his eyes still on the map.

It startled her, that a voice could be so loud yet so soft. No, she thought, no one will hurt the Great Family. No one will hurt the Great Family!

She turned to Maharet; Maharet was looking at her. And here we are, Jesse thought, at the opposite ends of this vine, Maharet and I.

A terrible pain welled in Jesse. A terrible pain. To be swept away from all things real, that had been irresistible, but to think that all things real could be swept away was unendurable.

During all her long years with the Talamasca, when she had seen spirits and restless ghosts, and poltergeists that could terrify their baffled victims, and clairvoyants speaking in foreign tongues, she had always known that somehow the supernatural could never impress itself upon the natural. Maharet had been so right! Irrelevant, yes, safely irrelevant—unable to intervene!

But now that stood to be changed. The unreal had been made real. It was absurd to stand in this strange room, amid these stark and imposing forms, and say, This cannot happen. This thing, this thing called the Mother, could reach out from behind the veil that had so long separated her from mortal eyes and touch a million human souls.

What did Khayman see when he looked at her now, as if he understood her. Did he see his daughter in Jesse?

"Yes," Khayman said. "My daughter. And don't be afraid. Mekare will come. Mekare will fulfill the curse. And the Great Family will go on."

Maharet sighed. "When I knew the Mother had risen, I did not guess what she might do. To strike down her children, to annihilate the evil that had come out of her, and out of Khayman and me and all of us who out of loneliness have shared this power—that I could not really question! What right have we to live? What right have we to be immortal? We are accidents; we are horrors. And though I want my life, greedily, I want it as fiercely as ever I wanted it—I cannot say that it is wrong that she has slain so many—"

"She'll slay more!" Eric said desperately.

"But it is the Great Family now which falls under her shadow," Maharet said. "It is their world! And she would make it her own. Unless . . ."

"Mekare will come," Khayman said. The simplest smile animated his face. "Mekare will fulfill the curse. I made Mekare what she is, so that she would do it. It is our curse now."

Maharet smiled, but it was vastly different, her expression. It was sad, indulgent, and curiously cold. "Ah, that you believe in such symmetry, Khayman."

"And we'll die, all of us!" Eric said.

"There has to be a way to kill her," Gabrielle said coldly, "without killing us. We have to think on this, to be ready, to have some sort of plan."

"You cannot change the prophecy," Khayman whispered.

"Khayman, if we have learned anything," Marius said, "it is that there is no destiny. And if there is no destiny then there is no prophecy. Mekare comes here to do what she vowed to do; it may be all she knows now or all she can do, but that does not mean that Akasha can't defend herself against Mekare. Don't you think the Mother knows Mekare has risen? Don't you think the Mother has seen and heard her children's dreams?"

"Ah, but prophecies have a way of fulfilling themselves," Khayman said. "That's the magic of it. We all understood it in ancient times. The power of charms is the power of the will; you might say that we were all great geniuses of psychology in those dark days, that we could be slain by the power of another's designs. And the dreams, Marius, the dreams are but part of a great design."

"Don't talk of it as if it were already done," Maharet said. "We have another tool. We can use reason. This creature speaks now, does she not? She understands what is spoken to her. Perhaps she can be diverted—"

"Oh, you are mad, truly mad!" Eric said. "You are going to speak to this monster that roamed the world incinerating her offspring!" He was becoming more frightened by the minute. "What does this thing know of reason, that inflames ignorant women to rise against their men? This thing knows slaughter and death and violence, that is all it has ever known, as your story makes plain. We don't change, Maharet. How many times have you told me. We move ever closer to the perfection of what we were meant to be."

"None of us wants to die, Eric," Maharet said patiently. But something suddenly distracted her.

At the same moment, Khayman too felt it. Jesse studied both of them, attempting to understand what she was seeing. Then she realized that Marius had undergone a subtle change as well. Eric was petrified. Mael, to Jesse's surprise, was staring fixedly at her.

They were hearing some sound. It was the way they moved their eyes that revealed it; people listen with their eyes; their eyes dance as they absorb the sound and try to locate its source.

Suddenly Eric said: "The young ones should go to the cellar immediately."

"That's no use," Gabrielle said. "Besides, I want to be here." She couldn't hear the sound, but she was trying to hear it.

Eric turned on Maharet. "Are you going to let her destroy us, one by one?"

Maharet didn't answer. She turned her head very slowly and looked towards the landing.

Then Jesse finally heard the sound herself. Certainly human ears couldn't hear it; it was like the auditory equivalent of tension without vibration, coursing through her as it did through every particle of substance in the room. It was inundating and disorienting, and though she saw that Maharet was speaking to Khayman and that Khayman was answering, she couldn't hear what they were saying. Foolishly, she'd put her hands to her ears. Dimly, she saw that Daniel had done the same thing, but they both knew it did no good at all.

The sound seemed suddenly to suspend all time; to suspend momentum. Jesse was losing her balance; she backed up against the wall; she stared at the map across from her, as if she wanted it somehow to sustain her. She stared at the soft flow of the lights streaming out of Asia Minor and to the north and to the south.

Some dim, inaudible commotion filled the room. The sound had died away, yet the air rang with a deafening silence.

In a soundless dream, it seemed, she saw the figure of the Vampire Lestat appear in the door; she saw him rush into Gabrielle's arms; she saw Louis move towards him and then embrace him. And then she saw the Vampire Lestat look at her—and she caught the flashing image of the funeral feast, the twins, the body on the altar. He didn't know what it meant! He didn't know.

It shocked her, the realization. The moment on the stage came back to her, when he had obviously struggled to recognize some fleeting image, as they had drawn apart.

Then as the others drew him away now, with embraces and kisses again—and even Armand had come to him with his arms out—he gave her the faintest little smile. "Jesse," he said.

He stared at the others, at Marius, at the cold and wary faces. And how white his skin was, how utterly white, yet the warmth, the exuberance, the almost childlike excitement—it was exactly as it had been before.

PART IV

THE QUEEN OF THE DAMNED

i

Wings stir the sunlit dust
of the cathedral in which
the Past is buried
to its chin in marble.

STAN RICE
from
"Poem on Crawling into Bed: Bitterness"
Body of Work (1983)

ii

In the glazed greenery of hedge,
and ivy,
and inedible strawberries
the lilies are white; remote; extreme.
Would they were our guardians.
They are barbarians.

STAN RICE
from
"Greek Fragments"
Body of Work (1983)

SHE sat at the end of the table, waiting for them; so still, placid, the magenta gown giving her skin a deep carnal glow in the light of the fire.

The edge of her face was gilded by the glow of the flames, and the dark window glass caught her vividly in a flawless mirror, as if the reflection were the real thing, floating out there in the transparent night.

Frightened. Frightened for them and for me. And strangely, for her. It was like a chill, the presentiment. For her. The one who might destroy all that I had ever loved.

At the door, I turned and kissed Gabrielle again. I felt her body collapse against me for an instant; then her attention locked on Akasha. I felt the faint tremor in her hands as she touched my face. I looked at Louis, my seemingly fragile Louis with his seemingly invincible composure; and at Armand, the urchin with the angel's face. Finally those you love are simply . . . those you love.

Marius was frigid with anger as he entered the room; nothing could disguise this. He glared at me—I, the one who had slain those poor helpless mortals and left them strewn down the mountain. He knew, did he not? And all the snow in the world couldn't cover it up. *I need you, Marius. We need you.*

His mind was veiled; all their minds were veiled. Could they keep their secrets from her?

As they filed into the room, I went to her right hand because she wanted me to. And because that's where I knew I ought to be. I gestured for Gabrielle and Louis to sit opposite, close, where I could see them. And the look on Louis's face, so resigned, yet sorrowful, struck my heart.

The red-haired woman, the ancient one called Maharet, sat at the opposite end of the table, the end nearest the door. Marius and Armand were on her right. And on her left was the young red-haired one, Jesse. Maharet looked absolutely passive, collected, as if nothing could alarm her.

But it was rather easy to see why. Akasha couldn't hurt this creature; or the other very old one, Khayman, who sat down now to my right.

The one called Eric was terrified, it was obvious. Only reluctantly did he sit at the table at all. Mael was afraid too, but it made him furious. He glowered at Akasha, as if he cared nothing about hiding his disposition.

And Pandora, beautiful, brown-eyed Pandora—she looked truly uncaring as she took her place beside Marius. She didn't even look at Akasha. She looked out through the glass walls, her eyes moving slowly, lovingly, as she saw the forest, the layers and layers of dim forest, with their dark streaks of redwood bark and prickling green.

The other one who didn't care was Daniel. This one I'd seen at the concert too. I hadn't guessed that Armand had been with him! Hadn't picked up the faintest indication that Armand had been there. And to think, whatever we might have said to each other, it was lost now forever. But then that couldn't be, could it? We would have our time together, Armand and I; all of us. Daniel knew it, pretty Daniel, the reporter with his little tape recorder who with Louis in a room on Divisadero Street had somehow started all of this! That's why he looked so serenely at Akasha; that's why he explored it moment by moment.

I looked at the black-haired Santino—a rather regal being, who was appraising me in a calculating fashion. He wasn't afraid either. But he cared desperately about what happened here. When he looked at Akasha he was awed by her beauty; it touched some deep wound in him. Old faith flared for a moment, faith that had meant more to him than survival, and faith that had been bitterly burnt away.

No time to understand them all, to evaluate the links which connected them, to ask the meaning of that strange image—the two red-haired women and the body of the mother, which I saw again in a glancing flash when I looked at Jesse.

I was wondering if they could scan my mind and find in it all the things I was struggling to conceal; the things I unwittingly concealed from myself.

Gabrielle's face was unreadable now. Her eyes had grown small and gray, as if shutting out all light and color; she looked from me to Akasha and back again, as if trying to figure something out.

And a sudden terror crept over me. Maybe it had been there all the time. They would never yield either. Something inveterate would prevent it, just as it had with me. And some fatal resolution would come before we left this room.

For a moment I was paralyzed. I reached out suddenly and took Akasha's hand. I felt her fingers close delicately around mine.

"Be quiet, my prince," she said, unobtrusively and kindly. "What you feel in this room is death, but it is the death of beliefs and strictures. Nothing more." She looked at Maharet. "The death of dreams, perhaps," she said, "which should have died a long time ago."

Maharet looked as lifeless and passive as a living thing can look. Her violet eyes were weary, bloodshot. And suddenly I realized why. They were human eyes. They were dying in her head. Her blood was infusing them over and over again with life but it wasn't lasting. Too many of the tiny nerves in her own body were dead.

I saw the dream vision again. The twins, the body before them. What was the connection?

"It is nothing," Akasha whispered. "Something long forgotten; for there are no answers in history now. We have transcended history. History is built on errors; we will begin with truth."

Marius spoke up at once:

"Is there nothing that can persuade you to stop?" His tone was infinitely more subdued than I'd expected. He sat forward, hands folded, in the attitude of one striving to be reasonable. "What can we say? We want you to cease the apparitions. We want you not to intervene."

Akasha's fingers tightened on mine. The red-haired woman was staring at me now with her bloodshot violet eyes.

"Akasha, I beg you," Marius said. "Stop this rebellion. Don't appear again to mortals; don't give any further commands."

Akasha laughed softly. "And why not, Marius? Because it so upsets your precious world, the world you've been watching for two thousand years, the way you Romans once watched life and death in the arena, as if such things were entertainment or theater, as if it did not matter—the literal fact of suffering and death—as long as you were enthralled?"

"I see what you mean to do," Marius said. "Akasha, you do not have the right."

"Marius, your student here has given me those old arguments," she answered. Her tone was now as subdued and eloquent of patience as his. "But more significantly, I have given them a thousand times to myself. How long do you think I have listened to the prayers of the world, pondering a way to terminate the endless cycle of human violence? It is time now for you to listen to what I have to say."

"We are to play a role in this?" Santino asked. "Or to be destroyed as the others have been destroyed?" His manner was impulsive rather than arrogant.

And for the first time the red-haired woman evinced a flicker of emotion, her weary eyes fixing on him immediately, her mouth tense.

"You will be my angels," Akasha answered tenderly as she looked at him. "You will be my gods. If you do not choose to follow me, I'll destroy you. As for the old ones, the old ones whom I cannot so easily dispatch"—she glanced at Khayman and Maharet again—"if they turn against me, they shall be as devils opposing me, and all humanity shall hunt them down, and they shall through their opposition serve the scheme quite well. But what you had before—a world to roam in stealth—you shall never have again."

It seemed Eric was losing his silent battle with fear. He moved as if he meant to rise and leave the room.

"Patience," Maharet said, glancing at him. She looked back at Akasha.

Akasha smiled.

"How is it possible," Maharet asked in a low voice, "to break a cycle of violence through more wanton violence? You are destroying the males of the human species. What can possibly be the outcome of such a brutal act?"

"You know the outcome as well as I do," Akasha said. "It's too simple and too elegant to be misunderstood. It has been unimaginable *until now.* All those centuries I sat upon my throne in Marius's shrine; I dreamed of an earth that was a garden, a world where beings lived without the torment that I could hear and feel. I dreamed of people achieving this peace without tyranny. And then the utter simplicity of it struck me; it was like dawn coming. The people who can realize such a dream are women; but only if all the men—or very nearly all the men—are removed.

"In prior ages, such a thing would not have been workable. But now it is easy; there is a vast technology which can reinforce it. After the initial purgation, the sex of babies can be selected; the unwanted unborn can be mercifully aborted as so many of both sexes are now. But there is no need to discuss this aspect of it, really. You are not fools, any of you, no matter how emotional or impetuous you are.

"You know as I know that there will be universal peace if the male population is limited to one per one hundred women. All forms of random violence will very simply come to an end.

"The reign of peace will be something the world has never known. Then the male population can be increased gradually. But for the conceptual framework to be changed, the males must be gone. Who can dispute that? It may not even be necessary to keep the one in a hundred. But it would be generous to do so. And so I will allow this. At least as we begin."

I could see that Gabrielle was about to speak. I tried to give her a silent signal to be quiet, but she ignored me.

"All right, the effects are obvious," she said. "But when you speak in terms of wholesale extermination, then questions of peace become ridiculous. You're abandoning one half of the world's population. If men and women were born without arms and legs, this might be a peaceful world as well."

"The men deserve what will happen to them. As a species, they will reap what they have sown. And remember, I speak of a temporary cleansing—a retreat, as it were. It's the simplicity of it which is beautiful. Collectively the lives of these men do not equal the lives of women who have been killed at the hands of men over the centuries. You know it and I know it. Now, tell me, how many men over the centuries have fallen at the hands of women? If you brought back to life every man slain by a woman, do you think these creatures would fill even this house?

"But you see, these points don't matter. Again, we know what I say is true. What matters—what is relevant and even more exquisite than the proposition itself—is that we now have the means to make it happen. I am indestructible. You are equipped to be my angels. And there is no one who can oppose us with success."

"That's not true," Maharet said.

A little flash of anger colored Akasha's cheeks; a glorious blush of red that faded and left her as inhuman looking as before.

"You are saying that *you* can stop me?" she asked, her mouth stiffening. "You are rash to suggest this. Will you suffer the death of Eric, and Mael, and Jessica, for such a point?"

Maharet didn't answer. Mael was visibly shaken but with anger not fear. He glanced at Jesse and at Maharet and then at me. I could feel his hatred.

Akasha continued to stare at Maharet.

"Oh, I know you, believe me," Akasha went on, her voice softening slightly. "I know how you have survived through all the years unchanged. I have seen you a thousand times in the eyes of others; I know you dream now that your sister lives. And perhaps she does—in some pathetic form. I know your hatred of me has only festered; and you reach back in your mind, all the way back, to the very beginning as if you could find there some rhyme or reason for what is happening now. But as you yourself told me long ago when we talked together in a palace of mud brick on the banks of the Nile River, there is no rhyme or reason. There is nothing! There are things visible and invisible; and horrible things can befall the most innocent of us all. Don't you see—this is as crucial to what I do now as all else."

Again, Maharet didn't answer. She sat rigid, only her darkly beautiful eyes showing a faint glimmer of what might have been pain.

"I shall *make* the rhyme or reason," Akasha said, with a trace of anger. "I shall *make* the future; I shall define goodness; I shall define peace. And

I don't call on mythic gods or goddesses or spirits to justify my actions, on abstract morality. I do not call on history either! I don't look for my mother's heart and brain in the dirt!"

A shiver ran through the others. A little bitter smile played on Santino's lips. And protectively, it seemed, Louis looked towards the mute figure of Maharet.

Marius was anxious lest this go further.

"Akasha," he said in entreaty, "even if it could be done, even if the mortal population did not rise against you, and the men did not find some way to destroy you long before such a plan could be accomplished—"

"You're a fool, Marius, or you think I am. Don't you think I know what this world is capable of? What absurd mixture of the savage and the technologically astute makes up the mind of modern man?"

"My Queen, I don't think you know it!" Marius said. "Truly, I don't. I don't think you can hold in your mind the full conception of what the world is. None of us can; it is too varied, too immense; we seek to embrace it with our reason; but we can't do it. You know a world; but it is not *the* world; it is the world you have selected from a dozen other worlds for reasons within yourself."

She shook her head; another flare of anger. "Don't try my patience, Marius," she said. "I spared you for a very simple reason. Lestat wanted you spared. And because you are strong and you can be of help to me. But that is all there is to it, Marius. Tread with care."

A silence fell between them. Surely he realized that she was lying. I realized it. She loved him and it humiliated her, and so she sought to hurt him. And she had. Silently, he swallowed his rage.

"Even if it could be done," he pressed gently, "can you honestly say that human beings have done so badly that they should receive such a punishment as this?"

I felt the relief course through me. I'd known he would have the courage, I'd known that he would find some way to take it into the deeper waters, no matter how she threatened him; he would say all that I had struggled to say.

"Ah, now you disgust me," she answered.

"Akasha, for two thousand years I have watched," he said. "Call me the Roman in the arena if you will and tell me tales of the ages that went before. When I knelt at your feet I begged you for your knowledge. But what I have witnessed in this short span has filled me with awe and love for all things mortal; I have seen revolutions in thought and philosophy which I believed impossible. Is not the human race moving towards the very age of peace you describe?"

Her face was a picture of disdain.

"Marius," she said, "this will go down as one of the bloodiest centuries in the history of the human race. What revolutions do you speak of, when millions have been exterminated by one small European nation on the whim of a madman, when entire cities were melted into oblivion by bombs? When children in the desert countries of the East war on other children in the name of an ancient and despotic God? Marius, women the world over wash the fruits of their wombs down public drains. The screams of the hungry are deafening, yet unheard by the rich who cavort in technological citadels; disease runs rampant among the starving of whole continents while the sick in palatial hospitals spend the wealth of the world on cosmetic refinements and the promise of eternal life through pills and vials." She laughed softly. "Did ever the cries of the dying ring so thickly in the ears of those of us who can hear them? Has *ever* more blood been shed!"

I could feel Marius's frustration. I could feel the passion that made him clench his fist now and search his soul for the proper words.

"There's something you cannot *see*," he said finally. "There is something that you fail to understand."

"No, my dear one. There is nothing wrong with my vision. There never was. It is you who fail to see. You always have."

"Look out there at the forest!" he said, gesturing to the glass walls around us, "Pick one tree; describe it, if you will, in terms of what it destroys, what it defies, and what it does not accomplish, and you have a monster of greedy roots and irresistible momentum that eats the light of other plants, their nutrients, their air. But that is not the truth of the tree. That is not the whole truth when the thing is seen as part of nature, and by nature I mean nothing sacred, I mean only the full tapestry, Akasha. I mean only the larger thing which embraces all."

"And so you will select now your causes for optimism," she said, "as you always have. Come now. Examine for me the Western cities where even the poor are given platters of meat and vegetables daily and tell me hunger is no more. Well, your pupil here has given me enough of that pap already—the idiot foolishness upon which the complacency of the rich has always been based. The world is sunk into depravity and chaos; it is as it always was or worse."

"Oh, no, not so," he said adamantly. "Men and women are learning animals. If you do not see what they have learned, you're blind. They are creatures ever changing, ever improving, ever expanding their vision and the capacity of their hearts. You are not fair to them when you speak of this as the most bloody century; you are not seeing the light that shines ever more radiantly on account of the darkness; you are not seeing the evolution of the human soul!"

He rose from his place at the table, and came round towards her on the left-hand side. He took the empty chair between her and Gabrielle. And then he reached out and he lifted her hand.

I was frightened watching him. Frightened she wouldn't allow him to touch her; but she seemed to like this gesture; she only smiled.

"True, what you say about war," he said, pleading with her, and struggling with his dignity at the same time. "Yes, and the cries of the dying, I too have heard them; we have all heard them, through all the decades; and even now, the world is shocked by daily reports of armed conflict. But it is the outcry against these horrors which is the light I speak of; it's the attitudes which were never possible in the past. It is the intolerance of thinking men and women in power who for the first time in the history of the human race truly want to put an end to injustice in all forms."

"You speak of the intellectual attitudes of a few."

"No," he said. "I speak of changing philosophy; I speak of idealism from which true realities will be born. Akasha, flawed as they are, they must have the time to perfect their own dreams, don't you see?"

"Yes!" It was Louis who spoke out.

My heart sank. So vulnerable! Were she to turn her anger on him—But in his quiet and refined manner, he was going on:

"It's their world, not ours," he said humbly. "Surely we forfeited it when we lost our mortality. We have no right now to interrupt their struggle. If we do we rob them of victories that have cost them too much! Even in the last hundred years their progress has been miraculous; they have righted wrongs that mankind thought were inevitable; they have for the first time developed a concept of the true family of man."

"You touch me with your sincerity," she answered. "I spared you only because Lestat loved you. Now I know the reason for that love. What courage it must take for you to speak your heart to me. Yet you yourself are the most predatory of all the immortals here. You kill without regard for age or sex or will to live."

"Then kill me!" he answered. "I wish that you would. But don't kill human beings! Don't interfere with them. Even if they kill each other! Give them time to see this new vision realized; give the cities of the West, corrupt as they may be, time to take their ideals to a suffering and blighted world."

"Time," Maharet said. "Maybe that is what we are asking for. Time. And that is what you have to give."

There was a pause.

Akasha didn't want to look again at this woman; she didn't want to listen to her. I could feel her recoiling. She withdrew her hand from Marius; she looked at Louis for a long moment and then she turned to Maharet as if it couldn't be avoided, and her face became set and almost cruel.

But Maharet went on:

"You have meditated in silence for centuries upon your solutions. What is another hundred years? Surely you will not dispute that the last century on this earth was beyond all prediction or imagining—and that the technological advances of that century can conceivably bring food and shelter and health to all the peoples of the earth."

"Is that really so?" Akasha responded. A deep smoldering hate heated her smile as she spoke. "This is what technological advances have given the world. They have given it poison gas, and diseases born in laboratories, and bombs that could destroy the planet itself. They have given the world nuclear accidents that have contaminated the food and drink of entire continents. And the armies do what they have always done with modern efficiency. The aristocracy of a people slaughtered in an hour in a snow-filled wood; the intelligentsia of a nation, including all those who wear eyeglasses, systematically shot. In the Sudan, women are still habitually mutilated to be made pleasing to their husbands; in Iran the children run into the fire of guns!"

"This cannot be all you've seen," Marius said. "I don't believe it. Akasha, look at me. Look kindly on me, and what I'm trying to say."

"It doesn't matter whether or not you believe it!" she said with the first sustained anger. "You haven't accepted what I've been trying to tell you. You have not yielded to the exquisite image I've presented to your mind. Don't you realize the gift I offer you? I would save you! And what are you if I don't do this thing! A blood drinker, a killer!"

I'd never heard her voice so heated. As Marius started to answer, she gestured imperiously for silence. She looked at Santino and at Armand.

"You, Santino," she said. "You who governed the Roman Children of Darkness, when they believed they did God's will as the Devil's henchmen—do you remember what it was like to have a purpose? And you, Armand, the leader of the old Paris coven; remember when you were a saint of darkness? Between heaven and hell, you had your place. I offer you that again; and it is no delusion! Can you not reach for your lost ideals?"

Neither answered her. Santino was horror-struck; the wound inside him was bleeding. Armand's face revealed nothing but despair.

A dark fatalistic expression came over her. This was futile. None of them would join her. She looked at Marius.

"Your precious mankind!" she said. "It has learned nothing in six thousand years! You speak to me of ideals and goals! There were men in my father's court in Uruk who knew the hungry ought to be fed. Do you know what your modern world is? Televisions are tabernacles of the miraculous and helicopters are its angels of death!"

"All right, then, what would your world be?" Marius said. His hands were trembling. "You don't believe that the women aren't going to fight for their men?"

She laughed. She turned to me. "Did they fight in Sri Lanka, Lestat? Did they fight in Haiti? Did they fight in Lynkonos?"

Marius stared at me. He waited for me to answer, to take my stand with him. I wanted to make arguments; to reach for the threads he'd given me and take it further. But my mind went blank.

"Akasha," I said. "Don't continue this bloodbath. Please. Don't lie to human beings or befuddle them anymore."

There it was—brutal and unsophisticated, but the only truth I could give.

"Yes, for that's the essence of it," Marius said, his tone careful again, fearful, and almost pleading. "It's a lie, Akasha; it's another superstitious lie! Have we not had enough of them? And now, of all times, when the world's waking from its old delusions. When it has thrown off the old gods."

"A lie?" she asked. She drew back, as if he'd hurt her. "What is the lie? Did I lie when I told them I would bring a reign of peace on earth? Did I lie when I told them I was the one they had been waiting for? No, I didn't lie. What I can do is give them the first bit of truth they've ever had! I am what they think I am. I am eternal, and all powerful, and shall protect them—"

"Protect them?" Marius asked. "How can you protect them from their most deadly foes?"

"What foes?"

"Disease, my Queen. Death. You are no healer. You cannot give life or save it. And they will expect such miracles. *All you can do is kill.*"

Silence. Stillness. Her face suddenly as lifeless as it had been in the shrine; eyes staring forward; emptiness or deep thought, impossible to distinguish.

No sound but the wood shifting and falling into the fire.

"Akasha," I whispered. "Time, the thing that Maharet asked for. A century. So little to give."

Dazed, she looked at me. I could feel death breathing on my face, death close as it had been years and years ago when the wolves tracked me into the frozen forest, and I couldn't reach up high enough for the limbs of the barren trees.

"You are all my enemies, aren't you?" she whispered. "Even you, my prince. You are my enemy. My lover and my enemy at the same time."

"I love you!" I said. "But I can't lie to you. I cannot believe in it! It is wrong! It is the very simplicity and the elegance which make it so wrong!"

Her eyes moved rapidly over their faces. Eric was on the verge of panic again. And I could feel the anger cresting in Mael.

"Is there not one of you who would stand with me?" she whispered. "Not one who would reach for that dazzling dream? Not even one who is ready to forsake his or her small and selfish world?" Her eyes fixed on Pandora. "Ah, you, poor dreamer, grieving for your lost humanity; would you not be redeemed?"

Pandora stared as if through a dim glass. "I have no taste for bringing death," she answered in an even softer whisper. "It is enough for me to see it in the falling leaves. I cannot believe good things can come from bloodshed. For that's the crux, my Queen. Those horrors happen still, but good men and women everywhere deplore them; you would reclaim such methods; you would exonerate them and bring the dialogue to an end." She smiled sadly. "I am a useless thing to you. I have nothing to give."

Akasha didn't respond. Then her eyes moved over the others again; she took the measure of Mael, of Eric. Of Jesse.

"Akasha," I said. "History is a litany of injustice, no one denies it. But when has a simple solution ever been anything but evil? Only in complexity do we find answers. Through complexity men struggle towards fairness; it is slow and clumsy, but it's the only way. Simplicity demands too great a sacrifice. It always has."

"Yes," Marius said. "Exactly. Simplicity and brutality are synonymous in philosophy and in actions. It is brutal what you propose!"

"Is there no humility in you?" she asked suddenly. She turned from me to him. "Is there no willingness to understand? You are so proud, all of you, so arrogant. You want your world to remain the same on account of your greed!"

"No," Marius said.

"What have I done that you should set yourselves so against me?" she demanded. She looked at me, then at Marius, and finally to Maharet. "From Lestat I expected arrogance," she said. "I expected platitudes and rhetoric, and untested ideas. But from many of you I expected more. Oh, how you disappoint me. How can you turn away from the destiny that awaits you? You who could be saviors! How can you deny what you have seen?"

"But they'd want to know what we really are," Santino said. "And once they did know, they'd rise against us. They'd want the immortal blood as they always do."

"Even women want to live forever," Maharet said coldly. "Even women would kill for that."

"Akasha, it's folly," said Marius. "It cannot be accomplished. For the Western world, not to resist would be unthinkable."

"It is a savage and primitive vision," Maharet said with cold scorn.

Akasha's face darkened again with anger. Yet even in rage, the prettiness of her expression remained. "You have always opposed me!" she said to Maharet. "I would destroy you if I could. I would hurt those you love."

There was a stunned silence. I could smell the fear of the others, though no one dared to move or speak.

Maharet nodded. She smiled knowingly.

"It is you who are arrogant," she answered. "It is you who have learned nothing. It is you who have not changed in six thousand years. It is your soul which remains unperfected, while mortals move to realms you will never grasp. In your isolation you dreamed dreams as thousands of mortals have done, protected from all scrutiny or challenge; and you emerge from your silence, ready to make these dreams real for the world? You bring them here to this table, among a handful of your fellow creatures, and they crumble. You cannot defend them. How could anyone defend them? And you tell us we deny what we see!"

Slowly Maharet rose from the chair. She leant forward slightly, her weight resting on her fingers as they touched the wood.

"Well, I'll tell you what I see," she went on. "Six thousand years ago, when men believed in spirits, an ugly and irreversible accident occurred; it was as awful in its own way as the monsters born now and then to mortals which nature does not suffer to live. But you, clinging to life, and clinging to your will, and clinging to your royal prerogative, refused to take that awful mistake with you to an early grave. To sanctify it, that was your purpose. To spin a great and glorious religion; and that is still your purpose now. But it was an accident finally, a distortion, and nothing more.

"And look now at the ages since that dark and evil moment; look at the other religions founded upon magic; founded upon some apparition or voice from the clouds! Founded upon the intervention of the supernatural in one guise or another—miracles, revelations, a mortal man rising from the dead!

"Look on the effect of your religions, those movements that have swept up millions with their fantastical claims. Look at what they have done to human history. Look at the wars fought on account of them; look at the persecutions, the massacres. Look at the pure enslavement of reason; look at the price of faith and zeal.

"And you tell us of children dying in the Eastern countries, in the name of Allah as the guns crackle and the bombs fall!

"And the war of which you speak in which one tiny European nation sought to exterminate a people. . . . In the name of what grand spiritual design for a new world was that done? And what does the world remember of it? The death camps, the ovens in which bodies were burnt by the thousands. The ideas are gone!

"I tell you, we would be hard put to determine what is more evil—religion or the pure idea. The intervention of the supernatural or the elegant simple abstract solution! Both have bathed this earth in suffering; both have brought the human race literally and figuratively to its knees.

"Don't *you* see? It is not man who is the enemy of the human species. It is the irrational; it is the spiritual when it is divorced from the material; from the lesson in one beating heart or one bleeding vein.

"You accuse us of greed. Ah, but our greed is our salvation. Because we know what we are; we know our limits and we know our sins; you have never known yours.

"You would begin it all again, wouldn't you? You would bring a new religion, a new revelation, a new wave of superstition and sacrifice and death."

"You lie," Akasha answered, her voice barely able to contain her fury. "You betray the very beauty I dream of; you betray it because you have no vision, you have no dreams."

"The beauty is out there!" Maharet said. "It does not deserve your violence! Are you so merciless that the lives you would destroy mean *nothing!* Ah, it was always so!"

The tension was unbearable. The blood sweat was breaking out on my body. I could see the panic all around. Louis had bowed his head and covered his face with his hands. Only the young Daniel seemed hopelessly enraptured. And Armand merely gazed at Akasha as if it were all out of his hands.

Akasha was silently struggling. But then she appeared to regain her conviction.

"You lie as you have always done," she said desperately. "But it does not matter whether you fight on my side. I will do what I mean to do; I will reach back over the millennia and I will redeem that long ago moment, that long ago evil which you and your sister brought into our land; I will reach back and raise it up in the eyes of the world until it becomes the Bethlehem of the new era; and peace on earth will exist at last. There is no great good that was ever done without sacrifice and courage. And if you all turn against me, if you all resist me, then I shall make of better mettle the angels I require."

"No, you will not do it," Maharet said.

"Akasha, please," Marius said. "Grant us time. Agree only to wait, to consider. Agree that nothing must come from this moment."

"Yes," I said. "Give us time. Come with me. Let us go together out there—you and I and Marius—out of dreams and visions and into the world itself."

"Oh, how you insult me and belittle me," she whispered. Her anger was turned on Marius but it was about to turn on me.

"There are so many things, so many places," he said, "that I want to show you! Only give me a chance. Akasha, for two thousand years I cared for you, I protected you . . ."

"You protected yourself! You protected the source of your power, the source of your evil!"

"I'm imploring you," Marius said. "I will get on my knees to you. A month only, to come with me, to let us talk together, to let us examine all the evidence . . ."

"So small, so selfish," Akasha whispered. "And you feel no debt to the world that made you what you are, no debt to give it now the benefit of your power, to alchemize yourselves from devils into gods!"

She turned to me suddenly, the shock spreading over her face.

"And you, my prince, who came into my chamber as if I were the Sleeping Beauty, who brought me to life again with your passionate kiss. Will you not reconsider? For my love!" The tears again were standing in her eyes. "Must you join with them now against me, too?" She reached up and placed her two hands on the sides of my face. "How can you betray me?" she said. "How can you betray such a dream? They are slothful beings; deceitful; full of malice. But your heart was pure. You had a courage that transcended pragmatism. You had your dreams too!"

I didn't have to answer. She knew. She could see it better perhaps than I could see it. And all I saw was the suffering in her black eyes. The pain, the incomprehension; and the grief she was already experiencing for me.

It seemed she couldn't move or speak suddenly. And there was nothing I could do now; nothing to save them; or me. I loved her! But I couldn't stand with her! Silently, I begged her to understand and forgive.

Her face was frozen, almost as if the voices had reclaimed her; it was as if I were standing before her throne in the path of her changeless gaze.

"I will kill you first, my prince," she said, her fingers caressing me all the more gently. "I want you gone from me. I will not look into your face and see this betrayal again."

"Harm him and that shall be our signal," Maharet whispered. "We shall move against you as one."

"And you move against yourselves!" she answered, glancing at Maharet. "When I finish with this one I love, I shall kill those you love; those who should have been dead already; I shall destroy all those whom I can destroy; but who shall destroy me?"

"Akasha," Marius whispered. He rose and came towards her; but she moved in the blink of an eye and knocked him to the floor. I heard him cry out as he fell. Santino went to his aid.

Again, she looked at me; and her hands closed on my shoulders, gentle and loving as before. And through the veil of my tears, I saw her smile sadly. "My prince, my beautiful prince," she said.

Khayman rose from the table. Eric rose. And Mael. And then the young ones rose, and lastly Pandora, who moved to Marius's side.

She released me. And she too rose to her feet. The night was so quiet suddenly that the forest seemed to sigh against the glass.

And this is what I've wrought, I who alone remained seated, looking not at any of them, but at nothing. At the small glittering sweep of my life, my little triumphs, my little tragedies, my dreams of waking the goddess, my dreams of goodness, and of fame.

What was she doing? Assessing their power? Looking from one to the other, and then back to me. A stranger looking down from some lofty height. And so now the fire comes, Lestat. Don't dare to look at Gabrielle or Louis, lest she turn it that way. Die first, like a coward, and then you don't have to see them die.

And the awful part is, you won't know who wins finally—whether or not she triumphs, or we all go down together. Just like not knowing what it was all about, or why, or what the hell the dream of the twins meant, or how this whole world came into being. You just won't ever know.

I was weeping now and she was weeping and she was that tender fragile being again, the being I had held on Saint-Domingue, the one who needed me, but that weakness wasn't destroying her after all, though it would certainly destroy me.

"Lestat," she whispered as if in disbelief.

"I can't follow you," I said, my voice breaking. Slowly I rose to my feet. "We're not angels, Akasha; we are not gods. To be human, that's what most of us long for. It is the human which has become myth to us."

It was killing me to look at her. I thought of her blood flowing into me; of the powers she'd given me. Of what it had been like to travel with her through the clouds. I thought of the euphoria in the Haitian village when the women had come with their candles, singing their hymms.

"But that is what it will be, my beloved," she whispered. "Find your courage! It's there." The blood tears were coursing down her face. Her lip trembled and the smooth flesh of her forehead was creased with those perfectly straight lines of utter distress.

Then she straightened. She looked away from me: and her face went blank and beautifully smooth again. She looked past us, and I felt she was reaching for the strength to do it, and the others had better act fast. I wished for that—like sticking a dagger into her; they had better bring her down now, and I could feel the tears sliding down my face.

But something else was happening. There was a great soft musical sound from somewhere. Glass shattering, a great deal of glass. There was a sudden obvious excitement in Daniel. In Jesse. But the old ones stood frozen, listening. Again, glass breaking; someone entering by one of the many portals of this rambling house.

She took a step back. She quickened as if seeing a vision; and a loud hollow sound filled the stairwell beyond the open door. Someone down below in the passage.

She moved away from the table, towards the fireplace. She seemed for all the world afraid.

Was that possible? Did she know who was coming, and was it another old one? And was that what she feared—that more could accomplish what these few could not?

It was nothing so calculated finally; I knew it; she was being defeated inside. All courage was leaving her. It was the need, the loneliness, after all! It had begun with my resistance, and they had deepened it, and then I had dealt her yet another blow. And now she was transfixed by this loud, echoing, and impersonal noise. Yet she did know who this person was, I could sense it. And the others knew too.

The noise was growing louder. The visitor was coming up the stairs. The skylight and the old iron pylons reverberated with the shock of each heavy step.

"But who is it!" I said suddenly. I could stand it no longer. There was that image again, that image of the mother's body and the twins.

"Akasha!" Marius said. "Give us the time we ask for. Forswear the moment. That is enough!"

"Enough for what!" she cried sharply, almost savagely.

"For our lives, Akasha," he said. "For *all* our lives!"

I heard Khayman laugh softly, the one who hadn't spoken even once.

The steps had reached the landing.

Maharet stood at the edge of the open doorway, and Mael was beside her. I hadn't even seen them move.

Then I saw who and what it was. The woman I'd glimpsed moving through the jungles, clawing her way out of the earth, walking the long miles on the barren plain. The other twin of the dreams I'd never understood! And now she stood framed in the dim light from the stairwell, staring straight at the distant figure of Akasha, who stood some thirty feet away with her back to the glass wall and the blazing fire.

Oh, but the sight of this one. Gasps came from the others, even from the old ones, from Marius himself.

A thin layer of soil encased her all over, even the rippling shape of her long hair. Broken, peeling, stained by the rain even, the mud still clung to her, clung to her naked arms and bare feet as if she were made of it, made of earth itself. It made a mask of her face. And her eyes peered out of the mask, naked, rimmed in red. A rag covered her, a blanket filthy and torn, and tied with a hemp rope around her waist.

What impulse could make such a being cover herself, what tender human modesty had caused this living corpse to stop and make this simple garment, what suffering remnant of the human heart?

Beside her, staring at her, Maharet appeared to weaken suddenly all over as if her slender body were going to drop.

"Mekare!" she whispered.

But the woman didn't see her or hear her; the woman stared at Akasha, the eyes gleaming with fearless animal cunning as Akasha moved back towards the table, putting the table between herself and this creature, Akasha's face hardening, her eyes full of undisguised hate.

"Mekare!" Maharet cried. She threw out her hands and tried to catch the woman by the shoulders and turn her around.

The woman's right hand went out, shoving Maharet backwards so that she was thrown yards across the room until she tumbled against the wall.

The great sheet of plate glass vibrated, but did not shatter. Gingerly Maharet touched it with her fingers; then with the fluid grace of a cat, she sprang up and into the arms of Eric, who was rushing to her aid.

Instantly he pulled her back towards the door. For the woman now struck the enormous table and sent it sliding northward, and then over on its side.

Gabrielle and Louis moved swiftly into the northwest corner, Santino and Armand the other way, towards Mael and Eric and Maharet.

Those of us on the other side merely backed away, except for Jesse, who had moved towards the door.

She stood beside Khayman and as I looked at him now I saw with amazement that he wore a thin, bitter smile.

"The curse, my Queen," he said, his voice rising sharply to fill the room.

The woman froze as she heard him behind her. But she did not turn around.

And Akasha, her face shimmering in the firelight, quavered visibly, and the tears flowed again.

"All against me, all of you!" she said. "Not a one who would come to my side!" She stared at me, even as the woman moved towards her.

The woman's muddy feet scraped the carpet, her mouth gaping and her hands only slightly poised, her arms still down at her sides. Yet it was the perfect attitude of menace as she took one slow step after another.

But again Khayman spoke, bringing her suddenly to a halt.

In another language, he cried out, his voice gaining volume until it was a roar. And only the dimmest translation of it came clear to me.

"Queen of the Damned . . . hour of worst menace . . . I shall rise to stop you. . . ." I understood. It had been Mekare's—the woman's—prophecy and curse. And everyone here knew it, understood it. It had to do with that strange, inexplicable dream.

"Oh, no, my children!" Akasha screamed suddenly. "It is not finished!"

I could feel her collecting her powers; I could see it, her body tensing, breasts thrust forward, her hands rising as if reflexively, fingers curled.

The woman was struck by it, shoved backwards, but instantly resisted. And then she too straightened, her eyes widening, and she rushed forward so swiftly I couldn't follow it, her hands out for the Queen.

I saw her fingers, caked with mud, streaking towards Akasha; I saw Akasha's face as she was caught by her long black hair. I heard her scream. Then I saw her profile, as her head struck the western window and shattered it, the glass crashing down in great dagged shards.

A violent shock passed through me; I could neither breathe nor move. I was falling to the floor. I couldn't control my limbs. Akasha's headless body was sliding down the fractured glass wall, the shards still falling around it. Blood streamed down the broken glass behind her. And the woman held Akasha's severed head by the hair!

Akasha's black eyes blinked, widened. Her mouth opened as if to scream again.

And then the light was going out all around me; it was as if the fire had been extinguished, only it hadn't, and as I rolled over on the carpet, crying, my hand clawing at it involuntarily, I saw the distant flames through a dark rosy haze.

I tried to lift my weight. I couldn't. I could hear Marius calling to me, Marius silently calling only my name.

Then I was rising, just a little, and all my weight pressed against my aching arms and hands.

Akasha's eyes were fixed on me. Her head was lying there almost within my reach, and the body lay on its back, blood gushing from the stump of the neck. Suddenly the right arm quivered; it was lifted, then it flopped back down to the floor. Then it rose again, the hand dangling. It was reaching for the head!

I could help it! I could use the powers she'd given me to try to move it, to help it reach the head. And as I struggled to see in the dimming light, the body lurched, shivered, and flopped down closer to the head.

But the twins! They were beside the head and the body. Mekare, staring at the head dully, with those vacant red-rimmed eyes. And Maharet, as if with the last breath in her, kneeling now beside her sister, over the body of the Mother, as the room grew darker and colder, and Akasha's face began to grow pale and ghostly white as if all the light inside were going out.

I should have been afraid; I should have been in terror; the cold was creeping over me, and I could hear my own choking sobs. But the strangest elation overcame me; I realized suddenly what I was seeing:

"It's the dream," I said. Far away I could hear my own voice. "The twins and the body of the Mother, do you see it! The image from the dream!"

Blood spread out from Akasha's head into the weave of the carpet; Maharet was sinking down, her hands out flat, and Mekare too had weakened and bent down over the body, but it was still the same image, and I knew why I'd seen it now, I knew what it meant!

"The funeral feast!" Marius cried. "The heart and the brain, one of you—take them into yourself. It is the only chance."

Yes, that was it. And they knew! No one had to tell them. They knew!

That was the meaning! And they'd all seen it, and they all knew. Even as my eyes were closing, I realized it; and this lovely feeling deepened, this sense of completeness, of something finished at last. Of something known!

Then I was floating, floating in the ice cold darkness again as if I were in Akasha's arms, and we were rising into the stars.

A sharp crackling sound brought me back. Not dead yet, but dying. And where are those I love?

Fighting for life still, I tried to open my eyes; it seemed impossible. But then I saw them in the thickening gloom—the two of them, their red hair catching the hazy glow of the fire; the one holding the bloody brain in her mud-covered fingers, and the other, the dripping heart. All but dead they were, their own eyes glassy, their limbs moving as if through water. And Akasha stared forward still, her mouth open, the blood gushing from her shattered skull. Mekare lifted the brain to her mouth; Maharet put the heart in her other hand; Mekare took them both into herself.

Darkness again; no firelight; no point of reference; no sensation except pain; pain all through the thing that I was which had no limbs, no eyes, no mouth to speak. Pain, throbbing, electrical; and no way to move to lessen it, to push it this way, or that way, or tense against it, or fade into it. Just pain.

Yet I was moving. I was thrashing about on the floor. Through the pain I could feel the carpet suddenly; I could feel my feet digging at it as if I were trying to climb a steep cliff. And then I heard the unmistakable sound of the fire near me; and I felt the wind gusting through the broken window, and I smelled all those soft sweet scents from the forest rushing into the room. A violent shock coursed through me, through every muscle and pore, my arms and legs flailing. Then still.

The pain was gone.

I lay there gasping, staring at the brilliant reflection of the fire in the glass ceiling, and feeling the air fill my lungs, and I realized I was crying again, brokenheartedly, like a child.

The twins knelt with their backs to us; and they had their arms around each other, and their heads were together, their hair mingling, as they caressed each other, gently, tenderly, as if talking through touch alone.

I couldn't muffle my sobs. I turned over and drew my arm up under my face and just wept.

Marius was near me. And so was Gabrielle. I wanted to take Gabrielle into my arms. I wanted to say all the things I knew I should say—that it was over and we had survived it, and it was finished—but I couldn't.

Then slowly I turned my head and looked at Akasha's face again, her face still intact, though all the dense, shining whiteness was gone, and she was as pale, as translucent as glass! Even her eyes, her beautiful ink black eyes were becoming transparent, as if there were no pigment in them; it had all been the blood.

Her hair lay soft and silken beneath her cheek, and the dried blood was lustrous and ruby red.

I couldn't stop crying. I didn't want to. I started to say her name and it caught in my throat. It was as if I shouldn't do it. I never should have. I never should have gone up those marble steps and kissed her face in the shrine.

They were all coming to life again, the others. Armand was holding Daniel and Louis, who were both groggy and unable yet to stand; and Khayman had come forward with Jesse beside him, and the others were all right too. Pandora, trembling, her mouth twisted with her crying, stood far apart, hugging herself as if she were cold.

And the twins turned around and stood up now, Maharet's arm around Mekare. And Mekare stared forward, expressionless, uncomprehending, the living statue; and Maharet said:

"Behold. The Queen of the Damned."

PART V

. . . WORLD WITHOUT END, AMEN

Some things lighten nightfall
and make a Rembrandt of a grief.
But mostly the swiftness of time
is a joke; on us. The flame-moth
is unable to laugh. What luck.
The myths are dead.
. . . .

STAN RICE
"Poem on Crawling into Bed: Bitterness"
Body of Work (1983)

MIAMI.

A vampire's city—hot, teeming, and embracingly beautiful. Melting pot, marketplace, playground. Where the desperate and the greedy are locked in subversive commerce, and the sky belongs to everyone, and the beach goes on forever; and the lights outshine the heavens, and the sea is as warm as blood.

Miami. The happy hunting ground of the devil.

That's why we are here, in Armand's large, graceful white villa on the Night Island, surrounded by every conceivable luxury, and the wide open southern night.

Out there, across the water, Miami beckons; victims just waiting: the pimps, the thieves, the dope kings, and the killers. The nameless ones; so many who are almost as bad as I am, but not quite.

Armand had gone over at sunset with Marius; and they were back now, Armand playing chess with Santino in the drawing room, Marius reading as he did constantly, in the leather chair by the window over the beach.

Gabrielle had not appeared yet this evening; since Jesse left, she was frequently alone.

Khayman sat in the downstairs study talking with Daniel now, Daniel who liked to let the hunger build, Daniel who wanted to know all about what it had been like in ancient Miletus, and Athens, and Troy. Oh, don't forget Troy. I myself was vaguely intrigued by the idea of Troy.

I liked Daniel. Daniel who might go with me later if I asked him; if I could bring myself to leave this island, which I have done only once since I arrived. Daniel who still laughed at the path the moon made over the water, or the warm spray in his face. For Daniel, all of it—her death even—had been spectacle. But he cannot be blamed for that.

Pandora almost never moved from the television screen. Marius had brought her the stylish modern garments she wore; satin shirt, boots to the knee, cleaving velvet skirt. He'd put the bracelets on her arms, and the rings on her fingers, and each evening he brushed her long brown hair. Sometimes he presented her with little gifts of perfume. If he did not open them for her, they lay on the table untouched. She stared the way Armand did at the endless progression of video movies, only now and then breaking off to go to the piano in the music room and play softly for a little while.

I liked her playing; rather like the Art of the Fugue, her seamless variations. But she worried me; the others didn't. The others had all recovered from what had happened, more quickly than I had ever imagined they could. She'd been damaged in some crucial way before it all began.

Yet she liked it here; I knew she did. How could she not like it? Even though she never listened to a word that Marius said.

We all liked it. Even Gabrielle.

White rooms filled with gorgeous Persian carpets and endlessly intriguing paintings—Matisse, Monet, Picasso, Giotto, Géricault. One could spend a century merely looking at the paintings; Armand was constantly changing them, shifting their positions, bringing up some new treasure from the cellar, slipping in little sketches here and there.

Jesse had loved it here too, though she was gone now, to join Maharet in Rangoon.

She had come here into my study and told me her side of it very directly, asking me to change the names she'd used and to leave out the Talamasca altogether, which of course I wouldn't do. I'd sat silently, scanning her mind as she talked, for all the little things she was leaving out. Then I'd poured it into the computer, while she sat watching, thinking, staring at the dark gray velvet curtains, and the Venetian clock; and the cool colors of the Morandi on the wall.

I think she knew I wouldn't do what she told me to do. She also knew it wouldn't matter. People weren't likely to believe in the Talamasca any more than they would ever believe in us. That is, unless David Talbot or Aaron Lightner came to call on them the way that Aaron had called on Jesse.

As for the Great Family, well, it wasn't likely that any of them would think it more than a fiction, with a touch here and there of truth; that is, if they ever happened to pick up the book.

That's what everybody had thought of *Interview with the Vampire* and my autobiography, and they would think it about *The Queen of the Damned* too.

And that's how it should be. Even I agree with that now. Maharet was right. No room for us; no room for God or the Devil; it should be metaphor—the supernatural—whether it's High Mass at St. Patrick's Cathedral, or Faust selling his soul in an opera, or a rock star pretending to be the Vampire Lestat.

Nobody knew where Maharet had taken Mekare. Even Eric probably didn't know now either, though he'd left with them, promising to meet Jesse in Rangoon.

Before she left the Sonoma compound, Maharet had startled me with a little whisper: "Get it straight when you tell it—the Legend of the Twins."

That was permission, wasn't it? Or cosmic indifference, I'm not sure which. I'd said nothing about the book to anyone; I'd only brooded on it in those long painful hours when I couldn't really think, except in terms of chapters: an ordering; a road map through the mystery; a chronicle of seduction and pain.

Maharet had looked worldly yet mysterious that last evening, coming to find me in the forest, garmented in black and wearing her fashionable paint, as she called it—the skillful cosmetic mask that made her into an alluring mortal woman who could move with only admiring glances through the real world. What a tiny waist she had, and such long hands, even more graceful, it seemed, for the tight black kid gloves she wore. So carefully she had stepped through the ferns and past the tender saplings, when she might have pushed the trees themselves out of her path.

She'd been to San Francisco with Jessica and Gabrielle; they had walked past houses with cheerful lights; on clean narrow pavements; where people lived, she'd said. How crisp her speech had been, how effortlessly contemporary; not like the timeless woman I had first encountered in the mountaintop room.

And why was I alone again, she'd asked, sitting by myself near the little creek that ran through the thick of the redwoods? Why would I not talk to the others, even a little? Did I know how protective and fearful they were?

They are still asking me those questions now.

Even Gabrielle, who in the main never bothers with questions, never says much of anything. They want to know when I'm going to recover, when I'm going to talk about what happened, when I'm going to stop writing all through the night.

Maharet had said that we would see her again very soon. In the spring perhaps we should come to her house in Burma. Or maybe she'd surprise us one evening. But the point was, we were never to be isolated from one another; we had ways to find each other, no matter where we might roam.

Yes, on that vital point at least everyone had agreed. Even Gabrielle, the loner, the wanderer, had agreed.

Nobody wanted to be lost in time again.

And Mekare? Would we see her again? Would she ever sit with us around a table? Speak to us with a language of gestures and signs?

I had laid eyes upon her only once after that terrible night. And it had been entirely unexpected, as I came through the forest, back to the compound, in the soft purple light just before dawn.

There had been a mist crawling over the earth, thinning above the ferns and the few scattered winter wild flowers, and then paling utterly into phosphorescence as it rose among the giant trees.

And the twins had come through the mist together, walking down into the creek bed to make their way along the stones, arms locked around each other, Mekare in a long wool gown as beautiful as her sister's, her hair brushed and shining as it hung down around her shoulders and over her breasts.

It seemed Maharet had been speaking softly in Mekare's ear. And it was Mekare who stopped to look at me, her green eyes wide and her face for one moment unaccountably frightening in its blankness, as I'd felt my grief like a scorching wind on my heart.

I'd stood entranced looking at her, at both of them, the pain in me suffocating, as if my lungs were being dried up.

I don't know what my thoughts were; only that the pain seemed unbearable. And that Maharet had made some little tender motion to me of greeting, and that I should go my way. Morning coming. The forest was waking all around us. Our precious moments slipping by. My pain had been finally loosened, like a moan coming out of me, and I'd let it go as I'd turned away.

I'd glanced back once to see the two figures moving eastward, down the rippling silver creek bed, swallowed as it were by the roaring music of the water that followed its relentless path through the scattered rocks.

The old image of the dream had faded just a little. And when I think of them now, I think not of the funeral feasts but of that moment, the two sylphs in the forest, only nights before Maharet left the Sonoma compound taking Mekare away.

I was glad when they were gone because it meant that we would be going. And I did not care if I ever saw the Sonoma compound again. My sojourn there had been agony, though the first few nights after the catastrophe had been the worst.

How quickly the bruised silence of the others had given way to endless analysis, as they strained to interpret what they'd seen and felt. How had the thing been transferred exactly? Had it abandoned the tissues of the brain as they disintegrated, racing through Mekare's bloodstream until it found the like organ in her? Had the heart mattered at all?

Molecular; nucleonic; solitons; protoplasm; glittering modern words! Come now, we are vampires! We thrive on the blood of the living; we kill; and we love it. Whether we need to do it or not.

I couldn't bear to listen to them; I couldn't bear their silent yet obsessive curiosity: *What was it like with her? What did you do in those few nights?* I couldn't get away from them either; I certainly hadn't the will to leave altogether; I trembled when I was with them; trembled when I was apart.

The forest wasn't deep enough for me; I'd roamed for miles through the mammoth redwoods, and then through scrub oaks and open fields and into dank impassable woods again. No getting away from their voices: Louis confessing how he had lost consciousness during those awful moments; Daniel saying that he had heard our voices, yet seen nothing; Jesse, in Khayman's arms, had witnessed it all.

How often they had pondered the irony—that Mekare had brought down her enemy with a human gesture; that, knowing nothing of invisible powers, she had struck out as any human might, but with inhuman speed and strength.

Had any of *her* survived in Mekare? That was what I kept wondering. Forget the "poetry of science" as Maharet had called it. That was what I wanted to know. Or had her soul been released at last when the brain was torn loose?

Sometimes in the dark, in the honeycombed cellar with its tin-plated walls and its countless impersonal chambers, I'd wake, certain that she was right there beside me, no more than an inch from my face; I'd feel her hair again; her arm around me; I'd see the black glimmer of her eye. I'd grope in the darkness; nothing but the damp brick walls.

Then I'd lie there and think of poor little Baby Jenks, as *she* had shown her to me, spiraling upwards; I'd see the varicolored lights enveloping Baby Jenks as she looked down on the earth for the last time. How could Baby Jenks, the poor biker child, have invented such a vision? Maybe we do go home, finally.

How can we know?

And so we remain immortal; we remain frightened; we remain anchored to what we can control. It all starts again; the wheel turns; we are *the* vampires; because there are no others; the new coven is formed.

LIKE a gypsy caravan we left the Sonoma compound, a parade of shining black cars streaking through the American night at lethal speed on immaculate roads. It was on that long ride that they told me everything—spontaneously and sometimes unwittingly as they conversed with one another. Like a mosaic it came together, all that had gone before. Even when I dozed against the blue velvet upholstery, I heard them, saw what they had seen.

Down to the swamplands of south Florida; down to the great decadent city of Miami, parody of both heaven and hell.

Immediately I locked myself in this little suite of tastefully appointed rooms; couches, carpet, the pale pastel paintings of Piero della Francesca; computer on the table; the music of Vivaldi pouring from tiny speakers hidden in the papered walls. Private stairway to the cellar, where in the steel-lined crypt the coffin waited: black lacquer; brass handles; a match and the stub of a candle; lining stitched with white lace.

Blood lust; how it hurt; but you don't need it; yet you can't resist it; and it's going to be like this forever; you never get rid of it; you want it even more than before.

When I wasn't writing, I lay on the gray brocade divan, watching the palm fronds move in the breeze from the terrace, listening to their voices below.

Louis begging Jesse politely to describe one more time the apparition of Claudia. And Jesse's voice, solicitous, confidential: "But Louis, it wasn't real."

Gabrielle missed Jesse now that she was gone; Jesse and Gabrielle had walked on the beach for hours. It seemed not a word passed between them; but then, how could I be sure?

Gabrielle was doing more and more little things to make me happy: wearing her hair brushed free because she knew I loved it; coming up to my room before she vanished with the morning. Now and then she'd look at me, probing, anxious.

"You want to leave here, don't you?" I'd ask fearfully; or something like it.

"No," she said. "I like it here. It suits me." When she got restless now she went to the islands, which weren't so very far away. She rather liked the islands. But that wasn't what she wanted to talk about. There was always something else on her mind. Once she had almost voiced it. "But tell me . . ." And then she'd stopped.

"Did I love her?" I asked. "Is that what you want to know? Yes, I loved her."

And I still couldn't say her name.

Mael came and went.

Gone for a week; here again tonight—downstairs—trying to draw

Khayman into conversation; Khayman, who fascinated everybody. First Brood. All that power. And to think, he had walked the streets of Troy.

The sight of him was continuously startling, if that is not a contradiction in terms.

He went to great lengths to appear human. In a warm place like this, where heavy garments are conspicuous, it isn't an easy thing. Sometimes he covered himself with a darkening pigment—burnt sienna mixed with a little scented oil. It seemed a crime to do so, to mar the beauty; but how else could he slice through the human crowd like a greased knife?

Now and then he knocked on my door. "Are you ever coming out?" he would ask. He'd look at the stack of pages beside the computer; the black letters: *The Queen of the Damned.* He'd stand there, letting me search his mind for all the little fragments, half-remembered moments; he didn't care. I seemed to puzzle him, but why I couldn't imagine. What did he want from me? Then he'd smile that shocking saintly smile.

Sometimes he took the boat out—Armand's black racer—and he let it drift in the Gulf as he lay under the stars. Once Gabrielle went with him, and I was tempted to listen to them, over all that distance, their voices so private and intimate. But I hadn't done it. Just didn't seem fair.

Sometimes he said he feared the memory loss; that it would come suddenly, and he wouldn't be able to find his way home to us. But then it had come in the past on account of pain, and he was so happy. He wanted us to know it; so happy to be with us all.

It seemed they'd reached some kind of agreement down there—that no matter where they went, they would always come back. This would be the coven house, the sanctuary; never would it be as it had been before.

They were settling a lot of things. Nobody was to make any others, and nobody was to write any more books, though of course they knew that was exactly what I was doing, gleaning from them silently everything that I could; and that I didn't intend to obey any rules imposed on me by anybody, and that I never had.

They were relieved that the Vampire Lestat had died in the pages of the newspapers; that the debacle of the concert had been forgotten. No provable fatalities, no true injuries; everybody bought off handsomely; the band, receiving my share of everything, was touring again under its old name.

And the riots—the brief era of miracles—they too had been forgotten, though they might never be satisfactorily explained.

No, no more revelations, disruptions, interventions; that was their collective vow; and please cover up the kill.

They kept impressing that upon the delirious Daniel, that even in a great festering urban wilderness like Miami, one could not be too careful with the remnants of the meal.

Ah, Miami. I could hear it again, the low roar of so many desperate humans; the churning of all those machines both great and small. Earlier I had let its voices sweep over me, as I'd lain stock-still on the divan. It was not impossible for me to direct this power; to sift and focus, and amplify an entire chorus of different sounds. Yet I drew back from it, unable yet to really use it with conviction, just as I couldn't use my new strength.

Ah, but I loved being near to this city. Loved its sleaze and glamour; the old ramshackle hotels and spangled high rises; its sultry winds; its flagrant decay. I listened now to that never ending urban music, a low throbbing hum.

"Why don't you go there, then?"

Marius.

I looked up from the computer. Slowly, just to needle him a little, though he was the most patient of immortal men.

He stood against the frame of the terrace door, with his arms folded, one ankle crossed over the other. The lights out there behind him. In the ancient world had there been anything like it? The spectacle of an electrified city, dense with towers glowing like narrow grids in an old gas fire?

He'd clipped his hair short; he wore plain yet elegant twentieth-century clothes: gray silk blazer and pants, and the red this time, for there was always red, was the dark turtleneck shirt.

"I want you to put the book aside and come join us," he said. "You've been locked in here for over a month."

"I go out now and then," I said. I liked looking at him, at the neon blue of his eyes.

"This book," he said. "What's the purpose of it? Would you tell me that much?"

I didn't answer. He pushed a little harder, tactful though the tone was.

"Wasn't it enough, the songs and the autobiography?"

I tried to decide what made him look so amiable really. Maybe it was the tiny lines that still came to life around his eyes, the little crinkling of flesh that came and went as he spoke.

Big wide eyes like Khayman's had a stunning effect.

I looked back at the computer screen. Electronic image of language. Almost finished. And they all knew about it; they'd known all along. That's why they volunteered so much information: knocking, coming in, talking, then going away.

"So why talk about it?" I asked. "I want to make the record of what happened. You knew that when you told me what it had been like for you."

"Yes, but for whom is this record being made?"

I thought of all the fans again in the auditorium; the visibility; and then those ghastly moments, at her side, in the villages, when I'd been a god without a name. I was cold suddenly in spite of the caressing warmth, the breeze that came in from the water. Had she been right when she called us selfish, greedy? When she'd said it was self-serving of us to want the world to remain the same?

"You know the answer to that question," he said. He drew a little closer. He put his hand on the back of my chair.

"It was a foolish dream, wasn't it?" I asked. It hurt to say it. "It could never have been realized, not even if we had proclaimed her the goddess and obeyed her every command."

"It was madness," he answered. "They would have stopped her; destroyed her; more quickly than she ever dreamed."

Silence.

"The world would not have *wanted* her," he added. "That's what she could never comprehend."

"I think in the end she knew it; no place for her; no way for her to have value and be the thing that she was. She knew it when she looked into our eyes and saw the wall there which she could never breach. She'd been so careful with her visitations, choosing places as primitive and changeless as she was herself."

He nodded. "As I said, you know the answers to your questions. So why do you continue to ask them? Why do you lock yourself here with your grief?"

I didn't say anything. I saw her eyes again. *Why can't you believe in me!*

"Have you forgiven me for all of it?" I asked suddenly.

"You weren't to blame," he said. "She was waiting, listening. Sooner or later something would have stirred the will in her. The danger was always there. It was as much an accident as the beginning, really, that she woke when she did." He sighed. He sounded bitter again, the way he'd been in the first nights after, when he had grieved too. "I always knew the danger," he murmured. "Maybe I wanted to believe she was a goddess; until she woke. Until she spoke to me. Until she smiled."

He was off again, thinking of the moment before the ice had fallen and pinned him helplessly for so long.

He moved away, slowly, indecisively, and then went out onto the terrace and looked down at the beach. Such a casual way of moving. Had the ancient ones rested their elbows like that on stone railings?

I got up and went after him. I looked across the great divide of black water. At the shimmering reflection of the skyline. I looked at him.

"Do you know what it's like, not to carry that burden?" he whispered. "To know now for the first time that I am free?"

I didn't answer. But I could most certainly feel it. Yet I was afraid for him, afraid perhaps that it had been the anchor, as the Great Family was the anchor for Maharet.

"No," he said quickly, shaking his head. "It's as if a curse has been removed. I wake; I think I must go down to the shrine; I must burn the incense; bring the flowers; I must stand before them and speak to them; and try to comfort them if they are suffering inside. Then I realize that they're gone. It's over, finished. I'm free to go wherever I would go and do whatever I would like." He paused, reflecting, looking at the lights again. Then, "What about you? Why aren't you free too? I wish I understood you."

"You do. You always have," I said. I shrugged.

"You're burning with dissatisfaction. And we can't comfort you, can we? It's *their* love you want." He made a little gesture towards the city.

"You comfort me," I answered. "All of you. I couldn't think of leaving you, not for very long, anyway. But you know, when I was on that stage in San Francisco . . ." I didn't finish. What was the use of saying it, if he didn't know. It had been everything I'd ever wanted it to be until the great whirlwind had descended and carried me away.

"Even though they never believed you?" he asked. "They thought you were merely a clever performer? An author with a hook, as they say?"

"They knew my name!" I answered. "It was *my* voice they heard. They saw *me* up there above the footlights."

He nodded. "And so the book, *The Queen of the Damned*," he said.

No answer.

"Come down with us. Let us try to keep you company. Talk to us about what took place."

"You saw what took place."

I felt a little confusion suddenly; a curiosity in him that he was reluctant to reveal. He was still looking at me.

I thought of Gabrielle, the way she would start to ask me questions and stop. Then I realized. Why, I'd been a fool not to see it before. They wanted to know what powers she'd given me; they wanted to know how much her blood had affected me; and all this time I'd kept those secrets locked inside. I kept them locked there now. Along with the image of those dead bodies strewn throughout Azim's temple; along with the memory of the ecstasy I'd felt when I'd slain every man in my path. And along with yet another awful and unforgettable moment: her death, when I had failed to use the gifts to help her!

And now it started again, the obsession with the end. Had she seen me lying there so close to her? Had she known of my refusal to aid her? Or had her soul risen when the first blow was struck?

Marius looked out over the water, at the tiny boats speeding towards the harbor to the south. He was thinking of how many centuries it had taken him to acquire the powers he now possessed. Infusions of her blood alone had not done it. Only after a thousand years had he been able to rise towards the clouds as if he were one of them, unfettered, unafraid. He was thinking of how such things vary from one immortal to another; how no one knows what power is locked inside another; no one knows perhaps what power is locked within oneself.

All very polite; but I could not confide in him or anyone just yet.

"Look," I said. "Let me mourn just a little while more. Let me create my dark images here, and have the written words for friends. Then later I'll come to you; I'll join you all. Maybe I'll obey the rules. Some of them, anyway, who knows? What are you going to do if I don't, by the way, and haven't I asked you this before?"

He was clearly startled.

"You are the damnedest creature!" he whispered. "You make me think of the old story about Alexander the Great. He wept when there were no more worlds to conquer. Will you weep when there are no more rules to break?"

"Ah, but there are always rules to break."

He laughed under his breath. "Burn the book."

"No."

We looked at each other for a moment; then I embraced him, tightly and warmly, and I smiled. I didn't even know why I'd done it, except that he was so patient and so earnest, and there had been some profound change in him as there had been in all of us, but with him it was dark and hurtful as it had been with me.

It had to do with the whole struggle of good and evil which he understood exactly the way I did, because he was the one who had taught me to understand it years ago. He was the one who had told me how we must wrestle forever with those questions, how the simple solution was not what we wanted, but what we must always fear.

I'd embraced him also because I loved him and wanted to be near to him, and I didn't want him to leave just now, angry or disappointed in me.

"You will obey the rules, won't you?" he asked suddenly. Mixture of menace and sarcasm. And maybe a little affection, too.

"Of course!" Again I shrugged. "What are they, by the way? I've forgotten. Oh, we don't make any new vampires; we do not wander off without a trace; we cover up the kill."

"You are an imp, Lestat, you know it? A brat."

"Let me ask you a question," I said. I made my hand into a fist and touched him lightly on the arm. "That painting of yours, *The Temptation of Amadeo,* the one in the Talamasca crypt . . ."

"Yes?"

"Wouldn't you like to have it back?"

"Ye gods, no. It's a dreary thing, really. My black period, you might say. But I do wish they'd take it out of the damned cellar. You know, hang it in the front hall? Some decent place."

I laughed.

Suddenly he became serious. Suspicious.

"Lestat!" he said sharply.

"Yes, Marius."

"You leave the Talamasca alone!"

"Of course!" Another shrug. Another smile. Why not?

"I mean it, Lestat. I'm quite serious. Do not meddle with the Talamasca. Do we understand each other, you and I?"

"Marius, you are remarkably easy to understand. Did you hear that? The clock's striking midnight. I always take my little walk around the Night Island now. Do you want to come?"

I didn't wait for him to answer. I heard him give one of those lovely forbearing sighs of his as I went out the door.

MIDNIGHT. The Night Island sang. I walked through the crowded galleria. Denim jacket, white T-shirt, face half covered by giant dark glasses; hands shoved into the pockets of my jeans. I watched the hungry shoppers dipping into the open doorways, perusing stacks of shining luggage, silk shirts in plastic, a sleek black manikin swathed in mink.

Beside the shimmering fountain, with its dancing plumes of myriad droplets, an old woman sat curled on a bench, paper cup of steaming coffee in her trembling hand. Hard for her to raise it to her lips; when I smiled as I passed she said in a quavering voice: "When you're old you don't need sleep anymore."

A soft whoozy music gushed out of the cocktail lounge. The young toughs prowled the video emporium; blood lust! The raucous zip and flash of the arcade died as I turned my head away. Through the door of the French restaurant I caught the swift beguiling movement of a woman lifting a glass of champagne; muted laughter. The theater was full of black and white giants speaking French.

A young woman passed me; dark skin, voluptuous hips, little pout of a mouth. The blood lust crested. I walked on, forcing it back into its cage. *Do not need the blood. Strong now as the old ones.* But I could taste it; I glanced back at her, saw her seated on the stone bench, naked knees jutting from her tight little skirt; eyes fixed on me.

Oh, Marius was right about it; right about everything. I was burning with dissatisfaction; burning with loneliness. I want to pull her up off that bench: *Do you know what I am!* No, don't settle for the other; don't lure her out of here, don't do it; don't take her down on the white sands, far beyond the lights of the galleria, where the rocks are dangerous and the waves are breaking violently in the little cove.

I thought of what *she* had said to us, about our selfishness, our greed! Taste of blood on my tongue. Someone's going to die if I linger here. . . .

End of the corridor. I put my key into the steel door between the shop that sold Chinese rugs made by little girls and the tobacconist who slept now among the Dutch pipes, his magazine over his face.

Silent hallway into the bowels of the villa.

One of them was playing the piano. I listened for a long moment. Pandora, and the music as always had a dark sweet luster, but it was more than ever like an endless beginning—a theme ever building to a climax which would never come.

I went up the stairs and into the living room. Ah, you can tell this is a vampire house; who else could live by starlight and the glow of a few scattered candles? Luster of marble and velvet. Shock of Miami out there where the lights never go out.

Armand still playing chess with Khayman and losing. Daniel lay under the earphones listening to Bach, now and then glancing to the black and white board to see if a piece had been moved.

On the terrace, looking out over the water, her thumbs hooked in her back pockets, Gabrielle stood. Alone. I went out to her, kissed her cheek, and looked into her eyes; and when I finally won the begrudging little smile I needed, then I turned and wandered back into the house.

Marius in the black leather chair reading the newspaper, folding it as a gentleman might in a private club.

"Louis is gone," he said, without looking up from the paper.

"What do you mean, gone?"

"To New Orleans," Armand said without looking up from the chessboard. "To that flat you had there. The one where Jesse saw Claudia."

"The plane's waiting," Marius said, eyes still on the paper.

"My man can drive you down to the landing strip," Armand said with his eyes still on the game.

"What is this? Why are you two being so helpful? Why should I go get Louis?"

"I think you should bring him back," Marius said. "It's no good his being in that old flat in New Orleans."

"I think you should get out and do something," Armand said. "You've been holed up here too long."

"Ah, I can see what this coven is going to be like, advice from all sides, and everyone watching everyone else out of the corner of an eye. Why did you ever let Louis go off to New Orleans anyway? Couldn't you have stopped him?"

I LANDED in New Orleans at two o'clock. Left the limousine at Jackson Square.

So clean it all was; with the new flagstones, and the chains on the gates, imagine, so the derelicts couldn't sleep on the grass in the square the way they'd done for two hundred years. And the tourists crowding the Café du Monde where the riverfront taverns had been; those lovely nasty places where the hunting was irresistible and the women were as tough as the men.

But I loved it now; always would love it. The colors were somehow the same. And even in this blasted cold of January, it had the old tropical feel to it; something to do with the flatness of the pavements; the low buildings; the sky that was always in motion; and the slanting roofs that were gleaming now with a bit of icy rain.

I walked slowly away from the river, letting the memories rise as if from the pavements; hearing the hard, brassy music of the Rue Bourbon, and then turning into the quiet wet darkness of the Rue Royale.

How many times had I taken this route in the old days, coming back from the riverfront or the opera house, or the theater, and stopping here on this very spot to put my key in the carriage gate?

Ah, the house in which I'd lived the span of a human lifetime, the house in which I'd almost died twice.

Someone up there in the old flat. Someone who walks softly yet makes the boards creak.

The little downstairs shop was neat and dark behind its barred windows; porcelain knickknacks, dolls, lace fans. I looked up at the balcony with its wrought-iron railings; I could picture Claudia there, on tiptoe, looking down at me, little fingers knotted on the rail. Golden hair spilling down over her shoulders, long streak of violet ribbon. My little immortal six-year-old beauty; *Lestat, where have you been?*

And that's what he was doing, wasn't he? Picturing things like that.

It was dead quiet; that is, if you didn't hear the televisions chattering behind the green shutters and the old vine-covered walls; and the raucous noise from Bourbon; a man and a woman fighting deep within a house on the other side of the street.

But no one about; only the shining pavements; and the shut-up shops; and the big clumsy cars parked over the curb, the rain falling soundlessly on their curved roofs.

No one to see me as I walked away and then turned and made the quick feline leap, in the old manner, to the balcony and came down silently on the boards. I peered through the dirty glass of the French doors.

Empty; scarred walls; the way Jesse had left them. A board nailed up here, as though someone had tried once to break in and had been found out; smell of burnt timbers in there after all these years.

I pulled down the board silently; but now there was the lock on the other side. Could I use the new power? Could I make it open? Why did it hurt so much to do it—to think of her, to think that, in that last flickering moment, I could have helped her; I could have helped head and body to come together again; even though she had meant to destroy me; even though she had not called my name.

I looked at the little lock. *Turn, open.* And with tears rising, I heard the metal creak, and saw the latch move. Little spasm in the brain as I kept my eye on it; and then the old door popped from its warped frame, hinges groaning, as if a draft inside had pushed it out.

He was in the hallway, looking through Claudia's door.

The coat was perhaps a little shorter, a little less full than those old frock coats had been; but he looked so very nearly like himself in the old century that it made the ache in me deepen unbearably. For a moment I couldn't move. He might as well have been a ghost there: his black hair full and disheveled as it had always been in the old days, and his green eyes full of melancholy wonder, and his arms rather limp at his sides.

Surely he hadn't contrived to fit so perfectly into the old context. Yet he *was* a ghost in this flat, where Jesse had been so frightened; where she'd caught in chilling glimpses the old atmosphere I'd never forget.

Sixty years here, the unholy family. Sixty years Louis, Claudia, Lestat.

Could I hear the harpsichord if I tried?—Claudia playing her Haydn; and the birds singing because the sound always excited them; and the collected music vibrating in the crystal baubles that hung from the painted glass shades of the oil lamps, and in the wind chimes even that hung in the rear doorway before the curving iron stairs.

Claudia. A face for a locket; or a small oval portrait done on porcelain and kept with a curl of her golden hair in a drawer. But how she would have hated such an image, such an unkind image.

Claudia who sank her knife into my heart and twisted it, and watched as the blood poured down my shirt. *Die, Father. I'll put you in your coffin forever.*

I will kill you first, my prince.

I saw the little mortal child, lying there in the soiled covers; smell of sickness. I saw the black-eyed Queen, motionless on her throne. And I had kissed them both, the Sleeping Beauties! *Claudia, Claudia, come round now, Claudia . . . That's it, dear, you must drink it to get well.*

Akasha!

Someone was shaking me. "Lestat," he said.

Confusion.

"Ah, Louis, forgive me." The dark neglected hallway. I shuddered. "I came here because I was so concerned . . . about you."

"No need," he said considerately. "It was just a little pilgrimage I had to make."

I touched his face with my fingers; so warm from the kill.

"She's not here, Louis," I said. "It was something Jesse imagined."

"Yes, so it seems," he said.

"We live forever; but they don't come back."

He studied me for a long moment; then he nodded. "Come on," he said.

We walked down the long hallway together; no, I did not like it; I did not want to be here. It was haunted; but real hauntings have nothing to do with ghosts finally; they have to do with the menace of memory; that had been my room in there; my room.

He was struggling with the back door, trying to make the old weathered frame behave. I gestured for him to go out on the porch and then I gave it the shove it needed. Locked up tight.

So sad to see the overgrown courtyard; the fountain ruined; the old brick kitchen crumbling, and the bricks becoming earth again.

"I'll fix it all for you if you want," I told him. "You know, make it like it was before."

"Not important now," he said. "Will you come with me, walk with me a little?"

We went down the covered carriageway together, water rushing through the little gutter. I glanced back once. Saw her standing there in her white dress with the blue sash. Only she wasn't looking at me. I was dead, she thought, wrapped in the sheet that Louis thrust into the carriage; she was taking my remains away to bury me; yet there she stood, and our eyes met.

I felt him tugging on me. "No good to stay here any longer," he said.

I watched him close the gate up properly; and then his eyes moved sluggishly over the windows again, the balconies, and the high dormers above. Was he saying farewell, finally? Maybe not.

We went together up to the Rue Ste. Anne, and away from the river, not speaking, just walking, the way we'd done so many times back then. The cold was biting at him a little, biting at his hands. He didn't like to put his hands in his pockets the way men did today. He didn't think it a graceful thing to do.

The rain had softened into a mist.

Finally, he said: "You gave me a little fright; I didn't think you were real when I first saw you in the hallway; you didn't answer when I said your name."

"And where are we going now?" I asked. I buttoned up my denim jacket. Not because I suffered from cold anymore; but because being warm felt good.

"Just one last place, and then wherever you wish. Back to the coven house, I should think. We don't have much time. Or maybe you can leave me to my meanderings, and I'll be back in a couple of nights."

"Can't we meander together?"

"Yes," he said eagerly.

What in God's name did I want? We walked beneath the old porches, past the old solid green shutters; past the walls of peeling plaster and naked brick, and through the garish light of the Rue Bourbon and then I saw the St. Louis Cemetery up ahead, with its thick whitewashed walls.

What did I want? Why was my soul aching still when all the rest of them had struck some balance? Even Louis had struck a balance, and we had each other, as Marius had said.

I was happy to be with him, happy to be walking these old streets; but why wasn't it enough?

Another gate now to be opened; I watched him break the lock with his fingers. And then we went into the little city of white graves with their peaked roofs and urns and doorways of marble, and the high grass crunching under our boots. The rain made every surface luminous; the lights of the city gave a pearl gleam to the clouds traveling silently over our heads.

I tried to find the stars. But I couldn't. When I looked down again, I saw Claudia; I felt her hand touch mine.

Then I looked at Louis again, and saw his eyes catch the dim and distant light and I winced. I touched his face again, the cheekbones, the arch beneath the black eyebrow. What a finely made thing he was.

"Blessed darkness!" I said suddenly. "Blessed darkness has come again."

"Yes," he said sadly, "and we rule in it as we have always done."

Wasn't that enough?

He took my hand—what did it feel like now?—and led me down the narrow corridor between the oldest, the most venerable tombs; tombs that went back to the oldest time of the colony, when he and I had roamed the swamps together, the swamps that threatened to swallow everything, and I had fed on the blood of roustabouts and cutthroat thieves.

His tomb. I realized I was looking at his name engraved on the marble in a great slanting old-fashioned script.

Louis de Pointe du Lac
1766–1794

He rested against the tomb behind him, another one of those little temples, like his own, with a peristyle roof.

"I only wanted to see it again," he said. He reached out and touched the writing with his finger.

It had faded only slightly from the weather wearing at the surface of the stone. The dust and grime had made it all the clearer, darkening each letter and numeral. Was he thinking of what the world had been in those years?

I thought of her dreams, her garden of peace on earth, with flowers springing from the blood-soaked soil.

"Now we can go home," he said.

Home. I smiled. I reached out and touched the graves on either side of me; I looked up again at the soft glow of the city lights against the ruffled clouds.

"You're not going to leave us, are you?" he asked suddenly, voice sharpened with distress.

"No," I said. I wished I could speak of it, all the things that were in the book. "You know, we were lovers, she and I, as surely as a mortal man and woman ever were."

"Of course, I know," he said.

I smiled. I kissed him suddenly, thrilled by the warmth of him, the soft pliant feel of his near human skin. God, how I hated the whiteness of my fingers touching him, fingers that could have crushed him now effortlessly. I wondered if he even guessed.

There was so much I wanted to say to him, to ask him. Yet I couldn't find the words really, or a way to begin. He had always had so many questions; and now he had his answers, more answers perhaps than he could ever have wanted; and what had this done to his soul? Stupidly I stared at him. How perfect he seemed to me as he stood there waiting with such kindness and such patience. And then, like a fool, I came out with it.

"Do you love me now?" I asked.

He smiled; oh, it was excruciating to see his face soften and brighten simultaneously when he smiled. "Yes," he said.

"Want to go on a little adventure?" My heart was thudding suddenly. It would be so grand if— "Want to break the new rules?"

"What in the world do you mean?" he whispered.

I started laughing, in a low feverish fashion; it felt so good. Laughing and watching the subtle little changes in his face. I really had him worried now. And the truth was, I didn't know if I could do it. Without her. What if I plunged like Icarus—?

"Oh, come now, Louis," I said. "Just a little adventure. I promise, I have no designs this time on Western civilization, or even on the attentions of two million rock music fans. I was thinking of something small, really. Something, well, a little mischievous. And rather elegant. I mean, I've been awfully good for the last two months, don't you think?"

"What on earth are you talking about?"

"Are you with me or not?"

He gave another little shake of his head again. But it wasn't a No. He was pondering. He ran his fingers back through his hair. Such fine black hair. The first thing I'd ever noticed about him—well, after his green eyes, that is—was his black hair. No, all that's a lie. It was his expression; the passion and the innocence and the delicacy of conscience. I just loved it!

"When does this little adventure begin?"

"Now," I said. "You have four seconds to make up your mind."

"Lestat, it's almost dawn."

"It's almost dawn *here*," I answered.

"What do you mean?"

"Louis, put yourself in my hands. Look, if I can't pull it off, you won't really be hurt. Well, not that much. Game? Make up your mind. I want to be off now."

He didn't say anything. He was looking at me, and so affectionately that I could hardly stand it.

"Yes or no."

"I'm probably going to regret this, but. . . ."

"Agreed then." I reached out and placed my hands firmly on his arms and I lifted him high off his feet. He was flabbergasted, looking down at me. It was as if he weighed nothing. I set him down.

"*Mon Dieu,*" he whispered.

Well, what was I waiting for? If I didn't try it, I'd never find out. There came a dark, dull moment of pain again; of remembering her; of us rising together. I let it slowly slip away.

I swung my arm around his waist. *Upwards now.* I lifted my right hand, but that wasn't even necessary. We were climbing on the wind that fast.

The cemetery was spinning down there, a tiny sprawling toy of itself with little bits of white scattered all over under the dark trees.

I could hear his astonished gasp in my ear.

"Lestat!"

"Put your arm around my neck," I said. "Hold on tight. We're going west, of course, and then north, and we're going a very long distance, and maybe we'll drift for a while. The sun won't set where we're going for some time."

The wind was ice cold. I should have thought of that, that he'd suffer from it; but he gave no sign. He was merely gazing upwards as we pierced the great snowy mist of the clouds.

When he saw the stars, I felt him tense against me; his face was perfectly smooth and serene; and if he was weeping the wind was carrying it away. Whatever fear he'd felt was gone now, utterly; he was lost as he looked upward; as the dome of heaven came down around us, and the moon shone full on the endless thickening plain of whiteness below.

No need to tell him what to observe, or what to remember. He always knew such things. Years ago, when I'd done the dark magic on him, I hadn't had to tell him anything; he had savored the smallest aspects of it all on his own. And later he'd said I'd failed to guide him. Didn't he know how unnecessary that had always been?

But I was drifting now, mentally and physically; feeling him a snug yet weightless thing against me; just the pure presence of Louis, Louis belonging to me, and with me. And no burden at all.

I was plotting the course firmly with one tiny part of my mind, the way she'd taught me to do it; and I was also remembering so many things; the first time, for example, that I'd ever seen him in a tavern in New Orleans. He'd been drunk, quarreling; and I'd followed him out into the night. And he had said in that last moment before I'd let him slip through my hands, his eyes closing:

"But who are you!"

I'd known I'd come back for him at sunset, that I'd find him if I had to search the whole city for him, though I was leaving him then half dead in the cobblestone street. I had to have him, had to. Just the way I had to have everything I wanted; or had to do everything I'd ever wanted to do.

That was the problem, and nothing she'd given me—not suffering, or power, or terror finally—had changed it one bit.

Four miles from London.

One hour after sunset. We lay in the grass together, in the cold darkness under the oak. There was a little light coming from the huge manor house in the middle of the park, but not much. The small deep-cut leaded windows seemed made to keep it all inside. Cozy in there, inviting, with all the book-lined walls, and the flicker of flames from those many fireplaces; and the smoke belching up from the chimneys into the foggy dark.

Now and then a car moved on the winding road beyond the front gates; and the beams would sweep the regal face of the old building, revealing the gargoyles, and the heavy arches over the windows, and the gleaming knockers on the massive front doors.

I have always loved these old European dwellings, big as landscapes; no wonder they invite the spirits of the dead to come back.

Louis sat up suddenly, looking about himself, and then hastily brushed the grass from his coat. He had slept for hours, inevitably, on the breast of the wind, you might say, and in the places where I'd rested for a little while, waiting for the world to turn. "Where are we?" he whispered, with a vague touch of alarm.

"Talamasca Motherhouse, outside London," I said. I was lying there with my hands cradling my head. Lights on in the attic. Lights on in the main rooms of the first floor. I was thinking, what way would be the most fun?

"What are we doing here?"

"Adventure, I told you."

"But wait a minute. You don't mean to go in there."

"Don't I? They have Claudia's diary in there, in their cellar, along with Marius's painting. You know all that, don't you? Jesse told you those things."

"Well, what do you mean to do? Break in and rummage through the cellar till you find what you want?"

I laughed. "Now, that wouldn't be very much fun, would it? Sounds more like dreary work. Besides, it's not really the diary I want. They can keep the diary. It was Claudia's. I want to talk to one of them, to David

Talbot, the leader. They're the only mortals in the world, you know, who really believe in us."

Twinge of pain inside. Ignore it. The fun's beginning.

For the moment he was too shocked to answer. This was even more delicious than I had dreamed.

"But you can't be serious," he said. He was getting wildly indignant. "Lestat, let these people alone. They think Jesse is dead. They received a letter from someone in her family."

"Yes, naturally. So I won't disabuse them of that morbid notion. Why would I? But the one who came to the concert—David Talbot, the older one—he fascinates me. I suppose I want to know. . . . But why say it? Time to go in and find out."

"Lestat!"

"Louis!" I said, mocking his tone. I got up and helped him up, not because he needed it, but because he was sitting there glowering at me, and resisting me, and trying to figure out how to control me, all of which was an utter waste of his time.

"Lestat, Marius will be furious if you do this!" he said earnestly, his face sharpening, the whole picture of high cheekbones and dark probing green eyes firing beautifully. "The cardinal rule is—"

"Louis, you're making it irresistible!" I said.

He took hold of my arm. "What about Maharet? These were Jesse's friends!"

"And what is she going to do? Send Mekare to crush my head like an egg!"

"You are really past all patience!" he said. "Have you learned anything at all!"

"Are you coming with me or not?"

"You're not going into that house."

"You see that window up there?" I hooked my arm around his waist. Now, he couldn't get away from me. "David Talbot is in that room. He's been writing in his journal for about an hour. He's deeply troubled. He doesn't know what happened with us. He knows something happened; but he'll never really figure it out. Now, we're going to enter the bedroom next to him by means of that little window to the left."

He gave one last feeble protest, but I was concentrating on the window, trying to visualize a lock. How many feet away was it? I felt the spasm, and then I saw, high above, the little rectangle of leaded glass swing out. He saw it too, and while he was standing there, speechless, I tightened my grip on him and went up.

Within a second we were standing inside the room. A small Elizabethan chamber with dark paneling, and handsome period furnishings, and a busy little fire.

Louis was in a rage. He glared at me as he straightened his clothes now with quick, furious gestures. I liked the room. David Talbot's books; his bed.

And David Talbot staring at us through the half-opened door to his study, from where he sat in the light of one green shaded lamp on his desk. He wore a handsome gray silk smoking jacket, tied at the waist. He had his pen in hand. He was as still as a creature of the wood, sensing a predator, before the inevitable attempt at flight.

Ah, now this was lovely!

I studied him for a moment; dark gray hair, clear black eyes, beautifully lined face; very expressive, immediately warm. And the intelligence of the man was obvious. All very much as Jesse and Khayman had described.

I went into the study.

"You'll forgive me," I said. "I should have knocked at the front door. But I wanted our meeting to be private. You know who I am, of course."

Speechless.

I looked at the desk. Our files, neat manila folders with various familiar names: "Théâtre des Vampires" and "Armand" and "Benjamin, the Devil." And "Jesse."

Jesse. There was the letter from Jesse's aunt Maharet lying there beside the folder. The letter which said that Jesse was dead.

I waited, wondering if I should force him to speak first. But then that's never been my favorite game. He was studying me very intensely, infinitely more intensely than I had studied him. He was memorizing me, using little devices he'd learned to record details so that he would remember them later no matter how great the shock of an experience while it was going on.

Tall, not heavy, not slender either. A good build. Large, very well-formed hands. Very well groomed, too. A true British gentleman; a lover of tweed and leather and dark woods, and tea, and dampness and the dark park outside, and the lovely wholesome feeling of this house.

And his age, sixty-five or so. A very good age. He knew things younger men just could not possibly know. This was the modern equivalent of Marius's age in ancient times. Not really old for the twentieth century at all.

Louis was still in the other room, but he knew Louis was there. He looked towards the doorway now. And then back to me.

Then he rose, and surprised me utterly. He extended his hand.

"How do you do?" he said.

I laughed. I took his hand and shook it firmly and politely, observing his reactions, his astonishment when he felt how cold my flesh was; how lifeless in any conventional sense.

He was frightened all right. But he was also powerfully curious; powerfully interested.

Then very agreeably and very courteously he said, "Jesse isn't dead, is she?"

Amazing what the British do with language; the nuances of politeness. The world's great diplomats, surely. I found myself wondering what their gangsters were like. Yet there was such grief there for Jesse, and who was I to dismiss another being's grief?

I looked at him solemnly. "Oh, yes," I said. "Make no mistake about it. Jesse is dead." I held his gaze firmly; there was no misunderstanding. "Forget about Jesse," I said.

He gave a little nod, eyes glancing off for a moment, and then he looked at me again, with as much curiosity as before.

I made a little circle in the center of the room. Saw Louis back there in the shadows, standing against the side of the bedroom fireplace watching me with such scorn and disapproval. But this was no time to laugh. I didn't feel at all like laughing. I was thinking of something Khayman had told me.

"I have a question for you now," I said.

"Yes."

"I'm here. Under your roof. Suppose when the sun rises, I go down into your cellar. I slip into unconsciousness there. You know." I made a little offhand gesture. "What would you do? Would you kill me while I slept?"

He thought about it for less than two seconds.

"No."

"But you know what I am. There isn't the slightest doubt in your mind, is there? Why wouldn't you?"

"Many reasons," he said. "I'd want to know about you. I'd want to talk to you. No, I wouldn't kill you. Nothing could make me do that."

I studied him; he was telling the truth completely. He didn't elaborate on it, but he would have thought it frightfully callous and disrespectful to kill me, to kill a thing as mysterious and old as I was.

"Yes, precisely," he said, with a little smile.

Mind reader. Not very powerful however. Just the surface thoughts.

"Don't be so sure." Again it was said with remarkable politeness.

"Second question for you," I said.

"By all means." He was really intrigued now. The fear had absolutely melted away.

"Do you want the Dark Gift? You know. To become one of us." Out of the corner of my eye I saw Louis shake his head. Then he turned his back. "I'm not saying that I'd ever give it you. Very likely, I would not. But do you want it? If I was willing, would you accept it from me?"

"No."

"Oh, come now."

"Not in a million years would I ever accept it. As God is my witness, no."

"You don't believe in God, you know you don't."

"Merely an expression. But the sentiment is true."

I smiled. Such an affable, alert face. And I was so exhilarated; the blood was moving through my veins with a new vigor; I wondered if he could sense it; did I look any less like a monster? Were there all those little signs of humanity that I saw in others of our kind when they were exuberant or absorbed?

"I don't think it will take a million years for you to change your mind," I said. "You don't have very much time at all, really. When you think about it."

"I will never change my mind," he said. He smiled, very sincerely. He was holding his pen in both hands. And he toyed with it, unconsciously and anxiously for a second, but then he was still.

"I don't believe you," I said. I looked around the room; at the small Dutch painting in its lacquered frame: a house in Amsterdam above a canal. I looked at the frost on the leaded window. Nothing visible of the night outside at all. I felt sad suddenly; only it wasn't anything as bad as before. It was just an acknowledgment of the bitter loneliness that had brought me here, the need with which I'd come, to stand in his little chamber and feel his eyes on me; to hear him say that he knew who I was.

The moment darkened. I couldn't speak.

"Yes," he said in a timid tone behind me. "I *know* who you are."

I turned and looked at him. It seemed I'd weep suddenly. Weep on account of the warmth here, and the scent of human things; the sight of a living man standing before a desk. I swallowed. I wasn't going to lose my composure, that was foolish.

"It's quite fascinating really," I said. "You wouldn't kill me. But you wouldn't become what I am."

"That's correct."

"No. I don't believe you," I said again.

A little shadow came into his face, but it was an interesting shadow. He was afraid I'd seen some weakness in him that he wasn't aware of himself.

I reached for his pen. "May I? And a piece of paper please?"

He gave them to me immediately. I sat down at the desk in his chair. All very immaculate—the blotter, the small leather cylinder in which he kept his pens, and even the manila folders. Immaculate as he was, standing there watching as I wrote.

"It's a phone number," I said. I put the piece of paper in his hand. "It's a Paris number, an attorney, who knows me under my proper name, Lestat de Lioncourt, which I believe is in your files? Of course he doesn't know the things about me you know. But he can reach me. Or, perhaps it would be accurate to say that I am always in touch with him."

He didn't say anything, but he looked at the paper, and he memorized the number.

"Keep it," I said. "And when you change your mind, when you want to be immortal, and you're willing to say so, call the number. And I'll come back."

He was about to protest. I gestured for silence.

"You never know what may happen," I told him. I sat back in his chair, and crossed my hands on my chest. "You may discover you have a fatal illness; you may find yourself crippled by a bad fall. Maybe you'll just start to have nightmares about being dead; about being nobody and nothing. Doesn't matter. When you decide you want what I have to give, call. And remember please, I'm not saying I'll give it to you. I may never do that. I'm only saying that when you decide you want it, then the dialogue will begin."

"But it's already begun."

"No, it hasn't."

"You don't think you'll be back?" he asked. "I think you will, whether I call or not."

Another little surprise. A little stab of humiliation. I smiled at him in spite of myself. He was a very interesting man. "You silver-tongued British bastard," I said. "How dare you say that to me with such condescension? Maybe I should kill you right now."

That did it. He was stunned. Covering it up rather well but I could still see it. And I knew how frightening I could look, especially when I smiled.

He recovered himself with amazing swiftness. He folded the paper with the phone number on it and slipped it into his pocket.

"Please accept my apology," he said. "What I meant to say was that I hope you'll come back."

"Call the number," I said. We looked at each other for a long moment; then I gave him another little smile. I stood up to take my leave. Then I looked down at his desk.

"Why don't I have my own file?" I asked.

His face went blank for a second; then he recovered again, miraculously. "Ah, but you have the book!" He gestured to *The Vampire Lestat* on the shelf.

"Ah, yes, right. Well, thank you for reminding me." I hesitated. "But you know, I think I should have my own file."

"I agree with you," he said. "I'll make one up immediately. It was always . . . just a matter of time."

I laughed softly in spite of myself. He was so courteous. I made a little farewell bow, and he acknowledged it gracefully.

And then I moved past him, as fast as I could manage it, which was quite fast, and I caught hold of Louis, and left immediately through the window, moving out and up over the grounds until I came down on a lonely stretch of the London road.

It was darker and colder here, with the oaks closing out the moon, and I loved it. I loved the pure darkness! I stood there with my hands shoved into my pockets looking at the faint faraway aureole of light hovering over London; and laughing to myself with irrepressible glee.

"Oh, that was wonderful; that was perfect!" I said, rubbing my hands together; and then clasping Louis's hands, which were even colder than mine.

The expression on Louis's face sent me into raptures. This was a real laughing fit coming on.

"You're a bastard, do you know that!" he said. "How could you do such a thing to that poor man! You're a fiend, Lestat. You should be walled up in a dungeon!"

"Oh, come on, Louis," I said. I couldn't stop laughing. "What do you expect of me? Besides, the man's a student of the supernatural. He isn't going to go stark raving mad. What does everybody expect of me?" I threw my arm around his shoulder. "Come on, let's go to London. It's a long walk, but it's early. I've never been to London. Do you know that? I want to see the West End, and Mayfair, and the Tower, yes, let's do go to the Tower. And I want to feed in London! Come on."

"Lestat, this is no joking matter. Marius will be furious. Everyone will be furious!"

My laughing fit was getting worse. We started down the road at a good clip. It was so much fun to walk. Nothing was ever going to take the place of that, the simple act of walking, feeling the earth under your feet, and the sweet smell of the nearby chimneys scattered out there in the blackness; and the damp cold smell of deep winter in these woods. Oh, it was all very lovely. And we'd get Louis a decent overcoat when we reached London, a nice long black overcoat with fur on the collar so that he'd be warm as I was now.

"Do you hear what I'm saying to you?" Louis said. "You *haven't* learned anything, have you? You're more incorrigible than you were before!"

I started to laugh again, helplessly.

Then more soberly, I thought of David Talbot's face, and that moment when he'd challenged me. Well, maybe he was right. I'd be back. Who said I couldn't come back and talk to him if I wanted to? Who said? But then I ought to give him just a little time to think about that phone number; and slowly lose his nerve.

The bitterness came again, and a great drowsy sadness suddenly that threatened to sweep my little triumph away. But I wouldn't let it. The night was too beautiful. And Louis's diatribe was becoming all the more heated and hilarious:

"You're a perfect devil, Lestat!" he was saying. "That's what you are! You are the devil himself!"

"Yes, I know," I said, loving to look at him, to see the anger pumping him so full of life. "And I love to hear you say it, Louis. I need to hear you say it. I don't think anyone will ever say it quite like you do. Come on, say it again. I'm a perfect devil. Tell me how bad I am. It makes me feel so good!"